Please renew/return this item by the last date shown.

So that your telephone call is charged at local rate,
please call the numbers as set out below:

	From Area codes 01923 or 020:	From the rest of Herts:
Renewals:	01923 471373	01438 737373
Enquiries:	01923 471333	01438 737333
Textphone:	01923 471599	01438 737599

L32   www.hertsdirect.org/librarycatalogue

MALORY
WORKS

Oxford University Press, Ely House, London W. 1

GLASGOW NEW YORK TORONTO MELBOURNE WELLINGTON
CAPE TOWN SALISBURY IBADAN NAIROBI DAR ES SALAAM LUSAKA ADDIS ABABA
BOMBAY CALCUTTA MADRAS KARACHI LAHORE DACCA
KUALA LUMPUR SINGAPORE HONG KONG TOKYO

MALORY

WORKS

EDITED BY

EUGÈNE VINAVER

Second Edition

LONDON
OXFORD UNIVERSITY PRESS
NEW YORK TORONTO
1971

SIR THOMAS MALORY

Born ? before 1410
Died 14 March 1471

The Works of Sir Thomas Malory, *edited by Eugène Vinaver, was first published in the Oxford Standard Authors in 1954 and reprinted in 1959, 1962, 1964, and 1966.*

This second edition, based on the revised text of Professor Vinaver's three-volume Oxford English Texts edition (Clarendon Press, 1967), was first published in 1969.

0-19-254163-3

PRINTED IN GREAT BRITAIN

O.S.A.

INTRODUCTION

OF Sir Thomas Malory's life little is known, and what is known does not contribute much to the understanding of his character. He was a soldier, at one time loyalist, at another rebel, and for several years a fugitive from justice. He belonged to an old Warwickshire family and both his father and grandfather had been persons of consequence in the county. In 1433 or 1434, when he was in his early twenties, he came into his father's estate at Newbold Revell; in 1436 he served in the train of Richard Beauchamp at Calais 'with one lance and two archers'; and in 1445 he was member of Parliament for Warwickshire. But if we are to believe the records, some five or six years later he became a hardened law-breaker. No doubt, at a time when legal process was not uncommonly used as a means of achieving private or political vengeance an innocent man might well find himself charged with any crime; but in Malory's case the charges are so multifarious that it is difficult to ignore them altogether. The records allege that he lay in ambush 'with other malefactors' with the intent of murdering the Duke of Buckingham; that he broke into the abbey of Blessed Mary of Coombe and did there steal money and valuables from the abbot's chest; that a few days later he returned and insulted the abbot; that on two occasions he stole the property and forced the wife of Hugh Smyth; that he frequently led extensive cattle-raids, and that he 'with others' extorted money by threat. Malory's denial of these charges was of no avail. Eight imprisonments, varying in length from a few days to two and a half years, are on record as well as two dramatic escapes: on 27 July 1451 he swam the moat at Coleshill prison, and in October 1454 broke out of jail at Colchester using with great skill a variety of deadly weapons—swords, daggers, and *langues-de-bœuf*.[1] His last recorded arrest took place in the winter of 1460.

Nothing is known about his release, but in the autumn of 1462 we find him among the knights who followed the Earl of Warwick on a military expedition to Northumberland. The purpose of the expedition was to raise the royal standard of Edward IV against the French and the Scots who at the instigation of Henry VI and Margaret of Anjou were threatening the peace of the realm. It is likely that Malory was with Warwick throughout the campaign and took part in the siege of Alnwick castle which lasted until 30 January 1463. When later on the long-pending breach between Warwick and Edward IV occurred and Warwick joined the Lancastrians, Malory probably did so too. We do

[1] *langue-de-bœuf*: a halberd with a spiked head shaped like an ox-tongue.

not know whether he took an active part in the insurrections which
followed the breach, but he was excluded from at least four general
pardons granted by Edward to the Lancastrians. The last of these
pardons was issued on 22 February 1470. Malory died on 14 March
1471, a month to the day before Warwick was killed at the battle of
Barnet, and his burial near Newgate suggests that he died a prisoner,
unpardoned by the king.

It was during this last imprisonment, probably his longest, that he
completed what he himself described as 'the whole book of King
Arthur and of his noble knights of the Round Table'—a series of
Arthurian romances which on 31 July 1485 appeared at Caxton's press
in Westminster under the title of *Le Morte Darthur*. According to the
Preface, Caxton was asked by 'many noble and dyvers gentylmen
of thys royame of Englond' why he had not hitherto produced a book
about King Arthur, a great English king who 'ought moost to be
remembred emonge us Englysshemen tofore al other Crysten kynges'.
This reminder, so Caxton tells us, coupled with his own conviction
that Arthur was not a fictitious character but a real king, prompted him
to publish such romances of King Arthur and his knights as had 'late
ben drawen oute bryefly into Englysshe'; not only as an account of
Arthur's reign, but as a record of 'the jentyl and vertuous dedes that
somme knyghtes used in tho dayes, by whyche they came to honour'.
The Preface refers to Malory as the author of the work, but does not
say who he was, and all that one can learn about him from *Le Morte
Darthur* is contained in a short paragraph at the end of the volume. In
bidding farewell to his readers Malory begs them to pray for his 'good
delyveraunce', declares that 'this book was ended the ninth yere of the
reygne of King Edward the Fourth' (i.e. in the year which began on
4 March 1469), and gives his name as 'Syr Thomas Maleore, knyght'.
But a manuscript of his works discovered in 1934 shows that his printer
had taken care to delete several passages of similar character. One of
these occurs in the manuscript at the end of *The Tale of King Arthur*
and sums up the author's strange destiny in the simplest terms: 'And
this booke endyth whereas sir Launcelot and sir Trystrams com to
courte. Who that woll make ony more lette hym seke other bookis of
kynge Arthure or of sir Launcelot or sir Trystrams; for this was drawyn
by a knyght presoner, sir Thomas Malleorré, that God send hym good
recover.'

It was this obscure knight-prisoner who 'drew' from the books of
King Arthur, of Lancelot and of Tristram the one work of real poetic
value in the whole field of modern Arthurian fiction. Arthurian
chivalry was to him something more concrete and specific than an
example of 'noble and virtuous deeds'. He thought of it primarily as an

example of loyalty to a great cause, and of Arthurian romance as a record of the heroic past of England. His first work, *The Tale of King Arthur and the Emperor Lucius*, which in the final arrangement was given second place, was based upon the English alliterative *Morte Arthur*. It was the story of Arthur's victorious campaign against the Emperor of Rome—an epic inspired by a long tradition of chronicles. But Malory soon discovered the attraction of chivalric adventures proper. In the French romances of the thirteenth century—those voluminous prose works to which he referred as his 'French books'—he found characters who, while they wore the same armour and fought as vigorously as did the heroes who had defended Arthur's kingdom, showed no patriotic ambition. The tasks they assumed, often at the instigation of Arthur himself, were at times more difficult and hazardous than those of any epic hero; yet they behaved throughout as though their sole intention had been to earn praise for their valour. For many long months, perhaps years, Malory followed their tracks, borrowing his material from such books as he could find—the *Suite du Merlin*, the *Tristan de Léonois*, and the prose *Lancelot* (which included *La Queste del Saint Graal* and *La Mort le Roi Artu*)—and occasionally supplementing these with his own comments on what he called 'the high order of knighthood'. But in his last and greatest work—*The Most Piteous Tale of the Morte Arthur*, based partly on the French romance and partly on an English stanzaic poem—the heroic ideal is revived again, this time in terms of the 'dolorous death and departing' of the great protagonists of Arthurian romance. The series ends as it began, with a tale of heroic deeds performed in the service of a great kingdom.

It was this collection that Sir Walter Scott once described as having been 'extracted at hazard, and without much art or combination, from the various French prose folios'. Since then many critics have spoken in Malory's defence, and some have even claimed with George Saintsbury that Malory, 'and he alone in any language, had made of this vast assemblage of stories one story, and one book'. In the light of more recent knowledge neither view would appear to be correct. The French Arthurian prose cycle with its various ramifications was not an 'assemblage of stories', but a singularly perfect example of thirteenth-century narrative art, subordinate to a well-defined principle of composition and maintaining in all its branches a remarkable sense of cohesion. It was an elaborate fabric woven out of a number of themes which alternated with one another like the threads of a tapestry: a fabric whose growth and development had been achieved not by a process of indiscriminate expansion, but by means of a consistent lengthening of each thread. Malory's adaptation, on the other hand, was far from possessing or even attempting the unity which is claimed for it by the critics. He never tried to reduce his French romances to 'one story'; the method he used was both more subtle and more drastic. With great consistency, though with varying degrees of success, he endeavoured to break up the complex structure of his sources and replace their slowly unfolding canvas of recurrent themes by a series of self-contained stories. It was a delicate and difficult process of un-ravelling, of collecting the various stretches of any given thread and letting it unwind itself with as few interruptions as possible. Some-times, as in certain parts of the romance of Arthur and Merlin (*The Tale of King Arthur*) and in the long and monotonous *Book of Sir Tristram*, Malory found himself defeated by the ingenuity of the French writers. But his successes were more impressive than his failures. If his *Noble Tale of Sir Launcelot* is, by modern standards, eminently readable, it is because it consists of three judiciously chosen short episodes which in the French *Lancelot* were hundreds of pages apart. Dismissing all the intervening matter, Malory makes these episodes into one 'tale': the tale of Lancelot and Lionel, which is concluded by a reunion at Arthur's court of all Lancelot's victims who have survived his great strokes. Still more significant is the handling of the story of Balin, the unhappy knight whose Dolorous Stroke lays waste two king-doms. In the French romance the story is an expansion of the theme of the Blighted Land which belongs to the *Queste del Saint Graal*. In Malory's version the Dolorous Stroke comes as a sequel to an event which occurs within the Balin episode itself; and because it can thus be understood without reference to any other work the whole perspective of the tale is altered: instead of a chain of events stretching far beyond any single romance there is a sequence which is complete in itself, a 'circle of destiny' drawn tightly and firmly around the protagonist's life.

The aesthetic principle involved in such changes is fundamental for the transition from medieval to modern fiction; and had Malory failed to grasp it he would also have failed to rescue his material from oblivion. The modern reader may be unaware of this; he may imagine that the survival of literature is determined by the importance of its message, the intrinsic interest of the matter, and its relation to human experience. The inability of such a reader to seize upon the real sources of aesthetic enjoyment is no more surprising than any similar discrepancy between the real and the conventional criteria of value. What is surprising is a fifteenth-century author's instinctive understanding of the principle of 'singleness' which underlies the normal structure of a modern work of fiction. Nowhere perhaps is Malory's comprehension of it more apparent than in his remodelling of the story of Arthur's death and of the destruction of the Round Table. The central theme is disengaged from all concomitant elements and freed from links with the other branches of the cycle. The events leading to the downfall of Arthur's kingdom are no longer interwoven with others, and the tragic destiny of Arthurian knighthood is divorced from the earlier account of how the 'worldly' knights failed in the quest for the Grail. The final catastrophe becomes a human drama conditioned from first to last by a clash of loyalties and explicable within its own limits. It is Lancelot's loyalty to Guinevere that causes him, in his anxiety to protect her, to destroy unwittingly the man he loves most—Gareth, Gawain's brother; and it is grief that turns Lancelot's truest friend, Gawain, into his sworn enemy and causes the mortal strife. Mordred's rebellion and the battle of Salisbury Plain are no longer treated as repercussions of extraneous events; they are links in the chain of human actions and feelings developed as the story progresses: fateful shadows arising from the depths of man's own noblest passions.

Perhaps none of this would have seemed real to us if so much of it were not conveyed in a form which in a very true sense creates its own substance, a prose both crisp and resonant, blending the majesty of epic eloquence with the freshness of living speech. How strange and yet how instructive the contrast between the appeal of the work to English readers and the neglect into which the Arthurian legend fell in the country where it had found its first poetic expression! France had all that fifteenth-century England had access to, and more; but she lacked a writer as powerful as Malory and as deeply attached to the 'noble tales' of Arthur and his knights. She was, and still is, more concerned with the way a story is told than with the story itself; and so her medieval traditions gave way to others, not because these were intrinsically greater, but because upon them was cast the same magic spell that had revived in English prose the quests of Arthurian knights, the epic grandeur of their grim battles, and the 'piteous tale' of the fall of Arthur's kingdom.

In the following pages I have reproduced the text of my second three-volume edition of *The Works of Sir Thomas Malory* published by the Clarendon Press in 1967, but without the Introduction, the critical apparatus, the Index, and the Bibliography. I have, however, included a revised glossary, brief summaries of my original Commentary on each romance, and explanatory notes on certain phrases and passages. The errors listed in vol. iii of the 1967 edition as 'corrigenda' have been removed, so that the text now offered approximates more than any I have so far published to a definitive edition; and it is all the more likely to be accurate since it has been proof-read by so careful a scholar as Mr. Barry Gaines to whom I wish to acknowledge my personal debt as well as that of all Malory's readers. The basis of the text is still the manuscript discovered in 1934 by Dr. W. F. Oakeshott in the Fellows' Library of Winchester College, a manuscript roughly contemporary with, but in many ways more authentic than Caxton's edition. I have emended it where necessary with the aid of the latter and of Malory's sources. Emendations based upon Caxton but not explicitly confirmed by Malory's sources are placed in square brackets; half-brackets ⌐ ⌐ are used for readings borrowed from Caxton and confirmed by the sources, and caret brackets ⟨ ⟩ for all other emendations. Square brackets are also used for the *lacunae* supplied from Caxton. The only type of alteration to which attention is not drawn is the occasional deletion of a word or a letter. In the section based upon the alliterative *Morte Arthure* (pp. 113–46) the sign ` ´ is introduced to distinguish alliterating lines. To facilitate reference to Caxton's edition his book-numbers appear at the top of each page, and his chapter-numbers in the outer margin. His Preface is prefixed to the text, but not his list of 'rubrics'.

In this as in the two Clarendon Press editions an attempt has been made to give the work the appearance of a modern novel, not that of a learned treatise. Hence the liberal use of paragraphing, the setting of dialogues in keeping with modern practice, and the endeavour to avoid a punctuation that strings sentences together by innumerable *ands* and so obscures Malory's preference for the short period falling into not more than three parts: a cadence thanks to which this 'noble and joyous book' seems to have preserved for us the inflections of the writer's own voice.

1970   E.V.

CONTENTS

Introduction   v

Caxton's Preface   xiii

THE TALE OF KING ARTHUR   1

    I. Merlin   3
    II. Balin or the Knight with the Two Swords   37
    III. Torre and Pellinor   59
    IV. The War with the Five Kings   76
    V. Arthur and Accolon   81
    VI. Gawain, Ywain and Marhalt   93

THE TALE OF THE NOBLE KING ARTHUR THAT WAS EMPEROR HIMSELF THROUGH DIGNITY OF HIS HANDS   111

A NOBLE TALE OF SIR LAUNCELOT DU LAKE   147

THE TALE OF SIR GARETH OF ORKNEY THAT WAS CALLED BEWMAYNES   175

THE BOOK OF SIR TRISTRAM DE LYONES   227

    I. Isode the Fair   229
    II. Lamerok de Galys   274
    III. La Cote Male Tayle   282
    IV. Tristram's Madness and Exile   294
    V. The Castle of Maidens   320
    VI. The Round Table   333
    VII. King Mark   353
    VIII. Alexander the Orphan   388
    IX. The Tournament at Surluse   399
    X. Joyous Gard   411
    XI. The Red City   432
    XII. The Tournament at Lonezep   440

XIII. Sir Palomides   466
XIV. Launcelot and Elaine   477
XV. Conclusion   506

THE TALE OF THE SANKGREAL BRIEFLY DRAWN OUT OF
FRENCH WHICH IS A TALE CHRONICLED FOR ONE OF
THE TRUEST AND ONE OF THE HOLIEST THAT IS IN
THIS WORLD   513
     I. The Departure   515
    II. The Miracles   524
   III. Sir Perceval   540
    IV. Sir Launcelot   551
     V. Sir Gawain   558
    VI. Sir Bors   564
   VII. Sir Galahad   577
  VIII. The Castle of Corbenic   593
    IX. The Miracle of Galahad   600

THE BOOK OF SIR LAUNCELOT AND QUEEN GUINEVERE   609
     I. The Poisoned Apple   611
    II. The Fair Maid of Astolat   621
   III. The Great Tournament   642
    IV. The Knight of the Cart   648
     V. The Healing of Sir Urry   663

THE MOST PITEOUS TALE OF THE MORTE ARTHUR SAUNZ
GUERDON   671
     I. Slander and Strife   673
    II. The Vengeance of Sir Gawain   685
   III. The Siege of Benwick   700
    IV. The Day of Destiny   707
     V. The Dolorous Death and Departing out of this world of
        Sir Launcelot and Queen Guinevere   718

Notes and Glossary   727

CAXTON'S PREFACE

AFTER that I had accomplysshed and fynysshed dyvers hystoryes as wel of contemplacyon as of other hystoryal and worldly actes of grete conquerours and prynces, and also certeyn bookes of ensaumples and doctryne, many noble and dyvers gentylmen of thys royame of Englond camen and demaunded me many and oftymes wherfore that I have not do made and enprynte the noble hystorye of the Saynt Greal and of the moost renomed Crysten kyng, fyrst and chyef of the thre best Crysten, and worthy, Kyng Arthur, whyche ought moost to be remembred emonge us Englysshemen tofore al other Crysten kynges.

For it is notoyrly knowen thorugh the unyversal world that there been nine worthy and the best that ever were, that is to wete, thre Paynyms, thre Jewes, and thre Crysten men. As for the Paynyms, they were tofore the Incarnacyon of Cryst, whiche were named, the fyrst Hector of Troye, of whome th'ystorye is comen bothe in balade and in prose, the second Alysaunder the Grete, and the thyrd Julyus Cezar, Emperour of Rome, of whome th'ystoryes ben wel knowen and had. And as for the thre Jewes whyche also were tofore th'Yncarnacyon of our Lord, of whome the fyrst was Duc Josué whyche brought the chyldren of Israhel into the londe of byheste, the second Davyd, kyng of Jerusalem, and the thyrd Judas Machabeus; of these thre the Byble reherceth al theyr noble hystoryes and actes. And sythe the sayd Incarnacyon have ben thre noble Crysten men stalled and admytted thorugh the unyversal world into the nombre of the nine beste and worthy, of whome was fyrst the noble Arthur, whos noble actes I purpose to wryte in thys present book here folowyng. The second was Charlemayn, or Charles the Grete, of whome th'ystorye is had in many places, bothe in Frensshe and Englysshe; and the thyrd and last was Godefray of Boloyn, of whos actes and lyf I made a book unto th'excellent prynce and kyng of noble memorye, Kyng Edward the Fourth.

The sayd noble jentylmen instantly requyred me t'emprynte th' ystorye of the sayd noble kyng and conquerour Kyng Arthur and of his knyghtes, wyth th'ystorye of the Saynt Greal and of the deth and endyng of the sayd Arthur, affermyng that I ought rather t'enprynte his actes and noble feates than of Godefroye of Boloyne or ony of the other eyght, consyderyng that he was a man borne wythin this royame and kyng and emperour of the same, and that there ben in Frensshe dyvers and many noble volumes of his actes, and also of his knyghtes.

To whome I answerd that dyvers men holde oppynyon that there was no suche Arthur and that alle suche bookes as been maad of hym ben but fayned and fables, bycause that somme cronycles make of hym no mencyon ne remembre hym noothynge, ne of his knyghtes.

Wherto they answerd, and one in specyal sayd, that in hym that shold say or thynke that there was never suche a kyng callyd Arthur myght wel be aretted grete folye and blyndenesse, for he sayd that there were many evydences of the contrarye. Fyrst, ye may see his sepulture in the monasterye of Glastyngburye; and also in Poly-cronycon, in the fifth book, the syxth chappytre, and in the seventh book, the twenty-thyrd chappytre, where his body was buryed, and after founden and translated into the sayd monasterye. Ye shal se also in th'ystorye of Bochas, in his book DE CASU PRINCIPUM, parte of his noble actes, and also of his falle. Also Galfrydus, in his Brutysshe book, recounteth his lyf. And in dyvers places of Englond many remem-braunces ben yet of hym and shall remayne perpetuelly, and also of his knyghtes : fyrst, in the abbey of Westmestre, at Saynt Edwardes shryne, remayneth the prynte of his seal in reed waxe, closed in beryll, in whych is wryton PATRICIUS ARTHURUS BRITANNIE GALLIE GERMANIE DACIE IMPERATOR; item, in the castel of Dover ye may see Gauwayns skulle and Cradoks mantel; at Wynchester, the Rounde Table; in other places Launcelottes swerde and many other thynges.

Thenne, al these thynges consydered, there can no man resonably gaynsaye but there was a kyng of thys lande named Arthur. For in al places, Crysten and hethen, he is reputed and taken for one of the nine worthy, and the fyrst of the thre Crysten men. And also he is more spoken of beyonde the see, moo bookes made of his noble actes than there be in Englond; as wel in Duche, Ytalyen, Spaynysshe, and Grekysshe, as in Frensshe. And yet of record remayne in wytnesse of hym in Wales, in the toune of Camelot, the grete stones and mervayllous werkys of yron lyeng under the grounde, and ryal vautes, which dyvers now lyvyng hath seen. Wherfor it is a mervayl why he is no more renomed in his owne contreye, sauf onelye it accordeth to the Word of God, whyche sayth that no man is accept for a prophete in his owne contreye.

Thenne, al these thynges forsayd aledged, I coude not wel denye but that there was suche a noble kyng named Arthur, and reputed one of the nine worthy, and fyrst and chyef of the Cristen men. And many noble volumes be made of hym and of his noble knyghtes in Frensshe, which I have seen and redde beyonde the see, which been not had in our maternal tongue. But in Walsshe ben many, and also in Frensshe, and somme in Englysshe, but nowher nygh alle. Wherfore, suche as have late ben drawen oute bryefly into Englysshe, I have, after the symple connynge that God hath sente to me, under the favour and correctyon of al noble lordes and gentylmen, enprysed to enprynte a book of the noble hystoryes of the sayd Kynge Arthur and of certeyn of his knyghtes, after a copye unto me delyverd, whyche copye Syr Thomas Malorye dyd take oute of certeyn bookes of Frensshe and reduced it into Englysshe.

And I, accordyng to my copye, have doon sette it in enprynte to the entente that noble men may see and lerne the noble actes of chyvalrye, the jentyl and vertuous dedes that somme knyghtes used in tho dayes, by whyche they came to honour, and how they that were vycious were punysshed and ofte put to shame and rebuke; humbly bysechyng al noble lordes and ladyes wyth al other estates, of what estate or degree they been of, that shal see and rede in this sayd book and werke, that they take the good and honest actes in their remembraunce, and to folowe the same; wherein they shalle fynde many joyous and playsaunt hystoryes and noble and renomed actes of humanyté, gentylnesse, and chyvalryes. For herein may be seen noble chyvalrye, curtosye, humanyté, frendlynesse, hardynesse, love, frendshyp, cowardyse, murdre, hate, vertue, and synne. Doo after the good and leve the evyl, and it shal brynge you to good fame and renommee.

And for to passe the tyme thys book shal be plesaunte to rede in, but for to gyve fayth and byleve that al is trewe that is conteyned herin, ye be at your lyberté. But al is wryton for our doctryne, and for to beware that we falle not to vyce ne synne, but t'exersyse and folowe vertu, by whyche we may come and atteyne to good fame and renommé in thys lyf, and after thys shorte and transytorye lyf to come unto everlastyng blysse in heven; the whyche He graunte us that reygneth in heven, the Blessyd Trynyté. AMEN.

Thenne, to procede forth in thys sayd book, whyche I dyrecte unto alle noble prynces, lordes and ladyes, gentylmen or gentylwymmen, that desyre to rede or here redde of the noble and joyous hystorye of the grete conquerour and excellent kyng, Kyng Arthur, somtyme kyng of thys noble royalme thenne callyd Brytaygne, I, Wyllyam Caxton, symple persone, present thys book folowyng whyche I have enprysed t'enprynte: and treateth of the noble actes, feates of armes of chyvalrye, prowesse, hardynesse, humanyté, love, curtosye, and veray gentylnesse, wyth many wonderful hystoryes and adventures.

THE TALE OF
KING ARTHUR

I. MERLIN

I (1)

[HIT befel in the dayes of Uther Pendragon, when he was kynge of all
Englond and so regned, that there was a myghty duke in Cornewaill
that helde warre ageynst hym long tyme, and the duke was called the
duke of Tyntagil. And so by meanes kynge Uther send for this duk,
chargyng hym to brynge his wyf with hym, for she was called a fair 5
lady and a passynge wyse, and her name was called Igrayne.

So whan the duke and his wyf were comyn unto the kynge, by the
meanes of grete lordes they were accorded bothe: the kynge lyked and
loved this lady wel, and he made them grete chere out of mesure
and desyred to have lyen by her. But she was a passyng good woman 10
and wold not assente unto the kynge.

And thenne she told the duke her husband and said,

'I suppose that we were sente for that I shold be dishonourcd.
Wherfor, husband, I counceille yow that we departe from hens
sodenly, that we maye ryde all nyghte unto oure owne castell.' 15

And in lyke wyse as she saide so they departed, that neyther the
kynge nor none of his counceill were ware of their departyng. Also
soone as kyng Uther knewe of theire departyng soo sodenly, he was
wonderly wrothe; thenne he called to hym his pryvy counceille and
told them of the sodeyne departyng of the duke and his wyf. Thenne 20
they avysed the kynge to send for the duke and his wyf by a grete
charge:

'And yf he wille not come at your somons, thenne may ye do your
best; thenne have ye cause to make myghty werre upon hym.'

Soo that was done, and the messagers hadde their ansuers; and that 25
was thys, shortly, that neyther he nor his wyf wold not come at hym.
Thenne was the kyng wonderly wroth, and thenne the kyng sette
hym playne word ageyne and badde hym be redy and stuffe hym and
garnysshe hym, for within forty dayes he wold fetche hym oute of the
byggest castell that he hath. Whanne the duke hadde thys warnynge 30
anone he wente and furnysshed and garnysshed two stronge castels of
his, of the whiche the one hyght Tyntagil and the other castel hyght
Terrabyl.

So his wyf dame Igrayne he putte in the castell of Tyntagil, and
hymself he putte in the castel of Terrabyl, the whiche had many yssues 35
and posternes oute. Thenne in all haste came Uther with a grete hoost
and leyd a syege aboute the castel of Terrabil, and ther he pyght many
pavelyons. And there was grete warre made on bothe partyes and
moche peple slayne.

Thenne for pure angre and for grete love of fayr Igrayne the kyng 40

Uther felle seke. So came to the kynge Uther syre Ulfius, a noble knyght, and asked the kynge why he was seke.

'I shall telle the,' said the kynge. 'I am seke for angre and for love of fayre Igrayne, that I may not be hool.'

5   'Wel, my lord,' said syre Ulfius, 'I shal seke Merlyn and he shalle do yow remedy, that youre herte shal be pleasyd.'

So Ulfius departed and by adventure he mette Merlyn in a beggars aray, and ther Merlyn asked Ulfius whome he soughte, and he said he had lytyl ado to telle hym.

10   'Well,' saide Merlyn, 'I knowe whome thou sekest, for thou sekest Merlyn; therfore seke no ferther, for I am he. And yf kynge Uther wille wel rewarde me and be sworne unto me to fulfille my desyre, that shall be his honour and profite more than myn, for I shalle cause hym to have all his desyre.'

15   'Alle this wyll I undertake,' said Ulfius, 'that ther shalle be nothyng resonable but thow shalt have thy desyre.'

'Well,' said Merlyn, 'he shall have his entente and desyre, and therfore,' saide Merlyn, 'ryde on your wey, for I wille not be long behynde.'

(2) 20   Thenne Ulfius was glad and rode on more than a paas tyll that he came to kynge Uther Pendragon and told hym he had met with Merlyn.

'Where is he?' said the kyng.

'Sir,' said Ulfius, 'he wille not dwelle long.'

Therwithal Ulfius was ware where Merlyn stood at the porche of 25 the pavelions dore, and thenne Merlyn was bounde to come to the kynge. Whan kyng Uther sawe hym he said he was welcome.

'Syr,' said Merlyn, 'I knowe al your hert every dele. So ye wil be sworn unto me, as ye be a true kynge enoynted, to fulfille my desyre, ye shal have your desyre.'

30   Thenne the kyng was sworne upon the four Evangelistes.

'Syre,' said Merlyn, 'this is my desyre: the first nyght that ye shal lye by Igrayne ye shal gete a child on her; and whan that is borne, that it shall be delyverd to me for to nourisshe thereas I wille have it, for it shal be your worship and the childis availle as mykel as the child is 35 worth.'

'I wylle wel,' said the kynge, 'as thow wilt have it.'

'Now make you redy,' said Merlyn. 'This nyght ye shalle lye with Igrayne in the castel of Tyntigayll. And ye shalle be lyke the duke her husband, Ulfyus shal be lyke syre Brastias, a knyghte of the dukes, and 40 I will be lyke a knyghte that hyghte syr Jordanus, a knyghte of the dukes. But wayte ye make not many questions with her nor her men, but saye ye are diseased, and soo hye yow to bedde and ryse not on the morne tyll I come to yow, for the castel of Tyntygaill is but ten myle hens.'

Soo this was done as they devysed. But the duke of Tyntigail aspyed hou the kyng rode fro the syege of Tarabil. And therfor that nyghte he yssued oute of the castel at a posterne for to have distressid the kynges hooste, and so thorowe his owne yssue the duke hymself was slayne or ever the kynge cam at the castel of Tyntigail. So after the deth of the 5 duke kyng Uther lay with Igrayne, more than thre houres after his deth, and begat on her that nygh⟨t⟩ Arthur; and or day cam, Merlyn cam to the kyng and bad hym make hym redy, and so he kist the lady Igrayne and departed in all hast. But whan the lady herd telle of the duke her husband, and by all record he was dede or ever kynge Uther 10 came to her, thenne she mervcilled who that myghte be that laye with her in lykenes of her lord. So she mourned pryvely and held hir pees.

Thenne alle the barons by one assent prayd the kynge of accord betwixe the lady Igrayne and hym. The kynge gaf hem leve, for fayne wold he have ben accorded with her; soo the kyng put alle the trust 15 in Ulfyus to entrete bitwene them. So by the entreté at the last the kyng and she met togyder.

'Now wille we doo wel,' said Ulfyus; 'our kyng is a lusty knyghte and wyveles, and my lady Igrayne is a passynge fair lady; it were grete joye unto us all and hit myghte please the kynge to make her his quene.' 20

Unto that they all well accordyd and meved it to the kynge. And anone, lyke a lusty knyghte, he assentid therto with good wille, and so in alle haste they were maryed in a mornynge with grete myrthe and joye.

And kynge Lott of Lowthean and of Orkenay thenne wedded 25 Margawse that was Gaweyns moder, and kynge Nentres of the land of Garlot wedded Elayne: al this was done at the request of kynge Uther. And the thyrd syster, Morgan le Fey, was put to scole in a nonnery, and ther she lerned so moche that she was a grete clerke of nygromancye. And after she was wedded to kynge Uryens of the lond of Gore that 30 was syre Ewayns le Blaunche Maynys fader.

Thenne quene Igrayne waxid dayly gretter and gretter. So it befel (3, 4, 5) after within half a yere, as kyng Uther lay by his quene, he asked hir by the feith she ought to hym whos was the child within her body. Thenne was she sore abasshed to yeve ansuer.   35

'Desmaye you not,' said the kyng, 'but telle me the trouthe, and I shall love you the better, by the feythe of my body!'

'Syre,' saide she, 'I shalle telle you the trouthe. The same nyghte that my lord was dede, the houre of his deth as his knyghtes record, ther came into my castel of Tyntigaill a man lyke my lord in speche and 40 in countenaunce, and two knyghtes with hym in lykenes of his two knyghtes Barcias and Jordans, and soo I went unto bed with hym as I ought to do with my lord; and the same nyght, as I shal ansuer unto God, this child was begoten upon me.'

'That is trouthe,' saide the kynge, 'as ye say, for it was I myself that cam in the lykenesse. And therfor desmay you not, for I am fader to the child,' and ther he told her alle the cause how it was by Merlyns counceil. Thenne the quene made grete joye whan she knewe who was
5 the fader of her child.

Sone come Merlyn unto the kyng and said,

'Syr, ye must purvey yow for the nourisshyng of your child.'

'As thou wolt,' said the kyng, 'be it.'

'Wel,' said Merlyn, 'I knowe a lord of yours in this land that is a
10 passyng true man and a feithful, and he shal have the nourysshyng of your child; and his name is sir Ector, and he is a lord of fair lyvelode in many partyes in Englond and Walys. And this lord, sir Ector, lete hym be sent for for to come and speke with you, and desyre hym yourself, as he loveth you, that he will put his owne child to nouris-
15 shynge to another woman and that his wyf nourisshe yours. And whan the child is borne lete it be delyverd to me at yonder pryvy posterne uncrystned.'

So like as Merlyn devysed it was done. And whan syre Ector was come he made fyaunce to the kyng for to nourisshe the child lyke as the
20 kynge desyred; and there the kyng graunted syr Ector grete rewardys. Thenne when the lady was delyverd the kynge commaunded two knyghtes and two ladyes to take the child bound in a cloth of gold, 'and that ye delyver hym to what poure man ye mete at the posterne yate of the castel.' So the child was delyverd unto Merlyn, and so he
25 bare it forth unto syre Ector and made an holy man to crysten hym and named hym Arthur. And so sir Ectors wyf nourysshed hym with her owne pappe.

Thenne within two yeres kyng Uther felle seke of a grete maladye. And in the meanewhyle hys enemyes usurpped upon hym and dyd a
30 grete bataylle upon his men and slewe many of his peple.

'Sir,' said Merlyn, 'ye may not lye so as ye doo, for ye must to the feld, though ye ryde on an hors-lyttar. For ye shall never have the better of your enemyes but yf your persone be there, and thenne shall ye have the vyctory.'
35 So it was done as Merlyn had devysed, and they caryed the kynge forth in an hors-lyttar with a grete hooste towarde his enemyes, and at Saynt Albons ther mette with the kynge a grete hoost of the North. And that day syre Ulfyus and sir Bracias dyd grete dedes of armes, and kyng Uthers men overcome the northeryn bataylle and slewe many
40 peple and putt the remenaunt to flight; and thenne the kyng retorned unto London and made grete joye of his vyctory.

And thenne he fyll passynge sore seke, so that thre dayes and thre nyghtes he was specheles; wherfore alle the barons made grete sorow and asked Merlyn what counceill were best.

'There nys none other remedye,' said Merlyn, 'but God wil have His wille. But loke ye al barons be bifore kynge Uther to-morne, and God and I shalle make hym to speke.'

So on the morne alle the barons with Merlyn came tofore the kyng. Thenne Merlyn said aloud unto kyng Uther, 5

'Syre, shall your sone Arthur be kyng after your dayes of this realme with all the appertenaunce?'

Thenne Uther Pendragon torned hym and said in herynge of them alle, 'I gyve hym Gods blissyng and myne, and byd hym pray for my soule, and righteuously and worshipfully that he clayme the croune 10 upon forfeture of my blessyng,' and therwith he yelde up the ghost.

And thenne was he enterid as longed to a kyng, wherfor the quene, fayre Igrayne, made grete sorowe and alle the barons.

Thenne stood the reame in grete jeopardy long whyle, for every lord that was myghty of men maade hym stronge, and many wende to 15 have ben kyng. Thenne Merlyn wente to the Archebisshop of Caunterbury and counceilled hym for to sende for all the lordes of the reame and alle the gentilmen of armes, that they shold to London come by Cristmas upon payne of cursynge, and for this cause, that Jesu, that was borne on that nyghte, that He wold of His grete mercy shewe 20 some myracle, as He was come to be Kynge of mankynde, for to shewe somme myracle who shold be rightwys kynge of this reame. So the Archebisshop, by the advys of Merlyn, send for alle the lordes and gentilmen of armes that they shold come by Crystmasse even unto London; and many of hem made hem clene of her lyf, that her prayer 25 myghte be the more acceptable unto God.

Soo in the grettest chirch of London—whether it were Powlis or not the Frensshe booke maketh no mencyon—alle the estates were longe or day in the chirche for to praye. And whan matyns and the first masse was done there was sene in the chircheyard ayenst the 30 hyhe aulter a grete stone four square, lyke unto a marbel stone, and in myddes therof was lyke an anvylde of stele a foot on hyghe, and theryn stack a fayre swerd naked by the poynt, and letters there were wryten in gold about the swerd that saiden thus: 'Whoso pulleth oute this swerd of this stone and anvyld is rightwys kynge borne of all 35 En⟨g⟩lond.' Thenne the peple merveilled and told it to the Archebisshop.

'I commande,' said th'Archebisshop, 'that ye kepe yow within your chirche and pray unto God still; that no man touche the swerd tyll the hyhe masse be all done.' 40

So whan all masses were done all the lordes wente to beholde the stone and the swerd. And whan they sawe the scripture som assayed suche as wold have ben kyng, but none myght stere the swerd nor meve hit.

'He is not here,' said the Archebisshop, 'that shall encheve the swerd, but doubte not God will make hym knowen. But this is my counceill,' said the Archebisshop, 'that we lete purvey ten knyghtes, men of good fame, and they to kepe this swerd.'

5   So it was ordeyned, and thenne ther was made a crye that every man shold assay that wold for to wynne the swerd. And upon Newe Yeers day the barons lete maake a justes and a tournement, that alle knyghtes that wold juste or tourneye there myght playe. And all this was ordeyned for to kepe the lordes togyders and the comyns, for the Arche-
10 bisshop trusted that God wold make hym knowe that shold wynne the swerd.

So upon New Yeres day, whan the servyce was done, the barons rode unto the feld, some to juste and som to torney. And so it happed that syre Ector that had grete lyvelode aboute London rode unto the
15 justes, and with hym rode syr Kaynus, his sone, and yong Arthur that was hys nourisshed broder; and syr Kay was made knyght at Alhalowmas afore. So as they rode to the justes-ward sir Kay had lost his suerd, for he had lefte it at his faders lodgyng, and so he prayd yong Arthur for to ryde for his swerd.

20   'I wyll wel,' said Arthur, and rode fast after the swerd.

And whan he cam home the lady and al were out to see the joustyng. Thenne was Arthur wroth and saide to hymself, 'I will ryde to the chircheyard and take the swerd with me that stycketh in the stone, for my broder sir Kay shal not be without a swerd this day.' So whan he
25 cam to the chircheyard sir Arthur alight and tayed his hors to the style, and so he wente to the tent and found no knyghtes there, for they were atte justyng. And so he handled the swerd by the handels, and lightly and fiersly pulled it out of the stone, and took his hors and rode his way untyll he came to his broder sir Kay and delyverd hym the swerd.
30 And as sone as sir Kay saw the swerd he wist wel it was the swerd of the stone, and so he rode to his fader syr Ector and said,

'Sire, loo here is the swerd of the stone, wherfor I must be kyng of thys land.'

When syre Ector beheld the swerd he retorned ageyne and cam to
35 the chirche, and there they alighte al thre and wente into the chirche, and anon he made sir Kay to swere upon a book how he came to that swerd.

'Syr,' said sir Kay, 'by my broder Arthur, for he brought it to me.'

'How gate ye this swerd?' said sir Ector to Arthur.
40   'Sir, I will telle you. When I cam home for my broders swerd I fond nobody at home to delyver me his swerd. And so I thought my broder syr Kay shold not be swerdles, and so I cam hyder egerly and pulled it out of the stone withoute ony payn.'

'Found ye ony knyghtes about this swerd?' seid sir Ector.

'Nay,' said Arthur.

'Now,' said sir Ector to Arthur, 'I understande ye must be kynge of this land.'

'Wherfore I?' sayd Arthur, 'and for what cause?'

'Sire,' saide Ector, 'for God wille have hit soo, for ther shold never 5 man have drawen oute this swerde but he that shal be rightwys kyng of this land. Now lete me see whether ye can putte the swerd theras it was and pulle hit oute ageyne.'

'That is no maystry,' said Arthur, and soo he put it in the stone. Therwithalle sir Ector assayed to pulle oute the swerd and faylled.   10

'Now assay', said syre Ector unto syre Kay. And anon he pulled at (6) the swerd with alle his myghte, but it wold not be.

'Now shal ye assay,' said syre Ector to Arthur.

'I wyll wel,' said Arthur, and pulled it out easily.

And therwithalle syre Ector knelyd doune to the erthe and syre Kay.   15

'Allas!' said Arthur, 'myne own dere fader and broder, why knele ye to me?'

'Nay, nay, my lord Arthur, it is not so. I was never your fader nor of your blood, but I wote wel ye are of an hyher blood than I wende ye were.' And thenne syre Ector told hym all how he was bitaken hym 20 for to nourisshe hym and by whoos commandement, and by Merlyns delyveraunce.

Thenne Arthur made grete doole whan he understood that syre Ector was not his fader.

'Sir,' said Ector unto Arthur, 'woll ye be my good and gracious lord 25 when ye are kyng?'

'Els were I to blame,' said Arthur, 'for ye are the man in the world that I am most beholdyng to, and my good lady and moder your wyf that as wel as her owne hath fostred me and kepte. And yf ever hit be Goddes will that I be kynge as ye say, ye shall desyre of me what I may 30 doo and I shalle not faille yow. God forbede I shold faille yow.'

'Sir,' said sire Ector, 'I will aske no more of yow but that ye wille make my sone, your foster broder syre Kay, se⟨ne⟩ceall of alle your landes.'

'That shalle be done,' said Arthur, 'and more, by the feith of my 35 body, that never man shalle have that office but he whyle he and I lyve.'

Therewithall they wente unto the Archebisshop and told hym how the swerd was encheved and by whome. And on twelfth day alle the barons cam thyder and to assay to take the swerd who that wold assay, but there afore hem alle ther myghte none take it out but Arthur. 40 Wherfor ther were many lordes wroth, and saide it was grete shame unto them all and the reame to be overgovernyd with a boye of no hyghe blood borne. And so they fell oute at that tyme, that it was put of tyll Candelmas, and thenne all the barons shold mete there ageyne; but

alwey the ten knyghtes were ordeyned to watche the swerd day and
nyght, and so they sette a pavelione over the stone and the swerd, and
fyve alwayes watched.

Soo at Candalmasse many moo grete lordes came thyder for to have
5　wonne the swerde, but there myghte none prevaille. And right as
Arthur dyd at Cristmasse he dyd at Candelmasse, and pulled oute the
swerde easely, wherof the barons were sore agreved and put it of in delay
till the hyghe feste of Eester. And as Arthur sped afore so dyd he at
Eester. Yet there were some of the grete lordes had indignacion that
10　Arthur shold be kynge, and put it of in a delay tyll the feest of Pentecoste. Thenne the Archebisshop of Caunterbury by Merlyns provydence lete purveye thenne of the best knyghtes that they myghte gete,
and suche knyghtes as Uther Pendragon loved best and moost trusted
in his dayes. And suche knyghtes were put aboute Arthur as syr
15　Bawdewyn of Bretayn, syre Kaynes, syre Ulfyus, syre Barsias; all these
with many other were alweyes about Arthur day and nyghte till the
feste of Pentecost.

(7)　And at the feste of Pentecost alle maner of men assayed to pulle at
the swerde that wold assay, but none myghte prevaille but Arthur, and
20　he pulled it oute afore all the lordes and comyns that were there. Wherfore alle the comyns cryed at ones,

'We wille have Arthur unto our kyng! We wille put hym no more
in delay, for we all see that it is Goddes wille that he shalle be our
kynge, and who that holdeth ageynst it, we wille slee hym.' And ther-
25　withall they knelyd at ones, both ryche and poure, and cryed Arthur
mercy bycause they had delayed hym so longe. And Arthur foryaf hem
and took the swerd bitwene both his handes and offred it upon the
aulter where the Archebisshop was, and so was he made knyghte of the
best man that was there. And so anon was the coronacyon made, and
30　ther was he sworne unto his lordes and the comyns for to be a true
kyng, to stand with true justyce fro thens forth the dayes of this lyf.

Also thenne he made alle lordes that helde of the croune to come in
and to do servyce as they oughte to doo. And many complayntes were
made unto sir Arthur of grete wronges that were done syn the dethe
35　of kyng Uther, of many londes that were bereved lordes, knyghtes,
ladyes, and gentilmen. Wherfor kynge Arthur maade the londes to be
yeven ageyne unto them that oughte hem.

Whanne this was done, that the kyng had stablisshed alle the countryes
aboute London, thenne he lete make syr Kay sencial of Englond, and
40　sir Baudewyn of Bretayne was made constable, and sir Ulfyus was
made chamberlayn, and sire Brastias was maade wardeyn to wayte
upon the Northe fro Trent forwardes, for it was that tyme the most
party the kynges enemyes. But within fewe yeres after Arthur wan alle
the North, Scotland, and alle that were under their obeissaunce, also

Walys. A parte of it helde ayenst Arthur, but he overcam hem al, as he
dyd the remenaunt, thurgh the noble prowesse of hymself and his
knyghtes of the Round Table.

Thenne the kyng remeved into Walys and lete crye a grete feste, (8)
that it shold be holdyn at Pentecost after the incoronacion of hym at 5
the cyté of Carlyon. Unto the fest come kyng Lott of Lowthean and of
Orkeney with fyve hondred knyghtes with hym; also ther come to the
feste kynge Uryens of Gore with four hondred knyghtes with hym;
also ther come to that feeste kyng Nayntres of Garloth with seven
hundred knyghtes with hym; also ther came to the feest the Kynge of 10
Scotland with sixe honderd knyghtes with hym, and he was but a yong
man. Also ther came to the feste a kyng that was called the Kyng with
the Honderd Knyghtes, but he and his men were passyng wel bisene
at al poyntes; also ther cam the kyng of Cardos with fyve honderd
knyghtes.   15

And kyng Arthur was glad of their comynge, for he wende that al
the kynges and knyghtes had come for grete love and to have done
hym worship at his feste, wherfor the kyng made grete joye and sente
the kynges and knyghtes grete presentes. But the kynges wold none
receyve, but rebuked the messagers shamefully and said they had no 20
joye to receyve no yeftes of a berdles boye that was come of lowe
blood, and sente hym word they wold none of his yeftes, but that they
were come to gyve hym yeftes with hard swerdys betwixt the neck and
the sholders; and therfore they came thyder, so they told to the messagers playnly, for it was grete shame to all them to see suche a boye to 25
have a rule of soo noble a reaume as this land was. With this ansuer the
messagers departed and told to kyng Arthur this ansuer, wherfor by
the advys of his barons he took hym to a strong towre with fyve
hondred good men with hym. And all the kynges aforesaid in a maner
leyd a syege tofore hym, but kyng Arthur was well vytailled.   30

And within fyftene dayes ther came Merlyn amonge hem into the
cyté of Carlyon. Thenne all the kynges were passyng gladde of Merlyn
and asked hym,

'For what cause is that boye Arthur made your kynge?'

'Syres,' said Merlyn, 'I shalle telle yow the cause, for he is kynge 35
Uther Pendragons sone borne in wedlok, goten on Igrayne, the dukes
wyf of Tyntigail.'

'Thenne is he a bastard,' they said al.

'Nay,' said Merlyn, 'after the deth of the duke more than thre houres
was Arthur begoten, and thirtene dayes after kyng Uther wedded 40
Igrayne, and therfor I preve hym he is no bastard. And, who saith nay,
he shal be kyng and overcome alle his enemyes, and or he deye he
shalle be long kynge of all Englond and have under his obeyssaunce
Walys, Yrland, and Scotland, and moo reames than I will now reherce.'

Some of the kynges had merveyl of Merlyns wordes and demed well that it shold be as he said, and som of hem lough hym to scorne, as kyng Lot, and mo other called hym a wytche. But thenne were they accorded with Merlyn that kynge Arthur shold come oute and speke 5 with the kynges, and to come sauf and to goo sauf, suche suraunce ther was made. So Merlyn went unto kynge Arthur and told hym how he had done and badde hym fere not, but come oute boldly and speke with hem, and spare hem not, but ansuere them as their kynge and chyvetayn, 'for ye shal overcome hem all, whether they wille or 10 nylle'.

(9)   Thenne kynge Arthur came oute of his tour and had under his gowne a jesseraunte of double maylle, and ther wente with hym the Archebisshop of Caunterbury, and syr Baudewyn of Bretayne, and syr Kay, and syre Brastias; these were the men of moost worship that 15 were with hym. And whan they were mette there was no mekenes but stoute wordes on bothe sydes, but alweyes kynge Arthur ansuerd them and said he wold make them to bowe and he lyved, wherfore they departed with wrath. And kynge Arthur badde kepe hem wel, and they bad the kynge kepe hym wel. Soo the kynge retornyd hym to 20 the toure ageyne and armed hym and alle his knyghtes.

'What will ye do?' said Merlyn to the kynges. 'Ye were better for to stynte, for ye shalle not here prevaille, though ye were ten so many.'

'Be we wel avysed to be aferd of a dreme-reder?' said kyng Lot.

With that Merlyn vanysshed aweye and came to kynge Arthur and 25 bad hym set on hem fiersly. And in the menewhyle there were thre honderd good men of the best that were with the kynges that wente streyghte unto kynge Arthur, and that comforted hym gretely.

'Syr,' said Merlyn to Arthur, 'fyghte not with the swerde that ye had by myracle til that ye see ye go unto the wers; thenne drawe it out and 30 do your best.'

So forthwithalle kynge Arthur sette upon hem in their lodgyng, and syre Bawdewyn, syre Kay, and syr Brastias slewe on the right hand and on the lyfte hand, that it was merveylle; and alweyes kynge Arthur on horsback leyd on with a swerd and dyd merveillous dedes of armes, 35 that many of the kynges had grete joye of his dedes and hardynesse. Thenne kynge Lot brake out on the bak syde, and the Kyng with the Honderd Knyghtes and kyng Carados, and sette on Arthur fiersly behynde hym.

With that syre Arthur torned with his knyghtes and smote behynd 40 and before, and ever sir Arthur was in the formest prees tyl his hors was slayne undernethe hym. And therwith kynge Lot smote doune kyng Arthur. With that his four knyghtes re⟨scow⟩ed hym and set hym on horsback; thenne he drewe his swerd Excalibur, but it was so bryght in his enemyes eyen that it gaf light lyke thirty torchys, and

therwith he put hem on bak and slewe moche peple. And thenne the
comyns of Carlyon aroos with clubbis and stavys and slewe many
knyghtes, but alle the kynges helde them togyders with her knyghtes
that were lefte on lyve, and so fled and departed; and Merlyn come unto
Arthur and counceilled hym to folowe hem no further.   5

So after the feste and journeye kynge Arthur drewe hym unto (10)
London. And soo by the counceil of Merlyn the kyng lete calle his
barons to counceil, for Merlyn had told the kynge that the sixe kynges
that made warre upon hym wold in al haste be awroke on hym and on
his landys; wherfor the kyng asked counceil at hem al. They coude no 10
counceil gyve, but said they were bygge ynough.

'Ye saye well,' said Arthur, 'I thanke you for your good courage;
but wil ye al that loveth me spcke with Merlyn? Yc knowe wel that he
hath done moche for me, and he knoweth many thynges. And whan he
is afore you I wold that ye prayd hym hertely of his best avyse.'   15

Alle the barons sayd they wold pray hym and desyre hym. Soo Merlyn
was sente for and fair desyred of al the barons to gyve them best
counceil.

'I shall say you,' said Merlyn, 'I warne yow al, your enemyes are
passyng strong for yow, and they are good men of armes as ben on 20
lyve. And by thys tyme they have goten to them four kynges mo and
a myghty duke, and onlesse that our kyng have more chyvalry with
hym than he may make within the boundys of his own reame, and
he fyghte with hem in batail, he shal be overcome and slayn.'

'What were best to doo in this cause?' said al the barons.   25

'I shal telle you,' said Merlyn, 'myne advys. Ther ar two bretheren
beyond the see, and they be kynges bothe and merveillous good men
of her handes: and that one hyghte kynge Ban of Benwic, and that
other hyght kyng Bors of Gaule, that is Fraunce. And on these two
kynges warrith a myghty man of men, the kynge Claudas, and stryveth 30
with hem for a castel; and grete werre is betwixt them. But this Claudas
is so myghty of goodes wherof he geteth good knyghtes that he putteth
these two kynges moost parte ⟨t⟩o the werse. Wherfor this is my
counceil: that our kyng and soverayne lord sende unto the kynges Ban
and Bors by two trusty knyghtes with letters well devysed, that and 35
they wil come and see] kynge Arthur and his courte to helpe hym in
hys warrys, that he wolde be sworne unto them to helpe hem in theire
warrys agaynst kynge Claudas. Now what sey ye unto thys counceyle?'
seyde Merlyon.

'Thys ys well councelde,' seyde the kynge.   40

And in all haste two barownes ryght so were ordayned to go on
thys message unto thes two kyngis, and lettirs were made in the most
plesauntist wyse accordynge unto kynge Arthurs desyre, and Ulphuns
and Brastias were made the messyngers; and so rode forth well horsed

and well i-armed and as the gyse was that tyme, and so passed the see
and rode towarde the cité of Benwyk. And there besydes were eyght
knyghtes that aspyed hem, and at a strayte passage they mette with
Ulphuns and Brastias and wolde a takyn them presoners. So they
5 preyde them that they myght passe, for they were messyngers unto
kyng Ban and Bors isente frome kynge Arthure.

'Therefore,' seyde the knyghtes, 'ye shall dey othir be presoners, for
we be knyghtes of kynge Claudas.'

And therewith two of them dressed their speris unto Ulphuns and
10 Brastias, and they dressed their sperys and ran togydir with grete
random. And Claudas his knyghtes brake theire spearis, and Ulphuns
and Brastias bare the two knyghtes oute of their sadils to the erth and
so leffte them lyynge and rode their wayes. And the other six knyghtes
rode before to a passage to mete with them ayen, and so Ulphuns and
15 Brastias othir two smote downe and so paste on hir wayes. And at the
fourthe passage there mette two for two and bothe were leyde unto
the erthe. So there was none of the eyght knyghtes but he was hurte
sore othir brused.

And whan they com to Benwyke hit fortuned both the kynges be
20 there, Ban and Bors. Than was hit tolde the two kyngis how there
were com two messyngers. And anone there was sente unto them two
knyghtes of worship, that one hyght Lyonses, lorde of the contrey of
ᴦPayarneᴸ, and sir Pharyaunce, a worshipfull knyght; and anone asked
them frome whens they com, and they seyde frome kyng Arthure, kynge
25 of Ingelonde. And so they toke them in theire armys and made grete
joy eche of othir. But anone as they wyste they were messyngers of
Arthurs there was made no taryynge, but forthwith they spake with
the kyngis. And they welcommed them in the moste faythfullyst wyse
and seyde they were moste welcom unto them before all the kynges
30 men lyvynge. And therewith they kyssed the lettirs and delyvird them.
And whan kynge Ban and Bors undirstoode them and the lettirs, than
were they more welcom than they were tofore.

And aft[i]r the haste of the lettirs they gaff hem thys answere that
they wolde fulfille th[e] desire of kyng Arthurs wrytynge, and bade sir
35 Ulphuns and sir Brastias tarry there as longe as they wolde, for they
shulde have such chere as myght be made for them in thys marchis.
Than Ulphuns and Brastias tolde the kynge⟨s⟩ of theire adventure at
the passagis for the eyght knyghtes.

'A ha,' seyde Ban and Bors, 'they were oure good frendis. I wolde I
40 had wyste of them, and they sholde nat so [have] ascaped.'

So thes two knyghtes had good chere and grete gyfftis as much as
they myght bere away, and had theire answere by mowth and by
wrytynge that the two kynges wolde com unto Arthure in all the haste
that they myght. So thes two knyghtes rode on afore and passed the see

and com to their lorde and tolde hym how they had spedde, wherefore
kyng Arthure was passyng glad and seyde,
'How suppose you, at what tyme woll thes two kynges be here?'
'Sir,' they seyde, 'before Allhalowmasse.'
    Than the kynge lette purvey for a grete feste, and also he lette cry 5
both turnementis and justis thorowoute all his realme, and the day
appoynted and sette at Allhalowmasse. And so the tyme drove on and
all thynges redy ipurveyed. Thes two noble kynges were entirde the
londe and comyn ovir the see with three hondred knyghtes full well
arayed both for the pees and also for the werre. And so royally they 10
were resceyved and brought towarde the cité of London. And so
Arthure mette them ten myle oute of London, and there was grete joy
made as couthe be thought.
    And on Allhalowmasse day at the grete feste sate in the halle the
three kynges, and sir Kay the Senesciall served in the halle, and sir 15
Lucas the Butler that was Duke Corneus son, and sir Grÿfflet that was
the son of God of Cardal: thes three knyghtes had the rule of all the
servyse that served the kyngis. And anone as they were redy and way-
she[n], all the knyghtes that wolde juste made hem redy. And be than
they were redy on horsebak there was seven hondred knyghtes. And 20
kynge Arthure, Ban, and Bors, with the Archebysshop of Caunterbyry,
and sir Ector, Kays fadir, they were in a place covirde with clothys of
golde lyke unto an halle, with ladyes and jantillwomen for to beholde
who dud beste and thereon to gyff a jugemente.
    And kyng Arthure with the two kyngis lette departe the seven 25 (11)
hondred knyghtes in two partyes. And there were three hondred
knyghtes of the realme of Benwyke and Gaule that turned on the othir
syde. And they dressed their shyldis and began to couche hir speyys,
many good knyghtes. So sir Grÿfflet was the first that sette oute, and
to hym com a knyght, hys name was sir Ladynas, and they com so 30
egirly togydir that all men had wondir, and they so sore fought that hir
shyldis felle on pecis and both horse and man felle to the erthe, and
both the Frensh knyght and the Englysh knyght lay so longe that all
men wente they had bene dede. Whan Lucas the Butler saw sir Grÿfflet
ly so longe, he horsed hym agayne anone, and they too ded many 35
mervelous dedis of armys with many bachelers.
    Also sir Kay com oute of a bushemente with fyve knyghtes with
hym, and they six smote othir six downe. But sir Kay dud that day
many mervaylous dedis of armys, that there was none that dud so welle
as he that day. Than there com Ladynas and Grastian, two knyghtes of 40
Fraunse, and dud passynge well, that all men praysed them. Than com
in sir Placidas, a good knyght, that mette with sir Kay and smote hym
downe horse and man, wherefore sir Grÿfflet was wroth and mette with
sir Placidas so harde that horse and man felle to the erthe. But whan

the fyve knyghtes wyst that sir Kay had a falle they were wroth oute of mesure and therewithall ech of them fyve bare downe a knyght.

Whan kynge Arthur and the two kynges saw hem begynne wexe wroth on bothe partyes, they leped on smale hakeneyes and lette cry
5 that all men sholde departe unto theire lodgynge. And so they wente home and unarmed them, and so to evynsonge and souper. And aftir souper the three kynges wente into a gardyne and gaff the pryce unto sir Kay and unto sir Lucas the Butler and unto sir Gryfflet. And than they wente unto counceyle, and with hem Gwenbaus, brothir unto
10 kynge Ban and Bors, a wyse clerke; and thidir wente Ulphuns, Brastias and Merlion. And aftir they had [ben] in her counceyle they wente unto bedde. And on the morne they harde masse, and to dyner and so to theire counceyle, and made many argumentes what were beste to do.

So at the laste they were concluded that Merlion sholde go with a
15 tokyn of kynge Ban, that was a rynge, unto hys men and kynge Bors, [and] Gracian and Placidas sholde go agayne and kepe their castels and theire contreyes, for kynge Ban of Benwyke and kynge Bors of Gaule had ordayned them all thynge. And so passed ⟨they⟩ the see and com to Benwyke. And whan the people saw ekynge Bannys rynge, and
20 Gracian and Placidas, they were glad and asked how theire kynge fared and made grete joy of their welfare. And accordyng unto theire soveraigne lordis desire, the m[e]n of warre made hem redy in all haste possible, so that they were fyftene thousand on horsebacke and foote, and they had grete plenté of vitayle by Merlions provisions. But
25 Gracian and Placidas were leffte at home to furnysh and garnysh the castel[s] for drede of kyng Claudas.

Ryght so Merlion passed the see well vitayled bothe by watir and by londe. And whan he com to the see he sente home the footemen agayne, and toke no mo with hym but ten thousand men on horsebake, the
30 moste party of men of armys; and so [s]hipped and passed the see into Inglonde and londed at Dovir. And thorow the wytte of Merlion he ledde the oste northwarde the pryvéyst wey that coude be thought, unto the foreste of Bedgrayne, and there in a valey lodged h[e]m secretely. Than rode Merlion to Arthure and to the two kynges, and
35 tolde hem how he had spedde, whereof they had grete mervayle that ony man on erthe myght spede so sone to go and com. So Merlion tolde them how ten thousandé were in the forest of Bedgrayne well armed at all poyntis.

Than was there no more to sey, but to horsebak wente all the oste as
40 Arthure had before provyded. So with twenty thousand he passed by nyght and day. Bu[t] there was made such an ordinaunce afore by Merlyon that there sholde no man of warre ryde nothir go in no contrey on this syde Trente watir but if he had a tokyn frome kynge Arthure, wherethorow the kynges enemyes durst nat ryde as they dud tofore to

aspye. And so wythin a litill whyle the three kyngis com to the forest (12)
of Bedgrayne and founde there a passynge fayre felyship and well
besene, whereof they had grete joy, and vitayle they wanted none.

Thys was the causis of the northir hoste, that they were rered for the
despite and rebuke that the ⌐six⌐ kyngis had at Carlyon. And tho six 5
kyngis by hir meanys gate unto them fyve othir kyngis, and thus they
began to gadir hir people. And ⟨now⟩ they swore nother for welle
nothyr wo they sholde nat lyve tyll they had destroyed Arthure, and
than they made an othe. And the first that began the othe was the
deuke of Can⌐benet⌐, that he wolde brynge with hym ⌐fyve⌐ thousand 10
men of armys, the which were redy on horsebakke. Than swore kynge
Brandegoris of Strangore that he wolde brynge with hym fyve thousand men of armys on horsebacke. Than swore kynge Clarivaus of
Northumbirlonde [that he] wolde brynge ⌐three⌐ thousand men of
armys with hym. Than swore the Kynge with the Hondred Knyghtes 15
that was a passynge good man and a yonge, that he wold brynge four
thousand good men of armys on horsebacke.

Than there swore kynge Lott, a passyng good knyght and fadir unto
sir Gawayne, that he wolde brynge fyve thousand good men of armys
on horsebak. Also the[re] swore kynge Uryens that was sir Uwaynes 20
fadir, of the londe of Goore, and he wolde brynge six thousand men of
armys on horsebak. Also there swore kynge Idres of Cornuwaile that
he wolde brynge fyve thousand men of armys on horsebake. Also there
swore kynge Cradilmans to brynge fyve thousand men on horsebacke.
Also there swore kyng Angwysshauns of Irelonde to brynge fyve 25
thousand men of armys on horsebak. Also there swore kynge Nentres
to brynge fyve thousand men on horsebak. Also there swore kynge
Carados to brynge fyve thousand men of armys on horsebak. So hir
hole oste was of clene men of armys: on horsebacke was fully fyffty
thousand, and on foote ten thousand of good mennes bodyes. 30

Than they were sone redy and mounted uppon horsebacke, and
sente forthe before the foreryders. For thes a eleven kynges in hir
wayes leyde a sege unto the castell of Bedgrayne; and so they departed
and drew towarde Arthure, and leffte a fewe to byde at the sege, for the
castell of Bedgrayne was an holde of kynge Arthurs and the men that 35
were within were kynge Arthurs men all.

So by Merlyons advice there were sente foreryders to skymme the (13)
contrey; and they mette with the foreryders of the Northe and made
hem to telle which way the oste com. And than they tolde kynge Arthure,
and by kynge Ban and Bors his counceile they lette brenne and destroy 40
all the contrey before them there they sholde ryde.

The Kynge of the Hondred Knyghtis that tyme mette a wondir
dreme two nyghtes before the batayle: that there blew a grete wynde
and blew downe hir castels and hir townys, and aftir that com a watir

and bare hit all away. And all that herde of that swevyn seyde hit was a tokyn of grete batayle. Than by counceile of Merlion, whan they wyst which wey the an eleven kynges wolde ryde and lodge that nyght, at mydnyght they sette uppon them as they were in their pavilions. But 5 the scowte-wacche by hir oste cryed:

'Lordis, to ⌐armes⌐! for here be oure enemyes at youre honde!'

(14)   Than kynge Arthur and kynge Ban and Bors with hir good and trusty knyghtes sette uppon them so fersely that he made them overthrowe hir pavilons on hir hedis. But the eleven kynges by manly 10 prouesse of armys toke a fayre champion, but there was slayne that morow tyde ten thousand good mennes bodyes. And so they had before hem a stronge passage; yet were there fyffty thousand of hardy men. Than hit drew toward day.

'Now shall ye do by myne advice,' seyde Merlyon unto the three 15 kyngis, and seyde: 'I wolde kynge Ban and Bors with hir felyship of ten thousand men were put in a woode here besyde in an inbusshemente and kept them prevy, and that they be leyde or the lyght of the day com, and that they stire nat tyll that ye and youre knyghtes a fought with hem longe. And whan hit ys daylyght, dresse youre batayle evyn 20 before them and the passage, that they may se all youre oste, for than woll they be the more hardy whan they se you but aboute twenty thousande, and cause hem to be the gladder to suffir you and youre oste to com over the passage.'

All the three kynges and the hole barownes seyde how Merlion de-25 vised passynge well, and so hit was done.

So on the morn whan aythir oste saw othir, they of the Northe were well comforted. Than Ulphuns and Brastias were delyvirde three thousand men of armys, and they sette on them fersely in the passage, and slew on the ryght honde and on the lyffte honde that hit was 30 wondir to telle. But whan the eleven kynges saw that there was so few a felyship that dud such dedis of armys, they were ashamed and sette on hem agayne fersely. And there was sir Ulphuns horse slayne, but he dud merveylously on foote. But the duke Es⌐t⌐anse of Can⌐benet⌐ and kynge Clarivaunce of Northehumbirlonde were allwey grevously set 35 on Ulphuns. Than sir Brastias saw his felow yfared so withall, he smote the duke with a spere, that horse and man felle downe. That saw kyng Claryvauns, and returne[d] unto sir Brastias, and eythir smote othir so that horse and man wente to the erthe. And so they lay longe astoned, and theire horse knees braste to the harde bone.

40   Than com sir Kay the Seneschall with six felowis with hym and dud passynge well. So with that com the eleven kyngis, and there was Gryfflette put to the erth horse and man, and Lucas the Butler horse and man, kynge Brandegoris and kynge Idres and kynge Angwyshaunce. Than wexed the medlee passyng harde on bothe parties. Whan sir

Kay saw sir Gryfflet on foote, he rode unto kynge Nentres and smote
hym downe, and ledde his horse unto sir Gryfflette and horsed hym
agayne. Also sir Kay with the same spere smote downe kynge Lotte and
hurte hym passynge sore. That saw the Kynge with the Hondred
Knyghtes and ran unto sir Kay and smote hym downe, and toke hys 5
horse and gaff hym kynge Lotte, whereof he seyde gramercy. Whan sir
Gryfflet saw sir Kay and sir Lucas de Butler on foote, he with a sherpe
spere grete and square rode to Pynnel, a good man of armys, and smote
horse and man downe, and than he toke hys horse and gaff hym unto
sir Kay.   10
    Than kynge Lotte saw kynge Nentres on foote, he ran unto Meliot
de la Roche and smote hym downe horse and man, and gaff ⟨unto⟩
kynge Nentres the horse and horsed hym agayne. Also the Kynge with
the Hondred Knyghtes saw kynge Idres on foote, he ran unto Gwyniarte
de Bloy and smote hym downe horse and man, and gaff kynge Idres 15
the horse and horsed hym agayne. Tha[n] kynge Lotte smote downe
Clarinaus de la Foreyste Saveage and gaff the horse unto duke Estans.
And so whan they had horsed the kyngis agayne, they drew hem all
eleven kynges togydir, and seyde they wolde be revenged of the damage
that they had takyn that day.   20
    The meanewhyle com in kyng Arthure with an egir countenans, and
founde Ulphuns and Brastias on foote, in grete percll of dethe, that
were fowle defoyled undir the horse feete. Than Arthure as a lyon ran
unto kynge Cradilment of North Walis and smote hym thorow the lyffte
syde, that horse and man felle downe. Than he toke the horse by the 25
reygne and lcd hym unto Ulphine and seyde,
    'Have this horse, myne olde frende, for grete nede hast thou of an
horse.'
    'Gramercy,' seyde Ulphuns.
    Than kynge Arthure dud so mervaylesly in armys that all men had 30
wondir. Whan the Kyng with the Hondred Knyghtes saw kynge
Cradilmente on foote, he ran unto sir Ector, sir Kayes fadir, that was
well ihorsed and smote horse and man downe, and gaff the horse unto
the kynge and horsed hym agayne. And whan kynge Arthure saw that
kynge ryde on sir Ectors horse he was wrothe, and with hys swerde he 35
smote the kynge on the helme, that a quarter of the helme and shelde
clave downe; and so the swerde carve downe unto the horse necke,
and so man and horse felle downe to the grounde. Than sir Kay com
unto kynge Morganoure, senesciall with the Kynge of the Hondred
Knyghtes, and smote hym downe horse and man, and ledde the horse 40
unto hys fadir, sir Ector.
    Than sir Ector ran unto a knyght that hyght Lardans and smote
horse and man downe, and lad the horse unto sir Brastias, that grete
nede had of an horse and was gretly defoyled. Whan Brastias behelde

Lucas the Butler that lay lyke a dede man undir the horse feete—and
ever sir Gryflet dud mercyfully for to reskow hym, and there were
allwayes fourtene knyghtes upon sir Lucas—and than sir Brastias
smote one of them on the helme, that hit wente unto his tethe; and he
5 rode unto another and smote hym, that hys arme flowe into the felde;
than he wente to the thirde and smote hym on the shulder, that sholdir
and arme flow unto the felde. And whan Gryfflet saw rescowis he
smote a knyght on the templis, that hede and helme wente of to the
erthe; and Gryfflet toke that horse and lad hym unto sir Lucas, and
10 bade hym mownte uppon that horse and revenge his hurtis—for sir
Brastias had slayne a knyght tofore—and horsed sir Lucas.

(15)   Than sir Lucas saw kynge Angwysschaunce that nygh⌐e⌐ had slayne
Maris de la Roche; and Lucas ran to hym with a sherpe spere that was
grete, and he gaff hym suche a falle that the horse felle downe to the
15 erthe. Also Lucas founde there on foote Bloyas de la Fla⌐un⌐dres and
sir Gwynas, two hardy knyghtes; and in that woodnes that Lucas was
in, he slew two bachelers and horsed them agayne. Than wexed the
batayle passynge harde one bothe partyes. But kynge Arthur was glad
that hys knyghtes were horsed agayne. And than they fought togiders,
20 that the noyse and the sowne range by the watir and woode. Wherefore kynge Ban and Bors made hem redy and dressed theire shyldis and
harneysse, and were so currageous that their enemyes shooke and
byverd for egirnesse.

All thys whyle sir Lucas, Gwynas, Bryaunte, and Bellias of Flaundres
25 helde stronge medlé agaynste six kynges, which were kynge Lott, kynge
Nentres, kynge Brandegoris, kynge Idres, kyng Uriens and kynge
Angwysshauns. So with the helpe of sir Kay and of sir Gryfflet they
helde thes six kyngis harde, that unneth they had ony power to deffende
them. But whan kynge Arthure saw the batayle wolde nat be ended
30 by no maner, he fared woode as a lyon and stirred his horse here and
there on the ryght honde and on the lyffte honde, that he stynted nat
tylle he had slayne twenty knyghtes. Also he wounded kynge Lotte
sore on the shulder, and made hym to leve that grownde, for sir
Kay with sir Gryfflet dud with kynge Arthure grete dedis of armys
35 there.

Than sir Ulphuns, Brastias and sir Ector encountirde agaynste the
duke Estans and kynge Cradilmante and kynge Clarivauns of Northhumbirlonde and kynge Carados and the Kynge with the Hondred
Knyghtes. So thes kynges encountird with thes knyghtes, that they
40 made them to avoyde the grounde. Than kynge Lotte made grete dole
for his damagis and his felowis, and seyde unto the kyngis,

'But if we woll do as I have devised, we all shall be slayne and destroyed. Lette me have the Kynge with the Hondred Knyghtes, and
kynge Angwysshaunce, and kynge Idres, and the duke of Can⌐benet⌐.

And we fyve kyngis woll have ten thousand men of armys with us,
and we woll go on one party whyle the six kynges holde the medlé with
twelve thousand. And whan we se that ye have foughtyn with hem
longe, than woll we com on freysshly; and ellis shall we never macche
them,' seyde kynge Lotte, 'but by thys means.'   5

So they departed as they here devised, and thes six kyngis made
theire party stronge agaynste kyng Arthure and made grete warre
longe in the meanewhyle.

Than brake the bushemente of kynge Banne and Bors; and Lionse
and Phariaunce had that advaunte-garde, and they two knyghtes mette 10
with kynge Idres [and his felaush.ip. And there began a grete medelé of
brekyng of speres and smytyng of swerdys with sleying of men and
horses, that kynge Idres] was nere discomfited. That saw kynge Angwysshaunce, and put Lyonses and Phariaunce in poynte of dethe, for
the duke ⌐of Canbenet⌐ com on with a grete felyship. So thes two 15
knyghtes were in grete daungere of their lyves, that they were fayne to
returne; but allweyes they rescowed hemselff and hir felyship merveylously. Whan kynge Bors saw tho knyghtes put on bak hit greved hym
sore. Than he com on so faste that his felyship semed as blak as inde.
Whan kynge Lotte had aspyed kynge Bors, he knew hym well, and 20
seyde,

'Jesu defende us frome dethe and horryble maymes, for I se well we
be in grete perell of dethe; for I se yondir a kynge, one of the moste
worshipfullyst ⌐men, and the⌐ best knyghtes of the worlde be inclyned unto his felyship.'   25

'What ys he?' seyde the Kynge with the Hu[n]dirde Knyghtes.

'Hit ys,' he seyde, 'kynge Bors of Gaule. I mervayle,' seyde he, 'how
they com unto this contrey withoute wetynge of us all.'

'Hit was by Merlions advice,' seyde a knyght.

'As for me,' seyde kynge Carados, 'I woll encountir with kynge Bors, 30
and ye woll rescow me whan myster ys.'

'Go on,' seyde they, 'for we woll all that we may.'

Than kynge Carados and hys oste rode on a softte pace tyll they com
as nyghe kynge Bors as a bowe-draught. Than eythir lette theire horsys
renne as faste as they myght. And Bleobris that was godson unto kynge 35
Bors, he bare his chyeff standard; that was a passyng good knyght.

'Now shall we se,' seyde kynge Bors, 'how thes northirne Bretons
can bere theire armys!'

So kynge Bors encountird with a knyght and smote hym thorowoute
with a spere, that he felle dede unto the erthe; and aftirwarde drew hys 40
swerde and dud mervaylous dedis of armys, that all partyes had grete
wondir thereof. And his knyght[es] fayled nat but dud hir parte. And
kynge Carados was smytten to the erthe. With that com the Kynge
with the Hondred Knyghtes and rescowed kynge Carados myghtyly

by force of armys, for he was a passynge good knyght and but a yonge
(16) man. Be than com into the felde kynge Ban as ferse as a lyon, with
bondis of grene and thereuppon golde.

'A ha,' seyde kynge Lott, 'we muste be discomfite, for yondir I se
5 the most valiante knyght of the worlde, and the man of moste renowne,
for such two brethirne as ys kynge Ban and kynge Bors ar nat lyvynge.
Wherefore we muste nedis voyde or dye, and but if we avoyde manly
and wysely there ys but dethe.'

So whan thes two kyngis, Ban and Bors, com into the batayle, they
10 com in so fersely that the strokis re[d]ounded agayne fro the woode
and the watir. Wherefore kynge Lotte wepte for pité and dole that he
saw so many good knyghtes take their ende. But thorow the grete force
of kynge Ban they made bothe the northirne batayles that were parted
hurteled togidirs for grete drede. And the three kynges and their
15 knyghtes slew on ever, that hit was pité to se and to beholde the multitude of peple that fledde.

But kyng Lott and the Kynge with the Hundred Knyghtes and
kynge Morganoure gadred the peple togydir passynge knyghtly, and
dud grete proues of armys, and helde the batayle all the day lyke harde.
20 Whan the Kynge with the Hundred Knyghtes behelde the grete damage
that kynge Ban [dyd] he threste unto hym with his horse and smote
hym an hyghe on the helme a grete stroke and stoned hym sore. Than
kynge Ban was wood wrothe with hym and folowed on hym fersely.
The othir saw that and caste up hys shelde and spored hys horse fore-
25 warde, but the stroke of kynge Ban downe felle and carve a cantell of the
shelde, and the swerde sloode downe by the hawbirke byhynde hys
backe and kut thorow the trappoure of stele and the horse evyn in
two pecis, that the swerde felle to the erth. Than the Kynge of the
Hundred Knyghtes voyded the horse lyghtly, and with hys swerde
30 he broched the horse of kynge Ban thorow and thorow. With that
kynge Ban voyded lyghtly frome the dede horse and smote at that
othir so egirly on the helme that he felle to the erthe. Also in that ire
he felde kynge Morganoure, and there was grete slawghtir of good
knyghtes and muche peple.
35 Be that tyme com into the prees kynge Arthure and founde kynge
Ban stondynge amonge the dede men and dede horse, fyghtynge on
foote as a wood lyon, that there com none nyghe hym as farre as he
myght reche with hys swerde but he caught a grevous buffette; whereof
kynge Arthure had grete pité. And kynge Arthure was so blody that
40 by hys shylde there myght no man know hym, for all was blode and
brayne that stake on his swerde and on hys shylde. And as kynge
Arthure loked besyde hym he sawe a knyght that was passyngely well
horsed. And therewith kynge Arthure ran to hym and smote hym on
the helme, that hys swerde wente unto his teeth, and the knyght sanke

downe to the erthe dede. And anone kynge Arthure toke hys horse by
the rayne and ladde hym unto kynge Ban and seyde,

'Fayre brothir, have ye thys horse, for ye have grete myster thereof,
and me repentys sore of youre grete damage.'

'Hit shall be sone revenged,' seyde kynge Ban, 'for I truste in God   5
myne hurte ys none suche but som of them may sore repente thys.'

'I woll welle,' seyde kynge Arthure, 'for I se youre dedys full actuall;
nevertheles I myght nat com to you at that tyme.'

But whan kynge Ban was mounted on horsebak, than there began
a new batayle whych was sore and harde, and passynge grete slaughtir.   10
And so thorow grete force kyng Arthure, kynge Ban, and kynge Bors
made hir knyghtes alyght to wythdraw hem to a lytyll wood, and so
over a litill ryvir; and there they rested hem, for on the nyght before
they had no grete reste in the felde. And than the eleven kyngis put
hem on an hepe all togydirs, as men adrad and oute of all comforte.   15
But there was no man that myght passe them; they helde hem so harde
togydirs bothe behynde and before that kynge Arthure had mervayle
of theire dedis of armys and was passynge wrothe.

'A, sir Arthure,' seyde kynge Ban and kynge Bors, 'blame hem nat,
for they do as good men ought to do. For be my fayth,' seyde kynge   20
Ban, 'they ar the beste fyghtynge men and knyghtes of moste prouesse
that ever y saw other herde off speke. And tho eleven kyngis ar men
of grete worship; and if they were longyng to you, there were no
kynge undir hevyn that had suche eleven kyngis nother off suche
worship.'   25

'I may nat love hem,' seyde kynge Arthure, 'for they wolde destroy
me.'

'That know we well,' seyde kynge Ban and kynge Bors, 'for they ar
your mortall enemyes, and that hathe bene preved beforehonde. And
thys day they have done theire parte, and that ys grete pité of their   30
wylfulnes.'

Than all the eleven kyngcs drew hem togydir, and than seyde Lott,
'Lordis, ye muste do othirwyse than ye do, othir ellis the grete losses
ys behynde: for ye may se what peple we have loste and what good
men we lese because we wayte allweyes on thes footemen; and ever in   35
sauyng of one of thes footemen we lese ten horsemen for hym. Therefore thys ys myne advise: lette us putte oure footemen frome us, for
hit ys nere nyght. For thys noble kynge Arthure woll nat tarry on the
footemen, for they may save hemselff: the woode ys nerehonde. And
whan we horsemen be togydirs, looke every of you kyngis lat make   40
such ordinaunce that none breke uppon payne of deth. And who that
seeth any man dresse hym to fle lyghtly, that he be slayne; for hit ys
bettir we sle a cowarde than thorow a coward all we be slayned. How
sey ye?' seyde kynge Lotte. 'Answere me, all ye kynges!'

'Ye say well,' seyde kynge Nentres. So seyde the Kynge with the Hondred Knyghtes; the same seyde kynge Carados and kynge Uryens; so seyde kynge Idres and kynge Brandegoris; so dud kyng Cradilmasse and the duke of Can ⌐benet;⌐ the same seyde kynge Claryaunce, and so
5 dud kynge Angwysshaunce, and swore they wolde never fayle other for lyff nothir for dethe, and whoso that fledde all they sholde be slayne. Than they amended their harneyse and ryghted their sheldis, and toke newe speris and sette hem on theire thyghes, and stoode stylle as hit had be a plumpe of woode.

(17) 10   Whan kynge Arthure and kynge Ban and Bors behelde them and all hir knyghtes, they preysed them much for their noble chere of chevalry, fo[r] the hardyeste fyghters that ever they herde other sawe.

So furthwith there dressed ⟨twenty-one⟩ knyghtes, and seyde unto the three kynges they wolde breke their batayle. And thes were their
15 namys: Lyonses, Phariaunce, Ulphuns, Brastias, Ector, Kayus, Lucas de Butler, Gryfflet la Fyse de Deu, Marrys de la Roche, Gwynas de Bloy, Bryaunte de la Foreyste Saveage, Bellaus, Morians of the Castel Maydyns, Flaundreus of the Castel of Ladyes, Annecians that was kynge Bors godson, a noble knyght, and Ladinas de la Rouse,
20 Emerause, Caulas, Graciens le Castilion, Bloyse de la Case, and sir Colgrevaunce de Goore.

All thes knyghtes rode on before with sperys on theire thyghes and spurred their horses myghtyly. And the eleven kyngis with parte of hir knyghtes rushed furthe as faste as they myght with hir sperys, and
25 there they dud on bothe partyes merveylous dedes of armys. So there com into the thycke of the prees Arthure, Ban, and Bors, and slew downeryght on bothe hondis, that hir horses wente in blood up to the fittlockys. But ever the eleven kyngis and the oste was ever in the visage of Arthure. Wherefore kynge Ban and Bors had grete mervayle
30 consyderyng the grete slaughter that there was; but at the laste they were dryven abacke over a litill ryver. With that com Merlion on a grete blacke horse and seyde unto kynge Arthure,

'Thou hast never done. Hast thou nat done inow? Of three score thousande thys day hast thou leffte on lyve but fyftene thousand!
35 Therefore hit ys tyme to sey "Who!" for God ys wroth with the for thou woll never have done. For yondir a eleven kynges at thys tyme woll nat be overthrowyn, but and thou tary on them ony lenger thy fortune woll turne and they shall encres. And therefore withdraw you unto youre lodgynge and reste you as sone as ye may, and rewarde
40 youre good knyghtes with golde and with sylver, for they have well deserved hit. There may no ryches be to dere for them, for of so fewe men as ye have there was never men dud more worshipfully in proues than ye have done to-day: for ye have macched thys day with the beste fyghters of the worlde.'

'That ys trouthe,' seyde kynge Ban and Bors.

Than Merlyon bade hem, 'Withdraw where ye lyste, for thys three yere I dare undirtake they shall nat dere you; and by that tyme ye shall hyre newe tydyngis.' Than Merlion seyde unto Arthure, 'These eleven kyngis have morc on hande than they are ware off, for the Sarezynes ar 5 londed in their contreies mo than fourty thousande, and brenne and sle and have leyde syege to the castell Wandesborow, and make grete destruccion: therefore drede you nat thys [thre] yere. Also, sir, all the goodis that be gotyn at this batayle lette hit be serched, and whan ye have hit in your hondis lette hit be geffyn frendly unto thes two 10 kyngis, Ban and Bors, that they may rewarde their knyghtes wythall: and that shall cause straungers to be of bettir wyll to do you servyse at nede. Also ye be able to rewarde youre owne knyghtcs at what tyme somever hit lykith you.'

'Ye sey well,' seyde Arthure, 'and as thou haste devised so shall hit 15 be done.'

Whan hit was delyverde to thes kynges, Ban and Bors, they gaff the godis as frely to theire knyghtes as hit was gevyn to them.

Than Merlion toke hys leve of kynge Arthure and of the two kyngis, for to go se hys mayster Bloyse that dwelled in Northhumbirlonde. And 20 so he departed and com to hys mayster that was passynge glad of hys commynge. And there he tolde how Arthure and the two kynges had spedde at the grete batayle, and how hyt was endyd, and tolde the namys of every kynge and knyght of worship that was there. And so Bloyse wrote the batayle worde by worde as Merlion tolde hym, 25 how hit hegan and by whom, and in lyke wyse how hit was ended and who had the worst. And all the batayles that were done in Arthurs dayes, Merlion dud hys mayster Bloyse wryte them. Also he dud wryte all the batayles that every worthy knyght ded of Arthurs courte.

So aftir this Merlion departed frome his mayster and com to kynge 30 Arthure that was in the castell of Bedgrayne, that was one of the castels that stondith in the foreyste of Sherewood. And Merlion was so disgysed that kynge Arthure knewe hym nat, for he was all befurred in blacke shepis skynnes, and a grete payre of bootis, and a boowe and arowis, in a russet gowne, and brought wylde gyese in hys honde. 35 And hit was on the morne aftir Candilmasse day. But kynge Arthure knew hym nat.

'Sir,' seyde Merlion unto the kynge, 'woll ye geff me a gyffte?'

'Wherefore,' seyde kynge Arthure, 'sholde I gyff the a gyffte, chorle?'

'Sir,' seyd Merlion, 'ye were bettir to gyff me a gyffte that ys nat in 40 youre honde than to lose grete rychesse. For here in the same place there the grete batayle was, ys grete tresoure hydde in the erthe.'

'Who tolde the so, chorle?'

'Sir, Merlyon tolde me so,' seyde he.

Than Ulphuns and Brastias knew hym well inowghe and smyled. 'Sir,' seyde thes two knyghtes, 'hit ys Merlion that so spekith unto you.'

Than kynge Arthure was gretly abaysshed and had mervayle of Merlion, and so had kynge Ban and Bors. So they had grete disporte at 5 hym.

Than in the meanewhyle there com a damesell that was an erlis doughter; hys name was Sanam and hir name was Lyonors, a passyng fayre damesell. And so she cam thidir for to do omage as other lordis ded aftir that grete batayle. And kynge Arthure sette hys love 10 gretly on hir, and so ded she uppon hym, and so the kynge had ado with hir and gate on hir a chylde. And hys name was Borre, that was aftir a good knyght and of the Table Rounde.

Than the[r] com worde that kynge Ryens of North Walis made grete warre on kynge Lodegreaunce of Camylarde, for the whiche 15 kynge Arthure was wrothe, for he loved hym welle and hated kyng Royns, for allwayes he was agenst hym.

(So by ordinauns of the three kynges ther were sente home unto Benwyke [all ⟨that⟩] wolde departe, for drede of kynge Claudas. Thes knyghtes: Pharyaunce, Anthemes, Graciens ⌜and Lyonses of⌝ Payarne 20 were the leders of them that sholde kepe the two kynges londis.)

(18)   And than kynge Arthure, kynge Ban and kynge Bors departed with hir felyship, a twenty thousand, and cam within seven dayes into the contrey of Camylarde; and there rescowed kynge Lodegraunce, and slew there muche people of kynge Ryons, unto the numbir of ten 25 thousand, and putte hem to flyght. And than had thes thre kynges grete chere of kynge Lodegraunce, and ⟨he⟩ thanked them of theire grete goodnes that they wolde revenge hym of his enemyes.

And there had Arthure the firste syght of queene Gwenyvere, the kyngis doughter of the londe of Camylarde, and ever afftir he loved 30 hir. And aftir they were wedded, as hit tellith in the booke.

So breffly to make an ende, they toke there leve to go into hir owne contreyes, for kynge Claudas dud grete destruction on their londis. Than seyde Arthure,

'I woll go with you.'

35   'Nay,' seyde the kyngis, 'ye shall nat at thys tyme, for ye have much to do yet in thys londe. Therefore we woll departe. With the grete goodis that we have gotyn in this londe by youre gyfftis we shall wage good knyghtes and withstonde the kynge Claudas hys malice, for, by the grace of God, and we have nede, we woll sende to you for suc-
40 cour. And ye have nede, sende for us, and we woll nat tarry, by the feythe of oure bodyes.'

'Hit shall nat nede,' seyde Merlion, 'thes two kynges to com agayne in the wey of warre; but I know well kynge Arthure may nat be longe frome you. For within a yere or two ye shall have grete nede, than shall

he revenge you of youre enemyes as ye have done on his. For thes
eleven kyngis shall dye all in one day by the grete myght and prouesse
of armys of two valyaunte knyghtes,'—as hit tellith aftir. Hir namys
[ben] Balyne le Saveage and Balan, hys brothir, that were merveylous
knyghtes as ony was tho lyvynge.   5
   Now turne we unto the eleven kynges that returned unto a cité that
hyght Surhaute, which cité was within kynge Uriens londe; and there
they refreysshed them as well as they myght, and made lechys serche for
their woundis and sorowed gretly for the deth of hir people. So with
that there com a messyngere and tolde how there was comyn into theyre 10
londis people that were lawles, as well as Sarezynes a fourty thousande,
and have brente and slayne all the people that they may com by withoute mercy, and have leyde sege unto the castell Wandesborow.
   'Alas!' seyde the eleven kyngis, 'here ys sorow uppon sorow, and if
we had nat warred agaynste Arthure as we have done, he wolde sone 15
a revenged us. And as for kynge Lodegreaunce, he lovithe Arthure
bettir than us; and as for kynge Royens, he hath ynow ado with kynge
Lodegreauns, for he hath leyde sege unto hym.'
   So they condescended togydir to kepe all the marchis of Cornuwayle,
of Walis, and of the Northe. So firste they put kynge Idres in the cité 20
of Nauntis in Bretayne with four thousand men of armys to wacche
bothe watir and the londe. Also they Ɡput in the cyté of Wyndesan
kynge Nauntres of Garlott with four thousand knyghtes to watche
both on water and on lond. Also theyꞌ had of othir men of warre mo
than eyght thousand for to fortefye all the fortresse in the marchys 25
of Cornuwayle. Also they put mo kyngis in all the marchis off Walis
and Scotlonde with many good men of armys, and so they kept hem
togydirs the space of three yere and ever alyed hem with myghty
kynges and dukis. And unto them felle kynge Royns of Northe Walis
which was a myghty kynge of men, and Nero that was a myghty man 30
of men. And all thys whyle they furnysshed and garnysshed hem of
good men of armys and vitayle and of all maner of ablemente that
pretendith to warre, to avenge hem for the batay[l]e of Bedgrayne, as
hit tellith in the booke of adventures.
   Than aftir the departynge of kynge Bans and Bors, kynge Arthure 35 (19)
rode unto the cité of Carlyon. And thydir com unto hym kynge Lottis
wyff of Orkeney in maner of a message, but she was sente thydir to
aspye the courte of kynge Arthure, and she com rychely beseyne with
hir four sonnes, Gawayne, Gaheris, Aggravayne and Gareth, with
many other knyghtes and ladyes, for she was a passynge fayre lady. 40
Wherefore the kynge caste grete love unto hir and desired to ly by her.
And so they were agreed, and [he] begate uppon hir sir Mordred. And
she was syster on the modirs syde Igrayne unto Arthure. So there she
rested hir a monthe, and at the last she departed.

Than the kynge dremed a mervaylous dreme whereof he was sore adrad. (But all thys tyme kynge Arthure knew nat [that] kynge Lottis wyff was his sister.) But thus was the dreme of Arthure: hym thought there was com into hys londe gryffens and serpentes, and hym thought
5 they brente and slowghe all the people in the londe; and than he thought he fought with them and they dud hym grete harme and wounded hym full sore, but at the laste he slew hem.

Whan the kynge waked, he was passynge hevy of hys dreme; and so to putte hit oute of thought he made hym redy with many knyghtes
10 to ryde on huntynge. And as sone as he was in the foreste, the kynge saw a grete harte before hym.

'Thys harte woll I chace,' seyde kynge Arthure.

And so he spurred hys horse and rode aftir longe, and so be fyne force oftyn he was lyke to have smytten the herte. Wherefore as the
15 kynge had chased the herte so longe that hys horse lost his brethe and felle downe dede, than a yoman fette the kynge another horse.

So the kynge saw the herte unboced and hys horse dede, he sette hym downe by a fowntayne, and there he felle downe in grete thought. And as he sate so hym thought he herde a noyse of howundis to the
20 som of thirty, and with that the kynge saw com towarde hym the strongeste beste that ever he saw or herde of. So thys beste wente to the welle and dranke, and the noyse was in the bestes bealy ⌜lyke unto the questyng of thirty coupyl houndes, but alle the whyle the beest dranke there was no noyse in the bestes bealy⌝. And therewith the
25 beeste departed with a grete noyse, whereof the kynge had grete mervayle. And so he was in a grete thought, and therewith he felle on slepe.

Ryght so there com a knyght on foote unto Arthure, and seyde, 'Knyght full of thought and slepy, telle me if thou saw any stronge
30 beeste passe thys way.'

'Such one saw I,' seyde kynge Arthure, 'that ys paste nye two myle. What wolde ye with that beeste?' seyde Arthure.

'Sir, I have folowed that beste longe and kylde myne horse, so wolde God I had another to folow my queste.'

35 Ryght so com one with the kyngis horse. And whan the knyght saw the horse he prayde the kynge to gyff hym the horse, 'for I have folowed this queste thys twelve-monthe, and othir I shall encheve hym othir blede of the beste bloode in my body.' (Whos name was kynge Pellynor that tyme folowed the questynge beste, and afftir hys
40 dethe sir Palomydes folowed hit.)
(20)   'Sir knyght,' seyd the kynge, 'leve that queste and suffir me to have hit, and I woll folowe hit anothir twelve-monthe.'

'A, foole!' seyde the kynge unto Arthure, 'hit ys in vayne thy desire, for hit shall never be encheved but by me other by my nexte kynne.'

And therewithe he sterte unto the kyngis horse and mownted into the sadyl and seyde, 'Gramercy, for this horse ys myne owne.'

'Well,' seyde the kynge, 'thou mayste take myne horse by force, but and I myght preve hit I wolde weete whether thou were bettir worthy to have hym or I.'

Whan the kynge herde hym sey so he seyde, 'Seke me here whan 5 thou wolte, and here nye thys welle thou shalte fynde me,' ⌐and soo passed on his weye.

Thenne the kyng sat in a study⌐ and bade hys men fecche another horse as faste as they myght. Ryght so com by hym Merlyon lyke a 10 chylde of fourtene yere of ayge and salewed the kynge and asked hym whye he was so pensyff.

'I may well [be] pensiff,' seyde the kynge, 'for I have sene the mervaylist syght that ever I saw.'

'That know I well,' seyde Merlyon, 'as welle as thyselff, and of all thy 15 thoughtes. But thou arte a foole to take thought for hit that woll nat amende the. Also I know what thou arte, and who was thy fadir, and of whom thou were begotyn: for kynge Uther was thy fadir and begate the on Igrayne.'

'That ys false!' seyde kynge Arthure. 'How sholdist thou know hit? 20 For thou arte nat so olde of yerys to know my fadir.'

'Yes,' seyde Merlyon, 'I know hit bettir than ye or ony man lyvynge.'

'I woll nat beleve the,' seyde Arthure, and was wrothe with the chylde.

So departed Merlyon, and com ayen in the lyknesse of an olde man 25 of four score yere of ayge, whereof the kynge was passynge glad, for he semed to be ryght wyse. Than seyde the olde man,

'Why ar ye so sad?'

'I may well be sad,' seyde Arthure, 'for many thynges. For ryght now there was a chylde here, and tolde me many thynges that mesemythe he 30 sholde nat knowe, for he was nat of ayge to know my fadir.'

'Yes,' seyde the olde man, 'the chylde tolde you trouthe, and more he wolde a tolde you and [y]e wolde a suffirde hym, but ye have done a thynge late that God ys displesed with you, for ye have lyene by youre syster and on hir ye have gotyn a childe that shall destroy you and all 35 the knyghtes of youre realme.'

'What ar ye,' seyde Arthure, 'that telle me thys tydyngis?'

'Sir, I am Merlion, and I was he in the chyldis lycknes.'

'A,' seyde the kynge, 'ye ar a mervaylous man! But I mervayle muche of thy wordis that I mou dye in batayle.'   40

'Mervayle nat,' seyde Merlion, 'for hit ys Goddis wylle that youre body sholde be punyss[h]ed for your fowle dedis. But I ought ever to be hevy,' seyde Merlion, 'for I shall dye a shamefull dethe, to be putte in the erthe quycke; and ye shall dey a worshipfull dethe.'

And as they talked thus, com one with the kyngis horse, and so the kynge mownted on hys horse, and Merlion on anothir, and so rode unto Carlyon. And anone the kynge askyd Ector and Ulphuns how he was begotyn, and they tolde hym how kynge Uther was hys fadir, and quene
5 Igrayne hys modir.

'So Merlion tolde me. I woll that my modir be sente for, that I myght speke with hir. And if she sey so hirselff, than woll I beleve hit.'

So in all haste the quene was sente for, [and she came] and she brought with hir Morgan le Fay, hir doughter, that was a fayre lady as
10 ony myght be. And the kynge welcommed Igrayne in the beste maner.
(21) Ryght so com in Ulphuns and seyde opynly, that the kynge and all myght hyre that were fested that day,

'Ye ar the falsyst lady of the wor[l]de, and the moste traytoures unto the kynges person.'

15 'Beware,' seyde kynge Arthure, 'what thou seyste : thou spekiste a grete worde.'

'Sir, I am well ware,' seyde Ulphuns, 'what I speke, and here ys my gloove to preve hit uppon ony man that woll sey the contrary : that thys quene Igrayne ys the causer of youre grete damage and of youre
20 grete warre, for and she wolde have uttirde hit in the lyff of Uther of the birth of you, and how ye were begotyn, than had ye never had the mortall warrys that ye have had. For the moste party of your barownes of youre realme knewe never whos sonne ye were, ne of whom ye were begotyn; and she that bare you of hir body sholde have made
25 hit knowyn opynly, in excusynge of hir worship and youres, and in lyke [wyse] to all the realme. Wherefore I preve hir false to God and to you and to all youre realme. And who woll sey the contrary, I woll preve hit on hys body.'

Than spake Igrayne and seyde, 'I am a woman and I may nat fyght;
30 but rather than I sholde be dishonoured, there wolde som good man take my quarell. But,' thus she seyde, 'Merlion knowith well, and ye, sir Ulphuns, how kynge Uther com to me into the castell of Tyntagyl in the lyknes of my lorde that was dede three owres tofore, and there begate a chylde that nyght uppon me, and aftir the thirtenth day
35 kynge Uther wedded me. And by his commaundemente, whan the chylde was borne, hit was delyvirde unto Merlion and fostred by hym. And so I saw the childe never aftir, nothir wote nat what ys hys name; for I knew hym never yette.'

Than Ulphuns seyde unto Merlion,
40 'Ye ar than more to blame than the queene.'

'Sir, well I wote I bare a chylde be my lorde kynge Uther, but I wote never where he ys becom.'

Than the kynge toke Merlion by the honde seyng thys wordis :
'Ys this my modir?'

'Forsothe, sir, yee.'

And therewith com in sir Ector, and bare wytnes how he fostred hym by kynge Uthers commaundemente. And therewith kyng Arthure toke his modir, quene Igrayne, in hys armys and kyssed her, and eythir wepte uppon other. Than the kynge lete make a feste that 5 lasted eyght dayes.

So on a day there com into the courte a squyre on horsebacke ledynge a knyght tofore hym, wounded to the deth, and tolde how there was a knyght in the foreste that had rered up a pavylon by a welle, 'that hath slayne my mayster, a good knyght: hys name was Myles. Where- 10 fore I besech you that my maystir may be buryed, and that som knyght may revenge my maystirs dethe.'

Than the noyse was grete of that knyghtes dethe in the courte, and every man seyde hys advyce. Than com Gryfflet that was but a squyre, and he was but yonge, of ⌐the ayge of the kyng Arthur⌐. So he be- 15 sought the kynge for all hys servyse that he had done hym to gyff hym the Order of Knyghthoode.

'Thou arte but yonge and tendir of ayge,' seyd kynge Arthure, 'for (22) to take so hyghe an orde[r] uppon you.'

'Sir,' seyde Gryfflet, 'I beseche you to make me knyght.'			20

'Sir,' seyde Merlion, 'hit were pité to lose Gryfflet, for he woll be a passynge good man whan he ys of ayge, and he shall abyde with you the terme of hys lyff. And if he aventure his body with yondir knyght at the fountayne, hit ys in grete perell if ever he com agayne, for he ys one of the beste knyghtes of the worlde and the strengyst man of armys.' 25

'Well,' seyde Arthure, 'at thyne owne desire thou shalt be made knyght.'

⌐So at the desyre of Gryflet the kynge made hym knyght.⌐

'Now,' seyde Arthure unto Gryfflet, 'sith I have made the knyght, thou muste gyff me a gyffte.'								30

'What ye woll,' seyde Gryfflet.

'Thou shalt promyse me by th[e] feyth of thy body, whan thou haste justed with that knyght at the fountayne, whether hit falle ye be on horsebak othir on foote, that ryght so ye shall com agayne unto me withoute makynge ony more debate.'						35

'I woll promyse you,' seyde Gryfflet, 'as youre desire ys.'

Than toke Gryfflet hys horse in grete haste and dressed hys shelde and toke a spere in hys honde, and so he rode a grete walop tylle he com to the fountayne. And thereby he saw a ryche pavilion, and thereby undir a cloth stood an horse well sadeled and brydyled, and on a tre 40 hynge a shelde of dyvers coloures, and a grete spere thereby. Than Gryfflet smote on the shylde with the butte of hys spere, that the shylde felle downe.

With that the knyght com oute of the pavilion and seyde,

'Fayre knyght, why smote ye downe my shylde?'

'Sir, for I wolde juste with you,' seyde Gryfflet.

'Sir, hit ys bettir ye do nat,' seyde the kynge, 'for ye ar but yonge and late made knyght, and youre myght ys nat to myne.'

5   'As for that,' seyde Gryfflet, 'I woll jouste with you.'

'That ys me loth,' seyde the knyght, 'but sitthyn I muste nedis, I woll dresse me thereto. Of whens be ye?' seyde the knyght.

'Sir, I am of kynge Arthurs courte.'

So the two knyghtes ran togydir, that Gryfflettis spere all to-shevirde.

10 And therewithall he smote Gryfflet thorow the shelde and the lyffte syde, and brake the spere, that the truncheon stake in hys body, and horse and man felle downe to the erthe.

(23)   Whan the knyght saw hym ly so on the grounde he alyght and was passyng hevy, for he wente he had slayne hym. And than he unlaced

15 hys helme and gate hym wynde; and so with the troncheon he sette hym on his horse and gate hym wynde, and so betoke hym to God and seyde, 'He had a myghty herte!' And seyde, 'If he myght lyve, he wolde preve a passyng good knyght,' and so rode forthe sir Gryfflet unto the courte, whereof passyng grete dole was made for hym. But

20 thorow good lechis he was heled and saved.

Ryght so com into the courte twelve knyghtes that were aged men, whiche com frome the Emperoure of Rome. And they asked of Arthure trwage for hys realme, othir ellis the Emperour wolde destroy hym and all hys londe.

25   'Well,' seyde kynge Arthure, 'ye ar messyngers: therefore ye may sey what ye woll, othir ellis ye sholde dye therefore. But thys ys myne answere: I owghe the Emperour no trewage, nother none woll I yelde hym, but on a fayre fylde I shall yelde hym my trwage, that shall be with a sherpe spere othir ellis with a sherpe swerde. And that shall

30 nat be longe, be my fadirs soule Uther!'

And therewith the messyngers departed passyngly wrothe, and kyng Arthure as wrothe; for in an evyll tyme com they. But the kynge was passyngly wrothe for the hurte of sir Gryfflet, and so he commaunded a prevy man of hys chambir that or hit were day his beste horse and

35 armoure 'and all that longith to my person be withoute the cité or to-morow day'. Ryght so he mette with his man and his horse, and so mownted up, and dressed his shelde and toke hys spere, and bade hys chambirlayne tary there tylle he com agayne.

And so Arthure rode a soffte pace tyll hit was day. And than was he

40 ware of thre chorlys chasyng Merlion and wolde have slayne hym. Than the kynge rode unto them and bade hem: 'Fle, chorlis!' Than they fered sore whan they sawe a knyght com, and fledde.

'A, Merlion!' seyde Arthure, 'here haddist thou be slayne for all thy crafftis, had nat I bene.'

'Nay,' seyde Merlyon, 'nat so, for I cowde a saved myselffe and I had wolde. But thou arte more nere thy deth than I am, for thou goste to thy dethe warde and God be nat thy frende.'

So as they wente thus talkynge, they com to the fountayne and the ryche pavilion there by hit. Than kynge Arthure was ware where sate a 5 knyght armed in a chayre.

'Sir knyght,' seyde Arthure, 'for what cause abydist thou here, that there may no knyght ryde thys way but yf he juste with the? I rede the to leve that custom.'

'Thys custom,' seyde the knyght, 'have I used and woll use magré 10 who seyth nay. And who that ys agreved with my custum lette hym amende hit.'

'That shall I amende,' seyde Arthure.

'And I shall defende the,' seyde the knyght.

And anone he toke hys horse, and dressed hys shelde and toke a 15 grete spere in hys honde, and they com togydir so harde that eythir smote other in mydde the shyldis, that all to-shevird theire speris. Therewith anone Arthure pulled oute his swerde.

'Nay, nat so,' seyde the knyght, 'hit ys bettir that we twayne renne more togydirs with sherpe sperys.' 20

'I woll well,' seyde Arthure, 'and I had ony mo sperys here.'

'I have inow,' seyde the knyght.

So there com a squyre and brought forthe two sperys, and Arthure chose one and he another. So they spurred theire horsis and com togydir with all theire myghtes, that eyther brake their sperys to their 25 hondis. Than Arthure sette honde on his swerde.

'Nay,' seyde the knyght, 'ye shall do bettir. Ye ar a passyng good juster as ever y mette withall, and onys for the hyghe Order of Knyght-hode lette us jouste agayne.'

'I assente me,' seyde Arthure. 30

And anone there was brought forth two grete sperys, and anone every knyght gate a spere; and therewith they ran togiders, that Arthures spere all to-shevirde. But this other knyght smote hym so harde in myddis the shelde that horse and man felle to the erthe. And there-with Arthure was egir, and pulde oute hys swerde, and seyde, 35

'I woll assay the, sir knyght, on foote, for I have loste the honoure on horsebacke,' seyde the kynge.

'Sir, I woll be on horsebacke stylle to assay the.'

Than was Arthure wrothe and dressed his shelde towarde hym with his swerde drawyn. Whan the knyght saw that he alyght, for hym 40 thought no worship to have a knyght at such avayle, he to be on horse-backe and hys adversary on foote, and so he alyght and dressed his shelde unto Arthure. And there began a stronge batayle with many grete strokis, and so they hew with hir swerdis, that the cantels flowe

unto the feldys, and muche bloode they bledde bothe, that all the place thereas they fought was ovirbledde with bloode. And thus they fought longe and rested them. And than they wente to the batayle agayne, and so hurteled togydirs lyke too rammes that aythir felle to the erthe.
5 So at the laste they smote togyders, that bothe hir [swerdys] mette evyn togyders. But kynge Arthurs swerde brake in two pecis, wherefore he was hevy.

Than seyde the knyght unto Arthure, 'Thou arte in my daungere, whethir me lyste to save the or sle the; and but thou yelde the to me as
10 overcom and recreaunte, thou shalt dey.'

'As for that,' seyde kynge Arthure, 'dethe ys wellcom to me whan hit commyth. But to yelde me unto the I woll nat!'

And therewithall the kynge lepte unto kynge Pellynore, and toke hym by the myddyll, and overthrew hym, and raced of hys helme. So
15 whan the knyght felte that, he was adradde, for he was a passynge bygge man of myght. And so forthewith he wrothe Arthure undir hym and raced of hys helme, and wolde have smytten off hys hede. And
(24) therewithall com Merlion and seyde,

'Knyght, holde thy honde, for and thou sle that knyght thou puttyst
20 thys realme in the gretteste damage that evir was realme: for thys knyght ys a man of more worshyp than thou wotist off.'

'Why, what ys he?' seyde the knyght.

'For hit ys kynge Arthure,' seyde Merlyon.

Than wolde he have slayne hym for drede of hys wratthe, and so he
25 lyffte up hys swerde. And therewith Merlion caste an inchauntemente on the knyght, that he felle to the erthe in a grete slepe. Than Merlion toke up kynge Arthure and rode forthe on the knyghtes horse.

'Alas!' seyde Arthure, 'what hast thou do, Merlion? Hast thou slayne thys good knyght by thy craufftis? For there lyvith nat so worshipffull
30 a knyght as he was. For I had levir than the stynte of my londe a yere that he were on lyve.'

'Care ye nat,' seyde Merlion, 'for he ys holer than ye: he ys but on slepe and woll awake within thys owre. I tolde you,' seyde Merlyon, 'what a knyght he was. Now here had ye be slayne had I nat bene. Also
35 there lyvith nat a bygger knyght than he ys one; and afftir this he shall do you goode servyse. And hys name ys kynge Pellinore, and he shall have two sonnes that shall be passyng good men as ony lyvynge: save one in thys worlde they shall have no felowis of prouesse and of good lyvynge, and hir namys shall be Percyvall and sir Lamorake of
40 Walis. And he shall telle you the name of youre owne son begotyn of youre syster, that shall be the destruccion of all thys realme.'

(25) Ryght so the kynge and he departed and wente unto an ermytage, and there was a good man and a grete leche. So the ermyte serched the kynges woundis and gaff hym good salves. And so the kyng was there

three dayes, and than wer his woundis well amended, that he myght ryde and goo; and so departed. And as they rode, kynge Arthur seyde, 'I have no swerde.'

'No force,' seyde Merlyon, 'hereby ys a swerde that shall be youre, and I may.'

So they rode tyll they com to a laake that was a fayre watir and brode. And in the myddis Arthure was ware of an arme clothed in whyght samyte, that helde a fayre swerde in that honde.

'Lo,' seyde Merlion, 'yondir ys the swerde that I spoke off.'

So with that they saw a damesell goynge uppon the laake.

⌈'What damoysel is that?' said Arthur.

'That is the Lady of the Lake,'⌉[1] seyde Merlion. 'There ys a grete roche, and therein ys as fayre a paleyce as ony on erthe, and rychely besayne. And thys damesel woll com to you anone, and than speke ye fayre to hir, that she may gyff you that swerde.'

So anone com this damesel to Arthure and salewed hym, and he hir agayne.

'Damesell,' seyde Arthure, 'what swerde ys that yondir that the arme holdith aboven the watir? I wolde hit were myne, for I have no swerde.'

'Sir Arthure,' seyde the damesel, 'that swerde ys myne, and if ye woll gyff me a gyffte whan I aske hit you, ye shall have hit.'

'Be my feyth,' seyde Arthure, 'I woll gyff you what gyffte that ye woll aske.'

'Well,' seyde the damesell, 'go ye into yondir barge, and rowe youreselffe to the swerde, and take hit and the scawberde with you. And I woll aske my gyffte whan I se my tyme.'

So kynge Arthur and Merlion alyght and tyed their horsis unto two treys; and so they wente into the barge. And whan they com to the swerde that the honde hylde, than kynge Arthure toke hit up by the hondils and bare hit with hym, and the arme and the honde wente undir the watir. And so he com unto the londe and rode forthe. And kynge Arthure saw a ryche pavilion.

'What signifieth yondir pavilion?'

'Sir, that ys the knyghtes pavilys that ye fought with laste, sir Pellynore; but he ys oute. He ys nat at home, for he hath had ado with a knyght of youres that hyght Egglame, and they had foughtyn togyddyr; but at the laste Egglame fledde, and ellis he had bene dede, and he hath chaced hym evyn to Carlion. And we shall mete with hym anone in the hygheway.'

'That ys well seyde,' seyde Arthure. 'Now have I a swerde I woll wage batayle with hym and be avenged on hym.'

'Sir,' seyde Merlion, 'nat so; for the knyght ys wery of fyghtynge and chasynge, that ye shall have no worship to have ado with hym. Also he woll nat lyghtly be macched of one knyght lyvynge, and

therefore hit ys my counceile: latte hym passe, for he shall do you
good servyse in shorte tyme, and hys sonnes afftir hys dayes. Also ye
shall se that day in shorte space that ye shall be ryght glad to gyff hym
youre syster to wedde for hys good servyse. Therefore have nat ado
5 with hym whan ye se hym.'
    'I woll do as ye avise me.'
    Than kynge Arthure loked on the swerde and lyked hit passynge well.
Than seyde Merlion,
    'Whethir lyke ye better the swerde othir the scawberde?'
10   'I lyke bettir the swerde,' seyde Arthure.
    'Ye ar the more unwyse, for the scawberde ys worth ten of the swerde;
for whyles ye have the scawberde uppon you ye shall lose no blood,
be ye never so sore wounded. Therefore kepe well the scawberde
allweyes with you.'
15   So they rode unto Carlion; and by the wey they mette with kynge
Pellinore. But Merlion had done suche a crauffte unto kynge Pellinore
saw nat kynge Arthure, and so passed by withoute ony wordis.
    'I mervayle,' seyde Arthure, 'that the knyght wold nat speke.'
    'Sir, he saw you nat; for had he seyne you, ye had nat lyghtly
20 parted.'
    So they com unto Carlion, whereof hys knyghtes were passynge
glad. And whan they herde of hys adventures, they mervayled that he
wolde jouparde his person so alone. But all men of worship seyde hit
was myrry to be under such a chyfftayne that wolde putte hys person in
25 adventure as other poure knyghtis ded.
(26)   So thys meanewhyle com a messyngere frome kynge Royns of
Northe Walis, and kynge he was of all Irelonde and of Iles. And this
was hys message, gretynge well kyng Arthure on thys maner of wyse,
sayng that kynge Royns had discomfite and overcom eleven kyngis,
30 and every of them dud hym omage. And that was thus to sey they gaff
theire beardes clene flayne off, as much as was bearde; wherefore the
messyngere com for kynge Arthures berde. For kynge Royns had
purfilde a mantell with kynges berdis, and there lacked one place of
the mantell; wherefore he sente for hys bearde, othir ellis he wolde
35 entir into his londis and brenne and sle, and nevir leve tylle he hathe
the hede and the bearde bothe.
    'Well,' seyde Arthure, 'thou haste seyde thy message, the whych ys
the moste orgulus and lewdiste message that evir man had isente unto
a kynge. Also thou mayste se my bearde ys full yonge yet to make off
40 a purphile. But telle thou thy kynge thus, that I owghe hym [none
homage] ne none of myne elders; but or hit be longe to, he shall do
me omage on bothe his knees, other ellis he shall lese hys hede, by
the fayth of my body! For thys ys the moste shamefullyste message
that ever y herde speke off. I have aspyed thy kynge never yette mette

with worshipfull man. But telle hym I woll have hys hede withoute he
do me omage.'

Than thys messyngere departed.

'Now ys there ony here that knowyth kynge Royns?'

Than answerde a knyght that hyght Naram: 'Sir, I know the kynge 5
well: he ys a passynge good man of hys body as fewe bene lyvynge
and a passynge proude man. And, sir, doute ye nat he woll make on you
a myghty puyssaunce.'

'Well,' seyde Arthure, 'I shall ordayne for hym in shorte tyme.'

Than kynge Arthure lette sende for all the children that were borne in 10 (27)
May-day, begotyn of lordis and borne of ladyes; for Merlyon tolde
kynge Arthure that he that sholde destroy hym and all the londe sholde
be borne on May-day. Wherefore he sente for hem all in payne of dethe,
and so there were founde many lordis sonnys and many knyghtes
sonnes, and all were sente unto the kynge. And so was Mordred sente 15
by kynge Lottis wyff. And all were putte in a shyppe to the se; and som
were four wekis olde and som lesse. And so by fortune the shyppe
drove unto a castelle, and was all to-ryven and destroyed the moste party,
save that Mordred was cast up, and a good man founde hym, and
fostird hym tylle he was fourtene yere of age, and than brought hym 20
to the courte, as hit rehersith aftirward and towarde the ende of the
MORTE ARTHURE.

So, many lordys and barownes of thys realme were displeased for hir
children were so loste; and many putte the wyght on Merlion more than
o[n] Arthure. So what for drede and for love, they helde their pece. 25

But whan the messynge com to the kynge Royns, than was he woode
oute of mesure, and purveyde hym for a grete oste, as hit rehersith
aftir in the BOOKE OF BALYNE LE SAVEAGE that folowith nexte aftir:
that was the adventure how Balyne gate the swerde.

II. BALIN OR THE KNIGHT WITH THE 30
TWO SWORDS

AFFTIR the deth of Uther regned Arthure, hys son, which had grete II (1)
warre in hys dayes for to gete all Inglonde into hys honde; for there
were many kyngis within the realme of Inglonde and of Scotlonde,
Walys and Cornuwayle. 35

So hit befelle on a tyme whan kynge Arthure was at London, ther
com a knyght and tolde the kynge tydyngis how the kynge Royns of
Northe Walis had rered a grete numbir of peple and were entred in the
londe and brente and slew the kyngis trew lyege people.

'Iff thys be trew,' seyde Arthure, 'hit were grete shame unto myne astate but that he were myghtyly withstonde.'

'Hit ys trouthe,' seyde the knyght, 'for I saw the oste myselff.'

'Well,' seyde the kynge, 'I shall ordayne to wythstonde hys malice.'

5 Than the kynge lette make a cry that all the lordis, knyghtes and jantilmen of armys sholde draw unto the castell called Camelot in tho dayes, and there the kynge wolde lette make a counceile generall and a grete justis. So whan the kynge was com thidir with all his baronage and logged as they semed beste, also there was com ⌐a damoisel¬ the

10 which was sente frome the grete Lady Lyle of Avilion. And whan she com before kynge Arthure she tolde fro whens she com, and how she was sente on message unto hym for thys causis. Than she lette hir mantell falle that was rychely furred, and than was she gurde with a noble swerde, whereof the kynge had mervayle and seyde,

15 'Damesel, for what cause ar ye gurte with that swerde? Hit besemyth you nought.'

'Now shall I telle you,' seyde the damesell. 'Thys swerde that I am gurte withall doth me grete sorow and comberaunce, for I may nat be delyverde of thys swerde but by a knyght, and he muste be a passynge

20 good man of hys hondys and of hys dedis, and withoute velony other trechory and withoute treson. And if I may fynde such a knyght that hath all thes vertues he may draw oute thys swerde oute of the sheethe. For I have bene at kynge Royns, for hit was tolde me there were passyng good knyghtes; and he and all his knyghtes hath assayde and

25 none can spede.'

'Thys ys a grete mervayle,' seyde Arthure. 'If thys be sothe I woll assay myselffe to draw oute the swerde, nat presumynge myselff that I am the beste knyght; but I woll begynne to draw youre swerde in gyvyng an insample to all the barownes, that they shall assay everych

30 one aftir othir whan I have assayde.'

Than Arthure toke the swerde by the sheethe and gurdil and pulled at hit egirly, but the swerde wolde nat oute.

'Sir,' seyd the damesell, 'ye nede nat for to pulle halffe so sore, for he that shall pulle hit oute shall do hit with litill myght.'

35 'Ye sey well,' seyde Arthure. 'Now assay ye all, my barownes.'

'But beware ye be nat defoyled with shame, trechory, nother gyle, for than hit woll nat avayle,' seyde the damesel, 'for he muste be a clene knyght withoute vylony and of jantill strene of fadir syde and of modir syde.'

40 The moste parte of all the barownes of the Rounde Table that were there at that tyme assayde all be rew, but there myght none spede. Wherefore the damesel made grete sorow oute of mesure and seyd,

'Alas! I wente in this courte had bene the beste knyghtes of the worlde withoute trechory other treson.'

'Be my faythe,' seyde Arthure, 'here ar good knyghtes as I deme as ony be in the worlde, but their grace ys nat to helpe you, wherefore I am sore displeased.'

Than hit befelle so that tyme there was a poore knyght with kynge (2) Arthure that had bene presonere with hym half a yere for sleyng of a 5 knyght which was cosyne unto kynge Arthure. And the name of thys knyght was called Balyne, and by good meanys of the barownes he was delyverde oute of preson, for he was a good man named of his body, and he was borne in Northehumbirlonde. And so he wente pryvaly into the courte and saw thys adventure whereoff hit reysed his herte, and 10 wolde assayde as othir knyghtes ded. But for he was poore and poorly arayde, he put hymselff nat far in prees. But in hys herte he was fully assured to do as well, if hys grace happed hym, as ony knyght that there was. And as the damesell toke [her] leve of Arthure and of all the barownes, so departynge, thys knyght Balyn called unto her and seyde, 15

'Damesell, I pray you of youre curteysy suffir me as well to assay as thes other lordis. Thoughe that I be pourely arayed yet in my herte mesemyth I am fully assured as som of thes other, and mesemyth in myne herte to spede ryght welle.'

Thys damesell than behelde thys poure knyght and saw he was a 20 lyckly man; but for hys poure araymente she thought he sholde nat be of no worship withoute vylony or trechory. And than she seyde unto that knyght,

'Sir, hit nedith nat you to put me to no more payne, for hit semyth nat you to spede thereas all thes othir knyghtes have fayled.' 25

'A, fayre damesell,' seyde Balyn, 'worthynes and good tacchis and also good dedis is nat only in araymente, but manhode and worship [ys hyd] within a mannes person; and many a worshipfull knyght ys nat knowyn unto all peple. And therefore worship and hardynesse ys nat in araymente.' 30

'Be God,' seyde the damesell, 'ye sey soth. Therefore ye shall assay to do what ye may.'

Than Balyn toke the swerde by the gurdyll and shethe and drew hit oute easyly, and whan he loked on the swerde hit pleased hym muche. Than had the kynge and all the barownes grete mervayle that Balyne 35 had done that aventure; many knyghtes had grete despite at hym.

'Sertes,' seyde the damesell, 'thys ys a passynge good knyght and the beste that ever y founde, and moste of worship withoute treson, trechory or felony. And many mervayles shall he do. Now, jantyll and curtayse knyght, geff me the swerde agayne.' 40

'Nay,' seyde Balyne, 'for thys swerde woll I kepe but hit be takyn fro me with force.'

'Well,' seyde the damesell, 'ye ar nat wyse to kepe the swerde fro me, for ye shall sle with that swerde the beste frende that ye have and the

man that ye moste love in the worlde, and that swerde shall be youre
destruccion.'

'I shall take the aventure,' seyde Balyn, 'that God woll ordayne for
me. But the swerde ye shall nat have at thys tyme, by the feythe of my
5 body!'

'Ye shall repente hit within shorte tyme,' seyde the damesell, 'for I
wolde have the swerde more for youre avauntage than for myne; for
I am passynge hevy for youre sake, for and ye woll nat leve that swerde
hit shall be youre destruccion, and that ys grete pité.'

10 So with that departed the damesell and grete sorow she made. And
anone afftir Balyn sente for hys horse and armoure, and so wolde departe frome the courte, and toke his leve of kynge Arthure.

'Nay,' seyde the kynge, 'I suppose ye woll nat departe so lyghtly
from thys felyship. I suppose that ye ar displesyd that I have shewed
15 you unkyndnesse. But blame me the lesse, for I was mysseinfourmed
ayenste you: but I wente ye had nat bene such a knyght as ye ar of
worship and prouesse. And if ye woll abyde in thys courte amonge my
felyship I shall so avaunce [you] as ye shall be pleased.'

'God thanke youre Hyghnesse,' seyde Balyne. 'Youre bounté may
20 no man prayse halff unto the valew, butt at thys tyme I muste nedis
departe, besechynge you allway of youre good grace.'

'Truly,' seyde the kynge, 'I am ryght wroth of youre departynge. But
I pray you, fayre knyght, that ye tarry nat longe frome me, and ye shall
be ryght wellcom unto me and to my barownes, and I shall amende all
25 mysse that I have done agaynste you.'

'God thanke youre good grace,' seyde Balyn, and therewith made
hym redy to departe. Than the moste party of the knyghtes of the
Rounde Table seyde that Balyne dud nat this adventure ⌜all⌝ on⌜l⌝y
by myght but by wycchecrauffte.

(3) 30   So the meanewhyle that thys knyght was makynge hym redy to
departe, there com into the courte the Lady of the Laake, and she com
on horsebacke rychely beseyne, and salewed kynge Arthure and there
asked hym a gyffte that he promysed her whan she gaff hym the swerde.

'That ys sothe,' seyde Arthure, 'a gyffte I promysed you, but I have
35 forgotyn the name of my swerde that ye gaff me.'

'The name of hit,' seyde the lady, 'ys Excalibir, that ys as muche to
sey as Kutte Stele.'

'Ye sey well,' seyde the kynge. 'Aske what ye woll and ye shall have
hit and hit lye in my power to gyff hit.'

40   'Well,' seyde thys lady, 'than I aske the hede of thys knyght that hath
wonne the swerde, othir ellis the damesels hede that brought hit. I
take no force though I have both theire hedis: for he slew my brothir,
a good knyght and a trew; and that jantillwoman was causer of my
fadirs deth.'

'Truly,' seyde kynge Arthure, 'I may nat graunte you nother of theire hedys with my worship; therefore aske what ye woll els, and I shall fulfille youre desire.'

'I woll aske none other thynge,' seyde the lady.

So whan Balyn was redy to departe, he saw the Lady of the Lake which by hir meanys had slayne hys modir; and he had sought hir three yere before. And whan hit was tolde hym how she had asked hys hede of kynge Arthure, he wente to hir streyght and seyde,

'Evyll be [y]e founde: ye wolde have myne hede, and therefore ye shall loose youres!'

And with hys swerde lyghtly he smote of hyr hede before kynge Arthure.

'Alas, for shame!' seyde the kynge. 'Why have ye do so? Ye have shamed me and all my courte, for thys lady was a lady that I was much beholdynge to, and hyder she com undir my sauffconduyghte. Therefore I shall never forgyff you that trespasse.'

'Sir,' seyde Balyne, 'me forthynkith of youre displeasure, for this same lady was the untrwyste lady lyvynge, and by inchauntement and by sorcery she hath bene the destroyer of many good knyghtes, and she was causer that my modir was brente thorow hir falschode and trechory.'

'For what cause soever ye had,' seyde Arthure, 'ye sholde have forborne in my presence. Therefore thynke nat the contrary: ye shall repente hit, for such anothir despite had I nevir in my courte. Therefore withdraw you oute of my courte in all the haste that ye may.'

Than Balyn toke up the hede of the lady and bare hit with hym to hys ostry, and there mette with hys squyre that was sory he had displeased kynge Arthure, and so they rode forthe oute of towne.

'Now,' seyde Balyne, 'we muste departe; therefore take thou thys hede and bere hit to my frendis and telle hem how I have spedde, and telle hem in Northhumbirlonde how my moste foo ys dede. Also telle hem how I am oute of preson, and what adventure befelle me at the getynge of this swerde.'

'Alas!' seyde the squyre, 'ye ar gretly to blame for to displease kynge Arthure.'

'As for that,' seyde Balyne, 'I woll hyghe me in all [the] haste that I may [to] mete with kyng Royns and destroy hym, othir ellis to dye therefore. And iff hit may happe me to wynne hym, than woll kynge Arthure be my good frende.'

'Sir, [wher] shall I mete with you?' seyde his squyre.

'In kynge Arthurs courte,' seyde Balyne.

So his squyre and he departed at that tyme. Than kynge Arthure and all the courte made grete dole and had grete shame of the Lady of the Lake. Than the kynge buryed hir rychely.

(4) So at that tyme there was a knyght, the which was the kynges son of Irelonde, and hys name was Launceor, the which was an orgulus knyght and accompted hymselff one of the beste of the courte. And he had grete despite at Balyne for the enchevynge of the swerde, that ony
5 sholde be accompted more hardy or more of prouesse, and he asked kynge Arthure licence to ryde afftir Balyne and to revenge the despite that he had done.

'Do youre beste,' seyde Arthur. 'I am ryght wrothe with Balyne. I wolde he were quytte of the despite that he hath done unto me and my
10 courte.'

Than thys Launceor wente to his ostré to make hym redy. So in the meanewhyle com Merlyon unto the courte of kynge Arthure, and anone was tolde hym the adventure of the swerde and the deth of the Lady of the Lake.

15 'Now shall I sey you,' seyde Merlion; 'thys same damesell that here stondith, that brought the swerde unto youre courte, I shall telle you the cause of hir commynge. She ys the falsist damesell that lyveth— she shall nat sey nay! For she hath a brothir, a passyng good knyght of proues and a full trew man, and thys damesell loved anothir knyght
20 that hylde her as paramoure. And thys good knyght, her brothir, mette with the knyght that helde hir to paramoure, and slew hym by force of hys hondis. And whan thys false damesell undirstoode this she wente to the lady Lyle of Avylion and besought hir of helpe to be revenged on hir owne brothir.

(5) 25 'And so thys lady Lyle of Avylion toke hir this swerde that she brought with hir, and tolde there sholde no man pulle hit oute of the sheethe but yf he be one of the beste knyghtes of thys realme, and he sholde be hardy and full of prouesse; and with that swerde he sholde sle hys brothir. Thys was the cause, damesell, that ye com into thys
30 courte. I know hit as well as ye. God wolde ye had nat com here; but ye com never in felyship of worshipfful folke for to do good, but all- wayes grete harme. And that knyght that hath encheved the swerde shall be destroyed thorow the swerde; for the which woll be grete damage, for there lyvith nat a knyght of more prouesse than he ys.
35 And he shall do unto you, my lorde Arthure, grete honoure and kyndnesse; and hit ys grete pité he shall nat endure but a whyle, for of his strengthe and hardinesse I know hym nat lyvynge hys macche.'

So thys knyght of Irelonde armed hym at all poyntes and dressed his
40 shylde on hys sholdir and mownted uppon horsebacke and toke hys glayve in hys honde, and rode aftir a grete pace as much as hys horse myght dryve. And within a litill space on a mowntayne he had a syght of Balyne, and with a lowde voice he cryde,

'Abyde, knyght! for ells ye shall abyde whethir ye woll other no.

And the shelde that ys tofore you shall nat helpe you,' seyde thys
Iryshe knyght, 'therefore com I affter you.'

'Peradventure,' seyde Balyne, 'ye had bene bettir to have holde you at
home. For many a man wenyth to put hys enemy to a rebuke, and ofte
hit fallith on hymselff. Outc of what courte be ye com fro ?' seyde Balyn. 5

'I am com frome the courte of kynge Arthure,' seyde the knyght of
Irelonde, 'that am com hydir to revenge the despite ye dud thys day
unto kynge Arthure and to his courte.'

'Well,' seyde Balyne, 'I se well I muste have ado with you, that me
forthynkith that I have greved kynge Arthure or ony of hys courte. 10
And youre quarell ys full symple,' seyde Balyne, 'unto me; for the
lady that ys dede dud to me grete damage, and ellis I wolde have bene
lothe as ony knyght that lyvith for to sle a lady.'

'Make you redy,' seyde the knyght Launceor, 'and dresse you unto
me, for that one shall abyde in the fylde.'   15

Than they fewtred their spearis in their restis and com togidirs as
muche as their horsis myght dryve. And the Irysh knyght smote Balyn
on the shylde that all wcnte to-shyvers of hys spere. And Balyne smote
hym agayne thorow the shylde, and [the] hawbirk perysshed, and so
bore hym thorow the body and over the horse crowpen; and anone 20
turned his horse fersely and drew oute hys swerde, and wyst nat that
he had slayne hym.

Than he saw hym lye as a dede corse, he loked aboute hym and was (6)
ware of a damesel that com rydynge full faste as the horse myght dryve,
on a fayre palferey. And whan she aspyed that Launceor was slayne 25
she made sorow oute of mesure and seyde,

'A! Balyne, two bodyes thou haste sla⟨in in⟩ one herte, and two
hertes in one body, and two soules thou hast loste.'

And therewith she toke the swerde frome hir love that lay dede, and
felle to the grounde in a swowghe. And whan she arose she made grete 30
dole oute of mesure, which sorow greved Balyn passyngly sore. And
he wente unto hir for to have tane the swerde oute of hir honde; but
she helde hit so faste he myght nat take hit oute of hir honde but yf he
sholde have hurte hir. And suddeynly she sette the pomell to the grounde,
and rove hirselff thorowoute the body.   35

Whan Balyne aspyed hir dedis he was passynge hevy in his herte and
ashamed that so fayre a damesell had destroyed hirselff for the love of
hys dethe. 'Alas !' seyde Balyn, 'me repentis sore the dethe of thys
knyght for the love of thys damesel, for there was muche tr[e]w love
betwyxte hem.' And so for sorow he myght no lenger beholde them, 40
but turned hys horse and loked towarde a fayre foreste.

And than was he ware by hys armys that there com rydyng hys
brothir Balan. And whan they were mette they put of hyr helmys and
kyssed togydirs and wepte for joy and pité. Than Balan seyde,

'Brothir, I litill wende to have mette with you at thys suddayne
adventure, but I am ryght glad of youre delyveraunce of youre dolerous
presonment: for a man tolde me in the Castell of Four Stonys that ye
were delyverde, and that man had seyne you in the courte of kynge
5 Arthure, and therefore I com hydir into thys contrey, for here I supposed to fynde you.'

And anone Balyne tolde hys brothir of hys adventure of the swerde
and the deth of the Lady of the Laake, and how kynge Arthure was
displeased with hym.

10 'Wherefore he sente thys knyght afftir me that lyethe here dede.
And the dethe of thys damesell grevith me sore.'

'So doth hit me,' seyde Balan, 'but ye must take the adventure that
God woll ordayne you.'   *Free will vs determination*

'Truly,' seyde Balyne, 'I am ryght hevy that my lorde Arthure ys
15 displeased with me, for he ys the moste worshypfullist kynge that
regnith now in erthe; and hys love I woll gete othir ellis I woll
putte my lyff in adventure. For kynge Ryons lyeth at the sege of the
Castell Terrable, and thydir woll we draw in all goodly haste to preve
oure worship and prouesse uppon hym.'

20 'I woll well,' seyde Balan, 'that ye so do; and I woll ryde with you
and put my body in adventure with you, as a brothir ought to do.'

(7)   'Now go we hense,' seyde Balyne, 'and well we beth mette.'

The meanewhyle as they talked there com a dwarff frome the cité of
Camelot on horsebacke as much as he myght, and founde the dede
25 bodyes; wherefore he made grete dole and pulled hys heyre for sorowe
and seyde,

'Which of two knyghtes have done this dede?'

'Whereby askist thou?' seyde Balan.

'For I wolde wete,' seyde the dwarff.

30 'Hit was I,' seyde Balyn, 'that slew this knyght in my defendaunte;
for hyder he com to chase me, and othir I muste sle hym other he me.
And this damesell slew hirself for his love, which repentith me. And
for hir sake I shall owghe all women the bettir wylle and servyse all
the dayes of my lyff.'

35 'Alas!' seyde the dwarff, 'thou hast done grete damage unto thyselff.
For thys knyght that ys here dede was one of the moste valyauntis men
that lyved. And truste well, Balyne, the kynne of thys knyght woll
chase you thorow the worlde tylle they have slayne you.'

'As for that,' seyde Balyne, 'the⟨m⟩ I fere nat gretely; but I am ryght
40 hevy that I sholde displease my lorde, kynge Arthure, for the deth of
thys knyght.'

So as they talked togydirs there com a kynge of Cornuwayle rydyng,
which hyght kyng Marke. And whan he saw thes two bodyes dede,
and undirstood howe they were dede, ⌐by⌐ the two knyghtes

Is Balin really upset about displeasing King Arthur.

aboven-seyde, ⌐thenne⌐ made the kynge grete sorow for the trew love
that was betwyxte them, and seyde, 'I woll nat departe tyll I have on
thys erth made a towmbe.' And there he pyght his pavylyons and sought
all the contrey to fynde a towmbe, and in a chirch they founde one was
fayre and ryche. And than the kyng lette putte h[e]m bothe in the erthe, 5
and leyde the tombe uppon them, and wrote the namys of hem bothe
on the tombe, how 'here lyeth Launceor, the kyngis son of Irelonde,
that at hys owne rekeyste was slayne by the hondis of Balyne', and how
'this lady Columbe and peramour to hym slew hirself with hys swerde
for dole and sorow.'   10

The meanewhyle as thys was adoynge, in com Merlion to kynge (8)
Marke and saw all thys doynge. *Sense of time*

'Here shall be,' seyde Merlion, 'in this same place the grettist bateyle
betwyxte two [knyghtes] that ever was or ever shall be, and the
trewyst lovers; and yette none of hem shall slee other.'   15

And there Merlion wrote hir namys uppon the tombe with lettirs of
golde, that shall feyght in that place: which namys was Launcelot du
Lake and Trystrams. *Foretelling*

'Thou [art] a merveylous man,' seyde kynge Marke unto Merlion,
'that spekist of such mervayles. Thou arte a boysteous man and an   20
unlyckly, to telle of suche dedis. What ys thy name?' seyde kynge
Marke.

'At thys tyme,' seyde Merlion, 'I woll nat telle you. But at that tyme
sir Trystrams ys takyn with his soveraigne lady, than shall ye here and
know my name; and at that tyme ye shall ⌐here⌐ tydynges that shall nat 25
please you. A, Balyne!' seyde Merlion, 'thou haste done thyselff grete
hurte that thou saved nat thys lady that slew herselff; for thou myghtyst
have saved hir and thou haddist wold.'

'By the fayth of my body,' seyde Balyne, 'I myght nat save hir, for
she slewe hirselff suddeynly.' *Where did he come from*   30

'Me repentis hit,' seyde Merlion; 'because of the dethe of that lady
thou shalt stryke a stroke moste dolerous that ever man stroke, excepte
the stroke of oure Lorde Jesu Cryste. For thou shalt hurte the trewyst
knyght and the man of moste worship that now lyvith; and thorow
that stroke three kyngdomys shall be brought into grete poverté,   35
miseri and wrecchednesse twelve yere. And the knyght shall nat be
hole of that wounde many yerys.'

Than Merlion toke hys leve.

'Nay,' seyde Balyn, 'nat so; for and I wyste thou seyde soth, I
wolde do so perleous a dede that I wolde sle myself to make the   40
a lyer.'

Therewith Merlion vanysshed away suddeynly, and than Balyn and
his brother toke their leve of kynge Marke.

'But first,' seyde the kynge, 'telle me youre name.'

'Sir,' seyde Balan, 'ye may se he beryth two swerdis, and thereby ye may calle hym the Knyght with the Two Swerdis.'

And so departed kynge Marke unto Camelot to kynge Arthure.

And Balyne toke the way to kynge Royns, and as they rode togydir
5 they mette with Merlion disgysed so that they knew hym nought.

'But whotherward ryde ye?' seyde Merlion.

'We had litill ado to telle you,' seyde thes two knyghtes. 'But what ys thy name?' seyde Balyn.

'At thys tyme,' seyde Merlion, 'I woll nat telle.'
10 'Hit ys an evyll sygne,' seyde the knyghtes, 'that thou arte a trew man, that thou wolt nat telle thy name.'

'As for that,' seyde Merlion, 'be as hit be may. But I can telle you wherefore ye ryde thys way: for to mete with kynge Royns. But hit woll nat avayle you withoute ye have my counceyle.'
15 'A,' seyde Balyn, 'ye ar Merlion. We woll be ruled by youre counceyle.'

'Com on,' seyde Merlion, 'and ye shall have grete worship. And loke that ye do knyghtly, for ye shall have nede.'

'As for that,' seyde Balyne, 'dred you nat, for we woll do what we
20 may.'
(9)   Than there lodged Merlion and thes two knyghtes in a woode amonge the levis besydes the hyghway, and toke of the brydyls of their horsis and putte hem to grasse, and leyde hem downe to reste tyll hit was nyghe mydnyght. Than Merlion bade hem ryse and make hem
25 redy: 'for here commyth the kynge nyghehonde, that was stoolyn away frome his oste with a three score horsis of hys beste knyghtes, and twenty of them rode tofore the lorde to warne the Lady de Vaunce that the kynge was commynge.' For that nyght kynge Royns sholde have lyen with hir.
30 'Which ys the kynge?' seyde Balyn.

'Abyde,' seyde Merlion, 'for here in a strete ⌈weye⌉ ye shall mete with hym.' And therewith he shewed Balyn and hys brothir the kynge.

And anone they mette with hym, and smote hym downe and wounded hym freyshly, and layde hym to the growunde. And there
35 they slewe on the ryght honde and on the lyffte honde mo than fourty of hys men; and the remanaunte fledde. Than wente they agayne unto kynge Royns and wolde have slayne hym, had he nat yelded hym unto hir grace. Than seyde he thus:

'Knyghtes full of prouesse, sle me nat! For be my lyff ye may wynne,
40 and by my dethe litill.'

'Ye say sothe,' seyde the knyghtes, and so leyde hym on an horse littur.

So with that Merlion vanysshed, and com to kynge Arthure aforehonde and tolde hym how hys moste enemy was takyn and discomfite.

'By whom?' seyde kynge Arthure.

'By two knyghtes,' seyde Merlion, 'that wolde fayne have youre lordship. And to-morow ye shall know what knyghtis they ar.'

So anone aftir com the Knyght with the Two Swerdis and hys brothir, and brought with them kynge Royns of Northe Waalis, and there 5 delyverde hym to the porters, and charged hem with hym. And so they two returned aghen in the dawnyng of the day.

Than kynge Arthure com to kynge Royns and seyde, 'Sir kynge, ye ar wellcom. By what adventure com ye hydir?'

'Sir,' seyde kynge Royns, 'I com hyder by an harde adventure.' 10

'Who wanne you?' seyde kynge Arthure.

'Sir,' seyde he, 'the Knyght with the Two Swerdis and hys brothir, which ar two mervayles knyghtes of prouesse.'

'I know hem nat,' seyde Arthure, 'but much am I beholdynge unto them.' 15

'A, sir,' seyde Merlion, 'I shall telle you. Hit ys Balyn that encheved the swerde, and his brothir Balan, a good knyght: there lyvith nat a bettir of proues, nother of worthynesse. And hit shall be the grettist dole of hym that ever y knew of knyght; for he shall nat longe endure.' 20

'Alas,' seyde kynge Arthure, 'that ys grete pité; for I am muche beholdynge unto hym, and I have evill deserved hit agayne for hys kyndnesse.'

'Nay, nay,' sede Merlion, 'he shall do much more for you, and that shall ye know in haste. But, sir, ar ye purveyde?' seyde Merlion. '[For 25 to-morn] the oste of kynge Nero, kynge Royns brothir, woll sette on you or none with a grete oste. And therefore make you redy, for I woll departe frome you.'

Than kynge Arthure made hys oste redy in ten batayles; and Nero (10) was redy in the fylde afore the Castell Terrable with a grete oste. And 30 he had ten batayles with many mo peple than kynge Arthure had. Than Nero had the vawarde with the moste party of the people. And Merlion com to kynge Lotte of the Ile of Orkeney and helde hym with a tale of the prophecy tylle Nero and his peple were destroyed. And there sir Kay the Senesciall dud passyngely well, that dayes of hys lyff 35 the worship wente never frome hym, and sir Hervis de Revel that dud merveylous dedys of armys that day with Arthur. And kynge Arthure slew that day twenty knyghtes and maymed fourty.

So at that tyme com in the Knyght with the Two Swerdis and his brothir, but they dud so mervaylously that the kynge and all the knyghtes 40 mervayled of them. And all they that behelde them seyde they were sente frome hevyn as angels other devilles frome helle. And kynge Arthure seyde hymself they were the doughtyeste knyghtes that ever he sawe, for they gaff such strokes that all men had wondir of hem.

So in the meanewhyle com one to kynge Lotte and tolde hym whyle he tarryed there how Nero was destroyed and slayne with all his oste.

'Alas,' seyde kynge Lotte, 'I am ashamed; for in my defaute there ys
5 [many a worshipful man slayne; for and we had ben togyders there had ben] none oste undir hevyn were able to have macched us. But thys faytoure with hys prophecy hath mocked me.'

All that dud Merlion, for he knew well that ⌈and⌉ kynge Lotte had bene with hys body at the first batayle, kynge Arthure had be slayne
10 and all hys peple distressed. And well Merlion knew that one of the kynges sholde be dede that day; and lothe was Merlion that ony of them bothe sholde be slayne, but of the tweyne he had levir kyng Lotte of Orkeney had be slayne than Arthure.

'What ys beste to do?' seyde kynge Lotte. 'Whether ys me bettir
15 to trete with kynge Arthur othir to fyght? For the gretter party of oure people ar slayne and distressed.'

'Sir,' seyde a knyght, 'sette ye on Arthure, for they ar wery and forfoughtyn, and we be freyssh.'

'As for me,' seyde kynge Lott, 'I wolde that every knyght wolde do
20 hys parte as I wolde do myne.'

Than they avaunced baners and smote togydirs and brused hir sperys. And Arthurs knyghtes with the helpe of the Knyght with Two Swerdys and hys brothir Balan put kynge Lotte and hys oste to the warre. But allwayes kynge Lotte hylde hym ever in the fore-fronte and
25 dud merveylous dedis of armys; for all his oste was borne up by hys hondys, for he abode all knyghtes. Alas, he myght nat endure, the whych was grete pité! So worthy a knyght as he was one, that he sholde be overmacched, that of late tyme before he had bene a knyght of kynge Arthurs, and wedded the syster of hym. And for because
30 that kynge Arthure lay by hys wyff and gate on her sir Mordred, there-fore kynge Lott helde ever agaynste Arthure.

So there was a knyght that was called the Knyght with the Strange Beste, and at that tyme hys ryght name was called Pellynore, which was a good man off prouesse as few in tho dayes lyvynge. And he
35 strake a myghty stroke at kynge Lott as he fought with hys enemyes, and he fayled of hys stroke and smote the horse necke, that he foundred to the erthe with kyng Lott. And therewith anone kynge Pellinor smote hym a grete stroke thorow the helme and hede unto the browis.

Than all the oste of Orkeney fledde for the deth of kynge Lotte, and
40 there they were takyn and slayne, all the oste. But kynge Pellynore bare the wyte of the dethe of kynge Lott, wherefore sir Gawayne revenged the deth of hys fadir the ten yere aftir he was made knyght, and slew kynge Pellynor hys owne hondis. Also there was slayne at that batayle twelve kynges on the syde of kynge Lott with Nero, and

were buryed in the chirch of Seynte Stevins in Camelot. And the remanent of knyghtes and other were buryed in a grete roche.

So at the enterement com kyng Lottis wyff, Morgause, with hir (11) four sonnes, Gawayne, Aggravayne, Gaheris, and Gareth. Also there com thydir kyng Uryens, sir Uwaynes fadir, and Morgan le Fay, his 5 wyff, that was kynge Arthurs syster. All thes com to the enterement. But of all the twelve kyngis kynge Arthure lette make the tombe of kynge Lotte passynge rychely, and made hys tombe by hymselff.

And than Arthure lette make twelve images of laton and cooper, and overgylte with golde in the sygne of the twelve kynges; and eche 10 one of hem helde a tapir of wexe in hir honde that brente nyght and day. And kynge Arthure was made in the sygne of a fygure stondynge aboven them with a swerde drawyn in hys honde, and all the twelve fygures had countenaunce lyke unto men that were overcom. All thys made Merlion by hys subtyle craufte. 15

And there he tolde the kynge how that whan he was dede thes tapers sholde brenne no lenger, 'aftir the adventures of the Sankgreall that shall com amonge you and be encheved.' Also he tolde kynge Arthure how Balyn, the worshipfull knyght, shall gyff the dolerouse stroke, whereof shall falle grete vengeaunce. 20

'A, where ys Balyne, Balan, and Pellinore?'

'As for kynge Pellinore,' seyde Merlion, 'he woll mete with you soone. And as for Balyne, he woll nat be longe frome you. But the other brothir woll departe: ye shall se hym no more.'

'Be my fayth,' seyde Arthur, 'they ar two manly knyghtes, and 25 namely that Balyne passith of proues off ony knyght that ever y founde, for much am I beholdynge unto hym. Wolde God he wolde abyde with me!'

'Sir,' seyde Merlion, 'loke ye kepe well the scawberd of Excaleber, for ye shall lose no bloode whyle ye have the scawberde uppon you, 30 thoughe ye have as many woundis uppon you as ye may have.'

So aftir for grete truste Arthure betoke the scawberde unto Morgan le Fay, hys sister. And she loved another knyght bettir than hir husbande, kynge Uriens, othir Arthure. And she wolde have had Arthure hir brother slayne, and therefore she lete make anothir scawberd for 35 Excaliber ⌐lyke it by enchauntement, and gaf the scawberd Excaliber to her lover⌐. And the knyghtes name was called Accolon, that aftir had nere slayne kynge Arthure. But after thys Merlion tolde unto kynge Arthure of the prophecy that there sholde be a grete batayle besydes Salysbiry, and Mordred hys owne sonne sholde be agaynste 40 hym. Also he tolde hym that Bagdemagus was his cosyne germayne, and unto kynge Uryens.

So within a day or two kynge Arthure was somwhat syke, and he (12) lette pycch hys pavilion in a medow, and there he leyde hym downe on a paylet to slepe; but he myght have no reste. Ryght so he herde a grete noyse of an horse, and therewith the kynge loked oute at the porche dore of the pavilion and saw a knyght commynge evyn by hym makynge grete dole.

'Abyde, fayre sir,' seyde Arthure, 'and telle me wherefore thou makyst this sorow.'

'Ye may litill amende me,' seyde the knyght, and so passed forth to the Castell of Meliot.

And anone aftir that com Balyne. And whan he saw kyng Arthur he alyght of hys horse and com to the kynge one foote and salewed hym.

'Be my hede,' seyde Arthure, 'ye be wellcom. Sir, ryght now com rydynge thys way a knyght makynge grete mone, and for what cause I can nat telle. Wherefore I wolde desire of you, of your curtesy and of your jantilnesse, to fecche agayne that knyght othir by force othir by his good wylle.'

'I shall do more for youre lordeship than that,' seyde Balyne, 'othir ellis I woll greve hym.'

So Balyn rode more than a pace and founde the knyght with a damesell undir a foreyste and seyde,

'Sir knyght, ye muste com with me unto kynge Arthure for to telle hym of youre sorow.'

'That woll I nat,' seyde the knyght, 'for hit woll harme me gretely and do you none avayle.'

'Sir,' seyde Balyne, 'I pray you make you redy, for ye muste go with me othir ellis I muste fyght with you and brynge you by for⌜c⌝e. And that were me lothe to do.'

'Woll ye be my warraunte,' seyde the knyght, 'and I go with you?'

'Yee,' seyde Balyne, 'othir ellis, by the fayth of my body, I woll dye therefore.'

And so he made hym redy to go with Balyne and leffte the damesell stylle. And as they were evyn before Arthurs pavilion, there com one invisible and smote the knyght that wente with Balyn thorowoute the body with a spere.

'Alas!' seyde the knyght, 'I am slayne undir youre conduyte with a knyght called ⌜Garlon⌝. Therefore take my horse that is bettir than youres, and ryde to the damesell and folow the queste that I was in as she woll lede you, and revenge my deth whan ye may.'

'That shall I do,' seyde Balyn, 'and that I make avow to God and knyghthode.'

And so he departed frome kynge Arthure with grete sorow.

So kynge Arthure lette bury this knyght rychely, and made mencion [on] his tombe how here was slayne Berbeus and by whom the trechory was done of the knyght ⌜Garlon⌝. But ever the damesell bare the truncheon of the spere with hir that sir Harleus le Berbeus was slayne withall.

So Balyne and the damescll rode into the foreyste and there mette (13) with a knyght that had bene an-hontynge. And that knyght asked Balyn for what cause he made so grete sorow.   5

'Me lyste nat to telle,' seyde Balyne.

'Now,' seyde the knyght, 'and I were armed as ye be, I wolde fyght with you but iff ye tolde me.'

'That sholde litell nede,' seyde Balyne, 'I am nat aferde to telle you,' and so tolde hym all the case how hit was.   10

'A,' seyde the knyght, 'ys thys all? Here I ensure you by the feyth of my body never to departe frome you whyle my lyff lastith.'

And so they wente to their ostré and armed hem and so rode forthe with Balyne. And as they com by an ermytage evyn by a chy[r]cheyerde, there com ⌜Garlon⌝ invisible and smote this knyght, Peryne de Mounte 15 Belyarde, thorowoute the body with a glayve.

'Alas,' seyde the knyght, 'I am slayne by thys traytoure knyght that rydith invisible.'

'Alas,' seyde Balyne, 'thy ys nat the first despite that he hath done me.'   20

And there the ermyte and Balyne buryed the knyght undir a ryche stone and a tombe royall. And on the morne they founde letters of golde wretyn how that sir Gawayne shall revenge his fadirs dethe ⌜kynge Lot⌝ on kynge Pellynore.

And anone aftir this Balyne and the damesell rode forth tylle they 25 com to a castell. And anone Balyne alyghte and wente in. And as sone as ⌜Balyne came⌝ with⌐in the castels yate⌐ the portecolys were lette downe at his backe, and there fell many men aboute the damesell and wolde have slayne hir. Whan Balyne saw that, he was sore greved for he myght nat helpe her. But than he wente up into a towre and lepte 30 over the wallis into the dyche and hurte nat hymselff. And anone he pulled oute his swerde and wolde have foughtyn with them. And they all seyde nay, they wolde nat fyght with hym, for they dud nothynge but the olde custom of thys castell, and tolde hym that hir lady was syke and had leyne many yeres, and she myght nat be hole but yf she 35 had bloode in a sylver dysshe full, of a clene mayde and a kynges doughter.

'And therefore the custom of thys castell ys that there shall no damesell passe thys way but she shall blede of hir bloode a sylver dysshefull.'   40

'Well,' seyde Balyne, 'she shall blede as much as she may blede, but I woll nat lose the lyff of hir whyle my lyff lastith.'

And so Balyn made hir to bleede by hir good wylle, but hir bloode holpe nat the lady. And so she and he rested there all that nyght and had good chere, and in the mornynge they passed on their wayes. And as hit tellith aftir in the SANKGREALL that sir Percivall his syster holpe that lady with hir blood, whereof she was dede.

(14)   Than they rode three or four dayes and nevir mette with adventure. And so by fortune they were lodged with a jantilman ⌐that was a ryche man and well at ease⌐. And as they sate at souper Balyn herde one complayne grevously by hym in a chambir.

'What ys thys noyse?' seyde Balyn.

'For sothe,' seyde his oste, 'I woll telle you. I was but late at a justynge and there I justed with a knyght that ys brothir unto kynge Pellam, and twyse 1 smote hym downe. And than he promysed to quyte me on my beste frende. And so he wounded thus my son that can nat be hole tylle I have of that knyghtes bloode. And he rydith all invisyble, but I know nat hys name.'

'A,' seyde Balyne, 'I know that knyghtes name, which ys ⌐Garlon⌐, and he hath slayne two knyghtes of myne in the same maner. Therefore I had levir mete with that knyght than all the golde in thys realme, for the despyte he hath done me.'

'Well,' seyde hys oste, 'I shall telle you how. Kynge Pellam off Lystenoyse hath made do cry in all the contrey a grete feste that shall be within thes twenty dayes, and no knyght may com there but he brynge hys wyff with hym othir hys paramoure. And that your enemy and myne ye shall se that day.'

'Than I promyse you,' seyde Balyn, 'parte of his bloode to hele youre sonne withall.'

'Than we woll be forewarde to-morne,' seyde he.

So on the morne they rode all three towarde kynge Pellam, and they had fyftene dayes journey or they com thydir. And that same day began the grete feste. And so they alyght and stabled their horsis and wente into the castell, but Balynes oste myght ⌐not⌐ be lette in because he had no lady. But Balyne was well receyved and brought unto a chambir and unarmed hym. And there was brought hym robis to his plesure, and wolde have had Balyn leve his swerde behynde hym.

'Nay,' seyde Balyne, 'that woll I nat, for hit ys the custom of my contrey a knyght allweyes to kepe hys wepyn with hym. Other ells,' seyde he, 'I woll departe as I ⌐c⌐am.'

Than they gaff hym leve with his swerde, and so he wente into the castell and was amonge knyghtes of worship and hys lady afore hym. So aftir this Balyne asked a knyght and seyde,

'Ys there nat a knyght in thys courte which his name ys ⌐Garlon⌐?'

'Yes, sir, yondir he goth, the knyght with the blacke face, for he ys the mervaylyste knyght that ys now lyvynge. And he destroyeth many good knyghtes, for he goth invisible.'

'Well,' seyde Balyn, 'ys that he?' Than Balyn avised hym longe, and thought: 'If I sle hym here, I shall nat ascape. And if I leve hym now, peraventure I shall never mete with hym agayne at such a stevyn, and muche harme he woll do and he lyve.' *Moral Dilemma*

And therewith thys ˹Garlon˺ aspyed that Balyn vysaged hym, so he com and slapped hym on the face with the backe of hys honde and seyde,

'Knyght, why beholdist thou me so? For shame, ete thy mete and do that thou com fore.' *Balin forced(?)*

'Thou seyst soth,' seyde Balyne, 'thys ys nat the firste spite that thou haste done me. And therefore I woll do that I come fore.' And rose hym up fersely and clave his hede to the sholdirs.

'Now geff me ˹the˺ troncheon,' seyde Balyn ˹to his lady˺, 'that he slew youre knyght with.'

And anone she gaff hit hym, for allwey she bare the truncheoune with hir. And therewith Balyn smote hym thorow the body and seyde opynly,

'With that troncheon thou slewyste a good knyght, and now hit stykith in thy body.' Than Balyn called unto hys oste and seyde, 'Now may ye fecche blood inowghe to hele youre son withall.'

So anone all the knyghtes rose frome the table for to sette on Balyne. And kynge Pellam hymself arose up fersely and seyde,

'Knyght, why hast thou slayne my brothir? Thou shalt dey therefore or thou departe.'

'Well,' seyde Balyn, 'do hit youreselff.'

'Yes,' seyde kyng Pellam, 'there shall no man have ado with the but I myselff, for the love of my brothir.'

Than kynge Pellam ˹caught in his hand˺ a grymme wepyn and smote egirly at Balyn, but he put hys swerde betwyxte hys hede and the stroke, and therewith hys swerde braste in sundir. And whan Balyne was wepynles he ran into a chambir for to seke a wepyn [and] fro chambir to chambir, and no wepyn coude he fynde. And allwayes kyng Pellam folowed afftir hym. And at the last he enterde into a chambir (which) was mervaylously dyght and ryche, and a bedde arayed with cloth of golde, the rychiste that myght be, and one lyyng therein. And thereby stoode a table of clene golde ˹with four pelours of sylver that bare up the table˺, and uppon the table stoode a mervaylous spere strangely wrought.

So whan Balyn saw the spere he gate hit in hys honde and turned to kynge Pellam and felde hym and smote hym passyngly sore with that spere, that kynge Pellam [felle] downe in a sowghe. And therewith the castell brake rooffe and wallis and felle downe to the erthe. And Balyn felle downe and myght nat styrre hande nor foote, and for the moste party of that castell was dede thorow the dolorouse stroke.

Ryght so lay kynge Pellam and Balyne three dayes.

Merlin? Strangely powerful spear.

(16) Than Merlion com thydir, and toke up Balyn and gate hym a good horse, for hys was dede, and bade hym voyde oute of that contrey.

'Sir, I wolde have my damesell,' seyde Balyne.

'Loo,' seyde Merlion, 'where she lyeth dede.'

5 And kynge Pellam lay so many yerys sore wounded, and myght never be hole tylle that Galaad the Hawte Prynce heled hym in the queste of the Sankgreall. For in that place was parte of the bloode of oure Lorde Jesu Cryste, which Joseph off Aramathy brought into thys londe. And there hymselff [lay] in that ryche bedde. And that was 10 the spere whych Longeus smote oure Lorde with to the herte. And kynge Pellam was nyghe of Joseph his kynne, and that was the moste worshipfullist man on lyve in tho dayes, and grete pité hit was of hys hurte, for thorow that stroke hit turned to grete dole, tray and tene.

Than departed Balyne frome Merlyon, 'for,' he seyde, 'nevir in thys 15 worlde we parte nother meete no more.' So he rode forthe thorow the fayre contreyes and citeys and founde the peple dede slayne on every syde, and all that evir were on lyve cryed and seyde,

'A, Balyne! Thou hast done and caused grete vengeaunce in thys contreyes! For the dolerous stroke thou gaff unto kynge Pellam thes 20 three contreyes ar destroyed. And doute nat but the vengeaunce woll falle on the at the laste!'

But whan Balyn was past tho contreyes he was passynge fayne, and so he rode eyght dayes or he mette with many adventure. And at the last he com into a fayre foreyst in a valey, and was ware of a towure. 25 And there besyde he mette with a grete horse tyed to a tree, and besyde there sate a fayre knyght on the grounde and made grete mournynge, and he was a lyckly man and a well made. Balyne seyde,

'God you save! Why be ye so hevy? Telle me, and I woll amende hit, and I may, to my power.'

30 'Sir knyght,' he seyde, 'thou doste me grete gryeff, for I was in ⌐mery⌐ thoughtes and now thou puttist me to more payne.'

Than Balyn went a litill frome hym and loked on hys horse, than herde Balyne hym sey thus:

'A, fayre lady! Why have ye brokyn my promyse? For ye promysed 35 me to mete me here by noone. And I may curse you that ever ye gaff me that swerde, for with thys swerde I woll sle myselff,' and pulde hit oute.

And therewith com Balyne and sterte unto hym and toke hym by the honde.

40 'Lette go my hande,' seyde the knyght, 'or ellis I shall sle the!'

'That shall nat nede,' seyde Balyn, 'for I shall promyse you my helpe to gete you youre lady and ye woll telle me where she ys.'

'What ys your name?' seyde the knyght.

'Sir, my name ys Balyne le Saveage.'

'A, sir, I know you well inowghe: ye ar the Knyght with the Two
Swerdis, and the man of moste proues of youre hondis lyvynge.'

'What ys youre name?' seyde Balyne.

'My name ys Garnysh of the Mownte, a poore mannes sonne, and
be my proues and hardynes a deuke made me knyght and gave me 5
londis. Hys name ys duke Harmel, and hys doughter ys [she that I love,
and she me, as I demed.'

'Hou fer is she hens?' sayd Balyn.

'But eleven myle,' said the knyghte.

'Now ryde we hens,' sayde these two knyghtes.   10

So they rode more than a paas tyll that they cam to a fayr castel wel
wallyd and dyched.

'I wylle into the castel,' sayd Balen, 'and loke yf she be ther.'

Soo he wente in and serched fro chamber to chambir and fond her
bedde, but she was not there. Thenne Balen loked into a fayr litil 15
gardyn, and under a laurel tre he sawe her lye upon a quylt of grene
samyte, and a knyght in her armes fast halsynge eyther other, and under
their hedes grasse and herbes. Whan Balen sawe her lye so with the
fowlest knyghte that ever he sawe, and she a fair lady, thenne Balyn
wente thurgh alle the chambers ageyne and told the knyghte how he 20
fond her as she had slepte fast, and so brought hym in the place there
she lay fast slepynge.

And whan Garnyssh beheld hir so lyeng, for pure sorou his mouth (17)
and nose brast oute on bledynge. And with his swerd he smote of bothe
their hedes, and thenne he maade sorowe oute of mesure and sayd, 25

'O, Balyn! Moche sorow hast thow brought unto me, for haddest
thow not shewed me that syght I shold have passed my sorow.'

'Forsoth,' said Balyn, 'I did it to this entent that it sholde better thy
courage, and that ye myght see and knowe her falshede, and to cause
yow to leve love of suche a lady. God knoweth I dyd none other but 30
as I wold ye dyd to me.'

'Allas,' said Garnysshe, 'now is my sorou doubel that I may not
endure, now have I slayne that I moost loved in al my lyf!'

And therwith sodenly he roofe hymself on his own swerd unto the
hyltys.   35

When Balen sawe that, he dressid hym thensward, lest folke wold
say he had slayne them, and so he rode forth. And within thre dayes
he cam by a crosse; and theron were letters of gold wryten that said:
'it is not for no knyght alone to ryde toward this castel.' Thenne sawe
he an old hore gentylman comyng toward hym that sayd,   40

'Balyn le Saveage, thow passyst thy bandes to come this waye,
therfor torne ageyne and it will availle the,' and he vanysshed awey
anone.

And soo he herd an horne blowe as it had ben the dethe of a best.

'That blast,' said Balyn, 'is blowen for me, for I am the pryse, and yet am I not dede.' Anone withal he sawe an honderd ladyes and many knyghtes that welcommed hym with fayr semblaunt and made hym passyng good chere unto his syght, and ledde hym into the castel, and
5 ther was daunsynge and mynstralsye and alle maner of joye. Thenne the chyef lady of the castel said,

'Knyghte with the Two Suerdys, ye must have adoo and juste with a knyght hereby that kepeth an iland, for ther may no man passe this way but he must juste or he passe.'
10 'That is an unhappy cust019me,' said Balyn, 'that a knyght may not passe this wey but yf he juste.'

'Ye shalle not have adoo but with one knyghte,' sayd the lady.

'Wel,' sayd Balyn, 'syn I shalle, therto I am redy; but traveillynge men are ofte wery and their horses to, but though my hors be wery
15 my hert is not wery. I wold be fayne ther my deth shold be.'

'Syr,' said a knyght to Balyn, 'methynketh your sheld is not good; I wille lene yow a byggar, therof I pray yow.'

And so he tooke the sheld that was unknowen and lefte his owne, and so rode unto the iland and put hym and his hors in a grete boote. And
20 whan he came on the other syde he met with a damoysel, and she said,

'O, knyght Balyn, why have ye lefte your owne sheld? Allas! ye have put yourself in grete daunger, for by your sheld ye shold have ben knowen. It is grete pyté of yow as ever was of knyght, for of thy
25 prowesse and hardynes thou hast no felawe lyvynge.'

'Me repenteth,' said Balyn, 'that ever I cam within this countrey; but I maye not torne now ageyne for shame, and what aventure shalle falle to me, be it lyf or dethe, I wille take the adventure that shalle come to me.'
30 And thenne he loked on his armour and understood he was wel
(18) armed, and therwith blessid hym and mounted upon his hors. Thenne afore hym he sawe come rydynge oute of a castel a knyght, and his hors trapped all reed, and hymself in the same colour. Whan this knyghte in the reed beheld Balyn hym thought it shold be his broder
35 Balen by cause of his two swerdys, but by cause he knewe not his sheld he demed it was not he.

And so they aventryd theyr speres and came merveillously fast togyders, and they smote other in the sheldes, but theire speres and theire cours were soo bygge that it bare doune hors and man, that they
40 lay bothe in a swoun, but Balyn was brysed sore with the falle of his hors, for he was wery of travaille. And Balan was the fyrst that rose on foote and drewe his swerd and wente toward Balyn, and he aroos and wente ageynst hym; but Balan smote Balyn fyrste, and he put up his shelde and smote hym thorow the shelde and tamyd his helme. Thenne

Balyn smote hym ageyne with that unhappy swerd and wel-nyghe had fellyd his broder Balan, and so they fought ther togyders tyl theyr brethes faylled.

Thenne Balyn loked up to the castel and sawe the towres stand ful of ladyes. Soo they went unto bataille ageyne and wounded everyche 5 other dolefully, and thenne they brethed oftymes, and so wente unto bataille that alle the place thereas they fought was blood reed. And att that tyme ther was none of them bothe but they hadde eyther smyten other seven grete woundes so that the lest of them myght have ben the dethe of the myghtyest gyaunt in this world. 10

Thenne they wente to batail ageyn so merveillously that doubte it was to here of that bataille for the grete blood shedynge; and their hawberkes unnaillcd, that naked they were on every syde. Atte last Balan, the yonger broder, withdrewe hym a lytel and leid hym doune. Thenne said Balyn le Saveage, 15

'What knyghte arte thow? For or now I found never no knyght that matched me.'

'My name is,' said he, 'Balan, broder unto the good knyght Balyn.'

'Allas!' sayd Balyn, 'that ever I shold see this day,' and therwith he felle backward in a swoune. 20

Thenne Balan yede on al four feet and handes, and put of the helme of his broder, and myght not knowe hym by the vysage, it was so ful hewen and bledde; but whan he awoke he sayd,

'O, Balan, my broder! Thow hast slayne me and I the, wherfore alle the wyde world shalle speke of us bothe.' 25

'Allas!' sayd Balan, 'that ever I sawe this day that thorow myshap I myght not knowe yow! For I aspyed wel your two swerdys, but bycause ye had another shild I demed ye had ben another knyght.'

'Allas!' saide Balyn, 'all that maade an unhappy knyght in the castel, for he caused me to leve myn owne shelde to our bothes destruction. 30 And yf I myght lyve I wold destroye that castel for ylle customes.'

'That were wel done,' said Balan, 'for I had never grace to departe fro hem syn that I cam hyther, for here it happed me to slee a knyght that kept this iland, and syn myght I never departe, and no more shold ye, broder, and ye myght have slayne me as ye have and escaped your- 35 self with the lyf.'

Ryght so cam the lady of the toure with four knyghtes and six ladyes and six yomen unto them, and there she herd how they made her mone eyther to other and sayd, 'We came bothe oute of one ⟨w⟩ombe, that is to say one moders bely, and so shalle we lye bothe in one pytte.' So 40 Balan prayd the lady of her gentylnesse for his true servyse that she wold burye them bothe in that same place there the bataille was done, and she graunted hem with wepynge it shold be done rychely in the best maner.

'Now wille ye sende for a preest, that we may receyve our sacrament and receyve the blessid body of oure Lord Jesu Cryst?'

'Ye,' said the lady, 'it shalle be done;' and so she sente for a preest and gaf hem her ryghtes.

5 'Now,' sayd Balen, 'whan we are buryed in one tombe and the mensyon made over us how two bretheren slewe eche other, there wille never good knyght nor good man see our tombe but they wille pray for our soules,' and so alle the ladyes and gentylwymen wepte for pyté.

Thenne anone Balan dyed, but Balyn dyed not tyl the mydnyghte 10 after. And so were they buryed bothe, and the lady lete make a mensyon of Balan how he was ther slayne by his broders handes, but she knewe not Balyns name.

(19) In the morne cam Merlyn and lete wryte Balyns name on the tombe with letters of gold that 'here lyeth Balyn le Saveage that was the 15 knyght with the two swerdes and he that smote the dolorous stroke.' Also Merlyn lete make there a bedde, that ther shold never man lye therin but he wente oute of his wytte. Yet Launcelot de Lake fordyd that bed thorow his noblesse.

And anone after Balyn was dede Merlyn toke his swerd and toke of 20 the pomel and set on another pomel. So Merlyn] bade a knyght that stood before hym to handyll that swerde, and he assayde hit and myght nat handyll hit. Than Merlion lowghe.

'Why lawghe ye?' seyde the knyght.

'Thys ys the cause,' seyde Merlion: 'there shall never man handyll 25 thys swerde but the beste knyght of the worlde, and that shall be sir Launcelot other ellis Galahad, hys sonne. And Launcelot with [t]hys swerde shall sle the man in the worlde that he lovith beste: that shall be sir Gawayne.'

And all thys he lette wryte in the pomell of the swerde.

30 Than Merlion lette make a brygge of iron and of steele into that ilonde, and hit was but halff a foote brode: 'and there shall never man passe that brygge nother have hardynesse to go over hit but yf he were a passynge good man withoute trechery or vylany.' Also the scawberd off Balyns swerde Merlion lefte hit on thys syde the ilonde, 35 that Galaad sholde fynde hit. Also Merlion lette make by hys suttelyté that Balynes swerde was put into a marbil stone stondynge upryght, as grete as a mylstone, and hoved allwayes above the watir, and dud many yeres. And so by adventure hit swamme downe by the streme unto the cité of Camelot, that ys in Englysh called Wynchester, and that 40 same day Galahad the Haute Prynce com with kynge Arthure, and so Galaad brought with hym the scawberde and encheved the swerde that was in the marble stone hovynge uppon the watir. And on Whytsonday he enchevyd the swerde, as hit ys rehersed in THE BOOKE OF THE SANKGREALL.

Sone aftir thys was done Merlion com to kynge Arthur and tolde hym of the dolerous stroke that Balyn gaff kynge Pellam, and how Balyn and Balan fought togydirs the merveyl[yste] batayle that evir was herde off, and how they were buryed bothe in one tombe.

'Alas!' seyde kynge Arthure, 'thys ys the grettist pité that ever I 5 herde telle off of two knyghtes, for in thys worlde I knewe never such two knyghtes.'

THUS ENDITH THE TALE OF BALYN AND BALAN, TWO BRETHIRNE THAT WERE BORNE IN NORTHHUMBIRLONDE, THAT WERE TWO PASSYNGE GOOD KNYGHTES AS EVER WERE IN THO DAYES. 10

EXPLICIT.

III. TORRE AND PELLINOR

I N the begynnyng of Arthure, aftir he was chosyn kynge by adventure III (1) and by grace, for the moste party of the barowns knew nat he was Uther Pendragon son but as Merlyon made hit opynly knowyn, but 15 yet many kyngis and lordis hylde hym grete werre for that cause. But well Arthur overcom hem all: the moste party dayes of hys lyff he was ruled by the counceile of Merlyon. So hit felle on a tyme kyng Arthur seyde unto Merlion,

'My barownes woll let me have no reste but nedis I muste take a 20 wyff, and I wolde none take but by thy counceile and advice.'

'Hit ys well done,' seyde Merlyon, 'that ye take a wyff, for a man of youre bounté and nobles scholde not be withoute a wyff. Now is there ony,' seyde Marlyon, 'that ye love more than another?'

'Ye,' seyde kyng Arthure, 'I love Gwenyvere, the kynges doughtir 25 of Lodegrean, of the londe of Camelerde, the whyche holdyth in his house the Table Rounde that ye tolde me he had hit of my fadir Uther. And this damesell is the moste valyaunte and fayryst that I know lyvyng, or yet that ever I coude fynde.'

'Sertis,' seyde M[e]rlyon, 'as of her beauté and fayrenesse she is one 30 of the fayrest on lyve. But and ye loved hir not so well as ye do, I scholde fynde you a damesell of beauté and of goodnesse that scholde lyke you and please you, and youre herte were nat sette. But thereas mannes herte is sette he woll be loth to returne.'

'That is trouthe,' seyde kyng Arthur. 35

But M[e]rlyon warned the kyng covertly that Gwenyver was nat holsom for hym to take to wyff. For he warned hym that Launcelot scholde love hir, and sche hym agayne, and so he turned his tale to the aventures of the Sankegreal.

Than Merlion desyred of the kyng for to have men with hym that scholde enquere of Gwenyver, and so the kyng gr[a]unted hym. And so Merlyon wente forthe unto kyng Lodegrean of Camylerde, and tolde hym of the desire of the kyng that he wolde have unto his wyff
5 Gwenyver, his doughter.

'That is to me,' seyde kyng Lodegreauns, 'the beste tydynges that ever I herde, that so worthy a kyng of prouesse and noblesse wol wedde my doug[h]ter. And as for my londis, I wolde geff hit hym yf I wyste hit myght please hym, but he hath londis inow, he nedith none.
10 But I shall sende hym a gyffte that shall please hym muche more, for I shall gyff hym the Table Rounde whych Uther, hys fadir, gaff me. And whan hit ys fullé complete there ys an hondred knyghtes and fyfty. And as for an hondred good knyghtes, I have myselff, but I wante fyfty, for so many hathe be slayne in my dayes.'
15 And so kynge Lodgreaunce delyverd hys doughtir Gwenyver unto Merlion, and the Table Rounde with the hondred knyghtes; and so they rode freysshly with grete royalté, what by watir and by londe, tyll
(2) that they com nyghe unto London. Whan kynge Arthure herde of the commynge of quene Gwenyver and the hondred knyghtes with the
20 Table Rounde, than kynge Arthure made grete joy for hir commyng and that ryche presente, and seyde opynly,

'Thys fayre lady ys passyngly wellcom to me, for I have loved hir longe, and therefore there ys nothynge so leeff to me. And thes knyghtes with the Table Rownde pleasith me more than ryght grete
25 rychesse.'

And in all haste the kynge lete ordayne for the maryage and the coronacion in the moste hono[r]ablyst wyse that cowude be devised.

'Now, Merlion,' seyde kynge Arthure, 'go thou and aspye me in all thys londe fyfty knyghtes which bene of moste prouesse and worship.'
30 So within shorte tyme Merlion had founde such knyghtes that sholde fulfylle twenty and eyght knyghtes, but no mo wolde he fynde. Than the Bysshop of Caunturbiry was [f]ette, and he blyssed the segis with grete royalté and devocion, and there sette the eyght and twenty knyghtes in her segis. And whan thys was done Merlion seyde,
35 'Fayre sirres, ye muste all aryse and com to kynge Arthure for to do hym omage; he woll the better be in wylle to maynteyne you.'

And so they arose and dud their omage. And whan they were gone Merlion founde in every sege lettirs of golde that tolde the knyghtes namys that had sitte[n] there, but two segis were voyde. And so anone
40 com in yonge Gawayne and asked the kynge a gyffte.

'Aske,' seyde the kynge, 'and I shall graunte you.'

'Sir, I aske that ye shall make me knyght that same day that ye shall wedde dame Gwenyver.'

'I woll do hit with a goode wylle,' seyde kynge Arthure, 'and do

unto you all the worship that I may, for I muste be reson ye ar my
nevew, my sistirs son.'

Forthwithall there com a poore man into the courte and brought (3)
with hym a fayre yonge man of eyghtene yere of ayge, rydynge uppon
a lene mare. And the poore man asked all men that he mette,   5
    'Where shall I fynde kynge Arthure?'
    'Yondir he ys,' seyde the knyghtes. 'Wolt tho[u] onythynge with
hym?'
    'Ye,' seyde the poore man, 'therefore I cam hydir.' And as sone as
he com before the kynge he salewed hym and seyde, 'Kynge Arthure,   10
the floure of all kyngis, I beseche Jesu save the! Sir, hit was tolde me
that [at] thys tyme of youre maryaige ye wolde gyff ony man the gyffte
that he wolde aske you excepte hit were unresonable.'
    'That ys trouthe,' seyde the kynge, 'such cryes I lette make, and that
woll I holde, so hit appayre nat my realme nor myne astate.'   15
    'Ye sey well and graciously,' seyde the pore man. 'Sir, I aske nothynge
elis but that ye woll make my sonne knyght.'
    'Hit ys a grete thynge thou askyst off me,' seyde the kynge. 'What
ys thy name?' seyde the kynge to the poore man.
    'Sir, my name ys Aryes the cowherde.'   20
    'Whethir commith thys of the other ells of thy sonne?' seyde the
kynge.
    'Nay, sir,' seyd Aryes, 'thys desyre commyth of my son and nat off
me. For I shall telle you, I have thirtene sonnes, and all they woll falle
to what laboure I putte them and woll be ryght glad to do laboure; 25
but thys chylde woll nat laboure for nothynge that my wyff and I may
do, but allwey he woll be shotynge, or castynge dartes, and glad for
to se batayles and to beholde knyghtes. And allwayes day and nyght
he desyrith of me to be made knyght.'
    'What ys thy name?' seyde the kynge unto the yonge man.   30
    'Sir, my name ys Torre.'
    Than the kynge behelde hym faste and saw he was passyn[g]ly well
vysaged and well made of hys yerys.
    'Well,' seyde kynge Arthure unto Aryes the cowherde, 'go fecche
all thy sonnes before me that I may see them.'   35
    And so the pore man dud. And all were shapyn muche lyke the poore
man, but Torre was nat lyke hym nother in shappe ne in countenaunce,
for he was muche more than ony of them.
    'Now,' seyde kynge Arthur unto the cowherde, 'where ys the
swerde he shall [b]e made knyght withall?'   40
    'Hyt ys here,' seyde Torre.
    'Take hit oute of the shethe,' sayde the kynge, 'and requyre me to
make you knyght.'
    Than Torre alyght of hys mare and pulled oute hys swerde, knelynge

and requyrynge the kynge to make hym knyght, and that he made hym knyght of the Table Rounde.

'As for a knyght I woll make you,' and therewith smote him in the necke with the swerde. 'Be ye a good knyght, and so I pray to God ye
5 may be, and if ye be of proues and worthynes ye shall be of the Table Rounde.'

'Now, Merlion,' seyde Arthure, 'whethir thys Torre shall be a goode man?'

'Yee, hardely, sir, he ought to be a good man for he ys com of good
10 kynrede as ony on lyve, and of kynges bloode.'

'How so, sir?' seyd the kynge.

'I shall telle you,' seyde Merlion. 'Thys poore man Aryes the cowherde ys nat his fadir, for he ys no sybbe to hym; for kynge Pellynore ys hys fadir.'

15 'I suppose nat,' seyde the cowherde.

'Well, fecch thy wyff before me,' seyde Merlion, 'and she shall nat sey nay.'

Anone the wyff was fette forth, which was a fayre houswyff. And there she answerde Merlion full womanly, and there she tolde the
20 kynge and Merlion that whan she was a mayde and wente to mylke hir kyne, 'there mette with me a sterne knyght, and half be force he had my maydynhode. And at that tyme he begate my sonne Torre, and he toke awey fro me my grayhounde that I had that tyme with me, and seyde he wolde kepe the grayhounde for my love.'

25 'A,' seyde the cowherde, 'I wente hit had nat be thus, but I may beleve hit well, for he had never no tacchys of me.'

Sir Torre seyde unto Merlion,

'Dishonoure nat my modir.'

'Sir,' seyde Merlion, 'hit ys more for your worship than hurte, for
30 youre fadir ys a good knyght and a kynge, and he may ryght well avaunce you and youre modir both, for ye were begotyn or evir she was wedded.'

'That ys trouthe,' seyde the wyff.

'Hit ys the lesse gryff unto me,' seyde the cowherde.

(4) 35 So on the morne kynge Pellynor com to the courte of kynge Arthure. And he had grete joy of hym and tolde hym of sir Torre, how he was hys sonne, and how he had made hym knyght at the requeste of the cowherde. Whan kynge Pellynor behelde sir Torre he plesed hym muche. So the kynge made Gawayne knyght, but sir Torre was the
40 firste he made at that feste.

'What ys the cause,' seyde kynge Arthure, 'that there ys two placis voyde in the segis?'

'Sir,' seyd Merlion, 'there shall no man sitte in tho placis but they that shall be moste of worship. But in the Sege Perelous there shall

nevir man sitte but one, and yf there be ony so hardy to do hit he shall
be destroyed, and he that shall sitte therein shall have no felowe.' And
therewith Merlyon toke kynge Pellinor by the honde, and in that one
hande nexte the two segis, and the Sege Perelous, he seyde in opyn
audiens, 'Thys [is] your place, for beste ar ye worthy to sitte thereinne 5
of ony that here ys.'

And thereat had sir Gawayne grete envy and tolde Gaherys hys
brothir,

'Yondir knyght ys putte to grete worship, whych grevith me sore,
for he slewe oure fadir kynge Lott. Therefore I woll sle hym,' seyde 10
Gawayne, 'with a swerde that was sette me that ys passynge trencheaunte.'

'Ye shall nat so,' seyde Gaheris, 'at thys tyme, for as now I am but
youre squyre, and whan I am made knyght I woll be avenged on hym;
and therefore, brothir, hit ys beste to suffir tyll another tyme, that we 15
may have hym oute of courte, for and we dud so we shall trouble thys
hyghe feste.'

'I woll well,' seyde Gawayne.

Than was thys feste made redy, and the kynge was wedded at (5)
Camelot unto dame Gwenyvere in the chirche of Seynte Stephyns with 20
grete solempnité. Than as every man was sette as hys degré asked,
Merlion wente to all the knyghtes of the Rounde Table and bade hem
sitte stylle, 'that none of you remeve, for ye shall se a straunge and a
mervailous adventure.'

Ryght so as they sate there com rennynge inne a whyght herte into 25
the hall, and a whyght brachet nexte hym, and thirty couple of blacke
rennynge houndis com afftir with a grete cry. And the herte wente
aboute the Rounde Table, and as he wente by the syde-bourdis the
brachet ever boote hym by the buttocke and pulde outte a pece, wherethorow the herte lope a grete lepe and overthrew a knyght that sate at 30
the syde-bourde. And therewith the knyght arose and toke up the
brachet, and so wente forthe oute of the halle and toke hys horse and
rode hys way with the brachett.

Ryght so com in the lady on a whyght palferey and cryed alowde unto
kynge Arthure and seyd, 'Sir, suffir me nat to have thys despite, for 35
the brachet ys myne that the knyght hath ladde away.'

'I may nat do therewith,' seyde the kynge.

So with thys there com a knyght rydyng all armed on a grete horse,
and toke the lady away with forse wyth hym, and ever she cryed and
made grete dole. So whan she was gone the kynge was gladde, for she 40
made such a noyse.

'Nay,' seyde Merlion, 'ye may nat leve hit so, thys adventure, so
lyghtly, for thes adventures muste be brought to an ende, other ellis
hit woll be disworshyp to you and to youre feste.'

'I woll,' seyde the kynge, 'that all be done by your advice.'

Than he lette calle sir Gawayne, for he muste brynge agayne the whyght herte.

'Also, sir, ye muste lette call sir Torre, for he muste brynge agay[ne] the brachette and the knyght, othir ellis sle hym. Also lette calle kynge Pellynor, for he must brynge agayne the lady and the knyght, othir ellis sle hym, and thes three knyghtes shall do mervayles adventures or they com agayne.'

Than were they called all three as hit ys rehersed afore and every of them toke their charge and armed them surely. But sir Gawayne had the firste requeste, and therefore we woll begynne at hym, and so forthe to thes other.

HERE BEGYNNITH THE FYRST BATAYLE THAT EVER SIR GAWAYNE DED AFTER HE WAS MADE KNYGHT.

(6) 15 Syr Gawayne rode more than a pace and Gaheris, his brothir, rode with hym in the stede of a squyre to do hym servyse. So as they rode they saw two knyghtes fyght on horseback passynge sore. So sir Gawayne and hys brothir rode betwyxte them and asked them for what cause they fought. So one of the knyghtes seyde,

'We fyght but for a symple mater, for we two be two brethirne and be begotyn of o[n]e man and of o[n]e woman.'

'Alas!' seyde sir Gawayne.

'Sir,' seyde the elther brother, 'there com a whyght herte thys way thys same day and many houndis chaced hym, and a whyght brachett was allwey nexte hym. And we undirstood hit was an adventure made for the hyghe feste of Arthure. And therefore I wolde have gone afftir to have wonne me worship, and here my yonger brothir seyde he wolde go aftir the harte for he was bygger knyght than I. And for thys cause we felle at debate, and so we thought to preff which of us was the bygger knyght.'

'Forsoth thys ys a symple cause,' seyde Gawayne, 'for uncouth men ye sholde debate withall, and no brothir with brothir. Therefore do be my counceyle: othir ellis I woll have ado with you bothe, other yelde you to me and that ye go unto kynge Arthure and yelde you unto hys grace.'

'Sir knyght,' seyde the two brethirne, 'we ar forfoughten and much bloode have we loste thorow oure wylfulnes, and therefore we wolde be loth to have ado with you.'

'Than do as I woll have you do,' seyde sir Gawayne.

'We agré to fulfylle youre wylle. But by whom shall we sey that we be thydir sente?'

'Ye may sey, by the knyght that folowith the queste of the herte. Now what ys youre name?' seyde Gawayne.

'Sir, my name ys Sorluse of the Foreyste,' seyde the elder.

'And my name ys,' seyde the yonger, 'Bryan of the Foreyste.'

And so they departed and wente to the kyngis courte, and sir Gawayne folowed hys queste. And as he folowed the herte by the cry of the howndis, evyn before hym there was a grete ryver; and the herte swam over.   5

And as sir Gawayn wolde a folowed afftir there stood a knyght on the othir syde and seyde, 'Sir knyght, com nat over aftir thys harte but if thou wolt juste with me.'

'I woll nat fayle as for that,' seyde sir Gawayne, 'to folow the queste that I am inne.'   10

And so made hys horse swymme over the watir. And anone they gate their glayves, and ran togydirs fulle harde, but Gawayne smote hym of hys horse and [turned hys horse and] than he bade hym yelde hym.

'Nay,' seyde the knyght, 'nat so, for thoughe ye have the better of 15
me on horsebak, I pray the, valyaunte knyght, alyght on foote and macche we togidir with oure swerdis.'

'What ys youre name?' seyde sir Gawayne.

'Sir, my name ys Alardyne of the Oute Iles.'

Than aythir dressed their shyldes and smote togydir, but sir Gawayne 20
smote hym so harde thorow the helme that hit wente to the brayne and the knyght felle downe dede.

'A,' seyde Gaherys, 'that was a myghty stroke of a yonge knyght.'

Than sir Gawayne and Gaherys ⌐rode more than a paas after the (7)
whyte herte, and lete slyppe at the herte thre couple of greyhoundes. 25
And so they chace the herte into a castel, and in the chyef place of the castel they slew the hert. Gawayne and Gaherys¬ folowed afftir. Ryght so there com a knyght oute of a chambir with a swerde drawyn in hys honde and slew two of the grayhoundes evyn in the syght of sir Gawayne, and the remanente he chaced with hys swerde oute of the 30
castell. And whan he com agayne he seyde,

'A, my whyght herte, me repentis that thou arte dede, for my soveraigne lady gaff the to me, and evyll have I kepte the, and thy dethe shall be evyl bought and I lyve.'

And anone he wente into hys chambir and armyd hym, and com 35
oute fersely. And there he mette with sir Gawayne and he seyde,

'Why have ye slayne my howndys? ⌐For they dyd but their kynde, and¬ I wolde that ye had wrokyn youre angir uppon me rather than uppon a dome beste.'

'Thou seyst trouth,' seyde the knyght. 'I have avenged me on thy 40
howndys, and so I woll on the or thou go.'

Than sir Gawayne alyght on foote and dressed hys shylde, and stroke togydirs myghtyly and clave their shyldis and stooned their helmys and brake their hawbirkes that their blo[de] thirled downe to their feete. So at the last sir Gawayne smote so harde that the knyght felle to the erthe, and than he cryed mercy and yelded hym and besought hym as he was a jantyll knyght to save hys lyff.

'Thou shalt dey,' seyd sir Gawayne, 'for sleynge of my howndis.'

5 'I woll make amendys,' seyde the knyght, 'to my power.'

But sir Gawayne wolde no mercy have, but unlaced hys helme to have strekyn of hys hede. Ryght so com hys lady oute of a chambir and felle over hym, and so he smote of hir hede by myssefortune.

'Alas,' seyde Gaherys, 'that ys fowle and shamefully done, for that
10 shame shall never frome you. Also ye sholde gyff mercy unto them that aske mercy, for a knyght withoute mercy ys withoute worship.'

So sir Gawayne was sore astoned of the deth of this fayre lady, that he wyst nat what he dud, and seyde unto the knyght,

'Aryse, I woll gyff the mercy.'

15 'Nay, nay,' seyd the knyght, 'I take no forse of thy mercy now, for thou haste slayne with vilony my love and my lady that I loved beste of all erthly t[h]ynge.'

'Me sore repentith hit,' seyde sir Gawayne, 'for I mente the stroke unto the. But now thou shalt go unto kynge Arthure and telle hym
20 of thyne adventure and how thou arte overcom by the knyght that wente in the queste of the whyght harte.'

'I take no force,' seyde the knyght, 'whether I lyve othir dey.' But at the last, for feare of dethe, he swore to go unto kynge Arthure, and he made hym to bere the one grehownde before hym on hys horse and
25 the other behynde hym.

'What ys youre name,' seyde sir Gawayne, 'or we departe?'

'My name ys,' seyde the knyght, 'Blamoure of the Maryse.'

(8)   And so he departed towarde Camelot. And sir Gawayne wente unto the castell and made hym redy to lye there all nyght and wolde have
30 unarmed hym.

'What woll ye do?' seyde Gaherys. 'Woll ye unarme you in thys contrey? Ye may thynke ye have many fooes in thys contrey.'

He had no sunner seyde the worde but there com in four knyghtes well armed and assayled sir Gawayne harde, and seyde unto hym,

35 'Thou new made knyght, thou haste shamed thy knyghthode, for a knyght withoute mercy ys dishonoured. Also thou haste slayne a fayre lady to thy grete shame unto the worldys ende, and doute the nat thou shalt have grete nede of mercy or thou departe frome us.'

And therewith one of hem smote sir Gawayne a grete stroke, that
40 nygh he felle to the erthe. And Gaherys smote hym agayne sore. And so they were assayled on the one syde and on the othir, that sir Gawayne and Gaherys were in jouparté of their lyves. And one with a bowe, an archer, smote sir Gawayne thorow the arme, that hit greved hym wondirly sore.

And as they sholde have bene slayne, there com four fayre ladyes and besought the knyghtes of grace for sir Gawayne. And goodly at the requeste of thes ladyes they gaff sir Gawayne and Gaherys their lyves and made them to yelde them as presoners. Than sir Gawayne and Gaherys made grete dole.   5

'Alas,' seyde sir Gawayne, 'myn arme grevith me sore, that I am lyke to be maymed,' and so made hys complaynte pyteuously.

So erly on the morne there com to sir Gawayne one of the four ladyes that had herd hys complaynte, and seyd,

'Sir knyght, what chere?'   10

'Nat good.'

'Why so? Hit ys youre owne defaute,' seyde the lady, 'for ye have done passynge foule for the sleynge of thys lady, the whych woll be grete vylony unto you. But be ye nat of kynge Arthurs?' seyde the lady.   15

'Yes, truly,' seyde syr Gawayne.

'What ys youre name, Sir?' seyde [the] lady, 'for ye muste telle or ye passe.'

'Fayre lady, my name ys sir Gawayne, the kynges son Lotte of Orkeney, and my modir ys kynge Arthurs sister.'   20

'Than ar ye nevew unto the kynge,' seyde the lady. 'Well,' seyde the lady, 'I shall so speke for you that ye shall have ⟨leve⟩ to go unto kynge Arthure for hys love.'

And so she departed and tolde the four knyghtes how the presonere was kynge Arthurs nevew, 'and hys name ys sir Gawayne, kynge Lottis 25
son of Orkeney.' So they gaff hym leve and toke hym the hartes hede with hym because hit was in the queste. And than they delyverde hym undir thys promyse, that he sholde bere the dede lady with hym on thys maner: the hede of her was hanged aboute hys necke, and the hole body of hir before hym on hys horse mane.   30

Ryght so he rode forthe unto Camelot. And anone as he was com Merlion dud make kynge Arthure that sir Gawayne was sworne to telle of hys adventure, and how he slew the lady, and how he wolde gyff no mercy unto the knyght, wherethorow the lady was slayne. Than the kynge and the quene were gretely displeased with sir Gawayne for the 35
sleynge of the lady, and there by ordynaunce of the queene there was sette a queste of ladyes uppon sir Gawayne, and they juged hym for ever whyle he lyved to be with all ladyes and to fyght for hir quarels; and ever that he sholde be curteyse, and never to refuse mercy to hym that askith mercy. Thus was sir Gawayne sworne uppon the four 40
Evaungelystis that he sholde never be ayenste lady ne jantillwoman but if he fyght for a lady and hys adversary fyghtith for another.

AND THUS ENDITH THE ADVENTURE OF SIR GAWAYNE THAT HE DUD AT THE MARIAGE OF ARTHURE.

(9)   Whan sir Torre was redy he mounted uppon horsebacke and rode afftir the knyght with the brachett. And so as he rode he mette with a dwarff suddeynly, that smote hys horse on the hede with a staff, that he reled bakwarde hys spere lengthe.

5   'Why dost thou so?' seyde sir Torre.

'For thou shalt nat passe thys way but if thou juste with yondir knyghtes of the pavilions.'

Than was sir Torre ware where were two pavilions, and grete spery[s] stood oute, and two shildes hangynge on treys by the pavilions.

10   'I may nat tarry,' seyd sir Torre, 'for I am in a queste that I muste nedys folow.'

'Thou shalt nat passe thys wey,' seyde the dwarff, and therewithall he blew hys horne. Than there com one armed on horsebacke and dressed hys shylde and com fast towarde sir Torre. And than he dressed

15   hym ayenste hem and so ran togydirs, and sir Torre bare hym frome hys horse, and anone the knyght yelded hym to hys mercy.

'But, sir, I have a felow in yondir pavilyon that woll have ado with you anone.'

'He shall be wellcom,' seyde sir Torre.

20   Than was he ware of another knyght commynge with grete rawndom, and eche of hem dressed to other, that mervayle hit was to se. But the knyght smote sir Torre a grete stroke in myddys the shylde, that his spere all to-shyverde. And sir Torre smote hym thorow the shylde benethe, that hit wente thorow the coste of the knyght; but the stroke

25   slew hym nat. And therewith sir Torre alyght and smote hym on the helme a grete stroke, and therewith the knyght yelded hym and besought hym of mercy.

'I woll well,' seyde sir Torre, 'but ye and youre felow muste go unto kynge Arthure and yelde you presoners unto hym.'

30   'By whom shall we sey we ar thydir sente?'

'Ye shall sey, by the knyght that wente in the queste of the knyght with the brachette. Now, what be your two namys?' seyde sir Torre.

'My name ys,' seyde that one, 'sir Phelot of Langeduke.'

'And my name ys,' seyde the othir, 'sir Petipace of Wynchilsee.'

35   'Now go ye forthe,' seyde sir Torre, 'and God spede you and me.'

Than cam the dwarff and seyde unto sir Torre,

'I pray you gyff me my bone.'

'I woll well,' seyde sir Torre, 'aske and ye shall have.'

'I aske no more,' seyde the dwarff, 'but that ye woll suffir me to do

40   you servyse, for I woll serve no more recreaunte knyghtes.'

'Well, take an horse,' seyde sir Torre, 'and ryde one with me.'

'For I wote,' seyde the dwarff, 'ye ryde afftir the knyght with the whight brachette, and I shall brynge you where he ys,' seyde the dwarff. And so they rode thorowoute a foreste; and at the laste they were

ware of two pavilions evyn by a pryory, ⌐with two sheldes⌐, and that
one shylde was enewed with whyght and that othir shylde was rede.

Therewith sir Torre alyght and toke the dwarff hys glayve, and so (10)
he com to the whyght pavilion. He saw three damesels lye in hyt
on a paylette slepynge; and so he wente unto the tother pavylyon and 5
founde a lady lyynge in hit slepynge, but therein was the whyght
brachett that bayed at hym faste. And than sir Torre toke up the
brachette and wente hys way and toke hit to the dwarffe.

And with the noyse the lady com oute of the pavilion, and all hir
damesels, and seyde,   10

'Woll ye take my brachette frome me?'

'Ye,' seyde sir Torre, 'this brachett have I sought frome kynge
Arthures courte hydir.'

'Well,' seyde the lady, 'sir knyght, ye shall nat go farre with hir but
that ye woll be mette with and greved.'   15

'I shall abyde what adventure that commyth by the grace of God,'
and so mownted uppon hys horse and passed on hys way towarde
Camelot.

But hit was so nere nyght he myght nat passe but litill farther.

'Know ye any lodgyng here nye?' seyde sir Torre.   20

'I know none,' seyde the dwarff, 'but here besydys ys an ermytaige,
and there ye muste take lodgynge as ye fynde.'

And within a whyle they com to the hermytage and toke such
lodgynge as was there, and as grasse and otis and brede for their horsis.
Sone hit was spedde, and full harde was their souper. But there they 25
rested them all nyght tylle on the morne, and herde a masse devoutely
and so toke their leve of the ermyte. And so sir Torre prayde the
ermyte to pray for hym, and he seyde he wolde, and betoke hym to
God. And so mownted uppon horsebacke and rode towardis Camelot
a longe whyle.   30

So with that they herde a knyght calle lowde that com afftir them,
and seyde,

'Knyght, abyde and yelde my brachette that thou toke frome my
lady!'

Sir Torre returned agayne and behelde hym how he was a semely 35
knyght and well horsed and armed at all poyntes. Than sir Torre
dressed hys shylde and toke hys glayve in hys hondys. And so they
com fersely on as freysshe men and droff both horse and man to the
erthe. Anone they arose lyghtly and drew hir swerdis as egirly as lyons,
and put their shyldis before them, and smote thorow their shyldys, 40
that the cantels felle on bothe partyes. Also they tamed their helmys,
that the hote bloode ran oute and the thycke mayles of their hawbirkes they carff and rooffe in sundir, that the hote bloode ran to the
erthe. And bothe they had many woundys and were passynge wery.

But sir Torre aspyed that the tothir knyght faynted, and than he sewed faste uppon hym and doubled hys strokis and stroke hym to the erthe on the one syde. Than sir Torre bade hym yelde hym.

'That woll I nat,' seyde Abelleus, 'whyle lastith the lyff and the soule 5 in my body, onles that thou wolte geff me the brachette.'

'That woll I nat,' seyde sir Torre, 'for hit was my queste to brynge agayne the brachette, thee, other bothe.'

(11)   With that cam a damesell rydynge on a palferey as faste as she myght dryve, and cryed with lowde voice unto sir Torre.

10   'What woll ye with me?' seyde sir Torre.

'I beseche the,' seyde the damesell, 'for kynge Arthurs love, gyff me a gyffte, I requyre the, jantill knyght, as thou arte a jantillman.'

'Now,' seyde sir Torre, 'aske a gyffte and I woll gyff hit you.'

'Grauntemercy,' seyde the damesell. 'Now I aske the hede of thys 15 false knyght Abelleus, for he ys the moste outerageous knyght that lyvith, and the grettist murtherer.'

'I am lothe,' seyde sir Torre, 'of that gyffte I have gyvyn you; but lette hym make amendys in that he hathe trespasced agayne you.'

'Now,' seyde the damesell, 'I may nat, for he slew myne owne brothir 20 before myne yghen that was a bettir knyght than he, and he had had grace; and I kneled halfe an owre before hym in the myre fo[r] to sauff my brothirs lyff that had done hym no damage, but fought with hym by adventure of armys, and so for all that I coude do he strake of hys hede. Wherefore I requyre the, as thou arte a trew knyght, to gyff me 25 my gyffte, othir ellis I shall shame the in all the courte of kynge Arthure; for he ys the falsyste knyght lyvynge, and a grete destroyer of men, and namely of good knyghtes.'

So whan Abellyus herde thys he was more aferde and yelded hym and asked mercy.

30   'I may nat now,' seyde sir Torre, 'but I sholde be founde false of my promyse, for erewhyle whan I wolde have tane you to mercy ye wolde none aske, but iff ye had the brachett agayne that was my queste.'

And therewith he toke off hys helme, and therewith he arose and fledde, and sir Torre afftir hym, and smote of hys hede quyte.

35   'Now, sir,' seyde the damesell, 'hyt ys nere nyght. I pray you come and lodge with me hereby at my place.'

'I woll well,' seyde sir Torre, 'for my horse and I have fared evyll syn we departed frome Camelot.'

And so he rode with her, and had passynge good chere with hir. 40 And she had a passyng fayre olde knyght unto hir husbande that made hym good chere and well easyd both hys horse and hym. And on the morne [he] herde hys masse and brake hys faste, and toke hys leve of the knyght and of the lady that besought hym to telle hys name.

'Truly,' he seyde, 'my name ys sir Torre, that was late made knyght,

and thys was the firste queste of armys that ever y ded, to brynge agayne
that thys knyght Abelleus toke away frome kynge Arthurs courte.'

'Now, fayre knyght,' seyde the lorde and the lady, 'and ye come here
in oure marchys, se here youre poore lodgynge, and hit shall be allwayes at youre commaundemente.'   5

So sir Torre departed and com to Camelot on the third day by
noone. And the kynge and the quene and all the courte was passynge
fayne of hys commynge, and made grete joy that he was com agayne,
for he wente frome the courte with litill succour but as kynge Pellynor,
hys fadir, gaff hym an olde courser, and kynge Arthur gaff hym armour 10
and swerde; other ellis had he none other succour, but rode so forthe
hymself alone. And than the kynge and the quene by Merlions advice
made hym swere to telle of hys adventures, and so he tolde and made
prevys of hys dedys as hit ys before reherced, wherefore the kynge and
the quene made grete joy.   15

'Nay, nay,' seyde Merlion, 'thys ys but japis that he hath do, for he
shall preve a noble knyght of proues as few lyvynge, and jantyl and
curteyse and of good tacchys, and passyng trew of hys promyse, and
never shall he outerage.'

Wherethorow Merlions wordis kynge Arthure gaff an erledom of 20
londis that felle unto hym. AND HERE ENDITH THE QUESTE OF SIR
TORRE, KYNGE PELLYNORS SONNE.

Than kynge Pellynore armed hym and mownted uppon hys horse, and (12)
rode more than a pace after the lady that the knyght lad away. And
as he rode in a foreyste he saw in a valey a damesell sitte by a well 25
and a wounded knyght in her armys, and kynge Pellynor salewed hir.
And whan she was ware of hym, she cryed on lowde and seyde, 'Helpe
me, knyght, for Jesuys sake!' But kynge Pellynore wolde nat tarry,
he was so egir in hys queste; and ever she cryed an hondred tymes aftir
helpe. Whan she saw he wolde nat abyde, she prayde unto God to 30
sende hym as much nede of helpe as she had, and that he myght feele
hit or he deyed. So, as the booke tellith, the knyght there dyed that
was wounded, wherefore for pure sorow the lady slew hirselff with
hys swerde.

As kynge Pellynore rode in that valey he mette with a poore man, 35
a laborer, ⟨and⟩ seyde,

'Sawyst thou ony knyght rydynge thys way ledyng a lady?'

'Ye, sir,' seyde the man. 'I saw that knyght and the lady that made
grete dole. And yondir beneth in a valey there shall ye se two pavilions,
and one of the knyghtes of the pavilions chalenged that lady of that 40
knyght, and seyde she was hys cosyne nere, wherefore he shold lede
hir no farther. And so they waged batayle in that quarell; that one seyde
he wolde have hir by force, and that other seyde he wold have the
rule of her, for he was hir kynnesman and wolde lede hir to hir kynne.'

So for thys quarell he leffte hem fyghtynge. 'And if ye woll ryde a pace ye shall fynde them fyghtynge, and the lady was leffte with two squyers in the pavelons.'

'God thanke the,' seyde kynge Pellynor.

5   Than he rode a walop tylle he had a syght of the two pavilons, and the two knyghtys fyghtynge. And anone he rode unto the pavilons and saw the lady how she was there, for she was hys queste, and seyde,

'Fayre lady, ye muste go with me unto the courte of kynge Arthure.'

'Sir knyght,' seyde the two squyres, 'yondir ar two knyghtes that
10 fyght for thys lady. Go ye thyder and departe them, and be ye agreed with them, and than may ye have hir at youre plesure.'

'Ye sey well,' seyde kynge Pellynor.

And anone he rode betwixte hem and departed them, and asked them their causis why they fought.

15 'Sir knyght,' seyde that one, 'I shall telle you. Thys lady ys my kynneswoman nye, my awntis doughtir, and whan I herde hir complayne that she was with hym magré hir hede, I waged batayle to fyght with hym.'

'Sir knyght,' seyde thys othir whos name was Outelake of Wente
20 londe, 'and thys lady I gate be my prouesse of hondis and armys thys day at Arthurs courte.'

'That ys nat trew,' seyde kynge Pellynor, 'for ye com in suddeynly thereas we were at the hyghe feste and toke awey thys lady or ony man myght make hym redy, and therefore hit was my queste to brynge her
25 agayne and you bothe, othir ellis that one of us to leve in the fylde. Therefore thys lady shall go with me, othir I shall dye therefore, for so have I promysed kynge Arthur. And therefore fyght ye no more, for none of you shall have parte of hir at thys tyme. And if ye lyst for to fyght for hir with me, I woll defende hir.'

30   'Well,' seyde the knyghtes, 'make you redy, and we shall assayle you with all oure power.'

And as kynge Pellynor wolde have put hys horse frome hym, sir Outelake roff hys horse thorow with a swerde, and seyde,

'Now art thou afoote as well as we ar.'

35   Whan kynge Pellynore aspyed that hys horse was ⌜slayne⌝, lyghtly he lepe frome hys horse, and pulled oute hys swerde, and put hys shylde afore hym and seyde,

'Knyght, kepe the well, for thou shalt have a buffette for the sleynge of my horse.'

40   So kynge Pellynor gaff hym such a stroke uppon the helme that he clave the hede downe to the chyne, and felle downe to the erthe dede.

(13) Than he turned hym to the other knyght that was sore wounded. But whan he saw that buffette he wolde nat fyght, but kneled downe and seyde,

'Take my cosyn, thys lady, with you, as ys youre queste, and I require you, as ye be a trew knyght, put hir to no shame nother vylony.'

'What?' seyde kynge Pellynore, 'woll ye nat fyght for hir?'

'No,' seyde the knyght, 'I woll nat fyght with such a knyght of proues as ye be.'   5

'Well,' seyde kynge Pellynore, 'I promyse you she shall have no vyllany by me, as I am trew knyght.'

'But now me wantis an horse,' seyde kynge Pellynor, 'but I woll have Outelakis horse.'

'Sir, ye shall nat nede,' seyde the knyght, 'for I shall gyff you such an   10
horse as shall please you, so that ye woll lodge with me, for hit ys nere nyght.'

'I woll well,' seyde kynge Pellynore, 'abyde with you all nyght.'

And there he had with hym ryght good chere and fared of the beste with passyng good wyne, and had myry reste that nyght.   15

And on the morne he harde masse and dyned. And so was brought hym a fayre bay courser, and kynge Pellynors sadyll sette uppon hym.

'Now, what shall I calle you,' seyde the knyght, 'inasmuch as ye have my cousyn at youre desyre of youre queste?'

'Sir, I shalle telle you: my name ys kynge Pellynor, kynge of the   20
Ilis, and knyght of the Table Rounde.'

'Now am I glad,' seyde the knyght, 'that such a noble man sholde have the rule of my cousyn.'

'Now, what ys youre name?' seyde kynge Pellynor. 'I pray you telle me.'   25

'Sir, my name ys sir Meliot de Logurs, and thys lady, my cosyn, hir name ys called Nenyve. And thys knyght that was in the other pavilion was my sworne brother, a passynge good knyght, and hys name ys Bryan of the Ilis, and he ys full lothe to do ony wronge or to fyght with ony man but if he be sore sought on.'   30

'Hit ys mervayle,' seyde kynge Pellynor, 'he wolde nat have ado with me.'

'Sir, he woll nat have ado with no man but if hit be at hys requeste.'

'I pray you brynge hym to the courte one of thes dayes,' seyde kynge Pellynor.   35

'Sir, we woll com togydirs.'

'Ye shall be wellcom,' seyde kynge Pellynore, 'to the courte of kynge Arthure, and ye shall be gretely alowed for youre commynge.'

And so he departed with the lady and brought her to Camelot.

But so as they rode in a valey, hit was full of stonys, and there the   40
ladyes horse stumbled and threw her downe, and hir arme was sore brused, that nerehonde she swooned for payne.

'Alas!' seyde the lady, 'myn arme ys oute of lythe, wherethorow I muste nedys reste me.'

'Ye shall well,' seyde kynge Pellynor.

And so he alyght undir a tre where was fayre grasse, and he put hys horse thereto, and so rested hem undir the tre and slepte tylle hit was ny nyght. And when he awooke he wolde have rydden forthe, but the
5 lady seyde,

'Ye may as well ryde backwarde as forewarde, hit ys so durke.'

So they abode stylle and made there theire lodgynge. Than kynge Pellynor put of hys armoure. Tha[n] so a litill tofore mydnyght they herde the trottynge of an horse. 'Be ye stylle,' seyde kynge Pellynor,
10 'for we shall hyre of som adventure.'

(14)   And therewith he armed hym. So ryght evyn before hym there mette two knyghtes, that one com frowarde Camelot, and that othir com from the Northe, and eyther salewed other and asked:

'What tydynges at Camelot?' seyde that one knyght.

15 'Be my hede,' ⌐seyde the other⌐, 'there have I bene and aspied the courte of kynge Arthure, and there ys such a felyship that they may never be brokyn, and well-nyghe all the world holdith with Arthure, for there ys the floure of chevalry. And now for thys cause am I rydyng into the Northe: to telle oure chyfftaynes of the felyship that ys withholdyn
20 with kynge Arthure.'

'As for that,' seyde the othir knyght, 'I have brought a remedy with me that ys the grettist poysen that ever ye herde speke off. And to Camelot woll I with hit, for we have a frende ryght nyghe the kynge, well cheryshed, that shall poysen kynge Arthur, for so hath he promysed
25 oure chyfftaynes, and receyved grete gyfftis for to do hit.'

'Beware,' seyde the othir knyght, 'of Merlion, for he knowith all thynges by the devylles craffte.'

'As for that, woll I nat lett,' seyde the knyght; and so they departed in sondir.

30   And anone aftir that kynge Pellynor made hym redy, and hys lady, and rode towarde Camelot. And as they com by the welle thereas the wounded knyght was and the lady, there he founde the knyght and the lady etyn with lyons other with wylde bestis, all save the hede, where-fore he made grete sorow and wepte passynge sore, and seyde,

35 'Alas! hir lyff myght I have saved, but I was so ferse in my queste that I wolde nat abyde.'

'Wherefore make ye such doole?' seyde the lady.

'I wote nat,' seyde kynge Pellinore, 'but my herte rwyth sore of the deth of hir that lyeth yondir, for she was a passyng fayre lady, and a
40 yonge.'

'Now, woll [ye] do by myne advise? Take this knyght and lette hym be buryed in an ermytage, and than take this ladyes hede and bere hit with you unto kynge Arthure.' So kynge Pellynor toke thys dede knyght on hys shyld and brought hym to the ermytage, and charged

the heremyte with the coorse, that servyse sholde be done for the
soule.

'And take ye hys harneyse for youre payne.'

'Hit shall be done,' seyde the hermyte, 'as I woll answere to God.'

And therewith they departed and com thereas the lady lay with a 5 (15)
fayre yalow here. That greved kynge Pellynore passynge sore whan
he loked on hit, for much hys herte caste unto that vysage. And so
by noone they com unto Camelot, and the kynge and the quene was
passyng fayne of hys commynge to the courte. And there he was made
to swere uppon the four Evangelistes to telle the trouthe of hys queste 10
frome the one ende to that other.

'A, kynge Pellynor,' seyde quene Gwenyver, 'ye were gretly to
blame that ye savcd nat thys ladyes lyff.'

'Madam,' seyde kynge Pellynore, 'ye were gretely to blame and ye
wolde nat save youre owne lyff and ye myght. But, self youre dis- 15
plesure, I was so furyous in my queste that I wolde nat abyde, and that
repentis me and shall do dayes of my lyff.'

'Truly ye ought sore to repente hit,' seyde Merlion, 'for that lady
was youre owne doughtir, begotyn of the lady of the Rule, and that
knyght that was dede was hir love and sholde have wedded hir, and he 20
was a ryght good knyght of a yonge man, and wolde a proved a good
man. An[d] to this courte was he commynge, and hys name was sir
Myles of the Laundis, and a knyght com behynde hym and slew hym
with a spere, and hys name was Lorayne le Saveage, a false knyght and
a cowherde. And she for grete sorow and dole slew hirselff with his 25
swerde, and hyr name was Alyne. And because ye wolde nat abyde and
helpe hir, ye shall se youre best frende fayle you whan ye be in the
grettist distresse that ever ye were othir shall be. And that penaunce
God hath ordayned you for that dede, that he that ye sholde truste
moste on of ony man on lyve, he shall leve you there ye shall be slayne.' 30

'Me forthynkith hit,' seyde kynge Pellynor, 'that thus shall me
betyde, but God may well fordo desteny.'

Thus whan the queste was done of the whyght herte the whych
folowed sir Gawayne, and the queste of the brachet whych folowed sir
Torre, kynge Pellynors son, and the queste of the lady that the knyghte 35
toke away, whych at that tyme folowed kynge Pellynor, than the
kynge stablysshed all the knyghtes and gaff them rychesse and londys;
and charged them never to do outerage nothir mourthir, and allwayes
to fle treson, and to gyff mercy unto hym that askith mercy, uppon
payne of forfiture [of their] worship and lordship of kynge Arthure for 40
evirmore; and allwayes to do ladyes, damesels, and jantilwomen and
wydowes [socour:] strengthe hem in hir ryghtes, and never to enforce
them, uppon payne of dethe. Also, that no man take no batayles in a
wrongefull quarell for no love ne for no worldis goodis. So unto thys

were all knyghtis sworne of the Table Rounde, both olde and younge,
and every yere so were the[y] sworne at the hyghe feste of Pentecoste.

EXPLICIT THE WEDDYNG OF KYNG ARTHUR.

IV. THE WAR WITH THE FIVE KINGS

IV (1) 5 So aftir thes questis of syr Gawayne, syr Tor and kynge Pellynore,
than hit befelle that Merlyon felle in dotage on the damesell that kynge
Pellynore brought to courte; and she was one of the damesels of the
Lady of the Laake, that hyght Nenyve. But Merlion wolde nat lette her
have no reste, but allwayes he wolde be wyth her. And ever she made
10 Merlion good chere tylle sche had lerned of hym all maner of thynges
that sche desyred; and he was assoted uppon hir, that he myght nat be
from hir.

So on a tyme he tolde to kynge Arthure that he scholde nat endure
longe, but for all his craftes he scholde be putte into the erthe quyk.
15 And so he tolde the kyng many thyngis that scholde befalle, but allwayes he warned the kyng to kepe well his swerde and the scawberde,
ᴦfor he told hym how the swerde and the scawberdeᴦ scholde be stolyn
by a woman frome hym that he moste trusted. Also he tolde kyng
Arthure that he scholde mysse hym:
20 'And yett had ye levir than all youre londis have me agayne.'
'A,' sayde the kyng, 'syn ye knowe of youre evil adventure, purvey
for hit, and putt hit away by youre crauftes, that mysseadventure.'
'Nay,' seyde Merlion, 'hit woll not be.'
He departed frome the kyng, and within a whyle the damesell of the
25 Lake departed, and Merlyon went with her evermore wheresomever
she yeode. And oftyntymes Merlion wolde have had hir prevayly away
by his subtyle crauftes. Than she made hym to swere that he sholde
never do none inchauntemente uppon hir if he wolde have his wil, and
so he swore. Than she and Merlyon wente over the see unto the londe
30 of Benwyke thereas kyng Ban was kyng, that had grete warre ayenste
kyng Claudas.

And there Merlion spake with kyng Bayans wyff, a fayre lady and a
good; hir name was Elayne. And there he saw yonge Launcelot. And
there the queene made grete sorowe for the mortal werre that kyng
35 Claudas made on hir lord [and on hir lond]is.

'Take none hevynesse,' seyde Merlyon, 'for this same chylde yonge
Launcelot shall within this twenty yere revenge you on kyng Claudas,
that all Crystendom shall speke of hit; and this same chylde shall be the
moste man of worship of the worlde. And his fyrst name ys Galahad,
40 that know I well,' seyde Merlyon, 'and syn ye have confermed hym
Launcelot.'

'That is trouth,' seyde the quene, 'his name was fyrst Galahad. A, Merlyon,' seyde the quene, 'shall I lyve to se my son suche a man of prouesse?'

'Yee, hardely, lady, on my perelle ye shall se hit, and lyve many wyntirs aftir.'   5

Than sone aftir the lady and Merlyon departed. And by weyes he shewed hir many wondyrs, and so come into Cornuayle. And allwayes he lay aboute to have hir maydynhode, and she was ever passynge wery of hym and wolde have bene delyverde of hym, for she was aferde of hym for cause he was a devyls son, and she cowde not be   10 skyfte of hym by no meane. And so one a tyme Merlyon ded shew hir in a roche whereas was a grete wondir and wrought by enchaunte- ment that went undir a grete stone. So by hir subtyle worchyng she made Merlyon to go undir that stone to latte hir wete of the mervayles there, but she wrought so there for hym that he come never oute for   15 all the craufte he coude do, and so she departed and leffte Merlyon.

And as kyng Arthure rode to Camelot and helde there a grete feste   (2) with myrth and joy, and sone aftir he returned unto Cardolle. And there come unto Arthure newe tydynges that the kyng of Denmarke and the kyng of Irelonde, that was his brothir, and the kyng of the   20 Vale and the kynge of Sorleyse and the kyng of the Ile of Longtaynse, all these fyve kynges with a grete oste was entirde into the londis of kyng Arthure and brent and slewe and distroyed clene byfore hem bothe the citeis and castels, that hit was pité to here.

'Alas!' seyde Arthure, 'yet had I never reste one monethe syne I was   25 kyng crowned of this londe. Now shall I never reste tylle I mete with tho kyngis in a fayre felde, that I make myne avow; for my trwe lyege peple shall nat be destroyed in my defaughte. Therefore go with me who so woll, and abyde who that wyll.'

Than kyng Arthure lette wryte unto kyng Pellynor and prayde hym   30 in all haste to make hym redy 'with suche peple as we myght lyghtlyeste arere,' and to hyghe hym aftir in haste. Than all the barownes were wrothe prevayly that the kynge wolde departe so suddaynly; but the kynge by no meane wolde abyde, but made wrytyng unto them that were nat ther and bade hyghe them aftir hym suche as were nat at that   35 tyme at that courte. Than the kynge come to quene Gwenyver and seyde unto her,

'Madame, make you redy, for ye shall go with me, for I may nat longe mysse you. Ye shall cause me to be the more hardy, what adven- ture so befalle me; yette woll I nat wyghte my lady to be in no jou-   40 pardye.'

'Sir,' she seyde, 'I am at youre commaundemente, and shall be redy at all tymes.'

So on the morne the kyng and the quene departed with suche

felyship as they had and come into the North, into a forerste besyde Humbir, and there lodged hem. So whan this worde come unto the fyve kynges abovynseyde that Arthure was besyde Humbir in a foreste, so there was a knyght, brothir unto one of the fyve kynges, that gaff 5 hem suche counseyle:

'Ye knowe well that sir Arthur hath the floure of chevalry of the worlde with hym, and hit preved by the grete batayle he did with the eleven kynges. And therefore hyghe ye unto hym nyght and day tyll that we be nyghe hym, for the lenger he taryeth the bygger he is, and 10 we ever the weyker. And he is so corageous of hymself that he is com to the felde with lytyll peple, and therefore lette us sette uppon hym or day, and we shall sle downe of his knyghtes that none shall helpe other of them.'

(3) Soo unto this counseyle these five kynges assented, and so they 15 passed forth with hir oste thorow North Walys and come uppon Arthure be nyght and sette uppon his oste as the kynge and his knyghtes were in theire pavylyons. So kynge Arthure was unarmed and leyde hym to reste with his quene Gwenyvere.

'Sir,' seyde sir Kayyus, 'hit is nat beste we be unarmed.'

20 'We shall have no nede,' seyde sir Gawayne and sir Gryflet that lay in a lytyll pavylyon by the kynge.

So with that they harde a grete noyse and many cryed 'Treson!'

'Alas!' seyde Arthure, 'we be betrayed! Unto armys, felowys!' than he cryed.

25 So they were armed anone at all poyntes. Than come there a wounded knyght unto the kynge and seyde,

'Sir, save youreself and my lady the quene, for oure oste is destroyed, and slayne is much of oure peple.'

So anone the kynge and the quene and the three knyghtes toke hir 30 horses and rode toward Humbir to passe over hit, and the watir was so rowghe that they were aferde to passe over hit.

'Now may ye chose,' seyde kynge Arthure, 'whethir ye woll abyde and take the adventure on this syde, for and ye be takyn they wol sle you.'

35 'Yet were me lever to dey in this watir than to falle in youre enemyes handis,' seyde the quene, 'and there to be slayne.'

And as they stode talkyng sir Kayus saw the fyve kynges commynge on horsebak by hemself alone, wyth hir sperys in hir hondis, evyn towarde hem.

40 'Lo,' seyde sir Kayus, 'yondir be tho fyve kynges. Lette us go to them and macche hem.'

'That were foly,' seyde sir Gawayne, 'for we ar but four, and they be fyve.'

'That is trouth,' seyde sir Gryfflette.

'No force,' seyd sir Kayus. 'I woll undirtake for two of the beste of hem, and than may ye three undirtake for all the othir three.'

And therewithall sir Kay lette his horse renne as faste as he myght to encountir with one of them, and strake one of the kynges thorow the shelde and also the body a fadom, that the kynge felle to the erthe 5 starke dede. That sawe sir Gawayne and ran unto anothir kyng so harde that he smote hym downe and thorow the body with a spere, that he felle to the erthe dede. Anone sir Arthure ran to anothir and smote hym thorow the body with a spere, that he fell to the erthe dede. Than sir Grymflet ran to the fourth kynge and gaff hym suche a falle 10 that his necke brake in sondir. Than sir Kay ran unto the fyfth kynge and smote hym so harde on the helme that the stroke clave the helme and hede to the erthe.

'That was well stryken,' seyde kynge Arthur, 'and worshipfully haste thou holde thy promyse; therefore I shall honoure the whyle that 15 I lyve.'

And therewithall they sette the quene in a barge into Humbir. But allwayes quene Gwenyvere praysed sir Kay for his dedis and seyde,

'What lady that ye love and she love you nat agayne, she were gretly to blame. And amonge all ladyes,' seyde the quene, 'I shall bere your 20 noble fame, for ye spake a grete worde and fulfylled hit worshipfully.'

And therewith the quene departed. Than the kynge and the three knyghtes rode into the forer[s]te, for there they supposed to here of them that were ascapid, and there founde the moste party of his peple, and tolde hem how the fyve kynges were dede. 25

'And therefore lette us holde us togedyrs tyll hit be day, and whan hir oste have aspyed that their chyfteynes be slayne they woll make such dole that they shall nat helpe hemself.'

And ryght as the kynge seyde, so hit was, for whan they founde the fyve kynges dede they made such dole that they felle downe of there 30 horsis. And therewithall com in kyng Arthure but with a fewe peple and slewe on the ryght honde and the lyffte honde, that well nye there ascaped no man, but all were slayne to the numbir of thirty thousand. And whan the batayle was all ended the kynge kneled downe and thanked God mekely. And than he sente for the quene. And anone she 35 was com and made grete joy of the overcommynge of that batayle.

Therewithall come one to kynge Arthure and tolde hym that kynge (4) Pellynore was within three myle with a grete oste. And [so he] seyde, 'Go unto hym and let hym undirstonde how we have spedde.' So within a whyle kyng Pellynore com with a grete oste and salewed the 40 peple and the kynge, and there was grete joy on every syde. Than the kynge let serch how many peple he had slayne, and there was founde but lytyll paste two hondred men slayne and eyght knyghtes of the Table Rounde in their pavylyons. Than the kynge lat rere and devyse, in the same place thereas the batayle was done and made, a fayre abbay, and endewed hit with grete lyvelode, and let calle hit the Abbay of La Beale Adventure.

But whan som of them come into there contrayes thereas the fyve
5 kynges were kynges, and tolde hem how they were slayne, there was made grete dole. And all the kynge Arthurs enemyes, as the kynge of North Walis and the kynges of the Northe, knewe of this batayle; they were passynge hevy. And so the kynge retourned unto Camelot in haste. And whan he was com to Camelot he called kyng Pellynore
10 unto hym and seyde,

'Ye undirstonde well that we have loste eyght knyghtes of the beste of the Table Rounde, and by youre advyse we muste chose eyght knyghtes of the beste we may fynde in this courte.'

'Sir,' seyde Pellynore, 'I shall counsayle you aftir my conceyte the
15 beste wyse. There ar in youre courte full noble knyghtes bothe of olde and yonge. And be myne advyse ye shall chose half of the olde and half of the yonge.'

'Whych be the olde?' seyde kynge Arthure.

'Sir, mesemyth kynge Uryence that hath wedded youre sistir Morgan
20 le Fay, and the Kynge of the Lake, and sir Hervyse de Revell, a noble knyght, and sir Galagars the fourthe.'

'This is well devysed,' seyde Arthure, 'and ryght so shall hit be. Now, whyche ar the four yonge knyghtes?'

'Sir, the fyrste is sir Gawayne, youre nevew, that is as good a knyght
25 of his tyme as is ony in this londe. And the secunde as mesemyth beste is sir Gryfflette le Fyse de Du, that is a good knyght and full desyrous in armys, and who may se hym lyve, he shall preve a good knyght. And the thirde as mesemyth ys well worthy to be one of the Table Rounde, sir Kay the Senesciall, for many tymes he hath done full worshipfully.
30 And now at youre laste batayle he dud full honorably for to undirtake to sle two kynges.'

'Be my hede,' seyde Arthure, 'ye sey soth. He is beste worthy to be a knyght of [the] Rounde Table of ony that is rehersed yet and he had done no more prouesse his lyve dayes.'

(5) 35   'Now,' seyde kynge Pellynore, 'chose you of two knyghtes that I shall reherce whyche is moste worthy, of sir Bagdemagus and sir Tor, my son; but for because he is my son I may nat prayse hym, but ellys and he were nat my son I durste say that of his age there is nat in this londe a better knyght than he is, nother of bettir condycions, and loth
40 to do ony wronge and loth to take ony wronge.'

'Be my hede,' seyde Arthure, 'he is a passyng good knight as ony ye spake of this day. That wote I well,' seyde the kynge, 'for I have sene hym proved; but he seyth but lytil, but he doth much more, for I know none in all this courte, and he were as well borne on his modir syde as he is on youre syde, that is lyke hym of prouesse and of myght. And therefore I woll have hym at this tyme and leve sir Bagdemagus tyll anothir tyme.'

So whan they were chosyn by the assent of the barouns, so were there founden in hir seges every knyghtes name that here ar reherced. 5 And so were they sette in hir seges, whereof sir Bagdemagus was wondirly wrothe that sir Tor was avaunced afore hym. And therefore soddeynly he departed frome the courte and toke his squyre with hym and rode longe in a foreste tyll they come to a crosse, and there he alyght and seyde his prayers devoutely. The meanewhyle his squyre 10 founde wretyn uppon the crosse that Bagdemagus sholde never retourne unto the courte agayne tyll he had wonne a knyght of the Table Rounde body for body.

'Loo,' seyde his squyer, 'here I fynde wrytyng of you; therefore I rede you, returne agayne to the courte.'   15

'That shall I never,' seyde Bagdemagus, 'tyll men speke of me ryght grete worship, and that I be worthy to be a kn[y]ght of the Rounde Table.'

And so he rode forth, and there by the way he founde a braunche of holy herbe that was the signe of the Sancgreall, and no knyght 20 founde no suche tokyns but he were a good lyver and a man of prouesse.

So as sir Bagdemagus rode to se many adventures, so hit happed hym to com to the roche thereas the Lady of the Lake had put Merlyon undir the stone, and there he herde hym make a grete dole; wherefore sir Bagdemagus wolde have holpyn hym, and wente unto the grete 25 stone, and hit was so hevy that an hondred men myght nat lyffte hit up. Whan Merlyon wyste that he was there, he bade hym leve his laboure, for all was in vayne: for he myght never be holpyn but by her that put hym there. And so Bagdemagus departed and dud many adventures and preved aftir a full good knyght, and come ayen to the courte and 30 was made knyght of the Rounde Table. So on the morne there befelle new tydyngis and many othir adventures.

V. ARTHUR AND ACCOLON

THAN hit befelle that Arthure and many of his knyghtes rode on (6) huntynge into a grete foreste. And hit happed kynge Arthure and 35 kynge Uryence and sir Accalon of Gawle folowed a grete harte; for they three were well horsed, and so they chaced so faste that within a whyle they three were more than ten myle from her felyshep. And at the laste they chaced so sore that they slewe hir horsis undirnethe them; and the horses were so fre that they felle downe dede. Than 40

were all three on foote and ever they saw the harte before them passynge wery and inboced.

'What shall we do?' seyde kynge Arthure, 'we ar harde bestadde.'

'Lette us go on foote,' seyde kynge Uryence, 'tyll we may mete with
5 somme lodgyng.'

Than were they ware of the harte that lay on a grete watir banke, and
a brachette bytyng on his throte; and mo othir houndis come aftir.
Than kynge Arthure blewe the pryce and dyght the harte. Than the
kynge loked aboute the worlde and sawe before hym in a grete water
10 a lytyll shippe all apparayled with sylke downe to the watir. And the
shippe cam ryght unto them and landed on the sandis. Than Arthure
wente to the banke and loked in and saw none erthely creature therein.

'Sirs,' seyde the kynge, 'com thens and let us se what is in this shippe.'

So at the laste they wente into the shippe all three, and founde hit
15 rychely behanged with cloth of sylke. So by that tyme hit was durke
nyght, there suddeynly was about them an hondred torchis sette uppon
all the shyppe-bordis, and hit gaff grete lyght. And therewithall there
come twelve fayre damesels and salued kynge Arthure on hir kneis,
and called hym be his name and seyde he was ryght wellcom, and suche
20 chere as they had he sholde have of the beste. Than the kynge thanked
hem fayre. Therewythall they ledde the kynge and his felawys into a
fayre chambir, and there was a clothe leyde rychely beseyne of all that
longed to a table, and there were they served of all wynes and metys
that they coude thynke of. But of that the kynge had grete mervayle,
25 for he never fared bettir in his lyff as for one souper.

And so whan they had souped at her leyser kyng Arthure was lad
into a chambir, a rycher besene chambir sawe he never none; and so
was kynge Uryence se[r]ved and lad into such anothir chambir; and
sir Accolon was lad into the thirde chambir passyng rychely and well
30 besayne. And so were they leyde in their beddis easyly, and anone
they felle on slepe and slepte merveylously sore all the nyght.

And on the morne kynge Uryence was in Camelot abedde in his
wyves armys, Morgan le Fay. And whan he woke he had grete mervayle how he com there, for on the evyn before he was two dayes
35 jurney frome Camelot. And whan kyng Arthure awoke he founde
hymself in a durke preson, heryng aboute hym many complayntes of
wofull knyghtes.

(7) 'What ar ye that so complayne?' seyde kyng Arthure.

'We bene here twenty knyghtes presoners, and som of us hath
40 layne here eyght yere, and som more and somme lesse.'

'For what cause?' seyde Arthure.

'We shall tell you,' seyde the knyghtes.

'This lorde of this castell his name is sir Damas, and he is the falsyst
knyght that lyvyth, and full of treson, and a very cowarde as [ony]

lyvyth. And he hath a yonger brothir, a good knyght of prouesse, and his name is sir Oughtlake. And this traytoure Damas, the elder brother, woll geff hym no parte of his londis but as sir Outlake kepyth thorow prouesse of his hondis. And so he kepith frome hym a full fayre maner and a rych, and therein sir Outlake dwellyth worshypfully 5 and is well beloved with all peple. And this sir Damas oure mayster is a[s] evyll beloved, for he is withoute mercy, and he is a cowarde, and grete warre hath bene betwyxte them. But Outlake hath ever the bettir, and ever he proferyth sir Damas to fyght for the lyvelode, body for body, but he woll nat of hit, other ellys to fynde a knyght to 10 fyght for hym. Unto that sir Damas hath grauntid to fynde a knyght, but he is so evyll beloved and hated that there is no knyght woll fyght for hym. And whan Damas saw this, that there was never a knyght wolde fyght for hym, he hath dayly layne a wayte wyth many a knyght with hym and takyn all the knyghtes in this contray to se and 15 aspye hir aventures: he hath takyn hem by force and brought hem to his preson. And so toke he us severally, as we rode on oure adventures, and many good knyghtes hath deyde in this preson for hunger, to the numbir of eyghtene knyghtes. And yf ony of us all that here is or hath bene wolde have foughtyn with his brother Outlake he wolde have 20 delyverde us; but for because this Damas ys so false and so full of treson we wolde never fyght for hym to dye for hit, and we be so megir for hungir that unnethe we may stonde on oure fete.'

'God delyver you for His grete mercy!'

Anone withall come a damesel unto Arthure and asked hym, 'What 25 chere?'

'I can nat sey,' seyde Arthure.

'Sir,' seyde she, 'and ye woll tyght for my lorde ye shall be delyverde oute of preson, and ellys ye ascape never with the lyff.'

'Now,' seyde Arthure, 'that is harde. Yet had I lever fyght with a 30 knyght than to dey in preson. Wyth this,' seyde Arthure, 'I may be delyverde and all thes presoners, I woll do the batayle.'

'Yes,' seyde the damesell.

'Than I am redy,' seyde Arthure, 'and I had horse and armoure.'

'Ye shall lak none,' seyde the damesell.   35

'Mesemethe, damesell, I shold have sene you in the courte of Arthure.'

'Nay,' seyde the damesell, 'I cam never there. I am the lordis doughter of this castell.'

Yet was she false, for she was one of the damesels of Morgan le Fay. 40 Anone she wente unto sir Damas and tolde hym how he wolde do batayle for hym, and so he sente for Arthure. And whan he com he was well coloured and well made of his lymmes, that all knyghtes that sawe hym seyde hit were pité that suche a knyght sholde dey in preson.

So sir Damas and he were agreed that he sholde fyght for hym uppon
this covenaunte, that all the othir knyghtes sholde be delyverde. And
unto that was sir Damas sworne unto Arthur and also he to do the
batayle to the uttermoste. And with that all the twenty knyghtes were
5 brought oute of the durke preson into the halle and delyverde, and so
they all abode to se the batayle.

(8)   Now turne we unto Accalon of Gaule, that whan he awoke he founde
hymself by a depe welles syde within half a foote, in grete perell of deth.
And there com oute of that fountayne a pype of sylver, and oute of that
10 pype ran water all on hyghe in a stone of marbil. Whan sir Accolon
sawe this he blyssed hym and seyde, 'Jesu, save my lorde kynge Arthure
and kynge Uryence, for thes damysels in this shippe hath betrayed us.
They were fendis and no women. And if I may ascape this mysadventure I shall distroye them, all that I may fynde of thes false damysels
15 that faryth thus with theire inchauntementes.'

And ryght with that there com a dwarf with a grete mowthe and a
flatte nose, and salewed sir Accalon and tolde hym how he cam fromme
quene Morgan le Fay.

'And she gretys yow well and byddyth you be of stronge herte, for
20 ye shall fyght to-morne wyth a knyght at the houre of pryme. And
therefore she hath sent the Excalebir, Arthurs swerde, and the scawberde, and she byddyth you as ye love her that ye do that batayle to the
uttirmoste withoute ony mercy, lyke as ye promysed hir whan ye
spoke laste togedir in prevyté. And what damesell that bryngyth her
25 the kynges hede whyche ye shall fyght withall, she woll make hir a
quene.'

'Now I undirstonde you,' seyde Accalon. 'I shall holde that I have
promysed her, now I have the swerde. Sir, whan sawe ye my lady
Morgan le Fay?'

30   'Ryght late,' seyde the dwarff.

Than Accalon toke hym in his armys and sayde, 'Recommaunde me
unto my lady the quene and telle hir all shall be done that I promysed
hir, and ellis I woll dye for hit. Now I suppose,' seyde Accalon, 'she
hath made all this crauftis and enchauntemente for this batayle.'

35   'Sir, ye may well beleve hit,' seyde the dwarff.

Ryght so there come a knyght and a lady wyth six squyers, and
salewed Accalon and prayde hym to aryse and com and reste hym at
his maner. And so Accalon mounted uppon a voyde horse and wente
with the [knyght] unto a fayre maner by a pryory, and there he had
40 passyng good chere.

Than sir Damas sente unto his brothir Outelake and bade make hym
redy be to-morne at the houre of pryme, and to be in the felde to fyght
with a good knyght; for he had founden a knyght that was redy to do
batayle at all poyntis. Whan this worde come to sir Outlake he was

passyng hevy, for he was woundid a lytyll tofore thorow bothe his
thyghes with a glayve, and he made grete dole; but as he was wounded
he wolde a takyn the batayle an honde.

So hit happed at that tyme, by the meanys of Morgan le Fay, Accalon
was with sir Oughtlake lodged. And whan he harde of that batayle and 5
how Oughtlake was wounded he seyde that he wolde fyght for hym
because that Morgan le Fay had sent hym Excaliber and the shethe for
to fyght with the k[n]yght on the morne. This was the cause sir Accalon
toke the batayle uppon hym. Than sir Outelake was passyng glad and
thanked sir Accalon with all his herte that he wolde do so muche for 10
hym. And therewithall sir Outlake sente unto his brother sir Damas
that he hadde a knyght redy that sholde fyght with hym in the felde
be the houre of pryme. So on the morne sir Arthure was armed and
well horsed, and asked sir Damas,

'Whan shall we to the felde?'   15

'Sir,' seyde sir Damas, 'ye shall hyre masse.'

And so Arthur herde a masse, and whan masse was done there com
a squyre ⌐on a grete hors¬ and asked sir Damas if his knyght were redy,
'for oure k[n]yght is redy in the felde.' Than sir Arthure mounted uppon horsebak. And there were all the knyghtes and comons of that 20
contray, and so by all their advyces there was chosyn twelve good men
of the contrey for to wayte uppon the two knyghtes.

And ryght as Arthure was on horsebak, there com a damesel fromme
Morgan le Fay and brought unto sir Arthure a swerde lyke unto
Excaliber and the scawberde, and seyde unto Arthure, 'She sendis 25
here youre swerde for grete love.' And he thanke hir and wente hit
had bene so; but she was falce, for the swerde and the scawberde was
counterfete and brutyll and false.

Than they dressed hem on two partyes of the felde and lette their (9)
horses ren so faste that aythir smote other in the myddis of the shelde, 30
and their sperys helde, that bothe horse and man wente to the erthe,
and than they stert up bothe and pulde oute their swerdis.

The meanewhyle that they were thus at the batayle com the Damesel
of the Lake into the felde that put Merlyon undir the stone. And she
com thidir for the love of kynge Arthur, for she knew how Morgan 35
le Fay had ordayned for Arthur shold have bene slayne that day, and
therefore she com to save his lyff.

And so they went egerly to the batayle and gaff many grete strokes.
But allwayes Arthurs swerde bote nat lyke Accalons swerde, and for
the moste party every stroke that Accalon gaff he wounded sir Arthure 40
sore, that hit was mervayle he stood, and allwayes his blood felle
frome hym faste. Whan Arthure behelde the grounde so sore bebledde
he was dismayde. And than he demed treson, that his swerde was
chonged, for his swerde bote nat steele as hit was wonte to do. Therefore

he dred hym sore to be dede, for ever hym semyd that the swerde
in Accalons honde was Excaliber, for at every stroke that Accalon
stroke he drewe bloode on Arthure.

'Now, knyght,' seyde Accolon unto Arthure, 'kepe the well frome
5 me!'

But Arthure answerde not agayne, but gaff hym suche a buffette on
the helme that he made hym to stowpe nyghe fallyng to the erthe. Than
sir Accalon wythdrewe hym a lytyll, and com on wyth Excaliber on
heyght, and smote sir Arthure suche a buffette that he fylle ny to the
10 erthe. Than were they bothe wrothe oute of mesure and gaff many sore
strokis.

But allwayes sir Arthure loste so muche bloode that hit was mervayle
he stoode on his feete, but he was so full of knyghthode that he endured
the payne. And sir Accolon loste nat a dele of blood; therefore he
15 waxte passynge lyght, and sir Arthure was passynge fyeble and [wente]
veryly to have dyed, but for all that he made countenaunce as he myght
welle endure and helde Accolon as shorte as he myght. But Accolon
was so bolde because of Excalyber that he wexed passyng hardy. But
all men that behelde hem seyde they sawe nevir knyght fyght so well
20 as Arthur ded, conciderynge the bloode that he had bled; but all that
peple were sory that thes two brethirne wolde nat accorde.

So allwayes they fought togedir as fers knyghtes, and at the laste
kynge Arthure withdrew hym a lytyll for to reste hym, and sir Accolon
callyd hym to batayle and seyde, 'Hit is no tyme for me to suffir the
25 to reste,' and therewith he come fersly uppon Arthure. But Arthur
therewith was wroth for the bloode that he had loste, and smote Accolon
on hyghe uppon the helme so myghtyly that he made hym nyghe falle
to the erthe; and therewith Arthurs swerde braste at the crosse and
felle on the grasse amonge the bloode, and the pomell and the sure
30 handyls he helde in his honde. Whan kynge Arthure saw that, he was
in grete feare to dye, but allwayes he helde up his shelde and loste no
grounde nother batyd no chere.

(10)   Than sir Accolon began with wordis of treson and seyde,

'Knyght, thou art overcom and mayste nat endure, and also thou art
35 wepynles, and loste thou haste much of thy bloode, and I am full loth
to sle the. Therefore yelde the to me recreaunte.'

'Nay,' seyde sir Arthur, 'I may nat so, for I promysed by the feythe
of my body to do this batayle to the uttermuste whyle my lyff lastith,
and therefore I had levir to dye with honour than to lyve with shame.
40 And if hit were possible for me to dye an hondred tymes, I had levir
to dye so oufte than yelde me to the. For though I lak wepon, yett
shall I lak no worshippe, and if thou sle me wepynles that shall be thy
shame.'

'Welle,' seyde Accolon, 'as for that shame I woll nat spare. Now

kepe the fro me, for thou art but a dede man!' And therewith Accolon
gaff hym such a stroke that he felle nyghe to the erthe, and wolde have
had Arthure to have cryed hym mercy. But sir Arthure preced unto
Accolon with his shelde and gaff hym wyth the pomell in his honde
suche a buffette that he reled three strydes abake.   5

Whan the Damesell of the Lake behelde Arthure, how full of
prouesse his body was, and the false treson that was wrought for hym
to have had hym slayne, she had grete peté that so good a knyght and
such a man of worship sholde so be destroyed. And at the nexte stroke
sir Accolon stroke at hym suche a stroke that by the damesels in-   10
chauntemente the swerde Excaliber fell oute of Accalons honde to
the erthe, and therewithall sir Arthure lyghtly lepe to hit and gate hit
in his honde, and forthwithall he knew hit that hit was his swerde
Excalyber.

'A,' seyde Arthure, 'thou haste bene frome me all to longe and muche   15
damage hast thou done me!'

And therewith he aspyed the scawberde by his syde, and suddaynly
he sterte to hym and pulled the scawberte frome hym and threw hit
frome hym as fer as he myght throw hit.

'A, sir knyght,' seyde kynge Arthur, 'this day haste thou done me   20
grete damage wyth this swerde. Now ar ye com unto youre deth, for
I shall nat warraunte you but ye shall be as well rewarded with this
swerde or ever we departe as ye have rewarded me, for muche payne
have ye made me to endure and much bloode have y loste.'

And therewith sir Arthure raced on hym with all his myght and   25
pulde hym to the erthe, and than raced of his helme and gaff hym suche
a buffette on his hede that the bloode com oute at his erys, nose, and
mowthe.

'Now woll I sle the!' seyde Arthure.

'Sle me ye may well,' seyde sir Accolon, 'and hit please you, for ye   30
ar the beste knyght that ever I founde, and I se well that God is with
you. But for I promysed,' seyde Accolon, 'to do this batayle to the
uttirmyst and never to be recreaunte while I leved, therefore shall I
never yelde me with my mowthe, but God do with my body what He
woll.'   35

Than sir Arthure remembirde hym and thought he scholde have sene
this knyght.

'Now telle me,' seyde Arthure, 'or I woll sle the, of what contrey
ye be and of what courte.'

'Sir knyght,' seyde sir Accolon, 'I am of the ryall courte of kyng   40
Arthure, and my name is Accolon of Gaule.'

Than was Arthure more dismayde than he was toforehonde, for
than he remembirde hym of his sistir Morgan le Fay and of the enchauntement of the shippe.

'A, sir k[n]yght, I pray you [telle me] who gaff you this swerde and by whom ye had hit.'

(11)   Than sir Accolon bethought hym and seyde, 'Wo worthe this swerde! for by hit I have gotyn my dethe.'

5   'Hit may well be,' seyde the kynge.

'Now, sir,' seyde Accolon, 'I woll tell you: this swerde hath bene in my kepynge the moste party of this twelve-monthe, and Morgan le Fay, kyng Uryence wyff, sente hit me yestirday by a dwarfe to the entente to sle kynge Arthure, hir brothir; for ye shall undirstonde that

10 kynge Arthur ys the man in the worlde that she hatyth moste, because he is moste of worship and of prouesse of ony of hir bloode. Also she lovyth me oute of mesure as paramour, and I hir agayne. And if she myght bryng hit aboute to sle Arthure by hir crauftis, she wolde sle hir husbonde kynge Uryence lyghtly. And than had she devysed to

15 have me kynge in this londe and so to reigne, and she to be my quene. But that is now done,' seyde Accolon, 'for I am sure of my deth.'

'Well,' seyde kyng Arthure, 'I fele by you ye wolde have bene kynge of this londe, yett hit had be grete damage to have destroyed your lorde,' seyde Arthure.

20   'Hit is trouthe,' seyde Accolon, 'but now I have tolde you the trouthe, wherefore I pray you tell me of whens ye ar and of what courte.'

'A, Accolon,' seyde kynge Arthure, 'now y let the wete that I am kynge Arthure that thou haste done grete damage t[o].'

Whan Accolon herd that he cryed on-lowde, 'Fayre swete lorde,

25 have mercy on me, for I knew you nat.'

'A, sir Accolon,' seyde kynge Arthur, 'mercy thou shalt have because I fele be thy wordis at this tyme thou knewest me nat, but I fele by thy wordis that thou haste agreed to the deth of my persone, and therefore thou art a traytoure; but I wyte the the lesse for my sistir

30 Morgan le Fay by hir false crauftis made the to agré to hir fals lustes. But I [shall] be sore avenged uppon hir, that all Crystendom shall speke of hit. God knowyth I have honoured hir and worshipped hir more than all my kyn, and more have I trusted hir than my wyff and all my kyn aftir.'

35   Than kynge Arthure called the kepers of the felde and seyde,

'Sirres, commyth hyder, for here ar we two knyghtes that have foughtyn unto grete damage unto us bothe, and lykly eche of us to have slayne other, and had ony of us knowyn othir, here had bene no batayle nothir no stroke stryken.'

40   Than all alowde cryed Accolon unto all the knyghtes and men that were [there,] and seyde,

'A, lordis! This knyght that I have foughten withall is the moste man of prouesse and of worship in the worlde, for hit is hymself kynge Arthure, oure al[ther] lyege lorde, and with myssehappe and

mysseadventure have I done this batayle with the lorde and kynge
that I am withholdyn withall.'

Than all the peple felle downe on her knees and cryed kynge (12)
Arthure mercy.

'Mercy shall ye have,' seyde Arthure. 'Here may ye se what soddeyn 5
adventures befallys ouftyn of arraunte knyghtes, how that I have
foughtyn with a knyght of myne owne unto my grete damage and his
bothe. But, syrs, because I am sore hurte and he bothe, and I had grete
nede of a lytyll reste, ye shall undirstonde this shall be the opynyon
betwyxte you two brethirne: 10

'As to the, sir Damas, for whom I have bene champyon and wonne
the felde of this knyght, yett woll I juge. Because ye, sir Damas, ar
called an [o]rgulus knyght and full of vylony, and nat worth of prouesse
of youre dedis, therefore woll I that ye geff unto youre brother all the
hole maner with the apportenaunce undir this fourme, that sir Oute- 15
lake holde the maner of you and yerely to gyff you a palfrey to ryde
uppon, for that woll becom you bettir to ryde on than uppon a courser.
Also I charge the, sir Damas, uppon payne of deth, that thou never
distresse no knyghtes araunte that ryde on their adventure, and also
that thou restore thyse twenty knyghtes that thou haste kepte longe 20
presoners of all theire harmys that they be contente for. And ony of
them com to my courte and complayne on the, be my hede, thou
shalt dye therefore!

'Also, sir Oughtlake, as to you, because ye ar named a good knyght
and full of prouesse and trew and jantyll in all youre dedis, this shall 25
be youre charge I woll gyff you: that in all goodly hast ye com unto me
and my courte, and ye shall be a knyght of myne, and if youre dedis be
thereaftir I shall so proferre you by the grace of God that ye shall in
shorte tyme be in ease as for to lyve as worshipfully as youre brother
Damas.'   30

'God thonke youre largenesse of youre grete goodnesse and of
youre bounté! I shall be frome hens forewarde in all tymes at your
commaundement. For, [sir,' said] sir Oughtlake, 'as God wolde, I was
hurte but late with an adventures knyght thorow bothe the thyghes,
and ellys had I done this batayle with you.'   35

'God wolde,' seyde sir Arthure, 'hit had bene so, for than had nat I
bene hurte as I am. I shall tell you the cause why: for I had nat bene
hurte as I am, had nat bene myne owne swerde that was stolyn frome
me by treson; and this batayle was ordeyned aforehonde to have slayne
me, and so hit was broughte to the purpose by false treson and by 40
enchauntment.'

'Alas,' seyde sir Outlake, 'that is grete pyté that ever so noble a man
as ye ar of your dedis and prouesse, that ony man or woman myght
fynde in their hertis to worche ony treson aghenst you.'

'I shall rewarde them,' seyde Arthure. 'Now telle me,' seyde Arthure, 'how far am I frome Camelot?'

'Sir, ye ar two dayes jurney.'

'I wolde be at som place of worship,' seyde sir Arthure, 'that I
5 myght reste me.'

'Sir,' seyde Outlake, 'hereby is a ryche abbey of youre elders foundacion, of nunnys, but three myle hens.'

So the kynge toke his leve of all the peple and mounted uppon horsebak and sir Accolon with hym. And whan they were com to the abbey
10 he lete fecch lechis and serchid his woundis and sir Accolons bothe. But sir Accolon deyed within four dayes, for he had bled so much blood that he myght nat lyve, but kynge Arthure was well recoverde. So whan Accolon was dede he lette sende hym in an horse-bere with six knyghtes unto Camelot, and bade 'bere hym unto my systir, Morgan
15 le Fay, and sey that I sende her hym to a present. And telle hir I have my swerde Excalyber and the scawberde.' So they departed with the body.

(13)   The meanewhyle Morgan le Fay had wente kynge Arthure had bene dede. So on a day she aspyed kynge Uryence lay on slepe on his bedde,
20 than she callyd unto hir a mayden of her counseyle and sayde,

'Go fecche me my lordes swerde, for I sawe never bettir tyme to sle hym than now.'

'A, madame,' seyde the damesell, 'and ye sle my lorde ye can never ascape.'

25 'Care the not,' sayde Morgan, 'for now I se my tyme is beste to do hit, and therefore hyghe the faste and fecche me the swerde.'

Than this damesell departed and founde sir Uwayne slepyng uppon a bedde in anothir chambir. So she wente unt[o] sir Uwayne and awaked hym and bade hym 'aryse and awayte on my lady youre modir, for she
30 woll sle the kynge youre fadir slepynge on his bedde, for I go to fecch his swerde.'

'Well,' seyde sir Uwayne, 'go on your way and lette me dele.'

Anone the damesell brought the quene the swerde with quakyng hondis. And lyghtly she toke the swerde and pullyd hit oute, and wente
35 boldely unto the beddis syde and awayted how and where she myght sle hym beste. And as she hevyd up the swerde to smyte, sir Uwayne lepte unto his modir and caught hir by the honde and seyde,

'A, fende, what wolt thou do? And thou were nat my modir, with this swerde I sholde smyte of thyne hede! A,' seyde sir Uwayne, 'men
40 seyde that Merlyon was begotyn of a fende, but I may sey an erthely fende bare me.'

'A, fayre son Uwayne, have mercy uppon me! I was tempted with a fende, wherefore I cry the mercy. I woll nevermore do so. And save my worship and discover me nat!'

'On this covenaunte,' seyde sir Uwayne, 'I woll forgyff you: so ye
woll never be aboute to do such dedis.'

'Nay, son, and that I make you assuraunce.'

Than come tydynges unto Morgan le Fay that Accolon was dede (14)
and his body brought unto the chirche, and how kyng Arthure had his 5
swerde ayen. But whan quenc Morgan wyste that Accolon was dede,
she was so sorowfull that nye hir herte to-braste, but bycause she wolde
nat hit were knowyn oute, she kepte hir countenaunce and made no
sembelaunte of dole. But welle sche wyste, and she abode tylle hir
brother Arthure come thydir, there sholde no golde go for hir lyff. 10
Than she wente unto the quene Gwenyvere and askid hir leve to ryde
into hir contrcy.

'Ye may abyde,' seyde the quene, 'tyll youre brother the kynge com
home.'

'I may nat, madame,' seyde Morgan le Fay, 'for I have such hasty 15
tydynges.'

'Well,' seyde the quene, 'ye may departe whan ye woll.'

So erely on the morne, or hit was day, she toke hir horse and rode all
that day and moste party of the nyght, and on the morne by none she
com to the same abbey of nonnys whereas lay kynge Arthure, and she 20
wyste ⟨welle⟩ that he was there. And anone she asked where he was,
and they answerde and seyde how he was leyde hym on his bedde to
slepe, 'for he had but lytyll reste this three nyghtes.'

'Well,' seyde she, 'I charge that none of you awake hym tyll I do.'

And than she alyght of hir horse and thought for to stele away 25
Excaliber, his swerde. And she wente streyte unto his chambir, and no
man durste disobey hir commaundement. And there she found Arthur
aslepe on his bedde, and Excalyber in his ryght honde naked. Whan she
sawe that, she was passyng hevy that she myght nat com by the
swer[d]e withoute she had awaked hym, and than she wyste welle she 30
had bene dede. So she toke the scawberde and went hir way to horsebak. When the kynge awoke and myssid his scawberde, he was wroth,
and so he asked who had bene there, and they seyde his sister, quene
Morgan le Fay, had bene there and had put the scawberde undir hir
mantell and is gone. 35

'Alas,' seyde Arthure, 'falsly have ye wacched me.'

'Sir,' seyde they all, 'we durst nat disobey your sistyrs commaunde-
mentc.'

'A,' seyde the kynge, 'lette fecch me the beste horse that may be
founde, and bydde sir Outlake arme hym in all hast and take anothir 40
good horse and ryde with me.'

So anone the kynge and sir Outlake were well armyd and rode aftir
this lady. And so they com be a crosse and founde a cowherde, and
they asked the pore man if there cam ony lady late rydynge that way.

'Sir,' seyde this pore man, 'ryght late com a lady rydynge this way with a fourty horses, ⌐and to yonder forest she rode. ˥'

And so they folowed faste, and within a whyle Arthur had a syght of Morgan le Fay. Than he chaced as faste as he myght. Whan she
5 aspyed hym folowynge her, she rode a grete pace thorow the foreste tyll she com to a playn. And whan she sawe she myght nat ascape she rode unto a lake thereby and seyde, 'Whatsoever com of me, my brothir shall nat have this scawberde!' And than she lete throwe the scawberde in the deppyst of the watir. So hit sanke, for hit was hevy
10 of golde and precious stonys.

Than she rode into a valey where many grete stonys were, and whan she sawe she muste be overtake, she shope hirself, horse and man, by enchauntemente unto grete marbyll stonys. And anone withall come kynge Arthure and sir Outlake whereas the kynge myght know his
15 sistir and her men and one knyght frome another.

'A,' seyde the kynge, 'here may ye se the vengeaunce of God! And now am I sory this mysaventure is befalle.'

And than he loked for the scawberde, but hit wold nat be founde; so he turned to the abbey there she come fro. So whan Arthure was
20 gone they turned all their lyknesse as she and they were before, and seyde,

'Sirs, now may we go where we wyll.'

(15)   Than seyde Morgan le Fay, 'Saw ye of Arthure, my brother?'

'Yee,' seyde hir men, 'and that ye sholde have founde, and we
25 myght a stered of one stede; for by his amyvestyall countenaunce [he] wolde have caused us to have fledde.'

'I beleve you,' seyde the quene.

So anone after as she rode she mette a knyght ledynge another knyght on horsebake before hym, bounde hande and foote, blynde-
30 felde, to have drowned hym in a fowntayne. Whan she sawe this knyght so bounde she asked,

'What woll ye do with that knyght?'

'Lady,' seyde he, 'I woll drowne hym.'

'For what cause?' she asked.
35   'For I founde hym with my wyff, and she shall have the same deth anone.'

'That were pyté,' seyde Morgan le Fay. 'Now, what sey ye, knyght? Is hit trouthe that he seyth of you?'

'Nay, truly, madame, he seyth nat ryght on me.'
40   'Of whens be ye,' seyde the quene, 'and of what contrey?'

'I am of the courte of kynge Arthure, and my name is Manessen, cosyn unto Accolon of Gaule.'

'Ye sey well, and for the love of hym ye shall be delyverde, and ye shal have youre adversary in the same case that ye were in.'

So this Manessen was loused, and the other kn[y]ght bounde. And anone Manessen unarmed hym and armede hymself in his harneyse, and so mounted on horsebak and the knyght afore hym, and so threw hym in the fountayne and so drowned hym. And than he rode unto Morgan aycn and asked if she wolde onythyng unto Arthure.   5

'Telle hym,' seyde she, 'that I rescewed the nat for the love of hym, but for the love of Accolon, and tell hym I feare hym nat whyle I can make me and myne in lyknesse of stonys, and lette hym wete I can do much more whan I se my tyme.'

And so she departed into the contrey of Gore, and there was she   10 rychely receyved, and made hir castels and townys stronge, for allwey she drad muche kyng Arthure.

VI. GAWAIN, YWAIN AND MARHALT

WHAN the kynge had well rested hym at the abbey ·he rode unto Camelot and founde his quene and his barownes ryght glad of his   15 commyng. And whan they herde of his stronge adventures, as hit is before rehersed, they all had mervayle of the falshede of Morgan le Fay. Many knyghtes wysshed hir brente. Than come Manessen to courte and tolde the kynge of his adventure.

'Well,' seyde the kyng, 'she is a kynde sister! I shall so be avengid on   20 hir and I lyve that all crystendom shall speke of hit.'

So on the morne there cam a damesell on message frome Morgan le Fay to the kynge, and she brought with hir the rycheste mantell that ever was scne in the courtc, for hit was sette all full of precious stonys as one myght stonde by another, and therein were the rycheste stonys   25 that ever the kynge saw. And the damesell seyde,

'Your sister sendyth you this mantell and desyryth that ye sholde take this gyfte of hir, and what thynge she hath offended she woll amende hit at your owne plesure.'

Whan the kyng behelde this mantell hit pleased hym much. He seyde   30 but lytyll. With that come the Damesell of the Lake unto the kynge   (16) and seyde,

'Sir, I muste speke with you in prevyté.'

'Sey on,' seyde the kynge, 'what ye woll.'

'Sir,' seyde this damesell, 'putt nat uppon you this mantell tylle ye   35 have sene more, and in no wyse lat hit nat com on you nother on no knyght of youres tyll ye commaunde the brynger thereof to putt hit uppon hir.'

'Well,' seyde the kynge, 'hit shall be as you counseyle me.'

And than he seyde unto the damesell that com frome his sister,   40

'Damesell, this mantell that ye have brought me, I woll se hit uppon you.'

'Sir,' she seyde, 'hit woll nat beseme me to were a kynges garmente.'

'Be my hede,' seyde Arthure, 'ye shall were hit or hit com on my bak other on ony mannys bak that here is.'

And so the kynge made to putt hit uppon hir. And forthwithall she fell downe deede and never spoke worde after, and brente to colys. Than was the kynge wondirly wroth more than he was toforehande, and seyde unto kynge Uryence,

'My sistir, your wyff, is allway aboute to betray me, and welle I wote other ye or my nevewe, your son, is accounseyle with hir to have me distroyed. But as for you,' seyde the kynge unto kynge Uryence, 'I deme nat gretly that ye be of counseyle, for Accolon confessed to me his owne mowthe that she wolde have distroyed you as well as me; therefore y holde you excused. But as for your son sir Uwayne, I holde hym suspecte. Therefore I charge you, putt hym oute of my courte.' So sir Uwayne was discharged.

And whan sir Gawayne wyste that, he made hym redy to go with hym, 'for whoso banyshyth my cosyn jarmayne shall banyshe me.' So they too departed and rode into a grete foreste, and so they com unto an abbey of monkys, and there were well logged. Butt whan the kynge wyste that sir Gawayne was departed frome the courte, there was made grete sorowe amonge all the astatis.

'Now,' seyde Gaherys, Gawaynes brother, 'we have loste two good knyghtes for the love of one.'

So on the morne they herde their masses in the abbey and so rode forth tyll they com to the grete foreste. Than was sir Gawayne ware in a valey by a turrette twelve fayre damesels and two knyghtes armed on grete horses, and the damesels wente to and fro by a tre. And than was sir Gawayne ware how there hynge a whyght shelde on that tre, and ever as the damesels com by hit they spette uppon hit and som threwe myre uppon the shelde. Than sir Gawayne and sir Uwayne wente and salewed them, and asked why they dud that dispyte to the shelde.

'Sir,' seyde the damesels, 'we shall telle you. There is a knyght in this contrey that owyth this whyght shelde, and he is a passyng good man of his hondis, but he hatyth all ladyes and jantylwomen, and therefore we do all this dyspyte to that shelde.'

'I shall sey you,' seyde sir Gawayne, 'hit besemyth evyll a good knyght to dispyse all ladyes and jantyllwomen; and peraventure thoughe he hate you he hath som cause, and peraventure he lovyth in som other placis ladyes and jantyllwomen and y⟨s⟩ belovyd agayne, and he be suche a man of prouesse as ye speke of. Now, what is his name?'

'Sir', they seyde, 'his name is sir Marhaus, the kynges son of Irelonde.'

'I knowe hym well,' seyde sir Uwayne, 'he is a passynge good knyght as ony on lyve, for I sawe hym onys preved at a justys where many knyghtes were gadird, and that tyme there myght no man withstonde hym.'

'A,' sayde sir Gawayne, 'damesels, methynke ye ar to blame, for hit is to suppose he that hyng that shelde there he woll nat be longe therefro, and than may tho knyghtes macche hym on horsebak. And that is more youre worshyp than thus to do, for I woll abyde no lenger to se a knyghtes shelde so dishonoured.'

And therewith sir Gawayne and sir Uwayne departed a lytyll fro them. And than ware they ware where sir Marhaus com rydynge on a grete horse streyte toward hem. And whan the twelve damesels sawe sir Marhaus they fledde to the turret as they were wylde, that som of hem felle by the way. Than that one of the knyghtes of the towre dressed his shylde and seyde on hyghe, 'Sir Marhaus, defende the!' And so they ran togedyrs that the knyght brake his spere on sir Marhaus, but Marhaus smote hym so harde that he brake his necke and his horse bak. That sawe the other knyght of the turret and dressed hym to Marhaus, that so egerly they mette that this knyght of the turret was smyte doune, horse and man, dede.

And than sir Marhaus rode unto his shylde and sawe how hit was defoyled, and sayde, 'Of this dispyte of parte I am avenged. But yet for hir love that gaff me this whyght shelde I shall were the and hange myne where that was.' And so he honged hit aboute his necke. Than he rode streyte unto sir Gawayne and to sir Uwayne and asked them what they dud there. They answerde hym and seyde they come frome kynge Arthurs courte for to se aventures.

'Welle,' seyde sir Marhaus, 'here am I redy, an adventures knyght that woll fulfylle any adventure that ye woll desyre.' And so departyd frome hem to fecche his raunge.

'Late hym go,' seyde sir Uwayne unto sir Gawayne, 'for he is a passynge good knyght os ony lyvynge. I wolde not be my wylle that ony of us were macched with hym.'

'Nay,' seyde sir Gawayne, 'nat so! Hit were shame to us and he were nat assayed, were he never so good a knyght.'

'Welle,' seyde sir Uwayne, 'I wolle assay hym before you, for I am weyker than ye, and yff he smyte me downe than may ye revenge me.'

So thes two knyghtes come togedir with grete raundom, that sir Uwayne smote sir Marhaus, that his spere braste in pecis on the shelde. And sir Marhaus smote hym so sore that horse and man he bare to the erthe, and hurte sir Uwayne on the lefte syde. Than sir Marhaus turned his horse and rode thidir as he com fro and made hym redy with his spere. Whan sir Gawayne saw that, he dressed his shelde, and than they feautirde their sperys, and they com togedyrs with all the myght of

(18, 19)

their horses, that eyther knyght smote other so harde in myddis the sheldis. But sir Gawaynes spere brake, but sir Marhaus speare helde, and therewith sir Gawayne and his horse russhed downe to the erthe.

And lyghtly sir Gawayne wan on his feete and pulde oute his swerde and dressed hym toward sir Marhaus on foote. And sir Marhaus saw that he pulde oute his swerde, and began to com to sir Gawayne on horsebak.

'Sir knyght,' sayde sir Gawayne, 'alyght on foote, or ellis I woll sle thyne horse.'

'Gramercy,' sayde sir Marhaus, 'of your jentylnesse! Ye teche me curtesy, for hit is nat commendable one knyght to be on horsebak and the other on foote.'

And therewith sir Marhaus sette his spere agayne a tre, and alyght and tyed his horse to a tre, and dressed his shelde, and eyther com unto other egirly and smote togedyrs with hir swerdys, that hir sheldis flew in cantellys, and they bresed their helmys and hawbirkes and woundid eyther other.

But sir Gawayne, fro hit was nine of the clok, wexed ever strenger and strenger, for by than hit cam to the howre of noone he had three tymes his myght encresed. And all this aspyed sir Marhaus and had grete wondir how his myght encreced. And so they wounded eyther other passyng sore. So whan hit was ⌐past noone, and whan it drew⌐ toward evynsonge, sir Gawayns strength fyebled and woxe passyng faynte, that unnethe he myght dure no lenger, and sir Marhaus was than bygger and bygger.

'Sir knyght,' seyde sir Marhaus, 'I have welle felt that ye ar a passynge goode knyght and a mervaylous man of myght as ever I felte ony whyle hit lastyth, and oure quarellys ar nat grete, and therefore hit were pyté to do you hurte, for I fele ye ar passynge fyeble.'

'A,' seyde sir Gawayne, 'jantyll knyght, ye say the worde that I sholde sey.'

And therewith they toke of her helmys and eyther kyssed other and there they swore togedyrs eythir to love other as brethirne. And sir Marhaus prayde sir Gawayne to lodge with hym that nyght. And so they toke their horsis and rode towarde sir Marhaus maner.

And as they rode by the way, 'Sir knyght,' seyde sir Gawayne, 'I have mervayle of you, so valyaunte a man as ye be of prouesse, that ye love no ladyes and damesels.'

'Sir,' seyde sir Marhaus, 'they name me wrongfully, for hit be the damesels of the turret that so name me and other suche as they be. Now shall I telle you for what cause I hate them: for they be sorsseres and inchaunters many of them, and be a knyght never so good of his body and as full of prouesse as a man may be, they woll make hym a starke cowerde to have the bettir of hym. And this is the pryncipall

cause that I hate them. And all good ladyes and jantyllwomen, I owghe
them my servyse as a knyght ought to do.'

For, as the booke rehersyth in Freynsch, there was this many knyghtes
that overmacched sir Gawayne for all his thryse double myghte that he
had: sir Launcelot de Lake, sir Trystrams, sir Bors de Gaynes, sir 5
Percivale, sir Pelleas, sir Marhaus; thes six knyghtes had the bettir of
sir Gawayne.

Than within a lytyll whyle they come to sir Marhaus place [which]
was in a lytyll pryory, and there they alyght, and ladyes and damesels
unarmed them and hastely loked to their hurtes, for they were all three 10
hurte. And so they had good lodgyng with sir Marhaus and good chere,
for whan he wyste that they were kynge Arthurs syster-sonnes he made
them all the chere that lay in his power. And so they sojourned there
a sevennyght and were well eased of their woundis, and at the laste
departed.   15

'Nay,' sayde sir Marhaus, 'we woll nat departe so lyghtly, for I woll
brynge you thorow the foreste.'

So they rode forth all three. And sir Marhaus toke with hym his
grettyste spere. And so they rode thorow the foreste, and rode day be
day well-nye a seven dayes or they founde ony aventure. So at the 20
laste they com into a grete foreste that was named the contrey and
foreste of Arroy, and the contrey is of stronge adventures.

'In this contrey,' seyde Marhaus, 'cam nevir knyght syn hit was
crystynde but he founde strange adventures.'

And so they rode and cam into a depe valey full of stonys, and thereby 25
they sawe a fayre streme of watir. Aboven thereby was the hede of the
streme, a fayre founteyne, and three damesels syttynge thereby. And
than they rode to them and ayther salewed othir. And the eldyst had
a garlonde of golde aboute her hede, and she was three score wyntir
of age or more, and hir heyre was whyght undir the garlonde. The 30
secunde damesell was of thirty wyntir of age, wyth a cerclet of golde
aboute her hede. The thirde damesel was but fiftene yere of age, and
a garlonde of floures aboute hir hede. Whan the sknyghtes had so beholde them they asked hem the cause why they sate at the fountayne.

'We be here,' seyde the damesels, 'for this cause: if we may se ony of 35
arraunte knyghtes to teche hem unto stronge aventures. And ye be
three knyghtes adventures and we be three damesels, and therefore
eche one of you muste chose one of us; and whan ye have done so, we
woll lede you unto three hyghewayes, and there eche of you shall chose
a way and his damesell with hym. And this day twelve moneth ye 40
muste mete here agayne, and God sende you the lyves, and thereto ye
muste plyght your trouth.'

'This is well seyde,' seyde sir Marhaus. 'Now shall everyche of us (20)
chose a damesell.'

'I shall tell you,' seyde sir Uwayne, 'I am yongyst and waykest of you bothe, therefore lette me have the eldyst damesell, for she hath sene much and can beste helpe me whan I have nede, for I have moste nede of helpe of you bothe.'

5　'Now,' seyde sir Marhaus, 'I woll have the damesell of thirty wyntir age, for she fallyth beste to me.'

"Well,' seyde sir Gawayne, 'I thanke you, for ye have lefft me the yongyst and the fayryste, and hir is me moste levyste.'

Than every damesell toke hir knyght by the reygne of his brydyll and
10　brought hem to the three wayes, and there was made promesse to mete at the fountayne that day twelve monthe and they were lyvynge. And so they kyssed and departed, and every k[n]yght sette his lady behynde hym. And sir Uwayne toke the way that lay weste, and sir Marhaus toke the way that lay sowthe, and sir Gawayne toke the way that lay northe.

15　Now woll we begyn at sir Gawayne that helde that way tyll that he com to a fayre maner where dwelled an olde knyght and a good householder. And there sir Gawayne asked the knyght if he knewe of any aventures.

'I shall shewe you to-morne,' seyde the knyght, 'mervelos adventures.'
20　So on the morne they rode all in same to the foreste of aventures tyll they com to a launde, and thereby they founde a crosse. And as they stood and hoved, there cam by them the fayreste knyght and the seme-lyest man that ever they sawe, but he made the grettyst dole that ever man made. And than he was ware of sir Gawayne and salewed hym,
25　and prayde to God to sende hym muche worshyp.

'As for that,' sayde sir Gawayne, 'gramercy. Also I pray to God sende you honoure and worshyp.'

'A,' sayde the knyght, 'I may lay that on syde, for sorow and shame commyth unto me after worshyppe.'

(21) 30　And therewyth he passed unto that one syde of the lawnde, and on that other syde saw sir Gawayne ten knyghtes that hoved and made hem redy with hir sheldis and with hir sperys agaynste that one knyght that cam by sir Gawayne. Than this one knyght feautred a grete spere, and one of the ten knyghtes encountird with hym. But this wofull
35　knyght smote hym so harde that he felle over his horse tayle. So this dolorous knyght served them all, that at the leste way he smote downe horse and man, and all he ded with one spere. And so whan they were all ten on foote they wente to the one knyght, and he stoode stone-stylle and suffyrde hem to pulle hym downe of his horse, and bounde
40　hym honde and foote, and tyed hym undir the horse bely, and so led hym with hem.

'A, Jesu,' seyde sir Gawayne, 'this is a dolefull syght to se the yondir knyght so to be entreted. And hit semyth by the knyght that he sufferyth hem to bynde hym so, for he makyth no resistence.'

'No,' seyde [his] hoste, 'that is trouth, for, and he wolde, they all were to weyke for hym.'

'Sir,' seyde the damesell unto sir Gawayne, 'mesemyth hit were your worshyp to helpe that dolerouse knyght, for methynkes he is one of the beste knyghtes that ever I sawe.'   5

'I wolde do for hym,' seyde sir Gawayne, 'but hit semyth he wolde have no helpe.'

'No,' seyde the damesell, 'methynkes ye have no lyste to helpe hym.'

Thus as they talked they sawe a knyght on the other syde of the launde all armed save the hede. And on the other syde there com a 10 dwarff on horsebak all armed save the hede, with a grete mowthe and a shorte nose. And whan the dwarff com nyghe he seyde, 'Where is this lady sholde mete us here?' And therewithall she com forth oute of the woode. And than they began to stryve for the lady, for the knyght seyde he wolde have hir [and the dwerf said he wold have her]. 15

'Woll we do welle?' seyde the dwarff. 'Yondir is a knyght at the crosse. Lette hit be putt uppon hym, and as he demeth hit, so shall hit be.'

'I woll well,' seyde the knyght.

And so they wente all three unto sir Gawayne and tolde hym where- 20 fore they strooff.

'Well, sirres, woll ye putt the mater in myne honde?'

'Ye, sir,' they seyde bothe.

'Now, damesell,' seyde sir Gawayne, 'ye shall stonde betwyxte them bothe, and whethir ye lyste bettir to go to he shall have you.' 25

And whan she was sette betwene hem bothe she lefte the knyght and went to the dwarff. And than the dwarff toke hir up and wente his way syngyng, and the knyght wente his way with grete mournyng.

Than com there two knyghtes all armed and cryed on hyght,

'Sir Gawayne, knyght of the courte of kynge Arthure! Make the 30 redy in haste and juste with me!'

So they ran togedirs, that eyther felle downe. And than on foote they drew there swerdis and dud full actually. The meanewhyle the other knyght went to the damesell and asked hir why she abode with that knyght, and seyde, 35

'If ye wolde abyde with me I wolde be your faythefull knyght.'

'And with you woll I be,' seyde the damesell, 'for I may nat fynde in my herte to be with hym, for ryght now here was one knyght that scomfyted ten knyghtes, and at the laste he was cowardly ledde away. And therefore let us two go whyle they fyght.' 40

And sir Gawayne fought with that othir knyght longe, but at the laste they accorded bothe. And than the knyght prayde sir Gawayne to lodge with hym that nyght. So as sir Gawayne wente with this knyght he seyde,

'What knyght is he in this contrey that smote downe the ten knyghtes? For whan he had done so manfully he suffirde hem to bynde hym hande and foote, and so led hym away.'

'A,' sayde the knyght, 'that is the beste knyght I trow in the worlde
5 and the moste man of prouesse. And hit is the grettyst pyté of hym as of ony knyght lyvynge, for he hath be served so as he was this tyme more than ten tymes. And his name hyght sir Pelleas; and he lovyth a grete lady in this contrey, and hir name is Ettarde. And so whan he loved hir there was cryed in this contray a grete justis three dayes, and all this
10 knyghtes of this contrey were there and jantyllwomen. And who that preved hym the beste knyght sholde have a passyng good ⌜swerd⌝ and a cerclet of golde, and that cerclet the knyght sholde geff hit to the fayryste lady that was at that justis.

'And this knyght sir Pelleas was far the beste of ony that was there,
15 and there were fyve hondred knyghtes, but there was nevir man that ever sir Pelleas met but he stroke hym downe other ellys frome his horse, and every day of three dayes he strake downe twenty knyghtes. And therefore they gaff hym the pryce. And furthewithall he wente thereas the lady Ettarde was and gaff her the cerclet and seyde opynly
20 she was the fayreste lady that there was, and that wolde he preve uppon ony knyght that wolde sey nay.

(22) 'And so he chose hir for his soveraygne lady, and never to love other but her. But she was so prowde that she had scorne of hym and seyde she wolde never love hym thoughe he wolde dye for hir; where-
25 fore all ladyes and jantyllwomen had scorne of hir that she was so prowde, for there were fayrer than she, and there was none that was there but and sir Pelleas wolde have profyrde hem love they wolde have shewed hym the same for his noble prouesse. And so this knyght promysed Ettarde to folow hir into this contray and nevir to leve her
30 tyll she lovid hym, and thus he is here the moste party nyghe her and logged by a pryory.

'And every weke she sendis knyghtes to fyght with hym, and whan he hath putt hem to the worse, than woll he suffir hem wylfully to take hym presonere because he wolde have a syght of this lady. And all-
35 wayes she doth hym grete dispyte, for somtyme she makyth hir knyghtes to tye hym to his horse tayle, and somtyme bynde hym undir the horse bealy. Thus in the moste shamfyllyste wyse that she can thynke he is brought to hir, and all she doth hit for to cawse hym to leve this contrey and to leve his lovynge. But all this cannat make hym to leve,
40 for, and he wolde a fought on foote, he myght have had the bettir of the ten knyghtes as well on foote as on horsebak.'

'Alas,' sayde sir Gawayne, 'hit is grete pyté of hym, and aftir this nyght I woll seke hym to-morow in this foreste to do hym all the helpe I can.'

So on the morow sir Gawayne toke his leve of his oste, sir Carados, and rode into the foreste. And at the laste he mette with sir Pelleas makynge grete mone oute of mesure; so eche of hem salewed other, and asked hym why he made suche sorow.

And as hit above rehersyth sir Pelleas tolde sir Gawayne: 'But all- 5 wayes I suffir her knyghtes to fare so with me as ye sawe yestirday, in truste at the laste to wynne hir love; for she knoweth well all hir knyghtes sholde nat lyghtly wynne me and me lyste to fyght with them to the uttirmoste. Wherefore and I loved hir nat so sore I had lever dye an hondred tymes, and I myght dye so ofte, rathir than I 10 wolde suffir that dispyte, but I truste she woll have pyté uppon me at the laste; for love causyth many a good knyght to suffir to have his entente, but alas, I am infortunate!'

And therewith he made so grete dole that unnethe he myght holde hym on his horse bak. 15

'Now,' sayde sir Gawayne, 'leve your mournynge, and I shall pro-myse you by the feyth of my body to do all that lyeth in my powere to gete you the love of your lady, and thereto I woll plyghte you my trouthe.'

'A,' seyde sir Pelleas, 'of what courte ar ye?' 20

'Sir, I am of the courte of kynge Arthure, and his sistir son, and kynge Lotte of Orkeney was my fadir, and my name is sir Gawayne.'

'And my name is sir Pelleas, born in the Iles, and of many iles I am lorde. And never loved I lady nother damesel tyll nowe. And, sir knyght, syn ye ar so nye cosyn unto kyng Arthure and ar a kynges 25 son, therefore betray me nat, but help me, for I may nevir com by hir but by som good knyght. For she is in a stronge castell here faste by, within this four myle, and over all this contrey she is lady off.

'And so I may never com to hir presence but as I suffir hir knyghtes to take me, and but if I ded so that I myght have a syght of hir, I had 30 bene dede longe ar this tyme. And yet fayre worde had I never none of hir. But whan I am brought tofore hir she rebukyth me in the fowlyst maner; and than they take me my horse and harneyse and puttyth me oute of the yatis, and she woll nat suffir me to ete nother drynke. And allwayes I offir me to be her presoner, but that woll she 35 nat suffir me; for I wolde desire no more, what paynes that ever I had, so that I myght have a syght of hir dayly.'

'Well,' seyde sir Gawayne, 'all this shall I amende, and ye woll do as I shall devyse. I woll have your armoure, and so woll I ryde unto hir castell and tell hir that I have slayne you, and so shall I com within hir 40 to cause hir to cheryshe me. And than shall I do my trew parte, that ye shall nat fayle to have the love of hir.'

And there, whan sir Gawayne plyght his trouthe unto sir Pelleas to (23) be trew and feythfull unto hym, so eche one plyght their trouthe to

other, and so they chonged horse and harneyse. And sir Gawayne departed and com to the castel where stood hir pavylyons withoute the ghate. And as sone as Ettarde had aspyed sir Gawayne she fledde in toward the castell. But sir Gawayne spake on hyght and bade hir
5 abyde, for he was nat sir Pelleas.

'I am another knyght that have slayne sir Pelleas.'

'Than do of your helme,' seyde the lady Ettarde, 'that I may se your vysage.'

So whan she saw that hit was nat sir Pelleas she made hym alyght
10 and lad hym into hir castell, and asked hym feythfully whethir he had slayne sir Pelleas, and he seyde yee. Than he tolde hir his name was sir Gawayne, of the courte of kynge Arthure and his sistyrs son, and how he had slayne sir Pelleas.

'Truly,' seyde she, 'that is grete pyté for he was a passynge good
15 knyght of his body. But of all men on lyve I hated hym moste, for I coude never be quytte of hym. And for ye have slayne hym I shall be your woman and to do onythynge that may please you.'

So she made sir Gawayne good chere. Than sir Gawayne sayde that he loved a lady and by no meane she wolde love hym.
20 'Sche is to blame,' seyde Ettarde, 'and she woll nat love you, for ye that be so well-borne a man and suche a man of prouesse, there is no lady in this worlde to good for you.'

'Woll ye,' seyde sir Gawayne, 'promyse me to do what that ye may do be the fayth of your body to gete me the love of my lady?'
25 'Yee, sir, and that I promyse you be my fayth.'

'Now,' seyde sir Gawayne, 'hit is yourself that I love so well; therefore holde your promyse.'

'I may nat chese,' seyde the lady Ettarde, 'but if I sholde be forsworne.'
30 And so she graunted hym to fulfylle all his desyre.

So hit was in the monthe of May that she and sir Gawayne wente oute of the castell and sowped in a pavylyon, and there was made a bedde, and there sir Gawayne and Ettarde wente to bedde togedyrs. And in another pavylyon she leyde hir damesels, and in the thirde
35 pavylyon she leyde parte of hir knyghtes, for than she had no drede of sir Pelleas. And there sir Gawayne lay with hir in the pavylyon two dayes and two nyghtes.

And on the thirde day on the morne erly sir Pelleas armed hym, for he hadde never slepte syn [sir Gawayne departed from hym, for] sir
40 Gawayne promysed hym by the feythe of his body to com to hym unto his pavylyon by the pryory within the space of a day and a nyght. Than sir Pelleas mounted uppon horsebak and com to the pavylyons that stood withoute the castell, and founde in the fyrste pavylyon three knyghtes in three beddis, and three squyres lyggynge at their

feete. Than wente he to the secunde pavylyon and founde four jantyllwomen lyggyng in four beddis. And than he yode to the thirde pavylyon
and founde sir Gawayne lyggyng in the bed with his lady Ettarde and
aythir clyppynge other in armys. And whan he sawe that, his hert well-
nyghe braste for sorow, and sayde, 'Alas, that ever a knyght sholde   5
be founde so false!'

And than he toke his horse and myght nat abyde no lenger for pure
sorow, and whan he had ryden nyghe half a myle he turned agayne
and thought for to sle hem bothe. And whan he saw hem lye so bothe
slepynge faste that unnethe he myght holde hym on horsebak for sorow,   10
and seyde thus to hymself: 'Though this knyght be never so false,
I woll never sle hym slepynge, for I woll never dystroy the hyghe
Ordir of Knyghthode,' and therewith he departed agayne. And or he
had rydden half a myle he returned agayne and thought than to sle hem
bothe, makynge the grettyst sorow that ever man made. And whan he   15
come to the pavylyons he tyed his horse to a tre and pulled oute his
swerde naked in his honde and wente to them thereas they lay. And
yet he thought shame to sle hem, and leyde the naked swerde overthawrte bothe their throtis, and so toke his horse and rode his way.
And whan sir Pelleas com to his pavylyons he tolde his knyghtes and   20
his squyers how he had spedde, and seyde thus unto them:

'For youre good and trew servyse ye have done me I shall gyff you
all my goodes, for I woll go unto my bedde and never aryse tyll I be
dede. And whan that I am dede, I charge you that ye take the herte oute
of my body and bere hit her betwyxte two sylver dysshes and telle her   25
how I sawe hir lye wyth that false knyght sir Gawayne.'

Ryght so sir Pelleas unarmed hymself and wente unto his bedde
makyng merveylous dole and sorow.

Than sir Gawayne and Ettarde awoke of her slepe and founde the
naked swerde overthawrte their throtis. Than she knew hit was the   30
swerde of sir Pelleas.

'Alas!' she seyde, 'Sir Gawayne, ye have betrayde sir Pelleas and me,
ᵣfor you told me you had slayne hym, and now I know well it is not so:
he is on lyve⟩. But had he bene so uncurteyse unto you as ye have bene
to hym, ye had bene a dede knyght. But ye have dissayved me, that all   35
ladyes and damesels may beware be you and me.' And therewith sir
Gawayne made hym redy and wente into the foreste.

So hit happed the Damesell of the Lake, Nynyve, mette with a
knyght of sir Pelleas that wente on his foote in this foreste makynge
grete doole, and she askede hym the cause; and so the wofull knyght   40
tolde her all how his mayster and lorde was betrayed thorow a knyght
and a lady, and how he woll never aryse oute of his bedde tyll he be
dede.

'Brynge me to hym,' seyde she anone, 'and y woll waraunte his

lyfe. He shall nat dye for love, and she that hath caused hym so to
love she shall be in as evylle plyte as he is or hit be longe to, for hit is
no joy of suche a proude lady that woll nat have no mercy of suche a
valyaunte knyght.'

5   Anone that knyght broute hir unto hym, and whan she sye hym lye
on his bedde she thought she sawe never so lykly a knyght. And therewith she threw an enchauntemente uppon hym, and he fell on slepe.
And than she rode unto the lady Ettarde and charged that no man
scholde awake hym tyll she come agayne. So within two owres she
10 brought the lady Ettarde thidir, and bothe the ladyes founde hym on
slepe.

'Loo,' seyde the Damesell of the Lake, 'ye oughte to be ashamed for
to murther suche a knyght,' and therewith she threw such an inchauntemente uppon hir that she loved hym so sore that well-nyghe she was
15 nere oute of hir mynde.

'A, Lorde Jesu,' seyde this lady Ettarde, 'how is hit befallyn unto me
that I love now that I have hatyd moste of ony man on lyve?'

'That is the ryghteuouse jugemente of God,' seyde the damesell.

And than anone sir Pelleas awaked and loked uppon Ettarde, and
20 wha[n] he saw hir he knew her, and than he hated hir more than ony
woman on lyve, and seyde,

'Away, traytoures, and com never in my syght!'

And whan she herde hym sey so she wepte and made grete sorow
oute of mynde.

(24) 25 'Sir knyght Pelleas,' seyde the Damesel of the Lake, 'take your
horse and com forthwith oute of this contrey, and ye shall love a lady
that woll love you.'

'I woll well,' seyde sir Pelleas, 'for this lady Ettarde hath done me
grete dispyte and shame;' and there he tolde hir the begynnyng and
30 endyng, and how he had never purposed to have rysen agayne tyll he
had bene dede. 'And now suche grace God hath sente me that I hate
hir as much as I have loved hir.'

'Thanke me therefore,' seyde the Lady of the Lake.

Anone sir Pelleas armed hym and toke his horse and commaunded
35 his men to brynge aftir his pavylyons and his stuffe where the Lady
of the Lake wolde assyngne them. So this lady Ettarde dyed for sorow,
and the Damesel of the Lake rejoysed sir Pelleas, and loved togedyrs
duryng their lyfe.

(25) Now turne we unto sir Marhaute that rode with the damesel of
40 thirty wynter of ayge southwarde. And so they come into a depe foreste,
and by fortune they were nyghted and rode longe in a depe way, and
at the laste they com unto a courtlage and there they asked herborow.
But the man of the courtlage wolde nat logge them for no tretyse that
they coude trete, but this much the good man seyde: 'And ye woll take

the adventure of youre herbourage, I shall bryng you there ye may be
herbourde.'

'What aventure is that [that] I shall have for my herborow?' seyde
sir Marhaute.

'Ye shall wete whan ye com there,' seyde the good man.   5

'Sir, what adventure so hit be, I pray the to brynge me thidir, for I
am wery, my damesel and my horse both.'

So the good man wente uppon his gate before hym in a lane, and
within an houre he brought hym untyll a fayre castell. And than the
pore man called the porter, and anone he was lette into the castell.   10
And so he tolde the lorde how he had brought hym a knyght arraunte
and a damesell wolde be lodged with hym. 'Lette hym in,' seyde the
lorde, 'for hit may happen he shall repente that they toke theire herborow here.' So sir Marhaute was let in with a torchelyght, and there
was a grete syght of goodly men that welcomed hym; and than his   15
horse was lad into a stable, and he and the damesel were brought into
the halle, and there stoode a myghty duke and many goodly men aboute
hym. Than this duke asked hym what he hyght, and fro whens he com,
and with whom he dwelte.

'Sir,' he seyde, 'I am a knyght of kynge Arthurs and knyght of the 20
Table Rounde, and my name is sir Marhaute, and borne I was in
Irelonde.'

'That me repentes,' seyde the duke, 'for I love nat thy lorde nother
none of thy felowys of the Table Rounde. And therefore ease thyself
this nyght as well as thou mayste, for as to-morne I and my six sonnes 25
shall macch with you.'

'Is there no remedy,' seyde sir Marhaute, 'but that I muste have ado
with you and your six sunnes at onys?'

'No,' seyde the duke, 'for this cause. I made myne avowe, for sir
Gawayne slew my sevynth sonne in a recountre, therefore I made   30
myne avow that there sholde never knyght of kynge Arthurs courte
lodge with me or com thereas I myght have ado with hym but I wolde
revenge me of my sonnes deth.'

'What is your name?' sayde sir Marhaute, 'I requyre you telle me,
and hit please you.'   35

'Wete thou well I am the duke of Southe Marchis.'

'A!' seyde sir Marhaute, 'I have herde seyde that ye have been longe
tyme a grete foo unto my lorde Arthure and unto his knyghtes.'

'That shall ye fele to-morne,' seyde the duke, 'and ye leve so longe.'

'Shall I have ado with you?' seyde sir Marhaute.   40

'Ye,' seyde the duke, 'thereof shalt thou not chose. And therefore
let take hym to his chambir and lette hym have all that tyll hym longis.'
So sir Marhaute departed and was led unto his chambir, and his damesel
was led in tyll hir chambir.

And on the morne the duke sente unto sir Marhaute and bade hym make hym redy. And so sir Marhaute arose and armed hym. And than there was a masse songe afore hym, and brake his faste, and so mounted on horsebak in the courte of the castell there they sholde do batayle.

5 So there was the deuke all ready on horsebak and clene armed, and his six sonnys by hym, and everyche had a spere in his honde. And so they encountirde whereas the deuke and his [two] sonnys brake her sperys uppon hym, but sir Marhaute hylde up his spere and touched none of hem.

(26) 10 Than come the four sonnes by couple, and two of them brake their sperys, and so dud the other two. And all this whyle sir Marhaute towched hem nat. Than sir Marhaute ran to the deuke and smote hym downe with his speare, that horse and man felle to the erthe, and so he served his sonnes. Than sir Marhaute alyght downe and bade the

15 deuke yelde hym, other he wolde sle hym. Than som of his sonnes recovirde and wolde have sette uppon sir Marhaute. Than sir Marhaute seyde, 'Sir deuke, cese thy sonnys, and ellys I woll do the uttirmust to you all.' Than the deuke sye he myght nat ascape the deth, he cryed to his sonnes and charged them to yelde them to sir Marhaute,

20 and than they kneled alle adowne and putt the pomels of their swerdis to the knyght, and so he receyvid them; and than they hove up their fadir on his feete. And so by their comunal assent promysed to sir Marhaute never to be fooys unto kynge Arthure, and thereuppon at Whytsonday next aftir to com, he and his sonnes, and there to putt

25 them in the kynges grace. Than sir Marhaute departed.

And within two dayes sir Marhautes damesel brought hym whereas was a grete turnemente that the lady Vawse had cryed, and who that dud beste sholde have a ryche cerclet of golde worth a thousand besauntis. And there sir Marhaute dud so nobely that he was re-

30 nomed, and had smeten doune forty knyghtes, and so the cerclet of golde was rewarded hym. Than he departed thens with grete honoure.

And so within sevennyght his damesel brought hym to an erlys place. His name was the erle Fergus that aftir was sir Trystrams knyght, and this erle was but a yonge man and late com to his londis, and there

35 was a gyaunte faste by hym that hyght Taulurd, and he had another brother in Cornuayle that hyght Taulas that sir Trystram slewe whan he was oute of his mynde. So this erle made his complaynte unto sir Marhaute that there was a gyaunte by hym that destroyed all his londis and how he durste nowhere ryde nother go for hym.

40 'Sir,' seyde he, 'whether usyth he to fyght on horsebak othir on foote?'

'Nay,' seyde the erle, 'there may no horse bere hym.'

'Well,' seyde sir Marhaute, 'than woll I fyght with hym on foote.'

So on the morne sir Marhaute prayde the erle that one of his men

myght brynge hym where the gyaunte was, and so one brought hym
where he syghe hym sytte undir a tre of hooly, and many clubbis of
ironne and gysernes aboute hym. So this knyght dressed hym to the
gyaunte and put his shylde before hym, and the gyaunte toke an ironne
club in his honde, and at the fyrste stroke he clave syr Marhautis shelde. 5
And there he was in grete perell, for the gyaunte was a sly fyghter. But
at the laste sir Marhaute smote of his ryght arme aboven the elbow.
Than the gyaunte fledde and the knyght affter hym, and so he drove hym
into a watir; but the gyaunte was so hyghe that he myght nat wade
aftir hym. And than sir Marhaute made the erle Fergus man to fecche 10
hym stonys, and with that stonys the knyght gave the gyaunte many
sore strokis tylle at the laste he made hym falle downe in the watir, and
so was he there dede.

Than sir Marhalte wente into the gyauntes castell, and there he
delyverde four-and-twenty knyghtes oute of the gyauntes preson and 15
twelve ladyes; and there he had grete rychesse oute of numbir, that
dayes of his lyff he was nevir poore man. Than he returned to the erle
Fergus, the whyche thanked hym gretly and wolde have yevyn hym
half his londys, but he wolde none take. So sir Marhaute dwellid with
the erle nye half a yere, for he was sore brused with the gyaunte. So at 20
the laste he toke his leve, and as he rode by the way with his damysel
he mette with sir Gawayne and wyth sir Uwayne.

So by adventure he mette with four knyghtes of Arthurs courte:
the fyrst was sir Sagramour le Desyrus, sir Ozanna le Cure Hardy,
sir Dodynas le Saveage, and sir Felotte of Lystynoyse; and there sir 25
Marhaute with one spere smote downe these four knyghtes and hurte
them sore. And so departed to mete at his day.

Now turne we unto sir Uwayne that rode westwarde with his dame- (27)
sell of three score wyntir of ayge. And there was a turnemente nyghe the
marche of Walys, and at that turnemente sir Uwayne smote doune 30
thirty knyghtes. Therefore was gyffyn hym the pryce, and that was a
jarfaucon and a whyght stede trapped with cloth of golde. So than sir
Uwayne ded many strange adventures by the meanys of the olde
damesel, and so she brought [hym] to a lady that was called the Lady
of the Roch, the whyche was curtayse. 35

So there was in that contrey two knyghtes that were brethirne, and
they were called two perelous knyghtes: that one hyght sir Edwarde of
the Rede Castell, and that other sir Hew of the Rede Castell, and these
two brethirne had dishcrytcd the Lady of the Roche of a baronnery of
londis by their extorsion. And as this knyghte was lodged with this 40
lady, she made hir complaynte to hym of thes two knyghtes.

'Madam,' seyde sir Uwayne, 'they ar to blame, for they do ayenste
the hyghe Order of Knyghthode and the oth that they made. And if hit
lyke you I woll speke with hem, because I am a knyght of kyng

Arthurs, and to entrete them with fayrenesse; and if they woll nat, I shall do batayle with hem for Goddis sake and in the defence of your ryght.'

'Gramercy,' seyde the lady, 'and thereas I may nat acquyte you,
5 God shall.'

So on the morne the two knyghtes were sente fore, that they sholde speke with the Lady of the Roche, and wete you well they fayled nat, for they com with an hondred horses. But whan this lady sawe them in suche maner so bygge she wolde nat suffir sir Uwayne to go oute to
10 them uppon no sureté ne of fayre langage, but she made hym to speke with them over a toure. But fynally thes two brethirne wolde nat be entreted, and answerde that they wolde kepe that they had.

'Well,' seyde syr Uwayne, 'than woll I fyght with one of you and preve that ye do this lady wronge.'

15 'That woll we nat,' seyde they, 'for and we do batayle we two woll fyght bothe at onys with one knyght. And therefore, yf ye lyste to fyght so, we woll be redy at what oure ye woll assygne, and yf ye wynne us in batayle, she to have hir londis agayne.'

'Ye say well,' seyde sir Uwayne. 'Therefore make you redy, and that
20 ye be here to-morne in the defence of this ladyes ryght.'

(28) So was there sykernesse made on bothe partyes, that no treson sholde be wrought. And so thes knyghtes departed and made them redy.

And that nyght sir Uwayne had grete chere, and on the morne he
25 arose erly and harde masse and brake his faste, and so rode into the playne withoute the gatis where hoved the two brethirne abydyng hym. So they ran togedyrs passynge sore, that sir Edwarde and sir Hew brake their sperys uppon sir Uwayne, and sir Uwayne smote sir Edwarde, that he felle over his horse and yette his spere braste nat.
30 And than he spurred his horse and com uppon sir Hew and overthrew hym. But they sone recoverde and dressed their shyldes and drew oute their swerdes, and bade sir Uwayne alyght and do his batayle to the utteraunce.

Than sir Uwayne devoyded his horse delyverly and put his shylde
35 before hym and drew his swerde, and so they threste togedyrs and eythir gave other grate strokis. And there thes two brethirne wounded sir Uwayne passyng grevously, that the Lady of the Roche wente he sholde have deyed. And thus they fought togedyrs fyve oures as men outraged of reson, and at the laste sir Uwayne smote sir Edwarde uppon
40 the helme suche a stroke that his swerde kerved unto his canellbone; and than sir Hew abated his corrage, but sir Uwayne presed faste to have slayne hym. That saw sir Hew and kneled adowne and yelded hym to sir Uwayne, and he of his jantylnesse resceyved his swerde and toke hym by the honde, and wente into the castell togedirs.

Than this Lady of the Roche was passyng glad, and sir Hew made
grete sorow for his brothirs deth. But this lady was restored ayen of
all hir londis, and sir Hew was commaunded to be at the courte of
kynge Arthure at the next feste of Pentecoste. So sir Uwayne dwelled
with this lady nyghe halfe a yere, for hit was longe or he myght be 5
hole of his grete hurtis. And so, whan hit drew nyghe the termeday
that sir Gawayne, sir Marhaute and sir Uwayne made to mete at the
crosseway, than every knyght drew hym thydir to holde his promyse
that they made. And sir Marhalte and sir Uwayne brought their damesels
with hem, but sir Gawayne had loste his damesel.   10

Ryght so at the twelve-monthis ende they mette all three knyghtes (29)
at the fountayne and theire damesels, but the damesell that sir Gawayne
had coude sey but lytyll worshyp of hym. So they departed frome the
damesels and rode thorowe a grete foreste, and there they mette with
a messyngere that com from kynge Arthurs courte that had sought 15
hem well-nyghe a twelve-monthe thorowoute all Ingelonde, Walis,
and Scotlonde, and charged yf ever he myght fynde sir Gawayne
and sir Uwayne to haste hem unto the courte agayne. And than were
they all glad, and so they prayde sir Marhaute to ryde with hem to the
kynges courte.   20

And so within twelve dayes they come to Camelot, and the kynge
was passyng glad of their commyng, and so was all the courte. Than
the kynge made hem to swere uppon a booke to telle hym all their
adventures that had befalle them that twelve-monthe before, and so
they ded. And there was sir Marhaute well knowyn, for there were 25
knyghtes that he had macched aforetyme, and he was named one of
the best knyghtes lyvyng.

So agayne the feste of Pentecoste cam the Damesell of the Laake
and brought with hir sir Pelleas, and at the hyghe feste there was grete
joustys. Of all knyghtes that were at that justis sir Pelleas had the pryce 30
and syr Marhaute was named next. But sir Pelleas was so stronge that
there myght but fewe knyghtes stonde hym a buffette with a spere.
And at the next feste sir Pelleas and sir Marhalt were made knyghtes
of the Rounde Table; for there were two segis voyde, for two knyghtes
were slayne that twelve-monthe.   35

And grete joy had kynge Arthure of sir Pelleas and of sir Marhalte,
but Pelleas loved never aftir sir Gawayne but as he spared hym for the
love of the kynge; but oftyntymes at justis and at turnementes sir
Pelleas quytte sir Gawayne, for so hit rehersyth in the booke of Frensh.

So sir Trystrams many dayes aftir fought with sir Marhaute in an 40
ilande. And there they dud a grete batayle, but the laste sir Trystrams
slew hym. So sir Trystrams was so wounded that unnethe he myght
recover, and lay at a nunrye half a yere.

And sir Pelleas was a worshypfull knyght, and was one of the four that enchéved the Sankgreal. And the Damesel of the Laake made by her meanes that never he had ado with sir Launcelot de Laake, for where sir Launcelot was at ony justis or at ony turnemente she wolde not suffir hym to be there that day but yf hit were on the syde of sir 5 Launcelot.

HERE ENDYTH THIS TALE, AS THE FREYNSHE BOOKE SEYTH, FRO THE MARYAGE OF KYNGE UTHER UNTO KYNG ARTHURE THAT REGNED AFTIR HYM AND DED MANY BATAYLES.

AND THIS BOOKE ENDYTH WHEREAS SIR LAUNCELOT AND SIR TRY- 10 STRAMS COM TO COURTE. WHO THAT WOLL MAKE ONY MORE LETTE HYM SEKE OTHER BOOKIS OF KYNGE ARTHURE OR OF SIR LAUNCELOT OR SIR TRYSTRAMS; FOR THIS WAS DRAWYN BY A KNYGHT PRESONER, SIR THOMAS MALLEORRÉ, THAT GOD SENDE HYM GOOD RECOVER. AMEN.

EXPLICIT.

THE TALE OF THE
NOBLE KING ARTHUR
THAT WAS
EMPEROR HIMSELF THROUGH
DIGNITY OF HIS HANDS

Hʏᴛ befelle whan kyng Arthur had wedded quene Gwenyvere and
fulfylled the Rounde Table, and so aftir his mervelous knyghtis and he
had venquyshed the moste party of his enemyes, than sone aftir com
sir Launcelot de Lake unto the courte, and sir Trystrams come that
tyme also, and than ⌐kyng Arthur helde a ryal feeste and Table Rounde⌐. 5
    So hit befelle that the Emperour Lucius, ⌐Procurour of the publyke
wele of Rome⌐, sente unto Arthure messyngers commaundynge hym
for to pay his trewage that his aunccettryes have payde before hym.
Whan kynge Arthure wyste what they mente he loked up with his
gray yghen and angred at the messyngers passyng sore. Than were 10
this messyngers aferde and knelyd stylle and durste nat aryse, they were
so aferde of his grymme countenaunce. Than one of the knyghtes
messyngers spake alowde and seyde,
    'Crowned kynge, myssedo no messyngers, for we be com at his
commaundemente, as servytures sholde.' 15
    Than spake the Conquerrour, 'Thou recrayed and coward knyghte,
why feryst thou my countenaunce? There be in this halle, and they were
sore aggreved, thou durste nat for a deukedom of londis loke in their
facis.'
    'Sir,' seyde one of the senatoures, 'so Cryste me helpe, I was so 20
aferde whan I loked in thy face that myne herte wolde nat serve for to
sey my message. But sytthen hit is my wylle for to sey myne erande, the
gretis welle Lucius, the Emperour of Roome, and commaundis the
uppon payne that woll falle to sende hym the trewage of this realme that
thy fadir Uther Pendragon payde, other ellys he woll bereve the all thy 25
realmys that thou weldyst, ⌐and thou as rebelle, not knowynge hym
as thy soverayne, withholdest and reteynest, contrary to the statutes
and decrees maade by the noble and worthy Julius Cezar, conquerour
of this realme⌐.'
    'Thow seyste well,' seyde Arthure, 'but for all thy brym wordys I 30
woll nat be to over-hasty, and therfore thou and thy felowys shall
abyde here seven dayes; and shall calle unto me my counceyle of my
moste trusty knyghtes and deukes and regeaunte kynges and erlys
and barowns and of my moste wyse doctours, and whan we have
takyn oure avysement ye shall have your answere playnly, suche as I 35
shall abyde by.'
    ⌐Than somme of the yonge knyghtes, heryng this their message,
wold have ronne on them to have slayne them, sayenge that it was a
rebuke to alle the knyghtes there beyng present to suffre them to saye
so to the kynge. And anone the kynge commaunded that none of them 40
upon payne of dethe to myssaye them ne doo them ony harme.⌐
    Than the noble kynge commaunded sir Clegis to loke that thes men

be seteled and served with the beste, that there be no deyntés spared uppon them, that nother chylde nor horse faught nothynge, 'for they ar full royall peple. And thoughe they have greved me and my courte, yet we muste remembir on oure worshyp.' So they were led into
5 chambyrs and served as rychely of deyntés that myght be gotyn. So the Romaynes had therof grete mervayle.

Than the kynge unto counsayle called his noble ⌐lordes and⌐ knyghtes, and within a towre there they assembled, the moste party of the knyghtes of the Rounde Table. Than the kynge commaunded
10 hem of theire beste counceyle.

'Sir,' seyde sir Cador of Cornuayle, 'as for me, I am nat hevy of this message, for we have be many dayes rested now. The lettyrs of Lucius the Emperoure lykis me well, for now shall we have warre and worshyp.'

'Be Cryste, I leve welle,' seyde the kyng, 'sir Cador, this message
15 lykis the. But yet they may nat be so answerde, for their spyteuous speche grevyth so my herte. That truage to Roome woll I never pay. Therefore counceyle me, my knyghtes, for Crystes love of Hevyn. For this muche have I founde in the cronycles of this londe, that ˋsir Belyne and sir Bryne, of my bloode elders´ that borne were in Bretayne, and
20 they hath ocupyed the empyreship eyght score wyntyrs; and aftir ˋConstantyne, oure kynnesman, conquerd hit,´ and ˋdame Elyneys son, of Ingelonde, was Emperour of Roome;´ and he ˋrecoverde the Crosse that Cryste dyed uppon.´ And thus was the Empyre kepte be my kynde elders, and thus have we evydence inowghe to the empyre of holé Rome.'

(2) 25 Than answerde kynge Angwysshaunce unto Arthure: 'Sir, thou oughte to be aboven all othir Crysten kynges for of knyghthode and of noble counceyle that is allway in the. And Scotlonde had never scathe syne ye were crowned kynge, and ˋwhan the Romaynes raynede uppon us they raunsomed oure elders´ and raffte us of oure lyves. ˋTherefore
30 I make myne avow unto mylde Mary´ and unto Jesu Cryste that I shall be avenged uppon the Romayns, and to farther thy fyght I shall brynge the ferce men of armys, fully twenty thousand of tyred men. I shall yeff hem my wages for to go and warre on the Romaynes and to dystroy hem, and all shall be within two ayges to go where the lykes.'
35 Than the kyng of Lytyll Brytayne sayde unto kynge Arthure, 'Sir answere thes alyauntes and gyff them their answere, and I shall somen my peple, and thirty thousand men shall ye have at my costis and wages.'

'Ye sey well,' seyde the kynge Arthure.

Than spake a myghty deuke that was lorde of Weste Walys: 'Sir, I
40 make myne avowe to God to be revenged on the Romaynes, and to have the vawarde, and there to ˋvynquyshe with vyctory the vyscounte of Roome.´ For onys ˋas I paste on pylgrymage all by the Poynte Tremble,´ than the vyscounte was in Tu⟨s⟩kayne, and toke up my knyghtys and raunsomed them unresonablé. And than ˋI complayned

me to the Potestate the Pope hymself,ʹ but I had nothynge ellys but plesaunte wordys; other reson at Roome myght I none have, and so I yode my way sore rebuked. And therefore to be avenged I woll arere of my wyghteste Walshemen, and of myne owne fre wagis brynge you thirty thousand.'   5

'Than sir Ewayne and his son Ider that were nere cosyns unto the Conquerrour, yet were they cosyns bothe twayne, and ʻthey helde Irelonde and Argayle and all the Oute Iles:ʹ 'Sir,' seyde they unto kynge Arthure, 'here we make oure avowes untoo Cryste manly to ryde into Lumbardy and so unto Melayne wallys, and so over the 10
Poynte Tremble ʻinto the vale of Vyterbe, and there to vytayle my knyghtes;ʹ and for to be avenged on the Romayns we shall bryng the thirty thousand of good mennys bodyes.'

Than leepe in yong ʻsir Launcelot de Laake with a lyght herteʹ and seyde unto kynge Arthure, 'Thoughe my londis marche nyghe thyne 15
enemyes, yet shall I make myne avow aftir my power that of good men of armys aftir my bloode thus many I shall brynge with me: twenty thousand helmys in haubirkes attyred that shall never fayle you whyles oure lyves lastyth.'

Than lowghe sir Bawdwyn of Bretayne and carpys to the kynge: 'I 20
make myne avow unto the vernacle noble for to brynge with me ten thousand good mennys bodyes that shall never fayle whyle there lyvis lastyth.'

'Now I thanke you,' seyde the kynge, 'with all my trew herte. I suppose by the ende be done and dalte the Romaynes had bene bettir 25
to have leffte their proude message.'

So whan the sevennyghte was atte an ende the Senatours besought the kynge to have an answere.

'Hit is well,' seyde the kynge. 'Now sey ye to youre Emperour that I shall in all haste me redy make with my keene knyghtes, and ʻby the 30
rever of Rome holde my Rounde Table.ʹ And I woll brynge with me the beste peple of fyftene realmys, and with hem ryde on the moun-taynes in the maynelondis, ʻand myne doune the wallys of Myllayne the proude,ʹ ʻand syth ryde unto Roome with my royallyst knyghtes.ʹ Now ye have youre answere, hygh you that ye were hense, and ʻfrome 35
this place to the porte there ye shall passe over;ʹ and I shall gyff you seven dayes to passe unto Sandwyche.

ʻ'Now spede you, I counceyle you, and spare nat youre horsis,ʹ ʻand loke ye go by Watlynge strete and no way ellys,ʹ and where nyght fallys on you, loke ye there abyde, be hit felle other towne, I take no 40
kepe; for hit longyth nat to none alyauntis for to ryde on nyghtes. And may ony be founde a spere-lengthe oute of the way and that ye be in the watir by the sevennyghtes ende, there shall no golde undir God pay for youre raunsom.'

'Sir,' seyde this senatoures, 'this is an harde conduyte. We beseche you that we may passe saufly.'

'"Care ye nat,' seyde the kynge, 'youre conduyte is able."'

Thus they passed fro Carleyle unto Sandwyche-warde that hadde
5 but seven dayes for to passe thorow the londe, and so sir Cador brought
hem on her wayes. But the senatours spared for no horse, but hyred
hem hakeneyes frome towne to towne, and `by the sonne was sette at
the seven dayes ende´ they com unto Sandwyche; so blythe were they
never. And so the same nyght they toke the watir and passed into
10 Flaundres, ⌐Almayn¬, and aftir that over the grete mountayne that
hyght Godarde, and so aftir thorow Lumbardy and thorow Tuskayne,
and sone aftir they come to the Emperour Lucius, and there they
shewed hym the lettyrs of kynge Arthure, and how he was the gast-
fullyst man that ever they on loked. Whan the Emperour Lucius hadde
15 redde the lettyrs and undirstoode them welle of theire credence, he
fared as a man were rased of his wytte:

'I wente that Arthure wold have obeyed you and served you ⌐hym-
self¬ unto your honde, for so he besemed, other ony kynge crystynde,
for to obey ony senatour that is sente fro my persone.'

20 '"Sir,' sayde the senatours, 'lette be suche wordis,´ for that we have
ascaped on lyve we may thonke God ever; for we wolde nat passe
ayen to do that message for all your brode londis. And therfore, sirres,
truste to our sawys, ye shall fynde hym your uttir enemye; and seke
ye hym and ye lyste, for into this londis woll he com, and that shall ye
25 fynde within this half-yere, for he thynkys to be Emperour hymself.
For he seyth ye have ocupyed the Empyre with grete wronge, for all his
trew auncettryes sauff his fadir Uther were Emperoures of Rome.

'And of all the soveraynes that we sawe ever he is the royallyst kynge
that lyvyth on erthe, for we sawe on Newerys day at his Rounde
30 Table nine kyngis, and the fayryst felyship of knyghtes ar with hym
that durys on lyve, and thereto of wysedome and of fayre speche and
all royalté and rychesse they fayle of none. Therefore, sir, be my
counsayle, rere up your lyege peple and sende kynges and dewkes to
loke unto your marchis, and that `the mountaynes of Almayne be
35 myghtyly kepte.'´

'Be Estir,' seyde the Emperour, 'I caste me for to passe Almayne
and so furth into Fraunce and there bereve hym his londis. I shall
brynge with me many gyauntys of Geene, that one of them shall be
worth an hondred of knyghtes, and perleous passage shall be surely
40 kepte with my good knyghtes.'

Than the Emperour sente furth his messyngers of wyse olde knyghtes
unto a contrey callyd `Ambage, and Arrage, and unto Alysundir,´
to Ynde, to Ermony that the rever of Eufrate rennys by, `and to
Assy, Aufryke, and Europe the large,´ `and to Ertayne, and Elamye,

to the Oute Yles,ʼ to Arrabé, to Egypte, to Damaske, and to Damyake,
and to noble deukis and erlys. Also the kynge of Capydos, and the
kyng of Tars, and of Turké, ʽand of Pounce, and of Pampoyle, and
oute of Preter Johanes londe,ʼ also the sowdon of Surre. And frome
Nero unto Nazareth, and frome Garese to Galely, there come Sarysyns   5
and becom sudgettis unto Rome. So they come glydyng in galyes. Also
ther come the kynge of Cypres, and ʽthe Grekis were gadirde and
goodly arayedʼ with the kynge of Macidony, and ʽof Calabe ᵢand of
Catelonde bothe kynges and deukes,ʼ and the kynge of Portyngale
with many thousande Spaynardis.   10

Thus all thes kynges and dukys and admyrallys noblys assembled
with syxtene kynges at onys, and so they com unto Rome with grete
multytude of peple. Whan the Emperour undirstood their comynge
he made redy all his noble Romaynes and all men of warre betwyxte
hym and Flaundyrs. Also he had gotyn with hym ʽfyffty gyauntys that 15
were engendirde with fendis,ʼ and all tho he lete ordeyne for to awayte
on his persone and for to breke the batayle of the frunte of Arthurs
knyghtes, but they were so muche of their bodyes that horsys myght
nat bere them. And thus the Emperour with all hys horryble peple
drew to passe Almayne to dystroy Arthures londys that he wan thorow 20
warre of his noble knyghtes.

And so Lucius ʽcom unto Cullayne, and thereby a castelle besegys,ʼ
and wanne hit within a whyle, and feffed hit with Saresyns. And thus
Lucius within a whyle destryed many fayre contrayes that Arthure had
wonne before of the myghty kynge Claudas. So this Lucius dispercled 25
abrode his oste syxty myle large, and commaunde hem to mete with
hym in Normandy, in the contray of Constantyne, ʽand at Barflete
there ye me abyde, for the douchery of Bretayne I shall thorowly
dystroy hit.ʼ

Now leve we sir Lucius and speke we of kyng Arthure that com-   30 (3)
maunded all that were undir his obeysaunce, aftir the utas of Scynte
Hyllary that all shulde be assembled for to holde a parlement at Yorke,
within the wallys. And there they concluded shortly to areste all the
shyppes of this londe, and within fyftene dayes to be redy at Sand-
wych.   35

ʽNow, sirrys,ʼ seyde Arthure,ʽI purpose me to passe many perelles
wayesʼ and to ocupye the Empyre that myne elders afore have claymed.
Therefore I pray you, counseyle me that may be beste and most
worshyp.ʼ

The kynges and knyghtes gadirde hem unto counsayle and were   40
condecended for to make two chyfftaynes, that was sir Baudwen of
Bretayne, an auncient and an honorable knyght, for to counceyle and
comforte; sir Cadore son of Cornuayle, that was at the tyme called sir
Constantyne, that aftir was kynge aftir Arthurs dayes. And there in

the presence of all the lordis the kynge res[yn]ed all the rule unto thes two lordis and quene Gwenyvere.

And sir Trystrams at that tyme beleft with kynge Marke of Cornuayle for the love of La Beale Isode, wherefore sir Launcelot was passyng
5 wrothe.

Than quene Gwenyver made grete sorow that the kynge and all the lordys sholde so be departed, and there she fell doune on a swone, and hir ladyes bare hir to her chambir. Than the kynge commaunded hem to God and belefte the quene in sir Constantynes and sir Baude-
10 wens hondis, and all Inglonde holy to rule as themselfe demed beste. And whan the kynge was an horsebak he seyde in herynge of all the lordis,

'If that I dye in this jurney, here I make the, sir Constantyne, my trew ayre, for thou arte nexte of my kyn save sir Cadore, thy fadir, and
15 therefore, if that I dey, I woll that ye be crowned kynge.'

Ryght so he sought and his knyghtes towarde Sandewyche where he founde before hym many galyard knyghtes, for there were the moste party of all the Rounde Table redy on tho bankes for to sayle whan the kynge lyked. Than in all haste that myght be they shypped their horsis
20 and harneyse and all maner of ordynaunce that fallyth for the werre, and tentys and pavylyons many were trussed, and so they shotte frome the bankes many grete caryckes and many shyppes of forestage with coggis and galeyes and spynnesse full noble with galeyes and galyottys, rowyng with many ores. And thus ʽthey strekyn forth into the stremys
25 many sadde hunderthes.ʼ

HERE FOLOWYTH THE DREME OF KYNGE ARTHURE.

(4) As the kynge was in his cog and lay in his caban, he felle in a slum-beryng and ʽdremed how a dredfull dragon dud drenche muche of his peple' and com fleyng one wynge oute of the weste partyes. And his
30 hede, hym semed, was enamyled with asure, and his shuldyrs shone as the golde, and his wombe was lyke mayles of a merveylous hew, and his tayle was fulle of tatyrs, and ʽhis feete were florysshed as hit were fyne sable.' And his clawys were lyke clene golde, ⌈and⌉ ʽan hydeouse flame of fyre there flowe oute of his mowth,' lyke as the londe and the
35 watir had flawmed all on fyre.

Than hym semed there com oute of the Oryent a grymly beare, all blak, in a clowde, and his pawys were as byg as a poste. He was all to-rongeled with lugerande lokys, and he was the fowlyst beste that ever ony man sye. He romed and rored so rudely that merveyle hit were to
40 telle.

ʽThan the dredfull dragon dressyd hym ayenste hym' and come in the wynde lyke a faucon, and freyshely strykis the beare. And agayne the gresly beare kuttis with his grysly tuskes, that his breste and his

bray⟨l⟩e was bloodé, and ⌐the reed blood¬ rayled all over the see. Than
the worme wyndis away and fleis uppon hyght and com downe with
such a sowghe, and towched the beare on the rydge that ˋfro the toppe
to the tayle was ten foote large.´ And so he rentyth the beare and brennys
hym up clene that all felle on pouder, both the fleysh and the bonys, 5
and so hit flotered abrode on the see.

  Anone the kynge waked ⌐and was sore abasshed¬ of his dreme, and
in all haste he sente for a philozopher and charged hym to telle what
sygnyfyed his dreme.

  'Sir,' seyde the phylozopher, 'the dragon thou dremyste of betokyns 10
thyne owne persone that thus here sayles with thy syker knyghtes;
and the coloure of his wyngys is thy kyngdomes that thou haste with
thy knyghtes wonne. And his tayle that was all to-tatered sygnyfyed
your noble knyghtes of the Rounde Table. And the beare that the
dragon slowe above in the clowdis ˋbetokyns som tyraunte that tur- 15
mentis thy peple,´ other thou art lyke to fyght with som gyaunt boldely
in batayle be thyself alone. Thereforc ˋof this dredfull dreme drede the
but a lytyll,´ and ˋcare nat now, sir conquerroure, but comfort⌐h¬
thyself.´´

  Than within a whyle they had a syght of the bankys of Normandy, 20
and at the same tyde the kynge aryved at Barfflete and founde there
redy many of his grete lordis, as he had commaunded at Crystemasse
before hymselfe.

  And than come there an husbandeman oute of the contrey and talkyth (5)
unto the kyng wondourfull wordys and sayde, 'Sir, here is ⌐besyde¬ a 25
⌐grete¬ gyaunte of Gene that turmentyth thy peple; mo than fyve
hundred and many mo of oure chyldren, ˋthat hath bene his sustynaunce all this seven wynters.´ Yet is the sotte never cesid, but in the
contrey of Constantyne he hath kylled ⌐and destroyed¬ all oure knave
chyldren, and this nyght he hath cleyghte the duches of Bretayne ˋas 30
she rode by a ryver with her ryche knyghtes,´ and ledde hir unto
yondir mounte to ly by hir whyle hir lyff lastyth.

  ˋ´Many folkys folowed hym, mo than fyve hundird´ barounes and
bachelers and knyghtes full noble, but ever she sh[r]yked wondirly
lowde, that the sorow of that lady cover shall we never. She was thy 35
cousyns wyff, sir Howell the Hende, a man that we calle nyghe of thy
bloode. Now, ˋas thou arte oure ryghtwos kynge, rewe on this lady´
and on thy lyege peple, and revenge us as a noble conquerroure sholde.'

  'Alas,' seyde kynge Arthure, 'this is a grete myscheffe! I had levir
than all the realmys I welde unto my crowne that ˋI had bene before 40
that freyke a furlonge way´ for to have rescowed that lady, and I wolde
have done my payne. Now, felow,' seyde Arthure, 'woldist thou ken
me where that carle dwellys? I trowe I shall trete with hym or I far
passe.'

'Sir Conquerrour,' seyde the good man, 'beholde yondir two fyrys, for there shalte thou fynde that carle beyonde the colde strendys, and tresoure oute of numbir there mayste thou sykerly fynde, more tresoure, as I suppose, than is in all Fraunce aftir.'

5 The kynge seyde, 'Good man, pees! and carpe to me no more. `Thy soth sawys have greved sore my herte.´ Than he turnys towarde his tentys and carpys but lytyll.

Than the kynge ⌈called to hym⌉ sir Kay in counceyle, and to sir Bedwere the bolde thus seyde he: 'Loke that ye two aftir evynsonge
10 be surely armed, and your beste horsis, for I woll ryde on pylgrymage prevayly, and none but we three. And whan my lordis is servyd we woll ryde `to Seynte Mychaels Mounte where mervayles ar shewed.´

Anone sir Arthure wente to his wardrop and caste on his armoure, bothe his gesseraunte and his basnet with his brode shylde. And so he
15 buskys hym tyll his stede that on the bente hoved. Than he stertes uppon loffte and hentys the brydyll, and stirres hym stoutly, and sone he fyndis his knyghtes two full clenly arayed. And than they trotted on stylly togedir over a blythe contray full of many myrry byrdis, and whan they com to the forlonde Arthure and they alyght on hir foote.
20 ⌈And the kynge commaunded them to tarye there.⌉

'Now fastenys,' seyde Arthure, 'oure horsis that none nyghe other, `for I woll seche this seynte be myself alone´ and speke wyth this maystir-man that kepys this mountayne.'

Than the kynge yode up to the creste of the cragge, and than he com-
25 forted hymself with the colde wynde; and than he yode forth by two welle-stremys, and there `he fyndys two fyres flamand full hyghe.´ And at that one fyre he founde a carefull wydow wryngande hir handys, syttande on a grave that was new marked. Than Arthure salued hir and she hym agayne, and asked hir why she sate sorowyng.

30 'Alas,' she seyde, ``carefull knyght! Thou carpys over lowde!´ Yon is a werlow woll destroy us bothe. I holde the unhappy. What doste thou on this mountayne? Thoughe here were suche fyffty, ye were to feyble for to macche hym all at onys. Whereto berys thou armoure? Hit may the lytyll avayle, for he nedys none other wepyn but his bare
35 fyste. Here is a douches dede, the fayryst that lyved; `he hath murthered that mylde withoute ony mercy;´ he forced hir by fylth of hymself, and so aftir slytte hir unto the navyll.'

'Dame,' seyde the kynge, 'I com fro the ⌈noble⌉ Conquerrour, sir Arthure, for to trete with that tirraunte for his lyege peple.'

40 'Fy on suche tretyse,' she seyde than, 'for he settys nought by the kynge nother by no man ellys. But and thou have brought Arthurs wyff, dame Gwenyvere, he woll be more blyther of hir than thou haddyste geffyn hym halfendele Fraunce. And but yf thou have brought hir, prese hym nat to nyghe. Loke what he hath done unto fyftene

kynges: he hath made hym a coote full of precious stonys, and the
bordoures thereof is the berdis ⟨of⟩ fyftene kynges, and they were of
the grettyst blood that dured on erthe. Othir farme had he none of
fyftene realmys. This presente was sente hym to this laste Crystemasse,
they sente hym in faythe for savyng of their peple. And for Arthurs 5
wyffe he lodgys hym here, for he hath more tresoure ˋthan ever had
Arthure or ony of his elders.´ And now thou shalt fynde hym at souper
with syx knave chyldirne, and there he hath made ˋpykyll and powder
with many precious wynes,´ and three fayre maydens that turnys the
broche that bydis to go to his bed, for they three shall be dede within 10
four oures ˋor the fylth is fulfylled that his fleyshe askys.´´

    'Well,' seyde Arthure, 'I woll fulfylle my message for alle your grym
wordis.'

    ˋ´Than fare thou to yondir fyre that flamys so hyghe,´ and there
thou shalt fynde hym sykerly for sothe.'   15

    Than he paste forth to the creste of the hylle ˋand syghe where he
sate at his soupere alone´ gnawyng on a lymme of a large man, and there
ˋhe beekys his brode lendys by the bryght fyre´ and brekelys hym
s⟨e⟩mys. And three damesels turned three brochis, and thereon was
twelve chyldir but late borne, and they were broched in maner lyke 20
birdis. Whan the kyng behylde that syght his herte was nyghe
bledyng for sorow. Than he haylesed hym with angirfull wordys:

    'Now He that all weldys geff the sorow, theeff, there thou syttes!
ˋFor thou art the fowlyste freyke that ever was fourmed,´ and fendly
thou fedyst the, the devill have thy soule! And ˋby what cause, thou 25
carle, hast thou kylled thes Crysten chyldern?´ ˋThou haste made
many martyrs by mourtheryng of this londis.´ Therefore thou shalt
have thy mede thorow Mychael that owyth this mounte. And also,
why haste thou slayne this fayre douches? Therefore dresse the,
doggys son, ˋfor thou shalt dye this day thorow the dynte of my 30
hondis.´

    ˋThan the gloton gloored and grevid full foule.´ He had teeth lyke
a grayhounde, he was the foulyst wyghte that ever man sye, and there
was never suche one fourmed on erthe, for there was never devil in
helle more horryblyer made: for he was ˋfro the hede to the foote fyve 35
fadom longe´ and large. And therewith sturdely he sterte uppon his
leggis and ˋcaughte a clubbe in his honde all of clene iron.´ ˋThan he
swappis at the kynge with that kyd wepyn.´ ˋHe cruysshed downe with
the club the coronal doune´ to the colde erthe. The kynge coverede
hym with his shylde and rechis a boxe evyn infourmede in the myddis 40
of his forehede, that the slypped blade unto the brayne rechis. Yet he
shappis at sir Arthure, but the kynge shuntys a lytyll and rechis hym a
dynte hyghe uppon the haunche, and there he swappis his genytrottys
in sondir.

Than he rored and brayed and yet angurly he strykes, and fayled of
sir Arthure and the erthe hittis, that he kutte into the swarffe a large
swerde-length and more. Than the kynge sterte up unto hym and
raught hym a buffette and kut his baly in sundir, that oute wente the
5 gore, that `the grasse and the grounde all foule was begone.´

`Than he kaste away the clubbe and caughte the kynge´ in his armys
and handeled the kynge so harde that he crusshed his rybbes. Than
the balefull maydyns wronge hir hondis and kneled on the grounde
and to Cryste called ʳfor helpe and comforte of Arthurˈ. With that
10 the warlow wrath Arthure undir, and so they waltyrde and tumbylde
over the craggis and busshys, and eythir cleyght other full faste in
their armys. And other whyles Arthure was aboven and other whyle
undir, and so ʳweltryng and walowynge they rolled doune the hylle,
andˈ they never leffte tyll they fylle thereas the floode marked. But
15 ever in the walterynge Arthure ʳsmyttes andˈ hittis hym with a shorte
dagger up to the hyltys, and in his fallynge there braste of the gyauntes
rybbys three evyn at onys.

And by fortune they felle thereas the two knyghtes aboode with
theire horsis. Whan sir Kay saw the kynge and the gyaunte so icelyght
20 togyder,

'Alas,' sayd sir Kay, 'we ar forfete for ever! Yondir is our lorde
overfallen with a fende.'

'Hit is nat so,' seyde the kynge, 'but helpe me, sir Kay, for this
corseynte have I clegged oute of the yondir clowys.'

25 'In fayth,' seyde sir Bedwere, 'this is a foule carle,' `and caughte the
corseynte oute of the kynges armys´ and there he seyde, 'I have mykyll
wondir, and Mychael be of suche a makyng, that ever God wolde
suffir hym to abyde in hevyn. `And if seyntis be suche that servys
Jesu,´ I woll never seke for none, be the fayth of my body!'

30 The kynge than lough at Bedwers wordis and seyde,

'This seynte have I sought nyghe unto my grete daungere. But
stryke of his hede and sette hit on a trouncheoune of a speare, and geff
hit to thy servaunte that is swyffte-horsed, and bere hit unto sir Howell
that is in harde bondis, and bydde hym be mery, for his enemy is
35 destroyed. And aftir in Barflete lette brace hit on a barbycan, that all
the comyns of this contrey may hit beholde.

'And than ye two go up ʳto the montaynˈ and fecche me my shelde,
my swerde, and the boystouse clubbe of iron, and yf ye lyste ony
tresoure, take what ye lyst, for there may ye fynde tresoure oute of
40 numbir. So I have the curtyll ʳand the clubbeˈ, I kepe no more. For
this was a freysh gyaunte and mykyll of strength, for I mette nat with
suche one this fyftene wyntir sauff onys in the mounte of Arrabé I
mette with suche another, but this was fersar; that had I nere founden,
had nat my fortune be good.'

Than the knyghtes fecched the clubbe and the coote and all the remenaunte, and toke with hem what tresoure that hem lyked. Than the
kynge and they sterte uppon their horsys, and so they rode fro thens
thereas they come fro.

And anone the clamoure was howge aboute all the contrey, and than 5
they wente with one voyse tofore the kynge and thanked God and
hym that their enemy was destroyed.

'All thanke ye God,' seyde Arthure, 'and no man ellys. Looke that
the gooddys be skyffted, that none playne of his parte.'

Than he commaunded his cosyn, sir Howell, to make a kyrke on 10
that same cragge in the worshyppe of Seynte Mychael.

On the morne frome Barflete remevyth the kynge with all his grete
batayle proudly arayed, and so they shooke over the stremys into a
fayre champayne, and thereby doune in a valey they pyght up hir
tentys. And evyn at the metewhyle come two messyngers, that one was 15
the marchall of Fraunce, that seyde to the kynge how the Emperour was
⌐entryd¹ into Fraunce, 'and hath destroyed much of oure marchis, and
is com into Burgayne, and many borowys hath destroyed, and hath
made grete slaughtir of your noble people. And where that he rydyth
all he destroyes. And now he is comyn into Dowse Fraunce, and there 20
he brennys all clene. Now all the ⟨dowseperys⟩, bothe deukys and
other, and the peerys of Parys towne, ar fledde downe into the Lowe
Contrey towarde Roone, and but yf thou helpe them the sunner they
muste yelde hem all at onys, bothe the bodyes and townys. They can
none othir succour, but nedys they muste yelde them in haste.' 25

Than `the kynge byddis sir Borce: 'Now bowske the blythe´ and (6)
sir Lyonel and sir Bedwere, loke that ye fare with sir Gawayne, my
nevew, with you, and take as many good knyghtes, and loke that ye
ryde streyte unto sir Lucius and sey I bydde hym in haste to remeve
oute of my londys. And yf he woll nat, so bydde hym dresse his batayle 30
and lette us redresse oure ryghtes with oure handis, and that is more
worshyppe than thus to overryde maysterlesse men.'

Than anone in all haste they dressed hem to horsebak, thes noble
knyghtes, and whan they com to the grene wood they sawe before
hem many prowde pavylyons of sylke of dyverse coloures that were 35
sette in a medow besyde a ryver, and the Emperoures pavylyon was in
the myddys with an egle displayed on loffte. Than thorow the wood
oure knyghtes roode tylle that they com unto the Emperoures tente.
But behynde them they leffte stuff of men of armys in a boyshemente;
and there he leffte in the boyshemente sir Lyonel and sir Bedwere. Sir 40
Gawayne and sir Borce wente with the message.

So they rode worthyly into the Emperoures tente and spoke bothe
at onys with hawté wordys: "Now geff the sorow, sir Emperour, and
all the sowdyars the aboute.´ For why ocupyest thou with wronge the

empyreship of'Roome? That is kynge Arthures herytage be kynde of his noble elders: there lakked none but Uther, his fadir. Therefore the kyng commaundyth the to ryde oute of his londys, other ellys to fyght for all and knyghtly hit wynne.'

5 'Ye sey well,' seyde the Emperour, 'as youre lorde hath you commaunded. But ⌈saye to⌉ your lorde I sende hym gretynge, but I have no joy of youre renckys thus to rebuke me and my lordys. But sey youre lorde I woll ryde downe by Sayne and wynne all that thereto longes, and aftir ryde unto Roone and wynne hit up clene.'

10 'Hit besemys the ylle,' seyde sir Gawayne, 'that ony such an elffe sholde bragge suche wordys, for I had levir than all Fraunce to fyght ayenste the.'

'Other I,' seyde sir Borce, 'than to welde all Bretayne other Burgayne the noble.'

15 'Than a knyght that hyght sir Gayus that was cosyn unto the Emperour, he seyde thes wordys: ⌈'Loo! how⌉ thes Englyshe Bretouns be braggars of kynde, for ye may see how ˋthey boste and bragge as they durste bete all the worlde.'ˊ

ˋThan grevid sir Gawayne at his grete wordys,ˊ and ˋwith his bowerly 20 bronde that bryght semedˊ he stroke of the hede of sir Gayus the knyght.

And so they turned their horsis and rode over watyrs and woodys into they com ny the busshemente there sir Lyonell and sir Bedwere were hovyng stylle. Than the Romaynes folowed faste on horsebak 25 and ˋon foote over a fayre champeyne unto a fayre wood.ˊ

Than turnys hym sir Borce wyth a freyshe wylle and sawe a gay knyght ⌈come fast on⌉, all floryshed in golde, that bare downe of Arthures knyghtes wondirfull many. Than sir Borce aspyed hym, he kaste in feautir a spere and gyrdis hym thorowoute the body, that his 30 guttys fylle oute and the knyght ⌈fylle doune⌉ to the grounde that gresly gronyd.

Than preced in a bolde barowne all in purpull arayed. He threste into the prece of kyng Arthures knyghtes and fruysshed downe many good knyghtes, and he was called Calleborne, the strengyste of Pavynes 35 Londis. And sir Borce turned hym to and ˋbare hym thorow the brode shylde and the brode of his breste,ˊ that he felle to the erthe as dede as a stone.

Than sir Feldenake the myghty that was a praysed man of armys, ˋhe gurde to sir Gawayne for greff of sir Gayusˊ and his other felowys, 40 and sir Gawayne was ware and drew Galantyne, his swerde, and hyt hym such a buffette that he cleved hym to the breste, and than he caughte his courser and wente to his ferys.

Than a rych man of Rome, one of the senatours, called to his felowys and bade hem returne, 'for yondir ar shrewed messengers and bolde

boosters. If we folow them ony farther the harme shall be owrys.'
And so the Romaynes returned lyghtly to theire tentys and tolde the
Emperour how they had spedde, and how the marchall of Rome was
slayne, and mo than fyve thousand in the felde dede.

But yet ore they wente and departe, 'oure bushemente brake on 5
bothe sydys' of the Romaynes, and there the bolde Bedwer and sir
Lyonel bare downe the Romaynes on every syde. There oure noble
knyghtes of mery Ingelonde bere hem thorow the helmys and bryght
sheldis and slew hem downe, and there the hole roughte returned unto
the Emperour and tolde hym at one worde his men were destroyed, 10
ten thousand, by batayle of tyred knyghtes, 'for they ar the brymmyst
men that evir we saw in felde.'

But allwayes sir Borce and sir Gawayne freyshly folowed on the
Romaynes evyn unto the Emperoures tentes. Than oute ran the Romaynes on every syde, bothe on horse and on foote, to many oute of 15
numbir. But sir Borce and sir Berel 'were formeste in the frunte and
freyshly faught' as ever dud ony knyghtes. But sir Gawayne was on
the ryght honde and dud what he myght, but there were so many
hym agaynste he myght nat helpe there his ferys, but was fayne to
turne on his horse othir his lyffe muste he lese. Sir Borce and sir Berell, 20
the good barounnes, fought as two boorys that myght no farther passe.
But at the laste, thoughe they loth were, they were yolden and takyn
and saved their lyves, yet the stale stoode a lytyll on fer with sir
Gawayne that made sorow oute of mesure for thes two lordys.

But than cam in a freysh knyght clenly arayed, sir Idres, sir Uwaynes 25
son, a noble man of armys. He brought fyve hondred good men in
haubirkes attyred, and whan he wyste sir Borce and sir Berel were
cesed of werre, 'Alas,' he sayde, 'this is to muche shame and overmuche losse! For with kynge Arthure, and he know that thes two
knyghtes bene thus loste, he woll never mery be tyll this be 30
revenged.'

'A, fayre knyght,' sayde sir Gawayne, 'thou moste nedis be a good
man, for so is thy fadir. I knowe full well thy modir. In Ingelonde was
thou borne. Alas, thes Romaynes this day have chaced us as wylde
harys, and they have oure noble chyfften takyn in the felde. There was 35
never a bettir knyght that strode uppon a steede. Loo 'where they lede
oure lordys over yondir brode launde.' I make myne avowe,' seyde
sir Gawayne, 'I shall never se my lorde Arthure but yf I reskew hem
that so lyghtly ar ledde us fro.'

'That is knyghtly spokyn,' seyde sir Idres, and pulde up her brydyls 40
and halowed over that champayne. There was russhynge of sperys
and swappyng of swerdis, and sir Gawayne with Galantyne, his swerde,
dud many wondyrs. Than he threste thorow the prece unto hym that
lad sir Bors, and bare hym thorow up to the hyltys, and lade away sir

Bors strayte unto his ferys. Than sir Idrus the yonge, sir Uwaynes son, he threste unto a knyght that had sir Berell, that the brayne and the blode clevid on his swerde.

There was a proude senatoure preced aftir sir Gawayne, and gaff 5 hym a grete buffet. That sawe sir Idres and aftir rydyth, and had slayne the senatour but that he yelded hym in haste. Yet he was loth to be yoldyn but that he nedys muste, and with that sir Idrus ledde hym oute of the prees unto sir Lyonel and unto sir Lovel, Idrus brothir, and commaunded hem to kepe hym on payne of theire hedis.

10 Than there began a passyng harde stoure, for the Romaynes ever wexed ever bygger. Whan sir Gawayne that aspyed he sente forth a knyght unto kyng Arthure. 'And telle hym what sorow we endure, and how we have takyn the chefe chaunceler of Rome. And Petur is presoner, a senatoure full noble, and odir proude pryncis, we knowe 15 nat theire namys. And pray hym, as he is oure lorde, to rescowe us betyme, for oure presoners may pay rychesse oute of numbir; and telle hym that I am wounded wondirly sore.'

Whan the messyngers com to the kyng and tolde hym thes wordys 'the kynge thanked Cryste clappyng his hondys.' 'And for thy trew 20 sawys, and I may lyve many wyntyrs, there was never no knyght better rewardid. But there is no golde undir God that shall save their lyvys, I make myne avow to God, and sir Gawayne be in ony perell of deth; for I had levir that the Emperour and all his chyff lordis were sunkyn into helle than ony lorde of the Rounde Table were byttyrly wounded.' 25 So forth the presoners were brought before Arthure, and he commaunded hem into kepyng of the conestablys warde, surely to be kepte as noble presoners. So within a whyle com in the foreryders, that is for to say sir Bors, sir Bedwere, sir Lyonell, and sir Gawayne that was sore wounded, with all hir noble felyshyp. They loste no man of worshyppe. 30 So anone the kyng lete rensake sir Gawayne anone in his syght and sayde,

'Fayre cosyn, me ruys of thyne hurtys! And yf I wyste hit myght glad thy hert othir fare the bettir with hit, I sholde presente the with hir hedys thorow whom thou art thus rebuked.'

35 'That were lytyll avayle,' sayde sir Gawayne, 'for theire hedys had they lorne, and I had wolde myself, and hit were shame to sle knyghtes whan they be yolden.'

Than was there joy and game amonge the knyghtes of Rounde Table, and spoke of the grete prouesse 'that the messyngers ded that day 40 thorow dedys of armys.'

So on the morne whan hit was day the kyng callyd unto hym sir Cador of Cornuayle, 'and sir Clarrus of Clereounte, a clene man of armys,' and sir Cloudres, sir Clegis, two olde noble knyghtes, and sir Bors, sir Berell, noble good men of armys, and also sir Bryan de les

Ylyes, and sir Bedwere the bolde, and also he called sir Launcelot in
heryng of all peple, and seyde,

'I pray the, sir, as thow lovys me, take hede to thes other knyghtes
and boldely lede thes presoners unto Paryse towne there for to be kepte
surely as they me love woll have, and yf ony rescowe befalle, moste I 5
affye the in me, as Jesu me helpe.'

Than sir Launcelot and sir Cador with thes other knyghtes attyred
oute of their felyshyp ten thousand be tale of bolde men arayed of the
beste of their company, and than they unfolde baners and let hem be
displayed.   10

Now turne we to the Emperour of Rome that wyste by a spye whethir (7)
this presoners sholde wende. He callyd unto hym sir Edolf and sir
Edwarde, two myghty kynges, and 'sir Sextore of Lybye, and senatours many,' and the kyng of Surré, and the senatoure of Rome
Sawtre. All thes turned towarde Troyes with many proved knyghtes to 15
betrappe the kynges sondismen that were charged with the presoners.

Thus ar oure knyghtes passed towarde Paryse. A busshemente lay
before them of sixty thousand men of armys.

'Now, lordis,' seyde sir Launcelot, 'I pray you, herkyns me a whyle.
I drede that in this woodys be leyde afore us many of oure enemyes.   20
Therefore be myne advyse sende we three good knyghtes.'

'I assente me,' seyde sir Cador, and all they seyde the same, and were
aggreed that sir Claryon and sir Clement the noble that they sholde
dyscover the woodys, bothe the dalys and the downys. So forth rode
thes three knyghtes and aspyed in the woodis men of armys rydyng on 25
sterne horsys. Than sir Clegys cryed on lowde, 'Is there ony knyght,
kyng, other cayser, that dare for his lordis love that he servyth recountir with a knyght of the Rounde Table? 'Be he kyng other knyght,
here is his recounter redy.'

'An erle hym answeryd angirly agayne' and seyde, 'Thy lorde   30
wenys with his knyghtes to wynne all the worlde! I trow your currage shall be aswaged in shorte tyme.'

'Fye on the, 'cowarde!' seyde sir Clegis, 'as a cowarde thou spekyste,'
for, by Jesu, myne armys ar knowyn thorowoute all Inglonde and
Bretayne, and I am com of olde barounes of auncetry noble, and sir   35
Clegis is my name, a knyght of the Table Rounde. And frome Troy
Brute brought myne elders.'

'Thou besemeste well,' seyde the kyng, 'to be one of the good be
thy bryght browys, but for all that thou canst conjeoure other sey,
there shall none that is here medyll with the this tyme.'   40

Than sir Clegis returned fro the ryche kyng and rode streyghte to
sir Launcelot and unto sir Cadore and tolde hem what he had seyne in
the woodis of the fayryste syght of men of armys to the numbir of
sixty thousand.

'And therefore, lordynges, fyght you behovys, ˋother ellys shunte for shame, chose whether ye lykys.ˊ

'Nay, be my fayth,' sayde sir Launcelot, 'to turne is no tyme, for here is all olde knyghtes of grete worshyp that were never shamed. Andˌas for
5 me and my cousyns of my bloode, we ar but late made knyghtes, yett wolde we be loth to lese the worshyp that oure eldyrs have deservyd.'

'Ye sey well,' seyde sir Cador and all these knyghtes; 'of youre knyghtly wordis comfortis us all. And I suppose here is none woll be glad to returne, and as for me,' seyde sir Cador, 'I had lever dye thisˏ
10 day than onys to turne my bak.'

'Ye sey well,' seyde sir Borce, 'lette us set on hem freyshly, and the worshyp shall be oures, and cause oure kyng to honoure us for ever and to gyff us lordshyppis and landys for oure noble dedys. And he that faynes hym to fyght, the devyl have his bonys! And who save ony
15 knyghtes for lycoure of goodys tylle all be done and know who shall have the bettir, he doth nat knyghtly, so Jesu me helpe!'

Than anone sir Launcelot and sir Cador, tho two myghty dukis, dubbed knyghtys worshyp to wynne. Joneke was the fyrste, a juster full noble; sir Hectimer and sir Alyduke, bothe of Inglonde borne;
20 ˋand sir Hamerel and sir Hardolf, full hardy men of armys;ˊ also sir Harry and sir Harygall that good men were bothe.

'Now, felowys,' seyde sir Launcelot and sir Cador the kene, 'com hydir, sir Bedwere and sir Berel, take with you ˋsir Raynolde and sir Edwarde that ar sir Roulondis chyldir,ˊ and loke that ye take kepe
25 to thes noble presoners. What chaunce so us betyde, save them and yourself. This commaundement we geff you as ye woll answere to oure soverayne lorde, and for ony stowre that ever ye se us bestadde ˋstondys in your stale and sterte ye no ferther.ˊ And yf hit befalle that ye se oure charge is to muche, than recover yourself unto som kydde castell,
30 and than ryde you faste unto oure kynge and pray hym of soccour, as he is oure kynde lorde.'

And than they fruyshed forth all at onys, ˋof the bourelyest knyghtes that ever brake brede,ˊ ˋwith mo than fyve hondred at the formyst frunte,ˊ and caste their spears in feawter all at onys, and save trumpettes
35 there was no noyse ellys. Than the Romaynes oste remeved a lytyll, and the lorde that was kynge of Lybye, that lad all the formyste route, he keste his spere in feautyr and bare his course evyn to sir Berel, and strake hym thorow the gorge, that he and his horse felle to the grounde, and so he was brought oute of his lyff.

40 'Alas,' sayde sir Cadore, 'now carefull is myne herte that now lyeth dede my cosyn that I beste loved.'

He alyght off his horse and toke hym in hys armys and ˋthere commaunded knyghtes to kepe well the corse.ˊ Than the kynge craked grete wordys on lowde and seyde,

'One of yon prowde knyghtes is leyde full lowe.'

'"Yondir kyng,' seyde sir Cador, 'carpis grete wordis.' But and I may lyve or this dayes ende 'I shall countir with yondir kynge, so Cryste me helpe!'

'Sir,' seyde sir Launcelot, 'meve you nat to sore, but take your spear in your honde and we shall you not fayle.'

Than sir Cador, sir Launcelot, and sir Bors, the good men of armys, thes three feawtyrd their sperys and threste into the myddys and ran thorowoute the grete oste twyse other three tymes, and whan their sperys were brokyn 'they swange oute their swerdis and slowe of noble men' of armys mo than an hondred, and than they rode ayen to theire ferys. Than alowde the kynge of Lybye cryed unto sir Cador,

'Well have ye revenged the deth of your knyght, for I have loste for one knyght an hondred by seven score.'

And therewith the batayle began to joyne, and grete slaughter there was on the Sarysens party, but thorow the noble prouesse of kyng Arthurs knyghtes ten were takyn and lad forth as presoners. That greved sore sir Launcelot, sir Cador, and sir Bors the brym. The kynge of Lybye behelde their dedis and sterte on a sterne horse and umbely-closed oure knyghtes and drove downe to the grounde many a good man, for there was sir Aladuke slayne, and also sir Ascamour sore wounded, and 'sir Herawde and sir Heryngale hewyn to pecis,' and sir Lovell was takyn, and sir Lyonell also, and nere had sir Clegis, sir Cleremonde had nat bene, with the knyghthode of sir Launcelot: tho newe made knyghtes had be slayne everych one.

Than sir Cador rode unto the kyng of Lybye with a swerde well stelyd and smote hym an hyghe uppon the hede, that the brayne folowed. 'Now haste thow,' seyde sir Cador, 'corne-boote agayne-warde, and the devyll have thy bonys that ever thou were borne!' Than the sowdan of Surré was wood wrothe, for the deth of that kynge grevid up hym at his herte, and recomforted his peple and sette sore on oure knyghtes.

Than sir Launcelot and sir Bors encountyrs with hym sone, and within a whyle, as tellyth the romaynes, they had slayne of the Sarazens mo than fyve thousand. And sir Kay the kene had takyn a captayne, and Edwarde had takyn two erlys, and the sawdon of Surré yeldid hym up unto sir Launcelot, and the senatur of Sautre yeldid hym unto sir Cador.

Whan the Romaynes and the Sarezens aspyed how the game yode they fledde with all hir myght to hyde there hedis. Than oure knyghtes folowed with a freysshe fare and slew downe of the Sarezens ᵊon every syde⌐.

And sir Launcelot ded so grete dedys of armys that day that sir Cador and all the Romaynes had mervayle of his myght, for there was nother kynge, cayser, nother knyght that day myght stonde hym ony buffette. Therefore was he honoured dayes of his lyff, for never ere or that day was he proved so well, for he and sir Bors and sir Lyonel was but late afore at an hyghe feste made all three knyghtes.

5 And thus were the Romaynes and the Sarezens slayne adowne clene, save a fewe were recovirde thereby into a lytyll castell. And than the noble renckys of the Rounde Table, thereas the felde was, toke up hir good bodyes of the noble knyghtes and garte sende them unto kyng Arthure into the erthe to be caste. So they all rode unto Paryse
10 and beleffte the presoners there with the pure proveste, and than they were delyverde into sure sauffgarde. Than every knyght toke a spere and dranke of the colde wyne, and than fersely in a brayde returned unto the kynge.

Whan the kynge his knyghtes sawe he was than mervelously re-
15 joyced and cleyght knyght be knyght in his armys and sayde, 'All the worshyp in the worlde ye welde! Be my fayth, there was never kyng sauff myselff that welded evir such knyghtes.'

'Sir,' seyde sir Cador, 'there was none of us that fayled othir, but of the knyghthode of sir Launcelot hit were mervayle to telle. And of his
20 bolde cosyns ar proved full noble knyghtes, but of wyse wytte and of grete strengthe of his ayge sir Launcelot hath no felowe.'

Whan the kyng herde sir Cador sey such wordys he seyde, 'Hym besemys for to do such dedis.' And sir Cadore tolde Arthure whyche of the good knyghtis were slayne: 'the kynge of Lybye, and he slew
25 the fyrste knyght on oure syde, that was sir Berell; and sir Aladuke was another, a noble man of armys, and sir Maurel and sir Mores that were two brethyrn, with sir Manaduke and sir Mandyff, two good knyghtes.'

Than the kynge ⌐wepte and¬ with a keverchoff wyped his iyen and sayde, 'Youre corrage and youre hardynesse nerehande had you
30 destroyed, for and ye had turned agayne ye had loste no worshyp, for I calle hit but foly to abyde whan knyghtes bene overmacched.'

'Not so,' sayde sir Launcelot, 'the shame sholde ever have bene oures.'

'That is trouthe,' seyde sir Clegis and sir Bors, 'for knyghtes ons
35 shamed recoverys hit never.'

(8) Now leve sir Arthure and his noble knyghtes and speke we of a senatoure that ascaped fro the batayle. Whan he com to Lucius the Emperour of Rome he seyde,

'Sir, withdraw the! What doste thou here in this marchis and to
40 overren poore peple? Thou shalt wynne nothyng ellys, and if thou dele with kynge Arthure and his doughty knyghtes thou wynnys naught ellys but grete strokys oute of mesure. For this day one of Arthurs knyghtes was worth in batayle an hondred of oures.'

'Fye on the,' seyde Lucyus, 'for cowardly thou spekyste! Yf my

harmys me greve, thy wordys greveth me muche more.' Than he called
to hym his counceyle, men of noble bloode. So by all theire advyse he
sent forth a knyght that hyght sir Leomye. He dressed his peple and
hyghe hym he bade, and take hym of the beste men of armys many sad
hundrethis, 'and go before, and we woll folow aftir'.   5

But the kynge of their commynge was prevely warned, and than
into Sessoyne he dressid his peple and forstalled the Romaynes from
the kyd castels and the walled townes. And there ˋsir Vyllers the
valyaunte made his avow evyn byfore the kyngeˊ to take other to sle
the vycounte of Rome, or ellys to dye therefore.   10

Than the kyng commaunded sir Cadore to take hede to the rerewarde: 'And take renkys of the Rounde Table that the beste lykes,
sauff sir Launcelot and sir Bors, with many mo othir. Sir Kay, sir
Clegis shall be there als, and sir Marroke, sir Marhaulte shall be with
me in fere, and all thes with mo other shall awayte uppon my persone.' 15

Thus kynge Arthure dispercled all his oste in dyverse partyes that
they sholde nat ascape, but to fyght them behovys.

Whan the Emperour was entyrd into the vale of Sessoyne he myght
se where kyng Arthure hoved in batayle with baners displayed. On
every syde was he besette, that he myght nat ascape but other to fyght 20
other to yelde hym, there was none other boote.

'Now I se well,' seyde sir Lucyus, 'yondir traytoure hath betrayed
me.'

Than he redressis his knyghtes on dyverse partyes, and sette up a
dragon with eglys many one enewed with sabyl, and than he lete blow 25
up with trumpettes and with tabours, that all the vale dyndled. And than
he lete crye on lowde, that all men myght here: 'Syrs, ye know well
that the honoure and worshyp hath ever folowyd the Romaynes. And
this day let hit nevir be loste for the defaughte of herte, for I se well
by yondyr ordynaunce this day shall dye much peple. And therefore 30
do doughtly this day, and the felde is ourys.'

Than anone the Welshe kyng was so nyghe that he herde sir
Lucyus. Than he dressed hym to the vycounte his avow for to holde.
His armys were full clene and therein was a dolefull dragon, and into
the vawarde he p⟨r⟩ykys hym with styff spere in honde, and there he 35
mette wyth ˋthe valyaunte Vyllers hymself that was vycounte of Rome,ˊ
and there he smote hym thorow the shorte rybbys with a speare, that
the bloode braste oute on every syde, and so fylle to the erthe and
never spake mo wordys aftir. Than the noble sir Uwayne boldely
approched and gyrde thorowoute the Emperoures batayle where was 40
the thyckest prece, and slew a grete lorde by the Emperours standard,
and than flow to the baner and strake hit thorowoute with his bryght
swerde, and so takyth hit fro hem and rydyth with hit away unto his
felyshyp.

Than sir Launcelot lepe forth with his stede evyn streyght unto sir Lucyus, and in his wey he smote thorow a kynge that stoode althirnexte hym, and his name was Jacounde, a Sarezen full noble. And than he russhed forth unto sir Lucyus and smote hym on the helme with his swerde, that he felle to the erthe; and syth he rode thryse over hym on a rowe, and so toke the baner of Rome and rode with hit away unto Arthure hymself. And all seyde that hit sawe there was never knyght dud more worshyp in his dayes.

Than dressed hym sir Bors unto a sterne knyght and smote hym on the umbrell, that his necke braste. Than he joyned his horse untyll a sterne gyaunte, and smote hym thorow bothe sydys, and yet he slewe in his way turnyng two other knyghtes.

Be than the bowemen of Inglonde and of Bretayne began to shote, and these other, Romaynes and Sarezens, shotte with dartis and with crosse-bowys. There began a stronge batayle on every syde and muche slaughter on the Romaynes party, and the Douchemen with quarels dud muche harme, for they were with the Romaynes with hir bowys of horne. And the grete gyauntes of Gene kylled downe many knyghtes, with clubbys of steele crusshed oute hir braynes. Also they sqwatte oute the braynes of many coursers.

Whan Arthure had aspyed the gyauntes workes he cryed on lowde that knyghtes myght here and seyde, 'Fayre lordys, loke youre name be nat loste! Lese nat youre worshyp for yondir bare-legged knavys, and ye shall se what I shall do as for my trew parte.' He toke there oute Excalyber `and gurdys towarde Galapas that grevid hym moste.´ `He kut hym of by the kneis clenly there in sondir:´ 'Now art thou of a syse,' seyde the kyng, 'lyke unto oure ferys,' and than he strake of his hede swyftely.

Than come in sir Cadore and sir Kay, sir Gawayne and good sir Launcelot, sir Bors, sir Lyonel, and sir Ector de Marys, and sir Ascamore the good knyght that never fayled his lorde, sir Pelleas and sir Marhault that were proved men of armys. All thes grymly knyghtes sette uppon the gyauntys, and `by the dyntys were dalte and the dome yoldyn´ they had felled hem starke dede of fyffty all to the bare erthe.

So forth they wente wyth the kynge, tho knyghtes of the Rounde Table. Was never kyng nother knyghtes dud bettir syn God made the worlde. They leyde on with longe swerdys and swapped thorow braynes. Shyldys nother no shene armys myght hem nat withstonde tyll they leyde on the erthe ten thousand at onys. Than the Romaynes reled a lytyl, for they were somwhat rebuked, but kyng Arthure with his pryce knyghtes preced sore aftir.

Than sir Kay, sir Clegis and sir Bedwere the ryche encountyrs with them by a clyffsyde, and there they three by good meanys slowe in that chace mo than fyve hondred. And also sir Kay roode unto a kyng of

Ethyopé and bare hym thorow, and as he turned hym agayne towarde
his ferys a tyrraunte strake hym betwyxte the breste and the bowellys,
and as he was hurte yet he turned hym agayne and smote the todir on
the hede, that to the breste hit raughte, and seyde, 'Thoughe I dey of
thy dente, thy praysyng shall be lytyll.'   5

Whan sir Clegys and sir Bedwere saw that sir Kay was hurt they
fared with the Romaynes as grayhoundis doth with harys. And than
they returned ayen unto noble kynge Arthure and tolde hym how they
had spedde.

'Sir kyng,' sayde sir Kay, 'I have served the longe. Now bryng me   10
unto som beryellys for my fadyrs sake, and commaunde me to dame
Gwenyvere, thy goodly quene, and grete well ʼmy worshypfull wyff
that wratthed me never,ʼ and byd hir for my love to worche for my
soule.'

Than wepte kynge Arthure for routhe at his herte and seyde, 'Thou 15
shalt lyve for ever, my herte thynkes.' And therewith the kynge hymself pulled oute the truncheoune of the speare and made lechis to seche
hym sykerly, and founde nother lyvir nor lungys nother bowelles that
were attamed. And than the kyng putte hym in hys owne tente with
syker knyghtes and sayde, 'I shall revenge thy hurte and I may aryght 20
rede.'

Than the kynge in this malyncoly metys with a kynge, and with
Excalyber he smote his bak in sundir. Than in that haste he metys
with anothir, and gurde hym in the waste thorow bothe sydes. Thus
he russhed here and there ʼthorow the thyckyst prees more than thirty 25
tymes.ʼ

Than sir Launcelot, sir Gawayne and sir Lovelys son gerde oute one
that one hande where Lucyus the Emperoure hymself in a launde
stoode. Anone as sir Lucyus sawe sir Gawayne he sayde all on hyght,
'Thou art welcom iwys, for thou sekyst aftir sorow. Here thou shalt 30
be sone overmacched!' Sir Launcelot was wroth at hys grymme wordys
and gurde to hym with his swerde aboven uppon hys bryght helme,
that the raylyng bloode felle doune to his feete.

And sir Gawayne wyth his longe swerde leyde on faste, that three
amerallys deyde thorow the dynte of his hondis. And so Lovel fayled 35
nat in the pres; he slew a kynge and a deuke that knyghtes were noble.
Than the Romaynes releved. Whan they sye hir lorde so hampred they
chaced and choppedde doune many of oure knyghtes good, and in
that rebukyng they bare the bolde Bedwere to the colde erthe, and
wyth a ranke swerde he was merveylously wounded. Yet sir Launcelot 40
and sir Lovel rescowed hym blyve.

With that come in kynge Arthure with the knyghtes of the Table
Rounde and rescowed the ryche men that never were lyke to ascape
at the tyme, for oftetymes thorow envy grete hardynesse is shewed

that hath bene the deth of many kyd knyghtes; for thoughe they speke fayre many one unto other, yet whan they be in batayle eyther wolde beste be praysed.

Anone as kynge Arthure had a syght of the Emperour Lucyus, for
5 kynge nother for captayne he taryed no lenger. And eythir with her swerdys swapped at othir. So sir Lucyus with his swerde hit Arthure overthwarte the nose and gaff hym a wounde nyghe unto the tunge. Sir Arthure was wroth and gaff hym another with all the myght that in his arme was leved, that frome the creste of his helme unto the bare
10 pappys hit wente adoune, and so ended the Emperour.

Than ˋthe kyng mette with sir Cadore, his kene cousyn,΄ and prayde hym, 'Kylle doune clene for love of sir Kay, my foster-brother, and for the love of sir Bedwer that longe hath me served. Therefore save none for golde nothir for sylver: for they that woll accompany them with
15 Sarezens, the man that wolde save them were lytyll to prayse. And therefore sle doune and save nother hethyn nothir Crystyn.'

ˋThan sir Cadore, sir Clegis, ⟨they⟩ caughte to her swerdys,΄ and sir Launcelot, sir Bors, sir Lyonel, sir Ector de Marys, they whyrled thorow many men of armys. And sir Gawayne, sir Gaherys, sir Lovell and sir
20 Florens, his brothir that was gotyn of sir Braundyles systir uppon a mountayne, all thes knyghtes russhed forth in a frunte with many mo knyghtes of the Rounde Table that here be not rehersid. They hurled over hyllys, valeyes, and clowys, and slow downe on every honde wondirfull many, ˋthat thousandis in an hepe lay thrumbelyng togedir.΄
25 But for all that the Romaynes and the Sarezens cowde do other speke to y⟨e⟩lde themself there was none saved, but all yode to the swerde. For evir kynge Arthure rode in the thyckeste of the pres and raumped downe lyke a lyon many senatours noble. He wolde nat abyde uppon no poure man for no maner of thyng, and ˋever he slow slyly and slypped
30 to another΄ tylle all were slayne to the numbir of a hondred thousand, and yet many a thousande ascaped thorow prevy frendys.

And than relevys the kynge with his noble knyghtes and rensaked over all the feldis for his bolde barouns. And tho that were dede were burryed as their bloode asked, and they that myght be saved there was
35 no salve spared nother no deyntés to dere that myght be gotyn for golde other sylver. And thus he let save many knyghtes that wente never to recover, but for sir Kayes recovir and of sir Bedwers the ryche was never man undir God so glad as hymself was.

Than the kynge rode streyte thereas the Emperoure lay, and garte
40 lyffte hym up lordely with barounes full bolde, and the sawdon of Surré and of Ethyopé the kyng, and of Egypte and of Inde two knyghtes full noble, wyth seventene other kynges were takyn up als, and also syxty senatours of Roome that were honoured full noble men, and all the elders. The kynge let bawme all thes with many good gummys and

setthen lette lappe hem in syxtyfolde of sendell large, and than lete lappe
hem in lede that for chauffynge other chongyng they sholde never
savoure, and sytthen ʽlete close them in chestys full clenly arayed,ʼ and
their bancrs abovyn on their bodyes, and their shyldys turned upwarde,
that eviry man myght knowe of what contray they were.   5

So on the morne they founde in the heth three senatours of Rome.
Whan they were brought to the kynge he seyde thes wordis:

'Now to save your lyvys I take no force grete, with that ye woll meve
on my message unto grete Rome and presente thes corses unto the
proude Potestate and aftir [shewe] hym my lettyrs and my hole entente. 10
And telle hem in haste they shall se me, and I trow they woll beware
how they bourde with me and my knyghtes.'

Than the Emperour hymself was dressed in a charyot, and every two
knyghtys in a charyot cewed aftir other, and the senatours com aftir
by cowplys in a corde.   15

'Now sey ye to the Potestate and all the lordys aftir that I sende hem
the trybet that I owe to Rome, for this is the trew trybet that I and myne
elders have loste this ten score wyntyrs. And sey hem as mesemes I have
sent hem the hole somme, and yf they thynke hit nat inowe, I shall
amende hit whan that I com. ʳAnd ferthermore I charge you to saye to   20
them never to demaunde trybute ne taxe of me ne of my londesꞋ, for
suche tresoure muste they take as happyns us here.'

So on the morne thes senatours rayked unto Rome, and within
eyghtene dayes they come to the Potestate and tolde hym how they
hadde brought ʽthe taxe and the trewage of ten score wynters' ʽbothe 25
of Ingelonde, Irelonde, and of all the Est londys.' 'For kyng Arthure
commaundys you nother trybet nother taxe ye never none aske uppon
payne of youre hedys, but yf youre tytil be the trewer than ever ought
ony of your elders. And for these causys ʽwe have foughtyn in Fraunce,
and there us is foule happed,' for all is chopped to the deth bothe the 30
bettir and the worse. Therefore I rede you store you wyth stuff, for war
is at honde. ʽFor in the moneth of May this myscheff befelle' ʽin the
contrey of Constantyne by the clere stremys,' and there he hyred us
with his knyghtes and heled them that were hurte that same day and
to bery them that were slayne.'   35

Now turne we to Arthure with his noble knyghtes that entryth   (9)
streyghte into Lushburne and so thorowe Flaundirs and than to
Lorayne. He laughte up all the lordshyppys, and sytthen he drew hym
into Almayne and unto Lumbardy the ryche, and ʽsette lawys in that
londe that dured longe aftir.' ʽAnd so into Tuskayne, and there the   40
tirrauntys destroyed,' ʽand there were captaynes full kene that kepte
Arthurs comyng,' and at streyte passages slew muche of his peple, and
there they vytayled and garnysshed many good townys.

But there was a cité kepte sure defence agaynste Arthure and his knyghtes, and therewith angred Arthure and seyde all on hyght, 'I woll wynne this towne other ellys many a doughty shall dye!' And than the kynge approched to the wallis withoute shelde sauff his bare harneys.

'Sir,' seyde sir Florence, 'foly thou workeste' for to nyghe so naked
5 this perleouse cité.'

'And thow be aferde,' seyde kyng Arthure, 'I rede the faste fle, 'for they wynne no worshyp of me but to waste their toolys;' for there 'shall never harlot have happe, by the helpe of oure Lord,' 'to kylle a crowned kynge that with creyme is anoynted.''

10 Than the noble knyghtes of the Rounde Table approched unto the cité and their horsis levys. They hurled on a frunte streyght unto the barbycans, and there they slewe downe all that before them stondys, and in that bray the brydge they wanne; and had nat the garnyson bene, they had wonne within the yatys and the cité wonne thorow wyght-
15 nesse of hondys. And than oure noble knyghtes withdrew them a lytyll and wente unto the kynge and prayde hym to take his ⟨herborgage⟩. 'And than he pyght his pavylyons of palle, and plantys all aboute' the sege, and there he lette sett up suddeynly many engynes.

Than the kynge called unto hym sir Florens and seyde these wordys:
20 'My folk ys wexen feble for wantynge of vytayle, and 'hereby be forestes full fayre, and thereas oure foomen many.' And I am sure they have grete store of bestes. And thyder shall thou go to forrey that forestes, and with the shall go sir Gawayne, 'and sir Wysharde with sir Walchere, two worshypfull knyghtes,' 'with all the wyseste men of the Weste
25 marchis.' 'Also sir Cleremount and sir Clegis that were comly in armys,' 'and the captayne of Cardyff that is a knyght full good.' Now go ye and warne all this felyshep that hit be done as I commaunde.'

So 'with that forth yode sir Florens, and his felyshyp was sone redy,' and so they rode thorow holtys and hethis, thorow foreste and over
30 hyllys. And than they com into a lowe medow that was full of swete floures, and there thes noble knyghtes bayted her ⌐horses⌐.

And in the ⌐b⌐ rekynge of the day sir Gawayne hente his hors won-dyrs for to seke. 'Than was he ware of a man armed walkynge a paase by a woodis ease' by a revers syde, and his shelde braced on his sholdir,
35 and he on a stronge horse rydys withoute man wyth hym save a boy alone that bare a grymme speare. The knyght bare in his shelde 'of golde glystrand three gryffons in sabyll' and charbuckkle, the cheff of sylver. Whan sir Gawayne was ware of that gay knyght, than he gryped a grete spere and rode streyght towarde hym on a stronge horse for to
40 mete with that sterne knyght where that he hoved. Whan sir Gawayne com hym nyghe, in Englyshe he asked hym what he was. And that other knyght answerde in his langage of Tuskayne and sayde,

'Whother pryckyst thou, pylloure, that profers the so large?' Thou ⌐getest⌐ no pray, prove whan the lykys, for 'my presoner thou shalt

be for all thy proude lokys.' 'Thou spekyste proudly,' seyde sir
Gawayne, 'but I counseyle the for all thy grymme wordis that ˇthou
grype to the thy gere or [gretter] grame falle.'

Than hir launcis ⌐and speres⌐ they handylde by crauff of armys, and (10)
com on spedyly with full syker dyntes, and there ˇthey shotte thorow 5
shyldys and mayles, and thorow there shene shuldyrs' they were
thorowborne the brede of an hande. ˇThan were they so wroth that
away wolde they never,' but rathly russhed oute their swerdys ˇand
hyttys on their helmys with hatefull dyntys,' ˇand stabbis at hir
stomakys with swerdys well steled.' ˇSo freysshly tho fre men fyghtes 10
on the grounde,' ˇwhyle the flamynge fyre flowe oute of hir helmys.'

Than sir Gawayne was grevid wondirly sore and swynges his ⌐good⌐
swerde Galantyne, and grymly he strykys, and clevys the knyghtes
shylde in sundir. And thorowoute the thycke haubirke made of sure
mayles, and the rubyes that were ryche, he russhed hem in sundir, that 15
men myght beholde the lyvir and longes. ˇThan groned the knyght for
his grymme woundis and gyrdis to sir Gawayne' and awkewarde hym
strykes, and brastyth the rerebrace and the vawmbrace bothe, and kut
thorow a vayne, that Gawayne sore greved, for ˇso worched his wounde
that his wytte chonged,' ·and therewithall his armure was all blody 20
berenne.

Than that knyght talked to sir Gawayne and ˇbade hym bynde up his
wounde, 'or thy ble chonge,' ˇfor thou all bebledis this horse and thy
bryght wedys,' ˇfor all the barbers of Bretayne shall nat thy blood
staunche.' For who that is hurte with this blaade bleed shall he ever.' 25

ˇ'Be God,' sayde sir Gawayne, 'hit grevys me but lytyll,' yet shalt
thou nat feare me for all thy grete wordis. ˇThow trowyste with thy
talkynge to tame my herte,' but yet thou betydys tene or thou parte
hense but thou telle me in haste who may stanche my bledynge.'

'That may I do, and I woll, so thou wolt succour me that I myght be 30
fayre crystynde and becom meke for my mysdedis. Now mercy I Jesu
beseche, and I shall becom Crysten and in God stedfastly beleve, ˇand
thou mayste for thy manhode have mede to thy soule.'

ˇ'I graunte,' seyde sir Gawayne, 'so God me helpe' to fullfyll all thy
desyre; thou haste gretly hit deservyd. So thou say me the soth, ˇwhat 35
thou sought here thus sengly thyself alone,' and what lorde or legeaunte
thou art undir.'

'Sir,' he seyde, 'I hyght Priamus, and a prynce is my fadir, and ˇhe
hath bene rebell unto Rome and overredyn muche of hir londis.' And
my fadir is com of Alysaundirs bloode that was overleder of kynges, 40
and of Ector also was he com by the ryght lyne; and many mo were of
my kynrede, bothe Judas Macabeus and deuke Josue. And ayre I am
althernexte of ˇAlysaundir and of Aufryke and of all the Oute Iles.'
ˇYet woll I beleve on thy Lorde that thou belevyst on,' and take the for,

thy labour tresour inow. `For I was so hauté in my herte I helde no man my pere,´ so was I sent into this werre by the assente of my fadir with seven score knyghtes, and now I have encountred with one hath geevyn [me of] fyghtyng my fylle. Therefore, sir knyght, for thy kynges sake
5 telle me thy name.'

'Sir,' seyde sir Gawayne, 'I am no knyght, but I have be brought up in the wardrope with the noble kyng Arthure wyntyrs and dayes for to take hede to his armoure and all his other wedis and to poynte all the paltokkys that longe to hymself `and to dresse doublettis for deukys
10 and erlys.´ `And at Yole he made me yoman and gaff me good gyfftys,´ more than `an hondred pounde and horse and harneyse rych.´ And yf I have happe ⟨to⟩ my hele to serve my lyege lorde I shall be well holpyn in haste.'

'A,' sayde sir Priamus, `'and his knavys be so kene, his knyghtes ar
15 passynge good.´ Now for thy Kynges love of Hevyn and for thy kyngys love, whether thou be knave other knyght, telle thou me thy name.'

'Be God,' seyde sir Gawayne, 'now woll I telle the soth. ⌐My name is syre Gawayn.⌐ `I am knowyn in his courte and kyd in his chambir´
20 `and rolled with the rychest of the Rounde Table,´ and I am a deuke dubbed wyth his owne hondis. `Therefore grucche nat, good sir, if me this grace is behappened:´ hit is the goodnesse of God that lente me this stength.'

'Now am I bettir pleased,' sayde sir Pryamus, 'than thou haddest
25 gyff me the Provynce ⌐and⌐ Perysie the ryche, for I had levir have be toryn with four wylde horse than ony yoman had suche a loose wonne of me, other els ony page other prycker sholde wynne of me the pryce in this felde gotyn. But now I warne the, sir knyght of the Rounde Table, here is by the deuke of Lorayne with his knyghtes, and `the
30 doughtyeste of Dolphyne landys with many Hyghe Duchemen,´ and many lordis of Lumbardy, and the garneson of Godarde, `and men of Westwalle, worshypfull kynges;´ and `of Syssoyne and of Southlonde Sarezyns many numbirde,´ and there named ar in rollys sixti thousand of syker men of armys.

35 'Therefore `but thou hyghe the fro this heth, hit woll harme us both,´ and sore be we hurte never lyke to recover. But `take thou hede ⟨to the⟩ haynxman that he no horne blow,´ for and he do, than loke that he be hewyn on pecis: `for here hovys at thy honde a hondred of good knyghtes´ that ar of my retynew and to awayte uppon my persone. `For
40 and thou be raught with that rought, raunsom nother rede golde´ woll they none aske.'

Than sir Gawayne rode over a water for to gyde hymself, and that worshypfull knyght hym folowed sore wounded. And so they rode tylle they com to their ferys that were baytand hir horsys in a low medow ˋwhere lay many lordys lenyng on there shyldys,ˊ ˋwith lawghyng and japyng and many lowde wordys.ˊ Anone as sir Wycharde was ware of sir Gawayne and aspyed that he was hurte ˋhe wente towarde hym wepyng and wryngyng his hondys.ˊ

Than sir Gawayne tolde hym ˋhow he had macchcd with that myghty 5 man of strengthe.ˊ 'Therefore greve yow nat, good sir, for thoughe my shylde be now thirled and my sholdir shorne, yett ˋthys knyght sir Pryamus hath many perelouse woundys.ˊ But he hath salvys, he seyth, that woll hele us bothe. But here is new note in honde nere than ye wene, fore by an houre aftir none I trow hit woll noy us all.' 10

Than sir Pryamus and sir Gawayne alyght bothe and lette hir horsys bayte in the fayre medow. ˋThan they lette brayde of hir basnettys and hir brode shyldys.ˊ Than eythir bled so muche that every man had wondir that ˋthey myght sitte in their sadyls or stonde uppon erthe.ˊ

'Now fecche me,' seyde sir Pryamus, 'my vyall that hangys by the 15 gurdyll of my haynxman, for ˋhit is full of the floure of the four good watyrsˊ that passis from Paradyse, ˋth⟨at⟩ mykyll fruyte in fallys that at one day fede shall us all.ˊ Putt that watir in oure fleysh where the syde is tamed, and we shall be hole within four houres.'

Than they lette clense their woundys with colde whyght wyne, and 20 than they lete anoynte them with bawme over and over, and holer men than they wcre within an houres space was never lyvyng syn God the worlde made. So whan they were clensed and hole ˋthey broched barellys and brought them the wyneˊ ˋwyth brede and brawne and many ryche byrdys.ˊ And whan they had etyn, ⌜than with a trompet they alle 25 assembled to counceylle, and⌝ sir Gawayne seyde, 'Lordynges, go to armys!' And whan they were armed and assembled togedyrs, ˋwith a clere claryon callys them togedirˊ to counceyle, and sir Gawayne of the case hem tellys.

'Now tell us, sir Pryamus, all the hole purpose of yondir pryce 30 knyghtes.'

'Sirs,' seyde sir Pryamus, 'for to rescow me they have made a vowe, other ellys ˋmanfully on this molde to be marred all at onys.ˊ ˋThis was the pure purpose, whan I passed thensˊ ˋat hir perellys, to preff me uppon payne of their lyvys.ˊ 35

ˋ'Now, good men,' seyde sir Gawayne, 'grype up your hertes,ˊ ˋand yf we g⟨et⟩tles go ⟨thus⟩ away hit woll greffe oure kynge.ˊ And sir Florens in this fyght shall here abyde for to kepe the stale as a knyght noble, ˋfor he was chosyn and charged in chambir with the kyngeˊ ˋchyfften of this chckke and cheyff of us all.ˊ ˋAnd whethir he woll 40 fyght other fle we shall folow aftir;ˊ for as for me, ˋfor all yondir folkys faare forsake hem shall I never.ˊ

ˋ'A, fadir!' seyde Florens, 'full fayre now ye speke,ˊ ˋfor I am but a fauntekyn to fraysted men of armys,ˊ and yf I ony foly do the faughte muste be youres. Therefore lese nat youre worshyp. My wytt is but symple, and ye ar oure allther governoure; therefore worke as ye lykys.'

'Now, fayre lordys,' seyde sir Pryamus, 'cese youre wordys, I warne
5 you betyme; for ye shall fynde in yondir woodys many perellus knyghtes. They woll putte furthty beyss to bayte you oute of numbir, and ye ar fraykis in this fryth nat paste seven hondred, ⸗and that is feythfully to fewe to fyght with so many,′ ⸗for harlottys and haynxmen wol helpe us but a lytyll,′ ⸗for they woll hyde them in haste for all their
10 hyghe wordys.′

'Ye sey well,' seyde sir Gawayne, 'so God me helpe!' 'Now, fayre sonne,' sayde sir Gawayne unto Florens, 'woll ye take youre felyshyp of the beste provyd men to the numbir of a hondred knyghtes and ⸗prestly prove yourself and yondir pray wynne?′

15 'I assent me with good hert,' seyde Florence.
(11) ⸗Than sir Florens called unto hym sir Florydas with fyve score knyghtes,′ ⸗and forth they flynged a faste tro⟨tt⟩e′ and the folke of the bestes dryvys. Than folowed aftir sir Florens with noble men of armys fully seven hondred, and one ⸗sir Feraunte of Spayne before on a fayre
20 stede′ ⸗that was fostred in Farmagos: the fende was his fadir.′ ⸗He flyttys towarde sir Florens and sayde, 'Whother flyest thou,′ false knyght?' Than ⸗sir Florens was fayne, and in feautyr castis his spere,′ ⸗and rydys towarde the rought and restys no lenger,′ and full but in the forehede he hyttys sir Feraunte and brake his necke-bone. Than
25 Feraunte ⸗his cosyn had grete care and cryed full lowde:′ 'Thou haste slayne a knyght and kynge anoynted that or this tyme founde never frayke that myght abyde hym a buffette. Therefore ye shall dey, there shall none of you ascape!'

'Fye on the,' seyde Florydas, 'thou eregned wrecche!'
30 And therewith to hym he flyngis with a swerde, that ⸗all the fleysshe of his flanke he flappys in sundir,′ that all the fylth of the freyke and many of his guttys fylle to the erthe.

⸗Than lyghtly rydis a raynke for to rescowe that barowne′ that was borne in the Rodis, and rebell unto Cryste. ⸗He preced in proudly and
35 aftir his pray wyndys.′ But ⸗the raynke Rycharde of the Rounde Table′ ⸗on a rede stede rode hym agaynste′ and threste hym thorow the shylde evyn to the herte. ⸗Than he rored full rudely, but rose he nevermore.′

⸗Than alle his feerys mo than fyve hondred′ ⸗felle uppon sir Florence and on his fyve score knyghtes.′ ⸗Than sir Florens and sir Florydas in
40 feautir bothe castys′ their spearys, and ⸗they felled fyve at the frunte at the fyrste entré,′ and sore they assayled our folke and brake browys and brestys and felde many adowne. ⸗Whan sir Pryamus, the pryse knyght, perceyved their gamys′ he yode to sir Gawyne and thes wordys seyde:

'Thy pryse men ar sore begone and put undir, for they ar oversette

with Sarezens mo than five hondred. Now wolde thou suffir me for
the love of thy God with a small parte of thy men to succoure hem
betyme?'

ˋ'Sir, grucch ye nat,' seyde sir Gawayne, 'the gre is there owne,ˊ ˋfor
they mowe have gyfftys full grete igraunted of my lorde.ˊ Therefore	5
lette them fyght whylys hem lystes, the freysh knyghtes; for som of
hem ˋfought nat their fylle of all this fyve wyntyr.ˊ Therefore ˋI woll
nat styrre wyth my stale half my steede lengthˊ ˋbut yf they be stadde
wyth more stuff than I se hem agaynste.'ˊ

So by that tyme was sir Gawayne ware by the woodys syde men	10
commynge woodly with all maner of wepon, for there rode ˋthe erle
of Ethelwolde havyng on eyther halfˊ many hole thousandys; ˋand the
deuke of Douchemen dressys hym aftirˊ and passis with Pryamus
knyghtes. Than Gawayne, the good knyght, he chered his knyghtes
and sayde,	15

ˋ'Greve you nat, good men, for yondir grete syght,ˊ and ˋbe nat
abaysshed of yondir boyes in hir bryghte weedis,ˊ ˋfor and we feyght
in fayth the felde is ourys!'ˊ

Than they haled up their brydyls and began walop, and by that they
com nygh by a londys length they jowked downe with her hedys many	20
jantyll knyghtes. A more jolyar joustynge was never sene on erthe.
ˋThan the ryche men of the Rounde Table ran thorow the thykkesteˊ
with hir stronge sperys, that many a raynke for that prouesse ran into
the grevys, and durste ˋno knavys but knyghtes kene of herteˊ fyght
more in this felde, but fledde.	25

ˋ'Be God,' seyde sir Gawayne, 'this gladys my herteˊ ˋthat yondir
gadlynges be gone, for they made a grete numbir.ˊ ˋNow ar they fewer
in the felde whan they were fyrst numbyrdˊ by twenty thousand, in
feyth, for all their grete boste.'

Than Jubeaunce of Geane, a myghty gyaunte, he feautred his speare	30
to sir Garrarde, a good knyght of Walys. He smote the Waylshe knyght
evyn to the herte. Than our knyghtes myghtyly meddeled wyth hir
myddylwarde. But anone at all assemble many Saresyns were destroyed,
ˋfor the soveraynes of Sessoyne were salved for ever.ˊ By that tyme ˋsir
Pryamus, the good prynce, in the presence of lordysˊ royall to his	35
penowne he rode and lyghtly hit hentys, ˋand rode with the royall
rought of the Rounde Table,ˊ and streyte all his retynew folowed hym
aftyr oute of the woode. They folowed as shepe oute of a folde, and
streyte they yode to the felde and stood by their kynde lorde. ˋAnd
sytthyn they sente to the deuke thes same wordis:ˊ	40

ˋ'Sir, we have bene thy sowdyars all this seven wynter,ˊ and now we
forsake the for the love of oure lyege lorde Arthure, ˋfor we may with
oure worshype wende where us lykys,ˊ for garneson nother golde have
we none resceyved.'

'Fye on you, the devyll have your bonys! For suche sowdyars I
sette but a lytyll.'

Than the deuke dressys his Dowchmen streyte unto sir Gawayne and
to sir Pryamus. So they two gryped their spearys, and at the gaynyste
5 in he gurdys, wyth hir noble myghtes. And there sir Pryamus ˅metyth
with the marquesse of Moyseslonde´ and smytyth hym thorow.

˅Than Chastelayne, a chylde of kyng Arthurs chambir,´ ˅he was a
warde of sir Gawaynes of the Weste marchis,´ ˅he chasis to sir Cheldrake that was a chyfteyne noble,´ and with his spere he smote thorow
10 Cheldrake, and so ˅that chek that chylde cheved by chaunce of armys.´
But than they chaced that chylde, that he nowhere myght ascape, for
one with a swerde the halse of the chylde he smote in too. Whan sir
Gawayne hit sawe he wepte wyth all his herte and inwardly he brente
for sorow.

15 But anone Gotelake, a good man of armys, ˅for Chastelayne the
chylde he chongyd his mode,´ ˅that the wete watir wente doune his
chykys.´ Than sir Gawayne dressis hym and to a deuke rydys, and sir
Dolphyn the deuke droff harde agaynste hym. But sir Gawayne hym
dressyth with a grete spere, that the grounden hede droff to his herte.
20 Yette he gate hit oute and ran to another one, sir Hardolf, an hardy man
of armys, and slyly in he lette hit slyppe thorow, and sodeynly he
fallyth to the erthe. Yet he slow in the slade of men of armys mo than
syxty with his hondys.

Than was sir Gawayne ware of the man that slew Chastelayne his
25 chylde, and ˅swyfftly with his swerde he smyttyth hym thorow.´

˅'Now and thou haddyst ascaped withoutyn scathe, the scorne had
bene oures!'´

And aftir sir Gawayne dressis hym unto the route and russhyth on
helmys, and rode streyte to the rerewarde and so his way holdyth, and
30 sir Pryamus hym allthernexte, gydynge hym his wayes. And there ˅they
hurtelyth and hewyth downe hethyn knyghtes many,´ and sir Florence
on the other syde dud what he myght. ˅There the lordys of Lorayne
and of Lumbardy both´ were takyn and lad away with oure noble
knyghtes. ˅For suche a chek oure lordys cheved by chaunce of that
35 were´ that they were so avaunced, for hit avayled hem ever.

Whan sir Florence and sir Gawayne had the felde wonne, than they
sente before fyve score of knyghtes, ˅and her prayes and hir presoners
passyth hem aftir.´ And sir Gawayne in a streyte passage he hovyth tyll
all the prayes were paste that streyte patthe that so sore he dredith. So
40 they rode tyll they the cité sawe, and ˅sothly the same day with asawte
hit was gotyn.´

Than sir Florence and sir Gawayne harborowed surely their peple,
and ˅sytthen turnys to a tente and tellyth the kynge´ ˅all the tale truly,
that day how they travayled´ and how his ferse men fare welle all.

'And fele of thy foomen ar brought oute of lyff, and many worshyp-full presoners ar yolden into oure handys. `But Chastelayne, thy chylde, is chopped of the hede,´ yette slewe he a cheff knyghte his owne hondys this day.'

'Now thanked be God,' sayde the noble kynge, 'but I mervayle 5 (12) muche of that bourely knyght that stondyth by the, for hym semys to be a straungere, for presonere is he none lyke.'

'Sir,' seyde sir Gawayne, 'this is a good man of armys: he macched me sore this day in the mournyng, and had nat his helpe bene ⟨dethe⟩ had I founden. And now is he yolden unto God and to me, sir kyng, 10 for to becom Crysten and on good beleve. And whan he is crystynde and in the fayth belevys, there lyvyth nat a bettir knyght nor a nobler of his hondis.'

Than the kynge in haste crystynde hym fayre and lette conferme hym Priamus, as he was afore, and lyghtly lete dubbe hym a deuke with his 15 hondys, and made hym knyght of the Table Rounde.

And anone the kynge lette cry asawte unto the towne, and there was rerynge of laddyrs and brekynge of wallys. `The payne that the peple had was pyté to se!´ `Than the duches hir dressed with damesels ryche,´ `and the countes of Clarysyn with hir clere maydyns,´ `they kneled in 20 their kyrtyls there the kynge hovyth´ `and besought hym of socoure for the sake of oure Lorde:´

'And sey us som good worde and cetyl thy peple `or the cité sud-deynly be with asawte wonne,´ for than shall dye many a soule that grevid the never.' 25

The kynge ⌜avalyd and⌝ lyffte up his vyser with a knyghtly coun-tenaunce, and kneled to hir myldely with full meke wordes and seyde,

`'Shall none myssedo you, madam, that to me longis,´ `for I graunte the chartyrs and to thy cheff maydyns,´ `unto thy chyldern and to thy 30 chyff men in chambir´ that to the longis. `But thy deuke is in daunger, my drede ys the lesse.´ But ye shall have lyvelode to leve by as to thyne astate fallys.'

`'Than Arthure sendyth on eche syde wyth sertayne lordis´ `for to cese of their sawte, for the cité was yolden, and therewith the deukeis 35 eldyst sonne com with the keyes and kneled downe unto the kynge and besought hym of his grace. `And there he cesed the sawte by assente of his lordis,´ `and the deuke was dressed to Dover with the kynges dere knyghtes´ `for to dwelle in daunger and dole dayes of his lyff.´ `Than the kynge with his crowne on his hede recoverde the cité´ and the 40 castell, `and the captaynes and connestablys knew hym for lorde,´ and there `he delyverde and dalte byfore dyverse lordis´ a dowré for the deuches and hir chyldryn. Than he made wardens to welde all that londis.

And so `in Lorayne and Lumbardy he lodged as a lorde in his owne,´ `and sette lawys in the londis as hym beste lyked.´ `And than at Lammas he yode, unto Lusarne he sought,´ `and lay at his leyser with lykynges inowe.´ `Than he mevys over the mountaynes and doth many
5 mervayles,´ `and so goth in by Godarte that Gareth sone wynnys.´ `Than he lokys into Lumbardy and on lowde spekyth:´
`"In yondir lykynge londis as lorde woll I dwelle."´
Sir Florence and sir Floridas that day passed with fyve hondred good men of armys unto the cité of Virvyn. They sought at the gaynyste and
10 `leyde there a buysshement as hem beste lykys.´ So there ⌐yssued¬ oute of that cité many hundretthis and skyrmysshed wyth oure foreryders as hem beste semed. `Than broke oute oure buysshemente and the brydge wynnys,´ and so rode unto their borowys with baners up dysplayed. There fledde much folke oute of numbir `for ferde of sir
15 Florence and his fers knyghtes.´ Than `they busked up a baner abovyn the gatis,´ and `of sir Florence in fayth so fayne were they never.´
The kynge than hovyth on an hylle and lokyth to the wallys and sayde, `"I se be yondir sygne the cité is wonne."´ Than he lete make a cry thorow all the oste that `uppon payne of lyff and lymme and also
20 lesynge of his goodys´ that no lyegeman that longyth to his oste sholde lye be no maydens ne ladyes nother no burgessis wyff that to the cité longis. So whan this conquerrour com into the cité he passed into the castell, and there he lendis and `comfortis the carefull men with many knyghtly wordis,´ and made there a captayne a knyght of his owne
25 contrey, and the commo⟨n⟩s accorded theretyll.
Whan the soveraygnes of Myllayne herde that the cité was wonne they sente unto kynge Arthure `grete sommys of sylver, syxty horsys well charged,´ and besought hym as soverayne to have ruthe of the peple, and seyde they wolde be sudgectes untyll hym for ever `and
30 yelde hym servyse and sewte surely for hir londys,´ `bothe for Plesaunce ⌐and Pavye¬ and Petresaynte and for the Porte Trembyll,´ and `so mekly to gyff ⌐yerly¬ for Myllayne a myllyon of golde,´ and `make homage unto Arthure all hir lyff tymes.´ `Than the kynge by his counceyle a conduyte hem sendys´ so to com in and know hym for
35 lorde.
`Than into Tuskayne he turned whan he tyme semed,´ and `there he wynnys towrys and townys full hyghe,´ and `all he wasted in his warrys there he away ryddys.´ `Than he spedys towarde Spolute with his spedfull knyghtys,´ `and so unto Vyterbe he vytayled his knyghtes,´
40 `and to the vale of Vysecounte he devysed there to lygge´ `in that vertuouse vale amonge vynys full.´ `And there he suggeournys, that soveraigne, with solace at his harte,´ for to wete whether the senatours wolde hym of succour beseke.
`But sone after, on a Saturday, sought unto kynge Arthure´ all the

senatoures that were on lyve and of the cunnyngyst cardynallis that dwelled in the courte, and ꞌprayde hym of pece and profird hym full large;ꞌ and besought hym as a soverayne ꞌmoste governoure undir God for to gyff them lycence' for syx wekys large, that they myght be assembled all, and than in the cité of Syon that is Rome callyd ꞌto crowne 5 hym there kyndly, with crysemed hondys,ꞌ with septure, forsothe, as an Emperoure sholde.

'I assente me,' seyde the kynge, 'as ye have devysed, and comly be Crystmas to be crowned, hereafter to reigne in my asstate and to kepe my Rounde Table ꞌwith the rentys of Rome to rule as me lykys;ꞌ and 10 than, as I am avysed, to gete me over the salte see with good men of armys to deme for His deth that for us all on the roode dyed.'

Whan the senatours had this answere, unto Rome they turned and made rydy for his corownemente in the moste noble wyse. And at the day assigned, as the romaynes me tellys, he was crowned Emperour 15 by the Poopys hondis, with all the royalté in the worlde to welde for ever. There they suggeourned that seson tyll aftir the tyme, and stabelysshed all the londys frome Rome unto Fraunce, and gaff londis and rentys unto knyghtes that had hem well deserved. There was none that playned on his parte, ryche nothir poore. Than he commaunded sir 20 Launcelot and sir Bors to take kepe unto their fadyrs landys that kynge Ban and kynge Bors welded and her fadyrs:

'Loke that ye take seynge in all your brode londis, and cause youre lyege men to know you as for their kynde lorde, and suffir never your soveraynté to be alledged with your subjectes, nother the soveraygne 25 of your persone and londys. Also the myghty kynge Claudas I gyff you for to parte betwyxte you evyn, for to mayntene your kynrede, that be noble knyghtes, so that ye and they to the Rounde Table make your repeyre.'

Sir Launcelot and sir Bors de Gaynys thanked the kynge fayre and 30 sayde their hertes and servyse sholde ever be his owne.

'Where art thou, Priamus? Thy fee is yet behynde. Here I make the and gyff the deukedom of Lorayne for ever unto the and thyne ayres; and whan we com into Ingelonde, for to purvey the of horse-mete, a fifty thousand quarterly, for to mayntene thy servauntes. So thou leve 35 not my felyship, this gyffte ys thyne owne.'

The knyght thankys the kynge with a kynde wylle and sayde, 'As longe as I lyve my servys is youre owne.'

Thus the kynge gaff many londys. There was none that wolde aske that myghte playne of his parte, for of rychesse and welth they had all at 40 her wylle. Than the knyghtes and lordis that to the kynge longis called a counsayle uppon a fayre morne and sayde,

'Sir kynge, we beseche the for to here us all. We are undir youre lordship well stuffid, blyssed be God, of many thynges; and also we have wyffis weddid. We woll beseche youre good grace to reles us to sporte us with oure wyffis, for, worshyp be Cryste, this journey is well overcom.'

'Ye say well,' seyde the kynge, 'for inowghe is as good as a feste, for
5 to attemte God overmuche I holde hit not wysedom. And therefore make you all redy and turne we into Ingelonde.'

Than there was trussynge of harneyse with caryage full noble. And the kynge toke his leve of the holy fadir the Pope and patryarkys and cardynalys and senatoures full ryche, and leffte good governaunce in
10 that noble cité and all the contrays of Rome for to warde and to kepe on payne of deth, that in no wyse his commaundement be brokyn. Thus he passyth thorow the contreyes of all partyes.

And so kyng Arthure passed over the see unto Sandwyche haven. Whan quene Gwenyvere herde of his commynge she mette with hym
15 at London, and so dud all other quenys and noble ladyes. For there was never a solempner metyng in one cité togedyrs, for all maner of rychesse they brought with hem at the full.

HERE ENDYTH THE TALE OF THE NOBLE KYNGE ARTHURE THAT WAS EMPEROURE HYMSELF THOROW DYGNYTÉ OF HIS HONDYS.
20 AND HERE FOLOWYTH AFFTIR MANY NOBLE TALYS OF SIR LAUNCELOT DE LAKE.

EXPLYCIT THE NOBLE TALE BETWYXT
KYNGE ARTHURE AND LUCIUS THE EMPEROUR OF ROME.

A NOBLE TALE
OF
SIR LAUNCELOT
DU LAKE

SONE aftir that kynge Arthure was com from Rome into Ingelonde, than all the knyghtys of the Rounde Table resorted unto the kynge and made many joustys and turnementes. And som there were that were but knyghtes encresed in armys and worshyp that passed all other of her felowys in prouesse and noble dedys, and that was well proved on many. 5

But in especiall hit was prevyd on sir Launcelot de Lake, for in all turnementes, justys, and dedys of armys, both for lyff and deth, he passed all other knyghtes, and at no tyme was he ovircom but yf hit were by treson other inchauntement. So this sir Launcelot encresed so mervaylously in worship and honoure; therefore he is the fyrste knyght 10 that the Frey[n]sh booke makyth me[n]cion of aftir kynge Arthure com frome Rome. Wherefore quene Gwenyvere had hym in grete favoure aboven all other knyghtis, and so he loved the quene agayne aboven all other ladyes dayes of his lyff, and for hir he dud many dedys of armys and saved her frome the fyre thorow his noble chevalry. 15

Thus sir Launcelot rested hym longe with play and game; and than he thought hymself to preve in straunge adventures, and bade his nevew, sir Lyonell, for to make hym redy, 'for we muste go seke adventures'. So they mounted on their horses, armed at all ryghtes, and rode into a depe foreste and so into a playne. 20

So the wedir was hote aboute noone, and sir Launcelot had grete luste to slepe. Than sir Lyonell aspyed a grete appyll-tre that stoode by an hedge, and seyde, 'Sir, yondir is a fayre shadow, there may we reste us and oure horsys.'

'Hit is trouthe,' seyde sir Launcelot, 'for this seven yere I was [not] 25 so slepy as I am nowe.'

So there they alyted and tyed there horsys unto sondry treis, and sir Launcelot layde hym downe undir this appyll-tre, and his helmet undir his hede. And sir Lyonell waked whyles he sl[e]pte. So sir Launcelot slepte passyng faste. 30

And in the meanewhyle com there three knyghtes rydynge, as faste fleynge as they myght ryde, and there folowed hem three but one knyght. And whan sir Lyonell hym sawe, he thought he sawe never so grete a knyght nother so well-farynge a man and well appareyld unto all ryghtes. So within a whyle this stronge knyght had overtakyn onc of 35 the three knyghtes, and there he smote hym to the colde erth, that he lay stylle; and than he rode unto the secunde knyght and smote hym so that man and horse felle downe. And so streyte unto the thirde knyght, and smote hym behynde his horse ars a spere-lengthe; and than he alyght downe and rayned his horse on the brydyll and bounde all three 40 knyghtes faste with the raynes of theire owne brydelys.

Whan sir Lyonell had sene hym do thus, he thought to assay hym and

made hym redy, and pryvaly he toke his horse and thought nat for to
awake sir Launcelot, and so mounted uppon his hors and overtoke the
strong knyght. He bade hym turne, and so he turned and smote sir
Lyonell so harde that hors and man he bare to the erth. And so he
5 alyght downe and bounde hym faste and threw hym overthwarte his
owne horse as he had served the other three, and so rode with hem tyll
he com to his owne castell. Than he unarmed them and bete them with
thornys all naked, and aftir put them in depe preson where were many
mo knyghtes that made grete dole.

(2) 10 So whan sir Ector de Marys wyste that sir Launcelot was paste oute
of the courte to seke adventures, he was wroth with hymsel[f] and
made hym redy to seke sir Launcelot. And as he had redyn longe in a
grete foreste, he mette with a man was lyke a foster.

'Fayre felow,' seyde sir Ector, 'doste thou know this contrey or ony
15 adventures that bene nyghe here honde?'

'Sir,' seyde the foster, 'this contrey know I well. And hereby within
this myle is a stronge maner and well dyked, and by that maner on the
lyffte honde there is a fayre fourde for horse to drynke off, and over
that fourde there growys a fayre tre. And thereon hongyth many fayre
20 shyldys that welded somtyme good knyghtes, and at the bo[le] of the
tre hongys a basyn of couper and latyne. And stryke uppon that basyn
with the butte of thy spere three tymes, and sone aftir thou shalt hyre
new tydynges; and ellys haste thou the fayreste [grace] that ever had
knyghte this many yeres that passed thorow this foreste.'

25 'Gramercy,' seyde sir Ector and departed. And com unto this tre and
sawe many fayre shyldys, and amonge them all he sawe hys brothirs
shylde, sir Lyonell, and many mo that he knew that were of his felowys
of the Rounde Table, the whyche greved his herte, and promysed to
revenge his brother. Than anone sir Ector bete on the basyn as he were
30 woode, and than he gaff his horse drynke at the fourde. And there com
a knyghte behynde hym and bade hym com oute of the water and make
hym redy. Sir Ector turned hym shortly, and in feawtir caste his spere
and smote the other knyght a grete buffette, that his horse turned twyse
abowte.

35 'That was well done,' seyde the stronge knyght, 'and knyghtly thou
haste strykyn me.'

And therewith he russhed his horse on sir Ector and caught hym
undir his ryght arme and bare hym clene oute of the sadyll, and so rode
with hym away into his castell and threw hym downe in myddyll of the
40 floure. [The name of this knyghte was sir Tarquyn.] Than this seyde
T⌈ar⌉quyn seyde unto sir Ector,

'For thou hast done this day more unto me than ony knyght dud this
twelve yere, now woll I graunte the thy lyff, so thou wolt be sworne to
be my trew presoner.'

'Nay,' sayde sir Ector, 'that woll I never promyse the but that I woll do myne advauntage.'

'That me repentis,' seyde sir Tᵣarᵣquyn. Than he gan unarme hym and bete hym with thornys all naked, and sytthyn put hym downe into a depe dongeon, and there he knewe many of his felowys.   5

But whan sir Ector saw sir Lyonell, than made he grete sorow.

'Alas, brother!' seyde sir Ector, 'how may this be, and where is my brothir sir Launcelot?'

'Fayre brother, I leffte hym on slepe, whan that I frome hym yode, undir an appil-tre, and what is becom of hym I can nat telle you.'   10

'Alas,' seyde the presoneres, 'but yf sir Launcelot helpe us we shall never be delyverde, for we know now no knyght that is able to macch with oure maystir Tarquyne.'

Now leve we thes knyghtes presoners, and speke we of sir Launce-   (3)
lot de Lake that lyeth undir the appil-tre slepyng. Aboute the none so   15
there com by hym four queenys of a grete astate; and for the hete sholde nat nyghe hem, there rode four knyghtes aboute hem and bare a cloth of grene sylke on four sperys betwyxte hem and the sonne. And the quenys rode on four whyghte mulys.

Thus as they rode they herde a grete horse besyde them grymly   20
nyghe. Than they loked and were ware of a slepynge knyght lay all armed undir an appil-tre. And anone as they loked on his face they knew well hit was sir Launcelot, and began to stryve for that knyght, and every of hem seyde they wolde have hym to hir love.

'We shall nat stryve,' seyde Morgan le Fay, that was kyng Arthurs   25
sister. 'I shall put an inchauntement uppon hym that he shall nat awake of all this seven owres, and than I woll lede hym away unto my castell. And whan he is surely within my holde, I shall take the inchauntement frome hym, and than lette hym chose whych of us he woll have unto peramour.'   30

So this enchauntemente was caste uppon sir Launcelot, and than they leyde hym uppon his shylde and bare hym so on horsebak betwyxte two knyghtes, and brought hym unto the Castell Charyot; and there they leyde hym in a chambir colde, and at nyght they sente unto hym a fayre dameselle with his souper redy idyght. Be that the enchauntement   35
was paste.

And whan she com she salewed hym and asked hym what chere.

'I can not sey, fayre damesel,' seyde sir Launcelot, 'for I wote not how I com into this castell but hit be by inchauntemente.'

'Sir,' seyde she, 'ye muste make good chere; and yf ye be suche a   40
knyght as is seyde ye be, I shall telle you more to-morn be pryme of the day.'

'Gramercy, fayre damesel,' seyde sir Launcelot, 'of your good wylle.'

And so she departed, and there he laye all that nyght withoute any comforte. And on the morne erly com thes four quenys passyngly well besene, and all they byddynge hym good morne, and he them agayne.

'Sir knyght,' the four quenys seyde, 'thou muste undirstonde thou art oure presonere, and we know the well that thou art sir Launcelot du
5 Lake, kynge Banis sonne. And because that we undirstonde youre worthynesse, that thou art the noblest knyght lyvyng, and also we know well there can no lady have thy love but one, and that is quene Gwenyvere, and now thou shalt hir love lose for ever, and she thyne. For hit behovyth the now to chose one of us four, for I am quene Morgan le *Wale*
10 Fay, quene of the londe of Gore, and here is the quene of North Galys, and the quene of Estlonde, and the quene of the Oute Iles. Now chose one of us, whyche that thou wolte have to thy peramour, other ellys to dye in this preson.'

'This is an harde case,' seyde sir Launcelot, 'that other I muste dye
15 other to chose one of you. Yet had I lever dye in this preson with worshyp than to have one of you to my peramoure, magré myne hede. And therefore ye be answeryd: I woll none of you, for ye be false enchaunters. And as for my lady, dame Gwenyvere, were I at my lyberté as I was, I wolde prove hit on youres that she is the treweste lady unto
20 hir lorde lyvynge.'

'Well,' seyde the quenys, 'ys this your answere, that ye woll refuse us?'

'Ye, on my lyff,' seyde sir Launcelot, 'refused ye bene of me.' *Lath*

So they departed and leffte hym there alone that made grete sorow.
(4) 25 So aftir that noone com the damesel unto hym with his dyner and asked hym what chere.

'Truly, damesel,' seyde sir Launcelot, 'never so ylle.'

'Sir,' she seyde, 'that me repentis, but and ye woll be ruled by me I shall helpe you oute of this dystresse, and ye shall have no shame nor
30 velony, so that ye wol⟨d⟩ [hold] my promyse.'

'Fayre damesel, I graunte you; but sore I am of thes quenys crauftis aferde, for they have destroyed many a good knyght.'

'Sir,' seyde she, 'that is soth, and for the renowne and bounté, that they here of you they woll have your love. And, sir, they sey youre
35 name is sir Launcelot du Lake, the floure of knyghtes, and they be passyng wroth with you that ye have refused hem. But, sir, and ye wolde promyse me to helpe my fadir on Tewysday next commynge, that hath made a turnemente betwyxt hym and the kynge of North Galys—for the laste Tewysday past my fadir loste the felde thorow
40 three knyghtes of Arthurs courte—and yf ye woll be there on Tewysday next commynge and helpe my fadir, and to-morne be pryme by the grace of God I shall delyver you clene.'

'Now, fayre damesell,' seyde sir Launcelot, 'telle me your fadyrs name, and than shall I gyff you an answere.'

'Sir knyght,' she seyde, 'my fadyrs name is kynge Bagdemagus, that was foule rebuked at the laste turnemente.'

'I knowe your fadir well,' seyde sir Launcelot, 'for a noble kyng and a good knyght, and by the fayth of my body, your fadir shall have my seyrvse, and you bothe at that [day].'   5

'Sir,' she seyde, 'gramercy, and to-morne loke ye be redy betymys, and I shall delyver you and take you your armoure, your horse, shelde and spere. And hereby wythin this ten myle is an abbey of whyght monkys, and there I pray you to abyde me, and thydir shall I brynge my fadir unto you.'   10

'And all this shall be done,' seyde sir Launcelot, 'as I am trew knyght.'

And so she departed and come on the morne erly and founde hym redy. Than she brought hym oute of twelve lockys, and toke hym his armour and his owne horse; and lyghtly he sadyld hym and toke his   15
spere in his honde, and so rode forth, and sayde,

'Damesell, I shall nat fayle, by the grace of God.'

And so he rode into a grete foreste all that day, and never coude fynde no hygheway. And so the nyght fell on hym, and than was he ware in a slade of a pavylyon of rede sendele. 'Be my feyth,' seyde sir   20
Launcelot, 'in that pavylyon woll I lodge all this nyght.' And so he there alyght downe, and tyed his horse to the pavylyon, and there he unarmed hym. And there he founde a bed, and layde hym therein, and felle on slepe sadly.

Than within an owre there com that knyght that ought the pavylyon. 25 (5)
He wente that his lemman had layne in that bed, and so he leyde hym adowne by sir Launcelot and toke hym in his armys and began to kysse hym. And whan sir Launcelot felte a rough berde kyssyng hym he sterte oute of the bedde lyghtly, and the othir knyght after hym. And eythir of hem gate their swerdys in their hondis, and oute at the   30
pavylyon dore wente the knyght of the pavylyon, and sir Launcelot folowed hym. And there by a lytyll slad sir Launcelot wounded hym sore nyghe unto the deth. And than he yelded hym to sir Launcelot, and so he graunted hym, so that he wolde telle hym why he com into the bed.   35

'Sir,' sayde the knyghte, 'the pavylyon is myne owne. And as this nyght I had assigned my lady to have slepte with hir, and now I am lykly to dye of this wounde.'

'That me repentyth,' seyde sir Launcelot, 'of youre hurte, but I was adrad of treson, for I was late begyled. And therefore com on your way 40
into youre pavylyon, and take youre reste, and as I suppose I shall staunche your bloode.'

And so they wente bothe into the pavylyon, and anone sir Launcelot staunched his bloode. Therewithall com the knyghtes lady that was a passynge fayre lady. And whan [she] aspyed that her lorde Belleus was sore wounded she cryed oute on sir Launcelot and made grete dole oute of mesure.

'Pease, my lady and my love,' seyde sir Belleus, 'for this knyght is a
5 good man and a knyght of aventures.' And there he tolde hir all the case how he was wounded. 'And whan that I yelded me unto hym he laffte me goodly, and hath staunched my bloode.'

'Sir,' seyde the lady, 'I require the, telle me what knyght thou art, and what is youre name.'

10 'Fayre lady,' he sayde, 'my name is sir Launcelot du Lake.'

'So me thought ever be youre speche,' seyde the lady, 'for I have sene you oftyn or this, and I know you bettir than ye wene. But now wolde ye promyse me of youre curtesye, for the harmys that ye have done to me and to my lorde, sir Belleus, that whan ye com unto kyng Arthurs
15 courte for to cause hym to be made knyght of the Rounde Table? For he is a passyng good man of armys and a myghty lorde of londys of many oute iles.'

'Fayre lady,' sayde sir Launcelot, 'latte hym com unto the courte the next hyghe feste, and loke ye com with hym, and I shall do my power;
20 and he preve hym doughty of his hondis he shall have his desyre.'

So within a whyle the nyght passed and the day shone. Than sir Launcelot armed hym and toke his horse, and so he was taughte to the abbey.

(6) And as sone as he come thydir the doughter of kyng Bagdemagus
25 herde a grete horse trotte on the pa[vy]mente, and she than arose and yode to [a] wyndowe, and there she sawe sir Launcelot. And anone she made men faste to take his horse frome hym, and lette lede hym into a stable; and hymself [was ledde] unto a chambir and unarmed hym. And this lady sente hym a longe gowne, and com hirself and made hym
30 good chere; and she seyde he was the knyght in the worlde that was moste welcom unto hir.

Than in all haste she sente for hir fadir Bagdemagus that was within twelve myle of that abbey, and afore evyn he come with a fayre fely-shyp of knyghtes with hym. And whan the kynge was alyght of his
35 horse he yode streyte unto sir Launcelotte his chambir, and there he founde his doughtir. And than the kynge toke hym in his armys and eythir made other good chere.

Than sir Launce lotmade his complaynte unto the kynge, how he was betrayed; and how he was brother unto sir Lyonell, whyche was de-
40 parted frome hym he wyste not where, and how his doughter had delyverde hym oute of preson. 'Therefore, whyle that I lyve, I shall do hir servyse and all hir kynrede.'

'Than am I sure of your helpe,' seyde the kyng, 'on Tewysday next commyng?'

'Yee, sir,' seyde sir Launcelot, 'I shall nat fayle you, for so have I promysed my lady youre doughter. But, sir, what knyghtes be tho of my lorde kyng Arthurs that were with the kyng of North Galys?'

'Sir, hit was sir Madore de la Porte and sir Mordred and sir Gahalantyne that all forfared my knyghtes, for agaynste hem three I nother 5 none of myne myght bere no strengthe.'

'Sir,' seyde sir Launcelot, 'as I here sey that the turnement shall be here within this three myle of this abbay. But, sir, ye shall sende unto me three knyghtes of youres suche as ye truste, and loke that the three knyghtes have all whyght sheldis and no picture on their shyldis, and 10 ye shall sende me another of the same sewte; and we four wyll oute of a lytyll wood in myddys of bothe partyes com, and we shall falle on the frunte of oure enemys and greve hem that we may. And thus shall I not be knowyn what maner a knyght I am.'

So they toke their reste that nyght. And this was on the Sonday, and 15 so the kynge departed and sente unto sir Launcelot three knyghtes with four whyght shyldys. And on the Tewysday they lodged hem in a lytyll leved wood besyde thereas the turnemente sholde be. And there were scaffoldys and ⌜holes⌝, that lordys and ladyes myght beholde and gyff the pryse.   20

Than com into the fylde the kynge of North Galys with nyne score helmys, and than the three knyghtis of kyng Arthurs stood by themself. Than com into the felde kynge Bagdemagus with four score helmys; and than they featured their sperys and come togydyrs with a grete daysshe. And there was slayne of knyghtes at the fyrste recountir 25 twelve knyghtes of kynge Bagdemagus parté, and syx of the kynge of North Galys syde and party; and kynge Bagdemagus his party were ferre sette asyde and bak.

Wyth that com in sir Launcelot, and he threste in with his spere in (7) the thyckyst of the pres; and there he smote downe with one spere fyve 30 knyghtes, and of four of them he brake their backys. And in that thrange he smote downe the kynge of North Galys, and brake his thygh in that falle. All this doynge of sir Launcelot saw the three knyghtes of Arthurs, and seyde, 'Yondir is a shrewde geste, therefore have here ons at hym.' So they encountred, and sir Launcelot bare hym downe horse and man 35 so that his sholdir wente oute of joynte.

'Now hit befallyth me,' seyde sir Mordred, 'to stirre me, for sir Mador hath a sore falle.' And than sir Launcelot was ware of hym, and gate a spere in his honde and mette with hym. And sir Mordred brake his spere uppon hym; and sir Launcelot gaff hym suche a buffette that the 40 arson of the sadill brake, and so he drove over the horse tayle, that his helme smote into the erthe a foote and more, that nyghe his nek was broke, and there he lay longe in a swowe.

Than com in sir Gahalantyne with a grete spere, and sir Launcelot

agaynste hym in all that they myght dryve, that bothe hir sperys to-
braste evyn to their hondys; and than they flange oute with her swerdes
and gaff many sore strokys. Than was sir Launcelot wroth oute of
mesure, and than he smote sir Gahalantyne on the helme, that his nose,
5 erys and mowthe braste oute on bloode; and therewith his hede hynge
low, and with that his horse ran away with hym, and he felle downe to
the erthe.

Anone therewithall sir Launcelot gate a speare in his honde, and or
ever that speare brake he bare downe to the erthe syxtene knyghtes, som
10 horse and man and som the man and nat the horse; and there was none
that he hitte surely but that he bare none armys that day. And than he
gate a spere and smote downe twelve knyghtes, and the moste party of
hem never throoff aftir. And than the knyghtes of the kyng of North
Galys party wolde jouste no more, and there the gre was gevyn to
15 kyng Bagdemagus.

So eythir party departed unto his owne, and sir Launcelot rode forth
with kynge Bagdemagus unto his castel. And there he had passynge
good chere bothe with the kyng and with his doughter, and they profyrde hym grete yefftes. And on the morne he toke his leve and tolde
20 the kynge that he wolde seke his brothir sir Lyonell that wente frome
hym whan he slepte. So he toke his horse and betaughte hem all to God,
and there he seyde unto the kynges doughter,

'Yf that ye have nede ony tyme of my servyse, I pray you let me
have knowlecche, and I shall nat fayle you, as I am trewe knyght.'

25 And so sir Launcelot departed, and by adventure he com into the
same foreste there he was takynge his slepe before; and in the myddys
of an hygheway he mette a damesel rydynge on a whyght palfray, and
there eythir salewed other.

'Fayre damesel,' seyde sir Launcelot, 'know y[e] in this contrey ony
30 adventures nere hande?'

'Sir knyght,' seyde the damesel, 'here ar adventures nyghe, and thou
durste preve hem.'

'Why sholde I not preve?' seyde sir Launcelot. 'For for that cause
com I hydir.'

35 'Welle,' seyde she, 'thou semyst well to be a good knyght, and yf
thou dare mete with a good knyght I shall brynge the where is the
beste knyght and the myghtyeste that ever thou founde, so thou wolte
telle me thy name and what knyght thou art.'

'Damesell, as for to telle you my name, I take no grete force. Truly,
40 my name is sir Launcelotte du Lake.'

'Sir, thou besemys well; here is adventures fast by that fallyth for the.
For hereby dwellyth a knyght that woll nat be overmacched for no man
I know but ye do overmacche hym. And his name is sir Tarquyn. And,
as I undirstonde, he hath in his preson of Arthurs courte good knyghtes

three score and four that he hath wonne with his owne hondys. But whan ye have done that journey, ye shall promyse me, as ye ar a trew knyght, for to go and helpe me and other damesels that ar dystressed dayly with a false knyght.'

'All youre entente, damesell, and desyre I woll fulfylle, so ye woll 5 brynge me unto this knyght.'

'Now, fayre knyght, com on youre way.'

And so she brought hym unto the fourde and the tre where hynge the basyn. So sir Launcelot lette his horse drynke, and sytthen he bete on the basyn with the butte of his spere tylle the bottum felle oute. And 10 longe dud he so, but he sye no man. Than he rode endlonge the gatys of that maner nyghe halfe an howre.

And than was he ware of a grete knyght that droffe an horse afore hym, and overthwarte the horse lay an armed knyght bounden. And ever as they com nere and nere sir Launcelot thought he sholde know 15 hym. Than was he ware that hit was sir Gaherys, Gawaynes brothir, a knyght of the Table Rounde.

'Now, fayre damesell,' seyde sir Launcelot, 'I se yondir a knyght faste ibounden that is a felow of myne, and brother he is unto sir Gawayne. And at the fyrste begynnynge I promyse you, by the leve of 20 God, for to rescowe that knyght. But yf his maystir sytte the bettir in his sadyl, I shall delyver all the presoners that he hath oute of daungere, for I am sure he hath two brethrene of myne presoners with hym.'

But by that tyme that eythir had sene other they gryped theyre sperys unto them. 25

'Now, fayre knyght,' seyde sir Launcelot, 'put that wounded knyghte of that horse and lette hym reste a whyle, and lette us too preve oure strengthis. For, as hit is enfourmed me, thou doyste and haste done me grete despyte, and shame unto knyghtes of the Rounde Table. And therefore now defende the !' 30

'And thou be of [the] Rounde Table,' seyde Terquyn, 'I de[fy] the and all thy felyshyp!'

'That is overmuche seyde,' sir Launcelot seyde, 'of the at thys tyme.'

And than they put there sperys in their restys and come togedyrs 35 (8) with hir horsis as faste as they myght ren; and aythir smote other in myddys of their shyldis, that both their horsys backys braste undir them, and the knyghtes were bothe astoned. And as sone as they myght they avoyded their horsys and toke their shyldys before them and drew oute their swerdys and com togydir egirly; and eyther gaff other many 40 stronge strokys, for there myght nothir shyldis nother harneyse holde their strokes.

And so within a whyle they had bothe many grymme woundys and bledde passyng grevously. Thus they fared two owres and more, trasyng and rasyng eyther othir where they myght hitte ony bare place. Than at the laste they were brethles bothe, and stode lenyng on her swerdys.

'Now, felow,' seyde sir Terquyne, 'holde thy honde a whyle, and
5 telle me that I shall aske of the.'

'Sey on,' seyde sir Launcelot.

Than sir Terquyn seyde, 'Thou art the byggyst man that ever I mette withall, and the beste-brethed, and as lyke one knyght that I hate abovyn all other knyghtes. So be hit that thou be not he, I woll lyghtly
10 acorde with the, and for thy love I woll delyver all the presoners that I have, that is three score and four, so thou wolde telle me thy name. And thou and I woll be felowys togedyrs and never to fayle the whyle that I lyve.'

'Ye sey well,' seyde sir Launcelot, 'but sytthyn hit is so that I have
15 thy frendeshyppe and may have, what knyght is that that thou hatyste abovyn all thynge?'

'Feythfully,' seyde sir Terquyn, 'his name is sir Launcelot de Lake, for he slowe my brothir sir Carados at the Dolerous Towre, that was one of the beste knyghtes on lyve; and therefore hym I excepte of alle
20 knyghtes, for may I hym onys mete, the tone shall make an ende, I make myne avow. And for sir Launcelottis sake I have slayne an hondred good knyghtes, and as many I have maymed all uttirly, that they myght never aftir helpe themself, and many have dyed in preson. And yette have I three score and four, and all [shal] be delyverde, so
25 thou wolte telle me thy name, so be hit that thou be nat sir Launcelot.'

'Now se I well,' seyde sir Launcelot, 'that suche a man I myght be, I myght have pease; and suche a man I myght[e be] that there sholde be mortall warre betwyxte us. And now, sir knyght, at thy requeste I woll that thou wete and know that I am sir Launcelot du Lake, kynge Bannys
30 son of Benwyke, and verry knyght of the Table Rounde. And now I defyghe the, and do thy beste!'

'A!' seyde sir Tarquyne, 'thou arte to me moste welcom of ony knyght, for we shall never departe tylle the tone of us be dede.'

Than they hurteled togedyrs as two wylde bullys, russhynge and
35 laysshyng with hir shyldis and swerdys, that somtyme they felle bothe on their nosys. Thus they foughte stylle two owres and more and never wolde have reste, and sir Tarquyne gaff sir Launcelot many woundys, that all the grounde thereas they faughte was all besparcled with bloode.

(9)   Than at the laste sir Terquyne wexed faynte and gaff somwhatt
40 abakke, and bare his shylde low for wery. That aspyed sir Launcelot, and lepte uppon hym fersly and gate hym by the bavoure of hys hel-mette and plucked hym downe on his kneis, and anone he raced of his helme and smote his necke in sundir. And whan sir Launcelot had done this he yode unto the damesell and seyde,

'Damesell, I am redy to go with you where ye woll have me, but I
have no horse.'

'Fayre, sir,' seyde this wounded knyght, 'take my horse, and than
lette me go into this maner and delyver all thes presoners.' So he toke
sir Gaheris horse and prayde hym nat to be greved.   5

'Nay, fayre lorde, I woll that ye have hym at your commaundemente,
for ye have bothe saved me and my horse. And this day I sey ye ar the
beste knyght in the worlde, for ye have slayne this day in my syght the
myghtyeste man and the beste knyght excepte you that ever I sawe.
But, fayre sir,' seyde sir Gaherys, 'I pray you telle me your name.'   10

'Sir, my name is sir Launcelot du Lake that ought to helpe you of
ryght for kynge Arthurs sake, and in especiall for my lorde sir Gawayne
his sake, youre owne brother. And whan that ye com within yondir
maner, I am sure ye shall fynde there many knyghtes of the Rounde
Table; for I have sene many of their shyldys that I know hongys on   15
yondir tre. There is sir Kayes shylde, ⌐and sir Brandeles shylde⌐, and
sir Galyhuddys shylde, and sir Bryan de Lystenoyse his shylde, and sir
Alydukis shylde, with many mo that I am nat now avysed of, and
sir Marhaus, and also my too brethirne shyldis, sir Ector de Marys and sir
Lyonell. Wherefore I pray you grete them all frome me and sey that I   20
bydde them to take suche stuff there as they fynde, that in ony wyse my
too brethirne go unto the courte and abyde me there tylle that I com,
for by the feste of Pentecoste I caste me to be there; for as at thys tyme
I muste ryde with this damesel for to save my promyse.'

And so they departed frome Gaherys; and Gaherys yode into the   25
maner, and there he founde a yoman porter kepyng many keyes. Than
sir Gaherys threw the porter unto the grounde and toke the keyes
frome hym; and hastely he opynde the preson dore, and there he lette
all the presoners oute, and every man lowsed other of their bondys. And
whan they sawe sir Gaherys, all they thanked hym, for they wente that   30
he had slayne sir Terquyne because that he was wounded.

'Not so, syrs,' seyde sir Gaherys, 'hit was sir Launcelot that slew hym
worshypfully with his owne hondys, and he gretys you all well and
prayeth you to haste you to the courte. And as unto you, sir Lyonell and
sir Ector de Marys, he prayeth you to abyde hym at the courte of kynge   35
Arthure.'

'That shall we nat do,' seyde his brethernc. 'We woll fynde hym and
we may lyve.'

'So shall I,' scyde sir Kay, 'fynde hym or I com to the courte, as I am
trew knyght.'   40

Than they sought the house thereas the armour was, and than they
armed them; and every knyght founde hys owne horse and all that
longed unto hym. So forthwith there com a foster with four horsys lade
with fatte venyson. And anone sir Kay seyde, 'Here is good mete for us

for one meale, for we had not many a day no good repaste.' And so that venyson was rosted, sodde, and bakyn; and so aftir souper som abode there all nyght. But sir Lyonell and sir Ector de Marys and sir Kay rode aftir sir Launcelot to fynde hym yf they myght.

(10) 5   Now turne we to sir Launcelot that rode with the damesel in a fayre hygheway.

'Sir,' seyde the damesell, 'here by this way hauntys a knyght that dystressis all ladyes and jantylwomen, and at the leste he robbyth them other lyeth by hem.'

10   'What?' seyde sir Launcelot, 'is he a theff and a knyght? And a ravyssher of women? He doth shame unto the Order of Knyghthode, and contrary unto his oth. Hit is pyté that he lyvyth! But, fayre damesel, ye shall ryde on before youreself, and I woll kepe myself in coverte; and yf that he trowble yow other dystresse you I shall be your rescowe

15 and lerne hym to be ruled as a knyght.'

So thys mayde rode on by the way a souffte amblynge pace, and within a whyle com oute a knyght on horseba[k] owte of the woode and his page with hym. And there he put the damesell frome hir horse, and than she cryed. With that com sir Launcelot as faste as he myght

20 tyll he com to the knyght, sayng,

'A, false knyght and traytoure unto knyghthode, who dud lerne the to distresse ladyes, damesels and jantyllwomen!'

Whan the knyght sy sir Launcelot thus rebukynge hym he answerde nat, but drew his swerde and rode unto sir Launcelot. And sir Launce-

25 lot threw his spere frome hym and drew his swerde, and strake hym suche a buffette on the helmette that he claffe his hede and necke unto the throte.

'Now haste thou thy paymente that longe thou haste deserved!'

'That is trouth,' seyde the damesell, 'for lyke as Terquyn wacched to

30 dystresse good knyghtes, so dud this knyght attende to destroy and dystresse ladyes, damesels and jantyllwomen; and his name was sir Perys de Foreste Savage.'

'Now, damesell,' seyde sir Launcelot 'woll ye ony more servyse of me?'

'Nay, sir,' she seyde, 'at thys tyme, but Allmyghty Jesu preserve you

35 wheresomever ye ryde or goo, for the curteyst knyght thou arte, and mekyste unto all ladyes and jantylwomen that now lyvyth. But one thyng, sir knyght, methynkes ye lak, ye that ar a knyght wyveles, that ye woll nat love som mayden other jantylwoman. For I cowde never here sey that ever ye loved ony of no maner of degré, and that is grete

40 pyté. But hit is noysed that ye love quene Gwenyvere, and that she hath ordeyned by enchauntemente that ye shall never love none other but hir, nother none other damesell ne lady shall rejoyce you; where[fore] there be many in this londe, of hyghe astate and lowe, that make grete sorow.'

'Fayre damesell,' seyde sir Launcelot, 'I may nat warne peple to speke
of me what hit pleasyth hem. But for to be a weddyd man, I thynke hit
nat, for than I muste couche with hir and leve armys and turnamentis,
batellys and adventures. And as for to sey to take my pleasaunce with
peramours, that woll I refuse: in prencipall for drede of God, for 5
knyghtes that bene adventures sholde nat be advoutrers nothir lecherous, for than they be nat happy nother fortunate unto the werrys;
for other they shall be overcom with a sympler knyght than they be
hemself, other ellys they shall sle by unhappe and hir cursednesse bettir
men than they be hemself. And so who that usyth peramours shall be 10
unhappy, and all thynge unhappy that is aboute them.'

And so sir Launcelot and she departed. And than he rode in a depe
foreste two dayes and more, and hadde strayte lodgynge. So on the
thirde day he rode on a longe brydge, and there sterte uppon hym
suddeynly a passyng foule carle. And he smote his horse on the nose, 15
that he turned aboute, and asked hym why he rode over that brydge
withoute lycence.

'Why sholde I nat ryde this way?' seyde sir Launcelotte, 'I may not
ryde besyde.'

'Thou shalt not chose,' seyde the carle, and laysshed at hym with a 20
grete club shodde with iron.

Than sir Launcelot drew his swerde and put the stroke abacke, and
clave his hede unto the pappys.

And at the ende of the brydge was a fayre vyllage, and all peple, men
and women, cryed on sir Launcelot and sayde, 'Sir knyght, a worse dede 25
duddyst thou never for thyself, for thou haste slayne the chyeff porter
of oure castell.' Sir Launcelot lete hem sey what they wolde, and streyte
he rode into the castelle.

And whan he come into the castell he alyght and tyed his horse to a
rynge on the walle. And there he sawe a fayre grene courte, and thydir 30
he dressid hym, for there hym thought was a fayre place to feyght in. So
he loked aboute hym and sye muche peple in dorys and in wyndowys
that sayde, 'Fayre knyghte, thou arte unhappy to com here!'

Anone withall there com uppon hym two grete gyauntis well armed (11)
all save there hedy[s], with two horryble clubbys in their hondys. Sir 35
Launcelot put his shylde before hym and put the stroke away of that
one gyaunte, and with hys swerde he clave his hede in sundir. Whan his
felowe sawe that, he ran away as he were woode, and sir Launcelot aftir
hym with all his myght, and smote hym on the shuldir and clave hym
to the navyll.   40

Than sir Launcelot wente into the halle, and there com afore hym
three score of ladyes and damesels, and all kneled unto hym and
thanked God and hym of his delyveraunce.

'For,' they seyde, 'the moste party of us have bene here this seven yere [theire] presoners, and we have worched all maner of sylke workys for oure mete, and we ar all grete jentylwomen borne. And blyssed be the tyme, knyght, that ever thou were borne, for thou haste done the moste worshyp that ever ded knyght in this worlde; that woll we beare

5 recorde. And we all pray you to telle us your name, that we may telle oure frendis who delyverde us oute of preson.'

'Fayre damesellys,' he seyde, 'my name is sir Launcelot du Laake.'

'A, sir,' seyde they all, 'well mayste thou be he, for ellys save yourself, as we demed, there myght never knyght have the bettir of thes two

10 jyauntis; for many fayre knyghtes have assayed, and here have ended. And many tymes have we here wysshed aftir you, and thes two gyauntes dredde never knyght but you.'

'Now may ye sey,' seyde sir Launcelot, 'unto your frendys, and grete them all fro me; and yf that I com in ony of your marchys, shew me

15 such chere as ye have cause. And what tresoure that there is in this castel I yeff hit you for a rewarde for your grevaunces. And the lorde that is ownere of this castel, I wolde he ressayved hit as is his ryght.'

'Fayre sir,' they seyde, 'the name of this castell is called Tyntagyll, and a deuke ought hit somtyme that had wedded fayre Igrayne, and so

20 aftir that she was wedded to Uther Pendragon, and he gate on hir Arthure.'

'Well,' seyde sir Launcelot, 'I undirstonde to whom this castel longith.'

And so he departed frome them and betaught hem unto God, and

25 than he mounted uppon his horse and rode into many strange contreyes and thorow many watyrs and valeyes, and evyll was he lodged. And at the laste by fortune hym happynd ayenste nyght to com to a fayre courtelage, and therein he founde an olde jantylwoman that lodged hym with goode wyll; and there he had good chere for hym and his

30 horse. And whan tyme was his oste brought hym into a garret over the gate to his bedde. There sir Launcelot unarmed hym and set his harneyse by hym and wente to bedde, and anone he felle on slepe.

So aftir there com one on horsebak and knokked at the gate in grete haste. Whan sir Launcelot herde this he arose up and loked oute at the

35 wyndowe, and sygh by the moonelyght three knyghtes com rydyng aftir that one man, and all three laysshynge on hym at onys with swerdys; and that one knyght turned on hem knyghtly agayne and defended hym.

'Truly,' seyde sir Launcelot, 'yondir one knyght shall I helpe, for

40 hit were shame for me to se three knyghtes on one, and yf [he] be there slayne I am partener of his deth.'

And therewith he toke his harneys and wente oute at a wyndowe by a shete downe to the four knyghtes. And than sir Launcelot seyde on hyght,

'Turne you, knyghtis, unto me, and leve this feyghtyng with that
knyght!'

And than they three leffte sir Kay and turned unto sir Launcelot, and
assayled hym on every honde. Than sir Kay dressid hym to have holpen
sir Launcelot.

'Nay, sir,' sayde he, 'I woll none of your helpe. Therefore, as ye woll
have my helpe, lette me alone with hem.'

Sir Kay for the plesure of that knyght suffyrd hym for to do his
wylle and so stoode on syde. Than anone within seven strokys sir
Launcelot had strykyn hem to the erthe. And than they all three
cryed,

'Sir knyght, we yelde us unto you as a man of myght makeles.'

'As to that, I woll nat take youre yeldyng unto me, but so that ye woll
yelde you unto thys knyght; and on that covenaunte I woll save youre
lyvys, and ellys nat.'

'Fayre knyght, that were us loth, for as for that knyght, we chaced
hym hydir, and had overcom hym, had nat ye bene. Therefore to yelde
us unto hym hit were no reson.'

'Well, as to that, avyse you well, for ye may chose whether ye woll
dye other lyve. For and ye be yolden hit shall be unto sir Kay.'

'Now, fayre knyght,' they seyde, 'in savyng of oure lyvys, we woll
do as thou commaundys us.'

'Than shall ye,' seyde sir Launcelot, 'on Whytsonday nexte commynge go unto the courte of kynge Arthure, and there shall ye yelde
you unto quene Gwenyvere and putte you all three in hir grace and
mercy, and say that sir Kay sente you thydir to be her presoners.'

'Sir,' they seyde, 'hit shall be done, by the feyth of oure bodyes, and
we be men lyvyng.'

And there they sware every knyght uppon his swerde, and so sir
Launcelot suffyrd hem to departe. And than sir Launcelot cnocked at
the gate with the pomell of his swerde; and with that come his oste, and
in they entyrd, he and sir Kay.

'Sir,' seyde his oste, 'I wente ye had bene in your bed.'

'So I was, but I arose and lepe oute at my wyndow for to helpe an
olde felowe of myne.'

So whan they come nye the lyght sir Kay knew well hit was sir
Launcelot, and therewith he kneled downe and thanked hym of all his
kyndenesse, that he had holpyn hym twyse frome the deth.

'Sir,' he seyde, 'I have nothyng done but that me ought for to do.
And ye ar welcom, and here shall ye repose you and take your reste.'

Whan sir Kay was unarmed he asked aftir mete. Anone there was
mete fette for hym and he ete strongly. And whan he had sowped they
wente to their beddys and were lodged togydyrs in one bed.

So on the morne sir Launcelot arose erly and leffte sir Kay slepyng.

And sir Launcelot toke sir Kayes armoure and his shylde and armed hym; and so he wente to the stable and sadylde his horse, and toke his leve of his oste and departed. Than sone aftir arose sir Kay and myssid sir Launcelot, and than he aspyed that he had his armoure and his
5 horse.

'Now, be my fayth, I know welle that he woll greve som of the courte of kyng Arthure, for on hym knyghtes woll be bolde and deme that hit is I, and that woll begyle them. And bycause of his armoure and shylde I am sure I shall ryde in pease.'

10 And than sone sir Kay departed and thanked his oste.
(12) Now turne we unto sir Launcelot that had ryddyn longe in a grete foreste. And at the laste he com unto a low contrey full of fayre ryvers, and fayre meedys; and before hym he sawe a longe brydge, and three pavylyons stood thereon, of sylke and sendell of dyverse hew. And
15 withoute the pavylyons hynge three whyght shyldys on trouncheouns of sperys, and grete longe sperys stood upryght by the pavylyons, and at every pavylyon dore stoode three freysh knyghtes.

And so sir Launcelot passed by hem and spake no worde. But whan he was paste the three knyghtes knew hym and seyde hit was the proude
20 sir Kay:

'He wenyth no knyght so good as he, and the contrary is oftyn proved. Be my fayth,' seyde one of the knyghtes, his name was sir Gawtere, 'I woll ryde aftir hym and assay hym for all his pryde; and ye may beholde how that I spede.'

25 So sir Gawtere armed hym and hynge his shylde uppon his sholdir, and mounted uppon a grete horse, and gate his speare in his honde, and wallopte aftir sir Launcelot. And whan he come nyghe hym he cryed, 'Abyde, thou proude knyght, sir Kay! for thou shalt nat passe all quyte.' So sir Launcelot turned hym, and eythir feautyrd their
30 sperys and com togedyrs with all their myghtes. And sir Gawters speare brake, but sir Launcelot smote hym downe horse and man.

And whan he was at the erthe his brethyrn seyde,

'Yondir knyght is nat sir Kay, for he is far bygger than he.'

'I dare ley my hede,' seyde sir Gylmere, 'yondir knyght hath slayne
35 sir Kay and hath takyn hys horse and harneyse.'

'Whether hit be so other no,' seyde sir Raynolde, 'lette us mounte on oure horsys and rescow oure brothir, sir Gawtere. For payne of deth, we all shall have worke inow to macche that knyght; for ever mese-myth by his persone hit is sir Launcelot other sir Trystrams other sir
40 Pelleas, the good knyght.

Than anone they toke their horsys and overtoke sir Launcelot. And sir Gylmere put forth his speare and ran to sir Launcelot, and sir Launcelot smote hym downe, that he lay in a sowghe.

'Sir knyght,' seyde sir Raynolde, 'thou arte a stronge man, and as I

suppose thou haste slayne my two bretherne, for the whyche rysyth
my herte sore agaynste the. And yf I myght wyth my worshyppe I
wolde not have ado with the, but nedys I muste take suche parte as they
do. And therefore, knyght, kepe thyselfe!'

And so they hurtylde togydyrs with all their myghtes and all to-she- 5
vird bothe there spearys, and than they drew hir swerdys and laysshed
togydir egirly. Anone there[with]all arose sir Gawtere and come unto
his brother sir Gyllymere, and bade hym aryse, 'and helpe we oure
brothir, sir Raynolde, that yondir merveylously macchyth yondir good
knyght.' Therewithall they hurteled unto sir Launcelot. And whan he 10
sawe them com he smote a sore stroke unto sir Raynolde, that he felle
of his horse to the grounde, and than he caste to the othir two bretherne,
and at two strokys he strake hem downe to the erthe. Wyth that sir
Raynolde gan up sterte with his hede all blody and com streyte unto
sir Launcelot.   15

'Now let be,' seyde sir Launcelot, 'I was not far frome the whan thou
were made knyght, sir Raynolde, and also I know thou arte a good
knyght, and lothe I were to sle the.'

'Gramercy,' seyde sir Raynolde, 'of your goodnesse, and I dare say
as for me and my bretherne, [we] woll nat be loth to yelde us unto you, 20
with that we know youre name; for welle we know ye ar not sir Kay.'

'As for that, be as be may. For ye shal yelde you unto dame Gwenyvere, and loke that ye be there on Whytsonday and yelde you unto hir
as presoners, and sey that sir Kay sente you unto hir.' Than they swore
hit sholde be done, and [so] passed forth sir Launcelot, and ecchone of 25
the bretherne halpe other as well as they myght.

So sir Launcelotte rode into a depe foreste, and there [by] hym in a (13)
slade he sey four knyghtes hovynge undir an oke, and they were of
Arthurs courte: one was sir Sagramour le Desyrus, and sir Ector de
Marys, and sir Gawayne, and sir Uwayne. And anone as these four 30
knyghtes had aspyed sir Launcelot they wende by his armys that hit had
bene sir Kay.

'Now, be my fayth,' seyde sir Sagramoure, 'I woll preve sir Kayes
myght,' and gate his spere in his honde and com towarde sir Launcelot.

Than sir Launcelot was ware of his commyng and knew hym well, 35
and featured his speare agaynste hym and smote sir Sagramoure so sore
that horse and man wente bothe to the erthe.

'Lo, my felowys,' seyde sir Ector, 'yondir may ye se what a buffette
he hath gyffen! Methynkyth that knyght is muche bygger than ever
was sir Kay. Now shall ye se what I may do to hym.'   40

So sir Ector gate his spere in his honde and walopte towarde sir
Launcelot, and sir Launcelot smote hym evyn thorow the shylde and
his sholdir, that man and horse wente to the erthe, and ever his spere
helde.

'Be my fayth,' sayde sir Uwayne, 'yondir is a stronge knyght, and I
am sure he hath slayne Kay. And I se be his grete strengthe hit woll be
harde to macche hym.'

And therewithall sir Uwayne gate his speare and rode towarde sir
5 Launcelot. And sir Launcelot knew hym well and lette hi⟨s⟩ horse
renne on the playne and gaff hym suche a buffette that he was astooned,
and longe he wyste nat where he was.

'Now se I welle,' seyde sir Gawayne, 'I muste encountir with that
knyght,' and dressed his shylde and gate a good speare in his honde
10 and lete renne at sir Launcelot with all his myght; and eyther knyght
smote other in myddys of the shylde. But sir Gawaynes spere braste,
and sir Launcelot charged so sore uppon hym that his horse reversed
up-so-downe, and muche sorow had sir Gawayne to avoyde his horse.
And so sir Launcelot passed on a pace and smyled and seyde, 'God
15 gyff hym joy that this spere made, for there cam never a bettir in my
honde.'

Than the four knyghtes wente echone to other and comforted eche
other and seyde,

'What sey ye by this geste,' seyde sir Gawayne, 'that with one spere
20 hath felde us all four?'

'We commaunde hym to the devyll,' they seyde all, 'for he is a man
of grete myght.'

'Ye may say hit well,' seyde sir Gawayne, 'that he [is] a man of myght,
for I dare ley my hede hit is sir Launcelot: I know hym well by his
25 rydyng.'

'Latte hym go,' seyde sir Uwayne, 'for whan we com to the courte
we shall wete.'

Than had they much sorow to gete their horsis agayne.

(14)   Now leve we there and speke we of sir Launcelot that rode a grete
30 whyle in a depe foreste. And as he rode he sawe a blak brachette sekyng
in maner as hit had bene in the feaute of an hurte dere. And therewith
he rode aftir the brachette and he saw lye on the grounde a large feaute
of bloode. And than sir Launcelot rode faster, and ever the brachette
loked behynde hir, and so she wente thorow a grete marys, and ever
35 sir Launcelot folowed.

And than was he ware of an olde maner, and thydir ran the brachette
and so over a brydge. So sir Launcelot rode over that brydge that was
olde and feble, and whan he com in the myddys of a grete halle there
he seye lye dede a knyght that was a semely man, and that brachette
40 lycked his woundis. And therewithall com oute a lady wepyng and
wryngyng hir hondys, and sayde,

'Knyght, to muche sorow hast thou brought me.'

'Why sey ye so?' seyde sir Launcelot. 'I dede never this knyght no
harme, for hydir by the feaute of blood this brachet brought me. And

therefore, fayre lady, be nat dyspleased with me, for I am full sore agreved for your grevaunce.'

'Truly, sir,' she seyde, 'I trowe hit be nat ye that hath slayne my husbonde, for he that dud that dede is sore wounded and is never lykly to be hole, that shall I ensure hym.'   5

'What was youre husbondes name?' seyde sir Launcelot.

'Sir, his name was called sir Gylberd the Bastarde, one of the beste knyghtys of the worlde, and he that hath slayne hym I know nat his name.'

'Now God sende you bettir comforte,' seyde sir Launcelot.   10

And so he departed and wente into the foreste agayne, and there he mette with a damesell the whyche knew hym well. And she seyde on lowde,

'Well be ye founde, my lorde. And now I requyre you of your knyghthode helpe my brother that is sore wounded and never styntyth   15 bledyng; for this day he fought with sir Gylberte the Bastarde and slew hym in playne batayle, and there was my brother sore wounded. And there is a lady, a sorseres, that dwellyth in a castel here bysyde, and this day she tolde me my brothers woundys sholde never be hole tyll I coude fynde a knyght wolde go into the Chapel Perelus, and there he sholde   20 fynde a swerde and a blody cloth that the woundid knyght was lapped in; and a pece of that cloth and that swerde sholde hele my brother, with that his woundis were serched with the swerde and the cloth.'

'This is a mervelouse thyng,' seyde sir Launcelot, 'but what is your brothirs name?'   *lady.*   25

'Sir,' she seyde, 'sir Melyot de Logyrs.'

'That me repentys,' seyde sir Launcelotte, 'for he is a felow of the 'Table Rounde, and to his helpe I woll do my power.'

Than she sayde, 'Sir, folow ye evyn this hygheway, and hit woll brynge you to the Chapel Perelus, and here I shall abyde tyll God sende   30 you agayne. And yf you spede nat I know no knyght lyvynge that may encheve that adventure.'

Ryght so sir Launcelot departed, and whan he com to the Chapell (15) Perelus he alyght downe and tyed his horse unto a lytyll gate. And as sone as he was within the chyrche-yerde he sawe on the frunte of the   35 chapel many fayre ryche shyldis turned up-so-downe, and many of tho shyldis sir Launcelot had sene knyghtes bere byforehande. With that he sawe by hym there stonde a thirty grete knyghtes, more by a yerde than any man that ever he had sene, and all they grenned and gnasted at sir Launcelot. And whan he sawe their countenaunce he   40 dredde hym sore, and so put his shylde before hym and toke his swerde in his honde redy unto batayle.

And they all were armed all in blak harneyse, redy with her shyldis and her swerdis redy drawyn. And as sir Launcelot wolde have gone

thorow them they skaterd on every syde of hym and gaff hym the way, and therewith he wexed bolde and entyrde into the chapel. And there he sawe no lyght but a dymme lampe brennyng, and than was he ware of a corpus hylled with a clothe of sylke. Than sir Launcelot stouped
5 doune and kutte a pese away of that cloth, and than hit fared undir hym as the grounde had quaked a lytyll; therewithall he feared.

And than he sawe a fayre swerde lye by the dede knyght, and that he gate in his honde and hyed hym oute of the chapell. Anone as ever he was in the chapell-yerde all the knyghtes spake to hym with grymly
10 voyces and seyde,

'Knyght, sir Launcelot, lay that swerde frome the or thou shalt dye!'

'Whether that I lyve other dye,' seyde sir Launcelot, 'with no wordys grete gete ye hit agayne. Therefore fyght for hit and ye lyst.'

Than ryght so he passed thorowoute them. And byyonde the
15 chapell-yarde there mette hym a fayre damesell and seyde,

'Sir Launcelot, leve that swerde behynde the, other thou wolt dye for hit.'

'I leve hit not,' seyde sir Launcelot, 'for no thretyng.'

'No,' seyde she, 'and thou dyddyste leve that swerde quene Gweny-
20 vere sholde thou never se.'

'Than were I a foole and I wolde leve this swerde.'

'Now, jantyll knyghte,' seyde the damesel, 'I requyre the to kysse me but onys.'

'Nay,' seyde sir Launcelot, 'that God me forbede.'

25 'Well, sir,' seyde she, 'and thou haddyst kyssed me thy lyff dayes had be done. And now, alas,' she seyde, 'I have loste all my laboure, for I ordeyned this chapell for thy sake and for sir Gawayne. And onys I had hym within me, and at that tyme he fought with this knyght that lyeth dede in yondir chapell, sir Gylberte the Bastarde, and at that tyme he
30 smote the lyffte honde of sir Gylberte. And, sir Launcelot, now I telle the: I have loved the this seven yere, [but] there may no woman have thy love but quene Gwenyver; and sytthen I myght nat rejoyse the nother thy body on lyve, I had kepte no more joy in this worlde but to have thy body dede. Than wolde I have bawmed hit and sered hit, and so to have
35 kepte hit my lyve dayes; and dayly I sholde have clypped the and kyssed the, dispyte of quene Gwenyvere.'

'Ye sey well,' seyde sir Launcelot, 'Jesu preserve me frome your subtyle crauftys!'

And therewithall he toke his horse and so departed frome hir. And
40 as the booke seyth, whan sir Launcelot was departed she toke suche sorow that she deyde within a fourtenyte; and hir name was called Hallewes the Sorseres, lady of the castell Nygurmous. And anone sir Launcelot mette with the damesel, sir Melyottis systir, and whan she sawe hym she clapped hir hondys and wepte for joy. And than they rode

into a castell thereby where lay sir Melyot, and anone as sir Launcelot
sye hym he knew hym, but he was passyng paale as the erthe for
bledynge. Whan sir Melyot saw sir Launcelot he kneled uppon his kneis
and cryed on hyghte:

'A, lorde, sir Launcelot, helpe me anone!'   5

Than sir Launcelot lepe unto hym and towched his woundys with
sir Gylbardys swerde, and than he wyped his woundys with a parte of
the bloody cloth that sir Gylbarde was wrapped in; and anone an holer
man in his lyff was he never.

And than there was grete joy betwene hem, and they made sir   10
Launcelot all the chere that they myghte. And so on the morne sir
Launcelot toke his leve and bade sir Melyot hyghe hym 'to the courte
of my lorde Arthure, for hit drawyth nyghe to the feste of Pentecoste.
And there, by the grace of God, ye shall fynde me.' And therewith they
departed.   15

And so sir Launcelot rode thorow many stronge contrayes, over (16)
mores and valeis, tyll by fortune he com to a fayre castell. And as he
paste beyonde the castell hym thought he herde bellys rynge, and than
he was warc of a faucon com over his hede fleyng towarde an hyghe
elme, and longe lunes aboute her feete. And she flowe unto the elme to 20
take hir perche, the lunes overcast aboute a bowghe; and whan she
wolde have tane hir flyght she hynge by the leggis faste. And sir
Launcelot syghe how ⟨s⟩he hynge, and behelde the fayre faucon perygot; and he was sory for hir. The meanewhyle cam a lady oute of a
castell and cryed on hyghe: 25

'A, Launcelot, Launcelot! as thow arte floure of all knyghtes, helpe
me to gete me my hauke; for and my hauke be loste my lorde wolde
destroy me, for I kepte the hauke and she slypped fro me. And yf my
lorde my husbande wete hit, he is so hasty that he wyll sle me.'

'What is your lordis name?' seyde sir Launcelot.   30

'Sir,' she seyde, 'his name is sir Phelot, a knyght that longyth unto
the kynge of North Galys.'

'Welle, fayre lady, syn that ye know my name and requyre me of
knyghthode to helpe, I woll do what I may to gete youre hauke; and
yet God knowyth I am an evyll clymber, and the tre is passynge hyghe, 35
and fewe bowys to helpe me withall.'

And therewith sir Launcelot alyght and tyed his horse to the same
tre, and prayde the lady to onarme hym. And so whan he was unarmed
he put of all his clothis unto his shurte and his breche, and with myght
and grete force he clambe up to the faucon and tyed the lunes to a grete 40
rotyn boysh, and threwe the hauke downe with the buysh.

And anone the lady gate the hauke in hir honde; and therewithall
com oute sir Phelot oute of the grevys suddeynly, that was hir husbonde, all armed and with his naked swerde in his honde, and sayde,

'A knyght, sir Launcelot, now I have founde the as I wolde,' he stondyng at the boole of the tre to sle hym.

'A, lady!' seyde sir Launcelot, 'why have ye betrayed me?'

'She hath done,' seyde sir Phelot, 'but as I commaunded hir, and
5 therefore there is none othir boote but thyne oure is com that thou muste dye.'

'That were shame unto the,' seyde sir Launcelot, 'thou an armed knyght to sle a nakyd man by treson.'

'Thou gettyste none other grace,' seyde sir Phelot, 'and therefore
10 helpe thyself and thou can.'

'Truly,' seyde sir Launcelot, 'that shall be thy shame; but syn thou wolt do none other, take myne harneys with the and hange my swerde there uppon a bowghe that I may gete hit, and than do thy beste [to] sle me and thou can.'

15 'Nay,' seyde sir Phelot, 'for I know the bettir than thou wenyste. Therefore thou gettyst no wepyn and I may kepe the therefro.'

'Alas,' seyde sir Launcelot, 'that ever a knyght sholde dey wepynles!'

And therewith he wayted above hym and undir hym, and over hym above his hede he sawe a rowgh spyke, a bygge bowghe leveles. And
20 therewith he brake hit of by the body, and than he com lowar, and awayted how his owne horse stoode, and suddenly he lepe on the farther syde of his horse froward the knyght. And than sir Phelot laysshed at hym egerly to have slayne hym, but sir Launcelot put away the stroke with the rowgh spyke, and therewith toke hym on the hede,
25 that downe he felle in a sowghe to the grounde. So than sir Launcelot toke his swerde oute of his honde and strake his necke in two pecys.

'Alas!' than cryed that lady, 'why haste thou slayne my husbonde?'

'I am nat causer,' seyde sir Launcelot, 'but with falshede ye wolde have had me slayne with treson, and now hit is fallyn on you bothe.'

30 And than she sowned as though she wolde dey. And therewith sir Launcelot gate all his armoure as well as he myght and put hit uppon hym for drede of more resseite, for he dredde hym that the knyghtes castell was so nyghe hym; and as sone as he myght he toke his horse and departed, and thanked God that he had escaped that harde adven-
35 ture.

(17) So sir Launcelot rode many wylde wayes thorowoute morys and mares, and as he rode in a valay, he sey a knyght chasyng a lady with a naked swerde to have slayne hir. And by fortune, as this knyght sholde have slayne thys lady, she cryed on sir Launcelot and prayde hym to
40 rescowe her.

Whan sir Launcelot sye that myschyff, he toke his horse and rode betwene hem, sayynge,

'Knyght, fye for shame, why wolte thou sle this lady? Shame unto the and all knyghtes!'

'What haste thou to do betwyxte me and my wyff? I woll sle her magré thyne hede.'

'That shall ye nat,' sayde sir Launcelot, 'for rather we woll have ado togydyrs.'

'Sir Launcelot,' seyde the knyght, 'thou doste nat thy parte, for thys 5
lady hath betrayed me.'

'Hit is not so,' seyde the lady, 'truly, he seyth wronge on me. And for bycause I love [and] cherysshe my cousyn jarmayne, he is jolowse betwyxte me and hym; and as I mutte answere to God there was never sene betwyxte us none suche thynges. But, sir,' seyde the lady, 'as thou 10 arte called the worshypfullyest knyght of the worlde, I requyre the of trewe knyghthode, kepe me and save me, for whatsomever he sey he woll sle me, for he is withoute mercy.'

'Have ye no doute: hit shalle nat lye in his power.'

'Sir,' seyde the knyght, 'in your syght I woll be ruled as ye woll have 15
me.'

And so sir Launcelot rode on the one syde and she on the other syde. And he had nat redyn but a whyle but the knyght bade sir Launcelot turne hym and loke behynde hym, and seyde, 'Sir, yondir com men of armys aftir [us] rydynge.' And so sir Launcelot turned hym and thought 20 no treson; and therewith was the knyght and the lady on one syde, and suddeynly he swapped of the ladyes hede. And whan sir Launcelot had aspyed hym what he had done, he seyde and so called hym: 'Traytoure, thou haste shamed me for evir!' And suddeynly sir Launcelot alyght of his horse and pulde oute his swerde to sle hym. And therewithall he 25 felle to the erthe and gryped sir Launcelot by the thyghes and cryed mercy.

'Fye on the,' seyde sir Launcelot, 'thou shamefull knyght! Thou mayste have no mercy: therefore aryse and fyghte with me!'

'Nay,' sayde the knyght, 'I woll never aryse tylle ye graunte me 30
mercy.'

'Now woll I proffyr the fayre: I woll unarme me unto my shyrte [and I woll have nothyng upon me but my sherte] and my swerde in my honde, and yf thou can sle me, quyte be thou for ever.'

'Nay, sir, that woll I never.' 35

'Well,' seyde sir Launcelot, 'take this lady and the hede, and bere [it] uppon the; and here shalt thou swere uppon my swerde to bere hit allwayes uppon thy bak and never to reste tyll thou com to my lady, quene Gwenyver.'

'Sir, that woll I do, by the feyth of my bo[d]y.' 40

'Now what is youre name?'

'Sir, my name is sir Pedy[v]ere.'

'In a shamefull oure were thou borne,' seyde sir Launcelot.

So sir Pedyvere departed with the lady dede and the hede togydir, and founde the quene with kynge Arthure at Wynchestir; and there he tolde all the trouthe.

'Sir knyght,' seyde the quene, 'this is an horryble dede and a shamefull, and a grete rebuke unto sir Launcelot, but natwythstondyng his worshyp is knowyn in many dyverse contreis. But this shall I gyff you in penaunce: make ye as good skyffte as ye can, ye shall bere this lady with you on horsebak unto the Pope of Rome, and of hym resseyve youre penaunce for your foule dedis. And ye shall nevir reste one nyght thereas ye do another, and ye go to ony bedde the dede body shall lye with you.'

This oth he there made and so departed. And as hit tellyth in the Frenshe booke, whan he com unto Rome the Pope there bade hym go agayne unto quene Gwenyver, and in Rome was his lady buryed by the Popys commaundement. And after thys knyght sir Pedyvere fell to grete goodnesse and was an holy man and an hermyte.

(18) Now turne we unto sir Launcelot du Lake that com home two dayes before the feste of Pentecoste, and the kynge and all the courte were passyng fayne. And whan Gawayne, sir Uwayne, sir Sagramoure, and sir Ector de Mares sye sir Launcelot in Kayes armour, than they wyste well that hit was he that smote hem downe all wyth one spere. Than there was lawghyng and smylyng amonge them, and ever now and now com all the knyghtes home that were presoners with sir Terquyn, and they all honoured sir Launcelot.

Whan sir Gaherys herde h[e]m speke he sayde, 'I sawe all the batayle from the begynnynge to the endynge,' and there he tolde kynge Arthure all how hit was and how sir Terquyn was the strongest knyght that ever he saw excep[t]e sir Launcelot; and there were many knyghtes bare hym recorde, three score. Than sir Kay tolde the kynge how sir Launcelot rescowed hym whan he sholde have bene slayne, and how 'he made the three knyghtes yelde hem to me and nat to hym'. And there they were all three and bare recorde.

'And by Jesu,' seyde sir Kay, 'sir Launcelot toke my harneyse and leffte me his, and I rode in Goddys pece and no man wolde have ado with me.'

Anone therewith com three knyghtes that fought with sir Launcelot at the longe brydge; and there they yelded them unto sir Kay, and sir Kay forsoke them and seyde he fought never with hem. 'But I shall ease your hertes,' seyde sir Kay, 'yondir is sir Launcelot that overcam you.' Whan they wyste that, they were glad. And than sir Melyot de Logrys com home and tolde hym and the kynge how sir Launcelot had saved hym frome the deth, and all his dedys was knowyn: how the quenys sorserers four had hym in preson, and how he was delyverde by the kynge Bagdemagus doughter.

Also there was tolde all the grete armys that sir Launcelot dud

betwyxte the two kynges, that ys for to say the kynge of North Galys
and kyng Bagdemagus : all the trouth sir Gahalantyne dud telle, and
sir Mador de la Porte, and sir Mordred, for they were at the same turnement. Than com in the lady that knew sir Launcelot whan that he
wounded sir Belleus at the pavylyon; and there at the requeste of sir 5
Launcelot sir Belleus was made knyght of the Rounde Table.

And so at that tyme sir Launcelot had the grettyste name of ony
knyght of the worlde, and moste he was honoured of hyghe and lowe.

EXPLICIT A NOBLE TALE OF SIR LAUNCELOT DU LAKE.

THE TALE OF
SIR GARETH OF ORKNEY
THAT WAS CALLED
BEWMAYNES

IN Arthurs dayes, whan he helde the Rounde Table moste plenoure, hit VII(1)
fortuned the kynge commaunded that the hyghe feste of Pentecoste
sholde be holden at a cité and a castell, in tho dayes that was called 5
Kynke Kenadonne, uppon the sondys that marched nyghe Walys. So
evir the kynge had a custom that at the feste of Pentecoste in especiall
afore other festys in the yere, he wolde nat go that day to mete unto
that he had herde other sawe of a grete mervayle. And for that custom
all maner of strange adventures com byfore Arthure, as at that feste 10
before all other festes.

And so sir Gawayne, a lytyll tofore the none of the day of Pentecoste,
aspyed at a wyndowe three men uppon horsebak and a dwarfe uppon
foote. And so the three men alyght, and the dwarff kepte their horsis,
and one of the men was hyghar than the tothir tweyne by a foote and 15
an half. Than sir Gawayne wente unto the kyng and sayde,

'Sir, go to your mete, for here at hande commyth strange adventures.'

So the kynge wente unto his mete with many other kynges, and
there were all the knyghtes of the Rounde Table, onles that ony were
presoners other slayne at recountyrs. Than at the hyghe feste evermore 20
they sholde be fulfylled the hole numbir of an hondred and fyffty, for
than was the Rounde Table fully complysshed.

Ryght so com into the halle two men well besayne and rychely, and
uppon their sholdyrs there lened the goodlyest yonge man and the
fayreste that ever they all sawe. And he was large and longe and brode 25
in the shuldyrs, well-vysaged, and the largyste and the fayreste handis
that ever may sye. But he fared as he myght nat go nothir bere hymself
but yf he lened uppon their shuldyrs. Anone as the kynge saw hym there
was made peas and rome, and ryght so they yode with hym unto the
hyghe deyse withoute seyynge of ony wordys. Than this yonge muche 30
man pullyd hym abak and easyly [stretched] streyghte upryght, seynge,

'The moste noble kynge, kynge Arthure! God you blysse and all your
fayre felyshyp, and in especiall the felyshyp of the Table Rounde. And
for this cause I come hydir, to pray you and requyre you to gyff me
three gyftys. And they shall nat be unresenablé asked but that ye may 35
worshypfully graunte hem me, and to you no grete hurte nother losse.
And the fyrste do[n]e and gyffte I woll aske now, and the tothir two
gyfftes I woll aske this day twelve-monthe, wheresomever ye holde
your hyghe feste.'

'Now aske ye,' seyde kyng Arthure, 'and ye shall have your askynge.' 40

'Now, sir, this is my petycion at this feste, that ye woll geff me mete

and drynke suffyciauntly for this twelve-monthe, and at that day I woll
aske myne other two gyfftys.'

'My fayre son,' seyde kyng Arthure, 'aske bettyr, I counseyle the,
for this is but a symple askyng; for myne herte gyvyth me to the gretly,
5 that thou arte com of men of worshyp, and gretly my conceyte fayleth
me but thou shalt preve a man of ryght grete worshyp.'

'Sir,' he seyde, 'thereof be as be may, for I have asked that I woll aske
at this tyme.'

'Well,' seyde the kynge, 'ye shall have mete and drynke inowe, I
10 nevir forbade hit my frynde nother my foo. But what is thy name,
I wolde wete?'

'Sir, I can nat tell you.'

'That is mervayle,' seyde the kynge, 'that thou knowyste nat thy
name, and thou arte one of the goodlyest yonge men that ever I saw.'

15 Than the kyng betoke hym to sir Kay the Styewarde, and charged
hym that he had of all maner of metys and drynkes of the beste, and
also that he had all maner of fyndynge as though he were a lordys
sonne.

'That shall lytyll nede,' seyde sir Kay, 'to do suche coste uppon hym,
20 for I undirtake he is a vylayne borne, and never woll make man, for and
he had be com of jantyllmen, he wolde have axed horse and armour, but
as he is, so he askyth. And sythen he hath no name, I shall gyff hym a
name whyche shall be called Beawmaynes, that is to say Fayre Handys.
And into the kychyn I shall brynge hym, and there he shall have fatte
25 browes every day that he shall be as fatte at the twelve-monthe ende
as a porke hog.'

Ryght so the two men departed and lefte hym with sir Kay that
(2) scorned and mocked hym. Thereat was sir Gawayne wroth. And in
especiall sir Launcelot bade sir Kay leve his mockyng, 'for I dare ley
30 my hede he shall preve a man of grete worshyp.'

'Lette be,' seyde sir Kay, 'hit may not be by reson, for as he is, so he
hath asked.'

'Yett beware,' seyde sir Launcelot, 'so ye gaff the good knyght
Brunor, sir Dynadans brothir, a name, and ye called hym La Cote Male
35 Tayle, and that turned you to anger aftirwarde.'

'As for that,' seyde sir Kay, 'this shall never preve none suche, for
sir Brunor desyred ever worshyp, and this desyryth ever mete and
drynke and brotthe. Uppon payne of my lyff, he was fosterde up in som
abbey, and howsomever hit was, they fayled mete and drynke, and so
40 hydir he is com for his sustynaunce.'

And so sir Kay bade gete hym a place and sytte downe to mete. So
Bewmaynes wente to the halle dore and sette hym downe amonge boyes
and laddys, and there he ete sadly. And than sir Launcelot aftir mete
bade hym com to his chambir, and there he sholde have mete and

drynke inowe, and so ded sir Gawayne; but he refused them all, for
he wolde do none other but as sir Kay commaunded hym, for no
profyr. But as towchyng sir Gawayne, he had reson to proffer hym
lodgyng, mete, and drynke, for that proffer com of his bloode, for he
was nere kyn to hym than he wyste off; but that sir Launcelot ded was   5
of his grete jantylnesse and curtesy.

So thus he was putt into the kychyn and lay nyghtly as the kychen
boyes dede. And so he endured all that twelve-monthe and never dyspleased man nother chylde, but allwayes he was meke and mylde. But
ever whan he saw ony justyng of knyghtes, that wolde he se and he   10
myght. And ever sir Launcelot wolde gyff hym golde to spende and
clothis, and so ded sir Gawayne. And where there were ony mastryes
doynge, thereat wolde he be, and there myght none caste barre nother
stone to hym by two yardys. Than wolde sir Kay sey, 'How lykyth you
my boy of the kychyn?'   15

So this paste on tyll the feste of Whytsontyde, and at that tyme the
kynge hylde hit at Carlyon, in the moste royallyst wyse that myght be,
lyke as he dud yerely. But the kyng wolde no mete ete uppon Whytsonday untyll he harde of som adventures.

Than com there a squyre unto the kynge and seyde, 'Sir, ye may go   20
to your mete, for here commyth a damesell with som strange adventures.' Than was the kyng glad and sette hym doune. Ryght so there
cam a damesell unto the halle and salewed the kyng and prayde hym
of succoure.

'For whom?' seyde the kynge. 'What is the adventure?'   25

'Sir,' she seyde, 'I have a lady of grete worshyp to my sustir, and she
is beseged with a tirraunte, that she may nat oute of hir castell. And
bycause here ar called the noblyst knyghtes of the worlde, I com to you
for succoure.'

'What is youre lady called, and where dwellyth she? And who is he   30
and what is his name that hath beseged her?'

'Sir kynge,' she seyde, 'as for my ladyes name that shall nat ye know
for me as at thys tyme, but I lette you wete she is a lady off grete worshyp and of grete londys; and as for that tyrraunte that besegyth her
and destroyeth hir londys, he is kallyd the Rede Kn[y]ght of the Rede   35
Laundys.'

'I know hym nat,' seyde the kyng.

'Sir,' seyde sir Gawayne, 'I know hym well, for he is one of the
perelest knyghtes of the worlde. Men sey that he hath seven mennys
strengthe, and from hym I ascapyd onys full harde with my lyff.'   40

'Fayre damesell,' seyde [the] kynge, 'there bene knyghtes here that
wolde do hir power for to rescowe your lady, but bycause ye woll not
telle hir name nother where she dwellyth, therfore none of my knyghtes
that here be nowe shall go with you be my wylle.'

'Than muste I seke forther,' seyde the damesell.

(3) So with thes wordys com Beawmaynes before the kyng whyle the damesell was there, and thus he sayde:

'Sir kyng, God tha[n]ke you, I have bene this twelve-monthe in your
5 kychyn and have had my full sustynaunce. And now I woll aske my other two gyfftys that bene behynde.'

'Aske on now, uppon my perell,' seyde the kynge.

'Sir, this shall be my fyrste gyffte of the two gyfftis: that ye woll graunte me to have this adventure of this damesell, for hit belongyth
10 unto me.'

'Thou shalt have it,' seyde the kynge, 'I graunte hit the.'

'Than, sir, this is that other gyffte that ye shall graunte me: that sir Launcelot du Lake shall make me knyght, for of hym I woll be made knyght and ellys of none. And whan I am paste I pray you lette hym
15 ryde aftir me and make me knyght whan I requyre hym.'

'All thys shall be done,' seyde the kynge.

'Fy on the,' seyde the damesell, 'shall I have none but one that is your kychyn knave?' Than she wexed angry and anone she toke hir horse.

20 And with that there com one to Bewmaynes and tolde hym his horse and armour was com for hym, and a dwarff had brought hym all thyng that neded hym in the rycheste wyse. Thereat the courte had muche mervayle from whens com all that gere. So whan he was armed there was none but fewe so goodly a man as he was.

25 And ryght so he cam into the halle and toke his leve of kyng Arthure and sir Gawayne and of sir Launcelot, and prayde hym to hyghe aftyr
(4) hym. And so he departed and rode afftyr the damesell, but there wente many aftir to beholde how well he was horsed and trapped in cloth of golde, but he had neyther speare nother shylde. Than sir Kay seyde all
30 opynly in the hall,

'I woll ryde aftir my boy of the kychyn to wete whether he woll know me for his bettir.'

'Yet,' seyde sir Launcelot and sir Gawayne, 'abyde at home.'

So sir Kay made hym redy and toke his horse and his speare and rode
35 aftir hym. And ryght as Beawmaynes overtoke the damesell, ryght so com sir Kay and seyde,

'Beawmaynes! What, sir, know ye nat me?'

Than he turned his horse and knew hit was sir Kay that had done all the dyspyte to hym, as ye have herde before. Than seyde Beawmaynes,
40 'Yee, I know you well for an unjantyll knyght of the courte, and therefore beware of me!'

Therewith sir Kay put his spere in the reest and ran streyght uppon hym, and Beawmaynes com as faste uppon hym with his swer[d]e [in his hand, and soo he putte awey his spere with his swerde,] and with a

foyne threste hym thorow the syde, that sir Kay felle downe as he had
bene dede. Than Beawmaynes alyght down and toke sir Kayes shylde
and his speare and sterte uppon his owne horse and rode his way.

All that saw sir Launcelot and so dud the damesell. And than he
bade his dwarff sterte uppon sir Kayes horse, and so he ded. By that sir 5
Launcelot was com, and anone he profyrde sir Launcelot to juste, and
ayther made hem redy and com togydir so fersly that eyther bare other
downe to the erthe and sore were they brused. Than sir Launcelot arose
and halpe hym frome his horse, and than Beawmaynes threw his shylde
frome hym and profyrd to fyght wyth sir Launcelot on foote.   10

So they russhed togydyrs lyke two borys, trasyng and traversyng
and foynyng the mountenaunce of an houre. And sir Launcelot felte
hym so bygge that he mervayled of his strengthe, for he fought more
lyker a gyaunte than a knyght, and his fyghtyng was so passyng durable
and passyng perelous. For sir Launcelot had so much ado with hym   15
that he dred hymself to be shamed, and seyde,

'Beawmaynes, feyght nat so sore! Your quarell and myne is nat grete
but we may sone leve of.'

'Truly that is trouth,' seyde Beawmaynes, 'but hit doth me good to
fele your myght. And yet, my lorde, I shewed nat the utteraunce.'   20

'In Goddys name,' seyde sir Launcelot, 'for I promyse you be the   (5)
fayth of my body I had as muche to do as I myght have to save myself
fro you unshamed, and therefore have ye no dought of none erthely
knyght.'

'Hope ye so that I may ony whyle stonde a preved knyght?'   25

'Do as ye have done to me,' seyde sir Launcelot, 'and I shall be your
warraunte.'

'Than I pray you,' seyde Beawmaynes, 'geff me the Order of
Knyghthod.'

'Sir, than muste ye tell me your name of ryght, and of what kyn ye 30
be borne.'

'Sir, so that ye woll nat dyscover me, I shall tell you my name.'

'Nay, sir,' seyde sir Launcelotte, 'and that I promyse you by the
feyth of my body, untyll hit be opynly knowyn.'

Than he seyde, 'My name is Garethe, and brothir unto sir Gawayne 35
of fadir syde and modir syde.'

'A, sir, I am more gladder of you than I was, for evir me thought ye
sholde be of grete bloode, and that ye cam nat to the courte nother for
mete nother drynke.'

Than sir Launcelot gaff hym the Order of Knyghthode; and than   40
sir Gareth prayde hym for to departe, and so he to folow the lady. So sir
Launcelot departed frome hym and come to sir Kay, and made hym
to be borne home uppon his shylde; and so he was heled harde with
the lyff. And all men scorned sir Kay, and in especiall sir Gawayne. And

sir Launcelot seyde that hit was nat his parte to rebuke no yonge man:
'For full lytyll knowe ye of what byrth he is com of, and for what cause
he com to the courte.'

And so we leve of sir Kay and turne we unto Beawmaynes. Whan
5 that he had overtakyn the damesell, anone she seyde,

'What doste thou here? Thou stynkyst all of the kychyn, thy clothis
bene bawdy of the grece and talow. What wenyste thou?' seyde the
lady, 'that I woll alow the for yondir knyght that thou kylde? Nay,
truly, for thou slewyst hym unhappyly and cowardly. Therefore turne
10 agayne, thou bawdy kychyn knave! I know the well, for sir Kay named
the Beawmaynes. What art thou but a luske, and a turner of brochis,
and a ladyll-waysher?'

'Damesell,' seyde sir Beawmaynes, 'sey to me what ye woll, yet woll
nat I go fro you whatsomever ye sey, for I have undirtake to kynge
15 Arthure for to encheve your adventure, and so shall I fynyssh hit to the
ende, other ellys I shall dye therefore.'

'Fye on the, kychyn knave! Wolt thou fynyssh myne adventure?
Thou shalt anone be mette withall, that thou woldyst nat for all the
broth that ever thou souped onys to loke hym in the face.'

20 'As for that, I shall assay,' seyde Beawmaynes.

So ryght thus as they rode in the wood there com a man fleyng all
that ever he myght.

'Whother wolt thou?' seyde Beawmaynes.

'A, lorde,' he seyde, 'helpe me, for hereby in a slade is six theffis that
25 have takyn my lorde and bounde hym sore, and I am aferde lest that
they woll sle hym.'

'Brynge me thydir,' seyde Beawmaynes.

And so they rode togydirs unto they com thereas was the knyght
bounden; and streyte he rode unto them and strake one to the deth, and
30 than another, and at the thirde stroke he slew the thirde, and than the
other three fledde. And he rode aftir them and ovetoke them, and than
they three turned agayne and assayled sir Beawmaynes harde, but at
the laste he slew them and returned and unbounde the knyght. And the
knyght thanked hym and prayde hym to ryde with hym to his castell
35 there a lytyll besyde, and he sholde worshypfully rewarde hym for his
good dedis.

'Sir,' seyde Beawmaynes, 'I woll no rewarde have. Sir, this day I was
made knyght of noble sir Launcelot, and therefore I woll no rewarde
have but God rewarde me. And also I muste folowe thys damesell.'

40 So whan he com nyghe to hir she bade hym ryde uttir, 'for thou
smellyst all of the kychyn. What wenyst thou? That I have joy of the
for all this dede? For that thou haste done is but myssehappe, but thou
shalt se sone a syght that shall make the to turne agayne, and that
lyghtly.'

Than the same knyght rode aftir the damesell and prayde hir to lodge with hym all that nyght. And because hit was nere nyght the damesell rode with hym to his castell and there they had grete chere. And at souper the knyght sette sir Beawmaynes afore the damesell.

'Fy, fy,' than seyde she, 'sir knyght, ye ar uncurtayse to sette a 5 kychyn page afore me. Hym semyth bettir to styke a swyne than to sytte afore a damesell of hyghe parage.'

Than the knyght was ashamed at hir wordys, and toke hym up and sette hym at a sydebourde and sate hymself before hym. So all that nyght they had good chere and myrry reste. And on the morne the 10 (6) damesell toke hir leve and thanked the knyght, and so departed and rode on hir way untyll they come to a grete foreste. And there was a grete ryver and but one passage, and there were redy two knyghtes on the farther syde to lette the passage.

'What sey[st th]ou?' seyde the damesell. 'Woll ye macche yondir two 15 knyghtis other ellys turne agayne?'

'Nay,' seyde sir Bewmaynes, 'I woll nat turne ayen, and they were six mo!'

And therewithall he russhed unto the watir, and in myddys of the watir eythir brake her sperys uppon other to their hondys. And than 20 they drewe their swerdis and smote egirly at othir. And at the laste sir Beawmaynes smote the othir uppon the helme, that his hede stoned, and therewithall he felle downe in the watir and there was he drowned. And than he spored his horse uppon the londe, and therewithall the tother knyght felle uppon hym [and] brake his speare. And so they 25 drew hir swerdys and fought longe togydyrs, but at the laste sir Beaw-maynes clevid his helme and his hede downe to the shuldyrs. And so he rode unto the damesell and bade hir ryde furth on hir way.

'Alas,' she seyde, 'that ever suche a kychyn payge sholde have the fortune to destroy such two knyghtes. Yet thou wenyste thou haste 30 done doughtyly? That is nat so; for the fyrste knyght his horse stumbled and there he was drowned in the watir, and never hit was be thy force nother be thy myghte. And the laste knyght, by myshappe thou camyste behynde hym, and by myssefortune thou slewyst hym.'

'Damesell,' seyde Beawmaynes, 'ye may sey what ye woll, but whom- 35 somever I have ado withall, I trust to God to serve hym or I and he departe, and therefore I recke nat what ye sey, so that I may wynne your lady.'

'Fy, fy, foule kychyn knave! Thou shalt se knyghtes that shall abate thy boste.'   40

'Fayre damesell, gyff me goodly langgage, and than my care is paste, for what knyghtes somever they be, I care nat, ne I doute hem nought.'

'Also,' seyde she, 'I sey hit for thyne avayle, for yett mayste thou turne ayen with thy worshyp; for and thou folow [me] thou arte but slayne, for I se all that evir thou doste is by mysseadventure and nat by preues of thy hondys.'

'Well, damesell, ye may sey what ye woll, but wheresomever ye go I woll folow you.'

5 So this Beawmaynes rode with that lady tyll evynsonge, and ever she chydde hym and wolde nat reste. So at the laste they com to a blak launde, and there was a blak hauthorne, and thereon hynge a baner, and on the other syde there hynge a blak shylde, and by hit stoode a blak speare, grete and longe, and a grete blak horse covered wyth sylk, (7) 10 and a blak stone faste by. Also there sate a knyght all armed in blak harneyse, and his name was called the Knyght of the Blak Laundis.

This damesell, whan she sawe that knyght, she bade hym fle downe that valey, for his hors was nat sadeled.

'Gramercy,' seyde Beawmaynes, 'for allway ye wolde have me a 15 cowarde.'

So whan the Blak Knyght saw hir he seyde, 'Damesell, have ye brought this knyght frome the courte of kynge Arthure to be your champyon?'

'Nay, fayre knyght, this is but a kychyn knave that was fedde in 20 kyng Arthurs kychyn for almys.'

Than sayde the knyght, 'Why commyth he in such aray? For hit is shame that he beryth you company.'

'Sir, I can not be delyverde of hym, for with me he rydyth magré my hede. God wolde,' seyde she, 'that ye wolde putte hym from me, other 25 to sle hym and ye may, for he is an unhappy knave, and unhappyly he hath done this day thorow myssehappe; for I saw hym sle two knyghtes at the passage of the watir, and other dedis he ded beforne ryght mervaylouse and thorow unhappynesse.'

'That mervayles me,' seyde the Blak Knyght, 'that ony man of 30 worshyp woll have ado with hym.'

'Sir, they knewe hym nat,' seyde the damesell, 'and for bycause he rydyth with me they wene that he be som man of worshyp borne.'

'That may be,' seyde the Blak Knyght; 'howbehit as ye say that he is no man of worshyp borne, he is a full lykly persone, and full lyke to be 35 a stronge man. But this muche shall I graunte you,' seyde the knyght, 'I shall put hym downe on foote, and his horse and harneyse he shall leve with me, for hit were shame to me to do hym ony more harme.'

Whan sir Beawmaynes harde hym sey thus, he seyde,

'Sir knyght, thou arte full large of my horse and harneyse! I lat the 40 wete hit coste the nought, and whether thou lyke well othir evyll, this launde woll I passe magré thyne hede, and horse ne harneyse gettyst thou none of myne but yf thou wynne hem with thy hondys. Therefore lat se what thou canste do.'

'Seyste thou that?' seyde the Blak Knyght. 'Now yelde thy lady fro the! For hit besemed never a kychyn knave to ryde with such a lady.'

'Thow lyest!' seyde Beawmaynes. 'I am a jantyllman borne, and of more hyghe lynage than thou, and that woll I preve o'n thy body!'

Than in grete wretth they departed their horsis and com togydyrs as 5 hit had bene thundir, and the Blak Knyghtes speare brake, and Beaw-maynes threste hym thorow bothe sydis. And therewith his speare brake and the truncheon was left stylle in his syde. But nevirtheles the Blak Knyght drew his swerde and smote many egir strokys of grete myght, and hurte Bewmaynes full sore. But at the laste the Blak Knyght, within 10 an owre and an half, he felle downe of his horse in a sowne and there dyed.

And than sir Bewmaynes sy hym so well horsed and armed, than he alyght downe and armed hym in his armour, and so toke his horse and rode aftir the damesell. Whan she sawe hym com she seyde, 15

'Away, kychyn knave, oute of the wynde, for the smelle of thy bawdy clothis grevyth me! Alas!' she seyde, 'that ever such a knave sholde by myssehappe sle so good a knyght as thou hast done! But all is thyne unhappynesse. But hereby is one that shall pay the all thy paymente, and therefore yett I rede the flee.' 20

'Hit may happyn me,' seyde Bewmaynes, 'to be betyn other slayne, but I warne you, fayre damesell, I woll nat fle away nothir leve your company for all that ye can sey; for ever ye sey that they woll sle me othir bete me, but howsomever hit happenyth I ascape and they lye on the grounde. And therefore hit were as good for you to holde you stylle 25 thus all day rebukyng me, for away wyll I nat tyll I se the uttermuste of this journay, other ellys I woll be slayne othir thorowly betyn.Therefore ryde on your way, for folow you I woll, whatsomever happyn me.'

Thus as they rode togydyrs they sawe a knyght comme dryvande by (8) them, all in grene, bothe his horse and his harneyse. And whan he com 30 nye the damesell he asked hir,

'Is that my brothir the Blak Knyght that ye have brought with you?'

'Nay, nay,' she seyde, 'this unhappy kychyn knave hath slayne thy brothir thorow unhappynes.'

'Alas!' seyde the Grene Knyght, '[that] is grete pyté that so noble a 35 knyght as he was sholde so unhappyly be slayne, and namely of a knavis honde, as ye say that he is. A, traytoure!' seyde the Grene Knyght, 'thou shalt dye for sleyng of my brothir! He was a full noble knyght, and his name was sir Perarde.'

'I defye the,' seyde sir Bewmaynes, 'for I lette the wete, I slew hym 40 knyghtly and nat shamfully.'

Therewythall the Grene Knyght rode unto an horne that was grene, and hit hynge uppon a thorne. And there he blew three dedly motis, and anone there cam two damesels and armed hym lyghtly. And than

he toke a grete horse, and a grene shylde, and a grene spere; and than
they ran togydyrs with all their myghtes and brake their sperys unto
their hondis.

And than they drewe their swerdys and gaff many sad strokys, and
5 eyther of them wounded other full ylle, and at the laste at an ovirtwarte
stroke sir Bewmaynes with his horse strake the Grene Knyghtes horse
uppon the syde, that he felle to the erthe. And than the Grene Knyght
voyded his horse delyverly and dressed hym on foote. That sawe Bewmaynes, and therewithall he alyght and they russhed togydyrs lyke two
10 myghty kempys a longe whyle, and sore they bledde bothe. Wyth that
come the damesell and seyde,

'My lorde the Grene Knyght, why for shame stonde ye so longe
fyghtynge with that kychyn knave? Alas! hit is shame that evir ye were
made knyght to se suche a lad to macche you as the wede growyth over
15 the corne.'

Therewith the Grene Knyght was ashamed, and therewithall he gaff
a grete stroke of myght and clave his shylde thorow. Whan Beawmaynes saw his shylde clovyn asundir he was a lytyll ashamed of that
stroke and of hir langage.

20 And than he gaff hym suche a buffette uppon the helme that he felle
on his kneis, and so suddeynly Bewmaynes pulde hym on the grounde
grovelynge. And than the Grene Knyght cryed hym mercy and yelded
hym unto Bewmaynes and prayde hym nat to sle hym.

'All is in vayne,' seyde Bewmaynes, 'for thou shalt dye but yf this
25 damesell that cam with me pray me to save thy lyff,' and therewithall
he unlaced his helme lyke as he wolde sle hym.

'Fye uppon the, false kychyn payge! I woll never pray the to save his
lyff, for I woll nat be so muche in thy daunger.'

'Than shall he dye,' seyde Beawmaynes.

30 'Nat so hardy, thou bawdy knave!' seyde the damesell, 'that thou
sle hym.'

'Alas!' seyde the Grene Knyght, 'suffir me nat to dye for a fayre
worde spekyng. Fayre knyght,' seyde the Grene Knyght, 'save my lyfe
and I woll forgyff the the deth of my brothir, and for ever to becom thy
35 man, and thirty knyghtes that hold of me for ever shall do you servyse.'

'In the devyls name,' seyde the damesell, 'that suche a bawdy kychyn
knave sholde have thirty knyghtes servyse and thyne!'

'Sir knyght,' seyde Bewmaynes, 'all this avaylyth the nought but yf
my damesell speke to me for thy lyff,' and therewithall he made a
40 semblaunte to sle hym.

'Lat be,' seyde the dameselle, 'thou bawdy kychyn knave! Sle hym
nat, for and thou do thou shalt repente hit.'

'Damesell,' seyde Bewmaynes, 'your charge is to me a plesure, and
at youre commaundemente his lyff shall be saved, and ellis nat.' Than

he sayde, 'Sir knyght with the grene armys, I releyse the quyte at this damesels requeste, for I woll nat make hir wroth, for I woll fulfylle all that she chargyth me.'

And than the Grene Knyght kneled downe and dud hym homage with his swerde. Than sayde the damesell,   5

'Me repentis of this Grene Knyghtes damage, and of your brothirs deth, the Blak Knyght, for of your helpe I had grete mystir; for I drede me sore to passe this foreste.'

'Nay, drede you nat,' seyde the Grene Knyght, 'for ye all shall lodge with me this nyght, and to-morne I shall helpe you thorow this forest.'   10

So they toke their horsys and rode to his maner that was faste by. And ever this damesell rebuked Bewmaynes and wolde nat suffir hym   (9) to sitte at hir table, but as the Grene Knyght toke hym and sate with hym at a syde table.

'Damesell, mervayle me thynkyth,' seyde the Grene Knyght, 'why   15 ye rebuke this noble knyghte as ye do, for I warne you he is a full noble man, and I knowe no knyght that is able to macche hym. Therefore ye do grete wronge so to rebuke hym, for he shall do you ryght goode servyse. For whatsomever he makyth hymself he shall preve at the ende that he is com of full noble blood and of kynges lynage.'   20

'Fy, fy!' seyde the damesell, 'hit is shame for you to sey hym suche worshyp.'

'Truly,' seyde the Grene Knyght, 'hit were shame to me to sey hym ony dysworshyp, for he hath previd hymself a bettir knyght than I am; and many is the noble knyght that I have mette withall in my dayes, and   25 never or this tyme founde I no knyght his macche.'

And so that nyght they yoode unto reste, and all nyght the Grene Knyght commaundede thirty knyghtes prevyly to wacche Bewmaynes for to kepe hym from all treson.

[And so on the morn] they all arose and herde their masse and brake   30 their faste. And than they toke their horsis and rode their way, and the Grene Knyght conveyed hem thorow the foreste. Than the Grene Knyght seyde,

'My lorde, sir Bewmaynes, my body and this thirty knyghtes shall be allway at your somouns, bothe erly and late at your callynge, and   35 whothir that ever ye woll sende us.'

'Ye sey well,' seyde sir Bewmaynes. 'Whan that I calle uppon you ye muste yelde you unto kynge Arthure, and all your knyghtes, if that I so commaunde you.'

'We shall be redy at all tymes,' seyde the Grene Knyght.   40

'Fy, fy uppon the, in the devyls name!' seyde the damesell, 'that ever [o]ny good knyght sholde be obedyent unto a kychyn knave!'

So than departed the Grene Knyght and the damesell, and than she seyde unto Bewmaynes,

'Why folowyste thou me, kychyn knave? Caste away thy shylde and thy spere and fle away. Yett I counseyle the betyme, or thou shalt sey ryght sone "Alas!" For and thou were as wyght as sir Launcelot, sir Trystrams or the good knyght sir Lamerok, thou shalt not passe a pace
5 here that is called the Pace Perelus.'

'Damesell,' seyde Bewmaynes, 'who is aferde let hym fle, for hit were shame to turne agayne syth I have ryddyn so longe with you.'

'Well,' seyde she, 'ye shall sone, whether y[e] woll or woll not.'

(10)   So within a whyle they saw a whyght towre as ony snowe, well
10 macchecolde all aboute and double-dyked, and over the towre gate there hynge a fyffty shyldis of dyvers coloures. And undir that towre there was a fayre medow, and therein was many knyghtes and squyres to beholde, scaffoldis and pavylons; for there, uppon the morne, sholde be a grete turnemente.

15   And the lorde of the towre was within his castell, and loked oute at a wyndow and saw a damesell, a dwarff, and a knyght armed at all poyntis.

'So God me helpe,' seyde the lorde, 'with that knyght woll I juste, for I se that he is a knyght arraunte.'

20   And so he armed hym and horsed hym hastely. Whan he was on horsebak with his shylde and his spere, hit was all rede, bothe his horse and his harneyse and all that to hym belonged. And whan that he com nyghe hym he wente hit had be his brother the Blak Knyght, and than lowde he cryed and seyde,

25   'Brothir, what do ye here in this marchis?'

'Nay, nay,' seyde the damesell, 'hit is nat he, for this is but a kychyn knave that was brought up for almys in kynge Arthurs courte.'

'Neverthelesse,' seyde the Rede Knyght, 'I woll speke with hym or he departe.'

30   'A,' seyde this damesell, 'this knave hathe slayne your brother, and sir Kay named hym Bewmaynes; and this horse and this harneyse was thy brothirs, the Blak Knyght. Also I sawe thy brothir the Grene Knyght overcom of his hondys. But now may ye be revenged on hym, for I may nevir be quyte of hym.'

35   Wyth this every knyght departed in sundir and cam togydir all that they myght dryve. And aythir of their horsis felle to the erthe. Than they avoyde theire horsis and put their shyldis before hem and drew their swerdys, and eythir gaff other sad strokys now here now there, trasyng, traversyng, and foynyng, rasyng and hurlyng lyke two borys,
40 the space of two owrys. Than she cryde on hyght to the Rede Knyght:

'Alas, thou noble Rede Knyght! Thynke what worshyp hath evermore folowed the! Lette never a kychyn knave endure the so longe as he doth!'

Than the Rede Knyght wexed wroth and doubled his strokes and

hurte Bewmaynes wondirly sore, that the bloode ran downe to the
grounde, that hit was wondir to see that stronge batayle. Yet at the
laste Bewmaynes strake hym to the erthe. And as he wolde have slayne
the Rede Knyght, he cryed,

'Mercy, noble knyght, sle me nat, and I shall yelde me to the wyth 5
fyffty knyghtes with me that be at my commaundemente, and forgyff
the all the dispyte that thou haste done to me, and the deth of my
brothir the Blak Knyght, and the wynnyng of my brothir the Grene
Knyght.'

'All this avaylyth nat,' seyde Beawmaynes, 'but if my damesell pray 10
me to save thy lyff.' And therewith he made semblaunte to stryke of
his hede.

'Let be, thou Bewmaynes, and sle hym nat, for he is a noble knyght,
and nat so hardy uppon thyne hede but that thou save hym.'

Than Bewmaynes bade the Rede Knyght to stonde up, 'and thanke 15
this damesell now of thy lyff.' Than the Rede Knyght prayde hym to se
his castell and to repose them all that nyght. So the damesell graunte
hym, and there they had good chere. But allwayes this damesell seyde
many foule wordys unto Bewmaynes, whereof the Rede Knyght had
grete mervayle. And all that nyght the Rede Knyght made three score 20
knyghtes to wacche Bewmaynes, that he sholde have no shame nother
vylony.

And uppon the morne they herde masse and dyned, and the Rede
Knyght com before Bewmaynes with his three score knyghtes, and
there he profyrd hym his omage and feawté at all tymes, he and his 25
knyghtes to do hym servyse.

'I thanke you,' seyde Bewmaynes, 'but this ye shall graunte me: whan
I calle uppon you, to com before my lorde, kynge Arthure, and yelde
you unto hym to be his knyghtes.'

'Sir,' seyde the Rede Knyght, 'I woll be redy and all my felyship at 30
youre somouns.'

So sir Bewmaynes departed and the damesell, and ever she rode
chydyng hym in the fowleste maner wyse that she cowde.

'Damesell,' seyde Bewmaynes, 'ye ar uncurteyse so to rebuke me as (11)
ye do, for mesemyth I have done you good servyse, and ever ye thretyn 35
me I shall be betyn wyth knyghtes that we mete, but ever for all your
boste they all lye in the duste or in the myre. And therefore y pray you,
rebuke me no more, and whan ye se me betyn or yoldyn as recreaunte,
than may you bydde me go from you shamfully, but erste, I let you
wete, I woll nat departe from you; for than I were worse than a foole 40
and I wolde departe from you all the whyle that I wynne worshyp.'

'Well,' seyde she, 'ryght sone shall mete the a knyght that shall pay
the all thy wagys, for he is the moste man of worshyp of the worlde
excepte kyng Arthure.'

'I woll well,' seyde Bewmaynes, 'the more he is of worshyp the more shall be my worshyp to have ado with hym.'

Than anone they were ware where was afore them a cyté rych and fayre, and betwyxte them and the cité, a myle and more, there was
5 a fayre medow that semed new mowyn, and therein was many pavylons fayre to beholde.

'Lo,' seyde the damesell, 'yondir is a lorde that owyth yondir cyté, and his custom is, whan the wedir is fayre, to lye in this medow, to juste and to turnay. And ever there is aboute hym fyve hondred
10 knyghtes and jantyllmen of armys, and there is all maner of gamys that ony jantyllman can devyse.'

'That goodly lorde,' seyde Bewmaynes, 'wolde I fayne se.'

'Thou shalt se hym tyme inowe,' seyde the damesell.

And so as she rode nere she aspyed the pavelon where the lorde
15 was.

'Lo!' seyde she, 'syeste thou yondir pavylyon that is all of the coloure of inde?' And all maner of thyng that there is aboute, men and women and horsis, trapped shyldis and sperys, was all of the coloure of inde. 'And his name is sir Parsaunte of Inde, the moste lordlyest knyght that
20 ever thou lokyd on.'

'Hit may well be,' seyde sir Bewmaynes, 'but be he never so stoute a knyght, in this felde I shall abyde tyll that I se hym undir his shylde.'

'A, foole!' seyde she, 'thou were bettir to flee betymes.'

'Why?' seyde Bewmaynes. 'And he be suche a knyght as ye make
25 hym he woll nat sette uppon me with all his men, for and there com no more but one at onys I shall hym nat fayle whylys my lyff may laste.'

'Fy, fy!' seyde the damesell, 'that evir suche a stynkyng kychyn knave sholde blowe suche a boste!'

'Damesell,' he seyde, 'ye ar to blame so to rebuke me, for I had lever
30 do fyve batayles than so to be rebuked. Lat hym com and than lat hym doo his worste.'

'Sir,' she seyde, 'I mervayle what thou art and of what kyn thou arte com; for boldely thou spekyst and boldely thou haste done, that have I sene. Therefore, I pray the, save thyself and thou may, for thyne horse
35 and thou have had grete travayle, and I drede that we dwelle ovirlonge frome the seege; for hit is hens but seven myle, and all perelous passage[s] we ar paste sauff all only this passage, and here I drede me sore last ye shall cacche som hurte. Therefore I wolde ye were hens, that ye were nat brused nothir hurte with this stronge knyght. But I lat you
40 wete this sir Persaunte of Inde is nothyng of myght nor strength unto the knyght that lyeth at the seege aboute my lady.'

'As for that,' seyde Bewmaynes, 'be as be may, for sytthen I am com so nye this knyght I woll preve his myght or I departe frome hym, and ellis I shall be shamed and I now withdrawe fro hym. And therefore,

damesell, have ye no doute: by the grace of God, I shall so dele with
this knyght that within two owrys after none I shall delyver hym, and
than shall we com to the seege be daylyght.'

'A, Jesu! mervayle have I,' seyde the damesell, 'what maner a man
ye be, for hit may never be other but that ye be com of jantyll bloode, 5
for so fowle and shamfully dud never woman revyle a knyght as I have
done you, and ever curteysly ye have suffyrde me, and that com never
but of jantyll bloode.'

'Damesell,' seyde Bewmaynes, 'a knyght may lytyll do that may nat
suffir a jantyllwoman, for whatsomever ye seyde unto me I toke none 10
hede to your wordys, for the more ye seyde the more ye angred me,
and my wretthe I wrekid uppon them that I had ado withall. [And therefore all] the mysseyyng that ye mysseyde me in my batayle furthered me
much and caused me to thynke to shew and preve myselffe at the ende
what I was, for peraventure, thoughe hit lyst me to be fedde in kynge 15
Arthures courte, I myght have had mete in other placis, but I ded hit
for to preve my frendys, and that shall be knowyn another day whether
that I be a jantyllman borne or none; for I latte yow wete, fayre
damesell, I have done you jantyllmannys servyse, and peraventure
bettir servyse yet woll I do or I departe frome you.'   20

'Alas!' she seyde, 'fayre Bewmaynes, forgyff me all that I have mysseseyde or done ayenste you.'

'With all my wyll,' seyde he, 'I forgeff hit you, for ye dud nothyng
but as ye sholde do, for all youre evyll wordys pleased me. Damesell,'
seyde Bewmaynes, 'syn hit lykyth you to sey thus fayre unto me, wote 25
ye well hit gladdyth myne herte gretly, and now mesemyth there is no
knyght lyvyng but I am able inow for hym.'

Wyth this sir Persaunte of Inde had aspyed them as they hoved in (12)
the fylde, and knyghtly he sente unto them whether he cam in warre or
in pece.   30

'Sey to thy lorde I take no force but whether as hym lyste.'

So the messyngere wente ayen unto sir Persaunte and tolde hym all
his answere.

'Well, than I woll have ado with hym to the utteraunce!' and so he
purveyede hym and rode ayenste hym.   35

Whan Bewmaynes sawe hym he made hym redy, and [there they]
mette with all theire myghtes togedir as faste as their horse myght ren,
and braste their spearys eythir in three pecis, and their horsis [rassed so
togyders that bothe their horsis] felle downe to the erthe. And delyverly
they avayded their horsis and put their shyldis before them and drew 40
their swerdys and gaff many grete strokys, that somtyme they hurled so
togydir that they felle grovelyng on the grounde.

Thus they fought two owres and more, that there shyldes and hawbirkes were all forhewyn, and in many placis [were they] wounded. So

at the laste sir Bewmaynes smote hym thorow the coste of the body, and than he retrayed hym here and there and knyghtly maynteyned his batayle longe tyme.

And at the laste, though hym loth were, Beawmaynes smote sir
5 Persaunte abovyn uppon the helme, that he felle grovelynge to the erthe, and than he lepte uppon hym overthwarte and unlaced his helme to have slayne hym. Than sir Persaunte yelded hym and asked hym mercy. Wyth that com the damesell and prayde hym to save his lyff.

10 'I woll well,' he seyde, 'for hit were pyté this noble knyght sholde dye.'

'Gramercy,' seyde sir Persaunte, 'for now I wote well hit was ye that slew my brother, the Blak Knyght, at the Blak Thorne. He was a full noble knyght! His name was sir Perarde. Also, I am sure that ye ar he
15 that wan myne other brother, the Grene Knyght: his name is sir Pertholepe. Also ye wan my brother the Rede Knyght, sir Perymones. And now, sir, ye have wonne me. This shall I do for to please you: ye shall have homage and feawté of me and of an hondred knyghtes to be allwayes at your commaundemente, to go and ryde where ye woll
20 commaunde us.'

And so they wente unto sir Persauntes pavylyon and dranke wyne and ete spycis. And afterwarde sir Persaunte made hym to reste uppon a bedde untyll supper tyme, and aftir souper to bedde ayen. So whan sir Bewmaynes was a-bedde—sir Persaunte had a doughter, a fayre
25 lady of eyghtene yere of ayge—and there he called hir unto hym and charged hir and commaunded hir uppon his blyssyng to go unto the knyghtis bed:

'And lye downe by his syde and make hym no strange chere but good chere, and take hym in your armys and kysse hym and loke
30 that this be done, I charge you, as ye woll have my love and my good wylle.'

So sir Persauntis doughter dud as hir fadir bade hir, and so she yode unto sir Bewmaynes bed and pryvyly she dispoyled hir and leyde hir downe by hym. And than he awooke and sawe her and asked her what
35 she was.

'Sir,' she seyde, 'I am sir Persauntis doughter that by the commaundemente of my fadir I am com hydir.'

'Be ye a pusell or a wyff?'

'Sir,' she seyde, 'I am a clene maydyn.'
40 'God deffende me,' seyde he, 'than that ever I sholde defoyle you to do sir Persaunte suche a shame! Therefore I pray you, fayre damesell, aryse oute of this bedde, other ellys I woll.'

'Sir,' she seyde, 'I com nat hydir by myne owne wyll, but as I was commaunded.'

'Alas!' seyde sir Bewmaynes, 'I were a shamefull knyght and I wolde do youre fadir ony dysworshyp.'

But so he kyste her, and so she departed and com unto sir Persaunte hir fadir and tolde hym all how she had sped.

'Truly,' seyde sir Persaunte, 'whatsomever he be he is com of full 5 noble bloode.'

And so we leve hem there tyll on the morne.

And so on the morne the damesell and sir Bewmaynes herde masse (13) and brake there faste and so toke their leve.

'Fayre damesell,' seyde sir Persaunte, 'whothirwarde ar ye away 10 ledynge this knyght?'

'Sir,' she seyde, 'this knyght is goynge to the Castell Daungerous thereas my systir is beseged.'

'Aha,' seyde sir Persaunte, 'that is the Knyght of the Rede Launde whyche is the moste perelyste knyght that I know now lyvynge and a 15 man that is wythouten mercy, and men sey that he hath seven mennes strength. God save you, sir Bewmaynes, frome that knyght, for he doth grete wronge to that lady, and that is grete pyté, for she is one of the fayreste ladyes of the worlde, and mesemyth that your damesell is hir sister. Ys nat your name Lyonet?' 20

'Sir, so I hyght, and my lady my sister hyght dame Lyones.'

'Now shall I tell you,' seyde sir Persaunte, 'this Rede Knyght of the Rede Laundys hath layne longe at that seege, well-nye this two yerys, and many tymes he myght have had hir and he had wolde, but he pro-longyth the tyme to this entente, for to have sir Launcelot du Lake to 25 do batayle with hym, or with sir Trystrams, othir sir Lamerok de Galys, other sir Gawayne, and this is his taryynge so longe at the sege. Now, my lorde,' seyde sir Persaunt of Inde, 'be ye stronge and of good herte, for ye shall have ado with a good knyght.'

'Let me dele,' seyde sir Bewmaynes. 30

'Sir,' seyde this damesell Lyonet, 'I requyre you that ye woll make this jantyllman knyght or evir he fyght with the Rede Knyght.'

'I woll, with all myne herte,' seyde sir Persaunte, 'and hit please hym to take the Order of Knyghthode of so symple a man as I am.'

'Sir,' seyde Bewmaynes, 'I thanke you for [your good will, for] I am 35 bettir spedde, for sertay[n]ly the noble knyghte sir Launcelot made me knyght.'

'A,' seyde sir Persaunte, 'of a more renomed man myght ye nat be made knyghte of, for of all knyghtes he may be called cheff of knyght-hode, and so all the worlde seythe that betwyxte three knyghtes is de- 40 parted clerely knyghthode, that is sir Launcelot du Lake, sir Trystrams de Lyones and sir Lamerok de Galys. Thes bere now the renowne, yet there be many other noble knyghtis, as sir Palomydes the Saresyn and sir Saphir, his brothir, also sir Bleobrys and sir Blamour de Ganys, his

brothir; also sir Bors de Ganys, and sir Ector de Marys, and sir Percivale de Galys. Thes and many mo bene noble knyghtes, but there be none that bere the name but thes three abovyn seyde. Therefore God spede you well,' seyde sir Persaunte, 'for and ye may macche that Rede
5 Knyght ye shall be called the fourth of the worlde.'

'Sir,' seyde Bewmaynes, 'I wolde fayne be of good fame and of knyghthode. And I latte you wete, I am com of good men, for I dare say my fadir was a nobleman. And so that ye woll kepe hit in cloce and this damesell, I woll tell you of what kynne I am com of.'

10 'We woll nat discover you,' seyde they bothe, 'tylle ye commaunde us, by the fayth we owe to Jesu.'

'Truly,' than sayde he, 'my name is sir Gareth of Orkenay, and kynge Lott was my fadir, and my modir is kyng Arthurs sistir, hir name is dame Morgawse. And sir Gawayne ys my brothir, and sir Aggra-
15 vayne and sir Gaherys, and I am yongeste of hem all. And yette wote nat kynge Arthure nother sir Gawayne what I am.'

(14) So the booke seyth that the lady that was beseged had worde of hir sisteris comyng by the dwarff, and a knyght with hir, and how he had passed all the perelus passages.

20 'What maner a man is he?' seyde the lady.

'He is a noble knyght, truly, madam,' seyde the dwarff, 'and but a yonge man, but he is as lykly a man as ever ye saw ony.'

'What is he, and of what kynne,' seyde the lady, 'is he com, and of whom was he made knyght?'

25 'Madam,' seyde the dwarff, 'he was kynges son of Orkeney, but his name I woll nat tell you as at this tyme; but wete you well, of sir Launcelot was he made knyght, for of none other wolde he be made knyght, and sir Kay named hym Bewmaynes.'

'How ascaped he,' seyde the lady, 'frome the brethyrn of sir Per-
30 saunte?'

'Madam,' he seyde, 'as a noble knyght sholde. First he slew two bretherne at a passage of a watir.'

'A!' seyde she, 'they were two good knyghtes, but they were murtherers. That one hyght sir Gararde le Breuse and that other hyght
35 sir Arnolde le Bruse.'

'Than, madam, he recountird at the Blak Knyght and slew hym in playne batayle, and so he toke his hors and his armoure and fought with the Grene Knyght and wanne hym in playne batayle. And in lyke wyse he served the Rede Knyght, and aftir in the same wyse he served the
40 Blew Knyght and wanne hym in playne batayle.'

'Than,' sayde the lady, 'he hath overcom sir Persaunte of Inde that is one of the noblest knyghtes of the worlde?'

'Trewly, madam,' seyde the dwarff, 'he hath wonne all the four bretherne and slayne the Blak Knyght, and yet he dud more tofore: he

overthrew sir Kay and leffte hym nye dede uppon the grounde. Also
he dud a grete batayle wyth sir Launcelot, and there they departed on
evyn hondis. And than sir Launcelot made hym knyght.'

'Dwarff,' seyde the lady, 'I am gladde of thys tydynges. Therefore
go thou unto an hermytage of myne hereby and bere with the of my 5
wyne in too flagons of sylver—they ar of two galons—and also two
caste of brede, with the fatte venyson ibake and deynté foules; and a
cuppe of golde here I delyver the that is ryche of precious stonys. And
bere all this to myne hermytage and putt hit in the hermytis hondis.

'And sytthyn go thou to my sistir and grete her welle, and com- 10
maunde me unto that jantyll knyght, and pray hym to ete and drynke
and make hym stronge, and say hym I thanke hym of his curtesy and
goodnesse that he wolde take uppon hym suche labur for me that
never ded hym bounté nother curtesy. Also pray hym that he be of
good herte and corrage hymself, for he shall mete with a full noble 15
knyght, but he is nother of curtesy, bounté, nother jantylnesse; for he
attendyth unto nothyng but to murther, and that is the cause I can nat
prayse hym nother love hym.'

So this dwarff departed and com to sir Persaunt where he founde the
damesell Lynet and sir Bewmaynes, and there he tolde hem all as ye 20
have herde. And than they toke their leve, but sir Persaunte toke an
amblynge hakeney and conveyed them on their wayes and than betoke
he them unto God.

And so within a lytyll whyle they com to the hermytage, and there
they dranke the wyne and ete the venyson and the foulys bakyn. And 25
so whan they had repasted them well the dwarff retourned ayen with
his vessell unto the castell. And there mette wyth hym the Rede Knyght
of the Rede Laundys and asked hym from whens he com and where
he had ben.

'Sir,' seyde the dwarff, 'I have bene with my ladyes sistir of the castell, 30
and she hath bene at kynge Arthurs courte and brought a knyght with
her.'

'Than I acompte her travayle but lorne, for though she had brought
with hir sir Launcelot, sir Trystrams, sir Lameroke, othir sir Gawayne,
I wolde thynke myself good inowe for them all.' 35

'Hit may well be,' seyde the dwarff, 'but this knyght hathe passed all
the perelouse passages and slayne the Blak Knyghte and other two mo,
and wonne the Grene Knyght, and Rede Knyght, and the Blew
Knyght.'

'Than is he one of thes four that I have before rehersyd?' 40
'He is none of thes,' seyde the dwarff, 'but he is a kynges son.'
'What is his name?' seyde the Rede Knyght of the Rede Laundis.
'That woll I nat tell you, but sir Kay on scorne named hym Bew-
maynes.'

'I care nat,' seyde the knyght, 'whatsomevir he be, for I shall sone delyver hym, and yf I overmacche hym he shall have a shamfull deth as many othir have had.'

'That were pyté,' seyde the dwarff, 'and hit is pyté that ye make suche
5 shamfull warre uppon noble knyghtes.'

(15)   Now leve we the knyght and the dwarff and speke we of Bewmaynes that all nyght lay in the hermytage. And uppon the morne he and the damesell Lynet harde their masse and brake their faste, and than they toke their horsis and rode thorowoute a fayre foreste. And than they
10 com to a playne and saw where was many pavylons and tentys and a fayre castell, and there was muche smoke and grete noyse.

And whan they com nere the sege sir Bewmaynes aspyed on grete trees, as he rode, how there hynge full goodly armed knyghtes by the necke, and their shyldis aboute their neckys with their swerdis and
15 gylte sporys uppon their helys. And so there hynge nyghe a fourty knyghtes shamfully with full ryche armys. Than sir Bewmaynes abated his countenaunce and seyde, 'What menyth this?'

'Fayre sir,' seyde the damesell, 'abate nat youre chere for all this syght, for ye muste corrage youreself, other ellys ye bene all shente.
20 For all these knyghtes com hydir to this sege to rescow my sistir dame Lyones, and whan the Rede Knyght of the Rede Launde had overcom hem he put them to this shamefull deth withoute mercy and pyté. And in the same wyse he woll serve you but yf ye quyte you the bettir.'

'Now Jesu defende me,' seyde sir Bewmaynes, 'frome suche vylans
25 deth and shondeshyp of harmys, for rathir than I sholde so be faryn withall I woll rather be slayne in playne batayle.'

'So were ye bettir,' seyde the damesell, 'for trust nat, in hym is no curtesy, but all goth to the deth other shamfull mourthur. And that is pyté,' seyde the damesell, 'for he is a full lykly man and a noble knyght
30 of proues, and a lorde of grete londis and of grete possessions.'

'Truly,' seyde sir Bewmaynes, 'he may be well a good knyght, but he usyth shamfull customys, and hit is mervayle that he enduryth so longe, that none of the noble knyghtes of my lorde Arthurs have nat dalte with hym.'

35   And than they rode unto the dykes and sawe them double-dyked wyth full warly wallys, [and there were lodged many grete lordes nyghe the wallys,] and there was grete noyse of mynstralsy. And the see bete uppon that one syde of the wallys where were many shyppis and marynars noyse with hale and how.

40   And also there was faste by a sygamoure tre, and thereon hynge an horne, the grettyst that ever they sye, of an olyvauntes bone, and this Knyght of the Rede Launde hath honged hit up there to this entente, that yf there com ony arraunte knyghte he muste blowe that horne and than woll he make hym redy and com to hym to do batayle.

'But, sir, pray you,' seyde the damesell, 'blow ye nat the horne tyll hit be hygh none, for now hit is aboute pryme, and now encresyth his myght, that as men say he hath seven mennys strength.'

'A! fy for shame, fayre damesell! Sey ye nevir so more to me, for and he were as good a knyght as ever was ony I shall never fayle hym in his moste myght, for other I woll wynne worshyp worshypfully othir dye knyghtly in the felde.'

And therewith he spored his horse streyte to the sygamoure tre and so blew the horne egirly that all the seege and the castell range thereoff. And than there lepe oute many knyghtes oute of their tentys and pavylyons, and they within the castell loked ovir the wallys and oute at wyndowis.

Than the Rede Knyght of the Rede Laundis armed hym hastely and too barouns sette on his sporys on his helys, and all was blood-rede: his armour, spere, and shylde. And an erle buckled his helme on his hede, and than they brought hym a rede spere and a rede stede. And so he rode into a lytyll vale undir the castell, that all that were in the castell and at the sege myght beholde the batayle.

'Sir,' seyde the damesell Lynet unto sir Bewmaynes, 'loke ye be glad and lyght, for yondir is your dedly enemy, and at yondir wyndow is my lady, my sistir dame Lyones.'

'Where?' seyde Bewmaynes.

'Yondir,' seyde the damesell, and poynted with her fyngir.

'That is trouth,' seyde Bewmaynes, 'she besemyth afarre the fayryst lady that ever I lokyd uppon, and truly,' he seyde, 'I aske no better quarell than now for to do batayle, for truly she shall be my lady and for hir woll I fyght.'

And ever he loked up to the wyndow with glad countenaunce, and this lady dame Lyones made curtesy to hym downe to the erth, holdynge up bothe her hondys. Wyth that the Rede Knyghte calle unto Bewmaynes and seyde,

'Sir knyght, leve thy beholdyng and loke on me, I counsayle the, for I warne the well, she is my lady, and for hir I have done many stronge batayles.'

'Geff thou so have done,' seyde Bewmaynes, 'mesemyth hit was but waste laboure, for she lovyth none of thy felyshyp, and thou to love that lovyth nat the is but grete foly. For and I undirstoode that she were nat ryght glad of my commynge I wolde be avysed or I dud batayle for hir; but I undirstonde by the segynge of this castell she may forbere thy felyshyp. And therefore wete thou well, thou Rede Knyght, I love hir and woll rescow hir, othir ellys to dye therefore.'

'Sayst thou that?' seyde the Rede Knyght. 'Mesemyth thou oughtyste of reson to beware by yondir knyghtes that thou sawyste hange on yondir treis.'

'Fy for shame!' seyde Bewmaynes, 'that ever thou sholdyst sey so or do so evyll, for in that thou shamest thyself and all knyghthode, and thou mayste be sure there woll no lady love the that knowyth the and thy wykked customs. And now thou wenyste that the syght of tho
5 honged knyghtes shulde feare me? Nay, truly, nat so! That shamefull syght cawsyth me to have courrage and hardynesse ayenst th[e] muche more than I wolde have agaynste the and thou were a well-ruled knyght.'

'Make the redy,' seyde the Rede Knyght, 'and talke no more with
10 me.'

Than they putt their sperys in the reste and com togedyrs with all the myght that they had bothe, and aythir smote other in the myddys of their shyldis, that the paytrels, sursynglys and crowpers braste, and felle to the erthe bothe, and the raynys of their brydyls in there hondys.
15 And so they lay a grete whyle sore astoned, that all that were in the castell and in the sege wente their neckys had bene broste.

Than many a straunger and othir seyde that the straunge knyght was a bygge man and a noble jouster, 'for or now we sawe never no knyght macche the Rede Knyght of the Rede Laundys.' Thus they seyde
20 bothe within and withoute.

Than lyghtly and delyverly they avoyded their horsis and putt their shyldis afore them and drew theire swerdys and ran togydyrs lyke two fers lyons, and eythir gaff othir suche two buffettys uppon their helmys that they reled bakwarde bothe two stredys. And than they
25 recoverde bothe and hew grete pecis of othyrs harneyse and their shyldys, that a grete parte felle in the fyldes.

(17) And than thus they fought tyll hit was paste none, and never wolde stynte tyll at the laste they lacked wynde bothe, and than they stoode waggyng, stagerynge, pantynge, blowynge, and bledyng, that all that
30 behelde them for the moste party wepte for pyté. So whan they had rested them a whyle they yode to batayle agayne, trasyng, traversynge, foynynge, and rasynge as two borys. And at som tyme they toke their bere as hit had bene two rammys and horled togydyrs, that somtyme they felle grovelynge to the erthe; and at som tyme they were so amated
35 that aythir toke others swerde in the stede of his owne.

And thus they endured tyll evynsonge, that there was none that behelde them myght know whethir was lyke to wynne the batayle. And theire armoure was so forhewyn that men myght se their naked sydys, and in other placis they were naked; but ever the nakyd placis they dud
40 defende. And the Rede Knyghte was a wyly knyght in fyghtyng, and that taught Bewmaynes to be wyse, but he abought hit full sore or he did asspye his fyghtynge.

And thus by assente of them both they grauntid aythir othir to reste, and so they sette hem downe uppon two mollehyllys there besydys the

fyghtynge place, and eythir of them unlaced othir helmys and toke the
colde wynde, for aythir of their pagis was faste by them to com whan
they called them to unlace their harneyse and to sette hem on agayne
at there commaundemente. And than sir Bewmaynes, whan his helme
was off, he loked up to the wyndowe, and there he sawe the fayre lady 5
dame Lyones, and she made hym suche countenaunce that his herte
waxed lyght and joly. And therewith he bade the Rede Knyght of the
Rede Laundis make hym redy, 'and lette us do oure batayle to the
utteraunce.'

'I woll well,' seyde the knyght. And than they laced on their helmys, 10
and avoyded their pagys, and yede togydyrs and fought freysshly. But
the Rede Knyght of the Rede Laundys awayted hym at an overthwarte and smote hym with[in the honde,] that his swerde felle oute of
his honde. And yette he gaff hym another buffette uppon the helme,
that he felle grovelynge to the erthe, and the Rede Knyghte felle over 15
hym for to holde hym downe.

Than cryed the maydyn Lynet on hyght and seyde,

'A, sir Bewmaynes! Where is thy corrayge becom? Alas! my lady
my sistir beholdyth the, and she shrekis and wepys so that hit makyth
myne herte hevy.'   20

Whan sir Bewmaynes herde hir sey so, he abrayded up with a grete
myght, and gate hym uppon hys feete, and lyghtly he lepe to his swerde
and gryped hit in his honde and dowbled his pace unto the Rede
Knyght, and there they fought a new batayle togydir.

But sir Bewmaynes than doubled his strokys and smote so thycke 25
that his swerde felle oute of his honde. And than he smote hym on the
helme, that he felle to the erthe, and sir Bewmaynes felle uppon hym
and unlaced his helme to have slayne hym. And than he yelded hym
and asked mercy and seyde with a lowde voyce,

'A, noble knyght! I yelde me to thy mercy!'   30

Than sir Bewmaynes bethought hym on his knyghtes that he had
made to be honged shamfully, and than he seyde,

'I may nat with my worship to save thy lyff for the shamefull de[the]s
that thou haste caused many full good knyghtes to dye.'

'Sir,' seyde the Rede Knyght, 'holde youre hande and ye shall knowe 35
the causis why I putte hem to so shamefull a deth.'

'Sey on!' seyde sir Bewmaynes.

'Sir, I loved onys a lady fayre, and she had hir bretherne slayne, and
she tolde me hit was sir Launcelot du Lake othir ellys sir Gawayne.
And she prayed me as I loved hir hertely that I wolde make hir a 40
promyse by the faythe of my knyghthode for to laboure in armys dayly
untyll that I had mette with one of them, and all that I myght overcom
I sholde put them to vylans deth. And so I ensured her to do all the
vylany unto Arthurs knyghtes, and that I sholde take vengeaunce

uppon all these knyghtes. And, sir, now I woll telle the that every day my stengthe encresyth tylle none untyll I have seven mennys strength.'

(18)   Than cam there many erlys and barowns and noble knyghtes and prayde that knyght to save his lyff, 'and take hym to your presoner.' And all they felle uppon their kneis and prayde hym of mercy that he wolde save his lyff.

'And, sir,' they all seyde, 'hit were fayrer of hym to take omage and feauté and lat hym holde his londys of you than for to sle hym, for by his deth ye shall have none advauntage, and his myssededys that be done may not be undone. And therefore make ye amendys for all partyes, and we all woll becom youre men and do you omage and feauté.'

'Fayre lordys,' seyde Bewmaynes, 'wete you well I am full loth to sle this knyght, neverthelesse he hath done passynge ylle and shamefully. But insomuche all that he dud was at a ladyes requeste I blame hym the lesse, and so for your sake I woll relece hym, that he shall have his lyff uppon this covenaunte: that he go into this castell and yelde hym to the lady, and yf she woll forgyff and quyte hym I woll well, with this he make hir amendys of all the trespasse that he hath done ayenst hir and hir landys. And also, whan that is done, that he goo unto the courte of kyng Arthur and that he aske sir Launcelot mercy and sir Gawayne for the evyll wylle he hath had ayenst them.'

'Sir,' seyde the Rede Knyght, 'all this woll I do as ye commaunde me, and syker assurraunce and borowys ye shall have.'

So whan the assurauns was made he made his omage and feauté, and all tho erlys and barouns with hym.

And than the mayden Lynet com to sir Bewmaynes and unarmed hym and serched his woundis and staunched the blood, and in lyke wyse she dud to the Rede Knyght of the Rede Laundis. And there they suggeourned ten dayes in there tentys. And ever the Rede Knyght made all his lordis and servauntys to do all the plesure unto sir Bewmaynes that they myght do.

And so within a whyle the Rede Knyghte yode unto the castell and putt hym in her grace, and so she resseyved hym uppon suffyciaunte sureté so that all her hertys were well restored of all that she coude complayne. And than he departed unto the courte of kynge Arthure, and there opynly the Rede Knyght putt hymself in the mercy of sir Launcelot and of sir Gawayne; and there he tolde opynly how he was overcom and by whom, and also he tolde all the batayles frome the begynnyng to the endynge.

'Jesu mercy!' seyde kynge Arthure and sir Gawayne, 'we mervayle muche of what bloode he is com, for he is a noble knyght.'

'Have ye no mervayle,' seyde sir Launcelot, 'for ye shall ryght well know that he is com of full noble bloode, and as for hys myght and

hardynesse, there bene but full few now lyvynge that is so myghty as
he is, and of so noble prouesse.'

'Hit semyth by you,' seyde kynge Arthure, 'that ye know his name
and frome whens he com.'

'I suppose I do so,' seyde sir Launcelot, 'or ellys I wolde not have 5
yeffyn hym the hyghe Order of Knyghthode, but he gaff me suche
charge at that tyme that I woll never discover hym untyll he requyre me,
or ellis hit be knowyn opynly by som other.'

Now turne we unto sir Bewmaynes that desyred [of] dame Lynet (19)
that he myght se hir lady.   10

'Sir,' she seyde, 'I wolde ye saw hir fayne.'

Than sir Bewmaynes all armed toke his horse and his spere and rode
streyte unto the castell, and whan he com to the gate he founde there
men armed, and pulled up the drawbrygge and drew the portcolyse.

Than he mervayled why they wolde nat suffir hym to entir, and than 15
he loked up to a wyndow and there he sawe fayre dame Lyones that
seyde on hyght,

'Go thy way, sir Bewmaynes, for as yet thou shalt nat have holy my
love unto the tyme that thou be called one of the numbir of the worthy
knyghtes. And therefore go and laboure in worshyp this twelve- 20
monthe, and than ye shall hyre newe tydyngis.'

'Alas! fayre lady,' seyde sir Bewmaynes, 'I have nat deserved that ye
sholde shew me this straungenesse. And I hadde wente I sholde have
had ryght good chere with you, and unto my power I have deserved
thanke. And well I am sure I have bought your love with parte of the 25
beste bloode within my body.'

'Fayre curteyse knyght,' seyde dame Lyonesse, 'be nat displeased,
nother be nat overhasty, for wete you well youre grete travayle nother
your good love shall nat be loste, for I consyder your grete laboure and
your hardynesse, your bounté and your goodnesse as me ought to do. 30
And therefore go on your way and loke that ye be of good comforte,
for all shall be for your worshyp and for the best; and, pardé, a twelve-
monthe woll sone be done. And trust me, fayre knyght, I shall be trewe
to you and never betray you, but to my deth I shall love you and none
other.'   35

And therewithall she turned frome the wyndowe, and sir Bewmaynes
rode awaywarde from the castell makynge grete dole. And so he rode
now here, now there, he wyste nat whother, tyll hit was durke nyght.
And than hit happened hym to com to a pore mannys house, and there
he was herborowde all that nyght. But sir Bewmaynes had no reste, but 40
walowed and wrythed for the love of the lady of that castell.

And so uppon the morne he toke his horse and rode untyll undyrn,
and than he com to a brode watir, [and thereby was a grete lodge.] And
there he alyght to slepe and leyde his hede uppon hys shylde and betoke

his horse to the dwarff and commaunded the dwarff to wacche all nyght.

Now turne we to the lady of the same castell that thought muche uppon Bewmaynes. And than she called unto hir sir Gryngamoure, hir
5 brother, and prayde hym in all maner, as he loved hir hertely, that he wolde ryde afftir sir Bewmaynes:

'And ever have ye wayte uppon hym tyll ye may fynde hym slepyng, for I am sure in his hevynesse he woll alyght adowne in som place and lay hym downe to slepe. And therefore have ye youre wayte uppon hym
10 in prevy maner, and take his dwarff and com your way wyth hym as faste as ye may[e or sir Bewmaynes awake:] for my sistir Lynet tellyth me that he can telle of what kynrede he is com of. And in the meane-whyle I and my sistir woll ryde untyll your castell to wayte whan ye brynge with you the dwarff, and than woll I have hym in examynacion
15 myself, for tyll that I know what is his ryght name and of what kynrede he is commyn shall I never be myrry at my herte.'

'Sistir,' seyde sir Gryngamour, 'all this shall be done aftir your entente.'

And so he rode all that other day and the nyght tyll he had lodged
20 hym. And whan he sawe sir Bewmaynes faste on slepe he com stylly stalkyng behynde the dwarff and plucked hym faste undir his arme and so rode his way with hym untyll his owne castell. And this sir Gryn-gamoure was all in blak, his armour and his horse and all that tyll hym longyth. But ever as he rode with the dwarff towarde the castell he
25 cryed untyll his lorde and prayde hym of helpe. And therewyth awoke sir Beawmaynes, and up he lepte lyghtly and sawe where the blak knyght rode his way wyth the dwarff, and so he rode oute of his syght.

(20) Than sir Bewmaynes put on his helme and buckeled on his shylde and toke his horse and rode afftir hym all that ever he myght, thorow
30 mores and fellys and grete sloughis, that many tymes his horse and he plunged over their hedys in depe myres, for he knewe nat the way but toke the gayneste way in that woodenesse, that many tymes he was lyke to peryshe. And at the laste hym happened to com to a fayre grene way, and there he mette with a poore man of the contray and asked hym
35 whether he mette nat with a knyght uppon a blak horse and all blak harneyse, and a lytyll dwarff syttynge behynde hym with hevy chere.

'Sir,' seyde the poore man, 'here by me com sir Gryngamoure the knyght with suche a dwarff, and therefore I rede you nat to folow hym, for he is one of the perelyst knyghtes of the worlde, and his castell is
40 here nerehonde but two myle. Therefore we avyse you, ryde nat aftir sir Gryngamour but yf ye owe hym good wylle.'

So leve we sir Bewmaynes rydyng toward the castell, and speke we of sir Gryngamoure and the dwarff. Anone as the dwarff was com to the castell dame Lyonesse and dame Lynet, hir systir, asked the dwarff

where was his mastir borne and of what lynage was he com. 'And but
yf thou telle me,' seyde dame Lyonesse, 'thou shalt never ascape this
castell but ever here to be presonere.'

'As for that,' seyde the dwarff, 'I feare nat gretly to telle his name
and of what kynne he is commyn of. Wete you well, he is a kynges son   5
and a quenys, and his fadir hyght kynge Lot of Orkeney, and his modir
is sistir to kyng Arthure, and he is brother to sir Gawayne, and his
name is sir Gareth of Orkenay. And now I have tolde you his ryght
name, I pray you, fayre lady, lat me go to my lorde agayne, for he woll
never oute of this contrey tyll he have me agayne; and yf he be angry   10
he woll do harme or that he be stynted, and worche you wrake in this
contrey.'

'As for that, be as be may.'

'Nay,' seyde sir Gryngamoure, 'as for that thretynge, we woll go
to dynere.'   15

And so they wayshed and wente to mete and made hem mery and
well at ease. Bycause the lady Lyonesse of the Castell Perelus was there,
they made the gretter joy.

'Truly, madam,' seyde Lynet unto hir sistir, 'well may he be a kyngys
son, for he hath many good tacchis: for he is curtyese and mylde, and   20
the most sufferynge man that ever I mette withall. For I dare sey there
was never jantyllwoman revyled man in so foule a maner a[s] I have
rebuked hym. And at all tymes he gaff me goodly and meke answers
agayne.'

And as they sate thus talkynge there cam sir Gareth in at the gate   25
with hys swerde drawyn in his honde and cryed alowde that all the
castell myght hyre:

'Thou traytour knyght, sir Gryngamoure! delyver me my dwarff
agayne, or by the fayth that I owghe to God and to the hygh Ordir of
Knyghthode I shall do the all the harme that may lye in my power!'   30

Than sir Gryngamour loked oute at a wyndow and seyde,

'Sir Gareth of Orkenay, leve thy bostyng wordys, for thou gettyst
nat thy dwarff agayne.'

'Than, cowarde knyght,' seyde Gareth, 'brynge hym with the, and
com and do batayle with me, and wynne hym and take hym.'   35

'So woll I do,' seyde sir Gryngamoure, 'and me lyste, but for all thy
grete wordys thou gettyst hym nat.'

'A, fayre lady,' seyde dame Lynet, 'I wolde he hadde his dwarff
agayne, for I wolde he were nat wroth: for now he hath tolde me all my
desyre, I kepe no more of the dwarff. And also, brother, he hath done   40
muche for me and delyverde me frome the Rede Knyght of the Rede
Laundis. And therefore, brother, I owe hym my servyse afore all
knyghtes lyvynge, and wete you well that I love hym byfore all othyr
knyghtes lyvynge, and full fayne I wolde speke with hym. But in no

wyse I wolde nat that he wyste what I were but as I were anothir
strange lady.'

'Well, sistir,' seyde sir Gryngamour, 'sythen that I know no[w] your
wyll I woll obey me now unto hym.' And so therewith he wente downe
5 and seyde, 'Sir Gareth, I cry you mercy, and all that I have myssedone
I woll amende hit at your wylle. And therefore I pray you that ye wolde
alyght and take suche chere as I can make you in this castell.'

'Shall I have my dwarff?' seyde sir Gareth.

'Yee, sir, and all the plesure that I can make you, for as sone as your
10 dwarff tolde me what ye were and of what kynde ye ar com and what
noble dedys ye have done in this marchis, than I repented me of my
dedys.'

Than sir Gareth alyght, and there com his dwarff and toke his horse.

'A, my felow!' seyde sir Gareth, 'I have had muche adventures for
15 thy sake!'

And so sir Gryngamoure toke hym by the honde and ledde hym into
(21) the halle where his owne wyff was. And than com forth dame Lyones
arayde lyke a prynces, and there she made hym passyng good chere and
he hir agayne, and they had goodly langage and lovely countenaunce.
20 And sir Gareth thought many tymes : 'Jesu, wolde that the lady of
this Castell Perelus were so fayre as she is!' And there was all maner of
gamys and playes, of daunsyng and syngynge, and evermore sir Gareth
behelde that lady. And the more he loked on her, the more he brenned
in love, that he passed hymself farre in his reson. And forth towardys
25 nyght they yode unto souper, and sir Gareth myght nat ete, for his love
was so hoote that he wyst nat where he was.

All thes lokys aspyed sir Gryngamour, and than aftir souper he
called his sistir dame Lyonesse untyll a chambir and sayde,

'Fayre sistir, I have well aspyed your countenaunce betwyxte you
30 and this knyght, and I woll, sistir, that ye wete he is a full noble knyght,
and yf ye can make hym to abyde here I woll do hym all the plesure
that I can, for and ye were bettir than ye ar, ye were well bewared uppon
hym.'

'Fayre brother,' seyde dame Lyonesse, 'I undirstonde well that the
35 knyght is a good knyght and com he is oute of a noble house. Natwith-
stondyng I woll assay hym bettir, howbehit I am moste beholde to hym
of ony erthely man, for he hath had grete labour for my love and passed
many dangerous passagis.'

Ryght so sir Gryngamour wente unto sir Gareth and seyde, 'Sir,
40 make ye good chere, for ye shall have none other cause, for this lady my
sistir is youres at all tymes, hir worshyp saved, for wete you well she
lovyth you as well as ye do hir and bettir, yf bettir may be.'

'And I wyste that,' seyde sir Gareth, 'there lyved nat a gladder man
than I wolde be.'

'Uppon my worshyp,' seyde sir Gryngamoure, 'truste unto my promyse. And as longe as hit lykyth you ye shall suggeourne with me, and this lady shall be wyth us dayly and nyghtly to make you all the chere that she can.'

'I woll well,' seyde sir Gareth, 'for I have promysed to be nyghe this 5
contray this twelve-monthe, and well I am sure kynge Arthure and other noble knyghtes woll fynde me where that I am wythin this twelve-monthe, for I shall be sought and founden yf that I be on lyve.'

And than sir Gareth wente unto the lady dame Lyonesse and kyssed hir many tymes, and eythir made grete joy of other, and there she 10
promysed hym hir love, sertaynly to love hym and none other dayes of hir lyff. Than this lady dame Lyonesse by the assent of hir brother tolde sir Gareth all the trouthe what she was, and how she was the same lady that he dud batayle fore, and how she was lady of the Castell Perelus. And there she tolde hym how she causid hir brother to take away 15
his dwarff, 'for this cause: to know the sertayne, what was your name (22)
and of what kyn ye were com.' And than she lette fette before hym hir systir Lynet that had ryddyn with hym many a wylsom way. Than was syr Gareth more gladder than he was tofore.

And than they trouthe-plyght other to love and never to fayle whyle 20
their lyff lastyth. And so they brente bothe in hoote love that they were acorded to abate their lustys secretly. And there dame Lyonesse counceyled sir Gareth to slepe in none other place but in the halle, and there she promysed hym to com to his bed a lytyll afore mydnyght.

This counceyle was nat so prevyly kepte but hit was undirstonde, for 25
they were but yonge bothe and tendir of ayge and had nat used suche craufftis toforne. Wherefore the damesell Lyonett was a lytyll dysplesed; and she thought hir sister dame Lyonesse was a lytyll overhasty that she myght nat abyde hir tyme of maryage, and for savyng of hir worshyp she thought to abate their hoote lustis. And she lete ordeyne by hir 30
subtyle craufftes that they had nat theire intentys neythir with othir as in her delytes untyll they were maryed.

And so hit paste on. At aftir souper was made a clene avoydaunce, that every lorde and lady sholde go unto his reste. But sir Gareth seyde playnly he wolde go no farther than the halle, for in suche placis, he 35
seyde, was convenyaunte for an arraunte knyght to take his reste in. And so there was ordayned grete cowchis and thereon fethir beddis, and there he leyde hym downe to slepe. And within a whyle came dame Lyonesse wrapped in a mantell furred with ermyne, and leyde hir downe by the sydys of sir Gareth. And therewithall he began to clyppe 40
hir and to kysse hir.

And therewithall he loked before hym and sawe an armed knyght with many lyghtes aboute hym, and this knyght had a longe gysarne in his honde and made a grymme countenaunce to smyte hym. Whan sir

Gareth sawe hym com in that wyse he lepte oute of his bedde and gate in his hande a swerde and lepte towarde that knyght. And whan the knyght sawe sir Gareth com so fersly uppon hym he smote hym with a foyne thorow the thycke of the thygh, that the wounde was a
5 shafftemonde brode and had cutte a-too many vaynes and synewys. And therewithall sir Gareth smote hym uppon the helme suche a buffette that he felle grovelyng, and than he lepe over hym and unlaced his helme and smote off his hede fro the body. And than he bled so faste that he myght not stonde, but so he leyde hym downe uppon his
10 bedde and there he sowned and lay as he had bene dede.

Than dame Lyonesse cryed alowde that sir Gryngamoure harde hit and com downe; and whan he sawe sir Gareth so shamfully wounded he was sore dyspleased and seyde,

'I am shamed that this noble knyght is thus dishonoured. Si⟨sti⟩r,'
15 seyde sir Gryngamour, 'how may this be that this noble knyght is thus wounded?'

'Brothir,' she seyde, 'I can nat telle you, for hit was nat done by me nother be myne assente, for he is my lorde and I am his, and he muste be myne husbonde. Therefore, brothir, I woll that ye wete I shame nat
20 to be with hym nor to do hym all the plesure that I can.'

'Sistir,' seyde Gryngamour, 'and I woll that ye wete hit and Gareth bothe that hit was never done by me, nother be myne assente this unhappy dede was never done.'

And there they staunched his bledyng as well as they myght, and
25 grete sorow made sir Gryngamour and dame Lyonesse. And forth-withall com dame Lyonett and toke up the hede in the syght of them all, and anoynted hit with an oyntemente thereas hit was smyttyn off, and in the same wyse [s]he ded to the othir parte thereas the hede stake. And than she sette hit togydirs, and hit stake as faste as ever hit
30 ded. And the knyght arose lyghtly up and the damesell Lyonett put hym in hir chambir.

All this saw sir Gryngamour and dame Lyonesse, and so ded sir Gareth, and well he aspyed that hit was dame Lyonett that rode with hym thorow the perelouse passages.
35 'A, well, damesell!' seyde sir Gareth, 'I wente ye wolde nat have done as ye have done.'

'My lorde sir Gareth,' seyde Lyonett, 'all that I have done I woll avowe hit, and all shall be for your worshyp and us all.'

And so within a whyle sir Gareth was nyghe hole and waxed lyght
40 and jocounde, and sange and daunced. Tha[n] agayne sir Gareth and dame Lyonesse were so hoote in brennynge love that they made their covenauntes at the tenth nyght aftir, that she sholde com to his bedde. And because he was wounded afore, he leyde his armour and his swerde nygh his beddis syde.

And ryght as she promysed she com. And she was nat so sone in his (23) bedde but she aspyed an armed knyght commynge towarde the bed, and anone she warned sir Gareth. And lyghtly thorow the good helpe of dame Lyonesse he was armed, and they hurled togydyrs with grete ire and malyce all aboute the halle. And there was grete lyght as hit had 5 be the numbir of twenty torchis bothe byfore and behynde. So sir Gareth strayned hym so that his olde wounde braste ayen on-bledynge. But he was hote and corragyous and toke no kepe, but with his grete forse he strake downe the knyght and voyded hys helme and strake of his hede.

Than he hew the hede uppon an hondred pecis, and whan he had done so he toke up all tho pecis and threw them oute at a wyndow into the dychis of the castell. And by this done he was so faynte that unnethis he myght stonde for bledynge, and by than he was allmoste unarmed he felle in a dedly sowne in the floure.

Than dame Lyonesse cryed, that sir Gryngamoure herde her, and whan he com and founde sir Gareth in that plyght he made grete sorow. And there he awaked sir Gareth and gaff hym a drynke that releved hym wondirly well. But the sorow that dame Lyonesse made there may no tunge telle, for she so fared with hirself as she wolde have dyed. 20

Ryght so come this damesell Lyonett before hem all, and she had sette all the gobbettis of the hede that sir Gareth had throwe oute at the wyndow, and there she anoynted hit as she dud tofore, and put them to the body in the syght of hem all.

'Well, damesell Lyonett,' seyde sir Gareth, 'I have nat deserved all 25 this dyspyte that ye do unto me.'

'Sir knyght,' she seyde, 'I have nothynge done but I woll avow hit, and all that I have done shall be to your worshyp and to us all.'

Than was sir Gareth staunched of his bledynge, but the lechis seyde there was no man that bare the lyff sholde heale hym thorowly of his 30 wounde but yf they heled them that caused the stroke by enchauntemente.

So leve we sir Gareth there wyth sir Gryngamour and his sisters, and turne we unto kyng Arthure that at the nexte feste of Pentecoste [helde his feste.] There cam the Grene Knyght and fyfty knyghtes with hym, 35 and yeldyd them all unto kynge Arthure. Than there com the Rede Knyghte, his brother, and yelded them to kynge Arthure wyth three score knyghtes with them. Also there com the Blew Knyght, his brother, and yelded hem to kyng Arthure. And the Grene Knyghtes name was sir Partholype, and the Rede Knyghtes name was sir Perymones, and 40 the Blew Knyghtes name was sir Persaunte of Inde.

Thes three bretherne tolde kynge Arthure how they were overcom by a knyght that a damesell had with hir, and she called hym sir Bewmaynes.

'Jesu!' seyde the kynge, 'I mervayle what knyght he is and of what lynage he is com. Here he was with me a twelve-monthe and poorely and shamefully he was fostred. And sir Kay i[n] scorne named hym Bewmaynes.'

5 So ryght as the kynge stode so talkyng with thes three bretherne there com sir Launcelot du Lake and tolde the kynge that there was com a goodly lorde with fyve hondred knyghtys with hym. Than the kynge was at Carlyon, for there was the feste holde, and thidir com to hym this lorde and salewed the kynge with goodly maner.

10 'What wolde ye?' seyde kynge Arthure, 'and what is your erande?'
'Sir,' he seyde, 'I am called the Rede Knyght of the Rede Laundis, but my name is sir Ironsyde; and, sir, wete you well, hydir I am sente unto you frome a knyght that is called sir Bewmaynes, for he wanne me in playne batayle hande for hande, and so ded never knyght but he
15 that ever had the bettir of me this twenty wyntir. And I am commaunded to yelde me to you at your wyll.'

'Ye ar welcom,' seyde the kynge, 'for ye have bene longe a grete foo of owres to me and to my courte, and now, I truste to God, I shall so entrete you that ye shall be my frende.'

20 'Sir, bothe I and thes fyve hondred knyghtes shall allwayes be at your sommons to do you suche servyse as may lye in oure powers.'

'Gramercy,' seyde kynge Arthure, 'I am muche beholdyng unto that knyght that hath so put his body in devoure to worshyp me and my courte. And as to the, sir Ironsyde, that is called the Rede Knyght of the
25 Rede Laundys, thou arte called a perelouse knyght, and yf thou wolte holde of me I shall worshyp the and make the knyght of the Table Rounde, but than thou muste be no man-murtherer.'

'Sir, as to that, I have made my promyse unto sir Bewmaynes nevermore to use such customs, for all the shamefull customs that I used I
30 ded hit at the requeste of a lady that I loved. And therefore I muste goo unto sir Launcelot and unto sir Gawayne and aske them forgyffnesse of the evyll wyll I had unto them; for all tho that I put to deth was all only for the love of sir Launcelot and of sir Gawayne.'

'They bene here,' seyde the kynge, 'before the. Now may ye sey to
35 them what ye woll.'

And than he kneled downe unto sir Launcelot and to sir Gawayne and prayde them of forgeffnesse of his enmyté that he had ayenste
(24) them. Than goodly they seyde all at onys,

'God forgyff you and we do. And we pray you that ye woll telle us
40 where we may fynde sir Bewmaynes.'

'Fayre lorde,' sayde sir Ironsyde, 'I can nat telle you, for hit is full harde to fynde hym: for such yonge knyghtes as he is, whan they be in their adventures, bene never abydyng in no place.'

But to sey the worshyp that the Rede Knyght of the Rede Laundys-

and sir Persaunte and his br[other] seyde by hym, hit was mervayle to
hyre.

'Well, my fayre lordys,' seyde kynge Arthure, 'wete you well I shall
do you honour for the love of sir Bewmaynes, and as sone as ever I may
mete with hym I shall make you all uppon a day knyghtes of the Table 5
Rounde. And as to the, sir Persaunte of Inde, thou hast bene ever called
a full noble knyght, and so hath evermore thy three bretherne bene
called. But I mervayle,' seyde the kynge, 'that I here nat of the Blak
Knyght, your brother. He was a full noble knyght.'

'Sir,' seyde Pertolype the Grene Knyght, 'sir Bewmaynes slew hym 10
in a recountir with hys spere. His name was sir Perarde.'

'That was grete pyté,' seyde the kynge, and so seyde many knyghtes,
for thes four brethyrne were full well knowyn in kynge Arthures courte
for noble knyghtes, for long tyme they had holdyn werre ayenste the
knyghtes of the Rownde Table.   15

Than Partolype the Grene Knyght tolde the kyng that at a passage
of the watir of Mortayse there encountird sir Bewmaynes with too
bretherne that ever for the moste party kepte that passage, and they
were two dedly knyghtes. And there he slew the eldyst brother in the
watir and smote hym uppon the hede suche a buffette that he felle 20
downe in the watir and there was he drowned. And his name was sir
Garrarde le Brewse. And aftir he slew the other brother uppon the
londe: hys name was sir Arnolde le Brewse.

So than the kynge [and they] wente to mete and were served in the (25, 26)
beste maner. And as they sate at the mete there com in the quene of 25
Orkenay with ladyes and knyghtes a grete numbir. And than sir
Gawayne, sir Aggravayne, and sir Gaherys arose and wente to hir
modir and salewed hir uppon their kneis and asked hir blyssynge,
for of twelve yere before they had not sene hir. Than she spake uppon
hyght to hir brother kynge Arthure: 30

'Where have ye done my yonge son, sir Gareth? For he was here
amongyst you a twelve-monthe, and ye made a kychyn knave of hym,
the whyche is shame to you all. Alas! Where have ye done myn owne
dere son that was my joy and blysse?'

'A, dere modir,' seyde sir Gawayne, 'I knew hym nat.'   35

'Nothir I,' seyde the kynge, 'that now me repentys, but, thanked be
God, he is previd a worshypfull knyght as ony that is now lyvyng of his
yerys, and I shall nevir be glad tyll that I may fynde [hym].'

'A, brothir!' seyde the quene, 'ye dud yourself grete shame whan ye
amongyst you kepte my son in the kychyn and fedde hym lyke an 40
hogge.'

'Fayre sistir,' seyde kynge Arthure, 'ye shall ryght well wete that I
knew hym nat, nother no more dud sir Gawayne, nothir his bretherne.
But sytthe hit is so,' seyde the kynge, 'that he thus is gone frome us all,

we muste shape a remedy to fynde hym. Also, sistir, mesemyth ye
myght have done me to wete of his commynge, and than, if I had nat
done well to hym, ye myght have blamed me. For whan he com to this
courte he cam lenynge uppon too mennys sholdyrs as though he myght
5 nat have gone. And than he asked me three gyfftys; and one he asked that
same day, and that was that I wolde gyff hym mete inowghe that twelve-
monthe. And the other two gyfftys he asked that day twelve-monthe,
and that was that he myght have the adventure of the damesel Lyonett;
and the thirde, that sir Launcelot sholde make hym knyght whan he
10 desyred hym. And so I graunted hym all [his] desyre. And many in this
courte mervayled that he desyred his sustynaunce for a twelve-monthe,
and thereby we demed many of us that he was nat com oute of a
noble house.'

   'Sir,' seyde the quene of Orkenay unto kynge Arthure her brother,
15 'wete you well that I sente hym unto you ryght well armed and horsed
and worshypfully besene of his body, and golde and sylver plenté to
spende.'

   'Hit may be so,' seyde the kyng, 'but thereof sawe we none, save that
same day that he departed frome us knyghtes tolde me that there com
20 a dwarff hyder suddeynely and brought hym armour and a good horse
full well and rychely beseyne. And thereat all we had mervayle, frome
whens that rychesse com. Than we demed all that he was com of men
of worshyp.'

   'Brother,' seyde the quene, 'all that ye sey we beleve hit, for ever
25 sytthen he was growyn he was [mervaylously wytted, and ever he was]
feythfull and trew of his promyse. But I mervayle,' seyde she, 'that sir
Kay dud mok and scorn hym and gaff hym to name Bewmaynes; yet
sir Kay,' seyde the quene, 'named hym more ryghteously than he wende,
for I dare sey he is as fayre an handid man ⌐and wel disposed¬, and he
30 be on lyve, as ony lyvynge.'

   'Sistir,' seyde Arthure, 'lat this langage now be stylle, and by the
grace of God he shall be founde and he be within this seven realmys.
And lette all this passe and be myrry, for he is preved to [be] a man of
worshyp, and that is my joy.'

(27) 35   Than seyde sir Gawayne and his bretherne unto kynge Arthure,
'Sir, and ye woll gyff us leve we woll go seke oure brother.'

   'Nay,' sayde sir Launcelot, 'that shall not nede.' And so seyde sir
Bawdwyn of Brytaygne. 'For as by oure advyse, the kynge shall sende
unto dame Lyonesse a messyngere and pray hir that she wolle come to
40 the courte in all haste that she may. And doute ye nat she woll com, and
than she may gyff you the beste counceyle where ye shall fynde sir
Gareth.'

   'This is well seyde of you,' seyde the kynge.

   So than goodly lettyrs were made, and the messyngere sente forth,

that nyght and day wente tyll he com to the Castell Perelous. And than
the lady, dame Lyonesse, was sente fore thereas she was with sir
Gryngamour, hir brother, and sir Gareth. And whan she undirstoode
this messyngere she bade hym ryde on his way unto kynge Arthure, and
she wolde com aftir in all the moste goodly haste.   5

Than she com unto sir Gryngamour and to sir Gareth, and tolde
hem all how kyng Arthure hadde sente for hir.

'That is because of me,' seyde sir Gareth.

'Now avyse ye me,' seyde dame Lyonesse, 'what I shall sey, and in
what maner I shall rule me.'   10

'My lady and my love,' seyde sir Gareth, 'I pray you in no wyse be
ye aknowyn where I am. But well I wote my modir is there and all my
bretherne, and they woll take uppon hem to seke me: I woll that they
do. But this, madam, I woll ye sey and avyse the kynge whan he ques-
tyons with you of me: than may ye sey this is your avyse, that and hit   15
lyke his good grace, ye woll do make a cry ayenst the Assumpcion of
Oure Lady, that what knyght that prevyth hym beste, he shall welde
you and all your lande. And yf so be that he be a wedded man that
wynnes the degré, he shall have a coronall of golde sette with stonys of
vertu to the valew of a thousand pound, and a whyght jarfawcon.'   20

So dame Lyonesse departed. And to com off and to breff this tale,
whan she com to kynge Arthure she was nobly resseyved, and there
she was sore questyonde of the kynge and of the quene of Orkeney.
And she answerde where sir Gareth was she coude not tell, but this
muche she seyde unto kynge Arthure: 25

'Sir, by your avyse I woll let cry a turnemente that shall be done
before my castell at the Assumpcion of Oure Lady; and the cry shall
be this, that you, my lorde Arthure, shall be there and your knyghtes,
and I woll purvey that my knyghtes shall be ayenste youres; and than
I am sure I shall hyre of sir Gareth.'   30

'This is well avysed,' seyde kynge Arthure.

And so she departed; and the kynge and she made grete provysion
to the turnemente.

Whan dame Lyonesse was com to the Ile of Avylyon—that was the
same ile thereas hir brother, sir Gryngamour, dwelled—than she tolde   35
hem all how she had done, and what promyse she had made to kynge
Arthure.

'Alas!' seyde sir Gareth, 'I have bene so sore wounded with unhappynesse sitthyn I cam into this castell that I shall nat be able to do at that
turnemente lyke a knyght; for I was never thorowly hole syn I was   40
hurte.'

'Be ye of good chere,' seyde the damesell Lyonett, 'for I undirtake
within this fyftene dayes to make you as hole and as lusty as ever ye
were.'

And than she leyde an oynemente and salve to hym as hit pleased hir, that he was never so freyshe nother so lusty as he was tho.

Than seyde the damesell Lyonett, 'Sende you unto sir Persaunte of Inde, and assumpne hym that he be redy there with hole assomons of
5 knyghtes, lyke as he made his promyse. Also that ye sende unto Ironsyde that is knyght of the Rede Laundys, and charge hym that he be there with you wyth his hole somme of knyghtes; and than shall ye be able to macche wyth kynge Arthure and his knyghtes.'

So this was done and all knyghtes were sente fore unto the Castell
10 Perelous. Than the Rede Knyght answerde and sayde unto dame Lyonesse and to sir Gareth,

'Ye shall undirstonde that I have bene at the courte of kynge Arthure, and sir Persaunte of Inde and his brotherne, and there we have done oure omage as ye comaunded us. Also,' seyde sir [Ironsyde], 'I have
15 takyn uppon me with sir Persaunte of Inde and his bretherne to holde party agaynste my lorde sir Launcelot and the knyghtes of that courte, and this have I done for the love of my lady, dame Lyonesse, and you, my lorde sir Gareth.'

'Ye have well done,' seyde sir Gareth, 'but wete ye well, we shall be
20 full sore macched with the moste nobleste knyghtes of the worlde: therefore we muste purvey us of good knyghtes where we may gete hem.'

'Ye sey well,' seyde sir Persaunte, 'and worshypfully.'

And so the cry was made in Ingelonde, Walys, Scotlonde, Irelonde,
25 and Cornuayle, and in all the Oute Iles, and in Bretayne and many contrayes, that at oure Lady Day, the Assumpsion next folowynge, [men] sholde com to the Castell Perelus besyde the Ile of Avylon, and there all knyghtes, whan they com there, sholde chose whethir them lyste to be on the tone party with the knyghtes of the Castell, other to
30 be with kyng Arthur on the tothir party. And two monthis was to the day that the turnamente sholde be.

And so many good knyghtys that were at hir large helde hem for the moste party all this tyme ayenste kynge Arthure and the knyghtes of the Rounde Table: and so they cam in the syde of [them of the] castell.
35 And sir Epynogrys was the fyrste, and he was the kynges son of Northumbirlonde; and sir Palamydes the Saresyn was another, and sir Safere and sir Segwarydes, hys bretherne—but they bothe were crystynde—and sir Malegryne, and sir Bryan de les Iles, a noble knyght, and sir Grummor and Grummorson, two noble knyghtes of Scotlond,
40 and sir Carados of the Dolowres Towre, a noble knyght, and sir Terquyne his brother, and sir Arnolde and sir Gauter, two bretherne, good knyghtes of Cornuayle.

Also there com sir Trystrams de Lyones, and with hym sir Dynas the Senesciall, and sir Saduk. But this sir Trystrams was nat at that tyme

knyght of the Rounde Table; but he was at that tyme one of the beste
knyghtes of the worlde. And so all thes noble knyghtes accompanyed
hem with the lady of the Castell, and with the Rede Knyght of the
Rede Laundys. But as for sir Gareth, he wolde nat take uppon hym but
as othir meane knyghtis.   5

Than turne we to kynge Arthure that brought wyth hym sir (28)
Gawayne, Aggravayne, Gaherys, his brethern; and than his nevewys, as
sir Uwayne le Blaunche Maynes, and sir Agglovale, sir Tor, sir Percivale
de Galys, sir Lamerok de Galys. Than com sir Launcelot du Lake with
his bretherne, nevewys, and cosyns, as sir Lyonell, sir Ector de Marys, 10
sir Bors de Gaynys, and sir Bleobrys de Gaynes, sir Blamour de Gaynys
and sir Galyhodyn, sir Galyhud, and many mo of sir Launcelottys
kynne; and sir Dynadan, sir La Cote Male Tayle, his brother, a knyght
good, and sir Sagramoure le Desyrus, sir Dodynas le Saveage; and all
the moste party of the Rounde Table.   15

Also there cam with kynge Arthure thes kynges: the kyng of Irelonde, kynge Angwysauns, and the kynge of Scotlonde, kynge Carados,
and kynge Uryens of the londe of Gore, and kynge Bagdemagus and
his son sir Mellyagauns, and sir Galahalte, the noble prynce,—all thes
prynces and erlys, barowns and noble knyghtes, as sir Braundyles, sir 20
Uwayne les Avoutres, and sir Kay, sir Bedyvere, sir Melyot de Logres,
sir Petypace of Wynchilsé, sir Gotlake—all thes com with kynge
Arthure and mo that be nat here rehersid.

Now leve we of thes knyghtes and kynges, and lette us speke of the
grete aray that was made within the castell and aboute the castell; for 25
this lady, dame Ly[o]nesse, ordayned grete aray uppon hir party for hir
noble knyghtys, for all maner of lodgynge and vytayle that cam by
londe and by watir, that there lacked nothynge for hir party, nother
for the othir party, but there was plenté to be had for golde and sylver
for kynge Arthure and all his knyghtes. And than there cam the 30
herbygeours frome kynge Arthure for to herborow hym and his
kyngys, deukis, erlys, barons, [and] knyghtes.

Than sir Gareth prayde dame Lyonesse and the Rede Knyght of the
Rede Laundys, and sir Persaunte and his bretherne, and sir Gryngamour, that in no wyse there sholde none of them telle his name, and 35
make no more of hym than of the leste knyght that there was: 'for,' he
seyde, 'I woll nat be knowyn of neythir more ne lesse, nothir at the
begynnynge nother at the endyng.'

Than dame Lyones seyde unto sir Gareth, 'Sir, I wolde leve with you
a rynge of myne; but I wolde pray you, as ye love me hertely, lette me 40
have hit agayne whan the turnemente is done: for that rynge encresyth
my beawté muche more than hit is of myself. And the vertu of my
rynge is this: that that is grene woll turne to rede, and that that is rede
woll turne in lyknesse to grene, and that that is blewe woll turne to

whyghte, and that that is whyght woll [turne] in lyknesse to blew; and so hit woll do of all maner of coloures; also who that beryth this rynge shall lose no bloode. And for grete love I woll gyff you this rynge.'

'Gramercy,' seyde sir Gareth, 'myne owne lady. For this rynge is
5 passynge mete for me; for hit woll turne all maner of lyknesse that I am in, and that shall cause me that I shall nat be knowyn.'

Than sir Gryngamour gaff sir Gareth a bay coursor that was a passynge good horse. Also he gaff hym good armour and sure, and a noble swerde that somtyme sir Gryngamours fadir wan uppon an
10 hethyn tyrraunte. And so thus every knyght made hym redy to that turnemente.

And kynge Arthure was commyn two dayes tofore the Assumpcion of Oure Lady; and there was all maner of royalté, of all maner of mynstralsy that myght be founde. Also there cam quene Gwenyvere and the
15 quene of Orkeney, sir Garethis mother.

And uppon the Assumpcion day, whan masse and matyns was done, there was herodys with trumpettis commaunded to blow to the felde. And so there com oute sir Epynogrys, the kynges son of Northumbirlonde, frome the castell; and there encountyrde with hym sir Sagra-
20 moure le Desyrous, and eythir of them brake there sperys to theire handis. And than com in sir Palomydes oute of the castell; and there encountyrd with hym sir Gawayne, and eythir of them smote other so harde that bothe good knyghtes and their horsis felle to the erthe. And than the knyghtes of eythir party rescowed other.

25 Than cam in sir Safer and sir Segwarydes, bretherne to Palamydes; and there encountyrd sir Aggravayne with sir Safer, and sir Gaherys encountyrd with sir Segwarydes. So sir Safer smote downe sir Aggravayne. And sir Malegryne, a knyght of the castell, encountyrd with sir Uwayne le Blaunche Maynes, and smote downe sir Malegryne, that he
30 had allmoste broke his necke.

(29)   Than sir Bryan de les Iles, and Grummor and Grummorson, knyghtes of the castell, encountyrde with sir Agglovale, and sir Tor smote them of the castell downe.

Than com in sir Carados of the Dolowres Towre, and sir Terquyne,
35 knyghtes of the castell; and there encountyrd with hem sir Percivale de Galys, and sir Lamerok, his brother; and there [encountryd sir Percivale with sir Carados, and eyther brake their speres unto their handes, and than sir Terquyne with sir Lamerok, and eyther] smote downe othir, hors and man, to the erthe; and eythir partyes rescowed other
40 and horsed them agayne.

And sir Arnolde and sir Gawter, knyghtes of the castell, encountird wyth sir Brandyles and sir Kay; and thes four knyghtes encountyrde myghtely, and brake their sperys to theyre handis.

Than com in sir Trystrams, sir Saduk, and sir Dynas, knyghtes of the

castell; and there encountyrd with sir Trystrams sir Bedyvere, and sir
Bedyvere was smyttyn to the erthe bothe horse and man. And sir
Sadoke encountyrde wyth sir Petypace, and there sir Sadoke was overthrowyn. And there sir Uwayne les Avoutres smote downe sir Dynas
the Senesciall.   5

Than com in sir Persaunte of Inde, a knyght of the castell; and there
encountyrde with hym sir Launcelot du Lake, and there he smote sir
Persaunte, horse and man, to the erthe. Than come in sir Pertolype
frome the castell; and there encountyrde with hym sir Lyonell, and
there sir Pertolype, the Grene Knyght, smote downe sir Lyonell,   10
brothir to sir Launcelot.

And all this was marked wyth noble herrodis, who bare hym beste,
and their namys.

And than com into the felde sir Perimones, the Grene Knyght, sir
Persauntis brothir, that was a knyght of the castell; and he encountyrde   15
wyth sir Ector de Marys, and aythir of hem smote other so harde that
hir sperys and horsys and they felle to the erthe.

And than com in the Rede Knyght of the Rede Laundis and sir
Gareth, frome the castell; and there encountyrde with hem sir Bors de
Gaynys and sir Bleobrys. And there the Rede Knyght and sir Bors   20
smote other so harde that hir sperys braste and their horsys felle
grovelynge to the erthe. Than sir Blamour brake another spere uppon
sir Gareth; but of that stroke sir Blamour felle to the erthe.

That sawe sir Galyhuddyn, and bade sir Gareth kepe hym; and sir
Gareth smote hym anone to the erthe. Than sir Galyhud gate a spere to   25
avenge his brother; and in the same wyse sir Gareth served hym. And
in the same maner sir Gareth served sir Dynadan and his brother, sir
La Kote Male Tayle, and sir Sagramoure le Desyrus, and sir Donyas le
Saveage: all these knyghtes he bare hem downe with one speare.

Whan kynge Anguyshauns of Irelonde sawe sir Gareth fare so, he   30
mervayled what knyght he was; for at one tyme he semed grene, and
another tyme at his gayne-commynge hym semed blewe. And thus at
every course that he rode too and fro he chonged whyght to rede and
blak, that there myght neyther kynge nother knyght have no redy
cognysshauns of hym.   35

Than kynge Anguyshaunce, the kynge of Irelonde, encountyrde
with sir Gareth, and there sir Gareth smote hym frome his horse,
sadyll and all. And than com in kynge Carados of Scotlonde, and sir
Gareth smote hym downe horse and man; and in the same wyse he
served kynge Uryens of the londe of Gore. And than come in sir Bag-   40
demagus, and sir Gareth smote hym downe horse and man to the
erthe; and kynge Bagdemagus son, sir Mellyagauns, brake a spere
uppon sir Gareth myghtyly and knyghtly.

And than sir Galahalte the noble prynce cryed on hyght:

'Knyght with the many coloures, well haste thou justed! Now make the redy, that I may juste with the!'

Sir Gareth herde hym, and gate a grete spere, and so they encountyrde togydir, and there the prynce brake his spere; but sir Gareth
5 smote hym uppon the buff syde of the helme, that he reled here and there, and had falle downe had nat his men recoverde hym.

'So God me helpe,' seyde kynge Arthure, 'that same knyght with the many coloures is a good knyght.' Wherefore the kynge called unto hym sir Launcelot and prayde hym to encountir with that knyght.
10 'Sir,' seyde sir Launcelot, 'I may well fynde in myne herte for to forbere hym as at this tyme, for he hath had travayle inowe this day. And whan a good knyght doth so well uppon som day, hit is no good knyghtes parte to lette hym of his worshyp, and namely whan he seyth a good knyghte hath done so grete labur. For peraventure,' seyde sir
15 Launcelot, 'his quarell is here this day, and peraventure he is beste beloved with this lady of all that bene here: for I se well he paynyth hym and enforsyth hym to do grete dedys. And therefore,' seyde sir Launcelot, 'as for me, this day he shall have the honour: thoughe hit lay in my power to put hym frome hit, yet wolde I nat.'
(30) 20 Than whan this was done there was drawynge of swerdys, and than there began a sore turnemente. And there dud sir Lameroke mervaylus dedys of armys; and bytwyxte sir Lameroke and sir Ironsyde, that was the Rede Knyght of the Rede Laundys, there was a stronge batayle. And sir Palomydes and sir Bleobrys, betwyxte them was full grete
25 batayle. And sir Gawayne and sir Trystrams mett; and there sir Gawayne had the worse, for he pulled sir Gawayne frome his horse, and there he was longe uppon foote and defouled.

Than com in sir Launcelot, and he smote sir Terquyn, and he hym. And than cam therein sir Carados, his brother, and bothe at onys they
30 assayled hym, and he as the moste noblyst knyght of the worlde worshypfully fought with hem bothe and helde them hote, that all men wondred of the nobles of sir Launcelot.

And than com in sir Gareth, and knew that hit was sir Launcelot that fought with tho perelous knyghtes, and parted them in sundir;
35 and no stroke wolde he smyte sir Launcelot. That aspyed sir Launcelot and demed hit sholde be the good knyght sir Gareth.

And than sir Gareth rode here and there and smote on the ryght honde and on the lyffte honde, that all folkys myght well aspye where that he rode. And by fortune he mette with his brother, sir Gawayne;
40 and there he put hym to the wors, for he put of his helme. And so he served fyve or six knyghtes of the Rounde Table, that all men seyde he put hym in moste payne and beste he dud his dever.

For whan sir Trystrams behylde hym how he fyrste justed and aftir fought so welle with a swerde, than he rode unto sir Ironsyde and to sir

Persaunte of Inde, and asked hem be their fayth what maner a knyght
yondir knyght is that semyth in so many dyvers coloures.

'Truly mesemyth,' seyde sir Trystrams, 'that he puttyth hymself in
grete payne, for he never sesyth.'

'Wote nat ye what he is?' seyde Ironsyde.   5

'No,' seyde sir Trystrams.

'Than shall ye knowe that this is he that lovyth the lady of the castell,
and she hym agayne. And this is he that wanne me whan I beseged the
lady of this castell; and this is he that wanne sir Persaunte of Inde and
his three brethirne.'   10

'What is his name?' seyde sir Trystrams, 'and of what bloode is he
com?'

'Sir, he was called in the courte of kynge Arthure Bewmaynes, but
his ryght name is sir Gareth of Orkeney, brother unto sir Gawayne.'

'By my hede,' seyde sir Trystrams, 'he is a good knyght and a   15
bygge man of armys: and yf he be yonge, he shall preve a full noble
knyght.'

'Sir, he is but a chylde,' he seyde, 'and of sir Launcelot he was made
knyght.'

'Therefore is he muche the bettir,' seyde sir Trystrams.   20

And than sir Trystrams, sir Ironsyde, and sir Persaunte and his
brethcrne rode togydyrs for to helpe sir Gareth. And than there was
many sadde strokis, and than sir Gareth rode oute on the tone syde to
amende his helme.

Than seyde his dwarff, 'Take me your rynge, that ye lose hit nat   25
whyle that ye drynke.' And so whan he had drunkyn he gate on hys
helme, and egirly toke his horse and rode into the felde, and leffte his
rynge with his dwarff: for the dwarf was glad the rynge was frome hym,
for than he wyste well he sholde be knowyn.

And whan sir Gareth was in the felde, all folkys sawe hym well and 30
playnly that he was in yealow colowres. And there he raced of helmys and
pulled downe knyghtes, that kynge Arthure had mervayle what knyght
he was. For the kynge sawe by his horse that hit was the same knyght,
'but byfore he was in so many coloures, and now he is but in one (31)
coloure, and that is yolowe.'   35

'Now goo,' seyde kynge Arthure unto dyvers herowdys, and bede
hem, 'Ryde aboute hym, and aspye yf ye can se what maner of knyght
he is; for I have spered of many knyghtes this day that is uppon his
party, and all sey that they knowe hym nought.'

But at the laste an herrowde rode nyghe sir Gareth as he coude, and 40
there he sawe wryten aboute his helme in golde, seyynge: 'This helme is
sir Garethis of Orkeney.' Than the heroude cryed as he were woode,
and many herowdys with hym:

'This is sir Gareth of Orkenay in the yealow armys!'

Thereby all the kynges and knyghtes of kynge Arthurs party behelde and awayted; and than they presed all knyghtes to beholde hym, and ever the herrowdys cryed and seyde: 'This is sir Gareth, kynge Lottys son of Orkeney!'

5 And whan sir Gareth aspyed that he was discoverde, than he dowbled his strokys and smote downe there sir Sagramoure and his brother sir Gawayne.

'A, brother,' seyde sir Gawayne, 'I wente ye wolde have smyttyn me.'

10 So whan he herde hym sey so, he thrange here and there, and so with grete payne he gate oute of the pres, and there he mette with his dwarff.

'A, boy!' seyde sir Gareth, 'thou haste begyled me fowle this day of my rynge. Geff hit me faste, that I may hyde my body withall!' And so he toke hit hym; and than they all wyst [not] where he was becom.

15 And sir Gawayne had in maner aspyed where sir Gareth rode, and than he rode aftir with all his myght. That aspyed sir Gareth and rode wyghtly into the [foreste]. For all that sir Gawayne coude do, he wyste nat where he was becom.

And whan sir Gareth wyste that sir Gawayne was paste, he asked the 20 dwarff of beste counsayle.

'Sir,' seyde the dwarff, 'mesemyth hit were beste, now that ye ar ascaped frome spyynge, that ye sende my lady, dame Lyones of the castell, hir rynge.'

'Hit is well avysed,' seyde sir Gareth. 'Now have hit here and bere 25 hit her, and sey that I recommaunde me unto hir good grace; and sey hir I woll com whan I may, and pray hir to be trewe and faythfull to me as I woll be to hir.'

'Sir,' seyde the dwarff, 'hit shall be done as ye commaunde me.'

And so he rode his way and dud his erande unto the lady. Than seyde 30 she, 'Where is my knyght, sir Gareth?'

'Madam, he bade me sey that he wolde nat be longe frome you.'

And so lyghtly the dwarff com agayne unto sir Gareth that wolde full fayne have had a lodgynge, for he had nede to be reposed.

And than fell there a thundir and a rayne, as hevyn and erthe sholde 35 go togydir. And sir Gareth was nat a lytyll wery, for of all that day he had but lytyll reste, nother his horse nor he. So thus sir Gareth rode longe in that foreste untyll nyght cam; and ever hit lyghtned and thundirde as hit had bene wylde. At the laste by fortune he cam to a (32) castell, and there he herde the waytis uppon the wallys. Than sir Gareth 40 rode unto the barbycan of the castell, and prayed the porter fayre to lette hym into the castell. The porter answerde ungoodly agayne and sayde,

'Thou gettyste no lodgynge here.'

'Fayre sir, sey not so, for I am a knyght of kynge Arthurs; and pray

the lorde and the lady of this castell to gyff me herborow for the love
of kynge Arthour.'

Than the porter wente unto the douches and tolde hir how there was
a knyght of kynge Arthures wolde have herborow.

'Latte hym in,' seyde the douches, 'for I woll see that knyght. And 5
for kynge Arthurs love he shall nat be herborowles.'

Than she yode up into a towre over a gate with tourchis ilyght. Whan
sir Gareth saw that lyght he cryed on hyghe:

'Whethir thou be lorde or lady, gyaunte other champyon, I take no
forse, so that I may have herborow as for this nyght: and yf hit be so 10
that I muste nedis fyght, spare me nat to-morne whan I have rested
me; for bothe I and myne horse be wery.'

'Sir knyght,' seyde the lady, 'ye speke knyghtly and boldely; but
wete you well the lorde of this castell lovyth nat kynge Arthure nother
none of hys courte, for my lorde hath ever bene ayenste hym. And 15
therefore thow were bettir nat to com within his castell; for and thou
com in this nyght, thou muste com undir this fourme, that wheresomever thou mete hym, by fylde other by strete, thou muste yelde the to
hym as presonere.'

'Madam,' seyde sir Gareth, 'what is your lorde and what is his name?' 20
'Sir, my lordys name is the deuke de la Rouse.'

'Well, madam,' seyde sir Gareth, 'I shal promyse you in what place
I mete youre lorde I shall yelde me unto hym and to his good grace,
with that I undirstonde that he woll do me no shame. And yf I undirstonde that he woll, I woll relece myself and I can with my spere and 25
my swerde.'

'Ye say well,' seyde the deuches.

Than she lette the drawbrygge downe; and so he rode into the halle
and there he alyght, and the horse was ladde into the stable. And in the
halle he unarmed hym and seyde,   30

'Madam, I woll nat oute of this halle this nyght. And whan hit is
daylyght, lat se who woll have ado with me; than he shall fynde me
redy.'

Than was he sette unto souper and had many good dysshis. Than sir
Gareth lyste well to ete, and full knyghtly he ete his mete and egirly. 35
Also there was many a fayre lady by hym, and som seyd they nevir
sawe a goodlyer man nothir so well of etynge. Than they made hym
passynge good chere; and shortly, whan he had souped, his bedde was
made there, and so he rested hym all nyght. And in the morne he herde
masse and brake hys faste, and toke his leve at the douches and at them 40
all, and thanked hir goodly of hir lodgyng and of hir good chere. And
than she asked hym his name.

'Truly, madam,' he seyde, 'my name is sir Gareth of Orkeney, and
som men call me Bewmaynes.'

Than knew she well hit was the same knyght that faught for dame Lyonesse.

So sir Gareth departed and rode up unto a mountayne, and there mette hym a knyght, his name was sir Bendaleyne. And he seyde to sir Gareth,

'Thou shalt nat passe this way, for other thou shalt juste with me othir ellys be my presonere.'

'Than woll I juste,' seyde sir Gareth.

And so they lette their horsis ren, and there sir Gareth smote hym thorowoute the body, and sir Bendelayne rode forth to his castell there besyde, and there dyed. So sir Gareth wolde have rested hym fayne. So hit happed hym to com to sir Bendalaynes castell. Than his knyghtys and servauntys aspyed that hit was he that had slayne there lorde. Than they armed twenty good men and com oute and assayled sir Gareth. And so he had no spere, but his swerde, and so he put his shylde afore hym, and there they brake ten sperys uppon hym. And they assayled hym passyngly sore, but ever sir Gareth defended hym as a knyght.

(33) So whan they sawe they myght nat overcom hym they rode frome hym, and toke their counceyle to sle his horse. And so they cam in uppon sir Gareth, and so with hir sperys they slewe his horse, and than they assayled hym harde. But whan he was on foote there was none that he raught but he gaff hym such a buffette that he dud never recover. So he slew hem by one and one tyll they were but four; and there they fledde. And sir Gareth toke a good horse that was one of theires and rode his way. Than he rode a grete pace tyll that he cam to a castell, and there he herde muche mournyng of ladyes and jantyllwomen. So at the laste there cam by hym a payge. Than he asked of hym,

'What noyse is this that I hyre within this castell?'

'Sir knyght,' seyde the payge, 'here be within this castell thirty ladyes, and all they be wydowys. For here is a knyght that waytyth dayly uppon this castell, and he is callyd the Browne Knyght wythoute Pyté, and he is the perelust knyght that now lyvyth. And therefore, sir,' seyde the payge, 'I rede you fle.'

'Nay,' seyde sir Gareth, 'I woll nat fle, though thou be aferde of hym.'

Than the payge saw where cam the Browne Knyght, and sayde, 'Lo yondir he commyth!'

'Lat me dele with hym,' seyde sir Gareth. And whan aythir of othir had a syghte, they let theire horsis ren, and the Browne Knyght brake his spere, and sir Gareth smote hym thorow the body, that he over-threwe [hym] to the grounde sterke dede. So sir Gareth rode into the castell and prayde the ladyes that he myght repose hym.

'Alas!' seyde the ladyes, 'ye may nat be lodged here.'

'Yes, hardely, make hym good chere,' seyde the payge, 'for this knyght hath slayne your enemy.'

Than they all made hym good chere as lay in theire power. But wete you well they made hym good chere, for they myght none other do, for they were but poore. And so on the morne he wente to masse and there he sawe the thirty ladyes knele and lay grovelynge uppon dyverse toumbis, makynge grete dole and sorow. Than sir Gareth knew well 5 that in tho tombis lay their lordys.

'Fayre ladyes,' seyde sir Gareth, 'ye muste at the next feste be at the courte of kynge Arthure, and sey that I, sir Gareth, sente you thydir.'

'Sir, we shall do your commaundemente,' seyde the ladyes.

So he departed; and by fortune he cam to a mountayne, and there 10 he founde a goodly knyght that bade hym 'Abyde, sir knyght, and juste with me!'

'What ar ye?' seyde sir Gareth.

'My name is,' he seyde, 'called deuke de la Rowse.'

'A, sir, ye ar the same knyght that I lodged onys within your castell, 15 and there I made promyse unto youre lady that I sholde yelde me to you.'

'A,' seyde the deuke, 'arte thou that proude knyght that profyrde to fyght with my knyghtes? Therefore make the redy, for I woll have ado wyth you.' 20

So they let their horsis renne, and there sir Gareth smote the deuke downe frome his horse: but the deuke lyghtly avoyded his horse and dressed his shylde and drew his swerde, and bade sir Gareth alyght and fyght with hym. So he dud alyght, and they dud grete batayle togedyrs more than an houre, and eythir hurte other full sore. But at the laste 25 sir Gareth gate the deuke to the erthe, and wolde have slayne hym; and than he yelded hym.

'Than muste ye go,' seyde sir Gareth, 'unto kynge Arthure, my lorde, at the next hyghe feste, and sey that I, sir Gareth, sente you thydir.'

'We shall do this,' seyde the deuke, 'and I woll do you omage and 30 feauté wyth an hondredsom of knyghtes with me, and all the dayes of my lyff to do you servyse where ye woll commaunde me.'

So the deuke departed, and sir Gareth stoode there alone. And as he (34) stoode he sey an armed knyght on horsebak commynge towarde hym. Than sir Gareth mownted uppon horsebak, and so withoute ony wordis 35 they ran togedir as thundir. And there that knyght hurte sir Gareth undir the syde with his spere, and than they alyght and drewe there swerdys and gaff grete strokys, that the bloode trayled downe to the grounde; and so they fought two owres. So at the laste there com the damesell Lyonette that som men calle the damesell Savyage. And she 40 com rydynge uppon an ambelynge mule, and there she cryed all on hygh:

'Sir Gawayne! leve thy fyghtynge with thy brothir, sir Gareth!'

And whan he herde hir sey so, he threwe away his shylde and his swerde, and ran to sir Gareth and toke hym in his armys, and sytthen kneled downe and asked hym mercy.

'What ar ye,' seyde sir Gareth, 'that ryght now were so stronge and so myghty, and now so sodeynly is yelde to me?'

5 'A, sir Gareth, I am your brother, sir Gawayne, that for youre sake have had grete laboure and travayle.'

Than sir Gareth unlaced hys helme, and kneled downe to hym and asked hym mercy. Than they arose bothe, and braced eythir othir in there armys, and wepte a grete whyle or they myght speke; and eythir 10 of them gaff other the pryse of the batayle, and there were many kynde wordys betwene them.

'Alas! my fayre brother,' seyde sir Gawayne, 'I ought of ryght to worshyp you, and ye were nat my brother, for ye have worshipte kynge Arthure and all his courte, for ye have sente mo worshypfull knyghtes 15 this twelve-monthe than fyve the beste of the Rounde Table hath done excepte sir Launcelot.'

Than cam the lady Savyaige, that was the lady Lyonet that rode with sir Gareth so long; and there she dud staunche sir Gareths woundis and sir Gawaynes.

20 'Now what woll ye do?' seyde the damesell Saveaige. 'Mesemyth hit were beste that kynge Arthure had wetynge of you bothe: for your horsis ar so brused that they may not beare.'

'Now, fayre damesell,' seyde sir Gawayne, 'I pray you ryde unto my lorde, myne unkle kynge Arthure, and tell hym what adventure is 25 betydde me here; and I suppose he woll nat tary longe.'

Than she toke hir mule and lyghtly she rode to kynge Arthure, that was but two myle thens. And whan she had tolde hir tydynges to the kynge, the kynge bade, 'Gete me a palferey!' And whan he was on horsebak he bade the lordys and ladyes com aftir and they wolde; and 30 there was sadelyng and brydelyng of quenys and prynces horsis, and well was he that sonneste myght be redy.

So whan the kynge cam there, he saw sir Gawayne and sir Gareth sitt uppon a lytyll hyllys syde. Than the kynge avoyded his horse, and whan he cam nye to sir Gareth he wolde a spokyn and myght nat, and 35 therewyth he sanke downe in a sowghe for gladnesse.

And so they sterte unto theire uncle and requyred hym of his good grace to be of good comforte. Wete you well the kynge made grete joy! And many a peteuous complaynte he made to sir Gareth, and ever he wepte as he had bene a chylde.

40 So with this com his modir, the quene of Orkeney, dame Morgawse, and whan she saw sir Gareth redyly in the vysage she myght nat wepe, but sodeynly felle downe in a sowne and lay there a grete whyle lyke as she had bene dede. And than sir Gareth recomforted hir in suche wyse that she recovirde and made good chere.

Than the kynge commaunded that all maner of knyghtes that were undir his obeysaunce sholde make their lodgynge ryght there, for the love of his two nevewys. And so hit was done, and all maner of purveya[n]s purveyde, that there lacked nothynge that myght be gotyn for golde nother sylver, nothir of wylde nor tame.   5

And than by the meanys of the damesell Saveaige sir Gawayne and sir Gareth were heled of their woundys; and there they suggeourned eyght dayes. Than seyde kynge Arthure unto the damesell Saveaige,

'I mervayle that youre sistyr, dame Lyonesse, comyth nat hydir to me; and in especiall that she commyth nat to vysyte hir knyght, my   10
nevewe, sir Gareth, that hath had so muche travayle for hir love.'

'My lorde,' seyde the damesell Lyonette, 'ye muste of your good grace holde hir excused, for she knowyth nat that my lorde sir Gareth is here.'

'Go ye than for hir,' seyde kynge Arthure, 'that we may be apoynted   15
what is beste to done accordynge to the plesure of my nevewe.'

'Sir,' seyde the damesell, 'hit shall be do.'

And so she rode unto hir sistir, and as lyghtly as she myght make hir redy she cam on the morne with hir brother, sir Gryngamour, and with hir fourty knyghtes. And so whan she was com she had all the   20
chere that myght be done bothe of the kynge and of many other knyghtes and also quenys. And amonge all thes ladyes she was named   (35)
the fayryst and pyereles. Than whan sir Gareth mette with hir, there was many a goodly loke and goodly wordys, that all men of worshyp had joy to beholde them.   25

Than cam kynge Arthure and many othir kynges, and dame Gwenyvere and quene Morgawse, his modir; and there the kynge asked his nevew, sir Gareth, whether he wolde have this lady as peramour, other ellys to have hir to his wyff.

'My lorde, wete you well that I love hir abovyn all ladyes lyvynge.'   30

'Now, fayre lady,' sayde kynge Arthure, 'what sey ye?'

'My moste noble kynge,' seyde dame Lyonesse, 'wete you well that my lorde, sir Gareth, ys to me more lever to have and welde as my husbonde than ony kyng other prynce that is crystyned; and if I may nat have hym, I promyse you I woll never have none. For, my lorde   35
Arthure,' seyde dame Lyonesse, 'wete you well he is my fyrste love, and he shall be the laste; and yf ye woll suffir hym to have his wyll and fre choyse, I dare say he woll have me.'

'That is trouthe,' seyde sir Gareth, 'and I have nat you and welde you as my wyff, there shall never lady nother jantyllwoman rejoyse me.'   40

'What, nevew?' seyde the kynge. 'Is the wynde in that dore? For wete you well I wolde nat for the stynte [of] my crowne to be causer to withdraw your hertys. And wete you well ye can nat love so well but I shall rather encrece hyt than discrece hit; and also ye shall have my love

and my lordeshyp in the uttirmuste wyse that may lye in my power.'
And in the same wyse seyde sir Garethys modir.

So anone there was made a provysion for the day of maryaige, and
by the kynges advyse hit was provyded that hit sholde be at Mychael-
5 masse folowyng, at Kyng Kenadowne, by the seesyde; for there is a
plenteuouse contrey. And so hit was cryed in all the placis thorow the
realme. And than sir Gareth sente his somons to all tho knyghtes and
ladyes that he had wonne in batayle tofore, that they sholde be at his
day of maryage at Kyng Kenadowne, by the seesyde.

10 And than dame Lyonesse and the damesell Lyonet wyth sir Gryngamour rode to their castell, and a goodly and a ryche rynge she gaff to
sir Gareth, and he gaff hir another. And kynge Arthure gaff hir a ryche
bye of golde, and so she departed. And kynge Arthure and his felyshyp
rode towarde Kyng Kenadowne; and sir Gareth brought his lady on the
15 way, and so cam to the kynge agayne, and rode wyth hym. Lorde, the
grete chere that sir Launcelot made of sir Gareth and he of hym! For
there was no knyght that sir Gareth loved so well as he dud sir
Launcelot; and ever for the moste party he wolde ever be in sir
Launcelottis company.

20 For evir aftir sir Gareth had aspyed sir Gawaynes conducions, he
wythdrewe hymself fro his brother sir Gawaynes felyshyp, for he was
evir vengeable, and where he hated he wolde be avenged with murther:
and that hated sir Gareth.

(36) So hit drew faste to Mychaelmas, that thydir cam the lady dame
25 Lyonesse, the lady of the Castell Perelus, and hir sistir, the damesell
Lyonet, with sir Gryngamour, her brother, with hem; for he had the
conduyte of thes ladyes. And there they were lodged at the devyse of
kynge Arthure.

And uppon Myghelmas day the bysshop of Caunturbyry made the
30 weddyng betwene sir Gareth and dame Lyonesse with grete solempnyté.
And kynge Arthure made sir Gaherys to wedde the damesell Saveage,
dame Lyonet. And sir Aggravayne kynge Arthure made to wedde dame
Lyonesseis neese, a fayre lady; hir name was dame Lawrell.

And so whan this solempnyté was done, than com in the Grene
35 Knyght, sir Pertolope, with thirty knyghtes; and there he dud omage
and feauté to sir Gareth, and all thes knyghtes to holde of hym for
evermore. Also sir Pertolope seyde,

'I pray you that at this feste I may be your chambirlayne.'

'With good wyll,' seyde sir Gareth, 'syth hit lyke you to take so
40 symple an offyce.'

Than com in the Rede Knyght wyth three score knyghtes with hym,
and dud to sir Gareth omage and feauté, and all tho knyghtes to holde
of hym for evermore. And than sir Perimones prayde sir Gareth to
graunte hym to be his chyeff butler at the hygh feste.

'I woll well,' seyde sir Gareth, 'that ye have this offyce and hit were bettir.'

Than com in sir Persaunte of Inde wyth an hondred knyghtes with hym, and there he dud omage and feauté, and all his knyghtes sholde do hym servyse and holde their londis of hym for evir. And there he 5 prayde sir Gareth to make hym his sewear cheyff at that hyghe feste.

'I woll well,' seyde sir Gareth, 'that ye have hit and hit were bettir.'

Than com in the deuke de la Rouse with an hondred knyghtes with hym; and there he dud omage and feauté to sir Gareth, and so to holde there londis of hym for evermore. And he requyred sir Gareth that he 10 myght serve hym of the wyne that day of the hyghe feste.

'I woll well,' seyde sir Gareth, 'and hit were bettir.'

Than cam the Rede Knyght of the Rede Laundis that hyght sir Ironsyde, and he brought with hym three hondred knyghtes; and there he dud omage and feauté, and all tho knyghtes to holde their londys of 15 hym for ever. And than he asked of sir Gareth to be his kerver.

'I woll well,' seyde sir Gareth, 'and hit please you.'

Than com into the courte thirty ladyes, and all they semed wydows; and tho ladyes brought with hem many fayre jantyllwomen, and all they kneled downe at onys unto kynge Arthure and unto sir Gareth; and 20 there all tho ladyes tolde the kynge how that sir Gareth had delyverde them fro the Dolorous Towre, and slew the Browne Knyght withoute Pyté: 'and therefore all we and oure ayres for evermore woll do omage unto sir Gareth of Orkeney.'

So than the kynges, quenys, pryncis, erlys, barouns, and many 25 bolde knyghtes wente to mete; and well may ye wete that there was all maner of plenté and all maner revels and game, with all maner of mynstralsy that was used tho dayes. Also there was grete justys three dayes, but the kynge wolde nat suffir sir Gareth to juste, because of his new bryde; for, as the Freynsh boke seyth, that dame Lyonesse desyred 30 of the kynge that none that were wedded sholde juste at that feste.

So the fyrste day there justed sir Lameroke de Gelys, for he [o]verthrewe thirty knyghtes and dud passyng mervelus dedis of armys. And than kynge Arthure made sir Persaunte and his bretherne knyghtes o[f] the Rounde Table to their lyvys ende, and gaff hem grete landys. 35

Also the secunde day there justed sir Trystrams beste, and he overthrew fourty knyghtes, and dud there mervelus dedis of armys. And there kynge Arthure made sir Ironsyde, that was the Rede Knyght of the Rede Laundys, a knyght of the Table Rounde to his lyvis ende, and gaff hym grete landis. 40

Than the thirde day there justed sir Launcelot, and he overthrew fyfty knyghtes and dud many dedis of armys, that all men wondird. And there kynge Arthure made the deuke de la Rowse a knyght of the Table Rounde to his lyvys ende, and gaff hym grete londis to spende.

But whan this justis was done, sir Lameroke and sir Trystrams departed suddeynly and wolde nat be knowyn; for the whych kyng
Arthure and all the courte was sore dysplesid.

And so they helde the courte fourty dayes with grete solempnyté.
5 And thus sir Gareth of Orkeney was a noble knyght, that wedded dame
Lyonesse of the Castell Parelus. And also sir Gaheris wedded her sistir,
dame Lyonette, that was called the damesell Saveaige. And sir Aggravayne wedded dame Lawrell, a fayre lady wyth grete and myghty londys,
wyth grete ryches igyffyn wyth them, that ryally they myght lyve tyll
10 theire lyvis ende.

AND I PRAY YOU ALL THAT REDYTH THIS TALE TO PRAY FOR HYM THAT
THIS WROTE, THAT GOD SENDE HYM GOOD DELYVERAUNCE SONE AND
HASTELY. AMEN.

HERE ENDYTH THE TALE OF SIR GARETH OF ORKENEY.

THE BOOK
OF
SIR TRISTRAM DE
LYONES

I. ISODE THE FAIR

THERE was a kynge that hyght Melyodas, and he was lorde of the contrey of Lyones. And this Melyodas was a lykly knyght as ony was that tyme lyvyng. And by fortune he wedded kynge Markis sister of Cornuayle, and she was called Elyzabeth, that was called bothe good and fayre.

And at that tyme kynge Arthure regned, and he was hole kynge of Ingelonde, Walys, Scotlonde, and of many othir realmys. Howbehit there were many kynges that were lordys of many contreyes, but all they helde their londys of kynge Arthure; for in Walys were two kynges, and in the Northe were many kynges, and in Cornuayle and in the Weste were two kynges; also in Irelonde were two or three kynges, and all were undir the obeysaunce of kynge Arthure; so was the kynge of Fraunce and the kyng of Bretayne, and all the lordshyppis unto Roome.

So whan this kynge Melyodas had bene with his wyff, wythin a whyle she wexed grete with chylde. And she was a full meke lady, and well she loved hir lorde and he hir agayne, so there was grete joy betwyxte hem.

So there was a lady in that contrey that had loved kynge Melyodas longe, and by no meane she never cowde gete his love. Therefore she let ordayne uppon a day as kynge Melyodas rode an-huntynge, for he was a grete chacer of dere, and there be enchauntemente she made hym chace an harte by hymself alone tyll that he com to an olde castell, and there anone he was takyn presoner by the lady that loved hym.

Whan Elyzabeth, kynge Melyodas his wyff, myssed hir lorde she was nyghe oute of hir wytte, and also, as grete with chylde as she was, she toke a jantylwoman with hir and ran into the fereste suddeynly to seke hir lorde. And whan she was farre in the foreste she myght no farther, but ryght there she gan to travayle faste of hir chylde, and she had many grymly throwys, but hir jantyllwoman halpe hir all that she myght.

And so by myracle of Oure Lady of Hevyn she was delyverde with grete paynes, but she had takyn suche colde for the defaute of helpe that the depe draughtys of deth toke hir, that nedys she muste dye and departe oute of thys worlde; there was none othir boote. Whan this quene Elyzabeth saw that she myght nat ascape she made grete dole and seyde unto hir jantylwoman,

'Whan ye se my lorde, kynge Melyodas, recommaunde me unto hym and tell hym what paynes I endure here for his love, and how I muste dye here for his sake for defawte of good helpe, and lat hym wete that I am full sory to departe oute of this worlde fro hym. Therefore pray
5 hym to be frende to my soule. Now lat me se my lytyll chylde for whom I have had all this sorow.'

And whan she sye hym she seyde thus: 'A, my lytyll son, thou haste murtherd thy modir! And therefore I suppose thou that arte a murtherer so yonge, thow arte full lykly to be a manly man in thyne
10 ayge; and bycause I shall dye of the byrth of the, I charge my jantyll-woman that she pray my lorde, the kynge Melyodas, that whan he is crystened let calle hym Trystrams, that is as muche to say as a sorowfull byrth.'

And therewith the quene gaff up the goste and dyed. Than the jantyll-
15 woman leyde hir undir an umbir of a grete tre, and than she lapped the chylde as well as she myght fro colde.

Ryght so there cam the barowns of kynge Melyodas folowyng aftir the quene. And whan they sye that she was dede and undirstode none
(2) othir but that the kynge was destroyed, than sertayne of them wolde
20 have slayne the chylde bycause they wolde have bene lordys of that contrey of Lyonesse. But than, thorow the fayre speche of the jantyll-woman and by the meanys that she made, the moste party of the barowns wolde nat assente thereto. But than they latte cary home the dede quene and muche sorow was made for hir.

25 Than this meanewhyle Merlyon had delyverde kynge Melyodas oute of preson on the morne aftir his quene was dede. And so whan the kynge was com home the moste party of the barowns made grete joy, but the sorow that the kynge made for his quene there myght no tonge tell. So than the kynge let entyre hir rychely, and aftir he let crystyn his
30 chylde as his wyff had commaunded byfore hir deth. And than he lette calle hym Trystrams, 'the sorowfull-borne chylde'.

Than kynge Melyodas endured aftir that seven yere withoute a wyff, and all this tyme Trystrams was forstred well. Than hit befelle that the kynge Melyodas wedded kynge Howellys of Bretaynes doughter, and
35 anone she had chyldirne by kynge Melyodas. Than was she hevy and wroth that hir chyldirne sholde nat rejoyse the contrey of Lyonesse, wherefore this quene ordayned for to poyson yong Trystrams.

So at the laste she let poyson be putt in a pees of sylver in the chambir where Trystrams and hir chyldir were togydyrs, unto that entente
40 that whan Trystrams were thirsty he sholde drynke that drynke. And so hit felle uppon a day the quenys son, as he was in that chambir, aspyed the pyese with poyson, and he wente hit had bene good drynke; and because the chylde was thirsty he toke the pyese with poyson and dranke frely, and therewith the chylde suddaynly braste and was dede.

So whan the quene of Mel⌐yod˥as wyste of the deth of hir sone, wete
you well that she was hevy; but yet the kynge undirstood nothynge of
hir treson. Notwythstondynge the quene wolde not leve by this, but
effte she lette ordeyne more poyson and putt hit in a pyese. And by
fortune kyng Mel⌐yod˥as, hir husbonde, founde the pyese with wyne   5
wherein was the poyson, and as he that was thirstelew toke the pyse
for to drynke; and as he wolde have drunken thereof the quene aspyed
hym and ran unto hym and pulde the pyse from hym sodeynly. The
kynge mervayled of hir why she ded so and remembred hym suddaynly
how hir son was slayne with poyson. And than he toke hir by the honde   10
and sayde,

'Thou false traytoures! Thou shalt telle me what maner of drynke
this is, other ellys I shall sle the!' And therewith he pulde oute his
swerde and sware a grete othe that he sholde sle hir but yf she tolde hym
the trouthe.   15

'A! mercy, my lorde,' she seyde, 'and I shall telle you all.' And than
she tolde hym why she wolde have slayne Trystrams, because her
chyldir sholde rejoyse his londe.

'Well,' seyde the kynge, 'and therefore ye shall have the lawe.'

And so she was dampned by the assente of the barownes to be   20
brente. And ryght as she was at the fyre to take hir excussion this same
yonge Trystrams kneled byfore his fadir kynge Mel⌐yod˥as and besought hym to gyff hym a done.

'I woll well,' seyde the kynge [ageyne].

Than seyde yonge Trystrams, 'Geff me the lyff of your quene, my   25
stepmodir.'

'That is unryghtfully asked,' seyde the kynge Melyodas, 'for thou
oughte of ryght to hate hir, for she wolde have slayne the with poyson,
and for thy sake moste is my cause that she sholde be dede.'

'Sir,' seyde Trystrams, 'as for that, I beseche you of your mercy that   30
ye woll forgyff hir. And as for my parte, God forgyff hir and I do. And
hit lyked so muche your hyghenesse to graunte me my boone, for
Goddis love I requyre you holde your promyse.'

'Sytthen hit is so,' seyde the kynge, 'I woll that ye have hir lyff,' and
sayde: 'I gyff hir you, and go ye to the fyre and take hir and do with   35
hir what ye woll.'

So thus sir Trystramys wente to the fyre, and by the commaundemente of the kynge delyverde hir frome the deth. But afftir that kynge
Mel⌐yod˥as wolde never have ado with hir as at bedde and at bourde.
But by the meanys of yonge Trystrams he made the kynge and hir   40
accorded, but than the kynge wolde nat suffir yonge Trystrams to
abyde but lytyll in his courte.

And than he lett ordayne a jantyllman that was well lerned and taught,   (3)
and his name was Governayle, and than he sente yonge Tristrams with

Governayle into Fraunce to lerne the langage and nurture and dedis of armys. And there was Trystrams more than seven yere. So whan he had lerned what he myght in tho contreyes, than he com home to his fadir kynge Melyodas agayne.

5 And so Trystrams lerned to be an harper passyng all other, that there was none suche called in no contrey. And so in harpynge and on instrumentys of musyke in his youthe he applyed hym for to lerne. And aftir, as he growed in myght and strength, he laboured in huntynge and in hawkynge—never jantylman more that ever we herde rede of. And

10 as the booke seyth, he began good mesures of blowynge of beestes of venery and beestes of chaace and all maner of vermaynes, and all the tearmys we have yet of hawkynge and huntynge. And therefore the booke of [venery, of hawkynge and huntynge is called the booke of] sir Trystrams.

15 Wherefore, as me semyth, all jantyllmen that beryth olde armys ought of ryght to honoure sir Trystrams for the goodly tearmys that jantylmen have and use and shall do unto the Day of Dome, that thereby in a maner all men of worshyp may discever a jantylman frome a yoman and a yoman frome a vylayne. For he that jantyll is woll drawe hym to

20 jantyll tacchis and to folow the noble customys of jantylmen.

Thus Trystrams enduryd in Cornewayle unto that he was stronge and bygge, unto the ayge of eyghtene yere. And than kyng Melyodas had grete joy of yonge Trystrams, and so had the quene, his wyff, for ever aftir in hir lyff, because sir Trystrams saved hir frome the fyre: she ded

25 never hate hym more afftir, but ever loved hym and gaff hym many grete gyfftys; for every astate loved hym where that he wente.

(4) Than hit befelle that kynge Angwysh of Irelonde sente unto kynge Marke of Cornwayle for his trwayge that Cornuayle had payde many wyntyrs, and ⟨at⟩ that tyme kynge Marke was behynde of the trwayge

30 for seven yerys.

And kynge Marke and his barownes gaff unto the messyngers of Irelonde thes wordis and answere that they wolde none pay, and bade the messyngers go unto their kynge Angwysh, 'and tell hym we woll pay hym no trwayge, but tell youre lorde, and he woll allwayes have

35 trwayge of us of Cornwayle, bydde hym sende a trusty knyght of his londe that woll fyght for his ryght, and we shall fynde another for to defende us.'

So the messyngers departed into Irelonde, and whan kynge Angwysh undyrstoode the answere of the messyngers he was wrothe. And than

40 he called unto hym sir Marhalt, the good knyght that was nobly proved and a knyght of the Rounde Table. And this Marhaltt was brother unto the quene of Irclonde. Than the kyng seyde thus:

'Fayre brother, sir Marhalt, I pray you go unto Cornewayle for my sake to do batayle for oure trwayge that we of ryght ought to have.

And whatsomevir ye spende, ye shall have suffyciauntely more than ye shall nede.'

'Sir,' seyde sir Marhalte, 'wete you well that I shall nat be loth to do batayle in the ryght of you and your londe with the beste knyght of Table Rounde, for I know them for the moste party what bene their 5 dedis. And for to avaunce my dedis and to encrece my worshyp I woll ryght gladly go unto this journey.'

So in all haste there was made purvyaunce for sir Marhalte, and he had all thynge that hym neded, and so he departed oute of Irelonde and aryved up in Cornwayle evyn by Castell of Tyntagyll. And whan kynge 10 Marke undirstood that he was there aryved for to fyght for Irelonde, than made kynge Marke grete sorow, whan he undirstood that the good knyght sir Marhalt was com; for they knew no knyght that durste have ado with hym, for at that tyme sir Marhalte was called one of the famuste knyghtes of the worlde.   15

And thus sir Marhalte abode in the see, and every day he sente unto kynge Marke for to pay the trwayge that was behynde seven yere, other ellys to fynde a knyght to fyght with hym for the trewayge. This maner of message sir Marhalte sente unto kynge Marke.

Than they of Cornwayle lete make cryes that what knyght that wolde 20 fyght for to save the trwayge of Cornwayle he shold be rewarded to fare the bettir, terme of his lyff. Than som of the barowns seyde to kynge Marke and counceyled hym to [sende to] the courte of kynge Arthure for to seke sir Launcelott du Lake that was that tyme named for the mervaylyste knyght of the worlde.   25

Than there were other barownes [that counceyled the kynge not to do] ⟨this⟩, and seyde that hit was laboure in vayne bycause sir Marhalte was a knyght of Rounde Table; therefore ony of hem wolde be loth to have ado with other, but yf hit were so that ony knyght at his owne rekeyste wolde fyght disgysed and unknowyn. So the kynge and all his 30 barownes assentyd that hit was no boote to seke aftir no knyght of the Rounde Table.

This meanewhyle cam the langayge and the noyse unto kynge Melyodas how that sir Marhalte abode faste by Tyntagyll, and how kynge Marke cowde fynde no maner of knyght to fyght for hym. So 35 whan yonge Trystrams herde of thys he was wroth and sore ashamed that there durste no knyght in Cornwayle have ado with sir Marhalte of Irelonde. Therewithall Trystrams wente unto his fadir kynge (5) Melyodas and asked hym counceyle what was beste to do for to recovir Cornwayle frome bondage.   40

'For as me semyth,' seyde Trystrams, 'hit were shame that sir Marhalte, the quenys brother of Irelonde, sholde go away onles that he were foughtyn withall.'

'As for that,' seyde kynge Melyodas, 'wete you well, sonne

Trystramys, that sir Marhalte ys called one of the beste knyghtes of
the worlde, and therefore I know no knyght in this contrey is able
to macche hym.'

'Alas,' seyde sir Trystrams, 'that I were nat made knyght! And yf sir
5 Marhalte sholde thus departe into Irelonde, God let me never have
worshyp: [and I were made knyght I shold matche hym.] And, sir,'
seyde Tristrams, 'I pray you, gyff me leve to ryde to kynge Mark. And
so ye woll nat be displesed, of kynge Marke woll I be made knyght.'

'I woll well,' seyde kynge Melyodas, 'that ye be ruled as youre corrage
10 woll rule you.'

Than Trystrams thanked his fadir, and than he made hym redy to
ryde into Cornwayle.

So in the meanewhyle there com ⌈a messager with⌉ lettyrs of love
fro kynge Faramon of Fraunces doughter unto syr Trystrams that were
15 peteuous lettyrs, but in no wyse Trystrams had no joy of hir lettyrs nor
regarde unto hir. Also she sente hym a lytyll brachet that was passynge
fayre. But whan the kynges doughter undirstoode that Trystrams wolde
nat love hir, as the booke seyth, she dyed ⌈for sorou⌉. And than the
same squyre that brought the lettyrs and the brachet cam ayen unto sir
20 Trystrams, as aftir ye shall [here] in the tale folowynge.

So aftir this yonge Trystrames rode unto hys eme, kynge Marke of
Cornwayle, and whan he com there he herde sey that there wolde no
knyght fyght with sir Marhalt.

'Sir,' seyde Trystrams, 'yf ye woll gyff me the Ordir of Knyghthode
25 I woll do batayle with sir Marhalte.'

'What are ye?' seyde the kynge, 'and frome whens be ye com?'

'Sir,' seyde Trystrames, 'I com frome kynge Melyodas that wedded
your systir, and a jantylman, wete you welle, I am.'

So kyng Marke behylde Trystrams and saw that he was but a yonge
30 man of ayge, but he was passyngly well made and bygge.

'Fayre sir,' seyde the kynge, 'what is your name and where were ye
borne?'

'Sir, my name is Trystrams, and in the contrey of Lyonesse was I
borne.'

35 'Ye sey well,' seyde the kynge, 'and yf ye woll do this batayle I shall
make you knyght.'

'Therefore cam I to you,' seyde Trystrams, 'and for none other cause.'

But than kynge Marke made hym knyght, and therewithall anone as
he had made hym knyght he sente unto sir Marhalte that he had founde
40 a yonge knyght redy for to take the batayle to the utteraunce.

'Hit may well be so,' seyde sir Marhalte, 'but tell kynge Marke I woll
nat fyght with no knyght but he be of blood royall, that is to seye owther
kynges son othir quenys son, borne of pryncis other of pryncesses.'

Whan kynge Marke undirstoode that, he sente for sir Trystrams de

Lyones and tolde hym what was the answere of sir Marhalte. Than
seyde sir Trystrams,

'Sytthen that he seyth so, lat hym wete that I am commyn of fadir
syde and modir syde of as noble bloode as he is; for, sir, now shall ye
know that I am kynge Mclyodas sonne, borne of your owne sistir dame 5
Elyzabeth that dyed in the foreste in the byrth of me.'

'A, Jesu!' seyde kynge Marke, 'ye ar welcom, fayre nevew, to me.'

Than in all the haste the kyng horsed sir Trystrams and armed hym
on the beste maner that myght be gotyn for golde othir sylver. And
than kynge Marke sente unto sir Marhalte and dud hym to wete that a 10
bettir man borne than he was hymself sholde fyght with hym, 'and his
name ys sir Trystrams de Lyones, begotyn of kynge Melyodas and
borne of kynge Markys sistir.' Than was sir Marhalte gladde and
blyeth that he sholde feyght with suche a jantylman.

And so by the assente of kynge Marke they lete ordayne that they 15
sholde fyght within an ilonde nyghe sir Marhaltes shyppis. And so was
sir Trystrames put into a vessell, bothe his horse and he and all that
to hym longed, bothe for his body and for his horse, that he lacked
nothyng. And whan kynge Marke and his barownes of Cornwayle
behelde how yonge sir Trystrams departed with suche a caryage to feyght 20
for the ryght of Cornwayle, there was nother man nother woman of
worshyp but they wepte to se and undirstonde so yonge a knyght to
jouparté hymself for theire ryght.

So, to shortyn this tale, whan syr Trystrams aryved within the ilonde (6)
he loked to the farther syde, and there he sawe at an ankyr six othir 25
shyppis nyghe to the londe, and undir the shadow of the shyppys,
uppon the londe, there hoved the noble knyght sir Marhalte of Irelonde. Than sir Trystrams commaunded to have his horse uppon the
londe. And than Governayle, his servaunte, dressed hys harneys at all
maner of ryghtes, and than sir Trystrams mounted uppon his horse. 30

And whan he was in his sadyll well apparayled, and his shylde dressed
uppon his sholdir, so sir Trystrams asked Governayle,

'Where is this knyght that I shall have ado withall?'

'Sir,' seyde Governayle, 'se ye hym nat? I wente that ye had sene
hym, for yondir he hovyth undir the umbir of his shyppys on horseback, 35
with his spere in his honde and his shylde uppon his sholdyr.'

'That is trouthe,' seyde sir Trystrams, 'now I se hym.'

Than he commaunded Governayle to go to his vessayle agayne, 'and
commaunde me unto myne eme, kynge Marke, and pray hym, yf that
I be slayne in this batayle, for to entere my body as hym semyth beste. 40
And as for me, lette hym wete I woll never be yoldyn for cowardyse,
and if I be slayne and fle nat, they have loste no trewayge for me. And
yf so be that I fle other yelde me as recreaunte, bydde myne eme bury
me never in Crystyn buryellys. And uppon thy lyff,' seyde sir Trystrams

unto Govirnayle, 'that thou com nat nyghe this ilonde tyll that thou see me overcom or slayne, other ellis that I wynne yondir knyght.'

(7) So they departed sore wepyng, And than sir Marhalte avysed sir Trystrames and seyde thus:

5 'Yonge knyght, sir Trystrams, what doste thou here? Me sore repentys of thy corrayge; for wete thou well, I have bene assayede with many noble knyghtes, and the beste knyghtes of this londe have bene assayed of myne hondys, and also the beste knyghtes of the worlde I have macched them. And therefore, be my counceyle, returne ayen

10 unto thy vessell.'

'A, fayre knyght and well proved,' seyde sir Trystrams, 'thou shalt well wete I may nat forsake the in this quarell. For I am for thy sake made knyght, and thou shalt well wete that I am a kynges sonne, borne and gotyn uppon a quene. And suche promyse I have made at my

15 nevewys requeste and myne owne sekynge that I shall fyght with the unto the uttirmuste and delyvir Cornwayle frome the olde trewage. And also wete thou well, sir Marhalte, that this ys the gretteste cause that thou coragyst me to have ado with the, for thou arte called one of the moste renomed knyghtes of the worlde. And bycause of that noyse

20 and fame that thou haste thou gevyst me corrayge to have ado with the, for never yett was I proved with good knyght. And sytthen I toke the Order of Knyghthode this day, I am ryght well pleased, and to me moste worshyp, that I may have ado wyth suche a knyght as thou arte. And now wete thou well, syr Marhalte, that I caste me to geete wor-

25 shyp on thy body. And yf that I be nat proved, I truste to God to be worshypfully proved uppon thy body, and to delyver the contrey of Cornwayle for ever fro all maner of trewayge frome Irelonde for ever.'

Whan sir Marhalte had herde hym sey what he wolde, he seyde thus

30 agayne:

'Fayre knyght, sytthen hit is so that thou castyste to wynne worshyp of me, I lette the wete worshyp may thou none loose by me gyff thou may stonde me three strokys. For I lat the wete, for my noble dedis proved and seyne kynge Arthure made me knyght of the Table

35 Rounde!'

Than they began to feauter there sperys, and they mette so fersly togydyrs that they smote aythir other downe, bothe horse and man. But sir Marhalte smote sir Trystrams a grete wounde in the syde with his spere.

40 And than they avoyded their horsis and pulde oute their swerdys, and threwe their shyldis afore them, and than they laysshed togydyrs as men that were wylde and corrageous. And whan they had strykyn togydyrs longe, that there armys fayled, than they leffte their strokys and foyned at brestys and vysours. And whan they sawe that hit myght

nat prevayle them, than they hurteled togedyrs lyke rammys to beare
eythir othir downe.

Thus they fought stylle togydirs more than halffe a day, and eythir
of them were wounded passynge sore, that the blood ran downe
ᒥfresshlyᒥ frome them uppon the grounde. By than sir Trystramys   5
wexed more fyerser than he dud, and sir Marhalte fyebled, and sir
Trystramys ever more well-wynded and bygger. And with a myghty
stroke he smote sir Marhalte uppon the helme suche a buffette that hit
wente thorow his helme and thorow the coyffe of steele and thorow the
brayne-panne, and the swerde stake so faste in the helme and in his   10
brayne-panne that sir Trystramys pulled three tymes at his swerde or
ever he myght pulle hit oute frome his hede.

And there sir Marhalte felle downe on his kneis, and the edge of his
swerde leffte in hys brayne-panne. And suddeynly sir Marhalte rose
grovelynge and threw his swerde and his shylde frome hym, and so he   15
ran to his shyppys and fledde his way. And sir Trystramys had ever his
shelde and his swerde, and whan sir Trystramys saw sir Marhalte
withdrow hym he seyde,

'A, sir knyght of the Rounde Table! Why withdrawyst thou the?
Thou doste thyself and thy kynne grete shame, for I am but a yonge   20
knyght: or now I was never preved. And rather than I sholde withdraw
me frome the, I had rathir be hewyn in pyese-mealys.'

Sir Marhalte answerde no worde, but yeode his way sore gronynge.

'Well, sir knyght,' seyde sir Trystrams, 'I promyse the thy swerde
and thy shylde shall be myne, and thy shylde shall I were in all placis   25
where I ryde on myne adventures, and in the syght of kyng Arthure and
all the Rounde Table.'

So sir Marhalte and hys felyshyp departed into Irelonde. And as sone   (8)
as he com to the kynge, his brother, they serched his woundis, and
whan his hede was serched a pyese of sir Trystrams swerde was therein   30
founden, and myght never be had oute of his hede for no lechecraffte.
And so he dyed of sir Trystramys swerde, and that pyse of the swerde
the quene, his sistir, she kepte hit for ever with hir, for she thought to
be revenged and she myght.

Now turne we agayne unto sir Trystrames that was sore wounded and   35
sore forbledde, that he myght nat within a lytyll whyle stonde. Whan
he had takyn colde ⟨he coude⟩ unnethe styrre hym of hys lymmes, and
than he sette hym downe sofftely uppon a lytyll hylle and bledde faste.
Than anone com Governayle, his man, with his vessell, and the kynge
and the moste party of his barownes com with procession ayenst sir   40
Trystrames.

And whan he was commyn unto the londe kynge Marke toke hym
in his armys, and he and sir Dynas the Senescyall lad sir Tristrames
into the castell of Tyntagyll; and than was he cerched in the beste maner

and leyde in his bed. And whan kynge Marke saw his woundys he
wepte hertely, and so dud all his lordys.

'So God me helpe,' seyde kynge Marke, 'I wolde nat for all my
londys that my nevew dyed.'

5   So sir Trystrames lay there a moneth and more, and ever he was lyke
to dey of the stroke that sir Marhalte smote hym fyrste wyth the spere;
for, as the Frenshe booke seyth, the spere-hede was invenymed, that sir
Trystrams myght nat be hole. Than was kynge Marke and all hys
barownes passynge hevy, for they demed none other but that sir
10   Trystrames sholde nat recover. Than the kynge lette sende for all
maner of lechis and surgeons, bothe unto men and women, and there
was none that wolde behote hym the lyff.

Than cam there a lady that was a wytty lady, and she seyde playnly
unto the kyng Marke and to sir Trystrames and to all his barownes that
15   he sholde never be hole but yf that sir Trystrames wente into the same
contrey that the venym cam fro, and in that contrey sholde he be
holpyn, other ellys never; thus seyde the lady unto the kynge. So whan
the kynge undirstood hit he lette purvey for syr Trystrames a fayre
vessell and well vytayled, and therein was putt sir Trystrames, and
20   Governayle wyth hym, and sir Trystrames toke his harpe with hym.
And so he was putt into the see to sayle into Irelonde.

And so by good fortune he aryved up in Irelonde evyn faste by a
castell where the kynge and the quene was. And at his aryvayle he sate
and harped in his bedde a merry lay: suche one herde they never none
25   in Irelonde before that tyme. And whan hit was tolde the kynge and
the quene of suche a syke knyght that was suche an harper, anone the
kynge sente for hym and lette serche hys woundys, and than he asked
hym his name. Than he answerde and seyde,

'I am of the contrey of Lyones, and my name is Tramtryste, that was
30   thus wounded in a batayle as I fought for a ladyes ryght.'

'So God me helpe,' seyde kynge An[g]wysh, 'ye shall have all the
helpe in this londe that ye may have here. But in Cornwayle but late I
had a grete losse as ever had kynge, for there I loste the beste knyght
of the worlde. His name was sir Marhalte, a full noble knyght and
35   knyght of the Table Rounde.'

And there he tolde sir Tramtryste wherefore sir Marhalte was slayne.
So sir Tramtryste made sembelaunte as he had bene sory, and bettir he
knew how hit was than the kynge.

(9)   Than the kynge for grete favour made Tramtryste to be put in his
40   doughtyrs awarde and kepyng, because she was a noble surgeon. And
whan she had serched hym she founde in the bottom of his wounde
that therein was poyson, and so she healed hym in a whyle.

And therefore sir Tramtryste kyste grete love to La Beale Isode, for
she was at that tyme the fayrest lady and maydyn of the worlde. And

there Tramtryste lerned hir to harpe and she began to have a grete
fantasy unto hym.

And at that tyme sir Palomydes ⌈the Sarasyn⌉ drew unto La Beale
Isode and profirde hir many gyfftys, for he loved hir passyngly welle.
All that aspyed Tramtryste, and full well he knew Palomydes for a   5
noble knyght and a myghty man. And wete you well sir Tramtryste had
grete despyte at sir Palomydes, for La Beale Isode tolde Tramtryste that
Palomydes was in wyll to be crystynde for hir sake. Thus was the[r]
grete envy betwyxte Tramtryste and sir Palomydes.

Than hit befelle that kynge Angwysh lett cry a grete justis and a grete   10
turnemente for a lady that was called the lady of the Laundys, and she
was ny cosyn unto the kynge. And what man wanne her, four dayes
[after] sholde wedde hir and have all hir londis. This cry was made in
Ingelonde, Walys, and Scotlonde, and also in Fraunce and in Bretayne.

So hit befelle uppon a day, La Beale Isode com unto Tramtryste and   15
tolde hym of this turnemente. He answerde and sayde,

'Fayre lady, I am but a feeble knyght, and but late I had bene dede,
had nat your good ladyshyp bene. Now, fayre lady, what wolde ye
that I sholde do in this mater? Well ye wote, my lady, that I may nat
juste.'   20

'A, Tramtryste!' seyde La Beale Isode, 'why woll ye nat have ado at
that turnamente? For well I wote that sir Palomydes woll be there and
to do what he may. And therefore, sir Tramtryste, I pray you for to be
there, for ellys sir Palomydes ys lyke to wynne the degré.'

'Madam, as for that, hit may be so, for he is a proved knyght and I   25
am but a yonge knyght and late made, and the fyrste batayle that ever I
ded hit myssehapped me to be sore wounded, as ye se. But and I wyste
that ye wolde be my bettir lady, at that turnemente woll I be, on this
covenaunte: so that ye woll kepe my counceyle and lette no creature
have knowlech that I shall juste but yourself and suche as ye woll to   30
kepe youre counceyle, my poure person shall [I] jouparté there for youre
sake, that peradventure sir Palomydes shall know whan that I com.'

Thereto seyde La Beale Isode, 'Do your beste, and as I can,' seyde La
Beale Isode, 'I shall purvey horse and armoure for you at my devyse.'

'As ye woll, so be hit,' seyde sir Tramtryste, 'I woll be at your   35
commaundemente.'

So at the day of justys there cam sir Palomydes with a blacke shylde
and he ovirthrew many knyghtes, that all people had mervayle; for he
put to the warre sir Gawayne, Gaherys, Aggravayne, Bagdemagus,
Kay, Dodynas le Savyaige, Sagramour le Desyrous, Guvrete le Petyte,   40
and Gryfflet le Fyse de Du—all thes the fyrste day sir Palomydes strake
downe to the erthe. And than all maner of knyghtes were adrad of sir
Palomydes, and many called hym the Knyght with the Blacke Shylde;
so that [day] sir Palomydes had grete worshyp.

Than cam kynge Angwyshe unto Tramtryste and asked hym why he wolde nat juste.

'Sir,' he seyde, 'I was but late hurte and as yett I dare nat aventure.'

Than there cam the same squyre that was sente frome the kynges
5 doughter of Fraunce unto sir Tramtryste, and whan he had aspyed sir Trystrames he felle flatte to his feete. And that aspyed La Beale Isode, what curtesy the squyre made to Tramtryste. And therewithall suddeynly sir Trystrames ran unto the squyre—his name was called Ebes le Renownys—and prayde hym hartely in no wyse to telle his name.

10 'Sir,' seyde Hebes, 'I woll nat discovir your name but yf ye commaunde me.'

(10) Than sir Trystramys asked hym what he dede in this contreys.

'Sir,' he seyde, 'I com hydir with sir Gawayne for to be made knyght, and yf hit please you of your hondis that I may be made knyght.'

15 'Well, awayte on me as to-morne secretly, and in the fylde I shall make you knyght.'

Than had La Beale Isode grete suspeccion unto Tramtryste that he was som man of worshyp preved, and therewith she comforted herselfe and kyste more love unto hym, for well she demed he was som
20 man of worshyp.

And so on the morne sir Palomydes made hym redy to com into the fylde, as he dud the fyrste day, and there he smote downe the Kynge with the Hondred Knyghtes and the Kynge of Scottis. Than had La Beale Isode ordayned and well arayde sir Tramtryste with whyght
25 horse and whyght armys, and ryght so she lette put hym oute at a prevy postren, and he cam so into the felde as hit had bene a bryght angell. And anone sir Palomydes aspyed hym, and therewith he feautred hys spere unto sir Trystramys and he agayne unto hym, and there sir Trystrams smote downe sir Palomydes unto the erthe.

30 And than there was a grete noyse of people: som seyde sir Palomydes had a fall, som seyde the knyght with the blacke shylde hath a falle. And wete you well La Beale Isode was passyng gladde. And than sir Gawayne and his felowys nine had mervayle who hit myght be that had smytten downe sir Palomydes. Than wolde there none juste with
35 Tramtryste, but all that there were forsoke hym, moste and leste.

Than sir Trystramys made Hebes a knyght and caused to put hymself forth, and dud ryght well that day. So aftir that sir Hebes helde hym with sir Trystrams.

And whan sir Palomydes had reseyved hys falle, wete ye well that he
40 was sore ashamed, and as prevayly as he myght he withdrew hym oute of the fylde. All that aspyed sir Tramtryste, and lyghtly he rode aftir sir Palomydes and overtoke hym and bade hym turne, for bettir he wolde assay hym or ever he departed. Than sir Palomydes turned hym and eythir laysshed at other with their swerdys; but at the fyrste stroke

sir Trystrames smote downe sir Palomydes and gaff hym suche a stroke uppon the hede that he felle to the erthe.

So than sir Trystrams bade hym yelde hym and do his commaundemente, other ellis he wolde sle hym. Whan sir Palomydes behylde hys countenaunce he drad his buffettes so that he graunted all his askynges. 5

'Well,' seyde sir Tramtryste, 'this shall be youre charge: fyrst, uppon payne of youre lyff, that ye forsake my lady, La Beale Isode, and in no maner of wyse that ye draw no more to hir; also, this twelve-monthe and a day that ye bere none armys nother none harneys of werre. Now promyse me this, othir here shalt thou dye.'   10

'Alas,' seyde sir Palomydes, 'for ever I am shamed!'

Than he sware as sir Trystrames had commaunded hym. So for dispyte and angir sir Palomydes kut of his harneyse and threw them awey.

And so sir Trystrames turned agayne to the castell where was La 15 Beale Isode, and by the way he mette wyth a damesell that asked aftir sir Launcelot that wan the Dolorous Garde; and this damesell asked sir Trystrames what he was, for hit was tolde her that hit was he that smote downe sir Palamydes by whom the ten knyghtes of Arthures were smyttyn downe. Than the damesell prayde sir Trystrames to telle 20 her what he was and whether that he were sir Launcelot du Lake, for she demed that there was no knyght in the worlde that myght do suche dedis of armys but yf hit were sir Launcelot.

'Wete you well that I am nat sir Launcelot, fayre damesell, for I was never of suche proues. But in God is all: He may make me as good 25 a knyght as that good knyght sir Launcelot is.'

'Now, jantyll knyght, put up thy vyser!'

And whan she behylde his vysage she thought she sawe never a bettir mannys vysayge nothir a bettir-farynge knyght. So whan the damesell knew sertaynly that he was nat sir Launcelot, than she toke 30 hir leve and departed frome hym.

And than sir Trystrames rode prevayly unto the posterne where kepte hym La Beale Isode, and there she made hym grete chere and thanked God of his good spede.

So anone within a whyle the kynge and the quene and all the courte 35 undirstood that hit was sir Tramtryste that smote downe sir Palamydes, and than was he muche made of, more than he was tofore. Thus was sir (11) Tramtryste longe there well cherysshed with the kynge and wyth the quene, and namely with La Beale Isode.

So uppon a day the quene and La Beale Isode made a bayne for sir 40 Tramtryste, and whan he was in his bayne the quene and Isode, hir doughter, romed up and downe in the chambir the whyles Governayle and Hebes attendede uppon Tramtryste. The quene behelde his swerde as hit lay uppon his bedde, and than at unhappis the quene drew oute

his swerde and behylde hit a long whyle. And bothe they thought hit a passynge fayre swerde, but within a foote and an halff of the poynte there was a grete pyese thereof outebrokyn of the edge. And whan the quene had aspyed that gappe in the swerde she remembirde hir of a
5 pyese of a swerde that was founde in the braynne-panne of sir Marhalte that was hir brother.

'Alas!' than seyde she unto hir doughter La Beale Isode, 'this is the same traytoure knyght that slewe my brother, thyne eme.'

Whan Isode herde her sey so she was passynge sore abaysshed, for
10 passynge well she loved Tramtryste and full well she knew the crewelnesse of hir modir the quene.

So anone therewithall the quene wente unto hir owne chambir and sought hir cofyr, and there she toke oute the pyese of the swerde that was pulde oute of sir Marhaltys brayne-panne aftir that he was dede.
15 And than she ran wyth that pyese of iron unto the swerde, ⌈and whanne she putte that pyese of stele and iron unto the swerde⌉ hit was as mete as hit myght be as whan hit was newe brokyn.

And than the quene gryped that swerde in hir honde fersely, and with all her myght she ran streyght uppon Tramtryste where he sate in
20 his bayne. And there she had ryved hym thorowe, had nat sir Hebes bene: he gate hir in his armys and pulde the swerde frome her, and ellys she had thriste hym thorowe. So whan she was lette of hir evyll wyll she ran to the kynge her husbonde and seyde,

'A, my lorde!' On hir kneys knelynge, she seyde, 'Here have ye in
25 your house that traytoure knyght that slewe my brother and your servaunte, the noble knyght sir Marhalte!'

'Who is that?' seyde the kynge, 'and where is he?'

'Sir,' she seyde, 'hit is sir Tramtryste, the same knyght that my doughter helyd.'

30 'Alas!' seyde the kynge, 'therefore I am ryght hevy, for he is a full noble knyght as ever I sawe in fylde. But I charge you,' seyde the kynge, 'that ye have nat ado with that knyght, but lette me dele with hym.'

Than the kynge wente into the chambir unto sir Tramtryste, and
35 than was he gone unto his owne chambir, and the kynge founde hym all redy armed to mownte uppon his horse. So whan the kynge sawe hym all redy armed to go unto horsebacke, the kynge seyde,

'Nay, Tramtryste, hit woll nat avayle to compare ayenste me. But thus muche I shall do for my worshyp and for thy love: in so muche as
40 thou arte wythin my courte, hit were no worship to sle the; therefore upon this conducion I woll gyff the leve for to departe frome this courte in savyté, so thou wolte telle me who was thy fadir and what is thy name, and also yf thou slewe sir Marhalte, my brother.'

(12)   'Sir,' seyde Tramtryste, 'now I shall tell you all the trouthe. My

fadyrs name ys sir Melyodas, kyng of Lyonesse, and my modir hyght
Elyzabeth, that was sister unto kynge Marke of Cornwayle. And my
modir dyed of me in the foreste, and because thereof she commaunded
or she dyed that whan I was crystened they sholde crystyn me Trystrames. And because I wolde nat be knowyn in this contrey I turned my 5
name and let calle me Tramtryste. And for the trwage of Cornwayle I
fought, for myne emys sake and for the ryght of Cornwayle that ye had
be possessed many yerys. And wete you well,' seyde sir Trystrames unto
the kynge, 'I dud the batayle for the love of myne uncle kynge Marke
and for the love of the contrey of Cornwayle, and for to encrece myne 10
honoure: for that same day that I fought with sir Marhalte I was made
knyght, and never or than dud I no batayle with no knyght. And
fro me he wente alyve and leffte his shylde and his swerde bchynde
hym.'

'So God me helpe!' seyde the kynge, 'I may nat sey but ye dud as a 15
knyght sholde do and as hit was youre parte to do for your quarell, and
to encrece your worshyp as a knyght sholde do. Howbehit I may nat
mayntayne you in this contrey with my worship but that I sholde displese many of my barownes and my wyff and my kynne.'

'Sir,' seyde sir Trystrames, 'I thanke you of your good lordeship 20
that I have had within here with you, and the grete goodnesse my lady
your doughter hath shewed me. And therefore,' seyde sir Trystramys,
'hit may so be that ye shall wynne more be my lyff than be my deth, for
in the partyes of Ingelonde hit may happyn I may do you servyse at
som season that ye shall be glad that ever ye shewed me your good 25
lordshyp. Wyth more I promyse you, as I am trewe knyght, that in all
placis I shall be my lady your doughtyrs servaunte and knyght in all
ryght and in wronge, and I shall never fayle her to do as muche as a
knyght may do. Also I beseche your good grace that I may take my
leve at my lady youre doughter and at all the barownes and knyghtes.' 30
'I woll [well],' seyde the kynge.

Than sir Trystrames wente unto La Beale Isode and toke his leve.
And than he tolde what he was, and how a lady tolde hym that he sholde
never be hole 'untyll I cam into this contrey where the poyson was
made, wherethorow I was nere my deth, had nat your ladyshyp bene.' 35

'A, janytll knyght!' seyde La Beale Isode, 'full wo I am of thy departynge, for I saw never man that ever I ought so good wyll to,' and
therewithall she wepte hertyly.

'Madam,' seyde sir Trystramys, 'ye shall undirstonde that my name
ys sir Trystrames de Lyones, gotyn of a kynge and borne of a quene. 40
And I promyse you faythfully, I shall be all the dayes of my lyff your
knyght.'

'Gramercy,' seyde La Beale Isode, 'and I promyse you there agaynste
I shall nat be maryed this seven yerys but by your assente, and whom

that ye woll I shall be maryed to hym and he woll have me, if ye woll
consente thereto.'

And than sir Trystrames gaff hir a rynge and she gaff hym another,
and therewith he departed and com into the courte amonge all the
5 barownes. And there he toke his leve at moste and leste, and opynly
he seyde amonge them all,

'Fayre lordys, now hit is so that I muste departe. If there be ony man
here that I have offended unto, or that ony man be with me greved, lette
hym complayne hym here afore me or that ever y departe, and I shall
10 amende hit unto my power. And yf there be ony man that woll proffir
me wronge other sey me wronge, other shame me behynde my backe,
sey hit now or ellys never, and here is my body to make hit good, body
ayenste body!'

And all they stood stylle—there was nat one that wolde sey one
15 worde. Yett were there som knyghtes that were of the quenys bloode
and of sir Marhaltys blood, but they wolde nat meddyll wyth hym.

(13)   So sir Trystramys departede and toke the see, and with good wynde
he aryved up at Tyntagyll in Cornwayle. And whan kynge Marke was
hole in hys prosperité there cam tydynges that sir Trystrames was
20 aryved, and hole of his woundis. Thereof was kynge Marke passynge
glad, and so were all the barownes.

And whan he saw hys tyme he rode unto his fadir, kynge Melyodas,
and there he had all the chere that the kynge and the quene coude make
hym. And than largely kynge Melyodas and his quene departed of their
25 londys and goodys to sir Trystrames. Than by the lysence of his fadir
he returned ayen unto the courte of kynge Marke.

And there he lyved longe in grete joy longe tyme, untyll at the laste
there befelle a jolesy and an unkyndenesse betwyxte kyng Marke and sir
Trystrames, for they loved bothe one lady, and she was an erlys wyff
30 that hyght sir Segwarydes. And this lady loved sir Trystrames passyngly well, and he loved hir agayne, for she was a passynge fayre lady
and that aspyed sir Trystrames well. Than kynge Marke undirstode
that and was jeluse, for kynge Marke loved hir passyngly welle.

So hit befelle uppon a day, this lady sente a dwarff unto sir Trys-
35 trames and bade hym, as he loved hir, that he wolde be with hir the
nexte nyght folowynge:

'Also she charged you that ye com nat to hir but yf ye be well armed.'
For her lorde was called a good knyght.

Sir Trystrames answerde to the dwarff and seyde,
40 'Recommaunde me unto my lady and tell hir I woll nat fayle, but I
shall be with her the terme that she hath sette me,' and therewith the
dwarff departed.

And kyng Marke aspyed that the dwarff was with sir Trystrames
uppon message frome Segwarydes wyff. Than kynge Marke sente for

the dwarff, and whan he was comyn he made the dwarff by force to tell hym all why and wherefore that he cam on message to sir Trystrames, and than he tolde hym.

'Welle,' seyde kyng Marke, 'go where thou wolte, and uppon payne of deth that thou sey no worde that thou spake with me.'   5

So the dwarff departed ⌐from the kynge⌐, and that same nyght that the steavyn was sette betwyxte Segwarydes wyff and sir Trystrames, so kynge Marke armed and made hym redy and toke two knyghtes of his counceyle with hym. And so he rode byfore for to abyde by the wayes for to wayte uppon sir Trystrames.   10

And as sir Trystrames cam rydynge uppon his way with his speare in his hande, kynge Marke cam hurlynge uppon hym and hys two knyghtes suddeynly, and all three smote hym with their sperys, and kynge Marke hurt sir Trystrames on the breste ryght sore. And than sir Trystrames feautred his spere and smote kynge Marke so sore that he russhed hym 15 to the erthe and brused hym, that he lay stylle in a sowne; and longe hit was or he myght welde hymselff. And than he ran to the one knyght and effte to the tothir, and smote hem to the colde erthe, that they lay stylle.

And there[with]all sir Trystrames rode forth sore wounded to the 20 lady and founde hir abydynge hym at a postern, and there she wel- (14) commed hym fayre, and eyther halsed other in armys. And so she lette putt up his horse in the beste wyse, and than she unarmed hym, and so they soupede lyghtly and wente to bedde with grete joy and plesaunce. And so in hys ragynge he toke no kepe of his greve wounde that kynge 25 Marke had gyffyn hym, and so sir Trystrames bledde bothe the over-shete and the neyther-sheete, and the pylowes and the hede-shete.

And within a whyle there cam one before, that warned her that hir lorde sir Segwarydes was nerehonde within a bowe-drawght. So she made sir Trystrames to aryse, and [so he] armed hym and toke his 30 horse and so departed. So by than was sir Segwarydes, hir lorde, com, and whan he founde hys bedde troubled and brokyn he wente nere and loked by candyll-lyght and sawe that there had leyne a wounded knyght.

'A, false traytoures!' he seyde, 'why haste thou betrayde me?' And 35 therewithall he swange oute a swerde and seyde, 'But yf thou telle me all ⌐who hath bene here⌐, now shalt thou dey!'

'A, my lorde, mercy!' seyde the lady, and helde up hir hondys, 'and sle me nat, and I shall tell you all who hath bene here.'

Than anone seyde Segwarydes, 'Sey and tell me the trouthe.'   40
Anone for drede she seyde,

'Here was sir Trystrames with me, and by the way, as he come to me-warde, he was sore wounded.'

'A, false traytoures! Where is he becom?'

'Sir,' she seyde, 'he is armed and departed on horsebacke nat yett hens halff a myle.'

'Ye sey well,' seyde Segwarydes.

Than he armed hym lyghtly and gate his horse and rode aftir sir
5 Trystrames the streyght wey unto Tyntagyll, and within a whyle he overtoke sir Trystrams. And than he [b]ade hym 'turne, false traytoure knyght!' And therewithall Segwarydes smote sir Trystrames with a speare, that hit all to-braste, and than he swange oute hys swerde and smote faste at sir Trystrames.

10 'Sir knyght,' seyde sir Trystrames, 'I counceyle you smyte no more! Howbehit for the wrongys that I have done you I woll forbere you as longe as I may.'

'Nay,' seyde Segwarydes, 'that shall nat be, for other thou shalt dye othir ellys I.'

15 Than sir Trystrames drew oute his swerde and hurled his horse unto hym freysshely, and thorow the waste of the body he smote sir Segwarydes, that he felle to the erthe in sowne.

And so sir Trystrames departed and leffte hym there. And so he rode unto Tyntagyll and toke hys lodgynge secretely, for he wolde nat be
20 know that he was hurte. Also sir Segwarydes men rode afftir theire master and brought hym home on his shylde; and there he lay longe or he were hole, but at the laste he recoverde.

Also kynge Marke wolde nat be a-knowyn of that he had done unto sir Trystramys whan he mette that nyght; and as for sir Trystramys, he
25 knew nat that kynge Marke had mette with hym. And so the kynge com ascawnce to sir Trystrames to comforte hym as he lay syke in his bedde. But as longe as kynge Marke lyved he loved never aftir sir Trystramys. So aftir that, thoughe there were fayre speche, love was there none.

And thus hit paste on many wykes and dayes, and all was forgyffyn
30 and forgetyn, for sir Segwarydes durste nat have ado with sir Trystrames because of his noble proues, and also because he was nevew unto kynge Marke. Therefore he lette hit overslyppe, for he that hath a prevy hurte is loth to have a shame outewarde.

(15) Than hit befelle uppon a day that the good knyghte sir Bleoberys de
35 Ganys, brother unto sir Blamore de Ganys and nye cosyne unto the good knyght syr Launcelot de Lake, so this sir Bleoberys cam unto the courte of kyng Marke, and there he asked kynge Marke to gyff hym a bone, 'what gyffte that I woll aske in this courte'.

Whan the kynge herde hym aske so he mervayled of his askynge, but
40 bycause he was a knyght of the Rounde Table and of a grete renowne, kynge Marke graunted hym his hole askynge. Than seyde sir Bleoberys, 'I woll have the fayreste lady in your courte that me lyste to chose.'

'I may nat say nay,' seyde kynge Marke. 'Now chose hir at your adventure.'

And so sir Bleoberys dud chose sir Segwarydes wyff, and toke hir by the honde, and so wente his way with her. And so he toke his horse, and made sette her behynde his squyer and rode uppon hys way.

Whan sir Segwarydes herde telle that his lady was gone with a knyght of kynge Arthures courte, than he armed hym and rode after 5 that knyght to rescow his lady. So whan sir Bleoberys was gone with this lady kynge Marke and all the courte was wroth that she was had away.

Than were there sertayne ladyes that knew that there was grete love betwene sir Trystrames and her, and also that lady loved sir Trystrames 10 abovyn all othyr knyghtes. Than there was one lady that rebuked sir Trystrams in the horrybelyst wyse, and called hym cowarde knyght, that he wolde for shame of hys knyghthode to se a lady so shamefully takyn away fro his uncklys courte; but she mente that eythir of hem loved other with entyre herte. But sir Trystrames answered her thus: 15

'Fayre lady, hit is nat my parte to have ado in suche maters whyle her lorde and husbonde ys presente here. And yf so be that hir lorde had nat bene here in this courte, than for the worshyp of this courte per-aventure I wolde have bene hir champyon. And yf so be sir Segwarydes spede nat well, hit may happyn that I woll speke with that good knyght 20 or ever he passe far fro this contrey.'

Than within a whyle com sir Segwarydes squyres and tolde in the [courte that] theyre master was betyn sore and wounded at the poynte of deth: as he wolde have rescowed his lady, sir Bleoberys overthrewe hym and sore hath wounded hym. Than was kynge Marke hevy thereof 25 and all the courte. Whan sir Trystrames herde of this he was ashamed and sore agreved, and anone he armed hym and yeode to horsebacke, and Governayle, his servaunte, bare his shylde and his spere.

And so as syr Trystrames rode faste he mette with sir Andret, his cosyn, that by the commaundement of kynge Marke was sente to 30 brynge forth two knyghtes of Arthures courte that rode by the contrey to seke their adventures. Whan sir Trystrames sawe sir Andret he asked hym,

'What tydynges?'

'So God me helpe,' seyde sir Andret, 'there was never worse with me, 35 for here by the commaundemente of kynge Marke I was sente to fecche two knyghtes of kynge Arthurs courte, and the tone bete me and wounded me and sette nought be my messayge.'

'Fayre cosyn,' seyde sir Trystrames, 'ryde on your way, and yf I may mete them hit may happyn I shall revenge you.'   40

So sir Andret rode into Cornwayle and sir Trystrames rode aftir the two knyghtes, whyche that one hyght sir Sagramoure le Desyrous an[d] that othir hyght sir Dodynas le Savyayge. So within a whyle sir Trys- (16) trames saw hem byfore hym, two lykly knyghtys.

'Sir,' seyde Governayle unto his maystir, 'I wolde counceyle you nat to have ado with them, for they be two proved knyghtes of Arthures courte.'

'As for that,' seyde sir Trystrames, 'have ye no doute but I woll have
5 ado with them bothe to encrece my worshyp, for hit is many day sytthe[n] I dud any armys.'

'Do as ye lyste,' seyde Governayle.

And therewythall anone sir Trystrames asked them from whens they come and whothir they wolde, and what they dud in those marchis. So
10 sir Sagramoure loked uppon sir Trystrames and had scorne of his wordys, and seyde to hym agayne,

'Sir, be ye a knyght of Cornwayle?'

'Whereby askyste thou?' seyde sir Trystrames.

'For hit is seldom seyne,' seyde sir Sagramoure, 'that ye Cornysshe
15 knyghtes bene valyaunte men in armys, for within thes two owres there mette with us one of you Cornysshe knyghtes, and grete wordys he spake, and anone with lytyll myght he was leyde to the erthe. And as I trow,' seyde sir Sagramoure, 'that ye wolde have the same hansell.'

'Fayre lordys,' seyde sir Trystrames, 'hit may so happe that I may
20 bettir wythstonde you than he ded, and whether ye woll or nylle, I woll have ado with you, because he was my cosyn that ye bete. And therefore here do your beste! And wete you well: but yf ye quyte you the bettir here uppon this grounde, one knyght of Cornwayle shall beate you bothe.'

25 Whan sir Dodynas le Savyaige herde hym sey so he gate a speare in hys honde and seyde, 'Sir knyght, kepe thyselff!' And than they departed and com togydirs as hit had bene thundir. And sir Dodynas spere braste in sundir, but sir Trystrames smote hym with a more myght, that he smote hym clene over the horse croupyn, and nyghe he
30 had brokyn his necke.

Whan sir Sagramoure saw hys felow have suche a falle he mervayled what knyght he was, but so he dressed his speare with all his myght, and sir Trystrames ayenste hym, and so they cam togydir as thundir. And there sir Trystrames smote sir Sagramour a stronge buffette, that he
35 bare hys horse and hym to the erthe, and in the fallynge he brake his thyghe.

So whan this was done sir Trystrames asked them,

'Fayre knyghtes, wyll ye ony more? Be there ony bygger knyghtys in the courte of kynge Arthure? Hit is to you shame to sey us knyghtes
40 of Cornwayle dishonour, for hit may happyn a Cornysh knyght may macche you.'

'That is trouthe,' seyde sir Sagramoure, 'that have we well proved. But I requyre you,' seyde sir Sagramour, 'telle us your name, be your feyth and trouthe that ye owghe to the Hyghe Order of Knyghthode.'

'Ye charge me with a grete thynge,' seyde sir Trystrames, 'and sytthyn ye lyste to wete, ye shall know and undirstonde that my name ys sir Trystrames de Lyones, kynge Melyodas son, and nevew unto kynge Marke.'

Than were they two knyghtes fayne that they had mette with sir Trys- 5 trames, and so they prayde hym to abyde in their felyshyp.

'Nay,' seyde sir Trystrames, 'for I muste have ado wyth one of your felawys. His name is sir Bleoberys de Ganys.'

'God spede yow well,' seyde sir Sagramoure and sir Dodynas.

So sir Trystrames departed and rode onwarde on his way. And than 10 was he ware before hym in a valay where rode sir Bleoberys wyth sir Segwarydes lady that rode behynde his squyre uppon a palfrey.

Than sir Trystrames rode more than a pace untyll that he had over- (17) take hym. Than spake sir Trystrames:

'Abyde,' he seyde, 'knyght of Arthures courte! Brynge agayne that 15 lady or delyver hir to me!'

'I woll do neyther nother,' seyde sir Bleoberys, 'for I drede no Cornysshe knyght so sore that me lyste to delyver her.'

'Why,' seyde sir Trystrames, 'may nat a Cornysshe knyght do as well as another knyght? Yes, this same day two knyghtes of youre 20 courte wythin this three myle mette with me, and or ever we departed they founde a Cornysshe knyght good inowe for them bothe.'

'What were their namys?' seyde sir Bleobrys.

'Sir, they tolde me that one hyght sir Sagramoure le Desyrous and that other hyght sir Dodynas le Saveayge.'   25

'A,' seyde sir Bleoberys, 'have ye mette with them? So God me helpe, they were two good knyghtes and men of grete worshyp, and yf ye have betyn them bothe ye muste nedis be a good knyght. Yf hit be so ye have beatyn them bothe, yet shall ye nat feare me, but ye shall beate me or ever ye have this lady.'   30

'Than defende you!' seyde sir Trystrames.

So they departed and com togydir lyke thundir, and eyther bare other downe, horse and man, to the erthe. Than they avoyded their horsys and lasshed togydyrs egerly with swerdys and myghtyly, now here now there, trasyng and traversynge on the ryght honde and on the lyffte 35 honde more than two owres. And somtyme they rowysshed togydir with suche a myght that they lay bothe grovelynge on the erthe. Than sir Bleoberys de Ganys sterte abacke and seyde thus:

'Now, jantyll knyght, a whyle holde your hondes and let us speke togydyrs.'   40

'Sey on what ye woll,' seyde sir Trystrames, 'and I woll answere you and I can.'

'Sir,' seyde Bleoberys, 'I wolde wete of whens ye were and of whom ye be com and what is your name.'

'So God me helpe,' seyde sir Trystrames, 'I feare nat to telle you my name. Wete you well, I am kynge Melyodas son, and my mother is kynge Markys sistir, and my name is sir Trystrames de Lyones, and kynge Marke ys myne uncle.'

5 'Truly,' seyde sir Bleoberys, 'I am ryght glad of you, for ye ar he that slewe [Marhalte] the knyght honde for honde in the ilonde for the trwayge of Cornwayle. Also ye overcom sir Palomydes, the good knyght, at the turnemente in Irelonde where he bete sir Gawayne and his nine felowys.'

10 'So God me helpe,' seyde sir Trystrames, 'wete you well I am the same knyght. Now I have tolde you my name, telle me yourys.'

'With good wyll. [Wete ye well] that my name is sir Bleoberys de Ganys, and my brother hyght sir Blamoure de Ganys that is callyd a good knyght, and we be sistyrs chyldyrn unto my lorde sir Launcelot
15 de Lake that we calle one of the beste knyghtes of the worlde.'

'That is trouthe,' seyde sir Trystrames, 'sir Launcelot ys called pereles of curtesy and of knyghthode, and for his sake,' seyde sir Trystramys, 'I wyll nat with my good wylle feyght no more with you, for the grete love I have to sir Launcelot.'

20 'In good feyth,' seyde sir Bleoberys, 'as for me, I wolde be loth to fyght with you, but sytthen ye folow me here to have thys lady I shall proffir you kyndenes and curtesy ryght here uppon this grounde. Thys lady shall be sette betwyxte us bothe, and who that she woll go unto of you and me, lette hym have hir in pees.'

25 'I woll well,' seyde sir Trystrames, 'for as I deme she woll leve you and com to me.'

'Ye shall preve anone,' seyde sir Bleoberys.

(18)   So whan she was sette betwyxte them she seyde thes wordys unto sir Trystrames:

30 'Wete thou well, sir Trystrames de Lyones, that but late thou was the man in the worlde that I moste loved and trusted, and I wente ye had loved me agayne above all ladyes. But whan thou sawyste this knyght lede me away thou madist no chere to rescow me, but suffirdyst my lorde sir Segwarydes to ryde after me. But untyll that tyme I wente
35 ye had loved me. And therefore now I forsake the and never to love the more.'

And therewithall she wente unto sir Bleoberys. Whan sir Trystrames saw her do so he was wondirly wroth with that lady and ashamed to com to the courte. But sir Bleoberys seyde unto sir Trystrames,

40 'Ye ar in the blame, for I hyre by this ladyes wordis that she trusted you abovyn all erthely knyghtes, and, as she seyth, ye have dysseyved hir. Therefore wete you well, there may no man holde that woll away, and rathir than ye sholde hertely be displesed with me, I wolde ye had her, and she wolde abyde with you.'

'Nay,' seyde the lady, 'so Jesu me helpe, I woll never go wyth hym, f[or] he that I loved and wente that he had loved me forsoke me at my nede. And therefore, sir Trystrames,' she seyde, 'ryde as thou com, for though thou haddyste overcom this knyght as thou were lykly, with the never wolde I have gone. And I shall pray thys knyght so fayre of 5 his knyghthode that or evir he passe thys contrey that he woll lede me to the abbey there my lorde sir Segwarydes lyggys.'

'So God me helpe,' seyde sir Bleoberys, 'I latte you wete this, good knyght sir Trystrames: because kynge Marke gaff me the choyse of a gyffte in this courte, and so this lady lyked me beste—natwythstond- 10 ynge she is wedded and hath a lorde—and I have also fulfylled my queste, she shall be sente unto hir husbande agayne, and in especiall moste for your sake, sir Trystrames. And she wolde go with you, I wolde ye had her.'

'I thanke you,' seyde sir Trystrames, 'but for her sake I shall beware 15 what maner of lady I shall love or truste. For had her lorde sir Seg-warydes bene away from the courte, I sholde have bene the fyrste that sholde a folowed you. But syth ye have refused me, as I am a trew knyght, I shall know hir passyngly well that I shall love other truste.'

And so they toke their leve and departed, and so sir Trystrames 20 rode unto Tyntagyll, and sir Bleoberys rode unto the abbey where sir Segwarydes lay sore wounded, and there he delyverde his lady and departed as a noble knyght.

So whan sir Segwarydes saw hys lady he was gretly comforted; and than she tolde hym that sir Trystrames had done grete batayle with sir 25 Bleoberys and caused hym to bryng her agayne. So that wordis pleased sir Segwarydes gretly, that sir Trystrames wolde do so muche; and so that lady tolde all the batayle unto kynge Marke betwexte sir Trys-tramys and sir Bleoberys.

So whan this was done kynge Marke caste all the wayes that he myght 30 (19) to dystroy sir Trystrames, and than imagened in hymselff to sende sir Trystramys into Irelonde for La Beale Isode. For sir Trystrames had so preysed her for hir beauté and hir goodnesse that kynge Marke seyde he wolde wedde hir; whereuppon he prayde sir Trystramys to take his way into Irelonde for hym on message. And all this was done to the 35 entente to sle sir Trystramys. Natwithstondynge he wolde nat refuse the messayge for no daunger nother perell that myght falle, for the pleasure of his uncle. So to go he made hym redy in the moste goodlyest wyse that myght be devysed, for he toke with hym the moste goodlyeste knyghtes that he myght fynde in the courte, and they were arayed aftir 40 the gyse that was used that tyme in the moste goodlyeste maner.

So sir Trystrames departed and toke the see with all his felyshyp. And anone as he was in the see a tempeste toke them and drove them into the coste of Ingelonde. And there they aryved faste by Camelot, and full fayne they were to take the londe. And whan they were londed sir Trystrames sette up his pavylyon uppon the londe of Camelot, and there he lete hange his shylde uppon the pavylyon.

And that same day cam two knyghtes of kynge Arthures: that one
5 was sir Ector de Marys, and that other was sir Morganoure. And thes two touched the shylde and bade hym com oute of the pavylyon for to juste and he wolde.

'Anone ye shall be answeryd,' seyde sir Trystramys, 'and ye woll tary a lytyll whyle.'

10 So he made hym redy, and fyrste he smote downe sir Ector and than sir Morganoure, all with one speare, and sore brused them. And whan they lay uppon the erthe they asked sir Trystramys what he was and of what contrey he was knyght.

'Fayre lordis,' seyde sir Trystrames, 'wete you well that I am of
15 Cornwayle.'

'Alas!' seyde sir Ector, 'now am I ashamed that ever ony Cornysshe knyght sholde overcom me!' And than for dispyte sir Ector put of his armoure fro hym and wente on foot and wolde nat ryde.

(20)   Than hit befelle that sir Bleoberys and sir Blamour de Ganys that
20 were brethyrn, they had assomned kynge Angwysshe of Irelonde for to com to kynge Arthurs courte uppon payne of forfeture of kyng Arthurs good grace; and yf the kynge of Irelonde come nat into that day assygned and sette, the kynge sholde lose his londys.

So by kynge Arthure hit was happened that day that nother he neythir
25 sir Launcelot myght nat be there where the jugemente sholde be yevyn, for kynge Arthure was with sir Launcelot at Joyous Garde. And so kynge Arthure assygned kynge Carados and the Kynge of Scottis to be there that day as juges.

So whan thes kynges were at Camelot kynge Angwysshe of Irelonde
30 was com to know hys accusers. Than was sir Blamour de Ganys there that appeled the kynge of Irelonde of treson, that he had slayne a cosyn of thers in his courte in Irelonde by treson. Than the kynge was sore abaysshed of his accusacion for why he was at the sommons of kyng Arthure, and or that he com at Camelot he wyste nat wherefore he was
35 sente fore.

So whan the kynge herde hym sey his wyll he undirstood well there was none other remedy but to answere hym knyghtly. For the custom was suche tho dayes that and ony man were appealed of ony treson othir of murthure he sholde fyght body for body, other ellys to fynde
40 another knyght for hym. And alle maner of murthers in tho dayes were called treson.

So whan kynge Angwysshe undirstood his accusyng he was passynge hevy, for he knew sir Blamoure de Ganys that he was a noble knyght, and of noble knyghtes comyn. So the kynge of Irelonde was but

symply purveyde of his answere. Therefore the juges gaff hym respyte
by the thirde day to gyff his answere. So the kynge departed unto his
lodgynge.

The meanewhyle there com a lady by sir Trystrames pavylyon
makynge grete dole.   5

'What aylyth you,' seyde sir Trystrames, 'that ye make suche dole?'

'A, fayre knyght!' seyde the lady, 'I am shamed onles that som good
knyght helpe me, for a grete lady of worshyp sent by me a fayre chylde
and a ryche unto sir Launcelot, and hereby there mette with me a
knyght and threw me downe of my palfrey and toke away the chylde   10
frome me.'

'Well, my lady,' seyde sir Trystramys, 'and for my lorde sir Launcelotes sake I shall gete you that chylde agayne, othir he shall beate me.'

And so sir Trystramys toke his horse and asked the lady whyche way
the knyght yoode. Anone she tolde hym, and he rode aftir. So within a   15
whyle he overtoke that knyght and bade hym turne and brynge agayne
the chylde.

Anone the knyght turned his horse and made hym redy to fyght, and   (21)
than sir Trystramys smote hym with a swerde such a buffet that he
tumbled to the erthe, and than he yelded hym unto sir Trystramys.   20

'Than com thy way,' seyde syr Trystrames, 'and brynge the chylde
to the lady agayne!'

So he toke his horse weykely and rode wyth sir Trystrames, and so by
the way he asked his name.

'Sir,' he seyde, 'my name is Breunys Sanze Pyté.'   25

So whan he had delyverde that chylde to the lady [he seyde],

'Sir, as in this the chylde is well remedyed.'

Than sir Trystramys lete hym go agayne, that sore repented hym
aftir, for he was a grete foo unto many good knyghtes of kyng Arthures
courte.   30

Than whan sir Trystrames was in his pavylyon Governayle, his man
com and tolde hym how that kynge Angwysh of Irelonde was com
thydir, and he was in grete dystresse; and there he tolde hym how he
was somned and appeled of murthur.

'So God me helpe,' seyde sir Trystrames, 'this is the beste tydynges   35
that ever com to me this seven yere, for now shall the kynge of Irelonde have nede of my helpe. For I dere say there is no knyght in this
contrey that is nat in Arthures courte that dare do batayle wyth sir
Blamoure de Ganys. And for to wynne the love of the kynge of Irelonde I woll take the batayle uppon me. And therefore, Governayle,   40
bere me this worde, I charge the, to the kynge.'

Than Governayle wente unto kynge Angwyshe of Irelonde and
salewed hym full fayre. So the kynge welcommed hym and asked what
he wolde.

'Sir,' he seyde, 'here is a knyght nerehonde that desyryth to speke wyth you, for he bade me sey that he wolde do you servyse.'

'What knyght is he?' seyde the kynge.

'Sir, hit [is] sir Trystrames de Lyones, that for the good grace ye
5 shewed hym in your londys he woll rewarde [you] in thys contreys.'

'Com on, felow,' seyde the kynge, 'with me anone, and brynge me unto sir Trystramys.'

So the kynge toke a lytyll hackeney and but fewe felyshyp with hym tyll that he cam unto sir Trystramys pavylyon. And whan sir Trys-
10 trames saw the kynge he ran unto hym and wolde have holdyn his styrope, but the kynge lepe frome his horse lyghtly, and eythir halsed othir in armys.

'My gracious lorde,' seyde sir Trystrames, 'grauntemercy of your grete goodnesse that ye shewed unto me in your marchys and landys!
15 And at that tyme I promysed you to do you servyse and ever hit lay in my power.'

'A, jantyll knyght,' seyde the kynge unto sir Trystrames, 'now have I grete nede of you, never had I so grete nede of no knyghtys helpe.'

'How so, my good lorde?' seyde sir Trystramys.
20 'I shall tyll you,' seyde the kynge. 'I am assumned and appeled fro my contrey for the deth of a knyght that was kynne unto the good knyght sir Launcelot, wherefore sir Blamour de Ganys, sir Bleoberys his brother, hath appeled me to fyght wyth hym other for to fynde a knyght in my stede. And well I wote,' seyde the kynge, 'thes that ar
25 comyn of kynge Banys bloode, as sir Launcelot and thes othir, ar passynge good harde knyghtes and harde men for to wynne in batayle as ony that I know now lyvyng.'

'Sir,' seyde sir Trystrames, 'for the good lordeshyp ye shewed unto me in Irelonde and for my lady youre doughtirs sake, La Beale Isode,
30 I woll take the batayle for you uppon this conducion, that ye shall graunte me two thynges: one is that ye shall swere unto me that ye ar in the ryght and that ye were never consentynge to the knyghtis deth. Sir,' than seyde sir Trystramys, 'whan I have done this batayle, yf God gyff me grace to spede, that ye shall gyff me a rewarde what thynge
35 resonable that I woll aske you.'

'So God me helpe,' seyde the kynge, 'ye shall have whatsomever ye woll.'

(22) 'Ye sey well,' seyde sir Trystramys, 'now make your answere that your champyon is redy, for I shall dye in your quarell rathir than to
40 be recreaunte.'

'I have no doute of you,' seyde the kynge, 'that and ye sholde have ado with sir Launcelot de Lake.'

'As for sir Launcelot, he is called the noblyst of the worlde of knyghtes, and wete you well that the knyghtes of hys bloode ar noble

men and drede shame. And as for sir Bleoberys, brother unto sir
Blamour, I have done batayle wyth hym; therefore, uppon my hede,
hit is no shame to calle hym a good knyght.'

'Sir, hit is noysed,' seyde the kynge, 'that sir Blamour is the hardyer
knyght.'   5

'As for that, lat hym be! He shall nat be refused and he were the beste
knyght that beryth shylde or spere.'

So kynge Angwysh departed unto kyng Carados and the kynges
that were that tyme as juges, and tolde them how that he had founde his
champyon redy. Than by the commaundementes of the kynges sir   10
Blamour de Ganys and sir Trystramys de Lyones were sente fore to
hyre their charge, and whan they were com before the juges there were
many kynges and knyghtes that behylde sir Trystrames and muche
speche they had of hym, because he slew sir Marhalte the good knyght
and because he forjusted sir Palomydes the good knyght.   15

So whan they had takyn their charge they withdrew hem to make
hem redy to do batayle. Than seyde sir Bleoberys to his brother sir
Blamoure,

'Fayre dere brother,' seyde he, 'remembir of what kynne we be com
of, and what a man is sir Launcelot de Lake, nother farther ne nere but 20
brethyrne chyldirne. And there was never none of oure kynne that
ever was shamed in batayle, but rathir, brothir, suffir deth than to be
shamed!'

'Brothir,' seyde sir Blamour, 'have ye no doute of me, for I shall
never shame none of my bloode. Howbe[it] I am sure that yondir   25
knyght ys called a passynge good knyght as of his tyme as ony in the
worlde, yett shall I never yelde me nother sey the lothe worde. Well
may he happyn to smyte me downe with his grete myght of chevalry,
but rather shall he sle me than I shall yelde me recreaunte.'

'God spede you well,' seyde sir Bleoberys, 'for ye shall fynde hym   30
the myghtyest knyght that ever ye had ado withall: I knowe hym, for
I have had ado with hym.'

'God me spede!' seyde sir Blamour.

And therewith he toke his horse at the one ende of the lystes, and sir
Trystramys at the othir ende of the lystes, and so they feautred their 35
sperys and com togedyrs as hit had be thundir, and there sir Trystrames
thorow grete myght smote doune sir Blamour and his horse to the
erthe.

Than anone sir Blamour avoyded his horse and pulled oute his
swerde and toke his shylde before hym and bade sir Trystrames alyght, 40
'for thoughe my horse hath fayled, I truste to God the erthe woll nat
fayle me!'

And than sir Trystrames alyght and dressed hym unto batayle, and
there they laysshed togedir strongely, rasynge, foynynge and

daysshynge many sad strokes, that the kynges and knyghtes had grete wondir that they myght stonde, for they evir fought lyke woode men. There was never seyne of two knyghtes that fought more ferselyer, for sir Blamour was so hasty he wolde have no reste, that all men wondirde
5 that they had brethe to stonde on their feete, that all the place was bloodé that they fought in. And at the laste sir Trystramys smote sir Blamour suche a buffette uppon the helme that he there synked downe uppon his syde, and sir Trystramys stood stylle and behylde hym.

(23) So whan sir Blamour myght speke he seyde thus:
10 'Sir Trystrames de Lyones, I requyre the, as thou art a noble knyght and the beste knyght that ever I founde, that thou wolt sle me oute, for I wolde nat lyve to be made lorde of all the erthe; for I had lever dye here with worshyp than lyve here with shame. And nedis, sir Trys-trames, thou muste sle me, other ellys thou shalt never wynne the fylde,
15 for I woll never sey the lothe worde. And therefore, yf [thou] dare sle me, sle me, I requyre the!'

Whan sir Trystrames herde hym sey so knyghtly, in his herte he wyste nat what to do with hym. Remembryng hym of bothe partyes, of what bloode he was commyn of, and for sir Launcelottis sake, he
20 wolde be loth to sle hym; and in the other party, in no wyse he myght nat chose but to make hym sey the lothe worde, othir ellys to sle hym.

Than sir Trystrames sterte abacke and wente to the kynges that were juges, and there he kneled downe tofore them and besought them of their worshyppis, and for kynge Arthurs love and for sir Launcellottis
25 sake, that they wolde take this mater in their hondis.

'For, my fayre lordys,' seyde sir Trystrames, 'hit were shame and pyté that this noble knyght that yondir lyeth sholde be slayne, for ye hyre well, shamed woll he nat be. And I pray to God that he never be slayne nother shamed for me. And as for the kynge whom I fyght fore,
30 I shall requyre hym, as I am hys trew champyon and trew knyght in this fylde, that he woll have mercy uppon this knyght.'

'So God me helpe,' seyde kyng Angwyshe, 'I woll for your sake, sir Trystrames, be ruled as ye woll have me, and I woll hartely pray the kynges that be here juges to take hit in there hondys.'
35 Than the kynges that were juges called sir Bleoberys to them and asked his advyce.

'My lordys,' seyde sir Bleoberys, 'thoughe my brother be beatyn and have the worse thorow myght of armys in his body, [I dare sey, though sir Trystrames hath beatyn his body], he hath nat beatyn his harte, and
40 thanke God he is nat shamed this day; and rathir than he be shamed I requyre you,' seyde sir Bleoberys, 'lat sir Trystrames sle hym oute.'

'Hit shall nat be so,' seyde the kynges, 'for his parte his adversary, bothe the kynge and the champyon, have pyté on sir Blamoure his knyghthode.'

'My lordys,' seyde sir Bleoberys, 'I woll ryght as ye woll.'

Than the kynges called the kynge of Irelonde and founde hym
goodly and tretable, and than by all their advyces sir Trystrames and
sir Bleoberys toke up sir Blamoure, and the two bretherne were made
accorded wyth kynge Angwyshe and kyssed togydir and made frendys 5
for ever.

And than sir Blamoure and sir Trystrames kyssed togedirs, and there
they made their othis that they wolde never none of them two brethirne
fyght wyth sir Trystrames, and sir Trystramys made them the same
othe. And for that jantyll batayle all the bloode of sir Launcelott loved 10
sir Trystrames for ever.

Than kynge Angwyshe and sir Trystrames toke their leve, and so he
sayled into Irelonde wyth grete nobles and joy. So whan they were in
Irelonde the kynge lete make hit knowyn thorowoute all the londe how
and in what maner sir Trystrames had done for hym. Than the quene 15
and all that there were made the moste of hym that they myght. But the
joy that La Beale Isode made of sir Trystrames there myght no tunge
telle, for of all men erthely she loved hym moste.

Than uppon a day kynge Angwyshe asked sir Trystrames why he (24)
asked nat his bone. Than seyde sir Trystrames,   20

'Now hit is tyme. Sir, this is all that I woll desyre, that ye woll gyff
La Beale Isode, youre doughter, nat for myself, but for myne uncle,
kyng Marke, [that] shall have her to wyff, for so have I promysed
hym.'

'Alas!' seyde the kynge, 'I had lever than all the londe that I have 25
that ye wolde have wedded hir yourself.'

'Sir, and I dud so, I were shamed for ever in this worlde and false of
my promyse. Therefore,' seyde sir Trystrames, 'I requyre you, holde
your promyse that ye promysed me, for this is my desyre: that ye woll
gyff me La Beale Isode to go with me into Cornwayle for to be wedded 30
unto kynge Marke, myne uncle.'

'As for that,' kynge Angwysshe seyde, 'ye shall have her with yow
to do with hir what hit please you, that is for to sey, if that ye lyste to
wedde hir yourselff, that is me leveste; and yf ye woll gyff hir unto
kyng Marke your uncle, that is in your choyse.'   35

So, to make shorte conclusyon, La Beale Isode was made redy to go
with sir Trystrames. And dame Brangwayne wente with hir for hir
chyff jantyllwoman with many other. Than [the] quene, Isodes modir,
gaff dame Brangwayne unto hir to be hir jantyllwoman.

And also she and Governayle had a drynke of the quene, and she 40
charged them that where kynge Marke sholde wedde, that same day
they sholde gyff them that drynke that kynge Marke sholde drynke to
La Beale Isode. 'And than,' seyde the quene, 'ayther shall love other
dayes of their lyff.'

So this drynke was gyvyn unto dame Brangwayne and unto Governayle. So sir Trystrames toke the see, and La Beale Isode. [And whan
they] were in their caban, hit happed so they were thyrsty. And than
they saw a lytyll flakette of golde stonde by them, and hit semed by the
5 coloure and the taste that hit was noble wyne. So sir Trystrames toke
the flaket in his honde and seyde,

'Madame Isode, here is a draught of good wyne that dame Brangwayne, your maydyn, and Governayle, my servaunte, hath kepte for
hemselff.'

10 Than they lowghe and made good chere and eyther dranke to other
frely, and they thought never drynke that ever they dranke so swete
nother so good to them. But by that drynke was in their bodyes they
loved aythir other so well that never hir love departed, for well nother
for woo. And thus hit happed fyrst, the love betwyxte sir Trystrames
15 and La Beale Isode, the whyche love never departed dayes of their lyff.

So than they sayled tyll that by fortune they com nye a castell that
hyght Plewre, and there they aryved for to repose them, wenynge to
them to have had good herborow.

But anone as sir Trystrames was within the castell they were takyn
20 presoners, for the custom of that castell was suche that who that rode
by that castell and brought ony lady wyth hym he muste nedys fyght
with the lorde that hyght Brewnour. And yf hit so were that Brewnor
wan the fylde, than sholde the knyght straunger and his lady be put to
deth, what that ever they were. And yf hit were so that the straunge
25 knyght wan the fylde of sir Brewnor, than sholde he dye and hys lady
bothe. So this custom was used many wyntyrs, wherefore hit was called
the Castell Plewre, that is to sey 'the wepynge castell'.

(25) Thus as sir Trystrames and La Beale Isode were in preson, hit
happynd a knyghte [and] a lady com unto them where they were to
30 chere them. Than seyde sir Trystrames unto the knyght and to the
lady,

'What is the cause the lorde of this castell holdyth us in preson? For
hit was never the custom of placis of worshyp that ever I cam in, whan
a knyght and a lady asked herborow, and they to receyve them, and
35 aftir to dystres them that be his gestys.'

'Sir,' seyde the knyght, 'this is the olde custom of this castell, that
whan a knyght commyth here he muste nedis fyght with oure lorde,
and he that is the wayker muste lose his hede. And whan that is done,
if his lady that he bryngyth be fowler than is oure lordys wyff, she muste
40 lose hir hede. And yf she be fayrer preved than ys oure lady, than shall
the lady of this castell lose her hede.'

'So God me helpe,' seyde sir Trystrames, 'this is a foule custom and a
shamfull custom. But one avauntage have I,' seyde sir Trystrames, 'I
have a lady is fayre ynowe, and I doute nat for lacke of beauté she shall

nat lose her hede. And rathir than I shall lose myne hede I woll fyght
for hit on a fayre fylde. Sir knyght and your fayre lady, I pray you, tell
your lorde that I woll be redy as to-morne, wyth my lady and myselff,
to do batayle if hit be so I may have my horse and myne armoure.'

'Sir,' seyde the knyght, 'I undirtake for youre desyre shall be spedde, 5
and therefore take your reste and loke that ye be up betymes, and make
you redy and your lady, for ye shall wante nothynge that you behovyth.'

And therewith he departed, and so on the morne betymys that same
knyght com to sir Trystramys and fecched hym oute and his lady, and
brought hym horse and armoure that was his owne, and bade hym 10
make hym redy to the fylde, for all the astatis and comyns of that
lordshyp were there redy to beholde that batayle and jugemente.

Than cam sir Brewnor, the lorde of the castell, with his lady in his
honde muffeled, and asked sir Trystrames where was his lady, 'for and
thy lady be feyrar than myne, with thy swerde smyte of my ladyes hede, 15
and yf my lady be fayrer than thyne, with my swerde I muste stryke of
hir hede. And if I may wynne the, yette shall thy lady be myne, and
thow shalt lese thy hede.'

'Sir,' seyde sir Trystrames, 'this is a foule custom and an horryble,
and rather than my lady sholde lose hir hede yett had I lever lose myne 20
hede.'

'Nay, nay!' seyde sir Brewnor, 'the ladyes shall be fyrste shewed
togydir, and that one shall have hir jugemente.'

'Nay, I wyll nat so,' seyde sir Trystrames, 'for here is none that woll
gyff ryghtuous jugemente. But I doute nat,' seyde sir Trystrames, 'my 25
lady is fayrer than youres, and that woll I make good with my hondys,
and who that woll sey the contrary, I woll preve hit on his hede!'

And therewyth sir Trystrames shewed forth La Beale Isode and
turned hir thryse aboute with his naked swerde in his honde. And so
dud sir Brewnor the same wyse to his lady. But whan sir Brewnor be- 30
helde La Beale Isode hym thought he saw never a fayrer lady, and than
he drad his ladyes hede sholde off. And so all the people that were there
presente gaff jugement that La Beale Isode was the fayrer lady and the
bettir made.

'How now?' seyde syr Trystrames. 'Mesemyth hit were pyté that my 35
lady sholde lose hir hede, but bycause thou and she of longe tyme have
used this wycked custom and by you bothe hath many good knyghtes
and fayre ladyes bene destroyed, for that cause hit were no losse to
destroy you bothe.'

'So God me helpe,' seyde sir Brewnor, 'for to sey the sothe, thy lady 40
is fayrer than myne, and that me sore repentys, and so I hyre the people
pryvyly sey, for of all women I sawe never none so fayre. And therefore, and thou wolt sle my lady, I doute nat I shall sle the and have thy
lady.'

'Well, thou shalt wyn her,' seyde sir Trystrames, 'as dere as ever knyght wanne lady. And bycause of thyne owne jugemente thou woldist have done to my lady if that she had bene fowler, and bycause of the evyll custom, gyff me thy lady,' seyde syr Trystrames.

5 And therewithall sir Trystrames strode unto hym and toke his lady frome hym, and with an awke stroke he smote of hir hede clene.

'Well, knyght,' seyde sir Brewnor, 'now haste thou done me a grete (26) dispyte. Now take thyne horse, and sytthen that I am ladyles, I woll wynne thy lady and I may.'

10 Than they toke their horsis and cam togydir as hit had bene thundir, and sir Trystrames smote sir Brewnor clene frome his horse. And lyghtly he rose up, and as sir Trystrames com agayne by hym he threste his horse thorowoute bothe shuldyrs, that his horse hurled here and there and felle dede to the grounde. And ever sir Brewnor ran aftir to

15 have slayne sir Trystrames, but he was lyght and nymell and voyded his horse. Yett, or ever sir Trystrames myght dresse his shylde and his swerde, he gaff hym three or four strokys.

Than they russhed togydyrs lyke two borys, trasynge and traversynge myghtyly and wysely as two noble knyghtes, for this sir Brewnor was

20 a proved knyght and had bene or than the deth of many good knyghtes. Soo thus they fought hurlynge here and there nyghe two owres, and aythir were wounded sore. Than at the laste sir Brewnor russhed uppon sir Trystrames and toke hym in his armys, for he trusted much to his strengthe. (Than was sir Trystrames called the strengyst knyght of the

25 worlde, for he was called bygger than sir Launcelotte, but sir Launcelot was bettir brethid.) So anone sir Trystrames threste sir Brewnor downe grovelyng, and than he unlaced his helme and strake of his hede.

And than all they [that] longed to the castell com to hym and dud

30 hym homage and feauté, prayng hym that he wolde abyde stylle there a lytyll whyle to fordo that foule custom. So this sir Trystrames graunted thereto.

So the meanewhyle one of the knyghtes rode unto sir Galahalte the Haute Prynce whyche was sir Brewnors son, a noble knyght, and tolde

35 hym what mysadventure his fadir had and his modir.

(27) Than cam sir Galahalt and the Kynge with the Hondred Knyghtes with hym, and this sir Galahalte profyrde to fyght wyth sir Trystrames hande for hande. And so they made hem redy to go unto batayle on horsebacke wyth grete corrayge. So anone they mette togydyrs so hard

40 that aythir bare othir adowne, horse and man, to the erthe. And whan they avoyded their horsis, as noble knyghtes they dressed their shyldis and drewe their swerdys wyth ire and rancoure, and they laysshed togydyr many sad strokys. And one whyle strykynge and another whyle foynynge, tracynge and traversynge as noble knyghtes.

Thus they fought longe, nerehonde halff a day, and aythir were sore wounded. So at the laste sir Trystrames wexed lyght and bygge, and doubled his strokys and drove sir Galahalt abacke on the tone sy[d]e and on the tothir, that he was nye myscheved, lyke to be slayne. So wyth that cam the Kynge wyth the Hondred Knyghtes, and all that 5 felyshyp wente freyshly uppon sir Trystrames. But whan sir Trystramys saw them comynge uppon hym, than he wyste well he myght nat endure, so as a wyse knyght of warre he seyde unto sir Galahalt the Haute Prynce,

'Syr, ye shew to me no kyndenesse for to suffir all your men to have 10 ado wyth me, and ye seme a noble knyght of your hondys. Hit is grete shame to you!'

'So God me helpe,' seyde sir Galahalt, 'there is none other way but thou muste yelde the to me other ellys to dye, sir Trystrames.'

'Sir, as for that, I woll rather yelde me to you than dye, for hit is 15 more for the myght of thy men than of thyne handys.'

And therewithall sir Trystrames toke his swerde by the poynte and put the pomell in his honde, and therewithall com the Kynge with the Hondred Knyghtes and harde began to assayle sir Trystrames.

'Lat be,' seyde sir Galahalt, 'that ye be nat so hardy to towche hym, 20 for I have gyffyn this knyght his lyff.'

'That ys your shame,' seyde the kynge, 'for he hath slayne youre fadir and your modir.'

'As for that,' seyde sir Galahalte, 'I may nat wyght hym gretly, for my fadir had hym in preso[n] and inforsed hym to do batayle with hym. 25 And my fadir hadde suche a custom, that was a shamefull custom, that what knyght and lady com thydir to aske herberow, his lady [must] nedis dye but yf she were fayrer than my modir; and if my fadir overcom that knyght he muste nedis dye. For sothe, this was a shamefull custom and usage, a knyght, for his herborow askynge, to have suche 30 herborage. And for this custom I wolde never draw aboute hym.'

'So God me helpe,' seyde the kynge, 'this was a shamefull custom.'

'Truly,' seyde sir Galahalt, 'so semyth me. And mesemyth hit had bene grete pyté that this knyght sholde have bene slayne, for I dare sey he is one of the noblyst knyghtes that beryth lyff but yf hit be sir 35 Launcelot du Lake.'

'Now, fayre knyght,' seyde sir Galahalte, 'I requyre you, telle me youre name and of whens ye ar and whethir thou wolte.'

'Sir,' he seyde, 'my name is sir Trystrames de Lyones, and frome kynge Marke of Cornwayle I was sente on messayge unto kyng Ang- 40 wyshe of Irelonde for to fecche his doughtyr to be his wyff, and here she is redy to go wyth me into Cornwayle, and her name is La Beale Isode.'

Than seyde sir Galahalte unto sir Trystramys,

'Well be ye founde in this marchis! And so ye woll promyse me to go unto sir Launcelot and accompany wyth hym, ye shall go where ye woll and youre fayre lady wyth you. And I shall promyse you never in all my dayes shall none suche custom be used in this castell as hath bene
5 used heretofore.'

'Sir,' seyde sir Trystrames, 'now I late you wete, so God me helpe, I wente ye had bene sir Launcelot du Lake whan I sawe you fyrste, and therefore I dred you the more. And, sir, I promyse you,' seyde sir Trystrames, 'as sone as I may I woll se sir Launcelot and infelyshyp
10 me with hym, for of all the knyghtes in the worlde I moste desyre his felyshyp.'

(28) And than sir Trystramys toke his leve whan he sawe his tyme, and toke the see.

And meanewhyle worde com to sir Launcelot and to sir Trys-
15 tramys that kynge Carados, the myghty kynge that was made lyke a gyaunte why⟨ght⟩, fought wyth sir Gawayne and gaff hym suche strokys that he sowned in his sadyll. And after that he toke hym by the coler and pulled hym oute of his sadyll and bounde hym faste to the sadyll-bowghe, and so rode his way with hym towarde his castell. And as he
20 rode, sir Launcelot by fortune mette with kynge Carados, and anone he knew sir Gawayne that lay bounde before hym.

'A!' seyde syr Launcelot unto sir Gawayne, 'how stondyth hit wyth you?'

'Never so harde,' seyde sir Gawayne, 'onles that ye helpe me. For,
25 so God me helpe, withoute ye rescow me I know no knyght that may but you other sir Trystrames,' wherefor sir Launcelot was hevy at sir Gawaynes wordys. And than sir Launcelot bade sir Carados,

'Ley downe that knyght and fyght with me!'

'Thow arte but a foole,' seyde sir Carados, 'for I woll serve the in the
30 same wyse.'

'As for that,' seyde sir Launcelot, 'spare me nat, for I warne the, I woll nat spare the.'

And than he bounde hym hande and foote and so threw hym to the grounde, and than he gate his speare in his honde of his squyre and
35 departed frome sir Launcelot to fecche his course. And so ayther mette with other and brake their speares to theire hondys. And than they pulled oute their swerdys and hurled togydyrs on horsebacke more than an owre. And at the laste sir Launcelot smote sir Carados suche a buffet on the helme that hit perysshed his brayne-panne. So than syr Launcelot
40 toke sir Carados by the coler and pulled hym undir his horse fete, and than he alyght and pulled of his helme and strake offe his hede. Than sir Launcelot unbownde sir Gawayne.

So this same tale was tolde to sir Galahalte and to syr Trystrames, and sayde, 'Now may ye hyre the nobles that folowyth sir Launcelot.'

'Alas!' seyde sir Trystrames, 'and I had nat this messayge in hande with this fayre lady, truly I wolde never stynte or I had founde sir Launcelot.'

Than syr Trystrames and La Beale Isode yeode to the see and cam into Cornwayle, and anone all the barownes mette with hym. And anone they were rychely wedded wyth grete nobley. But evir, as the Frenshe booke seyth, sir Trystrames and La Beale Isode loved ever togedyrs. 5 (29)

Than was there grete joustys and grete turnayynge, and many lordys and ladyes were at that feyste, and sir Trystrames was moste praysed of all other. So thus dured the feste longe. 10

And aftir that feste was done, within a lytyll whyle aftir, by the assente of two ladyes that were with the quene they ordayned for hate and envye for to distroy dame Brangwayne that was mayden and lady unto La Beale Isode. And she was sente into the foreste for to fecche herbys, and there she was [mette] and bounde honde and foote to a tre, and so she was bounden three dayes. And by fortune sir Palomydes founde dame Brangwayne, and there he delyverde hir from the deth and brought hir to a nunry there besyde for to be recoverde. 15

Whan Isode the quene myssed hir mayden, wete you well she was ryght hevy as evir any quene myght be, for of all erthely women she loved hir beste and moste, cause why she cam with her oute of her contrey. And so uppon a day quene Isode walked into the foreste to put away hir thoughtes, and there she wente hirselff unto a welle and made grete moone. And suddey[n]ly there cam sir Palomydes unto her, and herde all hir complaynte and seyde, 20 25

'Madame Isode, and ye wolde grauntc me my boone I shall brynge to you dame Brangwayne sauff and sounde.'

Than the quene was so glad of his profyr that suddaynly unavysed she graunte all his askynge. 30

'Well, madame,' seyde sir Palomydes, 'I truste to youre promyse, and yf ye woll abyde halff an owre here I shall brynge hir to you.'

'Sir, I shall abyde you,' seyde the quene.

Than sir Palomydes rode forth his way to that nunry, and lyghtly he cam agayne with dame Brangwayne; but by hir good wylle she wolde nat have comyn to the quene, for cause she stoode in adventure of hir lyff. Natwythstondynge, halff agayne hir wyll, she cam wyth sir Palomydes unto the quene, and whan the quene sawe her she was passyng glad. 35

'Now, madame,' seyde sir Palomydes, 'remembir uppon your promyse, for I have fulfylled my promyse.' 40

'Sir Palomydes,' seyde the quene, 'I wote nat what is your desyre, but I woll that ye wete, howbehit that I profyrde you largely, I thought none evyll, nother, I warne you, none evyll woll I do.'

'Madame,' seyde sir Palomydes, 'as at this tyme ye shall nat know my desyre.'

'But byfore my lorde, myne husbonde, there shall ye know that ye shall have your desyre that I promysed you.'

5   And than the quene rode home unto the kynge, and sir Palomydes rode with hir, and whan sir Palomydes com before the kynge he seyde,

'Sir kynge, I requyre the, as thou arte ryghtuous kynge, that ye woll juge me the ryght.'

10   'Telle me your cause,' seyde the kynge, 'and ye shall have ryght.'

(30)   'Sir,' seyde sir Palomydes, 'I promysed youre quene, my lady dame Isode, to brynge agayne dame Brangwayne that she had loste, uppon this covenaunte, that she sholde graunte me a boone that I wolde aske, and withoute grucchynge othir advysemente she graunted me.'

15   'What sey ye, my lady?' seyde the kynge.

'Hit is as he seyth, so God me helpe! To sey the soth,' seyde the quene, 'I promysed hym his askynge for love and joy I had to se her.'

'Welle, madame,' seyde the kynge, 'and yf'[ye] were hasty to graunte what boone he wolde aske, I wolde well that [ye] perfourmed [your]

20   promyse.'

Than seyde sir Palomydes, 'I woll that ye wete that I woll have youre quene to lede hir and to governe her whereas me lyste.'

Therewyth the kynge stoode stylle and unbethought hym of sir Trystrames and demed that he wolde rescowe her. And than hastely the

25   kynge answered and seyde,

'Take hir to the and the adventures withall that woll falle of hit, for, as I suppose, thou wolt nat enjoy her no whyle.'

'As for that,' seyde sir Palomydes, 'I dare ryght well abyde the adventure.'

30   And so, to make shorte tale, sir Palomydes toke hir by the honde and seyde,

'Madame, grucche nat to go with me, for I desyre nothynge but youre owne promyse.'

'As for that,' seyde the quene, 'wete thou well, I feare nat gretely to

35   go with the, howbehit thou haste me at avauntage uppon my promyse. For I doute nat I shall be worshypfully rescowed fro the.'

'As for that,' seyde sir Palomydes, 'be as hit be may.'

So quene Isode was sette behynde sir Palomydes and rode his way. And anone the kynge sente unto sir Trystrames, but in no wyse he

40   wolde nat be founde, for he was in the foreste an-huntynge; for that was allwayes hys custom, but yf he used armes, to chace and to hunte in the forestes.

'Alas!' seyde the kynge, 'now am I shamed forever, that be myne owne assente my lady and my quene shall be devoured.'

Than cam there forth a knyght that hyght Lambegus, and he was a knyght of sir Trystrames.

'My lorde,' seyde the knyght, 'syth that ye have suche truste in my lorde sir Trystrames, wete yow well for his sake I woll ryde aftir your quene and rescow her, other ellys shall I be beatyn.'   5

'Grauntemercy!' seyde the kynge. 'And I lyve, sir Lambegus, I shall deserve hit.'

And than sir Lambegus armed hym and rode aftir them as faste as he myght, and than wythin a whyle he overtoke hem. And than sir Palomydes lefte the quene and seyde,   10

'What arte thou?' seyde sir Palomydes, 'arte thou sir Trystrames?'

'Nay,' he seyde, 'I am his servaunte, and my name is sir Lambegus.'

'That me repentys,' seyde sir Palomydes, 'I had lever thou had bene sir Trystrames.'

'I leve you well,' seyde sir Lambegus, 'but whan thou metyste with   15
sir Trystrames thou shalt have bothe thy hondys full!'

And than they hurteled togydyrs and all to-braste their sperys, and than they pulled oute their swerdys and hewed on there helmys and hawbirkes. At the laste sir Palomydes gaff sir Lambegus suche a wounde that he felle doune lyke a dede man to the erthe. Than he loked aftir   20
La Beale Isode, and than she was gone he woste nat where. Wete you well that sir Palomydes was never so hevy!

So the quene ran into the foreste, and there she founde a welle and therein she had thought to have drowned herselff. And as good fortune wolde, there cam a knyght to her that had a castell there besyde, and his   25
name was sir Adtherpe. And whan he founde the quene in that myscheff he rescowed her and brought hir to his castell. And whan he wyste what [s]he was he armed hym and toke his horse, and seyde he wolde be avenged uppon sir Palomydes.

And so he rode unto the tyme he mette with hym, and there sir   30
Palomydes wounded hym sore. And by force he made hym to telle the cause why he dud batayle wyth hym, and he tolde hym how he ladde the quene La Beale Isode into hys owne castel.

'Now brynge me there,' seyde sir Palamydes, 'or thou shalt of myne handis die!'   35

'Sir,' seyde sir Adtherpe, 'I am so sore wounded I may nat folow, but ryde you this way and hit shall bryng you to my castell, and therein is the quene.'

Sir Palomydes rode tyll that he cam to the castell. And at a wyndow La Beale Isode saw sir Palomydes, than she made the yatys to be shutte   40
strongely. And whan he sawe he myght nat entir into the castell he put of his horse brydyll and his sadyll, and so put his horse to pasture and sette hymselff downe at the gate, lyke a man that was oute of his wytt that recked nat of hymselff.

(31)   Now turne we unto sir Trystrames, that whan he was com home and wyste that La Beale Isode was gone with sir Palomydes, wete you well he was wrothe oute of mesure.

'Alas!' seyde sir Trystrames, 'I am this day shamed!' Than he called
5 Gavernayle, his man, and seyde,

'Haste the that I were armed and on horsebacke, for well I wote sir Lambegus hath no myght nor strength to wythstonde sir Palomydes. Alas I had nat bene in his stede!'

So anone he was armed and horsed and rode aftir into the foreyste,
10 and within a whyle he founde his knyght sir Lambegus allmoste to deth wounded. And sir Trystrames bare hym to a foster and charged hym to kepe hym welle.

And than he rode forth and founde sir Adtherpe sore wounded; and he tolde all, and how the quene had drowned herselff 'had nat I bene,
15 and how for her sake I toke uppon me to do batayle with sir Palomydes.'

'Where is my lady?' seyde sir Trystrames.

'Sir,' seyde the knyght, 'she is sure inowe wythin my castell, and she can holde her within hit.'

'Grauntemercy,' seyde sir Trystrames, 'of thy grete goodnesse.'
20 And so he rode tyll that he cam nyghe his castell. And than sir Palomydes sate at the gate and sawe where sir Trystrames cam, and he sate as he had slepe, and his horse pastured afore hym.

'Now go thou, Governayle,' seyde sir Trystrames, 'and bydde hym awake and make hym redy.'
25 So Governayle rode unto hym and seyde,

'Sir Palomydes! aryse and take to thyne harneys!'

But he was in suche a study he herde nat what he seyde. So Governayle com agayne to sir Trystrames and tolde hym he slepe or ellys he was madde.
30 'Go thou agayne,' seyde sir Trystrames, 'and bydde hym aryse, and telle hym I am here, his mortall foo.'

So Governayle rode agayne, and putte uppon hym with the but of his spere and seyde,

'Sir Palomydes, make the redy, for wete thou welle sir Trystrames
35 hovyth yondir and sendyth the worde he is thy mortall foo.'

And therewithall sir Palomydes arose stylly withoute ony wordys, and gate hys horse anone and sadylled hym and brydylled hym; and lyghtly he lepe uppon hym and gate his spere in his honde. And aythir feautred their spearys and hurled faste togedyrs, and anone sir Trys-
40 trames smote downe sir Palomydes over his horse tayle. Than lyghtly sir Palomydes put his shylde before hym and drew his swerde.

And there began stronge batayle on bothe partyes, for bothe they fought for the love of on[e] lady. And ever she lay on the wallys and behylde them how they fought oute of mesure. And aythir were

wounded passynge sore, but sir Palomydes was muche sorer wounded;
for they fought thus trasynge and traversynge more than two owres,
that well nyghe for doole and sorow La Beale Isode sowned, and seyde,

'Alas! that one I loved and yet do, and the other I love nat, that they
sholde fyght! And yett hit were grete pyté that I sholde se sir Palo- 5
mydes slayne, for well I know by that the ende be done sir Palomydes is
but a dede man, bycause that he is nat crystened, and I wolde be loth
that he sholde dye a Sarezen.' And therewithall she cam downe and
besought hem for her love to fyght no more.

'A, madame,' seyde sir Trystrames, 'what meane you? Woll ye have 10
me shamed? For well ye know that I woll be ruled by you.'

'A, myne awne lorde,' seyde La Beale Isode, 'full well ye wote I
wolde nat your dyshonour, but I wolde that ye wolde for my sake spare
this unhappy Sarezen, sir Palomydes.'

'Madame,' seyde sir Trystrames, 'I woll leve for youre sake.' 15

Than seyde she to sir Palomydes, 'This shall be thy charge: thou shalt
go oute of this contrey whyle I am ⌐therin⌐.'

'Madame, I woll obey your commaundemente,' seyde sir Palomydes,
'whyche is sore ayenste my wylle.'

'Than take thy way,' seyde La Beale Isode, 'unto the courte of kynge 20
Arthure, and there recommaunde me unto quene Gwenyvere and tell
her that I sende her worde that there be within this londe but four
lovers, and that is sir Launcelot and dame Gwenyver, and sir Trystrames and quene Isode.'

And so sir Palomydes departed with grete hevynesse, and sir Trys- 25 (32)
trames toke the quene and brought her agayne unto kynge Marke. And
than was there made grete joy of hir home-commynge. Than who was
cheryshed but sir Trystrames!

Than sir Trystrames latte fecche home sir Lambegus, his knyght,
frome the forsters house; and hit was longe or he was hole, but so at the 30
laste he recoverde. And thus they lyved with joy and play a longe
whyle. But ever sir Andret, that was nye cosyn unto sir Trystrams, lay
in a [watche to] wayte betwyxte sir Trystrames and La Beale Isode for
to take hym and devoure hym.

So uppon a day sir Trystrames talked with La Beale Isode in a 35
wyndowe, and that aspyed sir Andred and tolde the kynge. Than kyng
Marke toke a swerde in his honde and cam to sir Trystrames and called
hym 'false traytowre', and wolde have stryken hym, but sir Trystrames
was nyghe hym and ran undir his swerde and toke hit oute of his honde.
And than the kynge cryed: 40

'Where ar my knyghtes and my men? I charge you, sle this traytowre!'

But at that tyme there was nat one that wolde meve for his wordys.

Whan sir Trystrames sawe there was none that wolde be ayenste hym

he shoke hys swerde to the kynge and made countenaunce as he wolde
have strykyn hym. And than kynge Marke fledde, and sir Trystrames
folowed hym and smote hym fyve or six strokys flatlynge in the necke,
that he made hym falle on the nose.

5 And than sir Trystrames yode his way and armed hym and toke his
horse and his men, and so he rode into the foreste. And there uppon
a day sir Trystrames mette with two bretherne that were wyth kynge
Marke knyghtes, and there he strake of the hede of the tone brother
and wounded that other to the deth, and he made hym to bere the hede
10 in his helme. And thirty mo he there wounded. And whan that knyght
com before the kynge to say hys message he dyed there before the
kynge and the quene. Than kyng Marke called his counceyle unto hym
and asked avyce of his barownes, what were beste to do with sir
Trystrames.

15 'Sir,' seyde the barowns, and in especiall sir Dynas the Senesciall, 'we
woll gyff you counceyle for to sende for sir Trystrames, for we woll that
ye wete many men woll holde with sir Trystrames and he were harde
bestadde. And, sir,' seyde sir Dynas the Senesciall, 'ye shall undirstonde
that sir Trystrames ys called peereles and makeles of ony Crystyn
20 knyght, and of his myght and hardynes we know none so good a
knyght but yf hit be sir Launcelot du Lake. And yff he departe frome
your courte and go to kyng Arthurs courte, wete you well he woll so
frende hym there that he woll nat sette by your malyce. And therefore,
sir, I counceyle you to take hym to your grace.'

25 'I woll well,' seyde the kynge, 'that he be sent fore, that we may
be frendys.'

Than the barounes sente for sir Trystrames undir theire conduyte,
and so whan sir Trystrames com to the kynge he was wellcom, and no
rehersall was made, and than there was game and play.

30 And than the kynge and the quene wente an-huntynge, and sir
(33) Trystrames. So the kynge and the quene made their pavylons and their
tentes in that foreste besyde a ryver, and there was dayly justyng and
huntyng, for there was ever redy thirty knyghtes to juste unto all that
cam at that tyme. And there by fortune com sir Lamorak de Galis and sir
35 Dryaunte. And there sir Dryaunte justed well, but at the laste he had a
falle. Than sir Lamorak profyrde, and whan he began he fared so wyth
the thirty knyghtes that there was nat one off them but he gaff a falle,
and som of them were sore hurte.

'I mervayle,' seyde kynge Marke, 'what knyght he is that doth suche
40 dedis of armys.'

'Sir,' seyde sir Trystrames, 'I know hym well for a noble knyght as
fewe now be lyvynge, and his name is sir Lamerake de Galys.'

'Hit were shame,' seyde the kynge, 'that he sholde go thus away
onles that he were manne-handeled.'

'Sir,' seyde sir Trystrames, 'mesemyth hit were no worshyp for a nobleman to have ado with hym, and for this cause : for at this tyme he hath done overmuche for ony meane knyght lyvynge. And as me semyth,' seyde sir Trystrames, 'hit were shame to tempte hym ony more, for his horse is wery and hymselff both [for the dedes of armes he 5 hath] done this day. Welle concidered, hit were inow for sir Launcelot du Lake.'

'As for that,' seyde kynge Marke, 'I requyre you, as ye love me and my lady the quene La Beale Isode, take youre armys and juste with sir Lameroke de Galis.'   10

'Sir,' seyde sir Trystrames, 'ye bydde me do a thynge that is ayenste knyghthode. And well I can thynke that I shall gyff hym a falle, for hit is no maystry : for my horse and y be freysshe, and so is nat his horse and he. And wete you well that he woll take hit for grete unkyndenes, for ever one good knyght is loth to take anothir at avauntage. But by- 15 cause I woll nat displase, as ye requyre me so muste I do and obey youre commaundemente.'

And so sir Trystrames armed hym and toke his horse and putte hym forth, and there sir Lameroke mette hym myghtyly. And what with the myght of his owne spere and of syr Trystrames spere sir Lameroke his 20 horse felle to the erthe, and he syttynge in the sadyll.

So as sone as he myght he avoyded the sadyll and his horse, and put his shylde afore hym, and drewe his swerde. And than he bade sir Trystrames, 'alyght, thou knyght, and thou darste !'

'Nay, sir !' seyde sir Trystrames, 'I woll no more have ado wyth you, 25 for I have done the overmuche unto my dyshonoure and to thy worshyppe.'

'As for that,' seyde sir Lamerok, 'I can the no thanke ; syn thou haste forjusted me on horsebacke I requyre the and I beseche the, and thou be sir Trystrames de Lyones, feyght with me on foote.'   30

'I woll nat,' seyde sir Trystrames, 'and wete you well my name is sir Trystrames de Lyones, and well I know that ye be sir Lameroke de Galis. And this have I done to you ayenst my wyll, but I was requyred thereto. But to sey that I woll do at your requeste as at this tyme, I woll nat have no more ado with you at this tyme, for me shamyth of that I 35 have done.'

'As for the shame,' seyde sir Lamerake, 'on thy party or on myne, beare thou hit and thou wyll : for thoughe a marys sonne hath fayled me now, yette a quenys sonne shall nat fayle the ! And therefore, and thou be suche a knyght as men calle the, I requyre the alyght and fyght 40 with me !'

'Sir Lameroke,' seyde sir Trystrames, 'I undirstonde your harte is grete, and cause why ye have to sey the soth, for hit wolde greve me and ony good knyght sholde kepe hym freyssh and than to stryke downe a wery knyght; for that knyght nother horse was never fourmed that allway may endure. And therefore,' seyde sir Trystrames, 'I woll nat have ado with you, for me forthynkes of that I have done.'

'As for that,' seyde sir Lameroke, 'I shall quyte you and ever I se my
5 tyme.'

(34) So he departed frome hym with sir Dryaunte, and by the way they mette with a knyght that was sente fro dame Morgan le Fay unto kynge Arthure. And this knyght had a fayre horne harneyste with golde, and the horne had suche a vertu that there myght no lady nothir jantyll-
10 woman drynke of that horne but yf she were trew to her husbande; and if she were false she sholde spylle all the drynke, and if she were trew to her lorde she myght drynke thereof pesiblé. And because of the quene Gwenyvere and in the dispyte of sir Launcelot this horne was sente unto kynge Arthure. And so by forse sir Lameroke made that
15 knyght to telle all the cause why he bare the horne, and so he tolde hym all hole.

'Now shalt thou bere this horne,' seyde sir Lamerok, 'to kynge Marke, othir chose to dye. For in the dyspyte of sir Trystrames thou shalt bere hit hym, that horne, and sey that I sente hit hym for to assay
20 his lady, and yf she be trew he shall preve her.'

So this knyght wente his way unt[o] kynge Marke and brought hym that ryche horne, and seyde that sir Lamerok sente hit hym, and so he tolde hym the vertu of that horne.

Than the kynge made his quene to drynke thereof, and an hondred
25 ladyes with her, and there were but four ladyes of all tho that dranke clene.

'Alas!' seyde kynge Marke, 'this is a grete dyspyte,' and swore a grete othe that she sholde be brente and the other ladyes also.

Than the barowns gadred them togedyrs and seyde playnly they
30 wolde nat have tho ladyes brente for an horne made by sorsery that cam 'frome the false sorseres and wycche moste that is now lyvyng'. For that horne dud never good, but caused stryff and bate, and allway in her dayes she was an enemy to all trew lovers.

So there were many knyghtes made their avowe that and evir they
35 mette wyth Morgan le Fay that they wolde shew her shorte curtesy. Also syr Trystrames was passyng wroth that sir Lameroke sent that horne unto kynge Marke, for welle he knew that hit was done in the dispyte of hym, and therefore he thought to quyte sir Lameroke.

Than sir Trystrames used dayly and nyghtly to go to quene Isode
40 evir whan he myght, and ever sir Andret, his cosyn, wacched hym nyght by nyght for to take hym with La Beale Isode.

And so uppon a nyght sir Andret aspyed his owre and the tyme whan sir Trystrames went to his lady. Than sir Andret gate unto hym twelve knyghtis, and at mydnyght he sette uppon sir Trystrames secretly and suddeynly. And there sir Trystrames was takyn nakyd a-bed with La Beale Isode, and so was he bounde hande and foote and kepte tyll day.

And than by the assent of kynge Marke and of sir Andret and of som of the barownes sir Trystramys was lad unto a chapell that stood uppon the see rockys, there for to take his jugemente. And so he was lad 5 bounden with forty knyghtes, and whan sir Trystrames saw that there was none other boote but nedis he muste dye, than seyde he,

'Fayre lordis! Remembir what I have done for the contrey of Corn-wayle, and what jouparté I have bene in for the wele of you all. For whan I fought ⌈for the trewage of Cornwayle⌉ with sir Marhalte, the 10 good knyght, I was promysed to be bettir rewarded, whan ye all refused to take the batayle. Therefore, as ye be good jantyll knyghtes, se me nat thus shamfully to dye, for hit is shame to all knyghthode thus to se me dye. For I dare sey,' seyde sir Trystrams, 'that I mette never with no knyght but I was as good as he or better.' 15

'Fye uppon the!' seyde sir Andrete, 'false traytur thow arte with thyne advauntage! For all thy boste thou shalt dye this day!'

'A, Andrete, Andrete!' seyde sir Trystrames, 'thou sholdyst be my kynnysman, and now arte to me full unfrendely. But and there were no more but thou and I, thou woldyst nat put me to deth.' 20

'No?' seyde sir Andred, and therewith he drew his swerde and wolde have slayne hym.

So whan sir Trystrames sye hym make that countenaunce he loked uppon bothe his hondis that were faste boundyn unto two knyghtes, and suddeynly he pulde them bothe unto hym and unwrayste his 25 hondis, and lepe unto his cosyn sir Andred, and wroth his swerde oute of his hondis. And than he smote sir Andret, that he felle downe to the erthe, and so he fought that he kylde ten knyghtys.

So than sir Trystrames gate the chapell and kepte hyt myghtyly. Than the crye was grete, and peple drew faste unto sir Andret, mo than 30 an hondred. So whan sir Trystramys saw the peple draw unto hym he remembyrd he was naked, and sparde faste the chapell dore and brake the barrys of a wyndow, and so he lepe oute and felle uppon the craggys in the see.

And so at that tyme sir Andret nothir none of his felowys myght nat 35 gete hym. But whan they were departed, Governayle and sir Lambegus (35) and sir Sentrayle de Lushon, that were sir Trystrames men, sought sore aftir their maystir whan they herde he was ascaped. And so on the rokkys they founde hym, and with towels pulde hym up. And than sir Trystrames asked where was La Beale Isode. 40

'Sir,' seyde Governayle, 'she is put in a lazar-cote.'

'Alas!' seyde sir Trystrames, 'that is a full ungoodly place for suche a fayre lady, and yf I may she shall nat be longe there.'

And so he toke hys men and wente thereas was La Beale Isode, and fette her away, and brought hir into a fayre foreste to a fayre maner; and so he abode there with hir. So now this good knyght bade his men departe, for at that tyme he myght nat helpe them, and so they departed all save Governayle.

5 And so uppon a day sir Trystrames yode into the foroste for to disporte hym, and there he felle on slepe. And so happynde there cam to sir Trystrames a man that he had slayne his brothir. And so whan this man had founde hym he shotte hym thorow the sholdir ⌐with an arow⌐, and anone sir Trystrames sterte up and kylde that man.

10 And in the meanetyme hit was tolde unto kynge Marke how sir Trystrames and La Beale Isode were in that same maner, and thydir he cam with many knyghtes to sle sir Trystrames. And whan he cam there he founde hym gone, and anone he toke La Beale Isode home with hym and kepte her strayte, that by no meane she myght never wryght 15 nor sende.

And whan sir Trystrames com toward the maner he founde the tracke of many horse, and loked aboute in the place and knew that his lady was gone. And than sir Trystrames toke grete sorow and endured with grete sorow and payne longe tyme, for the arow that he was hurte 20 wythall was envenomed.

So by the meane of La Beale Isode she ⟨b⟩ade a lady that was cosyn unto dame Brangwayne, and she cam unto sir Trystrames and tolde hym that he myght nat be hole by no meanys, 'for thy lady Isode may nat helpe the; therefore she byddyth you, haste you into Bretayne unto 25 kynge Howell, and there shall ye fynde his doughter that is called Isode le Blaunche Maynes, and there shall ye fynde that she shall helpe you.'

Than sir Trystrames and Governayle gate them shyppyng, and so sayled into Bretayne. And whan kyng Howell knew that hit was sir 30 Trystrames he was full glad of hym.

'Sir,' seyde sir Trystrames, 'I am com unto this contrey to have helpe of youre doughter, ⌐for hit is tolde me that there is none other may hele me but she⌐.'

And so ⌐within a whyle⌐ she heled hym.

(36) 35 There was an erle that hyght Grype, and thys erle made grete warre uppon ⌐the kynge and putte hym⌐ to the worse and beseged hym. And on a tyme sir Keyhydyns that was sonne to the kynge Howell, as he issewed oute he was sore wounded nyghe to the deth. Than Governayle wente to the kynge and seyde,

40 'Sir, I counceyle you to desyre my lorde sir Trystrames as in your nede to helpe you.'

'I woll do by youre counceyle,' seyde the kynge. And so he yode unto sir Trystrames and prayde hym as in his warrys to helpe hym, 'for my sonne sir Keyhidyns may nat go unto the fylde'.

'Sir', seyde sir Trystrames, 'I woll go to the fylde and do what I may.'

So sir Trystrames issued oute of the towne wyth suche felyshyp as he myght make, and ded suche dedys that all Bretayne spake of hym. And than at the laste by grete force he slew the erle Grype his owne hondys, and mo than an hondred knyghtes he slew that day.   5

And than sir Trystrames was resceyved into the cyté worshypfully with procession. Than kyng Howell enbraced hym in his armys and seyde,

'Sir Trystrames, all my kyngedom I woll resygne to you.'

'God defende!' seyde sir Trystrames, 'for I am beholdyn thereto for   10 your doughtyrs sake to do for you more than that.'

So by the grete meanes of the kynge and his sonne there grewe grete love betwyxte Isode and sir Trystrames, for that lady was bothe goode and fayre, and a woman of noble bloode and fame. And for because that sir Trystrames had suche chere and ryches and all other plesaunce that   15 he had allmoste forsakyn La Beale Isode.

And so uppon a tyme sir Trystrames aggreed to wed this Isode le Blaunche Maynes. And so at the laste they were wedded and solemply hylde their maryayge.

And so whan they were a-bed bothe, sir Trystrames remembirde hym   20 of his olde lady, La Beale Isode, and than he toke suche a thoughte suddeynly that he was all dismayde, and other chere made he none ᶦbutᶦ with clyppynge and kyssynge. As for ᴦother� fleyshely lustys, sir Trystrames had never ado with hir: suche mencion makyth the Freynshe booke. Also hit makyth mencion that the lady wente there   25 had be no plesure but kyssynge and clyppynge.

And in the meanetyme there was a knyght in Bretayne, his name was sir Suppynabyles, and he com over the see into Inglonde, and so he com into the courte of kynge Arthure. And there he mette with sir Launcelot du Lake and tolde hym of the maryayge of sir Trystrames.   30 Than seyde sir Launcelot,

'Fye upon hym, untrew knyght to his lady! That so noble a knyght as sir Trystrames is sholde be founde to his fyrst lady and love untrew, that is the quene of Cornwayle! But sey ye to hym thus,' seyde sir Launcelot, 'that of all knyghtes in the worlde I have loved hym [most   35 and had most joye of hym], and all was for his noble dedys. And lette hym wete that the love betwene hym and me is done for ever, and that I gyff hym warnyng: from this day forthe I woll be his mortall enemy.'

So departed sir Suppynabiles unto Bretayne agayne, and there he (37) founde sir Trystrames and tolde hym that he had bene in kynge   40 Arthures courte. Than sir Trystrames seyde,

'Herd ye onythynge of me?'

'So God me helpe,' seyde sir Suppynabyles, 'there I harde sir Launce-lot speke of you grete shame, and that ye ar a false knyght to youre lady. And he bade me do you to wyte that he woll be youre mortall foo in every place where he may mete you.'

'That me repentyth,' seyde sir Trystrames, 'for of all knyghtes I loved moste to be in his felyshyp.'

5 Than sir Trystrames was ashamed and made grete mone that ever any knyghtes sholde defame hym for the sake of his lady.

And so in this meanewhyle La Beale Isode made a lettir unto quene Gwenyvere complaynyng her of the untrouthe of sir Trystrames, how he had wedded the kynges doughter of Bretayne. So quene Gwenyver 10 sente hir another letter and bade her be of goode comforte, for she sholde have joy aftir sorow: for sir Trystrames was so noble a knyght called that by craftes of sorsery ladyes wolde make suche noble [men] to wedde them. 'But the ende,' quene Gwenyver seyde, 'shulde be thus, that he shall hate her and love you bettir than ever he dud.'

15 ## II. LAMEROK DE GALYS

So leve we sir Trystrames in Bretayne, and speke we of sir Lameroke de Galys, that as he sayled his shyppe felle on a rocke and disperysshed all save sir Lameroke and his squyer; for he swamme so myghtyly that fysshers of the Ile of Servayge toke hym up, and his squyer was 20 drowned. And the shypmen had grete laboure to save sir Lameroke his lyff for all the comforte that they coude do.

And the lorde of that ile hyght sir Nabon le Noyre, a grete myghty gyaunte, and thys sir Nabon hated all the knyghtes of kynge Arthures, and in no wyse he wolde do hem no favoure. And thes fysshers tolde 25 sir Lameroke all the gyse of syr Nabon, how there com never knyght of kynge Arthurs but he distroyed hym. And the laste batayle that ever he ded was wyth sir Nanowne le Petyte, and whan he had wonne hym he put hym to a shamefull deth in the despyte of kynge Arthure: he was drawyn lym-meale.

30 'That forthynkes me,' seyde sir Lamerok, 'for that knyghtes deth, for he was my cosyn, and yf I were at myne ease as well as ever I was, I wolde revenge his deth.'

'Pease,' seyde the fysshers, 'and make here no wordys! For or ever ye departe frome hens sir Nabon muste know that ye have bene here, 35 othir ellis we shall dye for your sake.'

'So that I be hole,' seyde sir Lameroke, 'of my mysse-ease that I have takyn in the see, I woll that ye telle hym that I am a knyght of kynge Arthures, for I was never ferde to renayne my lorde.'

(38) Now turne we unto sir Trystrams, that uppon a day he toke a lytyll 40 barget and hys wyff Isode le Blaunche Maynys wyth syr Keyhydyns, her

brother, to sporte hem on the costis. And whan they were frome the londe there was a wynde that drove hem into the coste of Walys uppon this Ile of Servage whereas was sir Lameroke.

And there the barget all to-rove, and there dame Isode was hurte, and as well as they myght they gate into the forest. And there by a welle 5 he sye sir Segwarydes, and a damesell with hym, and than aythir salewed other.

'Sir,' seyde sir Segwarydes, 'I know you well for sir Trystramys de Lyones, the man in the worlde that I have moste cause to hate, bycause ye departed the love betwene me and my wyff. But as for that,' seyde sir 10 Segwarydes, 'I woll never hate a noble knyght for a lyght lady, and therefore I pray you to be my frende, and I woll be yourys unto my power. For wete you well ye ar harde bestadde in this valey, and we shall have inowe ado ayther to succoure other.'

And so sir Segwarydes brought sir Trystrames to a lady thereby that 15 was borne in Cornwayle, and she tolde hym all the perels of that valay, how there cam never knyght there but he were takyn presonere or slayne.

'Wete you well, fayre lady,' seyde sir Trystrames, 'that I slewe sir Marhalte and delyverde Cornwayle frome the trewage of Irelonde. 20 And I am he that delyverde the kynge of Irelonde frome sir Blamoure de Ganys, and I am he that bete sir Palomydes, and wete you welle that I am sir Trystrames de Lyones that by the grace of God shall delyver this wofull Ile of Servage.'

So sir Trystrames was well eased that nyght. Than one tolde hym 25 there was a knyght of kynge Arthurs that wrakked on the rockes.

'What is his name?' seyde sir Trystrames.

'We wote nat,' seyde the fysshers, 'but he kepyth hit no counsel that he is a knyght of kynge Arthurs, and by the myghty lorde [of this yle] he settyth nought.' 30

'I pray you,' seyde sir Trystrames, 'and ye may, brynge hym hydir that I may se hym. And if he be ony of the noble knyghtes I know hym.'

Than the good lady prayde the fysshers to brynge hym to hir place. So on the morne they brought hym thydir in a fysshers garmente, and 35 as sone as sir Trystrames sy hym he smyled uppon hym and knew hym well. But he knew nat sir Trystrams.

'Fayre sir,' seyde sir Trystrams, 'mesemyth be youre chere that ye have bene desesed but late, and also methynkyth I sholde know you heretoforne.' 40

'I woll well,' seyde sir Lamerok, 'that ye have seyne me, for the nobelyst knyghtes of the Table Rownde have seyne me and mette with me.'

'Fayre sir,' seyde sir Trystrames, 'telle me youre name.'

'Sir, uppon a covenaunte I woll tell you, so that ye telle me whether that ye be lorde of thys ilonde or no, that is callyd sir Nabon le Noyre.'

'I am nat, nother I holde nat of hym, but I am his foo as well as ye be, and so shall I be founde or I departe of this ile.'

'Well,' seyde sir Lamerok, 'syn ye have seyde so largely unto me, my name is syr Lamerok de Galys, son unto kynge Pellynore.'

'Forsothe, I trow well,' seyde sir Trystrams, 'for and ye seyde other I know the contrary.'

'What ar ye,' seyde sir Lamerok, 'that knowith so me?'

'Forsothe, sir, I am sir Trystrames de Lyones.'

'A, sir, remembir ye nat of the fall ye dud gyff me onys, and aftir that ye refused to fyght on foote with me?'

'Sir, that was nat for no feare that [I had] of you, but me shamed at that tyme to have more ado with you, for as me semed ye had inowe ado. But, sir, wete you well, for my kyndenesse ye put many ladyes to a repreff whan ye sent the horne from Morgan le Fay unto kynge Marke. And hit sholde have gone to kynge Arthure, whereas ye dud that in dispyte of me.'

'Well,' seyde he, 'and hit were to do agayne, so wolde I do, for I had lever stryff and debate felle in kyng Markys courte rether than in kynge Arthurs courte, for the honour of bothe courtes be nat lyke.'

'As to that,' seyde sir Trystrams, 'I know well; but that, that was done for dispyte of me. But all youre malyce, I thanke God, hurte nat gretly. Therefore,' seyde sir Trystrames, 'ye shall leve all youre malyce and so woll I, and lette us assay how we may wynne worshyp betwene you and me uppon this gyaunte sir Nabon le Noyre, that is lorde of this ilonde, to destroy hym.'

'Sir,' seyde sir Lameroke, 'now I undirstonde youre knyghthode. Hit may nat be false that all men sey, for of youre bounté, nobles, and worshyp of all knyghtes ye ar pereles. And for your curtesy and jantylnes I shewed you unkyndnesse, and that now me repentyth.'

(39)   So in the meanetyme cam worde that sir Nabon had made a cry that all people sholde be at his castell the fifth day aftir, and the same day the sonne of Nabon sholde be made knyght, and all the knyghtes of that valey and thereaboute sholde be there to juste, and all tho of the realme of Logrys sholde be there to juste wyth them of Northe Walys.

And thydir cam fyve hondred knyghtes. And so they of the contrey brought thydir sir Lamerok and sir Trystrames and sir Keyhydyns and sir Segwarydes, for they durste none otherwyse do. And than Nabon lente sir Lamerok horse and armour at his owne desyre. And so sir Lamerok justed and dud suche dedis of armys that sir Nabon and all the people seyde there was never knyght that ever they sie that dud such dedis of armys. For, as the booke seyth, he forjusted all that were

there for the moste party of fyve hondred knyghtes, that none abode
hym in his sadyll.

Than sir Nabon profirde sir Lamerok to play his play with hym, 'for
I saw never one knyght do so muche uppon one day.'

'I woll well,' seyde sir Lameroke, 'play as I may, but I am wery and 5
sore brused.'

And there aythir gate a speare, but this sir Nabone wolde nat encountir with sir Lameroke, but smote his horse in the forhede and so
slew hym. And than sir Lameroke yode on foote, and turned his shylde
and drew his swerde, and there began stronge batayle on foote. But sir 10
Lameroke was so sore brused and shorte brethid that he traced and
traversed somwhat abacke.

'Fayre felow,' seyde sir Nabone, 'holde thy honde, and I shall shewe
the more curtesy than ever I shewyd knyght, because I have sene this
day thy noble knyghthode. And therefore stonde thou by, and I woll 15
wete whethir ony of thy felowys woll have ado with me.'

Whan sir Trystrames harde that he seyde,

'Sir Nabone, lende me horse and sure armoure, and I woll have ado
with you.'

'Well, felow,' seyde sir Nabone, 'go thou to yondir pavylyon and 20
arme the of the beste thou fyndyst there, and I shall play sone a
mervayles pley wyth the.'

Than seyde sir Trystrames,

'Loke ye play well, other ellys peraventure I shall lerne you a new
play.' 25

'That is well seyde,' seyde sir Nabone.

So whan sir Trystrames was armed as hym lyked beste and well
shylded and swerded, he dressed to hym on foote, 'for well I know that
sir Nabone wolde nat abyde a stroke with a speare, and therefore he
woll sle all knyghtes horse.' 30

'Now, fayre felow,' seyde sir Nabone, 'latte us play!'

And so they fought longe on foote, trasynge and traversynge,
smytynge and foynynge longe withoute ony reste. So at the laste sir
Nabone prayde hym to tell hym his name.

'Sir,' seyde he, 'my name ys sir Trystrames de Lyones, a knyght of 35
Cornwayle, whyche am undir kynge Marke.'

'A, thou arte wellcom!' seyde sir Nabone, 'for of all knyghtes I have
moste desyred to fyght wyth [the] othir ellys wyth sir Launcelot.'

And so they wente than egerly togydir, that at the laste sir Trystrames
slew sir Nabone. And so forthwithall he lepe to his sonne and strake 40
of his hede.

Than all the contrey seyde they wolde holde of sir Trystrames all the
whole valay of Servage.

'Nay,' seyde sir Trystrames, 'I woll nat so, for here is a worshypfull knyght, sir Lameroke de Galys, that for me he shall be lorde of this ile: for he hath done here grete dedis of armys.'

'Nay,' seyde sir Lameroke, 'I woll nat be lorde of this contrey, for I have nat deserved hit as well as ye. Therefore gyff ye hit where ye woll, for I woll [none] have.'

'Well,' seyde sir Trystrames, 'syn ye nother I woll nat have hit, lett us gyff hit unto hym that hath nat so well deserved hit.'

'Sir, do as ye lyste, for the gyffte is owres, for I woll none and I had deserved hit.'

And so by assente hit was yevyn unto sir Segwarydes. And he thanked them, and so was he lorde, and worshypfully he dud governe hem. And than sir Segwarydes delyvirde all the presoners and sette good governaunce in that valey.

And so he turned into Cornwayle and tolde kynge Marke and La Beale Isode how sir Trystrames had avaunced hym in the Ile of Servayge. And there he proclaymed in all Cornwayle of all the aventures of thes two knyghtes, and so was hit opynly knowyn. But full wo was La Beale Isode whan she herde telle that sir Trystrames had with hym Isode le Blaunche Maynys.

(40) So turne we unto sir Lamerok that rode towarde kynge Arthures courte.

(And so sir Trystramys wyff and sir Keyhydyns toke a vessell and sayled into Bretayne unto kynge Howell where they were wellcom. And whan they herde of thes adventures they mervayled of his noble dedys.)

Now turne we unto sir Lameroke that whan he was departed frome sir Trystrames he rode oute of the foreste tyll he cam to an ermytage. And whan the ermyte sawe hym he asked frome whens he com. 'Sir, I am com frome this valey.'

'That mervayle we off, for this twenty wyntir,' seyde the ermyte, 'I saw never knyght passe this contrey but he was other slayne other vylansely wounded or passe as a poore presonere.'

'Sir, tho evyll customys are fordone,' seyde sir Lameroke, 'for sir Trystrames hath slayne youre lorde sir Nabone and his sonne.'

Than was the ermyte glade and all his brethirne, for he seyde there was never suche a tirraunte amonge Crystyn men. 'And therefore,' seyde the ermyte, 'this valey and fraunchyse shall ever holde of sir Trystrames.'

So on the morne sir Lameroke departed, and as he rode he sawe four knyghtes fyght ayenste one, and that one knyght defended hym well, but at the laste the four knyghtes had hym downe. And than sir Lameroke wente betwexte them and asked them why they wolde sle that one knyght, and seyde hit was shame, four ayenste one.

'Thow shalt well wete,' seyde the four knyghtes, 'that he is false.'

'So that is your tale,' seyde sir Lameroke, 'and whan I here hym speke I woll sey as ye sey. Sir,' seyde sir Lameroke, 'how sey you? Can ye nat excuse you none otherwyse but that ye ar a false knyght?'

'Sir, yett can I excuse me bothe with my worde and with my hondys, and that woll I make good uppon one of the beste of them, my body 5 to his body.'

Than spake they all at onys: 'We woll nat jouparté oure bodyes, but wete thou welle,' they seyde, 'and kynge Arthure were here hymselff, hit sholde nat lye in his power to save his lyff.'

'That is seyde to largely,' seyde sir Lamerok, 'but many spekyth 10 behynde a man more than he woll seye to his face. And for because of youre wordis ye shall undirstonde that I am one of the symplyst of kynge Arthures courte, and in the worshyp of my lorde now do your beste, and in the dispyte of you I shall rescow hym!'

And than they layshed all at onys to syr Lameroke, but at two strokis 15 he had slayne two of them. Than the other two fled. So than sir Lamerok turned agayne unto that knyght and horsed hym and asked hym his name.

'Sir, my name is sir Froll of the Oute Ilys.'

And so he rode with sir Lameroke and bare hym company. And as 20 they rode by the way they sawe a semely knyght rydynge and commynge ayenst them, and all in whyght.

'A,' seyde sir Froll, 'yondir knyght justed but late wyth me and smote me downe, therefore I woll juste with hym.'

'Ye shall nat do so,' seyde sir Lamerok, 'be my counceyle. And ye 25 woll tell me your quarell, where ye justed at his requeste other he at youres.'

'Nay,' seyde sir Froll, 'I justed with hym at my requeste.'

'Sir, than woll I counceyle you, deale no more with hym, for, lyke his countenaunce, he sholde be a noble knyght and no japer: for 30 methynkys he sholde be of the Rounde Table.'

'As for that, I woll nat spare,' seyde sir Froll.

Than he cryed and seyde,

'Sir knyght, make the redy to juste!'

'That nedyth nat,' seyde the whyghte knyght, 'for I have no luste to 35 jape nother juste.'

So they feautred their sperys, and the whyght knyght overthrewe sir Froll and than he rode his way a soffte pace. Than sir Lameroke rode aftir hym and prayde hym to telle his name, 'for mesemyth ye sholde be of the felyshyp of the Rounde Table.'   40

'Sir, uppon a covenaunte, that ye woll nat telle my name, and also that ye woll tell me youres.'

'Sir, my name is sir Lamerok de Galis.'

'And my name is sir Launcelot du Lake.'

Than they putt up their swerdys and kyssed hertely togydirs, and aythir made grete joy of other.

'Sir,' seyde sir Lameroke, 'and hit please you I woll do you servyse.'

'God deffende, sir, that ony of so noble a blood as ye be sholde do
5 me servyse.' Than seyde sir Launcelot, 'I am in a queste that I muste do myselff alone.'

'Now God spede you!' seyde sir Lameroke.

And so they departed. Than sir Lamerok com to sir Froll and horsed hym agayne.

10 'Sir, what knyght is that?' seyde sir Froll.

'Sir, hit is nat for you to know, nother is no poynte of youre charge.'

'Ye ar the more uncurteyse,' seyde sir Froll, 'and therefore I woll departe felyshyp.'

'Ye may do as ye lyste, and yett be my company ye have savid the
15 fayryst floure of your garlonde.'

(41)   So they departed. Than wythin ⌐two or⌐ three dayes sir Lamerok founde a knyght at a welle slepynge, and his lady sate with hym and waked. Ryght so com sir Gawayne and toke the knyghtes lady and sette hir up behynde hys squyer. So sir Lamerok rode aftir sir Gawayne
20 and seyde,

'Sir, turne ayen!'

Than seyde sir Gawayne,

'What woll ye do with me? I am nevew unto kynge Arthure.'

'Sir, for that cause I woll forbeare you: othir ellys that lady sholde
25 abyde with me, ⟨other⟩ [els ye shold juste with me].'

Than sir Gawayne turned hym and ran to hym that ought the lady with his speare, but the knyght wyth pure myght smote downe sir Gawayne and toke his lady with hym.

And all this sye sir Lamerok and seyde to hymselff, 'but I revenge my
30 felow he woll sey me dishonoure in kynge Arthurs courte.' Than sir Lamerok returned and profyrde that knyght to fyght.

'Sir, I am redy,' seyde he.

And there they cam togedyrs with all theire myght, and sir Lamerok smote the knyght thorow bothe sydis that he fylle to the erthe dede.

35   Than that lady rode to that knyghtis brothir that hyght sir Bellyaunce le Orgulus that dwelled faste thereby and tolde hym how his brother was slayne.

'Alas!' seyde he, 'I woll be revenged.'

And so he horsed hym and armed hym, and within a whyle he over-
40 toke sir Lamerok and bade hym turne, 'and leve that lady, for thou and I muste play a new play: for thow haste slayne my brother sir Froll that was a bettir knyght than ever was thou.'

'Ye may well sey hit,' seyde sir Lamerok, 'but this day in the playne fylde I was founde the bettir knyght.'

So they rode togydyrs and unhorsed eche other, and turned their
shyldis and drew their swerdys, and fought myghtyly as noble knyghtes
preved the space of two owres. So than sir Bellyaunce prayde hym to
telle hym his name.

'Sir, my name is sir Lameroke de Galys.'   5

'A,' seyde sir Bellyaunce, 'thou arte the man in the worlde that I
moste hate, for I slew my sunnys for thy sake where I saved thy lyff,
and now thou haste slayne my brothir sir Froll. Alas, how sholde I be
accorded with the? Therefore defende the! Thou shalt dye! There is
none other way nor remedy.'   10

'Alas!' seyde sir Lameroke, 'full well me ought to know you, for ye
ar the man that moste have done for me.' And therewithall sir Lamerok
kneled adowne and besought hym of grace.

'Aryse up!' seyde sir Bellyaunce, 'other ellys thereas thou knelyste I
shall sle the!'   15

'That shall nat nede,' seyde sir Lameroke, 'for I woll yelde me to you,
nat for no feare of you nor of youre strength, but youre goodnesse
makyth me to lothe to have ado with you. Wherefore I requyre you,
for Goddis sake and for the honour of knyghthode, forgyff me all that
I have offended unto you.'   20

'Alas!' seyde sir Bellyaunce, 'leve thy knelynge, other ellys I shall
sle the withoute mercy.'

Than they yode agayne to batayle and aythir wounded othir, that all
the grounde was blody thereas they fought. And at the laste sir Bellyaunce withdrew hym abacke and sette hym downe a lytyll uppon an   25
hylle, for he was faynte for bledynge, that he myght nat stonde.

Than sir Lameroke threw his shylde uppon his backe and cam unto
hym and asked hym what chere.

'Well,' seyde sir Bellyaunce.

'A, sir, yett shall I shew you favoure in youre male ease.'   30

'A, knyght,' seyde sir Bellyaunce unto sir Lamerok, 'thou arte a foole,
for and I had the at suche avauntage as thou haste me, I sholde sle the.
But thy jantylnesse is so good and so large that I muste nedys forgyff
the myne evyll wyll.'

And than sir Lameroke kneled adowne and unlaced fyrst his um-   35
brere and than his owne, and than aythir kyssed othir with wepynge
tearys. Than sir Lamerok led sir Bellyaunce to an abbey faste by, and
there sir Lamerok wolde nat departe from sir Bellyaunce tylle he was
hole. And than they were sworne togydyrs that none of hem sholde
never fyght ayenste other.   40

So sir Lamerok departed and wente to the courte of Arthur.

III. LA COTE MALE TAYLE

HERE LEVYTH OF THE TALE OF SIR LAMEROK AND OF SYR TRYSTRAMYS,
AND HERE BEGYNNYTH THE TALE OF SYR LA COTE MALE TAYLE THAT WAS
A GOOD KNYGHT

IX (1) To the courte of kynge Arthure there cam a yonge man bygly made, and
he was rychely beseyne, and he desyred to be made a knyght of the
kynges. But his overgarmente sate overthwartely, howbehit hit was
ryche cloth of golde.

'What is youre name?' seyde kynge Arthure.

10 'Sir, my name is Br[e]wnor le Noyre, and within shorte space ye
shall know that I am comyn of goode kynne.'

'Hit may well be,' seyde sir Kay the Senesciall, 'but in mokkynge ye
shall be called "La Cote Male Tayle", that is as muche to sey "The
Evyll-Shapyn Cote".'

15 'Hit is a grete thynge that thou askyste,' seyde the kynge. 'But for
what cause weryst thou that ryche cote?'

'Hit is for som cause, sir,' he answerde. 'I had a fadir, a noble knyght,
and as he rode an-huntyng uppon a day hit happed hym to ley hym
downe to slepe, and there cam a knyght that had bene longe his enemy.

20 And whan he saw he was faste on slepe he all to-hew hym, and thys
same cote had my fadir on that tyme. And that makyth this coote to
sytte so evyll uppon me, for the strokes be on hit as I founde hit, and
never shall hit be amendid for me. Thus to have my fadyrs deth in
remembraunce I were this coote tyll I be revenged. And because ye ar

25 called the moste nobelyst kynge of the worlde, I com to you to make me
a knyght.'

'Sir,' seyde sir Lamerok and sir Gaheris, 'hit were well done to make
hym knyght, for hym besemyth well of persone and of countenaunce
that he shall preve a good knyght and a myghty. For, sir, and ye be

30 remembird, evyn suche one was sir Launcelot whan he cam fyrst into
this courte, and full fewe of us knew from whens he cam. And now is
he preved the man of moste worshyp in the worlde, and all your courte
and Rounde Table is by sir Launcelot worshypped and amended, more
than by ony knyght lyvynge.'

35 'That is trouthe,' seyde the kynge, 'and to-morow at youre requeste
I shall make hym knyght.'

So on the morne there was an harte founden, and thydir rode kyng
Arthure wyth a company of his knyghtes to sle that herte. And this
yonge man that sir Kay named La Cote Male Tayle was there leffte

40 behynde wyth quene Gwenyvere.

And by a suddeyne adventure there was an horryble lyon kepte in a
towre of stoon, and he brake lowse and cam hurlyng before the quene

and her knyghtes. And whan the quene sawe the lyon she cryed oute
and fledde and prayde hir knyghtes to rescow her. And there was none
but twelve knyghtes that abode, and all the other fledde. Than seyde
La Cote Male Tayle,

'Now I se that all cowherde knyghtes be nat dede,' and therewithall 5
he drew his swerde and dressed hym before the lyon. And that lyon
gaped wyde and cam uppon hym rawmpyng to have slayne hym, and
he agayne smote hym in the myddys of the hede, that hit claff in sundir
and so dayshed downe to the erthe.

And anone hit was tolde the quene how the yong ma[n] that sir Kay 10
named La Cote Male Tayle had slayne the lyon, and anone with that the
kynge com home and the quene tolde hym of that adventure. He was
well pleased and seyde,

'Uppon payne of myne hede, he shall preve a noble man and faythefull and trewe of his promyse!' 15

And so forthewithall the kynge made hym knyght.

'Now, sir,' seyde this yonge knyght, 'I requyre you and all the
knyghtes of the courte that ye calle me none other name but La Cote
Mele Tayle: insomuche that sir Kay hath so named me, so woll I be
called.' 20

'I assente me thereto,' seyde the kynge.

And so the same day there cam a damesell into the courte, and she (2)
brought wyth hir a grete blacke shylde with a whyght honde in the
myddis holdynge a swerde, and other pyctoure was there none in that
shylde. Whan kynge Arthure saw her he asked her from whens she cam 25
and what she wolde.

'Sir,' she seyde, 'I have rydden longe and many a day with this shylde
many wayes, and for this cause I am com to youre courte: for there was
a good knyght that ought this shylde, and this knyght had undirtake a
grete dede of armys to encheve hit. And so by myssefortune another 30
stronge knyght mette with hym by suddeyne aventure, and there they
fought longe, and aythir wounded othir passynge sore, and they were
so wery that they lefft that batayle on evyn honde. So this knyght that
ought the shylde sawe none other way but he muste dye, and than he
commaunded me to bere this shylde to the courte of kyng Arthure, he 35
requyrynge and prayynge som good knyght to take his shylde, and that
he wolde fulfylle the queste that he was in.'

'Now what sey ye to this queste?' seyde kynge Arthure. 'Is there here
ony of you that woll take uppon you to welde this shylde?'

Than was there nat one that wolde speke a worde. Than sir Kay toke 40
the shylde in his hondis and lyfft hit up.

'Sir knyght,' seyde the damesell, 'what is your name?'

'Wete you well my name is sir Kay the Senesciall that wydewhere is
knowyn.'

'Sir,' seyde the damesell, 'lay downe that shylde, for wyte thou well hit fallyth nat for you, for he muste be a bettir knyght than ye that shall welde this chylde.'

'Damesell,' seyde sir Kay, 'I toke youre shylde nat to that entente. But go whoso go woll, for I woll nat go with you.'

5

Than the damesell stood styll a grete whyle and behylde many of the knyghtes. Than spake this yonge knyght La Cote Male Tayle and seyde,

'Fayre damesell, I woll take this shylde and the adventure uppon me, and I wyste whothirward my jurney myght be. For because I was this day made knyght I wolde take this adventure uppon me.'

10

'What is youre name, fayre yonge man?' seyde the damesell.

'My name is,' he seyde, 'La Cote Male Tayle.'

'Well may thou be callyd so,' seyde the damesell, ' "the knyght wyth the evyll-shapyn coote"! But and thou be so hardy to take on the to beare that shylde and to folowe me, wete thou well thy skynne shall be as well hewyn as thy cote.'

15

'As for that,' seyde sir La Cote Male Tayle, 'whan I am so hewyn I woll aske you no salff to heale me withall!'

And forthwithall there com into the courte two squyers and brought hym grete horsis and his armoure and spearys. And anone he was armed and toke his leve.

20

'Sir, I woll nat,' seyde the kynge, 'be my wyll that ye toke uppon you this harde adventure.'

'Sir,' he seyde, 'this adventure is myne, and the fyrste that ever I toke uppon, and that woll I folow whatsomever com of me.'

25

Than that damesell departed, and so sir La Cote Male Tayle faste folowed afftir. And within a whyle he overtoke the damesell, and anone she mysseseyde hym in the fowlyst maner.

(3)   Than sir Kay ordayned sir Dagonet, kynge Arthurs foole, to folow aftir sir La Cote Male Tayle, and there sir Kay ordayned that sir Dagonet was horsed and armed, and bade hym folow sir La Cote Male Tayle and profyr hym to juste. And so he ded, and whan he sawe La Cote Male Tayle he cryed and bade make hym redy to juste. So sir La Cote Male Tayle smote sir Dagonet ovir his horse croupyn.

30

35   Than the damesell mocked La Cote Male Tayle and seyde,

'Fye for shame! Now arte thou shamed in kynge Arthurs courte, whan they sende a foole to have ado with the, and specially at thy fyrste justys.'

Thus she rode longe and chydde. And so within a whyle there cam sir Bleoberys, the good knyght, and there he justed with sir La Cote Male Tayle. And there syr Bleoberys smote hym so sore that horse and all felle to the erthe. Than sir La Cote Male Tayle arose up lyghtly and dressed his shylde and drew his swerde, and a wolde have done batayle to the uttraunce, for he was woode wroth.

40

'Nat so,' seyde sir Bleoberys de Ganys, 'as at this tyme I woll nat fyght uppon foote.'

Than the damesell Maledysaunte rebuked hym in the fowleste maner and bade hym 'turne agayne, cowarde!'

'A, damesell,' seyde he, 'I pray you of mercy of myssesay me no more, for my gryff is inow, though ye gryff me no more. Yet I calle me never the worse knyght, though a marys sonne hath fayled me, and also I counte myselff never the worse man for a falle of sir Bleoberys.'

So thus he rode with her two dayes, and by fortune there he encountred wyth sir Palomydes, the noble knyght, and in the same wyse sir Palomydes served hym as ded sir Bleoberys toforehonde. Than seyde the damesell,

'What doste thou here in my felyship? For thou canste nat sytte no knyght nother wythstonde hym one buffette but yf hit were sir Dagonet.'

'A, fayre damesell, I am nat the worse to take a falle of sir Palomydes. And yett grete dysworshyp have I none, for nother sir Bleoberys nother yett sir Palomydes woll not fyght with me on foote.'

'As for that,' seyde the damesell, 'wete you welle they have disdayne and scorne to alyght of their horsis to fyght with suche a lewde knyght as thou arte.'

So in the meanewhyle there com sir Mordred, sir Gawaynes brother, and so he felle in felyshyp with the damesell Maledysaunte.

And than they com before the Castell Orgulus, and there was suche a custom that there myght com no knyght by the castell but other he muste juste othir be presonere, othir at the leste to lose his horse and harneyse.

And there cam oute two knyghtes ayenste them, and sir Mordred justyd with the formyste, and that knyght of the castell smote sir Mordred downe of his horse. And than sir La Cote Male Tayle justed with that other, and ayther of hem smote downe other horsis to the erthe. And anone they avoyded their horsis and aythir of hem toke othirs horses.

And than sir La Cote Male Tayle rode unto that knyght that smote downe sir Mordred, and there La Cote Male Tayle wounded hym passynge sore and putte hym frome his horse, and ⟨he⟩ lay as he had bene dede.

So he turned unto hym that mette hym afore, and he toke the flyght towarde the castell, and sir La Cote Male Tayle rode aftir hym into the Castell Orgulus, and there sir La Cote Male Tayle slew hym.

And anone there cam an hondred knyghtys aboute hym, and all (4) assayled hym. And whan he sawe hys horse sholde be slayne he alyght and voyded his horse [and putte the brydel under his feete,] and so put hym oute of the gate. And whan he had so done he hurled in amonge them and dressed his backe untyll a ladyes chambir wall, thynkynge hymselff that he hadde lever dye there with worshyp than to abyde the rebukes of the Damesell Maledysaunte.

And so in the meanetyme, as he stood and fought, that lady that hylde that chambir wente oute slyly at a posterne, and withoute the gatys she founde sir La Cote Male Tayle his horse.

And lyghtly she gate hym by the brydyll and tyed hym to the posterne, and than she yode unto her chambir slyly agayne for to beholde how that one knyght faught ayenst an hondred knyghtes.

And whan she had beholde hym longe she wente to a wyndow behynde his backe and seyde,

'Thou knyght that fyghtyst wondirly well, but for all that at the laste thou muste nedys dye but yf thou can thorow thy myghty prouesse wynne unto yondir posterne: for there have I fastened th[y] horse to abyde the. But wete thou welle thou muste thynke on thy worshyp and thynke nat to dye, for thou mayste nat wynne unto that posterne withoute thou do nobely and myghtyly.'

Whan sir La Cote Male Tayle harde her sey so he gryped his swerde in his honde and put his shylde fayre before hym, and thorow the thyckyst pres he thryled thorow. And whan he cam to the porsterne he founde there redy four knyghtes, and at two the fyrste strokys he slew two of the knyghtes ⌜and the other fledde⌝, and so he wanne his horse and rode frome them.

And all hit was rehersed in kynge Arthurs courte, how he slew twelve knyghtes within the Castell Orgulus.

And so he rode on his way, and in the meanewhyle the damesell sayde unto sir Mordred,

'I wene my foolyssh knyght be othir slayne or takyn presonere.'

And than were they ware and saw hym com rydynge, and whan he was com to them he tolde all how he had spedde and escaped in the dispyte of all the castell, 'and som of the beste of hem woll telle no talys.'

'Thow gabbyst falsely,' seyde the damesell, 'that dare I make good! For as a foole and a dastarde to all knyghthode they have latte the passe.'

'That may ye preve,' seyde La Cote Male Tayle.

With that she sente a corroure of hers that allway rode with her, and so he rode thydir lyghtly and spurred how and in what wyse that knyght ascaped oute of that castell. Than all the knyghtes cursed hym and seyde he was a fende and no man, 'for he hath slayne here twelve of oure beste knyghtis, and we went [unto] this day that hit had bene to muche for sir Trystrames de Lyones othir for sir Launcelot de Lake. And in dyspyte and magré of us all he is departed frome us.'

And so hir curroure com agayne and tolde the damesell all how sir

La Cote Male Tayle spedde at the Castell Orgulus. Than she smote
downe the hede and seyde but lytyll.

'Be my hede,' seyde sir Mordred to the damesell, 'ye ar gretly to
blame so to rebuke hym, for I warne you playnly he is a good knyght,
and I doute nat but he shall preve a noble man. But as yette he may nat   5
sytte sure on horsebacke, for he that muste be a good horseman hit
muste com of usage and excercise. But whan he commyth to the strokis
of his swerde he is than noble and myghty. And that saw sir Bleoberys
and sir Palomydes; for wete you well they were wyly men of warre, for
they wolde know anone, whan they sye a yonge knyght, by his rydynge,   10
how they were sure to gyffe hym a falle frome his horse othir a grete
buffett. But for the moste party they wyll nat lyght on foote with
yonge knyghtes, for they ar myghtyly and strongely armed.

'For in lyke wyse syr Launcelot du Lake, whan he was fyrste made
knyght, he was oftyn put to the worse on horsebacke, but ever uppon   15
foote he recoverde his renowne and slew and defowled many knyghtes
of the Rounde Table. And therefore the rebukes that sir Launcelot ded
unto many knyghtes causyth them t[hat] be men of prouesse to beware,
for oftyn tyme I have seyne the olde preved knyghtes rebuked and
slayne by them that were but yonge begynners.'   20

Thus they rode sure talkyng by the wey togydyrs.

HERE THIS TALE OVERLEPYTH A WHYLE UNTO SIR LAUNCELOTT, that (5)
whan he was com to the courte of kynge Arthure than harde he telle of
the yonge knyghte sir La Cote Male Tayle, how he slew the lyon and
how he toke uppon hym the adventures of the blacke shylde, whyche   25
was named at that tyme the hardyest adventure of the worlde.

'So God me save!' seyde sir Launcelot unto many of his felowys.
'Hit was shame to all the good noble knyghtes to suffir suche a yonge
knyght to take so hyghe adventure on hym for his distruccion. For I
woll that ye wyte,' seyde sir Launcelot, 'that this damesell Maledy-   30
saunte hath borne that shylde many a day for to seche the moste proved
knyghtes. And that was she that sir Breunys Saunze Pité toke the
shylde frome, and aftir sir Trystrames de Lyones rescowed that
shylde frome hym and gaff hit to the damesell agayne, a lytyll afore
that tyme that sir Trystrames faught with my nevew sir Blamoure de   35
Ga[n]ys for a quarell that was betwyxte the kynge of Irelonde and
hym.'

Than many knyghtes were sory that sir La Cote Male Tayle was gone
forthe to that adventure.

'Truly,' seyde sir Launcelot, 'I caste me to ryde aftir hym.'   40

And so within seven dayes sir Launcelot overtoke sir La Cote Male
Tayle, and than he salewed hym and the damesell Maledysaunte. And
whan sir Mordred saw Launcelot, than he leffte their felyship, and so
sir Launcelot rode with hem all a day. And ever that damesell rebuked

sir La Cote Male Tayle, and than sir Launcelot answerde for hym. Than she leffte of and rebuked sir Launcelot.

So thys meanetyme sir Trystramys sente by a damesell a lettir unto sir Launcelot, excusynge hym of the weddynge of Isod le Blaunche
5 Maynes, and seyde in the lettir, as he was a trew knyght, he had never ado fleyshly with Isode le Blaunche Maynys. And passyng curteysly and jantely sir Trystrames wrote unto sir Launcelot, ever besechynge hym to be hys good frende and unto La Beall Isod of Cornwayle, and that sir Launcelot wolde excuse hym if that ever he saw her. And within
10 shorte tyme, by the grace of God, sir Trystramys seyd that he wolde speke with La Beall Isode and with hym ryght hastyly.

Than sir Launcelot departed frome the damesell and frome sir La Cote Male Tayle for to oversé that lettir and to wryte another lettir unto sir Trystram.
15 And in the meanewhyle sir La Cote Male Tale rode with the damesel untyll they cam to a castell that hyght Pendragon. And there were six knyghtes that stood afore hym and one of them profirde to fyght or to juste with hym. And so sir La Cote Male Tayle smote hym over hys horse croupe.
20 And than the fyve knyght[es] sette uppon hym all at onys with their spearys, and there they smote La Cote Male Tay[le] downe horse and man. And than they ded alyght suddeynly and sette their hondis uppon hym all at onys and toke hym presonere, [and so led hym unto the castel and kepte hym as prysoner.]
25 And on the morne sir Launcelot arose and delyverde the damesell with lettirs unto sir Trystram, and than he toke hys way aftir sir La Cote Male Tayle. And by the way uppon a brydge there was a knyght that profirde sir Launcelot to juste, and sir Launcelot smote hym downe. And than they faught uppon foote a noble batayle togydirs and a
30 myghty, and at the laste sir Launcelot smote hym downe grovelynge uppon hys hondys and hys kneys. And than that knyght yelded hym, and sir Launcelot resseyved hym fayre.

'Sir,' seyde the knyght, 'I requyre you telle me youre name, for muche my harte yevith unto you.'
35 'Nay,' seyd sir Launcelot, 'as at thys tyme I woll nat telle you my name onles that ye telle me youre name.'

'Sertaynly,' seyde the knyght, 'my name ys sir Neroveus, that was made knyght of my lorde sir Launcelot du Lake.'

'A, sir Neroveus de Lyle!' seyde sir Launcelot, 'I am ryght glad that
40 ye ar proved a good knyght, for now wyte you well my name ys sir Launcelot.'

'Alas!' seyde sir Neroveus, 'what have I done!' And therewithall he felle flatlynge to hys feete and wolde have kyste them, but sir Launcelot wolde nat suffir hym. And than aythir made grete joy of other, and

than sir Neroveus tolde sir Launcelot that he sholde nat go by the
Castell of Pendragon, 'for there ys a lorde, a myghty knyght, and many
myghty knyghtes with hym, and thys nyght I harde sey that they toke
a knyght presonere that rode with a damesell, and they sey he ys a
knyght of the Rounde Table.'   5

'A,' seyde sir Launcelot, 'that knyght ys my felow, and hym shall I (6)
rescowe and borow, or ellis lose my lyff therefore.'

And therewithall he rode faste tyll he cam before the Castell of Pen-
drag[on. And] anone therewithall there cam six knyghtes, and all
[made hem redy] to sette uppon sir Launcelot at onys. Than sir 10
[Launcelot feautryd his] speare and smote the formyst, that he br[ake
his bak in sonder], and three of them smote hym and three fa[yled. And
than sir Launcelot] passed thorow them, and lyghtly h[e torned in
ageyne and smote] anothir knyght thorow the brest [and thorowoute
the back] more than an elle, and there[withall his speare brak. Soo 15
than] all the remenaunte of the four k[nyghtes drewe their swerdes and
lasshed] at sir Launcelot, and at every s[troke sir Launcelot bestowed
so his] strokis that at four strokis sundry they avoyded their sadyls
passynge sore wounded, and furthwithall he rode hurlynge into the
castell.   20

And anone the lorde of that castell which was called sir Bryan de Les
Iles, whych was a noble man and a grete enemy to kynge Arthure, so
within a whyle he was armed and on horsebacke. And than they
feautred their spearis and hurled togydirs so strongly that bothe their
horsys russhed to the erthe. And than they avoyded their sadyls and 25
dressed their shyldis and drew their swerdis and flowe togydirs as wood
men, and there were many strokis a whyle.

At the laste sir Launcelot gaff sir Bryan such a buffette that he kneled
uppon hys knees, and than sir Launcelot russhed uppon hym with
grete force and pulled of his helme. And whan sir Bryan sy that he 30
sholde be slayne he yelded hym and put hym in hys mercy and in hys
grace.

Than sir Launcelot made hym to delyver all hys presoners that he
had within hys castell, and therein sir Launcelot founde of kynge
Arthurs knyghtes thirty knyghtes and forty ladyes, and so he delyverde 35
hem and than he rode his way. And anone as sir La Cote Male Tayle
was delyverde he gate hys horse and hys harneyse and hys damesell
Maledysaunte.

The meanewhyle sir Neroveus, that sir Launcelot had foughtyn
withall before at the brydge, he sente a damesell aftir sir Launcelot to 40
wete how [he] ⟨ha⟩d spedde at the castell of Pendragon. And than they
in the [castell mervey]led what knyght he was that was there whan
[sir Bryan and his] knyghtes delyverde all tho presoners.

'Syr, [have ye no mervei]le,' seyde the damesell, 'for the beste [knyght in this world] was here and ded thys jurnay, and wyte [ye wel,' she said, '⟨h⟩it was sir Launc]elot.'

Than was sir Bryan full glad, [and so was his lady and al]l hys knyghtes, that he sholde wynne [them. And whan the dame]sell and
5 sir La Cote Male Tayle [understood that ⟨h⟩it was s⟨i⟩r La]uncelot that had rydden with hem [in fel⟨y⟩ship, and that she reme]mbirde her how she had rebuked hym and called hym cowarde, than she was passyng hevy.

(7)   So than they toke their horsis and rode forthe a greate pace aftir sir
10 Launcelot, and within two myle they overtoke hym, and salewed hym and thanked hym. And anone the damesell cryed sir Launcelot mercy of hir evyll dede, and seyyng,

'For now I know ye ar the floure of all knyghthode of the worlde, and sir Trystram departe hit even betw[e]ne you. For God knowith,
15 be my good wyll,' seyde the damesell, 'that I have sought you, my lorde sir Launcelot, and sir Trystrams longe, and now I thanke God I have mette with you. And onys at Camelot I mette with sir Trystrams, and there he rescowed thys blacke shylde with the whyght honde holdyng a naked swerde that sir Brewnys Saunz Pité had takyn
20 frome me.'

'Now, fayre damesell,' seyde sir Launcelot, 'who tolde you my name?'

'Sir,' seyde she, 'there cam a damesel frome a knyght that ye fought withall at a brydge, and she tolde [me] that youre name was sir Launce-
25 lot du Lake.'

'Blame have she therefore,' seyde he, 'but her lorde, sir Neroveus, had tolde hir. But, damesell,' seyde sir Launcelot, 'uppon thys covenaunte I woll ryde with you, so that ye wyll nat rebuke thys knyght sir La Cote Male Tayle no more, for he ys a good knyght, and I doute nat but he
30 shall preve a noble man. And for hys sake and pité, that he sholde nat be destroyed, I folowed hym to succour hym in thys grete nede.'

'A, Jesu thanke you!' seyde the damesell, 'for now I woll sey unto you and to hym bothe, I rebuked hym never for none hate that I hated hym, but for grete love that I had to hym, for ever I supposed that he
35 had bene to yonge and to tendur of ayge to take uppon hym thys aventure. And therefore be my wyll I wolde have dryvyn hym away for jelosy that I had of hys lyff. For hit may be no yonge knyghtes dede that shall enchyve thys adventure to the ende.'

'Perdé!' seyd sir Launcelot, 'hit ys well seyde of you! And where ye
40 ar called the Damesell Maledysaunt, I woll calle you the Damesell Byeau-Pansaunte.'

And so they rode forth togydirs a grete whyle unto they cam unto the contreye of Surluse, and there they founde a fayre vyllayge wyth a stronge brydge lyke a fortresse. And whan sir Launcelot and they were

at the brydge there sterte forthe afore them of jantillmen and yomen
many that seyde,

'Fayre lordis! Ye may nat passe thys brydge and thys fortresse
because of that blacke shylde that I se one of you beare, and therefore
there shall nat passe but one of you at onys. Therefore chose you whych   5
of you shall entir within thys brydge fyrst.'

Than sir Launcelot profird hymselfe first to juste and entir within
thys brydge.

'Sir,' seyde sir La Cote Male [Tayle], 'I besech you to lette me entir
within thys fortresse. And if I may spede well I woll sende for you, and   10
if hit so be that I be slayne, there hit goth. And if I be takyn presonere,
than may you rescow me.'

'Sir, I am loth that ye sholde passe this passage first,' seyde sir
Launcelot.

'Sir,' seyde sir La Cote Male Tayle, 'I pray you lat me put my body   15
in that adventure.'

'Now go youre way,' seyde sir Launcelot, 'and Jesu be youre
spede!'

So he entird anone, and there mette with hym two brethirne, the
tone hyght sir Playne de Fors and that othir hyght sir Playne de Amoris.   20
And anone they justed with sir La Cote Male Tayle, and sir La Cote
Male Tayle smote downe sir Playne de Fors, and aftir he smote downe
sir Playne de Amoris.

And than they dressed their shyldis and swerdys and bade sir La Cote
Male Tayle alyght, and so he ded. And there was daysshynge and   25
foynynge with swerdis, and so they began to assayle othir full harde,
and they gaff sir La Cote Male Tayle many grete woundis uppon hed
and breste and uppon shuldirs. And as he mygh[t] ever amonge he gaff
sad strokis agayne, and than the two brethirne traced and traverced for
to be of both hondis of sir La Cote Male Tale, but he by fyne forse and   30
knyghtly proues gate hem afore hym. And whan he felte hym so
wounded than he doubled hys strokis and gaffe them so many woundis
that he felde hem to the erthe, and wolde have slayne them had they
nat yelded them.

And ryght so sir La Cote Male Tayle toke the beste horse that there   35
was of them three, and so he rode forth hys way to the othir fortres and
brydge. And there he mette with the thirde brother, hys name was sir
Plenoryus, a full noble knyght, and there they justed togydirs, and
aythir smote other downe, horse and man, to the erthe.

And than they avoyded their horsys and dressed their shyldis and   40
swerdis, and than they gaff many sad strokis. And one whyle the one
knyght was afore on the brydge, and another whyle the other. And thus
they faught two owres and more and never rested, and ever sir Launcelot and the damesell behylde them.

'Alas!' seyde the damesell, 'my knyght fyghttyth passynge sore and overlonge.'

'Now may ye se,' seyde sir Launcelot, 'that he ys a noble knyght, for to considir hys first batayle and his grevous woundis. And evyn forth-

5 withall, so wounded as he ys, hit ys mervayle that he may endure thys longe batayle with that good knyght.'

(8)   Thys meanewhyle sir La Cote Male Tayle sanke ryght downe uppon the erthe, what forwounded and forbled he myght nat stonde. Than the tothir knyght had pyté off hym and seyde,

10 'Fayre knyght, dysmay you nat, for had ye bene freysshe whan ye mette with me as I was, I wote well that I coude nat have endured you. And therefore, [for] youre noble dedys of armys, I shall shew to you kyndenes and jantilnes all that I may.'

And furthewithall thys noble knyght sir Plenoryus toke hym up in

15 hys armys and ledde hym into hys towre. And than he commaunded hym the wyne and made to serch hym and to stop hys bledynge woundys.

'Sir,' seyde sir La Cote Mal Tayle, 'withdraw you from me and hyghe you to yondir brydge agayne, for there woll mete with you another

20 maner a knyght than ever was I.'

'Why,' seyde sir Plenoryus, 'ys there behynde ony mo of youre felyship?'

'Ye, sir, wyte you well there ys a muche bettir knyght than I am.'

'What ys hys name?' seyde sir Plenoryus.

25 'Sir, ye shall nat know for me.'

'Well,' seyde the knyght, 'he shall be encountird withall, whatsom-ever he be.'

And anone he herde a knyght calle that seyde,

'Sir Plenoryus, where arte thou? Othir thou muste delyver me that

30 presoner that thou haste lad into thy towre, othir ellis com and do batayle with me!'

Than sir Plenoryus gate hys horse and cam, with a speare in hys honde, waloppynge towarde sir Launcelot. And than they began to feauter theire spearys, and cam togydir as thundir, and smote aythir

35 othir so myghtyly that their horsis felle downe undir them.

And than they avoyded their horsis and pulled oute their swerdis, and lyke too bullis they laysshed togydirs with grete strokis and foynys. But ever sir Launcelot recoverde grounde uppon hym, and sir Pleno-ryus traced to have gone aboute hym, but sir Launcelot wolde nat suffir

40 that, but bare hym backer and backer tylle he cam nye hys towre gate. And than seyde sir Launcelot,

'I know you well for a good knyght, but wyte thou well thy lyff and deth ys in my honde, and therefore yelde the to me and thy presonere!'

But he answerde no worde, but strake myghtyly uppon sir

Launcelotis helme, that the fyre sprange oute of hys yen. Than sir
Launcelot doubeled his strokes so thycke, and smote at hym so
myghtyly, that he made hym knele uppon his kneys. And therewithall
sir Launcelot lepe uppon hym and pulled hym grovelynge downe.

Than sir Plenoryus yelded hym and hys towre and all his presoners 5
at hys wylle. Than sir Launcelot receyved hym and toke hys trowthe.

And than he rode to the tothir brydge, and there sir Launcelot justed
with othir three of hys brethirn, that one hyght sir Pyllownes, and the
othir hyght sir Pellogres, and the thirde hyght sir Pelaundris. And first
uppon horsebacke sir Launcelot smote hem doune, and aftirwarde he 10
bete them on foote and made them to yelde them unto hym.

And than he returned ayen unto sir Plenoryus, and there he founde in
hys preson kynge Carados of Scotlonde and many other knyghtes, and
all they were delyverde.

And than sir La Cote Male Tale cam to sir Launcelot, and than sir 15
Launcelot wolde have gyvyn hym all thys fortresse and the brydges.

'Nay, sir,' seyde La Cote Male Tayle, 'I woll nat have sir Plenoryus
lyvelode. With that he wyll graunte you, my lorde sir Launcelot, to com
unto kynge Arthurs house and to be hys knyght and all hys brethirne,
I woll pray you, my lorde, to latte hym have hys lyvelode.'   20

'I woll well,' seyde sir Launcelot, 'with thys, that [he] woll com to the
courte of kynge Arthure and bycom hys man, and hys brethern fyve.
And as for you, sir Plenoryus, I woll undirtake,' seyde sir Launcelot,
'at the nexte feste, so there be a place voyde, that ye shall be knyght of
the Rounde Table.'   25

'Sir,' seyde sir Plenoryus, 'at the nexte feste of Pentecoste I woll be at
kynge Arthurs courte, and at that tyme I woll be gyded and ruled as
kynge Arthure and ye woll have me.'

Than sir Launcelot and sir La Cote Male Tayle reposed them there
untyll they were hole of hir woundis, and there they had myry chere 30
and good reste and many good gamys, and there were many fayre
ladyes.

And so in the meanewhyle cam sir Kay the Seneschall and sir Bran- (9)
diles, and anone they felyshipped with them, and so within ten dayes
they departed, the knyghtes of kynge Arthurs courte, from thes fortres. 35

And as sir Launcelot cam by the Castell of Pendragon, there he put
sir Bryan de Lese Iles from his londes, for because he wolde never be
withholde with kynge Arthur. And all the castell of Pendragon and all
the londis thereof he gaff to sir La Cote Male Tayle. And than sir
Launcelot sente for sir Neroveus that he made onys knyght, and he 40
made hym to have all the rule of that castell and of that contrey undir
sir La Cote Male Tayle. And so they rode unto kynge Arthurs courte
all hole togydirs.

And at Pentecoste nexte folowynge there was sir Plenoryus, and sir

La Cote Male Tayle was called otherwyse be ryght sir Brewne le Noyre. And bothe they were made knyghtes of the Rounde Table, and grete londis kynge Arthure gaff them.

And there sir Breune le Noyre wedded that damesell Maledysaunte, 5 and aftir she was called the lady Byeaue-Vyvante. But ever aftir for the more party he was called La Cote Male Tayle, and he preved a passyng noble knyght and a myghty, and many worshipfull dedys he ded aftir in hys lyff.

And sir Plenoryus preved a good knyght and was full of proues, and 10 all the dayes of theyre lyff for the moste party they awayted uppon sir Launcelot.

And sir Plenoryus brethirne were ever knyghtes of kynge Arthurs, and also, as the Freynshe booke makith mencion, sir La Cote Male Tayle revenged the deth of hys fadir.

15 ## IV. TRISTRAM'S MADNESS AND EXILE

(10) Now leve we here sir Launcelot de Lake and sir La Cote Male Tayle, and turne we unto sir Trystram de Lyones that was in Bretayne, that whan La Beall Isode undirstood that he was wedded she sente to hym by hir maydyn, dame Brangwayn, pyteuous lettirs as coude be thought 20 and made, and hir conclusyon was thus, that if hit pleased sir Trystram, to com to hir courte and brynge with hym Isode le Blaunche Maynys; and they shulde be kepte als well as herselff.

Than sir Trystram called unto hym sir Keyhydy⟨ns⟩ and asked hym whether he wolde go with hym into Cornwayle secretely. He answerde 25 hym and seyde that he was redy at all tymes. And than he lete ordayne prevayly a lityll vessell, and therein they sayled, sir Trystram, sir Keyhydyns, and dame Brangwayne and Governayle, sir Trystrams squyar.

So whan they were in the see a contraryous wynde blew them unto 30 the costis of North Walis, ny the Foreyste Perelus. Than seyde sir Trystrames,

'Here shall ye abyde me thes ten dayes, and Governayle, my squyer, with you. And if so be I com nat agayne by that day, take the nexte way into Cornwayle, for in thys foreyste ar many strange adventures, 35 as I have harde sey, and som of hem I caste to preve or that I departe. And whan I may I shall hyghe me aftir you.'

Than sir Trystrams and sir Keyhydyns toke their horsis and departed frome theire felyship. And so they rode within that foreyste a myle and more, and at the laste sir Trystramys saw before them a lykely 40 knyght syttyng armed by a well. And a stronge myghty horse stood passyng nyghe hym ityed to an oke, and a man hovyng and rydynge by hym, ledynge an horse lode with spearys. And thys knyght that sate at the well semyd by hys countenaunce to be passyng hevy. Than sir Trystramys rode nere hym and seyde,

'Fayre knyght! Why sitte you so droupynge? Ye seme to be a knyght arraunte by youre armys and harneys, and therefore dresse you to juste with one of us other with bothe!'

Therewithall that knyght made no wordes, but toke hys shylde and buckeled hit aboute hys necke, and lyghtly he toke hys horse and lepte uppon hym, and than he toke a grete speare of hys squyre and departed hys way a furlonge.

Than sir Keyhydyns asked leve of sir Trystrames to juste firste.

'Sir, do your beste!' seyde sir Trystrames.

So they mette togydirs, and there sir Keyhydi⟨ns⟩ had a falle and was sore wounded an hyghe abovyn the pappis. Than sir Trystramys seyde,

'Knyght, that ys well justed, now make you redy unto me!'

'Sir, I am redy,' seyde the knyght.

And anone he toke a grete speare and encountird with sir Trystramys. And there by fortune and by grete force that knyght smote downe sir Trystramys frome hys horse, and had a grete falle. Than sir Trystramys was sore ashamed, and lyghtly he avoyded hys horse and put hys shylde afore hys shulder and drew hys swerde, and than sir Trystramys requyred that knyght of hys knyghthode to alyghte uppon foote and fyght with hym.

'I woll well,' seyde the knyght.

And so he alyght uppon foote and avoyded hys horse and kest hys shylde uppon hys shuldir and drew oute hys swerde, and there they fought a longe batayle togydirs, nyghe two owrys.

Than sir Trystramys seyde,

'Fayre knyght, holde thyne honde a lityll whyle and telle me of whens thou arte and what ys thy name.'

'As for that,' seyde the knyght, 'I woll be avysed; but and ye woll telle me youre name, peradventure I woll telle you myne.'

'Now, fayre knyght,' he seyde, 'my name ys sir Trystram de Lyones.' (11)

'Sir, and my name ys sir Lamerok de Galys.'

'A, sir Lamerok!' seyde sir Trystram, 'well be we mette! And bethynke the now of the despite thou dedist me of the sendynge of the horne unto kynge Markis courte, to the entente to have slayne or dishonourde my lady, quene La Beall Isode. And therefore wyte thou well,' seyde sir Trystramys, 'the tone of us two shall dy or we departe.'

'Sir,' seyde sir Lamerok, 'that tyme that we were togydirs in the Ile of Servage ye promysed me bettir frendeship.'

So sir Trystramys wolde make no lenger delayes, but laysshed at sir Lamerok, and thus they faught longe tylle aythir were wery of other. Than sir Trystrams seyde unto sir Lamorak,

'In all my lyff mette I never with such a knyght that was so bygge and so well-brethed. Therefore,' sayde sir Trystramys, 'hit were pité that ony of us bothe sholde here be myscheved.'

'Sir,' seyde sir Lamerok, 'for youre renowne and your name I woll
5 that ye have the worship, and therefore I woll yelde me unto you.' And therewith he toke the poynte of hys swerde in hys honde to yelde hym.

'Nay,' seyde sir Trystrames, 'ye shall nat do so, for well I know youre profirs ⟨are⟩ more of your jantilnes than for ony feare or drede ye have of me.'

10 And therewithall sir Trystramys profferde hym hys swerde and seyde,

'Sir Lamerak, as an overcom knyght I yelde me to you as a man of moste noble proues that I ever mette!'

'Nay,' seyde sir Lamerok, 'I woll do you jantylnes: I requyre you, lat
15 us be sworne togydirs that never none of us shall aftir thys day have ado with other.'

And therewithall sir Trystrames and sir Lamorak sware that never none of hem sholde fyght agaynste othir, for well nother for woo.

(12) And thys meanewhyle com sir Palomydes, the good knyght,
20 folowyng the questyng beste that had in shap lyke a serpentis hede and a body lyke a lybud, buttokked lyke a lyon and footed lyke an harte. And in hys body there was such a noyse as hit had bene twenty couple of houndys questynge, and suche noyse that beste made wheresomever he wente. And thys beste evermore sir Palomydes folowed, for hit was
25 called hys queste.

And ryght so as he folowed this beste, hit cam by sir Trystram, and sone aftir cam sir Palomydes. And to breff thys mater, he smote downe sir Trystramys and sir Lamorak bothe with one speare, and so he departed aftir the Beste Glatyssaunte (that was called the Questynge
30 Beste), wherefore thes two knyghtes were passynge wrothe that sir Palomydes wold nat fyght with hem on foote.

Here men may undirstonde that bene men of worshyp that man was never fourmed that all tymes myght attayne, but somtyme he was put to the worse by malefortune and at som tyme the wayker knyght put
35 the byggar knyght to a rebuke.

Than sir Trystrams and sir Lamerok gate sir Kayhydyns uppon a shylde betwyxte them bothe and led hym to a fosters lodge. And there they gaff hym in charge to kepe hym well, and with hym they abode three dayes. Than thes two knyghtes toke their horsys and at a crosse
40 they departed.

And than seyde sir Trystramys to sir Lamorak,

'I requyre you, if ye hap to mete with sir Palomydes, say to hym that he shall fynde me at the same welle there we mette tofore, and there I, sir Trystramys, shall preve whether he be bettir knyght than I.'

And so ayther departed frome othir a sondry way, and sir Trystramys rode nyghe thereas was sir Keyhydyns, and sir Lamorak rode untyll he cam to a chapell, and there he put hys horse unto pasture.

And anone there cam sir Mellyagaunce that was kynge Bagdemagus sonne, and he there put hys horse to pasture, and was nat ware of sir 5 Lamerok. And than thys knyght sir Mellyagaunce made hys mone of the love that he had to quene Gwenyver, and there he made a wofull complaynte.

All thys harde sir Lamorak, and on the morne sir Lamorake toke hys horse and rode unto the foreyste, and there he mette with two knyghtes 10 hovyng undir the woodshaw.

'Fayre knyghtes,' seyde sir Lamerok, 'what do ye, hovynge here and wacchynge? And yff ye be knyghtes arraunte that wyll juste, lo I am redy!'

'Nay, sir knyght,' they seyde, 'we abyde nat here for to juste with 15 you, but we lye in a wayte uppon a knyght that slew oure brothir.'

'What knyght was that,' seyde sir Lamorak, 'that ye wolde [fayne] mete withall?'

'Sir,' they seyde, 'hit ys sir Launcelot that [slewe oure broder, and yf ever we maye mete with hym he shal not escape, but] we woll slee 20 [hym] and he com thys way.'

'Ye take uppon you a grete charge,' scyde sir Lamorake, 'for sir Launcelot ys a noble proved knyght.'

'As for that, sir, we doute nat, for there ys none of us but we ar good inowghe for hym.' 25

'I woll nat beleve that,' scyde sir Lamerok, 'for I harde never yet of no knyght dayes of oure lyff but sir Launcelot was to bygge for hym.'

Ryght as they talked sir Lameroke was ware how sir Launcelot com (13) rydynge streyte towarde them. Than sir Lamorak salewed hym and he hym agayne, and than sir Lamorak asked sir Launcelot if there were 30 onythynge that he myght do for hym in thys marchys.

'Nay,' seyde sir Launcelot, 'nat at thys tyme, I thanke you.'

Than ayther departed frome other, and sir Lamorake rode ayen thereas he leffte the two knyghtes, and than he founde them hydde in the leved woode. 35

'Fye on you!' seyde sir Lamerak, 'false cowardis! That pité and shame hit ys that ony of you sholde take the hyghe Order of Knyghthode!'

So sir Lamerok departed fro them, and within a whyle he mette with sir Mellyagaunce. And than sir Lamorak asked hym why he loved quene Gwenyver as he ded, 'for I was nat far frome you whan ye made 40 youre complaynte by the chapell.'

'Ded ye so?' seyde sir Mellyagaunce. 'Than woll I abyde by hit. I love quene Gwenyver!'

'What woll ye with hit?'

'I woll preve and make hit good that she ys the fayryste lady and moste of beauté in the worlde.'

'As to that,' seyde sir Lamerok, 'I say nay thereto, for quene Morgause of Orkeney, modir unto sir Gawayne, for she ys the fayryst lady
5 that beryth the lyff.'

'That ys nat so,' seyde sir Mellyagaunce, 'and that woll I preve with my hondis!'

'Wylle ye so?' seyde sir Lamorak. 'And in a bettir quarell kepe I nat to fyght.'

10 So they departed [ayther] frome othir in grete wratthe, and than they com rydyng togydir as hit had bene thundir, and aythir smote other so sore that their horsis felle backewarde to the erthe. And than they avoyded their horsys and dressed their shyldis and drew their swerdis, and than they hurteled togydirs as wylde borys, and thus they
15 fought a grete whyle. For sir Mellyagaunce was a good man and of grete myght, but sir Lamorak was harde byg for hym and put hym allwayes abacke, but aythir had wounded othir sore.

And as they stood thus fyghtynge, by fortune com sir Launcelot and sir Bleoberys, and than sir Launcelot rode betwyxte them and asked
20 them for what cause they fought so togydirs, 'and ye ar bothe of the courte of kynge Arthure.'

(14) 'Sir,' seyde sir Mellyagaunce, 'I shall telle you for what cause we do thys batayle. I praysed my lady, quene Gwenyvere, and seyde she was the fayryste lady of the worlde, and sir Lameroke seyde nay thereto, for
25 he seyde quene Morgause of Orkeney was fayrar than she and more of beauté.'

'A!' seyde sir ⟨Launcelot, 'sir⟩ Lamorak, why sayst thou so? Hit ys nat thy parte to disprayse thy prynces that thou arte undir obeysaunce and we all.' And therewithall sir Launcelot alyght on foote. 'And there-
30 fore make the redy, for I woll preve uppon the that quene Guenyver ys the fayryst lady and most of bounté in the worlde.'

'Sir,' seyde sir Lamerok, 'I am lothe to have ado with you in thys quarell, for every man thynkith hys owne lady fayryste, and thoughe I prayse the lady that I love moste, ye sholde nat be wrothe. For thoughe
35 my lady quene Gwenyver be fayryst in youre eye, wyte you well quene Morgause of Orkeney ys fayryst in myne eye, and so every knyght thynkith hys owne lady fayryste. And wyte you well, sir, ye ar the man in the worlde excepte sir Trystramys that I am moste lothyst to have ado withall, but and ye woll nedys have ado with me, I shall endure
40 you as longe as I may.'

Than spake sir Bleoberys and seyde,

'My lorde, sir Launcelot, I wyste you never so mysseadvysed as ye be at thys tyme, for sir Lamerok seyth to you but reson and knyghtly. For I warne you, I have a lady, and methynkith that she ys the fayryst

lady of the worlde. Were thys a grete reson that ye sholde be wrothe
with me for such langage? And well ye wote that sir Lamorak ys a
noble knyght as I know ony lyvynge, and he hath oughte you and all
us ever good wyll. Therefore I pray you, be fryndis!'

Than sir Launcelot seyde,   5

'Sir, I pray you, forgyve me myne offence and evyll wyll, and if I was
mysseadvysed I woll make amendis.'

'Sir,' seyde sir Lamerok, 'the amendis ys sone made betwyxte you and
me.'

And so sir Launcelot and sir Bleoberys departed, and sir Lamerok 10
and sir Mellyagaunce toke their horsis and aythir departed frome othir.

And within a whyle cam kyng Arthure and mette with sir Lamorak
and justed with hym, and there he smote downe sir Lamorak and
wounded hym sore with a speare. And so he rode frome hym, wherefore
sir Lamerok was wroth that he wolde nat fyght with hym on foote, 15
howbehit that sir Lamerok knew nat kynge Arthure.

Now levith of thys tale and spekith of sir Trystramys, that as he rode (15)
he mette with sir Kay the Senescyall, and there sir Kay asked sir
Trystramys of what contrey he was. He answerde and seyde he was of
the contrey of Cornwaile.   20

'Hit may well be,' seyde sir Kay, 'for as yet harde I never that evir
good knyght com oute of Cornwayle.'

'That ys well spokyn,' seyde sir Trystram, 'but and hit please you to
telle me your name, I pray you.'

'Sir, wyte you well that my name ys sir Kay the Senesciall.'   25

'A, sir, ys that youre name?' seyde sir Trystramys. 'Now wyte you
well that ye ar named the shamefullyst knyght of your tunge that now
ys lyvynge. Howbehit ye ar called a good knyght, but ye ar called
unfortunate and passyng overthwart of youre tunge.'

And thus they rode togydirs tylle they cam to a brydge, and there 30
was a knyght that wolde nat latte them passe tylle one of them justed
with hym. And so that knyght justed with sir Kay, and there he gaff sir
Kay a falle, and hys name was sir Tor, sir Lamerokes halff-brothir.

And than they two rode to their lodgynge, and there they founde sir
Braundiles, and sir Tor cam thydir anone aftir. And as they sate at hir 35
souper, thes four knyghtes, three of them spake all the shame by
Cornysh knyghtes that coude be seyde. Sir Trystramys harde all that
they seyde, and seyde but lytyll, but he thought the more. But at that
tyme he discoverde nat hys name.

And uppon the morne sir Trystrams toke hys horse and abode them 40
uppon their way. And there sir Brandiles p[ro]firde to juste with sir
Trystram, and there sir Trystram smote hym downe, horse and all,
to the erthe.

Than sir Tor le Fyze de Vaysshoure, he encountird with sir Trystram, and there sir Trystram smote hym downe. And than he rode hys way and sir Kay folowed hym, but he wolde none of hys felyship. Than sir Brandiles com to sir Kay and seyde,

'I wolde wyte fayne what ys that knyghtes name.'

'Com one with me,' seyde sir Kay, 'and we shall pray hym to telle us hys name.'

So they rode togydirs tyll they cam nyghe hym, and than they were ware where he sate by a welle and had put of hys helme to drynke at the welle. And whan that he saw them com he laced on hys helme lyghtly and toke hys horse to profir hem to juste.

'Nay!' seyde sir Braundyles, 'we justed late inowe with you, but we com nat in that entente, but we requyre you of knyghthod to telle us youre name.'

'My fayre lordys, sitthyn that hit ys youre [desyre], and now for to please you ye shall wyte that my name ys sir Trystram de Lyones, nevew unto kyng Mark of Cornwayle.'

'In goode tyme,' seyde sir Brandiles, 'and well be ye foundyn! And wyte you well that we be ryght glad that we have founde you, and we be of a felyship that wolde be ryght glad of youre company, for ye ar the knyght in the worlde that the felyship of the Rounde Table desyryth moste to have the company off.'

'God thank them all,' seyde sir Trystram, 'of hir grete goodnes, but as yet I fele well that I am nat able to be of their felyship, for I was never yet of such dedys of worthynes to be in the companye of such a felyship.'

'A,' seyde sir Kay, 'and ye be sir Trystrams, ye ar the man called now moste of proues excepte sir Launcelot, for he beryth nat the lyff crystynde nother hethynde that canne fynde such anothir knyght, to speke of hys proues and of his hondis and hys trouthe withall. For yet cowde there never creature sey hym dishonoure and make hit good.'

Thus they talked a grete whyle, and than they departed ayther frome other such wayes as hem semed beste.

(16) Now shall ye here what was the cause that kyng Arthure cam into the Foreyste Perelous, that was in North Walis, by the meanys of a lady. Her name was Aunowre, and thys lady cam to kynge Arthure at Cardyeff, and she by fayre promyses and fayre behestis made kynge Arthure to ryde with her into that foreyste Perelous. And she was a grete sorseres, and many dayes she had loved kynge Arthure, and bycause she wolde have had hym to lye by her she cam into that contrey.

So whan the kynge was gone with hir, many of hys knyghtes folowed aftir hym whan they myste hym, as sir Launcelot, sir Brandiles, and many other.

And whan she had brought hym to hir towre she desired hym to ly

by her, and than the kynge remembird hym of hy[s] lady and wolde nat
for no crauffte that she cowde do. Than every day she wolde make
hym ryde into that foreyste with hy⟨r⟩ owne knyghtes to the entente to
have had hym slayne; for whan thys lady Aunowre saw that she myght
nat have hym at her wylle, than she laboured by false meanys to have   5
destroyed kynge Arthure and slayne hym.

Than the Lady of the Lake, that was allwayes fryndely to kynge
Arthure, she undirstood by hir suttyle craufftes that kynge Arthure was
lykely to be destroyed. And therefore thys Lady of the Lake, that hyght
Nynyve, she cam into that foreyste to seke aftir sir Launcelot du Lake   10
othir ellis sir Trystramys for to helpe kynge Arthure, for as that same
day she knew well that kynge Arthur sholde be slayne onles that he had
helpe of one of thes two knyghtes.

And thus ⟨as⟩ she rode uppon a downe she mette with sir Trystram,
and anone as she saw hym she knew hym and seyde,   15

'A, my lorde, sir Trystram, well be ye mette, and blyssed be the tyme
that I have mette with you, for the same day and within thys [two]
owrys shall be done the dolefullyst dede that ever was done in thys
londe.'

'A, fayre damesell,' seyde sir Trystramys, 'may I amende hit?'   20

'Yee, sir, therefore comyth on with me in all the haste ye may, for
ye shall se the moste worshipfullyst knyght in the worlde harde
bestadde.'

Than seyde sir Trystramys, 'I am redy lo to helpe you and suche a
noble man as ye sey he ys.'   25

'Sir, hit ys nother better ne worse,' seyde the damesell, 'but the
noble kynge Arthure hymselff.'

'God deffende,' seyde sir Trystramys, 'that ever he shulde be in such
distresse!'

Than they rode togydirs a grete pace untyll they cam to a lityll turret   30
in a castell, and undirnethe that castel they saw a knyght stondynge
uppon foote fyghtyng with two knyghtes. And so sir Trystramys behelde them. And at the laste thes two knyghtes smote downe that one
knyght, and one of hem unlaced hys helme, and the lady Aunowre gate
kynge Arthurs swerde in her honde to have strykyn of his hede.   35

And therewithall com sir Trystramys as faste as he myght, and
seyyng, 'Traytoures! Leve that knyght anone!' And so sir Trystrams
smote the tone of hem thorow the body that he felle dede, and than he
russhed to the othir and smote hys backe in sundir.

And in the meanewhyle the Lady of the Lake cryed to kynge Arthur,   40
'Lat nat that false lady ascape!'

Than kynge Arthur overtoke hir and with the same swerde he smote
of her hede. And the Lady of the Lake toke up hir hede and hynge hit
at hir sadill-bowe by the heyre.

And than sir Trystramys horsed the kynge agayne and rode forth with hym, but he charged the Lady of the Lake nat to discover hys name as at that tyme. So whan the kynge was horsed he thanked hartely sir Trystramys and desired to wyte hys name, but he wolde nat telle
5 hym none other but that he was a poure knyght aventures. And so he bare kynge Arthure ⌐felyship⌐ tylle he mette with som of hys knyghtes.

And so within a whyle he mette with sir Ector de Marys, and he knew nat kynge Arthur nother yet sir Trystram, and he desired to juste with one of them. Than sir Trystrams rode unto sir Ector and
10 smote hym frome hys horse, and whan he had done so he cam agayne to [the] kynge and seyde,

'My lorde, yondir ys one of youre knyghtes, he may beare you felyshyp. And anothir day, ⟨by⟩ that dede that I have done for you I truste to God ye shall undirstonde that I wolde do you servyse.'
15 'Alas!' seyde kynge Arthure, 'lat me wyte what ye ar.'

'Nat at thys tyme,' seyde sir Trystramys. So he departed and leffte kynge Arthur and sir Ector togydirs.

(17) And than at a day sette sir Trystrams and sir Lamerok mette at a welle, and than they toke sir Keyhydyns at the fosters house, and so they rode
20 with hym to [the] ship where they leffte dame Brangwayne and Governayle. And so they sayled into Cornuayle all hole togydirs.

And by assente and by enformacion of dame Brangwayne, whan they were londed they rode unto sir Dynas the Senesciall, a trusty frynde of sir Trystramys, and so sir Dynas and dame Brangwayne rode to the
25 courte of kynge Marke and tolde the quene La Beall Isode that sir Trystramys was nyghe hir in the contrey. Than for verry pure joy La Beall Isode sowned, and whan she myght speke she seyde,

'Jantyll senesciall, helpe that I myght speke with hym, othir my harte woll braste!'
30 Than sir Dynas and dame Brangwayne brought sir Trystram and sir Keyhydyns prevaly into the courte, unto her chambir whereas La Beall Isode assygned them. And to telle the joyes that were betwyxte La Beall Isode and sir Trystramys, there ys no maker can make hit, nothir no harte can thynke hit, nother no penne can wryte hit, nother no
35 mowth can speke hit.

And as the Freynshe booke makith mension, at the firste tyme that ever sir Kayhidins saw La Beall Isode he was so enamered uppon hir that for very pure love he myght never withdraw hit. And at the laste, as ye shall hyre or the booke be ended, sir Keyhydyns dyed for the
40 love of Isode.

And than pryvaly he wrote unto her lettirs and baladis of the moste goodlyeste that were used in tho dayes. And whan La Beall Isode undirstoode hys lettirs she had pité of hys complaynte, and unavised she wrote another lettir to comforte hym withall.

And sir Trystram was all thys whyle in a turret, at the commaundemente of La Beall Isode, and whan she myght she yeode and come to
sir Trystram.

So on a day kynge Marke played at the chesse undir a chambir
wyndowe, and at that tyme sir Trystramys and sir Keyhydyns were 5
within the chambir over kynge Marke. And as hit myshapped, sir
Trystrams founde the lettir that sir Kayhydyns sente unto La Beall
Isode; also he had founde the lettir that she had sente unto sir Keyhydyns. And at the same tyme La Beall Isode was in the same chambir.

Than sir Trystramys com unto La Beall Isode and seyde,   10

'Madame, here ys a lettir that was sente unto you, and here ys the
lettir that ye sente unto hym that sente you that lettir. Alas! madame,
the good love that I have lovyd you, and many londis and grete rychesse
have I forsakyn for youre love! And now ye ar a traytouras unto me,
whych dothe me grete payne.   15

'But as for the, sir Keyhydyns, I brought the oute of Bretayne into
thys contrey, and thy fadir, kynge Howell, I wan hys londis. Howbehit
I wedded thy syster, Isode le Blaunche Maynes, for the goodnes she
ded unto me, and yet, as I am a trew knyght, she ys a clene maydyn for
me. But wyte thou well, sir Keyhydyns, for thys falshed and treson thou 20
hast done unto me, I woll revenge hit uppon the!' And therewithall
sir Trystram drew his swerde and seyde, 'Sir Keyhidyns, kepe the!'

And than La Beall Isode sowned to the erthe.

And whan sir Keyhydyns saw sir Trystrams com uppon hym, he
saw none other boote but lepte oute at a bay-wyndow evyn over 25
the hede where sate kynge Marke playyng at the chesse. And whan
the kynge saw one com hurlyng over hys hede he seyde,

'Felow, what arte thou, and what ys the cause thou lepe oute at that
wyndow?'

'My lorde kynge,' seyde sir Keyhydyns, 'hit fortuned me that I was 30
aslepe in the wyndow abovyn youre hede, and as I slepte I slumbirde,
and so I felle downe.'

Thus sir Keyhydyns excused hym, and sir Trystram drad hym leste (18)
he were discoverde unto the kyng that he was there. Wherefore he
drew hym to the strength of the towre and armed hym in such armour 35
as he had for to fyght with hem that wolde withstonde hym.

And so whan sir Trystram saw that there was no resistence agaynste
hym he sente Governayle for hys horse and hys speare, and knyghtly
he rode forth oute of the castell opynly that was callyd the Castell of
Tyntagyll.   40

And evyn at the gate he mette with sir Gyngalyn, Gawaynes sonne,
and anone sir Gyngalyn put hys speare in the reste and ran uppon sir
Trystram and brake hys speare. And sir Trystram at that tyme had but
a swerde, and gaff hym such a buffet uppon the helme that he fylle

downe frome hys sadill, and hys swerde slode adowne and carved asundir his horse necke. And so sir Trystramys rode hys way into the foreyste.

And all thys doynge saw kynge Marke, and than he sente a squyer 5 unto the hurte knyght and commaunded hym to com to hym, and so he ded. And whan kynge Marke wyst that hyt was sir Gyngalyn he well-commyd hym and gaff hym anothir horse, and so he asked hym what knyght was that encountyrde with hym.

'Sir,' seyde sir Gyngalyn, 'I wote nat what knyght hit was, but well 10 I wote he syeth and makith grete dole.'

Than sir Trystrames within a whyle mette with a knyght of hys owne—hys name was sir Fergus—and whan he had mette with hym he made such sorow that he felle downe of hys horse in a sowne, and in such sorow he was inne three dayes and three nyghtes. Than at the 15 laste sir Trystramys sente unto the courte by sir Fergus for to spurre what tydyngis.

And so as he rode by the way he mette with a damesell that cam frome sir Palomydes to know and seke how sir Trystramys ded. Than sir Fergus tolde her how he was allmoste oute of hys mynde.

20 'Alas!' seyde the damesell, 'where shall I fynde hym?'

'In suche a place,' seyde sir Fergus.

Than sir Fergus founde quene Isode syke in hir bedde, makynge the grettyste dole that ever ony erthly woman made.

And whan the damesell founde sir Trystramys she made grete dole, 25 bycause she myght nat amende hym; for the more she made of hym, the more was hys payne. And at the laste sir Trystram toke hys horse and rode awey frome her.

And than was hit three dayes or that she coude fynde hym, and than she broute hym mete and drynke, but he wolde none. And than another 30 tyme sir Trystramys ascaped away frome the damesell, and hit happened hym to ryde by the same castell where sir Palomydes and sir Trystramys dyd batayle, whan La Beall Isode departed them.

And there by fortune the damesell mette with sir Trystramys ayen, makynge the grettiste dole that ever erthely creature made, and she 35 yode to the lady of that castell and tolde of the myssadventure of sir Trystrames.

'Alas!' seyde the lady of that castell, 'where ys my lorde sir Trystramys?'

'Ryght here by youre castell,' seyde the damesell.

40 'In good tyme,' seyde the lady, 'ys he so nyghe me: he shall have mete and drynke of the beste. And an harpe I have of hys whereuppon he taught me, for of goodly harpyng he beryth the pryse of the worlde.'

So thys lady and damesell brought hym mete and drynke, but he ete lityll thereoff. Than uppon a nyght he put hys horse frome hym and unlaced hys armour, and so he yeode unto the wyldirnes and braste downe the treys and bowis.

And othirwhyle, whan he founde the harpe that the lady sente hym, than wolde he harpe and play thereuppon and wepe togydirs. And somtyme, whan he was in the wood, the lady wyst nat where he was. 5 Than wolde she sette hir downe and play uppon the harpe, and anone sir Trystramys wolde com to the harpe and harkyn thereto, and somtyme he wolde harpe hymselff.

Thus he there endured a quarter off a yere, and so at the laste he ran hys way and she wyst nat where he was becom. And than was he 10 naked, and waxed leane and poore of fleyshe. And so he felle in the felyshyppe of herdemen and shyperdis, and dayly they wolde gyff hym som of their mete and drynke, and whan he ded ony shrewde dede they wolde beate hym with roddis. And so they clypped hym with sherys and made hym lyke a foole.   15

And so uppon a day sir Dagonet, kynge Arthurs foole, cam into (19) Cornwayle with two squyers with hym, and as they rode thorow that foreyste they cam by a fayre welle where sir Trystramys was wonte to be. And the weddir was hote, and they alyght to drynke of that welle, and in the meanewhyle theyre horsys brake lowse.   20

Ryght so cam sir Trystramys unto them, and firste he sowsed sir Dagonet in that welle, and aftir that hys squyars, and thereat lowghe the shypperdis. And furthwithall he ran aftir their horsis and brought hem agayne one by one, and ryght so wete as they were he made them lepe up and ryde their wayes.   25

Thus sir Trystramys endured there an halff-yere naked, and wolde never com in towne [ne village]. So the meanewhyle the damesell that sir Palomydes sent to seke sir Trystram, she yode unto sir Palomydes and tolde hym off all the myschyff that sir Trystram endured.

'Alas!' seyde sir Palomydes, 'hit ys grete pité that ever so noble a 30 knyght sholde be so myscheved for the love of a lady. But nevertheles I woll go and seke hym and comforte hym and I may.'

Than a lytyll before that tyme La Beall Isode had commaunded sir Kayhydyns oute of the contrey of Cornwayle. So sir Keyhydyns departed with a dolerous harte, and by aventure he mette with sir 35 Palomydes, and they felyshyppyd togydirs, and aythir complayned to other of there hote love that they loved La Beall Isode.

'Now lat us,' seyde sir Palomydes, 'seke sir Trystramys that lovyth her as well as we, and let us preve whether we may recover hym.'

So they rode into the foreyste, and three dayes and three nyghtes they 40 wolde never take lodgynge, but ever sought sir Trystram. And uppon a tyme by adventure they mette with kynge Marke that was rydden frome hys men all alone. And whan they saw hym sir Palomydes knew hym, but sir Keyhydyns knew hym nat.

'A, false knyght!' seyde sir Palomydes, 'hit ys pité thou haste thy lyff, for thou arte a destroyer of all worshipfull knyghtes, and by thy myschyff and thy vengeaunce thou haste destroyed that moste noble knyght, sir Trystramys de Lyones. And therefore deffende the,' seyde
5 sir Palomydes, 'for thou shalt dye thys day!'

'That were shame,' seyde kynge Marke, 'for ye too ar armed and I am unarmed.'

'As for that,' seyde sir Palomydes, 'I shall fynde a remedy therefore: here ys a knyght with me, and thou shalt have hys harneyse.'
10 'Nay,' seyde kynge Marke, 'I woll nat have ado with you, for cause have ye none to me: for all the mysseease that sir Trystramys hath was for a lettir that he founde. For as for me, I ded to hym no displesure, and God knowith I am full sory for hys maledye and hys myssease.'

So whan the kynge had thus excused hymselff they were fryndys, and
15 kynge Marke wolde have had them unto the Castell of Tyntagyll. But sir Palomydes wolde nat, but turned unto the realme of Logrys, and sir Keyhydyns seyde that he wolde into Bretayne.

Now turne we unto sir Dagonet ayen, that whan he and hys squyers were uppon horsebacke he demyd that the shyperdis had sente that
20 foole to aray hem so bycause that they lawghed at them. And so they rode unto the kepers of the bestis and all to-bete them.

Whan sir Trystramys saw hem betyn that were wonte to gyff hym mete, he ran thydir and gate sir Dagonet by the hede, and there he gaff hym such a falle to the erthe and brusede hym so that he lay stylle. And
25 than he wraste hys swerde oute of hys honde, and therewith he ran to one of hys squyers and smote of hys hede, and hys othir squyer fled. And so sir Trystramys toke his way with the swerde in hys honde, rennynge as he had bene wyld woode.

Than sir Dagonet rode to kynge Marke and tolde hym how he had
30 spedde in the foreyste.

'And therefore,' seyde sir Dagonet, 'beware, kynge Marke, that thou com nat aboute that well in the foreyste, for there ys a foole naked. And that foole and I, foole, mette togydir, and he had allmoste slayne me.'

'A,' seyde kynge Marke, 'that ys sir Matto le Breune that felle oute of
35 hys wytte because he loste hys lady, for whan sir Gaherys smote downe sir Matto and wan hys lady of hym, never syns was he in his mynde, and that was grete pité, for he was a good knyght.'

(20)   Than sir Andred that was cousyn unto sir Trystram made a lady that was hys paramour to sey and to noyse hit that she was with sir Trys-
40 tramys or ever he dyed. And thys tale she brought unto kynge Markis house, that she buryed hym by a welle, and that or he dyed he besoughte kynge Marke to make hys cousyn, sir Andred, kynge of the contrey of Lyonas, of the whych sir Trystramys was lorde of. And all thys ded sir Andred bycause he wolde have had sir Trystramys londis.

And whan kynge Mark harde telle that sir Trystrames was dede he wepte and made grete dole. But whan quene Isode harde of thes tydyngis, she made such sorow that she was nyghe oute of hir mynde. And so uppon a day she thought to sl[e] hirselff and never to lyve aftir the deth of sir Trystramys.   5

And so uppon a day La Beall Isode gate a swerde pryvayly, and bare hit into her gardyne, and there she pyghte the swerde thorow a plumtre up to the hyltis so that hit stake faste, and hit stoode breste-hyghe. And as she wolde have renne uppon the swerde and to have slayne hirselff, all thys aspyed kynge Marke, how she kneled adowne and seyde,   10

'Sweyte Lorde Jesu, have mercy uppon me, for I may nat lyve aftir the deth of sir Trystram de Lyones, for he was my firste love and shall be the laste!'

And with thes wordis cam kynge Marke and toke hir in hys armys. And than he toke up the swerde and bare hir away with hym into a   15 towre, and there he made hir to be kepte, and wacched hir surely. And aftir that she lay longe syke, nyghe at the poynte of dethe.

So thys meanewhyle ran sir Trystramys naked in the foreyste with the swerde in hys honde, and so he cam to an ermytayge, and there he layde hym downe and slepte. And in the meanewhyle the ermyte stale   20 away the swerde and layde mete downe by hym. Thus was he kepte there a ten dayes, and at the laste he departed and com to the herdemen ayen.

And there was a gyaunte in that contrey that hyght Tauleas, and for feare of sir Trystram more than seven yere he durste never muche go at   25 large, but for the moste party he kepte hym in a sure castell of hys owne. And so thys Tauleas harde telle that sir Trystramys was dede by the noyse of the courte of kynge Marke. Than thys gyaunt Tauleas yode dayly at hys large.

And so he happyd uppon a day he cam to the herdemen wandrynge   30 and langeryng, and there he sette hym downe to reste amonge them. And in the meanewhyle there cam a knyght of Cornwayle that led a lady with hym, and hys name was sir Dynaunte. And whan the gyaunte saw hym he wente frome the herdemen and hydde hym under a tre.

And so the knyght cam to the well and there he alyght to repose hym.   35 And as sone as he was frome hys horse this gyaunte Tauleas com betwyxte thys knyght and hys horse and [toke the horse and] leped uppon hym, and so forthewith he rode unto sir Dynaunte and toke hym by the coler and pulled hym afore hym uppon hys horse, and wolde have stryken of hys hede.   40

Than the herdemen seyde unto sir Trystram,

'Helpe yondir knyght!'

'Helpe ye hym,' seyde sir Trystram.

'We dare nat,' seyde the herdemen.

Than sir Trystram was ware of the swerde of the knyght thereas hit lay, and so thydir he ran and toke up the swerde and smote to sir Tauleas, and so strake of hys hede, and so he yode hys way to the herdemen.

(21) 5 Than sir Dynaunte toke up the gyauntes hede and bare hit with hym unto kynge Marke, and tolde hym what adventure betydde hym in the foreyste and how a naked man rescowed hym frome the grymly gyaunte sir Tauleas.

'Where had ye thys aventure?' seyde kynge Marke.

10 'Forsothe,' seyde sir Dynaunte, 'at the fayre fountayne in the foreyst, where many adventures knyght[es] mete, and there ys the madde man.'

'Well,' seyde kynge Marke, 'I woll se that wood man.'

So within a day or too kynge Marke commaunded hys knyghtes and his hunters to be redy, and seyde that he wolde hunte on the morne.
15 And so uppon the morne he wente into that foreyste.

And whan the kynge cam to that welle he founde there lyyng a fayre naked man, and a swerde by hym. Than kynge Marke blew and straked, and therewith hys knyghtes cam to hym, and than he commaunded hys knyghtes to take the naked man with fayrenes, 'and brynge hym to my
20 castell'.

And so they ded savely and fayre, and keste mantels uppon sir Trystramys, and so lad hym unto Tyntagyll. And there they bathed hym and wayshed hym 'and gaff hym hote suppyngis, tylle they had brought hym well to hys remembraunce. But all thys whyle there was no creature
25 that knew sir Trystramys nothir what maner man he was.

So hyt befelle uppon a day that the quene La Beall Isode hard of such a man that ran naked in the foreyste, and how the kynge had brought hym home to the courte. Than La Beall Isode called unto her dame Brangwayne and seyde,

30 'Com on with me, for we woll go se thys man that my lorde brought frome the foreste the laste day.'

So they passed forth and spirred where was the syke man, and than a squyer tolde the quene that he was in the gardyne takyng hys reste to repose hym ayenst the sunne. So whan the quene loked uppon sir
35 Trystramys she was nat remembird of hym, but ever she seyde unto dame Brangwayne,

'Mesemys I shulde have sene thys man here before in many placis.'

But as sone as sir Trystramys sye her he knew her well inowe, and than he turned away hys vysage and wepte.

40 Than the quene had allwayes a lytyll brachett that sir Trystramys gaff hir the first tyme that ever she cam into Cornwayle, and never wold that brachet departe frome her but yf sir Trystram were nyghe thereas was La Beall Isode. And thys brachet was firste sente frome the kynges doughter of Fraunce unto sir Trystrams for grete love.

And anone thys lityll bracket felte a savoure of sir Trystram. He lepte
uppon hym and lycked hys learys and hys earys, and than he whyned
and quested, and she smelled at hys feete and at hys hondis and on all
the partyes of hys body that she myght com to.

'A, my lady!' seyde dame Brangwayne, 'Alas! I see hit ys myne owne   5
lorde sir Trystramys.'

And thereuppon La Beall Isode felle downe in a sowne and so lay a
grete whyle. And whan she myght speke she seyde,

'A, my lorde, sir Trystram! Blyssed be God ye have youre lyff! And
now I am sure ye shall be discoverde by thys lityll brachet, for she woll 10
never leve you. And also I am sure, as sone as my lorde kynge Marke do
know you he woll banysh you oute of the contrey of Cornwayle, othir
ellis he woll destroy you. And therefore, for Goddys sake, myne owne
lorde, graunte kynge Marke hys wyll, and than draw you unto the
courte off kynge Arthur, for there ar ye beloved. And ever whan I may 15
I shall sende unto you, and whan ye lyste ye may com unto me, and at
all tymys early and late I woll be at youre commaundement, to lyve as
poore a lyff as ever ded quyene or lady.'

'A, madame!' seyde sir Trystramys, 'go frome me, for much angur
and daunger have I as⟨say⟩ed for youre love.'   20

Than the quene departed, but the brachet wolde nat frome hym,   (22)
and therewithall cam kynge Marke, and the brachet sate uppon
hym and bayed at them all. And therewithall sir Andred spake and
sayde,

'Sir, thys ys sir Trystramys, I se well by that brachet.'   25

'Nay,' seyde the kynge, 'I can nat suppose that.'

Than the kyng asked hym uppon hys faythe what he was and what
was hys name.

'So God me helpe,' seyde he, 'my name ys sir Trystrames de Lyones.
Now do by me what ye lyst.'   30

'A,' sayde kynge Marke, 'me repentis of youre recoverynge.'

And so he lete calle hys barownes to geve jugemente unto sir Trystramys to the dethe. Than many of hys barownes wolde nat assente
thereto, and in especiall sir Dynas the Senesciall and sir Fergus. And so
by the avyse of them all sir Trystramys was banysshed oute of the 35
contrey for ten yere, and thereuppon he toke hys othe uppon a booke
before the kynge and hys barownys.

And so he was made to departe oute of the contrey of Cornwayle, and
there were many barownes brought hym unto hys shyp, that som were
of hys frendis and som were of hys fooys.   40

And in the meanewhyle there cam a knyght of kynge Arthurs, and
hys name was sir Dynadan, and hys commyng was for to seke aftir sir
Trystram. Than they shewed hym where he was, armed at all poyntis,
goyng to the shyp.

'Now, fayre knyght,' seyde sir Dynadan, 'or ye passe thys courte, that ye woll juste with me [I requyre the].'

'With a good wyll,' seyde sir Trystramys, 'and these lordes woll gyffe me leve.'

5   Than the barownes graunted thereto, and so they ranne togydir, and there sir Trystramys gaff sir Dynadan a falle. And than he prayde sir Trystram of hys jantylnes to gyff hym leve to go in hys felyshyp.

'Ye shall be ryght wellcom,' seyd he.

And than sir Trystramys and sir Dynadan toke their horsys and rode to
10 their shyppys togydir. And whan sir Trystramys was in the se he seyde,

'Grete well kyng Marke and all myne enemyes, and sey to hem I woll com agayne whan I may. And sey hym well am I rewarded for the fyghtyng with sir Marhalt, and delyverd all hys contrey frome servayge. And well am I rewarded for the fecchynge and costis of quene Isode
15 oute off Irelonde and the daunger that I was in firste and laste. And by the way commyng home what daunger I had to brynge agayne quene Isode frome the Castell Pleure! And well am I rewarded whan I fought with sir Bleoberys for sir Segwarydes wyff. And well am I rewarded whan I faught with sir Blamoure de Ganys for kyng Angwysh, fadir
20 unto La Beall Isode.

'And well am I rewarded whan I smote down the good knyght sir Lamerok de Galis at kynge Markes requeste. And well am I rewarded whan I faught with the Kynge with the Hondred Knyghtes and the kynge of North Galys, and both thes wolde have put hys londe in
25 servayge, and by me they were put to a rebuke. And well am I rewarded for the sleyng of Tauleas, the myghty gyaunte. And many othir dedys have I done for hym, and now have I my waryson!

'And telle kynge Marke that many noble knyghtes of the Rounde Table have spared the barownes of thys contrey for my sake. And also,
30 I am nat well rewarded whan I fought with the good knyght sir Palomydes and rescowed quene Isode frome hym. And at that tyme kynge Marke seyde afore all hys barownes I sholde have bene bettir rewarded.'

And furthewithall he toke the see.

(23) 35   And at the nexte londynge faste by the see there mette with sir Trystram and with sir Dynadan sir Ector de Marys and sir Bors de Ganys, and there sir Ector justed with sir Dynadan and he smote hym and hys horse downe. And than sir Trystram wolde have justed with sir Bors, and sir Bors seyde that he wolde nat juste with no Cornyssh
40 knyghtes, for they ar nat called men of worship. And all thys was done uppon a brydge.

And with thys cam sir Bleoberys and sir Dryaunte, and sir Bleoberys profird to juste with sir Trystram, [and there sir Trystram] smote downe sir Bleoberys. Than seyde sir Bors de Ganys,

'I wyste never Cornysh knyght of so grete a valure nor so valyaunte as that knyght that beryth the trappours enbrowdred with crownys.'

And than sir Trystram and sir Dynadan departed from them into a foreyst, and there mette them a damesell that cam for the love of sir Launcelot to seke aftir som noble knyghtes of kynge Arthurs courte for ₅ to rescow sir Launcelot. For he was ordayned for by the treson of quene Morgan le Fay to have slayne hym, and for that cause she ordayned thirty knyghtes to lye in wayte for sir Launcelot.

And thys damesell knew thys treson, and for thys cause she cam for to seke noble knyghtis to helpe sir Launcelot; for that nyght other the ₁₀ day affter sir Launcelot sholde com where thes thirty knyghtes were.

And so thys damesell mette with sir Bors and sir Ector and with sir Dryaunte, and there she tolde hem all four of the treson of Morgan le Fay. And than they promysed her that they wolde be nyghe her whan sir Launcelot shold mete with the thirty knyghtes. ₁₅

'And if so be they sette uppon hym, we woll do rescowis as we can.'

So the damesell departed, and by adventure she mette with sir Trystram and with sir Dynadan, and there the damesell tolde hem of all the treson that was ordayned for sir Launcelot. ₂₀

'Now, fayre damesell,' seyde sir Trystram, 'brynge me to that same place where they shold mete with sir Launcelot.'

Than seyde sir Dynadan,

'What woll ye do? Hit ys nat for us to fyght with thirty knyghtes, and wyte you well I woll nat thereoff! As to macche o knyght, two or three ₂₅ ys inow and they be men, but for to matche fiftene knyghtes, that I woll never undirtake.'

'Fy for shame!' seyde sir Trystram, 'do but youre parte!'

'Nay,' seyde sir Dynadan, 'I woll nat thereoff but iff ye woll lende me your shylde. For ye bere a shylde of Cornwayle, and for the cowardyse ₃₀ that ys named to the knyghtes of Cornwayle by youre shyldys ye bene ever forborne.'

'Nay,' sayde sir Trystram, 'I woll nat departe frome my shylde for her sake that gaff hit me. But one thyng,' seyde sir Trystram, 'I promyse the, sir Dynadan: but if thou wolte promyse me to abyde with me ₃₅ ryght here I shall sle the. For I desyre no more of the but answere one knyght. And yf thy harte woll nat serve the, stonde by and loke uppon!'

'Sir,' seyde sir Dynadan, 'I woll promyse you to looke uppon and to do what I may to save myselff, but I wolde I had nat mette with you.'

So than anone thes thirty knyghtes cam faste by thes four knyghtes, ₄₀ and they were ware of them, and aythir of other. And so thes thirty knyghtes lette ⟨them passe⟩ for thys cause, that they wolde nat wratth them if case be they had ado with sir Launcelot. And the four knyghtes lette them passe to thys entente, that they wolde se and beholde what they wolde do with sir Launcelot. And so the thirty knyghtes paste on and cam by sir Trystram and by sir Dynadan, and than sir Trystramys cryed on hyght:

'Lo here ys a knyght ayenste you for the love of sir Launcelot!'

5 And there he slew two with a speare and ten with hys swerde. And than cam in sir Dynadan and he ded passyng welle. And so of the thirty knyghtes there yoode but ten away, and they fledde.

And all thys batayle saw sir Bors de Ganys and hys three felowys, and than they saw well hit was the same knyght that justed with hem at the

10 brydge. Than they toke their horsys and rode unto sir Trystramys and praysed hym and thanked hym of hys good dedys. And they all desyred sir Trystram to go with them to their lodgynge, and he seyde he wold nat go to no lodgynge. Than they four knyghtes prayde hym to telle hys name.

15 'Fayre lordys,' seyde sir Trystramys, 'as at thys tyme I woll nat telle you my name.'

(24) Than sir Trystram and sir Dynadan rode forthe their way tylle they cam to shyperdis and to herdemen. And there they asked them if they knew ony lodgyng there nerehonde.

20 'Sir,' seyde the herdemen, 'hereby ys good herberow in a castell, but there ys such a custom that there shall no knyght herberow there but if he juste with two knyghtes, and if he be but o knyght he muste juste with two knyghtes. And as ye be, sone shall ye be macched.'

'There ys shrewde herberow!' seyde sir Dynadan. 'Lodge where ye

25 woll, for I woll nat lodge there.'

'Fye for shame!' seyde sir Trystramys, 'ar ye nat a knyght of the Table Rounde? Wherefore ye may nat with your worship reffuse your lodgynge.'

'Not so,' seyde the herdemen, 'for and ye be beatyn and have the

30 warse, ye shall nat be lodged there, and if ye beate them ye shall well be herberowed.'

'A,' seyde sir Dynadan, 'I undirstonde they ar two good knyghtes.'

Than sir Dynadan wolde nat lodge there in no maner but as sir Trystramys requyred hym of hys knyghthode, and so they rode thydir.

35 And to make shorte tale, sir Trystram and sir Dynadan smote hem downe bothe, and so they entirde into the castell and had good chere as they cowde thynke or devyse.

And whan they were unarmed and thought to be myry and in good reste, there cam in at the yatis sir Palomydes and sir Gaherys, requyryng

40 to have the custum of [the] castell.

'What aray ys thys?' seyde sir Dynadan, 'I wolde fayne have my reste.'

'That may nat be,' seyde sir Trystram. 'Now muste we nedis defende the custum of thys castell insomuch as we have the bettir of this lordes of thys castell. And therefor,' seyde sir Trystram, 'nedis muste ye make you redy.'

'In the devyls name,' seyde sir Dynadan, 'cam I into youre company!'

And so they made them redy, and sir Gaherys encountirde with sir Trystram, and sir Gaherys had a falle. And sir Palomydes encountirde 5 with sir Dynadan, and sir Dynadan had a falle: than was hit falle for falle. So than muste they fyght on foote, and that wolde nat sir Dynadan, for he was sore brused of that falle that sir Palomydes gaff hym.

Than sir Trystramys laced on sir Dynadans helme and prayde hym to helpe hym. 10

'I woll nat,' seyde sir Dynadan, 'for I am sore wounded of the thirty knyghtes that we had ado withall. But ye fare,' seyde sir Dynadan, 'as a man [that] were oute of hys mynde that wold caste hymselff away. And I may curse the tyme that ever I sye you, for in all the worlde ar nat such two knyghtes that ar so wood as ys sir Launcelot and ye, sir 15 Trystram! For onys I felle in the felyshyp of sir Launcelot as I have done now with you, and he sette me so a worke that a quarter of a yere I kept my bedde. Jesus deffende me,' seyde sir Dynadan, 'frome such two knyghtys, and specially frome youre felyshyp.'

Than seyde sir Trystram, 'I woll fyght with hem bothe!' And anone 20 sir Trystram bade hem com forthe bothe, 'for I woll fyght with you'.

Than sir Palomydes and sir Gaherys dressed and smote at hem bothe. Than sir Dynadan smote at sir Gaherys a stroke or two, and turned frome hym.

'Nay!' seyde sir Palomydes. 'Hit ys to much shame for us two 25 knyghtes to fyght with one!' And than he ded bydde sir Gaherys, 'Stonde asyde with that knyght that hath no lyste to fyght.'

Than they rode togydirs and fought longe, and at the laste sir Trystram doubled hys stroke and drove sir Palomydes abak more than three stryddys. And than by one assente sir Gaherys and sir Dynadan 30 wente betwyxt them and departed them in sundir.

And than by the assente of sir Trystramys they wolde have lodged togydirs, but sir Dynadan seyde he wold nat lodge in that castell. And than he cursed the tyme that ever he com in theyre felyship, and so he toke hys horse and hys harneyse and departed. 35

Than sir Trystram prayde the lordys of that castell to lende hym a man to brynge hym to a lodgyng. And so they ded, and overtoke sir Dynadan and rode to hir lodgynge, two myle thens, with a good man in a pryory; and there they were well at ease.

And that same nyght sir Bors and sir Bleoberys and sir Ector and sir 40 Dryaunt abode stylle in the same place thereas sir Trystram faught with [the] thirty knyghtes. And there they mette with sir Launcelot the same nyght, and had made promyse to lodge with sir Collgrevaunce the same nyght.

(25)   But anone as sir Launcelot harde of the shylde of Cornwayle, he wyste well hit was sir Trystram that had fought with hys enemyes, and than sir Launcelot praysed sir Trystram and called hym the man of moste worshyp in the worlde.

5   So there was a knyght in that pryory that hyght sir Pellynore, and he desyred to wete the name of sir Trystram, but in no wyse he coude nat. And so sir Trystram departed and leffte sir Dynadan in that pryory, for he was so wery and so sore brused that he myght nat ryde.

   Than thys knyght, sir Pellynore, seyde unto sir Dynadan,
10   'Sith that ye woll nat telle me that knyghtes name, I shall ryde affter hym and make hym to telle me hys name, other he shall dye therefore.'

   'Yet beware, sir knyght,' seyde sir Dynadan, 'for and ye folow hym ye woll repente hit.'

   So that knyght, sir Pellynor, rode aftir sir Trystram and requyred
15   hym of justis. Than sir Trystram smote hym downe and wounded hym thorow the shulder, and so he paste on hys way.

   And on the nexte day folowynge sir Trystram mette with pursy-vauntis, and they tolde hym that there was made a grete crye of turne-mente betwene kynge Carados of Scotlonde and the kynge of North
20   Galys, and aythir shulde juste agayne othir afore the Castell of Maydyns. And thes pursyvauntis sought all the contrey aftir good knyghtes, and in especiall kynge Carados lete make grete sykynge for sir Launcelot, and the kynge of North Galis lete seke specially for sir Trystramys de Lyones. And at that tyme sir Trystramys thought to be at that justis.

25   And so by adventure they mette with sir Kay the Senesciall and sir Sagramoure le Desirous, and sir Kay requyred syr Trystram to juste.

   And sir Trystram in a maner refused hym, bycause he wolde nat be hurte nothir brused ayenste the grete justis that shuld [be] before the Castell of Maydyns, and therefore he thought to reste hym and to repose
30   hym. And allway sir Kay cryed,

   'Sir knyght of Cornwayle, juste with me, othir ellys yelde the to me as recreaunte!'

   Whan sir Trystram herd hym sey so he turned unto hym, and than sir Kay refused hym and turned hys backe. Than sir Trystram sayde,
35   'As I fynde the, I shall take the!'

   Than sir Kay turned with evyll wyll, and sir Trystram smote sir Kay downe, and so he rode forthe.

   Than sir Sagramoure le Desirous rode aftir sir Trystram and made hym to juste with hym. And there sir Trystram smote downe sir Sagra-
40   moure frome hys horse and rode hys way.

   And the same day he mette with a damesell that tolde hym that he sholde wynne grete worshyp of a knyght aventures that ded much harme in all that contrey. Whan sir Trystramys herde her sey so he was glad to go with her to wyn worshyp. And so sir Trystram rode with that damesell a six myle. And than there mette with hym sir Gawayne, and therewithall sir Gawayne knew the damesell, that she was longynge to quyne Morgan le Fay. Than sir Gawayne undirstood that she lad that knyght to som myschyeff, and sayde,

'Fayre knyght, whothir ryde ye now with that damesell?'   5

'Sir,' seyde sir Trystram, 'I wote nat whothir I shall ryde, but as thys damesell woll lede me.'

'Sir,' seyde sir Gawayne, 'ye shall nat ryde with her, for she and her lady ded never goode but yll.'

And than sir Gawayne pulled oute hys swerde and seyde,   10

'Damesell, but yf thou telle me anone for what cause thou ledyst thys knyght, thou shalt dye for hit ryght anone, for I know all youre ladyes treson and yourys.'

'A, mercy, sir Gawayne,' seyde she, 'and yff ye woll save my lyff I woll telle you.'   15

'Say on,' seyde sir Gawayne, 'and thou shalt have thy lyff.'

'Sir,' she seyde, 'quene Morgan, my lady, hath ordayned a thirty ladyes to seke and aspye aftir sir Launcelot or aftir sir Trystram, and by the traynys of thes ladyes, who that may fyrste mete ony of thes two knyghtes, they shulde turne hem unto Morgan le Fayes castell, sayyng 20 that they sholde do dedys of worship. And yf ony of tho two knyghtes cam, there be thirty knyghtes liyng and wacchyng in a towre to wayte uppon sir Launcelot or uppon sir Trystramys.'

'Fy for shame,' seyde sir Gawayne, 'that evir such false treson sholde be wrought or used in a quene and a kyngys systir, and a kynge and a 25 quenys doughtir! Sir,' seyde sir Gawayne, 'wyll ye stonde with me, and (26) we woll se the malyce of thes knyghtes.'

'Sir,' seyde sir Trystram, 'go ye to them and hit please you, and ye shall se I woll nat fayle you, for hit ys not longe ago syn I and a felow mette with thirty [knyghtes] of the quenys felyship, and God spede us 30 so that we won away with worship.'

So than sir Gawayne and sir Trystram rode towarde the castell where Morgan le Fay was; and ever sir Gawayne demed that he was sir Trystram de Lyones, bycause he hard that two knyghtes had slayn and beatyn thirty knyghtes. And whan they cam afore the castell sir 35 Gawayne spake on hyght and seyde,

'Quene Morgan, sende oute youre knyghtes that ye have layde in wacche for sir Launcelot and for sir Trystram. Now,' seyde sir Gawayne, 'I know youre false treson, and all placis where that I ryde shall know of youre false treson. And now lat se,' seyde sir Gawayne, 40 'whethir ye dare com oute of youre castell, ye thirty knyghtes.'

Than the quene spake and all the thirty knyghtes at onys, and seyde,

'A, sir Gawayne, full well wotist thou what thou dost and seyst, for, pardé, we know the passyng well. But all that thou spekyst and doyst,

thou sayste hit uppon pryde of that good knyght that ys there with the. For there be som of us know the hondys of that good knyght overall well. And wyte thou well, sir Gawayne, ⌐hit is more for his sake than for thyn that we woll not come oute of this castel, for wete ye well, sir
5 Gawayne⌐, the knyght that beryth the armys of Cornwayle, we know hym and what he ys.'

Than sir Gawayne and sir Trystram departed and rode on their wayes a day or two togydirs, and there by adventure they mette with sir Kay and with sir Sagramour le Desyrous. And than they were glad of sir
10 Gawayne and he of them, but they wyst nat what he was with the shylde of Cornwayle but by demyng.

And thus they rode togydirs a day or too, and than they were ware of sir Breuse Saunz Pité chasyng a lady for to have slayne her, for he had slayn her paramour afore.

15 'Holde you all stylle,' seyde sir Gawayne, 'and shew none of you forth, and ye shall se me rewarde yonder false knyght: for and he aspye you, he ys so well horsed that he woll ascape away.'

And than sir Gawayne rode betwyxt sir Breuse and the lady and sayde, 'False knyght, leve her and have ado with me!'

20 So whan sir Brewse saw no man but sir Gawayne, he feautred hys speare, and sir Gawayne ayenste hym. And there sir Breuse overthrew sir Gawayne, and than he rode [over] hym and overtwarte hym twenty tymys to have destroyed hym.

And [whan] sir Trystram saw hym do so vylaunce a dede he hurled
25 oute ayenste hym, and whan sir Breuse hym saw with the shylde of Cornwayle he knew hym well that hit was sir Trystram. And then he fledde, and sir Trystrams folowed hym, and so sir Breuse was so horsed that he wente hys way quyte. And sir Trystram folowed hym longe affter, for he wolde fayne have bene avenged uppon hym.

30 And so whan he had longe chaced hym he saw a fayre well, and
(27) thydir he rode to repose hym, and tyed hys horse tylle a tre. And than he pulled of hys helme and waysshed hys vysayge and hys hondes, and so he felle on slepe.

And so in the meanewhyle cam a damesell that had sought sir Trys-
35 tram many wayes and dayes within thys londe. And whan she cam to the welle she loked uppon hym and had forgotyn hym as in remembraunce of sir Trystrames, but by hys horse she knew hym, that hyght Passe-Brewell, that had ben hys hors many yerys; for whan he was madde in the foreyste sir Fergus kepte hym. So thys lady, dame Brangwayne,
40 abode stylle tylle he was awake. And whan she saw hym awaked she salewed hym and he her agayne, for aythir knew other of olde acqueyn-taunce. Than she tolde sir Trystram how she had sought hym longe and brode, and there she tolde hym how she had lettirs frome the quene La Beall Isode. Then anone [sir Trystram redde them, and wete ye wel he

was gladde, for therein was many a pyteous complaynte. Than sir Trystram] seyde,

'Lady, dame Brangwayne, ye shall ryde with me tylle the turnemente be done at the Castell of Maydyns. And than shall ye beare lettirs and tydynges with you.'   5

And than sir Trystram toke hys horse and sought lodgynge, and there he mette with a good aunciaunte knyght and prayde hym to lodge with hym. Ryght so com Governayle unto sir Trystram that was glad of the commyng of the lady. And thys olde knyghtes name was sir Pellownes, and he tolde hym of the grete turnemente that shulde be at   10 the Castell of Maydyns:

'And there sir Launcelot and two and twenty knyghtes of hys blood have ordayne shyldis of Cornwayle.'

And ryght so there com one unto sir Pellownes and tolde hym that sir Persides de Bloyse was com home. Than that knyght hylde up hys   15 hondys and thanked God of hys commyng home, and there sir Pellownes tolde sir Trystram that of two yere afore he had nat sene hys son, sir Persydes.

'Sir,' seyde sir Trystramys, 'I know youre son well inowgh for a good knyght.'   20

And so one tyme sir Trystramys and sir Persydes com to their lodgyng both at onys, and so they unarmed h[e]m and put uppon them such clothyng as they had. And than thes two knyghtes ech wellcomyd other, and whan sir Persides undirstood that sir Trystram was of Cornwayle he seyde he was onys in Cornwayle: 25

'And there I justed before kynge Marke, and so hit happened me at that same day to overthrow ten knyghtis. And than cam to me sir Trystramys de Lyonas and overthrew me, and toke my lady fro me, and that shall I never forgete, but I shall remembir me and ever I se my tyme.'   30

'A,' sayde sir Trystram, 'now I undirstonde that ye hate sir Trystram. What deme you? [Wene ye] that sir Trystram ys nat able to withstonde youre malyce?'

'Yes,' seyde sir Persydes, 'I know well that sir Trystram ys a noble knyght and a muche bettir knyght than I am, yet I shall nat owghe hym   35 my good wyll.'

Ryght as they stood thus talkynge at a bay-wyndow of that castell, they sye many knyghtes ryde to and fro toward the turnemente. And than was sir Trystram ware of a lykly knyght rydyng uppon a grete black horse, and a blacke coverde shylde.   40

'What knyght ys that,' seyde sir Trystram, 'with the blacke shylde and the blacke horse?'

'I know hym well,' seyde sir Persydes, 'he ys one of the beste knyghtes of the worlde.'

'Than hit ys sir Launcelot,' seyde sir Trystramys.

'Nay,' seyde sir Persides, 'hit ys sir Palomydes that ys yett oncry-stynde.'

(28)   Than they saw muche people of the contrey salew sir Palomydes, and
5   seyde with a lowde voice,

'Jesu save the and kepe the, thou noble knyght sir Palomydes!'

And within a whyle aftir there cam a squyer of that castell that tolde sir Pellownes, that was lorde of that castell, that a knyght with a blacke shylde had smyttyn downe thirtene knyghtes.

10   'Now, fayre brother,' seyde sir Trystram unto sir Persydes, 'lat us caste on us lyght clokys, and lat us go se that play.'

'Not so,' seyde sir Persides, 'we woll nat go lyke knavys thydir, but we woll ryde lyke men and as good knyghtes to withstonde oure enemyes.'

15   So they armed them and toke their horsys and grete spearys, and thydir they rode thereas many knyghtes assayed themselff byfore the turnemente. And anone sir Palamydes saw sir Persides, and than he sente a squyar unto hym and seyde,

'Go thou to the yondir knyght with the grene shyld and therein a
20   lyon of gooldys, and say hym I requyre hym to juste with me, and telle hym that my name ys sir Palomydes.'

Whan sir Persides undirstood the rekeyst of sir Palomydes he made hym redy. And there anone they mette togydirs, but sir Persides had a falle.

25   Than sir Trystram dressed hym to be revenged uppon sir Palomydes. And that saw sir Palomydes that was redy, and so was nat sir Trystram, and toke hym at avauntayge and smote hym over hys horse tayle, whan he had no speare in hys reste.

Than sterte up sir Trystram and toke horse lyghtly, and was wrothe
30   oute of mesure, and sore ashamed of that falle. Than sir Trystramys sente unto sir Palomydes by Governayle and prayde hym to juste with hym at hys rekeyste.

'Nay,' seyde sir Palomydes, 'as at thys tyme I woll nat juste with that knyght, for I know hym bettir than he wenyth. And if he be wroth, he
35   may ryght hit to-morne at the Castell Maydyns, where he may se me and many other knyghtes.'

So with that cam sir Dynadan, and whan he saw sir Trystram wroth he lyste nat to jape, but seyde,

'Lo, sir Trystram, here may a man preve, be he never so good yet
40   may he have a falle; and he was never so wyse but he myght be over-sayne, and he rydyth well that never felle.'

So sir Trystram was passyng wrothe and seyde to sir Persides and to sir Dynadan,

'I woll revenge me!'

Ryght so as they stoode talkynge, there cam by sir Trystram a lykly knyght, rydyng passyng sobirly and hevyly, with a blacke shylde.

'What knyght ys that?' seyde sir Trystram unto sir Persides.

'I know hym well,' seyde sir Persides, 'for hys name ys sir Bryaunte of Northe Walis.'   5

And so he paste on amonge other knyghtes of North Walis. And there com in sir Launcelot de Lake with a shylde of the armys of Cornwayle, and he sente a squyer unto sir Bryaunte and requyred hym to juste with hym.

'Well,' seyde sir Bryaunte, 'sytthyn that I am requyred to juste, I woll 10 do what I may.'

And there sir Launcelot smote downe sir Bryaunte frome hys horse a grete falle. And than sir Trystram mervayled what knyght he was that bar the shylde of Cornwayle.

'Sir, whatsoever he be,' seyde sir Dynadan, 'I warraunte he ys of kyng 15 Bannys blode, whych bene knyghtes of the nobelyst proues in the worlde, for to accompte so many for so many.'

Than there cam in two knyghtes of North Galys, that one hyght sir Hew de la Mountayne, and the other sir Madok de la Mountayne, and they chalenged sir Launcelot footehote, sir Launcelot not refusynge 20 hem, but made hym redy, and with one grete speare he smote downe bothe over their horse taylis, and so sir Launcelot rode hys way.

'By the good Lorde,' seyde sir Trystram, 'he ys a good knyght that beryth the shylde of Cornwayle, and mesemyth he rydith on the beste 25 maner that ever I saw knyght ryde.'

Than the kynge of North Galis rode unto sir Palomydes and prayed him hartely for hys sake 'to juste with that knyght that hath done us of North Galis dispite.'

'Sir,' seyde sir Palomydes, 'I am full lothe to have ado with that 30 knyght, and cause why as to-morne the grete turnemente shall be. And therefore I wolde kepe myselff freyssh be my wyll.'

'Nay,' seyde the kynge of North Galis, 'I pray you, requyre hym of justis.'

'Sir,' seyde sir Palomydes, 'I woll juste at youre requeste, and requyre 35 that knyght to juste with me. And oftyn I have seyne a man at hys owne requeste have a grete falle.'

Than sir Palomydes sente unto sir Launcelot a squyre and requyred (29) hym to juste,

'Fayre felow,' seyde sir Launcelot, 'telle me thy lordis name.'   40

'Sir, my lordys name ys sir Palomydes, the good knyght.'

'In good owre,' seyde sir Launcelot, 'for there ys no knyght I saw thys seven yere that I had levir have ado withall.'

And so ayther knyghtes made them redy with two grete spearys.

'Nay,' seyde sir Dynadan, 'ye shall se that sir Palomydes woll quyte hym ryght well.'

'Hyt may be so,' seyde sir Trystram, 'but I undirtake that knyght with the shylde of Cornwayle shall gyff hym a falle.'

5 'I believe hit nat,' seyde sir Dynadan.

Ryght [so] they spurred their horsis and feautred their spearys, and aythir smote other. And sir Palomydes brake a speare uppon sir Launce-lot, and he sate and meved nat. But sir Launcelot smote hym so harde that he made hys horse to avoyde the sadill, and the stroke brake hys
10 shylde and the hawbarke, and had he nat fallyn he had be slayne.

'How now?' seyde sir Trystram. 'I wyst well by the maner of their rydynge bothe that sir Palomydes shulde have a falle.'

Ryght so sir Launcelot rode hys way, and rode to a well to drynke and repose hym. And they of North Galis aspyed hym whother he
15 wente. And than there folowed hym twelve knyghtes for to have myscheved hym for thys cause, that uppon the morne at the turne-mente at the Castell of Maydyns that he sholde nat wyn the victory.

So they com uppon sir Launcelot suddeynly, and unnethe he myght put on hys helme and take hys horse but they were in hondis with hym.
20 And than sir Launcelot gate hys speare in hys honde and ran thorow them, and there he slew a knyght and brake hys speare in hys body. Than he drew hys swerde and smote uppon the ryght honde and uppon the lyffte honde, that within a few strokis he had slayne other three knyghtes, and the remenaunte that abode he wounded hem sore, all that
25 ded abyde. Thus sir Launcelot ascaped fro hys enemyes of Northe Walis.

And than sir Launcelot rode hys way tylle a frynde, and lodged hym tylle on the morowe, for he wolde nat the firste day have ado in the turnemente bycause of hys grete laboure. And on the first day he was
30 with kynge Arthur, thereas he was sette on hye uppon a chafflet to d[i]scerne who was beste worthy of hys dedis. So sir Launcelot was with kynge Arthur and justed nat the first day.

V. THE CASTLE OF MAIDENS

HERE BEGYNNYTH THE TURNEMENT OF THE CASTEL MAYDYNS.
35 THE FYRSTE DAY.

(30) Now turne we unto sir Trystramys de Lyones that commaunded Governayle, hys servaunte, to ordayne hym a blacke shylde with none other remembraunce therein, and so sir Persides and sir Trystramys departed from sir Pellownes. And they rode erly toward the turne-
40 mente, and than they drew them to kynge Carydos syde of Scotlonde.

And anone knyghtes began the filde, what of the kynge of North
Galys syde and of kynge Carydos; and there began a grete party. Than
there was hurlyng and russhyng. Ryght so cam in sir Persides and sir
Trystram, and so they ded fare that day that they put the kyng of
North Galis abacke.   5

Than cam in sir Bleoberys de Ganys and sir Gaherys with them of
North Galis. And than was sir Persides smyttyn adowne and allmoste
slayne, for mo than forty horsemen wente over hym. For sir Bleoberys
ded grete dedes of armys, and sir Gaherys fayled hym not.

Whan sir Tristram behylde them and sye them do such dedis of   10
armys he mervayled what they were. Also sir Trystram thought shame
that sir Persides was so done to. And than he gate a grete speare in hys
honde, and rode to sir Gaherys and smote hym down frome hys
horse.

And than sir Bleoberys was wrothe, and gate a speare and rode   15
ayenste sir Trystram in grete ire. And there sir Trystram smote sir
Bleoberys frome hys horse. So than the Kynge with the Hondred
Knyghtes was wrothe, and he horsed sir Bleoberys and sir Gaherys
agayne, and there began a grete medlé. And ever sir Trystram hylde
them passyng shorte, and ever sir Bleoberys was passyng bysy upon   20
sir Trystram.

And there cam in sir Dynadan ayenst sir Trystram, and sir Trystram
gaff hym such a buffette that he sowned uppon hys horse. And so anone
sir Dynadan cam to sir Trystram and seyde,

'Sir, I know the bettir than thou wenyst, but here I promyse the my   25
trouth, I woll never com agaynst the more, for I promyse the that
swerde of thyne shall never com on my helme.'

So with that com sir Bleoberys, and sir Trystram gaff hym such a
buffett that downe he abaysshed hys hede; and than he raught hym so
sore by the helme that he pulled hym undir hys [hors] feete. And than 30
kyng Arthure blew to lodgyng. Than sir Tryström departed to hys
pavylion, and sir Dynadan rode with hym, and sir Persides.

And kynge Arthure than, and the kyngis uppon bothe partyes,
mervayled what knyght that was with the blacke shylde. Many knyghtis
seyde their avyse; and som knew hym for sir Trystram and hylde their 35
peace and wolde nat say. So that firste day kynge Arthure and all the
kynges and lordis that were juges gaff sir Trystram the pryce, howbehyt
they knew hym nat, but named hym the Knyght with the Blacke
Shylde.

Than uppon the morne sir Palomydes returned from the kynge of   40 (31)
Northe Galis, and rode to kynge Arthurs syde, where was kynge
Carados and the kynge of Irelonde, and sir Launcelottis kynne, and sir
Gawaynes kynne. So sir Palomydes sent the damesell unto sir Trystram
that he sente to seke hym whan he was oute of hys mynde in the foreyst,

and this damesell asked sir Trystramys what was hys name and what he was.

'As for that, telle sir Palomydes that he shall nat wete as at thys tyme, unto the tyme I have brokyn two spearis uppon hym. But lat hym wete
5 thys much, that I am the same knyght that he smote downe in the over-evenynge at the turnemente, and telle hym playnly on what party that he be, I woll be of the contrary party.'

'Sir,' seyde the damesell, 'ye shall undirstonde that sir Palomydes woll be on kynge Arthurs party where the moste noble knyghtes of the
10 worlde be.'

'In the name of God,' seyde sir Trystram, 'than woll I be with the kynge of Northe Galis, because of sir Palomydes woll be on kynge Arthurs syde, and ellis I wolde nat but for hys sake.'

So whan kyng Arthure was com they blew unto the fylde, and than
15 there began a grete party. And so kynge Carados justed with the Kynge with the Hondred Knyghtes, and there kynge Carados had a falle. Than was there hurlyng and russhynge. And ryght so com in knyghtes of kyng Arthurs, and they bare on bak the kynge of North Galis knyghtes.

Than sir Trystram cam in, and began so rowghly and so bygly that
20 there was none myght withstonde hym, and thus he endured longe. And at the laste by fortune he felle amonge the felyshyp of kyng Ban. So there fylle uppon hym sir Bors de Ganys, and sir Ector de Marys, and sir Blamour de Ganys, and many othir knyghtes.

And than sir Trystram smote on the ryght honde and on the lyffte
25 honde, that all lordis and ladyes spake of hys noble dedis. But at the last sir Trystram sholde have had the wars, had nat the Kynge with the Hondred Knyghtes bene. And than he cam with hys felyshyp and rescowed sir Trystram, and brought hym away frome the knyghtes that bare the shyldis of Cornwayle.

30 And than sir Trystram saw another felyship by themselff, and there was a forty knyghtes togydir, and sir Kay le Senescial was their governoure. Than sir Trystram rode in amongyst them, and there he smote downe sir Kay frome hys horse, and there he fared amonge tho knyghtis as a grehounde amonge conyes.

35 Than sir Launcelot founde a knyght that was sore wounded uppon the hede.

'Sir,' seyde sir Launcelot, 'who wounded you so sore?'

'Sir,' he seyde, 'a knyght that bearyth a blacke shylde. And I may curse the tyme that ever I mette with hym, for he ys a devyll and no
40 man.'

So sir Launcelot departed frome hym, and thought to mete with sir Trystram, and so he rode with hys swerde idrawyn in hys honde to seke sir Trystram. And than he aspyed hym hurlynge here and there, and at every stroke sir Trystram well-nyghe smote downe a knyght.

'A! mercy Jesu!' seyde sir Launcelot, 'syth the firste tyme that ever I bare armys saw I never one knyght do so mervaylous dedys of armys. And if I sholde,' seyde sir Launcelot to hymselff, 'sette uppon thys knyght now, I ded shame to myselff.'

And therewithall sir Launcelot put up hys swerde.   5

And than the Kynge with the Hondred Knyghtes, and an hondred mo of North Walis, sette uppon the twenty knyghtes of sir Launce-lottes kynne, and they twenty knyghtes hylde them ever togydir as wylde swyne, and none wolde fayle other. So sir Trystram, whan he behylde the nobles of thes twenty knyghtes, he mervayled of their good 10 dedys, for he saw by their fare and rule that they had levyr dye than to avoyde the fylde.

'Now, Jesu,' seyde sir Trystram, 'well may [h]e be called valyaunte and full of proues that hath such a sorte of noble knyghtes unto hys kynne. And full lyke ys he to be a nobleman that ys their leder and 15 governoure.'

He mente hit by sir Launcelot du Lake.

So whan sir Trystram had beholde them longe he thought s[h]ame to se two hondred knyghtes batteryng uppon twenty knyghtes. Than sir Trystram rode unto the Kynge with the Hondred Knyghtes and 20 seyde,

'Sir, leve your fyghtynge with tho twenty knyghtes, for ye wynne no worship of them, ye be so many and they so feaw. And wyte you well, they woll nat oute of the fylde, I se by their chere and countenaunce, [and] worship get you none and ye sle them. Therefore leve your 25 fyghtynge with them, for I, to encrese my worship, I woll ryde unto the twenty knyghtes and helpe them with all my myght and power.'

'Nay,' seyde the Kynge with the Hondred Knyghtes, 'ye shall nat do so. Now I se youre corayge and curtesye, I woll withdraw my knyghtes for youre plesure, for evermore o good knyght woll favoure another, 30 and lyke woll draw to lyke.'

Than the Kynge with the Hondred Knyghtes withdrew hys knyghtes. (32)

And all thys whyle and longe tofore sir Launcelot had wacched uppon sir Trystram in veary purpose to have felyshipped with hym. And than suddeynly sir Trystram, sir Dynadan and Governayle, hys 35 man, rode their way into the foreyste, that no man perceyved where they wente.

So than kynge Arthure blew unto lodgynge, and gaff the kynge of North Galis the pryce, bycause sir Trystram was uppon hys syde. Than sir Launcelot rode here and there as wode as a lyon that faughted hys 40 fylle, because he had loste sir Trystram, and so he returned unto kynge Arthure.

And than all the felde was in a noyse, that with the wynde hit myght be harde two myle how the lordys and ladyes cryed:

'The Knyght with the Blacke Shylde hath won the fylde!'

'Alas,' seyde kynge Arthure, 'where ys that knyght becom? Hit ys shame to all tho in the fylde so to lette hym ascape away frome you, but with jantylnes and curtesye ye myght have brought hym unto me to
5 thys Castell of Maydyns.'

Than kynge Arthur wente to hys knyghtes and comforted them, and seyde,

'My fayre felowis, be nat dismayde thoughe ye have loste the fylde thys day.' And many were hurte and sore wounded, and many were
10 hole. 'My felowys,' seyde kyng Arthur, 'loke that ye be of good chere, for to-morn I woll be in the fylde with you and revenge you of youre enemyes.'

So that nyght kynge Arthure and hys knyghtes reposed themselff.

So the damesell that com frome La Beall Isod unto sir Trystram, all
15 the whyle the turnement was a-doyng she was with quyene Gwenyvere, and ever the quene asked her for what cause she cam into that contrey.

'Madame,' she answerde, 'I com for none other cause but frome my [lady], La Beall Isode, to wete of youre wellfare.'
20 For in no wyse she wold nat telle the quene that she cam for sir Trystramys sake.

So thys lady, dame Brangwayn, toke hir leve of quene Gwenyver, and she rode aftir sir Trystram. And as she rode thorow the foreyste she harde a grete cry. Than she commaunded hir squyar to go into that
25 foreyste to wyte what was that noyse. And so he cam to a welle, and there he founde a knyght bounden tyll a tre, cryyng as he had bene woode, and his horse and hys harneys stondyng by hym.

And whan he aspyed the squyar, with a brayde he brake hymself lowse, and toke hys swerde in hys honde and ran to have slayne that
30 squyer. Than he toke hys horse and fledde to dame Brangwayne and tolde hir of hys adventure. Than she rode unto sir Trystramys pavylon, and tolde sir Trystram what adventure she had founde in the foreyste.

'Alas,' seyde sir Trystram, 'uppon my hede, there ys som good knyght at myschyff.'
35 Than sir Trystram toke hys horse and hys swerde, and rode thyder, and there he harde how the knyght complayned unto hymself and sayde,

'I, wofull knyght, sir Palomydes! What mysseadventure befallith me that thus am defoyled with falsehed and treson, thorow sir Bors and
40 sir Ector! Alas!' he seyde, 'why lyve I so longe?'

And than he gate his swerde in hys honde and made many straunge sygnes and tokyns, and so thorow the rageynge he threw hys swerd in that fountayne. Than sir Palomydes wayled and wrange hys hondys, and at the laste, for pure sorow, he ran into that fountayne and sought

aftir hys swerde. Than sir Trystram saw that, and ran uppon sir Palomydes and hylde hym in hys armys faste.

'What art thou,' seyde sir Palomydes, 'that holdith me so?'

'I am a man of thys foreyste that wold the none harme.'

'Alas!' seyde sir Palomydes, 'I may never wyn worship where sir 5
Trystram ys, for ever where he ys and I be, there gete I no worshyp.
And yf he be away, for the moste party I have the gre, onles that sir
Launcelot be there, othir ellis sir Lamerok.' Than sir Palomydes sayde,
'Onys in Irelonde sir Trystram put me to the wors, and anothir tyme
in Cornwayle and in other placis in thys londe.' 10

'What wolde ye do,' seyde sir Trystram, 'and ye had sir Trystram?'

'I wolde fyght with hym,' seyde sir Palomydes, 'and ease my harte
uppon hym. And yet, to say the sothe, sir Trystram ys the jantyllyste
knyght in thys worlde lyvynge.'

'Sir, what woll ye do?' seyde sir Trystram, 'woll ye go with me to 15
youre lodgyng?'

'Nay,' he seyde, 'to the Kynge with the Hondred Knyghtes, for he
rescowed me frome sir Bors de Ganys and sir Ector, and ellis had I bene
slayne traytourly.'

And sir Trystram seyde hym such kynde wordys that sir Palomydes 20
wente with hym to hys lodgynge. Than Governayle wente tofore and
charged dame Brangwayne to go oute of the way to hir lodgynge, 'and
byd ye sir Persides that he make hym no quarels.'

And so they rode togedirs tyll they cam to sir Trystramys pavylon,
and there had sir Palomydes all the chere that myght be had all that 25
nyght. But in no wyse sir Trystram myght nat be knowyn with sir
Palomydes. And so aftir souper they yeode to reste, and sir Trystram
for grete travayle slepte tylle hit was day. And sir Palomydes myght nat
slepe for angwysshe, and so in the dawnyng of the day he toke hys
horse prevayly and rode hys way unto Gaherys and to sir Sagramoure 30
le Desirous, where the[y] were in their pavylons, for they three were
felowis at the begynnynge of the turnemente.

And than uppon the morne the kynge blew unto the turnemente
uppon the third day.

So the kynge of Northe Galis and the Kynge of the Hondred 35 (33)
Knyghtes, they two encountird with kynge Carados and the kynge of
Irelonde. And there the Kynge with the Hondred Knyghtes smote
downe kyng Carados, and the kynge of North Galis smote downe the
kynge of Irelonde. So with that cam in sir Palomydes, and he made
grete worke, for by hys endented shylde he was well knowyn. So there 40
cam in kynge Arthur and ded grete dedis of armys togydirs, and put the
kynge of North Galis and the Kyng with the Hondred Knyghtes to the
wars.

So with [this] cam in sir Trystram with hys blak shylde, and anone

he justed with sir Palomydes, and there by fyne force sir Trystram smote
sir Palomydes over hys horse croupe. Than kynge Arthure cryed,

'Knyght with the blacke shylde, make the redy to me!'

And in the same wyse sir Trystram smote kynge Arthure.

5   And than by forse of kynge Arthurs knyghtes the kynge and sir
Palomydes were horsed agayne. Than kynge Arthur with a grete egir
harte, he gate a grete speare in hys honde, and there uppon the one syde
he smote sir Trystram over hys horse.

    Than foote-hote sir Palomydes cam uppon sir Trystram, as he was
10 uppon foote, to have overryddyn hym. Than sir Trystram was ware
off hym, and stowped a lytyll asyde, and with grete ire he gate hym by
the arme and pulled hym downe frome hys horse.

    Than sir Palomydes lyghtly arose, and [they] daysshed togydirs with
theire swerdys myghtyly, that many kynges, quenys, lordys and ladyes
15 stoode and behelde them. And at the last sir Trystram smote sir Palomydes uppon the helme three myghty strokes, and at every stroke that
he gaff he seyde,

'Have thys for sir Trystramys sake!'

And with that sir Palomydes felle to the erthe grovelynge.

20   Than cam the Kynge of the Hondred Knyghtes and brought sir
Trystram an horse, and so was he horsed agayne. And by that tyme
was sir Palomydes horsed, and with grete ire he justed uppon sir Trystram with hys speare as hit was in the reyste, and gaff hym a grete dayssh
with hys swerde. Than sir Trystram avoyded hys speare, and gate hym
25 by the nek with hys bothe hondis, and pulled hym clene oute of hys
sadle, and so he bare hym afore hym the lengthe of ten spearys, and
than he lete hym falle at hys adventure.

    Than sir Trystram was ware of kynge Arthure with a naked swerde
in hys honde, and with hys speare sir Trystram ran uppon kyng Arthure.
30 And than kyng Arthure boldely abode hym, and with hys swerde he
smote ato hys speare. And therewithall sir Trystram was astooned, and
so kynge Arthure gaff hym three or four strokis or he myght gete oute
hys swerde. And so sir Trystram drew hys swerde, and aythir of them
assayled othir passyng harde, and with that the grete prease departed.
35   Than sir Trystram rode here and there and ded hys grete payne, that
a twelve of the good knyghtes of the bloode of kynge Ban that were of
sir Launcelottis [kyn] that day sir Trystram smote downe, that all the
estatis mervayled of their grete dedis, and all people [cryede] uppon the
knyght with the blacke shylde.

(34) 40   So thys cry was so large that sir Launcelot harde hit, and than he
gate a grete speare in hys honde and cam towardis the cry. Than sir
Launcelot cryed,

'Knyght with the blacke shylde, make ye redy to juste with me!'

Whan sir Trystram harde hym sey so, he gate hys speare in hys honde, and ayther abeysed their hedys downe lowe and cam togydir as thundir, that sir Trystrams speare brake in pecis. And sir Launcelot by male-fortune stroke sir Trystram on the syde a depe wounde nyghe to the dethe. But yet sir Trystram avoyded nat hys sadyll, and so the speare brake therewithall. And yete sir Trystram gate oute hys swerde, and he 5 russhed to sir Launcelot and gaff hym three grete strokes uppon the helme, that the fyre sprange oute, that sir Launcelot abeysed hys hede low toward hys sadyll-bow. And so therewithall Trystram departed frome the fylde, for he felte hym so wounded that he wente he sholde have dyed. And sir Dynadan aspyed hym and folowed hym into the 10 foreyste.

Than sir Launcelot abode and ded mervaylous dedys.

So whan sir Trystram was departed by the foreystis syde, he alyght and unlaced hys harneys and freysshid hys wounde. Than wente sir Dynadan that he sholde have dyed, and wepte. 15

'Nay, nay,' seyde sir Trystram, 'never drede you, sir Dynadan, for I am harte-hole, and of thys wounde I shall sone be hole, by the mercy of God!'

And anone sir Dynadan was ware where cam sir Palomydes rydynge streyte uppon them. Than sir Trystram was ware that sir Palomydes 20 com to have destroyed hym, and so sir Dynadan gaff hym warnynge and seyde,

'Sir Trystram, my lorde, ye ar so sore wounded that ye may nat have ado with hym. Therefore I woll ryde agaynste hym and do to hym what I may, and yf I be slayne ye may pray for my soule. And so in the meane- 25 whyle ye may withdraw you and go into the castell or into the foreyste, that he shall nat mete with you.'

Sir Trystram smyled and seyde,

'I thanke you, sir Dynadan, ⌐of your good wylle⌐, but ye shall undir-stond that I am able to handyll hym.' 30

And anone hastely he armed hym, and toke hys horse and a grete speare in hys honde, and seyde to sir Dynadan 'Adew', and rode to-ward sir Palomydes a soffte pace.

Whan sir Palomydes saw hym he alyght and made a countenaunce to amende hys horse, but he ded hit for thys cause, for he abode sir 35 Gaherys that cam aftir hym. And whan he was com he rode towarde sir Trystram.

Than sir Trystram sente unto sir Palomydes and requyred hym to juste with hym; and if he smote downe sir Palomydes he wolde do no more to hym, and if sir Palomydes smote downe sir Trystram, he bade 40 hym do hys utteraunce. And so they were accorded and mette togydirs.

And sir Trystram smote downe sir Palomydes, that he had a vylaunce falle and lay stylle as he had bene dede. And than sir Trystram ran uppon sir Gaherys, and he wold nat have justed, but whethir he wolde or wolde nat sir Trystram smote hym over hys horse croupe, that he lay stylle. And sir Trystram rode hys way and lefft sir Persides hys squyar within the pavelons.

And sir Trystram and sir Dynadan rode to an olde knyghtes place to lodge them; and thys olde knyght had fyve sonnes at the turnement that prayde God hartely for their commynge home. And so, as the Freynshe booke sayeth, they com home all fyve well beatyn.

And whan sir Trystram departed into the foreyste sir Launcelot hylde allwayes the stowre lyke harde, as a man araged that toke none hede to hymselff. And wyte you well there was many a noble knyght ayenste hym. And whan kyng Arthure saw sir Launcelot do so mervaylous dedis of armys he than armed hym and toke hys horse and hys armour, and rode into the fylde to helpe sir Launcelot, and so many knyght[es] cam with kynge Arthur.

And to make shorte tale in conclusion, the kyng of North Galis and the Kynge of the Hondred Knyghtes were put to the wars. And bycause sir Launcelot abode and was the laste in the fylde, the pryse was gyvyn hym. But sir Launcelot, nother for kynge, quene, nother knyght, wolde thereoff. And where the cry was cryed thorow the fylde, 'Sir Launcelot hath wonne the filde thys day!'

Sir Launcelot made another cry contrary,

'Sir Trystram hath won the fylde, for he began firste, and lengyst hylde on, and so hathe he done the firste day, the secunde, and the thirde day!'

(35) Than all the astatis and degrees, hyghe and lowe, seyde [of] sir Launcelot grete worship for the honoure that he ded to sir Trystram, and for the honour doyng by sir Launcelot he was at that tyme more praysed and renowmed than [and] he had overthrowyn fyve hondred knyghtes. And all the peple hole for hys jantilnes, firste the astatis, hyghe and lowe, and after the comynalté, at onys cryed,

'Sir Launcelot hath won the gre, whosoever sayth nay!'

Than was sir Launcelot wrothe and ashamed, and so therewithall he rode to kynge Arthure.

'Alas,' seyde the kynge, 'we ar all dismayde that sir Trystram ys thus departed frome us! Pardé,' seyde kynge Arthur, 'he ys one of the nobelyst knyghtes that ever I saw holde speare in honde or swerde, and the moste curtayse knyght in hys fyghtyng. For full harde I sye hym bestad,' seyde kynge Arthure, 'whan he smote sir Palomydes upon the helme thryse, that he abaysshed hys helme with hys strokis. And also he seyde "here ys a stroke for sir Trystram", and thus he seyde thryse.'

Than kynge Arthure and sir Launcelot and sir Dodynas le Saveage toke their horsis to seke aftir sir Trystram. And by the meanys of sir Persides he had tolde kynge Arthure where sir Trystramys pavylyon was. But whan they cam there, sir Trystram and sir Dynadan was gone.

Than kynge Arthur and sir Launcelot was hevy and returned ayen to the Castell Maydyns makyng grete dole for the hurte of sir Trystram, and hys suddeyne departynge.

'So God me helpe,' seyde kynge Arthur, 'I am more hevy that I can nat mete with hym than I am for all the hurtys that all my knyghtes have had at the turnement.'

And so furthwith cam sir Gaherys and told kynge Arthur how sir Trystram had smytten downe sir Palomydes, and hit was at hys owne requeste.

'Alas,' seyde kynge Arthur, 'that was grete dishonoure to sir Palomydes, inasmuch as sir Trystram was so sore wounded. And may we all, kyngis and knyghtes and men of worship, sey that sir Trystram may be called a [noble] knyght and one of the beste knyghtes that ever y saw dayes of my lyff. For I woll that ye all, kyngis and knyghtes, know,' seyde kynge Arthur, 'that I never saw knyght do so mervaylously as he hath done thes three dayes, for he was the firste that began, and the lengyst that hylde on, save thys laste day; and thoughe he were hurte hit was a manly adventure of two noble knyghtes. And whan two noble men encountir, nedis muste the tone have the worse, lyke as God wyll suffir at that tyme.'

'Sir, as for me,' seyde sir Launcelot, 'for all the londys that ever my fadir leffte I wolde nat have hurt sir Trystram and I had knowyn hym at that tyme that I hurte hym: for I saw nat hys shylde. For and I had seyne hys blacke shylde, I wolde nat have medled with hym for many causis,' seyde sir Launcelot. 'For but late he ded as muche for me as ever ded knyght, and that ys well knowyn, that he had ado with thirty knyghtes and no helpe only save sir Dynadan. And one thynge shall I promyse you,' seyde sir Launcelot, 'sir Palomydes shall repente hit, as in hys unknyghtly delynge so for to folow that noble knyght that I be mysfortune hurte hym thus.'

So sir Launcelot seyd all the worship that myght be spokyn by sir Trystram.

Than kyng Arthure made a grete feste to all that wolde com.

And thus we lat passe kynge Arthure, and a lityll we woll turne unto sir Palomydes, that aftir he had a falle of sir Trystram he was nyghehonde araged oute of hys wytte for despite of sir Trystram, and so he folowed hym by adventure. And as he cam by a ryver, in hys woodnes he wolde have made hys horse to have lopyn over the watir, and the horse fayled footyng and felle in the ryver, wherefore sir Palomydes was adrad leste he shulde have bene drowned. And than he avoyde hys horse and swam to the londe, and lete hys horse go downe by adventure. And whan he cam to the londe he toke of hys harnys and sate romynge and cryynge as a man oute of hys mynde.

Ryght so cam a damessell evyn by sir Palomydes, that was sente [fro]

sir Gawayne and hys brothir unto sir Mordred that lay syke in the same
place with that olde knyght where sir Trystram was. For, as the booke
seythe, sir Persides hurte so sir Mordred a ten dayes afore, and had hit
nat bene for the love of sir Gawayne and hys brethirn, sir Persides had
5 slayne sir Mordred.

And so this damysell cam by sir Palomydes, and he and she had
langage togyder, whych pleased neythir of them. And so thys damesell
rode her wayes tyll she cam to that olde knyghtes place, and there she
tolde that olde knyght how she mette with the woodist knyght by
10 adventure that ever she mette withall.

'What bare he in hys shylde?' seyde sir Trystram.

'Sir, hit was endented with whyght and blacke,' seyde the damesell.

'A,' seyde sir Trystram, 'that was Palamydes, the good knyght. For
well I know hym,' seyde sir Trystram, 'for one of the beste knyghtes
15 lyvyng in thys realme.'

Than that olde knyght toke a lityll hakeney and rode for sir Palomydes, and brought hym unto hys owne maner. And full well knew sir
Trystram hym, but he sayde but lityll.

For at that tyme sir Trystram was walkyng uppon hys feete and well
20 amended of hi[s] hurtis, and allwayes whan sir Palomydes saw sir
Trystram he wolde beholde hym full mervaylously, and ever hym
semed that he had sene hym. Than wolde he sey unto sir Dynadan,

'And ever I may mete with sir Trystram, he shall nat escape myne
hondis.'

25 'I mervayle,' seyde sir Dynadan, 'that ye do boste behynde sir Trystram so, for hit ys but late that he was in youre hondys and ye in hys
hondis. Why wolde ye nat holde hym whan ye had hym? For I saw myselff twyse or thryse that ye gate but lytyll worship of sir Trystram.'

Than was sir Palomydes ashamed. So leve we them a lityll whyle in
30 the castell with the olde knyght sir Darras.

Now shall we speke of kynge Arthure, that seyde to sir Launcelot,

'Had nat ye bene, we had nat loste sir Trystram, for he was here dayly
unto the tyme ye mette with hym. And in an evyll tyme,' seyde kynge
Arthure, 'ye encountred with hym.'

35 'My lorde Arthure,' seyde sir Launcelot, 'ye shall undirstonde the
cause. Ye put now uppon me that I sholde be causer of hys departicion;
God knowith hit was ayenste my wyll! But whan men bene hote in
dedis of armys, oftyn hit ys seyne they hurte their frendis as well as their
foys. And, my lorde,' seyde sir Launcelot, 'ye shall undirstonde that sir
40 Trystram ys a man that I am ryght lothe to offende to, for he hath done
more for me than ever y ded for hym as yet.'

But than sir Launcelot mad brynge forthe a boke, and than seyde
sir Launcelot,

'Here we ar ten knyghtes that woll swere uppon thys booke never

to reste one nyght where we reste another thys twelve-month, untyll
that we fynde sir Trystram. And as for me,' seyde sir Launcelot, 'I
promyse you uppon thys booke that, and I may mete with hym, other
with fayrenes othir with fowlnes I shall brynge hym to thys courte,
other elles I shall dye therefore.'   5

And the namys of thes ten knyghtes that had undirtake thys queste
[were these folowynge]: first was sir Launcelot; sir Ector de Marys, sir
Bors de Ganys, and sir Bleoberys, sir Blamour de Ganys, sir Lucan de
Butler, sir Uwayne, sir Galyhud, sir Lyonel, and sir Galyodyn. So thes
ten noble knyghtes departed frome the courte of kynge Arthur, and so 10
they rode uppon theire queste togydirs tyll they com to a crosse where
departed four wayes, and there departed the felyship in four to seke sir
Trystram.

And as sir Launcelot rode, by adventure he mette with dame Brangwayne that was sente into that contrey to seke sir Trystram, and she 15
fled as faste as her palfrey myght go. So sir Launcelot mette with her
and asked why she fled.

'A, fayre knyght,' seyde dame Brangwayne, 'I fle for drede of my
lyff, for here folowith me sir Breuse Saunz Pité to sle me.'

'Holde you nyghe me,' seyde sir Launcelot.   20

And whan he sye sir Breuse Saunz Pité ⟨he⟩ cryed unto hym and
seyde,

'False knyght, destroyer of ladyes and damesels, now thy laste dayes
be com!'

Whan sir Breuse Saunce Pité saw sir Launcelottis shylde he knew hit 25
well, for at that tyme he bare nat the shylde of Cornwayle, but he bare
hys owne. And than sir Breuse returned and fled, and sir Launcelot
folowed aftir hym. But sir Breuse was so well horsed that whan hym
lyst to fle he myght fle whan he wolde and abyde whan he wolde. And
than sir Launcelot returned unto dame Brangwayne, and [she] thanked 30
sir Launcelot of hys curtesy and grete laboure.

Now woll we speke of sir Lucan de Butlere, that by fortune he cam (37)
rydynge to the same place thereas was sir Trystram, and in he cam for
none other entente but to aske herberow. Than the porter asked what
was hys name.   35

'Sir, telle youre lorde that my name ys sir Lucan de Butler, a knyght
of the Rounde Table.'

So the porter yode unto sir Darras, lorde of the place, and tolde hym
who was there to aske herberow.

'Nay, nay,' seyde sir Daname that was nevew unto sir Darras, 'sey   40
hym that he shall nat be lodged here. But lat hym wete that I, sir
Danam, woll mete with hym anone, and byd hym make hym redy.'

So sir Danam com forthe on horseback, and there they met togydirs
with spearys. And sir Lucan smote downe sir Danam over hys horse

croupe, and than he fled into that place, and sir Lucan rode aftir hym [and asked after hym] many tymys.

Than sir Dynadan seyde to sir Trystram,

'Hit ys shame to se the lordys cousyne of thys place defoyled.'

5   'Abyde,' seyde sir Trystram, 'and I shall redresse hit.'

And in the meanewhyle sir Dynadan was on horsebacke, and he justed with sir Lucan, and he smote sir Dynadan thorow the thycke of [the] thyghe, and so he rode hys way. And sir Trystram was wroth that sir Dynadan was hurte, and he folowed aftir and thought to avenge 10 hym. And within a whyle he overtoke sir Lucan and bade hym turne, and so they mette togydirs. And sir Trystram hurte sir Lucane passynge sore and gaff hym a falle.

So with that com sir Uwayne, a jantill knyght, and whan he saw sir Lucan so hurte he called to sir Trystram to juste.

15   'Fayre knyght,' seyde sir Trystram, 'telle me youre name, I requyre you.'

'Sir knyght, wite you well my name ys sir Uwayne, le Fyze de Roy Ureyne.'

'A,' seyde sir Trystram, 'be my wylle I wolde nat have ado with you 20 at no tyme.'

'Sir, ye shall nat do so,' seyde sir Uwayne, 'but ye shall have ado with me.'

And than sir Trystram saw none other boote but rode ayenste hym, and overthrew sir Uwayne and hurte hym in the syde, and so he de-25 parted unto hys lodgynge agayne.

And whan sir Danam undirstood that sir Trystram had hurte sir Lucan he wolde have ryddyn aftir hym for to have slayne hym. But sir Trystram wolde nat suffir hym. Than sir Uwayne lete ordayne an horse-litter, and brought sir Lucan to the abbay of Ganys. And the castell 30 thereby hyght the Castell off Ganys, of the whych sir Bleoberys was lorde. And at that castell sir Launcelot promysed all hys felowis there to mete in the queste of sir Trystram.

So whan sir Trystram was com to hys lodgynge, there cam a damsell that tolde sir Darras that three of his sunnys were slayne at that turne-35 mente, and two grevously wounded so that they were never lyke to helpe themselff: and all thys was done by a noble knyght that bare a blacke shylde, and that was he that bare the pryce.

Than cam one and tolde sir Darras that the same knyght was within hys courte that bare the blacke shylde. Than sir Darras yode unto sir 40 Trystramys chambir, and there he founde hys shylde and shewed hit to the damesell.

'A, sir,' seyde the damesell, 'thys same ys he that slewe youre three sunnys.'

Than withoute ony taryynge sir Darras put sir Trystram, sir

Palomydes, and sir Dynadan within a stronge preson, and there sir
Trystram was lyke to have dyed of grete syknes. And every day sir
Palomydes wolde repreve sir Trystram of olde hate betwyxt them, and
ever sir Trystram spake fayre and seyde lytyll. But whan sir Palomydes
se that sir Trystram was falle in syknes, than was he hevy for hym and 5
comforted hym in all the beste wyse he coude.

And, as the Freynshe booke sayth, there cam fourty knyghtes to sir
Darras that were of hys owne kynne, and they wolde have slayne sir
Trystram and hys felowis, but sir Darras wolde nat [suffre that,] but
ʳkepteˡ them in preson, and mete and drynke they had. 10

So sir Trystram endured there grete payne, for syknes had undirtake
hym, and that ys the grettist payne a presoner may have. For all the
whyle a presonere may have hys helth of body, he may endure undir
the mercy of God and in hope of good delyveraunce; but whan syknes
towchith a presoners body, than may a presonere say all welth ys hym 15
berauffte, and than hath he cause to wayle and wepe. Ryght so ded sir
Trystram whan syknes had undirtake hym, for than he toke such sorow
that he had allmoste slayne hymselff.

VI. THE ROUND TABLE

Now woll we speke and leve sir Trystram, sir Palomydes, and sir 20 (38)
Dynadan in preson, and speke we of othir knyghtes that sought aftir
sir Trystram many dyverse partyes of thys londe.

And some yode into Cornwayle, and by adventure sir Gaherys,
nevew unto kynge Arthure, cam unto kynge Marke. And there he was
well resseyved and sate at kynge Markys owne table and at hys owne 25
messe. Than kynge Marke asked sir Gaherys what tydynges there was
within the realme of Logrys.

'Sir,' seyde sir Gaherys, 'the kynge regnys as a noble knyght, and
now but late there was a grete justis and turnemente that ever y saw
within thys reallme of Logres, and the moste nobelyste knyghtes were 30
at that justis. But there was one knyght that ded mervaylously three
dayes, and he bare a blacke shylde, and on all the knyghtes that ever
y saw he preved the beste knyght.'

'That was,' seyde kynge Marke, 'sir Launcelot, other ellis sir Palomydes the paynym.' 35

'Not so,' seyde sir Gaherys, 'for they were both of the contrary party
agaynste the knyght with the blacke shylde.'

'Than was hit sir Trystram de Lyones,' seyde [the] kynge.

And therewithall he smote downe hys hede, and in hys harte he
feryd sore that sir Trystram sholde gete hym such worship in the 40

realme of Logrys wherethorow hymselff shuld nat be able to withstonde hym.

Thus sir Gaherys had grete chere with kynge Marke and with the quene. La Beall Isode was glad of his wordis, for well she wyste by hys dedis and maners that hit was sir Trystram.

And than the knyge made a feste royall, and to that feste cam sir Uwayne le Fyze de Roy Urayne (and som called hym sir Uwayne le Blaunche Maynes). And thys sir Uwayne chalenged all the knyghtes of Cornwayle. Than was the kynge wood wrothe that he had [no] knyghtes to answere hym.

Than sir Andred, nevew unto kynge Marke, lepe up and sayde,

'I woll encountir with sir Uwayne.'

Than he yode and armyd hym, and horsed hym in the beste maner. And there sir Uwayne mette with sir Andred and smote hym downe, that he sowned on the erthe. Than was kynge Marke sory and wrot[h]e oute of mesure that he had no knyght to revenge hys nevew, sir Andret. So the kynge called unto hym sir Dynas le Senesciall, and prayde hym for hys sake to take uppon hym for to juste with sir Uwayne.

'Sir,' seyd sir Dynas, 'I am full lothe to have ado with ony of the knyghtes of the Rounde Table.'

'Yet, for my love, take uppon you for to juste.'

So sir Dynas made hym redy to juste, and anone they encountirde togydirs with grete spearys. But sir Dynas was overthrowyn, horse and man, a grete falle. Who was wroth than but kynge Marke!

'Alas!' he seyde, 'have I no knyght that woll encounter with yondir knyght?'

'Sir,' seyde sir Gaherys, 'for youre sake I woll just.'

So sir Gaherys made hym redy, and whan he was armed he rode into the fylde. And whan sir Uwayne saw sir Gaherys shylde he rode to hym and seyde,

'Sir, ye do nat youre parte, for the firste tyme that ever ye were made knyght of the Rounde Table ye sware that ye shuld nat have ado with none of youre felyship wyttyngly. And, pardé, sir Gaherys, ye know me well inow by my shylde, and so do I know you by youre shylde. And thaughe ye wolde breke youre othe, I woll nat breke myne. For there ys nat one here nother ye that shall thynk I am aferde of you, but that I durst ryght well have ado with you. And yet we be syster sonnys!'

Than was sir Gaherys ashamed. And so therewithall every knyght wente their way, and sir Uwayne rode oute of the contrey.

Than kynge Marke armed hym and toke hys horse and hys speare with a squyar with hym, and than he rode afore sir Uwayne and suddeynly, at a gap, he ran uppon hym as he that was nat ware of hym.

And there he smote hym allmoste thorow the body, and so there leffte hym.

So within a whyle there cam sir Kay and founde sir Uwayne, and asked hym how he was hurte.

'I wote nat,' seyde sir Uwayne, 'why nother wherefore, but by treson, 5
I am sure, I gate thys hurte. For here cam a knyght suddeynly uppon me or that I was ware, and suddeynly hurte me.'

Than there was com sir Andred to seke kyng Marke.

'Thou traytoure knyght!' seyde sir Kay, 'and I wyst hit were thou that thus traytourely haste hurte thys noble knyght, thou shuldist never 10
passe my hondys!'

'Sir,' seyed sir Andred, 'I ded never hurte hym, and that I reporte me to hymselff.'

'Fy on you, false knyghtes of Cornwayle,' seyde sir Kay, 'for ye [are] naught worth!'   15

So sir Kay made cary sir Uwayne to the Abbay of the Black Crosse, and the[re] was he heled.

Than sir Gaherys toke hys leve of kyng Marke, but or he departed he seyde,

'Sir kynge, ye ded a fowle shame whan ye flemyd sir Trystram oute of 20
thys contrey, for ye nedid nat to have doughted no knyght and he had bene here.'

And so he departed.

Than there cam sir Kay the Senesciall unto kynge Marke, and there (39)
he had god chere shewynge outewarde.   25

'Now, fayre lordys,' seyde kynge Marke, 'woll ye preve ony adventure in this foreyste of Morrys, whych ys an harde adventure as I know ony?'

'Sir,' seyde sir Kay, 'I woll preve hit.'

And sir Gaherys seyde he wolde be avysed, for kynge Marke was 30
ever full of treson. And therewithall sir Gaherys departed and rode hys way. And by the same way that sir Kay sholde ryde, he leyde hym downe to reste, chargynge hys squyar to wayte uppon hym:

'And yf sir Kay comme, warne me whan he commyth.'

So within a whyle sir Kay com rydyng that way. And than sir 35
Gaherys toke hys horse and mette hym, and seyde,

'Sir Kay, ye ar nat wyse to ryde at the rekeyste of kynge Marke, for he delith all with treson.'

Than seyde sir Kay,

'I requyre you that we may preve well thys adventure.'   40

'I woll nat fayle you,' seyde sir Gaherys.

And so they rode that tyme tylle a lake that was that tyme called the Perelous Lake, and there they abode under the s[h]awe of the wood.

The meanewhyle kynge Marke within the castell of Tyntagyll

avoyded all hys barownes, and all othir, save such as were prevy with
hym, were avoyded oute of the chambir. And than he let calle hys
nevew, sir Andred, and bade arme hym and horse hym lyghtly, for by
that tyme hit was nyghe mydnyght. And so kynge Marke was armed
5 all in blacke, horse and all, and so at a prevy postern they two yssued
oute with their verlattes with them, and so rode tylle they cam to that
lake.

Than sir Kay aspyed them firste, and gate hys spear in hys honde,
and profirde to juste. And kynge Marke rode ayenst hym, and smote
10 ech other full harde, for the moone shone as the bryght day. And at that
justis sir Kayes horse felle downe, for hys horse was nat so bygge as the
kynges horse was, and sir Kayes horse bruced hym full sore.

Than sir Gaherys was wrothe that sir Kay had a falle. Than he cryed,
'Knyght, sitte thou faste in thy sadle, for I wolle revenge my felow!'
15 Than kynge Marke was aferde of sir Gaherys, and so with evyll
wylle kynge Marke rode ayenste hym, and sir Gaherys gaff hym such a
stroke that he felle downe. And so forthwithall sir Gaherys ran unto
sir Andred and smote hym frome hys horse quyte, that hys helme smote
in the erthe and nyghe had brokyn hys neke. And therewithall sir
20 Gaherys alyght, and gate up sir Kay, and than they yeode both on foote
to them, and bade them yelde them and telle their namys, othir ellis
they sholde dey. Than with grete payne sir Andred spake firste and
seyde,

'Hit ys kynge Marke of Cornwayle, therefore be ye ware what ye do.
25 And I am sir Andred, hys cousyn.'

'Fy on you bothe!' seyde sir Gaherys, 'for ye ar false traytours, and
false treson have ye wrought undir youre semble chere that ye made us.
For hit were pité that ye sholde lyve ony lenger,' seyde sir Gaherys.

'Save my lyff,' seyde kynge Marke, 'and I woll make amendys.
30 And concider that I am a kynge anoynted.'

'Hit were the more shame,' seyde sir Gaherys, 'to save thy lyff! For
thou arte a kynge anoynted with creyme, and therefore thou sholdist
holde with all men of worship. And therefore thou arte worthy to
dye.'

35 And so with that he laysshed at kynge Marke, and he coverde hym
with hys shylde and defended hym as he myght. And than sir Kay
laysshed at sir Andret. And therewithall kynge Marke yelded hym unto
sir Gaherys, and than he kneled adowne and made hys othe uppon the
crosse of the swerde that never whyle he lyved he wolde be ayenste
40 arraunte knyghtes. And also he sware to be good fryende unto sir
Trystram, if ever he cam into Cornwayle. And by that tyme sir Andret
was on the erthe, and sir Kay wolde have slayne hym.

'Lat be,' seyde sir Gaherys, 'sle hym nat, I pray you.'

'Sir, hit were pité,' seyde syr Kay, 'that he sholde lyve ony lenger, for

he ys cousyn nyghe unto sir Trystram, and ever he hath bene a traytoure unto hym, and by hym he was exhyled oute of Cornwayle. And
therefore I woll sle hym,' seyde sir Kay.

'Ye shall nat do so,' seyde sir Gaherys, 'for sytthyn I have yevyn the
kynge hys lyff, I pray you gyff hym hys lyffe.'   5

And therewithall sir Kay lete hym go.

And so they rode her wayes unto sir Dynas le Senesciall, for bycause
they harde sey that he loved well sir Trystram. So they reposed them,
and sone aftir they rode unto the realme of Logrys.

And so within a lityll while they mette with sir Launcelot that allwayes 10
had dame Brangwayne with hym, to that entente, he wente to have mette
the sunner with sir Trystram. And sir Launcelot asked what tydynges
in Cornwayle, and whethir they harde of sir Trystram. Sir Kay and sir
Gaherys answerde that they harde nat of hym, and so they tolde worde
by worde of their adventure. Than sir Launcelot smyled and seyde,   15

'Harde hit ys to take oute off the fleysshe that ys bredde in the
boone!'

And so they made hem myrry togydirs.

Now leve we of thys tale and speke we of sir Dynas that had within (40)
the castell a paramour, and she loved anothir knyght bettir than hym.   20
And so whan sir Dynas was oute an-huntynge, she slypped downe by a
towell, and toke with hir two brachettis, and so she yode to the knyght
that she loved [and he her ageyne.]

And whan sir Dynas cam home and myste hys paramoure and hys
brachettes, than was he the more wrother for hys brachettis, more than   25
for hys lady. So than he rode aftir the knyghte that had hys paramoure,
and bade hym turne and juste. So sir Dynas smote hym downe, that
with the falle he brake hys legge and hys arme. And than hys lady and
paramour cryed and seyde, 'Sir Dynas, mercy!' and she wolde love
hym bettir than ever she ded.   30

'Nay,' seyde sir Dynas, 'I shall never truste them that onys betrayeth
me, and therefore as ye have begunne so ende, for I woll nevir meddill
with you.'

And so sir Dynas departed and toke his brachettis with hym, and so
he rode to hys castell.   35

Now woll we turne unto sir Launcelot that was ryght hevy that he
cowth never hyre no tydynges of sir Trystram, for all this whyle he
was in preson with sir Darras, sir Palomydes, and sir Dynadan. Than
dame Brangwayne toke hyr leve to go into Cornwayle, and sir Launcelot, sir Kay and sir Gaherys rode to seke the contrey of Surluse.   40

Now spekith thys tale of sir Trystram and of hys two felowis, for
every day sir Palomydes brawled and seyde langayge ayenste sir
Trystram.

Than seyde sir Dynadan,

'I mervayle of the, sir Palomydes, whethir, and thou haddyst sir
Trystram here, I trow, thou woldiste do none harme. For and a wolff
and a sheepe were togydir in a preson, the wolff wolde suffir the sheepe
to be in pees. And wyte thou well,' seyde sir Dynadan, 'thys same ys
5 sir Trystram at a worde, and now mayst thou do thy beste with hym,
and latte se [yf ye] now skyffte hit with youre handys.'

Than was sir Palomydes abaysshed, and seyde lityll. Than seyde sir
Trystram to sir Palomydes,

'I have harde muche of youre magré ayenste me, but I woll nat
10 meddill with you at thys tyme be my wylle, bycause [I drede] the lorde
of this place that hath us in governaunce. For and I dred hym nat more
than I do the, sone hit sholde be skyffte.'

And so they peaced hemselff.

Ryght so cam in a damesell and seyde,

15 'Knyghtes, be of good chere, for ye ar sure of youre lyves, and that
I harde my lorde sir Darras sey.'

So than were they all glad, for dayly they wente to have dyed.

Than sone after thys sir Trystram fyll syke, that he wente to have
dyed. Than sir Dynadan wepte, and so ded sir Palomydes, undir them
20 bothe makynge grete sorow. So a damesell cam in to them and founde
them mournynge. Than she wente unto sir Darras and tolde hym how
the myghty knyght that bare the blacke shylde was lykly to dye.

'That shall nat be,' seyde sir Darras, 'for God deffende, whan
knyghtes com to me for succour, that I sholde suffir hem to dye within
25 my preson. Therefore,' seyde sir Darras, 'go fecche me that syke
knyght and hys felowis afore me.'

And whan sir Darras saw sir Trystram ibrought afore hym, he seyde,

'Sir knyght, me repentis of youre sykenes, for ye ar called a full
noble knyght, and so hit semyth by you. And wyte you well that hit
30 shall never be seyde that I, sir Darras, shall destroy such a noble knyght
as ye ar in preson, howbehit that ye have slayne three of my sunnes,
wherefore I was gretely agreved. But now shalt thou go and thy
felowys, and take youre horse and youre armour, for they have bene
fayre and clene kepte, and ye shall go where hit lykith you uppon this
35 covenaunte, that ye, knyght, woll promyse me to be good frynde to my
sunnys two that bene now on lyve, and also that ye telle me thy name.'

'Sir, as for [me], my name ys sir Trystram de Lyones, and in Cornwayle was I borne, and nevew I am unto kyng Marke. And as for the
dethe of youre two sunnes, I myght nat do withall. For and they had
40 bene the nexte kyn that I have, I myght have done none othirwyse; and
if I had slayne hem by treson other trechory, I had bene worthy to have
dyed.'

'All thys I co[n]sider,' seyde sir Darras, 'that all that ye ded was by
fors of knyghthode, and that was the cause I wolde nat put you to dethe.

But sith ye be sir Trystram the good knyght, I pray you hartyly to be
my good frynde and ⟨unto⟩ my sunnes.'

'Sir,' seyde sir Trystram, 'I promyse you by the faythe of my body,
ever whyle I lyve I woll do you servyse, for ye have done to us but as
a naturall knyght ought to do.'   5

Than sir Trystram reposed hym there a whyle tyll that he was
amended of hys syknes, and whan he was bygge and stronge they toke
their leve, and every knyght toke their horses and harneys, and so
departed and rode togydirs tyll they cam to a crosseway.

'Now, felowis,' seyde sir Trystram, 'here woll we departe in sundir.'   10
And bycause sir Dynadan had the firste adventure, of hym I woll
begyn.

So as sir Dynadan rode by a well, he founde a lady makyng grete dole.   (41)
'What aylith you?' seyde sir Dynadan.

'Sir knyght,' seyde the lady, 'I am the wofullyst lady of the worlde,   15
for within thys fyve dayes here com a knyght called sir Breuse Saunz
Pité, and he slewe myne owne brothir, and ever syns he hath kepte me
at hys owne wylle, and of all men in the worlde I hate hym moste. And
therefore I requyre you of knyghthode to avenge me, for he woll nat
tarry but be here anone.'   20

'Lat hym com!' seyde sir Dynadan. 'And bycause of honoure of all
women I woll do my parte.'

So with this cam sir Breuse, and whan he saw a knyght with his lady
he was wood wrothe, and than he seyde,

'Kepe the, sir knyght, from me!'   25

And so they hurled togydirs as the thundir, and aythir smote othir
passynge sore. But sir Dynadan put hym thorow the shuldir a grevous
wounde, and or ever sir Dynadan myght turne hym sir Breuse was gone
and fledde.

Than the lady prayde hym to brynge hyr to a castell there besyde but   30
four myle; and so sir Dynadan brought her there and she was wellcom,
for the lorde of that castell was hir uncle. And so sir Dynadan rode hys
way uppon hys adventure.

Now turnyth thys tale unto sir Trystram, that by adventure he cam
to a castell to aske lodgyng, wherein was quene Morgan le Fay. And   35
so whan sir Trystram was let into that castell he had good chere all that
nyght. And so uppon the morne, whan he wolde have departed, the
quene seyde,

'Wyte you well ye shall nat departe lyghtly, for ye ar here as a
presonere.'   40

'Jesu deffende me!' seyde sir Trystram, 'for I was but late a
presonere.'

'Now, fayre knyght,' seyde the quene, 'ye shall abyde with me tyll
that I wyte what ye ar, and frome whens ye cam.'

And ever the quene wolde sette sir Trystram on her one syde, and
her paramour on hir other syde, and evermore the quene wolde beholde
sir Trystram. And thereat thys othir knyght was jeleous, and was in
wyll suddeynly to have ronne uppon hym with a swerde, but he forbare
5 for shame. Than the quene seyde unto sir Trystram,

'Telle me your name, and I shall suffir you to departe whan ye
wyll.'

'Uppon that covenaunte, madame, I woll telle you: my name ys sir
Trystram de Lyones.'

10 'A!' seyde quene Morgan le Fay, 'and I had wyst that, thou sholdist
nat have departed so sone as thou shalte. But sitthyn I have made a
promyse, I wolde holde hit, with that thou wolte promyse me to beare
uppon the a shylde I shall delyver the [unto] the castell of the Harde
Roche, where kynge Arthure hath cryed a grete turnemente. And there
15 I pray you that ye woll be, and to do as much of dedys of armys for
me as ye may do. For at the Castell of Maydyns, sir Trystram, ye ded
mervaylous dedis of armys as ever I harde knyght do.'

'Madame,' seyde sir Trystram, 'let me se the shylde that I shall
beare.'

20 Than the shylde was brought forthe, and the fylde was gouldes with
a kynge and a quene therein paynted, and a knyght stondynge aboven
them with hys one foote standynge uppon the kynges hede and the
othir uppon the quenys hede.

'Madame,' seyde sir Trystram, 'thys ys a fayre shylde and a myghty,
25 but what signyfyeth this kynge and this quene and that knyght stondynge uppon bothe their hedis?'

'I shall telle you,' seyde Morgan le Fay. 'Hit signyfieth kynge
Arthure and que[ne] Gwenyver, and a knyght that holdith them bothe
in bondage and in servage.'

30 'Madame, who ys that knyght?' seyde sir Trystram.

'Sir, that shall ye nat wyte as at thys tyme,' seyde the quene.

But, as the Freynshe booke seyde, quene Morgan loved sir Launcelot
beste, and ever she desired hym, and he wolde never love her nor do
nothynge at her rekeyste, and therefore she hylde many knyghtes
35 togydir to have takyn hym by strengthe. And bycause that she demed
that sir Launcelot loved quene Gwenyver paramour and she hym
agayne, therefore dame Morgan ordayned that shylde to put sir Launcelot to a rebuke, to that entente, that kynge Arthure myght undirstonde the love betwene them.

40 So sir Trystram toke that shylde and promysed hir to beare hit at the
turnemente of the castell of Harde Rooche. But sir Trystram knew nat
of that shylde that hit was ordayned ayenste sir Launcelot, but aftir-
(42) warde he knew hit. So sir Trystram toke hys leve of the quene, and
toke the shylde with hym.

Than cam the knyght that hylde Morgan le Fay, whos name was sir Hemyson, and he made hym redy to folow sir Trystram.

'Now, fayre knyght,' seyde Morgan, 'ryde ye nat aftir that knyght, for ye shall wynne no worshyp of hym.'

'Fye on hym, coward knyght!' seyde sir Hemyson. 'For I wyste 5 nevir good knyght com oute of Cornwayle but yf hit were sir Trystram de Lyones.'

'Sir, what and that be he?'

'Nay, nay,' he seyde, 'he ys with La Beall Isode, and thys ys but a daffysshe knyght.' 10

'Alas, my fayre frynde, ye shall fynde hym the beste knyght that ever ye mette withall, for I know hym bettir than ye do.'

'Madame, for youre sake,' seyde sir Hemyson, 'I shall sle hym.'

'A! fayre frynde,' seyde the quene, 'me repentith that ye woll folow that knyght, for I feare me sore of your agayne-commynge.' 15

And so with thys the knyght rode hys way wood wrothe aftir sir Trystram as faste as he had be chaced with knyghtes.

So whan sir Trystram harde a knyght com aftir hym so faste, he returned aboute and saw a knyght commynge agaynste hym. And whan he cam nyghe to sir Trystram he cryed on hyght and seyde, 20

'Sir knyght, kepe the fro me!'

Than they russhed togydirs as hit had bene thundir. And sir Hemyson brused hys speare uppon sir Trystram, but hys harneys was so good that he myght nat hurte hym. And sir Trystram smote hym harder, and bare hym thorow the body, and fylle over hys horse croupe. Than sir 25 Trystram turned to have done more with hys swerde, but he sy so much bloode go frome hym that hym semed lyckly to dye. And so he departed frome hym, and cam to a fayre maner to an olde knyght, and there sir Trystram lodged.

Nowe leve we sir Trystram and speke we of the knyght that was 30 (43) wounded to the dethe. Than hys varlette alyght, and toke of hys helme, and than he asked hys lorde whether there were ony lyff in hym.

'There ys in me lyff,' seyde the knyght, 'but hit ys but lytyll, and therefore lepe thou up behynde me whan thou haste holpyn me up, and holde me faste that I falle nat, and brynge me to quene Morgan, for 35 the deepe drawghtes of dethe drawith to my harte, that I may nat lyve. For I wolde speke with her fayne or I dyed, for my soule woll be in grete perell and I dye.'

For with grete payne hys varlet brought hym to the castell, and there sir Hemyson fylle downe dede. Whan Morgan le Fay saw hym dede 40 she made grete sorow oute of reson, and than she lette dispoyle hym unto hys shurte, and so she lete put hym into a tombe. And aboute the tombe she lete wryte: He[re] lyeth sir Hemyson, slayne by the hondis of sir Trystram de Lyones.

Now turne we unto sir Trystram that asked the knyght, hys oste, if he saw late ony knyghtes aventures.

'Sir,' he seyde, 'here lodged the laste nyght sir Ector de Marys and a damesell with hym. And that damesell tolde me that he was one of the
5 beste knyghtes of the worlde.'

'That ys nat so,' seyde sir Trystram, 'for I know four bettir knyghtes of his owne blood. And the firste ys sir Launcelot du Lake, calle hym the beste knyght, and sir Bors de Ganys, sir Bleoberys de Ganys, and sir Blamour de Ganys, and also sir Gaherys.'

10 'Nay,' seyde hys oste, 'sir Gawayne ys the bettir knyght.'

'That ys nat so,' seyde sir Trystram, 'for I have mette with hem bothe, and I have felte sir Gaherys for the bettir knyght. And sir Lamorak, I calle hym as good as ony of them, excepte sir Launcelot.'

'Sir, why name ye nat sir Trystram?' sayde hys oste. 'For I accompte
15 hym as good a knyght as ony of them.'

'I knowe nat sir Trystram,' seyde sir Trystram.

Thus they talked and bourded as longe as them thought beste, and than wente to reste.

And on the morne sir Trystram departed and toke hys leve of hys
20 oste, and rode towarde the Roche Deure, and none adventure [had] ⟨he⟩ but that. And so he rested nat tylle he cam to the castell where he saw fyve hondred tentes.

(44) So the Kynge of Scottes and the Kynge of Irelonde hylde agaynste kynge Arthurs knyghtes, and there began a grete medlé.

25 So there cam in sir Trystram and ded mervaylous dedis of armys, for he smote downe many knyghtes, and ever he was before kynge Arthure with that shylde. And whan kynge Arthure saw that shylde he mervayled gretly in what entent hit was made. But que[ne] Gwenyver demed as hit was, wherefore she was hevy.

30 Than was there a damesell of quene Morgan in a chambir by kynge Arthure, and whan she harde kynge Arthure speke of that shylde, than she spake opynly unto kynge Arthure:

'Sir kynge, wyte you well thys shylde was ordayned for you, to warn you of youre shame and dishonoure that longith to you and youre
35 quene.'

And than anone that damesell pycked her away pryvayly, that no man wyste where she was becom. Than was kynge Arthure sad and wrothe, and asked frome whens com that damesell. And there was nat one that knew her nother wyst nat where she was becom.

40 Than quene Gwenyvere called to sir Ector de Marys, and there she made hyr complaynte to hym and seyde,

'I wote well thys shylde was made by Morgan le Fay in the dispite of me and of sir Launcelot, wherefore I drede me sore leste I shall be distroyed.'

And ever the kynge behylde sir Trystram that ded so mervaylous dedis of armys that he wondred sore what knyght hit myght be, and well he wyste hit was nat sir Launcelot. And also hit was tolde hym that sir Trystram was in Bretayne with Isode le Blaunche Maynys, for he demed, and he had bene in the realme of Logrys, sir Launcelot other 5 som of hys felowis that were in the queste of sir Trystram, that they sholde have founde hym or that tyme. So kynge Arthure had mervayle what knyght he myght be. And ever kynge Arthurs ye was on that shylde. And all that aspyed the quene and that made hir sore aferde.

Than ever sir Trystram smote downe knyghtes wondirly to beholde, 10 what uppon the ryght honde and uppon the lyffte honde, that unnethe no knyght myght withstonde hym. And the Kynge of Scottes and the Kynge of Irelonde began to withdraw them. Whan kynge Arthur aspyed that, he thought the knyght with the straunge shylde sholde nat ascape hym. Than he called unto sir Uwayne le Blaunche Maynes and 15 bade hym arme hym and make hym redy. So anone kyng Arthure and sir Uwayn dressed them before sir Trystram and requyred hym to telle where he hadde that shylde.

'Sir,' he seyde, 'I had hit of quene Morgan le Fay, suster to kynge Arthure.' 20

So here leuyth of this booke, for thit ys the firste booke of sir Trystram de Lyones. And the secunde boke begynnyth where sir Trystram smote downe kynge Arthure and sir Uwayne, bycause why he wolde nat telle hem wherefore that shylde was made. But to sey the soth, sir Trystram coude nat telle the 25 cause, for he knew hit nat.

'And yf hit be so ye can dyscryve what ye beare, ye ar worthy to X (1) beare armys.'

'As for that,' seyde sir Trystram, 'I woll answere you. For this shylde was yevyn me, not desyred, of quene Morgan le Fay. And as for [me], 30 I can nat dyscryve this armys, for hit is no poynte of my charge, and yet I truste to God to beare hit with worship.'

'Truly,' seyde kynge Arthure, 'ye ought nat to beare none armys but yf ye wyste what ye bare. But I pray you telle me youre name.'

'To what ententc?' seyde sir Trystram. 35

'For I wolde wete,' seyde kynge Arthure.

'Sir, ye shall nat wete for me at this tyme.'

'Than shall ye and I do batayle togydir.'

'Why,' seyde sir Trystram, 'woll ye do batayle with me but yf I telle you my name? For sothe, that lytyll nedyth you. And ye were a man 40 of worshyp ye wolde nat have ado with me, for ye have sene me this day have had grete travayle. And therefore ye ar no valyaunte knyght to aske batayle of me, consyderynge my grete travayle. Howbehit, I woll nat fayle you, and have ye no doute that I feare nat you. Though ye thynke ye have me at a grete avauntage, yet shall I ryght well endure you.'

And therewithall kynge Arthure dressid his shylde and his speare, 5 and sir Trystram ayenst hym, and they come egirly togydyrs. And there kynge Arthure brake his speare all to pecis on sir Trystrams shylde. But sir Trystram smote kynge Arthur agayne so sore that horse and man felle to the erthe, and there was kynge Arthure woundid on the lyfte syde a grete wounde and a perelous.

10 Whan sir Uwayne saw his lorde kynge Arthur ly on the erthe sore woundid, he was passynge hevy. And than he dressid his shylde and his speare, and cryed alowde unto sir Trystram and seyde,

'Knyght, defende the!'

So they come togydir as faste as their horse myght ren, and sir 15 Uwayne brused his speare all to pecis uppon sir Trystrams shylde. And sir Trystram smote hym harder and sorer with such a myght that he bare hym clene oute of his sadyll to the erthe. With that sir Trystram turned hys horse aboute and sayde to them,

'Fayre knyghtes, I had now no nede to juste with you, for I have had 20 inowghe to do this day.'

Than arose up kynge Arthure and went to sir Uwayne, and than he seyde to sir Trystrams,

'We have now as we have deservyd, for thorowe oure owne o[r]gulyté we demaunded batayle of you, and yet youre name we know 25 nat.'

'Neverthelesse, by Seynte Crosse,' seyde sir Uwayne, 'he is a stronge knyght, at myne advyse, as ony is lyvynge.'

Than sir Trystram departed, and in every place he asked aftir sir Launcelot. But in no place he cowde hyre of hym whether he were dede 30 other on lyve, wherefore sir Trystram made grete dole and sorowe.

So sir Trystram rode by a foreyste and than was he ware of a fayre toure by a marys on the tone syde, and on that other syde was a fayre medow, and there he sawe ten knyghtes fyghtynge togydirs. And ever the nere he cam, he saw how there was but one knyght ded batyle 35 ayenst a nine knyghtes, and that one knyght ded so mervaylousely that sir Trystram had grete wondir that ever one knyght myght do so grete dedis of armys. And than within a lytyll whyle he had slayne halff theire horsys and unhorsid them, and their horsys ran into the feldys and forestes.

40 Than sir Trystram had so grete pité of that one knyght that endured so grete payne, and ever hym thought hit sholde be sir Palomydes, by his shylde. So he rode unto the knyghtys and cryed unto them and bade them sease of that batayle, for they ded themself grete shame, so many knyghtes to feyght wyth one. Than answerde the maystir of tho

knyghtes, hys name was called sir Brunys Saunze Pyté, that was at that tyme the moste myschevuste knyght lyvynge, and seyde thus:

'Sir knyght, what have ye ado with us to medyll? And therefore, and ye be wyse, departe on youre way as ye cam, for this knyght shall nat scape us.'   5

'That were grete pyté,' seyde sir Trystram, 'that so good a knyght as he is sholde be slayne so cowardly. And therefore I make you ware I woll succour hym with all my puyssaunce.'

So sir Trystram alyght of hys horse, because they were on foote, (2) that they sholde nat sle his horse. And than sir Trystram dressyd his 10 shylde with hys swerde in his honde, and he smote on the ryght honde and on the lyffte honde passynge sore, that well-nye every stroke he strake downe a knyghte. And whan they aspyed his strokys they fledde, bothe sir Brunys Saunze Pyté and hys felyshyp, unto the towre, and sir Trystram folowed faste aftir wyth hys swerde in his honde, but 15 they ascaped into the towre and shut sir Trystram wythoute the gate.

And whan sir Trystram sawe that, he returned abacke unto sir Palomydes and founde hym syttynge undir a tre sore woundid.

'A, fayre knyght,' seyde sir Trystram, 'well be ye founde!'

'Gramercy,' seyde sir Palomydes, 'of youre grete goodnesse, for ye 20 have rescowed me of my lyff, and savyd me of my dethe.'

'What is your name?' seyde sir Trystram.

'Sir, my name ys sir Palomydes.'

'A, Jesu!' seyde sir Trystram, 'thou haste a fayre grace of me this day that I sholde rescowe the, and thou art the man in the worlde that I 25 moste hate! But now make the redy, for I shall do batayle with the!'

'What is your name?' seyde sir Palomydes.

'My name is sir Trystram, your mortall enemy.'

'Hit may be so,' seyde sir Palomydes, 'but ye have done overmuche for me this day that I sholde fyght with you, for inasmuche as ye have 30 saved my lyff hit woll be no worshyp for you to have ado with me; for ye ar freyshe and I am sore woundid. And therefore, and ye woll nedys have ado with me, assygne me a day, and than shall I mete with you withoute fayle.'

'Ye say well,' seyde sir Trystramys. 'Now I assygne you to mete me 35 in the medowe by the ryver of Camelot, where Merlyon sette the perowne.'

So they were agreed. Than sir Trystram asked sir Palomydes why the nine knyghtes ded batayle with hym.

'For this cause,' seyde sir Palomydes. 'As I rode uppon myne 40 adventures in a foreyste here besyde, I aspyed where lay a dede knyght, and a lady wepynge besydys hym. And whan I sawe her makynge suche doole, I asked her who slew her lorde. "Sir," she seyde, "the falsyste knyght of the worlde, and moste he is of vylany; and his name is sir

Br[e]wnes Saunze Pité." Than for pité I made the damesell to lepe on
her palferey, and I promysed her to be her waraunte and to helpe to
entyre hir lorde. And suddeynly, as I cam rydyng by this towre, there
come oute sir Brewnys Saunce Pité, and suddeynly he strake me fro my
5 horse. And or ever I myghte recovir my horse, this sir Brewnys slew
the damesell. And so I toke my horse agayne, and I was sore ashamyd,
and so began this medlé betwyxte us. And this is the cause wherefore
we ded this batayle.'

'Well,' seyde sir Trystram, 'now I undirstonde the maner of your
10 batayle. But in ony wyse, that ye have remembraunce of your promyse
that ye have made with me to do batayle this day fourtenyght.'

'I shall nat fayle you,' sayde sir Palomydes.

'Well,' seyde sir Trystram, 'as at this tyme I woll nat fayle you tylle
that ye be oute of the damage of your enemyes.'

15 So they amowntid uppon their horsys and rode togydyrs unto the
foreyste, and there they founde a fayre welle with clere watir burbelynge.

'Fayre sir,' seyde sir Trystramys, 'to drynke of that water I have
grete currage.'

20 And than they alyght of their horsys. And than were they ware
besyde them where stoode a grete horse tyed tylle a tre, and ever he
nayed. Than they aspyed farthermore, and than were they ware of a
fayre knyght armed undir a tre, lackynge no pece of harnes, save hys
helme lay undir his hede.

25 'By the good Lorde,' seyde sir Trystram, 'yondir lyeth a well-farynge
knyght. What is beste to do?' seyde sir Trystram.

'Awake hym!' seyde sir Palomydes.

So sir Trystram awakyd hym wyth the butte of hys speare. And so
the knyght arose up hastely, and put his helme uppon his hede, and
30 mowntyd uppon his horse, and gate a grete speare in his honde. And
withoute ony mo wordis he hurled unto sir Trystram and smote hym
clene from his sadyll to the erthe and hurte hym on the lyffte syde. Than
sir Trystram lay stylle in grete perell.

Than he waloppyd further and fette his course and come hurlynge
35 uppon sir Palomydes. And there he strake hym aparte thorow the body,
that he felle frome hys horse to the erthe. And than this straunge
knyght lefte them there and toke his way thorow the foreyste.

So wyth this sir Trystram and sir Palomydes were on foote, and gate
their horsys agayne, and aythir asked counceyle of other what was beste
40 to done.

'Be my hede,' seyde sir Trystram, 'I woll folow this stronge knyght
that thus hath shamed us.'

'Well,' seyde sir Palomydes, 'and I woll repose me here with a frende
of myne.'

'Beware,' seyde sir Trystram to sir Palomydes, 'loke that ye fayle nat that day that ye have sette with me, for, as I deme, ye woll nat holde your day, for I am muche bygger than ye ar.'

'As for that,' seyde sir Palomydes, 'be as be may, for I feare you nat. For and I be nat syke nother presoner, I woll nat fayle you, but I have 5 more doute of you that ye woll nat mete with me, for ye woll ryde aftir yondir stronge knyght, and yf ye mete with hym, hit is in adventure and ever ye scape his hondys.'

So sir Trystram and sir Palomydes departyd and ayther toke their wayes dyverse. 10

And so sir Trystram rode longe aftir this stronge knyght, and at the (3) laste he sye where lay a lady overtwarte a dede knyght.

'Fayre lady,' seyde sir Trystramys, 'who hath slayne your lorde?'

'Sir,' she seyde, 'here came a knyght rydynge, as my lorde and I restyd us here, and askyd hym of whens he was, and my lorde seyde 15 of kynge Arthurs courte. "Therefore," seyde the stronge knyght, "I woll juste with the, for I hate all tho that be of Arthurs courte." And my lorde that lyeth here dede amownted uppon hys horse, and the stronge knyght and my lorde recountyrd togydir, and there he smote my lorde thorowoute with his speare. And thus he hath brought me in 20 grete woo and damage.'

'That me repentys,' seyde sir Trystram, 'of youre grete hevynesse. But please hit you to tell me your husbondys name?'

'Sir, his name was sir Galardonne, that wolde have prevyd a good knyght.' 25

So departed sir Trystram frome that dolorous lady and had muche evyll lodgynge. Than on the thirde day sir Trystram mette with sir Gawayne and sir Bleoberys in a forcyste at a lodge, and ayther were sore wounded. Than sir Trystram askyd sir Gawayne and sir Bleoberys yf they mette with suche a knyght with suche a conyssaunce, wyth a 30 coverde shylde.

'Fayre knyght,' seyde these wounded knyghtes, 'such a knyght mette with us to oure damage. And fyrste he smote downe my felowe, sir Bleoberys, and sore woundid hym, bycause he bade me I sholde nat have ado with hym for why he was over stronge for me. That stronge 35 knyght toke his wordis at scorne, and seyde he seyde hit for mockery. And than they rode togedyrs, and so he hurte my felowe. And whan he had done so I myght nat for shame but I muste juste wyth hym. And at the fyrste course he smote me downe and my horse to the erthe, and there he had allmoste slayne me, and frome us he toke his horse 40 and departed. And in an evyll tyme we mette with hym!'

'Fayre knyghtes,' seyde sir Trystram, 'so he mette wyth me and with another knyght, sir Palomydes, and he smote us bothe downe with one speare and hurte us ryght sore.'

'Be my faythe,' sayde sir Gawayne, 'be my counceyle ye shall lette hym passe and seke hym no farther, for at the nexte feste of the Rounde Table, uppon payne of myne hede, ye shall fynde hym there.'

'Be my faythe,' sayde sir Trystram, 'I shall never reste tyll that I
5 fynde hym.'

And than syr Gawayne askyd hys name. [Than he sayde,
'My name is sir Trystram.'

And so ayther told other their names and than] aythir departed. And so sir Trystram rode his way. And by fortune in a medowe he mette
10 with sir Kay the Senescyall and with sir Dynadan.

'What tydynges,' seyde sir Trystram, 'with you knyghtes?'

'Nat good,' seyde these knyghtes.

'Why so?' seyde sir Trystram. 'I pray you tell me, for I ryde to seke a knyght.'

15 'What conyssaunce beryth he?' seyde sir Kay.

'He beryth,' seyde sir Trystram, 'a shylde covyrde close.'

'Be my hede,' seyde sir Kay, 'that is the same knyght that mette with us! For this nyght we were lodged hereby in a wydows house, and there was that knyght lodged. And whan he wyste we were of kynge
20 Arthurs courte, he spake grete vylony by the kynge, and specially by the quene Gwenyver. And than on the morne was waged batayle with hym for that cause. And at the fyrste recountir he smote me downe,' seyde sir Kay, 'fro myne horse, and hurte me passyngly sore. And whan my felowe, sir Dynadan, saw me smytten downe and hurte sore,
25 yet he wolde nat revenge me, but fledde fro me. And thus is he departed from us.'

And than sir Trystram asked what was their namys, and so ayther tolde other their namys. And so sir Trystram departed from sir Kay and frome sir Dynadan, and so he paste thorow a grete foreyste into a
30 playne tyll he was ware of a pryory. And there he reposyd hym with a good man six dayes.

(4)   And than he sente his squyer Gover[n]ayle and commaunded hym to go to a cité thereby to fecche hym newe harneyse, for hit was longe tyme afore that sir Trystram had bene refreysshed; for his harneyse was
35 brused and brokyn sore. And whan Governayle was com with his apparayle, he toke his leve at the wydow, and mownted uppon his horse and rode his way erly on the morne.

And by suddayne adventure he mette with sir Sagramour le Desyrus and wyth sir Dodynas le Saveayge. And this two knyghtes mette with
40 sir Trystram and questyonde with hym and askyd hym yf he wolde juste wyth hem.

'Fayre knyghtes,' sayde sir Trystram, 'with good wyll I wolde juste with you, but I have promysed a day isette nerehonde to do batayle wyth a stronge knyght, and therefore am I loth to have ado with you.

For and hit mysfortuned me to be hurte here, I sholde nat be able to do
my batayle whyche I promysed.'

'As for that,' sayde sir Sagramour, 'magré your hede ye shall juste
with us or ye passe frome us.'

'Well,' seyde sir Trystram, 'yf ye force me thereto I muste do what 5
I may.'

And than they dressed their shyldis and cam rennynge togydir with
grete ire. But thorow sir Trystrams grete force he strake sir Sagramoure frome his horse. Than he hurled his horse further and seyde to
sir Dodynas,   10

'Knyght, make the redy!'

And so, thorow fyne forse, sir Trystram strake downe sir Dodynas
frome hys horse. And whan he sawe hem ly on the erthe he toke his
brydyll and rode furth on his way, and his man Governayle with hym.

And anone as sir Trystram was paste, sir Sagramour and sir Dodynas 15
gate their horsys and mownted up lyghtly and folowed aftir sir Trystram. And whan sir Trystram sawe them com so faste aftir hym, he
returned his horse to them and asked them what they wolde.

'Methynkyth hit is nat longe ago sytthen I smote you downe to the
erthe at your owne desyre, and I wolde have ryddyn by you and ye 20
wolde have suffyrd me. But now mesemyth ye wolde do more batayle
with me.'

'That is trowthe,' seyde sir Sagramour and sir Dodynas, 'for we woll
be revengyd of the dyspyte that ye have done to us.'

'Fayre knyghtes,' seyde sir Trystram, 'that shall lytyll nede you, for 25
all that I ded to you, ye caused hit. Wherefore I requyre you of your
knyghthode, leve me as at this tyme, for I am sure, and I do batayle
with you, I shall nat ascape withoute grete hurtes, and, as I suppose, ye
shall nat ascape all lotles. And this is the cause why that I am so loth to
have ado wyth you, for I muste fyght within this three dayes with a 30
good knyght and a valyaunte as ony now is lyvynge. And yf I be hurte
I shall nat be able to do batayle with hym.'

'What knyght is that,' seyde sir Sagramoure, 'that ye shall fyght
wythall?'

'Sir, hit is a good knyght callyd sir Palomydes.'   35

'Be my hede,' seyde sir Sagramour and sir Dodynas, 'ye have a cause
to drede hym, for ye shall fynde hym a passynge good knyght and a
valyaunte. And bycause ye shall have ado wyth hym, we woll forbeare
you as at this tyme, and ellys ye sholde nat ascape us lyghtly. But, fayre
knyght,' sayde sir Sagramoure, 'telle us your name.'   40

'Syrrys, my name is sir Trystram.'

'A!' sayde sir Sagramoure and sir Dodynas, 'well be ye founde, for
muche worshyp have we harde of you.'

And than aythir toke leve of other and departed on there way.

(5)   And sir Trystram rode streyte to Camelot to the perowne that Merlyon had made tofore, where sir Launceor, that was the kynges son of Irelonde, was slayne by the hondys of sir Balyn. And in the same place was the fayre lady Columbe slayne that was love unto sir
5 Launceor, for aftir he was dede she toke hys swerde and threste hit thorow her body. And so by the crafte of Merlyon he made to entyre this knyght Launceor and his lady Columbe undir one stone. And at that tyme Merlyon profecied that in that same place sholde fyght two the beste knyghtes that ever were in kynge Arthurs dayes, and two of
10 the beste lovers.

So whan sir Trystram come to the towmbe of stone he loked aboute hym aftyr sir Palomydes. Than was he ware where come a semely knyght rydynge ayenst hym, all in whyght, and the coverde shylde. Whan he cam nyghe sir Trystram, he seyde on hyght,
15 'Ye be wellcom, sir knyght, and well and trewly have ye holdyn your promyse.'

And than they dressid their shyldis and spearys, and cam togydyrs with all her myghtes of their horsys. And they mette so fersely that bothe the horsys and knyghtes felle to the erthe, and as faste as they
20 myght avoyde there horsys and put their shyldis afore them, and they strake togedyrs wyth bryght swerdys as men that were of myght, and aythir woundid othir wondirly sore, that the bloode ran oute uppon the grasse. And thus they fought the space of four owres, that never one wolde speke to other. And of their harneys they had hewyn of many
25 pecis.

'A, lorde Jesu!' seyde Governayle, 'I mervayle gretely of the grete strokis my maystir hath yevyn to youre maystir.'

'Be my hede,' seyde sir Launcelottis servaunte, 'youre maystir hath not yevyn hym so many, but your maystir hath resseyvede so many
30 or more.'

'A, Jesu!' seyde Governayle, 'hit is to muche for sir Palomydes to suffir, other sir Launcelot. And yet pyté hit were that aythir of these good knyghtes sholde dystroy otheris bloode.'

So they stoode and wepte bothe, and made grete dole whan they
35 sawe their swerdys overcoverde with bloode of there bodyes. Than at the laste sir Launcelot spake and seyde,

'Knyght, thou fyghtyst wondir well as ever I sawe knyghte. Therefore, and hit please you, tell me your name.'

'Sir,' seyde sir Trystram, 'that is me loth to telle ony man my name.'
40 'Truly,' seyde sir Launcelot, 'and I were requyred, I was never loth to tell my name.'

'Ye say well,' seyde sir Trystram, 'than I requyre you to tell me your name.'

'Fayre knyght, my name is sir Launcelot du Lake.'

'Alas!' seyde sir Trystram, 'what have I done! For ye ar the man in
the worlde that I love beste.'

'Now, fayre knyght,' seyde sir Launcelot, 'telle me your name.'

'Truly, sir, I hyght sir Trystram de Lyones.'

'A, Jesu!' seyde sir Launcelot, 'what aventure is befall me!'　　5

And therewyth sir Launcelott kneled adowne and yeldid hym up his
swerde. And therewithall sir Trystram kneled adowne and yeldid hym
up his swerde, and so aythir gaff other the gre. And than they bothe
forthwithall went to the stone and set hem downe uppon hit and toke
of their helmys to keele them, and aythir kyste other an hondred tymes.　10

And than anone aftir they toke their horsis and rode to Camelot, and
there they mette with sir Gawayne and with sir Gaherys that had made
promyse to kynge Arthure never to com agayne to the courte tyll they
had brought sir Trystram with hem.

'Returne agayne,' sayde sir Launcelot, 'for youre queste is done, for　15 (6)
I have mette with sir Trystram. Lo, here is his owne person!'

Than was sir Gawayne glad and seyde to sir Trystram,

'Ye ar wellcom, for now have ye easid me gretly of my grete laboure.
For what cause,' seyde sir Gawayne, 'com ye into this contrey?'

'Fayre sir,' seyde sir Trystram, 'I come into this contrey because of　20
sir Palomydes, for he and I assigned at this day to have done batayle
togydyrs at the peroune, and I mervayle I hyre nat of hym. And thus
by adventure my lorde syr Launcelot and I mette togydirs.'

So wyth this come kynge Arthure, and when he wyste sir Trystram
was there, he yode unto hym, and toke hym by the honde, and seyde,　25

'Sir Trystram, ye ar as wellcom as ony knyght that ever com unto
this courte.'

And whan the kynge herde how sir Launcelot and he had foughtyn,
and aythir had wounded other wondirly sore, then the kynge made grete
dole. Than sir Trystram tolde the kynge how he com thydir to have ado　30
with sir Palomydes. And than he tolde the kynge how he had rescowed
hym from the nine knyghtes and sir Breunes Saunze Pité, and how he
founde a knyght lyynge by a welle, 'and that knyghte smote downe
bothe sir Palomydes and me, and hys shylde was coverde with a clothe.
So sir Palomydes leffte me, and I folowed aftir that knyght, and in many　35
placis I founde where he had slayne knyghtes and forjustyd many.'

'Be my hede,' seyde sir Gawayne, 'that same knyght smote me downe
and sir Bleoberys and hurte us sore bothe, he wyth the coverde shylde.'

'A!' sayde sir Kay, 'that same knyght smote me downe and hurte me
passynge sore.'　　40

'Jesu mercy!' seyde kynge Arthure, 'what knyght was that wyth the
coverde shylde?'

'We knew hym not,' seyde sir Trystram, and so seyde they all.

'No?' seyde kynge Arthure. 'Than wote I, for hit is sir Launcelot.'

Than they all lokyd uppon sir Launcelot and seyde,
'Sir, ye have begyled us all wyth youre coverde shylde.'
'Hit is not the fyrste tyme,' seyde kynge Arthure, 'he hath done so.'
'My lorde,' seyde sir Launcelot, 'truly, wete you well, I was the same
5 knyght that bare the coverde shylde, and bycause I wolde nat be
knowyn that I was of youre courte, I seyde no worshyp be youre
house.'

'That is trouthe,' seyde sir Gawayne, syr Kay and sir Bleoberys.

Than kynge Arthure toke sir Trystram by the honde and wente to
10 the Table Rounde. Than come quene Gwenyver and many ladyes with
her, and all tho ladyes seyde at one voyce,

'Wellcom, sir Trystram!'

'Wellcom!' seyde [the] damesels.

'Wellcom,' seyde kynge Arthur, 'for one of the beste knyghtes and
15 the jentyllyst of the wo[r]lde and the man of moste worship. For [of]
all maner of huntynge thou beryste the pryce, and of all mesures of
blowynge thou arte the begynnynge, of all the termys of huntynge and
hawkynge ye are the begynner, of all instirmentes of musyk ye ar the
beste. Therefore, jantyll knyghte,' seyde kynge Arthure, 'ye ar wellcom
20 to this courte. And also, I pray you,' seyde kynge Arthure, 'graunte me
a done.'

'Sir, hit shall be at youre commaundemente,' seyde sir Trystram.

'Well,' seyde kynge Arthure, 'I wyll desyre that ye shall abyde in my
courte.'

25 'Sir,' seyde sir Trystram, 'thereto me is lothe, for I have to do in
many contreys.'

'Not so,' seyde kynge Arthure, 'ye have promysed me, ye may not
say nay.'

'Sir,' seyde sir Trystram, 'I woll as ye woll.'

30 Than wente kynge Arthure unto the seges aboute the Rounde Table,
and loked on every syege whyche were voyde that lacked knyghtes.
And than the kynge sye in the syege of sir Marhalt lettyrs that seyde:
THIS IS THE SYEGE OF THE NOBLE KNYGHT SIR TRYSTRAMYS. And than
kynge Arthure made sir Trystram a knyght of the Rounde Table wyth
35 grete nobeley and a feste as myght be thought.

For sir Marhalte was slayne afore by the hondis of sir Trystram in an
ilonde, and that was well knowyn at that tyme in the courte of kynge
Arthure. For this sir Marhalte was a worthy knyght, and for evyll dedis
that he ded to the contreye of Cornwayle sir Trystram and he fought so
40 longe tyll they felle bledynge to the erthe, for they were so sore wounded
that they myght nat stonde for bledynge. And sir Trystram by fortune
recoverde, and sir Marhalte dyed thorow the stroke he had in the hede.

SO LEVE WE SIR TRYSTRAM AND TURNE WE UNTO KYNGE MARKE.

VII. KING MARK

THAN kynge Marke had grete dispyte at sir Trystram. And whan he (7)
chaced hym oute of Cornwayle (yette was he nevew unto kynge Marke,
but he had grete suspeccion unto sir Trystram bycause of his quene, La
Beall Isode, for hym semed that there was muche love betwene them 5
twayne), so whan sir Trystram was departed oute of Cornwayle into
Ingelonde, kynge Marke harde of the grete proues that sir Trystram
ded there, wyth the whyche he greved.

So he sente on his party men to aspye what dedis he ded, and the
quene sente pryvaly on hir party spyes to know what dedis he had done, 10
for full grete love was there betwene them. So whan the messyngers
were com home they tolde the trouthe as they herde, and how he passed
all other knyghtes but yf hit were sir Launcelot. Than kynge Marke was
ryght hevy of tho tydynges, and as glad was La Beale Isode.

Than grete dispyte kynge Marke had at hym, and so he toke wyth 15
hym two knyghtes and two squyers, and disgysed hymself, and toke his
way into Ingelonde to the entente to sle sir Trystram. And one of tho
knyghtes hyght sir Bersules, and the other knyght was callyd Amaunte.
So as they rode kynge Marke asked a knyght that he mette, where he
myght fynde kynge Arthure. 20

'Sir,' he seyde, 'at Camelot.'

Also he asked that knyght aftir sir Trystrams, whether [he] herde of
hym in the courte of kynge Arthure.

'Wete you well,' seyde that knyght, 'ye shall fynde sir Trystram there
for a man of worshyp moste that is now lyvynge, for thorow his proues 25
he wan the turnement at the Castell of Maydyns that stondyth by the
Roche Duie. And sytthen he hath wonne wyth his hondys thirty
knyghtes that were men of grete honoure. And the laste batayle that
ever he ded he fought with sir Launcelot, and that was a mervaylus
batayle. And by love and not by force sir Launcelotte brought sir 30
Trystram to the courte. And of hym kynge Arthure made passynge
grete joy, and so made hym knyght of the Table Rounde, and his seate
is in the same place where sir Marhalte the good knyghtes seate was.'

Than was kynge Marke passynge sory whan he harde of the honour
of sir Trystram, and so they departed. Than seyde kynge Marke unto 35
his two knyghtes,

'Now I woll tell you my counsell, for ye ar the men that I moste truste
on lyve. And I woll that ye wete my commynge hydir is to this entente,
for to destroy sir Trystram by som wylys other by treson, and hit shall
be harde and ever he ascape oure hondis.' 40

'Alas!' seyde sir Bersules, 'my lorde, what meane you? For and ye be
sette in such a way, ye ar disposed shamfully, for sir Trystram is the
knyght of worshyp moste that we knowe lyvynge. And therefore I

warne you playnly, I woll not consente to the deth of hym, and therefore I woll yelde hym my servyse and forsake you.'

Whan kynge Marke harde hym say so, suddeynly he drewe hys
swerde and seyde, 'A, traytoure!', and smote sir Bersules on the hede
5 that the swerde wente to his teithe. Whan sir Amant, his felow, sawe
hym do that vylaunce dede, and his squyers als[o, they] seyde to the
kynge,

'Hit was foule done and myschevously, wherefore we woll do you
no more servyse. And wete you well we woll appele you of treson afore
10 kynge Arthure.'

Than was kynge Marke wondirly wrothe, and wolde have ⌐slayne⌐
Amaunte, but he and the two squyers hylde them togydirs and sette
nought by his malyce. So whan kynge Marke sawe he myght nat be
revenged on them, he seyde thus unto the knyght Amante:

15 'Wyte thou well, and thou appeyche me of treson, I shall thereof
defende me afore kynge Arthure, but I requyre the that thou telle nat
my name that I am kynge Marke, whatsomevir com of me.'

'As for that,' seyde sir Amante, 'I woll nat discover your name.'

And so they departed. And sir Amante and his felowys toke the body
20 of sir Bersules and buryed hit.

(8)   Than kynge Marke rode tyll he com to a fountayne, and there he
rested hym by that fountayne, and stoode in a dwere whether he myght
ryde to kynge Arthurs courte other none, or to returne agayne to his
contrey.

25 And as he thus restyd hym by that fountayne, there cam by hym a
knyght well armed on horsebacke, and he alyght and tyed his horse and
sette hym downe by the brynke of the fountayne, and there he made
grete langoure and dole. And so he made the dolefullyst complaynte of
love that ever man herde, and all this whyle was he nat ware of kynge
30 Marke. And this was a grete complay[n]te: he cryed and wepte and
sayde,

'O, thou fayre quene of Orkeney, kynge Lottys wyff and modir unto
sir Gawayne and to sir Gaherys, and modir to many other, for thy
love I am in grete paynys!'

35   Than kynge Marke arose and wente nere hym and seyde,

'Fayre knyght, ye have made a piteuos complay[n]te.'

'Truly,' seyde the knyght, 'hit is an hondred parte more rufullyer
than myne herte can uttir.'

'I requyre you,' seyde kynge Marke, 'telle me youre name.'

40   'Sir, as for my name, I wyll not hyde hit from no knyght that beryth
a shylde. Sir, my name is sir Lameroke de Galys.'

But whan sir Lameroke herde kynge Marke speke, than wyste he
well by his speche that he was a Cornysh knyght.

'Sir knyght,' seyde sir Lameroke, 'I undirstonde by your tunge that

ye be of Cornewayle, wherein there dwellyth the shamfullist knyght of
a kynge that is now lyvynge, for he is a grete enemy to all good
knyghtes. And [that] prevyth well, for he hath chased oute of that
contrey sir Trystram that is the worshypfullyst knyght that now is
lyvynge, and all knyghtes spekyth of hym worship; and for the 5
jeleousnes of his quene he hath chaced hym oute of his contrey. Hit is
pité,' seyde sir Lameroke, 'that ony suche false kynge cowarde as kynge
Marke is shulde be macched with suche a fayre lady and a good as La
Beall Isode is, for all the wo[r]lde of hym spekyth shame, and of her
grete worshyp as ony quene may have.'   10

'I have nat ado in this mater,' seyde kynge Marke, ['neyther noughte
woll I speke thereof.'

'Well seyde,' seyde sir Lameroke.]

'But, sir, can you tell me ony tydyngis?'

'I can telle you,' seyde sir Lameroke, 'there shall be a grete turne- 15
mente in haste bysyde Camelot, at the Castell of Jagent. And the Kynge
wyth the Hondred Knyghtys and the kynge of Irelonde, as I suppose,
makyth that turnemente.'

Than cam there a knyght that was callyd sir Dynadan, and salewed
them bothe. And whan he wyste that kynge Marke was a knyght of 20
Cornwayle, he repreved hym for the love of kynge Marke a thousandfolde more than ded sir Lameroke. And so he profirde to juste with
kynge Marke. And he was full lothe thereto, but sir Dynadan egged
hym so that he justed wyth sir Lameroke. And sir Lameroke smote
kynge Marke so sore that he bare hym on his speare ende over his 25
horse tayle.

And than kynge Marke arose, and gate his horse agayne, and folowed
aftir sir Lameroke. But sir Dynadan wolde nat juste with sir Lameroke,
but he tolde kynge Marke that sir Lameroke was sir Kay the Senescyall.   30

'That is nat s[o,]' seyde kynge Marke, 'for he is muche bygger than
sir Kay.'

And so he folowed and overtoke hym and bade hym abyde.

'What woll ye do?' seyde sir Lameroke.

'Sir,' he seyde, 'I woll fyght wyth a swerde, for ye have shamed me 35
with a speare.'

And therewyth they daysshed togydyrs wyth swerdis. And sir
Lamerok suffyrde hym and forbare hym, and kynge Marke was passyng
besy and smote thycke strokys. Than sir Lameroke saw he wolde nat
stynte, he waxed somwhat wrothe, and doubled his strokys, for he was 40
of the nobelyste of the worlde. And he beete hym so on the helme that
his hede [henge] nyghe on the sadyll-bowe. Whan sir Lameroke saw
hym fare so, he sayde,

'Knyght, what chere? Mesemyth ye have nyghe youre fylle of

fyghtynge. Hit were pyté to do you ony more harme, for ye ar but a meane knyght. Therefore I gyff you leve to go where ye lyst.'

'Gramercy,' seyde kynge Marke, 'for ye and I be no macchis.'

Than sir Dynadan mocked kynge Marke and seyde,

5 'Ye ar nat able to macche a good knyght!'

'As for that,' seyde kynge Marke, 'at the fyrste tyme that [I] justed with this knyght, ye refused hym.'

'Thynke ye that a shame?' seyde sir Dynadan. 'Nay, sir, hit is ever worshyp to a knyght to refuse that thynge that he may nat ·attayne.

10 Therefore your worshyp had bene muche more to have refused hym as I ded, for I warne you playnly he is able to beate suche fyve as ye ar and I be: for ye knyghtis of Cornwayle ar no men of worshyp as other knyghtes ar, and bycause ye ar nat of worshyp, ye hate all men of worship, for never in your contrey was bredde suche a knyght as sir

15 Trystram.'

(9) Than they rode furth all togydyrs, kynge Marke, sir Lameroke and sir Dynadan, tylle that they com to a brygge, and at the ende thereof stood a fayre toure. Than saw they a knyght on horsebacke well armed, braundisshynge a speare, cryynge, and profyrde hymself to juste.

20 'Now,' seyde sir Dynadan unto kynge Marke, 'yondir ar too bretherne, that one hyght Alyne and that other hyght Tryan, that woll juste with ony that passyth this passayge. Now profyr youreself,' seyde sir Dynadan unto kynge Marke, 'for ever ye be leyde to the erthe.'

Than kynge Marke was ashamed, and therewith he feautyrde hys

25 speare and hurteled to sir Tryan, and aythir brake their spearys all to pecis, and passed thorow anone. Than sir Tryan sˑenˑte kyng Marke another speare to juste more, but in no wyse he wolde nat juste no more.

Than they com to the castell, all thre knyghtes, and prayde the lorde

30 of that castell of herborow.

'Ye ar ryght wellcom,' seyde the knyghtes of the castell, 'for the love of the lorde of this towre', the whyche hyght sir Torre le Fyze Aryes.

And than they com into a fayre courte well repayred, and so they had passynge good chere tyll the lyefftenaunte of that castell that hyght

35 Berluse aspyed kynge Marke of Cornwayle. Than seyde sir Berluse,

'Sir knyght, I know you well, better than ye wene, for ye ar kynge Marke that slew my fadir afore myne owne yghen, and me had ye slayn had I not ascapyd into a woode. But wyte you well, for the love of my lorde sir Torre, whyche is lorde of this castell, I woll nat at this tyme

40 nother hurte nor harme you, nothir none of your felyship. But wyte you well, whan ye ar paste this loggynge I shall hurte you and I may, for ye slew my [fader] traytourly and cowardly. But fyrste, fòr my lorde sir Torre, and for the·love of sir Lameroke the honorable knyght that here is lodgid, ye sholde have [none] evyll lodgynge. For hit [is] pyté

that ever ye sholde be in the company of good knyghtes, for ye ar the
moste vylaunce knyght of a kynge that is now lyvynge, for ye ar a
dystroyer of good knyghtes, and all that ye do is but by treson.'

Than was kynge Marke sore ashamyd and seyde but lytyll agayne. (10)
But whan sir Lameroke and sir Dynadan wyste that he was kynge 5
Marke they were sory of [his] felyshyp. So aftir supper they went to
lodgynge.

So on the morne they arose, and kynge Marke and sir Dynadan rode
togydyrs. And three myle of there mette with hem three knyghtes, and
sir Berluse was one, and other two of hys cosyns.   10

Whan sir Berluse saw kynge Marke he cryed on hyghte:
'Traytoure, kepe the from me, for wete thou well that I am sir
Berluse!'

'Sir knyght,' seyde sir Dynadan, 'I counceyle you as at this tyme
medyll nat wyth hym, for he is rydynge to kynge Arthure. And bycause 15
I promysed to conduyte hym to my lorde kynge Arthure, nedis muste I
take a parte wyth hym; howbehit I love nat his condision, and fayne
I wolde be from hym.'

'Well, sir Dynadan,' seyde sir Berluse, 'me repentys that ye woll take
party with hym, but now do youre beste!'   20

Than he hurteled to kynge Marke and smote hym sore uppon the
shylde, that he bare hym clene oute of his sadill to the erthe. That saw
sir Dynadan, and he feautyrd hys speare and ran to one of his felowys
and smote hym of hys sadyll. Than sir Dynadan turned his horse and
smote the thirde knyght in the same wyse, that he went to the erthe, 25
for this sir Dynadan was a good knyght on horsebacke.

And so there began a grete batayle, for sir Berluse and hys felowys
hylde them togydyrs strongely on foote. And so thorow the grete force
of sir Dynadan kynge Marke had sir Berluse at the erthe, and his two
felowys fled. And had nat sir Dynadan bene, kynge Marke wolde have 30
slayne hym; and so sir Dynadan rescowed hym of his lyff, for this
kynge Marke was but a murtherer.

And than they toke their horsys and departed, and lefte sir Berluse
there sore woundid. Than kynge Marke and sir Dynadan rode forth
a four leagis Englyshe tyll that they com to a brydge where hoved a 35
knyght on horsebacke, armyd redy to juste.

'Lo,' seyde sir Dynadan unto kynge Marke, 'yonder hovyth a knyght
that woll juste, for there shall none passe this brydge but he muste juste
with that knyght.'

'Ye say well,' seyde kynge Marke, 'for this justys fallyth for you.' 40

But sir Dynadan knew the knyght for a noble knyght, and fayne he
wolde have justyd, but he had levir that kynge Marke had justed with
hym. But by no meane kynge Marke wolde nat juste. Than sir Dynadan
myght nat refuse hym in no maner, and so ayther dressed their spearys

and their shyldys and smote togydyrs, that thorow fyne force sir Dynadan was smyttyn to the erthe. And lyghtly he arose up and gate his
horse and requyred that knyght to do batayle with swerdys. And he
answerde and seyde,

5 'Fayre knyght, as at this tyme I may nat have ado with you no more,
for the custom of this passage is suche.'

Than was sir Dynadan passynge wrothe that he myght nat be
revenged of that knyght, and so he departed. And in no wyse wolde
that knyght telle hys name, but ever sir Dynadan thought he sholde

10 know hym by his shylde that he sholde be sir Torre.

(11) So as they rode by the way kynge Marke than began to mocke sir
Dynadan, and seyde,

'I wente you knyghtes of the Rounde Table myght in no wyse fynde
youre macchis.'

15 'Ye sey well,' seyde sir Dynadan. 'As for you, on my lyff, [I] calle
you none of the good knyghtes. But syth ye have such dispyte at me, I
requere you to juste with me to preve my strengthe.'

'Nat so,' seyde kynge Marke, 'for I woll nat have ado with you in no
maner; but I requyre you of one thynge, that whan ye com to kynge

20 Arthures courte, discover nat my name, for I am sore there behatyd.'

'Hit is shame to you,' seyde sir Dynadan, 'that ye governe you so
shamfully, for I se by you ye ar full of cowardyse, and ye ar also a
murtherar, and that is the grettyst shame that ony knyght may have, for
nevir had knyght murthere[r] worshyp, nother never shall have. For I

25 sawe but late thorow my forse ye wolde have slayne sir Ber[lus]es, a
better knyght than ever ye were or ever shall be, and more of proues.'

Thus they rode forth talkynge tyll they com to a fayre place where
stoode a knyghte and prayde them to take their lodgynge with hym. So
at the requeste of that knyght they reposyd them there and made them

30 well at ease and had grete chere, for all araunte knyghtes to hym were
welcom, and specially all tho of kynge Arthurs courte.

Than sir Dynadan demaunded his oste what was the knyghtes name
that kepte the brydge.

'For what cause aske you?' seyde his oste.

35 'For hit is nat longe ago,' seyde sir Dynadan, 'sytthen he gaff me a
falle.'

'A, fayre knyght,' seyde his oste, 'thereof have ye no mervayle, for
he is a passynge good knyght, and his name is sir Torre, the sonne of
Aryes le Vaysshere.'

40 'A!' seyde sir Dynadan, 'was that sir Torre? Truly so ever me
thought.'

So ryght as they stood thus talkynge togydyrs they saw com rydynge
by them over a playne six knyghtes of the courte of kynge Arthure well
armyd at all poyntys; and by their shyldys sir Dynadan knew them well.

The fyrste was the good knyght sir Uwayne, the sonne of kynge Uryen.
The secunde was the noble knyght sir Brandyles. The thirde was
Ozanna le Cure Hardy. The fourth was sir Uwayne les Adventurys.
The fyfth was sir Agravayne, the sixth, sir Mordred, to brethirne to
sir Gawayne.   5

Whan sir Dynadan had aspyed thes six knyghtes he thought to hymself he wolde brynge kynge Marke by som wyle to juste with one of
them. And than anone they toke their horsys and ran aftir these six
knyghtes well-nye a three myle Englyshe. Than was kynge Marke ware
where they sate all six aboute a welle and ete and dranke suche metys as   10
they had, and their horsis walkynge and som tyed, and their shyldys
hynge in dyverse placis about them.

'Lo!' seyde sir Dynadan, 'yondir ar knyghtes arraunte that woll juste
with us.'

'God forbede,' seyde kynge Marke, 'for they be six, and we but   15
two.'

'As for that,' seyde sir Dynadan, 'lat us nat spare, for I woll assay the
formyst.'

And therewith he made hym redy. Whan kynge Marke sawe hym do
so, as faste as sir Dynadan rode towardis them, kynge Marke rode fro-   20
warde them with all his mayneall mayné.

So whan sir Dynadan saw that kynge Marke was gone, he sette the
speare oute of the reaste and threwe hys shylde uppon his backe and
cam rydynge to the felyshyp of the Rounde Table. And anone sir
Uwayne knew sir Dynadan, and welcomed hym, and so ded all his   25
felyshyp. And than they asked hym of aventures, and whether that he   (12)
sawe of sir Trystram othir sir Launcelot.

'So God me helpe,' seyde sir Dynadan, 'as for me, I sawe none of them
sytthyn we departed fro Camelot.'

'What knyght is that,' seyde sir Braundyles, 'that so sodeynly de-   30
parted frome you and rode over yondir fylde?'

'Sir, hit is a knyght of Cornwayle, and the moste orryble cowarde
that ever bestrode horse.'

'What is his name?' seyde all thos knyghtes.

'I wote nat,' seyde sir Dynadan.   35

So whan they had reposed them and spokyn togydyrs they toke there
horsys and rode to a castell where dwellyd an olde knyght that made
all knyghtes arraunte good chere.

So in the meanewhyle that they were talkynge, com into the castell
sir Gryfflet le Fyz de Deu. And there was he wellcom, and they all   40
askyd hym whethir he sye sir Launcelot other sir Trystram. He
answerde and seyde,

'I sawe hem nat sytthyn they departed frome Camelot.'

So as sir Dynadan walked and behylde the castell, thereby in a chambir he aspyed kynge Marke, and than he rebuked hym and asked why he departed so.

'Sir, for I durst nat abyde, for they were so many. But how ascaped ye?' seyde kynge Marke.

'Sir, they be better frendis than I went they had ben.'

'Who is captayne of this felyshyp?' seyde kynge Marke.

For to feare hym sir Dynadan seyde hit was sir Launcelot.

'A, Jesu!' seyde kynge Marke, 'myght ye knowe sir Launcelot by his shylde?'

'Ye,' seyde sir Dynadan, 'for he beryth a shylde of sylver and blacke bendis.'

All this he seyde to feare kynge Marke, for sir Launcelot was nat in the felyshyp.

'Now I pray you,' seyde kynge Marke, 'that ye woll ryde in my felyshyp.'

['That is me lothe to doo,' said sir Dynadan, 'bycause ye forsoke my felyshyp.'

Ryght so sir Dynadan went from kyng Marke and went to his own felyshyp]; and so they mownted uppon there horsys and rode on their wayes and talked of the Cornyshe knyght, for sir Dynadan tolde them that he was in the castell where they were lodged.

'Hit is well seyde,' seyde sir Gryfflet, 'for here have I brought sir Dagonet, kynge Arthurs foole, that is the beste felow and the meryeste in the worlde.'

'Woll ye than do well?' seyde sir Dynadan. 'I have tolde the Cornyshe knyght that here is sir Launcelot, and the Cornyshe knyght asked me what shylde he bare, and I tolde hym that he bare the same shylde that sir Mordred beryth.'

'Woll ye do well?' seyde sir Mordred. 'I am hurte and may nat well beare my shylde nother harneys, and therefore put my harneys and my shylde uppon sir Dagonet and let hym sette uppon the Cornyshe knyght.'

'That shall be done,' seyde sir Dagonet, 'be my fayth.'

And so anone sir Dagonet was armed in sir Mordredis harneys and hys shylde, and he was sette on a grete horse and a speare in his honde.

'Now,' seyde sir Dagonet, 'sette me to that knyght and I trowe I shall beare hym downe.'

So all thes knyghtes rode to a woodis syde and abode tyll kynge Marke cam by the way. Than they put forth sir Dagonet, and he cam on all the whyle his horse myght renne uppon kynge Marke. And whan he cam nye to kynge Marke he cryed as he were woode, and sayde,

'Kepe the, knyght of Cornwayle, for I woll sle the!'

And anone as kynge Marke behylde his shylde, he seyde to hymself, 'Yondyr is sir Launcelot. Alas, now am I destroyed!'

And therewithall he made his horse to ren and fledde as faste as he myght thorow thycke and thorow thynne. And ever sir Dagonet folowed aftir kynge Marke, cryynge and ratynge hym as a woode man, thorow a grete foreste.

Whan sir Uwayne and sir Brandules saw sir Dagonet so chace kynge 5 Marke, they lawghed all as they were wylde, and than they toke their horsys and rode aftir to se how sir Dagonet spedde, for theym behoved for no good that sir Dagonet were shente, for kynge Arthure loved hym passynge well and made hym knyght hys owne hondys. And at every turnemente he bega[n] to make kynge Arthure to lawghe. Than the 10 knyghtes rode here and there cryynge and chasynge aftir kynge Marke, that all the foreyste range of the noyse.

So kynge Marke by fortune rode by a welle, in the way where stood (13) a knyght arraunte on horsebacke, armed at all poyntys, with a grete spere in his honde. And whan he saw kyng Marke com fleynge he sayde 15 to the knyght,

'Returne agayne for shame and stonde with me, and I shall be thy waraunte.'

'A, fayre knyght,' seyde kynge Marke, 'lette me passe, for yondir commyth aftir me the beste knyght of the worlde, wyth the blacke 20 beanded shylde.'

'Fy, for shame,' seyde the knyght, 'for he is none of the worthy knyghtes. And yf he were sir Launcelot othir sir Trystram I shall nat doute to mete the bettyr of them bothe.'

Whan kyng Marke harde hym sey that worde, he returned his horse 25 and abode by hym. And than that stronge knyght bare a speare to sir Dagonet and smote hym so sore that he bare hym over his horse tayle, that nyghe he had brokyn his necke.

And anone aftir hym cam sir Braundules, and whan he sawe sir Dagonette have that falle he was passynge wrothe, and seyde,   30

'Kepe the, knyght!'

And so they hurled togydyrs wondir sore. But the knyghte smote sir Braundules so sore that he went to the erthe, horse and man. Sir Uwayne com aftir and sy all this.

'Jesu!' he seyde, 'yondyr is a stronge knyght!'   35

And than they feautred their spearys, and this knyght com so egirly that he smote downe sir Uwayne. Than cam sir Ozanna wyth the Hardy Harte, and he was smyttyn downe.

'Now,' seyde sir Gryfflet, 'be my counceyle lat us sende to yondir arraunte knyghte and wete whether he be of kynge Arthurs courte, for, 40 as I deme, hit is sir Lameroke de Galys.'

So they sente unto hym and prayde that stronge knyght to telle 'us his name', and whethir he were of kynge Arthurs courte other nat.

'As for my name, telle tho knyghtes I am a knyght arraunte as they ar, but my name they shall nat wete at this tyme. And lat them wete that I am no knyght of kynge Arthurs.'

And so the squyer rode ayen and tolde as he seyde.

5 'Be my hede,' seyde sir Aggravayne, 'he is one of the strongyst knyghtes that ever I saw, for he hathe overthrowyn three noble knyghtes, and nedis we muste encountyr with hym for shame.'

So sir Aggravayne feautred his speare, and that othir was redy and smote hym downe over his horse tayle to the erthe. And in the same 10 wyse he smote sir Uwayne les Avoutres, and also sir Gryfflot. Than had he served them all but sir Dynadan, for he was behynde, and sir Mordrede whyche sir Dagonet had his harneys.

So whan this was done this stronge knyght rode on his way a soffte pace, and kynge Marke rode aftir hym praysynge hym mykyll. But he 15 wolde answere no wordys but syghed wondirly sore, and hongynge downe his hede, takynge no hyde to his wordys. Thus they rode well-nye a three myle Englysh. And than this knyght callyd to hym a varlet and bade hym:

'Ryde untyll yondir fayre maner, and commaunde me to the lady of 20 that castell and place, and pray hir to sende me som refresshynge of good metys and drynkys. And yf she aske the what I am, telle her that I am the knyght that folowyth the Glatysaunte Beste.' (That is in Englysh to sey, the questynge beste, for the beste, wheresomever he yode, he quested in the bealy with suche a noyse as hit had bene a 25 thirty couple of howndis.)

Than the varlet wente his way and cam to the maner and salewed the lady, and tolde her frome whens he come. And whan [s]he undirstode that he cam fro the knyght that folowed the questynge beste,

'A! swete Lorde Jesu!' she seyde, 'whan shall I se that jantyll knyght, 30 my dere sonne sir Palomydes! Alas! woll he nat abyde with me?'

And therewith she sowned and wepte and made passynge grete dole. But allso sone as she myght she gaff the varlet mete all that he axed. And than the varlet returned unto sir Palomydes, for he was a varlet of kynge Markis. And as sone as he cam he tolde the knyghtes name was 35 sir Palomydes.

'I am well pleased,' seyde kynge Marke, 'but holde the stylle and sey nothynge.'

Than they alyght and sette them downe and reposed them a whyle. And anone wythall kynge Marke fylle on slepe. So whan sir Palomydes 40 sawe hym sounde on slepe he toke his horse and rode his way and seyde to them,

'I woll nat be in the company of a slepynge knyght.'

And so he rode a grete pace.

(14) Now turne we unto sir Dynadan that founde thes seven knyghtes

passynge hevy, and whan he wyste how that they had sped, ⌐as hevy
was he.⌐

'Sir Uwayne,' seyde sir Dynadan, 'I dare ley thereon my hede, hit is
sir Lameroke de Galys. I promyse you all I shall fynde hym, and he
may be founde in this contrey.'   5

And so sir Dynadan rode aftir this knyght, and so ded kynge Marke
that sought hym thorow the foreyste. And so as kynge Marke rode
aftir sir Palomydes he harde a noyse of a man that made grete dole.
Than kynge Marke rode as nye that noyse as he myght and as he durste.
Than was he ware of a knyght that was dissended of his horse, and he   10
had putte of his helme, and there he made a peteuous complay[n]te and
a dolerous of love.

Now leve we off, and talke we of sir Dynadan that rode to sekc sir
Palomydes. And as he cam wythin a foreyste, he mette with a knyght,
a chacer of deore.   15

'Sir,' seyde sir Dynadan, 'mette ye wyth ony knyght wyth as shylde
of sylver and lyons hedys?'

'Ye, fayre knyght,' seyde the other, 'with suche a knyght mette I
wyth but a whyle agone, and streyte yondir way he yeode.'

'Gramercy,' seyde sir Dynadan, 'for myght I fynde the tracke of his   20
horse, I sholde nat fayle to fynde that knyght.'

Ryght so as sir Dynadan rode in the evenynge late, he harde a dolefull noyse as hit were of a man. Than sir Dynadan rode towarde that
noyse, and whan he cam nyghe that noyse he alyght of his horse and
wente nere hym on foote. Than was he ware of a knyght that stoode   25
undir a tre, and his horse tyed by hym, and his helme off; and ever that
knyght made a dolefull complaynte as evir made knyght, and allwayes
he complayned of La Beale Isode, the quenc of Cornwayle, and sayde,

'A, fayre lady, why love I the? For thou arte fayryst of all othir, and
as yet shewdyst thou never love to me nother bounté. Pardé, and yet,   30
alas! muste I love the. And I may nat blame the, fayre lady, for myne
eyen caused me. And yet to love the I am but a foole, for the beste
knyght of the worlde lovyth the and ye hym agayne, that is sir Trystram
de Lyones. And the falsyst knyght and kynge of the worlde is your husbande, and the moste cowarde and full of treson is youre lorde kynge   35
Marke. And alas! so beawteuous a lady and pereles of all othir sholde be
matched with the moste vylaunce knyght of the worlde!'

And all this langage harde kynge Marke, what sir Palomydes seyde
by hym. Wherefore he was adrad, whan he sawe sir Dynadan, leste
that he had aspyed hym, and that he wolde tell sir Palomydes that he   40
was kynge Marke; wherefore he wythdrewe hym, and toke his horse
and rode to his men where he commaunded hem to abyde. And so he
rode as faste as he myght unto Camelot.

And the same day he founde there sir Amant, the knyght, redy that

afore kynge Arthure had appelyd hym of treson. And so lyghtly the
kynge commaunded them to do batayle. And by mysadventure kynge
Marke smote sir Amante thorow the body; and yet was sir Amaunte in
the ryghtuous quarell. And ryght so he toke his horse and departed
5 frome the courte for drede of sir Dynadan, that he wolde telle sir
Trystram and sir Palomydes what he was.

Than was there damesels that La Beale Isode had sente to sir Trystram
(15) that knew sir Amante well. Than by the lycence of kynge Arthure they
wente to hym and spake with hym, for whyle the truncheon of the
10 speare stake in his body he spake.

'A, fayre damesels,' seyde sir Amant, 'recommaunde me unto La
Beale Isode, and telle her that I am slayne for the love of her and of syr
Trystram.'

And there he tolde the damessels how cowardly kyng Marke had
15 slayne hym and sir Bersules, his felow:

'And for that dede I appeled hym of treson, and here am I slayne in
a ryghtuous quarell, and all was bycause sir Bersules and I wolde nat
consente by treson to sle the noble knyght sir Trystram.'

Than the two maydyns cryed alowde, that all the courte myght hyre,
20 and seyde,

'A, swete Jesu that knowyste all hydde thynges! Why sufferyst Thou
so false a traytoure to venqueyshe and sle a trewe knyght that faught
in a ryghteuous quarell!'

Than anone hit was spronge to the kynge and the quene and to all
25 the lordis that hit was kynge Marke that had slayne sir Amante and sir
Bersules aforehonde, wherefore they did there that batayle. Than was
kynge Arthure wrothe oute of mesure, and so was all other knyghtes.

But whan sir Trystram wyste all, he wepte for sorow for the losse of
sir Bersules and of sir Amante. Whan sir Launcelot aspyed sir Trystram
30 wepe he wente hastely to kynge Arthure and sayde,

'Sir, I pray you, gyff me leve to returne ayen yondir false kynge and
knyght.'

'I pray you,' seyde kynge Arthure, 'fetche hym agayne, but I wolde
nat ye slew hym, for my worshyp.'

35 Than sir Launcelot armed hym in all haste, and mownted uppon a
grete horse and toke a spere in his honde and rode aftir kynge Marke.
And frome thens a three myle Englysh sir Launcelot overtoke hym and
bade hym turne hym:

'Recreaunte kynge and knyght! For whethir thou wylte othir nylt,
40 thou shalt go with me to kynge Arthurs courte!'

Than kynge Marke returned and loked uppon sir Launcelot and
sayde,

'Fayre sir, what is your name?'

'Wyte you well my name is sir Launcelot, and therefore defende the!'

And whan kynge Marke knew that hit was sir Launcelot, and cam so
faste uppon hym with a speare, he cryed than alowde and seyde,

'I yelde me to the, sir Launcelot, honorable knyght.'

But sir Launcelot wolde nat hyre hym, but cam faste uppon hym.
Kynge Marke saw that, and made no deffence but tumbeled adowne ₅
oute of his sadyll to the erthe as a sak, and there he lay stylle and
cryed:

'Sir Launcelot, have mercy uppon me!'

'Aryse, recreaunte kynge and knyght!'

'Sir, I woll nat fyght,' seyde kynge Marke, 'but whother that ye woll ₁₀
I woll go wyth you.'

'Alas,' seyde sir Launcclotte, 'that I myght nat gyff the one buffette
for the love of sir Trystram and of La Beale Isode, and for tho two
knyghtes that thou haste slayne trayturly!'

And so he mownte uppon his horse and brought hym to kynge ₁₅
Arthure. And there kynge Marke alyght in that same place, and threwe
his helme frome hym uppon the erthe and his swerde, and felle flatte
to the erthe at kynge Arthurs feete, and put hym in his grace and
mercy.

'So God me helpe,' seyde kynge Arthure, 'ye ar wellcom in a maner, ₂₀
and in a maner ye ar nat wellcom. In this maner ye ar wellcom, that
[ye] com hydir magré your hede, as I suppose.'

'That is trouthe,' seyde kynge Marke, 'and ellys I had nat bene here
now, for my lorde sir Launcelot brought me hydir by fyne force, and
to hym am I yoldyn to as recreaunte.' ₂₅

'Well,' seyde kynge Arthure, 'ye ought to do me servyse, omayge
and feauté, and never wolde ye do me none, but ever ye have bene
ayenste me, and a dystroyer of my knyghtes. Now, how woll ye acquyte
you?'

'Sir,' seyde kynge Marke, 'ryght as youre lordshyp woll requyre me, ₃₀
unto my power I woll make a large amendys.' For he was a fayre speker,
and false thereundir.

Than for the grete plesure of sir Trystram, to make them two
accordid, the kynge withhylde kynge Marke as at that tyme and made
a brokyn love day betwene them. ₃₅

Now turne we agayne unto sir Palomydes, how sir Dynadan com- (16)
fortyd hym in all that he myght frome his grete sorowe.

'What knyght ar ye?' seyde sir Palomydes.

'Sir, I am a knyght arraunte as ye be, that have sought you longe by
your shylde.' ₄₀

'Here is my shylde,' seyde sir Palomydes, 'wete you well, and ye
wolde ought therewith, I woll deffende hit.'

'Nay,' seyde sir Dynadan, 'I woll nat have ado with you but in
good maner.'

'And yf ye wyll, ye shall fynde me sone redy.'

'Sir,' seyde sir Dynadan, 'whotherwarde ryde ye this way?'

'Be my hede,' seyde sir Palomydes, 'I wote nat whother, but as fortune ledyth me.'

5 'But harde ye other sawe ye ought of sir Trystram?'

'So God me helpe, of sir Trystram I bothe herde and sawe, and nat-forthan we love nat inwardly well togydyrs, yet at my myscheffe sir Trystram rescowed me fro my deth. And yet or he and I departed, by bothe oure assentys we assygned a day that we sholde have mette at the
10 stony grave that Merlyon sette besyde Camelot, and there to have done batayle togydyrs. Howbehit I was letted,' seyde sir Palomydes, 'that I myght nat holde my day, whyche grevyth me sore; but I have a layrge excuse, for I was presonere with a lorde and many other mo, and that shall sir Trystram well undirstonde that I brake hit of no feare of
15 cowardyse.'

And than sir Palomydes tolde sir Dynadan the same day that they sholde have mette.

'So God me helpe,' seyde sir Dynadan, 'that same day mette sir Launcelot and sir Trystram at the same grave of stone, and there was the
20 moste myghtyeste batayle that ever was sene in this londe betwyxte two knyghtes, for they fought more than fyve owres, and there they bothe bled so muche blood that all men mervayled that ever they myght endure hit. And so by bothe their assentys they were made frendys and sworne brethirne for ever, and no man cowde juge the bettir knyght.
25 And now is sir Trystram made a knyght of the Rounde Table, and he sytthyth in the syege of the noble knyght sir Marhalte.'

'Be my hede,' seyde sir Palomydes, 'sir Trystram ys farre bygger than is sir Launcelot, and the hardyer knyght.'

'Sir, have ye assayde them bothe?' seyde sir Dynadan.

30 'I have [sene] sir Trystramys myght,' seyde sir Palomydes, 'but never sir Launcelot, to my wyttynge, but at the fountayne where lay sir Launcelot on slepe. And there with one speare he smote downe sir Trystram and me,' [seyde] sir Palomydes. 'But at that tyme they knewe nat, but aftyrwarde.'

35 'Now, fayre knyght,' seyde sir Dynadan, 'as for sir Launcelot and sir [Trystram], lette them be, for the warre of them woll nat be lyghtly macchid of no knyghtes that I knowe lyvynge.'

'No,' seyde sir Palomydes, 'God deffende, but and I hadde a quarell to the bettir of them bothe, I wolde with as good a wyll fyght with
40 hem as with you.'

'Sir, I requere you,' seyde sir Dynadan, 'tell me your name, and in good fayth I shall holde you company tyll that we com to Camelot, and there shall ye have grete worshyp now at this grete turnemente, for there shall be quene Gwenyver and La Beale Isode of Cornwayle.'

'Wyte you well, sir knyght, for the love of La Beale Isode I woll be there, and ellis nat, but I woll nat have ado in kynge Arthurs courte.'

'Sir,' seyde sir Dynadan, 'I shall ryde with you and do you servyse, so ye woll tell me youre name.'   5

'Syr, ye shall undirstonde my name is Palomydes, brothir unto sir Saphyre, the good knyght, and sir Segwarydes. And we [b]e Sarezyns borne.'

'Sir, I thanke you,' seyde sir Dynadan, 'for I am glad that I knowe your name. And by me ye shall nat be hurte but rathir avaunced, and I   10 may, on my lyff. For ye shall wynne worshyp in the courte of kynge Arthure and be ryghte wellcom.'

And so they dressed on their helmys and put on there shyldis and mownted uppon their horsys and toke the brode way towarde Camelot. And than were they ware of a castell that was fayre and ryche and also   15 passynge stronge as ony was within this realme. So sir Palomydes seyde (17) to sir Dynadan,

'Here is a castell that I knowe well, and therein dwellyth quene Morgan le Fay, kynge Arthurs systyr. And kynge Arthure gaff hir this castell by the whyche he hath repented hym sytthyn a thousand tymes,   20 for sytthen kynge Arthur and she hath bene at debate and stryff; but this castell coude he never gete nother wynne of hir by no maner of engyne. And ever as she myght she made warre on kynge Arthure, and all daungerous knyghtes she wytholdyth with her for to dystroy all thos knyghtes that kynge Arthure lovyth. And there shall no knyght   25 passe this way but he muste juste with one knyght other wyth two other with three. And yf hit hap that kynge Arthurs knyghtes be beatyn, he shall lose his horse and harnes and all that he hath, and harde yf that he ascape but that he shall be presonere.'

'So God me helpe,' seyde sir Palomydes, 'this is a shamefull and a   30 vylaunce usage for a quene to use, and namely to make suche warre uppon her owne lorde that is called the floure of chevalry that is Crystyn othir hethyn, and with all my harte I woll destroy that shame-full custom. And I woll that all the worlde wyte she shall have no servyse of me. And yf she sende oute ony knyghtes, as I suppose she woll, to   35 juste, they shall have bothe there hondys full.'

'And I shall nat fayle you,' seyde sir Dynadan, 'unto my puyssaunce, uppon my lyff!'

So as they stoode on horsebacke afore the castell, there cam a knyght wyth a rede shylde and two squyers aftir hym; and he cam strayte unto   40 sir Palomydes and sayde,

'Fayre knyght arraunte, I requyre the for the love thou owyste unto knyghthode, that thou wylt not have ado here with this men of this castell.' (Thus sir Lamerok seyde.) 'For I cam hydir to seke this dede, and hit is my rekeyste. And therefore I beseche you, knyght, lette me deale, and yf I be beatyn, revenge me.'

'In the name of God,' seyde sir Palomydes, 'lat se how ye woll spede, and we shall beholde you.'

5 Than anone come furth a knyght of the castell and profyrde to juste with the knyght wyth the rede shylde. And anone they encountyrd togydyrs, and he with the rede shylde smote hym so harde that he bare hym over to the erthe. And therewith anone cam another knyght of the castell, and he was smyttyn so sore that he avoyded hys sadyll. And
10 furthwithall cam the thirde knyght, and the knyght with the rede shylde smote hym to the erthe. Than cam sir Palomydes and besought hym that he myght helpe hym to juste.

'Now, sir knyght,' he seyde, 'suffir me as at this tyme to have my wyll, for and they were twenty knyghtes I shall nat doute them.'

15 And ever there were uppon the wallys of the castell many lordys that cryed and seyde,

'Well have ye justed, knyght with the rede shylde!'

But as sone as the knyght had smyttyn hem downe, his squyers toke their horsys and avoyded there sadyls and brydyls of the horsis, and
20 turnede theym into the foreyste, and made the knyghtes to be kepte to the ende of the justys.

Ryght so cam forth of the castell the fourthe knyght, and freyshly profyrde to juste wyth the knyght with the rede shylde. And he was redy, and he smote hym so harde that horse and man felle to the erthe,
25 and the knyghtes backe brake with the falle, and his necke also.

'A, Jesu!' seyde sir Palomydes. 'That yondir is a passynge good knyght and the beste juster that ever I sawe.'

'Be my hede,' seyde sir Dynadan, 'he is as good as ever was sir Launcelot othir sir Trystram, what knyght soever he be.'

(18) 30 Than furthwithall cam a knyght oute of the castell with a shylde bended with blak and with whyght. And anone the knyght wyth the rede shylde and he encountyrd so harde that he smote the knyght of the castell thorowoute the bended shylde and thorow the body, and brake the horse backe.

35 'Fayre knyght,' sayde sir Palomydes, 'ye have overmuche on hande, therefore I pray you, lette me juste, for ye had nede to be reposed.'

'Why, sir,' seyde the knyght, 'seme ye that I am weyke and fyeble? A, sir, methynkyth ye proffir me grete wronge and shame whan I do well inowe, for I telle you now as I tolde you arste, and they were
40 twenty knyghtes I shall beate theym. And yf I be beatyn other slayne, than may ye revenge me. And yf ye thynke that I be wery, and ye have an appety[t]e to juste with me, I shall fynde [you] justynge inowghe.'

'Syr,' seyde he, 'I sayde hit nat because that I wolde juste with you, but mesemyth ye have overmuche on hande.'

'And therefore, and ye were jantyll,' sayde the knyght with the red shylde, 'ye wolde nat profyr me no shame. Therefore I requyre you to juste with me, and ye shall fynde that I am nat wery.'

'Syth ye requyre me,' seyde sir Palomydes, 'take kepe to youreselff.'

Than they two knyghtes com togydyrs as faste as their horsys myght ren, and the knyght smote sir Palomydes so sore on the shylde that the speare wente into hys syde and hurte hym a grete wounde and a perelous. And therewith sir Palomydes avoyded his sadyll. And that knyght turned unto sir Dynadan, and whan he sawe hym commynge he cryed alowde and sayde,

'Sir, I woll nat have ado with you!'

But for that he spared nat, but com strayte uppon [hym]. So sir Dynadan for shame put forth hys speare and all to-shyvirde hit uppon the knyght; but he smote sir Dynadan agayne so harde that he bare hym frome his horse. But he wolde nat suffyr his squyer to meddyll wyth there horsys, and bycause they were knyghtes arraunte.

Than he dressid hym agayne to the castell and justed with seven knyghtes mo, and there was none of hem that myght withstonde hym, but he bare them to the erthe. And of those a twelve knyghtes he slewe in playne justys four; and the eyght knyghtes he made them to swere on the crosse of a swerde that they sholde never use the evyll customs of the castell. And whan he made them to swere that othe, he lete them passe. And stoode the lordis and the ladyes on the castell wallys, cryynge and seynge:

'Knyght with the rede [shylde], ye have mervaylously well done as ever we sawe knyght do.'

And therewith come a knyght oute of the castell unarmed, and seyde,

'Knyght with the rede shylde, overmuche damage have ye done this same day! And therefore returne whother ye woll, for here ar no mo that woll have ado with the, for we repente sore that ever ye cam here, for by the is fordone all the olde customes of this castell.'

And with that worde he turned agayne into the castell, and shett the yatys. Than the knyght wyth the rede shylde turned and called his squyers, and so paste forth on his way and rode a grete pace.

And whan he was paste, sir Palomydes wente to sir Dynadan and seyde to hym,

'I had never suche a shame of one knyght that ever I mette, and therefore I caste me to ryde aftir hym and to be revenged uppon hym with my swerde, for on horsebacke I deme I shall gete no worshyp of hym.'

['Sir Palomydes,' seyde Dynadan, 'ye shalle not medle with hym by my counceil, for ye shale gete no worship of hym,] and for this cause: that ye have sene hym this day have had evermuche to done and overmuche travayled.'

'Be Allmyghty Jesu,' seyde sir Palomydes, 'I shall never be at ease tyll that I have had ado with hym.'

'Sir,' seyde sir Dynadan, 'I shall gyff you my beholdynge.'

'Well,' seyde sir Palomydes, 'than shall ye se how we shall redresse
5 oure myghtes.' So they toke there horsys of their varlettis and rode aftir the knyght with the rede shylde. And downe in a valay, besyde a fountayne, they were ware where he was alyght to repose hym, and had
(19) done of his helme for to drynke at the welle. Than sir Palomydes rode faste tyll he cam nyghe hym, and than he seyde,
10 'Knyght, remembir ye me, and of the same dede that ye ded to me late at the castell. Therefore redresse the, for I woll have ado with the.'

'Fayre knyght,' seyde sir Lamerok, 'of me ye wynne no worshyp, for ye have sene this [daye] that I have be travayled sore.'

'As for that,' seyde sir Palomydes, 'I woll nat lette, for wyte you well,
15 I woll be revenged.'

'Well,' seyde the knyght, 'I may happyn to endure you.'

And therewithall he mownted uppon his horse and toke a grete speare in his honde redy to juste.

'Nay,' seyde sir Palomydes, 'I woll nat juste, for I am sure at justynge
20 I gete no pryce.'

'Now, fayre knyght,' sayde he, 'hit wolde beseme a knyght to juste and to fyght on horsebacke.'

'Ye shall se what I woll do,' seyde sir Palomydes.

And therewith he alyght downe uppon foote, and dressed his shylde
25 afore hym and pulled oute his swerde. Than the knyght with the rede shylde descended downe frome his horse and dressed his shylde afore hym, and so he drewe oute his swerde. And than they come togydyrs a soffte pace, and wondirly they layshed togydyrs passynge thycke, the mowntenaunce of an owre, or ever they breethid. Than they trased and
30 traverced and wexed wondirly wrothe, and aythir behyght other deth. They hewe so faste wyth there swerdis that they kutte downe halff their shyldis, and they hewe togydyrs on helmys and mayles, that the bare fleysshe in som places stoode abovyn there harneys.

And whan sir Palomydes behylde his felowys swerde overheled
35 with his blood, hit greved hym sore. And som whyle they foyned and somwhyle they strake downe as wylde men. But at the laste sir Palomydes waxed wondir faynte bycause of his fyrste wounde that he had at the castell wyth a speare, for that wounde greved hym wondirly sore.

40 'Now, fayre knyght,' sayde sir Palomydes, 'mesemyth we have assayed ayther other passyngly well, and yf hit may please you [I requyre you] of your knyghthode to tell me your name.'

'Sir,' he sayde, 'that is me ryght loth, for ye have done me grete wronge and no knyghthode to proffir me batayle, consyderynge my

grete travayle. But and ye woll telle me youre name, I woll telle you
myne.'

'Sir, wyte you well, my name is sir Palomydes.'

'Than, sir, ye shall undirstonde my name is sir Lameroke de Galys,
sonne and ayre unto the good knyght and kynge, kynge Pellynore. 5
And sir Torre, the good knyght, is my halff brothir.'

Whan sir Palomydes had herde hym sey so, he kneled adowne and
asked mercy:

'For outrageously have I done to you this day, consyderynge the
grete dedis of armys I have sene you done, and shamefully and un- 10
knyghtly I have requyred you to do batayle with me.'

'A, sir Palomydes,' seyde sir Lamerok, 'overmuche have ye done and
seyde to me!'

And therewyth he pulled hym up wyth his bothe hondis, and seyde,

'Sir Palomydes, the worthy knyght, in all this londe is no bettir than 15
ye be, nor more of proues, and me repentys sore that we sholde fyght
togydirs.'

'So hit doth nat me,' seyde sir Palomydes, 'and yett I am sorer
wounded than ye be; but as for that, I shall sone be hole. But sertaynly
I wolde nat, for the fayryst castell in this londe, but yf ye and I had 20
mette: for I shall love you dayes of my lyff afore all other knyghtes
excepte my brother sir Saphir.'

'I say the same,' seyde sir Lameroke, 'excepte my brother sir Torre.'

Than cam sir Dynadan, and he made grete joy of sir Lamerok. Than
their squyers dressed bothe their shyldis and their harnes, and stopped 25
hir woundis. And thereby at a pryory they rested them all nyght.

Now turne we agayne, that whan sir Uwayne and sir Braundyles with (20)
his felowys cam to the courte of kynge Arthure, and they tolde the
kynge, sir Launcelot, and sir Trystram, how sir Dagonet, the foole,
chaced kynge Marke thorowoute the foreste, and how the stronge 30
knyght smote them downe all seven with one speare, than there was
grete lawghynge and japynge at kynge Marke and at sir Dagonet. But
all thos knyghtes coude nat telle what knyght hit was that rescowed
kynge Marke. Than they asked of kynge Marke yf that he knewe hym,
and he answerde and sayde,   35

'He named hymself the knyght that folowed the Questynge Beste,
and in that name he sent oute one of my varlettes to a place where was
his modir. And whan she harde from whens he cam she made passyng
grete dole, and so discoverde to my varlette his name, and seyde: "A,
my dere son, sir Palomydes, why wolt thou nat se me?" And therefore, 40
sir,' seyde kynge Marke, 'hit is to undirstonde his name is sir Palomydes,
a noble knyght.'

Than were all the seven knyghtys passynge glad that they knewe
his name.

Now turne we agayne, for on the morne they toke their horsys, bothe sir Lameroke, sir Palomydes, and sir Dynadan, wyth their squyers and varlettis, tylle they sawe a fayre castell that stoode on a mountayne well closyd, and thydir they rode.

5 And there they founde a knyght that hyght sir Galahalte, that was lorde of that castell. And there they had grete chere and were well eased.

'Sir Dynadan,' seyde sir Lameroke, 'what woll ye do?'

'Sir, I woll to-morne to the courte of kynge Arthure.'

10 'Be my hede,' seyde sir Palomydes, 'I woll nat ryde this three dayes, for I am sore hurte and muche have I bledde, and therefore I woll repose me here.'

'Truly,' seyde sir Lameroke, 'and I woll abyde here wyth you. And whan ye ryde, than woll I ryde, onles that ye tary overlonge; than woll 15 I take myne horse. Therefore I pray you, sir Dynadan, abyde ye and ryde with us.'

'Faythfully,' seyde sir Dynadan, 'I woll nat abyde, for I have suche a talente to se sir Trystram that I may nat abyde longe from hym.'

'A! sir Dynadan,' seyde sir Palomydes, 'now do I undirstonde that 20 ye love my mortall enemy, and therefore how sholde I truste you?'

'Wyte you well,' seyde sir Dynadan, 'I love my lorde sir Trystram abovyn all othir knyghtes, and hym woll I serve and do honoure.'

'So shall I,' seyde sir Lameroke, 'in all that I may with my power.'

So on the morne sir Dynadan rode unto the courte of kynge Arthur. 25 And by the way as he rode he sawe where stoode an arraunte knyght, and made hym redy for to juste.

'Nat so,' seyde sir Dynadan, 'for I have no wyll to juste.'

'Wyth me shall ye juste,' seyde the knyght, 'or that ye passe this way.'

'Sir, whether aske you justys of love othir of hate?'

30 The knyghte answerde and seyde,

'Wyte you well I aske hit for loove and nat of hate.'

'Hit may well be,' seyde sir Dynadan, 'but ye proffyr me harde love whan ye wolde juste with me wyth an harde speare! But, fayre knyght,' seyde sir Dynadan, 'sytthyn ye woll juste with me, mete wyth me in the 35 courte of kynge Arthure, and there I shall juste wyth you.'

'Well,' seyde the knyght, 'sytthyn ye woll not juste wyth me, I pray you tell me your name.'

'Sir knyght, my name ys sir Dynadan.'

'A, sir,' seyde that knyght, 'full well knowe I you for a good knyght 40 and a jantyll, and wyte you well, sir, I love you hertyly.'

'Than shall here be no justys,' seyde syr Dynadan, 'betwyxte us.'

So they departed.

And the same day he com to Camelot where lay kynge Arthure. And there he salewed the kynge and the quene, sir Launcelot and sir

Trystram; and all the courte was glad of sir Dynadans commynge home, for he was jantyll, wyse, and a good knyght. And in aspeciall sir Trystram loved sir Dynadan passyngly well.

Than the kynge askyd sir Dynadan what adventures he had sene.

'Sir,' seyde sir Dynadan, 'I have seyne many adventures, and of som kynge Marke knowyth, but nat all.'

Than the kynge herkened to sir Dynadan how he tolde that sir Palomydes and he were byfore the castell of Morgan le Fay, and how sir Lameroke toke the justys afore them, and how he forjusted twelve knyghtes and of them four he slew, and how aftir that 'he smote downe sir Palomydes and me bothe.'

'I may nat belyve that,' seyde the kynge, 'for sir Palomydes is a passynge good knyght.'

'That is verry trouthe,' seyde sir Dynadan, 'but yett I sawe hym bettyr preved hande for hande.'

And than he tolde the kynge of all that batayle, and how sir Palomydes was the more wayker and sorer was hurte, and more he loste of his blood than sir Lameroke.

'And withoute doute,' seyde sir Dynadan, 'had the batayle lasted ony lenger, sir Palomydes had be slayne.'

'A, Jesu!' seyde kynge Arthure, 'this is to me a grete mervayle.'

'Sir,' seyde sir Trystram, 'mervayle ye nothynge thereof, for, at myne advyce, there is nat a valyaunter knyght in the worlde lyvynge, for I know his myght. And now woll I say you, I was never so wery of knyght but yf hit were my lorde sir Launcelot. And there is no knyght in the worlde excepte sir Launcelot that I wolde ded so well as sir Lamerok.'

'So God me helpe,' seyde the kynge, 'I wolde fayne that knyght sir Lamerok wolde com to this courte.'

'Sir,' seyde sir Dynadan, 'he woll be here in shorte space and sir Palomydes bothe, but I feare me that sir Palomydes may nat yett travayle.'

So wythin three dayes after the kynge lete make a justenynge at a pryory frome the justys. And there made them redy many knyghtes of the Rounde Table, and sir Gawayne and his bretherne they made them redy to juste. But sir Launcelot, syr Trystram, nother sir Dynadan wolde nat juste, but suffyrd sir Gawayne for the love of kynge Arthure wyth his bretherne to wynne the degré yf they myght.

So on the morn they apparayled hem to juste; sir Gawayne and his four bretherne, they ded grete dedis of armys, and sir Ector de Marys ded mervaylously well. But sir Gawayne passed all that felyship, wherefore kynge Arthure and all the knyghtes gave sir Gawayne the honoure [at] the begynnynge.

Ryght so was kynge Arthure ware of a knyght and two squyers that

com oute of a foreystis syde wyth a covyrd shylde of lethir. Than he
cam in ⌐slyly⌐, and hurled here and there, and anone with one speare he
had smyttyn downe two knyghtes of the Rounde Table. And so wyth
his hurtelynge he loste the coverynge of his shylde. Than was the kynge
5 and all ware that he bare a rede shylde.

'A, Jesu!' seyde kynge Arthure, 'se where rydyth a strong knyght,
he wyth the rede shylde.'

And there was a noyse and a grete cry:

'Beware the knyght with the rede shylde!'

10 So wythin a lytyll whyle he had overthrowyn three bretherne of sir
Gawaynes.

'So God me helpe,' seyde kynge Arthur, 'mesemyth yondir is the
beste juster that ever I sawe.'

So he loked aboute and saw hym encountir with sir Gawayne, and
15 he smote hym downe with so grete force that he made his horse to
avoyde his sadyll.

'How now?' seyde the kynge to sir Gawayne. 'Methynkyth ye have
a falle! Well were me and I knew what knyght he were with the rede
shylde.'

20 'I know hym well inowghe,' seyde sir Dynadan, 'but as at this tyme
ye shall nat know his name.'

'Be my hede,' seyde sir Trystram, 'he justyth better than sir Palomydes, and yf ye lyste to know, his name is sir Lameroke de Galys.'

And as they stood thus, they saw sir Gawayne and he encountyrd
25 togedir agayne, and there he smote sir Gawayne from his horse and
brused hym sore. And in the syght of kynge Arthure he smote downe
twenty knyghtes besyde sir Gawayne, and so clyerly was the pryce
yevyn hym as a knyght piereles. Than slyly and mervaylously sir
Lameroke wythdrewe hym from all the felyshyp into the foreystys
30 syde. All this aspyed kynge Arthure, for his yghe went never frome
hym.

Than the kynge, sir Launcelot, and sir Trystram, and sir Dynadan
toke there hakeneyes and rode streyte aftir the good knyght sir
Lameroke de Galis, and there founde hym. And thus seyde [the]
35 kynge:

'A, fayre knyght, well be ye founde!'

Whan he sawe the kynge he put of his helme and salewed hym. And
whan he sawe sir Trystram he alyght adowne of his horse and ran to
[hym to] take hym by the ⌐thyes⌐; but sir Trystram wolde nat suffir
40 hym, but he alyght or that he cam and ayther toke othir in armys and
made grete joy of other.

Than the kynge was gladde and so was all the felyshyp of the Rounde
Table excepte sir Gawayne and his bretherne. And whan they wyste
that hit was sir Lameroke they had grete despyte of hym, and were

wondirly wrothe wyth hym that he had put hym to such a dishonoure
that day. Than he called to hym prevaly in counceyle all his bretherne,
and to them seyde thus:

'Fayre bretherne, here may ye se: whom that we hate kynge Arthure
lovyth, and whom that we love he hatyth. And wyte you well, my 5
fayre bretherne, that this sir Lamerok woll nevyr love us, because we
slew his fadir, kynge Pellynor, for we demed that he slew oure fadir,
kynge Lotte of Orkenay; and for the deth of kynge Pellynor sir
Lameroke ded us a shame to oure modir. Therefore I woll be revenged.'

'Sir,' seyde sir Gawaynes bretherne, 'lat se: devyse how ye woll be 10
revenged, and ye shall fynde us redy.'

'Well,' seyde sir Gawayne, 'holde ye styll and we shall aspye oure
tyme.'

Now passe we on oure mater and leve we sir Gawayne, and speke we (22)
of kynge Arthure, that on a day seyde unto kynge Marke, 15

'Sir, I pray you, gyff me a gyffte that I shall aske you.'

'Sir,' seyde kynge Marke, 'I woll gyff you what gyffte I may gyff
you.'

'Sir, gramercy,' seyde kynge Arthure, 'this woll I aske you, that ye be
good lorde unto sir Trystram, for he is a man of grete honoure, and 20
that ye woll take hym with you into Cornwayle and lat hym se his
fryndis, and there cherysh hym for my sake.'

'Sir,' seyde kynge Marke, 'I promyse you be my fayth and by the
fayth that I owe unto God and to you, I shall worship hym for youre
sake all that I can or may.' 25

'Sir,' seyde kynge Arthure, 'and I woll forgyff you all the evyll wyll
that ever I ought you, and ye swere that uppon a booke afore me.'

'Wyth a good wyll,' seyde kynge Marke.

And so he there sware uppon a booke afore hym and all his knyghtes,
and therewith kynge Marke and sir Trystram toke ayther othir by the 30
hondis harde knytte togydyrs. But for all this kynge Marke thought
falsely, as hit preved aftir; for he put sir Trystram in preson, and
cowardly wolde have slayne hym.

Than sone aftyr kynge Marke toke his leve to ryde into Cornwayle,
and sir Trystram made hym redy to ryde with hym, whereof the moste 35
party of the Rounde Table were wrothe and hevy. And in especiall sir
Launcelot and sir Lameroke and sir Dynadan were wrothe oute of
mesure, for well they wyste that kynge Marke wolde sle or destroy
sir Trystram.

'Alas!' seyde sir Dynadan, 'that my lorde sir Trystram shall departe!' 40
And sir Trystram toke suche a sorow that he was amased.

'Alas!' seyde sir Launcelot unto kynge Arthure, 'what have ye done?
For ye shall lose the man of moste worshyp that ever cam into youre
courte.'

'Sir, hit was his owne desyre,' seyde kynge Arthure, 'and therefore I myght nat do wythall, for I have done all that I can and made them at accorde.'

'Acorde?' seyde sir Launcelotte. 'Now fye on that accorde! For ye 5 shall here that he shall destroy sir Trystram other put hym into preson, for he is the moste cowarde and the vylaunste kynge and knyght that is now lyvynge.'

And therewith sir Launcelot departed and cam to kynge Marke and sayde to hym thus:

10 'Sir kynge, wyte [th]ou well the good knyght sir Trystram shall go with the. Beware, I rede the, of treson, for and thou myschyff that knyght by ony maner of falsehode or treson, by the fayth I awghe to God and to the Order of Knyghthode, I shall sle the myne owne hondis!'

15 'Sir Launcelot, overmuch have ye sayde unto me, and I have sworne and seyde over largely afore kynge Arthure, in hyrynge of all hys knyghtes, and overmuch shame hit were to me to breke my promyse.'

'Ye sey well,' seyde sir Launcelot, 'but ye ar called so false and full of felony that no man may beleve you. Pardé, hit is knowyn well for what 20 cause ye cam into this contrey: and for none other cause but to sle syr [Tristram.'

Soo with grete dole kynge Marke and sir Tristram rode togyders. For hit was by sir Tristrams wil and his meanes to goo with kyng Marke, and all was for the entente to see La Beale Isoud, for without 25 the syghte of her syr Tristram myght not endure.

(23) Now torne we ageyne unto syr Lamorak and speke we of his bretheren: syr Tor, whiche was kynge Pellenors fyrst sone and by-goten of Aryes wyf, the couherd, for he was a bastard; and sire Aglovale was his fyrste sone begoten in wedlok; syre Lamorak, Dornar, Per-30 cyvale, these were his sones to in wedlok.

So whanne kynge Marke and sire Tristram were departed from the courte there was made grete dole and sorowe for the departynge of sir Tristram. Thenne the kynge and his knyghtes made no manere of joyes eyghte dayes after.

35 And atte eyghte dayes ende ther cam to the courte a knyghte with a yonge squyer with hym, and whanne this knyghte was unarmed he went to the kynge and requyred hym to make the yonge squyer a knyghte.

'Of what lygnage is he come?' said kynge Arthur.

40 'Syre,' sayd the knyght, 'he is the sone of kynge Pellenore that dyd you somtyme good servyse, and he is broder unto syr Lamorak de Galys, the good knyghte.'

'Wel,' sayd the kynge, 'for what cause desyre ye that of me that I shold make hym knyghte?'

'Wete you wel, my lord the kynge, that this yonge squyer is broder to
me as wel as to sir Lamorak, and my name is Aglavale.'

'Syre Aglovayle,' sayd Arthur, 'for the love of sire Lamorak and for
his faders love he shalle be made knyghte to-morowe. Now telle me,'
said Arthur, 'what is his name?'   5

'Syre,' sayd the knyght, 'his name is Percyvale de Galys.'

Soo on the morne the kynge made hym knyght in Camelott. But the
kynge and alle the knyghtes thoughte hit wold be longe or that he
preved a good knyghte.

Thenne at the dyner, whanne the kynge was set at the table, and   10
every knyght after he was of prowesse, the kyng commaunded hym to
be sette amonge meane knyghtes; and soo was sire Percyvale sette as
the kynge commaunded.

Thenne was there a mayden in the quenes court that was come of
hyhe blood, and she was domme and never spak word. Ryght so she   15
cam streyght into the halle, and went unto sir Percyvale, and toke hym
by the hand and said alowde, that the kyng and all the knyghtes myght
here hit,

'Aryse, syr Percyvale, the noble knyght and Goddes knyght, and
go with me!'   20

And so he dyd, and there she broughte hym to the ryght syde of the
Sege Perillous and said,

'Fair knyghte, take here thy sege, for that sege apperteyneth to the
and to none other.'

Ryght soo she departed and asked a preste, and as she was confessid 25
and houseld thenne she dyed. Thenne the kynge and alle the courte
made grete joye of syr Percyvale.

Now torne we unto sir Lamorak that moche was there preysed. (24)
Thenne by the meane of sir Gawayn and his bretheren they sente for
her moder there besydes, fast by a castel besyde Camelot, and alle was 30
to that entente to slee sir Lamorak. The quene of Orkeney was there but
a whyle, but sir Lamorak wyst of ⟨her⟩ beynge and was ful fayne.

And for to make an ende of this matere, he sente unto her, and ther
betwixe them was a nyght assygned that sir Lamorak shold come to her.
Therof] was ware sir Gaherys, and rode afore the same nyght, and   35
wayted uppon sir Lamerok. And than he sy where he cam rydynge all
armed, and where he alyght and tyed his horse to a prevay postren,
and so he wente into a parler and unarmed hym. And than he wente
unto the quenys bed, and she made of hym passynge grete joy and he
of her agayne, for ayther lovid other passynge sore.   40

So whan sir Gaherys sawe his tyme he cam to there beddis syde all
armed, wyth his swerde naked, and suddaynly he gate his modir by the
heyre and strake of her hede. Whan sir Lameroke sawe the blood
daysshe uppon hym all hote, whyche was the bloode that he loved

passyng well, wyte you well he was sore abaysshed and dismayed of
that dolerous syght. And therewithall sir Lamerok lepte oute of the
bed in his shurte as a knyght dismayed, saynge thus:

'A, sir Gaherys, knyght of the Table Rounde! Fowle and evyll have
5 ye done, and to you grete shame! Alas, why have ye slayne youre
modir that bare you? For with more ryght ye shulde have slayne me!'

'The offence haste thou done,' seyde sir Gaherys. 'Natwithstondynge
a man is borne to offir his servyse, but yett sholdyst thou beware with
whom thou medelyst, for thou haste put my bretherne and me to a
10 shame; and thy fadir slew oure fadir, and thou to ly by oure modir is to
muche shame for us to suffir. And as for thy fadir, kynge Pellynor, my
brothir sir Gawayne and I slew hym.'

'Ye ded the more wronge,' seyde sir Lamerok, 'for my fadir slew nat
your fadir: hit was Balyn le Saveage! And as yett my fadyrs deth is nat
15 revenged.'

'Leve tho wordy[s],' seyde sir Gaherys, 'for and thou speke vylaunsly
I woll sle the, but bycause thou arte naked I am ashamed to sle the. But
wyte thou well, in what place I may gete the, I woll sle the! And now
is my modir quytte of the, for she shall never shame her chyldryn. And
20 therefore hyghe the and wythdrawe the and take thyne armour, that
thou were gone.'

So sir Lameroke saw there was none other boote, but faste armed
hym and toke his horse and roode his way makynge grete sorow; but
for shame and sorowe he wolde nat ryde to kynge Arthurs courte, but
25 rode another way.

But whan hit was knowyn that sir Gaherys had slayne his modir the
kynge was wrothe and commaunded hym to go oute of his courte.
Wyte you well sir Gawayne was wrothe that sir Gaherys had slayne
his modir and lete sir Lamerok ascape. And for this mater was the
30 kynge passynge wrothe and many other knyghtes.

'Sir,' seyde sir Launcelot, 'here is a grete myscheff fallyn by fellony
and by forecaste [treason], that your syster is thus shamfully islayne.
And I dare say hit was wrought by treson, and I dare say also that ye
shall lose that good knyght sir Lamerok. And I wote well, and sir
35 Trystram wyste hit, he wolde never com within your courte.'

'God deffende,' seyde kynge Arthur, 'that I sholde lese sir Lamerok
[or sir Trystram, for than tweyne of my chief knyghtes of the Table
Rounde were gone.'

'Sir,' seyde sir Launcelot, 'I am sure ye shall lose sir Lamerok,] for
40 sir Gawayne and his bretherne woll sle hym by one meane other by
another.'

'That shall I lette,' seyde kynge Arthur.

(25)   Now leve we of sir Lamerok and speke we of sir Gawayne and
his bretherne, sir Aggravayne and sir Mordred.

As they rode on their adventures they mette wyth a knyght flyynge sore wounded, and they asked hym what tydynges.

'Fayre knyghtes,' sayde he, 'here commyth a knyght aftir me that woll sle me.'

So wyth that come sir Dynadan fast rydynge to them by adventure, but he wolde promyse them none helpe. But sir Aggravayne and sir Mordred promysed to rescowe hym.

And therewithall come that knyght streyte unto them, and anone he profyrde to juste. That sawe sir Mordred and rode to hym and strake hym, but he smote sir Mordred over his horse tayle.

That sawe sir Aggravayne ⌐and streyghte he rode toward that knyght⌐. And ryght so as he served sir Mordred, so he served sir Aggravayne and [seyde],

'Wyte you well, syrrys bothe, that I am sir Brewnys Saunze Pité that hath done thus to you.'

And yet he rode over sir Aggravayne fyve or six tymes.

Whan sir Dynadan saw this, he muste nedis juste with hym for shame. And so sir Dynadan and he encountyrd togydyrs, but wyth pure strengthe sir Dynadan smote hym over hys horse tayle. Than he toke his horse and fledde. (For he was on foote one of the valyaunte knyghtes in Arthurs dayes, and a grete dystroyer of all good knyghtes).

Than rode sir Dynadan unto sir Mordred and unto sir Aggravayne.

'Sir knyght, well have ye done, and well have ye revenged us, where-fore we pray you tell us your name.'

'Fayre syrs, ye ought to knowe my name whyche is called sir Dynadan.'

Whan they undirstode that hit was sir Dynadan they were more wrothe than they were before, for they hated hym oute of mesure bycause of sir Lameroke. For sir Dynadan had suche a custom that he loved all good knyghtes that were valyaunte, and he hated all tho that were destroyers of good knyghtes. And there was none that hated sir Dynadan but tho that ever were called murtherers.

Than spake the hurte knyght that Brewnes Saunze Pité had chaced, his name was Dalan, and sayde,

'Yf thou be sir Dynadan, thou slewe my fadir.'

'Hit myght well be so,' seyde sir Dynadan, 'but than hit was in my deffence and at his requeste.'

'Be my hede,' seyde Dalyn, 'thou shalt dye therefore!'

And therewith he dressed his speare and his shylde. And to make shorte tale, sir Dynadan smote hym downe of his horse, that his necke was nye brokyn. And in the same wyse he smote sir Mordred and sir Aggravayne. And aftir, in the queste of the Sankgreal, cowardly and felonsly they slew sir Dynadan, whyche was a ⌐grete dammage, for he was a⌐ grete bourder and a passynge good knyght.

And so sir Dynadan rode to a castall that hyght Beall Valet, and there he founde sir Palamydes that was nat hole of the wounde that sir Lamerok gaff hym. And there sir Dynadan tolde sir Palomydes all the tydynges that he harde and sawe of sir Trystram, and how he was gone
5 with kynge Marke, and wyth hym he hath all his wyll and desyre. Therewith sir Palomydes wexed wrothe, for he loved La Beale Isode, and than he wyste well that sir Trystram enjoyed her.

(26) Now leve we sir Palomydes and sir Dynadan in the castell of Beale Valet, and turne we agayne unto kynge Arthure. There cam a knyght
10 oute of Cornwayle, his name was sir Fergus, a felow of the Rounde Table, and there he tolde the kynge and sir Launcelot good tydyngis of sir Trystram (and there was brought goodly letters), and how he leffte hym in the castell of Tyntagyll.

Than cam a damesell that brought goodly lettyrs unto kynge Arthure
15 and unto sir Launcelot, and there she had passynge good chere of the kynge and of the quene and of sir Launcelot. And so they wrote goodly lettyrs agayne. But sir Launcelot bade ever sir Trystram beware of kynge Marke, for ever he called hym in hys lettirs Kynge Foxe, as who sayth he faryth allwey with wylys and treson; whereof sir Trystram in
20 his herte thanked sir Launcelot.

Than the damesell wente unto La Beale Isode and bare hir lettirs frome the kyng and from sir Launcelot, whereof she was in grete joy.

'Fayre damesell,' seyde Isode, 'how faryth my lorde Arthure, and quene Gwenyver, and the noble knyght sir Launcelot?'
25 She answerd, and to make shorte tale, 'Muche the bettir that ye and sir Trystram bene in joy.'

'God rewarde them,' seyde Isode, 'for sir Trystram hath suffirde grete payne for me and I for hym.'

So the damesell departed and brought the lettirs to kynge Marke.
30 And whan he had rad them and undirstonde them, he was wroth wyth sir Trystram, for he demed that he had sente the damesell to kynge Arthure. For kynge Arthure and sir Launcelot in a maner thretned kynge Marke in ⟨t⟩his letters, and as kynge Marke red this lettyrs he demede treson by sir Trystram.
35 'Damesell,' seyde kynge Marke, 'woll ye ryde agayne and beare lettyrs frome me unto kynge Arthure?'

'Sir,' she seyde, 'I woll be at youre commaundement to ryde whan ye wyll.'

'Ye sey well,' seyde the kynge. 'Com ye agayne to-morne and fecche
40 youre lettyrs.'

Than she departed and cam to La Beall Isode and to sir Trystram and tolde hem how she sholde ryde agayne with lettyrs to kynge Arthure.

'Than we pray you,' seyde they, 'that whan ye have resceyved youre

lettyrs that ye wolde com by us, that we may se the prevyté of youre
lettirs.'

'All that I may do, madame, ye wote well I muste do for sir Trystram, for I have be longe his owne maydyn.'

So on the morne the damesell wente unto kynge Marke to have 5
resceyved his lettyrs and to departe.

'Damesell, I am nat avysed,' seyde kynge Marke, 'as at this tyme to
sende my lettyrs.'

But so pryvayly and secretely he sente lettirs unto kynge Arthure and
unto quene Gwenyver and unto sir Launcelot. So the varlet departed 10
and founde the kynge and the quene in Walys, at Carlyon. And as the
kynge and the quene was at masse the varlet cam wyth the lettyrs, and
whan masse was done the kynge and the quene opened the lettirs
prevayly. And to begyn, the kyngis lettirs spake wondirly shorte unto
kynge Arthur, and bade hym entermete with hymself and wyth hys 15
wyff, and of his knyghtes, for he was able to rule his wyff and his
knyghtes.

When kynge Arthure undirstode the lettir, he mused of many (27)
thynges, and thought of his systyrs wordys, quene Morgan le Fay, that
she had seyde betwyxte quene Gwenyver and sir Launcelot, and in this 20
thought he studyed a grete whyle. Than he bethought hym agayne how
his owne sistir was his enemy, and that she hated the quene and sir
Launcelot to the deth, and so he put that all oute of his thought.

Than kynge Arthur rad the letter agayne, and the lattir clause seyde
that kynge Marke toke sir Trystram for his mortall enemy, wherefore 25
he put kynge Arthure oute of doute he wolde be revenged of sir
Trystram. Than was kynge Arthure wrothe wyth kynge Marke.

And whan quene Gwenyver rad hir lettir and undirstode hyt, she was
wrothe oute of mesure, for the letter spake shame by her and by sir
Launcelot. And so prevayly she sente the lettir unto sir Launcelot. And 30
whan he wyste the entente of the letter he was so wrothe that he layde
hym downe on his bed to slepe, whereof sir Dynadan was ware, for hit
was his maner to be prevy with all good knyghtes. And as sir Launcelot
slepte, he stale the lettir oute of his honde and rad hit worde by worde,
and than he made grete sorow for angir. And sir Launcelot so wakened, 35
and wente to a wyndowe and redde the letter agayne, whyche made
hym angry.

'Syr,' seyde sir Dynadan, 'wherefore be ye angry? I pray you, discover your harte to me, for, pardé, ye know well that I wolde you but
well, for I am a poore knyght and a servyture unto you and to all good 40
knyghtes. For though I be nat of worship myself, I love all tho that
bene of worship.'

'Hit is trouthe,' seyde sir Launcelot, 'ye ar a trusty knyght, and for
grete truste I woll shewe you my counceyle.'

And whan sir Dynadan undirstoode hit well he seyde,

'Sir, thus is my counceyle: sette you ryght naught by thes thretenynges, for kynge Marke is so vylaunce a knyght that by fayre speche shall never man gete ought of hym. But ye shall se what I shall do: I woll make a lay for hym, and whan hit is made, I shall make an harpere to syng hit afore hym.'

And so anone he wente and made hit, and taught hit to an harpere that hyght Elyot, and whan he cowde hit he taught hit to many harpers. And so by the wyll of kynge Arthure and of sir Launcelot the harpers wente into Walys and into Cornwayle to synge the lay that sir Dynadan made by kynge Marke, whyche was the worste lay that ever harper songe with harpe or with ony other instrument.

(28)   Now turne we agayne unto sir Trystram and to kynge Marke. Now as sir Trystram was at a justys and at a turnemente hit fortuned he was sore hurte bothe with a speare and with a swerde, but yet allwayes he wan the gre. And for to repose hym he wente to a good knyght that dwelled in Cornwayle in a castell, whos name was sir Dynas the Senesciall.

So by myssefortune there come oute of Syssoyne a grete numbre of men of armys, and an hedeous oste, and they entyrd nye the castell of Tyntagyll; and hir captens name was sir Elyas, a good man of armys.

Whan kynge Marke undirstood his enemyes were entyrd into his londe he made grete dole and sorow, for in no wyse by his good wylle kynge Marke wolde nat sende for sir Trystram, for he hated hym dedly. So whan his counceyle was com, they devysed and caste many perellys of the grete strengthe of hir enemyes. And than they concluded all at onys, and seyde thus unto kynge Marke:

'Sir, wyte you well ye muste sende for sir Trystram, the good knyght, other ellys they woll never be overcom, for by sir Trystram they muste be foughtyn withall, other ellys we rowe ayenste the streme.'

'Well,' seyde kynge Marke, 'I woll do by youre counceyle.'

But yette he was full lothe thereto, but nede constrayned hym to sende for hym. And so he was sente fore in all haste that myght be, that he sholde com to kynge Marke. And whan he undirstoode that he had sente for hym, he bestrode a soffte ambular and rode to kynge Marke. And whan he was com the kynge seyde thus:

'Fayre nevew, sir Trystram, this is all: here be com oure enemyes off Sessoyne that ar here nyhonde, and without taryynge they muste be mette wyth shortly, other ellys they woll destroy this contrey.'

'Sir,' seyde sir Trystram, 'wyte you well all my power is at your commaundement. But, sir, this eyght dayes I may beare none armys, for my woundis be nat hole. And by that day I shall do what I may.'

'Ye say well,' seyde kynge Marke. 'Than go ye agayne and repose you and make you freysh, and I shall go mete the Sessoynes with all my power.'

So the kynge departed unto Tyntagyll and sir Trystram wente to repose hym.

And the kynge made a grete oste and departed them in three. 5 The fyrste parte ledde sir Dynas the Senescyall, and sir Andret led the secunde parte, and sir Arguys led the thirde parte, and he was of the bloode of kynge Marke. And the Sessoynes had three grete batayles and many good men of armys.

And so kynge Marke by the advyce of his knyghtes yssued oute of 10 the castell of Tyntagyll uppon his enemyes. And sir Dynas, the good knyght, rode oute afore and slewe two good knyghtes his owne hondis. And then began the batayles. And there was mervaylous brekynge of spearys and smytynge of swerdys, and bylled downe many good knyghtes. And ever was sir Dynas the Senesciall beste of kynge Markys 15 party.

And thus the batayle endured longe with grete mor[t]alyté, but at the laste kynge Marke and sir Dynas, were they never so loth, they were dryvyn to the castell of Tyntagyll with grete slaughter of people. And the Syssoynes folowed on faste, that ten of them were getyn wythin 20 the yatys and four slayne wyth the portecolyes.

Than kynge Marke sente for sir Trystram by a varlet agayne that tolde hym of all the mor[t]alyté. Than he sente the varlet agayne and bade hym:

'Telle kynge Marke that I woll com as sone as I am hole, for arste I 25 may do hym no goode.'

Than kynge Marke hadde hys answere.

And therewith cam Elyas, and bade the kynge yelde up the castell, 'for ye may not holde hit nowhyle.'

'Sir Elyas,' seyde kynge Marke, 'and yf I be nat the sonner rescowed, 30 I muste yelde up this castell.'

And anone the kynge sente ayen for rescow to sir Trystram. And by that tyme sir Trystram was nyghe hole, and he had getyn hym ten good knyghtes of kynge Arthurs, and wyth hem he rode unto Tyntagyll. 35

And whan he sawe the grete oste of Sessoynes he mervayled wondir gretly. And than sir Trystram rode by the woddys and by the dychis as secretely as he myght, tyll he cam ny the gatis. And anone there dressed a knyght to hym, whan he sawe that sir Trystram wolde have entird. Than sir Trystram ran to hym and smote hym downe dede. And so he 40 served three mo. And everyche of these ten knyghtes slewe a man of armys. So sir Trystram entyrde into the yatys of Tyntagyll.

And whan kynge Marke wyste that sir Trystram was com he was glad of his commynge, and so was all the felyship, and of hym they

(29) made grete joy. And on the morne Elyas the captayne cam and bade kynge Marke:

'Com oute and do batay[le], for now the good knyght sir Trystram is entyrd. And hit woll be shame,' seyde Elyas, 'for to kepe thy wallys.'

5 Whan kynge Marke undirstoode this he was wrothe and seyde no worde, but wente to sir Trystram and axed hym his counceyle.

'Sir,' seyde sir Trystram, 'woll ye that I gyff hym his answere?'

'I woll well,' seyde kynge Marke.

Than sir Trystram seyde thus to the messengere:

10 'Beare thy lorde worde frome the kynge and me and sey how that we woll do batayle to-mor[n]e wyth hym in the playne fylde.'

'Sir, what is your name?' seyde the messyngere.

'Sir, wyte [th]ou well my name is sir Trystram de Lyones.'

So therewithall the messyngere departed and tolde his lorde Elyas.

15 'Sir,' seyde sir Trystram, 'I pray o⟨f⟩ you gyff me leve to have the rule of youre oste to-morowe.'

'Sir, I pray you take the rule,' seyde kynge Marke.

Than sir Trystram lete devyse the batayle in what maner that they sholde be. So he lete his oste be departed in ⌈six⌉ batayles, and ordayned
20 sir Dynas the Senesciall to have the voward, and other good knyghtes to rule the remenaunte. And the same nyght sir Trystram gart bren all the Sessoynes shyppis unto the colde water. And anone, as Elyas wyst that, he seyde hit was of sir Trystrams doynge:

'For he castyth that we shall never ascape, modyrs sonne of us. There-
25 fore, fayre felowys, fyght frely to-morow, and myscomfort you nought for one knyght, for though he be the beste knyght of the worlde he may nat have ado with us all.'

Than they ordayned their batayles [in] four partyes, wondirly well apparayled and garnysshed [with] men of armys. Thus they wythin
30 issued oute, and they wythoute sette frely uppon them. And there sir Dynas ded grete dedis of armys; natforthan sir Dynas and his felyshyp were put to the wors.

So with that cam sir Trystram and slew two knyghtes with one speare. Than he slew on the ryght honde and on the lyffte honde, that
35 men mervayled that ever he myght do suche dedis of armys. And than he myght se somtyme the batayle was dryvyn a bow-draught frome the castell, and somtyme hit was at the yatys of the castell.

Than cam Elyas the captayne, russhynge here and there, and smote kynge Marke so sore uppon the helme that he made hym to avoyde his
40 sadyll. And than sir Dynas gate kynge Marke agayne to horsebacke.

And therewyth cam syr Trystram lyke a lyon, and there he mette wyth sir Elyas, and he smote hym so sore on the helme that he avayded his sad-yll. And thus they fought tylle hit was nyght, and for grete slaughtir of peple and for wounded peple every party withdrew to theire resseyte.

And whan kynge Marke was com wythin the castell of Tyntagyll he lacked of his knyghtes an hondred, and they withoute lacked two hondred. Than they serched the wounded men on bothe partyes, and than they wente to counceyle. And wyte you well eythir party were loth to fyght more, so that aythir myght ascape with their worshyp.   5

Whan Elyas the captayne undirstoode the deth of his men he made grete dole; also whan he knew that they were loth to go to batayle agayne, he was wrothe oute off mesure. Than Elyas sente unto kynge Marke in grete dispyte uppon hede whether he wolde fynde a knyght that wolde fyght with hym body for body, and yf that he myght sle   10 kynge Markis knyght, he to have the trewayge of Cornwayle yerely, and yf that his knyght sle ⌈hym⌉, 'I fully releace my clayme for ever.'

Than the messynge departed unto kynge Marke and tolde hym how that his lorde Elyas had sent hym worde to fynde a knyght to do batayle   15 wyth hym body for body. Whan kynge Marke undirstood the messynge he bade hym abyde and he sholde have his answere. Than callyd he all the batayle togydir to wyte what was beste counceyle, and they seyde all at onys,

'To fyght in a fylde we have no luste, for had nat bene the proues of   20 sir Trystram, hit hadde bene lykly that we never sholde have scaped. And therefore, sir, as we deme, hit were well done to fynde a knyght that wolde do batayle wyth hym, for he knyghtly proferyth.'

Natforthan whan all this was seyde they coude fynde no knyght that   (30) wolde do batayle with hym.   25

'Sir kynge,' seyde they all, 'here is no knyght that dare fyght with Elyas.'

'Alas!' seyde kynge Marke, 'than am I shamed and uttirly distroyed, onles that my nevew sir Trystram wolde take the batayle uppon hym.'   30

'Sir, wyte you well,' they seyde all, 'he had yesterday overmuche on hande, and he is wery and travayled and sore wounded.'

'Where is he?' seyde kynge Marke.

Than one answeryd and sayde, 'Sir, he lyeth in his bedde for to repose hym.'   35

'Alas!' seyde kynge Marke, 'but I have the succour of my nevew sir Trystram, I am utterly destroyed for ever.'

And therewithall one wente to sir Trystram there he lay, and tolde hym what kynge Marke seyde. And therewith sir Trystram arose lyghtly and put on hym a longe gowne, and cam afore the kynge and   40 the lordis. And whan he saw them so dismayed he axed them what tydynges.

'Never worse,' seyde the kynge. And therewyth he tolde hym all as ye have herde aforehonde. 'And as for you,' seyde the kynge, 'we may

aske no more of you for shame, for thorow youre hardynesse yestirday
ye saved all oure lyvys.'

'Sir,' seyde sir Trystram, 'now I undirstonde ye wolde have my
succour, and reson wolde that I sholde do all that lyyth in me to do,
5 savynge my worshyp and my lyff, howbe[hit] that I am sore brused and
hurte. And sytthyn sir Elyas proferyth so largely, I shall fyght with
hym. Other ellys I woll be slayne in the fylde, othir ellys delyver Cornwayle of the olde trewage. And therefore lyghtly calle his messyngere,
and he shall be answerde. For as yett my woundis bene grene, and they
10 woll be sorer hereaftir sevennyght than they be now, and therefore he
shall have his answere that I woll do batayle to-morne.'

Than was the messyngere brought before kynge Marke.

'Now herkyn, my felow,' seyde sir Trystram, 'go faste unto thy
lorde, and bid hym make trewe assurance on his party for the trwayge,
15 as the kynge here shall on his party. And than tell thy lorde that sir
Trystram, kynge Arthurs knyght and knyght of the Table Rounde,
wyll as to-morne mete with thy lorde on horsebak to do batayle as
longe as I may endure, and aftir that to do batayle with hym on foote
to the uttraunce.'

20 The messyngere behylde sir Trystram frome the top to the too, and
therewythall he departed. And so he cam to his lorde and tolde hym
how he was answere[d] of sir Trystram.

And therewithall was made ostage on bothe partyes, and made hit
as sure as hit myght be that whethirsomever party had the victory, so
25 for to ende. And than were bothe ostys assembeled on bothe partyes the
fylde wythoute the castell of Tyntagyll, and there was none that bare
armys but sir Trystram and sir Elyas.

So whan all the poyntemente was made they departed in sundir and
cam togydirs wyth all the myght that there horsys myght ren, that
30 ayther knyght smote othir so harde that bothe horsis and knyghtes
wente to the erthe. Natforthan they bothe arose lyghtly, and dressed
their shyldis on their sholdyrs with naked swerdys in their hondis, and
they daysshed togydirs so that hit semed a flamynge fyre aboute them.
Thus they traced and traversced, and hewe on helmys and hawberkes,
35 and cut away many cantellys of their shyldis, and aythir wounded othir
passynge sore, that the hoote blood ran freyshly uppon the erthe.

And by than they had foughtyn the mowntenaunce of an owre, sir
Trystram waxed faynte and wery, and bled sore, and gaff sore abak. That
sawe sir Elyas, and folowed fyersly uppon hym and wounded hym in
40 many placis. And ever sir Trystram traced and traverced and wente
froward hym here and there, and coverde hym with his shylde as he
myght all waykely, that all men sayde he was overcom; for sir Elyas
had gyvyn hym twenty strokes ayenste one. Than was there lawghynge
amonge the Sessoynes party, and grete dole on kynge Markis party.

'Alas,' seyde the kynge, 'we ar all shamed and destroyed for ever!'

For, as the booke seyth, sir Trystram was never so macched but yf hit were of sir Launcelot.

Thus as they stode and behylde bothe partyes, that one party laugh-   5
ynge and the othir party wepynge, sir Trystram remembird hym of his lady, La Beale Isode, that loked uppon hym, and how he was never lykly to com in hir presence. Than he pulled up his shylde that before hynge full lowe, and than he dressed hym unto sir Elyas and gaff hym many sad strokys, twenty ayenst one, and all to-brake his shylde and   10
his hawberke, that the hote bloode ran downe as hit had been rayne. Than began kynge Marke and all Cornyshemen to lawghe, and the other party to wepe.

And ever sir Trystram seyde to sir Elyas, 'Yelde the!'

And whan sir Trystram saw hym so stakir on the grounde, he seyde,   15
'Sir Elyas, I am ryght sory for the, for thou arte a passynge good knyght as ever I mette withall excepte sir Launcelot.'

And therewithall sir Elyas fell to the erthe and there dyed.

'Now what shall I do?' seyde sir Trystram unto kynge Marke, 'for this batayle ys at an ende.'   20

Than they [of Elyas party] departed, and kynge Marke toke of hem many presoners to redresse the harmys and the scathis, and the remenaunte he sente into her contrey to borow oute their felowys.

Than was sir Trystram serched and well healed. Yett for all this kynge Marke wolde have slayne sir Trystram, but for all that ever sir   25
Trystram saw other herde by kynge Marke, he wolde never beware of his treson; but evir he wolde be thereas La Beale Isode was.

Now woll we passe over this mater and speke we of the harpers that   (31)
sir Launcelot and sir Dynadan had sente into Cornwayle. And at the grete feste that kynge Marke made for the joy that the Sessoynes were   30
put oute of his contrey, than cam Elyas the harper with the lay that sir Dynadan had made, and secretly brought hit unto sir Trystram, and tolde hym the lay that sir Dynadan had made by kynge Marke. And whan sir Trystram harde hit, he seyde,

'O Lord Jesu! That sir Dynadan can make wondirly well and yll.   35
There he sholde make evyll!'

'Sir,' seyde Elyas, 'dare I synge this songe afore kynge Marke?'

'Yee, on my perell,' seyde sir Trystram, 'for I shall be thy waraunte.'

So at the mete in cam Elyas the harper amonge other mynstrels and began to harpe. And because he was a coryous harper men harde hym   40
synge the same lay that sir Dynadan made, whyche spake the moste vylany by kynge Marke and of his treson that ever man herde. And whan the harper had sunge his songe to the ende, kynge Marke was wondirly wrothe and sayde,

'Harper, how durste thou be so bolde, on thy hede, to synge this songe afore me?'

'Sir,' seyde Elyas, 'wyte thou well I am a mynstrell, and I muste do as I am commaunded of thos lordis that I beare the armys of. And, sir, 5 wyte you well that sir Dynadan, a knyght of the Table Rounde, made this songe and made me to synge hit afore you.'

'Thou seyste well,' seyde kynge Marke, 'and bycause thou arte a mynstrell thou shalt go quyte. But I charge the, hyghe the faste oute of my syght!'

10 So Elyas the harper departed and wente to sir Trystram and tolde hym how he had sped. Than sir Trystram let make lettyrs as goodly as he cowde to ⌈Launcelot⌉ and to sir Dynadan, and so he let conduyte the harper oute of the contrey. But to sey that kynge Marke was wondirly wrothe, [he was], for he demed that the lay that was songe afore 15 hym was made by sir Trystrams counceyle, wherefore he thought to sle hym and all his well-wyllers in that contrey.

VIII. ALEXANDER THE ORPHAN

(32) Now turne we to another mater that felle betwene kyng Marke and his brother that was called the good prynce Bodwyne, that all the 20 peple of the contrey loved hym passyng well.

So hit befelle on a tyme that the myscreauntys Sarezynes londid in the contrey of Cornwayle sone aftir the Sessoynes were departed. And whan the good prynce sir Bodwyne was ware of them where they were londed, than at the londynge he areysed the peple pryvayly and 25 hastyly.

And or hit were day he let put wylde fyre in three of his owne shyppis, and suddeynly he pulled up the sayle, and wyth the wynde he made tho shyppis to be drevyn amonge the navy of the Sarezynes. And to make a short tale, tho three shyppis sett on fyre all the shyppis, that 30 none were saved. And at the poynte of the day the good prynce Bodwyne with all his felyship set on the myscreauntys with showtys and cryes, and slew the numbir of forty thousand and lefft none on lyve.

Whan kynge Marke wyste this he was wondirly wrothe that his brother sholde wynne suche worship and honour. And bycause this 35 prynce was bettir beloved than he in all that contrey, and also this prynce Bodwyne lovid well sir Trystram, and therefore he thought to sle hym.

And thus, hastely and uppon hede, as a man that was full of treson, he sente for prynce Bodwyne and Anglydes, his wyff, and bade them 40 brynge their yonge sonne with hem, that he myght se hym; and all this

he ded to the entente to sle the chylde as well as his fadir, for he was
the falsist traytour that ever was borne. Alas, for the goodnes and for
hys good dedis this jantyll prynce Bodwyne was slayne!

So whan he cam wyth his wyff Anglydes the kynge made them fayre
semblaunte tylle they had dyned. And whan they had dyned kynge 5
Marke sente for his brother and seyde thus:

'Brothir, how sped you whan the myscreauntes aryved by you?
Mesemyth hit had bene your parte to have sente me worde, that I
myght have bene at that journey; for hit had bene reson that I had had
the honoure and nat you.'   10

'Sir,' seyde prince Bodwyne, 'hit was so that, and I had [taryed tyl
that I had] sente for you, tho myscreauntes had distroyed my contrey.'

'Thou lyeste, false traytoure!' seyde kynge Marke. 'For thou arte
ever aboute to wynne worship from me and put me to dishonoure, and
thou cherysht that I hate!'   15

And therewith he stroke hym to the herte wyth a dagger, that he
never aftir spake worde.

Than the lady Anglydes made grete dole and sowned, for she saw
her lorde slayne afore her face. Than was there no more to do, but
prynce Bodwyne was dispoyled and brought to his buryellys. But his 20
lady Anglydes pryvaly gate hir husbandis dubled and his shurte, and
that she kepte secretly.

Than was there muche sorow and cryynge, and grete dole made
betwyxt sir Trystram, sir Dynas, and sir Fergus. And so ded all
knyghtes that were there, for that prynce was passyngly well beloved. 25

So La Beall Isode sente for Anglydes, his wyff, and bade her avoyde
delyverly, other ellys hir yonge sonne Alysaundir le Orphelyne sholde
be slayne. Whan she harde this, she toke her horse and hir chylde and
rode away with suche poore men as durste ryde with hir.

Notwythstondynge, whan kynge Marke had done this dede, yet he 30 (33)
thought to do more vengeaunce, and with his swerde in his honde he
sought frome chambir to chambir for Anglydes and hir yonge sonne.
And whan she was myst he called a good knyght to hym that hyght sir
Sadoke, and charged hym in payne of dethe to fette agayne Anglydes
and hir yonge sonne.   35

So sir Sadoke departed, and rode aftir Anglydes, and within ten
myle he overtoke her and bade hir turne ayen and ryde with hym to
kynge Marke.

'Alas, fayre knyght!' she seyde, 'what shall ye wynne be my sunnys
deth, other ellys by myne? For I have overmuche harme, and to grete 40
a losse.'

'Madame,' seyde sir Sadoke, 'for your losse is grete dole and pité.
But, madame,' seyde sir Sadoke, 'wolde ye departe oute of this contrey
wyth youre sonne, and kepe hym tyll he be of ayge, that he may

revenge his fadyrs deth? Than wolde I suffir you to departe frome me,
so ye promyse me to revenge the deth of prynce Bodwyne.'

'A, jantyll knyght, Jesu thanke the! And yf ever my sonne Alysaundir le Orphelyne lyve to be a knyght, he shall have his fadirs dublet
5 and his shurte with the blody markes, and I shall gyff hym suche a
charge that he shall remember hit whylys he lyvyth.'

And therewithall departed sir Sadoke frome her, and ayther departed frome other. And whan sir Sadoke cam unto kynge Marke he
tolde hym faythfully that he had drowned yonge Alysaundir, her
10 sonne; and thereof kynge Marke was full glad.

Now turne we unto Anglydes that rode bothe nyght and day by
adventure oute off Cornwayle, and sylden and in feaw placis she rested,
but ever she drewe southwarde to the seesyde, tyll by fortune she cam
to a castell that is called Magowns, that now is called Arundell, in
15 Southsex. And the conestable of that castell welcomed Anglydes, and
seyde she was wellcom to her owne castell.

And so she was there worshypfully resceyved, for the conestable his
wyff was her ny cousyn. And the conestablys name was sir Bellyngere,
and he tolde Anglydes that the same castell was hers by ryght inery-
20 taunce.

Thus Anglydes endured yerys and wyntyrs, tyll Alysaundir was
bygge and stronge, and there was none so wyghty in all that contrey,
that there was no man myght do no maner of maystry afore hym.

(34)   Than uppon a day sir Bellyngere the constable cam to Anglydes
25 and seyde,

Madame, hit were tyme my lorde sir Alysaundir were made knyght,
for he is a stronge yonge man.'

'Sir,' seyde she, 'I wolde he were made knyght, but than muste I
gyff hym the moste charge that ever synfull modir gaff to hir childe.'

30   'As for that, do as ye lyste, and I shall gyff hym warnynge that he
shall be made knyght. And hit woll be well done that he be made
knyght at Oure Lady Day in Lente.'

'Be hit so,' seyde Anglydes, 'and I pray you, make ye redy therefore.'

So cam the conestable to Alysaundir, and tolde hym that he sholde
35 at oure Lady ⟨day⟩ of Lente be made a knyght.

'Sir, I thanke God and you,' seyde Alysaundir 'for this is the best
tydynges that ever cam to me.'

Than the conestable ordayned twenty of the grettyste jantylmennes
sunnys and the beste borne men of that contrey whyche sholde be made
40 knyghtes the same day that Alysaundir was made knyght. And so on
the same day that he and his twenty felowys were made knyghtes, at
the offerynge of the masse there cam this lady Anglydes unto her sonne
and seyde thus:

'A, my fayre swete sonne, I charge the uppon my blyssynge and of

the hyghe Order of Chevalry that thou takyste here this day, to take
hede what I shall sey and charge the wythall.'

And therewithall she pulled oute a blody dublet and a blody shurte
that was bebled with olde bloode. Whan Alysaundir saw this he sterte
abak, and waxed paale, and sayde,   5

'Fayre moder, what may this be or meane?'

'I shall tell the, fayre son. This was thyne owne fadyrs doublet and
shurte that he ware uppon hym that same tyme that he was slayne.'
And there she tolde hym why and wherefore. 'And for hys good dedis
kynge Marke slew hym with his dagger afore myne owne yghen. And   10
therefore this shall be youre charge that I gyff you at thys tyme. Now I (35)
requere the, and I charge the uppon my blyssynge and uppon the
hyghe Order of Knyghthode, that thou be revenged uppon kynge
Marke for the deth of thy fadir.'

And therewythall she sowned. Than Alysaundir lepte to his modir,   15
and toke her up in his armys, and sayde,

'Fayre modir, ye have gyvyn me a grete charge, and here I promyse
you I shall be avenged uppon kynge Marke whan that I may, and that
I promyse to God and to you.'

So this feste was ended, and the conestable by the avyce of Anglydes 20
let purvey that Alysaundir were well horsed and harneyste. Than he
justed with his twenty felowys that were made knyghtes with hym; but
for to make a shorte tale, he overthrewe all tho twenty, that none
myght withstonde hym a buffet.

Than one of tho knyghtes departed unto kynge Marke, and tolde all   25
how Alysaundir was made knyght and all the charge that his modir
gaff hym, as ye have harde aforetyme.

'Alas, false treson!' seyde kynge Marke. 'I wente that yonge traytoure had bene dede. Alas! whom may I truste?'

And therewithall kynge Marke toke a swerde in his honde, and   30
sought sir Sadoke from chambir to chambir to sle hym. Whan sir
Sadoke saw kynge Marke com with his swerde in his honde,

'Syr,' he seyde, 'beware, Marke, and com nat to nyghe me! For wyte
thou well that I saved Alysaundir his lyff, of the whyche I never
repente me, for thou falsely and cowardly slew his fadir, prynce Bod- 35
wyne, traytourly for his good dedis. Wherefore I pray Allmyghty Jesu
sende Alysaundir myght and power to be revenged uppon the. And
now beware, kynge Marke, of yonge Alysaundir, for he is made a
knyght.'

'Alas,' seyde kynge Marke, 'that ever I sholde hyre a traytoure sey   40
so afore me!'

And therewith four knyghtes of kynge Markes drew their swerdis
to sle sir Sadoke, but anone kynge Marke his knyghtes were slayne
afore hym. And sir Sadoke paste forthe into his chambir, and toke his

harneys and his horse and rode on his way, for there was nother sir
Trystram, sir Dynas, nother sir Fergus that wolde sir Sadoke ony
evyll wyll.

Than was kynge Marke wood wrothe, and thought to destroy sir
5 Alysaundir, for hym he dradde and hated moste of any man lyvynge.

Whan sir Trystram undirstood that Alysaundir was made knyght,
anone furthwithall he sent hym a lettir prayynge and chargynge hym
that he draw hym to the courte of kynge Arthure, and that he put hym
in the rule and in the hondis of sir Launcelot. So this lettyr was sente
10 unto sir Alysaundir from his cousyne, sir Trystram, and at that tyme
he thought to do after his commaundemente.

Than kynge Marke called a knyght that brought hym the tydynges
frome Alysaundir, and bade hym abyde stylle in that contrey.

'Sir,' seyde the knyght, 'so muste I do, for in myn owne contrey
15 dare I nat com.'

'No force,' seyde kynge Marke, 'for I shall gyff the here double as
muche londis as ever thou haddyste of thyne owne.'

But within shorte space sir Sadoke mette wyth that false knyght and
slew hym. Than was kynge Marke wood wrothe oute of mesure. Than
20 he sente unto quene Morgan le Fay and to the quene of Northe Galys,
prayynge them in his lettyrs that they two sorserers wolde sette all the
contrey envyrone with ladyes that were enchauntours, and by suche
that were daungerous knyghtes, as sir Malagryne and sir Brewnys
Saunze Pyté, that by no meane Alysaundir le Orphelyne shulde
25 never ascape, but other he sholde be takyn or slayne. And all this
ordynaunce made kynge Marke to distroy sir Alysaunder.

(36)   Now turne we unto sir Alysaundir, that at his departyng his modir
toke with hym his fadyrs blody sherte, and so he bare hit with hym tyll
his deth day in tokenynge to thynke uppon his fadyrs deth.

30   So was Alysaundir purposed to ryde to London, by the counceyle of
sir Trystram, to sir Launcelot. And [by] fortune he went aftir the
seesyde, and rode wronge. And there he wan at a turnemente the g[r]e,
that kynge Carados made, and there he smote downe kynge Carados
and twenty of his knyghtes, and also sir Saffir, a good knyght that was
35 sir Palomydes brother.

And all this sawe a damesell, and went to Morgan le Fay, and tolde
hir how she saw the beste knyght juste that ever she sawe; and ever as
he s[mo]te downe knyghtes, he made them to swere to were none
harneyse of a twelve-monthe and a day.

40   'This is well seyde,' seyde Morgan le Fay, 'for that is the knyght that
I wolde fayne se.'

And so she toke her palfrey and rode a grete whyle, and than she
rested her in her pavylyon. So there cam four knyghtes, two of them
were armed, and two were unarmed, and they tolde Morgan le Fay

there namys. The fyrste was Elyas de Gomeret the secunde Car de Gomeret; tho two were armed. And the other two were of Camyl-yarde, cousyns unto quene Gwenyver. And that one hyght sir Gye, and that othir hyght sir Garaunte; tho two were unarmed. And this four knyghtes tolde Morgan le Fay how a yonge knyght had smytten them downe afore a castell. 5

'For the maydyn of that castell seyde that he was but late made knyght, and yonge. But as we suppose, but yf hit were sir Trystram othir sir Launcelot other ellys sir Lameroke the good knyght, [there is none] that myght sytte hym a buffette with a speare.' 10

'Well,' seyde Morgan le Fay, 'I shall mete wyth that knyght or hit be longe tyme and he dwelle in that contrey.'

So turne we to the damesell of the castell, that whan Alysaundir le Orphelyne had forjusted the four knyghtes she called hym to her and seyde thus: 15

'Sir knyght, wolte thou for my sake juste and fyght wyth a knyght of this contrey, that is and hath bene longe an evyll neyghboure to me? His name is sir Malegryne, and he woll nat suffir me to be maryde in no maner.'

'Damesell,' seyde sir Alysaundir, 'and he com the whyle that I am here, I woll fyght with hym.' 20

And therewithall she sente for hym, for he was at her commaunde-mente. And whan ayther had a syght of other, they made hem redy for to juste. And so they cam togydyr egirly, and this sir Malegryne brused his speare uppon sir Alysaundir, and he smote hym agayne so harde that he bare hym quyte from his horse ⌐to the erthe⌐. But this Malegryne devoyded, and lyghtly arose and dressed his shylde and drew his swerde, and bade hym alyght: 25

'For wyte thou well, sir knyghte, thoughe thou have the bettir on horsebacke, thou shalt fynde that I shall endure the lyke a knyght on foote.' 30

'Ye sey well!' seyde sir Alysaundir. And so he avoyded his horse and bytoke hym to his varlet. And than they russhed togydyrs lyke two boorys, and leyde on their helmys and shyldis longe tyme by the space of three owrys, that never man coude sey whyche was the bettir knyght. And in the meanewhyle cam Morgan le Fay to the damesell of the castell, and they behylde the batayle. 35

But this sir Malagryne was an olde rooted knyght, and he was called one of the daungerous knyghtes of the worlde to do batayle on foote, but on horsebacke there was many bettir. And ever this Malagryne awayted to sle sir Alysaundir, and so wounded hym wondirly sore that hit was mervayle that ever he myght stonde, for he had bled so muche; for this sir Alysaundir fought ever wyldely and nat wyttyly, and that othir was a fel[on]ous knyght and awayted hym, and smote hym sore. 40

And somtyme they russhed togydyrs with their shyldis lyke two boorys other rammys, and felle grovelynge bothe to the erthe.

'Now, sir knyght,' seyde sir Malegryne, 'holde thyne honde a whyle, and telle me what thou arte.'

5 'That woll I nat,' seyde sir Alysaundir, 'but yf me lyst well. But tell me thy name, and why thou kepyste thys contrey, other ellys thou shalt dye of my hondis.'

'Sir, wyte thou well,' seyde sir Malagryne, 'that for this maydyns love, of this castell, I have slayne ten good knyghtes by myssehap, and 10 by outerage [and] orgulyté of myselff I have slayne othir ten knyghtes.'

'So God helpe me,' seyde sir Alysaundir, 'this is the fowlyste confession that ever I harde knyght make, and hit were pité that thou sholdiste lyve ony lenger. And therefore, kepe the! For, as I am a trewe knyght, other thou shalt sle me, other ellys I shall sle the!'

15 Than they laysshed togydyrs fyersely. And at the laste sir Alysaundir smote hym to the erthe, and than he raced of his helme and smote of his hede.

And whan he had done this batayle he toke his horse and wolde have mownted uppon his horse, but he myght nat tor taynte. And than he 20 seyde,

'A, Jesu, succoure me!'

So by that com Morgan le Fay and bade hym be of good comforte. And so she layde hym, this Alysaundir, in an horse-lettir, and so led hym into the castell, for he had no foote to stonde uppon the erthe; for 25 he had sixtene grete woundis, and in especiall one of them was lyke to be his deth.

(37) Than quene Morgan le Fay serched his woundis and gaff hym suche an oynement that he sholde have dyed. And so on the morne whan she cam to hym agayne, he complayned hym sore. And than she put another 30 oynemente uppon hym, and than he was oute of his payne.

Than cam the damesell of the castell and seyde unto Morgan le Fay,

'I pray you helpe me that this knyght myght wedde me, for he hath wonne me with his hondis.'

35 'Ye shall se,' seyde Morgan le Fay, 'what I shall sey.'

Than this quene Morgan le Fay wente to sir Alysaundir and bade hym in ony wyse that he shulde refuse this lady, 'and she desyre to wed you; for she is nat for you'.

So this damesell cam and desired of hym maryage.

40 'Damesell,' seyde sir Alysaundir, 'I thanke you, but as yet I caste me nat to mary in this contrey.'

'Sir,' she seyde, 'sytthyn ye woll nat mary me, I pray you, insomuche as ye have wonne me, that ye woll gyff me to a knyght of this contrey that hath bene my frende and loved me many yerys.'

'Wyth all myne herte,' seyde sir Alysaundir, 'I woll assente thereto.'
Than was the knyght sente fore, and his name was sir Geryne le
Grose. And anone he made them honde-faste and wedded them.

Than cam quene Morgan le Fay to sir Alysaundir and bade hym
aryse, and so put hym in an horse-lytter. And so she gaff hym suche   5
a drynke that of three dayes and three nyghtes he waked never, but
slepte. And so she brought hym to hir owne castell that at that tyme
was called La Beale Regarde. Than Morgan le Fay com to sir Alysaundir and axed hym yf he wolde fayne he hole.

'Madame, who wolde be syke and he myght be hole?'   10

'Well,' seyde Morgan, 'than shall ye promyse me by youre knyghthode that this twelve-monthe and a day ye shall nat passe the compace
of this castell, and ye shall lyghtly be hole.'

'I assent me,' seyde sir Alysaundir.

And there he made hir a promyse and was sone hole. And whan sir   15
Alysaundir was hole, he repented hym of his othe, for he myght nat
be revenged uppon kynge Marke.

Ryght so there cam a damesell that was cousyn nyghe to the erle of
Pase, and she was cousyn also unto Morgan le Fay; and by ryght that
castell of La Beale Regarde sholde have bene hers by trew enhery-   20
taunce. So this damesell entyrd into this castell where lay sir Alysaundir, and there she founde hym uppon his bedde passynge hevy and
all sad.

'Sir knyght,' seyde the damesell, 'and ye wolde be myrry, I cowde   (38)
tell you good tydyngis.'   25

'Well were me,' seyde sir Alysaundir, 'and I myght hyre of good
tydynges, for now I stonde as a presonere be my promyse.'

'Sir,' she seyde, 'wyte you well that ye be a presonere and wois than
ye wene, for my lady, my cousyn, quene Morgan, kepyth you here for
none other entente but for to do hir plesure whan hit lykyth hir.'   30

'A, Jesu defende me,' seyde sir Alysaundir, 'frome suche pleasure!
For I had levir kut away my hangers than I wolde do her ony suche
pleasure!'

'As Jesu me helpe,' seyde the damesell, 'and ye wolde love me and
be ruled by me, I shall make your delyveraunce with your worship.'   35

'Telle me now by what meane, and ye shall have my love.'

'Fayre knyght,' sayde she, 'this castell ought of ryght to be myne.
And I have an uncle [the whiche] is a myghty erle, and he is erle of the
Pace; and of all folkis he hatyth [moste] Morgan le Fay. And I shall
sende unto hym and pray hym for my sake to destroy this castell for   40
the evyll customys that bene used therein, and than woll he com and
sette fyre on every parte with wylde fyre. And so shall I gete you at a
prevy postren, and there shall ye have your horse and youre harneis.'

'Fayre damesell, ye sey passynge well.'

'And than may ye kepe the rome of this castell this twelve-monthe and a day, and than breke ye nat youre othe.'

'Truly, fayre damesell,' seyde sir Alysaundir, 'ye say sothe.'

And than he kyssed hir and ded to her plesaunce as hit pleased them
5 bothe at tymes and leysers.

So anone she sente unto hir uncle and bade hym com to destroy that castell; for, as the booke seyth, he wolde have destroyed that castell aforetyme, had nat that damesell bene.

Whan the erle undirstode hir letteris, he sente her worde on suche a
10 day he wolde com and destroy that castell. So whan that day cam, sir Alysaundir yode to a postren where he sholde fle into the gardyne, and there he sholde fynde his armoure and his horse.

So whan the day cam that was sette, thydir cam the erle of the Pase wyth four hondred knyghtes and sette on fyre all the partyes of the
15 castell, that or they seased they leffte nat one stone stondynge.

And all this whyle that this fyre was in the castell, he abode in the gardyne. And whan the fyre was done, he let crye that he wolde kepe that pyce of erthe, thereas the castell of La Beale Regarde was, a twelve-monthe and a day frome all maner of knyghtes that wolde com.

20 So hit happed there was a deuke Aunsyrus, and he was of the kynne of sir Launcelot. And this knyght was a grete pylgryme, for every thirde yere he wolde be at Jerusalem; and bycause he used all his lyff to go in pylgrymage, men called hym deuke Aunserus the Pylgryme. And this deuke had a doughter that hyght Alys, that was a passynge fayre
25 woman; and bycause of her fadir she was called Alys le Beall Pylgryme.

And anone as she harde of this crye, she wente unto kyng Arthurs [courte] and seyde opynly, in hyrynge of many knyghtes, that what knyght may overcom that knyght that kepyth the pyce of erthe 'shall have me and all my londis'.

30 Whan knyghtes of the Rounde Table harde hir sey thus, many of them were glad, for she was passynge fayre and ryche, and of grete rentys.

Ryght so she lete crye in castellys and townys as faste on her syde as sir Alysaundir ded on his syde. Than she dressed hir pavylion streyte by
35 the pyese of erthe that sir Alysaundir kepte.

So she was nat so sone there but there cam a knyght of kynge Arthurs courte that hyght sir Sagramour le Desyrous, and he profyrde to juste wyth sir Alysaundir. And so they encountyrd, and he bruse his speare uppon sir Alysaundir. But sir Alysaundir smote hym so sore that he
40 avoyded his arson of his sadyll to the erthe.

Whan La Beale Alys sawe hym juste so well, she thought hym a passyng goodly knyght on horsebacke. And than she lepe oute of hir pavylyon and toke sir Alysaundir by the brydyll, and thus she seyde:

'Fayre knyght! Of thy knyghthode, shew me thy vysayge.'

'That dare I well,' seyde sir Alysaundir, 'shew my vysayge.'

And than he put of his helme, and whan she sawe his vysage she seyde,

'A, swete Fadir Jesu! The I muste love, and never othir.'

'Than shewe me youre vysage,' seyde he.   5

And anone she unwympeled her, and whan he sawe her he seyde,   (39)

'A, Lorde Jesu! Here have I founde my love and my lady! And therefore, fayre lady, I promyse you to be youre knyght, and none other that beryth the lyff.'

'Now, jantyll knyghte,' seyde she, 'telle me youre name.'   10

'Madame, my name is sir Alysaundir le Orphelyne.'

'A, sir,' seyde she, 'syth ye lyst to know my name, wyte you well my name is Alys la Beale Pellaron. And whan we be more at oure hartys ease, bothe ye and I shall telle of what bloode we be com.'

So there was grete love betwyxt them.   15

And as they thus talked, there cam a knyght that hyght sir Harleuse le Berbuse, and axed parte of sir Alysaundirs spearys. Than sir Alysaundir encountred with hym, and at the fyrste sir Alysaundir smote hym over his horse croupe. And than there cam another knyght that hyght sir Hewgon, and sir Alysaundir smote hym downe as he ded   20 that othir. Than sir Hewgan profirde batayle on foote, and anone sir Alysaundir overthrewe hym within three strokys; and than he raced of his helme and there wolde have slayne hym, had he nat yelded hym. So than sir Alysaundir made bothe tho knyghtes to swere to were none armour of a twelve-monthe and a day. Than sir Alysaundir alyght, and 25 wente to reste hym and to repose hym.

Than the damesell that halpe sir Alysaundir oute of the castell, in her play tolde Alys alltogydir how he was presoncre in the castell of La Beall Regarde; and there she tolde her how she gate hym oute of preson.   30

'Sir,' seyde Alys la Beall Pillaron, 'mesemyth ye ar muche beholdynge to this mayden.'

'That is trouthe,' seyde sir Alysaundir.

And there Alys tolde of what bloode she was com, and seyde,

'Sir, wyte you well that I am of the bloode of kynge Ban, tha[t] was 35 fadir unto sir Launcelot.'

'Iwys, fayre lady,' seyde sir Alysaundir, 'my modir tolde me my fadir was brothir unto a kynge, and I am nye cousyn unto sir Trystram.'

So this meanewhyle cam three knyghtes; that one hyght sir Vayns, and that other hyght Harvis le Marchis, and the thirde hyghte Peryne 40 de la Mountayne. And with one speare sir Alysaundir smote them downe all three, and gaff them suche fallys that they had no lyst to fyght uppon foote. So he made them to swere to were none armys of a twelve-monthe.

So whan they were departed sir Alysaundir behylde his lady Alys on horsebak as she stoode in hir pavylion, and than was he so enamered uppon her that he wyst nat whether he were on horsebacke other on foote. Ryght so cam the false knyght sir Mordred and sawe sir Aly-
5 saundir was so afonned uppon his lady, and therewithall he toke hys horse by the brydyll and lad hym here and there, and had caste to have lad hym oute of that place to have shamed hym.

So whan the damesell that halpe hym oute of that castell sawe how shamefully he was lad, anone she lete arme her and sette a shylde uppon
10 her shuldir. And therewith she amownted uppon his horse and gate a naked swerde in hir honde, and she threste unto Alysaundir with all hir myght, and she gaff hym suche a buffet that hym thought the fyre flowe oute of his yghen.

And whan sir Alysaundir felte that stroke he loked aboute hym and
15 drew his swerde. And whan she sawe that, she fledde, and so ded sir Mordred into the foreyste. And the damesell fled into the pavylyon.

So whan sir Alysaundir undirstood hymselff how the false knyght wolde have shamed hym had nat the damesell bene, than was he wroth with hymselff that sir Mordred had so ascaped his hondis. But than sir
20 Alysaundir and his lady Alys had good game at the damesell, how sadly she smote hym uppon the helme.

Than sir Alysaundir justed thus day be day, and on foote ded many batayles with many knyghtes of kynge Arthurs courte, and with many knyghtes straungers, that for to tell batayle by batayle hit were over-
25 muche to reherse. For every day in that twelve-monthe he had to do wyth one knyght owther wyth another, and som day with three or four, and there was never knyght that put hym to the warre.

And at the twelve-monthes ende he departed with his lady La Beall Pyllerowne. And the damesell wolde never go frome hym, and so they
30 wente into their contrey of Benoy and lyved there in grete joy.

(40) But, as the booke tellyth, kynge Marke wolde never stynte tylle he had slayne hym by treson. And by Alis he gate a chylde that hyght Bellengerus le Beuse, and by good fortune he cam to the courte of kynge Arthure and preved a good knyght. And he revenged his
35 fadirs deth, for this false kynge Marke slew bothe sir Trystram and sir Alysaundir falsely and felonsly.

And hit happed so that sir Alysaundir had never grace ne fortune to com to kynge Arthurs courte; for and he had com to sir Launcelot, all knyghtes seyde that knew hym that he was one of the strengyste
40 knyghtes that was in kynge Arthurs dayes. And grete dole was made for hym.

SO LETTE WE HYM PASSE AND TURNE WE TO ANOTHER TALE.

IX. THE TOURNAMENT AT SURLUSE

So hit befelle that sir Galahalte the Haute Prynce, lorde of the contrey of Surluse, whereof cam oute many good knyghtes—and this noble prince was a passynge good man of armys, and ever he hylde a noble felyship togydirs—and than he cam to kynge Arthurs courte and tolde 5 hym his entente, how this was his wyll: he had let cry a justys in the contrey of Surluse, the whyche contrey was within the bandis of kynge Arthur, and there he asked leve to crye a justys.

'I woll gyff you leve,' seyde kynge Arthur, 'but wyte you well I may not be there myselff.'   10

'Sir,' seyde quene Gwenyver, 'please hit you to gyff me leve to be at that justis?'

'Wyth ryght a good wyll,' seyde kynge Arthur, 'for sir Galahalte, the good prynce, shall have you in governaunce.'

'Sir, as ye wyll, so be hit.' Than the quene seyde, 'I woll take with 15 me suche knyghtes as lykyth me beste.'

'Do as ye lyste,' seyde kynge Arthure.

So anone she commaunded sir Launcelot to make hym redy with suche knyghtes as hym thought beste.

So in every goode towne and castell off this londe was made a crye 20 that in the contrey of Surluse sir Galahalte shulde make a justis that sholde laste seven dayes, and how the Hawte Prince, with the helpe of quene Gwenyvers knyghtes, sholde juste agayne all maner of men that commyth. Whan this crye was knowyn, kynges and pryncces, deukes, erlys and barownes and noble knyghtes made them redy to be at that 25 justys.

And at the day of justenynge there cam in sir Dynadan disgysed, and ded many grete dedis of armys. Than at the requeste of quene Gweny- (41) ver and of kynge Bagdemagus sir Launcelot com into the thrange, but he was disgysed; that was the cause that feaw folke knew hym. And 30 there mette wyth hym sir Ector de Marys, his owne brother, and ayther brake their spearys uppon other to their handis. And than aythir gate another speare, and than sir Launcelot smote downe sir Ector, his owne brother.

That sawe sir Bleoberys, and he smote sir Launcelot uppon the 35 helme suche a buffet that he wyste nat well where he was. Than sir Launcelot smote sir Bleoberys so sore uppon the helme that his hed bowed downe bakwarde, and he smote hym efft another stroke, and therewith he avoyded his sadyll. And so he rode by and threste in amonge the thykkyst.   40

Whan the kynge of North Galys saw sir Ector and sir Bleoberys ley on the grounde, than was he wrothe, for they cam on his party agaynste them of Surluse. So the kynge of North Galys ran unto sir Launcelot and brake a speare uppon hym all to pecis. And therewith sir Launcelot overtoke the kynge of North Galys and smote hym such a buffet on the helme with his swerde that he made hym to avoyde the arson of his sadyll. And anone the kynge was horsed agayne.

5 So kynge Bagdemagus and the kynge of Northe Galys aythir party hurled to other, and than began a stronge medlé, but they of Northe Galys were muche bygger than the other.

So whan sir Launcelot saw his party go so to the warre, he thrange oute to the thyckyst with a bygge swerde in his honde. And there he

10 smote downe on the ryght honde and on the lyffte hond, and pulled downe knyghtes and russhed of helmys, that all men had wondir that ever knyght myght do suche dedis of armys.

Whan sir Mellyagaunce that was sonne unto kynge Bagdemagus saw how sir Launcelot fared, and whan he undirstood that hit was he, he

15 wyste well that he was disgysed for his sake. Than sir Mellyagaunce prayde a knyght to sle sir Launcelotes horse, other with swerde or speare.

And at that tyme, kynge Bagdemagus mette with another knyght that hyght Sauseyse, a good knyght, and sayde,

20 'Now, fayre knyght sir Sauseyse, encountir with my sonne, sir Mellyagaunce, and gyff hym layrge pay, for I wolde that he were well beatyn of thy hondis, that he myght departe oute of this felyship.'

And than sir Sauseyse encountyrd with sir Mellyagaunce, and aythir smote other adowne. And than they fought on foote. And there sir

25 Sauseyse had wonne sir Mellyagaunce, had there nat com rescowys.

So than the Haute Prynce blewe to lodgynge, and every knyght unarmed hym and wente to the grete feyste.

Than in the meanewhyle there came a damesell to the Haute Prynce and complayned that there was a knyght that hyght sir Gonereyes that

30 withhylde all her londis. And so the knyght was there presente, and keste his glove to hir or to ony that wolde fyght in hir name. So the damesell toke up the glove all hevyly for the defaute of a champyon. Than there cam a varlet to her and seyde,

'Damesell, woll ye do aftir me?'

35 'Full fayne,' seyde the damesell.

'Than go ye unto suche a knyght that lyeth here besyde in an ermy-tage, and that knyght folowyth the questynge beeste, and pray hym to take the batayle uppon hym. And anone he woll graunte you.'

So anone she toke her palferey, and within a whyle she founde that

40 knyght whyche was called sir Palomydes. And whan she requyred hym he armed hym and rode with her and made her go to the Haute Prynce and to aske leve for hir knyght to do batayle.

'I woll well,' seyde the Haute Prynce.

Than the knyghtes made them redy and cam to the fylde to juste on

horsebacke, and aythir gate a grete speare in his honde, and so mette
togydirs so hard that theire spearis all to-shevird. And anone they
flange oute their swerdis, and sir Palomydes smote sir Gonereyse
downe to the erthe. And than he raced of his helme and smote of his
hede. Than they wente to souper.   5

And this damesell loved sir Palomydes as her paramour, but the
booke seyth she was of his kynne.

So than sir Palomydes disgysed hymselff in this maner: in his shylde
he bare the questynge beste, and in all his trapours. And whan he was
thus redy he sente to the Haute Prynce to gyff hym leve to juste with   10
othir knyghtes, but he was adouted of syr Launcelot. Than the Haute
Prynce sente hym worde agayne that he sholde be wellcom, and that sir
Launcelot sholde nat juste wyth hym. Than sir Galahalte the Haute
Prynce lete cry that what knyght somever smote downe sir Palomydes
sholde have his damesell to hymselff to his demaynes.   15

HERE BEGYNNYTH THE SECUNDE DAY. And anone as sir Palomydes (42)
came into the fylde, sir Galahalte the Haute Prynce was at the raunge
ende, and mette wyth sir Palomydes and he with hym with two grete
spearys. And they cam so harde togydyrs that their spearys all to-
shevirde. But sir Galahalte smote hym so harde that he bare hym   20
bakwarde over his horse, but yet he loste nat his styroppis. Than they
pulled oute their swerdis, and laysshed togydirs many sad strokis, that
many worshypfull knyghtes leffte their busynes to beholde them. But
at the laste sir Galahalte smote a stroke of myght unto sir Palomydes
sore uppon the helme; but the helme was so harde that the swerde   25
myght nat byghte, but slypped and smote of the hede of his horse.

But whan sir Galahalte saw the good knyght sir Palomydes fall to the
erthe, he was ashamed of that stroke. And therewithall he alyght
adowne of his owne horse, and prayde sir Palomydes to take that
horse of his gyffte and to forgyff hym that dede.   30

'Sir,' seyde sir Palomydes, 'I thanke you of youre grete goodnes, for
ever of a man of worship a knyght shall never have disworshyp.'

And so he mownted uppon that horse, and the Haute Prynce had
another horse anone.

'Now,' seyde the Haute Prynce, 'I releace to you that maydyn, for   35
ꞁyeꞁ have wonne her.'

'A,' sayde sir Palomydes, 'the damesell and I be at youre commaundement.'

So they departed, and sir Galahalte ded grete dedis of armys. And
ryght so cam sir Dynadan and encountyrd wyth sir Galahalte, and aythir 40
cam on other so faste that their spearys brake to there hondis. But sir
Dynadan had wente the Haute Prynce had bene more weryar than he
was, and than he smote many sad strokes at the Haute Prynce. But whan
sir Dynadan saw he myght nat gete hym to the erthe, he seyde,

'My lorde, I pray you, leve me and take anothir.'

So the Haute Prynce knew nat sir Dynadan, but leffte hym goodly for his fayre wordis, and so they departed. But another knyght there cam and tolde the Haute Prynce that hit was sir Dynadan.

5   'Iwys,' seyde the Haute Prynce, 'therefore am I hevy that he is so ascaped fro me, for with his mokkis and his japys now shall I never have done with hym.'

And than sir Galahalte rode faste aftyr hym and bade hym,

'Abyde, sir Dynadan, for kynge Arthurs sake!'

10   'Nay,' seyde sir Dynadan, 'so God me helpe, we mete no more togydyrs this day!'

Than in that haste sir Galahalte mett with sir Mellyagaunce, and he smote hym so in the throte that and he had fallyn his necke had be brokyn. And with the same speare he smote downe anothir

15 knyght.

Than cam in they of the Northe Galys and many straungers with them, and were lyke to have put them of Surluse to the worse, for sir Galahalte the Haute Prynce had overmuche in honde. So there cam the good knyght sir Symounde the Valyaunte with forty knyghtes and bete

20 them all abacke.

Than quene Gwenyver and sir Launcelot let blow to lodgynge, and every knyght unarmed hym and dressed them to the feste.

(43)   So whan sir Palomydes was unarmed he axed lodgynge for hymselff and the damesell, and anone the Haute Prynce commaunded them to

25 lodgynge. And he was nat so sone in his lodgynge but there cam a knyght that hyght Archade: he was brothir unto sir Gomoryes that sir Palomydes slewe afore in the damesels quarell. And this knyght Archede called sir Palomydes traytoure, and appeled hym for the deth of his brother.

30   'By the leve of the Haute Prynce,' seyde sir Palomydes, 'I shall answere the.'

Whan sir Galahalte undirstood there quarell he bade them go to the dyner:

'And as sone as ye have dyned, loke that aythir knyght be redy in the

35 fylde.'

So whan they had dyned they were armed bothe and toke their horsys. And the quene and the prynce and sir Launcelot were sette to beholde them. And so they let ren their horsis, and there sir Palomydes and sir Archade mette, and he bare sir Archade on his speare ende over

40 his horse tayle. And than sir Palomydes alyght and drewe his swerde, but sir Archade myght nat aryse. And there sir Palomydes raced of his helme and smote of his hede. Than the Haute Prynce and quene Gwenyver went to souper.

Than kynge Bagdemagus sente away his sonne Mellyagaunce,

bycause sir Launcelot sholde nat mete with hym; for he hated sir Launcelot, and that knewe he nat.

Now BEGYNNYTH THE THIRDE DAY OF JUSTIS. And at that day kynge (44) Bagdemagus made hym redy, and there cam agaynste hym kynge Marsyll that had in gyffte an ilonde of sir Galahalte the Haute Prynce. 5 And this ilonde was called Pomytayne.

Than hit befelle thus that kynge Bagdemagus and kynge Marsyll of Pomytayne mett togydir wyth spearys, and kynge Marsyll had suche a buffet that he felle over his horse croupe. Than cam therein a knyght of kynge Marsyls to revenge his lorde, and kynge Bagdemagus smote 10 hym downe, horse and man, to the erthe.

So there came an erle that hyght sir Arrowse, and sir Breuse, and an hondred knyghtes wyth hem of Pometaynes, and the kynge of Northe Galys was with hem, and all they were agaynste them of Surluse. And than there began a grete batayle, and many knyghtes were caste undir 15 their horse fyete. And ever kynge Bagdemagus ded beste, for he fyrste began and ever he was lengyste that helde on. But sir Gaherys, Gawaynes brother, smote ever at the face of kynge Bagdemagus, and at the laste he smote downe sir Gaherys, horse and man.

And by aventure sir Palomydes mette with sir Blamour de Ganys, 20 brother unto sir Bleoberys, and ayther smote other with grete spearis, that bothe horse and men felle to the erthe. But sir Blamour had [suche a falle that he had] allmoste broke his necke, for the blood braste oute at the nose, mowthe, and earys. Than cam in deuke Chalens of Claraunce, and undir his governaunce there cam a knyght that hyght sir 25 Elys la Noyre, And there encountyrd with hym kynge Bagdemagus, and he smote sir Elys, that he made hym to avoyde his arson of his sadyll.

So this deuke Chalence of Claraunce ded there grete dedis of armys, and so late as he cam in the thirde day there ded no man so well excepte kynge Bagdemagus and sir Palomydes. And the pryce was gyvyn that 30 day unto kynge Bagdemagus, and than they blew unto lodgyng and unarmed them and wente to the feyste.

Ryght so cam in sir Dynadan and mocked and japed wyth kynge Bagdemagus, that all knyghtes lowghe at hym, for he was a fyne japer and lovynge unto all good knyghtes. 35

So anone as they had dyned, there cam a varlet beerynge four spearys on his backe, and he cam to sir Palomydes and seyde thus:

'Here is a knyght by that hath sente the choyse of four spearys, and requyryth you for youre ladyes sake to take that one halff of thes spearys and juste with hym in the fylde.' 40

'Telle hym,' seyde sir Palomydes, ' "I woll nat fayle you".'

So sir Galahalte seyde, 'Make you redy!' So quene Gwenyver, the Haute Prynce, and sir Launcelot, they were sette in scaffoldis [to gyve the jugement of these two knyghtis].

Than sir Palomydes and the straunge knyght ran togydirs and brake there spearys to their hondys. And anone aythir of them toke another speare and shyvyrd them in pecis. And than ayther toke a gretter speare, and than the knyght smote downe sir Palomydes, horse and
5 man, and as he wolde have passed over hym the knyghtes horse stombeled and felle downe uppon sir Palomydes. Than they drewe theire swerdis, and laysshed togydirs wondirly sore.

Than the Haute Prynce and sir Launcelot seyde they saw never two knyghtes fyght bettir; but ever the straunge knyght doubled his
10 strokys and put sir Palomydes abak.

And therewithall the Haute Prynce cryed 'Whoo!'

And than they wente to lodgynge, and whan they were unarmed anone they knew hym for sir Lamerok. And whan Launcelot knew sir Lamerok he made muche of hym; for of all erthely men he loved
15 hym beste excepte sir Trystram. Than quene Gwenyver comended hym, and so did all good knyghtes, ⟨and⟩ made muche of hym, excepte sir Gawaynes brethirne. Than quene Gwenyvir seyde unto sir La⌐uncelot⌐,

'Sir, I requyre you that and ye juste ony more, that ye juste wyth none
20 of the blood of my lorde kynge Arthur.'

And so he promysed he wolde nat as at that tyme.

(45) HERE BEGYNNYTH THE FOURTH DAY. Than cam into the fylde the Kynge with the Hondred Knyghtes, and all they of Northe Galys, and deuke Chalens of Claraunce, and kynge Marsyll of Pometayne. And
25 there cam sir Saphir, sir Palomydes brother, and he tolde hym tydynges of hys fadir and of his modir.

'And his name was called [the] erle ⟨de la Plaunche⟩, and so I appeled hym afore the kynge, for he made warre uppon oure fadir and modir. And there I slewe hym in playne batayle.'

30 So they two wente into the fylde, and the damesell wyth hem. And there cam to encounter agayne them sir Bleoberys de Ganys and sir Ector de Marys. And sir Palomydes encountyrd wyth sir Bleoberys, and aythir smote other downe. In the same wyse ded sir Saphir and sir Ector, and tho two couplys ded batayle on foote.

35 Than cam in sir Lamerok, and he encountyrd with the Kynge of the Hondred Knyghtes and smote hym quyte over his horse tayle. And in the same wyse he served the kynge of Northe Galys, and also he smote downe kynge Marsyll. And so or ever he stynte he smote downe wyth his speare and with his swerde thirty knyghtys. Whan deuke Chalens
40 saw sir Lamerok do so grete proues he wolde nat meddyll with hym for shame. And than he charged all his knyghtes in payne of deth that 'none of you towche hym, for hit were shame to all goode knyghtes and that knyght were shamed'.

Than the two kynges gadird them togydirs, and all they sett uppon

sir Lameroke. And he fayled them nat, but russhed here and there and
raced of many helmys, that the Haute Prince and quene Gwenyver
seyde they sawe never knyght do suche dedis of armys on horsebacke.

'Alas!' seyde sir Launcelot to kynge Bagdemagus, 'I woll arme me
and helpe sir Lamerok.'   5

'And I woll ryde wyth you,' seyde kynge Bagdemagus.

And whan they two were horsed they cam to sir Lamerok that stood
amonge thirty knyghtes, and well was hym that myght reche hym a
buffet; and ever he smote agayne myghtyly. Than cam there into the
pres sir Launcelot, and he threwe downe sir Mador de la Porte, and   10
with the troncheon of that speare he threwe downe many knyghtes.
And kynge Bagdemagus smote on the lyffte honde and on the ryght
honde mervaylusly well. And than tho three kynges fledde abak.

And therewithall sir Galahalte lat blow to lodgynge; and all herrowdis
gaff sir Lamerok the pryce.   15

And all this whyle fought sir Palomydes, and sir Bleoberys, and sir
Safer, and sir Ector on foote, and never was there four knyghtes more
evynner macched. And anone they were departed, and had unto their
lodgynge, and unarmed; and so they wente to the grete feste.

But whan sir Lamerok was com unto the courte quene Gwenyver   20
enbraced hym in her armys and seyde,

'Sir, well have ye done this day!'

Than cam the Haute Prynce, and he made of hym grete joy, and so
ded sir Dynadan, for he wepte for joy. But the joy that sir Launcelot
made of sir Lamerok there myght no tonge telle. Than they wente   25
unto reste.

And so on the morne the Haute Prynce sir Galahalte blew unto the
fylde.

HERE BEGYNNYTH THE FYFTH DAY. So hit befell that sir Palomydes   (46)
cam in the morne-tyde, and profyrde to juste thereas kynge Arthur was 30
in a castell there besydys Surluse. And there encountyrd with hym a
worshypfull deuke that hyght Adrawns, and there sir Palomydes smote
hym over his horse croupyn. And this deuke was uncle unto kynge
Arthure.

Than sir Elyce, his sonne, rode unto sir Palomydes, and so he servid 35
sir Elyse in the same wyse. Whan sir Gawayne sawe this he was wrothe.
Than he toke his horse and encountird with sir Palomydes, and sir
Palomydes smote hym so harde that he wente to the erthe, horse and
man. And for to make a short tale, he smote downe his three breth.erne,
that is for to say sir Mordred, sir Gaherys, and sir Aggravayne.   40

'A, Jesu!' seyde kynge Arthure, 'this is a grete dispyte that suche a
Saryson shall smyte downe my blood!'

And therewithall kynge Arthure was wrothe and thought to have
made hym redy to juste. That aspyed sir Lamerok, that kynge Arthure

and his blood was so discomfite. And anone he was redy and axed sir Palomydes if he wolde ony more juste.

'Why sholde I nat juste?' seyde sir Palomydes.

So they hurled togydirs and brake their spearys, and all to-shyvird
5 them, that all the castell range of their dyntys. Than aythir gate a gretter speare, and they cam so fyersly togydir that sir Palomydes speare brake, and sir Lamerokes hylde. And therewythall sir Palomydes loste his spurrys, and so he lay upryght on his horse backe. But sir Palomydes recoverde agayne and toke his damesell, and so sir Saffir and he wente
10 their way.

So whan he was departed the kynge cam to sir Lamerok and thankyd hym of his goodnes and prayde hym to tell hym his name.

'Syr,' seyde sir Lamerok, 'wyte you well I owghe you my servyse, but as at this tyme I woll nat abyde here, for I se off myne enemyes
15 many aboute you.'

'Alas!' seyde kynge Arthure, 'nowe wote I well hit is sir Lamerok de Galys. A, sir Lamerok, abyde wyth me! And be my crowne, I shall never fayle the: and nat so hardy in sir Gawaynes hede, nothir none of his bretherne, to do the wronge.'
20 'Sir, grete wronge have they done me and you bothe.'

'That is trouthe,' seyde kynge Arthur, 'for they slew their owne modir, my sistir. Hit had bene muche fayrer and bettir that ye hadde wedded her, for ye ar a kynges sonne as well as they.'

'A, Jesu, mercy!' seyde sir Lamerok. 'Her deth shall I never forgete,
25 and if hit were nat at the reverence of youre hyghnes, I sholde be revenged uppon sir Gawayne and his bretherne.'

'Truly,' seyde kynge Arthour, 'I woll make you at acorde.'

'Sir,' seyde sir Lamerok, 'as at this tyme I may nat abyde with you, for I muste to the justis where is sir Launcelot and the Haute Prynce
30 sir Galahalte.'

So there was a damesell that was doughtir unto kynge Baudas; and there was a Sarazen knyght that hyght sir Corsabryne, and he loved the damesell and in no wyse he wolde suffir her to be maryed. For ever this Corsabryne [n]oysed her and named her that she was
35 oute of her mynde, and thus he lette her that she myght nat be maryed.
(47)   So by fortune this damesell harde telle that sir Palomydes ded muche for damesels. And anone she sente hym a pensell and prayde hym to fyght with sir Corsabroyne for her love, and he sholde have her and all her londis, and of her fadirs that sholde falle aftir hym.
40   Than the damesell sente unto sir Corsabryne and bade hym go unto sir Palomydes that was a paynym as well as he, and she gaff hym warn-ynge that she had sente hym her pensell; and yf he myght overcom sir Palomydes she wolde wedde hym.

Whan sir Corsabryne wyste of her dedis, than was he wood wrothe.

And anone he rode unto Surluse where the Haute Prynce [was], and there he founde sir Palomydes redy, the whyche had the pensell. And so there they waged batayle aythir with othir afore sir Galahalte.

'Well,' seyde the Haute Prynce, 'this day muste noble knyghtes juste, and at aftir dyner we shall se how ye can do.'   5

Than they blew to justys. And in cam sir Dynadan and mette with sir Geryne, a good knyght, and he threw hym downe over his horse croupen. And sir Dynadan overthrew four knyghtes mo, and there he dede grete dedis of armys, for he was a good knyght. But he was a grete skoffer and a gaper, and the meryste knyght amonge felyship that 10 was that tyme lyvynge: and he loved every good knyght and every good knyght loved hym.

So whan the Haute Prynce saw sir Dynadan do so well, he sente unto sir Launcelot and bade hym stryke hym adowne:

'And [whan that ye have done] so, brynge hym afore me and quene 15 Gwenyver.'

Than sir Launcelot ded as he was requyred. Than cam sir La[morak] and smote downe many knyghtes, and raced of helmys, and droff all the knyghtes afore hym, and sir Launcelot smote adowne sir Dynadan and made his men to unarme hym. And so brought hym to the quene, and 20 tho the Haute Prynce lowghe at sir Dynadan, that they myght nat stonde.

'Well,' seyde sir Dynadan, 'yet have I no shame, for the olde shrew sir Launcelot smote me downe.'

So they wente to dyner, all the courte, and had grete disporte at sir Dynadan.   25

So whan the dyner was done, they blew to the fylde to beholde sir Palomydes and sir Corsabryne. Syr Palomydes pyght his pensell in myddys of the fylde, and than they hurled togydirs with her spearys as hit were thundir, and they smote aythir other to the erthe. And than they pulled oute there swerdis and dressed their shyldis and laysshed 30 togydirs myghtyly as myghty knyghtes, that well-nyghe there was no pyse of harneyse wolde holde them, for this Corsabryne was a passynge felownse knyght. Than Corsabryne seyde,

'Sir Palomydes, wolt thou release me yondir damesell and the pensell?'

Than was he wrothe oute of mesure, and gaff sir Palomyde[s] suche 35 a buffet that he kneled on his kne. Than sir Palomydes arose lyghtly and smote hym uppon the helme, that he fell upryght to the erthe. And therewithall he raced of his helme and seyde,

'Yelde the, Corsabryne, or thou shalt dye!'

'Fye on the,' seyde sir Corsabryne, 'and do thy warste!'   40

Than he smote of his hede. And therewithall cam a stynke of his body, whan the soule departed, that there myght nobody abyde the savoure. So was the corpus had away and buryed in a wood, bycause he was a pay[n]ym.

Than they blew unto lodgynge, and sir Palomydes was unarmed. Than he wente unto quene Gwenyver, to the Haute Prynce, and to sir Launcelot.

'Sir,' seyde the Haute Prynce, 'here have ye seyne this day a grete myracle by Corsabryne, what savoure was there whan the soule departed frome the body. Therefore we all requyre you to take the baptyme uppon you, and than all knyghtes woll sette the more be you.'

'Sir,' seyde sir Palomydes, 'I woll that ye all knowe that into this londe I cam to be crystyned, and in my harte I am crystynde, and crystynde woll I be. But I have made suche a vowe that I may nat be crystynde tyll I have done seven trewe bataylis for Jesus sake, and than woll I be crystynde. And I truste that God woll take myne entente, for I meane truly.'

Than sir Palomydes prayde quene Gwenyver and the Haute Prynce [to soupe with hym]; and so he ded bothe sir Launcelot and sir Lamerok and many other good knyghtes.

So on the morne they herde there masse, and blewe to the [felde,] and than many worshipfull knyghtes made them redy.

(48) HERE BEGYNNYTH THE SYXTH DAY. Than cam therein sir Gaherys, and there encountyrd with hym sir Ossayse of Surluse, and sir Gaherys smote hym over his horse croupe. And than ayther party encountyrd with othir, and there were many [speres broken and many] knyghtes caste undir fyete.

So there cam in sir Darnarde and sir Agglovale, that were bretherne unto sir Lamerok, and they mette with other two knyghtes, and aythir smote other so harde that all four knyghtes and horsis fell to the erthe.

Whan sir Lamerok saw his two bretherne downe he was wrothe oute of mesure; and than he gate a grete speare in his honde, and therewithall he smote downe four good knyghtes, and than his speare brake. Then he pulled oute his swerde and smote aboute hym on the ryght honde and on the lyffte honde, and raced of helmys and pulled downe knyghtes, that all men mervayled of suche dedis of armys as he ded, for he fared so that many knyghtes fledde. Than he horsed his bretherne agayne and sayde,

'Bretherne, ye ought to be ashamed to falle so of your horsis! What is a knyght but whan he is on horsebacke? For I sette nat by a knyght whan he is on foote, for all batayles on foote ar but pyllours in batayles, for there sholde no knyght fyghte on foote but yf hit were for treson or ellys he were dryvyn by forse to fyght on foote. Therefore, bretherne, sytte faste in your sadyls, or ellys fyght never more afore me!'

So with that cam in the deuke Chalence of Claraunce. And there encountyrd with hym the erle of Ulbawys of Surluse, and aythir of hem smote other downe. Than the knyghtes of bothe partyes horsed their

lordis agayne, for sir Ector and sir Bleoberys were on foote waytynge
on the deuke Chalence, and the Kynge with the Hondred Knyghtes was
with the erle of Ulbawes.

So wyth that cam sir Gaherys and laysshed to the Kynge wyth the
Hondred Knyghtes and he to hym agayne. Than cam the deuke 5
Chalence and departed them. So they blew to lodgynge, and the
knyghtes unarmed them and drewe them to there dyner.

And at the myddys of his dynar in cam sir Dynadan and began to
rayle. And than he behelde the Haute Prynce that hym semed wrothe
with som faute that he sawe: for he had a condission that he loved no 10
fysshe, and bycause [he] was served with fysshe and hated hit, therefore
he was nat myrry. And whan sir Dynadan had aspyed the Haute
Prynce he aspyed where was a fysshe with a grete hede, and anone that
he gate betwyxte two disshis and served the Haute Prynce with that
fysshe. And than he sayde thus: 15

'Sir Galahalte, well may I lykkyn you to a wolff, for he woll never ete
fysshe, but fleysshe.'

And anone the Haute Prynce lowghe at his wordis.

'Well, well,' seyde sir Dynadan to sir Launcelot, 'what devyll do ye
in this contrey? For here may no meane knyghtes wynne no worship 20
for the.'

'I ensure the, sir Dynadan,' seyde sir Launcelot, 'I shall no more
mete with the, nother with thy grete speare, for I may nat sytte in my
sadyll whan thy speare hittyth me. And I be happy, I shall beware of
thy boyteous body that thou beryst. Well,' seyde sir Launcelot, 'make 25
good wacche [e]ver. God forbode that ever we mete but hit be at a
dysshe of mete!'

Than lowghe the quene and the Haute Prynce, that they myght nat
sytte at their table, and thus they made grete joy tyll on the morne.
And than they harde masse, and blew to the fylde, and quene Gwenyver 30
and all astatys were sette, a[nd] jouges armed clene with their shyldis
to kepe the ryghtes.

Now BEGYNNYTH THE SEVENTH BATAYLE. Here cam in the deuke (49)
Cambynes and there encountyrd with hym sir Arystaunce that was
cownted a good knyght, and they mette so harde that aythir bare other 35
adowne, horse and man. Than there cam in the erle Lambayle and
halpe the deuke agayne to horsebacke.

Than there cam in sir Ossayse of Surluse, and he smote the erle
Lambayle downe frome his horse. And so they began grete dedis of
armys, and many spearys were brokyn and many knyghtes were caste 40
to the erthe. Than the kynge of Northe Galys and the erle Ulbawes
smote togydyrs, that all the jouges thought hit was mortall deth.

This meanewhyle quene Gwenyver and the Haute Prynce and sir
Launcelot made there sir Dynadan to make hym redy to juste.

'I woll,' seyde sir Dynadan, 'ryde into the fylde, but than one of you twayne woll mete with me.'

'Perdeus,' seyde the Haute Prynce and sir Launcelot, 'ye may se how we sytte here as jouges with oure shyldis, and allway may ye beholde
5 where we sytte here or nat.'

So sir Dynadan departed and toke his horse, and mette with many knyghtes and ded passyngly well. And as he was departed, sir Launcelot disgysed hymselff and put uppon his armour a maydyns garmente freysshely attyred. Than sir Launcelot made sir Galyhodyn to lede hym
10 thorow the raunge, and all men had wondir what damesell was that. And so as sir Dynadan cam into the raunge, sir Launcelot, that was in the damesels aray, gate sir Galyhodyns speare and ran unto sir Dynadan.

And allwayes he loked up thereas sir Launcelot was, and than he sawe one sytte in the stede of sir Launcelot armed. But whan sir
15 Dynadan saw a maner of a damesell, he dradde perellys lest hit sholde be sir Launcelot disgysed. But sir Launcelot cam on hym so faste that he smote sir Dynadan over his horse croupe. And anone grete coystrons gate sir Dynadan, and into the foreyste there besyde, and there they dispoyled hym unto his sherte and put uppon hym a womans
20 garmente and so brought hym into fylde; and so the[y] blew unto lodgyng, and every knyght wente and unarmed them.

And than was sir Dynadan brought in amonge them all, and whan quene Gwenyver sawe sir Dynadan ibrought in so amonge them all, than she lowghe, that she fell downe; and so dede all that there was.
25 'Well,' seyde sir Dynadan, 'sir Launcelot, thou arte so false that I can never beware of the.'

Than by all the assente they gaff sir Launcelot the pryce; the next was sir Lameroke de Galys, and the thirde was sir Palomydes; the fourth was kynge Bagdemagus. So thes four knyghtes had the pryce. And there
30 was grete joy and grete nobelay in all the courte.

And on the morne quene Gwenyver and sir Launcelot departed unto kynge Arthur; but in no wyse sir Lamerok w[ol]de nat go wyth them.

'Sir, I shall undirtake,' seyde sir Launcelot, 'that, and ye woll go wyth us, kynge Arthure shall charge sir Gawayne and his bretherne
35 never to do you hurte.'

'As for that,' sayde sir Lamerok, 'I woll nat truste to sir Gawayne, nother none of his bretherne. And wyte you well, sir La[uncelot], and hit were nat for my lorde kynge Arthurs sake, I shuld macche sir Gawayne and his bretherne well inowghe. But for to sey that I shall
40 truste them, that shall I never. And there[fore] I pray you recommaunde me unto kynge Arthure and all my lordys of the Rounde Table, and in what place that ever I com I shall do you all servyse to my power. And, sir, yet hit is but late that I revenged them whan they were put to the [werse] by sir Palomydes.'

Tha[n] sir Lameroke departed frome sir Launcelot and all the felyship, and aythir of them wepte at her departynge.

Now turne we from this mater and speke of sir Trystram, of (50)
whom this booke is pryncipall off. And leve we the kynge and
the quene, and sir Launcelot, and sir Lamerok.   5

X. JOYOUS GARD

And here begynnyth the treson of kynge Marke that he
ordayned agayne sir Trystram.

And there was cryed by the costys of Cornwayle a grete turnemente
and justus, and all was done by sir Galahalt the Haute Prynce and kynge   10
Bagdemagus to the entente to sle syr Launcelot other ellys uttirly to
destroy hym and shame hym, bycause sir Launcclot had evermore the
hygher degré. Therefore this prince and this kynge made this justys
ayenst sir Launcelot.

And thus her counceyle was discoverde unto kynge Marke, whereof   15
he was glad. Than kynge Marke unbethought hym that he wolde have
sir Trystram unto the turnemente disgysed, that no man sholde knowe
hym, to that entente that the Haute Prynce sholde wene that sir
Trystram were sir Launcelot.

And so at that justys cam in sir Trystram, and at that tyme sir   20
Launcelot was not there. But whan they sawe a knyght disgysed do
suche dedis of armys, they wente hit had bene sir Launcelot, and in
especiall kynge Marke seyde hit was sir Launcclot playnly.

Than they sette uppon hym, bothe kynge Bagdemagus and the
Haute Prynce, and there knyghtes seyde that hit was wondir that ever   25
sir Trystram myght endure that payne. Notwythstondynge for all the
payne that they ded hym, he wan the degré at that turnemente; and
there he hurte many knyghtes and brused them, [and they hurte hym
and brused hym] wondirly sore.

So whan the justys was all done they knewe well that he was sir   30
Trystram de Lyones, and all they that were on kynge Markis party were
glad that sir Trystram was hurte, and all the remenaunte were sory of
his hurte, for sir Trystrams was nat so behated as was sir Launcelot,
nat wythin the realme of Ingelonde.

Than cam kynge Marke unto sir Trystrams and sayde,   35
'Fayre nevew, I am hevy of your hurtys.'
'Gramercy, my lorde,' seyde sir Trystram.
Than kynge Marke made hym to be put in an horse letter in grete
tokenynge of love and sayde,

'Fayre cousyne, I shall[e be] your leche myselff.'

And so he rode forth wyth sir Trystram and brought hym into a castell by daylyght. And than kynge Marke made sir Trystram to ete, and aftir that he gaff hym a drynke; and anone as he hadde drunke he
5 felle on slepe. And whan hit was nyght he made hym to be caryed to another castell, and there he put hym in a stronge preson, and a man and a woman to gyff hym his mete and his drynke. So there he was a grete whyle.

Than was sir Trystram myssed, and no creature wyst where he was
10 becam. And whan La Beall Isode harde how he was myste, pryvayly she wente unto sir Sadocke and prayde hym to aspye where was sir Trystram. And whan sir Sadocke knew how sir Trystram was myste he sought and made spyes for hym.

And than he aspyed that kynge Marke had put the good knyght in
15 preson by his owne assente and the traytoure of Magouns. Than sir Sadocke toke with hym too of his cousyns and he layde them and hymself anone in a bushemente faste by the castell of Tyntagyll in armys.

And as by fortune there cam rydyng kynge Marke and four of his nevewys and a sertayne of the traytoures of Magouns. So whan sir
20 Sadocke aspyed them he brake oute of bushemente and sette there uppon them. And whan that kynge Marke aspyed sir Sadocke he fledde as faste as he myght, and there sir Sadocke slew all the four nevewys of kynge Marke, his cousyns. But these traytoures of Magouns smote one of sir Sadockes cousyns a grete wounde in the necke, but sir Sadocke
25 smote other twayne to the deth.

Than sir Sadocke rode uppon his way unto the castell that was called Lyonas, and there he aspyde of the treson and felony of kynge Marke. So off that castell they rode wyth sir Sadocke tyll they cam to a castel that hyght Arbray, and there in the towne they founde sir Dynas the
30 Senesciall that was a good knyght. But whan sir Sadock had tolde sir Dynas of all the treson of kynge Marke, than he defyed suche a kynge and seyde he wolde gyff up all his londis that hylde of hym.

And whan he seyde thes wordis all maner knyghtes seyde as sir Dynas sayde. Than by his advyse and of sir Sadockes he let stuff all the
35 townys and castels wythin the contrey of Lyones and assemble all that they cowde make.

(51) Now turne [we] unto kynge Marke, that whan he was ascaped frome sir Sadocke he rode unto the castell of Tyntagyll, and there he made a grete cry and noyse, and cryed unto harneyse all that myght bere armys.
40 Than they sought and founde where was dede four cousyns of kynge Marke, and the traytoure of Magouns. Than the kynge lette entyre them in a chapell.

Than kynge Marke lette cry in all the contrey that hylde of hym to go unto armys, for he undirstood that to the warre he muste nedis.

So whan kynge Marke harde and undirstood how sir Dynas and sir Sadok were arysyn in the cuntrey of Lyones, he reme[mb]ird of treson and wyeles, and so thus he ded lete make and countirfete lettirs from the Pope, and dede make a straunge clarke to brynge tho lettyrs unto kynge Marke, the whyche lettyrs specifyed that kynge Marke sholde make 5 hym redy, uppon payne of cursynge, wyth his oste to com to the Pope to helpe hym to go to Jerusalem for to make warre uppon the Saresyns.

So whan this clarke was com by the meane of the kynge, anone therewyth kynge Marke sente that clarke unto sir Trystram and bade hym sey thus, that and he wolde go warre uppon the myscreauntes he 10 sholde go oute of preson and have all his power with hym.

Whan sir Trystram undirstood this lettir, than he sayde thus to the clerke:

'A, kynge Marke, ever haste thou bene a traytoure and ever wolt be! But thou, clerke,' seyde sir Trystram, 'sey thou thus unto kynge Marke: 15 syne the Pope hath sente for hym, bid hym go thidir hymselff. For telle hym, traytoure kynge as he is, I woll nat go at his commaundemente! Gete oute of preson as well as I may, for I se I am well rewarded for my trewe servyse.'

Than the clarke returned agayne unto kynge Mark and tolde hym of 20 the answere of sir Trystram.

'Well,' seyde kynge Marke, 'yet shall he be begyled.'

And anone he wente unto hys chambir and countirfeted lettyrs, [and the lettyrs] specifyed that the Pope desyred sir Trystram to com hymself to make warre uppon the myscreauntes. 25

So whan the clerke cam agayne unto sir Trystram and toke hym thes lettyrs he aspyed they were of kynge Markes countirfetynge and sayde,

'A, kynge Marke! False hast thou ever bene, and so wolt thou ende!'

Than the clarke departed frome sir Trystram and cam unto kynge Marke agayne. And so by than there was com four wounded knyghtes 30 within the castell of Tyntagyll, and one of them his necke was nyghe brokyn in twayne, and another had his arme nyghe strykyn away; the thirde was boren thorow with a speare; the fourthe had his thyghe stryken in twayne. And whan they cam afore kynge Marke they cryed and sayde, 35

'Kynge, why fleyste thou nat? For all this contrey ys clyerly arysen ayenste the.'

Than was kynge Marke wrothe oute of mesure.

And so in the meanewhyle there cam into the contrey sir Percivale de Galys to seke aftir sir Trystram. And whan sir Percivale harde that sir 40 Trystram was in preson, he made clerly the delyveraunce of hym by his knyghtly meanys. And whan he was so delyverde he made grete joy of sir Percivale, and so ded ech one of other. Than sir Trystram seyde unto sir Percivale,

'And ye woll abyde in this marchis, I woll ryde with you.'

'Nay,' seyde sir Percivale, 'in thes contreyes I may nat tary, for I muste nedis into Wales.'

So sir Percivale departed frome sir Trystram and streyte he rode unto
5 kynge Marke and tolde hym how he had delyvered sir Trystram. And also he tolde the kynge that he had done hymselff grete shame for to preson sir Trystram so, 'for he is now the knyght of moste reverence in the worlde lyvynge, and wyte you well that the noblyste knyghtes of the worlde lovyth sir Trystram. And yf he woll make warre uppon you,
10 ye may nat abyde hit.'

'That is trouthe,' seyde kynge Marke, 'but I may nat love sir Trystram, bycause he lovyth my quene, La Beall Isode.'

'A, fy for shame!' seyde sir Percivale. 'Sey ye never so more! For ar nat ye uncle unto sir Trystram? And by youre neveaw ye sholde never
15 thynke that so noble a knyght as sir Trystram is, that he wolde do hymselff so grete vylany to holde his unclys wyff. Howbehit,' seyde sir Percivale, 'he may love youre quene synles, because she is called one of the fayryst ladyes of the worlde.'

Than sir Percivale departed frome kynge Marke, but yet he bethought
20 hym of more treson, notwithstondynge he graunted unto sir Percivale never by no maner of meanys to hurte sir Trystram.

So anone kynge Marke sente unto sir Dynas the Senesciall that he sholde put downe all the people that he had raysed, for he sente hym an othe that he wolde go hymselff unto the Pope of Rome to warre uppon
25 the myscreauntes, 'and I trow that is fayrer warre than thus to areyse people agaynste youre kynge.'

And anone as sir Dynas undirstood that he wolde go uppon the myscreauntys, than sir Dynas, in all the haste that myght be, he putte downe all his people. And whan the people were departed every man
30 to his home, than kynge Marke aspyed where was sir Trystram wyth La Beall Isode, and there by treson kynge Marke lete take hym and put hym in preson, contrary to his promyse that he made unto sir Percivale.

Whan quene Isode undirstode that sir Trystram was in preson agayne,
35 she made grete sorow as ever made lady or jantyllwoman. Than sir Trystram sente a lettir unto La Beall Isode and prayde hir to be his good lady, and sayde, yf hit pleased her to make a vessell redy for her and hym, he wolde go wyth her unto the realme of Logrys, that is this londe.

40 Whan La Beall Isode undirstood sir Trystrams [letters] and his entente she sente hym another and bade hym be of good comforte, for she wolde do make the vessell redy and all maner of thynge to purpose. Than La Beall Isode sente unto sir Dynas and to sir Sadok and prayde hem in ony wyse to take kynge Marke and put hym in preson unto the

tyme that she and sir Trystram were departed unto the realme of Logrys.

Whan sir Dynas the Senesciall undirstood the treson of kynge Marke he promysed her to do her commaundemente, and sente her worde agayne that kynge Marke sholde be put in preson. And so as they devysed hit was done, and than sir Trystram was delyverde oute of preson. And anone in all haste quene Isode and sir Trystram wente and toke there counceyle, and so they toke wyth them what them lyste beste, and so they departed.

Than La Beall Isode and sir Trystram toke their vessell and cam by watir into this londe. And so they were nat four dayes in this londe but there was made a crye of a justys and turnement that kynge Arthure let make. Whan sir Trystram harde tell of that turnement he disgysed hymselff and La Beall Isode and rode unto that turnemente. And whan he cam there he sawe many knyghtes juste and turney, and so sir Trystram dressed hym to the raunge. And to make shorte conclusyon, he overthrewe fourtene knyghtes of the Rounde Table.

Whan sir Launcelot saw thes knyghtes of the Rounde Table thus overthrowe he dressed hym to sir Trystram, and that sawe La Beall Isode, how sir Launcelot was commyn into the fylde. Than she sente unto sir Launcelot a rynge to lat hym wete hit was sir Trystram de Lyones. Whan sir Launcelot undirstood that he was sir Trystram he was full glad and wolde nat juste. And than sir Launcelot aspyed whydir syr Trystram yeode, and aftir hym he rode, and than aythir made grete joy of other.

And so sir Launcelot brought sir Trystram and Isode unto Joyus Garde that was his owne castell, and he had wonne hit with his owne hondis. And there sir Launcelot put them in, to welde hit for their owne. And wyte you well that castell was garnyshed and furnysshed for a kynge and a quene royall there to have suggeourned. And sir Launcelot charged all his people to honoure them and love them as they wolde do hymselff.

So sir Launcelot departed unto kynge Arthure, and than he tolde quene Gwenyver how he that justed so well at the laste turnemente was sir Trystram, and there he tolde her how that he had with hym La Beall Isode, magré kynge Mark. And so quene Gwenyvere tolde all this to kynge Arthure, and whan kynge Arthure wyste that sir Trystram was ascaped and commyn from kynge Marke and had brought La Beall Isode with hym, than was he passyng glad. So bycause of sir Trystram kynge Arthure let make a cry that on Mayday shulde be a justis byfore the castell of Lonezep, and that castell was faste by Joyus Garde.

And thus kynge Arthure devysed that all the knyghtes of this londe, of Cornwayle, and of North Walys, shulde juste ayenste all thes

contreyis: Irelonde and Scotlonde and the remenaunte of Walys, and the
contrey of Goore and Surluse, and of Lystenoyse, and they of Northumbirlonde, and all those that hylde londis of kynge Arthurs a this
halff the se. So whan this crye was made many knyghtes were glad and
5 many were sad.

'Sir,' seyde sir Launcelot unto kynge Arthure, 'by this cry that ye
have made ye woll put us that bene aboute you in grete jouparté, for
there be many knyghtes that hath envy to us. Therefore whan we shall
mete at the day of justis there woll be harde skyffte for us.'

10 'As for that,' seyde kynge Arthure, 'I care nat. There shall we preve
whoo shall be beste of his hondis.'

So whan sir Launcelot undirstood wherefore kynge Arthure made
this justenynge, than he made suche purvyaunce that La Beall Isode
sholde beholde the justis in a secrete place that was honeste for her
15 astate.

Now turne we unto sir Trystram and to La Beall Isode, how they
made joy togydrys dayly with all maner of myrthis that they coude
devyse.

And every day sir Trystram wolde go ryde an-huntynge, for he was
20 called that tyme the chyeff chacer of the worlde and the noblyst blower
of an horne of all maner of mesures. For, as bookis reporte, of sir
Trystram cam all the good termys of venery and of huntynge, and all
the syses and mesures of all blowyng wyth an horne; and of hym we
had fyrst all the termys of hawkynge, and whyche were bestis of chace
25 and bestis of venery, and whyche were vermyns; and all the blastis that
longed to all maner of game: fyrste to the uncoupelynge, to the sekynge,
to the fyndynge, to the rechace, to the flyght, to the deth, and to strake;
and many other blastis and termys, that all maner jantylmen hath cause
to the worldes ende to prayse sir Trystram and to pray for his soule.
30 AMEN, SAYDE SIR THOMAS MALLEORRÉ.

(53)   So on a day La Beall Isode seyde unto sir Trystram,
'I mervayle me muche that ye remembir nat youreselff how ye be
here in a straunge contrey, and here be many perelous knyghtes, and
well ye wote that kynge Marke is full of treson. And that ye woll ryde
35 thus to chace and to hunte unarmed, ye myght be sone destroyed.'

'My fayre lady and my love, mercy! I woll no more do so.'

So than sir Trystram rode dayly an-huntynge armed, and his men
berynge his shylde and his speare.

So on a day, a lytil afore the moneth o May, sir Trystram chaced an
40 harte passynge egirly, and so the harte passed by a fayre welle. And than
sir Trystram alyght and put of his helme to drynke of that burbely
welle, and ryght so he harde and sawe the questynge beste commynge
towarde the welle. So whan sir Trystram saw that beste he put on his

helme, for he demed he sholde hyre of sir Palomydes; for that beste
was hys queste. Ryght so sir Trystram saw where cam a knyghte armed
uppon a noble courser, and so he salewed hym.

So they spake of many thynges, and this knyghtes name was sir
Brewnys Saunze Pité. And so anone with that there cam unto them sir 5
Palomydes, and aythir salewed other and spake fayre to other.

'Now, fayre knyghtes,' seyde sir Palomydes, 'I can tell you tydynges.'
'What is that?' seyde tho knyghtes.

'Sirris, wyte you well that kynge Marke of Cornwayle is put in
preson by his owne knyghtes, and all was for the love of sir Trystram, 10
for kynge Marke had put sir Trystram twyse in preson, and onys sir
Percivale delyverde hym, and at the laste tyme La Beall Isode delyverde
sir Trystram and wente clyerly away wyth hym into this realme. And
all this whyle kynge Marke is in preson. And this be trouthe,' seyde sir
Palomydes, 'we shall hyre hastely of sir Trystram. And as for to say 15
that I love La Beall Isode peramoures, I dare make good that I do, and
that she hath my servyse abovyn all other ladyes and shall have all the
terme of my lyff.'

And ryght so as they stoode thus talkynge, they sawe afore them
where cam a knyght all armed on a grete horse, and his one man bare 20
hys shylde and the othir his speare. And anone as that knyght aspied
h[e]m he gate his shylde and his speare and dressed hym to juste.

'Now, fayre felowys,' seyde sir Trystram, 'yondir ys a knyghte woll
juste wyth us. Now lette us se whyche of us shall encountir wyth hym,
for I se well he is of the courte of kynge Arthur.' 25

'Hit shall nat be longe ar he be mette wythall,' seyde sir Palomydes,
'for I f[o]nde never no knyght in my queste of this glatissynge beste
but, and he wolde juste, I never yet refused hym.'

'Sir, as well may I,' seyde sir Brewnes Saunz Pité, 'folow that beste
as ye.' 30

'Than shall ye do batayle wyth me,' seyde sir Palomydes.

So sir Palomydes dressed hym unto that othir knyght whyche hyght
sir Bleoberis, that was a noble knyght and nygh kynne unto sir Launcelot. And so they mette so harde that sir Palomydes felle to the erthe,
horse and man. Than sir Bleoberys cryed alowde and seyde thus: 35

'Make redy, thou false traytoure knyght, sir Brewnys Saunze Pité!
For I woll have ado wyth the to the uttraunce for the noble knyghtes
and ladyes that thou haste betrayde!'

Whan sir Brewnys harde hym sey so, he toke his horse by the brydyll
and fledde his way ⸢as faste as ever his hors myghte renne.⸣ Whan sir 40
Bleoberys saw hym fle he felowed faste after thorow thycke and thorow
thynne.

And by fortune, as sir Brewnys fled, he saw evyn afore hym three
knyghtes of the Table Rounde, that one hyght sir Ector de Marys and

the other hyght sir Percivale de Galys, the thirde hyght sir Harry de
Fyze Lake, a good knyght and an hardy. And as for sir Percivale, he
was called that tyme as of his ayge one of the beste knyghtes of the
worlde and the beste assured. So whan sir Brewnys saw these knyghtes
5   he rode strayte unto them and cryed and prayde them of rescowys.

'What nede have ye?' seyde sir Ector.

'A, fayre knyghtes!' seyde sir Brewnys, 'here folowyth me the moste
traytour knyght and the moste coward and moste of vylany, and his
name is sir Brewnys Saunze Pité. And if he may gete me he woll sle me
10 wythoute mercy and pyté.'

'Than abyde ye with us,' seyde sir Percivale, 'and we shall warraunte.'

And anone were they ware of sir Bleoberys whyche cam rydyng all
that he myght. Than sir Ector put hymselff fyrste forthe to juste afore
them all. And whan sir Bleoberys saw that they were four knyghtes and
15 he but hymselff, he stoode in a dwere whethir he wolde turne other
holde his way.

Than he seyde to hymselff, 'I am a knyght of the Table Rounde, and
rathir than I sholde shame myne othe and my bloode I woll holde my
way whatsomever falle thereoff.'

20 And than sir Ector dressed his speare, and smote aythir other passyng
sore, but sir Ector felle to the erthe. That saw sir Percivale, and he
dressed his horse towarde hym all that he myght dryve. But syr
Percyvale had suche a stroke that horse and man felle bothe to the
erthe.

25 Whan sir Harry saw that they were bothe to the erthe, than he seyde
to hymselff, 'Never was sir Brewnes of suche proues.' So sir Harry
dressed his horse, and they mette togydyrs so strongly that bothe the
horsys and the knyghtes felle to the erthe, but sir Bleoberys horse
began to recover agayne.

30 That saw sir Brewnys and cam hurtelynge and smote hym over and
over, and wolde have slayne hym as he lay on the grounde. Than sir
Harry arose lyghtly and toke the brydyll of sir Brewnys horse and
sayde,

'Fy for shame! Stryke never a knyght whan he is at the erthe! For
35 this knyght may be called no shamefull knyght of his dedis, for on this
grounde he hath done worshypfully, and put to the warre passynge
good knyghtes.'

'Therefore woll I nat let,' seyde sir Brewnys.

'Thou shalt nat chose,' seyde sir Harry, 'as at this tyme!'

40 So whan sir Brewnys saw that he myght nat have hys wylle he spake
fayre. Than sir Harry let hym go, and than anone he made his horse to
renne over sir Bleoberys and rosshed hym to the erthe lyke to have
slayne hym. Whan sir Harry saw hym do so vylaunsly he cryed and
sayde,

'Traytoure knyght, leve of, for shame!'

And as sir Harry wolde have takyn his horse to fyght wyth syr
Brewnys, than sir Brewnys [ranne upon hym] as he was halff uppon his
horse, and smote hym downe, horse and man, and had slayne nere sir
Harry, the good knyght. That saw sir Percyvale, and than he cryde,   5

'Traytur knyght, what doste thou?'

And whan sir Percyvale was uppon his horse sir Brewnys toke his
horse and fledde all that ever he myght, and sir Percyvale and sir Harry
folowed hym faste, but ever the lenger they chaced the farther were they
behynde. Than they turned agayne and cam to sir Ector de Marys and   10
to sir Bleoberys. Than sayde sir Bleoberys,

'Why have ye so succoured that false traytoure knyght?'

'Why,' sayde sir Harry, 'what knyght is he? For well I wote hit is
a false knyght,' seyde sir Harry, 'and a cowarde and a felons knyght.'

'Sir,' seyde sir Bleoberys, 'he is the moste cowarde knyght, and a   15
devowrer of ladyes, and also a distroyer of kynge Arthurs knyghtes as
grete as ony ys now lyvynge.'

'Sir, what is youre name?' seyde sir Ector.

'My name is', he seyde, 'sir Bleoberys de Ganys.'

'Alas, fayre cousyn!' seyde sir Ector, 'forgyff me, for I am sir Ector 20
de Marys.'

Than sir Percyvale and sir Harry made grete joy of sir Bleoberys, but
all they were hevy that sir Brewnys Saunze Pité had ascaped them,
whereof they made grete dole.

Ryght so as they stood there cam sir Palomydes; and whan he saw   25 (54)
the shylde of sir Bleoberys ly on the erthe, than sayde sir Palomydes,

'He that owyth that shylde lette hym dresse hym to me, for he smote
me downe here faste by at a fountayne, and therefore I woll fyght wyth
hym on foote.'

'Sir, I am redy,' seyde sir Bleoberys, 'here to answere the, for wyte 30
thou well, sir knyght, hit was I, and my name ys sir Bleoberys de
Ganys.'

'Well art thou mette,' seyde sir Palomydes, 'and wyte thou well my
name ys sir Palomydes the Saresyn.'

(And aythir of them hated other to the dethe.)   35

'Sir Palomydes,' seyde sir Ector, 'wyte thou well there is nother
[th]ou nothir no knyght that beryth the lyff that sleyth ony of oure
bloode but he shall dye for hit. Therefore, and thou lyst to fyght, go
and syke sir Launcelot othir ellys sir Trystram, and there shalt thou
fynde thy matche.'   40

'Wyth them have I mette,' seyde sir Palomydes, 'but I had never no
worshyp of them.'

'Was there never no maner of knyght,' seyde sir Ector, 'but they too
that ever matched you?'

'Yes,' seyde sir Palomydes, 'there was the thirde; as good a knyght as ony of them, and of his ayge he was the beste, for yet founde I never his pyere. For and he myght have lyved tyll he had bene more of ayge, an hardyer man there lyvith nat than he wolde have bene, and his name 5 was sir Lamorak de Galys. And as he had justed at a turnemente, there he overthrewe me and thirty knyghtes mo, and there he wan the gre. And at his departynge there mette hym sir Gawayne and his bretherne, and wyth grete payne they slewe hym felounsly, unto all good knyghtes grete damage!'

10 And anone as sir Percyvale herde that his brothir was dede, sir Lamerok, he felle over his horse mane sownynge, and there he made the grettyste dole and sorow that ever made any noble knyght. And whan sir Percyvale arose he seyde,

'Alas, my good and noble brother, sir Lamorak, now shall we never 15 mete! And I trowe in all the wyde worlde may nat a man fynde suche a knyght as he was of his ayge. And hit is to muche to suffir the deth of oure fadir kynge Pellynor, and now the deth of oure good brother sir Lamorak!'

So in this meanewhyle there cam a varlet frome the courte of kynge 20 Arthure and tolde hem of the grete turnemente that sholde be at Lonezep, and how this londis, Cornwayle [and] No[r]the Galys, shulde juste ayenst all that wolde com of other co⟨n⟩tereyes.

(55) Now turne we unto sir Trystram, that as he rode an-huntynge he mette wyth sir Dynadan that was commyn into the contrey to seke sir 25 Trystram.

And anone sir Dynadan tolde sir Trystram his name, but sir Trystram wolde nat tell his name, wherefore sir Dynadan was wrothe.

'For suche a folyshe knyght as ye ar,' seyde sir Dynadan, 'I saw but late this day lyynge by a welle, and he fared as he slepte. And there he 30 lay lyke a fole grennynge and wolde nat speke, and his shylde lay by hym. and his horse also stood by hym. And well I wote he was a lovear.'

'A, fayre sir,' seyde sir Trystram, 'ar nat ye a lovear?'

'Mary, fye on that crauffte!' seyde sir Dynadan.

'Sir, that is yevell seyde,' [seyde] sir Trystram, 'for a knyght may 35 never be of proues but yf he be a lovear.'

'Ye say well,' seyde sir Dynadan. 'Now I pray you telle me youre name, syth ye be suche a lovear; othir ellys I shall do batayle with you.'

'As for that,' seyde sir Trystram, 'hit is no reson to fyght wyth me but yf I telle you my name. And as for my name, ye shall nat wyte as at 40 this tyme for me.'

'Fye for shame! Ar ye a knyght and dare nat telle youre name to me? Therefore, sir, I woll fyght with you!'

'As for that,' seyde sir Trystram, 'I woll be avysed, for I woll nat do batayle but yf me lyste. And yf I do batayle wyth you,' seyde sir Trystram, 'ye ar nat able to withstonde me.'

'Fye on the, cowarde!' seyde sir Dynadan.

And thus 'as they h[o]ved stylle they saw a knyght com rydynge agaynste them.   5

'Lo,' seyde sir Trystram, 'se where commyth a knyght rydynge whyche woll juste wyth you.'

Anone as sir Dynadan behylde hym he seyde,

'Be my fayth! That same is the doted knyght that I saw lye by the welle, nother slepynge nother wakynge.'   10

'Well,' seyde sir Trystram, 'I know that knyght well, wyth the coverde shylde of assure, for he is the kynges sonne of Northumbirlonde. His name is sir Epynogrys, and he is as grete a lover as I know, and he lovyth the kynges doughter of Walys, a full fayre lady.   15 And now I suppose,' seyde sir Trystram, 'and ye requyre hym, he woll juste wyth you, and than shall ye preve whether a lover be bettir knyght or ye that woll nat love no lady.'

'Well,' seyde sir Dynadan, 'now shalt thou se what I shall do.'

And therewythall sir Dynadan spake on hyght and sayde,   20

'Sir knyght, make the redy to juste wythe me, for juste ye muste nedis, for hit is the custom of knyghtes arraunte for to make a knyght to juste, woll he othir nell he.'

'Sir,' seyde sir Epynogrys, 'ys that the rule and custom of you?'

'As for that,' seyde sir Dynadan, 'make the redy, for here is for   25 me!'

And therewythall they spurred their horsys and mette togydirs so harde that sir Epynogrys smote downe sir Dynadan. And anone sir Trystram rode to sir Dynadan and sayde,

'How now? Mesemyth the lover hath well sped.'   30

'Fye on the, cowarde!' seyde sir Dynadan. 'And yf thou be a good knyght, revenge me!'

'Nay,' seyde sir Trystram, 'I woll nat juste as at this tyme, but take youre horse and let us go hens.'

'God defende me,' seyde sir Dynadan, 'frome thy felyshyp, for I   35 never spedde well syns I mette wyth the.'

And so they departed.

'Well,' seyde sir Trystram, 'peraventure I cowde tell you tydynges of sir Trystram.'

'Godde save me,' seyde sir Dynadan, 'from thy felyshyp! For sir   40 Trystram were mykyll the warre and he were in thy company.'

And they departed.

'Sir,' seyde sir Trystram, 'yet hit may happyn that I may mete wyth yow in othir placis.'

So rode sir Trystram unto Joyus Garde, and there he harde in that towne grete noyse and cry.

'What is this noyse?' seyde sir Trystram.

'Sir,' seyde they, 'here is a knyght of this castell that hath be longe
5 amonge us, and ryght now he is slayne with two knyghtes, and for none other cause but that oure knyght seyde that sir Launcelot was bettir knyght than sir Gawayne.'

'That was a symple cause,' seyde sir Trystram, 'for to sle a good knyght for seyynge well by his maystir.'

10 'That is lytyll remedy to us,' seyde the men of the towne. 'For and sir Launcelot had bene hyre, sone we sholde have bene revenged uppon tho false knyghtes.'

Whan sir Trystram harde them sey so, he sente for his shylde and his speare. And lyghtly so wythin a whyle he had overtake them and made
15 them turne and amende that they had myssedone.

'What amendis woldiste thou have?' seyde the one knyght.

And therewyth they toke there course, and aythir mette other so harde that sir Trystram smote downe that knyght over his horse tayle. Than the othir knyght dressed hym to sir Trystram, and in the same
20 wyse he served the othir knyght.

And than they gate of their horsis as well as they myght and dressed their swerdis and their shyldis to do batayle to the utteraunce.

'Now, knyghtes,' seyde sir Trystram, 'woll ye telle me of whens ye be and what is youre namys? For suche men ye myght be ye
25 shulde harde ascape my hondis, and also ye myght be suche men and of such a cuntré that for all youre yevell dedis ye myght passe quyte.'

'Wyte thou well, sir knyght,' seyde they, 'we feare nat muche to telle the oure namys, for my name is sir Aggravayne, and my name is sir
30 Gaherys, brethirne unto the good knyght sir Gawayne, and we be nevewys unto kynge Arthure.'

'Well,' seyde sir Trystram, 'for kynge Arthurs sake I shall lette you passe as at this tyme. But hit is shame,' seyde sir Trystram, 'that sir Gawayne and ye be commyn of so grete blood, that ye four bretherne
35 be so named as ye be: for ye be called the grettyste distroyers and murtherars of good knyghtes that is now in the realme of Ingelonde. And as I have harde say, sir Gawayne and ye, his brethirne, amonge you slew a bettir knyght than ever any of you was, whyche was called the noble knyght sir Lamorak de Galys. And hit had pleased God,' seyde
40 sir Trystram, 'I wolde I had bene by hym at his deth day.'

'Than shuldist thou have gone the same way,' seyde sir Gaherys.

'Now, fayre knyghtes, than muste there have bene many mo good knyghtes than ye of youre bloode.'

And therewythall sir Trystram departed frome them towarde Joyus

Garde. And whan he was departed they toke there horsis, and the tone seyde to the tothir,

'We woll overtake hym and be revenged uppon hym in the despyte of sir Lamerok.'

So whan they had overtakyn sir Trystram, sir Aggravayne bade hym, 'Turne, traytoure knyght!'   5 (56)

'Ye sey well!' seyde sir Trystram.

And therewythall he pulled oute his swerde and smote sir Aggravayne suche a buffet uppon the helme that he tumbeled downe of his horse in a sowne, and he had a grevous wounde. And than he turned to 10 sir Gaherys, and sir Trystram smote hys swerde and his helme togydir wyth suche a myght that sir Gaherys felle oute of his sadyll.

And so sir Trystram rode unto Joyus Garde, and there he alyght and unarmed hym. So sir Trystram tolde La Beall Isode of all this adventure as ye have harde toforne, and whan she harde hym tell of sir 15 Dynadan,

'Sir,' she seyde, 'is nat that he that made the songe by kynge Marke?'

'That same is he,' seyde sir Trystram, 'for he is the beste bourder and japer that I know, and a noble knyght of his hondis, and the beste felawe that I know, and all good knyghtis lovyth his felyship.'   20

'Alas, sir,' seyde she, 'why brought ye hym nat wyth you hydir?'

'Have ye no care,' seyde sir Trystram, 'for he rydyth to seke me in this contrey, and therefore he woll nat away tyll he have mette wyth me.'

And there sir Trystram tolde La Beall Isode how sir Dynadan hylde 25 ayenste all lovers.

Ryght so cam in a varlette and tolde sir Trystram how there was com an arraunte knyght into the towne wyth suche a coloures uppon his shylde.

'Be my fayth, that is sir Dynadan,' seyde sir Trystram. 'Therefore, 30 madame, wote ye what ye shall do: sende ye for hym, and I woll nat be seyne. And ye shall hyre the myrryeste knyght that ever ye spake wythall, and the maddyst talker. And I pray you hertaly that ye make hym good chere.'

So anone La Beall Isode sente unto the towne and prayde sir Dyna- 35 dan that he wolde com into the castell and repose hym there wyth a lady.

'Wyth a good wyll!' seyde sir Dynadan.

And so he mownted uppon his horse and rode into the castell, and there he alyght and was unarmed and brought into the halle.   40

And anone La Beall Isode cam unto hym and aythir salewed other. Than she asked hym of whens that he was.

'Madame,' seyde sir Dynadan, 'I am of the courte of kynge Arthure, and a knyght of the Table Rounde, and my name is sir Dynadan.'

'What do ye in this contrey?' seyde La Beall Isode.

'For sothe, madame, I seke after sir Trystram, the good knyght, for hit was tolde me that he was in this contrey.'

'Hit may well be,' seyde La Beall Isode, 'but I am nat ware of hym.'

5 'Madame,' seyde sir Dynadan, 'I mervayle at sir Trystram and mo other suche lovers. What aylyth them to be so madde and so asoted uppon women?'

'Why,' seyde La Beall Isode, 'ar ye a knyght and ar no lovear? For sothe, hit is grete shame to you, wherefore ye may nat be called a good
10 knyght by reson but yf ye make a quarell for a lady.'

'God deffende me!' seyde sir Dynadan, 'for the joy of love is to shorte, and the sorow thereof [and what cometh thereof] is duras over longe.'

'A!' sayde La Beall Isode, 'say ye nevermore so, for hyre faste by
15 was the good knyght sir Bleoberys de Galys that fought wyth ⌜three⌝ knyghtes at onys for a damesell, and he wan her afore the kynge off Northumbirlonde. And that was worshypfully done,' seyde La Beall Isode.

'For sothe, hit was so,' seyde sir Dynadan, 'for I knowe hym well for
20 a good knyght and a noble, and commyn he is of noble bloode, and all be noble knyghtes of the blood of sir Launcelot de Lake.'

'Now I pray you, for my love,' seyde La Beall Isode, 'wyll ye fyght for me wyth three knyghtes that doth me grete wronge? And insomuche as ye bene a knyght of kynge Arthurs, I requyre you to do
25 batayle for me.'

Than sir Dynadan seyde,

'I shall sey you ye be as fayre a lady as evir I sawe ony, and much fayrer than is my lady quene Gwenyver, but wyte you well, at one worde, I woll nat fyght for you wyth three knyghtes, Jesu me defende!'
30 Than Isode lowghe, and had good game at hym. So he had all the chyre that she myght make hym, and there he lay all that nyght.

And on the morne early sir Trystram armed hym, and La Beall Isode gaff hym a good helme, and than he promysed her that he wolde mete wyth sir Dynadan. And so they two wolde ryde togedyrs unto Lone-
35 zep, where the turnemente sholde be, 'and there shall I make redy for you, where ye shall se all the feyght'.

(57) So departed sir Trystram wyth two squyers that bare his shylde and his speare[s] that were grete and longe. So aftir that sir Dynadan departed and rode his way a grete shake untyll he had overtakyn sir
40 Trystram. And whan sir Dynadan had overtakyn hym he knew hym anone, and hated the felyshyp of hym of all othir knyghtes.

'A!' seyde sir Dynadan, 'arte thou that cowherd knyght that I mette wyth yestirday? Well, kepe the! for thou shalt juste wyth me, magré thyne hede!'

'Well,' seyde sir Trystram, 'and I am passynge lothe to juste.'

And so they lette there horsis renne, and sir Trystram myste of hym a purpose, and sir Dynadan brake his speare al to-shyvyrs. And therewythall sir Dynadan dressed hym to drawe oute his swerde.

'Not so, sir,' seyde sir Trystram, 'why ar ye so wrothe? I am nat 5 disposid to fyght at this tyme.'

'Fye on the, cowarde!' seyde sir Dynadan. 'Thou shamyste all knyghtes!'

'As for that,' seyde sir Trystram, 'I care nat, for I woll wayte uppon you and be undyr youre proteccion, for cause ye ar so good a knyght 10 that ye may save me.'

'God delyver me of the!' seyde sir Dynadan. 'For thou arte as goodly a man of armys and of thy persone as ever I sawe, and also the moste cowarde that ever I saw. What wolt thou do wyth grete spearys and suche wepen as thou caryeste with the?' 15

'Sir, I shall yeff them,' seyde sir Trystram, 'to som good knyght whan I com to the turnemente; and yf I se that you do beste, sir, I shall gyff them to you.'

So thus as they rode talkynge they saw where cam an arraunte knyght afore them that dressed hym to juste. 20

'Lo,' seyde sir Trystram, 'yondir is one that woll juste. Now dresse you to hym.'

'A, shame betyde the!' seyde sir Dynadan.

'Nay, nat so,' seyde sir Trystram, 'for that knyght semyth a shrewe.'

'Than shall I,' seyde sir Dynadan. 25

And so they dressed there shyldis and there spearys, and there they mett togydirs so harde that the othir knyght smote downe sir Dynadan frome his horse.

'Lo,' seyde sir Trystram, 'hit had bene bettir ye had lefft.'

'Fye on the, cowarde!' seyde sir Dynadan. 30

And than he sterte up and gate his swerde in his honde and proffyrd to do batayle on foote.

'Whether in love other in wrathe?' seyde the other knyght.

'Sir, lat us do batayle in love,' seyde sir Dynadan.

'What is youre name?' seyde that knyght. 'I pray you telle me.' 35

'Sir, wyte you well my name is sir Dynadan.'

'A, sir Dynadan,' seyde that knyght, 'and my name is sir Gareth, yongyst brothir unto sir Gawayne.'

Than aythir made of other grete chere, for this sir Gareth was the beste knyght of all the brethirne, and he preved a good knyght. Than 40 they toke their horsys and there they spoke of sir Trystram, how suche a cowarde he was; and every worde sir Trystram harde, and lowgh them to scorne. Than were they ware where cam a knyght afore them well horsed and well armed, and he made hym redy to juste.

'Now, fayre knyght,' sayde sir Trystram, 'loke betwyxte you who shall juste wyth yondir knyght, for I warne you I woll nat have ado wyth hym.'

'Than shall I,' seyde sir Gareth.

5 And so they encountyrd togydyrs, and there that knyght smote downe sir Gareth over his horse croupe.

'How now?' seyde sir Trystram unto sir Dynadan. 'Now dresse you and revenge the good knyght sir Gareth.'

'That shall I nat,' seyde sir Dynadan, 'for he hath strykyn downe a 10 muche bygger knyght than I am.'

'A, sir Dynadan,' seyde sir Trystram, 'now I se and fele that youre harte faylyth you. And therefore now shall ye se what I shall do.'

And than sir Trystram hurtelyd unto that knyght and smote hym quyte frome his horse. And whan sir Dynadan saw that he mervayled 15 gretly, and than he demed that hit was sir Trystram. And anone this knyght that was on foote pulled oute his swerde to do batayle.

'Sir, what is youre name?' seyde sir Trystram.

'Wyte you well,' seyde that knyght, 'my name is sir Palomydes.'

'A, sir knyght, whyche knyght hate ye moste in the worlde?' seyde 20 sir Trystram.

'For sothe,' seyde he, 'I hate sir Trystram moste to the deth, for and I may mete wyth hym the tone of us shall dye.'

'Ye sey well,' seyde sir Trystram. 'And now wyte you well that my name is sir Trystram de Lyones, and now do your warste!'

25 Whan sir Palomydes saw hym sey so he was astoned, and than he seyde thus:

'I pray you, sir Trystram, forgyff me all my evyll wyll! And yf I lyve I shall do you servyse afore all the knyghtes that bene lyvynge. And thereas I have owed you evyll wyll me sore repentes. I wote nat 30 what eylyth me, for mesemyth that ye ar a good knyght; and that ony other knyght that namyth hymselff a good knyght sholde hate you, me sore mervaylyth. And there I requyre you, sir Trystram, take none displaysure at myne unkynde wordis.'

'Sir Palomydes,' seyde sir Trystram, 'ye sey well. And well I wote ye 35 ar a good knyght, for I have seyne you preved, and many grete entirpryses ye have done and well enchyeved them. Therefore,' seyde sir Trystrams, 'and ye have ony yevyll wyll to me, now may ye ryght hit, for I am redy at youre hande.'

'Nat so, my lorde sir Trystram, for I woll do you knyghtly servyse in 40 all thynge as ye woll commaunde me.'

'Sir, ryght so I woll take you,' seyde sir Trystram.

And so they rode forthe on their wayes talkynge of many thynges. Than seyde sir Dynadan,

'A, my lorde sir Trystram! Fowle have ye mocked me, for God

knowyth I came into this contrey for youre sake, and by the advyce of my lorde sir Launcelot, and yet wolde he nat tell me the sertaynté of you where I sholde fynde you.'

'Truly,' seyde sir Trystram, 'and sir Launcelot wyste beste where I was, for I abyde in his owne castell.'   5

And thus they rode untyll they were ware of the cᵣaᵣsteᵣlᵣl of   (58)
Lonezep, and than were they ware of foure hondred tentes and pavelouns, and mervaylous grete ordynaunce.

'So God me helpe,' seyde sir Trystram, 'yondir I se the grettyste ordynaunce that ever I sawe.'   10

'Sir,' seyde sir Palomydes, 'mesemyth that there [was] a[s] grete [an] ordynaunce at the Castell of Maydyns uppon the roche where ye wan the pryce, for I saw myself where ye forjusted thirty knyghtes.'

'Sir,' seyde sir Dynadan, 'and in Surluce, at the turnemente that sir Galahalte of the Longe Iles made, whyche there dured seven dayes; for   15
there was as grete a gaderynge as is hyre, for there were many nacions.'

'Syr, who was the beste there?' seyde sir Trystram.

'Sir, hit was sir Launcelot du Lake, and the noble knyght sir Lamerok de Galys.'

'Be my fayth,' sayde sir Trystram, 'and sir Launcelot were there, I   20
doute nat,' seyde sir Trystram, 'but he wan the worshyp, so he had nat bene overmacched wyth many knyghtes. And of the deth of sir Lamorak,' seyde sir Trystram, 'hit was over grete pité, for I dare say he was the clennyst-myghted man and the beste-wynded of his ayge that was on lyve. For I knew hym that he was one of the best knyghtes   25
that ever I mette wythall but yf hit were sir Launcelot.'

'Alas,' seyde sir Dynadan and sir Trystram, 'that full wo is us for his deth! And yf they were nat the cousyns of my lorde kynge Arthure that slew hym, they sholde dye for hit, all that were concentynge to his dethe.'   30

'And for suche thynges,' seyde sir Trystrams, 'I feare to drawe unto the courte of kynge Arthure. Sir, I woll that ye were hit,' seyde sir Trystram unto sir Gareth.

'As for that, I blame you nat,' seyde sir Gareth, 'for well I undirstonde the vengeaunce of my brethirne, sir Gawayne, sir Aggravayne,   35
sir Gaherys, and sir Mordred. But as for me,' seyde sir Gareth, 'I meddyll nat of their maters, and therefore there is none that lovyth me of them. And for cause that I undirstonde they be murtherars of good knyghtes I lefte there company, and wolde God I had bene besyde sir Gawayne whan that moste noble knyght sir Lamorake was slayne!'   40

'Now, as Jesu be my helpe,' seyde sir Trystram, 'hit is passyngly well sayde of you, for I had lever,' sayde sir Trystrams, 'than all the golde betwyxte this and Rome I had bene there.'

'Iwysse,' seyde sir Palomydes, 'so wolde I, and yet had I never the

gre at no justis nothir turnemente and that noble knyght sir Lamorak
had be there, but other on horsebak othir ellys on foote he put me ever
to the wars. And that day that sir Lamorak was slayne he ded the moste
dedis of armys that ever I saw knyght do in my lyeff, and whan he was
5 gyvyn the gre be my lorde kynge Arthure, sir Gawayne and his three
bretherne, sir Aggravayne, sir Gaherys and sir Mordred, sette uppon
sir Lamorak in a pryvy place, and there they slew his horse. And so
they faught with oym on foote more than three owrys bothe byfore
hym and behynde hym, and so sir Mordrede gaff hym his dethis wounde
10 behynde hym at his bakke, and all to-hewe hym: for one of his squyers
tolde me that sawe hit.'

'Now fye uppon treson!' seyde sir Trystram, 'for hit sleyth myne
harte to hyre this tale.'

'And so hit dothe myne,' seyde sir Gareth, 'bretherne as they be
15 myne.'

'Now speke we of othir dedis,' seyde sir Palomydes, 'and let hym be,
for his lyff ye may nat gete agayne.'

'That is the more pité!' seyde sir Dynadan. 'For sir Gawayne and his
bretherne, excepte you, sir Gareth, hatyth all good knyghtes of the
20 Rounde Table for the moste party. For well I wote, ⟨as⟩ they myght,
prevayly they hate my lorde sir Launcelot and all his kyn, and grete
pryvay dispyte they have at hym. And sertaynly that is my lorde sir
Launcelot well ware of, and that causyth hym the more to have the
good knyghtes of his kynne aboute hym.'

(59) 25 'Now, sir,' seyde sir Palomydes, 'let us leve of this mater and let us
se how we shall do at this turnemente. And, sir, by myne advyce, lat us
four holde togydyrs ayenst all that woll com.'

'Nat be my counceyle,' seyde sir Trystram, 'for I se by their pavy-
louns there woll be four hondred knyghtes. And doute ye nat,' seyde
30 sir Trystram, 'but there woll be many good knyghtes, and be a man
never so valyaunte nother so bygge but he may be overmatched. And
so have I seyne knyghtes done many, and whan they wente beste to
have wonne worshyp they loste hit; for manhode is nat worthe but
yf hit be medled with wysdome. And as for me,' seyde sir Trystram,
35 'hit may happen I shall kepe myne owne hede as well as another.'

So thus they rode untyll they cam to Humbir banke where they harde
a crye and a dolefull noyse. Than were they ware in the wynde where
cam a ryche vessell heled over with r[e]de sylke, and the vessell londed
faste by them. Therewith sir Trystram alyght and his knyghtes, and so
40 sir Trystram wente afore and entird into that vessell. And whan he
cam in he saw a fayre bedde rychely coverde, and thereuppon lay a
semely dede knyght all armed sauff the hede, ⟨and⟩ was all bloody wyth
dedly woundys uppon hym, whych semed to be a passynge good
knyght.

'Jesu, how may this be,' seyde sir Trystram, 'that this knyght is thus slayne?'

And anone sir Trystram was ware of a lettir in the dede knyghtes honde.

'Now, maystir marynars,' seyde sir Trystram, 'what meanyth this 5 lettir?'

'Sir,' seyde they, 'in that lettir shall ye hyre and knowe how he was slayne, and for what cause, and what was his name. But, sir,' seyde the marynars, 'wyte you well that no man shall take that lettir and rede hit but yf he be a good knyght, and that he woll faythfully promyse 10 to revenge his dethe, and ellis shall there no knyght se that lettir opyn.'

'And wyte you well,' seyde sir Trystram, 'that som of us may revenge his dethe as well as another; and yf hit so be as ye marynars sey, his dethe shall be revenged.' 15

And therewythall sir Trystram toke the lettir oute of the knyghtes honde, and than he opened hit and rad hit, and thus hit specifyed:

'Harmaunce, kyng and lorde of the Rede Cité, I sende to all knyghtes arraunte, recommaundynge unto you, noble knyghtes of Arthurs courte, that I beseche them all amonge them to fynde one knyght that 20 woll fyght for my sake with two bretherne that I brought up off nought, and felounsly and traytourly they slewe me. Wherefore I beseche one good knyght to revenge my dethe, and [he] that revengyth my dethe I woll that he have my Rede Cité and all my castels.'

'Sir,' seyde the marynars, 'wyte you well, this knyght and kynge that 25 hyre lyeth was a full worshypfull man and of grete proues, and full [well] he loved all maner of knyghtes arraunte.'

'So God me helpe,' seyde sir Trystram, 'here is a pyteuous cause, and full fayne I wolde take this entirpryse, but I have made suche a promyse that nedis I muste be at this grete justys and turnement, othir ellys I am 30 shamed. For well I wote for my sake in aspeciall my lorde kynge Arthure made this justis and turnemente in this contrey, and well I wote that many worshypfull people woll be hyre at this turnemente for to se me; and therefore I feare to take this entirpryse uppon me, that I shall nat com agayne betyme to this justys.' 35

'Sir,' seyde sir Palomydes, 'I pray you gyff me this entirpryse, and ye shall se me enchyeve hit worshypfully, other ellys I shall dye in this quarell.'

'Well,' seyde sir Trystram, 'and this entirpryse I gyff hit you, wyth this, that ye be with me at this turnemente whyche shall be as this day 40 sevennyght.'

'Sir,' seyde sir Palomydes, 'I promyse you I shall be wyth you by that day, and I be unslayne and unmaymed.'

So departed sir Trystram, sir Gareth, and sir Dynadan, and so leffte (60)

sir Palomydes in the vessell. And so sir Trystram behylde the marynars
how they sayled overlonge Humbir.

And whan sir Palomydes was oute of there syght they toke their
horsys and loked aboute them, and than were they ware of a knyght
5 that cam rydynge agaynste them unarmed, and nothynge but a swerde
aboute hym. And whan he cam nyghe, this knyght salewed them and
they hym agayne.

'Now, fayre knyghtes,' seyde that knyght, 'I pray you, insomuche as
ye be knyghtes arraunte, that ye woll com and se my castall and take
10 suche as ye fynde there; I pray you hertely!'

'Wyth a good wyll,' seyde sir Trystram.

And so they rode with hym untyll his castell, and there they were
brought into the halle whyche was well apparayled, and so they were
there unarmed and sette at a borde. And whan this knyght sawe sir
15 Trystram, anone he knew hym and wexed passynge pale and wrothe
at sir Trystram. And whan sir Trystram sawe his oste make suche chere
he mervayled and sayde,

'Sir, myne oste, what chere make you?'

'Wyte thou well,' sayde he, 'I fare muche the warre that I se the, for I
20 know the for sir Trystram de Lyones. For thou slewyste my brother,
and therefore I gyff the warnynge that I woll sle the and ever I may
gete the at large!'

'Sir knyght,' seyde sir Trystram, 'I am never advysed that ever I slew
ony brother of yourys, and yf ye say that I ded hit I woll make amendys
25 unto my power.'

'I woll no mendys have,' seyde the knyght, 'but kepe the frome me!'

So whan he hadde dyned sir Trystram asked his armys and departed.
And so they rode on there wayes, and wythin a myle way sir Dynadan
saw where cam a knyght armed and well horsed, wyth a whyghte
30 shylde.

'Sir Trystram,' seyde sir Dynadan, 'take kepe to youreselff, for I dare
undirtake yondir commyth your oste that woll have ado wyth you.'

'Lat hym com,' seyde sir Trystram, 'I shall abyde hym as I may.'

And whan the knyght cam nyghe to sir Trystram he cryed and bade
35 hym abyde and kepe hym.

And anone they hurteled togydyrs, but sir Trystram smote the other
knyght so sore that he bare hym over his horse croupen. Than the
knyght arose lyghtly and toke his horse agayne and rode fyersly to sir
Trystram and smote hym twyse other thryse harde uppon the helme.

40 'Sir knyght,' seyde sir Trystram, 'I pray you leve of and smyte me
no more, for I wolde be lothe to deale with you and I myght chose, for
I have of your mete and drynke in my body.'

And for all that he wolde nat leve. Than sir Trystram gaff hym suche
a buffette uppon the helme that he felle up-so-downe from his horse,

that the bloode braste oute at the ventayles of his helme, and so he lay
stylle lykly to be dede. Than sir Trystram sayde,

'Me repentys of this buffette that I smote so sore, for as I suppose
he is dede.'

And so they lefft hym and rode on their wayes. So whan they had   5
ryddyn awhyle they sawe com rydynge agayenst them two full lyckely
knyghtes, well armed and well horsed, and goodly servauntes aboute
them. And that one knyght hyght sir Berraunt le Apres, and he was
called the Kynge with the Hondred Knyghtes, and the other was sir
Segwarydes, that were renomed two noble knyghtes.   10

So as they cam aythir by other, the kynge loked uppon sir ⌐Dynadan⌐,
and at that tyme sir Dynadan had sir Trystrams helme uppon his
shuldir, whyche ⌐helme the kynge⌐ had seyne tofore with the quene of
North Galys, and that quene the kynge loved as peramour. And that
helme the quene of Northe Galys gaff to La Beall Isode, and quene   15
Isode gaff hit to sir Trystram.

'Sir knyght,' seyde sir Berraunte, 'where had ye that helme?'

'What wolde ye?' seyde sir Dynadan.

'For I woll have ado wyth you,' seyde the kynge, 'for the love of her
that ought this helme. And therefore kepe you!'   20

So they cam togydir wyth all there myghtes of their horsis. And there
the Kynge with the Hondred Knyghtes smote downe sir Dynadan and
his horse, and than he commaunded his servaunte to take that helme off
and kepe hit. So the varlet wente to unbuckyll his helme.

'What wolt thou do?' seyde sir Trystrams. 'Leve that helme!'   25

'To what entente,' seyde the kynge, 'wyll ye meddyll with that
helme?'

'Wyte you well,' seyde sir Trystram, 'that helme shall nat departe fro
me tyll hit be derrer bought.'

'Than make you redy!' seyde sir Berraunte unto sir Trystram.   30

So they hurteled togydyrs, and there sir Trystram smote hym downe
over his horse tayle; and than the kynge arose lyghtly and gate his
horse agayne, and than he strake fyersly at sir Trystram many grete
strokys. And than he gaff sir Berraunte such a buffette upon the helme
that he felle downe over his horse sore astonyed.   35

'Lo!' seyde sir Dynadan, 'that helme is unhappy to us twayne, for I
had a falle for hit, and now, sir kynge, have ye another falle.'

Than sir Segwarydes asked,

'Who shall juste wyth me?'

'I pray you,' seyde sir Gareth unto sir Dynadan, 'let me have this   40
justys.'

'Sir,' seyde sir Dynadan, 'I pray you hertely take hit as for me!'

'That is no reson,' seyde sir Trystram, 'for this justys shulde have
bene youres.'

'At a worde,' seyde sir Dynadan, 'I woll nat thereof.'

Than sir Gareth dressed hym unto sir Segwarydes, and there sir Segwarydes smote sir Gareth and his horse to the erthe.

'Now,' seyde sir Trystram unto sir Dynadan, 'juste ye with yondir
5　knyght.'

'I woll nat thereof,' seyde sir Dynadan.

'Than woll I,' seyde sir Trystram.

And than sir Trystram ranne unto hym and gaff hym a falle, and so they leffte hem on foote.

10　And sir Trystram rode unto Joyus Garde. And there sir Gareth wolde nat of his curtesy have gone into his castell, but sir Trystram wolde nat suffir hym to departe, and so they alyght and unarmed them and had grete chere. But whan sir Dynadan cam afore La Beall Isode he cursed her that ever he bare sir Trystrams helme, and there he tolde her how
15　sir Trystram had mocked hym. Than there was lawghynge and japynge at sir Dynadan, that they wyste nat what to do wyth hym.

XI. THE RED CITY

(61)　Now woll we leve them myrry wythin Joyus Garde and speke we of sir Palomydes, the whyche sayled evynlongis Humbir untyll that he
20　came unto the see costys, and thereby was a fayre castell. And at that tyme hit was erly in the mornynge, afore day. Than the marynars wente unto sir Palomydes that slepte faste.

'Sir knyght,' seyde the marynars, 'ye muste aryse, for here is a castell that ye muste go into.'

25　'I assente me,' seyde sir Palomydes.

And therewithall he aryved, and than he blew his horne that the marynars had yevyn hym. And whan they in the castell harde that horne they put oute many knyghtes; and there they stood uppon the wallys and sayde with one voyse,

30　'Wellcom be ye to this castell!'

And than hit waxed clyere day, and sir Palomydes entyrde into the castell. And within a whyle he was served with many dyverse metys. Than sir Palomydes harde aboute hym muche wepyng and grete dole.

'What may this meane?' seyde sir Palomydes. 'For I love nat to hyre
35　suche a sorowfull noyse, and therefore I wolde knowe what hit meaned.'

Than there cam a knyght afore hym, his name was sir Ebell, that seyde thus:

'Wyte you well, sir knyght, this dole and sorow is made here every
40　day, and for this cause. We had a kynge that hyght Harmaunce, and he

was kynge of the Rede Cité, and this kynge that was oure lorde was a
noble knyght, layrge and lyberall of his expence. And in all the worlde
he loved nothynge so muche as he ded arraunte knyghtes of kynge
Arthurs courte, and all justynge, huntynge, and all maner of knyghtly
gamys; for so good a kynge and knyght had never the rewle of poore 5
peple. And bycause of his goodnes and jantyll demeanys we bemoone
hym, and ever shall. And all kyngis and astatys may beware by oure
lorde: for he was destroyed in his owne defaute; for had he cheryshed
his owne bloode, he had bene a lyvis kynge and lyved with grete ryches
and reste; but all astatys may beware by owre kynge. But alas,' 10
seyde sir Ebell, 'that ever we sholde gyff all other warnynge by his
dcthe!'
    'Telle me,' seyde sir Palomydes, 'how and in what maner was your
lorde slayne, and by whom.'
    'Sir,' seyde sir Ebell, 'oure kynge brought up of chyldir two men 15
that now ar perelous knyghtes, and thes two knyghtes oure kynge had
them so in favour that he loved no man nother trusted no man of his
owne bloode, nother none other that was aboute hym. And by thes
two knyghtes oure kynge was governed, and so they ruled hym
peasably and his londys, and never wolde they suffir none of his bloode 20
to have no rule with oure kynge. And also he was so fre and so jeantyll,
and they so false and so dysseyvable, that they ruled hym peasabely.
And that aspyed the lordis of oure kynges bloode, and departed frome
hym unto their owne lyeffloode.
    'And whan thos traytours undirstood that they had dryvyn all the 25
lordis of his bloode frome hym, than were they nat pleased wyth suche
rewle, but ever thought to have more. And as ever hit is an olde sawe,
"Gyeff a chorle rule and thereby he woll nat be suffysed", for whatsomever he be that is rewled by a vylayne borne, and the lorde of the soyle
be a jantylman born, that same vylayne shall destroy all the jeauntylmen 30
aboute hym. Therefore all the astatys and lordys, of what astate ye be,
loke ye beware whom ye take aboute you. And therefore, sir, and ye be
a knyght of kynge Arthurs courte remembir this tale, for this is the
ende and conclusyon:
    'My lorde and kynge rode unto the foreyste hereby by the advyse of 35
thes two traytoures, and there he chaced at the rede deare, armed at all
peacis full lyke a good knyght. And so for labour he waxed drye, and
than he alyght and dranke at a well. And whan he was alyght, by the
assente of thes two traytoures, the tone whyche hyght Helyus he suddeynly smote oure kynge thorow the body wyth a speare. And so they 40
leffte hym there; and whan they were departed, than by fortune I cam
to the welle and founde my lorde and kynge wounded to the deth. And
whan I harde his complaynte I lat brynge hym to the watirs syde, and
in that same shyppe I put hym on lyve. And whan my lorde kynge

Harmaunce was in that vessell he requyred me for the trewe feythe I
owed unto hym for to wryte a lettir in this maner:

(62)   ' "Recommaunde me unto kynge Arthure and to all his noble
knyghtys arraunte, besechynge them all that, insomuche as I, kynge
5   Harmaunce, kynge of the Rede Cité, thus I am slayne by felony and
treson thorow two knyghtes of myne owne bryngynge up and of myne
owne makynge, besechynge som worshypfull knyght to revenge my
dethe, insomuch as I have bene ever to my power well-wyllynge unto
kynge Arthurs courte. And who that woll adventure his lyff for my sake
10   to revenge my deth and sle thes two traytoures in one batayle, I, kynge
Harmaunce, kynge of the Red Cité, frely woll gyff hym all my londis
and rentes that ever I welded in my lyeff."

'And this lettir,' seyde sir Ebell, 'I wrote be my lordis commaundemente, and than he resceayved his Creature. And whan he was dede, he
15   commaunded me, or ever he were colde to put that lettir faste in his
honde, and than he commaunded me to sende forthe that same vessell
downe by Humbir streyme, and that I sholde gyeff thes marynars in
commaundemente never to stynte tyll they cam unto Lonezep, where
all the noble knyghtes shall assemble at this tyme: "And there shall
20   som good knyght have pité of me and revenge my deathe, for there was
never knyght nother lorde falselyar nothir traytourlyar slayne than I
am hyere wounded unto my dethe." Thus was the complaynte of oure
kynge Harmaunce.

'Now,' seyde sir Ebell, 'ye knowe all how oure lorde was betrayed.
25   And therefore we requyre you for Goddis sake have pité uppon his
dethe, and worshypfully than may ye welde all his londis. For we all
wyte well, and ye may sle tho two traytours, the Rede Cité and all that
be therein woll take you for their kyndely lorde.'

'Truly,' seyde sir Palomydes, 'hit grevyth myne harte for to hyre you
30   tell this dolefull tale, and to say the trouthe I saw that same lettir that
ye speke of, and one of the beste knyghtes of the worlde rad that same
lettir to me that ye speake of, and by his commaundemente I cam hydir
to revenge your kynges deathe. And therefore have done and let me
wyte where I shall fynde tho traytoures, for I shall never be at ease in
35   my harte tyll I be in handis wyth them.'

'Sir,' seyde Ebell, 'than take youre shyppe agayne, and that shyppe
muste brynge you unto the Delectable Ile, faste by the Rede Cité. And
we in this castell shall pray for you and abyde youre agayne-commynge.
For this same castell, and ye sped well, muste nedis be youres. For oure
40   kynge Harmaunce lette make this castell for the love of tho two traytoures, and so we kepte hit with stronge honde, and therefore full sore
ar we thretened.'

'Wote ye what ye shall do,' seyde Palomydes. 'Whatsomevir com of
me, loke ye kepe well thys castell, for and hit myssefortune me so to be

slayne in this queste, I am sure there woll com one of the beste knyghtis of the worlde for to revenge my dethe, and that is sir Trystram de Lyones, othir ellis sir Launcelot de Lake.'

Than sir Palomydes departed frome that castell. And as he cam nyghe the shyppe, there cam oute of a shyppe a goodly knyght armed ayenste 5 hym wyth his shylde on his shuldir, and his honde uppon his swerde. And anone as he cam nyghe unto sir Palomydes, he seyde,

'Sir knyght, what seke you hyre? Leeve this queste, for hit is myne, and myne hit was or hit were youres, and therefore I woll have hit.'

'Sir knyght,' seyde sir Palomydes, 'hit may well be that this queste 10 was youres or hit was myne. But whan the lettir was takyn oute of the dede knyghtes honde, at that tyme by lyklyhode there was no knyght had undirtake to revenge the kynges dethe. And so at that tyme I promysed to avenge his dethe, and so I shall, other ellys I am shamed.'

'Ye say well,' seyde the knyght, 'butte wyte you well, than woll I 15 fyght wyth you, and whether of us be bettir knyght lat hym take the batayle on honde.'

'I assente me,' seyde sir Palomydes.

And than they dressed their shyldis and pulled oute their swerdis, and laysshed togydyrs many sad strokys as men of myght. And this fyght- 20 ynge lasted more than an owre. But at the laste sir Palomydes waxed bygge and bettir-wynded, and than he smote that knyght suche a stroke that he kneled on his kneis. Than that knyght spake on hyght and sayde,

'Jeantyll knyght, holde thy honde!' 25

And therewyth sir Palomydes wythdrewe his honde. Than thys knyght seyde,

'Sir, wyte you well ye ar bettir worthy to have this batayle than I, and I requyre you of knyghthode telle me youre name.'

'Sir, my name is sir Palomydes, a knyght of kynge Arthurs and of the 30 Table Rounde, whyche am com hydir to revenge [the dethe of] thys same dede [kynge].'

'Sir, well be ye founde,' seyde the knyght to sir Palomydes, 'for of (63) all knyghtes that bene on lyve, excepte three, I had levyste have you. And the fyrste is sir Launcelot du Lake, and the secunde ys sir Trys- 35 tram de Lyones, and the thyrde is my nyghe cousyn, the good knyght sir Lamorak de Galys. And I am brothir unto kynge Harmaunce that is dede, and my name is sir Hermynde.'

'Ye sey well,' seyde sir Palomydes, 'and ye shall se how I shall spyede; and yff I be there slayne go ye unto my lorde sir Launcelot 40 other ellys to my lorde sir Trystram, and pray them to revenge my dethe. For as for sir Lamorak, hym shall ye never se in this worlde.'

'Alas!' seyde sir Hermynde, 'how may that be that he is slayne?'

'By sir Gawayne and his bretherne,' seyde sir Palomydes.

'So God me helpe,' seyde sir Hermynde, 'there was nat one for one that slew hym!'

'That is trouthe,' seyde sir Palomydes, 'for they were four daungerus knyghtes that slew hym, that was sir Gawayne, sir Aggravayne, sir Gaherys and sir Mordred. But sir Gareth, the fifth brothir, was awey, the beste knyght of them all.'

And so sir Palomydes tolde sir Hermynde all the maner and how they slew sir Lamorak all only by treson.

So sir Palomyde toke his shyppe and drove up to the Delectable Ile. And in the meanewhyle sir Hermynde, the kynges brothir, he aryved up at the Rede Cité, and there he tolde them how there was com a knyght of kynge Arthurs to avenge kynge Harmaunce dethe: 'and his name ys sir Palomydes, the good knyght, that for the moste party he folowyth the beste glatyssaunte.'

Than all the cité made grete joy, for muche had they harde of sir Palomydes and of his noble prouesse. So they lette ordayne a messyngere and sente unto the two bretherne and bade them to make them redy, for there was a knyght com that wolde fyght wyth them bothe. So the messyngere wente unto them where they were at a castell there besyde, and there he tolde them how there was a knyght comyn of kynge Arthurs to fyght with them bothe at onys.

'He is wellcom,' seyde they, 'but is hit sir Launcelot other ony of his bloode?'

'Sir, he is none of that bloode,' seyde the messyngere.

'Than we care the lesse,' seyde the two brethirne, 'for none of the bloode of sir Launcelot we kepe nat to have ado wythall.'

'Sir, wyte you well,' seyde the messyngere, 'his name is sir Palomydes, that yet is uncrystened, a noble knyght.'

'Well,' seyde they, 'and he be now uncrystynde he shall never be crystynde.'

So they appoynted to be at the cité within two dayes. And whan sir Palomydes was comyn to the cité they made passaynge grete joy of hym. And than they behylde hym and thought he was well made and clenly and bygly, and unmaymed of his lymmys, and neyther to yonge nother to olde; and so all the people praysed hym.

And though he were nat crystynde, yet he belyved in the beste maner and was full faythefull and trew of his promyse, and wellcondyssyonde; and bycause he made his avow that he wolde never be crystynde unto the tyme that he had enchyeved the beste glatysaunte, the whyche was a full wondirfull beyste and a grete sygnyfycasion; for Merlyon prophesyed muche of that byeste. And also sir Palomydes avowed never to take full Crystyndom untyll that he had done seven batayles within lystys.

So wythin the thirde day there cam to the cité thes two brethirne:

the tone hyght sir Helyus and [the other hyght] Helake, the whyche
were men of grete prouesse; howbehit that they were falsse and full of
treson, and but poore men born, yet were they noble knyghtes of their
handys. And with them they brought fourty knyghtes, of theire hondis
noble men, to that entente that they shulde be bygge inowghe for the 5
Rede Cité. Thus cam the two bretherne wyth grete bobbaunce and
pryde, for they had put the Rede Cité in grete feare and damage. Than
they were brought to the lystes, and sir Palomydes cam into the place
and seyde thus:

'Be ye the two brethirne, Helyus and Helake, that slew youre kynge 10
and lorde sir Harmaunce by felony and treson, for whom that I am
comyn hydir to revenge his dethe?'

'Wyte [th]ou well, sir,' seyde Helyus and sir Helake, 'that we ar the
same knyghtes that slewe kynge Harmaunce. And wyte thou well,
thou sir Palomydes Sarezyn, that we shall so handyll the or that thou 15
departe that thou shalt wysshe that thou haddyst be crystynde.'

'Hit may well be,' seyde sir Palomydes, 'but as yet I wolde nat dye
or that I were full crystynde. And yette so aferde am I nat of you bothe
but that I shall dye a bettir Crystyn man than ony of you bothe. And
doute ye nat,' seyde sir Palomydes, 'ayther ye other I shall be leffte 20
dede in this place.'

So they departed in grete wreath; and the two bretherne cam ayenst (64)
sir Palomydes, and he ayenste them, as faste as their horsis myght ren.
And by fortune sir Palomydes smote sir Helake thorow his shylde and
thorow his breste more than a fadom.   25

All this whyle sir Helyus hylde up his speare, and for pryde and
orgule he wolde nat smyte sir Palomydes wyth his speare. But whan he
saw his brothir lye on the erthe and saw he myght nat helpe hymsclff,
than he seyde unto sir Palomydes,

'Kepe the!'   30

And therewyth he cam hurtelynge unto sir Palomydes with his
speare, and smote hym quyte frome his horse. So sir Helyus rode over
sir Palomydes twyse or thryse; and therewyth sir Palomydes was
ashamed, and gate the horse of sir Helyus by the brydyll, and therewithall the horse arered, and sir Palomydes halpe aftir, and so they felle 35
to the erthe.

But anone sir Helyus starte up lyghtly, and there he smote sir Palomydes a grete stroke uppon the helme, that he kneled uppon his kne;
and than they laysshed togydyrs many sad strokis and trased and
traversed now bakwarde, now sydelynge, hurtelynge togydyrs lyke 40
two borys, and that same tyme they felle bothe grovelynge to the
erthe.

Thus [they] fought stylle withoute ony reposynge two owres and
never brethid. And than sir Palomydes wexed faynte and wery, and sir

Helyus waxed passynge stronge and doubeled his strokes and drove sir Palomydes ovirtwarte and endelonge all the fylde.

Than whan they of the cité saw sir Palomydes in this case they wepte and cryed and made grete dole, and the other party made as grete joy.

5 'Alas,' seyde the men of the cité, 'that this noble knyght shulde thus be slayne for oure kynges sake!'

And as they were thus wepynge and cryynge, sir Palomydes, whyche had suffyrde an hondred strokes, and wondir hit was that he stoode on his fyete, so at the laste sir Palomydes loked aboute as he myght

10 weyakly unto the comyn people how they wepte for hym, and than he seyde to hymselff, 'A, fye for shame, sir Palomydes! Why hange ye youre hede so lowe?' And therewith he bare up his shylde and loked sir Helyus in the vysoure and smote hym a grete stroke uppon the helme and aftir that anothir and anothir, and than he smote sir Helyus

15 with suche a myght that he felde hym to the erthe grovelynge. And than he raced of hys helme frome his hede and so smote of his hede from the body.

And than were the people of the cité the myryest people that myght be. So they brought hym to his lodgynge with grete solempnyté, and

20 there all the people becam his men. And than sir Palomydes prayde them all to take kepe unto all the lordeship of kyng Harmaunce:

'For, fayre sirrys, wyte you well, I may nat as at this tyme abyde with you, for I muste in all haste be wyth my lorde kynge Arthure at the castel of Lonezep.'

25 Than were people full hevy at his departynge, for all the cité profyrd sir Palomydes the thirde parte of their goodis so that he wolde abyde wyth hem. But in no wyse as at that tyme he ne wolde abyde. And so sir Palomydes departed, and cam unto the castell thereas sir Ebell was lyefftenaunte. And whan they in the castell wyste how sir Palomydes

30 had sped there was a joyfull mayné.

And so sir Palomydes departed and cam to the castell of Lonezep; and whan he knew that sir Trystram was nat there he toke hys way over Humbir and cam unto Joyus Garde where was sir Trystram and La Beall Isode.

35 So sir Trystram had commaunded that what knyght arraunte cam within Joyus Garde, as in the towne, that they sholde warne sir Trystram. So there cam a man of the towne and tolde sir Trystram how there was a knyght in the towne, a passyng goodly man.

'What maner of man ys he?' seyde sir Trystram, 'and what sygne

40 beryth he?'

And anone he tolde hym all the tokyns of hym.

'Be my fayth, that ys sir Palomydes,' seyde sir Dynadan.

'For sothe hit may well be,' seyde sir Trystram. 'Than go ye, sir Dynadan, and fecche hym hydir.'

Than sir Dynadan wente unto sir Palomydes, and there aythir made othir grete chere, and so they lay togydirs that nyght. And on the morn erly cam sir Trystram and sir Gareth, and toke them in their beddis; and so they arose and brake their faste.

And than sir Trystram dressed sir Palomydes unto the fyldis and 5 (65) woodis, and so they were accorded to repose them in the foreyste. And whan they had played them a grete whyle they rode unto a fayre well. And anone they were ware of an armed knyght cam rydynge agaynste them, and there ayther salewed other.

Than this armed knyght spake to sir Trystram and asked what were 10 those knyghtes that were lodged in Joyus Garde.

'I wote nat what they ar,' seyde sir Trystram.

'But what knyghtes be ye? For mesemyth ye be no knyghtes arraunte, because ye ryde unarmed.'

'Sir, whethir we be knyghtes or nat, we lyste nat to telle the oure 15 name.'

'Why wolt thou nat tell me thy name?' seyde that knyght. 'Than kepe the, for thou shalt dye of myne hondis!'

And therewithall he gate his speare and wolde have ronne sir Trystram [thorow]. That saw sir Palomydes, and smote his horse traveyse 20 in myddys the syde, that he smote horse and man spyteuously to the erthe. And therewyth sir Palomydes alyght and pulled oute his swerde to have slayne hym.

'Lat be,' seyde sir Trystram, 'sle hym nat, for the knyghte is but a foole and hit were shame to sle hym. But take away his speare,' seyde 25 sir Trystram, 'and lat hym take his horse and go where that he wyll.'

So whan this knyght arose he groned sore of the falle, and so he gate his horse, and whan he was up he turned his horse and requyred sir Trystram and sir Palomydes to telle hym what knyghtes they were.

'Now wyte thou well,' seyde sir Trystram, 'my name is sir Trystram 30 de Lyones, and this knyghtes name is sir Palomydes.'

Whan he wyste what he hyght he toke his horse wyth the spurrys, bycaus they shulde nat aske hym his name, and so he rode faste away thorow thicke and thorow thynne. Than cam there by them a knyght with a bended shylde of assure, his name was sir Epynogrys, and he 35 cam a grete walop.

'Whother ar ye away?' sayde sir Trystram.

'My fayre lordis,' seyde sir Epynogrys, 'I folow the falsiste knyght that beryth the lyeff, wherefore I requyre you telle me whethyr ye sye hym, for he beryth a shylde with a case of rede over hit.' 40

'So God me helpe,' seyde sir Trystram, 'suche a knyght departed frome us nat a quarter of an owre agone, and therefore we pray you to telle us his name.'

'Alas,' seyde sir Epynogrys, 'why let ye hym ascape from you? And

he is so grete a foo untyll all arraunte knyghtys, whos name is sir
Brewnys Saunze Pieté.'

'A, fy for shame!' seyde sir Palomydes, 'and alas that ever he ascapyd
myne hondis, for he ys the man in the worlde whom I hate moste.'

5　　Than eviry knyght made grete sorow to othir, and so sir Epynogrys
departed and folowed the chace aftir hym. Than sir Trystram and hys
three felowys rode towarde Joyus Garde, and there sir Trystram
talked unto sir Palomydes of his batayle, and how that he had sped at
the Rede Cité. And as ye have harde afore, so was hyt ended.

10　　'Truly,' seyde sir Trystram, 'I am glad ye have well sped, fo[r] ye
have done worshypfully. Well,' seyde sir Trystram, 'we muste for-
warde as to-morne.'

And than he devysed how hit shulde be; and there sir Trystram
devysed to sende his two pavelons to set hem faste by the well of

15　Lonezep, 'and therein shall be the quene La Beall Isode'.

'Ye sey well,' seyde sir Dynadan.

But whan sir Palomydes herde of that his harte was ravysshed oute of
mesure: notwythstondynge he seyde but lytyll. So whan they cam to
Joyus Garde sir Palomydes wolde nat have gone into the castell, but as

20　sir Trystram lad hym by the honde into Joyus Garde. And whan sir
Palomydes saw La Beall Isode he was so ravysshed that he myght
unnethe speke. So they wente unto mete, but sir Palomydes myght nat
ete, and there was all the chire that myght be had.

And so on the morn they were apparayled for to ryde towarde

25　Lonezep.

XII. THE TOURNAMENT AT LONEZEP

So syr Trystram had three squyars, and La Beall Isode had three
jantyllwomen, and bothe the quene and they were rychely apparayled;
and other people had they none with them but varlettes to beare their

30　shyldis and their spearys. And thus they rode forthe. And as they rode
they saw afore them a route of knyghtes, and that was sir Galyhodyn
with twenty knyghtes with hym.

'Now, fayre fealowys,' seyde sir Galyhodyn, 'yondir commyth four
knyghtes, and a ryche and a well fayre lady; and I am in wyll to take that

35　fayre lady from them.'

'Sir, that is nat beste,' seyde one of them, 'but sende ye to them and
awyte what they woll say.'

And so they ded, and anone there cam a squyer unto sir Trystram
and asked them whether they wolde juste other ellys to lose that lady.

40　'Nat so,' seyde sir Trystram, 'but telle your lorde and bydde hym
com as many as we bene, and wynne her and take her.'

'Sir,' seyde sir Palomydes, 'and hit please you, lat me have this dede, and I shall undirtake them all four.'

'Sir, I woll that ye have hit,' seyde sir Trystram, 'at youre pleasure.'

'Now go and telle your lorde sir Galyhodyn that this knyght woll encountir with hym and his felowys.'　　　　　5

So this squyer departed and tolde sir Galyhodyn.　　　　　(66)

Than he dressed his shylde and put forth a speare and sir Palomydes [another, and there sir Palomydes] smote sir Galyhodyn so harde that horse and man bothe yode to the erthe, and there he had an horryble falle.　　　　　10

And than cam another knyght, and the same wyse he served hym; and so he served the thirde and the fourthe, that he smote them over their horse croupes. And allwayes sir Palomydes speare was hole.

Than cam there six knyghtes mo of sir Galyhodynes men and wolde have bene avenged uppon sir Palomydes.　　　　　15

'Lat be,' seyde sir Galyhodyn, 'nat so hardy! None of you all meddyll with this knyght, for he is a man of grete bounté and honoure, and yf he wolde do his uttermuste ye ar nat all able to deale wyth hym.'

And ryght so they hylde them styll, and ever sir Palomydes was redy to juste. And whan he sawe they wolde no more he rode unto sir　20 Trystram.

'A, sir Palomydes! Ryght well have ye done and worshypfully, as a good knyght sholde.'

(So this sir Galyhodyn was nyghe kyn unto sir Galahalte the Haute Prynce, and this sir Galyhodyn was a kynge within the contrey of　25 Surluse.)

So as sir Trystram with his three felowys and La Beall Isode rode, they saw afore them four knyghtes, and every knyght had his speare in his honde. The fyrst was sir Gawayne, the secunde was sir Uwayne, the thirde was sir Sagramour le Desyrus, and the fourthe was sir Dodynas　30 le Saveage. And whan sir Palomydes behylde them, that the four knyghtes were redy to juste, he prayde sir Trystram to gyff hym leve to have ado with them also longe as he myght holde hym on horsebak.

'And yf that I be smyttyn downe, I pray you revenge me.'　　　　　35

'Well,' seyde syr Trystram, 'and ye ar nat so fayne to have worship but I wolde as fayne encrease youre worshyp.'

And wythall sir Gawayne put forthe his speare and sir Palomydes another, and so they cam egirly togydyrs, that sir Palomydes smote hym so harde that sir Gawayne felle to the erthe, horse and all. And in the　40 same wyse he served sir Uwayne and sir Dodynas and sir Sagramour, and all thes four knyghtes sir Palomydes smote them downe with dyverse spearys.

And than sir Trystram departed towarde Lonezep, and whan they

were departed than cam thydir sir Galyhodyn with his twenty knyghtes
unto sir Gawayne, and there he tolde hym all how he had sped.

'Be my trouthe,' seyde sir Gawayne, 'I mervayle what knyghtes they
ben that ar so arayed all in grene.'

5   'And that knyght uppon the whyghte horse smote me downe,'
seyde sir Galyhodyn, 'and three of my felowys.'

'So ded he me,' seyde sir Gawayne, 'and my three felowys. And well
I wote,' seyde sir Gawayne, 'that other he uppon the whyghte horse ys
sir Trystram othir ellys sir Palomydes, and that well-beseyne lady is
10 quene Isode.'

And as they talked thus of one thynge and of other, and in the meanewhyle sir Trystram passed on tyll that he cam to the welle where his
pavylyons were sette. And there they alyghted, and there they sawe
many pavylons and grete aray.

15 Than sir Trystram leffte there sir Palomydes and sir Gareth with La
Beall Isode, and sir Trystram and sir Dynadan rode unto Lonezep to
herkyn tydynges, and sir Trystram rode uppon sir Palomydes whyghte
horse. And whan he cam into the castell sir Trystram harde a grete
horne blowe, and to the horne drewe many knyghtes.

20 Than sir Trystrams asked a knyght,

'What meanyth the blaste of that horne?'

'Sir,' seyde that knyght, 'hit is for all tho that shall holde ayenste
kynge Arthure at this turnemente: the fyrst ys the kynge of Irelonde,
and the kynge of Surluse, and the kynge of Lystenoyse, the kynge of
25 Northumbirlonde, and the kynge of the beste parte of Walys, with
many other contreys.'

And all thes drewe them to a counceyle to undirstonde what governaunce they shall be of. But the kyng of Irelonde his name was sir
Marhalte, that was fadir unto the good knyght sir Marhalte that sir
30 Trystram slew; and he had the speache, that sir Trystram myght
hyre:

'Now, lordis and felowis, lat us loke to oureselff, for wyte you well
kynge Arthure ys sure of many good knyghtes, other ellys he wolde
nat with feaw knyghtes have ado with us. Therefore, be my rede, lat
35 every knyght have a standarde and a cognyssaunce by hymselff, that
every knyght may draw to his naturall lorde. And than may every
kynge and captayne helpe his knyght yf he have nede.'

Whan sir Trystram had harde all their counceyle he rode unto kynge
(67) Arthure for to hyre his counceyle. But sir Trystram was nat so sone
40 com unto the place but sir Gawayne and sir Galyhodyn wente unto
kynge Arthure and tolde hym that that same grene knyght in the grene
harneyse with the whyghte horse 'smote us two downe and six of oure
felowys this same day'.

'Well,' seyde kynge Arthure.

And than he called sir Trystram to hym and asked what was his name.

'As for that,' seyde sir Trystram, 'ye shall holde me excused: as at this tyme ye shall nat know my name.'

And there sir Trystram returned and rode his way.

'I have mervayle,' seyde kynge Arthure, 'that yondir knyght woll [nat] tell me his name. But go ye, sir Grytflet, and pray hym to speke with me betwyxt us twayne.'

Than sir Grytflet rode aftir hym and overtoke hym and seyde that kynge Arthure prayde hym to speake with hym.

'Sir, uppon this covenaunte,' seyde sir Trystram, 'I woll turne agayne, so that ye woll ensure me that the kynge woll nat desyre to hyre my name.'

'I shall undirtake hit,' seyde sir Grytflet, 'that he woll nat gretly desyre of you.'

So they rode togydirs tyll they cam to kynge Arthure.

'Now, fayre sir,' seyde kynge Arthure, 'what is the cause ye woll nat tell me your name?'

'Sir,' seyde sir Trystram, 'withoute a cause I wolde nat hyde my name.'

'Well, uppon what party woll ye holde?' seyde kynge Arthure.

'Truly, my lorde,' seyde sir Trystram, 'I wote nat yet on what party I woll be on untyll I com to the fylde. And thereas my harte gyvyth me, there woll I holde me. But to-morow ye shall se and preve on what party I shall com.'

And therewithall he returned and went to his pavelons. And uppon the morne they armed them all in grene and cam into the fylde. And there yonge knyghtys began to juste and ded many worshypfull dedis.

Than spake sir Gareth unto sir Trystram and prayde hym to gyff hym leve to breake his speare, for hym thought shame to beare his speare hole agayne.

Whan sir Trystram had harde hym sey so, he lowghe and sayde,

'I pray you, do youre beste!'

Than sir Gareth gate his speare and profirde to juste. And that sawe a knyght that was neveaw unto the Kynge with the Hondred Knyghtes; his name was sir Selyses, a good knyght and a good man of armys. So this Selyses dressed hym unto sir Gareth, and they two mette togydirs so harde that ayther smote other downe, horse and man, to the erthe.

And so they were bothe hurte and brused, and there they lay tyll the Kynge with the Hondred Knyghtes halpe up sir Selyses, and sir Trystram and sir Palomydes halpe up sir Gareth ayen, and so they rode wyth hym to their pavylons. And than they pulled of his helme, and whan La Beall Isode sawe sir Gareth brused so in the face she asked hym what ayled hym.

'Madame,' sayde sir Gareth, 'I had a grete buffette, and I suppose I gaff anothir, but none of my fealowys, God thanke hem, wolde rescowe me.'

'Perdeus,' seyde sir Palomydes, 'hit longyth nat to none of us at this day to juste, for there hath nat this day justed no preved knyghtes. And whan the other party saw that ye profyrd yourself to juste, they sente a passyng good knyght unto you, for I know hym well: his name is sir Selyses. And worshypfully ye mette with hym, and neyther of you ar dishonoured. And therefore refreyshe yourselff, that ye may be redy and hole to juste to-morne.'

'As for that,' seyde sir Gareth, 'I shall nat fayle you and I may bestryde myne horse.'

(68) 'Now, sirs, uppon what party is hyt beste,' seyde sir Trystram, 'to be withall to-morne?'

'Sir,' seyde sir Palomydes, 'ye shall have myne advyse to be ayenst kynge Arthure as to-morne, for on his party woll be sir Launcelot and many good knyghtes of his blood with hym; and the mo men of worship that they be, the more worshyp shall we wynne.'

'That is full knyghtly spokyn,' seyde sir Trystram, 'and so shall hit be ryght as y[e] counceyle me.'

'In the name of God,' seyde they all.

So that nyght they were reposed with the beste. And in the morne whan hit was day they were arayed all in grene trapurs, bothe shyldis and spearys, and La Beall Isode in the same coloure, and her three damesels. And ryght thes four knyghtes cam into the fylde endlynge and thorow, and so they lad La Beall Isode thidir as she sholde stande and beholde all the justes in a bay-wyndow; but allwayes she was wympled, that no man myght se her vysayge. And than thes four knyghtes rode streyte unto the party of the Kynge of Scottis.

Whan kynge Arthure had seyne hem do all this he asked sir Launcelot what were this knyghtes and this quene.

'Sir,' seyde sir Launcelot, 'I can nat tell you, for no sertayne. But yf sir Trystram be in this contrey or sir Palomydes, sir, wyte you well hit be they, and there is quene La Beall Isode.'

Than kynge Arthure called unto hym sir Kay and seyde,

'Go ye lyghtly and wyte how many knyghtes there bene hyre lackynge of the Table Rounde, for by the segis ye may know.'

So went sir Kay and saw by the wrytynge in the syeges that there lacked ten knyghtes, and thes were hir namys: sir Trystram, sir Palo-mydes, sir Percivall, sir Gareth, sir Gaherys, sir Epynogrys, sir Mor-dred, sir Dynadan, sir La Cote Male Tayle, and sir Pelleas, the noble knyght.

'Well,' seyde kynge Arthur, 'som of thes, I dare undirtake, ar here this day ayenste us.'

Than cam therein two bretherne, cousyns unto sir Gawayne: that one hyght sir Edwarde and that other hyght sir Sadok, the whyche were two good knyghtes.

And they asked of kynge Arthure that they myght have the fyrste justis, for they were of Orkeney.   5

'I am pleased,' seyde kynge Arthure.

Than sir Edwarde encountirde with the kynge of Scottis, in whos party was sir Trystram and sir Palomydes. And this sir Edwarde of Orkeney smote the Kynge of Scottis quyte frome his horse, a grete falle. And sir Sadoke smote the kynge of Northe Walys downe and   10 gaff hym a wondir grete falle, that there was a grete cry on kynge Arthurs party.

And that made sir Palomydes passyngly wrothe, and so sir Palomydes dressed his shylde and his speare, and wyth all hys myght he mette with sir Edwarde of Orkeney and smote hym so harde that his   15 horse had no myght to stonde on his fyete, and so he hurled downe to the erthe. And than with the same speare sir Palomydes smote downe Sadok over his horse croupe.

'A, Jesu!' seyde kyng Arthure, 'what knyght ys that arayed so all in grene? For he justyth myghtyly.'   20

'Wyte you well,' seyde sir Gawayne, 'he ys [a] good knyght, and yet shall ye se hym juste bettir or he departe. And yet shall ye se a more bygger knyght in the same colour than he is. For that same knyght,' seyde sir Gawayne, 'that smote downe ryght now my two cousyns, he smote me downe within thes two dayes, and seven felowys mo.'   25

This meanewhyle as they stood thus talkynge, there cam into the place sir Trystram uppon a blacke horse. And or ever he stynte he smote downe with one speare four good knyghtes of Orkeney that were of the kynne of sir Gawayne. And sir Gareth and sir Dynadan everyche of them smote downe a good knyght.   30

'A, Jesu!' seyde Arthure, 'yondir knyght uppon the bl[a]cke horse dothe myghtyly and mervaylously well.'

'Abyde you!' seyde sir Gawayne. 'That knyght on the blak horse began nat yet.'

Than sir Trystrams made to horse the two knyghtes agayne that sir   35 Edwarde and sir Sadok had unhorsed at the begynnynge. And than sir Trystram drew his swerde and rode unto the thyckyst prease ayenste them of Orkeney, and there he smote downe knyghtes and raced off helmys and pulled away their shyldis and hurteled downe many of their knyghtes. And so he fared that kynge Arthure and all knyghtes had   40 grete mervayle to se ony o knyght do so muche dedis of armys.

And sir Palomydes fayled nat uppon the other syde, that he so mervaylously ded and well that all men had wondir; for kynge Arthure lykened sir Trystram, that was on the blak horse, unto a wood lyon:

and he lykened sir Palomydes, uppon the whyght horse, unto a wood lybarde, and sir Gareth and sir Dynadan unto egir wolvis.

But the custom was suche amonge them that none of the kyngys wolde helpe other, but all the felyshyp of every standarde to helpe
5 other as they myght. But ever sir Trystram ded so muche dedis of armys that they of Orkeney wexed wery of hym and so withdrew them unto Lonezep.

(69)   Than was the cry of herowdys and all maner of comyn people, 'The grene knyght hathe done mervaylously and beatyn all them of
10 Orkeney!'

And there herowdis numbird that sir Trystram, that was uppon the blacke horse, had smytten downe with spearys and swerdis thirty knyghtes, and sir Palomydes had smyttyn downe twenty knyghtes; and the moste party of thes fifty knyghtes were of the house of kynge
15 Arthure and preved knyghtes.

'So God me helpe,' seyde kynge Arthur unto sir Launcelot, 'this is a grete shame [to us] to se four knyghtes beate so many knyghtes of myne. And therefore make you redy, for we woll have ado with them!'

'Sir,' seyde sir Launcelot, 'wyte you well that there ar two passynge
20 good knyghtes, and grete worship were hit nat to us now to have ado with them, for they ar gretly travayled.'

'As for that,' seyde kynge Arthure, 'I woll be avenged. And therefore take with you sir Bleoberys and sir Ector de Marys, and I woll be the fourthe,' seyde kynge Arthure.

25 'Well, sir,' seyde sir Launcelot, 'ye shall fynde me redy, and my brother sir Ector and my cousyn sir Bleoberys.'

And so whan they were redy and on horsebacke, 'Now chose,' seyde kynge Arthure unto sir Launcelot, 'whom that ye woll encountir wythall.'

30 'Sir,' seyde sir Launcelot, 'I woll counter wyth the grene knyght uppon the blacke horse.' (That was sir Trystram.) 'And my cousyn sir Bleoberys shall macche the grene knyght uppon the whyght horse.' (That was sir Palomydes.) 'And my brother sir Ector shall macche wyth the grene knyght uppon the dunne horse.' (That was sir Gareth.)

35 'Than muste I,' seyde kynge Arthur, 'have ado with the grene knyght uppon the gresylde horse,' and that was sir Dynadan.

'Now every man take kepe to his felow!' seyde sir Launcelot.

And so they trotted on togydyrs, and there encountirde sir Launcelot ayenst sir Trystram, and they smote ayther othir so sore that horse and
40 man yeode to the erthe. But sir Launcelot wente that hit had be sir Palomydes, and so they passed utter.

And than sir Bleoberys encountyrd wyth sir Palomydes, and he smote hym so harde uppon the shylde that sir Palomydes and his whyght horse rosteled to the erthe. Than sir Ector smote sir Gareth so

harde that downe he felle frome his horse. And than noble kynge
Arthure he encountyrd wyth sir Dynadan, and kynge Arthure smote
hym quyte frome his horse. And than the noyse turned awhyle and
seyde,

'The grene knyghtes were felde downe!'   5

Whan the kyng of Northe Galys saw that sir Trystram was on foote,
and than he remembyrd hym how grete dedis of armys they had done,
than he made redy many knyghtes. For the custom and the cry was
suche that what knyght were smytten downe and myght nat be horsed
agayne by his felowys othir by his owne strengthe, that as that day he   10
sholde be presonere unto the party that smote hym downe.

So there cam in the kynge of Northe Galys, and he rode streyte unto
sir Trystram. And whan he cam nyghe hym he alyght delyvirly and
toke sir Trystram hys horse and seyde thus:

'Noble knyght, I know the nat, nothir of what contrey ye be, but for   15
the noble dedis that ye have done this day take there my horse and let
me do as well as I may; for, as Jesu be my helpe, ye ar bettir worthy to
have myne horse than myselff.'

'Grauntemercy!' seyde sir Trystram. 'And yf I may, I shall quyte you.
And loke that ye go nat far frome us, and as I suppose I shall wynne   20
you sone another horse.'

And therewythall sir Trystram mounte uppon his horse, and anone
he mette wyth kynge Arthure and he gaff hym suche a buffet that
kynge Arthure had no power to kepe his sadyll. And than sir Trystram
gaff the kynge of Northe Galys kynge Arthurs horse. Than was there   25
grete prease aboute kynge Arthure for to horse hym agayne. [But sire
Palomydes wold not suffre kynge Arthur to be horsed ageyne,] but
ever sir Palomydes smote on the ryght honde and on the lyffte honde
and raced of helmys myghtyly as a noble knyght.

And this meanewhyle sir Trystram rode thorow the thyckyste   30
prece and smote downe knyghtes on the ryght honde and on the lyffte
honde and raced of helmys, and so passed forthe unto his pavelouns
and leffte sir Palomydes on foote. And than sir Trystram chonged his
horse and disgysed hymselff all in rede, horse and harnes.

And whan quene Isode saw sir Trystram unhorsed and she wyst nat   35 (70)
where he was becom, than she wepte hartely. But sir Trystram, whan
he was redy, cam daysshynge lyghtly into the fylde, and than La Beall
Isode aspyed hym. And so he ded grete dedis of armys wyth one speare
that was grete, for sir Trystram smote downe fyve knyghtes or ever he
stynted.   40

Than sir Launcelot aspyed hym redyly that hit was sir Trystram, and
than he repented hym of that he had smyttyn hym downe. And so sir
Launcelot wente oute of the prees to repose hym, and lyghtly he cam
agayne.

And so whan sir Trystram was com into the prees, thorow his grete forse he put sir Palomydes uppon his horse, and sir Gareth and sir Dynadan, and than they began to do mervaylously. But sir Palomydes nothir none of his two felowys knew nat who had holpen them to 5 horsebak. But ever sir Trystram was nyghe them and knew them and they nat hym, because he had chonged into rede armour. And all this whyle sir Launcelot was away.

So whan La Beall Isode aspyed sir Trystram agayne uppon his horse bak she was passynge glad, and than she lowghe and made good chere. 10 And as hit happened, sir Palomydes loked up toward her; she was in the wyndow, and sir Palomydes aspyed how she lawghed. And there-wyth he toke suche a rejoysynge that he smote downe, what wyth his speare and wyth hys swerde, all that ever he mette, for thorow the syght of her he was so enamered in her love that he semed at that tyme 15 that and bothe sir Trystram and sir Launcelot had bene bothe ayenste hym they sholde have wonne no worshyp of hym. And in his harte, as the booke saythe, sir Palomydes wysshed that wyth his worshyp he myght have ado wyth sir Trystram before all men, bycause of La Beall Isode.

20 Than sir Palomydes began to double his strengthe, and he ded so mervaylously all men had wondir; and ever he kaste up his yee unto La Beall Isode. And whan he saw her make suche chere he fared lyke a lyon, that there myght no man wythstonde hym. And than sir Trystram behylde hym how he styrred aboute, and seyde unto sir Dynadan,

25 'So God me helpe, sir Palomydes ys a passynge ⌈good knyghte and a⌉ well endurynge, but suche dedis sawe I hym never do, nother never erste herde I tell that ever he ded so muche in one day.'

'Sir, hit is his day,' seyde sir Dynadan, and he wolde sey no more unto sir Trystram, but to hymself he seyde thus: 'And sir Trystram 30 knew for whos love he doth all this dedys of armys, sone he wolde abate his corrage.'

'Alas,' seyde sir Trystram, 'that sir Palomydes were nat crystynde!'

So seyde kynge Arthur, and so seyde all that behylde them. Than all people gaff hym the pryse as for the beste knyght that day, and he 35 passed sir Launcelot othir ellys sir Trystram.

'Well,' seyde sir Dynadan to hymselff, 'all this worshyp that sir Palomydes hath here thys day, he may thanke the quene Isode: for had she bene away this day, had nat sir Palomydes gotyn the pryse.'

Ryght so cam into the fylde sir Launcelot du Lake, and sawe and 40 harde the grete noyse and the grete worshyp that sir Palomydes had. He dressed hym ayenst sir Palomydes wyth a grete speare and a longe, and thought to have smyttyn hym downe. And whan sir Palomydes saw sir Launcelot com uppon hym so faste, he toke his horse wyth the spurrys and ran uppon hym as faste wyth his swerde. And as sir

Launcelot sholde have strykyn hym, he smote the speare on syde and
smote hit a-too wyth his swerde. And therewyth sir Palomydes russhed
unto sir Launcelot and thought to have put hym to shame, and wyth his
swerde he smote of his horse nek that sir Launcelot rode uppon. And
than sir Launcelot felle to the erthe.   5

Than was the cry huge and grete, how sir Palomydes the Saresyn
hath smyttyn downe sir Launcelots horse. Ryght so there were many
knyghtes wrothe wyth sir Palomydes bycause he had done that dede,
and helde there ayenste hit, and seyde hyt was unknyghtly done in a
turnemente to kylle an horse wylfully, othir ellys that hit had bene done   10
in playne batayle lyff for lyff.

Whan sir Ector de Marys saw sir Launcelot, his brothir, have suche (71)
a dispyte and so sette on foote, than he gate a speare egirly and ran
ayenst sir Palomydes, and he smote hym so harde that he bare sir
Palomydes quyte frome his horse. That sawe sir Trystram, and he   15
smote downe sir Ector de Marys quyte frome his horse. Than sir
Launcelot dressed his shylde uppon his shuldir, and wyth his swerde
naked in his honde, and so he cam streyte uppon sir Palomydes:

'Wyte thou well thou haste done me this day the grettyste dispyte
that ever ony worshipfull knyght ded me in turnemente othir in justys,   20
and therefore I woll be avenged uppon the. And therefore take kepe to
youreselff!'

'A, mercy, noble knyght,' seyde sir Palomydes, 'of my dedis! And,
jantyll knyght, forgyff me myne unknyghtly dedis, for I have no power
nothir myght to wythstonde you. And I have done so muche this day   25
that well I wote I ded never so muche nothir never shall do so muche in
my dayes. And therefore, moste noble knyght of the worlde, I requyre
the spare me as this day, and I promyse you I shall ever be youre
knyght whyle I lyve, for and yf ye put me from my worshyp now, ye
put me from the grettyst worship that ever I had or ever shall have.'   30

'Well,' seyde sir Launcelot, 'I se, for to say the sothe, ye have done
mervaylously well this day, and I undirstonde a parte for whos love
ye do hit, and well I wote that love is a grete maystry. And yf my lady
were here, as she is nat, wyte you well, sir Palomydes, ye shulde nat
beare away the worshyp! But beware youre love be nat discoverde, for   35
and sir Trystram may know hit, ye woll repente hit. And sytthyn my
quarell is nat here, ye shall have this day the worshyp as for me;
consyderynge the grete travayle and payne that ye have had this day,
hit were no worship for me to put you frome hit.'

And therewythall sir Launcelot suffyrd sir Palomydes to departe.   40
Than sir Launcelot by grete forse and myght gate his horse agayne
magré twenty knyghtes.

So whan sir Launcelot was horsed he ded many mervaylouse dedis
of armys, and so ded sir Trystram, and sir Palomydes in lyke wyse.

Than sir Launcelot smote adowne wyth a speare sir Dynadan, and the kynge of Scotlonde, and the kynge of Northe Walys, and the kynge of Northumbirlonde, and the kynge of Lystenoyse. So than sir Launcelot and his felowys smote downe well-nye a fourty knyghtes.

5 Than cam the kynge of Irelonde and the kynge of the Streyte Marchis to rescowe sir Trystram and sir Palomydes, and there began a grete medlé, and many knyghtys were smyttyn downe on bothe partyes. And allwayes sir Launcelot spared sir Trystram, and he spared hym, and sir Palomydes wolde nat meddyll wyth sir Launcelot.

10 And so there was hurlynge here and there, and than kynge Arthure sente oute many knyghtes of the Table Rounde, and sir Palomydes was ever in the formyste frunte; and sir Trystram ded so strongly that the kynge and all othir had mervayle.

And than the kynge let blowe to lodgynge, and bycause sir Palo-
15 mydes beganne fyrste, and never he wente nor rode oute of the fylde to repose hym, but ever he was doynge on horsebak othir on foote, and lengyst durynge, kynge Arthure and all the kynges gaff sir Palomydes the honoure and the gre as for that day.

Than sir Trystram commaunded sir Dynadan to fecche the quene
20 La Beall Isode and brynge her to his two pavelons by the well. And so sir Dynadan ded as he was commaunded, but whan sir Palomydes undirstoode and knew that sir Trystram was he that was in the rede armour and on the rede horse, wyte you well that he was glad, and so was sir Gareth and sir Dynadan, for all they wente that sir Trystram
25 had be takyn presonere.

And than every knyght drew to his inne. And than kynge Arthure and every kynge spake of th[o] knyghtes, but of all men they gaff sir Palomydes the pryce, and all knyghtes that knew sir Palomydes had wondir of his dedis.

30 'Sir,' seyde sir Launcelot unto kynge Arthure, 'as for sir Palomydes, and he be the grene knyght, I dare say as for this day he is beste worthy to have the gre, for he reposed hym never, nor never chaunged hys wedis, and he began fyrste and lengyste hylde on. And yet well I wote,' seyde sir Launcelot, 'that there was a better knyght than he, and that
35 ye shall preve or we departe fro them, [on payne] of my lyff.'

Thus they talked on aythir party, and so sir Dynadan rayled wyth sir Trystram and sayde,

'What the devyll ys uppon the this day? For sir Palomydes strengthe
(72) fyeblede never this day, but ever he doubled. And sir Trystram fared
40 all this day as he had bene on slepe, and therefore I calle hym a coward.'

'Well, sir Dynadan,' seyde sir Trystram, 'I was never called cowarde or now of earthely knyght in my lyff. And wyte thou well, sir Dynadan, ⌜I calle myself never the more coward⌝ though sir Launcelot gaff me a falle, for I outecepte hym of all knyghtes. And doute ye nat, sir

Dynadan, and sir Launcelot have a quarell good, he is to over good for ony knyght that now ys lyvynge, and yet of his sufferaunce, larges, bounté and curtesy I calle hym a knyght pyerles.'

And so sir Trystram was in maner wrothe wyth sir Dynadan. But all this langayge sir Dynadan saydc because he wolde angur sir Trystram for to cause hym to wake hys sp⟨e⟩retes, for well knew sir Dynadan that, and sir Trystram were thorowly wrothe, sir Palomydes shulde wynne no worship uppon the morne. And for thys entente sir Dynadan seyde all this raylynge langage ayenste sir Trystram.

'Truly,' seyde sir Palomydes, 'as for sir Launcelot, of noble knyght-hode and of his curtesy, proues, and jantylnes I know nat his piere. For this day,' seyde sir Palomyde[s], 'I ded full uncurteysly unto sir Launcelot, and ful unknyghtly. And full knyghtly and curteysly he ded to me agayne, for and he had bene so unjantyll to me as I was to hym, this day had I wonne no worshyp. And therefore,' seyde sir Palomydes, 'I shall be sir Launcelottis knyght whyles that I lyve.'

And all this was talkynge off in all the howsis of the kynges, and all kynges and lordis and knyghtes seyde, of clyere knyghthode and of pure strengthe and of bounté and of curtesy sir Launcelot and sir Trystram bare the pryce of all knyghtes that ever were in kyng Arthurs dayes, and there were no knyghtes in kynge Arthurs dayes that ded halff so many dedis of armys as they two ded. As the booke seyth, no ten knyghtes ded nat halff the dedis that they ded, and there was never knyght in there dayes that requyred sir Launcelot othir ellys sir Trystram of ony queste, so hit were nat to there shame, but they parformed there desyre.

So on the morne sir Launcelot departed, and sir Trystram was redy, (73) and La Beall Isode wyth sir Palomydes and sir Gareth. And so they rode all in grene, full freysshely besayne, unto the foreyste. And sir Trystram laffte sir Dynadan slepynge in his bedde. And so as they rode hit happened the kynge and sir Launcelot stode in a wyndow and saw sir Trystram rydc and La Beall Isode.

'Sir,' seyde sir Launcelot, 'yondir rydyth the fayreste lady of the worlde excepte youre quene, dame Gwenyver.'

'Who ys that?' seyde kynge Arthure.

'Sir,' seyde he, 'hit is quene Isode that, outetake my lady youre quene, she ys makeles.'

'Take youre horse,' seyde kynge Arthure, 'and aray you at all ryghtes as I woll do, and I promyse you,' seyde the kynge, 'I woll se her.'

And anone they were armed and horsed, and aythir toke a speare and rode unto the foreyste.

'Sir,' seyde sir Launcelot, 'hit is nat good that ye go to nyghe them, for wyte you well ther ar two as good knyghtes as ony now ar lyvynge. And therefore, sir, I pray you, be nat to hasty; for peradventure there woll be som knyghtes that woll be displeased and we com suddeynly uppon them.'

'As for that,' seyde kynge Arthure, 'I woll se her, for I take no forse whom I gryeve.'

5 'Sir,' seyde sir Launcelot, 'ye put youreselff in grete jupardé.'

'As for that,' seyde the kynge, 'we woll take the adventure.'

Ryght so anone the kynge rode evyn to her and [salewed her and] seyde, 'God you save!'

'Sir,' she seyde, 'ye ar wellcom.'

10 Than the kynge behylde her, and lyked her wondirly well. So wyth that cam sir Palomydes unto kynge Arthure and seyde,

'Thou uncurteyse knyght, what sekyst thou here? For thou art uncurteyse to com uppon a lady thus suddeynly. Therefore wythdrawe the!'

15 But kynge Arthure toke none hede of sir Palomydes wordys, but ever he loked stylle uppon quene Isode. Than was sir Palomydes wrothe, and therewyth he toke a speare and cam hurtelynge uppon kynge Arthure and smote hym downe with a speare, a grete falle.

Whan sir Launcelot saw that despyte of sir Palomydes, he seyde to 20 hymselff,

'I am lothe to have ado wyth yondir knyght, and nat for his owne sake, but for sir Trystrams. And of one thynge I am sure of hym: yf I smyte downe sir Palomydes I muste have ado wyth sir Trystram, and that were to muche to macche them bothe for me alone, for they ar two 25 noble knyghtes. Natwythstondynge, whethir I lyve or dye, nedys muste I revenge my lorde Arthure, and so I woll, whatsomever befalle me.'

And ⌐therewyth sir Launcelot cryed to sir Palomydes, 'Kepe the from me!' and¬ therewythall sir Launcelot and sir Palomydes russhed 30 togydyrs wyth two spearys strongly. But [sir Launcelot smote] sir Palomydes so harde that he wente quyte oute of his sadyll and had a grete falle.

Whan sir Trystram saw sir Palomydes have that falle, he seyde to sir Launcelot,

35 'Sir knyght, kepe the! For I muste juste [with] the.'

'As for to juste wyth me,' seyde sir Launcelot, 'I woll nat fayle you for no drede that I have of you. But I am lothe to have ado wyth you and I myght chose, for I woll that ye wyte that I muste revenge my speciall lorde and my moste bedrad frynde that was unhorsed unwarely 40 and unknyghtly. And therefore, sir, thoughe I revenge that falle, take ye no displesure, for he is to me suche a frynde that I may nat se hym shamed.'

Anone sir Trystram undirstood by hys persone and by his knyghtly wordis hit was sir Launcelot du Lake, and truly sir Trystram demed that hit was kynge Arthure that sir Palomydes had smyttyn downe. And than sir Trystram put hys speare frome hym, and gate sir Palomydes agayne on his horse backe; and sir Launcelot gate kynge Arthure agayne to horsebacke, and so departed.

'So God me helpe,' seyde sir Trystram unto sir Palomydes, 'ye ded 5 nat worshypfully whan ye smote downe that knyght so suddeynly as ye ded. And wyte you well ye ded youreselff grete shame, for the knyghtes came hyddir of there jantylnes to se a fayre lady, and that ys every good knyghtes parte to beholde a fayre lady, and ye had nat ado to play suche maystryes for my lady. Wyte thou well hit woll turne to 10 angir, for he that ye smote downe was kynge Arthure, and that othir was the good knyght sir Launcelot. But I shall nat forgete,' seyde sir Trystram, 'the wordys of sir Launcelot whan that he called hym a man of grete worshyp, and thereby I wyste that hit was kynge Arthure. And as for sir Launcelot, and there had bene an hondred knyghtes in the 15 medow, he wolde nat a refused them, and yet he seyde he wolde refuse me. And by that agayne I knew that hit was sir Launcelot, for ever he forberyth me in every place and shewyth me grete kyndenes. And of all knyghtes—I outetake none, say what men wyll say—he bearyth the floure: assay hym whosomever wyll, and he be well angred and that 20 hym lyst to do his utteraunce wythoute ony favoure, I know hym nat on lyve but sir Launcclot ys over harde [for] hym, take hym bothe on horsebacke and on foote.'

'Sir, I may never belyeve,' seyde sir Palomydes, 'that kynge Arthure woll ryde so pryvaly as a poure arraunte knyght.'   25

'A!' sayd sir Trystrams, 'ye know nat my lorde kynge Arthure, for all knyghtes may lerne to be a knyght of hym. And therefore ye may be sory,' seyde sir Trystram, 'of youre unknyghtly dedys done to so noble a knyght.'

'And a thynge, sir, be done, hit can nat be undone,' seyde sir 30 Palomydes.

Than sir Trystram sente quene Isode unto her lodgynge into the pryory, there to beholde all the turnemente.

Than there was a cry unto all knyghtes made, that whan they herde (74) the horne blow they sholde make justes as they ded the fyrste [daye]. 35 And lyke as the brethirne sir Edwarde and sir Sadok began the justys the fyrste day, sir Uwayne, the kyngis son Uryen, and sir Lucanere de Butlere, began the justis the secunde day.

And at the fyrste encountir sir Uwayne smote downe the kynge of Scottys, and sir Lucanere ran ayenste the kynge of Walys, and they 40 brake there spearys all to pecis, and they were so fyrse bothe that they hurteled there horsys togydir that bothe felle to the erthe. Than they off Orkeney horsed agayne sir Lucanere.

And than cam in syr Trystram de Lyones and smote downe sir

Uwayne and sir Lucanere; and sir Palomydes smote downe othir two knyghtes. And than cam sir Gareth and smote downe othir two good knyghtes. Than seyde kynge Arthure unto sir Launcelott,

'A! se yondir three knyghtes do passyngly well, and namely the
5 fyrste that justed.'

'Sir,' seyde sir Launcelot, 'that knyght began nat yet, but ye shall se hym do mervaylously.'

And than cam into the place the knyghtes of Orkeney, and than they began to do many dedys of armys. Whan sir Trystram saw them so
10 begyn he seyde to sir Palomydes:

'How feele ye youreselff? May ye do this day as ye ded yestirday?'

'Nay,' seyde sir Palomydes, 'I feele myselff so wery and so sore brused of the dedis of yestirday that I may nat endure as I ded.'

'That me repentyth,' seyde sir Trystram, 'for I shall lacke you this
15 day.'

'But helpe youreselff,' seyde sir Palomydes, 'and truste nat to me, for I may nat do as I ded.'

And all thes wordis seyde sir Palomydes but to begyle sir Trystram. Than seyde sir Trystram unto sir Gareth,

20 'Than muste I truste uppon you, wherefore, I pray you, be nat farre fro me to rescow me and nede be.'

'Sir, I shall nat fayle you,' seyde sir Gareth, 'in all that I may do.'

Than sir Palomydes rode by hymselff, and than in despyte of sir Trystram he put hymselff in the thyckyst prees amonges them of
25 Orkeney. And there he ded so mervaylous dedis of armys that all men had wondir of hym, for there myght none stonde hym a stroke.

Whan sir Trystram saw sir Palomydes do suche dedys he mervayled and sayde to hymselff,

'Methynkyth he is wery of my company.'

30 So sir Trystram behylde hym a grete whyle and ded but lytyll ellys, for the noyse and cry was so grete that sir Trystram mervayled frome whens cam the strengthe that sir Palomydes had there.

'Sir,' seyde sir Gareth unto sir Trystram, 'remembir ye nat of the wordis that sir Dynadan seyde to you yestirday, whan he called you
35 cowarde? Pardé, sir, he seyde hit for none ylle, for ye ar the man in the worlde that he lovyth beste, and all that he seyde was for youre worshyp. And therefore,' seyde sir Gareth, 'lat me know this day what ye be. And wondir ye nat so uppon sir Palomydes, for he forsyth hymselff to wynne all the honoure frome you.'

40 'I may well beleve hit,' seyde sir Trystram, 'and sytthyn I undir-stonde his yevil wyll and hys envy, ye shall se, yf that I enforce myselff, that the noyse shall be leffte that is now uppon hym.'

Than sir Trystram rode into the thyckyst of the prees, and than he ded so mervaylously well and ded so grete dedis of armys that all men

seyde that sir Trystram ded dowble so muche dedys of armys as ded
sir Palomydes aforehande. And than the noyse wente clene frome sir
Palomydes, and all the people cryed uppon sir Trystram and seyde,
   'A, Jesu, a l Se how sir Trystram smytyth wyth hys speare so many
knyghtes to the erthe! And se,' seyde they all, 'how many knyghtes he 5
smytyth downe wyth his swerde, and how many knyghtes he racith
of there helmys and there shyldys!'
   And so he bete all of Orkeney afore hym.
   'How now?' seyde sir Launcelot unto kynge Arthure. 'I tolde you
that thys day there wolde a knyght play his pageaunte. For yondir 10
rydyth a knyght: ye may se he dothe all knyghtly, for he hath strengthe
and wynde inowe.'
   'So God me helpe,' seyde kynge Arthure to sir Launcelot, 'ye sey
sothe, for I sawe never a bettir knyght, for he passyth farre sir
Palomydes.'   15
   'Sir, wyte you well,' seyde sir Launcelot, 'hit muste be so of ryght,
for hit is hymselff that noble knyght sir Trystram.'
   'I may ryght well belyeve hit,' seyde kynge Arthure.
   But whan sir Palomydes harde the noyse and the cry was turned
frome hym, he rode oute on the tone syde and behylde sir Trystram. 20
And whan he saw hym do so mervaylously well he wepte passyngly
sore for dispyte, for he wyst well than he sholde wyn no worshyp that
day; for well knew sir Palomydes, whan sir Trystram wolde put forthe
his strengthe and his manhode, that he sholde gete but lytyll worshyp
that day.   25
   Than cam kynge Arthure and the kynge of Northe Galys and sir (75)
Launcelot du Lake; and sir Bleoberys and sir Bors de Ganys and sir
Ector de Marys, thes three knyghtes cam into the fylde wyth sir Launcelot. And so they four ded so grete dedys of armys that all the noyse
began uppon sir Launcelot. And so they bete the kynge of Walys 30
and the kynge of Scottys far abacke, and made them to voyde the
fylde.
   But sir Trystram and sir Gareth abode stylle in the fylde and endured
all that ever there cam, that all men had wondir that ever ony knyght
endured so many grete strokys. But ever sir Launcelot and hys kynnes- 35
men forbare sir Trystram and sir Gareth.
   Than seyde kynge Arthure, 'Ys that sir Palomydes that enduryth
so well?'
   'Nay,' seyde sir Launcelot, 'wyte you well hit ys the good knyght
sir Trystram, for yondir ye may se sir Palomydes beholdyth and hovyth 40
and doth lytyll or naught. And, sir, ye shall undirstonde that sir
Trystram wenyth this day to beate us all oute of the fylde. And as for
me,' seyde sir Launcelot, 'I shall nat mete hym, mete hym whoso wyll.
But, sir,' seyde sir Launcelot, 'ye may se how sir Palomydes hovyth

yondir as thoughe he were in a dreame, and wyte you well he ys full hevy that sir Trystram doyth suche dedys of armys.'

'Than ys he but a foole,' seyde kynge Arthure, 'for never yet was sir Palomydes suche a knyght, nor never shall be of suche proues. And yf he have envy at sir Trystram,' seyde kynge Arthure, 'and commyth in wyth hym uppon his syde, he ys a false knyght.'

And as the kynge and sir Launcelot thus spake, sir Trystram rode pryvayly oute of the prees, that no man aspyed hym but La Beall Isode and sir Palomydes, for they two wolde nat leve off there yghesyght of hym. And whan sir Trystram cam to his pavylons he founde sir Dynadan in hys bedde aslepe.

'Awake!' seyde sir Trystram, 'for ye ought to be ashamed so to slepe whan knyghtes have ado in the fylde.'

Than sir Dynadan arose lyghtly and sayde,

'Sir, what wyll ye do?'

'Make you redy,' seyde sir Trystram, 'to ryde wyth me into the fylde.'

So whan sir Dynadan was armed he loked uppon sir Trystrames helme and on hys shylde, and whan he saw so many strokys uppon his helme and uppon hys shylde he seyde,

'In good tyme was I thus aslepe, for had I bene wyth you I muste nedys for shame have folowed wyth you, more for shame than for any proues that ys in me, for I se well now be thy strokys that I sholde have bene truly beatyn as I was yestirday.'

'Leve youre japys,' seyde sir Trystram, 'and com of, that we were in the fylde agayne.'

'What?' sayde sir Dynadan, 'ys youre harte up now? Yestirday ye fared as ye had dremed.'

So than sir Trystram was arayed all in blacke harneys.

'A, Jesu!' seyde sir Dynadan, 'what ayleth you thys day? Mesemyth that ye be more wyldar than ye were yestirday.'

Than smyled sir Trystram and seyde to sir Dynadan,

'Awayte well uppon me: yf ye se me ovirmacched, and loke that ever ye be byhynde me, and I shall make you redy way, by Goddys grace!'

So they toke there horsys.

And all thys aspyed sir Palomydes, bothe the goynge and the comynge, and so ded La Beall Isode, for she knew sir Trystram passynge well.

(76) Than sir Palomydes sawe that sir Trystram was disgysed, and thought to shame hym. And so he rode unto a knyght that was sore wounded, that sate undir a thorne a good way frome the fylde.

'Syr knyght,' seyde sir Palomydes, 'I pray you to lende me youre armour and youre shylde, for myne ys overwell knowyn in thys fylde,

and that hath done me grete damayge. And ye shall have myne armour
and my shylde that ys as sure as youres.'

'I woll well,' seyde the knyght, 'that ye have myne armoure and also
my shylde. Yf they may do you ony avayle, I am well pleased.'

So sir Palomydes armed hym hastely in that knyghtes armour and 5
hys shylde that shone lyke ony crystall or sylver, and so he cam rydynge
into the fylde. And than there was nothir sir Trystram nothir none of
hys party nothir of kynge Arthurs that knew sir Palomydes.

And as sone as he was com into the fylde sir Trystram smote downe
three knyghtes, evyn in the syght of sir Palomydes. And than he rode 10
ayenste sir Trystram, and aythir mette othir wyth grete spearys, that
they all to-braste to there hondys. And than they daysshed togedir
wyth swerdys egirly.

Tha[n] sir Trystram had mervayle what knyght he was that ded
batayle so myghtyly wyth hym. Than was sir Trystram wrothe, for he 15
felte hym passynge stronge, and he demed that he cowde nat have ado
wyth the remenaunte of the knyghtes bycause of the stren[g]the of
sir Palomydes.

So they laysshed togydyrs and gaff many sad strokys togydyrs, and
many knyghtys mervayled what knyght he was that so encountred wyth 20
the blak knyght, sir Trystram. And full well knew La Beall Isode that
hit was sir Palomydes that faught wyth sir Trystram, for she aspyed all
in her wyndow where that she stood, how sir Palomydes chaunged hys
harnes wyth the wounded knyght. And than she began to wepe so
hertely for the dyspyte of sir Palomydes that well-nyghe there she 25
sowned.

Than cam in sir Launcelot wyth the knyghtes of Orkeney; and whan
the todir party had aspyed sir Launcelot they cryed and seyde, 'Returne,
for here commyth sir Launcelot!'

So there cam in a knyght unto sir Launcelot and seyde,   30

'Sir, ye muste nedis fyght wyth yondyr knyght in the blak harneyes'
—whyche was sir Trystram—'for he hath allmoste overcom that good
knyghte that fyghtyth wyth hym wyth the sylver shylde'—whyche was
sir Palomydes.

Than sir Launcelot rode betwyxte them, and sir Launcelot seyde 35
unto sir Palomydes,

'Sir knyghte, let me have this batayle, for ye have nede to be reposed.'

Sir Palomydes knew well sir Launcelot, and so ded sir Trystram, but
bycause sir Launcelot was farre hardyer knyght and bygger than sir
Palomydes, he was ryght glad to suffir sir Launcelot to fyght wyth sir 40
Trystram. For well wyste he that sir Launcelot knew nat sir Trystram,
and therefore he hoped that sir Launcelot sholde beate other shame sir
Trystram, and thereof sir Palomydes was full fayne.

And so sir Launcelot laysshed at sir Trystram many sad strokys. But sir Launcelot knew nat sir Trystram, but sir Trystram knew well sir Launcelot. And thus they faught longe togydyrs, whyche made La Beall Isode well-nyghe oute of her mynde for sorow.

Than sir Dynadan tolde sir Gareth how that knyght in the blak harneys was there lorde sir Trystram, 'and that othir ys sir Launcelot that fyghtyth wyth hym, that muste nedys have the bettyr of hym, for sir Trystram hath had overmuche travayle this day.'

'Than lat us smyte hym downe,' seyde sir Gareth.

'So hit is beste that we do,' seyde sir Dynadan, 'rathir than sir Trystrams sholde be shamed, for yondir hovyth the straunge knyghte wyth the sylver shylde to falle uppon sir Trystram yf nede be.'

And so furthwythall sir Gareth russhed uppon sir Launcelot and gaff hym a grete stroke uppon the helme, that he was astoned. And than cam in sir Dynadan wyth hys speare, and he smote sir Launcelot suche a buffet that horse and man yode to the erthe and had a grete falle.

'Now, fye for shame!' seyde sir Trystram unto sir Gareth and sir Dynadan, 'why ded ye so to-smyte adowne soo good a knyght as he ys, and namely whan I had ado wyth hym? A, Jesu! ye do youreself grete shame and hym no disworshyp, for I hylde hym resonabely hote, though ye had nat holpyn me.'

Than cam sir Palomydes whyche was disgysed, and smote downe sir Dynadan frome hys horse. Than sir Launcelot, bycause sir Dynadan had smyttyn hym downe aforehonde, therefore he assayled sir Dynadan passynge sore. And sir Dynadan deffended hym myghtyly, but well undirstood sir Trystram that sir Dynadan myght nat endure ayenste sir Launcelot, wherefore sir Trystram was sory.

Than cam sir Palomydes freysshe uppon sir Trystram. And whan he saw sir Palomydes com so freyshly he thought to delyver hym at onys, bycause that he wolde helpe sir Dynadan that stoode in perell wyth sir Launcelot. Than sir Trystram hurteled unto sir Palomydes and gaff hym a grete buffet, and than sir Trystram gate sir Palomydes and pulled hym downe undirnethe his horse feete.

And than sir Trystram lyghtly lepe up and leffte sir Palomydes and wente betwyxte sir Launcelot and sir Dynadan, and than they began to do batayle togydyrs. And ryght so sir Dynadan gate sir Trystrams horse and seyde on hyght, that sir Launcelot myght hyre:

'My lorde sir Trystram, take youre horse!'

And whan sir Launcelot harde hym name sir Trystram, 'A, Jesu! what have I done?' seyde sir Launcelot, 'for now am I dishonoured'; and seyde, 'A, my lorde sir Trystram, why were ye now disgysed? Ye have put youreself this day in grete perell. But I pray you to pardon me, for and I had knowyn you we had nat done this batayle.'

'Sir,' seyde sir Trystrams, 'this is nat the fyrste kyndenes and goodnes that ye have shewed unto me.'

And anone they were horsed bothe agayne. So all the peple on that one syde gaff sir Launcelot the honoure and the gre, and all the people on the othir syde gaff sir Trystram the honoure and the gre. But sir Launcelot seyde nay thereto: 'For I am nat worthy to have this honoure, for I woll reporte me to all knyghtes that sir Trystram hath bene 5 lenger in the fylde than I, and he hath smyttyn downe many mo knyghtes this day than I have done. And therefore I woll gyff sir Trystram my voyse and my name, and so I pray all my lordys and felowys so to do.'

Than there was the hole voyse of kyngys, deukes and erlys, barons 10 and knyghtes that sir Trystram de Lyones 'thys day ys preved the beste knyght'.

Than they blewe unto lodgynge. And quene Isode was lad unto her (77) pavelons; but wyte you well she was wrothe oute of mesure wyth sir Palomydes, for she saw all his treson frome the begynnynge to the 15 endynge. And all thys whyle neythir sir Trystram, sir Gareth, nothir sir Dynadan knew nat of the treson of sir Palomydes. But aftirward ye shall hyre how there befelle the grettyst debate betwyxte sir Trystram and sir Palomydes that myght be.

So whan the turnemente was done sir Trystram, sir Gareth and 20 sir Dynadan rode wyth La Beall Isode to his pavelons, and ever sir Palomydes rode wyth them in there company, disgysed as he was. But whan sir Trystram had aspyed hym that he was the same knyght wyth the shylde of sylver that hylde hym so hote that day, than seyde Trystram,   25

'Sir knyght, wyte thou well here ys none that hath nede of youre felyshyp. And therefore I pray you departe frome us.'

Than sir Palomydes answered agayne, as though he had nat knowyn sir Trystram,

'Wyte you well, sir knyght, that frome this felyshyp woll I nat 30 departe, for one of the beste knyghtys of the worlde commaunded me to be in this company, and tyll that he discharge me of my servyse I woll nat be discharged.'

So by his langayge sir Trystram knew that hit was sir Palomydes, and seyde,   35

'A, sir, ar ye such a knyght? Ye have be named wronge! For ye have ben called ever a jantyll knyght, and as this day ye have shewed me grete unjantylnes, for ye had allmoste brought me to my dethe. But as for you, I suppose I sholde have done well inowghe, but sir Launcelot with you was overmuche, for I know no knyght lyvynge but sir 40 Launcelot ys to over good for hym and he woll do hys utteryst.'

'Alas,' seyde sir Palomydes, 'ar ye my lorde sir Trystram?'

'Yee, sir, and that know you well inow.'

'Be my knyghthod,' seyde sir Palomydes, 'untyll now I knew you nat, for I wente that ye had bene the kynge off Irelonde, for well I wote that ye bare his armys.'

'I bare his armys,' seyde sir Trystram, 'and that woll I abyde bye, for I wanne them onys in a fylde of a full noble knyght whos name was sir
5 Marhalte. And wyth grete payne I wan that knyght, for there was none othir recover. But sir Marhalte dyed thorow false lechis, and yet was he never yoldyn to me.'

'Sir,' seyde sir Palomydes, 'I wente that ye had bene turned uppon sir Launcelottys party, and that caused me to turne.'
10 'Ye sey well,' seyde sir Trystram, 'and so I take you and forgyff you.'

So than they rode to there pavelons. And whan they were alyghte they unarmed them and wysshe there facis and there hondys, and so yode unto mete and were set at there table.

But whan La Beall Isode saw sir Palomydes she chaunged than her
15 coloures; for wrathe she myght nat speake. Anone sir Trystram aspyed her countenaunce and seyde,

'Madame, for what cause make ye us such chere? We have bene sore travayled all thys day.'

'Myne owne lorde,' [seyde] La Beall Isode, 'for Goddys sake, be ye
20 nat displeased wyth me, for I may none othirwyse do. I sawe thys day how ye were betrayed and nyghe brought unto youre dethe. Truly, sir, I sawe every dele, how and in what wyse. And therefore, sir, how sholde I suffir in youre presence suche a felonne and traytoure as ys sir Palomydes? For I saw hym wyth myne yen, how he behylde you whan ye
25 wente oute of the fylde. For ever he hoved stylle uppon his horse tyll that he saw you com agaynewarde; and than furthwythall I saw hym ryde to the hurte knyght, and chaunged hys harneys with hym, and than streyte I sawe hym how he sought you all the fylde, and anone as he had founde you he encountred wyth you, and wylfully sir Palo-
30 mydes ded batayle wyth you. And as for hym, sir, [I] was nat gretly aferde, but I drad sore sir Launcelot whyche knew nat you.'

'Madame,' seyde sir Palomydes, 'ye may say what ye woll, I may nat contrary you, but, be my knyghthod, I knew nat my lorde sir Trystram.'

'No forse,' seyde sir Trystram unto sir Palomydes, 'I woll take youre
35 exscuse, but well I wote ye spared me but a lytyll. But no forse! All ys pardonned as on my party.'

Than La Beall Isode hylde downe her hede and seyde no more at that tyme.

(78)   And therewythall two knyghtes armed come unto the pavelon, and
40 there they alyghte bothe and cam in armed at all pecis.

'Fayre knyghtes,' seyde sir Trystram, 'ye ar to blame to com thus armed at all pecis uppo[n] me whyle we ar at oure mete. And yf ye wolde onythynge wyth us whan we were in the fylde, there myght ye have eased youre hertys.'

'Not so, sir,' seyde the tone of tho knyghtes, 'we com nat for that entente, but wyte you well, sir Trystram, we be com as youre frendys. And I am comyn hydir for to se you, and this knyght ys comyn for to se youre quene Isode.'

Than seyde sir Trystram, 'I requyre you, do of your helmys, that I may se you.'

'Sir, that woll we do at youre desyre,' seyde the knyghtes.

And whan their helmys were of, sir Trystram thought that he sholde know them. Than spake sir Dynadan prevayly unto sir Trystram,

'That is my lorde kynge Arthure, and that other that spake to you fyrst ys my lorde sir Launcelot.'

'A, madame, I pray you aryse,' seyde sir Trystram, 'for here ys my lorde, kynge Arthure.'

Than the kynge and the quene kyssed, and sir Launcelot and sir Trystram enbraced aythir other in armys, and than there was joy wythoute mesure. And at the requeste of La Beall Isode the kynge and sir Launcelot were unarmed, and than there was myry talkynge.

'Madame,' seyde kynge Arthur, 'hit is many a day ago sytthyn I desyred fyrst to se you, for ye have bene praysed so fayre a lady. And now I dare say ye ar the fayryste that ever I sawe, and sir Trystram ys as fayre and as good a knyght as ony that I know. And therefore mesemyth ye ar well besett togydir.'

'Sir, God thanke you!' seyde sir Trystram and la Beall Isode. 'Of youre goodnes and of youre larges ye ar pyerles.'

And thus they talked of many thyngys and of all the hole justes.

'But for what cause,' seyde kynge Arthure, 'were ye, sir Trystram, ayenst us? And ye ar a knyght of the Table Rounde, and of ryght ye sholde have bene with us.'

'Sir,' seyde sir Trystram, 'here ys sir Dynadan and sir Gareth, youre owne nevew, caused me to be ayenst you.'

'My lorde Arthure,' seyde sir Gareth, 'I may well beare ⌐the blame⌐, for my bak ys brode inowghe. But for sothe, hit was sir Trystrams awne dedis.'

'Be God, that may I repente,' seyde sir Dynadan, 'for thys unhappy sir Trystram brought us to this turnemente, and many grete buffettys he hath caused us to have!'

Than the kynge and sir Launcelot ⌐lowghe⌐, that unnethe they myght sytte.

'But what knyght was that,' seyde kynge Arthure, 'that hylde you so shorte?'

'Sir,' seyde sir Trystram, 'here he syttyth at this table.'

'What?' seyde kyng Arthure, 'was hit sir Palomydes?'

'Sir, wyte you well that hit was he,' seyde La Beall Isode.

'So God me helpe,' seyde kynge Arthure, 'that was unknyghtly done of you as of so good a knyght, for I have harde many people calle you a curtayse knyght.'

'Sir,' seyde sir Palomydes, 'I knew nat sir Trystram, for he was so disgysed.'

5 'So God helpe me,' seyde sir Launcelot, 'hit may well be, for I knew hym nat myselff.'

'But I mervayled whye ye turned on oure party.'

'Sir, hit was done for the same cause,' seyde sir Launcelot.

'Syr, as for that,' seyde sir Trystram, 'I have pardouned hym, and I 10 wolde be ryght lothe to leve hys felyshyp, for I love ryght well hys company.'

And so they leffte of and talked of other thynges. And in the evenynge kynge Arthure and sir Launcelot departed unto their lodgynge. But wyte you well sir Palomydes had grete envy hartely, for all that nyght 15 he had never reste in his bed, but wayled and wepte oute of mesure.

So on the morne sir Trystram, sir Gareth and sir Dynadan arose early and went unto sir Palomydes chambir, and there they founde hym faste aslepe, for he had all nyght wacched. [And it] was sene uppon his chekes that he had wepte full sore.

20 'Say ye nothynge,' seyde sir Trystram, 'for I am sure he hath takyn angir and sorow for the rebuke that I gaff hym and La Beall Isode.'

(79)   Than sir Trystram let calle sir Palomydes and bade hym make redy, for hit was tyme to go to the fylde. And anon they armed them, and clothed them all in rede, bothe La Beall Isode and all the felyshyp, and 25 so they lad her passynge freysshly thorow the fylde into the pryory where was hir lodgynge.

And anone they harde three blastes blowe, and every kynge and knyght dressed hym to the fylde. And the fyrste that was redy to juste was sir Palomydes and sir Kaynes le Straunge, a knyght of the Table 30 Rounde, and so they two encountyrd togydyrs. But sir Palomydes smote sir Kaynes so harde that he bare hym quyte over his horse croupe. And furthewithall sir Palomydes smote downe anothir knyght and brake his speare, and than pulled oute hys swerde and ded wondirly well. And than the noyse began gretly uppon sir Palomydes.

35 'Lo,' seyde kynge Arthure, 'yondir sir Palomydes begynnyth to play his play. So God me helpe,' seyde kynge Arthur, 'he is a passynge goode knyght.'

And ryght as they stood talkynge thus, in cam sir Trystram as thundir, and he encountird wyth sir Kay le Senesciall, and there he 40 smote hym downe quyte frome his horse. And wyth that same speare he smote downe three knyghtes more. And than he pulled oute his swerde and ded mervaylously. Than the noyse and the cry chonged fro sir Palomydes and turned unto sir Trystram. And than all the people cryed,

'A, Trystram! A, Trystram!'

And than was sir Palomydes clene forgotyn.

'How now?' seyde sir Launcelot unto kynge Arthure, 'yondyr rydyth a knyght that playyth his pageauntes.'

'So God me help,' seyde kynge Arthure, 'ye shall se this day that yondir two knyghtes shall do here wondirs.'

'Sir,' seyde sir Launcelot, 'the tone knyghte waytyth uppon the tother and enforsyth hymselff thorow envy to passe sir Trystram, and he knowyth nat the prevy envy of sir Palomydes. For, sir, all that sir Trystram doth is thorow clene knyghthod.'

And than sir Gareth and sir Dynadan ded ryght well that day, that kynge Arthure spake of them grete worshyp, and [the] kynges and the knyghtes on sir Trystrams syde ded passynge well and hylde them truly togydyrs.

Than kynge Arthure and sir Launcelot toke their horsys and dressed them to the fylde amonge the thyckeste of the prees. And there sir Trystram unknowyn[g] smote downe kynge Arthur, and than sir Launcelot wolde have rescowed hym, but there were so many uppon sir Launcelot that they pulled hym downe from his horse. And than the kynge of Irelonde and the Kynge of Scottes with their knyghtes ded their payne to take kynge Arthure and sir Launcelot presoners. Whan sir Launcelot harde them sey so, he fared as hit had bene an hungry lyon, for he fared so that no knyght durst nyghe hym.

Than cam sir Ector de Marys, and he bare a speare ayenst sir Palomydes and braste hit uppon hym all to-shyvyrs. And than sir Ector cam agayne and gaff sir Palomydes suche a daysshe with a swerde that he stowped adowne uppon his sadyll-bowe. And forthwythall sir Ector pulled downe sir Palomydes undir his horse fyete, and than he ⌐gate⌐ sir Launcelot ⌐an horse and brought hit to hym and badde hym mounte upon hym⌐. But sir Palomydes lepe before and gate the horse by the brydyll and lepe into the sadyll.

'So God me helpe,' seyde sir Launcelot, 'ye ar bettir worthy to have that horse than I.'

Than sir Ector brought sir Launcelot another horse.

'Grauntemercy,' seyde sir Launcelot unto his brother.

And so, whan he was horsed agayne, with one speare he smote downe four good knyghtes, and than sir Launcelot gate kynge Arthure a good horse. Than kynge Arthure and sir Launcelot wyth a feawe of his knyghtes of sir Launcelottis kynne ded mervaylouse dedis of armys; for that tyme, as the booke recordyth, sir Launcelot smote downe and pulled downe thirty knyghtes.

Natwithstondynge the other parté hylde them so faste togydir tha[t] kynge Arthure and his knyghtes were overmacched. And whan sir Trystram saw that, what laboure kynge Arthure and his knyghtes, and

in especiall the grete noble dedis that sir Launcelott ded with hys owne
(80) hondis, than sir Trystram called unto hym sir Palomydes, sir Gareth
and sir Dynadan, and seyde thus to them:

'My fayre fealowys, wyte you well that I woll turne unto kynge
5 Arthure[s] party, for I saw never so feawe men do so well. And hit
woll be shame unto us that bene knyghtes of the Rounde Table to se
oure lorde kynge Arthure and that noble knyght, sir Launcelot, to be
dishonoured.'

'Sir, hit wyll be well do,' seyde sir Gareth and sir Dynadan.
10 'Sir, do your beste,' seyde sir Palomydes, 'for I woll nat chaunge my
party that I cam in wythall.'

'That is for envy of me,' seyde sir Trystram, 'but God spede you well
in your journey!'

And so departed sir Palomydes frome them.
15 Than sir Trystram, sir Gareth and sir Dynadan turned with sir
Launcelot. And than sir Launcelot smote downe the kynge of Irelonde
quyte frome his horse, and he smote downe the kyng of Scottes and the
kynge [of] Walys. And than the kynge Arthure ran unto sir Palomydes
and smote hym quyte frome his horse. And than sir Trystram bare
20 downe all that ever he mette wythall, and sir Gareth and sir Dynadan
ded there as noble knyghtes. And anone all the todir party began to fle.

'Alas,' seyde sir Palomydes, 'that ever I sholde se this day! For now
I have loste all the worshyp that I wan.'

And than sir Palomydes wente hys way waylynge, and so wythdrewe
25 hym tylle he cam to a welle. And there he put his horse from hym and
ded of his armoure and wayled and wepte lyke as he had bene a wood
man.

Than they gaff the pryce unto sir Trystram many knyghtes, and there
were many mo that gaff the pryce unto sir Launcelot.
30 'Now, fayre lordys, I thanke you of youre honoure that ye wolde
gyff me, but I pray you hartely that ye woll gyff youre voyce unto sir
Launcelot, for, be my fayth, I woll gyff sir Launcelot my voyce,' seyde
sir Trystram.

But sir Launcelot wolde none of hit, and so the pryce was gyffyn
35 betwyxte them bothe; and so every man rode to his lodgynge. And sir
Bleoberys and sir Ector rode wyth sir Trystram and La Beall Isode unto
her pavelons.

Than as sir Palomydes was at the welle waylynge and wepynge, there
cam fleynge the kynge of Walys and of Scotlonde, and they sawe sir
40 Palomydes in that rayge.

'Alas,' seyde they, 'so noble a man as ye be sholde be in this aray!'

And than the kynge gate sir Palomydes horse agayne, and made hym
to arme hym and mownte uppon his horse agayne, and so he rode wyth
them makyng grete dole.

So whan sir Palomydes cam nygh sir Trystram and La Beall Isode pavelons, than sir Palomydes pray[de] the two kynges to abyde hym there the whyle that he spake wyth sir Trystram. And whan he cam to the porte of the pavelon sir Palomydes seyde an hyghe,

'Where art thou, sir Trystram de Lyones?'   5

'Sir,' seyde sir Dynadan, 'that ys sir Palomydes.'

'What, sir Palomydes, woll ye nat com nere amonge us?'

'Fye on the, traytoure!' seyde sir Palomydes, 'for wyte thou well, and hit were daylyght as hit is nyght, I sholde sle the myn awne hondis. And yf ever I may gete the,' seyde sir Palomydes, 'thou shalt dye for 10 this dayes dede.'

'Sir Palomydes,' seyde sir Trystram, 'ye wyte me wyth wronge, for, had ye done as I ded, ye sholde have had worshyp. But sytthyn ye gyff me so large warnynge, I shall be well ware of you.'

'Fye on the, traytoure!' seyde sir Palomydes, and therewythall he 15 departed.

Than on the morne sir Trystram and La Beall Isode, sir Bleoberys, sir Ector de Marys, sir Gareth, and sir Dynadan, what by londe and by watir, they brought La Beall Isode unto Joyus Garde, and there they reposed them a sevennyght and made all the myrthis and desportys 20 that they cowde devyse. And kynge Arthure and his knyght[es] drew unto Camelot.

And sir Palomydes rode wyth the two kynges, and ever he made the grettyst dole that ony man cowde thynke, for he was nat all only so dolorous for the departynge frome La Beall Isode, but he was as sorow- 25 ful a parte to go frome the felyshyp of sir Trystram. For he was so kynde and so jantyll that whan sir Palomydes remembyrd hym [thereof] he myght never be myrry.

So at the sevennyghtes ende sir Bleoberys [and] sir Ector departed (81) frome sir Trystram and frome the quene, and thes two knyghtes had 30 grete gyfftys. And ever sir Gareth and sir Dynadan abode wyth sir Trystram.

And whan sir Bleoberys and sir Ector were comyn thereas quene Gwenyver was lodged in a castell by the sesyde (and thorow the grace of God the quene was recovirde of hir malady), than she asked the two 35 knyghtes fro whens they cam. And they seyde they cam frome sir Trystram and frome La Beall Isode.

'How doth sir Trystram,' seyde the quene, 'and La Beall Isode?'

'Truly, madame,' seyde tho knyghtes, 'he doth as a noble knyght shulde do. And as for the quene, she is pyerles of all ladyes; for to 40 speake of her beauté, bounté, and myrthe, and of hir goodnes, we sawe never hir macche as far as we have ryddyn and gone.'

'A, mercy Jesu!' seyde quene Gwenyvir, 'thus seyth all folkys that hath sene her and spokyn wyth her. God wolde,' seyde she, 'that I had parte of her condycions! And was now myssefortuned me of my syknesse whyle that turnemente endured, for, as I suppose, I shall never se in all my lyff such asemblé of noble knyghtes and fayre ladyes.'

And than the knyghtes tolde the quene how sir Palomydes wan the
5 gre the fyrste day wyth grete nobles, 'and the secunde day sir Trystram wan the gre, and the thirde day sir Launcelot wan the gre.'

'Well,' seyde quene Gwenyvir, 'who ded beste all three dayes?'

'So God me help,' seyde thes knyghtes, 'sir Launcelot and sir Trystram had there leste dishonour. And wyte you well sir Palomydes ded
10 passyngly well and myghtyly, but he turned ayenste the party that he cam in wythall, and that caused hym to loose a grete parte of his worshyp, for hit semed that sir Palomydes ys passynge envyous.'

'Than shall he never wynne worshyp,' seyde the quene, 'for and hyt happyn an envyous man onys to wynne worshyp, he shall be dis-
15 honoured twyse therefore. And for this cause all men of worshyp hate an envyous man and woll shewe hym no favoure, and he that ys curteyse and kynde and jantil hath favoure in every place.'

XIII. SIR PALOMIDES

(82) Now leve we of this mater and speke we of sir Palomydes that rode
20 and lodged wyth the two kynges all that nyght. And on the morne sir Palomydes departed frome the two kynges, whereof they were hevy. Than the Kynge of Irelonde lente a man of his to sir Palomydes and gaff hym a grete courser. And the Kynge of Scotlonde gaff hym grete gyfftes, and fayne they wolde have had hym abyde wyth them, but he
25 wolde nat in no wyse.

And so he departed and rode as adventures wolde gyde hym tyll hitte was nyghe none. And than in a foreyste by a well sir Palomydes saw where lay a fayre wounded knyght, and his horse bounden by hym. And that knyght made the grettyst dole that ever he herde man make,
30 for ever he wepte and therewyth syghed as he wolde dye.

Than sir Palomydes rode nere hym and salewed hym myldely and sayde,

'Fayre knyght, why wayle you so? Lat me lye downe by you and wayle also, for dowte ye nat, I am muche more hevyar than ye ar. For I
35 dare say,' seyde sir Palomydes, 'that my sorow ys an hondred-folde more than youres ys. And therefore lat us complayne aythir to other.'

'Fyrst,' seyde the woundid knyght, 'I requyre you telle me youre name. For and thou be none of the noble knyghtes ⌈of the Rounde Table⌉, thou shalt never know my name, whatsomever com of me.'
40 'Fayre knyght,' seyde sir Palomydes, 'suche as I am, be hit bettir be

hit worse, wyte thou well that my name ys sir Palomydes, sunne and ayre unto kynge Asclabor, and sir Saphir and sir Segwarydes ar my two brethirne. And wyte thou well, as for myselff, I was never crystynde, but my two brethirne ar truly crystynde.'

'A, noble knyght!' seyde that woundid knyght, 'well ys me that I 5 have mette wyth you. And wyte you well that my name ys sir Epynogrys, the kynges sonne of Northumbirlonde. Now sytte ye downe,' seyde sir Epynogrys, 'and let us aythir complayne to othir.'

Than sir Palomydes alyght and tyed his horse faste. And thus sir Palomydes began hys complaynte and sayde,   10

'Now shall I tell you what wo I endure. I love the fayryst quene and lady that ever bare lyff, and wyte you well her name ys La Beall Isode, kynge Markes wyff of Cornwayle.'

'That ys grete foly,' seyde sir Epynogrys, 'for to love quene Isode. For one of the beste knyghtes of the worlde lovyth her, that ys sir 15 Trystram de Lyones.'

'That ys trouthe,' seyde sir Palomydes, 'for no man knowyth that mater bettir than I do. For I have bene in sir Trystrams felyshyp this moneth and more, and wyth La Beall Isode togydyrs. And, alas!' seyde sir Palomydes, 'unhappy man that I am, now have I loste the felyshyp 20 of sir Trystram and the love of La Beall Isode for ever, and I am never lykly to se her more. And sir Trystram and I bene aythir to othir mortall enemyes.'

'Well,' seyde sir Epynogrys, 'syth that ye loved La Beall Isode, loved she ever you agayne by onythynge that ye cowde wyte, othir ellys ded 25 ye ever rejoyse her in ony plesure?'

'Nay, be my knyghthode,' seyde sir Palomydes, 'for I never aspyed that ever she loved me more than all the worlde ded, nor never had I pleasure wyth her, but the laste day she gaff me the grettyst rebuke that ever I had, whyche shall never go fro my harte. And yet I well deservyd 30 that rebuke, for I ded nat knyghtly, and therefore I have loste the love of her and of sir Trystram for ever. And I have many tymes enforsed myselff to do many dedis of armys for her sake, and ever she was the causer of my worship-wynnynge. And alas! now have I loste all the worshyp that ever I wanne, for never shall befalle me suche proues as I 35 had in the felyshyp of sir Trystram.'

'Nay, nay,' seyde sir Epynogrys, 'youre sorow ys but japys to my (83) sorow; for I rejoysed my lady and wan her wyth myne hondis and loste her agayne: alas that day! And fyrst thus I wan her: my lady was an erlys doughtir, and as the erle and two knyghtes cam home fro the 40 turnement of Lonezep, for her sake I sette uppon this erle myselff and on his two knyghtes, and my lady there beynge presente. And so by fortune there I slew the erle and one of the knyghtes, and the othir knyght fledde. And so that nyght I had my lady.

'And on the morne, as she and I reposed us at this wellesyde, than cam there to me an arraunte knyght, his name was sir Helyor le Prewse, an hardy knyght, and he chalenged me to fyght for my lady. And than we wente to batayle, fyrst uppon horsebacke and aftir uppon foote, but
5 at the laste sir Helyor wounded me so that he lefft me for dede, and so he toke my lady with hym. And thus my sorow ys more than youres, for I have rejoysed, and ye nevir rejoysed.'

'That ys trouthe,' seyde sir Palomydes, 'but syth I can nat recover myselff, I shall promyse you, yf I can mete with sir Helyor, that I shall
10 gete to you your lady agayne, other ellys he shall beate me.'

Than sir Palomydes made sir Epynogrys to take his horse, and so they rode untyll an ermytage, and there sir Epynogrys rested hym. And in the meanewhyle sir Palomydes walked prevayly oute to reste hym under the levis, and there besydes he sawe a knyght com rydynge wyth
15 a shylde that he had sene sir Ector de Marys beare aforehonde. And there cam aftir hym a ten knyghtes, and so thes knyghtes hoved undir the levys for hete.

And anone aftir, there cam a knyght with a grene shylde and therein a whyght lyon, ledynge a lady uppon a palfrey. Than this knyght with
20 the shylde he semed to be maystir of the ten knyghtes, and he rode fyersly aftir sir Helyor, for hit was he that hurte sir Epynogrys. And whan he cam nygh sir Helyor he bade hym deffende his lady.

'I woll deffende her,' seyde sir Helyor, 'unto my power!'

And so they ran togydirs so myghtyly that ayther smote other downe,
25 horse and all, to the erth. And than they wan up lyghtly and drewe swerdys and dressed their shyldis, and laysshed togydyrs wondir fyersly more than an owre. And all this sir Palomydes saw and behylde.

But ever at the laste the knyght with sir Ectors shylde was far bigger, and at the laste he smote downe sir Helyor. And than that knyght
30 unlaced his helme to have strykyn off his hede. And than he cryed mercy and prayed hym to save his lyff and bade hym take his lady.

Than sir Palomydes dressed hym up, bycause he wyste well that that same lady was sir Epynogrys lady, and he had promysed hym to helpe hym. Than sir Palomydes went streyte to that lady and toke her by the
35 honde and asked her whether she knew a knyght whyche was called sir Epynogrys.

'Alas,' she seyde, 'that evir I knew hym other he me! For I have for his sake loste my worshyp and also hys lyff; that greveth me moste of all.'

'Nat so, fayre lady!' sayde sir Palomydes. 'Commyth on with me, for
40 here ys sir Epynogrys in this ermytage.'

'A, well ys me,' seyde that lady, 'and he be on lyve!'

Than cam the tother knyght and seyde, 'Whythir wolt thou with that lady?'

'I woll do wyth her what me lyste,' seyde sir Palomydes.

'Wyte thou well,' seyde that knyght, 'thou spekyst over large, thoughe thou semyst thou haste me at avauntayge, bycause thou sawyst me do batayle but late. Thou wenyst, sir knyght, to have that lady away fro me so lyghtly? Nay, thynke hit never! And thou were as good a knyght as ys sir Launcelot or sir Trystram other ellys sir Palomydes,   5 but thou shalt wyn her more derar than ever ded I.'

And so they wente unto batayle uppon foote, and there they gaff many sad strokys togydir, and aythir wounded other wondirly sore. And thus they faught togydir styll more than an owre. Than sir Palomydes had mervayle what knyght he myght be that was so stronge and 10 so well-brethid durynge, and at the laste thus seyde sir Palomydes:

'Knyght, I requyre the telle me thy name!'

'Wyte thou well,' seyde that knyght, 'I dare telle the my name, so that thou wolt tell me thy name.'

'I woll,' seyde sir Palomydes.   15

'Truly,' seyde that knyght, 'and my name ys sir Saphir, sonne of kynge Asclabor, and sir Palomydes and sir Segwarydes ar my bretherne.'

'Now, and wyte thou well, my name ys sir Palomydes!'

Than sir Saphir kneled adowne uppon his kneis and prayde hym of mercy, and than they unlaced their helmys and aythir kyssed other 20 wepynge. And the meanewhyle sir Epynogrys rose of his bedde and harde them by the strokys, and so he armed hym to helpe sir Palomydes yf nede were. Than sir Palomydes toke the lady by the honde and   (84) brought her to sir Epynogrys, and there was grete joy betwyxte them, for aythir sowned for jou whan they were mette.   25

'Now, fayre knyght and lady,' sayde sir Saphir, 'hit were pité to departe you too, and therefore Jesu sende you joy ayther of othir!'

'Grauntemercy, jantyll knyght,' seyde sir Epynogrys, 'and muche more thanke to my lorde sir Palomydes that thus hath thorow his proues made me to gete my lady.'   30

Than sir Epynogrys requyred sir Palomydes and sir Saffir, [his] brother, to ryde with hym unto his castell for the sauffgarde of his persone.

'Syr,' seyde sir Palomydes, 'we woll be redy to conduyte you, because that ye ar sore woundid.'   35

And so was sir Epynogrys and hys lady horsed uppon a soffte ambler, and than they rode unto his castell. And there they had grete chere and grete joy, as ever sir Palomydes and sir Saffir had in their lyvys.

So on the morne sir Saphir and sir Palomydes departed and rode but as fortune lad them, and so they rode all that day untyll aftir noone. 40 And at the laste they harde a grete wepyng and a grete noyse downe in a maner.

'Sir,' seyde sir Saffir, 'lette us wyte what noyse this ys.'

'I woll well,' seyde sir Palomydes.

And so they rode tyll that they co[m] to a fayre gate of a maner, and there sate an olde man sayynge his prayers and beadis.

Than sir Palomydes and sir Saphir alyght and leffte their horsis and wente within the gatys. And there they saw full goodly men wepynge
5 many.

'Now, fayre sirrys', seyde sir Palomydes, 'wherefore wepe ye and make thys sorow?'

And anone one of tho knyghtes of the castel behylde sir Palomydes and knew hym, and than he wente to his felowys and sayde,
10 'Fayre fealowys, wyte you well all, we have within this castell the same knyght that slew oure lorde at Lonezep, for I know hym well for sir Palomydes.'

Than they wente unto harneys, all that myght beare harneys, som on horsebak and som uppon foote, to the numbir of three score. And
15 whan they were redy they cam freyss[h]ly uppon sir Palomydes and uppon sir Sap⟨h⟩ir wyth a grete noyse, and sayde thus:

'Kepe the, sir Palomydes, for thou arte knowyn! And be ryght thou muste be dede, for thou haste slayne oure lorde, and therefore wyte thou well we may do the none other favoure but sle the. And therefore
20 deffende the!'

Than sir Palomydes and sir Saphir, the tone sette his bak to the todir and gaff many sad strokes, and also toke many grete strokes. And thus they faught wyth twenty knyghtes and forty jantyllmen and yomen nyghe a two owres. But at the laste, though they were never so lothe,
25 sir Palomydes and sir Saphir were takyn and yoldyn and put in a stronge preson.

And within three dayes twelve knyghtes passed uppon h[e]m, and they founde sir Palomydes gylty, and sir Saphir nat gylty, of the lordis deth. And whan sir Saphir shulde be delyverde there was grete dole
30 betwyxte his brother and hym. And many peteous complayntis that was made at her departicion, there ys no maker can reherse the tenth parte.

'Now, fayre brother, lat be youre doloure,' seyde sir Palomydes, 'and youre sorow, for and I be ordeyned to dy a shamfull dethe, well-
35 com be hit. But and I had wyste of this deth that I am demed unto, I sholde never have bene yoldyn.'

So departed sir Saphir, his brother, with the grettyst sorow that ever made knyght.

And on the morne they of the castell ordayned twelve knyghtes for
40 to ryde wyth sir Palomydes unto the fadir of the same knyght that sir Palomydes slew. And so they bounde his leggys undir an olde steedis bealy, and than they rode wyth sir Palomydes unto a castell by the seesyde that hyght Pylownes, and there sir Palomydes shulde have his just⌜yse⌝: thus was their ordynaunce.

And so they rode wyth sir Palomydes faste by the castell of Joyus
Garde, and as they passed by that castell there cam rydynge one of that
castell by them that knew sir Palomydes. And whan that knyght saw
hym lad bounden uppon a croked courser, than the knyght asked sir
Palomydes for what cause he was so lad.   5

'A, my fayre felow and knyght,' seyde sir Palomydes, 'I ryde now
towarde my dethe for the sleynge of a knyght at the turnemente of
Lonezep. And yf I had [not] departed frome my lorde sir Trystram as I
ought [not] to have done, now myght I have bene sure to have had my
lyff saved. But I pray you, sir knyght, recommaunde me unto my lorde 10
sir Trystram and unto my lady quene Isode, and sey to them, yf ever
I trespast to them, I aske them forgyffnes. And also, I beseche you,
recommaunde me unto my lorde kynge Arthure and to all the felyshyp of the Rounde Table, unto my power.'

Than that knyght wepte for pité, and therewyth he rode unto Joyus 15
Garde as faste as his horse myght renne, and lyghtly that knyght
descended downe of his horse and went unto sir Trystram, and there
he tolde hym all as ye have harde. And ever the knyght wepte as he
were woode.

Whan sir Trystram knew how sir Palomydes wente to his dethward 20 (85)
he was hevy to hyre thereof and sayde,

'Howbehit that I am wrothe wyth hym, yet I woll nat suffir hym to
dye so shamefull a dethe, for he ys a full noble knyght.'

And anone sir Trystram asked his armys, and whan he was armed
he toke his horse and two squyars wyth hym and rode a grete pace 25
thorow a foreyste aftir sir Palomydes, the nexte way unto the castell
Pelownes where sir Palomydes was jowged to his dethe.

And as the twelve knyghtes lad hym byfore them, there was the
noble knyght sir Launcelot whyche was alyght by a welle, and had
tyed hys horse tyll a tre, and had takyn of hys helme to drynke of that 30
welle. And whan he sawe suche a route whyche semed knyghtes, sir
Launcelot put on his helme and suffyrd them to passe by hym; and
anone he was ware of sir Palomydes bounden and lad shamfully towarde his dethe.

'A, Jesu!' seyde sir Launcelot, 'what mysseadventure ys befallyn 35
hym that he ys thus lad towarde hys dethe? Yet, pardeus,' seyde sir
Launcelot, 'hit were shame to me to suffir this noble knyght thus to
dye and I myght helpe hym. And therefore I woll helpe hym whatsomever com of hit, other ellys I shall dye for hys sake!'

And than sir Launcelot mounted on hys horse and gate hys speare in 40
hys honde and rode aftyr the twelve knyghtes whyche lad sir Palomydes.

'Fayre knyghtes,' seyde sir Launcelot, 'whother lede ye that knyght?
For hit besemyth hym full evyll to ryde bounden.'

Than thes twelve knyghtes returned suddeynly there horsis and seyde to sir Launcelot,

'Sir knyght, we counceyle you nat to meddyll of this knyght, for he hath deserved deth, and unto deth he ys jouged.'

5 'That me repentyth,' seyde sir Launcelot, 'that I may nat borow hym wyth fayrenes, for he ys over good a knyght to dye such a shamefull dethe. And therefore, fayre knyghtes,' seyde sir Launcelot, 'than kepe you as well as ye can! For I woll rescow that knyght, othir ellys dye for hit.'

10 Than they began to dresse there spearys, and sir Launcelot smote the formyste downe, horse and man, and so he served three mo wyth one spere. And than that speare braste, and therewythall sir Launcelot drewe his swerde, and than he smote on the ryght honde and on the lyffte honde. And so wythin a whyle he leffte none of tho knyghtes, but 15 he had leyde them to the erthe, and the moste party of them were sore wounded.

And than sir Launcelot toke the beste horse and lowsed sir Palomydes and sette hym uppon that horse, and so they returned agayne unto Joyus Garde.

20 And than was sir Palomydes ware of sir Trystram how he cam rydynge. And whan sir Launcelot sy hym he knew hym well; but sir Trystram knew nat hym, because he had on his shuldir a gylden shylde. So sir Launcelot made hym redy to juste wyth sir Trystram, because he sholde nat wene that he were sir Launcelot. Than sir Palomydes cryed 25 on lowde to sir Trystram and seyde,

'A, my lorde! I requyre you, juste nat wyth this knyght, for he hath saved me frome my dethe.'

Whan sir Trystram harde hym sey so he cam a soffte trottynge pace towarde hym. And than sir Palomydes seyde,

30 'My lorde, sir Trystram, muche am I beholdynge unto you of youre grete goodnes, that wolde proffir youre noble body to rescow me undeserved, for I have greatly offended you. Natwythstondynge,' seyde sir Palomydes, 'here mette we wyth this noble knyght that worshypfully and manly rescowed me frome twelve knyghtes, and smote them 35 downe all and sore wounded hem.'

(86) 'Fayre knyght,' seyde sir Trystram unto sir Launcelot, 'of whens be ye?'

'I am a knyght arraunte,' seyde sir Launcelot, 'that rydyth to seke many dedis.'

'Sir, what ys youre name?' seyde sir Trystram.

40 'Sir, as at this tyme I woll nat telle you.' Than sir Launcelot seyde unto sir Trystram and to sir Palomydes, 'Now ar ye mette togydirs aythir wyth other, and now I woll departe frome you.'

'Nat so,' seyde sir Trystram, 'I pray you and requyre you of knyghthod to ryde wyth me unto my castell.'

'Wyte you well,' seyde sir Launcelot, 'I may nat ryde wyth you, for I have many dedis to do in other placys, that at this tyme I may nat abyde wyth you.'

'A, mercy Jesu!' seyde sir Trystram, 'I requyre you, as ye be a trewe knyght to the Order of Knyghthode, play you wyth me this nyght.'   5

Than sir Trystram had a graunte of sir Launcelot; howbehit, thoughe he had nat desyred hym, he wolde have rydden with hem, other sone a com aftir hym. For sir Launcelot cam for none other cause into that contrey but for to se sir Trystram.

And whan they were com wythin Joyus Garde they alyght, and there   10
horsis were lad into a stable, and than they unarmed them. For sir Launcclot, as sone as his helme was of, sir Trystram and sir Palomydes knew hym. Than sir Trystram toke sir Launcelot in his armys, and so ded La Beall Isode, and sir Palomydes kneled downe uppon his kneis and thanked sir Launcelot. And whan he sawe sir Palomydes knele he   15
lyghtly toke hym up and seyde thus:

'Wyte thou well, sir Palomydes, that I, and ony knyght in this londe of worshyp, muste of verry ryght succoure and rescow so noble a knyght as ye ar preved and renowmed thorougheoute all this realme, enlonge and overtwarte.'   20

Than was there grete joy amonge them. And the ofter that sir Palomydes saw La Beall Isode, the hevyar he waxed day be day.

Than sir Launcelot wythin three or four dayes departed, and wyth hym rode sir Ector de Marys and sir Dynadan, and sir Palomydes was leffte there wyth sir Trystram a two monethis and more. But ever sir   25
Palomydes faded and mourned, that all men had merveyle whercfore he faded so away.

So uppon a day, in the dawnynge, sir Palomydes wente into the foreste by hymselff alone; and there he founde a welle, and anone he loked into the well and in the watir he sawe his owne vysayge, how he   30
was discolowred and defaded, a nothynge lyke as he was.

'Lorde Jesu, what may this meane?' seyde sir Palomydes. And thus he seyde to hymselff: 'A, Palomydes, Palomydes! Why arte thou thus defaded, and ever was wonte to be called one of the fayrest knyghtes of [the] worlde? Forsothe, I woll no more lyve this lyff, for I love that I   35
may never gete nor recover.'

And therewythall he leyde hym downe by the welle, and so began to make a ryme of La Beall Isode and of sir Trystram. And so in the meanewhyle sir Trystram was ryddyn into the same foreyste to chace an harte of grece; but sir Trystram wolde nat ryde an huntynge never-   40
more unarmed bycause of sir Brewnys Saunze Pité. And so sir Trystram rode into the foreyste up and downe, and as he rode he harde one synge mervaylowsly lowde; and that was sir Palomydes whyche lay by the welle.

And than sir Trystram rode sofftly thydir, for he demed that there was som knyght arraunte whyche was at the welle. And whan sir Trystram cam nyghe he descended downe frome hys horse and tyed his horse faste tyll a tre. And so he cam nere on foote, and sone aftir he was
5 ware where lay sir Palomydes by the welle and sange lowde and myryly. And ever the complayntys were of La Beall Isode, whyche was mervaylously well seyde, and pyteuously and full dolefully ⌐made⌐. And all the hole songe sir Trystram harde worde by worde, and whan he had herde all sir Palomydes complaynte, he was wrothe oute of mesure, and
10 thought for to sle hym thereas he lay.

Than sir Trystram remembyrde hymselff that sir Palomydes was unarmed, and of so noble a name that sir Palomydes had, and also the noble name that hymselff had. Than he made a restraynte of his angir, and so he wente unto sir Palomydes a soffte pace and seyde,
15 'Sir Palomydes, I have harde youre complay[n]te and of youre treson that ye have owed me longe, and wyte you well, therefore ye shall dye! And yf hit were nat for shame of knyghthode thou sholdyst nat ascape my hondys, for now I know well thou haste awayted me wyth treson. And therefore,' seyde sir Trystram, 'tell me how thou wolt acquyte
20 the.'

'Sir, I shall acquyte me thus: as for quene La Beall Isode, thou shalt wyte that I love her abovyn all other ladyes in this worlde, and well I wote hit shall befalle by me as for her love as befelle on the noble knyght sir Kayhydyns that dyed for the love of La Beall Isode. And
25 now, sir Trystram, I woll that ye wyte that I have loved La Beall Isode many a longe day, and she hath bene the causer of my worshyp. And ellys I had bene the moste symplyste knyght in the worlde, for by her, and bycause of her, I have wonne the worshyp that I have; for whan I remembred me of quene Isode I wanne the worshyp wheresomever I
30 cam, for the moste party. And yet I had never rewarde nother bounté of her dayes of my lyff, and yet I have bene her knyght longe gwardonles. And therefore, sir Trystram, as for ony dethe I drede nat, for I had as lyeff dye as lyve. And yf I were armed as ye ar, I shulde lyghtly do batayle with the.'
35 'Sir, well have ye uttyrd youre treson,' seyde sir Trystram.

'Sir, I have done to you no treson,' seyde sir Palomydes, 'for love is fre for all men, and thoughe I have loved your lady, she ys my lady as well as youres. Howbehyt that I have wronge, if ony wronge be, for ye rejoyse her and have youre desyre of her; and so had I nevir, nor never
40 [am] lyke to have, and yet shall I love her to the uttermuste dayes of my lyff as well as ye.'

(87) Than seyde sir Trystram, 'I woll fyght with you to the utteryste!'

'I graunte,' seyde sir Palomydes, 'for in a bettir quarell kepe I never to fyght. For and I dye off youre hondis, of a bettir knyghtes hondys myght I never be slayne. And sytthyn I undirstonde that I shall never rejoyse La Beall Isode, I have as good wyll to dye as to lyve.'

'Tha[n] sette ye a day,' seyde sir Trystram, 'that we shall do batayle.'

'Sir, this day fyftene dayes,' seyde sir Palomydes, 'I woll mete with you hereby, in the medow undir Joyus Garde.'   5

'Now fye for shame!' seyde sir Trystram. 'Woll ye sette so longe a day? Lat us fyght to-morne.'

'Nat so,' seyde sir Palomydes, 'for I am megir, and have bene longe syke for the love of La Beall Isode. And therefore I woll repose me tyll I have my strengthe agayne.'   10

So than sir Trystram and sir Palomydes promysed faythefully to mete at the welle that day fyftene dayes.

'But now I am remembred,' seyde sir Trystram to sir Palomydes, 'that ye brake me onys a promyse whan that I rescowed you frome sir Brewnys Saunze Pité and nyne knyghtes. And than ye promysed to   15
mete me at the perowne and the grave besydis Camelot, whereas that tyme ye fayled of youre promyse.'

'Wyte you well,' seyde sir Palomydes unto sir Trystram, 'I was at that day in preson, that I myght nat holde my promyse. But wyte you well,' seyde sir Palomydes, 'I shall promyse you now and kepe   20
hit.'

'So God me helpe,' seyde sir Trystram, 'and ye had holden youre promyse this worke had nat bene here now at this tyme.'

Ryght so departed sir Trystram and sir Palomydes. And so sir Palomydes toke his horse and hys harneys, and so he rode unto kynge   25
Arthurs courte. And there he gate hym four knyghtes and four sargeauntes of armys, and so he returned agayne unto Joyus Garde.

And so in the meanewhyle sir Trystram chaced and hunted at all maner of venery. And aboute three dayes afore the batayle that shulde be, as sir Trystram chaced an harte, there was an archer shotte at the   30
harte, and by mysfortune he smote sir Trystram in the thyk of the thyghe, and the same arrow slew sir Trystrams horse undir hym.

Whan sir Trystram was so hurte he was passynge hevy; and wyte you well he bled passynge sore. And than he toke another horse and rode unto Joyus Garde with grete hevynes, more for the promyse that he had   35
made unto sir Palomydes to do batayle with hym wythin three dayes aftir [than for ony hurte]. Wherefore there was nother man nother woman that coude chere hym [wyth onythynge that they coude make to hym], for ever he demed that sir Palomydes had smytten hym so, because he sholde nat be able to do batayle with hym at the day   40
appoynted. But in no wyse there was no knyght aboute sir Trystram   (88)
that wolde belyeve that sir Palomydes wolde hurte hym, nother by his owne hondis nothir by none other consentynge.

And so whan the fyftenth day was com sir Palomydes cam to the

welle wyth four knyghtes wyth hym of kynge Arthurs courte and three
sargeauntes of armys. And for this entente sir Palomydes brought tho
knyght[es] with hym and the sargeauntes of armys, for they sholde
beare recorde of the batayle betwyxt sir Trystram and hym. And one
5 sargeaunte brought in his helme, and the tother his speare, and the
thirde his swerde. So sir Palomydes cam into the fylde and there he
abode nyghe two owres, and than he sente a squyar unto sir Trystram
and desyred hym to com into the fylde to holde his promyse.

Whan the squyar was com unto Joyus Garde, anone as sir Trystram
10 harde of his commynge he commaunded that the squyar shulde com to
his presence thereas he lay in his bedde.

'My lorde sir Trystram,' seyde sir Palomydes squyar, 'wyte you well,
my lorde sir Palomydes abydyth you in the fylde, and he wolde wyte
whether ye wolde do batayle or nat.'

15   'A, my fayre brother,' seyde sir Trystram, 'wyte you well that I am
ryght hevy for this tydyngis. But telle youre lorde sir Palomydes, and I
were well at ease, I wolde nat lye here, nothir he sholde have had no
nede to sende for me and I myght othir ryde or go. And for thou shalt
se that I am no lyar'—sir Trystram shewed hym his thyghe, and the
20 depnes of the wounde was syx inchis depe. 'And now thou haste sene
my hurte, telle thy lorde that this is no fayned mater, and tell hym that
I had levir than all the golde that kynge Arthure hath that I were hole.
And lat hym wyte that as for me, as sone as I may ryde I shall seke hym
endelonge and overtwarte this londe; and that I promyse you as I am a
25 trew knyght. And yf ever I may mete hym, telle youre lorde sir Palomydes he shall have of me hys fylle of batayle.'

And so the squyar departed. And whan sir Palomydes knew that sir
Trystram was hurte, than he seyde thus:

'Truly, I am glad of his hurte, and for this cause: for now I am sure
30 I shall have no shame. For I wote well, and we had medled, I sholde
have had harde handelynge of hym, and by lyklyhode I muste nedys
have had the worse. For he is the hardyeste knyght in batayle that
now ys lyvynge excepte sir Launcelot.'

And than departed sir Palomydes whereas fortune lad hym. And
35 within a moneth sir Trystram was hole of his hurte, and than he toke
hys horse and rode frome contrey to contrey, and all straunge adventures he encheved wheresomever he rode. And allwayes he enquyred
for sir Palomydes, but off all that quarter of somer sir Trystram coude
never mete with sir Palomydes.

40   But thus as sir Trystram soughte and enquyred aftir sir Palomydes,
sir Trystram enchevyd many grete batayles, wherethorow all the
noyse and brewte felle to sir Trystram, and the name ceased of sir
Launcelot. And therefore sir Launcelottis bretherne and his kynnysmen wolde have slayne sir Trystram bycause of his fame. But whan sir

Launcelot wyste how hys kynnysmen were sette, he seyde to them
opynly,

'Wyte you well that and ony of you all be so hardy to wayte my lorde
sir Trystram wyth ony hurte, shame, or vylany, as I am trew knyght, I
shall sle the beste of you all myne owne hondis. Alas, fye for shame, 5
sholde ye for his noble dedys awayte to sle hym! Jesu defende,' seyde
sir Launcelot, 'that ever ony noble knyght as sir Trystram ys sholde be
destroyed wyth treson.'

So of this noyse and fame sprange into Cornwayle and unto them of
Lyones, whereof they were passynge glad and made grete joy. And 10
than they of Lyones sente lettyrs unto sir Trystram of recommendacion,
and many greate gyfftys to mayntcne sir Trystrams astate. And ever
betwene sir Trystram resorted unto Joyus Garde whereas La Beall
Isode was, that lovid hym ever.

XIV. LAUNCELOT AND ELAINE   15

As the booke of Frenshe makyth mencion, afore the tyme that sir
Galahad was begotyn or borne, there cam in an ermyte unto kynge 20
Arthure uppon Whitsonday, as the knyghtes sate at the Table Rounde.
And whan the ermyte saw the Syege Perelous he asked the kynge and
all the knyghtes why that syege was voyde. Than kynge Arthure for all
the knyghtes answerde and seyde.

'There shall never none sytte in that syege but onc, but if he be 25
destroyed.'

Than seyde the ermyte, 'Sir, wote ye what he ys?'

'Nay,' seyde kynge Arthure and all the knyghtes, 'we know nat who
he ys yet that shall sytte there.'

'Than wote I,' seyde the ermyte. 'For he that shall sytte there ys yet 30
unborne and unbcgotyn, and this same yere he shall be bygotyn that
shall sytte in that Syege Perelous, and he shall wynne the Sankgreall.'
Whan this ermyte had made this mencion he departed frome the courte
of kynge Arthure.

And so aftir this feste sir Laucelot rode on his adventure tyll on a 35
tyme by adventure he paste over the Pounte de Corbyn. And there he
saw the fayryste towre that ever he saw, and thereundir was a fayre
lytyll towne full of people. And all the people, men and women, cryed
at onys,

'Wellcom, sir Launcelot, the floure of knyghthode! For by the we
shall be holpyn oute of daungere!'

'What meane ye,' seyde sir Launcelot, 'that ye cry thus uppon me?'

'A, fayre knyght,' seyde they all, 'here is wythin this towre a
5 dolerous lady that hath bene there in paynes many wyntyrs and dayes,
for ever she boyleth in scaldynge watir. And but late,' seyde all the
people, 'sir Gawayne was here, and he myght nat helpe her, and so he
leffte her in payne stylle.'

'Peradventure so may I,' seyde sir Launcelot, 'leve her in payne as
10 well as sir Gawayne.'

'Nay,' seyde the people, 'we know well that hit y[s] ye, sir Launcelot,
that shall delyver her.'

'Well,' seyde sir Launcelot, 'than telle me what I shall do.'

And so anone they brought sir Launcelot into the towre. And whan
15 he cam to the chambir thereas this lady was, the doorys of iron un-
loked and unbolted, and so sir Launcelot wente into the chambir that
was as hote as ony styew. And there sir Launcelot toke the fayryst lady
by the honde that ever he sawe, and she was as naked as a nedyll. And
by enchauntemente quene Morgan le Fay and the quene of Northe
20 Galys had put her there in that paynes, bycause she was called the
fayryst lady of that contrey; and there she had bene fyve yere, and never
myght she be delyverde oute of her paynes unto the tyme the beste
knyght of the worlde had takyn her by the honde.

Than the people brought her clothis, and whan sche was arayed sir
25 Launcelot thought she was the fayryst lady that ever he saw but yf hit
were quene Gwenyver. Than this lady seyde to sir Launcelot,

'Sir, if hit please you, woll ye go wyth me hereby into a chapel, that
we may gyff lovynge to God?'

'Madame,' seyde sir Launcelot, 'commyth on wyth me, and I woll
30 go with you.'

So whan they cam there they gaff thankynges to God, all the people
bothe lerned and lewde, and seyde,

'Sir knyght, syn ye have delyverde this lady ye muste delyver us also
frome a serpente whyche ys here in a tombe.'

35 Than sir Launcelot toke hys shylde and seyde,

'Sirrys, brynge me thydir, and what that I may do to the plesure of
God and of you I shall do.'

So whan sir Launcelot com thydir he saw wrytten uppon the tombe
wyth lettyrs of golde that seyde thus:

40 'HERE SHALL COM A LYBARDE OF KYNGES BLOOD AND HE SHALL SLE
THIS SERPENTE. AND THIS LYBARDE SHALL ENGENDIR A LYON IN THIS
FORAYNE CONTREY WHYCHE LYON SHALL PASSE ALL OTHER KNYGHTES.'

Soo whan sir Launcelot had lyffte up the tombe there came oute an
orryble and a fyendely dragon spyttynge wylde fyre oute of hys

mowthe. Than sir Launcelotte drew his swerde and faught wyth that
dragon longe, and at the laste wyth grete payne sir Launcelot slew
that dragon.

And therewythall com kynge Pelles, the good and noble kynge, and
salewed sir Launcelot and he hym agayne.   5

'Now, fayre knyght,' seyde the kynge, 'what is youre name? I requyre you of youre knyghthode telle ye me.'

'Sir,' seyde sir Launcelot, 'wyte you well my name ys sir Launcelot (2)
du Lake.'

'And my name ys kynge Pelles, kynge of the forayne contré and   10
cousyn nyghe unto Joseph of Aramathy.'

And than aythir of them made muche of othir, and so they wente
into the castell to take there repaste. And anone there cam in a dove at
a wyndow, and in her mowthe there semed a lytyll ⌐senser¬ of golde,
and therewythall there was suche a savour as all the spycery of the   15
worlde had bene there. And furthwythall there was uppon the table
all maner of meates and drynkes that they coude thynke uppon.

So there came in a damesell passynge fayre and yonge, and she bare
a vessell of golde betwyxt her hondis; and thereto the kynge kneled
devoutly and seyde his prayers, and so ded all that were there.   20

'A, Jesu!' seyde sir Launcelot, 'what may this meane?'

'Sir,' seyde the kynge, 'this is the rychyst thynge that ony man hath
lyvynge, and whan this thynge gothe abrode the Rounde Table shall be
brokyn for a season. And wyte you well,' seyde the kynge, 'this is the
Holy Sankgreall that ye have here seyne.'   25

So the kynge and sir Launcelot lad there lyff the moste party of that
day togydir. And fayne wolde kynge Pelles have found the meane that
sir Launcelot sholde have ley by his doughter, fayre Eleyne, and for this
entente: the kynge knew well that sir Launcelot shulde gete a pusyll
uppon his doughtir, whyche shulde be called sir Galahad, the good   30
knyght by whom all the forayne cuntrey shulde be brought oute of
daunger; and by hym the Holy Grayle sholde be encheved.

Than cam furth a lady that hyght dame Brusen, and she seyde unto
the kynge,

'Sir, wyte you well sir Launcelot lovyth no lady in the worlde but   35
all only quene Gwenyver. And therefore worche ye be my counceyle,
and I shall make hym to lye wyth youre doughter, and he shall nat wyte
but that he lyeth by quene Gwenyver.'

'A, fayre lady,' sayde the kynge, 'hope ye that ye may brynge this
mater aboute?'   40

'Sir,' seyde she, 'uppon payne of my lyff, latte me deale.'

For thys dame Brusen was one of the grettyst enchaunters that was
that tyme in the worlde.

And so anone by dame Brusens wytte she made one to com to sir

Launcelot that he knew well, and this man brought a rynge frome
quene Gwenyver lyke as hit had com frome her, [and suche one as she
was wonte for the moste parte to were]. And whan sir Launcelot saw
that tokyn, wyte you well he was never so fayne.

5 'Where is my lady?' seyde sir Launcelot.

'In the castell of Case,' seyde the messyngere, 'but fyve myle hens.'

Than thought sir Launcelot to be there the same nyght. And than
this dame Brusen, by the commaundemente of kynge Pelles, ⟨s⟩he
let sende Elayne to this castell wyth fyve and twenty knyghtes, unto
10 the castell of Case.

Than sir Launcelot ayenst nyght rode unto the castell, and there
anone he was receyved worshypfully wyth suche people, to his semynge,
as were aboute quene Gwenyver secrete. So whan sir Launcelot was
alyght he asked where the quene was. So dame Brusen seyde she was in
15 her bed.

And than people were avoyded and sir Launcelot was lad into her
chambir. And than dame Brusen brought sir Launcelot a kuppe of
wyne, and anone as he had drunken that wyne he was so asoted and
madde that he myght make no delay but wythoute ony let he wente
20 to bedde. And so he wente that mayden Elayne had bene quene
Gwenyver. And wyte you well that sir Launcelot was glad, and so was
that lady Eleyne that she had gotyn sir Launcelot in her armys, for well
she knew that that same nyght sholde be bygotyn sir Galahad uppon
her, that sholde preve the beste knyght of the worlde.

25 And so they lay togydir untyll underne of the morne; and all the
wyndowys and holys of that chambir were stopped, that no maner of
day myght be seyne. And anone sir Launcelot remembryd hym and
(3) arose up and wente to the wyndow, and anone as he had unshutte the
wyndow the enchauntemente was paste. Than he knew hymselff that
30 he had done amysse.

'Alas!' he seyde, 'that I have lʳyˡved so longe, for now am I shamed.'

And anone he gate his swerde in his honde and seyde,

'Thou traytoures! What arte thou that I have layne bye all this
nyght? Thou shalt dye ryght here of myne hondys!'

35 Than this fayre lady Elayne skypped oute of her bedde all naked and
[kneled downe afore sir Launcelot and] seyde,

'Fayre curteyse knyght sir Launcelot,' knelynge byfore hym, 'ye
ar comyn of kynges bloode, and therefore I requyre you have mercy
uppon me! And as thou arte renowmed the moste noble knyght of the
40 worlde, sle me nat, for I have in my wombe bygetyn of the that shall
be the moste nobelyste knyght of the worlde.'

'A, false traytoures! Why haste thou betrayed me? Telle me anone,'
seyde sir Launcelot, 'what thou arte.'

'Sir,' she seyde, 'I am Elayne, the doughter of kynge Pelles.'

'Well,' seyde sir Launcelot, 'I woll forgyff you.'

And therewyth he toke her up in his armys and kyssed her, for she was a fayre lady and thereto lusty and yonge, and wyse as ony was that tyme lyvynge.

'So God me helpe,' seyde sir Launcelot, 'I may nat wyte [thys to] you; but her that made thys enchauntemente uppon me and betwene you and me, and I may fynde her, that same lady dame Brusen shall lose her hede for her wycchecrauftys, for there was never knyght disceyved as I am this nyght.'

And than she seyde, 'My lorde, sir Launcelot, I beseche you, se me as sone as ye may, for I have obeyde me unto the prophesye that my fadir tolde me. And by hys commaundemente to fullfyll this prophecie I have gyvyn the the grettyst ryches and the fayryst floure that ever I had, and that is my maydynhode that I shall never have agayne. And therefore, jantyll knyght, owghe me youre good wyll.'

And so sir Launcelot arayed hym and armed hym and toke hys leve myldely at that yonge lady Eleyne. And so he departed and rode to the castell of Corbyn where her fadir was.

And as faste as her tyme cam she was delyverde of a fayre chylde, and they crystynd hym Galahad. And wyte yow well that chylde was well kepte and well norysshed, and he was so named Galahad bycause sir Launcelot was so named at the fountayne stone (and aftir that the Lady of the Lake confermed hym sir Launcelot du Lake).

Than aftir the lady was delyverde and churched, there cam a knyght unto her, hys name was sir Bromell la Pleche, the whyche was a grete lorde. And he had loved that lady Eleyne longe, and he evermore desyred to wedde her. And so by no meane she coude put hym off, tylle on a day she seyde to sir Bromell,

'Wyte you well, sir knyght, I woll nat love you, for my love ys sette uppon the beste knyght of the worlde.'

'Who ys that?' seyde sir Bromell.

'Sir,' she seyde, 'hit ys sir Launcelot du Lake that I love and none other, and therefore wowe ye me no lenger.'

'Ye sey well,' seyde sir Bromell, 'and sythyn ye have tolde me so muche ye shall have lytyll joy of sir Launcelot, for I shall sle hym wheresomever I mete hym!'

'Sir,' seyde this lady Elayne, 'do to hym no treson, and God forbede that ye spare hym.'

'Well, my lady,' seyde sir Bromell, 'and I shall promyse you this twelve-monthe ⟨and a⟩ day I shall kepe Le Pounte Corbyn for sir Launcelot sake, that he shall nothir com nother go unto you but I shall mete wyth hym.'

Than as hit fell by fortune and adventure, sir Bors de Ganys that was nevew unto sir Launcelot com over that brydge; and there sir Bromell and sir Bors justed, and sir Bors smote sir Bromell suche a buffette that he bare hym over his horse croupe.

And than sir Bromell, as an hardy man, pulled oute his swerde and dressed hys shylde to do batayle wyth sir Bors. And anone sir Bors
5 alyght and voyded his horse, and there they daysshed togydyrs many sad strokys. And longe thus they faught, and at the laste sir Bromell was leyde to the erthe, and there sir Bors began to unlace his helme to sle hym. Than sir Bromell cryed hym mercy and yeldyd hym.

'Uppon this covenaunte thou shalt have thy lyff,' seyde sir Bors, 'so
10 thou go unto my lorde sir Launcelot uppon Whytsonday nexte commynge and yelde the unto hym as a knyght recreaunte.'

'Sir, I woll do hit,' seyde sir Bromell.

And so he sware uppon the crosse of the swerde, and so he lete hym departe. And sir Bors rode unto kynge Pelles that was wythin Corbyne,
15 and whan the kynge and Elayne, hys doughter, knew that sir Bors was nevew unto sir Launcelot they made hym grete chere. Than seyde dame Elayne,

'We mervayle where sir Launcelot ys, for he cam never here but onys that ever I sawe.'

20 'Madame, mervayle ye nat,' seyde sir Bors, 'for this halff yere he hath bene in preson wyth quene Morgan le Fay, kynge Arthurs systir.'

'Alas,' seyde dame Eleyne, 'that me sore repentyth!'

And ever sir Bors behylde that chylde in her armys, and ever hym semed hit was passynge lyke sir Launcelot.

25 'Truly,' seyde dame Elayne, 'wyte you well, this chylde he begate uppon me.'

Than sir Bors wept for joy, and there he prayde to God that hit myght preve as good a knyght as hys fadir was.

And so there cam in a whyght dowve, and she bare a lytyll sensar
30 of golde in her mowthe, and there was all maner of metys and drynkis. And a mayden bare that Sankgreall, and she seyde there opynly,

'Wyte you well, sir Bors, that this chylde, sir Galahad, shall sytte in the Syege Perelous and enchyve the Sankgreall, and he shall be muche bettir than ever was his fadir, sir Launcelot, that ys hys owne
35 fadir.'

And than they kneled adowne and made there devocions, and there was suche a savoure as all the spycery in the worlde had bene there. And as the dowve had takyn her flyght the mayden vanysshed wyth the Sankgreall as she cam.

40 'Sir,' seyde sir Bors than unto kynge Pelles, 'this castell may be named the Castell Adventures, for here be many stronge adventures.'

'That is sothe,' seyde the kynge, 'for well may thys place be called the adventures place. For there com but feaw knyghtes here that goth away wyth ony worshyppe; be he never so stronge, here he may be

preved. And but late ago sir Gawayne, the good knyght, gate lytyll
worshyp here. For I lat you wyte,' seyde kynge Pelles, 'here shall no
knyght wynne worshyp but yf he be of worshyp hymselff and of good
lyvynge, and that lovyth God and dredyth God. And ellys he getyth
no worshyp here, be he never so hardy a man.'   5

'That is a wondir thynge,' seyde sir Bors, 'what ye meane in thys
contrey, for ye have many straunge adventures. And therefore woll I
lye in thys castell thys nyght.'

'Sir, ye shall nat do so,' seyde kynge Pelles, 'be my counceyle, for
hit ys harde and ye ascape wythoute a shame.'   10

'Sir, I shall take the adventure that woll fall,' seyde sir Bors.

'Than I counceyle you,' seyde the kynge, 'to be clene confessed.'

'As for that,' seyde sir Bors, 'I woll be shryvyn wyth a good wyll.'

So sir Bors was confessed. And for all women sir Bors was a vergyne
sauff for one, that was the doughter of kynge Braundegorys, and on her   15
he gate a chylde whyche hyght Elayne. And sauff for her sir Bors was a
clene mayden.

And so sir Bors was lad unto bed in a fayre large chambir, and many
durres were shutte aboute the chambir. Whan sir Bors had aspyde all
tho durrys he avoyded all the people, for he myght have nobody   20
wyth hym. But in no wyse sir Bors wolde unarme hym, but so he
leyde hym downe uppon the bed.

And ryght so he saw a lyght com, that he myght well se a speare
grete and longe that cam streyte uppon hym poyntelynge, and sir
Boors semed that the hede of the speare brente lyke a tapir. And anone,   25
or sir Bors wyste, the speare smote hym in the shuldir an haunde-brede
in depnes, and that wounde grevid sir Boors passyng sore, and than
he layde hym downe for payne.

And anone therewythall cam a knyght armed wyth hys shylde on
hys shuldir and hys swerde in hys honde, and he bade sir Bors, 'Aryse,   30
sir knyght, a[nd] fyght wyth me!'

'I am sore hurte, but yet I shall nat fayle the!'

And than sir Bors sterte up and dressed his shylde, and than they
laysshed togydyrs myghtyly a grete whyle; and at the laste sir Bors
bare hym bakwarde tyll that he cam to a chambir dore, and there that   35
knyght yode into that chambir and rested hym a grete whyle. And whan
he had reposed hym he cam oute fyersly agayne and began new
batayle wyth sir Bors myghtyly and strongely. Than sir Bors thought   (5)
he sholde no more go into that chambir to reste hym, and so sir Bors
dressed hym betwyxte the knyght and the chambir dore. And there sir   40
Bors smote hym downe, and than that knyght yelded hym.

'What ys youre name?' seyde sir Bors.

'Sir, my name ys sir Bedyvere of the Streyte Marchys.'

So sir Bors made hym to swere at Whytsonday nexte commynge to com to the courte of kynge Arthure, 'and yelde you there as presonere and as an overcom knyght by the hondys of sir Bors.'

So thus departed sir Bedyvere of the Strayte Marche. And than sir Bors layde hym downe to reste. And anone he harde muche noyse in that chambir, and than sir Bors aspyed that there cam in, he wyst nat whethir at durrys or at wyndowys, shotte of arowys and of quarellys so thyk that he mervayled, and many felle uppon hym and hurte hym in the bare placys.

And than sir Bors was ware where cam in an hedyous lyon. So sir Bors dressed hym to that lyon, and anone the lyon beraufte hym hys shylde, and with hys swerde sir Bors smote of the lyons hede.

Ryght so furthwythall he sawe a dragon in the courte, passynge parelous and orryble, and there semyd to hym that there were lettyrs off golde wryttyn in hys forhede, and sir Bors thought that the lettyrs made a sygnyfycacion of 'kynge Arthure'. And ryght so there cam an orryble lybarde and an olde, and there they faught longe and ded grete batayle togydyrs. And at the laste the dragon spytte oute of hys mowthe as hit had bene an hondred dragons; and lyghtly all the smale dragons slew the olde dragon and tore hym all to pecys.

And anone furthwythall there cam an olde man into the halle, and he sette hym downe in a fayre chayre, and there semed to be two addirs aboute hys nek. And than the olde man had an harpe, and there he sange an olde lay of Joseph of Aramathy how he cam into this londe. And whan he had sungen this olde man bade sir Bors go frome thens, 'for here shall ye have no mo adventures; yet full worshypfully have ye encheved this, and bettir shall ye do hyreaftir'.

And than sir Bors semed that there cam the whyghtyst dowve that ever he saw, wyth a lytyll goldyn sensar in her mowthe. And anone therewythall the tempeste ceased and passed away that afore was mervaylous to hyre. So was all that courte full of good savoures.

Than sir Bors saw four fayre chyldren berynge four fayre tapirs, and an olde man in the myddys of this chyldyrn wyth a sensar in hys one honde and a speare in hys othir honde, and that speare was called the Speare of Vengeaunce.

(6) 35   'Now,' seyde that olde man to sir Bors, 'go ye to youre cousyn sir Launcelot and telle hym this adventure had be moste convenyent for hym of all earthely knyghtes, but synne ys so foule in hym that he may nat enchyve none suche holy dedys; for had nat bene hys synne, he had paste all the knyghtes that ever were in hys dayes. And telle thou sir Launcelot, of all worldly adventures he passyth in manhode and proues all othir, but in this spyrytuall maters he shall have many hys bettyrs.'

And than sir Bors sawe four jantyllwomen com by hym, pourely beseyne: and he saw where that they entirde into a chambir where was

grete lyght as hit were a somers lyght. And the women kneled downe
before an auter of sylver wyth four pyloures, as hit had bene a bysshop
whyche kneled afore the table of ⌐sylver⌐. And as sir Bors loked over
hys hede he saw a swerde lyke sylver, naked, hovynge over hys hede,
and [the] clyernes thereof smote in hys yghen, that as at that tyme sir 5
Bors was blynde.

And there he harde a voyce whyche seyde, 'Go hens, thou sir Bors,
for as yet thou arte nat worthy for [to] be in thys place!' And than he
yode bakwarde tylle hys bedde tylle on the morne.

And so on the morne kyng Pelles made grete joy of sir Bors, and 10
than he departed and rode unto Camelot. And there he founde sir
Launcelot and tolde hym of the adventures that he had sene wyth
kynge Pelles at Corbyn.

And so the noyse sprange in kynge Arthurs [courte] that sir Launcelot had gotyn a chylde uppon Elayne, the doughter of kynge Pelles, 15
wherefore quene Gwenyver was wrothe, and she gaff many rebukes to
sir Launcelot and called hym false knyght. And than sir Launcelot tolde
the quene all, and how he was made to lye by her, 'in the lyknes of you,
my lady the quene'; and so the quene hylde sir Launcelot exkused.

And as the booke seythe, kynge Arthure had bene in Fraunce and 20
hadde warred uppon the myghty kynge Claudas and had wonne
muche of hys londys. And whan the kynge was com agayne he lete
cry a grete feste, that all lordys and ladyes of all Ingelonde shulde be
there but yf hit were suche as were rebellyous agaynste hym.

And whan dame Elayne, the doughter of kynge Pelles, harde of 25 (7)
thys feste she yode to her fadir and requyred hym that he wolde gyff her
leve to ryde to that feste. The kynge answerde and seyde,

'I woll that ye go thydir. But in ony wyse, as ye love me and woll have
my blyssynge, loke that ye be well beseyne in the moste rychest wyse,
and loke that ye spare nat for no coste. Aske and ye shall have all 30
that nedyth unto you.'

Than by the advyce of dame Brusen, her mayden, all thynge was
appareyled unto the purpose, that there was never no lady rychelyar
beseyne. So she rode wyth twenty knyghtes and ten ladyes and jantyllwomen, to the numbir of an hondred horse. And whan she cam to 35
Camelott kynge Arthure and quene Gwenyver seyde wyth all the
knyghtes that dame Elayne was ⌐the fayrest and⌐ the beste beseyne
lady that ever was seyne in that courte.

And anone as kynge Arthure wyste that she was com he mette her and
salewed her, and so ded the moste party of all the knyghtes of the 40
Rounde Table, both sir Trystram, sir Bleoberys and sir Gawayne, and
many mo that I woll nat reherse.

But whan sir Launcelot sye her he was so ashamed, [and] that bycause
he drew hys swerde to her on the morne aftir that he had layne by her,

that he wolde nat salewe her nother speke wyth her. And yet sir
Launcelot thought that she was the fayrest woman that ever he sye in
his lyeff dayes.

But whan dame Elayne saw sir Launcelot wolde nat speke unto her
5 she was so hevy she wente her harte wolde have to-braste; for wyte you
well, oute of mesure she loved hym. And than dame Elayne seyde unto
her woman, dame Brusen,

'The unkyndenes of sir Launcelot sleyth myne harte nere!'

'A! peas, madame,' seyde dame Brusen, 'I shall undirtake that this
10 nyght he shall lye wyth you, and ye woll holde you stylle.'

'That were me lever,' seyde dame Elayne, 'than all the golde that
ys abovyn erthe.'

'Lat me deale,' seyde dame Brewsen.

So whan dame Eleyne was brought unto the quene aythir made
15 other goode chere as by countenaunce, but nothynge wyth there hartes.
But all men and women spake of the beauté of dame Elayne.

And than hit was ordayned that dame Elayne shulde slepe in a chambir
nygh by the quene, and all undir one rooff. And so hit was done as
the kynge commaunded. Than the quene sente for sir Launcelot and
20 bade hym com to her chambir that nyght, 'other ellys,' seyde the quene,
'I am sure that ye woll go to youre ladyes bedde, dame Elayne, by
whome ye gate Galahad'.

'A, madame!' seyde sir Launcelot, 'never say ye so, for that I ded was
ayenste my wylle.'

25 'Than,' seyde the quene, 'loke that ye com to me whan I sende for
you.'

'Madame,' seyde sir Launcelot, 'I shall nat fayle you, but I shall be
redy at youre commaundement.'

So this bargayne was nat so sone done and made betwene them but
30 dame Brusen knew hit by her crauftes and tolde hit unto her lady dame
Elayne.

'Alas!' seyde she, 'how shall I do?'

'Lat me deale,' seyde dame Brusen, 'for I shall brynge hym by the
honde evyn to youre bedde, and he shall wyne that I am quene Gweny-
35 vers messyngere.'

'Than well were me,' seyde dame Elayne, 'for all the worlde I love
nat so muche as I do sir Launcelot.'

(8)   So whan tyme com that all folkys were to bedde, dame Brusen cam
to sir Launcelottes beddys syde and seyde,

40 'Sir Launcelot du Lake, slepe ye? My lady quene Gwenyver lyeth
and awaytyth uppon you.'

'A, my fayre lady!' seyde sir Launcelot, 'I am redy to go wyth you
whother ye woll have me.'

So Launcelot threwe uppon hym a longe gowne, and so he toke his

swerde in hys honde. And than dame Brusen toke hym by the fyngir
and lad hym to her ladyes bedde, dame Elayne, and than she departed
and leaffte them there in bedde togydyrs. And wyte you well this lady
was glad, and so was sir Launcelot, for he wende that he had had another
in hys armys.   5

Now leve we them kyssynge and clyppynge, as was a kyndely
thynge, and now speke we of quene Gwenyver that sente one of her
women that she moste trusted unto sir Launcelotys bedde. And whan
she cam there she founde the bedde colde, and he was nat therein; and
so she cam to the quene and tolde her all.   10

'Alas!' seyde the quene, 'where is that false knyght becom?'

So the quene was nyghe oute of her wytte, and than she wrythed and
waltred as a madde women, and myght nat slepe a four or a five owres.

Than sir Launcelot had a condicion that he used of custom to clatir
in his slepe and to speke oftyn of hys lady, quene Gwenyver. So sir   15
Launcelot had awayked as longe as hit had pleased hym, and so by
course of kynde he slepte and dame Elayne bothe. And in his slepe he
talked and claterde as a jay of the love that had bene betwyxte quene
Gwenyver and hym, and so as he talked so lowde the quene harde hym
thereas she lay in her chambir. And whan she harde hym so clattir she   20
was wrothe oute of mesure, ᶠand for anger and payne wist not what to
do� 1, and than she cowghed so lowde that sir Launcelot awaked. And
anone he knew her hemynge, and than he knew welle that he lay by
the quene Elayne, and therewyth he lepte oute of hys bedde as he had
bene a wood man, in hys shurte, and anone the quene mette hym in   25
the floure; and thus she seyde:

'A, thou false traytoure knyght! Loke thou never abyde in my
courte, and lyghtly that thou voyde my chambir! And nat so hardy,
thou false traytoure knyght, that evermore thou com in my syght!'

'Alas!' seyde sir L[a]uncelot.   30

And therewyth he toke suche an hartely sorow at her wordys that he
felle downe to the floure in a sowne. And therewythall quene Gwenyver
departed.

And whan sir Launcelot awooke oute of hys swoghe, he lepte oute
at a bay-wyndow into a gardyne, and there wyth thornys he was all to-   35
cracched of his vysage and hys body, and so he ranne furth he knew
nat whothir, and was as wylde [woode] as ever was man. And so he
ran two yere, and never man had grace to know hym.

Now turne we unto quene Gwenyver and to the fayre lady Elayne,   (9)
that whan dame Elayne harde the quene so rebuke sir Launcelot, and   40
how also he sowned and how he lepte oute of the bay-wyndow, than
she seyde unto quene Gwenyver,

'Madame, ye ar gretly to blame for sir Launcelot, for now have ye
loste hym, for I saw and harde by his countenaunce that he ys madde

for ever. And therefore, alas! madame, ye have done grete synne and youreselff grete dyshonoure, for ye have a lorde royall of youre owne, and therefore hit were youre parte for to love hym; for there ys no quene in this worlde that hath suche another kynge as ye have. And
5　yf ye were nat, I myght have getyn the love of my lorde sir Launcelot; and a grete cause I have to love hym, for he hadde my maydynhode and by hym I have borne a fayre sonne whose [name] ys sir Galahad. And he shall be in hys tyme the beste knyght of the worlde.'

'Well, dame Elayne,' seyde the quene, 'as sone as hit ys daylyght I
10　charge you to avoyde my courte. And for the love ye owghe unto sir Launcelot discover not hys counceyle, for and ye do, hit woll be hys deth!'

'As for that,' seyde dame Elayne, 'I dare undirtake he ys marred for ever, and that have you made. For nother ye nor I ar lyke to rejoyse
15　hym, for he made the moste pyteuous gronys whan he lepte oute at yondir bay-wyndow that ever I harde man make. Alas!' seyde feyre Elayne, and 'Alas!' seyde the quene, 'for now I wote well that we have loste hym for ever!'

So on the morne dame Elayne toke her leve to departe and wolde no
20　lenger abyde. Than kynge Arthur brought her on her way wyth mo than an hondred knyghtes thorowoute a foreyste. And by the way she tolde sir Bors de Ganys all how hit betydde that same nyght, and how sir Launcelot lepte oute at a wyndow araged oute of hys wytte.

'Alas!' than seyde sir Bors, 'where ys my lorde sir Launcelot becom?'
25　'Sir,' seyde dame Eleyne, 'I wote nere.'

'Now, alas!' seyde sir Bors, 'betwyxt you bothe ye have destroyed a good knyght.'

'As for me, sir,' seyde dame Elayne, 'I seyde nevir nother dede thynge that shulde in ony wyse dysplease hym. But wyth the rebuke,
30　sir, that quene Gwenyver gaff hym I saw hym sowne to the erthe. And whan he awoke he toke [hys swerd in] hys honde, naked save hys shurte, and lepe oute at a wyndow wyth the greselyest grone that ever I harde man make.'

'Now farewell,' seyde [sir Bors] unto [dame Elayne], 'and holde my
35　lorde kynge Arthure wyth a tale as longe as ye can, for I woll turne agayne unto quene Gwenyver and gyff her an hete. And I requyre you, as ever ye woll have my servyse, make good wacche and aspye yf ever hit may happyn you to se my lorde sir Launcelot.'

'Truly,' seyde dame Elayne, 'I shall do all that I may do, for I wolde
40　[as fayne knowe and wete where he is become as you or ony of his kynne, or quene Gwenyver; and cause grete ynough have I thereto as well as ony other. And wete ye well,' sayde fayre Elayne to sir Bors, 'I wolde] lose my lyff for hym rathir than he shulde be hurte.'

'Madame,' seyde dame Brusen, 'lat sir Bors departe and hyghe hym

as faste as he may to seke sir Launcelot, for I warne you, he ys clene oute
of hys mynde, and yet he shall be welle holpyn and but by myracle.'

Than wepte dame Elayne, and so ded sir Bors de Ganys, and anone
they departed. And sir Bors rode streyte unto quene Gwenyver, and
whan she saw sir Bors she wepte as she were wood.   5

'Now, fye on youre wepynge!' seyde sir Bors de Ganys. 'For ye wepe
never but whan there ys no boote. Alas!' seyde sir Bors, 'that ever sir
Launcelot or ony of hys blood ever saw you, for now have ye loste
the beste knyght of oure blood, and he that was all oure leder and oure
succoure. And I dare say and make hit good that all kynges crystynde   10
nother hethynde may nat fynde suche a knyght, for to speke of his
noblenes and curtesy, wyth hys beauté and hys jantylnes. Alas!' seyde
sir Bors, 'what shall we do that ben of hys bloode?'

'Alas!' seyde sir Ector de Marys, and 'Alas!' seyde sir Lyonell.

And whan the quene harde hem sey so she felle to the erthe in a dede 15 (10)
sowne. And than sir Bors toke her up and dawed her, and whan she
awaked she kneled afore tho three knyghtes and hylde up bothe (her)
hondys and besought them to seke hym: 'And spare nat for no goodys
but that he be founden, for I wote well that he ys oute of hys mynde.'

And sir Bors, sir Ector and sir Lyonell departed frome the quene,   20
for they myght nat abyde no lenger for sorow. And than the quene sente
them tresoure inowe for there expence, and so they toke there horsys
and there armour and departede. And than they rode frome contrey to
contrey, in forestes and in wyldirnessys and in wastys, and ever they
leyde waycche bothe at forestes and at all maner of men as they rode   25
to harkyn and to spare aff[t]ir hym, as he that was a naked man in his
shurte wyth a swerde in hys honde.

And thus they rode nyghe a quarter of a yere, longe and overtwarte,
and never cowde hyre worde of hym, and wyte you well these three
knyghtes were passynge sory. And so at the laste sir Bors and hys   30
felowys mette wyth a knyght that hyght sir Melyon de Tartare.

'Now, fayre knyght,' seyde sir Bors, 'whothir be ye away?' (For
they knew aythir other aforetyme.)

'Sir,' seyde sir Mellyon, 'I am in the way to the courte of kynge
Arthure.'   35

'Than we pray you,' seyde sir Bors, 'that ye woll telle my lorde
Arthure and my lady quene Gwenyver and all the felyshyp of the
Rounde Table that we can nat in no wyse here telle where sir Launcelot
ys becom.'

Than sir Mellyon departed from them and seyde that he wolde telle   40
the kynge and the quene and all the felyshyp of the Rounde Table as
they had desyred hym. And whan sir Mellyon cam to the courte he
tolde the kynge and the quene and all the felyship as they had desyred
hym, how sir Bors had seyde of sir Launcelot.

Than sir Gawayne, sir Uwayne, sir Sagramoure le Desyrous, sir Agglovale and sir Percyvale de Galys toke uppon them by the grete desyre of the kynge, and in especiall by the quene, to seke all Inglonde, Walys and S[c]otlonde to fynde sir Launcelot. And wyth them rode eyghtene knyghtes mo to beare them felyshyppe, and wyte you well they lakked no maner of spendynge; and so were they three and twenty knyghtes.

Now turne we unto sir Launcelot and speke we of hys care and woo, and what payne he there endured; for colde, hungir and thyrste he hadde plenté.

And thus as these noble knyghtes rode togydyrs they by assente departed; and than they rode by two and by three, and by four [and] by fyve, and ever they assygned where they sholde mete.

And so sir Agglovale and sir Percyvale rode togydir unto there modir whyche was a quene in tho dayes. And whan she saw her two sunnes, for joy she wepte tendirly, and than she seyde,

'A, my dere sonnes! Whan youre fadir was slayne he leffte me four sonnes of the whyche now be two slayne. And for the dethe of my noble sonne sir Lamorak shall myne harte never be glad!'

And than she kneled downe uppon her knees tofore sir Agglovale and sir Percyvale and besought them to abyde at home wyth her.

'A, my swete modir,' seyde sir Percyvale, 'we may nat, for we be comyn of kynges bloode of bothe partis. And therefore, modir, hit ys oure kynde to haunte armys and noble dedys.'

'Alas! my swete sonnys,' than she seyde, 'for youre sakys I shall fyrste lose my lykynge and luste, and than wynde and wedir I may nat endure, what for the [dethe] of kynge Pellynor, youre fadir, that was shamefully slayne by the hondys of sir Gawayne and hys brothir, sir Gaherys! And they slew hym nat manly, but by treson. And alas! my dere sonnes, thys ys a pyteuous complaynte for me off youre fadyrs dethe, conciderynge also the dethe of sir Lamorak that of knyghthod had but feaw fealowys. And now, my dere sonnes, have this in youre mynde.'

And so there was but wepynge and sobbynge in the courte whan they sholde departe, and she felle in sownynge in the myddys of the courte.

(11) And whan she was awaked, aftir them she sente a squyar wyth spendynge inowghe. And so whan the squyar had overtake them they wolde nat suffir hym to ryde wyth them, but sente hym home agayne to comforte there modir, prayynge her mekely of her blyssynge.

And so he rode agayne, and so hit happened hym to be benyghtyd. And by mysfortune he cam to a castel where dwelled a barowne, and whan the squyar was com into the castell the lorde asked hym from whens he cam and whom he served.

'My lorde,' seyde the squyar, 'I serve a good knyght that ys called sir Agglovale.'

The squyar sayde hit to good entente, wenynge unto hym to have be more forborne for sir Agglovales sake than he [had] seyde he had served the quene, hys modir.   5

'Well, my felow,' seyde the lorde of the castell, 'for sir Agglovalys sake thou shalt have evyll lodgynge, for sir Agglovale slew my brother. And therefore thou shalt have thy dethe in party of paymente.'

And than that lorde commaunded hys men to have hym away and to sle hym. And so they ded, and than they pulled hym oute of the castell   10 and there they slewe hym wythoute mercy. And ryght so on the morne com sir Agglovale and sir Percyvale rydynge by a churche-yearde where men and women were busy and behylde the dede squyar, and so thought to bury hym.

'What ys that there,' seyde sir Agglovale, 'that ye beholde so faste?'   15
Anone a good woman sterte furth and seyde,

'Fayre knyght, here lyeth a squyar slayne shamefully this nyght.'

'How was he slayne, fayre modir?' sayde sir Agglovale.

'My fayre lorde,' seyde the woman, 'the lorde of thys castell lodged this squyar thys nyght. And because he seyde he was servaunte unto   20 a good knyght whyche is wyth kynge Arthure, whos name ys sir Agglovale, therefore the lorde commaunded to sle hym, and for thys cause ys he slayne.'

'Gramercy,' seyde sir Agglovale, 'and ye shall se hys deth lyghtly revenged! For I am that same knyght for whom thys squyar was slayne.'   25

Than sir Agglovale called unto hym sir Percyvale and bade hym alyght lyghtly. And anone they betoke there men their horsys, and so they yode on foote into the castell. And as sone as they were wythin the castell gate sir Agglovale bade the porter go unto hys lorde and tell his lorde 'that I am here, sir Agglovale, for whom my squyar was   30 slayne thys nyght'.

And anone as this porter had tolde hys lorde, 'He ys welcom!' seyde sir Goodwyne. And anone he armed hym and cam into the courte and seyde,

'Whyche of you ys sir Agglovale?'   35

'Here I am, loo! But for what cause slewyst thou thys nyght my modyrs squyar?'

'I slew hym,' seyde sir Goodwyne, 'bycause of the, for thou slewyste my brother sir Gawdelyne.'

'As for thy brother,' seyde sir Agglovale, 'I avow I slew hym, for he   40 was a false knyght and a betrayer of ladyes and of good knyghtes. And for the dethe of my squyar,' seyde sir Agglovale, ⌐'I defye the!'¬

And anone they laysshed togydyrs as egirly as hit had bene two lyons.

And sir Percyvale he faught wyth all the remenaunte that wolde fyght, and wythin a whyle sir Percyvale had slayne all that wolde withstonde hym, for sir Percyvale deled so hys strokys that were so rude that there durste no man abyde hym. And wythin a whyle sir
5 Agglovale had sir Goodwyne at the erthe, and there he unlaced hys helme and strake of hys hede. And than they departed and toke their horsys; and than they let cary the dede squyar unto a pryory, and there they entered hym.

(12) And whan thys was done they rode in many contreys ever inquyrynge
10 aftir sir Launcelot. But they coude never hyre of hym. And at the laste they com to a castell that hyght Cardycan, and there sir Percyvale and sir Agglovale were lodged togydyrs.

And prevaly, aboute mydnyght, sir Percyvale com to sir Agglovales squyar and seyde,
15 'Aryse and make the redy, for ye and I woll ryde away secretely.'

'Sir,' seyde the squyar, 'I wolde full fayne ryde with you where ye wolde have me, but and my lorde, youre brother, take me he woll sle me.'

'As for that, care not, for I shall be youre warraunte.'
20 And so sir Percyvale rode tyll hyt was aftir none, and than he cam uppon a brydge of stone, and there he founde a knyght whyche was bounden wyth a chayne faste aboute the waste unto a pylloure of stone.

'A, my fayre knyght,' seyde that boundyn knyght, 'I requyre the of knyghthode, lowse my bondys of!'
25 'Sir, what knyght ar ye?' seyde sir Percyvale. 'And for what cause ar ye bounden?'

'Sir, I shall telle you,' seyde that knyght. 'I am a knyght off the Table Rounde, and my name ys sir Persydes. And thus by adventure I cam thys way, and here I lodged in thys castell at the brydge foote. And
30 therein dwellyth an uncurteyse lady, and bycause she proffyrd me to be her paramoure and I refused her, she sette her men uppon me suddeynly or ever I myght com to my wepyn. Thus they toke me and bounde me, and here I wote well I shall dye but yf som man of worshyp breke my bondys.'
35 'Sir, be ye of good chere!' seyde sir Percyvale. 'And bycause ye ar a knyght of the Rounde Table as well as I, I woll truste to God to breke youre bondys.'

And therewyth sir Percyvale pulled oute hys swerde and strake at the chayne wyth suche a myght that he cutte a-to the chayne and thorow
40 sir Parsydes hawbirke, and hurte hym a lytyll.

'A, Jesu!' seyde sir Parsydes, 'that was a myghty stroke as ever I felte of mannes hande! For had nat the chayne be, ye had slayne me.'

And therewithall sir Parsydes saw a knyght whyche cam oute of the castell as faste as ever he myght flynge.

'Sir, beware! For yondyr commyth a knyght that woll have ado with you.'

'Lat hym com!' seyde sir Percyvale.

And so mette that knyght in myddys the brydge, and sir Percyvale gaff hym suche a buffette that he smote hym quyte frome hys horse 5
and over a parte of the brydge, that and there had nat bene a lytyll vessell undir the brydge, that knyght had bene drowned.

And than sir Percyvale toke the knyghtes horse and made sir Persydes to mounte uppon hym. And so they two rode unto the castell and bade the lady delyver sir Persydes servauntys, othir ellys he wolde 10
sle all that ever he founde. And so for feare she delyverde them all.

Than was sir Percyvale ware of a lady that stoode in that towre.

'A, madame,' seyde sir Percyvale, 'what use and custom ys that in a lady to destroy good knyghtes but yf they woll be youre paramour? Perdé, this [is] a shamefull custom of a lady, and yf I had nat a grete 15
mater to do in my honde I shulde fordo all youre false customys!'

And so sir Parsydes brought sir Percyvale unto hys owne castell, and there he made hym grete chere all that nyght. And on the morne, whan sir Percyvale had harde a masse and broke hys faste, he bade sir Parsydes ryde unto kynge Arthure: 20

'And telle ye the kynge how that ye mette wyth me, and telle you my brother, sir Agglovale, how I rescowed you. And byd hym seke nat aftir me, for I am in the queste to syke sir Launcelot du Lake. And thoughe he seke me, he shall nat fynde me. And tell hym I woll never se hym nothir the courte tylle that I have founde sir Launcelot. Also 25
telle sir Kay the Senescyall and syr Mordred that I truste to Jesu to be of as grete worthynes as aythir of them, for tell them that I shall never forgete their mokkys and scornys that day that I was made knyght; and telle them I woll never se that courte tylle men speke more worshyp of me than ever they ded of ony of them bothe.'   30

And so sir Parsydes departed frome sir Percyvale, and than he rode unto kynge Arthure and tolde of sir Percyvale. And whan sir Agglovale harde hym speke of hys brothir sir Percyvale,

'Forsothe,' he seyde, 'he departed fro me unkyndly.'

'Sir,' seyde sir Parsydes, 'on my lyff, he shall preve a noble knyght 35 (13)
as ony now ys lyvynge.'

And whan he saw sir Kay and sir Mordred, sir Parsydes sayde thus:

'My fayre lordys, sir Percyvale gretyth you well bothe, and he sente you worde by me that he trustyth to God or ever he com to courte 40
agayne to be of as grete nobles as ever were you bothe, and mo men to speke of his noblenesse than ever spake of youres.'

'Hyt may well be,' seyde sir Kay and sir Mordred, 'but at that tyme he was made knyght he was full unlykly to preve a good knyght.'

'As for that,' seyde kynge Arthure, 'he muste nedys preve a good knyght, for hys fadir and hys bretherne were noble knyghtes all.'

And now woll we turne unto sir Percyvale that rode longe. And in a foreyste he mette wyth a knyght wyth a brokyn shylde and a brokyn helme. And as sone as aythir saw other they made them redy to juste, and so they hurled togydyrs wyth all ⌐the¬ myghtes ⌐of their horses¬, and they mette togydyrs so hard that sir Percyvele was smyttyn to the erthe. And than sir Percyvale arose delyverly, and keste hys shylde on hys shuldir and drew hys swerde, and bade the other knyght alyght and do batayle unto the uttirmuste.

'Well, sir, wyll ye more yet?' seyde that knyght.

And therewyth he alyght, and put hys horse from hym. And than they cam togydir an easy pace and laysshed togydyrs with noble swerdys. And somtyme they stroke and somtyme they foyned, that ayther gaff other many sad strokys and woundys. And thus they faught nerehande halffe a day and never rested but lytyll, and there was none of them bothe that hadde leste woundys but he had fyftene, and they bledde so muche that hyt was mervayle they stoode on their feete. But thys knyght that faught wyth sir Percyvale was a proved knyght and a wyse-fyghtynge knyght, and sir Percyvale was yonge and stronge, nat knowynge in fyghtynge as the othir was. Than sir Percyvale spake fyrste and seyde,

'Sir knyght, holde thy honde a whyle, for we have foughtyn over longe for a symple mater and quarell. And therefore I requyre the tell me thy name, for I was never ar thys tyme thus macched.'

'So God me helpe,' seyde that knyght, 'and never or this tyme was there never knyght that wounded me so sore as thou haste done, and yet have I foughtyn in many batayles. And now shall thou wyte that I am a knyght of the Table Rounde, and my name ys sir Ector de Marys, brother unto the good knyght sir Launcelot du Lake.'

'Alas!' sayde sir Percyvale, 'and my name ys sir Percyvale de Galys whyche hath made my qu[e]ste to seke sir Launcelott. And now am I syker that I shall never fenyshe my queste, for ye have slayne me with youre hondys.'

'Hit is nat so,' seyde sir Ector, 'for I am slayne by youre hondys, and may not lyve. And therefore I requyre you,' seyde sir Ector unto sir Percyvale, 'ryde ye here faste by to a pryory, and brynge me a preste, that I may resseyve my Savyoure, for I may nat lyve. And whan ye com to the courte of kynge Arthure tell nat my brother, sir Launcelot, how that ye slew me, for than woll he be youre mortall enemy, but ye may sey that I was slayne in my queste as I sought hym.'

'Alas!' seyde sir Percyvale, 'ye sey that thynge that never woll be, for I am so faynte for bledynge that I may unnethe stonde. How sholde I than take my horse?'

Than they made bothe grete dole oute of mesure.   (14)

'This woll nat ·avayle,' seyde sir Percyvale. And than he kneled downe and made hys prayer devoutely unto Allmyghty Jesu, for he was one of the beste knyghtes of the worlde at that tyme, in whom the verrey fayth stoode moste in.   5

Ryght so there cam by the holy vessell, the Sankegreall, wyth all maner of swetnesse and savoure, but they cowde nat se redyly who bare the vessell. But sir Percyvale had a glemerynge of the vessell and of the mayden that bare hit, for he was a parfyte mayden. And furthwithall they were as hole of hyde and lymme as ever they were in their lyff.   10 Than they gaff thankynges to God with grete myldenesse.

'A, Jesu!' seyde sir Percyvale, 'what may thys meane that we be thus heled, and ryght now we were at the poyynte of dyynge?'

'I woote full well,' seyde sir Ector, 'what hit is. Hit is an holy vessell that is borne by a mayden, and therein ys a parte of the bloode of oure 15 Lorde Jesu Cryste. But hit may nat be sene,' seyde sir Ector, 'but yff hit be by ⟨an holy⟩ man.'

'So God me helpe,' seyde sir Percyvale, 'I saw a damesell, as me thought, all in whyght, with a vessell in bothe her hondys, and furth-withall I was hole.'   20

So than they toke their horsys and their harneys, and mended hyt as well as they myght that was brokyn; and so they mounted up and rode talkynge togydyrs. And there sir Ector de Marys tolde sir Percy-vale how he had sought hys brother, sir Launcelot, longe, and never cowde hyre wytynge of hym: 25

'In many harde adventures have I bene in thys queste!'

And so aythir tolde othir of there grete adventures.

And now leve we of a whyle of sir Ector and of sir Percyvale, and XII (1) speke we of sir Launcelot that suffird and endured many sharpe showres, that ever ran wylde woode frome place to place, and lyved by fruyte 30 and suche as he myght gete and dranke watir two yere. And other clothynge had he but lytyll, but his shurte and his breke.

And thus as sir Launcelott wandred here and there, he cam into a fayre medow where he founde a pavelon. And thereby uppon a tre hynge a whyght shylde, and two swerdys hynge thereby, and two 35 spearys lened thereby to a tre. And whan sir Launcelot saw the swerdys, anone he lepte to the tone swerde, and clyched that swerde in hys honde and drew hitte oute. And than he laysshed at the shylde, that all the medow range of the dyntys, that he gaff such a noyse as ten knyghtes hadde fought togydyrs.   40

Than cam furth a dwarff, and lepe unto sir Launcelot, and wolde have had the swerde oute of his honde. And than sir Launcelot toke hym

by the bothe shuldrys and threw hym unto the grounde, that he felle
uppon hys nek and had nygh brokyn hit. And therewythall the dwarff
cryede helpe.

Than there com furth a lykly knyght and well apparaylede in scarlet
5 furred with menyvere. And anone as he saw sir Launcelot he demed that
he shulde be oute of hys wytte, and than he seyde wyth fayre speche,

'Good man, ley downe that swerde! For as mesemyth thou haddyst
more nede of a slepe and of warme clothis than to welde that swerde.'

'As for that,' seyde sir Launcelot, 'com nat to nyghe, for and thou
10 do, wyte thou well I woll sle the!'

And whan the knyght of the pavylon saw that, he starte bakwarde
into hys pavylon. And than the dwarffe armed hym lyghtly, and so the
knyght thought by force and myght to have takyn the swerde fro sir
Launcelot. And so he cam steppynge uppon hym, and whan sir
15 Launcelot saw hym com so armed wyth hys swerde in hys honde,
than sir Launcelot flowghe to hym wyth suche a myght, and smote
hym uppon the helme suche a buffet, that the stroke troubled his
brayne, and therewythall the swerde brake in three. And the knyght
felle to the erthe and semed as he had bene dede, the bloode brastynge
20 oute of his mowthe, nose, and eares.

And than sir Launcelot ran into the pavelon, and russhed evyn into
the warme bedde. And there was a lady that lay in that bedde; and
anone she gate her smokke, and ran oute of the pavylon, and whan
she sawe her lorde lye at the grounde lyke to be dede, than she cryed
25 and wepte as she had bene madde. And so wyth her noyse the knyght
awaked oute of his sowghe, and loked up weykly wyth his yen.

And than he asked where was that madde man whyche had yevyn
hym suche a buffette, 'for suche a one had I never of mannes honde!'

'Sir,' seyde the dwarff, 'hit is nat youre worshyp to hurte hym, for
30 he ys a man oute of his wytte; and doute ye nat he hath bene a man of
grete worshyp, and for som hartely sorow that he hath takyn he ys
fallyn madde. And mesemyth,' seyde the dwarff, 'that he resembelyth
muche unto sir Launcelot, for hym I sawe at the turnemente of Lonezep.'

35 'Jesu defende,' seyde that knyght, 'that ever that noble knyght, sir
Launcelot, sholde be in suche a plyght! But whatsomever he be,'
seyde that knyght, 'harme woll I none do hym.'

And this knyghtes name was sir Blyaunte, the whyche seyde unto
the dwarff,

40 'Go thou faste on horsebak unto my brother, sir Selyvaunte, whyche
ys in the castell Blanke, and telle hym of myne adventure, and byd
hym brynge wyth hym an horse-lytter. And than woll we beare thys
knyght unto my castell.'

(2)   So the dwarff rode faste, and he cam agayn and brought sir Selyvaunte

wyth hym, and six men wyth an horse-lytter. And so they toke up
the fethir bedde wyth sir Launcelot, and so caryed all away wyth
hem unto the castell Blanke, and he never awaked tylle he was wythin
the castell. And than they bounde hys handys and hys feete, and gaff
hym good metys and good drynkys, and brought hym agayne to hys 5
strengthe and his fayrenesse. But in hys wytte they cowde nat brynge
hym, nother to know hymselff. And thus was sir Launcelot there more
than a yere and an halff, honestely arayed and fayre faryn wythall.

Than uppon a day thys lorde of that castell, sir Blyaunte, toke hys
armys on horsebak wyth a speare to seke adventures. And as he rode in 10
a foreyste there mette hym to knyghtes adventures: that one was sir
Brewnys Saunze Pité, and hys brother, sir Bartelot. And thes two ran
bothe at onys on sir Bleaunte and brake theyre spearys uppon hys body.
And than they drewe there swerdys and made grete batayle, and
foughte longe togydyrs. But at the laste sir Blyaunte was sore wounded 15
and felte hymselffe faynte, and anone he fledde on horsebak towarde
hys castell.

And as they cam hurlyng undir the castell, there was sir Launcelot at
a wyndow, and saw how two knyghtes layde uppon sir Blyaunte wyth
there swerdys. And whan sir Launcelot saw that, yet as woode as he 20
was he was sory for hys lorde, sir Blyaunte. And than in a brayde sir
Launcelot brake hys chaynes of hys leggys and of hys armys, and in the
breakynge he hurte hys hondys sore; and so sir Launcelot ran oute at a
posterne, and there he mette wyth tho two knyghtes that chaced syr
Blyaunte. And there he pulled downe sir Bartelot wyth his bare hondys 25
frome hys horse, and therewythall he wrothe oute the swerde oute of
hys honde, and so he lepe unto sir Brewse and gaff hym suche a buffette
upon the hede that he tumbeled bakwarde over hys horse croupe.

And whan sir Bartelot saw hys brother have suche a buffet he gate
a speare in hys honde, and wolde have renne sir Launcelot thorow. 30
And that saw sir Blyaunte and strake of the hande of sir Bartelot. And
than sir Brewse and sir Bartelot gate there horsis and fledde away as
faste as they myght.

So whan sir Selyvaunte cam and saw what sir Launcelot had done
for hys brother, than he thanked God, and so ded hys brother, that 35
ever they ded hym ony good. But whan sir Blyaunte sawe that sir
Launcelot was hurte wyth the brekynge of hys irons, than was he h[e]vy
that ever he bounde hym.

'I pray you, brother, sir Selyvaunte, bynde hym no more, for he ys
happy and gracyous.'   40
Than they made grete joy of sir Launcelot, and [they bounde hym
no more. And] so he bode thereaff⟨t⟩ir an halff yere and more.

And so on a morne sir Launcelot was ware where cam a grete bore
wyth many houndys afftir hym, but the boore was so bygge ther

myght no houndys tary hym. And so the hunters cam aftir, blowynge there hornys, bothe uppon horsebacke and som uppon foote, and than sir Launcelot was ware where one alyght and tyed hys horse tylle a tre
(3) and lened hys speare ayenst the tre. So there cam syr Launcelot and
5 founde the horse, and a good swerde tyed to the sadyll bowe, and anone sir Launcelot lepe into the sadyll and gate that speare in hys honde, and than he rode faste aftir the boore.

And anone he was ware where he sate, and his ars to a roche, faste by an ermytayge. And than sir Launcelot ran at the boore wyth hys
10 speare and all to-shyvird his speare. And therewyth the boore turned hym lyghtly, and rove oute the longys and the harte of the horse, that sir Launcelot felle to the erthe; and, or ever he myght gete frome hys horse, the bore smote hym on the brawne of the thyghe up unto the howghe-boone. And than sir Launcelot was wrothe, and up he gate
15 uppon hys feete, and toke hys swerde and smote of the borys hede at one stroke.

And therewythall cam oute the ermyte and saw hym have suche a wounde. Anone he meaned hym, and wolde have had hym home unto his ermytage. But whan sir Launcelot harde hym speake, he was so
20 wrothe wyth hys wounde that he ran uppon the ermyte to have slayne hym. Than the ermyte ran away, and whan sir Launcelot myght nat overgete hym he threw his swerde aftir hym, for he myght no farther for bledynge. Than the ermyte turned agayne and asked sir Launcelot how he was hurte.

25 'A, my fealow,' seyde sir Launcelot, 'this boore hath byttyn me sore!'
'Than com ye wyth me,' seyde the ermyte, 'and I shall heale you.'
'Go thy way,' seyde sir Launcelot, 'and deale nat wyth me!'
Than the ermyte ran his way, and there he mette wyth a goodly knyght ⌜wyth many men⌝.
30 'Sir,' seyde the ermyte, 'here is faste by my place the goodlyest man that ever I sawe, and he ys sore wounded wyth a boore, and yet he hath slayne the bore. But well I wote,' seyde the good man, 'and he be nat holpyn, he shall dye of that wounde, and that were grete pité.'

Than that knyght at the desyre of the ermyte gate a carte, and therein
35 he put the boore and sir Launcelot; for he was so fyeble that thei myght ryght easyly deale with hym. And so sir Launcelot was brought unto the ermytayge, and there the ermyte healed hym of hys wounde. But the ermyte myght nat fynde hym his sustenaunce, and so he empeyred and wexed fyeble bothe of body and of hys wytte: for defaute of suste-
40 naunce he waxed more wooder than he was aforetyme.

And than uppon a day sir Launcelot ran his way into the foreyste; and by the adventure he com to the cité of Corbyn where dame Elayne was, that bare Galahad, sir Launcelottys sonne. And so whan he was entyrde into the towne he ran thorow the towne to the castell; and than

all the yonge men of that cité ran aftir sir Launcelot, and there they
threwe turvis at hym and gaff hym many sad strokys. And ever as sir
Launcelot myght reche ony of them, he threw them so that they wolde
never com in hys hondes no more, for of som he brake the leggys
and armys.   5

And so he fledde into the castell, and than cam oute knyghtes and
squyars and rescowed sir Launcelot. Whan they behylde hym and
loked uppon hys persone, they thought they never sawe so goodly a
man. And whan they sawe so many woundys uppon hym, they demed
that he had bene a man of worshyp. And than they ordayned hym   10
clothis to hys body, and straw and lytter undir the gate of the castell to
lye in. And so every day they wolde throw hym mete and set hym
drynke, but there was but feaw that wolde brynge hym mete to hys
hondys.

So hit befelle that kyng Pelles had a neveaw whos name was Caster; 15 (4)
and so he desyred of the kynge to be made knyght, and at hys owne
rekeyste the kynge made hym knyght at the feste of Candylmasse. And
whan sir Castor was made knyght, that same day he gaff many gownys.
And than sir Castor sente for the foole, whych was sir Launcelot; and
whan he was com afore sir Castor, he gaff sir Launcelot a robe of   20
scarlet and all that longed unto hym. And whan sir Launcelot was so
arayed lyke a knyght, he was the semelyeste man in all the courte, and
none so well made.

So whan he sye hys tyme he wente into the gardyne, and there he
layde hym downe by a welle and slepte. And so at aftir none dame   25
Elayne and her maydyns cam into the gardyne to sporte them. And as
they romed up and downe one of dame Elaynes maydens aspyed where
lay a goodly man by the welle slepynge.

'Peas,' seyde dame Elayne, 'and sey no worde, but shew me that man
where he lyeth.'   30

So anone she brought dame Elayne where he lay. And whan that
she behylde hym, anone she felle in remembraunce of hym and knew
hym veryly for sir Launcelot. And therewythall she felle on wepynge
so hartely that she sanke evyn to the erthe. And whan she had thus
wepte a grete whyle, than she arose and called her maydyns and seyde 35
she was syke. And so she yode oute of the gardyne as streyte to her
fadir as she cowde, and there she toke hym by herselff aparte; and than
she seyde,

'A, my dere fadir! now I have nede of your helpe, and but yf that
ye helpe me now, farewell my good dayes forever!'   40

'What ys that, doughter?' seyde kynge Pelles.

'In youre gardyne I was to sporte me, and there, by the welle, I founde
sir Launcelot du Lake slepynge.'

'I may nat byleve hit!' seyde kynge Pelles.

'Truly, sir, he ys there!' she seyde. 'And mesemyth he shulde be yet distracke oute of hys wytte.'

'Than holde you stylle,' seyde the kynge, 'and lat me deale.'

Than the kynge called unto hym suche as he moste trusted, a four
5 persones, and dame Elayne, hys doughter, and dame Brusen, her servaunte. And whan they cam to the welle and behylde sir Launcelot, anone dame Brusen seyde to the kynge,

'We muste be wyse how we deale wyth hym, for thys knyght ys oute of hys mynde, and yf we awake hym rudely, what he woll do we
10 all know nat. And therefore abyde ye a whyle, and I shall throw an inchauntemente uppon hym, that he shall nat awake of an owre.'

And so she ded, and than the kynge commaunded that all people shulde avoyde, that none shulde be in that way thereas the kynge wolde com. And so whan thys was done thes four men and thes ladyes
15 layde honde on sir Launcelot, and so they bare hym into a towre, and so into a chambir where was the holy vessell of the Sankgreall. And byfore that holy vessell sir Launcelot was layde. And there cam an holy man and unhylled that vessell, and so by myracle and by vertu of that holy vessell sir Launcelot was heled and recoverde.

20 And as sone as he was awaked he groned and syghed, and complayned
(5) hym sore of hys woodnes and strokys that he had had. And as sone as sir Launcelot saw kynge Pelles and dame Elayne, he waxed ashamed and seyde thus:

'A, Lorde Jesu, how cam I hydir? For Goddys sake, my fayre lorde,
25 lat me wyte how that I cam hydir.'

'Sir,' seyde dame Elayne, 'into thys contrey ye cam lyke a mased man, clene oute of youre wytte. And here have ye ben kepte as a foole, and no cryature here knew what ye were, untyll by fortune a mayden of myne brought me unto you whereas ye lay slepynge by a well. And
30 anone as I veryly behylde you [I knewe you]. Than I tolde my fadir, and so were ye brought afore thys holy vessell, and by the vertu of hit thus were ye healed.'

'A, Jesu, mercy!' seyde sir Launcelot. 'Yf this be sothe, how many be there that knowyth of my woodnes?'

35 'So God me helpe,' seyde dame Elayne, 'no mo but my fadir, and I, and dame Brusen.'

'Now, for Crystes love,' seyde sir Launcelot, 'kepe hit counceyle and lat no man knowe hit in the worlde! For I am sore ashamed that I have be myssefortuned, for I am banysshed the contrey of [Logrys for
40 ever.' (That is for to sey the contrey of] Inglonde).

And so sir Launcelot lay more than a fourtenyght or ever that he myght styrre for sorenes. And than uppon a day he seyde unto dame Elayne thes wordis:

'Fayre lady Elayne, for youre sake I have had muche care and

angwyshe, hit nedyth nat to reherse hit, ye know how. Natwythstondynge I know well I have done fowle to you whan that I drew my
swerde to you to have slayne you uppon the morne aftir whan that I
had layne wyth you. And all was for the cause that ye and dame Brusen
made me for to lye be you magry myne hede. And as ye sey, sir Galahad, 5
your sonne, was begotyn.'

'That ys trouthe,' seyde dame Elayne.

'Than woll ye for my sake,' seyde sir Launcelot, 'go ye unto youre
fadir and gete me a place of hym wherein I may dwelle? For in the courte
of kynge Arthure may I never com.'   10

'Sir,' seyde dame Eleyne, 'I woll lyve and dye wyth you, only for
youre sake; and yf my lyff myght nat avayle you and my dethe myght
avayle you, wyte you well I wolde dye for youre sake. And I woll to
my fadir, and I am ryght sure there ys [no]thynge that I can desyre of
hym but I shall have hit. And wher ye be, [my] lorde sir Launcelot,   15
doute ye nat but I woll be wyth you, wyth all the servyse that I may do.'

So furthwythall she wente to her fadir and sayde,

'Sir, my lorde sir Launcelot desyreth to be hyre by you in som castell
off youres.'

'Well, doughter,' seyde the kynge, 'sytthyn hit is his desyre to abyde 20
in this marchis, he shall be in the castell of Blyaunte, and there shall ye
be wyth hym, and twenty of the fayryste yonge ladyes that bene in
thys contrey, and they shall be all of the grettyst blood in this contrey;
and ye shall have twenty knyghtes wyth you. For, doughter, I woll that
ye wyte we all be honowred by the blood of sir Launcelot.'   25

Than wente dame Elayne unto sir Launcelot and tolde hym all how (6)
her fadir had devysed. Than cam a knyght whyche was called sir
Castor, that was neveaw unto kynge Pelles, and he cam unto sir Launcelot and asked hym what was hys name.

'Sir,' seyde sir Launcelot, 'my name ys Le Shyvalere Ill Mafeete, 30
that ys to sey "the knyght that hath trespassed".'

'Sir,' seyde sir Castor, 'hit may well be so, but ever mesemyth youre
name shulde be sir Launcelot du Lake, for or now I have seyne you.'

'Sir,' seyde sir Launcelot, 'ye ar nat jantyll, for I put a case that my
name were sir Launcelot and that hyt lyste me nat to dyscover my   35
name, what shulde hit greve you here to kepe my counsell and ye nat
hurte thereby? But wyte you well, and ever hit lye in my power, I shall
greve you, and ever I mete with you in my way!'

Than sir Castor kneled adowne and besought sir Launcelot of
mercy: 'for I shall never uttir what ye be whyle that ye ar in thys 40
partyes.'

Than sir Launcelot pardowned hym. And so kynge Pelles wyth
twenty knyghtes and dame Elayne wyth her twenty ladyes rode unto
the castel of Blyaunte that stood in an ilonde beclosed envyrowne

wyth a fayre watir depe and layrge. And whan they were there sir
Launcelot lat calle hit the Joyus Ile; and there was he called none otherwyse but Le Shyvalere Mafete, 'the knyght that hath trespast'.

Than sir Launcelot lete make hym a shylde all of sable, and a quene
5 crowned in the myddis of sylver, and a knyght clene armed knelynge
afore her. And every day onys, for ony myrthis that all the ladyes
myght make hym, he wolde onys every day loke towarde the realme
of Logrys, where kynge Arthure and quene Gwenyver was, and than
wolde he falle uppon a wepyng as hys harte shulde to-braste.

10 So hit befelle that tyme sir Launcelot harde of a justynge faste by,
wythin three leagis. Than he called unto hym a dwarff, and he bade
hym go unto that justynge:

'And or ever the knyghtes departe, loke that thou make there a cry,
in hyrynge of all knyghtes, that there ys one knyght in Joyus Ile,
15 whyche ys the castell of Blyaunte, and sey that hys name ys Le Shyvalere
Mafete, that woll juste ayenst knyghtes all that woll com. And who that
puttyth that knyght to the wars, he shall have a fayre maydyn and a
jarfawcon.'

(7) So whan this cry was cryed, unto Joyus Ile drew the numbir of fyve
20 hondred knyghtes. And wyte you well there was never seyne in kynge
Arthurs dayes one knyght that ded so muche dedys of armys as sir
Launcelot ded tho three dayes togydyrs. For, as the boke makyth truly
mencyon, he had the bettir of all the fyve hondred knyghtes, and there
was nat one slayne of them. And aftir that sir Launcelot made them all
25 a grete feste.

And in the meanewhyle cam sir Percyvale de Galys and sir Ector de
Marys undir that castell whyche was called the Joyus Ile. And as they
behylde that gay castell they wolde have gone to that castell, but they
myght nat for the brode watir, and brydge coude they fynde none.
30 Than were they ware on the othir syde where stoode a lady wyth a
sparhawke on her honde, and sir Percyvale called unto her and asked
that lady who was in that castell.

'Fayre knyghtes,' she seyde, 'here wythin thys castell ys the fayryste
lady in thys londe, and her name is dame Elayne. Also we have in thys
35 castell one of the fayryste knyghtes and the myghtyest man that ys,
I dare sey, lyvynge, and he callyth hymselff Le Shyvalere Mafete.'

'How cam he into thys marchys?' seyde sir Percyvale.

'Truly,' seyde the damesell, 'he cam into thys contrey lyke a madde
man, wyth doggys and boyes chasynge hym thorow the cyté of
40 Corbyn, and by the holy vessell of the Sankgreall he was brought into
hys wytte agayne. But he woll nat do batayle wyth no knyght but by
undirne or noone. And yf ye lyste to com into the castell,' seyde the
lady, 'ye muste ryde unto the farther syde of the castell, and there shall
ye fynde a vessell that woll beare you and youre horse.'

Than they departed and cam unto the vessell; and than sir Percyvale alyght, and sayde unto sir Ector de Marys,

'Ye shall abyde me hyre untyll that I wyte what maner a knyght he ys. For hit were shame unto us, inasmuche as he ys but one knyght, and w[e] shulde bothe do batayle wyth hym.'   5

'Do as ye lyste,' seyde syr Ector, 'and here I shall abyde you untyll that I hyre off you.'

Than passed sir Percyvale the water, and whan he cam to the castell gate he seyde unto the porter,

'Go thou to [the] good knyght of this castell and telle hym hyre ys   10 com an arraunte knyght to juste wyth hym.'

Than the porter yode in and cam agayne and bade hym ryde into the comyn place 'thereas the justynge shall be, where lordys and ladyes may beholde you'.

And so anone as sir Launcelot had a warnynge he was sone redy, and   15 there sir Percyvale and sir Launcelot were com bothe. They encountirde wyth suche a myght, and there spearys were so rude, that bothe the horsys and the knyghtys fell to the grounde. Than they avoyded there horsys, and flange oute there noble swerdys, and hew away many cantels of there shyldys, and so hurteled togydyrs lyke two borys.   20 And aythir wounded othir passynge sore, and so at the laste sir Percyvale spake fyrste, whan they had foughtyn there longe more than two owres.

'Now, fayre knyght,' seyde sir Percyvale, 'I requyre you of youre knyghthode to telle me youre name, for I mette never wyth suche   25 another knyght.'

'Sir, as for my name,' seyde sir Launcelot, 'I woll nat hyde hyt frome you, but my name ys Le Shyvalere Mafete. Now telle me your name,' seyde sir Launcelot, 'I requyre you.'

'Truly,' seyde sir Percyvale, 'my name ys sir Percyvale de Galys,   30 that was brothir unto the good knyght sir Lamorak de Galys, and kynge Pellynor was oure fadir, and sir Agglovale ys my brothir.'

'Alas!' seyde sir Launcelot, 'what have I done to fyght wyth you whyche ar a knyght of the Table Rounde! And somtyme I was youre [felawe].'   35

And therewythall sir Launcelot kneled downe uppon hys kneys   (8) and threwe away hys shylde and hys swerde frome hym. Whan sir Percyvale sawe hym do so he mervayled what he meaned, and than he seyde thus:

'Sir knyght, whatsomever ⟨y⟩e be, I requyre you uppon the hyghe   40 Order of Knyghthode to telle me youre trewe name.'

Than he answerde and seyde, 'So God me helpe, my name ys sir Launcelot du Lake, kynge Bannys son of Benoy.'

'Alas!' than seyde sir Percyvale, 'what have I now done? For I was

sente by the quene for to seke you, and so I have sought you nygh thys
two yere, and yondir ys sir Ector de Marys, youre brothir, whyche
abydyth me on the yondir syde of the watyr. And therefore, for Goddys
sake,' seyde sir Percyvale, 'forgyffe me myne offencys that I have here
5 done.'

'Sir, hyt ys sone forgyvyn,' seyde sir Launcelot.

Than sir Percyvale sente for sir Ector de Marys, and whan sir
Launcelot had a syght of hym he ran unto hym and toke hym in hys
armys; and than sir Ector kneled downe, and aythir wepte uppon othir,
10 that all men had pité to beholde them.

Than cam forthe dame Elayne. And she made them grete chere as
myght be made, and there she tolde sir Ector and sir Percyvale how
and in what maner sir Launcelot cam into that contrey and how he was
heled. And there hyt was knowyn how longe sir Launcelot was with sir
15 Blyaunte and wyth sir Selyvaunte, and how he fyrste mette wyth them,
[and how he] departed frome them bycause he was hurte wyth a boore,
and how the ermyte healed hym off hys grete wounde, and how that
he cam to the cité of Corbyn.

(9)   Now leve we sir Launcelot in Joyus Ile wyth hys lady, dame Elayne,
20 and sir Per[cy]vayle and sir Ector playynge wyth them, and now turne
we unto sir Bors de Ganys and unto sir Lyonell that had sought sir
Launcelot long, nye by the space of two yere, and never coude they
hyre of hym. And as they thus rode, by adventure they cam to the house
of kynge Brandegorys, and there sir Bors was well knowyn, for he had
25 gotyn a chylde uppon the kynges doughtir fyftene yere tofore, and hys
name was Elyne le Blanke. And whan sir Bors sawe that chylde he
lyked hym passynge well. And so thoo knyghtes had good chere of
kynge Brandegorys. [And on the morne sir Bors came afore kynge
Brandegorys] and seyde,

30 'Here ys my sonne Elyne le Blanke, and syth hyt ys so, I wyll
that ye wyte I woll have hym wyth me unto the courte of kynge
Arthur.'

'Sir,' seyde the kynge, 'ye may well take hym wyth you, but he ys as
yet over tendir of ayge.'

35 'As for that,' seyde sir Bors, 'yet I woll have hym wythe me and
brynge hym to the howse of moste worshyp in the worlde.'

So whan sir Bors shulde departe there was made grete sorow for the
departynge of Helyne le Blanke. But at the laste they departed, and
wythin a whyle they cam unto Camelot whereas was kynge Arthure.
40 And so whan kynge Arthure undirstoode that Helyne le Blanke was sir
Bors son and neveaw unto kynge Brandegorys, than kynge Arthure let
make hym knyghte of the Rounde Table. And so he preved a good
knyghte and an adventurus.

AND NOW WOLL WE TO OURE MATER OF SIR LAUNCELOT.

So hyt befelle on a day that sir Ector and sir Percyvale cam unto sir
Launcelot and asked of hym what he wolde do, and whethir he wolde
go wyth them unto kynge Arthure.

'Nay,' seyde sir Launcelott, 'that may I nat do by no meane, for I 5
was so vengeabely deffended the courte that I caste me never to com
there more.'

'Sir,' seyde sir Ector, 'I am youre brothir, and ye ar the man in the
worlde that I love moste. And yf I undirstoode that hyt were youre
dysworshyp, ye may undirstonde that I wolde never counceyle you 10
thereto. But kynge Arthure and all hys knyghtes, and in especiall quene
Gwenyver, makyth suche dole and sorow for you that hyt ys mervayle
to hyre and se. And ye muste remembir the grete worshyp and renowne that ye be off, how that ye have bene more spokyn of than ony
othir knyght that ys now lyvynge; for there ys none that beryth the 15
name now but ye and sir Trystram. And therefore, brother,' seyde sir
Ector, 'make you redy to [ryde to] the courte wyth us. And I dare sey
and make hyt good,' seyde sir Ector, 'hyt hath coste my lady the quene
twenty thousand pounds the sekynge of you.'

'Welle, brothir,' seyde sir Launcelot, 'I woll do aftir youre counceyle 20
and ryde wyth you.'

So than they toke [their horses] and made redy, and anone they toke
there leve at kynge Pelles and at dame Elayne. And whan sir Launcelot
shulde departe dame Elayne mad grete sorow.

'My lorde, sir Launcelot,' seyde dame Elayne, 'thys same feste of 25
Pentecoste shall youre sonne and myne, Galahad, be made knyght, for
he ys now fully fyftene wynter olde.'

'Madame, do as ye lyste,' seyde sir Launcelot, 'and God gyff hym
grace to preve a good knyght.'

'As for that,' seyde dame Elayne, 'I doute nat he shall preve the beste 30
man of hys kynne excepte one.'

'Than shall he be a good man inowghe,' seyde sir Launcelot.

So anone they departed, and wythin fyftene dayes journey they cam (10)
unto Camelot, that ys in Englyshe calle[d] Wynchester. And whan sir
Launcelot was com amonge them, the kynge and all the knyghtes 35
made grete joy of hys homecommynge.

And there sir Percyvale and sir Ector de Marys began and tolde the
hole adventures: how sir Launcelot had bene oute of hys mynde in the
tyme of hys abcence, and how he called hymselff Le Shyvalere Mafete,
'the knyght that had trespast'; and in three dayes wythin Joyus Ile sir 40
Launcelot smote downe fyve hondred knyghtes. And ever as sir Ector
and sir Percyvale tolde thes talys of sir Launcelot, quene Gwenyver
wepte as she shulde have dyed. Than the quene made hym grete chere.

'A, Jesu!' seyde kynge Arthure, 'I mervayle for what cause ye, sir

Launcelot, wente oute of youre mynde. For I and many othir deme hyt was for the love of fayre Elayne, the doughtir of kynge Pelles, by whom ye ar noysed that ye have gotyn a chylde, and hys name ys Galahad. And men sey that he shall do many mervaylouse thyngys.'

5 'My lorde,' seyde sir Launcelot, 'yf I ded ony foly I have that I sought.'

And therewythall the kynge spake no more. But all sir Launcelottys kynnesmen knew for whom he wente oute of hys mynde. And than there was made grete feystys, and grete joy was there amonge them. 10 And all lordys and ladyes made grete joy whan they harde how sir Launcelot was com agayne unto the courte.

(11)   Now woll we leve of thys mater, and speke we off sir ⌐Trys-tram⌐ and of sir Palomydes that was the Sarezen uncrystynde.

XV. CONCLUSION

15 Whan sir Trystram was com home unto Joyus Garde frome hys adventures—and all thys whyle that sir Launcelot was thus myste, two yere and more, sir Trystram bare the brewte and renowne thorow all the realme of Logyrs, and many stronge adventures befelle hym, and full well and [manly and] worshypfully he brought hem to an ende— 20 so whan he was com home La Beall Isode tolde [hym] off the grete feste that sholde be at Pentecoste nexte folowynge. And there she tolde hym how sir Launcelot had bene myssed two yere, and all that whyle he had bene oute of hys mynde, and how he was holpyn by the holy vessell of the Sankgreall.

25 'Alas!' seyde sir Trystram, 'that caused som debate betwyxte hym and quene Gwenyver.'

'Sir,' seyde dame Isode, 'I knowe hyt all, for quene Gwenyver sente me a lettir all how hyt was done, for because I sholde requyre you to seke hym. And now, blessyd be God,' seyde La Beall Isode, 'he ys hole 30 and sounde and comyn ayen to the courte.'

'A, Jesu! thereof am I fayne,' seyde sir Trystram. 'And now shall ye and I make us redy, for bothe ye and I woll be at that feste.'

'Sir,' seyde dame Isode, 'and hyt please you, I woll nat be there, for thorow me ye bene marked of many good knyghtes, and that causyth 35 you for to have muche more laboure for my sake than nedyth you to have.'

'Than woll I nat be there,' seyde sir Trystram, 'but yf ye be there.'

'God deffende,' seyde La Beall Isode, 'for than shall I be spokyn of shame amonge all quenys and ladyes of astate; for ye that ar called one 40 of the nobelyste knyghtys of the worlde and a knyght of the Rounde

Table, how may ye be myssed at that feste? For what shall be sayde of
you amonge all knyghtes? "A! se how sir Trystram huntyth and
hawkyth, and cowryth wythin a castell wyth hys lady, and forsakyth
us. Alas!" shall som sey, "hyt ys pyté that ever he was knyght, or ever
he shulde have the love of a lady." Also, what shall quenys and ladyes 5
say of me? "Hyt ys pyté that I have my lyff, that I wolde holde so
noble a knyght as ye ar frome hys worshyp."'

'So God me helpe,' seyde sir Trystram unto La Beall Isode, 'hyt
ys passyngly well seyde of you and nobely counceyled. And now I
well undirstonde that ye love me. And lyke as ye have counceyled me 10
I woll do a parte thereaftir, but there shall no man nor chylde ryde
wyth me but myselff alone. And so I woll ryde on Tewysday next
commynge, and no more harneyse of warre but my speare and my
swerde.'

And so whan the day come sir Trystram toke hys leve at La Beall 15 (12)
Isode, and she sente wyth hym four knyghtys; and wythin halff a myle
he sente them agayne. And within a myle way aftir sir Trystram sawe
afore hym where sir Palomydes had stryken downe a knyght and allmoste wounded hym to the dethe. Than sir Trystram repented hym
that he was nat armed, and therewyth he hoved stylle. And anone as 20
sir Palomydes saw sir Trystram he cryed on hyght,

'Sir Trystram, now be we mette, for or we departe we shall redresse
all oure olde sorys!'

'As for that,' seyde sir Trystram, 'there was never yet no Crystyn man
that ever myght make hys boste that ever I fledde from hym. And wyte 25
thou well, sir Palomydes, thou that arte a Sarezen shall never make thy
boste that ever sir Trystram de Lyones shall fle fro the!'

And therewyth sir Trystram made hys horse to ren, and wyth all hys
myght he cam streyte uppon sir Palomydes and braste hys speare uppon
hym at an hondred pecis. And furthwythall sir Trystram drewe hys 30
swerde, and than he turned hys horse and stroke togydyrs six grete
strokys uppon hys helme. And than sir Palomydes stode stylle and
byhylde sir Trystram and mervayled gretely at hys woodnes and of hys
foly.

And than sir Palomydes seyde unto hymselff, 'And thys sir Trystram 35
were armed, hyt were harde to cese hym frome hys batayle, and yff I
turne agayne and sle hym I am shamed wheresomevir I go.'

Than sir Trystram spake and seyde,

'Thou cowarde knyght, what castyste thou to do? And why wolt
thou nat do batayle wyth me? For have thou no doute I shall endure 40
the and all thy malyce!'

'A, sir Trystram!' seyde sir Palomydes, 'full well thou wotyste I may
nat have ado wyth the for shame, for thou arte here naked and I am
armede, and yf that I sle the, dyshonoure shall be myne. And well thou

wotyste,' seyde sir Palomydes unto sir Trystram, 'I knowe thy strengthe and thy hardynes to endure ayenste a goode knyght.'

'That ys trouthe,' seyde sir Trystram, 'I undirstonde thy valyauntenesse.'

5   'Ye say well,' seyde sir Palomydes. 'Now, I requyre you, telle me a questyon that I shall sey unto you.'

'Than telle me what hyt ys,' seyde sir Trystram, 'and I shall answere you of the trouthe, as God me helpe.'

'Sir, I put a case,' seyde sir Palomydes, 'that ye were armed at all 10 ryghtes as well as I am, and I naked as ye be, what wolde ye do to me now, be youre trewe knyghthode?'

'A,' seyde sir Trystram, 'now I undirstonde the well, sir Palomydes, for now muste I sey myne owne jugemente! And, as God me blysse, that I shall sey shall nat be seyde for no feare that I have of the, sir 15 Palomydes. But thys ys all: wyte thou well, sir Palomydes, as at thys tyme thou sholdyst departe from me, for I wolde nat have ado wyth the.'

'No more woll I,' seyde sir Palomydes. 'And therefore ryde furth on thy way!'

20   'As for that,' seyde sir Trystram, 'I may chose othir to ryde othir to go. But, sir Palomydes,' seyde sir Trystram, 'I mervayle greatly of one thynge, that thou arte so good a knyght, that thou wolt nat be crystynde, and thy brothir, sir Saffir, hath bene crystynde many a day.'

(13)   'As for that,' seyde sir Palomydes, 'I may nat yet be crystyned for 25 a vowe that I have made many yerys agone. Howbehyt in my harte and in my soule I have had many a day a good beleve in Jesu Cryste and hys mylde modir Mary, but I have but one batayle to do, and were that onys done I wolde be baptyzed.'

'Be my hede,' seyde sir Trystram, 'as for one batayle, thou shalt nat 30 seke hyt longe. For God deffende,' seyde sir Trystram, 'that thorow my defaute thou sholdyste lengar lyve thus a Sarazyn. For yondyr ys a knyght that ye have hurte and smyttyn downe: now helpe me than that I were armed in hys armoure, and I shall sone fullfyll thyne avowys.'

'As ye wyll,' seyde sir Palomydes, 'so shall hyt be.'

35   So they rode bothe unto that knyght that sate uppon a banke, and than sir Trystram salewed hym, and he waykely salewed hym agayne.

'Sir knyght,' seyde sir Trystram, 'I requyre you telle me youre ryght name.'

'Syr,' he seyde, 'my ryght name ys sir Galleron off Galowey, and a 40 knyght of the Table Rounde.'

'So God me helpe,' seyde sir Trystram, 'I am ryght hevy of youre hurtys! But thys ys all: I muste pray you to leane me youre hole armoure, for ye se that I am unarmed, and I muste do batayle wyth thys knyght.'

'Sir, ye shall have hyt wyth a good wyll. But ye muste beware, for
I warne you that knyght ys an hardy knyght as ever I mette wythall.
But, sir,' seyde sir Galeron, 'I pray you, telle me youre name, and what
ys that knyghtes name that hath beatyn me?'

'Sir, as for my name, wyte you well [yt] ys sir Trystram de Lyones, 5
and as for hym, hys name ys sir Palomydes, brothir unto the good
knyght sir Sapher, and yet ys sir Palomydes uncrystynde.'

'Alas!' seyde sir Galleron, 'that ys grete pyté that so good a knyght
and so noble a man off armys sholde be uncrystynde.'

'So God me helpe,' seyde sir Trystram, 'owthyr he shall sle me, othir 10
I hym, but that he shall be crystynde or ever we departe in sundir.'

'My lorde, sir Trystram,' seyde sir Galleron, 'youre renowne and
worshyp ys well knowyn thorow many realmys, and God save you
thys day frome senshyp and shame!'

Than sir Trystram unarmed sir Galleron, the whyche was a noble 15
knyght and had done many dedys of armys; and he was a large knyght
of fleyshe and boone. And whan he was unarmed he stood on hys feete,
for he was sore brused in the backe wyth a speare; yet as well as sir
Galleron myght he armed sir Trystram.

And than sir Trystram mounted uppon hys horse, and in hys honde 20
he gate sir Galleron hys speare; and therewythall sir Palomydes was
redy. And so they cam hurtelynge togydyrs, and aythir smote othir in
myddys off there shyldys. And therewythall sir Palomydes speare brake,
and sir Trystram smote downe sir Palomydes, horse and man, to the
erthe.   25

And than sir Palomydes, as sone as he myght, avoyded hys horse,
and dressed hys shylde, and pulled oute hys swerde. That sawe sir
Trystram, and therewythall he alyght and tyed hys horse to a tre. And (14)
than they cam togydyrs egirly as two wylde borys, and so they layshed
togydyrs, trasynge and traversynge as noble men that offten had bene 30
well proved in batayle. But ever sir Palomydes dred passynge sore
the myght of sir Trystram, and therefore he suffyrd hym to breeth
hym, and thus they faught more than two owrys. But oftyntymes sir
Trystram smote suche strokys at sir Palomydes that he made hym to
knele, and sir Palomydes brake and kutte many pecis of sir Trystrams 35
shylde, and than sir Palomydes wounded sir Trystram passynge sore,
for he was a well fyghtynge man.

Than sir Trystram waxed wood wrothe oute off mesure, and russhed
uppon sir Palomydes wyth suche a myght that sir Palomydes felle
grovelynge to the erthe. And therewythall he lepe up lyghtly uppon 40
hys feete, and than sir Trystram wounded sore sir Palomydes thorow
the shuldir. And ever sir Trystram fought stylle in lyke harde, and sir
Palomydes fayled hym nat but gaff hym many sad strokys agayne. And
at the laste sir Trystram doubeled hys strokys uppon hym, and by

fortune sir Trystram smote sir Palomydes swerde oute of hys honde, and yf sir Palomydes had stouped for hys swerde he had bene slayne. And than sir Palomydes stood stylle and behylde hys swerde wyth a sorowfull harte.

5 'How now?' sayde sir Trystram. 'For now I have the at avauntayge,' seyde sir Trystram, 'as thou haddist me thys day, but hyt shall never be seyde in no courte nor amonge no good knyghtes that sir Trystram shall sle ony knyght that ys wepynles. And therefore take thou thy swerde, and lat us make an ende of thys batayle!'

10 'As for to do thys batayle,' seyde sir Palomydes, 'I dare ryght well ende hyt. But I have no grete luste to fyght no more, and for thys cause,' seyde sir Palomydes: 'myne offence ys to you nat so grete but that we may be fryendys, for all that I have offended ys and was for the love of La Beall Isode. And as for her, I dare say she ys pyerles of all 15 othir ladyes, and also I profyrd her never no maner of dyshonoure, and by her I have getyn the moste parte of my worshyp. And sytthyn I ⟨ha⟩d [o]ffended never as to her owne persone, and as for the offence that I have done, hyt was ayenste youre owne persone, and for that [o]ffence ye have gyvyn me thys day many sad strokys (and som I have 20 gyffyn you agayne, and now I dare sey I felte never man of youre myght nothir so well-brethed but yf hit were sir Launcelot du Laake), wherefore I requyre you, my lorde, forgyff me all that I have offended unto you! And thys same day have me to the nexte churche, and fyrste lat me be clene conffessed, and aftir that se youreself that I be truly 25 baptysed. And than woll we all ryde togydyrs unto the courte of kynge Arthure, that we may be there at the nexte hyghe feste folowynge.'

'Than take youre horse,' seyde sir Trystram, 'and as ye sey, so shall hyt be; and all my evyll wyll God forgyff hyt you, and I do. And hereby wythin thys myle ys the suffrygan of Carlehylle whyche shall 30 gyff you the sacramente of baptyme.'

And anone they toke there horsys, and sir Galleron rode wyth them, and whan they cam to the suffrygan sir Trystram tolde hym there desyre. Than the suffrygan let fylle a grete vessell wyth watyr, and whan he had halowed hy the than conffessed clene sir Palomydes. 35 And sir Trystram and sir Galleron were hys two godfadyrs.

And than sone afftyr they departed and rode towarde Camelot where that kynge Arthure and quene Gwenyvir was, and the moste party of all the knyghtes of the Rounde Table were there also. And so the kynge and all the courte were ryght glad that sir Palomydes was crystynde.

40 And that same feste in cam sir Galahad that was son unto sir Launcelot du Lake, and sate in the Syge Perelous. And so therewythall they departed and dysceyvirde, all the knyghtys of the Rounde Table.

And than sir Trystram returned unto Joyus Garde, and sir Palomydes folowed aftir the questynge beste.

HERE ENDYTH THE SECUNDE BOKE OFF SYR TRYSTRAM DE LYONES, WHYCHE DRAWYN WAS OUTE OF FREYNSHE BY SIR THOMAS MALLEORRÉ, KNYGHT, AS JESU BE HYS HELPE. AMEN.

BUT HERE YS NO REHERSALL OF THE THIRDE BOOKE.

BUT HERE FOLOWYTH THE NOBLE TALE OFF THE SANKEGREALL, 5 WHYCHE CALLED YS THE HOLY VESSELL AND THE SYGNYFYCACION OF BLYSSED BLOODE OFF OURE LORDE JESU CRYSTE, WHYCHE WAS BROUGHT INTO THYS LONDE BY JOSEPH OFF ARAMATHYE.

THEREFORE ON ALL SYNFULL, BLYSSED LORDE, HAVE ON THY KNYGHT MERCY. AMEN.

10

THE TALE OF
THE SANKGREAL

BRIEFLY DRAWN OUT OF FRENCH
WHICH IS A TALE CHRONICLED
FOR ONE OF THE TRUEST
AND ONE OF THE HOLIEST THAT
IS IN THIS WORLD

I. THE DEPARTURE

At the vigyl of Pentecoste, whan all the felyship of the Table Rownde were com unto Camelot and there harde hir servyse, so at the laste the tablys were sette redy to the meete, ryght so entird into the halle a full fayre jantillwoman on horsebacke that had ryddyn full faste, for hir 5 horse was all beswette. Than she there alyght and com before the kynge and salewed hym, and he seyde,

'Damesell, God you blysse!'

'Sir,' seyde she, 'for Goddis sake telle me where ys sir Launcelot.'

'He ys yondir, ye may se hym,' seyde the kynge. 10

Than she wente unto sir Launcelot and seyde,

'Sir Launcelot, I salew you on kynge Pelles behalff, and I also requyre you to com with me hereby into a foreste.'

Than sir Launcelot asked her with whom she dwelled.

'I dwelle,' she seyde, 'with kynge Pelles.' 15

'What woll ye with me?' seyde sir Launcelot.

'Ye shall know,' she seyde, 'whan ye com thydir.'

'Well,' seyde he, 'I woll gladly go with you.'

So sir Launcelot bade hys squyre sadyll hys horse and brynge hys armys in haste. So he ded hys commandemente. Than com the quene 20 unto sir Launcelot and seyde,

'Woll ye leve us now alone at thys hyghe feste?'

'Madam,' seyde the jantyllwoman, 'wyte you well he shall be with you to-morne by dyner tyme.'

'If I wyste,' seyde the quene, 'that he sholde nat be here with us to- 25 morne, he sholde nat go with you be my good wyll!'

Ryght so departed sir Launcelot, and rode untyll that he com into a foreste and into a grete valey where they sye an abbey of nunnys. And there was a squyre redy, and opened the gatis, and so they entird and descended of their horsys. And anone there cam a fayre felyship aboute 30 sir Launcelot and wellcomed hym, [and were passyng gladde of his comynge]; and than they ladde hym unto the abbas chambir and unarmed hym.

And ryght so he was ware uppon a bed lyynge two of hys cosyns, sir Bors and sir Lyonell. And anone he waked them, and whan they 35 syghe hym they made grete joy.

'Sir,' seyde sir Bors unto sir Launcelot, 'what adventure hath brought you hidir? For we wende to have founde you to-morne at Camelot.'

'So God me helpe,' seyde sir Launcelot, 'a jantillwoman brought 40 me hydir, but I know nat the cause.'

So in the meanewhyle that they thus talked togydir, there com in twelve nunnes that brought with hem Galahad, the whych was passynge fayre and welle made, that unneth in the worlde men myght nat fynde hys macche. And all tho ladyes wepte.

5 'Sir,' seyd they all, 'we brynge you hyre thys chylde the whycch we have norysshed, and we pray you to make hym knyght, for of a more worthyer mannes honde may he nat resceyve the Order of Knyghthode.'

Sir Launcelot behylde thys yonge squyer and saw hym semely and 10 demure as a dove, with all maner of goode fetures, that he wende of hys ayge never to have seene so fayre a fourme of a man. Than seyde sir Launcelot,

'Commyth thys desyre of hymselff?'

He and all they seyde 'Yes'.

15 'Than shall he,' seyde sir Launcelot, 'resseyve the Order of Knyghthode at the reverence of the hyghe feste.'

So that nyght sir Launcelot had passyng good chere. And on the mor[n]e at the howre of pryme at Galahaddis desyre he made hym knyght, and seyde,

20 'God make you a good man, for of beauté faylith you none as ony
(2) that ys now lyvynge. Now, fayre sir,' seyde sir Launcelot, 'woll ye com with me unto the courte of kynge Arthure?'

'Nay,' seyde he, 'I woll nat go with you at thys tyme.'

Than he departed frome them and toke hys two cosynes with hym.
25 And so they com unto Camelot by the owre of undirne on Whytsonday. So by that tyme the kynge and the quene was gone to the mynster to here their servyse. Than the kynge and the quene were passynge glad of sir Bors and sir Lyonel, and so was all the felyshyp.

So whan the kynge and all the knyghtes were com frome servyse
30 the barownes aspyed in the segys of the Rounde Table all aboute wretyn with golde lettirs:

'HERE OUGHT TO SITTE HE', and 'HE OUGHT TO SITTE HYRE'.

And thus they wente so longe tylle that they com to the Sege Perelous, where they founde lettirs newly wrytten of golde, whych seyde:

35 'FOUR HONDRED WYNTIR AND FOUR AND FYFFTY ACOMPLYVYSSHED AFTIR THE PASSION OF OURE LORDE JESU CRYST OUGHTE THYS SYEGE TO BE FULFYLLED.'

Than all they seyde,

'Thys ys a mervaylous thynge and an adventures!'

40 'In the name of God!' seyde sir Launcelot, and than accounted the terme of the wrytynge, frome the byrth of oure Lorde untyll that day.

'Hit semyth me,' seyd sir Launcelot, 'that thys syge oughte to be fulfylled thys same day, for thys [ys] the Pentecoste after the four hondred and four and fyffty yere. And if hit wolde please all partyes,

I wolde none of thes lettirs were sene thys day tyll that he be com that
ought to enchyve thys adventure.'

Than made they to ordayne a cloth of sylke for to cover thes lettirs
in the Syege Perelous. Than the kynge bade haste unto dyner.

'Sir,' seyde sir Kay the Stywarde, 'if ye go now unto youre mete ₅
ye shall breke youre olde custom of youre courte, for ye have nat
used on thys day to sytte at your mete or that ye have sene some
adventure.'

'Ye sey sothe,' seyde the kynge, 'but I had so grete joy of sir Launcelot and of hys cosynes whych bene com to the courte hole and sounde, 10
that I bethought me nat of none olde custom.'

So as they stood spekynge, in com a squyre that seyde unto the
kynge,

'Sir, I brynge unto you mervaylous tydynges.'

'What be they?' seyde the kynge.   15

'Sir, there ys here bynethe at the ryver a grete stone whych I saw
fleete abovyn the watir, and therein I saw stykynge a swerde.'

Than the kynge seyde, 'I woll se that mervayle.'

So all the knyghtes wente with hym. And whan they cam unto [the]
ryver they founde there a stone fletynge, as hit were of rede marbyll, 20
and therein stake a fayre ryche swerde, and the pomell thereof was of
precious stonys wrought with lettirs of golde subtylé. Than the
barownes redde the lettirs whych seyde in thys wyse:

'NEVER SHALL MAN TAKE ME HENSE BUT ONLY HE BY WHOS SYDE I
OUGHT TO HONGE AND HE SHALL BE THE BESTE KNYGHT OF THE WORLDE.' 25

So whan the kynge had sene the lettirs he seyde unto sir Launcelot,

'Fayre sir, thys swerde ought to be youres, for I am sure ye be the
beste knyght of the worlde.'

Than sir Launcelot answerde full sobirly,

'Sir, hit ys nat my swerde; also, I have no hardines to sette my honde 30
thereto, for hit longith nat to hange be my syde. Also, who that
assayth to take hit and faylith of that swerde, he shall resseyve a
wounde by that swerde that he shall nat be longe hole afftir. And I
woll that ye weyte that thys same day shall the adventure of the Sankgreall begynne, that ys called the holy vessell.'   35

'Now, fayre nevew,' seyde the kynge unto sir Gawayne, 'assay ye for (3)
my love.'

'Sir,' he seyde, 'sauff youre good grace, I shall nat do that.'

'Sir,' seyde the kynge, 'assay to take the swerde for my love and at
my commaundemente.'   40

'Sir, youre commaundemente I woll obey.'

And therewith he toke the swerde by the handyls, but he myght nat
stirre hit.

'I thanke you,' seyde the kynge.

'My lorde sir Gawayne,' seyde sir Launcelot, 'now wete you well thys swerde shall touche you so sore that ye wolde nat ye had sette youre honde thereto for the beste castell of thys realme.'

'Sir,' he seyde, 'I myght nat withsey myne unclis wyll.'

5   But whan the kynge herde thys he repented hit much and seyde unto sir Percyvall,

'Sir, woll ye assay for my love?'

And he assayed gladly for to beare sir Gawayne felyship, and therewith he sette to hys honde on the swerde and drew at hit strongely, but
10 he myght nat meve hytte. Than were there [no] mo that durste be so hardy to sette their hondis thereto.

'Now may ye go to youre dyner,' seyde sir Kay unto the kynge, 'for a mervalous adventure have ye sene.'

So the hynge and all they wente unto the courte, and every knyght
15 knew hys owne place and sette hym therein. And yonge men that were good knyghtes served them. So whan they were served and all syegis fulfylled sauff only the Syege Perelous, anone there befelle a mervaylous adventure: that all the doorys and wyndowes of the paleyse shutte by themselff. Natforthan the halle was nat gretly durked, and therewith
20 they abaysshed bothe one and other. Than kynge Arthure spake fyrste and seyde,

'Be God, fayre felowis and lordis, we have sene this day mervayles! But or nyght I suppose we shall se gretter mervayles.'

In the meanewhyle com in a good olde man and an awnciente,
25 clothed all in whyght, and there was no knyght knew from whens he com. And with hym he brought a yonge knyght, and bothe on foote, in rede armys, withoute swerde other shylde sauff a scawberd hangynge by hys syde. And thes wordys he seyde:

'Pees be with you, fayre lordys!'

30 Than the olde man seyde unto kynge Arthure, 'Sir, I brynge you here a yonge knyght the whych ys of kynges lynage and of the kynrede of Joseph of Aramathy, whereby the mervayles of this courte and of stronge realmys shall be fully complevysshed.'

(4) The kynge was ryght glad of hys wordys and seyde unto the good man,
35 'Sir, ye be ryght wellcom, and the yonge knyght with you.'

Than the olde man made the yonge man to unarme hym. And he was in a cote of rede sendell, and bare a mantell uppon hys sholder that was furred with ermyne, and put that uppon hym.

And the olde knyght seyde unto [the] yonge knyght,

40 'Sir, swith me.'

And anone he lad hym to the Syege Perelous where besyde sate sir Launcelot, and the good man lyffte up the clothe and founde there the lettirs that seyde thus:

'THYS YS THE SYEGE OF SIR GALAHAD THE HAWTE PRYNCE.'

'Sir,' seyde the olde knyght, 'weyte you well that place ys youres.'

And than he sette hym downe surely in that syge, and than he seyde unto the olde man,

'Now may ye, sir, go youre way, for well have ye done in that that ye were commaunded. And recommaunde me unto my grauntesyre, kynge 5 Pelles, and unto my lorde kynge Pecchere, and sey hem on my behalff I shall com and se hem as sone as ever y may.'

So the good man departed. And there mette hym twenty noble squyers, and so toke their horsys and wente their wey.

Than all the knyghtes of the Table Rounde mervayled gretly of sir 10 Galahad that he durst sitte there and was so tendir of ayge, and wyst nat frome whens he com but all only be God. All they seyde,

'Thys ys he by whom the Sankgreall shall be encheved, for there sate never none but he there but he were myscheved.'

Than sir Launcelot behylde hys sonne and had grete joy of hym. Than 15 sir Bors tolde hys felowis,

'Uppon payne of my lyff thys yonge knyght shall com to grete worship!'

So thys noyse was grete in all the courte, that hit cam unto the quene. And she had mervayle what knyght hit myght[e be] that durste adven- 20 ture hym to sytte in that Sege Perelous.

Than som seyde he resembled much unto sir Launcelot.

'I may well suppose,' seyde the quene, 'that sir Launcelot begate hym on kynge Pelles doughter, whych made hym to lye by her by enchaunte- mente, and hys name ys Galahad. I wolde fayne se hym,' seyde the 25 quene, 'for he muste nedys be a noble man, for so hys fadir ys that hym begate: I reporte me unto all the Table Rounde.'

So whan the mete was done, that the kynge and all were rysen, the kyng yode to the Sege Perelous and lyfft up the clothe and founde there the name of sir Galahad. And than he shewed hit unto sir Gawayne 30 and seyde,

'Fayre nevew, now have we amonge us sir Galahad, the good knyght that shall worship us all. And uppon payne of my lyff he shall encheve the Sankgreall, ryght as sir Launcelot had done us to undirstonde.'

Than cam kynge Arthure unto sir Galahad and seyde, 'Sir, ye be ryght 35 wellcom, for ye shall meve many good knyghtes to the queste of the Sankgreall, and ye shall enchyve that many other knyghtes myght never brynge to an ende.'

Than the kynge toke hym by the honde and wente downe frome the paleyes to shew Galahad the adventures of the stone.   40

Than the quene harde thereof and cam aftir with many ladyes, and (5) ⟨so they⟩ shewed her the stone where hit hoved on the watir.

'Sir,' seyde the kynge unto sir Galahad, 'here ys a grete mervayle as ever y sawe, and ryght good knyghtes have assayde and fayled.'

'Sir,' seyde sir Galahad, 'hit ys no mervayle, for thys adventure ys nat theyrs but myne. And for the sureté of thys swerde I brought none with me, but here by my syde hangith the scawberte.'

And anone he leyde hys honde on the swerde, and lyghtly drew hit
5 oute of the stone, and put hit in the sheethe, and seyde unto the kynge, 'Now hit goth ⌐better than hit dyd aforehand.'¬

'Sir,' seyde the kynge, 'a shylde God may sende you.'

'Now have I the swerde that somtyme was the good knyghtes Balyns le Saveaige, and he was a passynge good knyght of hys hondys; and
10 with thys swerde he slew hys brothir Balan, and that was grete pité, for he was a good knyght. And eythir slew othir thorow a dolerous stroke that Balyn gaff unto kynge Pelles, the whych ys nat yett hole, nor naught shall be tyll that I hele hym.'

So therewith the kynge ⌐and all¬ had aspyed com rydynge downe the
15 ryver a lady on a whyght palferey a grete paace towarde them. Than she salewed the kynge and the quene and asked if that sir Launcelot were there, and than he answerd hymselff and seyde,

'I am here, my fayre lady!'

Than she seyde all with wepynge chere,
20 'A, sir Launcelot! How youre grete doynge ys chonged sytthyn thys day in the morne!'

'Damesell, why sey ye so?'

'Sir, I say you sothe,' seyde the damesell, 'for ye were thys day in the morne the best knyght of the worlde. But who sholde sey so now, he
25 sholde be a lyer, for there ys now one bettir than ye be, and well hit ys preved by the adventure of the swerde whereto ye durst nat sette to your honde. And that ys the change of youre name and levynge. Wherefore I make unto you a remembraunce that ye shall nat wene frome hensforthe that ye be the best knyght of the worlde.'

30 'As towchyng unto that,' seyde sir Launcelot, 'I know well I was never none of the beste.'

'Yes,' seyde the damesell, 'that were ye, and ar yet, of ony synfull man of the worlde. And, sir kynge, Nacien the eremeyte sende[th] the worde that the shall befalle the grettyst worship that ever befelle kynge in
35 Bretayne, and I sey y[o]u wherefore: for thys day the Sankegreall appered in thy house and fedde the and all thy felyship of the Rounde Table.'

So she departed and wente the same way that she cam.

(6) 'Now,' seyde the kynge, 'I am sure at this quest of the Sankegreall
40 shall all ye of the Rownde Table departe, and nevyr shall I se you agayne holé togydirs, therefore ones shall I se you togydir in the medow, all holé togydirs! Therefore I woll se you all holé togydir in the medow of Camelot, to juste and to turney, that aftir youre dethe men may speke of hit that such good knyghtes were here, such a day, holé togydirs.'

As unto that counceyle and at the kynges rekeyst they accorded all, and toke on the harneyse that longed unto joustenynge. But all thys mevynge of the kynge was for thys entente, for to se Galahad preved; for the kynge demed he sholde nat lyghtly com agayne unto the courte aftir thys departynge.   5

So were they assembled in the medowe, both more and lasse.

Than sir Galahalt by the prayer of the kynge and the quene dud on a noble jesseraunce uppon hym, and also he dud on hys helme, but shylde wolde he take none for no prayer of the kynge. So than sir Gawayne and othir knyghtes prayde hym to take a speare. Ryght so he dud. So   10 the quene was in a towure with all hir ladyes for to beholde that turne-ment.

Than sir Galahad dressed hym in myddys of the medow and began to breke spearys mervaylously, that all men had wondir of hym, for he there surmownted all othir knyghtes. For within a whyle he had de-   15 fowled many good knyghtes of the Table Rounde sauff all only tweyne, that was sir Launcelot and sir Persyvale.

Than the kynge at the quenys desyre made hym to alyght and to un-   (7) lace hys helme, that the quene myght se hym in the vysayge. Whan she avysed hym she seyde,   20

'I dare well sey sothely that sir Launcelot begate hym, for never two men resembled more in lyknesse. Therefore hit ys no mervayle thoughe he be of grete proues.'

So a lady that stood by the quene seyde,

'Madam, for Goddis sake, ought he of ryght to be so good a knyght?'   25

'Ye, forsothe,' seyde the quene, 'for he ys of all partyes comyn of the beste knyghtes of the worlde and of the hyghest lynage: for sir Launce-lot ys com but of the eyghth degré frome oure Lorde Jesu Cryst, and thys sir Galahad ys th[e] nyneth degré frome oure Lorde Jesu Cryst. Therefore I dare sey they be the grettist jantillmen of the worlde.'   30

And than the kynge and all the astatis wente home unto Camelot, and so wente unto evynsong to the grete monester. And so aftir uppon that to sowper, and every knyght sette in hys owne place as they were toforehonde.

Than anone they harde crakynge and cryynge of thundir, that hem   35 thought the palyse sholde all to-dryve. So in the myddys of the blast entyrde a sonnebeame, more clerer by seven tymys than ever they saw day, and all they were alyghted of the grace of the Holy Goste. Than began every knyght to beholde other, and eyther saw other, by their semynge, fayrer than ever they were before. Natforthan there was no   40 knyght that myght speke one worde a grete whyle, and so they loked every man on other as they had bene doome.

Than entird into the halle the Holy Grayle coverde with whyght samyte, but there was none that myght se hit nother whom that bare hit. And there was all the halle fulfylled with good odoures, and every knyght had such metis and drynkes as he beste loved in thys worlde.

And whan the Holy Grayle had bene borne thorow the hall, than the holy vessell departed suddeynly, that they wyst nat where hit becam. Than had they all breth to speke, and than the kyng yelded thankynges to God of Hys good grace that He had sente them.

'Sertes,' sey[de] the kynge, 'we ought to thanke oure Lorde Jesu Cryste gretly that he hath shewed us thys day at the reverence of thys hyghe feste of Pentecost.'

'Now,' seyde sir Gawayne, 'we have bene servyd thys day of what metys and drynkes we thought on. But one thyng begyled us, that we myght nat se the Holy Grayle: hit was so preciously coverde. Wherefore I woll make here a vow that to-morne, withoute longer abydynge, I shall laboure in the queste of the Sankgreall, and that I shall holde me oute a twelve-month and a day or more if nede be, and never shall I returne unto the courte agayne tylle I have sene hit more opynly than hit hath bene shewed here. And iff I may nat spede I shall returne agayne as he that may nat be ayenst the wylle of God.'

So whan they of the Table Rounde harde sir Gawayne sey so, they arose up the moste party and made such avowes as sir Gawayne hathe made. Anone as kynge Arthur harde thys he was gretly dysplesed, for he wyst well he myght nat agaynesey their avowys.

'Alas!' seyde kynge Arthure unto sir Gawayne, 'ye have nygh slayne me for the avow that ye have made, for thorow you ye have berauffte me the fayryst and the trewyst of knyghthode that ever was sene togydir in ony realme of the worlde. For whan they departe frome hense I am sure they all shall never mete more togydir in thys worlde, for they shall dye many in the queste. And so hit forthynkith nat me a litill, for I have loved them as well as my lyff. Wherefore hit shall greve me ryght sore, the departicion of thys felyship, for I have had an olde custom to have hem in my felyship.'

(8)　　And therewith the teerys felle in hys yen, and than he seyde,

'Sir Gawayne, ⌐Gawayne⌐! Ye have sette me in grete sorow, for I have grete doute that my trew felyshyp shall never mete here more agayne.'

'A, sir,' sayde sir Launcelot, 'comforte youreself! For hit shall be unto us a grete honoure, and much more than we dyed in other placis, for of dethe we be syker.'

'A, Launcelot!' seyde the kynge, 'the grete love that I have had unto you all the dayes of my lyff makith me to sey such dolefull wordis! For there was never Crysten kynge that ever had so many worthy men at hys table as I have had thys day at the Table Rounde. And that ys my grete sorow.'

Whan the quene, ladyes, and jantillwomen knew of thys tydynges they had such sorow and hevynes that there myght no tunge telle, for tho knyghtes had holde them in honoure and charité. But aboven all othir quene Gwenyver made grete sorow.

'I mervayle,' seyd she, 'that my lorde woll suffir hem to departe fro hym.'   5

Thus was all the courte trowbled for the love of the departynge of these knyghtes, and many of tho ladyes that loved knyghtes wolde have gone with hir lovis. And so had they done, had nat an olde knyght com amonge them in relygious clothynge and spake all on hyght and seyde,

'Fayre lordis whych have sworne in the queste of the Sankgreall, thus   10
sendith you Nacien the eremyte worde that none in thys queste lede lady nother jantillwoman with hym, for hit ys nat to do in so hyghe a servyse as they laboure in. For I warne you playne, he that ys nat clene of hys synnes he shall nat se the mysteryes of oure Lorde Jesu Cryste.'

And for thys cause they leffte thes ladyes and jantillwomen.   15

So aftir thys the quene com unto sir Galahad and asked hym of whens he was and of what contrey. Than he tolde hir of whens he was. 'And sonne unto sir Launcelot?' ⌈she seyde⌉. As to that ⌈he⌉ seyde nother yee nother nay.

'So God me helpe,' seyde the quene, 'ye dar[f] nat shame, for he ys   20
the goodlyest knyght, and of the beste men of the worlde commyn, and of the strene, of all partyes, of kynges. Wherefore ye ought of ryght to be of youre dedys a passyng good man. And sertayne,' she seyde, 'ye resemble hym much.'

Than sir Galahad was a lityll ashamed and seyde,   25

'Madame, sithyn ye know in sertayne, wherefore do ye aske hit me? For he that ys my fadir shall be knowyn opynly and all betymys.'

And than they wente unto reste them. And in honoure of the hyghnes of knyghthod ⌈of⌉ sir Galahad he was ledde into kynge Arthures chambir, and there rested in hys owne bedde. And as sone as hit was   30
day the kynge arose, for he had no reste of all that nyght for sorow. Than he wente unto sir Gawayne and unto sir Launcelot that were arysen for to hyre masse, and than the kynge agayne seyde,

'A, Gawayne, Gawayne! Ye have betrayed me, for never shall my courte be amended by you. But ye woll never be so sory for me as I am   35
for you!'

And therewith the terys began to renne downe by hys vysayge, and therewith the kynge seyde,

'A, curteyse knyght, sir Launcelot! I requyre you that ye counceyle me, for I wolde that thys queste were at an ende and hit myght be.'   40

'Sir,' seyde sir Launcelot, 'ye saw yestirday so many worthy knyghtes there were sworne that they may nat leve hit in no maner of wyse.'

'That wote I well,' seyde the kynge, 'but hit shall so hevy me at their departyng that I wote well there shall no maner of joy remedy me.'

And than the kynge and the quene wente unto the mynster. So anone sir Launcelot and sir Gawayne commaunded hir men to brynge hir armys, and whan they all were armed sauff hir shyldys and her helmys, than they com to their felyship whych were all redy in the same wyse
5 for to go to the monastery to hyre their masse and servyse.

Than aftir servyse the kynge wolde wete how many had undirtake the queste of the Holy Grayle; than founde they be tale an hondred and fyffty, and all tho were knyghtes of the Rounde Table.

And than they put on their helmys and departed and recommaunded
10 them all hole unto the kynge and quene. And there was wepyng and grete sorow.

Than the quene departed into the chambir and holde hir there, that no man shold perceyve hir grete sorowys. Whan sir Launcelot myssed the quene he wente tyll hir chambir, and whan she saw hym she cryed
15 alowde and seyde,

'A, sir Launcelot, Launcelot! Ye have betrayde me and putte me to the deth, for to leve thus my lorde!'

'A, madam, I pray you be nat displeased, for I shall com agayne as sone as I may with my worship.'

20 'Alas,' seyde she, 'that ever I syghe you! But He that suffird dethe uppon the Crosse for all menkynde, He be unto you good conduyte and saufté, and all the hole felyshyp!'

Ryght so departed sir Launcelot and founde hys felyship that abode hys commyng, and than they toke their horsys and rode thorow the
25 strete of Camelot. And there was wepyng of ryche and poore, and the kynge turned away and myght nat speke for wepyng.

So within a whyle they rode all togydirs tyll that they com to a cité, and a castell that hyght Vagon. And so they entird into the castell, and the lorde thereof was an olde man that hyght Vagon, and good of hys
30 lyvyng, and sette opyn the gatis and made hem all the chere that he myght.

And so on the morne they were all accorded that they sholde departe everych from othir. And on the morne they departed with wepyng chere, and than every knyght toke the way that hym lyked beste.

35   II. THE MIRACLES

(9) Now rydith Galahad yet withouten shylde, and so rode four dayes withoute ony adventure, and at the fourthe day aftir evynsonge he com to a whyght abbay. And there was he resceyved with grete reverence and lad untyll a chambir, and there was he unarmed.

40   And than was he ware of two knyghtes of the Table Rounde, on[e] was sir Bagdemagus, and sir Uwayne, and whan they sy hym they wen[t]

to sir Galahad and made of hym grete solace. And so they wente unto
supper.

'Sirs,' seyde sir Galahad, 'what adventure brought you hydir?'

'Sir,' they seyde, 'hit ys tolde us that in thys place ys a shylde that no
man may bere hit aboute his necke but he be myscheved other dede   5
within three dayes, other maymed for ever. But, sir,' seyde kynge Bagdemagus, 'I shall beare hit to-morne for to assay thys adventure.'

'In the name of God!' seyde sir Galahad.

'Sir,' seyde Bagdemagus, 'and I may nat encheve the adventure of
thys shylde ye shall take hit uppon you, for I a[m] sure ye shall nat   10
fayle.'

'Sir, I ryght well agré me thereto, for I have no shylde.'

So on the morne they arose and herde masse. Than syr Bagdemagus
asked where the adventures shylde was. Anone a munke ledde hym behynde an awter where the shylde hynge as whyght as ony snowe, but   15
in the myddys was a rede crosse.

'Syrres,' seyde t[he] monke, 'thys shylde oughte nat to be honged
aboute the nek of no knyght but he be the worthyest knyght of the
worlde. Therefore I counceyle you, knyghtes, to be well avysed.'

'Well,' seyde sir Bagdemagus, 'I wote well I am nat the beste knyght,   20
but I shall assay to bere hit,' and so bare hit oute of the monaster. Than
he seyde unto sir Galahad, 'And hit please you to abyde here styll tylle
that ye wete how that I spede.'

'Sir, I shall abyde you,' seyde sir Galahad.

Than kynge Bagdemagus toke with hym a good squyre, to brynge   25
tydynges unto sir Galahad how he spedde. Than they rode two myle
and com to a fayre valey before an ermytayge, and than they saw a
knyght com frome that partyes in whyght armour, horse and all, and he
com as faste as hys horse myght renne, and hys speare in hys reeste.
Than sir Bagdemagus dressed hys speare ayenste hym and brake hit   30
uppon the whyght knyght, but the othir stroke hym so harde that he
braste the mayles and threste hym thorow the ryght sholdir, for the
shylde coverde hym nat as at that tyme. And so he bare hym frome hys
horse, and therewith he alyght and toke hys whyght shylde frome hym,
saynge,   35

'Knyght, thou hast done thyselff grete foly, for thys shylde ought nat
to be borne but by hym that shall have no pere that lyvith.'

And than he com to Bagdemagus squyre and bade hym 'bere thys
shylde to the good knyght sir Galahad that thou leffte in the abbey, and
grete hym well by me.'   40

'Sir,' seyde the squyre, 'what ys youre name?'

'Take thou none hede of my name,' seyde the k[nyghte], 'for hit ys
nat for ⌈the⌉ to know, nother none erthely man.'

'Now, fayre sir,' seyde the squyre, 'at the reverence of Jesu Cryst, telle me be what cause thys shylde may nat be borne but if the berer thereof be myscheved.'

'Now syn thou hast conjoured me,' seyde the knyght, 'thys shelde behovith unto no man but unto sir Galahad.'

5　　Than the squyre wente unto Bagdemagus and asked hym whethir he were sore wounded or none.

'Ye forsothe,' seyde he, 'I shall ascape harde frome the dethe.'

Than he fette hys horse and ledde hym with a grete payne tylle they cam unto the abbay. Than he was takyn downe sofftely and unarmed 10 and leyde in hys bedde and loked there [to] hys woundys. And as the booke tellith, he lay there longe and ascaped hard with the lyff.

(10)　　'Sir Galahad,' seyde the squyre, 'that knyght that wounded Bagdemagus sende you gretyng, and bade that ye sholde bere thys shylde wherethorow grete adventures sholde befalle.'

15　　'Now blyssed be good fortune!' seyde sir Galahad.

And than he asked hys armys and mownted uppon hys horse backe and hanged the whyght shylde aboute hys necke and commaunded hem unto God. So sir Uwayne seyde he wolde beare hym felyshyp if hit pleased hym.

20　　'Sir,' seyde sir Galahad, 'that may ye nat, for I must go alone, save thys squyre shall bere me felyship.'

And so departed sir Uwayne. Than within a whyle cam sir Galahad thereas the whyght knyght abode hym by the ermytayge, and everych salewed other curteysly.

25　　'Sir,' seyde sir Galahad, 'by thys shylde bene many mervayles fallen.'

'Syr,' seyde the knyght, 'hit befelle aftir the Passion of oure Lorde Jesu Cryste two and thirty yere that Joseph of Aramathy, that jantyll knyght the whych toke downe oure Lorde of the holy Crosse, at that 30 tyme he departed frome Jerusalem with a grete party of hys kynrede with hym. And so he labourde tyll they com to a cité whych hyght Sarras. And that same owre that Joseph com to Sarras, there was a kynge that hyght Evelake that had grete warre ayenst the Sarezens, and in especiall ayenste one Sarezyn the whych was kynge Evelakes cousyn, 35 a ryche kynge and a myghty, whych marched nyghe hys londe, and hys name was called Tholomé la Feyntis. So on a day thes two mette to do batayle.

'Than Josephé, the sonne of Aramathy, wente to kyng Evelake and tolde hym he sholde be discomfite and slayne but he leffte hys beleve of 40 the olde law and beleeve uppon the new law. And anone he shewed hym the ryght beleve of the Holy Trynyté, for the whyche he agreed unto with all hys herte.

'And there thys shylde was made for kyng Evelake in the name of Hym that dyed on the Crosse. And than thorow hys goodly belyeve he

had the bettir of kynge Tholomé. For whan kynge Evelake was in the
batayle there was a clothe sette afore the shylde, and whan he was in the
grettist perell he lett put awey the cloth, and than hys enemyes saw a
vigoure of a man on the crosse, wherethorow they all were discomfite.

'And so hit befelle that a man of kynge Evelakes was s[m]ytten hys ₅
honde off, and bare that honde in hys other honde. And Josephé called
that man unto hym and bade hym with good devocion touche the
crosse. And as sone as that man had towched the crosse with hys honde
hit was as hole as ever hit was tofore.

'Than sone afftir the[re] felle a grete mervayle, that the crosse of the ₁₀
shylde at one tyme vanysshed, that no man wyste where hit becam. And
than kynge Evelake was baptyzed, and the moste party of all the people
of that cité.

'So sone aftir Josephé wolde departe, and kynge Evelake wolde
nedys go with hym whethir he wolde or nolde. And so by fortune they ₁₅
com into thys londe that at that tyme was called Grete Bretayne, and
there they founde a grete felon paynym that put Josephé into preson.
And so by fortune that tydynges com unto a worthy man that hyght
Mondrames, and he assembled all hys people for the grete renowne
he had herde of Josephé. And so he com into the londe of Grete ₂₀
Bretaygne and disheryted thys fellon paynym, and confounded hym,
and therewith delyverde Josephé oute of preson. And after that all
the people withturned to the Crystyn feythe.

'So nat longe afftir Josephé was leyde in hys dedly bedde, and whan (₁₁)
kyng Evelake saw that, he had muche sorow, and seyde, "For thy love ₂₅
I leffte my contrey, and syth ye sholl departe frome me oute of thys
worlde, leve me som toky[n] that I may thynke on you."

'Than Josephé seyde, "That woll I do full gladly. Now brynge me
youre shylde that I toke you whan ye wente into batayle ayenst kyng
Tholomé."   ₃₀

'Than Josephé bledde sore at the nose, that he myght nat by no
meane be staunched, and there, uppon that shylde, he made a crosse of
hys owne bloode and seyd,

' "Now may ye se a remembraunce that I love you, for ye shall never
se thys shylde but ye shall thynke one me. And hit shall be allwayes as ₃₅
freysh as hit ys now, and never shall no man beare thys shylde aboute
hys necke but he shall repente hit, unto the tyme that Galahad, the
good knyght, beare hit. And laste of my lynayge have hit aboute hys
necke, that shall do many mervaylous dedys."

' "Now," seyde kyng Evelake, "where shall I put thys shylde, that ₄₀
thys worthy knyght may have hit?"

' "Sir, ye shall leve hit thereas Nacien the ermyte shall put hit afftir
hys dethe, for thydir shall that good knyght com the fiftenth day afftir
that he shall reseyve the Order of Knyghthode.".

'And so that day that they sette ys thys tyme that he have hys shylde. And in the same abbay lyeth Nacien the eremyte.'

And than the whyght knyght vanyshed.

Anone as the squyre had herde thes wordis he alyght of hys hakeney and kneled downe at Galahadys feete, and prayde hym that he myght go ⌜with hym⌝ tyll he had made hym knyght.

'If I wolde ⟨have ony felyshyp I wolde⟩ nat refuse you.'

'Than woll ye make me a knyght?' seyde the squyre. 'And that Order, by the grace of God, shall be well besette in me.'

So sir Galahad graunted hym and turned ayen unto the abbay there they cam fro, and there men made grete joy of sir Galahad.

And anone as he was alyght there was a munke brought hym unto a tombe in a chircheyarde, 'where ys such a noyse that who hyryth hit veryly shall nyghe be madde other lose hys strengthe. And, sir, we deme hit ys a fyende.'

(12)   'Now lede me thydir,' seyd sir Galahad.

And so they dud, all armed sauff hys helme.

'Now,' seyde the good man, 'go to the tombe and lyffte hit up.'

And so he dud, and herde a grete noyse; and pyteuously he seyde, that all men myght hyre,

'Sir Galahad, the servaunte of Jesu Crist, com thou nat nyghe me, for thou shalt make me go agayne there where I have bene so longe.'

But sir Galahad was nothynge aferde, but heve up the stone. And there com oute a fowle smoke, and aftir that he saw the fowlyst vygoure lepe thereoute that ever he saw in the lyknes of a man. And than he blyssed hym and wyst well hit was a fyende. Than herde he a voyce sey,

'Sir Galahad, I se there envyrowne aboute the so many angels that my power may nat deare the!'

Ryght so sir Galahad saw a body all armed lye in that tombe and besyde hym a swerde.

'Now, fayre brothir,' seyde sir Galahad, 'lette remeve thys body. For he ys nat worthy to lye within thys chyrcheyarde, for he was a false Crysten man.'

And therewithall they departed and wente to the abbay. And anone as he was unarmed a good man cam and set hym downe by hym and seyd,

'Sir, I shall telle you what betokenyth of that ye saw in the tombe. Sir, that that coverde the body, hit betokenyth the duras of the worlde, and the grete synne that oure Lorde founde in the worlde. For there was suche wrecchydnesse that the fadir loved nat the sonne, nother the sonne loved nat the fadir. And that was one of the causys that oure Lorde toke fleysh and bloode of a clene maydyn; for oure synnes were so grete at that tyme that well-nyghe all was wyckednesse.'

'Truly,' seyde sir Galahad, 'I beleve you ryght well.'

So sir Galahad rested hym there that nyght, and uppon the morne he made the squyre a knyght and asked hym hys name and of what kynred he was com.

'Sir,' he seyde, 'men calle me Melyas de Lyle, and I am the sonne of 5 the kynge of Denmarke.'

'Now, fayre sir,' seyde Galahad, 'sitthyn that ye be com of kynges and quenys, now lokith that knyghthode be well sette in you, for ye ought to be a myrroure unto all chevilry.'

'Sir,' seyde sir Melyas, 'ye sey sothe. But, sir, sytthyn ye have made 10 me a knyght ye muste of ryght graunte me my first desyre that ys resonable.'

'Ye say soth,' seyde sir Galahad, 'I graunte hit you.'

'Grauntmercy, myne owne lorde,' seyde he, 'and that ye woll suffir me to ryde with you in thys queste of the Sankgreall tyll that som 15 adventure departe us.'

'I graunte you, sir.'

Than men brought sir Melias hys armour and his speare and hys horse. And so sir Galahad and he rode forth all that wyke or ever they founde ony adventure. And than uppon a Munday in the mornynge, 20 as they were departed frome an abbay, they com to a crosse whych departed two wayes, and in that crosse were letters wretyn that seyd thus:

'NOW YE KNYGHTES ARRAUNTE WHICH GOTH TO SEKE KNYGHTES ADVENTURYS, SE HERE TWO WAYES: THAT ONE WAY DEFENDITH THE 25 THAT THOU NE GO THAT ⌐W⌐AY, FOR HE SHALL NAT GO OUTE OF THE WAY AGAYNE BUT IF HE BE A GOOD MAN AND A WORTHY KNYGHT. AND IF THOU GO ON THE LYFFTE HONDE THOU SHALL NAT THERE LYGHTLY WYNNE PROUESSE, FOR THOU SHALT IN THYS WAY BE SONE ASSAYDE.'

'Sir,' seyde Melyas unto sir Galahad, 'if hit lyke you to suffir me to 30 take the way on the lyffte honde ⌐lette me⌐, for I shall well preve my strength.'

'Hit were bettir,' seyde sir Galahad, 'ye rode nat that way, for I deme I sholde bettir ascape in that way, better than ye.'

'Nay, my lorde, I pray you lette me have that adventure.'   35

'Take hit in Goddys name,' seyde sir Galahad.

NOW TURNYTH THE TALE UNTO SYR MELYAS DE LYLE.

And than rode sir Melyas into an olde foreyste, and therin he roode (13) two dayes and more. And than he cam into a fayre medow, and there was a fayre lodge of bowys. And than he aspyed in that lodge a chayre 40 wherein was a crowne of golde, ryche and subtyly wrought. Also there was clothys coverde uppon the erthe, and many delycious metis sette thereon.

So sir Melyas behylde thys adventure and thought hit mervaylous, but he had no hungir. But of the crowne of golde he toke much kepe, and therewith he stowped downe and toke hit up, and rode hys way with hit. And anone he saw a knyght com rydyng aftir hym and seyde,

5 'Knyght, sette downe that crowne whych ys nat youres, and therefore defende you!'

Than sir Melyas blyssed hym and seyde, 'Fayre Lorde of Hevyn, helpe and save thy new-made knyght!'

And than they lette their horses renne as faste as they myght, and so 10 they smote togydirs. But the othir knyght smote sir Melyas thorow hawbirke and thorow the lyff[t] syde, that he felle to the erth nyghe dede, and than he toke hys crowne and yode hys way. And sir Melyas lay stylle and had no power to styrre hym. So in the meanewhyle by fortune com sir Galahad and founde hym there in perell of dethe. And 15 than he seyde,

'Sir Melyas, who hath wounded you? Therefore hit had bene bettir to have ryddyn the other way.'

And whan sir Melyas herde hym speke, 'Sir,' he seyde, 'for Goddys love, lat me nat dye in thys foreyst, but brynge me to the abbey here 20 besyde, that I may be confessed and have my ryghtes.'

'Hit shall be done,' seyde sir Galahad. 'But where ys he that hath wounded you?'

So with that sir Galahad herde on amonge the levys cry on hyght, 'Knyght, kepe the from me!'

25 'A, sir!' seyde sir Melyas, 'beware, for that y[s] he that hath slayne me.'

Sir Galahad answerde and seyde,

'Sir knyght, com on your perell!'

Than aythir dressed to other and com as fast as they myght dryve. 30 And sir Galahad smote hym so that hys speare wente thorow his shuldir, and smote hym downe of hys horse, and in the fallyng sir Galahaddis speare brake. So with that com oute another knyght oute of the grene levys and brake a spere uppon sir Galahad or ever he myght turne hym. Than sir Galahad drew oute hys swerde and smote 35 the lyffte arme off, that hit felle to the erthe; and than he fledde and sir Galahad sewed faste aftir hym.

And than he turned agayne unto sir Melyas, and there he alyght and dressed hym softely on hys horse tofore hym, for the truncheon of hys speare was in hys body. And sir Galahad sterte up behynde hym and 40 hylde hym in hys armys, and so brought hym to the abbay, and there unarmed hym and brought hym to hys chambir. And than he asked hys Saveoure, and whan he had reseyved Hym he seyde unto sir Galahad,

'Syr, latte dethe com whan hit pleasith Hym.'

And therewith he drew the truncheon of the speare oute of hys body,

and than he sowned. Than com there an olde monke whych somtyme
had bene a knyght, and behylde sir Melyas. And anone he ransaked
hym, and than he seyde unto sir Galahad,

'I shall heale hym of hys play, by the grace of God, within the terme
of seven wykes.'   5

Than was sir Galahad glad and unarmed hym and seyde he wolde
abyde there stylle all that nyght.

Thus dwelled he there three dayes, and than he asked sir Melyas how
hit stood with hym. Than he seyde he was turned into helpynge, God
he thanked.   10

'Now woll I departe,' sir Galahad seyde, 'for I have much on honde, (14)
for many good knyghtes be fulle bysy aboute hit. And thys knyght and
I were in the same quest of the Sankgreal.'

'Sir,' seyde a good man, 'for hys synne he was th[u]s wounded. And
I mervayle,' seyde the good man, 'how ye durste take uppon you so   15
rych a thynge as the hyghe Order of Knyghthode ys withoute clene
confession. That was the cause that ye were bittirly wounded, for the
way on the ryght hande betokenyd the hygheway of oure Lorde Jesu
Cryst, and the way of a good trew lyver. And the othir way betokenyth
the way of synnars and of myssebelevers. And whan the devyll saw   20
your pryde and youre persumpcion for to take you to the queste of the
Sankgreal, and that made you to be overthrowyn, for hit may nat
be encheved but by vertuous lyvynge.

'Also the wrytyng on the crosse was a significac[y]on of hevynly
dedys, and of knyghtly dedys in Goddys workys, and no knyghtes   25
dedys in worldly workis; and pryde ys hede of every synne: that
caused thys knyght to departe fromc sir Galahad. And where thou toke
the crowne of golde thou ded syn in covetyse and in theffte. All this
was no knyghtly dedys. And so, sir Galahad, the holy knyght which
fought with the two knyghtes, [the two knyghtes] signyfycth the two 30
dedly synnes whych were holy in thys knyght, sir Melias; and they
myght nat withstonde you, for ye ar withoute dedly synne.'

So now departed sir Galahad frome thens and betaughte hem all unto
God. Than sir Melias seyde,

'My lorde, syr Galahad, as sone as I may ryde I shall seke you.'   35

'God sende you helthe!' seyde sir Galahad.

And so he toke hys horse and departed and rode many journeyes
forewarde and bakwarde, and departed frome a place that hyght
Abblasowre and had harde no masse, [the whiche he was wonte ever to
here or ever he departed oute of ony castel or place, and kepte that for 40
a customme.] Than sir Galahad com to a mountayne where he founde
a chapell passyng olde, and founde therein nobody, for all was desolate.
And there he kneled before the awter and besought God of good counceyle, and so as he prayde he harde a voyce that seyd,

'Go thou now, thou adventurous knyght, to the Castell of Madyns, and there do thou away the wycked customes!'

(15)   Whan sir Galahad harde thys he thanked God and toke hys horse, and he had nat ryddyn but a whyle but he saw in a valey before hym
5 a stronge castell with depe dychys, and there ran besyde hyt a fayre ryver that hyght Sevarne. And there he mette with a man of grete ayge, and ayther salewed other, and sir Galahad asked hym the castels name.

'Fayre sir,' seyde he, 'hit ys the Castell of Maydyns. That ys a cursed
10 castell and all they that be conversaunte therein, for all pité ys oute thereoff, and all hardynes and myschyff ys therein. Therefore I counceyle you, sir knyght, to turne agayne.'

'Sir,' sir Galahad seyde, 'wete you welle that I shall nat turne agayne.' Than loked sir Galahad on hys armys that nothyng fayled hym, and
15 than he putte hys shylde before hym. And anone there mette hym seven fayre maydyns the whych seyde unto hym,

'Sir knyght, ye ryde here in grete foly, for ye have the watir to passe over.'

'Why shold I nat passe the watir?' seyde sir Galahad.
20   So rode he away frome hem and mette with a squyre that seyde,

'Knyght, thoo knyghtes in the castell defyeth you and defendith you ye go no farther tyll that they wete what ye wolde.'

'Fayre sir,' seyde sir Galahad, 'I com for to destroy the wycked custom of thys castell.'
25   'Sir, and ye woll abyde by that ye shall have inowghe to do.'

'Go ye now,' seyde sir Galahad, 'and hast my nedys.'

. Than the squyre entird into the castell, and anone aftir there com oute of the castell seven knyghtes, and all were brethirne. And whan they saw sir Galahad they cryed,
30   'Knyght, kepe the! For we assure you nothyng but dethe.'

'Why,' seyd Galahad, 'woll ye all have ado with me at onys?'

'Yee,' seyde they, 'thereto mayste thou truste!'

Than Galahad put forth hys speare and smote the formyst to the erthe, that nerehonde he brake hys necke. And therewithall the other
35 six smote hym on hys shylde grete strokes, that their sperys brake. Than sir Galahad drew oute hys swerde and sette uppon hem so harde that hit was mervayle, and so thorow grete force he made hem for to forsake the fylde. And sir Galahad chased hem tylle they entird into the castell and so passed thorow the castell at another gate.
40   And anone there mette [sir Galahalte] an olde man clothyd in relygyous clothynge and seyde,

'Syr, have here the kayes of thys castell.'

Than sir Galahad openyd the gatis and saw so muche people in the stretys that he myght nat numbir hem. And all they seyde,

'Sir, ye be wellcom, for longe have we abydyn here oure delyveraunce!'

Then com to hym a jantillwoman and seyde,

'Sir, thes knyghtes be fledde, but they woll com agayne thys nyght,
and here to begyn agayne their evyll custom.'   5

'What woll ye that I do?' seyde sir Galahad.

'Sir,' seyde the jantilwoman, 'that ye sende aftir all the knyghtes
hydir that holde their londys of thys castell, and make hem all to swere
for to use the customs that were used here of olde tyme.'

'I woll well,' seyde sir Galahad.   10

And there she brought hym an horne of ivery boundyn with golde
rychely, and seyde,

'Sir, blow thys horne whiche woll be harde two myles aboute.'

Whan sir Galahad had blowyn the horne he sette hym downe uppon
a bedde. Than com a pryste to Galahad and seyde,   15

'Sir, hit ys past a seven yere agone that thes seven brethirne com into
thys castell and herberowde with the lorde of this castell that hyght
the dyuke Lyanowre, and he was lorde of all this contrey. And whan
they had aspyed the dyukes doughter that was a full fayre woman, than
by there false covyn they made a bate betwyxte hemselff. And the deuke 20
of hys goodnes wolde have departed them, and there they slew hym and
hys eldyst sonne. And than they toke the maydyn and the tresoure of
the castell, and so by grete force they helde all the knyghtes of the
contrey undir grete servayge and trewayge, [robbynge and pyllynge
the poure comyn peple.] So on a day the deukes doughter seyde to   25
them,

' "Ye have done grete wronge to sle my fadir and my brothir and
thus to holde oure londys. Natforthan," she seyde, "ye shall nat holde
thys castell many yerys, for by one knyght ye shall all be overcom."
Thus she prophecyed seven yerys agone.   30

' "Well," seyde the seven knyghtes, "sytthyn ye sey so, there shall
never lady nother knyght passe thys castell but they shall abyde magré
their hedys other dye therefore tyll that knyght be com by whom we
shall lose thys castell."

'And therefore hit ys called the Maydyns Castell, for they have de-   35
voured many maydyns.'

'Now,' seyde sir Galahad, 'ys she here for whom thys castell was
loste?'

'Nay, sir,' seyde the pryste, 'she was dede within three nyghtes aftir
that she was thus forsed, and sytthen have they kepte their yonger   40
syster whych enduryth grete payne with mo other ladyes.'

By thys were the knyghtes of the contrey com, and than he made hem
to do omage and feawté to the dukes doughter and sette them in grete
ease of harte.

And in the morne there com ⌜one⌝ and tolde sir Galahad how that sir Gawayne, sir Gareth and sir Uwayne had slayne the seven brethirne.

'I supposse well,' seyde sir Galahad, and toke hys armoure and hys horse, and commaunded hem unto God.

5 HERE LEVITH THE TALE OF SIR GALAHAD AND SPEKITH OF SIR GAWAYNE.

(16)   Now seyth the tale, aftir sir Gawayne departed he rode many journeys both towarde and frowarde, and at the last [he] com to the abbey where sir Galahad had the whyght shylde. And there sir Gawayne lerned the way to sewe aftir sir Galahad, and so he rode to the abbey
10 where Melyas lay syke. And there sir Melyas tolde sir Gawayne of the mervaylous adventures that sir Galahad dud.

'Sertes,' seyde sir Gawayne, 'I am nat happy that I toke nat the way that he wente. For and I may mete with hym I woll nat departe from hym lyghtly, for all mervaylous adventures sir Galahad enchevith.'

15 'Sir,' seyde one of the munkes, 'he woll nat of youre felyship.'

'Why so?' seyde sir Gawayne.

'Sir,' seyd he, 'for ye be wycked and synfull, and he ys full blyssed.'

So ryght as they thus talked there com in rydynge sir Gareth, and than they made grete joy aythir of other. And on the morne they herde
20 masse and so departed, and by the way they mett with sir Uwayne le Avowtres. And the[re] sir Uwayne tolde sir Gawayne that he had mette with none adventures syth he departed frome the courte.

'Nother yet we,' seyd sir Gawayne.

And so ayther promysed othir of tho three knyghtes nat to departe
25 whyle they were in that queste but if suddayne fortune caused hyt. So they departed and rode by fortune tyll that they cam by the Castell of Maydyns. And there the seven brethirn aspyed the three knyghtes and seyde,

'Sytthyn we be flemyd by one knyght from thys castell, we shall
30 destroy all the knyghtes of kyng Arthurs that we may overcom, for the love of sir Galahad.'

And therewith the seven knyghtes sette uppon hem three knyghtes. And by fortune sir Gawayne slew one [of] the brethren, and ech one of hys felowys overthrew anothir, and so ⌜s⌝lew all the remenaunte.

35   And than they toke the wey undir the castell, and there they loste the way that sir Galahad rode. And there everych of hem departed from other.

And syr Gawayne rode tyll he com to an ermytayge, and there he founde the good man seyynge hys evynsonge of oure Lady. And there
40 sir [Gawayne] asked herberow for charité, and the good man graunted hym gladly. Than the good man asked hym what he was.

'Sir,' he seyde, 'I am a knyght of kynge Arthures that am in the queste of the Sankgreall, and my name ys sir Gawayne.'

'Sir,' seyde the good man, 'I wolde wete how hit stondith betwyxte God and you.'

'Sir,' seyd sir Gawayne, 'I wyll with a good wyll shew you my lyff if hit please you.' There he tolde the eremyte how a monke of an abbay 'called me wycked knyght'. 5

'He myght well sey hit,' seyde the eremyte, 'for whan ye were made first knyght ye sholde have takyn you to knyghtly dedys and vertuous lyvyng. And ye have done the contrary, for ye have lyved myschevously many wyntirs. And sir Galahad ys a mayde and synned never, and that ys the cause he shall enchyve where he goth that ye nor none 10 suche shall never attayne, nother none in youre felyship, for ye have used the moste untrewyst lyff that ever I herd knyght lyve. For sertes, had ye nat bene so wycked as ye ar, never had the seven brethirne be slayne by you and youre two felowys: for sir Galahad hymself alone bete hem all seven the day toforne, but hys lyvyng ys such that he 15 shall sle no man lyghtly.

'Also I may sey you that the Castell of Maydyns betokenyth the good soulys that were in preson before the Incarnacion of oure Lorde Jesu Cryste. And the seven knyghtes betokenyth the seven dedly synnes that regned that tyme in the worlde. And I may lyckyn the good 20 knyght Galahad unto the Sonne of the Hyghe Fadir that lyght within a maydyn and bought all the soules oute of thralle: so ded sir Galahad delyver all the maydyns oute of the woofull castell. Now, sir Gawayne,' seyde the good man, 'thou muste do penaunce for thy synne.'

'Sir, what penaunce shall I do?' 25

'Such as I woll gyff the,' seyde the good man.

'Nay,' seyd sir Gawayne, 'I may do no penaunce, for we knyghtes adventures many tymes suffir grete woo and payne.'

'Well,' seyde the good man, and than he hylde hys pece.

And on the morne than sir Gawayne departed frome the ermyte 30 and bytaught hym unto God. And by adventure he mette wyth sir Agglovale and sir Gryfflet, two knyghtes of the Rounde Table, and so they three rode four dayes withoute fyndynge of ony adventure. And at the fifth day they departed and everych hylde as felle them by adventure. 35

Here levith the tale of syr Gawayne and hys felowys and spekith of sir Galahad.

So whan sir Galahad was departed frome the Castell of Maydyns he (17) rode tyll he com to a waste forest, and there he mette with sir Launcelot and sir Percivale. But they knew hym nat, for he was new dysgysed. 40 Ryght so hys fadir, sir Launcelot, dressed hys speare and brake hit uppon sir Galahad, and sir Galahad smote hym so agayne that he bare downe horse and man. And than he drew his swerde and dressed hym unto sir Percyvall and smote hym so on the helme that hit rooff to the coyff of steele, and had nat the swerde swarved sir Percyvale had be slayne. And with the stroke he felle oute of hys sadyll.

So thys justis was done tofore the ermytayge where a recluse dwelled.
5 And whan she saw sir Galahad ryde she seyde,

'God be with the, beste knyght of the worlde! A, sertes,' seyde she all alowde, that sir Launcelot and Percyvall myght hyre, 'and yondir two knyghtes had knowyn the as well as I do, they wolde nat have encountird with the.'

10 Whan sir Galahad herde hir sey so he was adrad to be knowyn, and therewith he smote hys horse with his sporys and rode a grete pace toward them. Than percyved they bothe that he was sir Galahad, and up they gate on their horsys and rode faste aftir hym. But within a whyle he was oute of hir syght, and than they turned agayne wyth
15 hevy chere and seyde,

'Lat us spyrre som tydynges,' seyde Percyvale, 'at yondir rekles.'

'Do as ye lyst,' seyde sir Launcelot.

So whan sir Percyvale com to the recluse she knew hym well ynoughe and sir Launcelot both.

20 But syr Launcelot rode overthwarte and endelonge a wylde foreyst and hylde no patthe but as wylde adventure lad hym. And at the last he com to a stony crosse whych departed two wayes in waste londe, and by the crosse was a stone that was a marble, but hit was so durke that sir Launcelot myght nat wete what hyt was. Than sir Launcelot
25 loked besyde hym and saw an olde chapell, and there he wen[d]e to have founde people.

And anone sir Launcelot fastenyd hys horse tylle a tre, and there he dud of hys shylde and hynge hyt uppon a tre, and than he wente to the chapell dore and founde hit waste and brokyn. And within he founde a
30 fayre awter full rychely arayde with clothe of clene sylke, and there stoode a clene fayre candyllstykke whych bare six grete candyls therein, and the candilstyk was of sylver; and whan sir Launcelot saw thys lyght he had grete wylle for to entir into the chapell, but he coude fynde no place where he myght entir. Than was he passyng hevy and
35 dysmayed, and returned ayen and cam to hys horse, and dud of hys sadyll and brydyll and leete hym pasture hym, and unlaced hys helme and ungerde hys swerde and layde hym downe to slepe uppon hys shylde tofore the crosse.

(18)   And so he felle on slepe; and half wakyng and half slepynge he saw
40 commyng by hym two palfreyes, all fayre and whyght, whych bare a lytter, and therein lyyng a syke knyght. And whan he was nyghe the crosse he there abode stylle. All thys sir Launcelot sye and behylde hit, for he slepte nat veryly, and he herde hym sey,

'A, sweete Lorde! Whan shall thys sorow leve me, and whan shall

the holy vessell com by me wherethorow I shall be heled? For I have
endured thus longe for litill trespasse, a full grete whyle!'

Thus complayned the knyght and allways sir Launcelot harde hit.
So with that sir Launcelot sye the candyllstyk with the ⌐six⌐ tapirs cam
before the crosse, and he saw nobody that brought hit. Also there cam 5
a table of sylver and the holy vessell of the Sankgreall which sir Launcelot had sene toforetyme in kynge Pe⌐scheo⌐rs house. And therewith the
syke knyght sette hym up, and hylde up both hys hondys, and seyde,

'Fayre swete Lorde whych ys here within the holy vessell, take hede
unto me, that I may be hole of thys malody!   10

And therewith on hys hondys and kneys he wente so nyghe that he
towched the holy vessell and kyst hit, and anone he was hole. And
than he seyde,

'Lorde God, I thanke The, for I am helyd of thys syknes!'

So whan the holy vessell had bene there a grete whyle hit went unto 15
the chapell with the chaundeler and the lyght, so that sir Launcelot
wyst nat where hit was becom; for he was overtakyn with synne, that
he had no power to ryse agayne the holy vessell. Wherefore aftir that
many men seyde hym shame, but he toke repentaunce aftir that.

Than the syke knyght dressed hym up and kyssed the crosse. Anone 20
hys squyre brought hym hys armys and aske[d] hys lorde how he ded.

'Sertes,' seyde he, 'I thanke God, ryght well! Thorow the holy vessell
I am heled. But I have mervayle of thys slepyng knyght that he had no
power to awake whan thys holy vessell was brought hydir.'

'I dare well sey,' seyde the squyre, 'that he dwellith in som dedly 25
synne whereof he was never confessed.'

'Be my fayth,' seyde the knyght, 'whatsomever he be, he ys unhappy.
For as I deme he ys of the felyship of the Rounde Table whych ys
entird in the queste of the Sankgreall.'

'Sir,' seyde the squyre, 'here I have brought you all youre armys 30
save youre helme and youre swerde, and therefore, be myne assente,
now may ye take thys knyghtes helme and his swerde.'

And so he dud. And whan he was clene armed he toke there sir
Launcelottis horse, for he was bettir than hys, and so departed they
frome the crosse.   35

Than anone sir Launcelot waked and sett hym up and bethought (19)
hym what he had sene there and whether hit were dremys or nat.
Ryght so harde he a voyse that seyde,

'Sir Launcelot, more harder than ys the stone, and more bitter than
ys the woode, and more naked and barer than ys the lyeff of the fygge- 40
tre! Therefore go thou from hens, and withdraw the from thys holy
places!'

And whan sir Launcelot herde thys he was passyng hevy and wyst
nat what to do. And so departed sore wepynge and cursed the tyme that

he was bor[n]e, for than he demed never to have worship more. For tho wordis wente to hys herte, tylle that he knew wherefore he was called so.

Than sir Launcelot wente to the crosse and founde hys helme, hys
5 swerde, and hys ⌐horse⌐ away. And than he called hymselff a verry wrecch and moste unhappy of all knyghtes, and there he seyde,

'My synne and my wyckednes hath brought me unto grete dishonoure! For whan I sought worldly adventures for worldely desyres I ever encheved them and had the bettir in every place, and never was
10 I discomfite in no quarell, were hit ryght were hit wronge. And now I take uppon me the adventures to seke of holy thynges, now I se and undirstonde that myne olde synne hyndryth me and shamyth me, that I had no power to stirre nother speke whan the holy bloode appered before me.'

15 So thus he sorowed tyll hit was day, and harde the fowlys synge; than somwhat he was comforted. But whan sir Launcelot myssed his horse and hys harneyse than he wyst well God was displesed with hym. And so he departed frome the crosse on foote into a fayre foreyste, and so by pryme he cam to an hyghe hylle and founde an ermytage and an ermyte
20 therein whych was goyng unto masse.

And than sir Launcelot kneled downe and cryed on oure Lorde mercy for hys wycked workys. So whan masse was done sir Launcelot called hym, and prayde hym for seynte charité for to hyre hys lyff.

'With a good wylle,' seyde the good man, and asked hym whethir he
25 was of kyng Arthurs and of the felyship of the Table Rounde.

'Ye, forsoth, sir, and my name ys sir Launcelot du Lake, that hath bene ryght well seyde off. And now my good fortune ys chonged, for I am the moste wrecch of the worlde.'

The ermyte behylde hym and had mervayle whye he was so abaysshed.
30 'Sir,' seyde the ermyte, 'ye ought to thanke God more than ony knyght lyvynge, for He hath caused you to have more worldly worship than ony knyght that ys now lyvynge. And for youre presumpcion to take uppon you in dedely synne for to be in Hys presence, where Hys fleyssh and Hys blood was, which caused you ye myght nat se hyt with
35 youre worldely yen, for He woll nat appere where such synners bene but if hit be unto their grete hurte other unto their shame. And there is no knyght now lyvynge that ought to yelde God so grete thanke os ye, for He hath yevyn you beauté, bownté, semelynes, and grete strengthe over all other knyghtes. And therefore ye ar the more beholdyn
40 unto God than ony other man to love Hym and drede Hym, for youre strengthe and your manhode woll litill avayle you and God be agaynste you.'

(20) Than sir Launcelot wepte with hevy harte and seyde,

'Now I know well ye sey me sothe.'

'Sir,' seyde the good man, 'hyde none olde synne frome me.'

'Truly,' seyde sir Launcelot, 'that were me full lothe to discover, for thys fourtene yere I never discoverde one thynge that I have used, and that may I now wyghte my shame and my disadventure.'

And than he tolde there the good man all hys lyff, and how he had 5 loved a quene unmesurabely and oute of mesure longe.

'And all my grete dedis of armys that I have done for the moste party was for the quenys sake, and for hir sake wolde I do batayle were hit ryght other wronge. And never dud I batayle all only [for] Goddis sake, but for to wynne worship and to cause me the bettir to be be- 10 loved, and litill or nought I thanked never God of hit.' Than sir Launcelot seyde, 'Sir, I pray you counceyle me.'

'Sir, I woll counceyle you,' seyde the ermyte, '[yf] ye shall ensure me by youre knyghthode ye shall no more com in that quenys felyship as much as ye may forbere.' 15

And than sir Launcelot promysed hym that he nolde, by the faythe of hys body.

'Sir, loke that your harte and youre mowth accorde,' seyde the good man, 'and I shall ensure you ye shall have the more worship than ever ye had.' 20

'Holy fadir,' seyde sir Launcelot, 'I mervayle of the voyce that seyde to me mervayles wordes, as ye have herde toforehonde.'

'Have ye no mervayle,' seyde the good man, 'thereoff, for hit semyth well God lovith you. For men may undirstonde a stone ys harde of kynde, and namely one more than another, and that ys to 25 undirstonde by the, sir Launcelot, for thou wolt nat leve thy synne for no goodnes that God hath sente the. Therefore thou arte more harder than ony stone, and woldyst never be made neyssh nother by watir nother by fyre, and that ys the hete of the Holy Goste may nat entir in the. 30

'Now take hede, in all the worlde men shall nat fynde one knyght to whom oure Lorde hath yevyn so much of grace as He hath lente the, for He hathe yeffyn the fayrenes with semelynes; also He hath yevyn the wytte and discression to know good frome ille. He hath also yevyn prouesse and hardinesse, and gevyn the to worke so largely that thou 35 hast had the bettir all thy dayes of thy lyff wheresomever thou cam. And now oure Lorde wolde suffir the no lenger but that thou shalt know Hym whether tho[u] wolt other nylt. And why the voyce called the bitterer than the woode, for wheresomever much synne dwellith there may be but lytyll swettnesse; wherefore thou art lykened to an olde 40 rottyn tre.

'Now have I shewed the why thou art harder than the stone and bitterer than the tre; now shall I shew the why thou art more naked and barer than the fygge-tre. Hit befelle that oure Lorde on Palme Sonday

preched in Jerusalem, and there He founde in the people that all hard-
nes was herberowd in them, and there He founde in all the towne nat
one that wolde herberow Hym. And than He wente oute of the towne
and founde in myddis the way a fygge-tre which was ryght fayre and
5 well garnysshed of levys, but fruyte had hit none. Than oure Lorde
cursed the tre that bare no fruyte; that betokenyth the fyg-tre unto
Jerusalem that had levys and no fruyte. So thou, sir Launcelot, whan
the Holy Grayle was brought before the, He founde in the no fruyte,
nother good thought nother good wylle, and defouled with lechory.'
10 'Sertes,' seyde sir Launcelot, 'all that ye have seyde ys trew, and
frome hensforewarde I caste me, by the grace of God, never to be so
wycked as I have bene but as to sew knyghthode and to do fetys of
armys.'

Than thys good man joyned sir Launcelot suche penaunce as he
15 myght do and to sew knyghthode, and so assoyled hym, and prayde
hym to abyde with hym all that day.

'I woll well,' seyde sir Launcelot, 'for I have nother helme, horse, ne
swerde.'

'As for that,' seyde the good man, 'I shall helpe you or to-morne at
20 evyn of an horse and all that longith unto you.'

And than sir Launcelot repented hym gretly of hys myssededys.

HERE LEVITH THE TALE OF SIR LAUNCELOT AND BEGYNNYTH OF SIR
PERCYVALE DE GALIS.

III. SIR PERCEVAL

XIV(1) 25 Now seyth the tale that whan sir Launcelot was ryddyn aftir sir Galahad, the whych had all thes adventures aboven seyd, sir Percivale
turned agayne unto the recluse where he demed to have tydynges of
that knyght that sir Launcelot folowed.

And so he kneled at hir wyndow, and the recluse opened hit and
30 asked sir Percivale what he wolde.

'Madam,' he seyde, 'I am a knyght of kyng Arthurs courte and my
name ys sir Percivale de Galis.'

Whan the recluse herde his name she had grete joy of hym, for
mykyll she loved hym toforn passyng ony other knyght; she ought so
35 to do, for she was hys awnte. And than she commaunded the gatis to
be opyn, and there he had grete chere, as grete as she myght make hym
or ly in hir power.

So on the morne sir Percyvale wente to the recluse and asked her if
she knew that knyght with the whyght shylde.

40 'Sir,' seyde she, 'why woll ye wete?'

'Truly, madam,' seyde sir Percyvale, 'I shall never be well at ease tyll that I know of that knyghtes felyship and that I may fyght with hym, for I may nat leve hym so lyghtly, for I have the shame as yette.'

'A, sir Percyvale!' seyde she, 'wolde ye fyght with hym? I se well ye have grete wyll to be slayne, as youre fadir was thorow outerageousnes slayne.'   5

'Madam, hit semyth by your wordis that ye know me.'

'Yee,' seyde she, 'I well oughte to know you, for I am youre awnte, allthoughe I be in a poore place. For som men called me somtyme the Quene of the Wast Landis, and I was called the quene of moste rychesse in the worlde. And hit pleased me never so much my rychesse as doth   10 my poverté.'

Than Percyvale wepte for verry pité whan he knew hit was hys awnte.

'A, fayre nevew,' seyde she, 'whan herde you tydynges of youre modir?'   15

'Truly,' seyde he, 'I herde none of hir, but I dreme of hir muche in my slepe, and therefore I wote nat whethir she be dede other alyve.'

'Sertes, fayre nevew, youre modir ys dede, for aftir youre departynge frome her she toke such a sorow that anone as she was confessed she dyed.'   20

'Now God have mercy on hir soule!' seyde sir Percyvale. 'Hit sore forthynkith me; but all we muste change the lyff. Now, fayre awnte, what ys that knyght? I deme hit be he that bare the rede armys on Whytsonday.'

'Wyte you well,' seyde she, 'that this ys he, for othirwyse ought he   25 nat to do but to go in rede armys. And that same knyght hath no peere, for he worchith all by myracle, and he shall never be overcom of none erthly mannys hande.

'Also Merlyon made the Rounde Table in tokenyng of rowndnes of (2) the worlde, for men sholde by the Rounde Table undirstonde the   30 rowndenes signyfyed by ryght. For all the worlde, crystenyd and hethyn, repayryth unto the Rounde Table, and whan they ar chosyn to be of the felyshyp of the Rounde Table they thynke hemselff more blessed and more in worship than they had gotyn halff the worlde.

'And ye have sene that they have loste hir fadirs and hir modirs and   35 all hir kynne, and hir wyves and hir chyldren, for to be of youre felyship. Hit ys well seyne be you, for synes ye departed from your modir ye wolde never se her, ye founde such felyship at the Table Rounde.

'Whan Merlyon had ordayned the Rounde Table he seyde, "By them whych sholde be felowys of the Rounde Table the trouth of the Sanke-   40 greall sholde be well knowyn." And men asked hym how they myght know them that sholde best do and to encheve the Sankgreall. Than he seyde, "There sholde be three whyght bullis sholde encheve hit, and the two sholde be maydyns and the thirde sholde be chaste. And one of thos three shold passe hys fadir as much as the lyon passith the lybarde, both of strength and of hardines."

'They that herde Merlion sey so seyde thus: "Sitthyn there shall be such a knyght, thou sholdyst ordayne by thy craufftes a syge, that no
5 man shold sytte in hit but he all only that shold passe all other knyghtes." Than Merlyon answerde that he wold so do, and than he made the Syge Perelous [in] whych Galahad sate at hys mete on Whyttsonday last past.'

'Now, Madam,' seyde sir Percyvale, 'so much have I herde of you
10 that be my good wyll I woll never have ado with sir Galahad but by wey of goodnesse. And for Goddis love, fayre awnte, can ye teche me whe[re] I myght fynde hym? For much I wolde love the felyship of hym.'

'Fayre nevew,' seyde she, 'ye muste ryde unto a castell, the whych ys
15 called Gooth, where he hath a cousyn jermayne, and there may ye be lodged thys nyght. And as he techith you, sewith afftir as faste as ye can; and if he can telle you no tydynges of hym, ryde streyte unto the castell of Carbonek where the Maymed Kyng ys lyyng, for there shall ye hyre trew tydynges of hym.'

(3) 20 Than departed sir Percivale frome hys awnte, aythir makyng grete sorow. And so he rode tyll aftir evynsonge, and than he herde a clock smyte. And anone he was ware of an house closed well with wallys and depe dyches, and there he knocke at the gate. And anone he was lette in, and ⌐he alyght and⌐ was ledde unto a chamber and sone [u]narmed.
25 And there he had ryght good chere all that nyght.

And on the morne he herde hys masse, and in the monestery he founde a preste redy at the awter, and on the ryght syde he saw a pew closed with iron, and behynde the awter he saw a ryche bedde and a fayre, as of cloth of sylke and golde. Than sir Percivale aspyed that
30 therein was a man or a woman, for the visayge was coverde. Than he leffte of hys lokynge and herd hys servyse.

And whan hit cam unto the sakarynge, he that lay within the perclose dressyd hym up and uncoverde hys hede, and than hym besemed a passyng olde man, and he had a crowne of golde uppon hys hede, and
35 hys shuldirs were naked and unhylled unto hys navyll. And than sir Percyvale aspyed hys body was full of grete woundys, both on the shuldirs, armys, and vysayge. And ever he hylde up hys hondys agaynst oure Lordis Body and cryed,

'Fayre swete Lorde Jesu Cryste, forgete nat me!'
40 And so he lay nat downe, but was allway in hys prayers and orysons, and hym semed to be of the ayge of three hondred wynter. And whan the masse was done the pryste toke oure Lordys Body and bare hit unto the syke kynge. And whan he had used hit he ded of hys crowne and commaunded the crowne to be sett on the awter.

Than sir Percyvale asked one of the brethirn what he was. 'Sir,' seyde the good man, 'ye have herde much of Joseph of Aramathy; how he was sent ⌐by Jesu Cryst⌐ into thys londe for to teche and preche the holy Crysten faythe, and therefor he suffird many persecucions the whych the enemyes of Cryst ded unto hym. And in the cité of Sarras he 5 converted a kynge whos name was Evelake, and so the kyng cam with Joseph into thys londe, and ever he was bysy to be thereas the Sank-greall was. And on a tyme he nyghed hit so nyghe that oure Lorde was displeased with hym, but ever he folowed hit more and more tyll God stroke hym allmoste blynde. Than thys k[ynge] cryed mercy and 10 seyde,

' "Fayre Lorde, lat me never dye tyll the good knyght of my blood of the ninth degré ⌐be com⌐, that I may se hym opynly that shall encheve the Sankgreall, and that I myght kysse hym."

'Whan the kynge thus had made hys prayers he herde a voyce that 15 (4) seyde, "Herde ys thy prayers, for thou shalt nat dye tylle he hath kyssed the. And whan that knyght shall com the clerenes of youre yen shall com agayne, and thou shalt se opynly, and thy woundes shall be heled, and arst shall they never close."

'And thus befelle of kynge Evelake, and thys same kynge hath lyved 20 four hondred yerys thys holy lyff, and men sey the knyght ys in thys courte that shall heale hym. Sir,' seyde the good man, 'I pray you telle me what knyght that ye be, and if that ye be of the Rownde Table.'

'Yes, forsoth, and my name ys sir Percyvale de Galis.'

And whan the good man undirstood hys name he made grete joy of 25 hym. And than sir Percyvale departed and rode tylle the owre of none. And he mette in a valey aboute twenty men of armys whych bare in a beere a knyght dedly slayne. And whan they saw sir Percyvale they [asked] hym of whens he was, and he seyde,

'Of the courte of kynge Arthur.'   30

Than they cryed at onys, 'Sle hym!'

Than sir Percivale smote the firste to the erth and hys horse uppon hym, and than seven of the knyghtes smote uppon hys shylde at onys and the remenaunte slew hys horse, that he felle to the erth, and had slayne hym other takyn hym, had nat the good knyght s[ir] Galahad 35 with the rede armys com there by adventure into tho partys. And whan he saw all tho knyghtes uppon one knyght he seyde,

'Save me that knyghtes lyve!'

And than he dressed hym towarde the twenty men of armys as faste as hys horse myght dryve, with hys speare in hys reaste, and 40 smote the formyste horse and man to the erth. And whan his speare was brokyn he sette hys honde to hys swerde and smote on the ryght honde and on the lyffte honde, that hit was mervayle to se; and at every stroke he smote downe one or put hym to a rebuke, so that they wolde fyght no more, but fledde to a thyk foreyst, and sir Galahad folowed them.

And whan sir Percyvale saw hym chace them so, he made grete sorow that hys horse was away. And than he wyst well hit was sir
5 Galahad, and cryed alowde and seyde,

'Fayre knyght, abyde and suffir me to do you thankynges, for much have ye done for me.'

But ever sir Galahad rode fast, that at the last he past oute of hys syght. And as fast as sir Percyvale myght he wente aftir hym on foote,
10 cryyng. And than he mette with a yoman rydyng uppon an hakeney which lad in hys ryght honde a grete steede blacker than ony beré.

'A, fayre frende,' seyde sir Percivale, 'as ever y may do for you, and to be youre knyght in the first place ye woll requyre me, that ye woll lende me that blacke steed, that I myght overtake a knyght which
15 [rydeth] before me.'

'Sir,' seyde the yoman, 'that may I nat do, for the horse is such a mannys horse that [and I lente hit you or ony man that] he wolde sle me.'

'Alas,' seyde sir Percivale, 'I had never so grete sorow as I have for losyng of yondir knyght.'
20 'Sir,' seyde the yoman, 'I am ryght hevy for you, for a good horse wolde beseme you well, but I dare nat delyver you thys horse but if ye wolde take hym frome me.'

'That woll I nat,' seyde sir Percivale.

And so they departed, and sir Percivale sette hym downe under a tre
25 and made sorow oute of mesure. And as he sate there cam a knyght
(5) rydynge on the horse that the yoman lad, and he was clene armyd. And anone the yoman com rydynge and pryckyng aftir as fast as he myght and asked sir Percivale if he saw ony knyght rydyng on hys blacke steede.
30 'Ye, sir, forsothe. Why aske ye me, sir?'

'A, sir! that steede he hath benomme me with strengthe, wherefore my lorde woll sle me in what place somever he fyndith me.'

'Well,' seyde sir Percyvale, 'what woldist thou that I ded? Thou seest well that I am on foote. But and I had a good horse I sholde soone
35 brynge hym agayne.'

'Sir,' syde the yoman, 'take my hakeney and do the beste ye can, and I shall sew you on foote to wete how that ye shall spede.'

Than sir Percivale bestrode the hakeney and rode as faste as he myght, and at the last he saw that knyght. And than he cryde,
40 'Knyght, turne agayne!'

And he turned and set hys speare ayenst sir Percivale, and he smote the hackeney in myddis the breste, that he felle downe ⌈dede⌉ to the erthe. And there he had a grete falle and the other rode hys way. And than sir Percivale was wood wrothe and cryed,

'Abyde, wycked knyght! Cowarde and false-harted knyght, turne ayen, and fyght with me on foote!'

But he answerd nat, but past on hys way. Whan sir Percivale saw he wolde nat turne he kest away shylde, helme and swerde, and seyde,

'Now am I a verry wreche, cursed and moste unhappy of all other 5 knyghtes!'

So in thys sorow there he abode all that day tyll hit was nyght, and than he was faynte and leyde hym downe and slepte tyll hit was mydnyght. And than he awaked and saw before hym a woman whych seyde unto hym ryght fyersely,   10

'Sir Percivale, what dost thou here?'

'I do nother good nother grete ille.'

'If thou wolt ensure me,' seyde she, 'that thou wolt fulfylle my wylle whan I somon the, I shall lende the myne owne horse whych shall bere the whother thou wolt.'   15

Sir Percivale was glad of hir profer and ensured hir to fulfylle all hir desire.

'Than abydith me here, and I shall go fecche you an horse.'

And so she cam sone agayne and brought an horse with her that was [i]nly black. Whan sir Percyvale behylde that horse he mervaylde that 20 he was so grete and so well apparayled. And natforthan he was so hardy he lepte uppon hym and toke none hede off hymselff.

And anone as he was uppon hym he threst to hym with hys spurres, and so rode by a foreste; and the moone shoone clere, and within an owre and lasse he bare hym four dayes journey thense untyll he com to 25 a rowghe watir whych rored, and that horse wolde have borne hym into hit.

And whan sir Percivale cam nye the brymme he saw the watir so (6) boysteous he doutted to passe over hit, and than he made a sygne of the crosse in hys forehed. Whan the fende felte hym so charged he 30 shooke of sir Percivale, and he wente into the watir cryynge ˹and roryngeˡ and makyng grete sorowe, and hit semed unto hym that the watir brente. Than sir Percivale perceyved hit was a fynde, the whych wolde have broughte hym unto perdicion. Than he commended hymselff unto God, and prayde oure Lorde to kepe hym frome all suche 35 temptacions.

And so he prayde all that nyght tylle on the morne that hit was day, and anone he saw he was in a wylde mounteyne whych was closed with the se nyghe all aboute, that he myght se no londe aboute hym whych myghte releve hym, but wylde bestes. And than he wente downe into 40 a valey, and there he saw a serpente brynge a yonge lyon by the necke, and so he cam by sir Percivale.

So with that com a grete lyon cryynge and romyng aftir the serpente. And as fast as sir Percivale saw thys he hyghed hym thydir, but

the lyon had overtake the serpente and began batayle with hym. And than sir Percivale thought to helpe the lyon, for he was the more naturall beste of the two, and therewith he drew hys swerde and sette hys shylde afore hym, and there he gaff the serpente suche a buffett that he
5 had a dedely wounde. Whan the lyon saw that, he made no sembelaunte to fyght with hym but made hym all the chere that a beest myghte make a man.

Whan sir Percivale perceyved hit he kyst downe his shylde whych was brokyn, and than he dud of hys helme for to gadir wynde, for he
10 was gretly chaffed with the serpente; and the lyon wente allwey aboute hym fawnynge as a spaynell, and than he stroked hym on the necke and on the sholdirs and thanked God of the feliship of that beste.

And aboute noone the lyon toke hys lityll whelpe and trussed hym and bare hym there he com fro. Than was sir Percivale alone. And as
15 the tale tellith, he was at that tyme, one of the men of the worlde whych moste beleved in oure Lorde Jesu Cryste, for in tho dayes there was but fewe folkes at that tyme that beleved perfitely; for in tho dayes the sonne spared nat the fadir no more than a straunger.

And so sir Percivale comforted hymselff in oure Lorde Jesu and be-
20 sought Hym that no temptacion sholde brynge hym oute of Goddys servys, but to endure as His trew champyon. Thus whan sir Percyvale had preyde he saw the lyon com towarde hym and cowched downe at his feet. And so all that nyght the lyon and he slepte togydirs.

And whan sir Percivale slepte he dremed a mervaylous dreme; that
25 two ladyes mette with hym, and that one sate uppon a lyon, and that other sate uppon a serpente; and that one of hem was yonge, and that other was olde, and the yongist, hym thought, seyde,

'Sir Percyvale, my lorde salewith [the] and sende[th] the worde thou aray the and make the redy, for to-morne thou muste fyght with the
30 stronge[st] champion of the worlde. And if thou be overcom thou shalt nat be quytte for losyng of ony of thy membrys, but thou shalt be shamed for ever to the worldis ende.'

And than he asked her what was hir lorde, and she seyde 'the grettist lorde of the worlde'. And so she departed suddeynly, that he wyst nat
(7) 35 where. Than com forth the tothir lady, that rode uppon the serpente, and she seyde,

'Sir Percivale, I playne unto you of that ye have done unto me, and I have nat offended unto you.'

'Sertes, madam,' seyde he, 'unto you nor no lady I never offended.'
40 'Yes,' seyde she, 'I shall sey you why. I have noryshed in thys place a grete whyle a serpente whych pleased me much ⌐and served me a grete whyle⌐. And yestirday ye slew hym as he gate hys pray. Sey me for what cause ye slew hym, for the lyon was nat youres.'

'Madam, I know well the lyon was nat myne, but for the lyon ys

more of jantiller nature than the serpente, therefore I slew hym, and
mesemyth I dud nat amysse agaynst you. Madam,' seyde he, 'what
wolde ye that I dud?'

'I wolde,' seyde she, 'for the amendis of my beste that ye becam my
man.'   5

And than he answerde and seyde,

'That woll I nat graunte you.'

'No?' seyde she. 'Truly, ye were never but my servaunte syn ye
resseyved the omayge of oure Lorde Jesu Cryste. Therefore I you ensure, in what place that I may fynde you withoute kepyng, I shall take   10
you as he that somtyme was my man.'

And so she departed fro sir Percivale and leffte hym slepynge, whych
was sore travayled of hys avision. And on the morne he arose and
blyssed hym, and he was passynge fyeble.

Than was sir Percivale ware in the see where com a shippe saylyng   15
toward hym, and sir Percivale wente unto the ship and founde hit
coverde within and withoute with whyght samyte. And at the helme
stoode an olde man clothed in a surplyse, in lyknes of a pryste.

'Sir,' seyde sir Percivale, 'ye be wellcom.'

'God kepe you,' seyde the good man. 'And of whense be ye?'   20

'Sir, I am of kynge Arthurs courte and a knyght of the Rounde
Table, whych am in the queste of the Sankgreall, and here I am in
grete duras and never lyke to ascape oute of thys wyldernes.'

'Doute ye nat,' seyde the good man, 'and ye be so trew a knyght as
the Order of Shevalry requyrith, and of herte as ye ought to be, ye   25
shold nat doute that none enemy shold ⟨s⟩lay you.'

'What ar ye?' seyde sir Percyvale.

'Sir, I am of a strange contrey, and hydir I com to comforte you.'

'Sir,' seyde sir Percivale, 'what signifieth my dreme that I dremed
thys nyght?' And there he tolde hym alltogydir.   30

'She which rode uppon the lyon, hit betokenyth the new law of Holy
Chirche, that is to undirstonde fayth, good hope, belyeve and baptyme;
for she semed yonger [than] that othir hit ys grete reson, for she was
borne in the Resurreccion and the Passion of oure Lorde Jesu Cryste.
And for grete love she cam to the to warne the of thy grete batayle that 35
shall befalle the.'

'With whom,' seyde sir Percivale, 'shall I fyght?'

'With the moste douteful champion of the worlde, for, as the lady
seyde, but if thou quyte the welle thou shalt nat be quytte by losyng of
one membir, but thou shalt be shamed to the worldis ende. And she   40
that rode on the serpente signifieth the olde law, and that serpente
betokenyth a fynde. And why she blamed the that thou slewyst hir
servaunte, hit betokenyth nothynge ⟨aboute⟩ the serpente ye slewe; that
betokenyth the devyll that thou rodist on to the roche. And whan thou

madist a sygne of the crosse, there thou slewyst hym and put away hys power. And whan she asked the amendis and to becom hir man, than thou saydist nay, that was to make the beleve on her and leve thy baptym.'

5 So he commaunded sir Percivale to departe, and so he lepte over the boorde, and the shippe and all wente away he wyste nat whydir. Than he wente up into the roche and founde the lyon whych allway bare hym felyship, and he stroked hym uppon the backe and had grete joy of hym.

(8) Bi that sir Percivale had byddyn there tyll mydday he saw a shippe
10 com saylyng in the see as all the wynde of the worlde had dryven hit, and so hit londid undir that rocche. And whan sir Percivale saw thys he hyghed hym thydir and founde the shippe coverde with sylke more blacker than ony beré, and therein was a jantillwoman of grete beauté, and she was clothe rychly, there myght be none bettir. And whan she
15 saw sir Percivale she asked hym who brought hym into thys wyldernesse 'where ye be never lyke to passe hense, for ye shall dye here for hunger and myscheff'.

'Damesell,' seyde sir Percivale, 'I serve the beste man of the worlde, and in Hys servyse He woll nat suffir me to dye, for who that knoᵉcklith
20 shall entir, and who that askyth shall have; and who that sekith Hym, He hydyth Hym not unto Hys wordys.'

But than she seyde, 'Sir Percivale, wote ye what I am?'

'Who taught you my name?' now seyde sir Percivale.

'I knowe you bettir than ye wene: I com but late oute of the Waste
25 Foreyste where I founde the Rede Knyght with the whyghte shylde.'

'A, fayre damesell,' seyde he, 'that knyght wolde I fayne mete withall.'

'Sir knyght,' seyde she, 'and ye woll ensure me by the fayth that ye owghe unto knyghthode that ye shall do my wyll what tyme I somon you, and I shall brynge you unto that knyght.'

30 'Yes,' he seyde, 'I shall promyse you to fullfylle youre desyre.'

'Well,' seyde she, 'now shall I telle you. I saw hym in the Waste Foreyste chasyng two knyghtes unto the watir whych ys callede Mortayse, and they drove into that watir for drede of dethe. And the two knyghtes passed over, and the Rede Knyght passed aftir, and there hys
35 horse was drowned, and he thorow grete strengthe ascaped unto the londe.'

Thus she tolde hym, and sir Percivale was passynge glad thereoff. Than she asked hym if he had ete ony mete late.

'Nay, madam, truly I yeete no mete nyghe thes three dayes, but late
40 here I spake with a good man that fedde me with hys good wordys ᵉand holy¹ and refreyshed me gretly.'

'A, sir knyght, that same man,' seyde she, 'ys an inchaunter and a multiplier of wordis, for and ye belyve hym, ye shall be playnly shamed and dye in thys roche for pure hunger and be etyn with wylde bestis.

And ye be a yonge man and a goodly knyght, and I shall helpe you and ye woll.'

'What ar ye,' seyde sir Percivale, 'that proferyth me thus so grete kyndenesse?'

'I am,' seyde she, 'a jantillwoman that am diseryte, whych was the rychest woman of the worlde.'

'Damesell,' seyde sir Percivale, 'who hath disheryte you? For I have grete pité of you.'

'Sir,' seyde she, 'I dwelled with the grettist man of the worlde, and he made me so fayre and so clere that there was none lyke me. And of that grete beawté I had a litill pryde, more than I oughte to have had. Also I sayde a worde that plesed hym nat, and than he wolde nat suffir me to be no lenger in [his] company. And so he drove me frome myne herytayge and disheryted me for ever, and he had never pité of me nother of none of my counceyle nother of my courte. And sitthyn, sir knyght, hit hath befallyn me to be so overthrowyn and all myne, yet I have benomme hym som of hys men and made hem to becom my men, for they aske never nothynge of me but I gyff hem that and much more. Thus I and my servauntes wer⟨r⟩e ayenste hym nyght and day, therefore I know no good knyght nor no good man but I gete hem on my syde and I may. And for that I know that ye ar a good knyght I beseche you to helpe me, and for ye be a felowe of the Rounde Table, wherefore ye ought nat to fayle no jantillwoman which ys disherite and she besought you of helpe.'

Than sir Percivale promysed her all the helpe that he myght, and than she thanked hym.

And at that tyme the wedir was hote. Than she called unto her a jantillwoman and bade hir brynge forth a pavilion. And so she ded and pyghte hit uppon the gravell.

'Sir,' seyde she, 'now may ye reste you in thys hete of thys day.'

Than he thanked her, and she put of hys, helme and hys shylde. And there he slepte a grete whyle.

And so he awoke and asked her if she had ony mete, and she seyde 'Yee, ye shall have inowghe.'

And anone there was leyde a table, and so muche meete was sette thereon that he had mervayle, for there was all maner of meetes that he cowde thynke on. Also he dranke there the strengyst wyne that ever he dranke, hym thought, and therewith he was chaffett a lityll more than he oughte to be. With that he behylde that jantilwoman, and hym thought she was the fayryst creature that ever he saw.

And than sir Percivale profird hir love and prayde hir that she wolde be hys. Than she refused hym in a maner whan he requyred her, for cause he sholde be the more ardente on hir. And ever he sesed nat to pray hir of love. And whan she saw hym well enchaffed, than she seyde,

'Sir Percivale, wyte you well I shall nat fulfylle youre wylle but if ye swere frome henseforthe ye shall be my trew servaunte, and to do nothynge but that I shall commaunde you. Woll ye ensure me thys as ye be a trew knyght?'

5 'Yee,' seyde he, 'fayre lady, by the feythe of my body!'

'Well,' seyde she, 'now shall ye do with me what ye wyll, and now, wyte you well, ye ar the knyght in the worlde that I have moste desyre to.'

And than two squyres were commaund[ed] to make a bedde in
10 myddis of the pavelon, and anone she was unclothed and leyde therein. And than sir Percivale layde hym downe by her naked. And by adventure and grace he saw hys swerde ly on the erthe nake[d], where in the pomell was a rede crosse and the sygne of the crucifixe [ther]in, and bethought hym on hys knyghthode and hys promyse made unto the
15 good man tofornehande, and than he made a sygne in the forehed of hys. And therewith the pavylon turned up-so-downe and than hit chonged unto a smooke and a blak clowde. And than he drad sore and cryed alowde,

(10)   'Fayre swete Lorde Jesu Cryste, ne lette me nat be shamed, which
20 was nyghe loste had nat Thy good grace bene!'

And than he loked unto her shippe and saw her entir therein, which seyde,

'Syr Percivale, ye have betrayde me.'

And so she wente with the wynde, rorynge and yellynge, that hit
25 semed all the water brente after her.

Than sir Percivale made grete sorow and drew hys swerde unto hym and seyde,

'Sitthyn my fleyssh woll be my mayster I shall punyssh hit.'

And therewith he rooff hymselff thorow the thygh, that the blood
30 sterte aboute hym, and seyde,

'A, good Lord, take thys in recompensacion of that I have myssedone ayenste The, Lorde!'

So than he clothed hym and armed hym and called hymself wrecche of all wrecchis: 'How nyghe I was loste, and to have lost that I sholde
35 never have gotyn agayne, that was my virginité, for that may never be recoverde aftir hit ys onys loste.'

And than he stopped hys bledyng woundes with a pece of hys sherte. Thus as he made hys mone he saw the same shippe com fro the Oryente that the good man was in the day before. And thys noble knyght was
40 sore ashamed of hymselff, and therewith he fylle in a sowne. And whan he awooke he wente unto hym waykely, and there he salewed the good man.

And than he asked sir Percivale, 'How haste thou done syth I departed?'

'Sir,' seyde [he], 'here was a jantillwoman and ledde [me] into dedly synne.'

And there he tolde hym alltogidirs.

'Knew ye nat that mayde?' seyde the good man.

'Sir,' seyde he, 'nay, but well I wote the fynde sente hir hydir to shame me.'

'A, good knyght,' seyde he, 'thou arte a foole, for that jantillwoman was the mayster fyende of helle, which hath pousté over all other devyllis. And that was the olde lady that thou saw in thyne avision rydyng on the serpente.'

Than he tolde sir Percivale how oure Lorde Jesu Cryste bete hym oute of hevyn for hys synne, whycch was the moste bryghtist angell of hevyn, and therefore he loste hys heritaige. 'And that was the champion that thou fought withall, whych had overcom the, had nat the grace of God bene. Now, sir Percivale, beware and take this for an insample.'

And than the good man vanysshed. Than sir Percivale toke hys armys and entirde into the shippe, and so he departed from thens.

SO LEVITH THYS TALE AND TURNYTH UNTO SIR LAUNCELOT.

IV. SIR LAUNCELOT

WHAN the eremyte had kepte sir Launcelot three dayes than the eremyte gate hym an horse, a helme and a swerde, and than he departed ⟨and rode⟩ untyll the owre of none. And than he saw a litill house, and whan he cam nere he saw a lityll chapell. And there besyde he sye an olde man which was clothed all in whyght full rychely. And than sir Launcelot seyde,

'Sir, God save you!'

'Sir, God kepe you,' seyde the good man, 'and make you a good knyght.'

Than sir Launcelot alyght and entird into the chapell, and there he saw an olde man dede and in a whyght sheʳ|ʳte of passyng fyne clothe.

'Sir,' seyde the good man, 'this man ought nat to be in such clothynge as ye se hym in, for in that he brake the othe of hys order, for he hath bene more than an hondred wynter a man of religions.' And than the good man and sir Launcelot ⌐went into the chapell⌐; and the good man toke a stole aboute hys neck and a booke, and than he conjoured on that booke. And with that they saw the fyende in an hydeous fygure, that there was no man so hardé-herted in the worlde but he sholde a bene aferde. Than seyde the fyende,

'Thou haste travayle me gretly. Now telle me what thou wolte with me.'

'I woll,' seyde the good man, 'that thou telle me how my ⌐felawe⌐ becam dede, and whether he be saved or dampned.'

5   Than he seyde with an horrible voice,

'He ys nat lost, but he ys saved!'

'How may that be?' seyde the good man. 'Hit semyth me that he levith nat well, for he brake hys order for to were ˌa sherte where he ought to were none, and who that trespassith ayenst oure [ordre] doth
10 nat well.'

'Nat so,' seyde the fyende. 'Thys man that lyeth here was com of grete lynage. And there was a lorde that hyght the erle de Vale that hylde grete warre ayenste thys mannes nevew which hyght Aguaurs. And so thys Aguaurs saw the erle was bygger than he. Than he wente
15 for to take counceyle of hys uncle which lyeth dede here ⌐as ye may se,⌐ and than he wente oute of hys ermytaige for to maynteyne his nevew ayenste the myghty erle. And so hit happed that thys man that lyeth dede ded so muche by hys wysedom and hardines that the erle was take
(2) and three of hys lordys by force of thys dede man. Than was there pees
20 betwyxte thys erle and thys Aguaurs, and grete sureté that the erle sholde never warre agaynste hym more.

'Than this dede man that here lyeth cam to thys ermytayge agayne. And than the erle made two of hys nevews for to be avenged uppon this man. So they com on a day and founde thys dede man at the saker-
25 ynge of hys masse. And they abode hym tyll he had seyde masse, and than they sette uppon hym and drew oute their swerdys to have slayne hym, but there wolde no swerde byghte on hym more than uppon a gadde of steele, for the Hyghe Lorde which he served, He hym preserved. Than made they a grete fyre and dud of all hys clothys and
30 the heyre of hys backe. And than thys dede man ermyte seyde unto them,

' "Wene ye to bren me? Hit shall nat lyghe in youre power, nother to perish me as much as a threde, and there were ony on my body."

' "No?" seyde one of them. "Hit shall be assayde."

35 'And than they dispoyled hym, and put uppon hym hys sherte, and kyste hym in a fyre. And there he lay all that day tyll hit was nyght in that fyre and was nat dede. And so in the morne than com I and founde hym dede, but I founde neyther threde nor skynne tamed. So toke they hym oute of the fyre with grete feare and leyde hym here as ye may se.
40 And now may ye suffir me to go my way, for I have seyde you the sothe.'

And than he departed with a grete tempest. Than was the good man and sir Launcelot more gladder than they were tofore. And than sir Launcelot dwelled with that good man that nyght.

'Sir,' seyde the good man, 'be ye nat sir Launcelot du Lake?'

'Ye, sir,' seyde he.

'Sir, what seke you in thys contrey?'

'I go, sir, to seke the adventures of the Sankgreall.'

'Well,' seyde he, 'seke ye hit ye may well, but thoughe hit were here 5
ye shall have no power to se hit, no more than a blynde man that sholde
se a bryght swerde. And that ys longe on youre synne, and ellys ye
were more abeler than ony man lyvynge.'

And than sir Launcelot began to wepe. Than seyde the good man,
'Were ye confessed synne ye entred into the queste of the Sankgreall?' 10

'Ye, sir,' seyde sir Launcelot.

Than uppon the morne whan the good man had songe hys masse,
than they buryed the dede man.

'Now,' seyde sir Launcelot, 'fadir, what shall I do?'

'Now,' seyde the good man, 'I requyre you take thys hayre that was 15
thys holy mannes and put hit nexte thy skynne, and hit shall prevayle
the gretly.'

'Sir, than woll I do hit,' seyde sir Launcelot.

'Also, sir, I charge the that thou ete no fleysshe as longe as ye be in
the queste of Sankgreall, nother ye shall drynke no wyne, and that ye 20
hyre masse dayly and ye may com thereto.'

So he toke the hayre and put hit uppon hym, and so departed at
evynsonge, and so rode into a foreyste. And there he mette with a
jantillwoman rydyng uppon a whyght palferey, and than she asked
hym,   25

'Sir knyght, whother ryde ye?'

'Sertes, damesell,' seyde sir Launcelot, 'I wote nat whothir I ryde
but as fortune ledith me.'

'A, sir Launcelot,' seyde she, 'I wote what adventure ye seke, for ye
were beforetyme nerar than ye be now, and yet shall ye se hit more 30
opynly than ever ye dud, and that shall ye undirstonde in shorte tyme.'

Than sir Launcelot asked her where he myght be harberowde that
nyght.

'Ye shall none fynde thys day nor nyght, but to-morne ye shall fynde
herberow goode, and ease of that ye bene in doute off.'   35

And than he commaunded hir unto God, and so he rode tylle that he
cam to a crosse and toke that for hys oste as for that nyght. And so he (3)
put hys horse to pasture and ded of hys helme and hys shylde and made
hys prayers unto the crosse that he never falle in dedely synne agayne.
And so he leyde hym downe to slepe.   40

And anone as he was on slepe hit befylle hym there a vision; that
there com a man afore hym all bycompast with sterris, and that man
had a crowne of golde on hys hede. And that man lad in hys felyship
seven kynges and two knyghtes, and all thes worshipt the crosse,

knelyng uppon their kneys, holdyng up their hondys towarde the
hevyn, and all they seyde:

'Swete Fadir of Hevyn, com and visite us, and yelde unto everych of
us as we have deserved.'

5   Than loked sir Launcelot up to the hevyn and hym semed the clowdis ded opyn, and an olde man com downe with a company of angels
and alyghte amonge them and gaff unto everych hys blyssynge and
called them hys servauntes and hys good and trew knyghtes. And whan
thys olde man had seyde thus he com to one of the knyghtes and seyde,

10   'I have loste all that I have besette in the, for thou hast ruled the
ayenste me as a warryoure and used wronge warris with vayneglory for
the pleasure of the worlde more than to please me, therefore thou
shalt be confounded withoute thou yelde me my tresoure.'

All thys avision saw sir Launcelot at the crosse, and on the morne he
15   toke hys horse and rode tylle mydday. And there by adventure he
mette the same knyght that toke hys horse, helme and hys swerde whan
he slepte, whan the Sankgreall appered afore the crosse. So whan sir
Launcelot saw hym he salewede hym nat fayre, but cryed on hyght,

'Knyght, kepe the, for thou deddist me grete unkyndnes.'

20   And than they put afore them their spearis, and sir Launcelot com so
fyersely that he smote hym and hys horse downe to the erthe, that he
had nyghe brokyn hys neck. Than sir Launcelot toke the knyghtes
horse that was hys owne beforehonde, and descended frome the horse
he sate uppon, and mownted uppon hys horse, and tyed the knyghtes
25   owne horse to a tre, that he myght fynde that horse whan he was rysen.

Than sir Launcelot rode tylle nyght, and by adventure he mette an
ermyte, and eche of hem salewd other. And there he reste with that
good man all nyght and gaff hys horse suche as he myght gete. Than
seyde the good man unto sir Launcelot,

30   'Of whens be ye?'

'Sir,' seyde he, 'I am of Arthurs courte, and my name ys sir Launcelot
de Lake, that am in the queste of the Sankegreall. And therefor, sir, I
pray you counceile me of a vision that I saw thys nyght.' And so he
tolde h[y]m all.

(4) 35   'Lo, sir Launcelot,' seyde the good man, 'there myght thou undirstonde the hyghe lynayge that thou arte com off; ⟨th⟩at thyne avision
betokenyth.

'Aftir the Passion of Jesu Cryste fourty yere, Joseph of Aramathy
preched of the victory of kynge Evelake, that he had in hys batayles the
40   bettir of hys enemyes. And of the seven kynges and the two knyghtes
the firste of hem ys called Nappus, an holy man, and the secunde hyght
Nacien in remembraunce of hys grauntesyre, and in hym dwelled oure
Lorde Jesu Cryst. And the third was called Hellyas le Grose, and the
fourth hyght Lysays, and the fifth hyght Jonas; he departed oute of hys

contrey and wente into Walis and toke there the doughter of Manuell, whereby he had the londe Gaule. And he com to dwelle in thys contrey, and of hym com kynge Launcelot, thy grauntesyre, whych were wedded to the kynges doughter of Irelonde, and he was as worthy a man as thou arte. And of hym cam kynge Ban, thy fadir, whych was the 5 laste of the seven kynges. And by the, sir Launcelot, hit signyfieth that the angels seyde thou were none of the seven felysschip. And the last was the ninth knyght, he was signyfyed to a lyon, for he sholde passe all maner of erthely knyghtes : that ys sir Galahad whych thou gate on kynge Pelles doughter. And thou ought to thanke God more than ony 10 othir man lyvyng, for of a synner erthely thou hast no pere as in knyghthode nother never shall have. But lytyll thanke hast thou yevyn to God for all the grete vertuys that God hath lente the.'

'Sir,' seyde sir Launcelot, 'ye sey that good knyght ys my sonne?'

'That ought thou to know,' seyde the good man, 'for thou knew the 15 doughter of kyng Pelles fleyshly, and on her thou begatist sir Galahad, and that was he that at the feste of Pentecoste sate in the Syge Perelous. And therefore make thou hit to be knowyn opynly that he ys of thy begetyn[ge]. And ꞀI counceyle the,꞉ in no place prees nat uppon hym to have ado with hym, for hit woll nat avayle no knyght to have ado with 20 hym.'

'Well,' seyde sir Launcelot, 'mesemyth that good knyght shold pray for me unto the Hyghe Fadir, that I falle nat to synne agayne.'

'Truste thou well,' seyde the good man, 'thou faryst muche the better for hys prayer, for the sonne shall nat beare the wyckednesse of the 25 Ꞁfader, nor the fader꞉ shall nat beare the wyckednesse of theꞀ sonne, but every man shall beare hys owne burdou. And therefore beseke thou only God, and He woll helpe the in all thy nedes.'

And than sir Launcelot and he wente to supere. And so leyde hem to reste, and ꞀtheꞀ heyre prycked faste Ꞁsir Launcelots skynneꞀ and greved 30 hym sore, but he toke hyt mekely and suffirde the payne. And so on the morne he harde hys masse and toke hys armys and so toke hys leve, and (5) mownted uppon hys horse and rode into a foreyst and helde no hygheway.

And as he loked before hym he sye a fayre playne, and besyde that a 35 fayre castell, and before the castell were many pavelons of sylke and of dyverse hew. And hym semed that he saw there fyve hondred knyghtes rydynge on horsebacke, and there was two partyes : they that were of the castell were all on black horsys and their trappoures black, and they that were withoute were all on whyght horsis and trappers. So there 40 began a grete turnemente, and every[che] hurteled with other, that hit mervayled sir Launcelot gretly. And at the laste hym thought they of the castell were putt to the wars.

Than thought sir Launcelot for to helpe there the wayker party in increasyng of hys shevalry. And so sir Launcelot threste in amonge the party of the castell and smote downe a knyght, horse and man, to the erthe, and than he russhed here and there and ded many mervaylous dedis of armys. And than he drew oute hys swerde and strake many knyghtes to the erth, that all that saw hym mervayled that ever one knyght myght do so grete dedis of armys.

But allwayes the whyght knyghtes hylde them nyghe aboute sir Launcelot for to tire hym and wynde hym, and at the laste, ⌐as a man may not ever endure⌐, sir Launcelot ⌐waxed so faynt of fyghtyng and travaillyng, and⌐ was so wery of hys grete dedis, that he myght nat lyffte up hys armys for to gyff one stroke, that he wente never to have borne armys.

And than they all toke and ledde hym away into a foreyste and there made hym to alyght to reeste hym. And than all the felyship of the castell were overcom for the defaughte of hym. Than they seyd all unto sir Launcelot,

'Blessed be God that ye be now of oure felyship, for we shall holde you in oure preson.'

And so they leffte hym with few wordys, and than sir Launcelot made grete sorowe:

'For never or now was I never at turnemente nor at justes but I had the beste. And now I am shamed, and am sure that I am more synfuller than ever I was.'

Thus he rode sorowyng, and halff a day oute of dispayre, tyll that he cam into a depe valey.

And whan sir Launcelot sye he myght nat ryde up unto the mountayne, he there alyght undir an appyll-tre. And there he leffte hys helme and hys shylde, and put hys horse unto pasture. And than he leyde hym downe to slepe.

And than hym thought there com an olde man afore hym whych seyde,

'A, Launcelot, of evill, wycked fayth and poore beleve! Wherefore ys thy wyll turned so lyghtly toward dedly synne?'

And whan he had seyde thus he vanysshed away, and sir Launcelot wyst nat where he becom.

Than he toke hys horse and armed hym. And as he rode by the hygheway he saw a chapell where was a recluse, which had a wyndow, that she myght se up to the awter. And all a⌐loude⌐ she called sir Launcelot for that he semed a knyght arraunte.

And than he cam, and she asked hym what he was, and of what place, and where aboute he wente to seke. And than he tolde hir alltogydir worde by worde, and the trouth how hit befelle hym at the turnemente, and aftir that he tolde hir hys avision that he had that nyght in hys slepe, ⌐and prayd her to telle hym what hit myght mene⌐.

'A, Launcelot,' seyde she, 'as longe as ye were knyght of erthly
knyghthode ye were the moste mervayloust man of the worlde, and
moste adventurest. Now,' seyde the lady, 'sitthen ye be sette amonge
the knyghtis of hevynly adventures, if adventure falle ⟨you contrary at
that turnamente yet⟩ have ye no mervayle; for that turnamente yestir-   5
day was but a tokenynge of oure Lorde. And natforethan there was
none enchauntemente, for they at the turnemente were erthely knyghtes.
The turnamente was tokyn to se who sholde have moste knyghtes, of
⟨E⟩liazar, the sonne of kynge Pelles, or Argustus, the sonne of kynge
Harlon. But ⟨E⟩liazar was all clothed in whyght, and Argustus were   10
coverde in blacke. And what thys betokenyth I shall telle you.

'The day of Pentecoste, whan kynge Arthure hylde courte, hit befelle
that erthely kynges and erthely knyghtes toke a turnemente togydirs,
that ys to sey the queste of the Sankgreall. Of thes [the] erthely knyghtes
[were they] which were clothed all in blake, and the coveryng betok-   15
enyth the sy[n]nes whereof they be nat confessed. And they with the
coverynge of whyght betokenyth virginité, and they that hath chosyn
chastité. And thus was the queste begonne in them. Than thou behelde
the synners and the good men. And whan thou saw the synners overcom tho[u] enclyned to that party for bobbaunce and pryde of the   20
worlde, and all that muste be lefftc in that queste; for in thys queste
thou shalt have many felowis and thy bettirs, for thou arte so feble of
evyll truste and good beleve. Thys made hit whan thou were [there]
where they toke the and ladde the into the foreyste.

'And anone there appered the Sankgreall unto the whyght knyghtes,   25
but thou were so fyeble of good ⌐beleve and⌐ fayth that thou myght nat
abyde hit for all the techyng of the good man before. But anone thou
turned to the synners, and that caused thy mysseaventure, that thou
sholde know go[o]d frome vayneglory of the worlde; hit ys nat worth
a peare. And for grete pryde thou madist grete sorow that thou haddist   30
nat overcom all the whyght knyghtes. Therefore God was wrothe with
you, for in thys queste God lovith no such dedis. And that made the
avision to say to the that thou were of evyll faythe and of poore by-
lyeve, the which woll make the ⌐to falle into the⌐ depe pitte of helle, if
thou kepe the nat the better.   35

'Now have I warned the of thy vayneglory and of thy pryde, that
thou haste many tyme arred ayenste thy Maker. Beware of everlastynge payne, for of all erthly knyghtes I have moste pité of the, for I
know well thou haste nat thy pere of ony erthly synfull man.'

And so she commaunded sir Launcelot to dyner.   40

And aftir dyner he toke hys horse and commaunde her to God, and
so rode into a depe valey. And there he saw a ryver ⟨that⟩ hygh⟨t⟩
Mortays. And thorow the watir he muste nedis passe, the whych was
hedyous. And than in the name of God he toke hit wit[h] good herte.

And whan he com over he saw an armed knyght, horse and man all black as a beré. Withoute ony worde he smote sir Launcelottis horse to the dethe. And so he paste on and wyst nat where he was becom.

And than he toke hys helme and hys shylde, and thanked God of hys
5 adventure.

HERE LEVITH THE TALE OF SIR LAUNCELOT AND SPEKITH OF SIR [GAWAYNE].

V. SIR GAWAIN

XVI (1) WHAN sir Gawayne was departed frome hys felyship he rode longe
10 withoute ony adventure, for he founde nat the tenthe parte of aventures as they were wonte to have. For sir Gawayne rode frome Whytsontyde tylle Mychaellmasse, and founde never adventure that pleased
hym.

So on a day hit befelle that Gawayne mette with sir Ector de Maris,
15 and aythir made grete joy of othir. And so they tolde everyche othir,
and complayned them gretely, that they coude fynde none adventure.

'Truly,' seyde sir Gawayne, 'I am ny wery of thys queste, and lothe
I am to folow further in straunge contreyes.'

'One thynge mervaylith me muche,' seyde sir Ector. 'I have mette
20 with twenty knyghtes that be felowys of myne, and all they complayne
as I do.'

'I have mervayle,' seyd sir Gawayne, 'where that sir Launcelot, you[r]
brothir, ys.'

'Truly,' seyde sir Ector, 'I can nat hyre of hym, nother of sir Galahad,
25 sir Percivale, and sir Bors.'

'Lette hem be,' seyde sir Gawayne, 'for they four have no peerys.
And if one thynge were nat [in] sir Launcelot he had none felow of an
erthely man; but he ys as we be but if he take the more payne uppon
hym. But and thes four be mette togydyrs they woll be lothe that ony
30 man mete with hem; for and they fayle of Sankgreall, hit ys in waste of
all the remenaunte to recover hit.'

Thus sir Ector and sir Gawayne rode more than eyght dayes. And on
a Satirday they founde an auncyant chapell which was wasted, that
there semed no man nor woman thydir repayred. And there they alyght
35 and sette their sperys at the dore. And so they entirde into the chapell
and there made their orysons a grete whyle.

And than they sette hem downe in the segys of the chapell, and as
they spake of one thynge and of othir, for hevynesse they felle on slepe.
And there [befelle] hem bothe mervaylous adventures.

40 Sir Gawayne hym semed he cam into a medow full of herbis and
floures, and there he saw a rake of bullis, an hundrith and fyffty, that

were proude and black, save three of hem was all whyght, and one had
a blacke spotte. And the othir two were so fayre and so whyght that
they myght be no whytter. And thes three bullis which were so fayre
were tyed with two stronge cordis. And the remnaunte of the bullis
seide amonge them,

'Go we hens to seke bettir pasture!'

And so som wente and som com agayne, but they were so megir
that the[y] myght nat stonde upryght. And of the bullys that were so
whyght that one com agayne and no mo. But whan thys whyght bulle
was com agayne and amonge thes other, there rose up a grete crye for
lacke of wynde [that] fayled them. And so they departed, one here and
anothir there.

Thys avision befelle sir Gawayne that nyght.

But to sir Ector de Mares befelle another avision, the contrary. For
hit semed hym that hys brothir, sir Launcelot, and he alyght oute
of a chayre and lepte uppon two horsis. And the one s[a]yde to the
othir,

'Go we to seke that we shall nat fynde.'

And hym thought thatt a man bete sir Launcelot and dispoyled hym,
and clothed hym in another aray whych [was] all fulle of knottis, and
sette hym uppon an asse. And so he rode tylle that he cam unto the
fayryst welle that ever he saw. And there sir Launcelot alyght and
[wolde have dronke] of that welle; and whan he stowped to drynke of
that watir the watir sanke frome hym. And whan sir Launcelot saw
that, he turned and wente thidir as ⟨he had⟩ com fro. And in the meanewhyle he trowed that hymself, sir Ector, rode tylle that ⟨he⟩ com to
a ryche mannes house where there was a weddynge. And there he saw
a kynge whych seyd,

'Sir knyght, here ys no place for you.'

And than he turned agayne unto the chayre that he cam fro.

And so within a whyle both sir Gawayne and sir Ector awaked, and
ayther tolde other of their avision, whych mervayled hem gretly.

'Truly,' seyde sir Ector, 'I shall never be myrry tyll I hyre tydynges
of my brothyr sir Launcelot.'

So as they sate thus talkynge they saw an honde shewynge unto the
elbow, and was coverde with rede samyte, and uppon that a brydill
nat ryght ryche, that hylde within the fyste a grete candill whych brenned ryght clere; and so passed before them and entird into the chapell,
and than vanyshed away they wyste nat whydir.

And anone com downe a voice which seyde,

'Knyghtes full of evyll fayth and of poore beleve, thes two thynges
have fayled you, and therefore ye may nat com to the aventures of the
Sankgreall!'

Than first spake sir Gawayne and seyde,

'Sir Ector, have ye herde thes wordys?'

'Ye truly,' seyde sir Ector, 'I herde all. Now go we,' seyde sir Ector, 'unto som ermyte that woll telle us of oure avision, for hit semyth me we laboure all in waste.'

5   And so they departe and rode into a valey, and there they mette with a squyre which rode on an hakeney, and anone they salew hym fayre.

'Sir,' seyde sir Gawayne, 'can thou teche us to ony ermyte?'

'Sir, here ys on[e] in a litill mountayne, but hit ys so rowghe there may no horse go thydir. And therefore ye muste go on foote. And
10 there ye shall fynde a poore house, and therein ys Nacien [the] ermyte, whych ys the holyeste man in thys contrey.'

And so they departed eythir frome othir. And than in a valey they mette with a knyght all armed which profirde hem to fyght and juste as sone as he saw them.

15 'In the name of God,' seyde Gawayne, 'for sitthyn I departed frome Camelot there was none that profirde me to juste but onys.'

'And now, sir,' seyde sir Ector, 'lat me juste with hym.'

'Nay, ye shall nat, but if I be betyn. Hit shall nat than forthynke me if ye go to hym ⌐after me¬.'

20 And than aythir enbraced other to juste, and so they cam togydirs as faste as the⌐ir horses¬ myght renne, that they braste their shyldis and mayles, and that one more than the tother. But sir Gawayne was wounded in the lyffte syde, and thys other knyght was smytten thorow the breste, that the speare com oute on that other syde. And so they
25 felle bothe oute of their sadyls, and in the fallynge they brake both their spearys.

And anone sir Gawayne arose and sette hys honde to hys swerde and caste hys shylde before hym. But all for naught was hit, for the knyght had no power to aryse agayne hym. Than seyde sir Gawayne,
30 'Ye muste yelde you as an overcom man, other ellis I muste sle you!'

'A, sir knyght!' he seyde, 'I am but dede! Therefore, for Goddys sake and of youre jantilnes, lede me here unto an abbay, that I may resceyve my Creature.'

'Sir,' seyde sir Gawayne, 'I know no house of religion here nyghe.'
35 'Sir, sette me on an horse tofore you, and I shall teche you.'

So sir Gawayne sette hym up in the sadyll, and he lepe up behynde hym to sustayne hym. And so they cam to the abbay, and there were well resceyved. And anone he was unarmed and resceyve hys Creature.

Than he prayde sir Gawayne to drawe oute the truncheon of the
40 speare oute of hys body. Than sir Gawayne asked hym what he was.

'Sir,' he seyde, 'I am of kynge Arthurs courte, and was a felow of the Rounde Table, and we were sworne togydir. And now, sir Gawayne, thou hast slayne me. And my name ys sir Uwayne le Avoutres, that somtyme was sone unto kynge Uryen, and I was in the queste of the

Sankgreall. And now forgyff the God, for hit shall be ever rehersed that the tone sworne brother hath slayne the other.'

'Alas,' seyde sir Gawayne, 'that ever thys mysadventure befelle me!' (3)

'No force,' seyde sir Uwayne, 'sytthyn I shall dye this deth, of a much more worshipfuller mannes hande myght I nat dye. But whan ye 5 com to the courte recommaunde me unto my lorde Arthur, and to all them that be leffte on lyve. And for olde brothirhode thynke on me.'

Than began sir Gawayne to wepe, and also sir Ector. And than sir Uwayne bade hym draw oute the truncheon of the speare, and than sir Gawayne drew hit oute, and anone departed the soule frome the body. 10 Than sir Gawayne and sir Ector buryed hym as them ought to bury a kynges sonne and made hit wrytyn uppon hys tombe what was hys name and by whom he was slayne.

Than departed sir Gawayne and sir Ector as hevy as they myght for their mysseadventure. And so rode [tyl that] they com to the rowghe 15 mountayne, and there they tyed their horsis and wente on foote to the ermytayge.

And whan they were com up they saw a poore house, and besyde the chapell a litill courtelayge where Nacien the ermyte gadred wortis to hys mete, as he whych had tasted none other mete of a grete whyle. 20 And whan he saw the arraunte knyghtes he cam to them and salewed them and they hym agayne.

'Fayre lordis,' seyde he, 'what adventure brought you hydir?'

Than seyde sir Gawayne, 'to speke with you for to be confessed.'

'Sir,' seyde the ermyte, 'I am redy.'   25

Than they tolde hym so muche that he wyste welle what they ware, and than he thought to counceyle them if he myght.

Than began sir Gawayne and tolde hym of hys avision that he had in the chapell. And Ector tolde hym all as hit ys before reherced.

'Sir,' seyde [the ermyte unto] sir Gawayne, 'the fayre medow and 30 the rak therein ought to be undirstonde the Rounde Table, and by the medow oughte to be undirstonde humilité and paciens; tho be the thynges which bene allwey grene and quyk. For that men mowe no tyme overcom humilité and pacience, therefore was the Rounde Table founden, and the shevalry hath ben at all tymes so hyghe by the frater- 35 nité which was there that she myght nat be overcom: for men seyde she was founded in paciens and in humilité. At the rack ete an hondred and fyffty bullys, but they ete nat in the medowe, for if they had, their hartes sholde have bene sette in humilité and paciens; and the bullis were proude and blacke sauff only three.   40

'And by the bullys ys undirstonde the felyshyp of the Rounde Table whych for their synne and their wyckednesse bene blacke; blackenes ys as much to sey withoute good vertues or workes. And the three bulles whych were whyght sauff only one had bene spotted? The too whyght

betokenythe sir Galahad and sir Percivale, for they be maydyns and clene withoute spotte, and the thirde, that had a spotte, signifieth sir Bors de Gaynes, which trespassed but onys in hys virginité. But sithyn he kepyth hymselff so wel in chastité that all ys forgyffyn hym and hys
5 myssededys. And why tho three were tyed by the neckes, they be three knyghtes in virginité and chastité, and there ys no pryde smytten in them.

'And the blacke bullis whych seyde, "go we hens", they were tho whych at Pentecoste at the hyghe feste toke uppon hem [to go] in the
10 queste of the Sankgreall withoute confession: they myght nat entir in the medow of humilité and paciens. And therefore they turned into waste contreyes: that signifieth dethe, for there shall dye many off them. For everych of them shall sle othir for synne, and they that shall ascape shall be so megir that hit shall be mervayle to se them. And of the three
15 bullis withoute spotte the one shall com agayne and the other two never.'
(4)   Than spake Nacien unto sir Ector: 'Soth hit ys that sir Launcelot and ye com downe of one chayre; the chayer betokenyth maystership and lordeship which ye too cam downe fro. But ye two knyghtes,' sayde the ermyte, 'ye go to seke that ye shall nat fynde, that ys the Sankgreall, for
20 hit ys the secrete thynges of oure Lorde Jesu Cryste. But what ys to meane that sir Launcelot felle doune of hys horse? He hath leffte hys pryde and takyn to humilité, for he hath ⌐cryed¬ mercy lowde for hys synne and sore repented hym, and oure Lorde hath clothed hym in Hys clothynge whych ys full of knottes, that ys the hayre that he werith
25 dayly. And the asse that he rode uppon ys a beest of humilité (for God wolde nat ryde uppon no styede nother uppon no palferey), in an ex-emple that an asse betokenyth mekenes, that thou saw sir Launcelot ryde [on] in thy slepe.

'A[nd] the welle whereat the watir sanke frome hym whan he sholde
30 have takyn thereoff? (And whan he saw he myght nat have hit he re-turned from whens he cam, for the welle betokenyth the hyghe grace of God; for the more men desyre hit to take hit, the more shall be their desire.) So whan he cam nyghe the Sankgreall he meked hym so that he hylde hym nat the man worthy to be so nyghe the holy vessell, for he
35 had be so defoyled in dedly synne by the space of many yere. Yett whan he kneled downe to drynke of the welle, there he saw grete provydence of the Sankgreall; and for he hath served so longe the devyll he shall have ⌐vengeaunce¬ four and twenty dayes, for that he hath bene the devillis servaunte four and twenty yerys. And than sone aftir he shall
40 returne to Camelot oute of thys contrey, and he shall sey a party such thyngis as he hath founde.

'Now woll I telle you what betokenyth the hande with the candill and the brydyll: that ys to undirstonde the Holy Goste where charité ys ever; and the brydyll signifieth abstinens, for whan she ys brydeled

in a Crysten mannes herte s[he] holdith hym so shorte that he fallith
nat in dedly synne. And the candyll which shewith clernesse and lyght
signyfieth the ryght way of Jesu Cryste.

'And whan ⌐He⌐ wente He seyde, "Knyghtes of pore fayth and of
wycked beleve, thes three thynges fayled: charité, abstinaunce and 5
trouthe. Therefore ye may nat attayne thys adventure of the Sankgreall." '

'Sertes,' seyde sir Gawayne, 'full sothly have ye seyde, that I se hit (5)
opynly. Now I pray you telle me why we mette nat with so many
adventures as we were wonte to do?'   10

'I shall telle you gladly,' seyde the good man. 'The adventure of the
Sankgreall whych be in shewynge now, [ye and many other have undertaken the quest of hit and fynde hit not,] for hit apperith nat to no synners (wherefore mervayle ye nat thou[gh] ye fayle thereoff and many
othir, for ye bene an untrew knyght and a grete murtherar), and to good 15
men signifieth othir thynges than murthir. For I dare sey, as synfull as
ever sir Launcelot hath byn, sith that he wente into the queste of the
Sankgreal he slew never man nother nought shall, tylle that he com to
Camelot agayne; for he hath takyn [upon] hym to forsake synne. And
nere were that he ys nat stable, but by hys thoughte he ys lyckly to 20
turne agayne, he sholde be nexte to enchev[c] hit sauff sir Galahad, hys
sonne; but God knowith hys thought and hys unstablenesse. And yett
shall he dye ryght an holy man, and no doute he hath no felow of none
erthly synfull man lyvyng.'

'Sir,' seyde sir Gawayne, 'hit semyth me by youre wordis that for 25
oure synnes hit woll nat avayle us to travayle in thys queste.'

'Truly,' seyde the good man, 'there bene an hondred such as ye bene
shall never prevayle but to have shame.'

And whan they had herde thes wordis they commaunded hym unto
God. Than the good man called sir Gawayne and seyde,   30

'Hit ys longe tyme passed sith that ye were made knyght and never
synnes servyd thou thy Maker, and now thou arte so olde a tre that in
the ys neythir leeff, nor grasse, nor fruyte. Wherefore bethynke the that
thou yelde to oure Lorde the bare rynde, sith the fende hath the levis
and the fruyte.'   35

'Sir,' seyde sir Gawayne, 'and I had leyser I wolde speke with you,
but my felow sir Ector ys gone and abithe me yondir bynethe the hylle.'

'Well,' seyde the good man, 'thou were better to be counceyled.'

Than departed sir Gawayne and cam to sir Ector, and so toke their
horsis and rode tylle that they com to a fosters house, which herber- 40
owde them ryght welle. And on the morne departed frome hir oste and
rode longe or they cowthe fynde ony adventure.

Now turnyth thys tale unto syr Bors de Ganys.

VI. SIR BORS

(6) WHAN sir Bors was departed frome Camelot he mette with a religious man rydynge on an asse, and anone sir Bors salewed hym. And anone the good man knew that he was one of the knyghtes arraunte that was
5 in the queste of the Sankgreall.

'What ar ye?' seyde the good man.

'Sir,' seyde he, 'I am a knyght that fayne wolde be counceyled, that ys entirde into the queste of the Sankgreall. For he shall have much erthly worship that may bryng hit to an ende.'

10 'Sertes,' seyde the good man, 'that ys sothe withoute fayle, for he shall be the beste knyght of the worlde and the fayryst of the felyship. But wyte you welle there shall none attayne hit but by clennes, that ys pure confession.'

So rode they togydir tyll that they com unto a litill ermytayge, and
15 there he prayde sir Bors to dwelle all that nyght. And he so put of hys armoure and prayde hym that he myght be confessed, ⌐and so they went into the chappel and there he was clene confessed.⌐ And so they ete brede and dranke watir togydir.

'Now,' seyde the good man, 'I pray the that thou ete none other tyll
20 that thou sitte at the table where the Sankgreall shall be.'

'Sir,' seyde he, 'I agré me thereto. But how know ye that I shall sytte there?'

'Yes,' seyde the good man, 'that know I well, but there shall be but fewe of youre felowis with you.'

25 'All ys wellcomme,' seyde sir Bors, 'that God sendith me.'

'Also,' seyde the good man, 'insteede of a shurte, and in sygne of chastisemente, ye shall were a garmente. Therefore I pray you do of all your clothys and youre shurte.'

And so he dud. And than he toke hym a scarlet cote so that sholde be
30 hys instede of hys sherte tylle he had fulfilled the queste of the Sanke-greall. And thys good man founde hym in so mervales a lyffe and so stable that he felte he was never gretly correpte in fleysshly lustes but in one tyme that he begat Elyan le Blanke.

Than he armyd hym and toke hys leve, and so departed. And so a
35 litill frome thens he loked up into a tre and there he saw a passynge grete birde uppon that olde tre. And hit was passyng drye, withoute leyffe; so she sate above and had birdis whiche were dede for hungir. So at the laste he smote hymselffe with hys beke which was grete and sherpe, and so the grete birde bledde so faste that he dyed amonge hys
40 birdys. And the yonge birdys toke lyff by the bloode of the grete birde.

Whan sir Bors saw thys he wyste well hit was a grete tokenynge; for whan he saw the grete birde arose nat, than he toke hys horse and yode hys way.

And so by aventure, by evynsonge tyme, he cam to a stronge towre and an hyghe, and there was he herberowde gladly. And whan he was (7) unarmed they lad hym into an hyghe towre where was a lady, yonge, lusty and fayre, and she resceyved hym with grete joy and made hym to sitte down by her. And anone he was sette to supper with fleyssh 5 and many deyntees.

But whan sir Bors saw that, he bethought hym on hys penaunce and bade a squyre to brynge hym watir. And so he brought hym, and he made soppis therein and ete them.

'A,' seyde the lady, 'I trow ye lyke nat youre mete.' 10

'Yes truly,' seyde sir Bors, 'God thanke you, madam, but I may nat ete none other mete to-day.'

Than she spake no more as at that tyme, for she was lothe to displease hym. Than aftir supper they spake of one thynge and of othir. So with that there cam a squyre and seyde, 15

'Madam, ye muste pirvey you to-morne for a champion, for ellis youre syster woll have thys castell and also youre londys, excepte ye can fynde a knyght that woll fyght to-morne in youre quarell ayenste sir Prydam le Noyre.'

Than she made grete sorow and seyde, 'A, Lorde God! wherefore 20 graunted ye me to holde my londe whereof I sholde now be disherited withoute reson and ryght?'

And whan sir Bors herde hir sey thus he seyde, 'I shall comforte you.'

'Sir,' seyde she, 'I shall telle you: there was here a kynge that hyghte Anyawse whych hylde all thys londe in hys kepynge. So hit myssehap- 25 ped he loved a jantillwoman a grete dele elder than I. And so he toke her all this londe in hir kepynge and all hys men to governe, and she brought up many evyll custums whereby she put to dethe a grete party of his kynnesmen. And whan he saw that, he commaunded her oute of this londe and bytoke hit me, and all thys londe in my demenys. But 30 anone as that worthy kynge was dede thys other lady began to warre uppon me, and hath destroyed many of my men and turned hem ayenste me, that I have well-nyghe no man leffte me, and I have naught ellis but thys hyghe towre that she leffte me. And yet she hath promysed me to have thys towre withoute I can fynde a knyght to 35 fyght with her champion.'

'Now telle me,' seyde sir Bors, 'what ys that Prydam le Noyre?'

'Sir, he ys the moste douted man of thys londe.'

'Than may ye sende hir worde that ye have founde a knyght that shall fyght with that Prydam le Noyre in Goddis quarelle and youres.' 40

So that lady was than glad and sente her worde that she was purveyde. And so that nyght sir Bors had passyng good chere, but in no bedde he wolde com but leyde hym on the floore, nor never wolde do otherwyse tyll that he had mette with the queste of the Sankegreall.

(8)   And anone as he was aslepe hym befelle a vision: that there cam two
birdis, that one whyght as a swanne and that other was merveylous
blacke; but he was nat so grete as was that other, but in the lyknes of a
raven. Than the whyght birde cam to hym and seyde,

5   'And thou woldist gyff me mete and serve me, I sholde gyff the all
the ryches of the worlde, and I shall make the as fayre and as whyght as
I am.'

So the whyght birde departed. And than cam the blacke birde to
hym and seyde,

10   'And thou serve me to-morow and have me in no dispite, thoughe
I be blacke. For wyte thou well that more avaylith myne blaknesse
than the odirs whyghtnesse.'

And than he departed. Than he had anothir vision: that he cam to a
grete place which semed a chapell, and there he founde a chayre sette,

15 on the lyffte syde which was ⟨a⟩ worme-etyn and fyeble tre besyde hit,
and on the ryght honde were two floures lyke a lylye, and that one
wolde a benomme the tother theyre whyghtnes. But a good man departed them, that they towched none othir, and than oute of eche
floure com oute many floures and fruyte grete plenté. Than hym

20 thought the good man seyde,

'Sholde nat he do grete foly that wolde lette thes two floures perishe
for to succoure the rottyn tre that hyt felle nat to the erthe?'

'Sir,' seyde he, 'hit semyth me that thys wood myght nat avayle.'

'Now kepe the,' seyde the good man, 'that thou never se such
25 adventure befalle the.'

Than he awaked and made a sygne of the crosse in myddys of the
forehede, and so he arose and clothed hym. And anone there cam the
lady of the place, and she salewed hym and he her agayne, and so
wente to a chapell and herd their servyse.

30   And anone there cam a company of knyghtes that the lady had sente
for, to lede sir Bors unto the batayle. Than asked he his armys, and
whan he was armed she prayde hym to take a lytyll morsell to dyne.

'Nay, madam,' seyde he, 'that shall I nat do tylle I have done my
batayle, by the grace of God.'

35   And so he lepe uppon hys horse and departed, and all the knyghtes
and men with hym.

And as sone as thes two ladyes mette togydir, she which sir Bors
sholde fyght for, she playned hir and seyde,

'Madam, ye have done grete wronge to beryve me my landis that
40 kyng Anyauss gaff me, and full lothe I am there sholde be ony batayle.'

'Ye shall nat chose,' seyde the other, 'othir ellis lat your knyght
withdraw hym.'

Than there was the cry made, which party had the bettir of tho two
knyghtes, that hys lady sholde rejoyse all the londys.

Than departed the one knyght here and the other there. Than they cam togydirs with such raundom that they perced their shildes and their habergeons, and their spearis flye in pecis, and they sore wounded. Than hurteled they togydyrs so that they beete eche other to the erthe and theire horsis betwene their leggis. And anone they arose and sette 5 handis to their swerdys and smote eche one other uppon their hedys, that they made grete woundis and depe, that the blode wente oute of hyre bodyes. For there founde sir Bors gretter deffence in that knyght more than he wente; for thys sir Prydam was a passyng good knyght and [he] wounded sir Bors full evyll, and he hym agayne. But ever sir 10 Pridam hylde the stowre inlyche harde. That perceyved sir Bors and suffird hym tylle he was nyghe ataynte, and than he ranne uppon hym more and more, and the other wente backe for drede of dethe.

So in hys withdrawyng he felle upryght, and sir Bors drew hys helme so strongely that he rente hit frome hys hede, and gaff hym 15 many sadde strokes with the flatte of hys swerde uppon the visayge and bade hym yelde hym or he sholde sle hym. Than he cryed hym mercy and seyde,

'Fayre knyght, for Goddis love, sle me nat, and I shall ensure the never to warre ayenste thy lady, but be allway towarde hir.' 20

So sir Bors gaffe hym hys lyff, and anone the olde lady fledde with all hir knyghtes. Than called sir Bors all tho that hylde landis of hys (9) lady, and seyde he sholde destroy them but if they dud such servyse unto her as longed to their londys. So they dud her omayge, and they that wolde nat were chaced oute of their londis, that hit befelle that the 25 yonge lady com to her astate agayne be the myghty prouesse of sir Bors de Ganys.

So whan all the contrey was well sette in pease, than sir Bors toke hys leve and departed, and she thanked hym gretly and wolde have gyffyn hym grete gyfftes, but he refused hit. 30

Than he rode all that day tylle nyght, and so he cam to an herberow to a lady which knew hym well inowghe and made of hym grete joy. So on the morne as sone as the day appered, sir Bors departed from thens, and so rode into a foreyste unto the owre of mydday.

And there befelle hym a mervaylous aventure. So he mette at the 35 departynge of the two ⌜w⌝ayes two knyghtes that lad sir Lyonell, hys brothir, all naked, bowndyn uppo[n] a stronge hakeney, and his hondis bounden tofore hys breste; and everych of them helde in theyre hondis thornys wherewith they wente betynge hym so sore that the bloode trayled downe more than in an hondred placis of hys body, so that he 40 was all bloodé tofore and behynde. But he seyde never a worde as he whych was grete of herte. [He] suffird all that they ded to hym as thoughe he had felte none angwysh.

And anone sir Bors dressed hym to rescow hym that was his brothir.

And so he loked uppon the other syde of hym and sawe a knyght which brought a fayre jantillwoman, and wolde a sette her in the thycke of the foreyste for to have be the more surer oute of the way from hem that sought her. And she whych was nothynge assured cryde with an
5 hyghe voice,

'Seynte Mary, succour youre mayde!'

And anone as she syghe sir Bors she demed hym a knyght of the Rounde Table, [whereof she hoped to have some comforte.] Than she conjoured hym, by the faythe that he ought unto Hym 'in whos ser-
10 vyse thou arte entred [and for the feythe ye owe to the hyghe Ordre of Knyghthode, and] for kynge Arthures sake, which I suppose made the knyght, that thou helpe me and suffir me nat to be shamed of this knyght'.

Whan sir Bors herde hir say thus, he had so much sorow that he
15 wyst nat what to do : 'For if I latte my brothir be in adventure he muste be slayne, and that wold I nat for all the erthe; and if I helpe nat the mayde she ys shamed, and shall lose hir virginité which she shall never gete agayne'. Than lyffte he up hy syghen and seyde wepynge, 'Fayre swete Lorde Jesu Cryst, whos creature I am, kepe me sir Lyonell, my
20 brothir, that thes knyghtes sle hym nat, and for pité of you and for mylde Maryes sake, I shall succour thys mayde.'

(10) Than dressed he hym unto the knyght which had the jantillwoman, and than he cryed, 'Sir knyght, let youre honde of youre maydyn, or ye be but dede!'

25 And than he sette downe the mayden, and was armed at all pycis sauff he lacked his speare. Than he dressed hys shylde and drew ⌐oute⌐ his swerde. And sir Bors smote hym so harde that hit wente thorow hys shylde and habirgeon on the lyffte sholdir, and thorow grete strengthe he bete hym downe to the erthe. And at the pullyng oute of sir Bors
30 spere he there sowned. Than cam sir Bors to the mayde and seyde,

'How semyth hit you ? Of thys knyght be ye delyverde at thys tyme ?'

'Now, sir,' seyde she, 'I pray you lede me thereas this knyght had me.'

'So shall I do gladly.'

And toke the horse of the wounded knyght and sette the jantil-
35 woman uppon hym, and so brought hir as she desired.

'Sir knyght,' seyde she, 'ye have bettir spedde than ye wente, for and I had loste my maydynhode fyve hondred men sholde have dyed there-fore.'

'What knyght was he that had you in the foreyst ?'

40 'Be my fayth, he ys my cosyne. So wote I never [with] what engyne the fynde enchaffed hym, for yestirday he toke me fro my fadir pre-vayly, for I, nother none of my fadirs men, myssetrusted hym nat. And iff he had had my maydynhode he had dyed for the synne of hys body, and shamed and dishonoured for ever.'

Thus as she stood talkyng with hym there cam twelve knyghtes sekyng aftir hir. And anone she tolde hem all how sir Bors had dely-verde hir. Than they made grete joy and besought hym to com to her fadir, a grete lorde, and he sholde be ryght wellcom.

'Truly,' seyde sir Bors, 'that may nat be at thys tyme, for I have a   5 grete aventure to do in this contrey.'

So he commaunde hem to God, and departed. Than sir Bors rode after sir Lyonell, hys brothir, by the trace of their horsis.

Thus he rode sekyng a grete whyle, and anone he overtoke a man clothed in a religious wede, and rode on a stronge blacke horse, 10 blacker than a byry, and seyde,

'Sir knyght, what seke you?'

'Sir,' seyde he, 'I seke my brother that I saw erewhyle betyn with two knyghtes.'

'A, sir Bors, discomforte you nat, nor falle nat into no wanhope, for 15 I shall telle you tydyngis such as they be, for truly he ys dede.'

Than shewed he hym a new-slayne body lyyng in a buyssh, and hit semed hym well that hyt was the body of sir Lyonell, hys brothir. And than he made suche sorow that he felle to the erthe in a sowne, and so lay a grete whyle there. And whan he cam to hymselff he seyde, 20

'Fayre brother, sytthe the company of you and me ar departed, shall I never have joy in my herte. And now He whych I have takyn unto my mayster, He be my helpe.'

And whan he had seyde thus he toke the body lyghtly in hys armys and put hit upon the harson of hys sadyll, and than he seyde to the man, 25

'Can ye shew me ony chapell nyghe whcre that I may bury thys body?'

'Com one,' seyde [he], 'here ys one faste hye.'

And so longe they rode tylle they saw a fayre towre, and afore hit there semed an olde, fyeble chapell; and than they alyght bothe and put hym in the tombe of marble. 30

'Now leve we hym here,' seyde the good man, 'and go we to oure (11) herberow tylle to-morow we com hyre agayne to do hym servyse.'

'Sir,' seyd sir Bors, 'be ye a pryest?'

'Ye forsothe,' seyde he.

'Than I pray you telle me a dreme that befelle me the laste nyght.' 35

'Say on,' seyde he.

So he begon so much to telle hym of the grete birde in the foreyste, and aftir tolde hym of hys birdys, one whyght and another blacke, and of the rottyn tre and of the whyght floures.

'Sir, I shall telle you a parte now, and the othir dele to-morow. The 40 whyght fowle betokenyth a jantillwoman fayre and ryche whych loved the paramours and hath loved the longe. And if that thou warne hir love she shall dy anone—if thou have no pité on her. That signifieth the grete birde which shall make the to warne hir. Now for no feare

that thou haste, ne for no drede that thou hast of God, thou shalt nat
warne hir; for thou woldist nat do hit for to be holdyn chaste, for to
conquere the loᵗosᵗe of the vayneglory of the worlde; for that shall
befalle the now, and thou warne hir, that sir Launcelot, the good knyght,
5 thy cousyn, shall dye. And than shall men sey that thou arte a man-sleer,
both of thy brothir sir Lyonell and of thy cousyn sir Launcelot, whych
th[o]u myght have rescowed easyly, but thou wentist to rescow a
mayde which perteyned nothynge to the. Now loke thou whether hit
had bene gretter harme of thy brothers dethe, other ellis to have suffirde
10 her to have loste hir maydynhode.' Than seyde he, 'Now hast thou
harde the tokyns of thy dreme?'

'Ye,' seyd sir Bors.

'Than ys hit in thy defaughte if sir Launcelot, thy cousyn, dye.'

'Sir,' seyde sir Bors, 'that were me lothe, for there ys ⌐noᵗthynge in
15 the worlde but I had levir do [hit] than to se my lorde sir Launcelot
dye in my defaught.'

'Chose ye now the tone or that other.'

Than he ladde hym into the hygh towre, and there he founde knyghtes
and ladyes that seyde he was welcom. And so they unarmed hym, and
20 whan he was in his dublette they brought hym a mantell furred with
ermyne and put hit aboute hym. So they made hym such chere that he
had forgotyn hys sorow [and anguysshe and only sette his herte in
these delytes and deyntees, and tooke no thought more for his brother
sir Lyonell neyther of sir Launcelot du Lake, his cosyn]. And anone cam
25 oute of a chambir unto hym the fayryst lady that ever he saw, and more
rycher beseyne than ever was quene Guenyver or ony other astate.

'Lo,' seyde they, 'sir Bors, here ys the lady unto whom we owghe all
oure servyse, and I trow she be the rychyst lady and the fayryste of the
worlde, whych lovith you beste aboven all other knyghtes, for she woll
30 have no knyght but you.'

And whan he undirstood that langayge he was abaysshed. Notforthan she salewed hym and he her; and than they sate downe togydirs and
spake of many thyngis, insomuch that she besought hym to be hir love,
for she had loved hym aboven all erthly men and she sholde make hym
35 rycher than evyr was man of hys ayge.

Whan sir Bors undirstood hir wordis he was ryght evyll at ease, but
in no wyse he wolde breke his chastité, and so he wyst nat how to
answere her.

(12)   'Alas, sir Bors!' seyde she, 'woll ye nat do my wylle?'

40   'Madam,' seyde he, 'there ys no lady in thys worlde whos wylle I
wolde fullfylle as of thys thynge. She ought nat desire hit, for my
brothir lyeth dede, which was slayne ryght late.'

'A, sir Bors,' seyde she, 'I have loved you longe for the grete beauté
I have sene in you and the grete hardynesse that I have herde of you,

that nedys ye muste lye be me to-nyght, therefore I pray you graunte
me.'

'Truly,' seyde he, 'I shall do hit in no maner wyse.'

Than anone she made hym such sorow as thoughe she wolde have
dyed. 5

'Well, sir Bors,' seyd she, 'unto thys have ye brought me, nyghe to
myne ende.' And therewith she toke hym by the hande and bade hym
beholde her, 'and ye shall se how I shall dye for youre love.'

And he seyd than, 'I shall hit never se.'

Than she departed and wente up into an hyghe batilment and lad 10
with her twelve jantilwomen, and whan they were above one of the
jantillwomen cryed,

'A, sir Bors, jantill knyght! Have mercy on us all, and suffir my lady
to have hir wyll; and if ye do nat, we muste suffir dethe with oure lady
for to falle downe of this hyghe towre. And if ye suffir us thus to dye 15
for so litill a thynge all ladys and jantillwomen woll sey you dishonoure.'

Than loked he upwarde and saw they semed all ladyes of grete astate
and rychely and well beseyne. Than had he of hem grete pité; natforthat he was nat uncounceyled in hymselff that levir he had they all had 20
loste their soules than he hys soule. And with that they felle all at onys
unto the erthe, and whan he saw that, he was all abaysshed and had
thereof grete mervayle. And with that he blyssed hys body and hys
vysayge.

And anone he harde a grete noyse and a grete cry as all the fyndys of 25
helle had bene aboute hym. And therewith ⌐he sawe⌐ nother towre,
lady, ne jantillwomen, nother no chapell where he brought hys brothir
to. Than hylde he up both hys hondis to the hevyn and seyde, 'Fayre
swete Lorde Fadir and God in hevyn, I am grevously ascaped!'

And than he toke hys armys and hys horse and set hym on hys way. 30
And anone he herde a clocke smyte on hys ryght honde, and thydir he
cam to an abbay which was closed with hyghe wallis, and there was he
lette in. And anone they supposed that he was one of the knyghtes of
the Rounde Table that was in the queste of the Sankgreall, so they led
hym into a chambir and unarmed hym. 35

'Sirs,' seyde sir Bors, 'if there be ony holy man in thys house, I pray
you lette me speke with hym.'

Than one of hem lad hym unto the abbotte which was in a chapell.
And than sir Bors salewed hym and he hym agayne.

'Sir,' seyde sir Bors, 'I am a knyght arraunte,' and tolde hym the 40
adventures whych he had sene.

'Sir knyght,' seyde the abbotte, 'I wote nat what ye be, for I went
that a knyght of youre ayge myght nat have be so stronge in the grace
of oure Lorde Jesu Cryste. Natforthan ye shall go unto youre reste, for

I woll nat counceyle thys day, hit ys to late. And to-morow I shall
counceyle you as I can.'

(13)   And that nyght was sir Bors served rychely. And on the morne erly
he harde masse, and than the abbot cam to hym and bade hym good-
5   morow, and sir Bors to hym agayne. And than he tolde hym he was
felow of the queste of the Sangreall, and how he had charge of the
holy man to ete brede and watir.

'Than oure Lorde shewed Hym unto you in the lyknesse of a fowle,
that suffirde grete anguysshe for us whan He was putte uppon the
10   Crosse, and bledde Hys herte blood for mankynde; there was the tokyn
and the lyknesse of the Sankgreall that appered afore you, for the blood
that the grete fowle bledde reysyd the chykyns frome dethe to lyff. And
by the bare tre betokenyth the worlde, whych ys naked and nedy,
withoute fruyte, but if hit com of oure Lorde.

15   'Also, the lady for whom ye fought for. And kyng Anyauss, whych
was lorde thereto, betokenyth Jesu Cryste, which ys Kyng of the worlde.
And that ⟨y⟩e fought with the champion for the lady, thus hit betokenyth: whan ⟨y⟩e toke the batayle for the lady, by her shall ye undirstonde the ⌜newe⌝ law of oure Lord Jesu Cryst and Holy Chirche, and
20   by the othir lady ye shall undirstonde the olde lawe and the fynde
which all day warryth ayenst Holy Chirch; therefore ye dud youre
batayle with ryght, for ye be Jesu Crystes knyght[es,] therefore ye
oughte to be defenders of Holy Chirche. ⌜And by the blak birde myght
ye understande Holy Chirche⌝ whych seyth, "I am blacke," but he ys
25   fayre. And by the whyght birde may men undirstonde the fynde, and
I shall telle you how the swan ys whyght withoutefurth and blacke
within: hit ys ipocresye, which ys with[oute] yalew or pale, and semyth
withouteforth the servauntis of Jesu Cryste, but they be withinfurthe
so horrible of fylth and synne, and begyle the worlde so evyll.

30   'Also whan the fynde apperith to you in lyknesse of a man o[f] religion and blamed the that thou lefft thy brothir for a lady, and he lede
the where thou semed thy brothir was slayne—but he ys yette on lyve—
and all was for to putte the in erroure, and to brynge the into wanhope
and lechery, for he knew thou were tendir-herted, and all was for thou
35   sholdist nat fynde the aventure of the Sankgreall. And the thirde
fowle betokenyth the stronge batayle ayenste the fayre ladyes whych
were all devyls.

'Also the dry tre and the whyght lylyes: the sere tre betokenyth thy
brothir sir Lyonell, whych ys dry withoute vertu, and therefore men
40   oughte to calle hym the rotyn tre, and the worme-etyn tre, for he ys a
murtherer and doth contrary to the Order off Knyghthode. And the
two whyght floures signifieth two maydyns; the one ys a knyght which
y⟨e⟩ wounded the other day, and the other is the jantillwoman whych
ye rescowed. And why the other floure drew nye the tother, that was

the knyght which wolde have defowled her and hymselff bothe. And, sir Bors, ye had bene a grete foole and in grete perell for to have sene tho two flowris perish for to succoure the rottyn tre, for and they had synned togydir, they had be dampned; and for ye rescowed them bothe, men myght calle you a verry knyght and the servaunte of Jesu Cryste.'   5

Than wente sir Bors frome thens and commaunded the abbotte to (14) God. And than he rode all that day, and herberowde with an olde lady.

And on the morne he rode to a castell in a valey, and there he mette with a yoman goyng a grete pace toward a foreyste.

'Sey me,' seyde sir Bors, 'canst thou telle me of ony adventure?'   10

'Sir,' seyde he, 'here shall be undir thys castell a grete and a mervay- lous turnemente.'

'Of what folkys shall hit be?' seyde sir Bors.

'The erle of Playns shall be on the tone party, and the ladyes nevew off Hervyn on the todir party.'   15

Than sir Bors thought to be there, to assay iff he myght mete with hys brothir sir Lyonell, or ony other of hys felyship whych were in the queste of the Sankgreall, than turned to an ermytayge that was in the entré of the foreysst. And whan he was com thydir he founde there sir Lyonell, his brother, which sate all (un)armed at the entré 20 of the chapell dore for to abyde there herberow tylle on the morne that the turnement sholde be.

And whan sir Bors saw hym he had grete joy of hym, that no man cowde telle of gretter joy. And than he alyght of his horse and seyde, 'Fayre swete brothir, whan cam ye hydir?'   25

And as sir Lyonell saw hym he seyde, 'A, sir Bors, ye may nat make none avaunte, but as for you I myght have bene slayne. Whan ye saw two knyghtes lede me away beatynge me, ye leffte me to succour a jantillwoman, and suffird me in perell of deth. For never arste ne ded no brothir to another so grete an untrouthe. And for that myssedede I 30 ensure you now but dethe, for well have ye deserved hit. Therefor kepe you frome me frome hens forewarde! And that shall ye fynde as sone as I am armed.'

Whan sir Bors undirstode his brothirs wratth he kneled downe tofore hym to the erthe, and cryed hym mercy, holdyng up both hys 35 hondis, and prayde hym to forgyff hym hys evyll wylle.

'Nay, nay,' seyde sir Lyonell, 'that shall never [be] and I may have the hygher hande, that I make myne avow to God. Thou shalt have dethe, for hit were pité ye leved any lenger.'

Ryght so he wente in and toke hys harneyse, and lyghte uppon his 40 horse and cam tofore hym and seyde,

'Sir Bors, kepe the fro me, for I shall do to the as I wolde do to a felon other a traytoure. For ye be the untrewyst knyght that ever cam oute of so worthy an house as was kyng Bors de Ganis, which was oure fadir. Therefore sterte uppon thy horse, and so shalt thou be moste at thyne avauntayge. And but if thou wylt, I woll renne uppon the thereas thou arte on foote, and so the shame shall be myne and the harme youres, but of that shame recke I nought.'

5 Whan sir Bors sye that he must fyght with his brothir othir ellis to dye, he wyst nat what to do; so hys herte counceyled hym nat thereto, inasmuch as sir Lyonell was hys elder brothir, wherefore he oughte to bere hym reverence. Yette kneled he adowne agayne tofore sir Lyonelles horse feete and seyde,

10 'Fayre swete brothir, have mercy uppon me and sle me nat, and have in remembraunce the grete love which oughte to be betwene us two.'

So whatsomever sir Bors seyde to sir Lyonell he rought nat, for the fynde had brought hym in suche a wylle that he sholde sle hym. So whan sir Lyonell saw he wolde none other do nor wolde nat ryse to

15 gyff hym batayle he russhed over hym so that he smote sir Bors with his horse feete upwarde to the erthe, and hurte hym so sore that he sowned for distresse which he felte in hymselff to have dyed withoute confession. So whan sir Lyonell saw thys he alyght of hys horse to have smytten of hys hede, and so he toke hym by the helme and wolde

20 have rente hit frome hys hede. Therewith cam the ermyte rennynge unto hym, which was a good man and of grete ayge, and well had herde all the wordis ⌜that were betwene them⌝. He lepe betwene them,

(15) and so felle downe uppon sir Bors, and seyde unto sir Lyonell,

'A, jantyll knyght! have mercy uppon me and uppon thy brothir,

25 for if thou sle hym thou shalt be dede of that synne, and that were grete sorow, for he ys one of the worthyest knyghtes of the worlde and of beste condicions.'

'So God me helpe, sir pryste, but if ye fle from hym I shall sle you, and he shall never the sunner be quytte.'

30 'Sertes,' seyde the good man, 'I had levir ye sle me than hym, for as for my dethe shall nat be grete harme, nat halff so much as for his woll be.'

'Well,' seyd sir Leonell, 'I am agreed,' and sette his honde to his swerde, and smote hym so harde that hys hede yode off bacwarde.

35 And natforthan he rescowed hym nat of hys evyll wyll, but toke hys brothir by the helme and unlaced hit to have smytten off hys hede, and had slayne hym had nat a felowe of hys of the Rounde Table com whos name was called sir Collegrevaunce, a felow of the Rounde Table, that com thydyr as oure Lordis wyll wolde.

40 And whan he saw the good man slayne he mervayled much what hit myght be; and than he behylde sir Lyonell that wolde have slayne hys brothir, ⌜and knewe⌝ sir Bors which he loved ryght well. Than sterte he adowne and toke sir Lyonell by the shuldirs, and drew hym strongely abacke frome sir Bors, and seyde to sir Lyonell,

'Woll ye sle youre brothir, the worthyest knyght one of the worlde?
That sholde no good man suffir.'

'Why,' so seyde sir Lyonell, 'woll ye lette me thereoff? For if ye
entirmete thereoff, I shall sle you to, and hym thereafftir!'

'Why,' seyde sir Colgrevaunce, 'ys thys sothe that ye woll sle hym?'   5

'Yee, sle hym woll I, whoso seyth the contrary! For he hath done so
muche ayenst me that he hath well deserved hit.'

And so ran uppon hym, and wolde have smytten of the hede. And
so sir Colgrevaunce ran betwixte them and seyde,

'And ye be so hardy to do so more, we two shall meddyll togidirs!'   10

So whan sir Lyonell undirstood his wordis he toke his shylde tofore
hym and asked hym what that he was.

'Sir, my name ys sir Collgrevaunce, one of his felowis.'

Than sir Lyonell defyed hym, and so he sterte uppon hym and gaff
hym a grete stroke thorow the helme. Than he drew his swerde—for   15
he was a passyng good knyght—and defended hym ryght manfully.

And so longe dured there the batayle that sir Bors sate up all ang-
wyshlye and behylde sir Collegrevaunce, the good knyght, that fought
with his brother for his quarell. Thereof he was full hevy, and thought
if sir Collgrevaunce slew hys brothir that he sholde never have joy;   20
also, and if hys brothir slew sir Collgrevaunce, 'the same shame
sholde ever be myne'.

Than wolde he have rysen to have departed them, but he had nat so
much myght to stonde one foote. And so he abode so longe that sir
Collgrevaunce was overthrowyn, for thys sir Lyonell was of grete   25
chevalry and passyng hardy; for he had perced the hawbirke and the
helme so sore that h[e] abode but deth; for he had lost much blood
that hit was mervayle that he myght stonde upryght. Than behylde he
sir Bors whych sate dressyng upward hymselff, which seyde,

'A, sir Bors! Why cam ye nat to rescowe me oute of perell of dethe   30
wherein I have putte me to succour you which were ryght now nyghe
dethe?'

'Sertes,' seyde sir Lyonell, 'that shall nat avayle you, for none of you
shall be othirs warraunte, but ye shall dye both of my honde!'

Whan sir Bors herde that he seyde so muche, he arose and put on   35
hys helme. And than he perceyved fi[r]st the ermyte-pryste whych was
slayne; than made he a mervaylous sorow uppon hym. Than sir Coll-   (16)
grevaunce cryed offtyn uppon sir Bors and seyde,

'Why, woll ye lat me dye here for your sake? No forse, sir! If hit
please you that I shall dy, the deth shall please me the bettir, for to save   40
a worthyer man myght I never ressayve the dethe.'

With that worde sir Lyonell smote of the helme frome hys hede; and
whan sir Collgrevaunce saw that he myght nat ascape, than he seyde,

'Fayre swete Jesu Cryste, that I have myssedo, have mercy uppon my soule! For such sorow that my harte suffirthe for goodnes and for almes-dede that I wolde have done here, be to me a lyegemente of penaunce unto my sowle helthe!'

And so at thes wordis sir Lyonell smote hym so sore that he bare
5 hym dede to the erthe. And whan he had slayne sir Collgrevaunce he ran uppon hys brothir as a fyndely man, and gaff hym such a stroke that he made hym stoupe. And ⌈he,⌉ as he that was full of humilité, prayde hym for Goddis love to leve his batayle, 'for if hit befelle, fayre brothir, if that I sle you other ye me, we both shall dye for that
10 synne'.

'So God me helpe, I shall never have othir mercy, and I may have the bettir honde.'

'Well,' seyde sir Bors, and drew hys swerde, all wepyng, and seyde, 'fayre brother, God knowith myne entente, for ye have done full evyll
15 thys day to sle an holy pryste which never trespasced. Also ye have slayne a jantill knyght, and one of oure felowis. And well wote ye that I am nat aferde of you gretely, but I drede the wratthe of God; and thys ys an unkyndely werre. Therefore God shew His myracle uppon us bothe, and God have mercy uppon me, thoughe I defende my lyff
20 ayenst my brothir.'

And so with that sir Bors lyffte up hys honde and wolde have smyttyn
(17) hys brothir. And with that he harde a voice whych seyde,

'Fle, sir Bors, and towche hym nat, othir ellis thou shalt sle hym!'

Ryght so alyght a clowde betwyxte them in lykenes of a fayre and a
25 mervaylous flame, that bothe hir two shyldis brente. Than were they sore aferde and felle both to the erthe and lay there a grete whyle in a sowne. And whan they cam to themselff sir Bors saw that hys brothir had none harme. Than he hylde up both his hondys, for he drad last God had takyn vengeaunce uppon hym. So with that he harde a voyce
30 that seyde,

'Sir Bors, go hens and beare felyship no lenger with thy brothir, but take thy way anone ryght to the see, for sir Percivale abydith the there.'

Than he seyde to his brother, 'For Goddis love, fayre swete brothir, forgyffe me my trespasse!'

35 Than he answerd and seyde, 'God forgyff you, and I do gladly.'

So sir Bors departed frome hym, and rode the next way to the se. And at the last, by fortune, he cam to an abbay which was nyghe the see, and that nyght he rested hym there.

And as he slepte, there cam a voyse and bade hym go to the see.
40 Than he sterte up and made a signe of the crosse ⌈in the myddes of his forhede⌉, and toke hym to hys harnes, and made redy hys horse. And at a brokyn wall he rode oute, and by fortune he cam to the see. And uppon the see-stronde he founde a shyppe that was coverde all with whyght samyte.

Than he alyghte and betoke hym to Jesu Cryste. And as sone as he
was entird, the shippe departed into the see, and to hys semyng hit
wente fleyng, but hit was sone durked, that he myght know no man.
Than he layde hym downe and slept tyll hit was day.

And whan he was waked he sawe in myddis of the shippe a knyght 5
lye all armed sauff hys helme, and anone he was ware hit was sir Percivale de Galys. And than he made of hym ryght grete joy, but sir
Percivale was abaysshed of hym and asked what he was.

'A, fayre sir,' seyde sir Bors, 'know ye me nat?'

'Sertes,' seyde he, 'I mervayle how ye cam hydir but if oure Lorde 10
brought you hydir Hymselff.'

Than sir Bors smyled, and ded off hys helme, and anone sir Percyvale
knew hym. And ayther made grete joy of othir, that hit was mervayle
to hyre. Than sir Bors tolde hym how he cam into the ship, and by
whos amonyshment. And aythir told other of their temptacions, as ye 15
have herde toforehonde.

So wente they dᵣowneward¹ in the see, one whyle backwarde,
another while foreward, and every man comforted other, and ever
they were in theyre prayers. Than seyde sir Percivale,

'We lak nothynge but sir Galahad, the good knyght.' 20

Now turnyth the tale unto sir Galahad.

VII. SIR GALAHAD

Now seyth the tale, whan sir Galahad had rescowed sir Percyvale XVII(1)
frome the twenty knyghtes he rode tho into a waste foreyste wherein
he dud many journeyes and founde many adventures which he brought 25
all to an ende, whereof the tale makith here no mencion.

Than he toke hys way to the see; and on a day, as hit befelle, as he
passed by a castell there was a wondir turnemente. But they withoute
had done so much that they within were put to the worse, and yet were
they within good knyghtes inow. 30

So whan sir Galahad saw tho within were at so grete myschyff that
men slew hem at the entré of the castell, than he thought to helpe them,
and put a speare furthe, and smote the firste, that he flowe to the erthe
and the speare yode in pecis. Than he drew hys swerde and smote
thereas they were thyckyst; and so he dud wondirfull dedys of armys, 35
that all they mervayled.

And so hyt happynde that sir Gawayne and sir Ector de Marys were
with the knyghtes withoute. But than they aspyed the whyght shylde
with the rede crosse, and anone that one seyde to that othir,

'Yondir ys the good knyght sir Galahad, the Haute Prynce. Now, 40 forsothe, methynkith he shall be a grete foole that shall mete with hym to fyght.'

But at the last by aventure he cam by sir Gawayne and smote hym so sore that he clave hys helme and the coyff of iron unto the hede, that
5 sir Gawayne felle to the erthe; but the stroke was so grete that hit slented downe and kutte the horse sholdir in too. So whan sir Ector saw sir Gawayne downe, he drew hym asyde and thought hit no wysedom for to abyde hym, and also for naturall love, for because he was hys uncle.

10 Thus thorow hys hardynesse he bete abacke all the knyghtes withoute, and than they within cam oute and chaced them all aboute. But whan sir Galahad saw there wolde none turne agayne, he stale away prevayly, and no man wyste where he was becom.

'Now, be my hede,' seyde sir Gawayne unto sir Ector, 'now ar the
15 wondirs trew that was seyd of sir Launcelot, that the swerd which stake in the stone shulde gyff me such a buffette that I wold nat have hit for the beste castell in the worlde. And sothely now hit ys preved trew, for never ar had I such a stroke of mannys honde.'

'Sir,' seyde sir Ector, 'mesemyth youre queste ys done, and myne ys
20 nat done.'

'Well,' seyde he, 'I shall seke no farther.'

Than was sir Gawayne borne into the castell, and unarmed hym and leyde hym in a rych bedde, and a leche was founde to hele hym. And sir Ector wolde nat departe frome hym tyll he was nyghe hole.

25 And so this good knyght sir Galahad rode so faste that he cam that nyght to the castell of Carbonecke. And so hit befelle hym that he was benyghted and cam unto an armytayge. So the good man was fayne whan he saw he was a knyght arraunte.

So whan they were at reste, there befelle a jantillwoman com and
30 cnokkede at the dore and called sir Galahad. And so the good man cam to the dore to wete what she wolde. Than she called the ermyte sir Ulphyne and seyde,

'I am a jantillwoman that wolde fayne speke with the knyght which ys within you.'

35 Than the good man awaked sir Galahad and bade hym aryse 'and speke with a jantyllwoman that semyth she hath grete nede of you'.

Than sir Galahad ⌐wente to hir⌐ and asked hir what she wolde.

'Sir Galahad,' seyde she, 'I woll that ye arme you and lyght uppon thys horse and sew me, for I shall shew you within thys three dayes
40 the hyghest adventure that ever ony knyght saw.'

So anone sir Galahad armed hym and toke hys horse, and commended the e[r]myte to God.

And so he bade the jantillwoman to ryde, and he wolde folow thereas
(2) she lyked. So she rode as faste as hir palferey myght bere her, tyll that

she cam to the see whych was called Collybye. And by nyght they com
unto a castell in a valey, closed with a rennyng watir, whych had
stronge wallis and hyghe.

And so she entird into the castell with sir Galahad, and there had he
grete chere, for the lady of that castell was the damesels lady. So was 5
he unarmed. Than seyde the damesell,

'Madame, shall we abyde here all thys day?'

'Nay,' seyde she, 'but tylle he hath dyned and slepte a litill.'

And so he ete and slepte a whyle, and this mayde than called hym
and armed hym by torchelyght. And whan the mayden was horsed and 10
he bothe, the lady toke sir Galahad a fayre shylde and ryche, and so
they departed frome the castell and rode tylle they cam to the see. And
there they founde the shippe that sir Bors and sir Percivale was in,
whych seyde on the shipbourde,

'Sir Galahad, ye be wellcom, for we have abydyn you longe!'   15

And whan he herde them he asked them what they were.

'Sir,' seyde she, 'leve youre horse hyre, and I shall leve myne also.'

And toke hir sadils and hir brydyls with them, and made a crosse on
them, and so entird into the ship. And the two knyghtes resceyved
them bothe with grete joy, and everych knew other.   20

And so the wynde arose and drove hem thorow the see into a mervayles place, and within a whyle hit dawed. Than dud sir Galahad of
hys helme and hys swerde, and asked of hys felowis from whens com
that fayre shippe.

'Trewly,' seyde they, 'ye wote as well as we, but hit com of Goddis 25
grace.'

And than they tolde everych to othir of all theyre harde aventures,
and of her grete temptacions.

'Truly,' seyd sir Galahad, 'ye ar much bounden to God, for ye have
escaped ryght grete adventures. Sertes, had nat this jantillwoman bene, 30
I had nat come hydir at thys tyme. For as for you two, I wente never
to have founde you in thys straunge contreys.'

'A, sir Galahad,' seyde sir Bors, 'if sir Launcelot, your fadir, were
here, than were we well at ease, for than mesemed we fayled nothynge.'

'That may nat be,' seyd sir Galahad, 'but if hit pleased our Lorde.' 35

By than the shipp had renne frome the londe of Logrys many myles.
So by adventure hit aryved up bytwyxte two rocchis, passynge grete
and mervaylous, but there they myght nat londe, for there was a
swalowe of the see, save there was another shippe, and uppon hit
they myght go withoute daungere.   40

'Now go we thydir,' seyde the jantillwoman, 'and there shall we se
adventures, for so ys oure Lordys wylle.'

And wan they com thyder they founde the shippe ryche inowghe,
but they founde nother man nor woman therein. But they founde in

the ende of the shippe two fayre lettirs wrytten, which seyde a dredefull worde and a mervaylous:

'THOU MAN WHYCH SHALT ENTIR INTO THYS SHIPPE, BEWARE THAT
THOU BE IN STEDEFASTE BELEVE, FOR I AM FAYTHE. AND THEREFORE
5 BEWARE HOW THOU ENTIRST BUT IF THOU BE STEDFASTE, FOR AND
THOU FAYLE THEREOF I SHALL NAT HELPE THE.'

And than seyde the jantillwoman:

'Sir Percivale,' seyde she, 'wote ye what I am?'

'Sertes,' seyde he, 'nay. Unto my wytynge I saw you never arst.

10 'Wyte ye well,' seyde she, 'I am thy syster, whych was doughter unto
kynge Pellynor, and therefore wete you welle ye ar the man that I
moste love. And if ye be nat in perfite belyve of Jesu Cryste, entir nat
in no maner of wyse for than sholde ye perish the shippe; for he ys so
perfite he woll suffir no synner within hym.'

15 So whan sir Percyvale undirstode she was hys verry syster he was
inwardly glad and seyde,

'Fayre sister, I shall entir in, for if I be a myssecreature other an
untrew knyght, there shall I perische.'

(3) So in the meanewhyle sir Galahad blyssed hym and entirde thereinne,
20 and so nexte the jantillwoman, and than sir Bors, and than sir Percyvale.
And whan they were in, hit was so mervaylous fayre and ryche [that
they mervaylede]. And amyddis the shippe was a fayre bedde. And
anone sir Galahad wente thereto and founde thereon a crowne of
sylke. And at the feete was a swerde, rych and fayre, and hit was
25 drawyn oute of the sheeth ˥half˥ a foote and more.

And the swerde was of dyverse fassions; and the pomell was of
stoone, and there was in hym all maner of coloures that ony man
myght fynde, and every of the coloures had dyverse vertues. And the
scalis of the hauffte were of two rybbis of two dyverse bestis; that one
30 was a serpente whych ys coversaunte in Calydone and ys calle there the
serpente of the fynde, and the boone of hym ys of such vertu that
there ys no hande that handelith hym shall never be wery nother hurte;
and the other bone ys of a fyssh whych ys nat ryght grete, and hauntith
the floode of Eufrate, and that fyssh ys called Ertanax. And the bonys
35 be of such maner of kynde that who that handelyth hym shall have so
muche wyll that he shall never be wery, and he shall nat thynke on joy
nother sorow that he hath had, but only that thynge that he beholdith
before hym.

'AND AS FOR THYS SWERDE, THERE SHALL ˥NEVER˥ MAN BEGRYPE
40 HYM, THAT YS TO SEY, THE HAND, BUT ONE; AND HE SHALL PASSE ALL
OTHIR.'

'In the name of God,' seyde sir Percivale, 'I shall assay to handyll hit.'
So he sette hys honde to the swerde, but he myght nat begrype hit.
'Be my faythe,' seyde he, 'now have I fayled.'

Than sir Bors sette to hys hande and fayled.

Than sir Galahad behylde the swerde and saw lettirs lyke bloode
that seyde:

'LAT SE WHO DARE DRAW ME OUTE OF MY SHEETH BUT IF HE BE MORE
HARDYER THAN ONY OTHER, FOR WHO THAT DRAWITH M[E] OUTE,   5
WETE YOU WELLE HE SHALL NEVER BE SHAMED OF HYS BODY NOTHER
WOUNDED TO THE DETHE.'

'Perfay,' seyde sir Galahad, 'I wolde draw thys swerde oute of the
sheethe, but the offendynge ys so grete that I shall nat se[tt]e my hande
thereto.'   10

'Now, sirs,' seyde the jantillwoman, 'the drawynge of thys swerde ys
warned to all sauff all only to you. Also thys shippe aryved into [the]
realme of Logrys, and that tyme was dedly warre betwene kyng Labor,
which was fadir unto the Maymed Kynge, and kynge Hurlaine, whych
was a Saresyn. But than was he newly crystened, and so aftirwarde   15
hylde hym one of the worthyest men of the worlde.

'And so uppon a day hit befelle that kynge Labor and kyng Hurlaine
had assembeled theire folke uppon the see, where thys shippe was
aryved. And there kynge Hurlaine was discomfite, and hys men slayne.
And he was aferde to be dede and fledde to thys shippe, and there   20
founde this swerde, and drew hit, and cam oute and founde kynge
Labor, the man of the worlde of all Crystyn in whom there is the
grettist faythe. And whan kynge Hurlaine ˹saw kynge Labor he
dressid this swerde˺ and smote hym uppon the helme so harde that
he clave hym and hys horse to the ˹erthe˺ with the firste stroke of   25
hys swerde.

'And hit was in the realme of Logris, and so befelle there grete pes-
tilence, and grete harme to bothe reallmys; for there encresed nother
corne, ne grasse, nother well-nye no fruyte, ne in the watir was founde
no fyssh. Therefore men calle hit—the londys of the two marchys—the   30
Waste Londe, for that dolerous stroke.

And whan kynge Hurleine saw thys swerde so kerveyynge, he
turned agayne to fecch the scawberd. And so cam into thys shippe and
entird, and put up the swerde in the sheethe, and as sone as he had done
hit he felle downe dede afore the bedde. Thus was the swerde preved   35
that never man drew hit but he were dede or maymed. So lay he here
tyll a maydyn cam into the shippe and caste hym oute, for there was no
man so hardy in the worlde to entir in that [shippe] for the defens.'

And than behylde they the scawberte, hit besemyd to be of a ser-   (4)
pentis skynne, and thereon were lettirs of golde and sylver. And the   40
gurdyll was but porely to com to, and nat able to susteyne such a
ryche swerde. And the lettirs seyde:

'HE WHYCH SHALL WELDE ME OUGHT TO BE MORE HARDY THAN
ONY OTHER, IF HE BEARE ME AS TRULY AS ME OUGHTE TO BE BORNE.

FOR THE BODY OF HYM WHICH I OUGHT TO HANGE BY, HE SHALL NAT
BE SHAMED IN NO PLACE WHYLE HE YS GURDE WITH THE GURDYLL.
NOTHER NEVER NONE BE SO HARDY TO DO AWAY THYS GURDYLL, FOR
HIT OUGHT NAT TO BE DONE AWAY BUT BY THE HONDIS OF A MAYDE,
5 AND THAT SHE BE A KYNGIS DOUGHTER AND A QUENYS. AND SHE MUST
BE A MAYDE ALL THE DAYES OF HIR LYFF, BOTH IN WYLL AND IN WORKE;
AND IF SHE BREKE HIR VIRGINITÉ SHE SHALL DY THE MOSTE VYLAYNES
DETH THAT EVER DUD ONY WOMAN.'

'Sir,' seyde sir Percivale, 'turne thys swerde that we may se what ys
10 on the other syde.'

And hit was rede os bloode, with blacke lettirs as ony cole that seyde:
'HE THAT SHALL PRAYSE ME MOSTE, MOSTE SHALL HE FYNDE ME TO
BLAME AT A GRETE NEDE. AND TO WHOM I SHOLDE BE MOSTE DEBONAYRE
SHALL I BE MOST FELON. AND THAT SHALL BE AT ONE TYME ONLY.'

15 'Fayre brother,' seyde she to sir Percyvale, 'hit befelle afftir a fourty
yere aftir the Passion of our Lorde Jesu Cryste, that Nacien, th⟨e⟩
brothir-in-law of kyng Mordr[a]i[ns], was bore in a towne, more than
fourtene dayes journey frome his contray, by the commaundemente of
oure Lorde, into an yle into the partyes of the Weste that men clepith
20 the Ile of Turnaunce.

'So befelle hit, he founde thys shippe at the entré of a roche, and he
founde the bedde and the swerde, as we have ⌐herd⌐ now. Natforthan
he had nat so much hardynesse to draw hit. And there he dwelled an
eyght dayes, and at the nynyth day there felle a grete wynd whych de-
25 parted hym oute of the ile, and brought hym to another ile by a roche.
And there he founde the grettist gyaunte that ever man myght see.
And therewith cam that horrible gyaunte to sle hym, and than he loked
aboute hym, and myght nat fle, also he had nothyng wherewith to
defende hym. But at the laste he ran to the swerde, and whan he saw
30 hit naked he praysed hit muche, and than he shooke hit, and therewith
hit brake in the myddys.

' "A," seyde Nacien, "the thynge that I moste praysed ought I now
moste to blame!"

'And therewith he threw the pecis of this swerde over hys bedde, and
35 aftir that he lepe over the bourde to fyght with the gyaunte, and slew
hym. And anone he entirde into the shyppe agayne, and the wynde
arose and drove hym thorow the see, that by adventure he cam to
another shippe where kynge Mordrayns was, whych had bene tempted
full evyll with the fynde, in the Porte of Perelous Roche.

40 'And whan that one saw that other they made grete joy aythir of
othir. And so they tolde eche other of their adventure, and how the
swerde fayled hym at hys moste nede. So whan Mordrayns saw the
swerde he praysed hit muche, "but the brekyng was do by wyckednesse
of thyselffward, for thou arte in som synne".

'And there he toke the swerde and sette the pecis togydirs, and they were as fayre isowdred as ever they were tofore. And than he put the swerde in the sheeth ayen, and leyde hit downe on the bedde. Than herde they a voyce that seyde,

' "Go ye oute of thys shippe a litill whyle and entir into that othir for 5 drede ye falle in dedly synne. For and ye be founde in dedely synne ye may nat ascape but perishe!"

'And so they wente into the othir shippe. And as Nacyen wente over the bourde he was smytten with a swerde on the ryght foote, that he felle downe noselynge to the shippe-bourde. And therewith he seyde, 10

' "A, Good Lorde, how am I hurte!"

'Than there cam a voice that seyde, "Take thou that for thy forfette that thou dyddist in drawynge of this swerde! Therefore thou hast ressayved a wounde, for thou were never worthy to handyll hit: the wrytynge makith mencion." ' 15

'In the name of God!' seyde sir Galahad, 'ye ar ryght wyse of thes wor⟨d⟩es.'

'Sir,' seyde she, 'there was a kynge that hyght Pelleaus, which men (5) called the Maymed Kynge, and whyle he myght ryde he supported much Crystyndom and Holy Chyrche. So uppon a day he hunted in a 20 woode of hys owne whych lasted unto the see, so at the laste he loste hys howndys and hys knyghtes sauff only one.

'And so he and his knyght wente tyll that they cam toward Irelonde, and there he founde the shippe. And whan he saw the lettirs and undirstood them, yet he entird, for he was ryght perfite of lyff. But hys 25 knyght had no hardynes to entir. And there founde he thys swerde, and drew hit oute as much as ye may se. So therewith entirde a spere wherewith he was smytte⟨n⟩ thorow both thyghes. And never sith myght he be heled, ne nought shall tofore we com to hym. Thus,' seyde she, 'was kyng Pelles, youre grauntesyre, maymed for hys hardynes.' 30

'In the name of God, damesell!' seyde sir Galahad.

So they wente towarde the bedde to beholde all aboute hit. And abovyn the bed there hynge two swerdys, also there were spyndelys whych were whyght as snowe, and othir that were rede as bloode, and othir abovyn grene as ony emerawde. Of these three colowres were 35 thes spyndyls, and of naturall coloure within, and withoute ony pay[n]tynge.

'Thes spyndyls,' seyde the damesell, 'was whan synfull Eve cam to gadir fruyte, for which Adam and she were put oute of Paradyse. She toke with her the bowgh whych the appyll hynge on, than perseyved 40 she that the braunche was freysh and grene, and she remembird of the losse which cam of the tre. Than she thought to kepe the braunche as longe as she myght, and for she had no coffir to kepe hit in, she put hit in the erthe. So by the wylle of oure Lorde the braunche grew to

a grete tre within a litill whyle, and was as whyght as ony snowe, braunchis, bowis, and levys: that was a tokyn that a maydyn planted hit. But affter that oure Lorde com to Adam and bade hym know hys wyff fleyshly, as nature requyred. So lay Adam with hys wyff undir the
5 same tre, and anone the tre which was whyght felle to grene os ony grasse, and all that com oute of hit. And in the same tyme that they medled togydirs Abell was begotyn.

'Thus was the tre longe of grene coloure. And so [hit] befelle many dayes aftir, undir the same tre, Cayme slew Abell, whereof befelle grete
10 mervayle, for a[s] Abell had ressayved dethe undir the grene tre, he loste the grene colour and becam rede; and that was in tokenyng of blood. And anone all the plantis dyed thereoff, but the tre grewe and waxed mervaylusly fayre, and hit was the moste fayryst tre and the most delectable that ony man myght beholde and se; and so ded the
15 plantes that grewe oute of hit tofore that Abell was slayne undir hit.

'And so longe dured the tre tyll that Salamon, kynge Davythys sonne, regned and hylde the londe aftir his fadir. So thys Salamon was wyse, and knew all the vertues of stonys and treys; also he knew the course of the stirres, and of many other dyvers thynges. So this Salamon
20 had an evyll wyff, wherethorow he wente there had be no good woman borne, and therefore he dispysed them in hys bookis. So there answerde a voice that seyde to hym thus:

' "Salamon, if hevynesse com to a man by a woman, ne rek tho[u] never, for yet shall there com a woman whereof there shall com gretter
25 joy to a man an hondred tymes than thys hevynesse gyvith sorow. And that woman shall be borne of thy lynayge."

'So whan Salamon harde thes wordis, he hylde hymself but a foole. Tha⟨n⟩ preff had he by olde bookis the trouthe. Also the Holy Goste shewed hym the commynge of the glorius Virgyne Mary.

30 'Than asked he the voyce if hit sholde be in the yarde of hys lynayge.
' "Nay," seyde the voyce, "but there shall com a Man which shall be a mayde, and laste of youre bloode, and He shall be as good a knyght
(6) as deuke Josue, thy brother-in-law. Now have I sertefyed the of that thou stondist in doute."

35 'Than was Salamon gladde that there shulde com ony suche of hys lynayge, but ever he mervayled and studyed who that sholde be, and what hys name myght be. So hys wyff perceyved that he studyed, and thought she wolde know at som season. And so she wayted hir tyme and cam to hym and asked hym. And there he tolde her alltogydir how
40 the voice had tolde hym.

' "Well," seyde she, "I shall lette make a shippe of the beste wood and moste durable that ony man may fynde."

'So Salamon sente for carpenters, of all the londe the beste. And whan they had made the shippe the lady seyde to Salamon,

' "Sir, syn hit ys so that thys knyght oughte to passe all knyghtes of chevalry whych hath bene tofore hym and shall com affitir hym, moreover I shall lerne you," seyde she, "ye shall go into oure Lordis temple where ys kyng Davith his swerde, youre fadir, whych ys the mervaylouste and the sherpyste that ever was takyn in ony knyghtes 5 hondys. Therefore take ye that, and take off the pomelle, and thereto make ye a pomell of precious stonys; late hit be so suttelly made that no man perceyve hit but that they beth all one. And aftir make there an hylte so mervaylously that no man may know hit, and aftir that make a mervaylous sheethe. And whan ye have made all thys I shall lette make 10 a gurdyll thereto, such one as shall please me."

'So all thys kyng Salamon ded lat make as she devised, bothe the shippe and all the remenaunte. And whan the shippe was redy in the see to sayle, the lady lete make a grete bedde and mervaylous ryche, and sette hir uppon the beddis hede coverde with ⌐sylke¬, and leyde the 15 swerde at the feete. And the gurdyls were of hempe.

'And therewith the kynge was ryght angry.

' "Sir, wyte you welle that I have none so hyghe a thynge whych were worthy to susteyne ⌐soo hyghe a swerde. And a mayde shall brynge other knyghtes thereto, but I wote not whan hit shall be ne 20 what tyme.¬"

'And there she lete make a coverynge to the shippe of clothe of sylke, that sholde never rotte for no manner of wedir. Than thys lady wente and made a carpynter to com to the tre whych Abelle was slayne undir. 25

' "Now," seyde she, "carve me oute of thys tre as much woode as woll make me a spyndill."

' "A, madam," seyde he, "thys ys the tre which oure firste modir planted."

' "Do hit," seyd she, "other ellis I shall destroy the." 30

'Anone as he began to worke, there com oute droppis of blood; and than wolde he a leffte, but she wolde nat suffir hym. And so he toke as muche woode as myght make a spyndyll, and so she made hym to take as muche of the grene tre, and so of the whyght tre. And whan thes three spyndyls were shapyn she made hem to be fastened uppon the 35 syler of the bedde. So whan Salamon saw thys he seyde to hys wyff,

' "Ye have done mervaylously, for thoughe all the worlde were here ryght now, they cowde nat devise wherefore all thys was made but oure Lorde Hymselff. And thou that haste done hit wote nat what hit shall betokyn." 40

' "Now lat hyt be," seyde she, "for ye shall hyre peraventure tydynges sonner than ye wene." '

NOW HERE YS A WONDIR TALE OF KYNG SALAMON AND OF HYS WYFF.

'That nyght lay Salamon before the shippe with litill felyship. And (7)

whan he was on slepe hym thought there com from hevyn a grete company of angels, and alyght into the shippe, and toke water whych was brought by an angell in a vessell of sylver, and besprente all the shippe.

'And aftir he cam to the swerde and drew lettirs o[n] the hylte. And aftir wente to the shippe-bourde and wrote there other lettirs whych seyde: "Thou man that wolte entir within me, beware that thou be fulle in the faythe, for I ne am but Fayth and Belyve."

'Whan Salamon aspyed thos lettirs he was so abaysshed that he dirst nat entir, and so he drew hym abacke, and the shippe was anone shovyn in the see. He wente so faste that he had loste the syght of hym within a litill whyle. And than a voyce seyde,

' "Salamon, the laste knyght of thy kynred shall reste in ⌈t⌉hys bedde."

'Than wente Salamon and awaked hys wyff, and tolde her the adventures of thys shipp.'

Now seyth the tale that a grete whyle [the] three felowis behylde the bed and the three spyndyls. Than they were at a sertayne that they were of naturall coloures withoute ony payntynge. Than they lyfft up a cloth which was above the grounde, and there founde a rych purse be semyng. And sir Percivale toke hit and founde therein a wrytte, and so he rad hit, and devysed the maner of the spyndils and of the ship: whens hit cam, and by whom hit was made.

'Now,' seyde sir Galahad, 'where shall we fynde the jantillwoman that shall make new gurdyls to the swerde?'

'Fayre sirres,' seyde Percivallis syster, 'dismay you nat. For, by the leve of God, I shall lette make a gurdyll to the swerde, such one as sholde longe thereto.'

And than opynde she a boxe and toke oute gurdils which were semely wrought [with] goldyn thredys, and uppon that were sette full precius stonys, and a ryche buckyll of golde.

'Lo, lordys,' she seyde, 'here ys a gurdill that ought to be sette aboute the swerde. And wete you well the grettist parte of thys gurdyll was made of my hayre, whych somme tyme I loved well, whyle that I was woman of the worlde. But as sone as I wyste that thys adventure was ordayned me, I clipped off my heyre and made thys gurdyll.'

'In the name of God, ye be well ifounde!' seyde sir Bors. 'For serteyse ye have put us oute off grete payne, wherein we sholde have entirde ne had your tydyngis ben.'

Than wente the jantillwoman and sette hit on the gurdyll of the swerde.

'Now,' seyde the felyship, 'what ys the name of the swerde, and what shall we calle hit?'

'Truly,' seyde she, 'the name of the swerde ys the Swerde with the Straunge Gurdyls, and the s[h]eeth, Mevear of Blood. For no man that

hath blood in hym ne shall never see that one party of the sheth whych
was made of the tree of lyff.'

Than they seyde, 'Sir Galahad, in the name of Jesu Cryste, we pray
you to gurde you with thys swerde which hath bene desyred so much
in the realme of Logrys.'   5

'Now latte me begynne,' seyde Galahad, 'to grype thys swerde for
to gyff you corrayge. But wete you well hit longith no more to me than
hit doth to you.'

And than he gryped aboute hit with his fyngirs a grete dele, and
than she gurte hym aboute the myddyll with the swerde.   10

'Now recke I nat though I dye, for now I holde me one of the beste
blyssed maydyns of the worlde, whych hath made the worthyest knyght
of the worlde.'

'Damesell,' seyde sir Galahad, 'ye have done so muche that I shall
be your knyght all the dayes of my lyff.'   15

Than they wente frome that ship and wente to the other. And anone
the wynde droff hem into the see a grete pace, but they had no vytayle.
So hit befelle that they cam on the morne to a castell that men calle
Carteloyse, that was in the marchys of Scotlonde. And whan they had
passed the porte the jantillwoman seyde,   20

'Lordys, here be men aryven that, and they wyst that [y]e were of
kynge Arthurs courte, ye shulde be assayled anone.'

'Well, damesell, dismay you nat,' seyde sir Galahad, 'for He that
cast us oute of the rocche shall delyver us frome hem.'

So hit befelle, as they talked thus togydir, there cam a squyre by   25 (8)
them and asked what they were.

'Sir, we ar of kyng Arthu[r]s howse.'

'Ys that sothe?' seyde he. 'Now, be my hede,' seyd he, 'ye be evyll
arayde.'

And than turned agayne unto the chyff fortresse, and within a whyle   30
they harde an horne blow. Than a jantillwoman cam to hem and asked
them of whens they were. Anone they tolde her.

'Now, fayre lordys,' she seyde, 'for Goddys love, turnyth agayne if
ye may, for ye be com to youre dethe.'

'Nay, forsoth,' they seyde, 'we woll nat turne agayne, for He shulde 35
helpe us into whos servyse we were entred in.'

So as they stoode talkynge there cam ten knyghtes well armed, and
bade hem yelde othir ellis dye.

'That yeldyng,' seyde they, 'shall be noyous unto you.'

And therewith they lete their horsis renne, and sir Percivale smote the 40
firste, that he bare hym to the erthe, and toke hys horse and bestrode
hym. And the same wyse dud sir Galahad, and al[so] sir Bors served
another so; for they had no horse in that contrey, for they lefft their
horsys whan they toke their shippe.

And so, whan they were horsed, than began they to sette uppon them, and they of the castell fledde into stronge fortressis, and thes three knyghtes aftir them into the castell; and so alyght on foote, and with their swerdis slew them downe, and gate into the halle.

5 Than whan they behelde the grete multitude of the people that they had slayne, they helde themself grete synners.

'Sertes,' seyde sir Bors, 'I wene, and God had loved them, that we sholde nat have had power to have slayne hem thus. But they have done so muche agayne oure Lorde that He wolde nat suffir hem to
10 regne no lenger.'

'Yee say nat so,' seyde Galahad. 'First, if they mysseded ayenst God, the vengeaunce ys nat owris, but to Hym which hath power there-off.'

So cam there, oute of a chambir, a good man, which was a preste and
15 bare Goddis body in a cuppe. And whan he saw hem whych lay dede in the halle he was abaysshed. Anone sir Galahad ded of hys ⌐helme⌐ and kneled adowne, and so dud hys two felowis.

'Sir,' seyde they, 'have ye no drede of us, for we bene of kynge Arthurs courte.'

20 Than asked the good man how they were slayne so suddaynly. And they tolde hym.

'Truly,' seyde the good man, 'and ye myght lyve as longe as the worlde myght endure, ne myght ye have done so grete almys-dede as this.'

25 'Sir,' seyde sir Galahad, 'I repente me gretely inasmuch as they were crystynde.'

'Nay, repente you nat,' seyde he, 'for they were nat crystynde. And I shall telle you how that I know of thys castell. Here was a lorde erle whos name was Hernox, nat but one yere. And he had three sonnys,
30 good knyghtes of armys, and a doughter, the fayrist jantillwoman that men knew. So tho three knyghtes loved their syster so sore that they brente in love. And so they lay by her, magré her hede. And for she cryed to hir fadir they slew her, and toke their fadir and put hym in preson and wounded hym nye to the deth. But [a] cosyn of hers res-
35 cowed hym.

'And than ded they grete untrouthe, for they slew clerkis and prestis, and made bete downe chapellis that oure Lordys servyse myght nat be seyde. And thys same day her fadir sente unto me for to be confessed and howseled. But such shame had never man as I had
40 thys same day with the three bretherne; but the olde erle made me to suffir, for he seyde they shold nat longe endure, for three servauntes of oure Lorde sholde destroy them. And now hit ys brought to an ende, and by thys may you wete that oure Lorde ys nat displesed with youre dedis.'

'Sertes,' seyde sir Galahad, 'and hit had nat pleased oure Lorde, never sholde we have slayne so many men in so litill a whyle.'

And they brought the erle Hernox oute of preson into the myddis of the hall, the which knew well sir Galahad, and yet he sye hym never before but by revelacion of oure Lorde. Than began he to wepe ryght ₅ (9) tendirly, and seyde,

'Longe have I abyddyn youre commynge! But for Goddis love, holdith me in youre armys, that my soule may departe oute of my body in so good a mannys armys as ye be.'

'Full gladly,' seyde sir Galahad.   10

And than one seyde on hyght, that all folke harde,

'Sir Galahad, well hast thou ben avenged on Goddis enemyes. Now behovith the to go to the Maymed Kynge as sone as thou mayste, for he shall ressayve by the helth whych he hath abyddyn so longe.'

And therewith the soule departed frome the body. And sir Galahad ₁₅ made hym to be buryed as hym ought to be.

Ryght so departed the three knyghtes, and sir Percivallis syster with them. And so they cam into a waste foreyst, and there they saw afore them a whyght herte which four lyons lad. Than they toke hem to assente for to folow aftir to know whydir they repayred.   20

And so they rode aftir a grete pase tyll that they cam to a valey. And thereby was an ermytayge where a good man dwelled, and the herte and the lyons entirde also. Whan they saw all thys they turned to the chapell and saw the good man in a relygious wede and in the armour of oure Lorde, for he wolde synge masse of the Holy Goste.   25

And so they entird in and herde masse; and at the secretis of the masse they three saw the herte become a man, which mervayled hem, and sette hym uppon the awter in a ryche se⌜g⌝e, and saw the four lyons were chaunged: one to the fourme of man, and another to the fourme of a lyon, and the t[h]irde to an egle, and the fourth was changed to an 30 oxe. Than toke they her se⌜g⌝e where the harte sate, and wente out thorow a glasse wyndow; and there was nothynge perisshed nother brokyn.

And they harde ⌜a voyce⌝ say: 'In such maner entred the Sonne of God into the wombe of Maydyn Mary, whos virginité ne was perisshed, 35 ne hurte.'

And whan they harde thes wordis, they felle downe to the erthe and were astoned. And therewith was a grete clerenesse. And whan they were com to theirselff agayne, they wente to the good man and prayde hym that he wolde sey them the trouthe of that vision.   40

'Why, what thynge have ye sene?'

Anone they tolde hym all.

'A, lordys,' seyde he, 'ye be wellcom, for now wote I well ye beth the good knyghtes whych shall brynge the Sankgreall to an ende; for

ye bene they unto whom oure Lorde shall shew grete secretis. And well ought oure Lorde be signifyed to an harte. For the harte, whan he ys olde, he waxith yonge agayne in his whyght skynne. Ryght so commyth agayne oure Lorde frome deth to lyff, for He lost erthely
5 fleysshe, that was the dedly fleyssh whych He had takyn in the wombe of the Blyssed Virgyne Mary. And for that cause appered oure Lorde as a whyght harte withoute spot.

'And the four that were with hym ys to undirstonde the four Evaun-gelistis, which sette in wrytynge a parte of Jesu Crystes dedys, that He
10 dud somtyme whan He was amonge you an erthely man. For wete you welle never arst ne myght no knyght knowe the trouthe; for oftyn-tymes or thys hath oure Lorde shewed Hym unto good men and to good knyghtes in lyknesse of an herte, but I suppose frome henseforthe ye shall se hit no more.'

15 And than they joyed much, and dwelled there all day. And uppon the morne, whan they had herde masse, they departed and commended the good man to God. And so they cam to a castell, and passed. So there cam a knyght armed aftir them and seyde,

(10) 'Lordys, thys jantillwoman that ye lede with you, ys she a mayde?'
20 'Ye, sir,' seyde she, 'a mayde I am.'

Than he toke hir by the brydyll and seyde,

'By the Holy Crosse, ye shall nat ascape me tofore ye have yolden the custum of thys castell.'

'Lat her go!' seyde sir Percivale. 'Ye be nat wyse, for a mayde, in
25 what place she commythe, ys fre.'

So in the meanewhyle there cam oute a ten or twelve knyghtes armed oute of the castell, and with hem cam jantillwomen the which hylde a dyssh of sylver. And than they seyde,

'Thys jantillwoman muste yelde us the custom of thys castell.'
30 'Why,' seyde sir Gallahad, 'what ys the custom of thys castell?'

'Sir,' seyde a knyght, 'what mayde passith hereby, sholde hylde thys dyshe full of bloode of hir ryght arme.'

'Blame have he,' seyde Galahad, 'that brought up such customs! And so God save me, also sure mow ye be that of this jantillwom[a]n
35 shall ye fayle whyle that I have hele.'

'So God me helpe,' seyde sir Percivale, 'I had lever be slayne.'

'And I also,' seyde sir Bors.

'Be my fayth,' seyde the knyght, 'than shall ye dye, for ye mow nat endure ayenste us, thoughe ye were the beste knyghtes of the worlde.'
40 Than lette they ren ech horse to other, and thes three knyghtes bete the ten knyghtes, and than set their hondis to their swerdis and bete them downe. Than there cam oute of the castell a sixty knyghtes armed.

'Now, fayre lordis,' seyde thes three knyghtes, 'have mercy on youreselff, and have nat ado with us.'

'Nay, fayre lordes,' seyde the knyghtes of the castell, 'we counceyle you to withdrawe you, for ye ben the beste knyghtes of the worlde, and therefore do no more, for ye have done inow. We woll lat you go with thys harme, but we muste nedys have the custum.'

'Sertes,' seyde sir Galahad, 'for noughte speke ye.'   5

'Well,' sey they, 'woll ye dye?'

'Sir, we be nat yet com thereto', seyde sir Galahad.

Than began they to meddyll togydirs. And sir Galahad with the straunge gurdyls drew his swerde and smote on the ryght honde and on the lyffte honde, and slew whom that ever abode hym, and dud so   10 mervaylously that ⌜there was none that sawe hym⌝ they ⌜wend he had ben none erthely man, but a monstre.⌝ And hys two felowis holpe hym passyngly well, and so they helde their journey everych inlycke harde tyll hit was nyghe nyght. Than muste they nedis departe.

So there cam a good knyght and seyde to thes three knyghtes,   15

'If ye woll com in to-nyght and take such herberow as here ys, ye shall be ryght wellcom. And we shall ensure you by the fayth of oure bodyes and as we be trew knyghtes to leve you in such astate to-morow as here we fynde you, withoute ony falsehode. And as sone as ye know of the custom, we dare sey ⌜y⌝e woll accorde therefore.'   20

'For Goddis love,' seyde the jantyllwoman, 'go we thydir, and spare nat for me.'

'Well, go we!' seyde sir Galahad.

And so they entird into the castell, and whan they were alyght they made grete joy of hem. So within a whyle the three knyghtes asked the   25 custom of the castell, and wherefore hit was used.

'Sir, what hit ys we woll sey you the sothe. There ys in this castell a   (11) jantillwoman, whych both we and thys castell ys hers, and many other. So hit befelle many yerys agone, there happened on her a malodye, and whan she had lyene a grete whyle she felle unto a mesell. And no leche   30 cowde remedye her, but at the laste an olde man sayde, and she myght have a dysshfulle of bloode of a maydyn, and a clene virgyne in wylle and in worke, and a kynges doughter, that bloode sholde be her helth for to anoynte her withall. And for thys thynge was thys custom made.'

'Now,' seyde sir Percivallis sister, 'fayre knyghtes, I se well that this   35 jantillwoman ys but dede withoute helpe, and therefore lette me blede.'

'Sertes,' seyde sir Galahad, 'and ye blede so muche ye mo⟨u⟩ dye.'

'Truly,' seyd she, 'and I dye for the helth of her I shall gete me grete worship and soule helthe, and worship to my lynayge; and better ys one harme than twayne. And therefore there shall no more batayle   40 be, but to-morne I shall ⌜yelde⌝ you youre custom of this castell.'

And than there was made grete joy over there, ⌜more than⌝ was made tofore, for ellis had there bene mortall warre uppon the morne; natwithstondynge she wolde none other, whether they wolde or nolde.

So that nyght were thes three felowis eased with the beste, and on the morne they harde masse. And sir Percivalis sister bade them brynge forth the syke lady. So she was brought forth, whych was full evyll at ease. Than seyde she,

5   'Who shall lette me bloode?'

So one cam furthe and lette her bloode. And she bled so muche that the dyssh was fulle. Than she lyfft up her honde and blyssed her and seyde to thys lady,

'Madame, I am com to my dethe for to hele you. Therefore, for
10 Goddis love, prayeth for me!'

And with that she felle in a sowne. Than sir Galahad and his two felows sterte up to her, and lyffte hir up, and staunched hir blood, but she had bled so muche that she myght nat lyve. So whan she was awaked she seyde,

15 'Fayre brothir sir Percivale, I dye for the helynge of this lady. And whan I am dede, I requyre you that ye burye me nat in thys contrey, but as sone as I am dede putte me in a boote at the nexte haven, and lat me go as aventures woll lede me. And as sone as ye three com to the cité of Sarras, there to enchyeve the Holy Grayle, ye shall fynde me
20 undir a towre aryved. And the[re] bury me in the spirituall palyse. For I shall telle you for trouthe, there sir Galahad shall be buryed, and ye bothe, in the same place.'

Whan sir Percivale undirstoode thes wordis he graunted hir all wepyn[g]ly. And than seyde a voice unto them,

25 'Lordis, to-morow, at the owre of pryme, ye three shall departe everych frome other, tylle the aventure brynge you unto the Maymed Kynge.'

Than asked she her Saveoure, and as sone as she had reseyved Hym the soule departed frome the body. So the same day was the lady heled
30 whan she was anoynted with hir bloode.

Than sir Percivale made a lettir of all that she had holpe them as in stronge aventures, and put hit in hir [r]yght honde. And so leyde hir in a barge, and coverde hit with blacke sylke. And so the wynde arose and droff the barge frome the londe, and all maner of knyghtes behylde
35 hit tyll hit was oute of ther syght.

Than they drew all to the castell, and furthewith there fylle a tempeste suddeyne of thundir and lyghtnynge and rayne, as all the erthe wolde a brokyn. So halff the castell turned up-so-downe. So hyt passyd evynsonge or the tempest were seased.

40 Than they saw tofore hem a knyght armed and wounded harde in the body and in the hede, whych seyde,

'A, Good Lord, succour me, for now hit ys nede!'

So after thys knyght there cam another knyght and a dwarff which cryed to h⟨y⟩m afarre,

'Stonde, ye may nat ascape!'

Than the wounded knyght hylde up hys hondys, and prayde God he myght nat dye in suche tribulacion.

'Truly,' seyde sir Galahad, 'I shall succour hym, for His sake that he callith on.'   5

'Sir,' seyde sir Bors, 'I shall do hit, for hit ys nat for you, for he ys but one knyght.'

'Sir,' seyde he, 'I graunte you.'

So sir Bors toke hys ⌜horse⌝ and commaunded hym to God, and rode after to rescow the wounded knyght.   10

NOW TURNE WE TO SIR GALAHAD AND TO SIR PERCIVALL.

Now turnyth the tale unto sir Galahad and sir Percivall, that were in   (12)
a chapell all nyght in hir prayers, for to save hem sir Bors.

So on the morow they dressed them in their harneys toward the castell, to wete what was fallyn of them ⌜therein⌝. And whan they cam   15
there, they founde nother man nother woman that he ne was dede by the vengeaunce of oure Lorde. So with that they harde a voice that seyde,

'Thys vengeaunce ys for bloode-shedynge of maydyns!'

Also they founde at the ende of the c⌜h⌝a⌜pp⌝el a chircheyarde, and   20
therein they myght se a sixti fayre tumbis. And that place was fayre and so delectable that hit semed hem there had bene no tempeste. And there lay the bodyes of all the good maydyns which were martirde for the syke lady. Also they founde there namys of ech lady, and of what bloode they were com off. And all were of kyngys bloode, and ⌜twelve⌝   25
of them were kynges doughtirs.

Than departed they and wente into a foreyste.

'Now,' seyde sir Percivale unto sir Galahad, 'we muste departe, and therefore pray we oure Lorde that we may mete togydirs in shorte tyme.'

Than they ded of their helmys and kyssed togydir and sore wepte at   30
theyre departynge.

NOW TURNYTH THYS TALE UNTO SIR LAUNCELOTT.

VIII. THE CASTLE OF CORBENIC

Now seyth the tale that whan sir Launcelot was com to the watir of   (13)
Mortays as hit ys reherced before, he was in grete perell. And so he   35
leyde hym downe and slepte, and toke the aventure that God wolde sende hym. So whan he was aslepe there cam a vision unto hym that seyde,

'Sir Launcelot, aryse up and take thyne armour, and entir into the firste shippe that thou shalt fynde!'   40

And whan he herde thes wordys he sterte up and saw grete clerenesse aboute hym, and than he lyffte up hys honde and blyssed hym. And so toke hys armys and made hym redy.

And at the laste he cam by a stronde and founde a shippe withoute
5 sayle other ore. And as sone as he was within the shippe, there he had the moste swettnes that ever he felte, and he was fulfylled with all thynge that he thought on other desyred. Than he seyde,

'Swete Fadir, Jesu Cryste! I wote natt what joy I am in, for thys passith all erthely joyes that ever I was in.'

10 And so in thys joy [he] leyde hym downe to the shippe-bourde and slepte tyll day. And whan he awooke he founde there a fayre bed, and therein lyynge a jantillwoman dede, which was sir Percivalles sister. And as sir Launcelot avised her, he aspyed in hir ryght honde ⌐a wrytte¬ whych he rad, that tolde hym all the aventures that ye have herde
15 before, and of what lynayge she was com.

So with thys jantillwoman sir Launcelot was a moneth and more. If ye wold aske how he lyved, for He that fedde the ⌐peple¬ of Israel with manna in deserte, so was he fedde; for every day, whan he had seyde hys prayers, he was susteyned with the grace of the Holy Goste.

20 And so on a ⌐nyght¬ he wente to play hym by the watirs syde, for he was somwhat wery of the shippe. And than he lystened and herde an ⌐hors¬ com and one rydyng uppon hym, and whan he cam nyghe hym semed a knyght, and so he late hym passe and wente theras the ship was. And there he alyght and toke the sadyll and the brydill, and
25 put the horse frome hym, and so wente into the shyppe.

And than sir Launcelot dressed hym unto the shippe and seyde,
'Sir, ye be wellcom!'
And he answerd, and salewed hym agayne and seyde,
'Sir, what ys youre name? For much my herte gevith unto you.'
30 'Truly,' seyde he, 'my name ys sir Launcelot du Lake.'
'Sir,' seyde he, 'than be ye wellcom! For ye were the begynner of me in thys worlde.'
'A, sir, ar ye sir Galahad?'
'Ye, forsothe.'
35 And so he kneled downe and askyd hym hys blyssynge. And aftir that toke of hys helme and kyssed hym, and there was grete joy betwyxte them, for no tunge can telle what joy was betwyxte them. And there every of them tolde othir the aventures that had befalle them syth that they departed frome the courte.

40 And anone as sir Galahad saw the jantillwoman dede in the bedde he knew her well, and seyde grete worship of hir, that she was one of the beste maydyns lyvyng and hit was grete pité of hir dethe.

But whan sir Launcelot herde how the mervayles swerde was gotyn and who made hit, and all the mervayles rehersed afore, than he prayd

sir Galahad that he wolde shew hym the swerde. And so he brought
hit forth and kyssed the pomell and the hiltis and the scawberde.

'Truly,' seyde sir Launcelot, 'never arste knew I of so hyghe adventures done, and so mervalous stronge.'

So dwelled sir Launcelot [and] Galahad within that shippe halff [a   5
yere, and served God dayly and] nyghtly with all their power. [And
often they aryved in yles ferre] frome folke, where th[ere repayred
none but wylde beestes, and ther] they founde many [straunge adventures and peryllous which they] brought to an end. [But for tho adventures were with wylde beestes] and nat in the q[uest of the Sancgreal,   10
therfor the tale ma]kith here [no] menci[on therof; for it wolde be to
longe to telle of alle tho adventures that befelle] them.

So aftir, [on a Mondaye, hit befelle that they aryved in the] edge of a   (14)
forey[ste tofore a crosse. And thenne sawe they a knyghte] armed all in
[whyte, and was rychely horsed, and ledde in his] ryght hond [a whyte   15
hors. And so he cam to the shyp and] salewed the two knyghtes in the
Hyghe Lordis behalff, and seyde unto sir Galahad,

'Sir, ye have bene longe inowe with youre fadir. Therefor com oute
of the shippe, and take thys horse, and go where the aventures shall
lede you in the queste of the Sankgreall.'   20

Than he wente to hys fadir and kyste hym swetely and seyde,

'Fayre swete fadir, I wote nat whan I shall se you more tyll I se the
body of Jesu Cryste.'

'Now, for Goddis love,' seyde sir Launcelot, 'pray to the Fadir that
He holde me stylle in Hys servyse.'   25

And so he toke hys horse, and there they hard a voyce that seyde,

'Every of you thynke for to do welle, for nevermore shall one se
another off you before the dredefull day of doome.'

'Now, my sonne, sir Galahad, sith we shall departe and nother of us
se other more, I pray to that Hyghe Fadir, conserve me and you bothe.'   30

'Sir,' seyde sir Galahad, 'no prayer avaylith so much as youres.'

And therewith sir Galahad entird into the foreyste. And the wynde
arose and drove sir Launcelot more than a moneth thorow the se,
where he sleped but litill, but prayde to God that he myght se som
tydynges of the Sankgreall.   35

So hit befelle on a nyght, at mydnyght, he aryved before a castell, on
the backe [syde whiche was ry]ch and fayre, and there was a posterne
[opened toward the see, and was open] withoute ony kepynge, save
two [lyons kept the entré; and the moon]e shone ryght clere. A[none
sir Launcelot herd a voyce that] seyde,   40

'Launcelot, go oute [of this shyp, and entre into the castel] where
thou shalte [see a grete parte of thy desyre.'

Thenne he ran] to hys armys and [so armed hym, and so wente to
the gate and] saw the lyons. [Thenne sette he hand to his suerd and

dr]ew hit. So there cam [a dwerf sodenly and smote hym th]e arme so
sore [that the suerd felle oute of his hand. Then] herde he a voice [say,
'O, man of evylle feyth and poure byleve]! Wherefore trustist thou
more on thy harneyse than in thy Maker? For He myght more avayle
5 the than thyne armour, in what servyse that thou arte sette in.'
    Than seyde sir Launcelot,
'Fayre Fader, Jesu Cryste! I thanke The of Thy grete mercy that
Thou reprevyst me of my myssedede. Now se I that Thou holdiste me
for one of Thy servauntes.'
10   Than toke he hys swerde agayne and put hit up in hys sheethe, and
made a crosse in hys forehede, and cam to the lyons. And they made
sembelaunte to do hym harme. Natwithstondynge he passed by them
withoute hurte, and entird into the castell to the chyeff fortresse. And
there were they all at reste.
15   Than sir Launcelot entred so armed, for he founde no gate nor
doore but hit was opyn. And at the laste he founde a chambir whereof
the doore was shutte, and he sett hys honde thereto to have opened hit,
(15) but he myght nat. Than he enforced hym myckyll to undo the doore.
Than he lystened and herde a voice whych sange so swetly that hit
20 semede none erthely thynge, and hym thought the voice seyde,
'Joy and honoure be to the Fadir of Hevyn.'
    Than sir Launcelot kneled adowne tofore the chambir dore, for well
wyst he that there was the Sankgreall within that chambir. Than seyde
he,
25 'Fayre swete Fadir, Jesu Cryste! If ever I dud thynge that plesed
The, Lorde, for Thy pité ne have [me] nat in dispite for my synnes
done byforetyme, and that Thou shew me somthynge of that I seke.'
    And with that he saw the chambir dore opyn, and there cam oute a
grete clerenesse, that the house was as bryght as all the tourcheis of
30 the worlde had bene there. So cam he to the chambir doore and wolde
have entird. And anone a voice seyde unto hym,
'Sir Launcelot, flee and entir nat, for thou ought nat to do hit! For
and if thou entir thou shalt forthynke hit.'
    Than he withdrew hym aback ryght hevy.
35 Than loked he up into the myddis of the chambir and saw a table of
sylver, and the holy vessell coverde with rede samyte, and many
angels aboute hit, whereof one hylde a candyll of wexe brennynge and
the other hylde a crosse and the ornementis of an awter. And before
the holy vessell he saw a good man clothed as a pryste, and hit semed
40 that he was at the sakerynge of the masse. And hit semed to sir Launcelot that above the prystis hondys were three men, whereof the two
put the yongyste by lyknes betwene the prystes hondis; and so he
lyffte ⟨hym⟩ up ryght hyghe, and hit semed to shew so to the peple.
    And than sir Launcelot mervayled nat a litill, for hym thought the

pryste was so gretly charged of the vygoure that hym semed that he sholde falle to the erth. And whan he saw none aboute hym that wolde helpe hym, than cam he to the dore a grete pace and seyde,

'Fayre Fadir, Jesu Cryste, ne take hit for no synne if I helpe the good man whych hath grete nede of helpe.'   5

Ryght so entird he into the chambir and cam toward the table of sylver, and whan he cam nyghe hit he felte a breeth that hym thought hit was entromedled with fyre, which smote hym so sore in the vysayge that hym thought hit brente hys vysayge. And therewith he feile to the erthe and had no power to aryse, as he that ⌜was so araged that⌝   10
had loste the power of hys body and hys hyrynge and syght. Than felte he many hondys whych toke hym up and bare hym oute of the chambir doore and leffte hym there semynge dede to all people.

So uppon the morow, whan hit was fayre day, they within were rysen and founde sir Launcelot lyynge before the chambir doore. All   15
thcy mervayled how that he com in. And so they loked uppon hym, and felte hys powse to wete whethir were ony lyff in hym. And so they founde lyff in hym, but he myght nat stonde nother stirre no membir that he had.

And so they toke hym by every parte of the body and bare hym into   20
a chambir and leyde hym in a rych bedde farre frome folke. And so he lay four dayes.

Than one seyde he was on lyve, and another seyde nay, he was dede.

'In the name of God,' seyde an olde man, 'I do you veryly to wete he ys nat dede, but he ys as fulle of lyff as the strengyst of ⌜you⌝ all.   25
Therefore I rede you all that he be well kepte tylle God sende lyff in hym agayne.'

So in such maner they kepte sir Launcelot four-and-twenty dayes   (16)
and also many nyghtis, that ever he lay stylle as a dede man. And at the twenty-fifth day befylle hym aftir mydday that he opened hys yen.   30
And whan he saw folke he made grete sorow and seyde,

'Why have ye awaked me? For I was more at ease than I am now. A, Jesu Cryste, who myght be so blyssed that myght se opynly Thy grete mervayles of secretnesse there where no synner may be?'

'Wh⌜at⌝ have ye sene?' seyde ⌜they aboute hym⌝.   35

'⌜I have sene,' seyde⌝ he, 'grete mervayles that no tunge may telle, and more than ony herte can thynke. And had nat my synne bene beforetyme, ellis I had sene muche more.'

Than they tolde hym how he had layne there four-and-twenty dayes and nyghtes.   40

Than hym thought hit was ponyshemente for the four-⌜and-twenty⌝ yere that he had bene ⌜a⌝ synner, wherefore oure Lorde put hym in penaunce the four-⌜and-twenty⌝ dayes and nyghtes. Than loked Launcelot tofore hym and saw the hayre whych he had borne nyghe a yere; for that he forthoughte hym ryght muche that he had brokyn his promyse unto the ermyte whych he had avowed to do.

Than they asked how [hit] stood with hym.

'Forsothe,' seyde he, 'I am hole of body, thanked be oure Lorde.
5 Therefore, for Goddis love, telle me where I am.'

Than seyde they all that he was in the castell of Carbonek.

Therewith com a jantillwoman and brought hym a shirte of small lynen clothe; but he chaunged nat there, but toke the hayre to hym agayne.

10 'Sir,' seyde they, 'the queste of the Sankgreall ys encheved now ryght in you, and never shall ye se of Sankgreall more than ye have sene.'

'Now I thanke God,' seyde sir Launcelot, 'for Hys grete mercy of that I have sene, for hit suffisith me. For, as I suppose, no man in thys
15 worlde have lyved bettir than I have done to enchyeve that I have done.'

And therewith he toke the hayre and clothed hym in hit, and aboven that he put a lynen ⌐shirte⌐, and aftir that a roobe of scarlet, freyssh and new. And whan he was so arayed they mervayled all, for they knew hym well that he was sir Launcelot, the good knyght. And than they
20 seyde all,

'A, my lorde sir Launcelott, ye be he?'

And he seyde, 'Yee truly, I am he.'

Than cam worde to the kynge Pelles that the knyght that had layne so longe dede was the noble knyght sir Launcelot. Than was the
25 kynge ryght glad and wente to se hym, and whan sir Launcelot saw hym com he dressed hym ayenste hym, and than made the kynge grete joy of hym.

And there the kynge tolde hym tydynges how his fayre doughter was dede. Than sir Launcelot was ryght hevy and seyde,

30 'Me forthynkith of the deth of youre doughter, for she was a full fayre lady, freyshe and yonge. And well I wote she bare the beste knyght that ys now on erthe, or that ever was syn God was borne.'

So the kynge hylde hym there four dayes, and on the morow he toke hys leve at kynge Pelles and at all the felyship, and thanked them
35 of the grete laboure.

Ryght so as they sate at her dyner in the chyff halle, hit befylle that the Sangreall had fulfylled the table with all metis that ony harte mygh[t] thynke. And as they sate they saw all the doorys of the paleyse and wyndowes shutte withoute mannys honde. So were they all
40 abaysshed. So a knyght whych was all armed cam to the chyeff dore, and knocked and cryed,

'Undo!'

But they wolde nat, and ever he cryed,

'Undo!'

So hit noyed hem so much that the kynge hymselff arose and cam to
a wyndow there where the knyght called. Than he seyde,

'Sir knyght, ye shall nat enter at thys tyme, whyle the Sankgreall ys
hyre. And therefore go ye into anothir fortresse, for ye be none of the
knyghtes of the Quest, but one of them whych have servyd the fyende,   5
and haste leffte the servyse of oure Lorde.'

Than was he passynge wroth at the kynges wordis.

'Sir knyght,' seyde the kynge, 'syn ye wolde so fayne entir, telle me
of what contrey ye be.'

'Sir,' he seyde, 'I am of the realme of Logrys, and my name ys sir   10
Ector de Marys, brother unto my lorde sir Launcelot.'

'In the name of God,' seyde the kynge, 'me forthynkis ⟨sore⟩ [of
that I have] seyde, for youre brother ys hereinne.'

Whan sir Ector undirstood that hys brother was there, for he was
the man in the worlde that he moste drad and loved, than he seyde,   15

'A, good lorde, now dowblith my sorow and shame! Full truly
seyde the good man of the hylle unto sir Gawayne and to me of oure
dremys.'

Than wente he oute of the courte as faste as hys horse myght, and
so thorowoute the castell.   20

Than kyng Pelles cam to sir Launcelot and tolde hym tydynges of   (17)
hys brothir. Anone he was sory therefore that he wyst nat what to do.
So sir Launcelot departed and toke hys armys and seyde he wold go se
the realme of Logris whych ⟨he⟩ had nat sene afore in a yere, and
therewith commaunded the kynge to God.   25

And so rode thorow many realmys, and at the laste he com to a
whyght abbay, and there they made hym that nyght grete chere. And
on the morne he arose and hard masse, and afore an awter he founde a
ryche tombe which was newly made. And than he toke hede and saw
the sydys wryten with golde which seyde,   30

'Here lyeth kyng Bagdemagus of Gore, which kynge Arthurs nevew
slew,' and named hym sir Gawayne.

Than was nat he a litill sory, for sir Launcelot loved hym muche
more than ony other (and had hit bene ony other than sir Gawayne he
sholde nat ascape frome the dethe), and seyde to hymselff,   35

'A, lorde God! Thys ys a grete hurte unto kynge Arthurs courte,
the losse of suche a man!'

And than he departed and cam to the abbey where sir Galahad dud
the aventure of the tombis and wan the whyght shylde with the rede
crosse. And there had he grete chere all that nyght, and on the morne   40
he turned to Camelot where he founde kynge Arthure and the quene.

But many of the knyghtes of Rounde Table were slayne and destroyed, more than halff; and so three of them were com home, sir Ector,
Gawayne, and Lyonell, and many other that nedith nat now to

reherce. And all the courte were passyng glad of sir Launcelot, and the kynge asked hym many tydyngis of hys sonne sir Galahad.

And there sir Launcelot tolde the kynge of hys aventures that befelle hym syne he departed. And also he tolde hym of the aventures of sir 5 Galahad, sir Percivale, and sir Bors whych that he knew by the lettir of the ded mayden, and also as sir Galahad had tolde hym.

'Now God wolde,' seyde the kynge, 'that they were all three here!'

'That shall never be,' seyde sir Launcelot, 'for two of hem shall ye never se. But one of them shall com home agayne.'

10 Now levith thys tale and spekith of sir Galahad.

IX. THE MIRACLE OF GALAHAD

(18) Now seyth the tale that sir Galahad rode many journeys in vayne, and at the last he com to the abbay where kynge Mordrayns was. And whan he harde that, he thoughte he wolde abyde to se hym.

15 And so uppon the morne, whan he had herd masse, sir Galahad com unto kynge Mordrayns. And anone the kyng saw hym, whych had layne blynde of longe tyme, and than he dressed hym ayenste hym and seyde,

'Sir Galahad, the servaunte of Jesu Cryste and verry knyght, whos 20 commynge I have abyddyn longe, now enbrace me and lette me reste on thy breste, so that I may reste betwene thyne armys! For thou arte a clene virgyne above all knyghtes, as the floure of the lyly in whom virginité is signified. And thou arte the rose which ys the floure of all good vertu, and in colour of fyre. For the fyre of the Holy Goste ys 25 takyn so in the that my fleyssh, whych was all dede of oldenes, ys becom agayne yonge.'

Whan sir Galahad harde thes wordys, than he enbraced hym and all hys body. Than seyde he,

'Fayre Lorde Jesu Cryste, now I have my wylle! Now I requyre 30 The, in thys poynte that I am in, that Thou com and visite me.'

And anone oure Lorde herde his prayere, and therewith the soule departed frome the body. And than sir Galahad put hym in the erthe as a kynge oughte to be, and so departed, and cam into a perelous foreyste where he founde the welle which boyled with grete wawis, 35 as the tale tellith tofore.

And as sone as sir Galahad sette hys honde thereto hit seased, so that hit brente no more, and anone the hete departed away. And cause why that hit brente, hit was a sygne of lechory that was that tyme muche used. But that hete myght nat abyde hys pure virginité. And so thys was takyn in the contrey for a miracle, and so ever afftir was hit called Galahaddis Welle.

So by aventure he com unto the contrey of Gore, and into the abbey where sir Launcelot had bene toforehonde and founde the tombe of kynge Bagdemagus. But he was fownder thereoff, for there was the ₅ tombe of Joseph of Aramathyys son and the tombe of Symyan, where sir Launcelot had fayled. Than he loked into a croufte undir the mynstir, and there he sawe a tombe which [brente] full mervaylously.

Than asked he the brethirne what hit was.

'Sir', seyde they, 'a mervalous aventure that may nat be brought to ₁₀ an ende but by hym that passith of bounté and of knyghthode all them of the Rounde Table.'

'I wolde,' seyde sir Galahad, 'that ye wolde brynge me thereto.'

'Gladly,' seyde they, and so ledde hym tyll a cave. And so he wente downe uppon grecis and cam unto the tombe. And so the flamyng ₁₅ fayled, and the fyre staunched which many a day had bene grete.

Than cam there a voice whych seyde,

'Much ar ye beholde to thanke God which hath gyven you a good owre, that ye may draw oute the soulis of erthely payne and to putte them into the joyes of Paradyse. Sir, I am of youre kynred, which hath ₂₀ dwelled in thys hete thys three hondred wyntir and four-and-fifty to be purged of the synne that I ded ayenste Aramathy Joseph.'

Than sir Galahad toke the body in his armys and bare hit into the mynster. And that nyght lay sir Galahad in the abbay; and on the morne he gaff hym hys servyse and put hym in the erthe byfore ₂₅ the hyghe awter.

So departed he frome thens, and commended the brethirn to God. (19) And so he rode fyve dayes tylle that he cam to the Maymed Kynge.

And ever folowed sir Percivale the fyve dayes [askynge] where he had bene, and so one tolde hym how the aventures of Logrus were ₃₀ encheved. So on a day hit befelle that he cam oute of a grete foreyste, and there mette they at travers with sir Bors which rode alone. Hit ys no rede to aske if they were glad! And so he salewed them, and they yelded to hym honoure and good aventure, and everych tolde other how they had spedde. Than seyde sir Bors, ₃₅

'Hit ys more than a yere and a halff that I ne lay ten tymes where men dwelled, but in wylde forestis and in mownteaynes. But [God] was ever my comforte.'

Than rode they a grete whyle tylle they cam to the castell of Carbonek. And whan they were entirde within, kynge Pelles knew hem. ₄₀ So there was grete joy, for he wyste well by her commynge that they had fulfylled the [quest of the] Sankgreall. Than Elyazar, kynge Pelles sonne, brought tofore them the brokyn swerde wherewith Josephe was stryken thorow the thyghe. Than sir Bors sette his honde thereto

to say if he myght have sowded hit agayne, but hit wolde nat be. Than
he toke hit to sir Percivale, but he had no more power thereto than he.

'Now have ye hit agayne,' seyde sir Percivale unto sir Galahad, 'for
and hit be ever encheved by ony bodily man, ye muste do hit.'

5 And than he toke the pecis and set hem togydirs, and semed to them
as hit had never be brokyn, and as well as hit was firste forged. And
whan they within aspyed that the aventure of the swerde was encheved,
than they gaff the swerde to sir Bors, for hit myght no bettir be sette,
for he was so good a knyght and a worthy man.

10 And a litill before evyn the swerde arose, grete and merevaylous,
and was full of grete hete, that many men felle for drede. And anone
alyghte a voyce amonge them and seyde,

'They that ought nat to sitte at the table of oure Lorde Jesu Cryste,
avoyde hens! For now there shall verry knyghtes be fedde.'

15 So they wente thense, all sauf kyng Pelles and Elyazar, hys sonne,
which were holy men, and a mayde whych was hys nyce. And so
⟨there abode⟩ thes three knyght⟨es⟩ and thes three; elles were no mo.
And anone they saw knyghtes all armed that cam in at the halle dore,
and ded of their helmys and armys, and seyde unto sir Galahad,

20 ['Sir,] we have hyghed ryght muche for to be with you at thys table
where the holy mete shall be departed.'

Than seyde he, 'Ye be wellcom! But of whens be ye?'

So three of them seyde they were of Gaule, and other three seyde
they were of Irelonde, and other three seyde they were of Danemarke.

25 And so as they sate thus, there cam oute a bedde of tre of a chambir,
which four jantillwomen broughte; and in the bedde lay a good man
syke, and had a crowne of golde uppon his hede. And there, in the
myddis of the paleyse, they sette hym downe and wente agayne. Than
he lyffte up hys hede and seyde,

30 'Sir Galahad, good knyght, ye be ryght wellcom, for much have y
desyred your commyng! For in such payne and in such angwysh as I
have ⟨no man ellis myght have⟩ suffird longe. But now I truste to God
the terme ys com that my payne shall be alayed, and ⌐so I shall⌐ sone
passe oute of thys worlde, so as hit was promysed me longe ago.'

35 And therewith a voice seyde, 'There be two amonge you that be
nat in the queste of the Sankgreall, and therefore departith!'

(20) Than kynge Pelles and hys sunne departed. And therewithall besemed
them that there cam an olde man and four angelis frome hevyn, clothed
in lyknesse of a byshop, and had a crosse in hys honde. And thes four

40 angels bare hym up in a chayre and sette hym downe before the table of
sylver whereuppon the Sankgreall was. And hit semed that he had in
myddis of hys forehede lettirs which seyde, 'Se you here Joseph, the
firste bysshop of Crystendom, the same which oure Lorde succoured
in the cité of Sarras in the spirituall palleys'. Than the knyghtes

mervayled, for that bysshop was dede more than three hondred yere
tofore.

'A, knyghtes,' seyde he, 'mervayle nat, for I was somtyme an erthely
man.'

So with that they harde the chambir dore opyn, and there they saw 5
angels; and two bare candils of wexe, and the thirde bare a towell, and
the fourth a speare which bled mervaylously, that the droppis felle
within a boxe which he hylde with hys othir hande. And anone they
sette the candyls uppon the table, and the thirde the towell uppon
the vessell, and the fourth the holy speare evyn upryght uppon the 10
vessell.

And than the bysshop made sembelaunte as thoughe he wolde have
gone to the sakeryng of a masse, and than he toke an obley which was
made in lyknesse of brede. And at the lyftyng up there cam a vigoure in
lyknesse of a chylde, and the vysayge was as rede and as bryght os ony 15
fyre, and smote hymselff into the brede, that all they saw hit that the
brede was fourmed of a fleyshely man. And than he put hit into the
holy vessell agayne, and than he ded tha[t] longed to a preste to do
masse.

And than he wente to sir Galahad and kyssed hym, and bade hym go 20
and kysse hys felowis. And so he ded anone.

'Now,' seyde he, 'the servauntes of Jesu Cryste, ye shull be fedde
afore thys table with swete metis that never knyghtes yet tasted.'

And whan he had seyde he vanysshed away. And they sette hem at
the table in grete drede and made their prayers. Than loked they and 25
saw a man com oute of the holy vessell that had all the sygnes of the
Passion of Jesu Cryste bledynge all opynly, and seyde,

'My knyghtes and my servauntes and my trew chyldren which bene
com oute of dedly lyff into the spirituall lyff, I woll no lenger cover me
frome you, but ye shall se now a parte of my secretes and of my hydde 30
thynges. Now holdith and resseyvith the hyghe order and mete whych
ye have so much desired.'

Than toke He hymselff the holy vessell and cam to sir Galahad. And
he kneled adowne and resseyved hys Saveoure. And aftir hym so
ressayved all hys felowis, and they thought hit so sweete that hit was 35
mervaylous to telle. Than seyde He to sir Galahad,

'Sonne, wotyst thou what I holde betwyxte my hondis?'

'Nay,' seyde he, 'but if ye telle me.'

'Thys ys,' seyde He, 'the holy dysshe wherein I ete the lambe on
Estir Day, and now hast thou sene that thou moste desired to se. But 40
yet hast thou nat sene hit so opynly as thou shalt se hit in the cité of
Sarras, in the spirituall paleyse. Therefore thou must go hense and
beare with the thys holy vessell, for this nyght hit shall departe frome
the realme of Logrus, and hit shall nevermore be sene here. And

knowyst thou wherefore? For he ys nat served nother worshipped to hys ryght by hem of thys londe, for they be turned to evyll lyvyng, and therefore I shall disherite them of the honoure whych I have done them. And therefore go ye three ⌐to-morne⌐ unto the see, where ye shall
5 fynde youre shippe redy, and with you take the swerde with the stronge gurdils, and no mo with you but sir Percivale and sir Bors. Also I woll that ye take with you off thys bloode of thys speare for to anoynte the Maymed Kynge, both his legges and hys body, and he shall have hys heale.'

10 'Sir,' seyde Galahad, 'why shall nat thys other felowis go with us?'
'For thys cause: for ryght as I departe my postels one here and anothir there, so I woll that ye departe. And two of you shall dy in my servyse, and one of you shall com agayne and telle tydynges.'
Than gaff He hem Hys blyssynge and vanysshed away.
(21) 15 And sir Galahad wente anone to the speare which lay uppon the table and towched the bloode with hys fyngirs, and cam aftir to the maymed knyght and anoynted his legges and hys body. And therewith he clothed hym anone, and sterte uppon hys feete oute of hys bedde as an hole man, and thanked God that He had heled hym. And anone he
20 leffte the worlde and yelded hymselffe to a place of religion of whyght monkes, and was a full holy man.
And that same nyght, aboute mydnyght, cam a voyce amonge them which seyde,
'My sunnes, and nat my chyeff sunnes, my frendis, and nat my
25 ⌐werryours⌐, go ye hens where ye hope beste to do, and as I bade you do.'
'A, thanked be Thou, Lorde, that Thou wolt whyghtsauff to calle us Thy sunnes! Now may [we] well preve that we have nat ⌐lost⌐ oure paynes.'
30 And anone in all haste they toke their harneyse and departed; but the three k⌐nyght⌐es of Gaule (one of hem hyght Claudyne, kynge Claudas sonne, and the other two were grete jantillmen) than prayde sir Galahad to every[che] of them, that and they com to kynge Arthurs courte, 'to salew my lorde sir Launcelot, my fadir, and hem all of the
35 Rounde Table', [and prayde hem, and] they com on that party, nat to forgete hit.
Ryght so departed sir Galahad, and sir Percivale and sir Bors with hym, and so they rode three dayes. And than they com to a ryvage and founde the shippe whereof the tale spekith of tofore. And whan they
40 com to the bourde they founde in the myddys of ⟨the bedde⟩ the table of sylver, whych they had lefft with the Maymed Kynge, and the Sankgreall whych was coverde with rede samyte. Than were they glad to have such thyngis in their felyship. And so they entred and made grete reverence thereto, and sir Galahad felle on hys kneys and prayde

longe tyme to oure Lorde, that at what tyme that he asked, he myght passe oute of this worlde. And so longe he prayde tyll a voice seyde,

'Sir Galahad, thou shalt have thy requeste, and whan thou askyst the deth of thy body thou shalt have hit, and than shalt thou have the 5 lyff of thy soule.'

Than sir Percivale harde hym a litill, and prayde hym of felyship that was betwene them [to telle hym] wherefore he asked such thynges.

'Sir, that shall I telle you,' seyde sir Galahad. 'Thys othir day, whan we sawe a parte of the adventures of the Sangreall, I was in such joy of 10 herte that I trow never man was [that was] erthely. And therefore I wote well, whan my body ys dede, my soule shall be in grete joy to se the Blyssed Trinité every day and the majesté of oure Lorde Jesu Cryste.'

And so longe were they in the shippe that they seyde to sir Galahad, 15 'Sir, in thys bedde ye oughte to lyghe, for so seyth the lettirs.'

And so he layde hym downe, and slepte a grete whyle. And whan he awaked he loked tofore hym and saw the cité of Sarras. And as they wolde have londed they saw the shyp wherein sir Percivall had putte hys syster in. 20

'Truly,' seyde sir Percivall, 'in the name of God, well hath my syster holden us covenaunte.'

Than toke they oute of the shyppe the table of sylver; and he toke hit to sir Percivale and to sir Bors to go tofore, and sir Galahad com behynde, and ryght so they wente into the cité. And at the gate of the 25 cité they saw an olde man croked, and anone sir Galahad called hym and bade hym 'helpe to bere thys hevy thynge'.

'Truly,' seyde the olde man, 'hit ys ten yere ago that I myght nat go but with crucchis.'

'Care thou nat,' seyde sir Galahad, 'aryse up and shew thy good wyll!' 30 And so he assayde, and founde hymselff as hole as ever he was. Than ran he to the table and toke one parte ayenst sir Galahad.

Anone rose there a grete noyse in the cité that a crypple was made hole by knyghtes merveylous that entird into the cité. Than anone aftir the three knyghtes wente to the watir and brought up into the 35 paleyse sir Percivallis syster, and buryed her as rychely as them oughte a kynges doughter.

And whan the kynge of that contrey knew that and saw that felyship (whos name was Estorause), he asked them of whens they were, and what thynge hit was that they had brought uppon the table of sylver. 40 And they told hym the trouth of the Sankgreall, and the power whych God hath sette there.

Than thys kynge was a grete tirraunte, and was com of the lyne of paynymes, and toke hem and put hem in preson in a depe hole. But as (22)

sone as they were there our Lord sente them the Sankgreall, thorow whos grace they were allwey fullfylled whyle they were in preson.

So at the yerys ende hit befelle that thys kynge lay syke and felte that he sholde dye. Than he sente for the three knyghtes, and they cam
5 afore hym, and he cryed hem mercy of that he had done to them; and they forgave hym goodly, and he dyed anone.

Whan the kynge was dede all the cité stoode dyssemayde and wyst nat who myght be her kynge. Ryght so as they were in counceyle, there com a voice downe amonge them and bade hem chose the yongyst
10 knyght of three to be her kynge, 'for he shall well maynteyne you and all youris'.

So they made sir Galahad kynge by all the assente of the hole cité, and ellys they wolde have slayne hym. And whan he was com to ⌜beholde⌝ hys ⌜londe⌝ he lete make abovyn the table of sylver a cheste of
15 golde and of precious stonys that coverde the holy vessell, and every day erly thes three knyghtes wolde com before hit and make their prayers.

Now at the yerys ende, and the selff Sonday aftir that sir Galahad had borne the crowne of golde, he arose up erly and hys felowis, and cam
20 to the paleyse, and saw tofore hem the holy vessell, and a man knelyng on his kneys in lykenesse of a bysshop that had aboute hym a grete feliship of angels, as hit had bene Jesu Cryste hymselff. And than he arose and began a masse of oure Lady. And so he cam to the sakerynge, and anone made an ende. He called sir Galahad unto hym and seyde,
25 'Com forthe, the servaunte of Jesu Cryste, and thou shalt se that thou hast much desired to se.'

And than he began to tremble ryght harde whan the dedly fleysh began to beholde the spirituall thynges. Than he hylde up his hondis towarde hevyn and seyde,
30 'Lorde, I thanke The, for now I se that that hath be my desire many a day. Now, my Blyssed Lorde, I wold nat lyve in this wrecched worlde no lenger, if hit myght please The, Lorde.'

And therewith the good man toke oure Lordes Body betwyxte hys hondis and profird hit to sir Galahad, and he resseyved hit ryght
35 gladly and mekely.

'No[w] wotist thou what I am?' seyde the good man.

'Nay, sir,' seyde sir Galahad.

'I am Joseph, the sonne of Joseph of Aramathy, which oure Lorde hath sente to the to bere the felyship. And wotyst thou wherefore He
40 hathe sente me more than ony other? For thou hast resembled ⟨me⟩ in to thynges: that thou hast sene, that ys the mervayles of the Sankgreall, ⟨and⟩ for thou hast bene a clene mayde as I have be and am.'

And whan he had seyde thes wordis ⌜sir Galahad⌝ wente to sir Percivale and kyssed hym and commended hym to God. And so he wente to sir Bors and kyssed hym and commended hym to God and seyde,

'My fayre lorde, salew me unto my lorde sir Launcelot, my fadir, and as sone as ye se hym bydde hym remembir of this worlde unstable.'

And therewith he kneled downe tofore the table and made hys 5 prayers. And so suddeynly departed hys soule to Jesu Cryste, and a grete multitude of angels bare hit up to hevyn evyn in the syght of hys two felowis.

Also thes two knyghtes saw cam frome hevyn an hande, but they sy nat the body, and so hit cam ryght to the vessell and toke hit, and the 10 speare, and so bare hit up into hevyn. And sythen was there never man so hardy to sey that he hade sey⌈ne⌉ the Sankgreal.

So whan sir Percivale and sir Bors saw sir Galahad dede they made (23) as much sorow as ever ded men. And if they had nat bene good men they myght lyghtly have falle in dispayre. And so people of the contrey 15 and cité, they were ryght hevy. But so he was buryed, and as sone as he was buryed sir Percivale yelded hym to an ermytayge oute of the cité, and toke religious clothyng. And sir Bors was allwey with hym, but he chonged never hys seculer clothyng, for that he purposed hym to go agayne into the realme of Logrus. 20

Thus a yere and two monethis lyved sir Percivale in the ermytayge a full holy lyff, and than passed oute of the worlde. Than sir Bors lat bury hym by hys syster and by sir Galahad in the spiritualités.

So whan sir Bors saw that he was in so farre contreyes as in the partis of Babilonye, he departed frome the cité of Sarras and armed hym and 25 cam to the see, and entird into a shippe. And so hit befelle hym, by good adventure, he cam unto the realme of Logrus, and so he rode a pace tylle he com to Camelot where the kynge was.

And than was there made grete joy of hym in all the courte, for they wente he had bene loste forasmuch as he had bene so longe oute 30 of the contrey. And whan they had etyn the kynge made grete clerkes to com before hym, for cause they shulde cronycle of the hyghe adventures of the good knyghtes. So whan sir Bors had tolde hym of the hyghe aventures of the Sankgreall such as had befalle hym and his three felowes, which were sir Launcelot, Percivale and sir Galahad and 35 hymselff, than sir Launcelot tolde the adventures of the Sangreall that he had sene. And all thys was made in grete bookes and put up in almeryes at Salysbury.

And anone sir Bors seyde to sir Launcelot,

'Sir Galahad, youre owne sonne, salewed you by me, and aftir you 40 my lorde kynge Arthure and all the hole courte, and so ded sir Percivale. For I buryed them both myne owne hondis in the cité of Sarras. Also, sir Launcelot, sir Galahad prayde you to remembir of thys unsyker worlde, as ye behyght hym whan ye were togydirs more than halffe a yere.'

'Thys ys trew,' seyde sir Launcelot, 'now I truste to God hys prayer shall avayle me.'

Than sir Launcelot toke sir Bors in hys armys and seyde,

'Cousyn, ye ar ryght wellcom to me! For [all that ever I may do for
5 you and for yours, ye shall fynde my poure body redy atte all tymes whyle the spyryte is in hit, and that I promyse you feythfully, and never to fayle. And wete ye well, gentyl cousyn sir Bors,] ye and I shall never departe in sundir whylis oure lyvys may laste.'

'Sir,' seyde he, 'as ye woll, so woll I.'

10   THUS ENDITH THE TALE OF THE SANKGREAL THAT WAS BREFFLY DRAWY[N] OUTE OF FREYNSHE—WHICH YS A TALE CRONYCLED FOR ONE OF THE TREWYST AND OF THE HOLYEST THAT YS IN THYS WORLDE— BY SIR THOMAS MALEORRÉ, KNYGHT.

O BLESSED JESU HELPE HYM THOROW HYS MYGHT! AMEN.

THE BOOK
OF SIR LAUNCELOT
AND
QUEEN GUINEVERE

I. THE POISONED APPLE

So aftir the quest of the Sankgreall was fulfylled and all knyghtes that were leffte on lyve were com home agayne unto the Table Rownde— as the BOOKE OF THE SANKGREALL makith mencion—than was there grete joy in the courte, and enespeciall kynge Arthure and quene 5 Gwenyvere made grete joy of the remenaunte that were com home. And passyng gladde was the kynge and the quene of sir Launcelot and of sir Bors, for they had bene passynge longe away in the queste of the Sankgreall.

Than, as the booke seyth, sir Launcelot began to resorte unto quene 10 Gwenivere agayne and forgate the promyse and the perfeccion that he made in the queste; for, as the booke seyth, had nat sir Launcelot bene in his prevy thoughtes and in hys myndis so sette inwardly to the quene as he was in semynge outewarde to God, there had no knyght passed hym in the queste of the Sankgreall. But ever his thoughtis prevyly 15 were on the quene, and so they loved togydirs more hotter than they dud toforehonde, and had many such prevy draughtis togydir that many in the courte spake of hit, and in especiall sir Aggravayne, sir Gawaynes brothir, for he was ever opynne-mowthed.

So hit befelle that sir Launcelot had many resortis of ladyes and 20 damesels which dayly resorted unto hym, [that besoughte hym] to be their champion. In all such maters of ryght sir Launcelot applyed hym dayly to do for the plesure of oure Lorde Jesu Cryst, and ever as much us he myght he withdrew hym fro the company of quene Gwenyvere for to eschew the sclawndir and noyse. Wherefore the quene waxed 25 wrothe with sir Launcelot.

So on a day she called hym to hir chambir and seyd thus:

'Sir Launcelot, I se and fele dayly that youre love begynnyth to slake, for ye have no joy to be in my presence, but ever ye ar oute of thys courte, and quarels and maters ye have nowadayes for ladyes, maydyns 30 and jantillwomen, [more] than ever ye were wonte to have beforehande.'

'A, madame,' seyde sir Launcelot, 'in thys ye must holde me excused for dyvers causis: one ys, I was but late in the quest of the Sankgreall, and I thanke God of Hys grete mercy, and never of my deservynge, that I saw in that my queste as much as ever saw ony synfull man 35 lyvynge, and so was hit tolde me. And if that I had nat had my prevy thoughtis to returne to you[r]e love agayne as I do, I had sene as grete mysteryes as ever saw my sonne sir Galahad, Percivale, other sir Bors. And therefore, madam, I was but late in that queste, and wyte you well, madam, hit may nat be yet lyghtly forgotyn, the hyghe servyse 40 in whom I dud my dyligente laboure.

'Also, madame, wyte you well that there be many men spekith of oure love in thys courte and have you and me gretely in awayte, as thes sir Aggravayne and sir Mordred. And, madam, wyte you well I drede them more for youre sake than for ony feare I have of them
5 myselffe, for I may happyn to ascape and ryde myselff in a grete nede where, madame, ye muste abyde all that woll be seyde unto you. And than, if that ye falle in ony distresse thorowoute wyllfull foly, than ys there none other helpe but by me and my bloode.

'And wyte you well, madam, the boldenesse of you and me woll
10 brynge us to shame and sclaundir, and that were me lothe to se you dishonoured. And that is the cause I take uppon me more for to do for damesels and maydyns than ever y ded toforne, that men sholde undirstonde my joy and my delite ys my plesure to have ado for damesels and maydyns.'

(2) 15 All thys whyle the quene stoode stylle and lete sir Launcelot sey what he wolde; and whan he had all seyde she braste oute of wepynge, and so she sobbed and awepte a grete whyle. And whan she myght speke she seyde,

'Sir Launcelot, now I well understonde that thou arte a false, recrayed
20 knyght and a comon lechourere, and lovyste and holdiste othir ladyes, and of me thou haste dysdayne and scorne. For wyte thou well, now I undirstonde thy falsehede I shall never love the more, and loke thou be never so hardy to com in my syght. And ryght here I dyscharge the thys courte, that thou never com within hit, and I forfende the my
25 felyship, and uppon payne of thy hede that thou se me nevermore!'

Ryght so sir Launcelot departed with grete hevynes, that unneth he myght susteyne hymselff for grete dole-makynge.

Than he called sir Bors, Ector de Maris and sir Lyonell, and tolde hem how the quene had forfende hym the courte, and so he was in
30 wyll to departe into hys owne contrey.

'Fayre sir,' seyde Bors de Ganys, 'ye shall departe oute of thys londe by myne advyce, for ye muste remembir you what ye ar, and renomed the moste nobelyst knyght of the worlde, and many grete maters ye have in honde. And women in their hastynesse woll do oftyntymes that
35 aftir hem sore repentith. And therefore, be myne advyce, ye shall take youre horse and ryde to the good ermytayge here besyde Wyndesore, that somtyme was a good knyght, hys name ys sir Brastias. And there shall ye abyde tyll that I sende you worde of bettir tydynges.'

'Brother,' seyde sir Launcelot, 'wyte you well I am full loth to de-
40 parte oute of thys reallme, but the que[ne] hath defended me so hyghly that mesemyth she woll never be my good lady as she hath bene.'

'Sey ye never so,' seyde sir Bors, 'for many tymys or this she hath bene wroth with you, and aftir that she was the first [that] repented hit.'

'Ye sey well,' seyde sir Launcelot, 'for now woll I do by your counceyle and take myne horse and myne harneyse and ryde to the ermyte
sir Brastias, and there woll I repose me tille I hyre som maner of
tydynges frome you. But, fayre brother, in that ye can, gete me the love
of my lady quene Gwenyvere.'   5

'Sir,' seyde sir Bors, 'ye nede nat to meve me of such maters, for
well ye wote, I woll do what I may to please you.'

And than sir Launcelot departed suddeynly, and no creature wyst
where he was becom but sir Bors. So whan sir Launcelot was departed
the quene outewarde made no maner of sorow in shewyng to none of   10
his bloode nor to none other, but wyte ye well, inwardely, as the
booke seythe, she toke grete thought; but she bare hit oute with a
proude countenaunce, as thoughe she felte no thought nother daungere.

So the quene lete make a pryvy dᵣynᵉere in London unto the knyghtes   (3)
of the Rownde Table, and all was for to shew outwarde that she had   15
as grete joy in all other knyghtes of the Rounde Table as she had in sir
Launcelot. So there was all only at that dyner sir Gawayne and his
b[r]ethern, that ys for to sey, sir Aggravayne, sir Gaherys, sir Gareth
and sir Mordred. Also there was sir Bors de Ganis, sir Blamour de
Ganys, sir Bleobris de Ganys, sir Galihud, sir Eliodyn, sir Ector de   20
Maris, sir Lyonell, sir Palamydes, sir Safyr, his brothir, sir La Cote
Male Tayle, sir Persaunte, sir Ironsyde, sir Braundeles, sir Kay le
Senysciall, sir Madore de la Porte, sir Patrise, a knyght of Irelonde, sir
Alyduke, sir Ascamoure and sir Pynell le Saveayge, whych was
cosyne to sir Lameroke de Galis, the good knyght that sir Gawayne   25
and hys brethirn slew by treson.

And so thes four-and-twenty knyghtes sholde dyne with the quene
in a prevy place by themselff, and there was made a grete feste of all
maner of deyntees. But sir Gawayne had a custom that he used dayly
at mete and at supper: that he loved well all maner of fruyte, and in   30
especiall appyls and pearys. And therefore whosomever dyned other
fested sir Gawayne wolde comonly purvey for good fruyte for hym.
And so ded the quene; for to please sir Gawayne she lette purvey for
hym all maner of fruyte.

For sir Gawayne was a passyng hote knyght of nature, and thys sir   35
Pyonell hated sir Gawayne bycause of hys kynnesman sir Lamorakes
dethe; and therefore, for pure envy and hate, sir Pyonell enpoysonde
sertayn appylls for to enpoysen sir Gawayne.

So thys was well yet unto the ende of mete, and so hit befylle by
myssefortune a good knyght, sir Patryse, which was cosyn unto sir   40
Mador de la Porte, toke an appyll, for ⟨he⟩ was enchaffed with hete of
wyne. And hit myssehapped hym to take a poysonde apple. And whan
he had etyn hit he swall sore tylle h[e] braste, and there sir Patryse
felle downe suddeynly dede amonge hem.

Than every knyght lepe frome the bourde ashamed and araged for wratthe oute of hir wittis, for they wyst nat what to sey; considerynge quene Guenyvere made the feste and dyner they had all suspeccion unto hir.

5 'My lady the quene!' seyde sir Gawayne. 'Madam, wyte you that thys dyner was made for me and my felowis, for all folkes that knowith my condicion undirstonde that I love well fruyte. And now I se well I had nere be slayne. Therefore, madam, I drede me leste ye woll be shamed.'

10 Than the quene stood stylle and was so sore abaysshed that she wyst nat what to sey.

'Thys shall nat so be ended,' seyde sir Mador de la Porte, 'for here have I loste a full noble knyght of my bloode, and therefore uppon thys shame and dispite I woll be revenged to the utteraunce!'

15 And there opynly sir Mador appeled the quene of the deth of hys cousyn sir Patryse.

Than stood they all stylle, that none wolde speke a worde ayenste hym, for they all had grete suspeccion unto the quene bycause she lete make that dyner. And the quene was so abaysshed that she cowde none 20 otherwayes do but wepte so hartely that she felle on a swowghe. So with thys noyse and crye cam to them kynge Arthure, and whan he (4) wyste of the trowble he was a passyng hevy man. And ever sir Madore stood stylle before the kynge and appeled the quene of treson. (For the custom was such at that tyme that all maner of [s]hamefull deth was 25 called treson.)

'Fayre lordys,' seyd kynge Arthure, 'me repentith of thys trouble, but the case ys so I may nat have ado in thys mater, for I muste be a ryghtfull juge. And that repentith me that I may nat do batayle for my wyff, for, as I deme, thys dede com never by her. And therefor I sup- 30 pose she shall nat be all distayned, but that somme good knyght shall put hys body in jouperté for my quene rather than she sholde be brente in a wronge quarell. And therefore, sir Madore, be nat so hasty; for, perdé, hit may happyn she shall nat be all frendeles. And therefore desyre thou thy day of batayle, and she shall purvey hir of som good 35 knyght that shall answere you, other ellis hit were to me grete shame and to all my courte.'

'My gracious lorde,' seyde sir Madore, 'ye muste holde me excused, for thoughe ye be oure kynge, in that degré ye ar but a knyght as we ar, and ye ar sworne unto knyghthode als welle as we be. And therefore 40 I beseche you that ye be nat displeased, for there ys none of all thes four-and-twenty knyghtes that were bodyn to thys dyner but all they have grete suspeccion unto the quene. What sey ye all, my lordys?' seyde sir Madore.

Than they answerde by and by and seyde they coude nat excuse the quene for why she made the dyner, and other hit muste com by her other by her servauntis.

'Alas,' seyde the quene, 'I made thys dyner for a good entente and never for none evyll, so Allmyghty Jesu helpe me in my ryght, as I was never purposed to do such evyll dedes, and that I reporte me unto 5 God.'

'My lorde the kynge,' seyde sir Madore, 'I requyre you, as ye beth a ryghteuous kynge, gyffe me my day that I may have justyse.'

'Well,' seyde the kynge, 'thys day fiftene dayes, loke thou be redy armed on horsebak in the medow besydes Wynchestir. And if hit so 10 falle that there be ony knyght to encountir ayenste you, there may you do youre beste, and God spede the ryght. And if so befalle that there be no knyght redy at that day, than muste my quene be brente, and there she shall be redy to have hir jugemente.'

'I am answerde,' seyde sir Mador.   15

And every knyght yode where hym lyked. So whan the kynge and the quene were togidirs the kyng asked the quene how this case befelle. Than the [quene] seyde, 'Sir, as Jesu be my helpe!' She wyst nat how, nother in what manere.

'Where ys sir Launcelot?' seyde kynge Arthure. 'And he were here 20 he wolde nat grucche to do batayle for you.'

'Sir,' seyde the quene, 'I wote nat where he ys, but hys brother and hys kynessmen deme that he be nat within thys realme.'

'That me repentith,' seyde kyng Arthure, 'for and he were here, he wolde sone stynte thys stryffe. Well, than I woll counceyle you,' seyde 25 the kyng, 'that ye go unto sir Bors and pray hym for to [do] batayle for you for sir Launcelottis sake, and uppon my lyff he woll nat refuse you. For well I se,' seyde the kynge, 'that none of the four-and-twenty knyghtes, that were at your dyner where sir Patryse was slayne, that woll do batayle for you, nother none of hem woll sey well of you, and 30 that shall be grete sclaundir to you in thys courte.'

'[Allas,' seyde the quene, 'and I may not do withalle,] but now I mysse sir Launcelot, for and he were here he wolde sone putte me in my hartis ease.'

'What aylith you,' seyde the kynge, 'that ye can nat kepe sir Launcelot 35 uppon youre syde? For wyte you well,' seyde the kynge, 'who that hath sir Launcelot uppon his party hath the moste man of worship in thys worlde uppon hys syde. Now go youre way,' seyde the kynge unto the quene, 'and requyre sir Bors to do batayle for you for sir Launcelottis sake.'

                                                                          40

So the quene departed frome the kynge and sente for sir Bors into (5) the chambir. And whan he cam she besought hym of succour.

'Madam,' seyde he, 'what wolde ye that I ded? For I may nat with my worship have ado in thys mater, because I was at the same dyner,

for drede of ony of tho knyghtes wolde have you in suspeccion. Also, madam,' seyde sir Bors, 'now mysse ye sir Launcelot, for he wolde nat a fayled you in youre ryght nother in youre wronge, for whan ye have bene in ryght grete daungers he hath succoured you. And now ye
5 have drevyn hym oute of thys contrey by whom ye and all we were dayly worshipped by. Therefore, madame, I mervayle how ye dare for shame to requyre me to do onythynge for you, insomuche ye have enchaced oute of your courte by whom we were up borne and honoured.'

'Alas, fayre knyght,' seyde the quene, 'I put me holé in youre grace,
10 and all that ys amysse I woll amende as ye woll counceyle me.' And therewith she kneled downe uppon both hir kneys and besought sir Bors to have mercy uppon her, 'other ellis [I] shall have a shamefull dethe, and thereto I never offended.'

Ryght so cam kynge Arthure and founde the quene knelynge. And
15 than sir Bors toke hir up and seyde,

'Madam, ye do me grete dishonoure.'

'A, jantill knyght,' seyde the kynge, 'have mercy uppon my quene, curteyse knyght, for I am now in sertayne she ys untruly defamed. And therefore, curteyse knyght,' the kynge seyde, 'promyse her to do
20 batayle for her, I requyre you, for the love ye owghe unto sir [Launcelot.'

'My lord,' seyde sir] Bors, 'ye requyre me the grettist thynge that ony man may requyre me. And wyte you well, if I graunte to do batayle for the quene I shall wretth many of my felyship of the Table Rounde.
25 But as for that,' seyde sir Bors, 'I woll graunte for my lorde sir Launcelottis sake, and for youre sake: I woll at that day be the quenys champyon onles that there com by adventures a better knyght than I am to do batayle for her.'

'Woll ye promyse me this,' seyde the kynge, 'by youre fayth?'
30 'Yee, sir,' seyd sir Bors, 'of that I shall nat fayle you nother her but if there com a bettir knyght than I am: than shall he have the batayle.'

Than was the kynge and the quene passynge gladde, and so departed and thanked hym hertely.

Than sir Bors departed secretly uppon a day and rode unto sir
35 Launcelot thereas he was with sir Brastias, and tolde hym of all thys adventure.

'A, Jesu,' sir Launcelot seyde, 'thys ys com happely as I wolde have hit. And therefore I pray you make you redy to do batayle, but loke that ye tarry tylle ye se me com as longe as ye may. For I am sure sir
40 Madore ys an hote knyght whan he ys inchaffed, for the more ye suffyr hym the hastyer woll he be to batayle.'

'Sir,' seyde sir Bors, 'latte me deale with hym. Doute ye nat ye shall have all youre wylle.'

So departed sir Bors frome hym and cam to the courte agayne.

Than was hit noysed in all the courte that sir Bors sholde do batayle
for the quene, wherefore many knyghtes were displeased with hym that
he wolde take uppon hym to do batayle in the quenys quarell; for
there were but fewe knyghtes in all the courte but they demed the
quene was in the wronge and that she had done that treson. So sir Bors 5
answered thus to hys felowys of the Table Rounde:

'Wete you well, my fayre lordis, hit were shame to us all and we
suffird to se the moste noble quene of the worlde to be shamed opynly,
consyderyng her lorde and oure lorde ys the man of moste worship
crystynde, and he hath ever worshipped us all in all placis.'   10

Many answerd hym agayne: 'As for oure moste noble kynge
Arthure, we love hym and honoure hym as well as ye do, but as
for quene Gwenyvere, we love hir nat, because she ys a destroyer
of good knyghtes.' ·

'Fayre lordis,' seyde sir Bors, 'mesemyth ye sey nat as ye sholde sey, 15
for never yet in my dayes knew I never ne harde sey that ever she was
a destroyer of good knyghtes, but at all tymes, as far as ever I coude
know, she was a maynteyner of good knyghtes; and ever she hath
bene large and fre of hir goodis to all good knyghtes, and the moste
bownteuous lady of hir gyffti[s] and her good grace that ever I saw 20
other harde speke off. And therefore hit were shame to us all and to
oure moste [noble] kynges wyff whom we serve [and we suffred her]
to be shamefully slayne. And wete you well,' seyde sir Bors, 'I woll
nat suffir hit, for I dare sey so much, for the quene ys nat gylty of sir
Patryseys dethe: for she ought hym never none evyll wyll nother none 25
of the four-and-twenty knyghtes that were at that dyner, for I dare sey
for good love she bade us to dyner and nat for no male engyne. And
that, I doute nat, shall be preved hereafftir, for howsomever the game
goth, there was treson amonge us.'

Than som seyde to sir Bors, 'We may well belyve youre wordys.' 30
And so somme were well pleased and som were nat.

So the day com on faste untyll the evyn that the batayle sholde [be]. (6)
Than the quene sente for sir Bors and asked hym how he was disposed.

'Truly, madame,' seyde he, 'I am disposed in lykewyse as I promysed
you, that ys to sey I shall natt fayle you onles there by aventure com a 35
bettir knyght than I am to do batayle for you. Than, madam, I am of
you discharged of my promyse.'

'Woll ye,' seyde the que[ne], 'that I telle my lorde the kyng thus?'

'Doth as hit pleasith you, madam.'

Than the quene yode unto the kyng and tolde the answere of sir 40
Bors.

'Well, have ye no doute,' seyde the kynge, 'of sir Bors, for I calle
hym now that ys lyvynge one of the nobelyst knyghtes of the worlde,
and moste perfitist man.'

And thus hit paste on tylle the morne, and so the kynge and the quene and all maner of knyghtes that were there at that tyme drewe them unto the medow bysydys Wynchester where the batayle [shold be]. And so whan the kynge was com with the quene and many knyghtes of the Table Rounde, so the quene was than put in the conestablis awarde and a grete fyre made aboute an iron stake, that an sir Mador de la Porte had the bettir, she sholde there be brente; for such custom was used in tho dayes: for favoure, love, nother affinité there sholde be none other but ryghtuous jugemente, as well uppon a kynge as uppon a knyght, and as well uppon a quene as uppon another poure lady.

So thys meanewhyle cam in sir Mador de la Porte and toke hys [othe] before the kynge, how that the que[ne] ded thys treson untill hys cosyn sir Patryse, 'and unto myne othe I woll preve hit with my body, honde for hande, who that woll sey the contrary.'

Ryght so cam in sir Bors de Ganys and seyde that as for quene Gwenivere, 'she ys in the ryght, and that woll I make good that she ys nat culpable of thys treson that is put uppon her.'

'Than make the redy,' seyde sir Madore, 'and we shall preve whethir thou be in the ryght or I!'

'Sir Madore,' seyde sir Bors, 'wete you well, I know you for a good knyght. Natforthan I shall nat feare you so gretly but I truste to God I shall be able to withstonde youre malyce. But thus much have I promised my lorde Arthure and my lady the quene, that I shall do batayle for her in thys cause to the utteryste, onles that there com a bettir knyght than I am and discharge me.'

'Is that all?' seyde sir Madore. 'Othir com thou off and do batayle with me, other elles sey nay.'

'Take youre horse,' seyde sir Bors, 'and, as I suppose, I shall nat tarry long but ye shall be answerde.'

Than ayther departed to their tentis and made hem redy to horsebacke as they thought beste. And anone sir Madore cam into the fylde with hys shylde on hys shulder and hys speare in hys honde, and so rode aboute the place cryyng unto kyng Arthure,

'Byd youre champyon com forthe and he dare!'

Than was sir Bors ashamed, and toke hys horse and cam to the lystis ende. And than was he ware where cam frome a woode there fast by a knyght all armed uppon a whyght horse with a straunge shylde of straunge armys, and he cam dryvyng all that hys horse myght renne. And so he cam to sir Bors and seyd thus:

'Fayre knyght, I pray you be nat displesed, for here muste a bettir knyght than ye ar have thys batayle. Therefore I pray you withdraw you, for wyte you well I have had thys day a ryght grete journey and thys batayle ought to be myne. And so I promysed you whan I spake

with you laste, and with all my herte I thanke you of youre good
wylle.'

Than sir Bors rode unto kynge Arthure and tolde hym how there
was a knyght com that wolde have the batayle to fyght for the quene.

'What knyght ys he?' seyde the kyng.   5

'I wote nat,' seyde sir Bors, 'but suche covenaunte he made with me
to be here thys day. Now, my lorde,' seyde sir Bors, 'here I am discharged.'

Than the kynge called to that knyght and asked hym if he wolde   (7)
fyght for the quene.   10

Than he answerd and seyde, 'Sir, therefore com I hyddir. And therefore, sir kynge, tarry me no lenger, for anone as I have fynysshed thys
batayle I muste departe hens, for I have to do many batayles elswhere.
For wyte you well,' seyde that knyght, 'thys ys dishonoure to you and
to all knyghtes of the Rounde Table to se and know so noble a lady and   15
so curteyse as quene Gwenyvere ys, thus to be rebuked and shamed
amongyst you.'

Than they all mervayled what knyght that myght be that so toke
[the batayle] uppon hym, for there was nat one that knew hym but
if hit were sir Bors. Than seyde sir Madore de la Porte unto the   20
kynge,

'Now lat me wete with whom I shall have ado.'

And than they rode to the lystes ende, and there they cowched their
spearis and ran togydirs with all their myghtes. And anone sir Madors
speare brake all to pecis, but the othirs speare hylde and bare sir   25
Madors horse and all backwarde to the erthe a grete falle. But myghtyly
and delyverly he avoyded his horse from hym and put hys shylde before
hym and drew hys swerde and bade the othir knyght alyght and do
batayle with hym on foote.

Than that knyght descended downe frome hys horse and put hys   30
shylde before hym and drew hys swerde. And so they cam egirly unto
batayle, and aythir gaff othir many sadde strokes, trasyng and traversyng and foynyng togydir with their swerdis as hit were wylde boorys,
thus fyghtyng nyghe an owre; for thys sir Madore was a stronge knyght
and myghtyly preved in many strange batayles. But at the laste thys   35
knyght smote sir Madore grovelynge uppon the erthe, and the [knyghte]
stepte nere hym to have pulde sir Madore flatlynge uppon the grounde.
And therewith sir Madore arose, and in hys rysyng he smote that
knyght thorow the thyk of the thyghes, that the bloode braste oute
fyersly.   40

And whan he felte hymself so wounded and saw hys bloode, he lete
hym aryse uppon hys feete, and than he gaff hym such a buffette uppon
the helme that he felle to the erthe flatlyng. And therewith he strode to
hym to have pulled of hys helme of hys hede. And so sir Madore

prayde that knyght to save hys lyff. And so he yeldyd hym as overcom, and releaced the quene of hys quarell.

'I woll nat graunte the thy lyff,' seyde that knyght, 'only that thou frely reales the quene for ever, and that no mencion be made uppon sir
5 Patryseys tombe that ever quene Gwenyver consented to that treson.'

'All thys shall be done,' seyde sir Madore. 'I clerely discharge my quarell for ever.'

Than the knyghtes parters of the lystis toke up sir Madore and led hym tylle hys tente. And the othir knyght wente strayte to the stayre-
10 foote where sate kynge Arthure. And by that tyme was the quene com to the kyng and aythir kyssed othir hartely.

And whan the kynge saw that knyght he stowped downe to hym and thanked hym, and in lyke wyse ded the quene. And the kynge prayde hym to put of his helmet and to repose hym and to take a soppe of
15 wyne.

And than he putte of hys helmette to drynke, and than every knyght knew hym that hit was sir Launcelot. And anone as the kyng wyst that, he toke the quene in hys honde and yode unto sir Launcelot and seyde,

'Sir, grauntemercy of youre grete travayle that ye have had this day
20 for me and for my quyene.'

'My lorde,' seyde sir Launcelot, 'wytte you well y ought of ryght ever [to be] in youre quarell and in my ladyes the quenys quarell to do batayle, for ye ar the man that gaff me the hygh Order of Knyghthode, and that day my lady, youre quene, ded me worshyp. And ellis had I
25 bene shamed, for that same day that ye made me knyght, thorow my hastynes I loste my swerde, and my lady, youre quene, founde hit, and lapped hit in her trayne, and gave me my swerde whan I had nede thereto; and ells had I bene shamed amonge all knyghtes. And there-fore, my lorde Arthure, I promysed her at that day ever to be her
30 knyght in ryght othir in wronge.'

'Grauntemercy,' seyde the kynge, 'for this journey. And wete you well,' seyde the kynge, 'I shall acquyte youre goodnesse.'

And evermore the quene behylde sir Launcelot, and wepte so tendirly that she sanke allmoste to the grownde for sorow that he had done to
35 her so grete kyndenes where she shewed hym grete unkyndenesse. Than the knyghtes of hys bloode drew unto hym, and there aythir of them made grete joy of othir. And so cam all the knyghtes of the Table Rounde that were there at that tyme and wellcommed hym.

And than sir Madore was [had to] lechecraufftc, and sir Launcelot
40 was heled of hys play. And so there was made grete joy, and many merthys there was made in that courte.

(8)   And so hit befelle that the Damesell of the Lake that hyght Nynyve, whych wedded the good knyght sir Pelleas, and so she cam to the courte, for ever she ded grete goodnes unto kynge Arthure and to all

hys knyghtes thorow her sorsery and enchauntementes. And so whan
she herde how the quene was greved for the dethe of sir Patryse, than
she tolde hit opynly that she was never gylty, and there she disclosed
by whom hit was done, and namcd hym sir Pynel, and for what cause
he ded hit. There hit was opynly knowyn and disclosed, and so the   5
quene was [excused]. And thys knyght sir Pynell fledde unto hys contrey, and was opynly knowyn that he enpoysynde the appyls at that
feste to that entente to have destroyed sir Gawayne, bycause sir Gawayne
and hys brethirne destroyed sir Lamerok de Galys which sir Pynell
was cosyn unto.   10

Than was sir Patryse buryed in the chirche of Westemynster in a
towmbe, and thereuppon was wrytten: HERE LYETH SIR PATRYSE OF
IRELONDE, SLAYNE BY SIR PYNELL LE SAVEAIGE THAT ENPOYSYNDE
APPELIS TO HAVE SLAYNE SIR GAWAYNE, AND BY MYSSEFORTUNE SIR
PATRYSE ETE ONE OF THE APPLIS, AND THAN SUDDEYNLY HE BRASTE.   15
Also there was wrytyn uppon the tombe that quene Gwenyvere was
appeled of treson of the deth of sir Patryse by sir Madore de la Porte,
and there was made the mencion how sir Launcelot fought with hym
for quene Gwenyvere and overcom hym in playne batayle. All thys
was wretyn uppon the tombe of sir Patryse in excusyng of the quene. 20

And than sir Madore sewed dayly and longe to have the quenys
good grace, and so by the meanys of sir Launcelot he caused hym to
stonde in the quenys good grace, and all was forgyffyn.

II. THE FAIR MAID OF ASTOLAT

THUS hit passed untyll oure Lady day of the Assumpcion. Within a   25
fiftene dayes of that feste the kynge lete crye a grete justyse and a
turnement that sholde be at that day at Camelott, otherwyse called
Wynchester. And the kyng lete cry that he and the Kynge of Scottes
wolde juste ayenst all th[at] wolde [come].

And whan thys cry was made, thydir cam many good knyghtes, that   30
ys to sey the kynge of North Galis, and kynge Angwysh of Irelonde,
and the Kynge with the Hondred Knyghtes, and syr Galahalte the
Haute Prynce, and the kynge of Northumbirlonde, and many other
noble deukes and erlis of other dyverse contreyes.

So kynge Arthure made hym redy to departe to hys justis, and   35
wolde have had the quene with hym; but at that tyme she wolde nat,
she seyde, for she was syke and myght nat ryde.

'That me repentith,' seyde the kynge, 'for thys seven yere ye saw nat
such a noble felyship togydirs excepte the Whytsontyde whan sir
Galahad departed frome the courte.'
                                                                  40

'Truly,' seyde the quene, 'ye muste holde me excused. Y may nat be there.'

And many demed the quene wolde nat be there because of sir Launcelot, for he wolde nat ryde with the kynge; for he seyde he was nat
5 hole of the play of sir Madore. Wherefore the kynge was hevy and passynge wroth, and so he departed towarde Wynchestir with hys felyship.

And so by the way the kynge lodged at a towne that was called Astolot, that ys in Englysh Gylforde, and there the kynge lay in the
10 castell. So whan the kynge was departed the quene called sir Launcelot unto her and seyde thus:

'Sir, ye ar gretly to blame thus to holde you behynde my lorde. What woll youre enemyes and myne sey and deme? "Se how sir Launcelot holdith hym ever behynde the kynge, and so the quene doth
15 also, for that they wolde have their plesure togydirs." And thus woll they sey,' seyde the quene.

(9) 'Have ye no doute, madame,' seyde sir Launcelot. 'I alow youre witte. Hit ys of late com syn ye were woxen so wyse! And there[fore], madam, at thys tyme I woll be ruled by youre counceyle, and thys
20 nyght I woll take my reste, and to-morow betyme I woll take my way towarde Wynchestir. But wytte you well,' seyde sir Launcelot unto the quene, 'at that justys I woll be ayenste the kynge and ayenst all hys felyship.'

'Sir, ye may there do as ye lyste,' seyde the quene, 'but be my coun-
25 ceyle ye shall nat be ayenst youre kynge and your felyshyp, for there bene full many hardé knyghtes of youre bloode.'

'Madame,' seyde sir Launcelot, 'I shall take the adventure that God woll gyff me.'

And so uppon the morne erly he harde masse and dyned, and so he
30 toke hys leve of the quene and departed. And than he rode so muche unto the tyme he com to Astolott, and there hit happynd hym that in the evenyng-tyde he cam to an olde barownes place that hyght sir Barnarde of Astolot. And as sir Launcelot entird into hys lodgynge, kynge Arthure aspyed hym as he dud walke in a gardeyne besyde the
35 castell: he knew hym welle inow.

'Well, sirs,' seyde kynge Arthure unto hys knyghtes that were by hym besyde the castell, 'I have now aspyed one knyght,' he seyde, 'that woll play hys play at the justys, I undirtake.'

'Who ys that?' seyde the knyghtes.
40 'At thys tyme ye shall nate wyte for me!' seyde the kynge and smyled, and wente to hys lodgynge.

So whan sir Launcelot was in hys lodgyng and unarmed in hys chambir, the olde barown, sir Barnarde, com to hym and wellcomed hym in the beste maner. But he knew nat sir Launcelot.

'Fayre sir,' seyde sir Launcelot tylle hys oste, 'I wolde pray you to
lende me a shylde that were nat opynly knowyn, for myne ys well
knowyn.'

'Sir,' seyde hys oste, 'ye shall have youre desire, for mesemyth ye
bene one of the lyklyest knyghtes that ever y sawe, and therefore, sir, 5
I shall shew you freynship.' And seyde, 'Sir, wyte you well I have two
sunnes that were but late made knyghtes. And the eldist hyght sir
Tirry, and he was hurte that same day he was made knyght, and he
may nat ryde; and hys shylde ⌐ye shalle have⌐, for that ys nat knowyn,
I dare sey, but here [and] in no place [else].' And hys yonger sonne 10
hyght sir Lavayne. 'And if hit please you, he shall ryde with you unto
that justis, for he ys of hys ayge stronge and wyght. For much my
herte gyvith unto you, that ye sholde be a noble knyght. And therefore
I praye you to telle me youre name,' seyde sir Barnarde.

'As for that,' seyd sir Launcelot, 'ye muste holde me excused as at 15
thys tyme. And if God gyff me grace to spede well at the justis I shall
com agayne and telle you my name. But I pray you in ony wyse lete me
have your sonne, sir Lavayne, with me, and that I may have hys
brothers shylde.'

'Sir, all thys shall be done,' seyde sir Barnarde. 20

So thys olde barown had a doughtir that was called that tyme the
Fayre Maydyn off Astolot, and ever she behylde sir Launcelot wondirfully.

(And, as the booke sayth, she keste such a love unto sir Launcelot
that she cowde never withdraw hir loove, wherefore she dyed. And her 25
name was Elayne le Blanke.)

So thus as she cam to and fro, she was so hote in love that [she]
besought sir Launcelot to were uppon hym at the justis a tokyn of
hers.

'Damesell,' seyde sir Launcelot, 'and if I graunte you that, ye may 30
sey that I do more for youre love than ever y ded for lady or jantillwoman.'

Than he remembird hymselff that he wolde go to the justis disgysed,
and because he had never aforne borne no maner of tokyn of no
damesell, he bethought hym to bere a tokyn of hers, that none of hys 35
bloode thereby myght know hym. And than he seyde,

'Fayre maydyn, I woll graunte you to were a tokyn of youres uppon
myne helmet. And therefore what ys hit? Shewe ye hit me.'

'Sir,' she seyde, 'hit ys a rede sleve of myne, of scarlet, well embrow-
dred with grete perelles.' 40

And so she brought hit hym. So sir Launcelot resseyved hit and
seyde,

'Never dud I erste so much for no damesell.'

Than sir Launcelot betoke the fayre mayden hys shylde in kepynge, and prayde her to kepe hit untill tyme that he com agayne. And so that nyght he had myrry reste and grete chere, for thys damesell Elayne was ever aboute sir Launcelot all the whyle she myght be suffirde.

(10) So uppon a day, on the morne, kynge Arthure and all hys knyghtis
5 departed, for there the kyng had tarryed three dayes to abyde hys noble knyghtes. And so whan the kynge was rydden, sir Launcelot and sir Lavayne made them redy to ryde, and aythir of them had whyght shyldis, and the rede sleve sir Launcelot lete cary with hym.

And so they toke their leve at sir Barnarde, the olde barowne, and at
10 hys doughtir, the fayre mayden, and than they rode so longe tylle that they cam to Camelot, that tyme called Wynchester. And there was grete pres of kyngis, deukes, erlis, and barownes, and many noble knyghtes. But there sir Launcelot was lodged pryvaly by the meanys of sir Lavayne with a ryche burgeyse, that no man in that towne was ware
15 what they were. And so they reposed them there tyll oure Lady day of the Assumpcion that the grete justes sholde be.

So whan trumpettis blew unto the fylde and kynge Arthur was sette on hyght uppon a chafflet to beholde who ded beste (but, as the Freynshe booke seyth, the kynge wold nat suffir sir Gawayne to go
20 frome hym, for never had sir Gawayne the bettir and sir Launcelot were in the fylde, and many tymes was sir Gawayne rebuked so whan sir Launcelot was in the fylde in ony justis dysgysed), than som of the kyngis, as kynge Angwysh of Irelonde and the Kynge of Scottis, were that tyme turned to be uppon the syde of kynge Arthur. And than the
25 othir party was the kynge of North Galis, and the Kynge with the Hondred Knyghtis, and the kynge of Northhumbirlonde, and sir Galahalte the Halte Prynce. But thes three kyngis and thys duke was passynge wayke to holde ayenste Arthurs party, for with hym were the nobelyst knyghtes of the worlde.

30 So than they withdrew them, aythir party frome othir, and every man made hym redy in his beste maner to do what he myght. Than sir Launcelot made hym redy and put the rede slyeve uppon hys helmette and fastened hit faste. And so sir Launcelot and sir Lavayne departed oute of Wynchestir pryvayly and rode untyll a litill leved woode
35 behynde the party that hylde ayenste kynge Arthure party. And there they hylde hem stylle tylle the partyes smote togydirs. And than cam in the Kynge o[f] Scottis and the kynge of Irelonde on kynge Arthurs party, and ayenste them cam in the kynge of Northumbirlonde and the Kynge with the Hondred Knyghtes.

40 And there began a grete medlé, and there the kynge of Scottis smote downe the kynge of Northumbirlonde, and the Kynge with the Hondred Knyghtes smote downe kynge Angwysh of Irelonde. Than sir Palamydes, that was one Arthurs party, he encountird with sir Galahalte, and ayther of hem smote downe othir, and aythir party halpe

their lordys [on] horseback agayne. So there began a stronge assayle on bothe partyes.

And than com in sir Braundyles, sir Sagramoure le Desyrous, sir Dodynas le Saveayge, sir Kay la Senesciall, sir Gryffelet le Fyze de Dᶦieᶦu, sir Lucan de Butlere, sir Bedwere, sir Aggravayne, sir Ga- 5 herys, sir Mordred, sir Melyot de Logrys, sir Ozanna le Cure Hardy, sir Saphyr, sir Epynogrys, sir Gallerowne of Galeway. All thes fiftene knyghtes, that were knyghtes of the Rounde Table, so thes with mo other cam in togydir and bete abacke the kynge off Northumbirlonde and the kynge of North Walys.   10

Whan sir Launcelot saw thys, as he hoved in the lytyll leved wood, than he seyde unto sir Lavayne,

'Se yondir ys a company of good knyghtes, and they holde them togydirs as borys that were chaced with doggis.'

'That ys trouth,' seyde sir Lavayne.   15

'Now,' seyde sir Launcelot, 'and ye woll helpe a lityll, ye shall se the (11) yonder felyship that chacith now thes men on oure syde, that they shall go as faste backwarde as they wente forewarde.'

'Sir, spare ye nat for my parte,' seyde sir Lavayne, 'for I shall do what I may.'   20

Than sir Launcelot and sir Lavayne cam in at the thyckyst of the prees, and there sir Launcelot smote downe sir Brandeles, sir Sagramour, sir Dodynas, sir Kay, sir Gryfflet, and all thys he ded with one speare. And sir Lavayne smote downe sir Lucan de Butlere and sir Bedwere. And than sir Launcelot gate another grete speare, and there 25 he smote downe sir Aggravayne and sir Gaherys, sir Mordred, sir Melyot de Logrys; and sir Lavayne smote downe sir Ozanna le Cure Hardy. And than sir Launcelot drew hys swerde, and there he smote on the ryght honde and on the lyf[t] honde, and by grete forse he unhorsed sir Safir, sir Epynogrys, and sir Galleron. And than the knyghtes of the 30 Table Rounde withdrew them abacke aftir they had gotyn their horsys as well as they myght.

'A, mercy Jesu!' seyde sir Gawayne. 'What knyght ys yondir that doth so mervaylous dedys in that fylde?'

'I wote what he ys,' seyde the kyn[g], 'but as at thys tyme I woll nat 35 name hym.'

'Sir,' seyde sir Gawayne, 'I wolde sey hit were sir Launcelot by hys rydynge and hys buffettis that I se hym deale. But ever mesemyth hit sholde nat be he, for that he beryth the rede slyve uppon hys helmet; for I wyst hym never beare tokyn at no justys of lady ne jantillwoman.' 40

'Lat hym be,' seyde kynge Arthure, 'for he woll be bettir knowyn and do more or ever he departe.'

Than the party that was ayenst kynge Arthur were well comforted, and than they hylde hem togydirs that befornhande were sore rebuked.

Than sir Bors, sir Ector de Marys [and] sir Lyonell, they called unto them the knyghtes of their blood, as sir Blamour de Ganys, sir Bleoberys, sir Alyduke, sir Galyhud, sir Galyhodyn, sir Bellyngere le Bewse. So thes nine knyghtes of sir Launcelottis kynne threst in
5 myghtyly, for they were all noble knyghtes, and they of grete hate and despite [that they had unto hym] thought to rebuke sir Launcelot and sir Lavayne, for they knew hem nat.

And so they cam hurlyng togydirs and smote downe many knyghtes of North Walys and of Northumbirlonde. And whan sir Launcelot
10 saw them fare so, he gate a grete speare in hys honde; and there encountird with hym all at onys, sir Bors, sir Ector, and sir Lyonell. And they three smote hym at onys with their spearys, and with fors of themselff they smote sir Launcelottis horse revers to the erthe. And by myssefortune sir Bors smote sir Launcelot thorow the shylde into the
15 syde, and the speare brake and the hede leffte stylle in the syde.

Whan sir Lavayne saw hys mayster lye on the grounde he ran to the Kynge of Scottis and smote hym to the erthe; and by grete forse he toke hys horse and brought hym to sir Launcelot, and magré them all he made hym to mownte uppon that horse. And than sir Launcelot gate
20 a speare in hys honde, and there he smote sir Bors, horse and man, to the erthe; and in the same wyse he served sir Ector and sir Lyonell; and sir Lavayne smote downe sir Blamour de Gaynys. And than sir Launcelot drew hys swerde, for he felte hymselff so sore hurte that he wente there to have had hys deth. And than he smote sir Bleoberis such a
25 buffet on the helmet that he felle downe to the erthe in a sowne, and in the same wyse he served sir Alyduke and sir Galyhud. And sir Lavayne smote downe sir Bellyngere that was [sone] to Alysaunder le Orphelyn.

And by thys was done, was sir Bors horsed agayne and in cam with
30 sir Ector and sir Lyonell, and all they three smote with their swerdis uppon sir Launcelottis helmet. And whan he felte their buffettis, and with that hys wounde greved hym grevously, tha[n] he thought to do what he myght whyle he cowde endure. And than he gaff sir Bors such a buffette that he made hym bowghe hys hede passynge lowe; and
35 therewithall he raced of hys helme, and myght have slayne hym, but whan he saw ⟨his⟩ vysayge so pulde hym downe. And in the same wyse he served sir Ector and sir Lyonell; for, as the booke seyth, he myght have slayne them, but whan he saw their visages hys herte myght nat serve hym thereto, but leffte hem there.
40   ⌜And than afterward he hurled into the thyckest prees of them alle, and dyd there the merveyloust dedes of armes that ever man sawe⌝, and ever sir Lavayne with hym. And there sir Launcelot with hys swerde smote downe and pulled downe, as the Freynsh booke seyth, mo than thirty knyghtes, and the moste party were of the Table

Rounde. And there sir Lavayne dud full well that day, for he smote
downe ten knyghtes of the Table Rounde.

'Mercy Jesu,' seyde sir Gawayne unto kynge Arthur, 'I mervayle (12)
what knyght that he ys with the rede sleve.'

'Sir,' seyde kyng Arthure, 'he woll be knowyn or ever he departe.'   5

And than the kynge blew unto lodgynge, and the pryce was gyvyn
by herowdis unto the knyght with the whyght shylde that bare the
rede slyve. Than cam the kynge of North Galys, and the kynge of
Northhumbirlonde, and the Kynge with the Hondred Knyghtes, and
sir Galahalte the Haute Prince, [and] seyde unto sir Launcelot,   10

'Fayre knyght, God you blysse, for muche have ye done for us thys
day. And therefore we pray you that ye woll com with us, that ye may
resceyve the honour and the pryce as ye have worshypfully deserved hit.'

'Fayre lordys,' seyde sir Launcelot, 'wete you well, gyff I have deserved thanke I have sore bought hit, and that me repentith hit, for I   15
am never lyke to ascape with the lyff. Therefore, my fayre lordys, I
pray you that ye woll suffir me to departe where me lykith, for I am sore
hurte. And I take no forse of none honoure, for I had levir repose me
than to be lorde of all the worlde.'

And therewithall he groned pyteuously and rode a grete walop   20
awaywarde from them untyll he cam undir a woodys evyse. And whan
he saw that he was frome the fylde nyghe a myle, that he was sure he
myght nat be seyne, than he seyde with an hyghe voyce and with a
grete grone,

'A, jantill knyght, sir Lavayne! Helpe me that thys truncheoune   25
were oute of my syde, for hit stykith so sore that hit nyghe sleyth me.'

'A, myne owne lorde,' seyde sir Lavayne, 'I wolde fayne do that
myght please you, but I drede me sore, and I pulle oute the truncheoune, that ye shall be in perelle of dethe.'

'I charge you,' seyde sir Launcelot, 'as ye love me, draw hit oute!'   30

And therewithall he descended frome hys horse, and ryght so ded sir
Lavayne; and forthwithall he drew the truncheoune oute of hys syde,
and gaff a grete shryche and a gresly grone, that the blood braste oute,
nyghe a pynte at onys, that at the laste he sanke downe uppon hys arse
and so sowned downe, pale and dedly.   35

'Alas,' seyde sir Lavayne, 'what shall I do?'

And than he turned sir Launcelot into the wynde, and so he lay
there nyghe halff an owre as he had bene dede. And so at the laste sir
Launcelot caste up hys yghen and seyde,

'A, sir Lavayne, helpe me that I were on my horse! For here ys   40
faste by, within thys two myle, a jantill ermyte that somtyme was a full
noble knyght and a grete lorde of possessyons. And for grete goodnes
he hath takyn hym to wyllfull poverté and forsakyn myghty londys.
And hys name ys sir Bawdwyn of Bretayne, and he ys a full noble

surgeon and a good leche. Now lat se and helpe me up that I were
there, for ever my harte gyvith me that I shall never dye of my cousyne
jermaynes hondys.'

And than with grete payne sir Lavayne holpe hym uppon hys horse,
5 and than they rode a grete walop togydirs, and ever sir Launcelot
bled, that hit ran downe to the erthe. And so by fortune they cam to an
ermytayge [whiche] was undir a woode, and a grete clyff on the othir
syde, and a fayre watir rennynge undir hit. And than sir Lavayne bete
on the gate with the but of hys speare and cryed faste,
10 'Lat in, for Jesus sake!'

And anone there cam a fayre chylde to hem and asked them what
they wolde.

'Fayre sonne,' seyde sir Lavayne, 'go and pray thy lorde the ermyte
for Goddys sake to late in here a knyght that ys full sore wounded. And
15 thys day, telle thy lorde, I saw hym do more dedys of armys than ever
I herde sey that ony man ded.'

So the chylde wente in lyghtly, and than he brought the ermyte
whych was a passynge lycly man. Whan sir Lavayne saw hym he prayde
hym for Goddys sake of succour.
20 'What knyght ys he?' seyde the ermyte. 'Ys he of the house of
kynge Arthure or nat?'

'I wote nat,' seyde sir Lavayne, 'what he ys, nother what ys hys
name, but well I wote I saw hym do mervaylously thys day as of
dedys of armys.'
25 'On whos party was he?' seyde the ermyte.

'Sir,' seyde sir Lavayne, 'he was thys day ayenste kynge Arthure, and
there he wanne the pryce of all the knyghtis of the Rounde Table.'

'I have seyne the day,' seyde the ermyte, 'I wolde have loved hym
the worse bycause he was ayenste my lorde kynge Arthure, for some-
30 tyme I was one of the felyship, but now I thanke God I am othirwyse
disposed. But where ys he? Lat me se hym.'

(13)   Than sir Lavayne brought the ermyte to hym. And whan the ermyte
behylde hym as he sate leenynge uppon hys sadyll-bowe, ever bledynge
spiteuously, and ever the knyght ermyte thought that he sholde know
35 hym; but he coude nat brynge hym to knowlech bycause he was so
pale for bledyng.

'What knyght ar ye?' seyde the ermyte, 'and where were ye borne?'

'My fayre lorde,' seyde sir Launcelot, 'I am a straungere and a
knyght aventures that laboureth thorowoute many realmys for to
40 wynne worship.'

Than the ermyte avysed hym bettir, and saw by a wounde on hys
chyeke that he was sir Launcelot.

'Alas,' seyde the ermyte, 'myne owne lorde! Why layne you youre
name from me? Perdeus, I ought to know you of ryght, for ye ar the

moste nobelyst knyght of the worlde. For well I know you for sir
Launcelot.'

'Sir,' seyde he, 'syth ye know me, helpe me, and ye may, for Goddys
sake! For I wolde be oute of thys payne at onys, othir to deth othir to
lyff.'   5

'Have ye no doute,' seyde the ermyte, 'for ye shall lyve and fare
ryght well.'

And so the ermyte called to hym two of hys servauntes, and so they
bare hym into the ermytayge, and lyghtly unarmed hym and leyde hym
in hys bedde. And than anone the ermyte staunched hys bloode and   10
made hym to drynke good wyne, that he was well refygowred and
knew hymselff. For in thos dayes hit was nat the gyse as ys nowadayes; for there were none ermytis in tho dayes but that they had bene
men of worship and of prouesse, and tho ermytes hylde grete house-
holdis and refreysshed people that were in distresse.   15

Now turned we unto kynge Arthure and leve we sir Launcelot in
the ermytayge. So whan the kyngis were togydirs on both partyes, and
the grete feste sholde be holdyn, kynge Arthure asked the kynge of
North Galis and their felyshyp where was that knyght that bare the
rede slyve.   20

'Lat brynge hym before me, that he may have hys lawde and honoure
and the pryce, as hit ys ryght.'

Than spake sir Galahalte the Haute Prynce and the Kynge with the
Hondred Knyghtes, and seyde,

'We suppose that knyght ys myscheved so that he ys never lyke to se   25
you nother none of us all. And that ys the grettyst pyté that ever we
wyste of ony knyght.'

'Alas,' seyde kynge Arthure, 'how may thys be? Ys he so sore hurte?
But what ys hys name?' seyde kynge Arthure.

'Truly,' seyde they all, 'we know nat hys name, nother frome whens   30
he cam, nother whother he wolde.'

'Alas,' seyde the kynge, 'thys ys the warste tydyngis that cam to me
thys seven yere! For I wolde nat for all the londys I welde to knowe
and wyte hit were so that that noble knyght were slayne.'

'Sir, knowe ye ought of hym?' seyde they all.   35

'As for that,' seyde kynge Arthure, 'whethir I know hym other
none, ye shall nat know for me what man he ys but Allmyghty Jesu
sende me good tydyngis of hym.'

And so seyde they all.

'Be my hede,' seyde sir Gawayne, 'gyff hit so be that the good   40
knyght be so sore hurte, hit ys grete damage and pité to all thys londe,
for he ys one of the nobelyst knyghtes that ever I saw in a fylde handyll
speare or swerde. And iff he may be founde I shall fynde hym, for I am
sure he ys nat farre frome thys contrey.'

'Sir, ye beare you well,' seyde kynge Arthure, 'and ye [maye] fynde hym, onles that he be in such a plyte that he may nat welde hymselff.'

'Jesu defende!' seyde sir Gawayne. 'But wyte well, I shall know what he ys and I may fynde hym.'

5 Ryght so sir Gawayne toke a squyre with hym uppon hakeneyes and rode all-aboute Camelot within six or seven myle, but so⟨ne⟩ he com agayne and cowde here no worde of hym. Than within two dayes kynge Arthure and all the felyshyp returned unto London agayne. And so as they rode by the way hyt happened sir Gawayne at Astolot 10 to lodge with sir Barnarde thereas was sir Launcelot lodged.

And so as sir Gawayne was in hys chamber to repose hym, sir Barnarde, the olde barowne, cam in to hym, and hys doughtir Elayne, to chere hym and to aske hym what tydyngis, and who ded beste at the turnemente of Wynchester.

15 'So God me helpe,' seyde sir Gawayne, 'there were two knyghtes that bare two whyght shyldys, but one of them bare a rede sleve uppon hys hede, and sertaynly he was the beste knyght that ever y saw juste in fylde. For I dare sey,' seyde sir Gawayne, 'that one knyght with the rede slyve smote downe fourty knyghtes of the Rounde Table, and 20 his felow ded ryght well and worshipfully.'

'Now blyssed be God,' seyde thys Fayre Maydyn of Astolate, 'that that knyght sped so welle! For he ys the man in the worlde that I firste loved, and truly he shall be the laste that ever I shall love.'

'Now, fayre maydyn,' seyde sir Gawayne, 'ys that good knyght 25 youre love?'

'Sertaynly, sir,' she seyde, 'he ys my love.'

'Than know ye hys name?' seyde sir Gawayne.

'Nay, truly, sir,' seyde the damesell, 'I know nat hys name nothir frome whens he com, but to sey that I love hym, I promyse God and 30 you I love hym.'

'How had ye knowlecch of hym firste?' seyde sir Gawayne.

(14) Than she tolde hym, as ye have harde before, and how hir fadir betoke hym her brother to do hym servyse, and how hir fadir lente hym her brothirs, sir Tyrryes, shylde: 'and here with me he leffte hys 35 owne shylde.'

'For what cause ded he so?' seyde sir Gawayne.

'For thys cause,' seyde the damesell, 'for hys shylde was full well knowyn amonge many noble knyghtes.'

'A, fayre damesell,' seyde sir Gawayne, 'please hit you to lette me 40 have a syght of that shylde?'

'Sir,' she seyde, 'hit ys in my chambir, coverde wyth a case, and if ye woll com with me ye shall se hit.'

'Nat so,' seyde sir Barnarde to hys doughter, 'but sende ye for that shylde.'

So whan the shylde was com sir Gawayne toke of the case, and whan he behylde that shylde [he] knew hyt anone that hit was sir Launcelottis shylde and hys owne armys.

'A, Jesu mercy!' seyde sir Gawayne, 'now ys my herte more hevyar than ever hit was tofore.'

'Why?' seyde thys mayde Elayne.

'For I have a grete cause,' seyde sir Gawayne. 'Ys that knyght that owyth thys shylde youre love?'

'Yee truly,' she sayde, 'my love ys he. God wolde that I were hys love!'

'So God me spede,' seyde sir Gawayne, 'fayre damesell, ye have ryght, for and he be youre love, ye love the moste honorabelyst knyght of the worlde and the man of moste worship.'

'So methought ever,' seyde the damesell, 'for never ar that tyme no knyght that ever I saw loved I never none a[r]ste.'

'God graunte,' seyde sir Gawayne, 'that aythir of you may rejoyse othir, but that ys in a grete aventure. But truly,' seyde sir Gawayne unto the damesell, 'ye may sey ye have a fayre grace, for why I have knowyn that noble knyght thys four-and-twenty yere, and never or that day I nor none othir knyght, I dare make good, saw never nother herde say that ever he bare tokyn or sygne of no lady, jantillwoman, nor maydyn at no justis nother turnemente. And therefore, fayre maydyn, ye ar much beholdyn to hym to gyff hym thanke. But I drede me,' seyde sir Gawayne, 'that ye shall never se hym in thys worlde, and that ys as grete pité as ever was of ony erthely man.'

'Alas,' seyde she, 'how may thys be? Ys he slayne?'

'I say nat so,' seyde sir Gawayne, 'but wete you well he ys grevously wounded, by all maner of sygnys, and by meanys of syght more lycklyer to be dede than to be on lyve. And wyte you well he ys the noble knyght sir Launcelot, for by thys shylde I know hym.'

'Alas!' seyde thys Fayre Maydyn of Astolat, 'how may thys be? And what was hys hurte?'

'Truly,' seyde sir Gawayne, 'the man in the worlde that loved beste hym hurte hym. And I dare sey,' seyde sir Gawayne, 'and that knyght that hurte hym knew the verry sertaynté that he had hurte sir Launcelot, hit were the moste sorow that ever cam to hys herte.'

'Now, fayre fadir,' seyde than Elayne, 'I requyre you gyff me leve to ryde and seke hym, othir ellis I wote well I shall go oute of my mynde. For I shall never stynte tyll that I fynde hym and my brothir, sir Lavayne.'

'Do ye as hit lykith you,' seyde hir fadir, 'for sore me repentis of the hurte of that noble knyght.'

Ryght so the mayde made hyr redy and departed before sir Gawayne makynge grete dole. Than on the morne sir Gawayne com to kynge

Arthure and tolde hym all how he had founde sir Launcelottis shylde in the kepynge of the Fayre Mayden of Astolat.

'All that knew I aforehande,' seyde kynge Arthure, 'and that caused me I wolde nat suffir you to have ado at the grete justis; for I aspyed
5 hym whan he cam untyll hys lodgyng, full late in the evenyng, into Astolat. But grete mervayle have I,' seyde kynge Arthure, 'that ever he wolde beare ony sygne of ony damesell, for ar now I never herde sey nor knew that ever he bare ony tokyn of none erthely woman.'

'Be my hede, sir,' seyde sir Gawayne, 'the Fayre Maydyn of Astolat
10 lovith hym mervaylously well. What hit meanyth I cannat sey. And she ys ryddyn aftir to seke hym.'

So the kynge and all com to London, and there Gawayne all opynly disclosed hit to all the courte that hit was sir Launcelot that justed beste.
(15) And whan sir Bors harde that, wyte you well he was an hevy man, and
15 so were all hys kynnysmen. But whan the quyene wyst that hit was sir Launcelot that bare the rede slyve of the Fayre Maydyn of Astolat, she was nygh ought of her mynde for wratthe. And than she sente for sir Bors de Ganys in all haste that myght be. So whan sir Bors was com before the quyene she seyde,

20 'A, sir Bors! Have ye nat herde sey how falsely sir Launcelot hath betrayed me?'

'Alas, madame,' seyde sir Bors, 'I am aferde he hath betrayed hymselff and us all.'

'No forse,' seyde the quene, 'though he be distroyed, for he ys a
25 false, traytoure knyght.'

'Madame,' seyde sir Bors, 'I pray you sey ye no more so, for wyte you well I may nat here no such langayge of hym.'

'Why so, sir Bors?' seyde she. 'Shold I nat calle hym traytoure whan he bare the rede slyve uppon hys hede at Wynchester at the grete
30 justis?'

'Madame,' seyde sir Bors, 'that slyeve-berynge repentes me, but I dare say he dud beare hit to none evyll entent, but for thys cause he bare the rede slyve that none of hys blood shold know hym. For or than we nother none of us all never knew that ever he bare tokyn or
35 sygne of maydyn, lady, nothir jantillwoman.'

'Fy on hym!' seyde the quene. 'Yet for all hys pryde and bobbaunce, there ye proved youreselff better man than he.'

'Nay, madam, sey ye nevermore so, for he bete me and my felowys, and myght have slayne us and he had wolde.'

40 'Fy on hym!' seyde the quene. 'For I harde sir Gawayne say before my lorde Arthure that hit were mervayle to telle the grete love that ys betwene the Fayre Maydyn of Astolat and hym.'

'Madam,' seyde sir Bors, 'I may nat warne sir Gawayne to sey what hit pleasith hym, but I dare sey, as for my lorde sir Launcelot, that he lovith no lady, jantillwoman, nother mayden, but as he lovith all inlyke muche. And therefore, madam,' seyde sir Bors, 'ye may sey what ye wyll, but wyte you well I woll hast me to syke hym and fynde hym wheresumever he be, and God sende me good tydyngis of hym!'

And so leve we them there, and speke we of sir Launcelot that lay 5 in grete perell. And so as thys fayre madyn Elayne cam to Wynchester she sought there all aboute, and by fortune sir Lavayne, hir brothir, was ryddyn to sporte hym to enchaff hys horse. And anone as thys maydyn Elayne saw hym she knew hym, and than she cryed on-lowde tylle hym, and whan he herde her he com to her. And anone with that 10 she asked hir brother,

'How dothe my lorde, sir Launcelot?'

'Who tolde you, syster, that my lordys name was sir Launcelot?'

Than she tolde hym how sir Gawayne by hys shylde knew hym.

So they rode togydirs tyll that they cam to the ermytayge, and anone 15 she alyght. So sir Lavayne brought her in to sir Launcelot, and whan she saw hym ly so syke and pale in hys bed she myght nat speke, but suddeynly she felle downe to the erthe in a sowghe. And there she lay a grete whyle. And when she was releved she shryked and seyde,

'My lord, sir Launcelot! Alas, whyghe lye ye in thys plyte?'   20

And than she sowned agayne. And than sir Launcelot prayde sir Lavayne to take hir up, 'and brynge hir hydir to me'. And whan she cam to herselff sir Launcelot kyste her and seyde,

'Fayre maydyn, why fare ye thus? For ye put me to more payne. Wherefore make ye no such chere, for and ye be com to comforte me, 25 ye be ryght wellcom; and of thys lytyll hurte that I have I shall be ryght hastely hole, by the grace of God. But I mervayle,' seyde sir Launcelot, 'who tolde you my name.'

And so thys maydyn tolde hym all how sir Gawayne was lodged with hir fader, 'and there by youre shylde he dyscoverde youre name.' 30

'Alas!' seyde sir Launcelot, 'that repentith me that my name ys knowyn, for I am sure hit woll turne untyll angir.'

And than sir Launcelot compaste in hys mynde that sir Gawayne wolde telle quene Gwenyvere how he bare the rede slyve and for whom, that he wyst well wolde turne unto grete angur.   35

So thys maydyn Elayne never wente frome sir Launcelot, but wacched hym day and nyght, and dud such attendaunce to hym that the Freynshe booke seyth there was never woman dyd never more kyndlyer for man. Than sir Launcelot prayde sir Lavayne to make aspyes in Wynchester for sir Bors if he cam there, and tolde hym by what tokyns he 40 sholde know hym: by a wounde in hys forehede.

'For I am sure,' seyde sir Launcelot, 'that sir Bors woll seke me, for he ys the same good knyght that hurte me.'

Now turne we unto sir Bors de Ganys, that cam untyll Wynchestir (16)

to seke aftir hys cosyne sir Launcelot. And whan he cam to Wynchester sir Lavayne leyde wacche for sir Bors. And anone he had
warnyng of hym, and so he founde hym, and anone he salewed hym
and tolde hym frome whens he com.

5 'Now, fayre knyght,' seyde sir Bors, 'ye be wellcom, and I requyre
you that ye woll brynge me to my lorde sir Launcelot.'

'Sir,' seyde sir Lavayne, 'take youre horse, and within thys owre ye
shall se hym.'

So they departed and com to the ermytayge. And whan sir Bors saw
10 sir Launcelot lye in hys bedde, dede pale and discoloured, anone sir Bors
loste hys countenaunce, and for kyndenes and pité he myght nat speke
but wepte tendirly a grete whyle. But whan he myght speke he seyde
thus:

'A, my lorde sir Launcelot, God you blysse and sende you hasty
15 recoveryng! For full hevy am I of my mysfortune and of myne unhappynesse. For now I may calle myselff unhappy, and I drede me that
God ys gretely [displeasyd] with me, that He wolde suffir me to have
such a shame for to hurte you that ar all oure ledar and all oure worship;
and therefore I calle myselff unhappy. Alas, that ever such a caytyff
20 knyght as I am sholde have power by unhappines to hurte the moste
noblyst knyght of the worlde! Where I so shamefully sette uppon you
and overcharged you, and where ye myght have slayne me, ye saved me;
and so ded nat I, for I and all oure bloode ded to you their utteraunce.
I mervayle,' seyde sir Bors, 'that my herte or my bloode wolde serve
25 me. Wherefore, my lorde sir Launcelot, I aske you mercy.'

'Fayre cousyn,' seyde sir Launcelot, 'ye be ryght wellcom, and wyte
you well, overmuche ye se[y] for the plesure of me whych pleasith me
nothynge, for why I have the same isought; for I wolde with pryde
have overcom you all. And there in my pryde I was nere slayne, and
30 that was in myne owne defaughte; for I myght have gyffyn you warnynge of my beynge there, and [than] had I had no hurte. For hit ys an
olde-seyde sawe, "there ys harde batayle thereas kynne and frendys
doth batayle ayther ayenst other", for there may be no mercy, but
mortall warre. Therefore, fayre cousyn,' seyde sir Launcelot, 'lat
35 thys langage overpasse, and all shall be wellcom that God sendith.
And latte us leve of thy[s] mater and speke of som rejoysynge, for
thys that ys done may nat be undone; and lat us fynde a remedy
how sone that I may be hole.'

Than sir Bors lenyd uppon hys beddys syde and tolde sir Launcelot
40 how the quene was passynge wrothe with hym, 'because ye ware the
rede slyve at the grete justes'. And there sir Bors tolde hym all how sir
Gawayne discoverde hit 'by youre shylde' that he leffte with the Fayre
Madyn of Astolat.

'Than ys the quene wrothe?' seyde sir Launcelot. 'Therefore am I

ryght hevy, but I deserved no wrath, for all that I ded was bycause I
wolde nat be knowyn.'

'Sir, ryght so excused I you,' seyde sir Bors, 'but all was in vayne, for
she seyde more largelyer to me than I to you sey now. But, sir, ys thys
she,' seyde sir Bors, 'that ys so busy aboute you, that men calle the 5
Fayre Maydyn of Astolat?'

'Forsothe, she hit ys,' seyde sir Launcelot, 'that by no meany[s] I
cannat put her fro me.'

'Why sholde ye put her frome you?' seyde sir Bors. 'For she ys a
passyng fayre damesell, and well besayne and well taught. And God 10
wolde, fayre cousyn,' seyde sir Bors, 'that ye cowde love her, but as to
that I may nat nother dare nat counceyle you. But I se well,' seyde sir
Bors, 'by her dylygence aboute you that she lovith you intyerly.'

'That me repentis,' seyde sir Launcelot.

'Well,' seyde sir Bors, 'she ys nat the first that hath loste hir payne 15
uppon you, and that ys the more pyté.'

And so they talked of many mo thynges.

And so within three or four dayes sir Launcelot wexed bygge and
lyght. Than sir [Bors] tolde sir [Launcelot] how there was sworne a (17)
grete turnement betwyxt kyng Arthure and the kynge of North Galis, 20
that sholde be uppon Allhalowmasse day, besydes Wynchestir.

'Is that trouth?' seyde sir Launcelot. 'Than shall ye abyde with me
stylle a lityll whyle untyll that I be hole, for I fele myself resonabely
bygge and stronge.'

'Blessed be God!' seyde sir Bors.   25

Than they were there nyghe a moneth togydirs, and ever thys maydyn Elayne ded ever hir dylygence and labour both nyght and day unto
sir Launcelot, that there was never chylde nother wyff more mekar
tyll fadir and husbande than was thys Fayre Maydyn of Astolat;
wherefore sir Bors was gretly pleased with her.   30

So uppon a day, by the assente of sir Lavayne, sir Bors, and sir
Launcelot, they made the ermyte to seke in woodys for diverse erbys,
and so sir Launcelot made fayre Elayne to gadir erbys for hym to make
hym a bayne. So in the meanewhyle sir Launcelot made sir Lavayne to
arme hym at all pecis, and there he thought to assay hymselff uppon 35
horsebacke with a speare, whether he myght welde hys armour and
hys speare for hys hurte or nat.

And so whan he was uppon hys horse he steyred hym freyshly, and
the horse was passyng lusty and frycke because he was nat laboured of
a moneth before. And than sir Launcelot bade sir Lavayne gyff hym 40
that grete speare, and so sir Launcelot cowchyd that speare in the
reeste. The courser lepte myghtyly whan he felte the spurres, and he
that was uppon hym, [whiche] was the nobelyst horseman of the
worlde, strayned hym myghtyly and stabely, and kepte stylle the speare

in the reeste. And therewith sir Launcelot strayned hymselff so straytly, with so grete fors, to gete the courser forewarde that the bottom of hys wounde braste both within and withoute, and therewithall the bloode cam oute so fyersely that he felte hymselff so feble that he
5 myght nat sitte uppon hys horse. And than sir Launcelot cryed unto sir Bors,

'A, sir Bors and sir Lavayne, helpe! For I am com unto myne ende!'

And therewith he felle downe on the one syde to the erth lyke a dede coorse. And than sir Bors and sir Lavayne cam unto hym with sorow-
10 makynge oute of mesure. And so by fortune thys mayden, Elayne, harde their mournynge; and than she cam, and whan she founde sir Launcelot there armed in that place she cryed and wepte as she had bene wood. And than she kyssed hym and ded what she myght to awake hym, and than she rebuked her brothir and sir Bors, and called
15 hem false traytours, and seyde,

'Why wolde ⟨ye⟩ take hym oute of hys bed? For and he dye, I woll appele you of hys deth!'

And so with that cam the ermyte, sir Bawdewyn of Bretayne, and whan he founde sir Launcelot in that plyte he seyde but lityll, but wyte
20 you well he was wroth. But he seyde, 'Lette us have hym in', and anone they bare hym into the ermytage and unarmed hym, and leyde hym in hys bedde; and evermore hys wounde bled spiteuously, but he stirred no lymme off hym. Than the knyght armyte put a thynge in hys nose and a litill dele of watir in hys mowthe, and than sir Launcelot waked of
25 hys swowghe. And than the ermyte staunched hys bledyng, and whan sir Launcelot myght speke he asked why he put his lyff so in jouperté.

'Sir,' seyde sir Launcelot, 'because I wente I had be stronge inowghe, and also sir Bors tolde me there sholde be at [Al]halowmasse a grete justis betwyxte kynge Arthure and the kynge of Northe Galys. And
30 therefore I thought to assay myselff, whether I myght be there or not.'

'A, sir Launcelot,' seyde the ermyte, 'youre harte and youre currayge woll never be done untyll youre laste day! But ye shall do now be my counceyle: lat sir Bors departe frome you, and lat hym do at that turnemente what he may; and, by the grace of God,' seyde the knyght
35 ermyte, 'be that the turnemente be done and he comyn hydir agayne, sir, ye shall be hole, so that ye woll be governed by me.'

(18) Than sir Bors made hym redy to departe frome hym, and sir Launcelot seyde,

'Fayre cousyn, sir Bors, recommaunde me unto all tho ye owght
40 recommaunde me unto, and I pray you enforce youreself at that justis that ye may be beste, for my love. And here shall I abyde you, at the mercy of God, tyll youre agayne-commynge.'

And so sir Bors departed and cam to the courte of kynge Arthure, and tolde hem in what place he leffte sir Launcelot.

'That me repentis!' seyde the kynge. 'But syn he shall have hys lyff, we all may thanke God.'

And than sir Bors tolde the quene what jouperté sir Launcelot was in whan he wolde asayde hys horse:

'And all that he ded was for the love of you, because he wolde a bene 5 at thys turnemente.'

'Fy on hym, recreayde knyght!' seyde the quene. 'For wyte you well I am ryght sory and he shall have hys lyff.'

'Madam, hys lyff shall he have,' seyde sir Bors, 'and who that wolde otherwyse, excepte you, madame, we that ben of hys blood wolde 10 helpe to shortyn their lyves! But, madame,' seyde sir Bors, 'ye have ben oftyntymes displeased with my lorde sir Launcelot, but at all tymys at the ende ye founde hym a trew knyght.'

And so he departed. And than every knyght of the Rounde Table that were there that tyme presente made them redy to that justes at 15 Allhalowmasse. And thidir drew many knyghtes of diverse contreyes. And as Halowmasse drew nere, thydir cam the kynge of North Galis, and the Kynge with the Hondred Knyghtes, and sir Galahalt the Haute Prynce of Surluse. And thider cam kynge Angwysh of Irelonde, and the Kynge of Northumbirlonde, and the Kynge of Scottis. So thes 20 three kynges com to kynge Arthurs party.

And so that day sir Gawayne ded grete dedys of armys and began first; and the herowdis nombirde that sir Gawayne smote downe twenty knyghtes. Than sir Bors de Ganys cam in the same tyme, and he was numbir[de] he smote downe twenty knyghtes; and therefore the 25 pryse was gyvyn betwyxt them bothe, for they began firste and lengist endured. Also sir Gareth, as the boke seyth, ded that day grete dedis of armys, for he smote downe and pulled downe thirty knyghtes; but whan he had done that dedis he taryed nat, but so departed, and therefore he loste hys pryse. And sir Palamydes ded grete dedis of armys 30 that day, for he smote downe twenty knyghtes; but he departed suddeynly, and men demed that he and sir Gareth rode togydirs to som maner adventures.

So whan thys turnement was done sir Bors departed, and rode tylle he cam to sir Launcelot, hys cousyne. And than he founde hym walkyng 35 on hys feete, and there aythir made grete joy of other.

And so he tolde sir Launcelot of all the justys, lyke as ye have herde.

'I mervayle,' seyde sir Launcelot, 'that sir Gareth, whan he had done such dedis of armys, that he wolde nat tarry.'

'Sir, thereof we mervayled all,' seyde sir Bors, 'for but if hit were 40 you, other the noble knyght sir Trystram, other the good knyght sir Lamorake de Galis, I saw never knyght bere so many knyghtes and smyte downe in so litill a whyle a[s] ded sir Gareth. And anone as he was gone we all wyst nat where he becom.'

'Be my hede,' seyde sir Launcelot, 'he ys a noble knyght and a myghty man and well-brethed; and yf he were well assayed,' seyd sir Launcelot, 'I wolde deme he were good inow for ony knyght that beryth the lyff. And he ys jantill, curteyse and ryght bownteuous, meke
5 and mylde, and in hym ys no maner of male engynne, but playne, faythfull an trew.'

So than they made hem redy to departe frome the ermytayge. And so uppon a morne they toke their horsis, and this Elayne le Blanke with hem. And whan they cam to Astolat there were they well lodged and had
10 grete chere of sir Barnarde, the olde baron, and of sir Tirré, hys sonne.

And so uppon the morne, whan sir Launcelot sholde departe, fayre Elayne brought hir fadir with her, and sir Lavayne, and sir Tyrré, and than thus she sayde:

(19) 'My lorde, sir Launcelot, now I se ye woll departe frome me. Now,
15 fayre knyght and curtayse knyght,' seyde she, 'have mercy uppon me, and suffir me nat to dye for youre love.'

'Why, what wolde you that I dud?' seyde sir Launcelot.

'Sir, I wolde have you to my husbande,' seyde Elayne.

'Fayre damesell, I thanke you hartely,' seyde sir Launcelot, 'but
20 truly,' seyde he, 'I caste me never to be wedded man.'

'Than, fayre knyght,' seyde she, 'woll ye be my paramour?'

'Jesu deffende me!' seyde sir Launcelot. 'For than I rewarded youre fadir and youre brothir full evyll for their grete goodnesse.'

'Alas! Than', seyde she, 'I muste dye for youre love.'
25 'Ye shall nat do so,' seyde sir Launcelot, 'for wyte you well, fayre mayden, I myght have bene maryed and I had wolde, but I never applyed me yett to be maryed. But bycause, fayre damesell, that ye love me as ye sey ye do, I woll for youre good wylle and kyndnes shew to you som goodnesse. That ys thys, that wheresomever ye woll
30 besette youre herte uppon som good knyght that woll wedde you, I shall gyff you togydirs a thousand pounde yerly, to you and to youre ayris. This muche woll I gyff you, fayre mayden, for youre kyndnesse, and allweyes whyle I lyve to be youre owne knyght.'

'Sir, of all thys,' seyde the maydyn, 'I woll none, for but yff ye woll
35 wedde me, other to be my paramour at the leste, wyte you well, sir Launcelot, my good dayes ar done.'

'Fayre damesell,' seyde sir Launcelot, 'of thes two thynges ye muste pardon me.'

Than she shryked shirly and felle downe in a sowghe; and than
40 women bare hir into her chambir, and there she made overmuche sorowe. And than sir Launcelot wolde departe, and there he asked sir Lavayne what he wolde do.

'Sir, what sholde I do,' seyde sir Lavayne, 'but folow you, but if ye dryve me frome you or commaunde me to go frome you.'

Than cam sir Barnarde to sir Launcelot and seyde to hym,
'I cannat se but that my doughtir woll dye for youre sake.'

'Sir, I may nat do withall,' seyde sir Launcelot, 'for that me sore
repentith, for I reporte me to youreselff that my profir ys fayre. And me
repentith,' seyde sir Launcelot, 'that she lovith me as she dothe, for I   5
was never the causer of hit; for I reporte me unto youre sonne, I never
erly nother late profirde her bownté nother fayre behestes. And as for
me,' seyde sir Launcelot, 'I dare do that a knyght sholde do, and sey
that she ys a clene mayden for me, bothe for dede and wylle. For I am
ryght hevy of hir distresse. For she ys a full fayre maydyn, goode and   10
jentill, and well itaught.'

'Fadir,' seyde sir Lavayne, 'I dare make good she ys a clene maydyn
as for my lorde sir Launcelot; but she doth as I do, for sythen I saw
first my lorde sir Launcelot I cowde never departe frome hym, nother
nought I woll, and I may folow hym.'   15

Than sir Launcelot toke hys leve, and so they departed and cam to
Wynchestir. And whan kynge Arthur wyst that sir Launcelot was com
hole and sownde, the kynge made grete joy of hym; and so ded sir
Gawayne and all the knyghtes of the Rounde Table excepte sir Aggravayne and sir Mordred. Also quene Gwenyver was woode wrothe with   20
sir Launcelot, and wolde by no meanys speke with hym, but enstraunged
herselff frome hym. And sir Launcelot made all the meanys that he
myght for to speke with the quene, but hit wolde nat be.

Now speke we of the Fayre Maydyn of Astolat that made such
sorow day and nyght that she never slepte, ete, nother dranke, and ever   25
she made hir complaynte unto sir Launcelot. So whan she had thus
endured a ten dayes, that she fyebled so that she muste nedis passe oute
of thys worlde, than she shrove her clene and resseyved hir Creature.
And ever she complayned stylle uppon sir Launcelot. Than hir gostly
fadir bade hir leve such thoughtes. Than she seyde,   30

'Why sholde I leve such thoughtes? Am I nat an erthely woman?
And all the whyle the brethe ys in my body I may complayne me, for
my belyve ys that I do none offence, thou[gh] I love an erthely man,
unto God, for He fourmed me thereto, and all maner of good love
comyth of God. And othir than good love loved I never sir Launcelot   35
du Lake. And I take God to recorde, I loved never none but hym, nor
never shall, of erthely creature; and a clene maydyn I am for hym and
for all othir. And sitthyn hit ys the sufferaunce of God that I shall dye
for so noble a knyght, I beseche The, Hyghe Fadir of Hevyn, have
mercy uppon me and my soule, and uppon myne unnumerable paynys   40
that I suffir may be alygeaunce of parte of my synnes. For, Swete
Lorde Jesu,' seyde the fayre maydyn, 'I take God to recorde I was
never to The grete offenser nother ayenste Thy lawis but that I loved
thys noble knyght, sir Launcelot, oute of mesure. And of myselff,

Good Lorde, I had no myght to withstonde the fervent love, where-fore I have my deth!'

And than she called hir fadir, sir Bernarde, and hir brothir, sir Tirry, and hartely she prayd hir fadir that hir brothir myght wryght a lettir 5 lyke as she ded endite, and so hir fadir graunted her. And whan the lettir was wryten, worde by worde lyke as she devised hit, than she prayde hir fadir that she myght be wacched untylle she were [dede]. 'And whyle my body ys hote lat thys lettir be put in my ryght honde, and my honde bounde faste to the letter untyll that I be colde. And 10 lette me be put in a fayre bed with all the rychyste clothys that I have aboute me, and so lat my bed and all my rychyst clothis be ledde with m[e] in a charyat unto the nexte place where the Temmys ys; and there lette me be put within a barget, and but one man with me, such as ye truste, to stirre me thidir; and that my barget be coverde with blacke 15 samyte over and over. And thus, fadir, I beseche you, lat hit be done.'

So hir fadir graunte her faythfully all thynge sholde be done lyke as she had devised. Than hir fadir and hir brothir made grete dole for he⟨r⟩. And whan thys was done anone she dyed.

20 And whan she was dede the corse and the bedde all was lad the nexte way unto the Temmys, and there a man and the corse, and all thynge as she had devised, was put in the Temmys. And so the man stirred the bargett unto Westmynster, and there hit rubbed and rolled too and fro a grete whyle or ony man aspyed hit.

(20) 25 So by fortune kynge Arthure and quene Gwenyver were talkynge togydirs at a wyndow, and so as they loked into the Temmys they aspyed that blacke barget and had mervayle what hit mente. Than the kynge called sir Kay and shewed hit hym.

'Sir,' seyde sir Kay, 'wete you well, there ys som new tydynges.'

30 'Therefore go ye thidir,' seyde the kynge to sir Kay, 'and take with you sir Braundiles and sir Aggr[a]vayne, and brynge me redy worde what ys there.'

Than thes three knyghtes departed and cam to the barget and wente in. And there they founde the fayryst corse lyyng in a ryche bed that 35 ever ⟨y⟩e saw, and a poore man syttynge in the bargettis ende, and no worde wolde [he] speke. So thes three knyghtes returned unto the kynge agayne and tolde hym what they founde.

'That fayre corse woll I se,' seyde the kynge.

And so the kynge toke the quene by the honde and wente thydir.

40 Than the kynge made the barget to be holde faste, and than the kynge and the quene wente in with sertayne knyghtes with them, and there he saw the fayryst woman ly in a ryche bed, coverde unto her myddyll with many rych clothys, and all was of cloth of golde. And she lay as ‹she had smyled.

Than the quene aspyed the lettir in hir ryght hande and tolde the kynge. Than the kynge toke hit and seyde,

'Now am I sure thys lettir woll telle us what she was, and why she ys com hyddir.'

So than the kynge and the quene wente oute of the bargette, and so commaunded a sertayne to wayte uppon the barget. And so whan the kynge was com to hys chambir he called many knyghtes aboute hym and seyde that he wolde wete opynly what was wryten within that lettir. Than the kynge brake hit and made a clerke to rede hit, and thys was the entente of the lettir:

'Moste noble knyght, my lorde sir Launcelot, now hath dethe made us two at debate for youre love. And I was youre lover, that men called the Fayre Maydyn of Astolate. Therefore unto all ladyes I make my mone, yet for my soule ye pray and bury me at the leste, and offir ye my masse-peny: thys ys my laste requeste. And a clene maydyn I dyed, I take God to wytnesse. And pray for my soule, sir Launcelot, as thou arte pereles.'

Thys was all the substaunce in the lettir. And whan hit was rad the kynge, the quene and all the knyghtes wepte for pité of the dolefull complayntes. Than was sir Launcelot sente for, and whan he was com kynge Arthure made the lettir to be rad to hym. And whan sir Launcelot harde hit worde by worde, he seyde,

'My lorde Arthur, wyte you well I am ryght hevy of the deth of thys fayre lady. And God knowyth I was never causar of her deth be my wyllynge, and that woll I reporte me unto her owne brothir that here ys, sir Lavayne. I woll nat say nay,' seyde sir Launcelot, 'but that she was both fayre and good, and much I was beholdyn unto her, but she loved me oute of mesure.'

'Sir,' seyde the quene, 'ye myght have shewed hir som bownté and jantilnes whych myght have preserved hir lyff.'

'Madame,' seyde sir Launcelot, 'she wolde none other wayes be answerde but that she wolde be my wyff othir ellis my paramour, and of thes two I wolde not graunte her. But I proffird her, for her good love that she shewed me, a thousand pound yerely to her and to her ayres, and to wedde ony maner of knyght that she coude fynde beste to love in her harte. For, madame,' seyde sir Launcelot, 'I love nat to be constrayned to love, for love muste only aryse of the harte selff, and nat by none constraynte.'

'That ys trouth, sir,' seyde the kynge, 'and with many knyghtes love ys fre in hymselffe, and never woll be bonde; for where he ys bonden he lowsith hymselff.'

Than seyde the kynge unto sir Launcelot, 'Sir, hit woll be youre worshyp that ye oversé that she be entered worshypfully.'

'Sir,' seyde sir Launcelot, 'that shall be done as I can beste devise.'

And so many knyghtes yode thyder to beholde that fayre dede mayden, and so uppon the morn she was entered rychely. And sir Launcelot offird her masse-peny; and all tho knyghtes of the Table Rounde that were there at that tyme offerde with sir Launcelot. And than the
5 poure m[a]n wente agayne wyth the barget.

Than the quene sent for sir Launcelot and prayde hym of mercy for why that she had ben wrothe with hym causeles.

'Thys ys nat the firste tyme,' seyde sir Launcelot, 'that ye have ben displese with me causeles. But, madame, ever I muste suffir you, but
10 what sorow that I endure, ye take no forse.'

So thys passed on all that wynter, with all maner of huntynge and hawkynge; and justis and turneyes were many betwyxte many grete lordis. And ever in all placis sir Lavayn gate grete worshyp, that he was nobely defamed amonge many knyghtis of the Table Rounde.
(21) 15   Thus hit past on tylle Crystemasse, and than every day there was justis made for a dyamonde: who that justed best shulde have a dyamounde. But sir Launcelot wolde nat juste but if hit were a grete justes cryed; but sir Lavayne justed there all the Crystemasse passyngly well, and was beste praysed, for there were but feaw that ded so well.
20 Wherefore all maner of knyghtes demed that sir Lavayn sholde be made knyght of the Table Rounde at the next feste of Pentecoste.

III. THE GREAT TOURNAMENT

So at afftir Crystemas kynge Arthure lete calle unto hym many knyghtes, and there they avysed togydirs to make a party and a grete turnemente and justis. And the kynge of North Galys seyde to kynge
25 Arthure he wolde have on hys party kyng Angwysh of Irelonde and the Kynge wyth the Hondred Knyghtes and the kynge of Northhumbirlonde and sir Galahalt the Haute Prynce. So thes four kynges and this myghty deuke toke party ayenste kynge Arthure and the knyghtes
30 of the Rounde Table.

And the cry was made that the day off justys shulde be [be]sydes Westemynster, uppon Candylmasse day, whereof many knyghtes were glad and made them redy to be at that justys in the freysshyste maner.

Than quene Gwenyver [sente] for sir Launcelot and seyd thus:
35   'I warne you that ye ryde no more in no justis nor turnementis but that youre kynnesmen may know you, and at thys justis that shall be ye shall have of me a slyeve of golde. And I pray you for my sake to force yourselff there, that men may speke you worshyp. But I charge you, as ye woll have my love, that ye warne your kynnesmen that ye
40 woll beare that day the slyve of golde uppon your helmet.'

'Madame,' seyde sir Launcelot, 'hit shall be done.'

And othir made grete joy of othir. And whan sir Launcelot saw hys tyme he tolde sir Bors that he wolde departe, and no mo wyth hym but sir Lavayne, unto the good ermyte that dwelled in the foreyst of Wyndesore, whos name was sir Brastias. And there he thought to repose hym and to take all the reste that he myght, because he wolde be 5 freysh at that day of justis.

So sir Launcelot and sir Lav[ayne] departed, that no creature wyste where he was becom but the noble men of hys blood. And whan he was com to the ermytayge, wyte you well he had grete chyre. And so dayly sir Launcelot used to go to a welle by the ermytage, and there he 10 wolde ly downe and se the well sprynge and burble, and somtyme he slepte there.

So at that tyme there was a lady that dwelled in that forcyste, and she was a grete hunteresse, and dayly she used to hunte. And ever she bare her bowghe with her, and no men wente never with her, but allwayes 15 women, and they were all shooters and cowde well kylle a dere at the stalke and at the treste. And they dayly beare bowys, arowis, hornys and wood-knyves, and many good doggis they had, bothe for the strenge and for a bate.

So hit happed the lady, the huntresse, had abated her dogge for the 20 bowghe at a barayne hynde, and so [this barayne hynde] toke the flyght over hethys and woodis. And ever thys lady and parte of her women costed the hynde, and checked hit by the noyse of the hounde to have mette with the hynde at som watir. And so hit happened that that hynde cam to the same welle thereas sir Launcelot was by that welle 25 slepynge and slumberynge.

And so the hynde, whan he cam to the welle, for heete she wente to soyle, and there she lay a grete whyle. And the dogge cam aftir and unbecaste aboute, for she had lost the verray parfyte fewte of the hynde. Ryght so cam that lady, the hunteres, that knew by her dogge 30 that the hynde was at the soyle by that welle, and thyder she cam streyte and founde the hynde. And anone as she had spyed hym she put a brode arow in her bowe and shot at the hynde, and so she overshotte the hynde, and so by myssefortune the arow smote sir Launcelot in the thycke of the buttok over the barbys.   35

Whan sir Launcelot felte hym so hurte he whorled up woodly, and saw the lady that had smytten hym. And whan he knew she was a woman he sayde thus:

'Lady, or damesell, whatsomever ye be, in an evyll tyme bare ye thys bowe. The devyll made you a shoter!'   40

'Now, mercy, fayre sir!' seyde the lady, 'I am a jantillwoman that (22) usyth here in thys foreyste huntynge, and God knowyth I saw you nat but as here was a barayne hynde at the soyle in thys welle. And I wente I had done welle, but my hande swarved.'

'Alas,' seyde sir Launcelot, 'ye have myscheved me.'

And so the lady departed. And sir Launcelot, as he myght, pulled oute the arow and leffte the hede stylle in hys buttok, and so he wente waykely unto the ermytayge, evermore bledynge as he wente. And whan sir Lavayne and the ermyte aspyed that sir Launcelot was so sore hurte, wyte you well they were passyng hevy. But sir Lavayne wyst nat how that he was hurte nothir by whom. And than were they wrothe oute of mesure. And so wyth grete payne the ermyte gate oute the arow-hede oute of sir Launcelottis buttoke, and muche of hys bloode he shed; and the wounde was passynge sore and unhappyly smytten, for hit was on such a place that he myght nat sytte in no sadyll.

'A, mercy Jesu!' seyde sir Launcelot, 'I may calle myselff the moste unhappy man that lyvyth, for ever whan I wolde have faynyst worshyp there befallyth me ever som unhappy thynge. Now, so Jesu me helpe,' seyde sir Launcelot, 'and if no man wolde but God, I shall be in the fylde on Candilmas day at the justys, whatsomever falle of hit.'

So all that myght be gotyn to hele sir Launcelot was had. So whan the day was com sir Launcelot lat devise that he was arayed, and sir Lavayne and he and their horsis, as they had ben Sar[a]syns. And so they departed and cam nyghe to the fylde.

So the kynge of North Galys he had an hondred knyghtes with hym, and the kynge of Northehumbirlonde brought with hym an hondred good knyghtes, and kynge Angwysh of Irelonde brought with hym an hondred good knyghtes redy to juste. And sir Galahalte the Haute Prynce brought with hym an hondred good knyghtes, and the Kynge wyth the Hondred Knyghtes brought with hym as many, and all the[s]e were proved good knyghtes.

Than cam in kynge Arthurs party, and in cam wyth hym the kynge of Scottes, and an hondred knyghtes with hym, and kynge Uryence of Goore brought with hym an hondred knyghtes, and kynge Howell of Bretayne he brought wyth hym an hondred knyghtes, and deuke Chalaunce of Claraunce brought with hym an hondred knyghtes. And kynge Arthure hymselff cam into the fylde with two hondred knyghtes, and the moste party were knyghtes of the Rounde Table that were all proved noble men. And there were olde knyghtes set on skaffoldys for to jouge with the quene who ded beste.

(23)　Than they blew unto the fylde. And there the kynge off North Galis encountred wyth the kynge of Scottes, and there the kynge of Scottis had a falle; and the kynge of Irelonde smote downe kynge Uryence, and the kynge of Northhumbirlonde smote downe kynge Howell of Bretayne, and sir Galahalte the Haute Prynce smote downe deuke Chalaunce of Claraunce. And than kynge Arthure was wood wrothe, and ran to the Kynge wyth the Hondred Knyghtes, and so kynge Arthure smote hym downe. And aftir wyth that same speare he smote downe other three knyghtes, and than hys speare brake, and ded passyngly well.

So therewith cam in sir Gawayne and sir Gaherys, sir Aggravayne and sir Mordred, and there everych of them smote downe a knyght and sir Gawayne smote downe four knyghtes. And than there began a grete medlé, for than cam in the knyghtes of sir Launcelottys blood and sir Gareth and sir Palomydes wyth them, and many knyghtes of the Rounde Table; and they began to holde the four kynges and the myghty deuke so harde that they were ny discomfyte. But thys sir Galahalte the Haute Prynce was a noble knyght, and by hys myghty proues of armys he hylde the knyghtes of the Rounde Table strayte.

So all thys doynge saw sir Launcelot, and than he cam into the fylde wyth sir Lavayne with hym, as hit had bene thunder. And than anone sir Bors and the knyghtes of hys bloode aspyed sir Launcelot anone and seyde unto them all,

'I warne you, beware of hym with the slyve of golde uppon hys hede, for he ys hymselff my lorde sir Launcelot.'

And for grete goodnes sir Bors warned sir Gareth.

'Sir, I am well payde,' seyde sir Gareth, 'that I may know hym.'

'But who ys he,' seyde they all, 'that rydith with hym in the same aray?'

'Sir, that ys the good and jantyll knyght sir Lavayne,' seyde sir Bors.

So sir Launcelot encountred with sir Gawayne, and there by force sir Launcelot smote downe sir Gawayne and his horse to the erthe. And so he smote downe sir Aggravayne and sir Gaherys, and also he smote downe sir Mordred, and all this was wyth one speare. Than sir Lavayne mette with sir Palomydes, and aythir mette other so harde and so fersely that both theire horsis felle to the erthe. And than were they horsed agayne.

And than mette sir Launcelot with sir Palomydes, and there sir Palomydes had a falle. And so sir Launcelot, or ever he stynte, and as faste as he myght get spearys, he smote downe thirty knyghtes, and the moste party were knyghtes of the Rounde Table. And ever the knyghtes of hys bloode wythdrew them, and made hem ado in othir placis where sir Launcelot cam nat.

And than kynge Arthure was wrotthe whan he saw sir Launcelot do suche dedis, and than the kynge called unto hym sir Gawayne, sir Gaherys, sir Aggravayne, sir Mordred, sir Kay, sir Gryfflet, sir Lucan de Butlere, sir Bedyvere, sir Palomydes and sir Safyre, hys brothir. And so the kynge wyth thes nine knyghtes made them redy to sette uppon sir Launcelot and uppon sir Lavayne.

And all thys aspyed sir Bors and sir Gareth.

'Now I drede me sore,' seyde sir Bors, 'that my lorde sir Launcelot woll be harde macched.'

'Now, be my hede,' seyde sir Gareth, 'I woll ryde unto my lorde sir Launcelot for to helpe hym whatsomever me betyde. For he ys the same man that made me knyght.'

'Sir, ye shall nat do so,' seyde sir Bors, 'be my counceyle, onles that ye were disgysed.'

'Sir, ye shall se me sone disgysed,' seyde sir Gareth.

And therewithall he had aspyed a Waylshe knyght where he was to repose hym, for he was sore hurte before of sir Gawayne. And unto hym sir Gareth rode and prayde hym of hys knyghthode to lende hym hys shylde for hys.

'I woll well,' seyde the Waylshe knyght.

And whan sir Gareth had hys shylde—the booke seythe h[it] was gryne, wyth a maydyn whych semed in hit—than sir Gareth cam dryvynge unto sir Launcelot all that ever he myght, and seyde,

'Sir knyght, take kepe to thyselff, for yondir commyth kynge Arthur with nine noble knyghtes wyth hym, to put you to a rebuke. And so I am com to beare you felyshyp for the olde love ye have shewed unto me.'

'Grauntemercy,' seyde sir Launcelot.

'But, sir,' seyde sir Gareth, 'encountir ye with sir Gawayne, and I shall encountir with sir Palomydes, and lat sir Lavayne macche with the noble kynge Arthur. And whan we have delyverde them lat us three holde us sadly togydirs.'

So than cam in kynge Arthure wyth hys nine knyghtes with hym, and sir Launcelot encountred with sir Gawayne and gaff hym suche a buffette that the arson of hys sadyll braste, and sir Gawayne felle to the erthe. Than sir Gareth encountred with sir Palomydes, and he gaff hym such a buffet that bothe hys horse and he daysshed to the erthe. Than encountred kynge Arthure wyth sir Lavayne, and there aythir of them smote other to the erthe, horse and all, that they lay bothe a grete whyle.

Than sir Launcelot smote downe sir Aggravayne and sir Gaherys and sir Mordred; and sir Gareth smote downe sir Kay, sir Safir and sir Gryfflet.

And than sir Lavayne was horsed agayne, and he smote downe sir Lucan de Butlere and sir Bedyvere, and than there began grete thrange of good knyghtes. Than sir Launcelot hurled here and there, and raced and pulled of helmys, that at that tyme there myght none sytte hym a buffette with speare nothir with swerde.

And sir Gareth ded such dedys of armys that all men mervayled what knyght he was with the gryne shylde, for he smote downe that day and pulled downe mo than thirty knyghtes. And, as the Freynshe booke sayth, sir Launcelot mervayled, whan he behylde sir Gareth do such dedis, what knyght he myght be. And sir Lavayne smote and pulled downe mo than twenty knyghtes. And yet, for all thys, sir

Launcelot knew nat sir Gareth; for and sir Trystram de Lyones other sir Lamorak de Galys had ben on lyve, sir Launcelot wolde have demed he had bene one of them twayne.

So ever as sir Launcelot, sir Gareth and sir Lavayne fought on the tone syde, sir Bors, sir Ector de Marys, sir Lyonell, sir Bleoberys, sir 5 Galyhud, sir Galyhodyn and sir Pelleas and many mo other of kynge Banys blood faught uppon another party and hylde the Kynge wyth the Hondred Knyghtes and the kynge of Northhumbirlonde ryght strayte.

So thys turnemente and justis dured longe tylle hit was nere nyght, (24) for the knyghtes of the Rounde Table releved ever unto kynge Ar- 10 thure; for the kyng was wrothe oute of mesure that he and hys knyghtes myght nat prevayle that day. Than sayde sir Gawayne to the kynge,

'Sir, I mervayle where ar all thys day sir Bors de Ganys and hys fely-shyp of sir Launcelottis blood, that of all thys day they be nat aboute you. And therefore I deme hit ys for som cause,' seyde sir Gawayne. 15

'Be my hede,' seyde sir Kay, 'sir Bors ys yondir all thys day uppon the ryght honde of thys fylde, and there he and his blood dothe more worshypfully than we do.'

'Hit may well be,' seyde sir Gawayne, 'but I drede me ever of gyle. For o[n] payne of my lyff, that same knyght with the rede slyve of 20 golde ys hymselff sir Launcelot, for I se well by hys rydynge and by hys greate strokis. And the othir knyght in the same colowres ys the good yonge knyght sir Lavayne, and that knyght with the grene shylde ys my brothir sir Gareth, and yet he hath disgysed hymselff, for no man shall make hym be ayenste sir Launcelot, bycause he made hym knyght.' 25

'By my hede,' seyde kynge Arthure, 'neveaw, I belyeve you. And therefore now telle me what ys youre beste counceyle.'

'Sir,' seyde sir Gawayne, 'my counceile ys to blow unto lodgynge. For and he be sir Launcelot du Lake and my brothir sir Gareth wyth hym, wyth the helpe of that goode yonge knyght, sir Lavayne, truste me 30 truly, hit woll be no boote to stryve wyth them but if we sholde falle ten or twelve uppon one knyght, and that were no worshyp, but shame.'

'Ye say trouthe,' seyde the kynge, 'hit were shame for us, so many as we be, to sette uppon them ony more. For wyte you well,' seyde kynge Arthure, 'they be three good knyghtes, and namely that knyght 35 with the slyve of golde.'

And anone they blew unto lodgyng, but furthwithall kynge Arthure lete sende unto the four kyngis and to the myghty deuke and prayde hem that the knyght with the slyve of golde departe nat frome them but that the kynge may speke with hym. Than furthwithall kynge 40 Arthur alyght and unarmed hym and toke a lytyll hakeney and rode after sir Launcelot, for ever he had a spy uppon hym. And so he founde hym amonge the four kyngis and the deuke, and there the kynge prayde hem all unto suppere, and they seyde they wolde with good wyll. And whan they were unarmed kynge Arthure knew sir Launcelot, sir Gareth and sir Lavayne.

'A, sir Launcelot,' seyde kynge Arthure, 'thys day ye have heted me and my knyghtes!'

5 And so they yode unto kynge Arthurs lodgynge all togydir, and there was a grete feste and grete revell. And the pryce was yevyn unto sir Launcelot, for by herowdys they named hym that he had smytten downe fifty knyghtys, and sir Gareth fyve-and-thirty knyghtes, and sir Lavayne four-and-twenty.

10 Than sir Launcelot tolde the kynge and the quene how the lady hunteras shotte hym in the foreyste of Wyndesore in the buttok wyth a brode arow, and how the wounde was at that tyme six inchys depe and inlyke longe.

Also kynge Arthure blamed sir Gareth because he leffte hys fely-
15 shyp and hylde with sir Launcelot.

'My lorde,' seyde sir Garethe, 'he made me knyght, and whan I saw hym so hard bestad, methought hit was my worshyp to helpe hym. For I saw hym do so muche dedis of armys, and so many noble knyghtes ayenste hym, that whan I undirstode that he was sir Launcelot du Lake
20 I shamed to se so many good knyghtes ayenste hym alone.'

'Now, truly,' seyde kynge Arthur unto sir Gareth, 'ye say well, and worshypfully have ye done, and to youreself grete worshyp. And all the dayes of my lyff,' seyde kynge Arthure unto sir Gareth, 'wyte you well I shall love you and truste you the more bettir. For ever hit ys,'
25 seyde kynge Arthure, 'a worshypfull knyghtes dede to help and succoure another worshypfull knyght whan he seeth hym in daungere. For ever a worshypfull man woll be lothe to se a worshypfull man shamed, and he that ys of no worshyp and medelyth with cowardise never shall he shew jantilnes nor no maner of goodnes where he seeth a man in
30 daungere, for than woll a cowarde never shew mercy. And allwayes a good man woll do ever to another man as he wolde be done to hymself.'

So than there were made grete festis unto kyngis and deukes, and revell, game, and play, and all maner of nobeles was used. And he that was curteyse, trew, and faythefull to hys frynde was that tyme
35 cherysshed.

IV. THE KNIGHT OF THE CART

(25) AND thus hit passed on frome Candylmas untyll [after] Ester, that the moneth of May was com, whan every lusty harte begynnyth to blossom and to burgyne. For, lyke as trees and erbys burgenyth and florysshyth
40 in May, in lyke wyse every lusty harte that ys ony maner of lover spryngith, burgenyth, buddyth, and florysshyth in lusty dedis. For hit

gyvyth unto all lovers corrayge, that lusty moneth of May, in somthynge to constrayne hym to som maner of thynge more in that moneth
than in ony other monethe, for dyverce causys: for than all erbys and
treys renewyth a man and woman, and in lyke wyse lovers callyth to
their mynde olde jantylnes and olde servyse, and many kynde dedes 5
that was forgotyn by neclygence.

For, lyke as wynter rasure dothe allway arace and deface grene sum-
mer, so faryth hit by unstable love in man and woman, for in many
persones there ys no stabylité: for [w]e may se all day, for a lytyll
blaste of wyntres rasure, anone we shall deface and lay aparte trew 10
love, for lytyll or nowght, that coste muche thynge. Thys ys no wysedome nother no stabylité, but hit ys fyeblenes of nature and grete
disworshyp, whosomever usyth thys.

Therefore, lyke as May moneth flowryth and floryshyth in every
mannes gardyne, so in lyke wyse lat every man of worshyp florysh hys 15
herte in thys worlde: firste unto God, and nexte unto the joy of them
that he promysed hys feythe unto; for there was never worshypfull
man nor worshypfull woman but they loved one bettir than anothir;
and worshyp in armys may never be foyled. But firste reserve the honoure to God, and secundely thy quarell muste com of thy lady. And 20
such love I calle vertuouse love.

But nowadayes men can nat love sevennyght but they muste have all
their desyres. That love may nat endure by reson, for where they bethe
sone accorded and hasty, heete sone keelyth. And ryght so faryth the
love nowadayes, sone hote sone colde. Thys ys no stabylyté. But the 25
olde love was nat so. For men and women coude love togydirs seven
yerys, and no lycoures lustis was betwyxte them, and than was love
trouthe and faythefulnes. And so in lyke wyse was used such love in
kynge Arthurs dayes.

Wherefore I lykken love nowadayes unto sommer and wynter: for, 30
lyke as the tone ys colde and the othir ys hote, so faryth love nowadayes. And therefore all ye that be lovers, calle unto youre remembraunce the monethe of May, lyke as ded quene Gwenyver, for whom
I make here a lytyll mencion, that whyle she lyved she was a trew lover,
and therefor she had a good ende.   35

So hit befelle in the moneth of May, quene Gwenyver called unto XIX (1)
her ten knyghtes of the Table Rounde, and she gaff them warnynge
that early uppon the morn she wolde ryde on-maynge into woodis and
fyldis besydes Westemynster:

'And I warne you that there be none of you but he be well horsed, 40
and that ye all be clothed all in gryne, othir in sylke othir in clothe.
And I shall brynge with me ten ladyes, and every knyght shall have a
lady be hym. And every knyght shall have a squyar and two yomen,
and I woll that all be well horsed.'

So they made hem redy in the freysshyst maner, and thes were the namys of the knyghtes: sir Kay le Senesciall, sir Aggravayne, sir Braundyles, sir Sagramour le Desyrous, sir Dodynas le Savayge, sir Ozanna le Cure Hardy, sir Ladynas of the Foreyst Savayge, sir Per-
5 saunte of Inde, sir Ironsyde that was called the Knyght of the Rede Laundes, and sir Pelleas the Lovear. And thes ten knyghtes made them redy in the freysshyste maner to ryde wyth the quyne.

And so uppon the morne or hit were day, in a May mornynge, they toke their horsys wyth the quene and rode on-mayinge in wodis and
10 medowis as hit pleased hem, in grete joy and delytes. For the quene had caste to have bene agayne with kynge Arthur at the furthest by ten of the clok, and so was that tyme her purpose.

Than there was a knyght whych hyght sir Mellyagaunce, and he was sonne unto kynge Bagdemagus, and this knyght had that tyme a
15 castell of the gyffte of kynge Arthure within seven myle of Westemyn-ster. And thys knyght sir Mellyagaunce loved passyngly well quene Gwenyver, and so had he done longe and many yerys. And the booke seyth he had lay[n] in awayte for to stele away the quene, but evermore he forbare for bycause of sir Launcelot; for in no wyse he wolde
20 meddyll with the quene and sir Launcelot were in her company othir ellys and he were nerehonde.

And that tyme was such a custom that the quene rode never wythoute a grete felyshyp of men of armys aboute her. And they were many good knyghtes, and the moste party were yonge men that wolde have
25 worshyp, and they were called the Quenys Knyghtes. And never in no batayle, turnement nother justys they bare none of hem no maner of knowlecchynge of their owne armys but playne whyght shyldis, and thereby they were called the Quenys Knyghtes. And whan hit happed ony of them to be of grete worshyp by hys noble dedis, than at the
30 nexte feste of Pentecoste, gyff there were ony slayne or dede (as there was none yere that there fayled but there were som dede), than was there chosyn in hys stede that was dede the moste men of worshyp that were called the Quenys Knyghtes. And thus they cam up firste or they were renowmed men of worshyp, both sir Launcelot and all the
35 reme[n]aunte of them.

But thys knyght sir Mellyagaunce had aspyed the quene well and her purpose, and how sir Launcelot was nat wyth her, and how she had no men of armys with her but the ten noble knyghtis all rayed in grene for maiynge. Than he purveyde hym a twenty men of armys
40 and an hondred archars for to destresse the quene and her knyghtes; for he thought that tyme was beste seson to take the quene.

(2)   So as [the quene] was oute on-mayynge wyth all her knyghtes whych were bedaysshed wyth erbis, mossis and floures in the freysshyste maner, ryght so there cam oute of a wood sir Mellyagaunte with an

eyght score men, all harneyst as they shulde fyght in a batayle of areste, and bade the quene and her knyghtis abyde, for magré their hedis they shulde abyde.

'Traytoure knyght,' seyd quene Gwenyver, 'what caste thou to do? Wolt thou shame thyselff? Bethynke the how thou arte a kyngis sonne 5 and a knyght of the Table Rounde, and thou thus to be aboute to dishonoure the noble kyng that made the knyght! Thou shamyst all knyghthode and thyselffe and me. And I lat the wyte thou shalt never shame me, for I had levir kut myne owne throte in twayne rather than thou sholde dishonoure me!' 10

'As for all thys langayge,' seyde sir Mellyagaunte, 'be as hit be may. For wyte you well, madame, I have loved you many a yere, and never ar now cowde I gete you at such avayle. And therefore I woll take you as I fynde you.'

Than spake all the ten noble knyghtes at onys and seyde, 15

'Sir Mellyagaunte, wyte thou well thou ar aboute to jouparté thy worshyp to dishonoure, and also ye caste to jouparté oure persones. Howbehit we be unarmed and ye have us at a grete avauntayge—for hit semyth by you that ye have layde wacche uppon us—but rather than ye shulde put the quene to a shame and us all, we had as lyff to departe 20 frome owre lyvys, for and we othyrwayes ded we were shamed for ever.'

Than seyde sir Mellyagaunt, 'Dresse you as well as ye can, and kepe the quene!'

Than the ten knyghtis of the Rounde Table drew their swerdis, and thes othir lat ren at them wyth their spearys. And the ten knyghtes 25 manly abode them and smote away their spearys, that no speare ded them no harme. Than they laysshed togydirs wyt[h] swerdis, and anone sir Kay, sir Sagramoure, sir Aggravayne, sir Dodynas, sir Ladynas and sir Ozanna were smytten to the erthe with grymly woundis. Than sir Braundiles and sir Persaunte, sir Ironsyde and sir Pelleas faught 30 longe, and they were sore wounded, for thes ten knyghtes, or ever they were leyde to the grounde, slew fourty men of the boldyste and the beste of them.

So whan the quene saw her knyghtes thus dolefully wounded and nedys muste be slayne at the laste, than for verry pyté and sorow she 35 cryed and seyde,

'Sir Mellyagaunte, sle nat my noble knyghtes and I woll go with the uppon thys covenaunte: that thou save them and suffir hem no more to be hurte, wyth thys that they be lad with me wheresomever thou ledyst me. For I woll rather sle myselff than I woll go wyth the, onles 40 that thes noble knyghtes may be in my presence.'

'Madame,' seyde sir Mellyagaunt, 'for your sake they shall be lad wyth you into myne owne castell, with that ye woll be reuled and ryde with me.'

Than the quene prayde the four knyghtes to leve their fyghtynge, and she and they wolde nat departe.

'Madame,' seyde sir Pelleas, 'we woll do as ye do, for as for me, I take no force of my lyff nor deth.'

5 For, as the Freynshe booke seyth, sir Pelleas gaff such buffettis there that none armoure myght holde hym.

(3) Than by the quenys commaundemente they leffte batayle and dressed the wounded knyghtes on horsebak, som syttyng and som overtwarte their horsis, that hit was pité to beholde. And than sir Mellyagaunt

10 charged the quene and all her knyghtes that none of hir felyshyp shulde departe frome her, for full sore he drad sir Launcelot du Lake, laste he shulde have ony knowlecchynge. And all this aspyed the quene, and pryvaly she called unto her a chylde of her chambir whych was swyfftely horsed of a grete avauntayge.

15 'Now go thou,' seyde she, 'whan thou seyst thy tyme, and beare thys rynge unto sir Launcelot du Laake, and pray hym as he lovythe me that he wo[ll] se me and rescow me, if ever he woll have joy of me. And spare nat thy horse,' seyde the quyene, 'nother for watir nother for londe.'

20 So thys chyld aspyed hys tyme, and lyghtly he toke hys horse with spurres and departed as faste as he myght. And wan sir Mellyagaunte saw hym so fle, he undirstood that hit was by the quyenys commaundemente for to warne sir Launcelot. Than they that were beste horsed chaced hym and shotte at hym, but frome hem all the chylde wente

25 delyverly.

And than sir Mellyagaunte sayde unto the quyne,

'Madame, ye ar aboute to betray me, but I shall ordayne for sir Launcelot that he shall nat com lyghtly at you.'

And than he rode wyth her and all the felyshyp in all the haste that

30 they myght. And so by the way sir Mellyagaunte layde in buyshemente of the beste archars that he [myghte gete in his countré to the numbre] of a thirty to awayte uppon sir Launcelot, chargynge them that yf they saw suche a maner a knyght com by the way uppon a whyght horse, 'that in ony wyse ye sle hys horse, but in no maner have ye ado wyth

35 hym bodyly, for he ys over hardé to be overcom'. So thys was done, and they were com to hys castell; but in no wyse the quene wolde never lette none of the ten knyghtes and her ladyes oute of her syght, but allwayes they were in her presence. For the booke sayth sir Mellyagaunte durste make no mastryes for drede of sir Launcelot, insomuche

40 he demed that he had warnynge.

So whan the chylde was departed fro the felyshyp of sir Mellyagaunte, wythin a whyle [he] cam to Westemynster, and anone he founde sir Launcelot. And whan he had tolde hys messayge and delyverde hym the quenys rynge,

'Alas!' seyde sir Launcelot, 'now am I shamed for ever, onles that I may rescow that noble lady frome dishonour!' Than egirly he asked hys armys.

And ever the chylde tolde sir Launcelot how the ten knyghtes faught mervaylously, and how sir Pelleas, sir Ironsyde, sir Braundyles 5 and sir Persaunte of Inde fought strongely, but namely sir Pelleas, there myght none harneys holde hym; and how they all faught tylle they were layde to the [erthe], and how the quene made apoyntemente for to save their lyvys and to go wyth sir Mellyagaunte.

'Alas!' seyde sir Launcelot, 'that moste noble lady, that she shulde 10 be so destroyed! I had lever,' seyde sir Launcelot, 'than all Fraunce that I had bene there well armed.'

So whan sir Launcelot was armed and uppon hys horse he prayde the chylde of the quynys chambir to warne sir Lavayne how suddeynly he was departed and for what cause. 'And pray hym, as he lovyth me, 15 that he woll hyghe hym aftir me, and that he stynte nat untyll he com to the castell where sir Mellyagaunt abydith, for there,' seyde sir Launcelot, 'he shall hyre of me, and I be a man lyvynge!'

Than sir Launcelot rode as faste as he myght, and the booke seyth he (4) toke the watir at Westmynster Brydge and made hys horse swymme 20 over the Temmys unto Lambyth. And so within a whyle he cam to the same place thereas the ten noble knyghtes fought with sir Mellyagaunte.

And than sir Launcelot folowed the trak untyll that he cam to a woode, and there was a strayte way, and there the thirty archers bade 25 sir Launcelot 'turne agayne and folow no longer that trak'.

'What commaundementis have ye,' seyde sir Launcelot, 'to cause me, that am a knyght of the Rounde Table, to leve my ryght way?'

'Thys wayes shalt thou leve, othir ellis thou shalte go hit on thy foote, for wyte thou well thy horse shall be slayne.' 30

'That ys lytyll maystry,' seyde sir Launcelot, 'to sle myne horse! But as for myselff, whan my horse ys slayne I gyff ryght nought of you, nat and ye were fyve hundred mo!'

So than they shotte sir Launcelottis horse and smote hym with many arowys. And than sir Launcelot avoyded hys horse and wente on 35 foote, but there were so many dychys and hedgys betwyxte hem and hym that he myght nat meddyll with none of hem.

'Alas, for shame!' seyde sir Launcelot, 'that ever one knyght shulde betray anothir knyght! But hyt ys an oldeseyde saw: "A good man ys never in daungere but whan he ys in the daungere of a cowhard." ' 40

Than sir Launcelot walked on a whyle, and was sore acombird of hys armoure, hys shylde, and hys speare. Wyte you well he was full sore anoyed! And full lothe he was for to leve onythynge that longed unto hym, for he drad sore the treson of sir Mellyagaunce.

Than by fortune there cam [by hym] a charyote that cam thydir to feche wood.

'Say me, carter,' seyde sir Launcelot, 'what shall I gyff the to suffir me to lepe into thy charyote, and that thou wolte brynge me unto a castell within thys two myle?'

'Thou shalt nat entir into thys caryot,' seyde the carter, 'for I am sente for to fecche wood.'

'Unto whom?' seyde sir Launcelot.

'Unto my lorde, sir Mellyagaunce,' seyde the carter.

'And with hym wolde I speke,' seyde sir Launcelot.

'Thou shalt nat go with me!' seyde the carter.

Whan sir Launcelot lepe to hym and gaff hym backwarde with hys gauntelet a reremayne, that he felle to the erthe starke dede, than the tothir carter, hys felow, was aferde and wente to have gone the same way. And than he sayde,

'Fayre lorde, sauff my lyff, and I shall brynge you where ye woll.'

'Than I charge the,' seyde sir Launcelot, 'that thou dryve me and thys charyote unto sir Mellyagaunce yate.'

'Than lepe ye up into the charyotte,' seyde the carter, 'and ye shall be there anone.'

So the carter drove on a grete walop, and sir Launcelottes hors folowed the charyot, with mo than forty arowys in hym.

And more than an owre and an halff quene Gwenyver was a-waytyng in a bay-wyndow. Than one of hir ladyes aspyed an armed knyght stondyng in a charyote.

'A! se, madam,' seyde the lady, 'where rydys in a charyot a goodly armed knyght, and we suppose he rydyth unto hangynge.'

'Where?' seyde the quene.

Than she aspyed by hys shylde that hit was sir Launcelot, and than was she ware where cam hys horse after the charyotte, and ever he trode hys guttis and hys paunche undir hys feete.

'Alas!' seyde the quene, 'now I may preve and se that well ys that creature that hath a trusty frynde. A ha!' seyde quene Gwenyver, 'I se well that ye were harde bestad whan ye ryde in a charyote.' And than she rebuked that lady that lykened sir Launcelot to ryde in a charyote to hangynge: 'Forsothe hit was fowle-mowthed,' seyde the quene, 'and evyll lykened, so for to lyken the moste noble knyght of the worlde unto such a shamefull dethe. A! Jesu deffende hym and kepe hym,' sayde the quene, 'frome all myschevous ende!'

So by thys was sir Launcelot comyn to the gatis of that castell, and there he descended down and cryed, that all the castell myght rynge:

'Where arte thou, thou false traytoure sir Mellyagaunte, and knyght of the Table Rownde? Com forth, thou traytour knyght, thou and all

thy felyshyp with the, for here I am, sir Launcelot du Lake, that shall
fyght with you all!'

And therewithall he bare the gate wyde opyn uppon the porter, and
smote hym undir the ere wyth hys gauntelet, that hys nekke braste in
two pecis. Whan sir Mellyagaunce harde that sir Launcelot was comyn   5 (5)
he ranne unto the quene and felle uppon hys kne and seyde,

'Mercy, madame, for now I putte me holé in you[r] good grace.'

'What ayles you now?' seyde quene Gwenyver. 'Pardé, I myght
well wete that some good knyght wolde revenge me, thoughe my
lorde kynge Arthure knew nat of thys your worke.'   10

'A! madame,' seyde sir Mellyagaunte, 'all thys that ys amysse on my
party shall be amended ryght as youreselff woll devyse, and holy I put
me in youre grace.'

'What wolde ye that I ded?' seyde the quene.

'Madame, I wolde no more,' seyde sir Mellyagaunt, 'but that ye   15
wolde take all in youre owne hondys, and that ye woll rule my lorde
sir Launcelot. And such chere as may be made hym in thys poure
castell ye and he shall have untyll to-morn, and than may ye and all
they returne ayen unto Westmynster. And my body and all that I have
I shall put in youre rule.'   20

'Ye sey well,' seyde the quene, 'and bettir ys pees than evermore
warre, and the lesse noyse the more ys my worshyp.'

Than the quene and hir ladyes wente downe unto sir Launcelot that
stood wood wrothe oute of mesure [in the inner courte] to abyde
batayle, and ever he seyde,   25

'Thou traytour knyght, com forthe!'

Than the quene cam unto hym and seyde,

'Sir Launcelot, why be ye so amoved?'

'A! madame,' seyde sir Launcelot, 'why aske ye me that questyon?
For mesemyth ye oughte to be more wrotther than I am, for ye have   30
the hurte and the dishonour. For wyte you well, madame, my hurte ys
but lytyll in regard for the sleyng of a marys sonne, but the despite
grevyth me much more than all my hurte.'

'Truly,' seyde the quene, 'ye say trouthe, but hartely I thanke you,'
seyde the quene. 'But ye muste com in with me pesyblé, for all thynge   35
ys put in myne honde, and all that ys amysse shall be amended, for the
knyght full sore repentys hym of thys mysadventure that ys befallyn
hym.'

'Madame,' seyde sir Launcelot, 'syth hit ys so that ye be accorded
with hym, as for me I may nat agaynesay hit, howbehit sir Mellya-   40
gaunte hath done full shamefully to me and cowardly. And, madame,'
seyde sir Launcelot, 'and I had wyste that ye wolde have bene so
lyghtly accorded with hym I wolde nat a made such haste unto you.'

'Why say ye so?' seyde the quene. 'Do ye forthynke youreselff of' youre good dedis? Wyte you well,' seyde the quene, 'I accorded never with hym for no favoure nor love that I had unto hym, but of every shamefull noyse of wysedom to lay adoune.'

'Madame,' seyde sir Launcelot, 'ye undirstonde full well I was never
5 wyllynge nor glad of shamefull sclaundir nor noyse. And there ys nother kynge, quene ne knyght that beryth the lyffe, excepte my lorde kynge Arthur and you, madame, that shulde lette me but I shulde make sir Mellyagaunte harte full colde or ever I departed frome hense.'

'That wote I well,' seyde the quene, 'but what woll ye more? Ye
10 shall have all thynge ruled as ye lyste to have hit.'

'Madame,' seyde sir Launcelot, 'so ye be pleased! As for my parte, ye shall sone please me.'

Ryght so the quene toke sir Launcelot by the bare honde, for he had put of hys gauntelot, and so she wente wyth hym tyll her chambir, and
15 than she commaunded hym to be unarmed.

And than sir Launcelot asked the quene where were hir ten knyghtes that were wounded with her. Than she shewed them unto hym, and there they made grete joy of the commyng of sir Launcelot, and he made grete sorow of their hurtis. And there sir Launcelot tolde them
20 how cowardly and traytourly he sette archers to sle hys horse, and how he was fayne to put hymselff in a charyotte. And thus they complayned everyche to other, and full fayne they wolde have ben revenged, but they kepte the pees bycause of the quene.

Than, as the Freynsh booke saythe, sir Launcelot was called many
25 dayes aftyr 'le Shyvalere de Charyotte', and so he ded many dedys and grete adventures.

And so we leve of here of la Shyvalere le Charyote, and turne we to thys tale.

So sir Launcelot had grete chere with the quene. And than he made
30 a promyse with the quene that the same nyght he sholde com to a wyndow outewarde towarde a gardyne, and that wyndow was barred with iron, and there sir Launcelot promysed to mete her whan all folkes were on slepe.

So than cam sir Lavayne dryvynge to the gatis, seyyng, 'Where ys
35 my lorde sir Launcelot?' And anone he was sente fore, and whan sir Lavayne saw sir Launcelot, he seyde, 'A, my lorde! I founde howe ye were harde bestadde, for I have founde your hors that ys slayne with arowys.'

'As for that,' seyde sir Launcelot, 'I praye you, sir Lavayne, speke ye of
40 othir maters and lat thys passe, and ryght hit anothir tyme and we may.'
(6) Than the knyghtes that were hurt were serched, and soffte salves were layde to their woundis, and so hit passed on tyll souper-tyme. And all the chere that myght be made them there was done unto the

quene and all her knyghtes. And whan season was they wente unto their chambirs, but in no wyse the quene wolde nat suffir her wounded knyghtes to be fro her, but that they were layde inwyth draughtes by hir chambir, uppon beddis and paylattes, that she myght herselff se unto them that they wanted nothynge.　　　　5

So whan sir Launcelot was in hys chambir whych was assygned unto hym, he called unto hym sir Lavayne and tolde hym that nyght he must speke with hys lady, quene Gwenyver.

'Sir,' seyde sir Lavayne, 'let me go with you, and hyt please you, for I drede me sore of [the] treson of sir Mellyagaunte.'　　　　10

'Nay,' seyde sir Launcelot, 'I thanke you, but I woll have nobody wyth me.'

Than sir Launcelot toke hys swerde in hys honde and prevaly wente to the place where he had spyed a ladder toforehande, and that he toke undir hys arme, and bare hit thorow the gardyne and sette hit up to　15 the wyndow. And anone the quene was there redy to mete hym.

And than they made their complayntes to othir of many dyverce thyngis, and than sir Launcelot wysshed that he myght have comyn in to her.

'Wyte you well,' seyde the quene, 'I wolde as fayne as ye that ye　20 myght com in to me.'

'Wolde ye so, madame,' seyde sir Launcelot, 'wyth youre harte that I were with you?'

'Ye, truly,' seyde the quene.

'Than shall I prove my myght,' seyde sir Launcelot, 'for youre love.'　25

And than he sette hys hondis uppon the barrys of iron and pulled at them with suche a myght that he braste hem clene oute of the stone wallys. And therewithall one of the barres of iron kutte the brawne of hys hondys thorowoute to the bone. And than he lepe into the chambir to the quene.　　　　30

'Make ye no noyse,' seyde the quene, 'for my wounded knyghtes lye here fast by me.'

So, to passe uppon thys tale, sir Launcelot wente to bedde with the quene and toke no force of hys hurte honde, but toke hys plesaunce and hys lykynge untyll hit was the dawnyng of the day; for wyte you　35 well he slept nat, but wacched. And whan he saw hys tyme that he myght tary no lenger, he toke hys leve and departed at the wyndowe, and put hit togydir as well as he myght agayne, and so departed untyll hys owne chambir. And there he tolde sir Lavayne how that he was hurte. Than sir Lavayne dressed hys honde [and staunched] hit and　40 put uppon hit a glove, that hit sholde nat be aspyed. And so they lay longe a-bed in the mornynge tylle hit was nine of the clok.

Than sir Mellyagaunte wente to the quenys chambir and founde her ladyes there redy clothed.

'A! Jesu mercy,' seyde sir Mellyagaunte, 'what ayles you, madame, that ye slepe thys longe?'

And therewithall he opened the curtayn for to beholde her. And than was he ware where she lay, and all the hede-sheete, pylow, and
5 over-shyte was all bebled of the bloode of sir Launcelot and of hys hurte honde. Whan sir Mellyagaunt aspyed that blood, than he demed in her that she was false to the kynge and that som of the wounded knyghtes had lyene by her all that nyght.

'A ha, madame!' seyde sir Mellyagaunte, 'now I have founde you a
10 false traytouras unto my lorde Arthur, for now I preve well hit was nat for nought that ye layde thes wounded knyghtis within the bondys of youre chambir. Therefore I calle you of tresoun afore my lorde kynge Arthure. And now I have proved you, madame, wyth a shamefull dede; and that they bene all false, or som of them, I woll make hit good, for
15 a wounded knyght thys nyght hath layne by you.'

'That ys false,' seyde the quene, 'that I woll report me unto them.'

But whan the ten knyghtes harde of sir Mellyagaunteys wordys, than they spake all at onys and seyd,

'Sir Mellyagaunte, thou falsely belyest my lady, the quene, and that
20 we woll make good uppon the, any of us. Now chose whych thou lyste of us, whan we ar hole of the woundes thou gavyst us.'

'Ye shall nat! Away with youre proude langayge! For here ye may all se that a wounded knyght thys nyght hath layne by the quene.'

25 Than they all loked and were sore ashamed whan they saw that bloode. And wyte you well sir Mellyagaunte was passyng glad that he had the quene at suche avauntayge, for he demed by that to hyde hys owne treson.

And so in thys rumour com in sir Launcelot and fownde them at
30 a grete affray.

(7) 'What aray ys thys?' seyde sir Launcelot.

Than sir Mellyagaunce tolde hem what he had founde, and so he shewed hym the quenys bed.

'Now truly,' seyde sir Launcelot, 'ye ded nat youre parte nor
35 knyghtly, to touche a quenys bede whyle hit was drawyn and she lyyng therein. And I daresay,' seyde syr Launcelot, 'my lorde kynge Arthur hymselff wolde nat have displayed hir curtaynes, and she beyng within her bed, onles that hit had pleased hym to have layne hym downe by her. And therefore, sir Mellyagaunce, ye have done unworshypfully
40 and shamefully to youreselff.'

'Sir, I wote nat what ye meane,' seyde sir Mellyagaunce, 'but well I am sure there hath one of hir hurte knyghtes layne with her thys nyght. And that woll I prove with myne hondys, that she ys a traytoures unto my lorde kynge Arthur.'

'Beware what ye do,' seyde sir Launcelot, 'for and ye say so and wyll preve hit, hit woll be takyn at youre handys.'

'My lorde sir Launcelot,' seyde sir Mellyagaunce, 'I rede you beware what ye do; for thoughe ye ar never so good a knyght, as I wote well ye ar renowmed the beste knyght of the wor[l]de, yet shulde ye be avysed to do batayle in a wronge quarell, for God woll have a stroke in every batayle.' 5

'As for that,' seyde sir Launcelot, 'God ys to be drad! But as to that I say nay playnly, that thys nyght there lay none of thes ten knyghtes wounded with my lady, quene Gwenyver, and that woll I prove with myne hondys that ye say untrewly in that. Now, what sey ye?' seyde sir Launcelot. 10

'Thus I say,' seyde sir Mellyagaunce, 'here ys my glove that she ys a traytoures unto my lorde kynge Arthur, and that thys nyght one of the wounded knyghtes lay wyth her.'

'Well, sir, and I resceyve youre glove,' seyde sir Launcelot. 15

And anone they were sealed with their synattes, and delyverde unto the ten knyghtes.

'At what day shall we do batayle togydirs?' seyde sir Launcelot.

'Thys day eyght dayes,' seyde sir Mellyagaunce, 'in the fylde besydys Westemynster.' 20

'I am agreed,' seyde sir Launcelot.

'But now,' seyde sir Mellyagaunce, 'sytthyn hit ys so that we muste nedys fyght togydirs, I pray you as ye betthe a noble knyght, awayte me wyth no treson nother no vylany the meanewhyle, nother none for you.' 25

'So God me helpe,' seyde sir Launcelot, 'ye shall ryght well wyte that I was never of no such condysions. For I reporte me to all knyghtes that ever have knowyn me, I fared never wyth no treson, nother I loved never the felyshyp of hym that fared with treson.' 30

'Than lat us go unto dyner,' seyde sir Mellyagaunce, 'and aftir dyner the quene and ye may ryde all unto Westemynster.'

'I woll well,' seyde sir Launcelot.

Than sir Mellyagaunce seyde unto sir Launcelot, 'Sir, pleasyth you to se esturys of thys castell?' 35

'With a good wyll,' seyde sir Launcelot.

And than they wente togydir frome chambir to chambir, for sir Launcelot drad no perellis: for ever a man of worshyp and of proues dredis but lytyll of perels, for they wene that every man be as they bene. But ever he that faryth with treson puttyth oftyn a trew man in grete daungere. And so hit befelle uppon sir Launcelot that no perell dred: as he wente with sir Mellyagaunce he trade on a trappe, and the burde rolled, and there sir Launcelot felle downe more than ten fadom into a cave full off strawe. 40

And than sir Mellyagaunce departed and made no fare, no more than he that wyste nat where he was. And whan sir Launcelot was thus myssed they mervayled where he was becomyn, and than the quene and many of them demed that he was departed, as he was wonte to do, 5 suddaynly. For sir Mellyagaunce made suddaynly to put on syde sir Lavaynes horse, that they myght all undirstonde that sir Launcelot were departed suddaynly.

So tha⟨n⟩ hit passed on tyll afftir dyner, and than sir Lavayne wolde nat stynte untyll that he had horse-lytters for the wounded knyghtes, 10 that they myght be caryed in them. And so with the quene bothe ladyes and jantylwomen and [other] rode unto Westemynster, and there the knyghtes tolde how sir Mellyagaunce had appeled the quene of hyghe treson, and how sir Launcelot resceyved the glove of hym, 'and thys day eyght dayes they shall do batayle before you.'

15 'Be my hede,' seyde kynge Arthure, 'I am aferde sir Mellyagaunce hath charged hymselff with a grete charge. But where is sir Launcelot?' seyde the kynge.

'Sir, we wote nat where he ys, but we deme he ys ryddyn to som ad-venture, as he ys offtyntymes wonte to do, for he had sir Lavaynes horse.' 20 'Lette hym be,' seyde the kynge, 'for he woll be founden but if he be betrapped wyth som treson.'

(8) Thus leve we sir Launcelot liyng within that cave in grete payne. And every day there cam a lady and brought hys mete and hys drynke, and wowed hym every day to have layne by her, and ever sir Launcelot 25 seyde her nay.

Than seyde she, 'Sir, ye ar nat wyse, for ye may never oute of this preson but if ye have my helpe. And also youre lady, quene Gwenyver, shall be brente in youre defaute onles that ye be there at the day of batayle.'

30 'God deffende,' seyde sir Launcelot, 'that she shulde be brente in my defaught! And if hit be so,' seyde sir Launcelot, 'that I may nat be there, hit shall be well undirstonde, bothe at the kynge and the quene and with all men of worship, that I am dede, syke othir in preson. For all men that know me woll say for me that I am in som evyll case and I 35 be nat that day there. And thus well I undirstonde that there ys som good knyght, othir of my blood other som other that lovys me, that woll take my quarell in honde. And therefore,' seyde sir Launcelot, 'wyte you well, ye shall nat feare me, and if there were no mo women in all thys londe but ye, yet shall nat I have ado with you.'

40 'Than ar ye shamed,' seyde the lady, 'and destroyed for ever.'

'As for worldis shame, now Jesu deffende me! And as for my dis-tresse, hit ys welcom, whatsomever hit be that God sendys me.'

So she cam to hym agayne the same day that the batayle shulde be and seyde,

'Sir Launcelot, bethynke you, for ye ar to hard-harted. And therefore, and ye wolde but onys kysse me, I shulde delyver you and your
armoure, and the beste horse that was within sir Mellyagaunce stable.'

'As for to kysse you,' seyde sir Launcelot, 'I may do that and lese no
worshyp. And wyte you well, and I undirstood there were ony dis-   5
worshyp for to kysse you, I wold nat do hit.'

And than he kyssed hir. And anone she gate hym up untyll hys
armour, and whan he was armed she brought hym tylle a stable where
stoode twelve good coursers, and bade hym to chose of the beste.
Than sir Launcelot loked uppon a whyght courser and that lyked hym   10
beste, and anone he commaunded hym to be sadeled with the beste
sadyll of warre, and so hit was done. Than he gate hys owne speare in
hys honde and hys swerde by hys syde, and than he commaunded the
lady unto God and sayde,

'Lady, for thys dayes dede I shall do you servyse, if ever hit lye in my   15
power.'

Now leve we here sir Launcelot, all that ever he myght walop, and   (9)
speke we of quene Gwenyver that was brought tyll a fyre to be brente;
for sir Mellyagaunce was sure, hym thought, that sir Launcelotte
sholde nat be at that batayle, and therefore he ever cryed uppon sir   20
Arthur to do hym justyse othir ellys brynge forth sir Launcelot. Than
was the kynge and all the courte full sore abaysshed and shamed that the
quene shulde have be brente in the defaute of sir Launcelot.

'My lorde, kynge Arthur,' seyde sir Lavayne, 'ye may undirstonde
that hit ys nat well with my lorde sir Launcelot, for and he were on   25
lyve, so he be nat syke other in preson, wyte you well he wolde have
bene here. For never harde ye that ever he fayled yet hys parte for whom
he solde do batayle fore. And therefore,' seyde sir Lavayne, 'my lorde
kynge Arthur, I beseche you that ye woll gyff me lycence to do batayle
here thys day for my lorde and mayster, and for to save my lady the   30
quene.'

'Grauntemercy, jantill sir Lavayne,' seyde kynge Arthur, 'for I dare
say all that sir Mellyagaunce puttith uppon my lady the quene ys wronge.
For I have spokyn with all the ten wounded knyghtes, and there ys
nat one of them, and he were hole and able to do batayle, but he wolde   35
prove uppon sir Mellyagaunce body [that it is fals that he puttith upon
my] ⟨lady⟩.'

'And so shall I,' seyde sir Lavayne, 'in the deffence of my lorde sir
Launcelot, and ye woll gyff me leve.'

'And I gyff you leve,' seyde kynge Arthur, 'and do youre beste, for   40
I dare well say there ys som treson done to sir Launcelot.'

Than was sir Lavayn armed and horsed, and delyverly at the lystes
ende [he rode] to perfourme hys batayle. And ryght as the herrowdis
shuld cry: 'Lechés les alere!' ryght so com sir Launcelot dryvyng with

all the myght of hys horse. And than kynge Arthure cryed: 'Whoo!'
and 'Abyde!'

And than was sir Launcelot called tofore kynge Arthur, and there he
tolde opynly tofor the kynge all how that sir Mellyagaunce had served
5 hym firste and laste. And whan the kynge and quene and all the lordis
knew off the treson of sir Mellyagaunte, they were all ashamed on hys
behalffe. Than was the quene sente fore and sette by the kynge in the
grete truste of hir champion.

And than sir Launcelot and sir Mellyagaunte dressed them togydir
10 wyth spearys as thunder, and there sir Launcelot bare hym quyte over
hys horse croupe. And than sir Launcelot alyght and dressed hys shylde
on hys shuldir and toke hys swerde in hys honde, and so they dressed
to eche other and smote many grete strokis togydir. And at the laste sir
Launcelot smote hym suche a buffet uppon the helmet that he felle on
15 the tone syde to the erthe.

And than he cryed uppon hym lowde and seyde, 'Moste noble knyght,
sir Launcelot, save my lyff! For I yelde me unto you, and I requyre you,
as ye be a knyght and felow of the Table Rounde, sle me nat, for I
yelde me as overcomyn, and whethir I shall lyve or dey, I put me in
20 the kynges honde and youres.'

Than sir Lancelot wyst nat what to do, for he had lever than all the
good in the worlde that he myght be revenged uppon hym. So sir
Launcelot loked uppon the quene, gyff he myght aspye by ony sygne
or countenaunce what she wolde have done. And anone the quene
25 wagged hir hede uppon sir Launcelot, as ho seyth 'sle hym'. And full
well knew sir Launcelot by her sygnys that she wolde have hym dede.

Than sir Launcelot bade hym, 'Aryse, for shame, and perfourme
thys batayle with me to the utteraunce!'

'Nay,' seyde sir Mellyagaunce, 'I woll never aryse untyll that ye
30 take me as yolden and recreaunte.'

'Well, I shall proffir you a large proffir,' seyde sir Launcelot, 'that ys
for to say I shall unarme my hede and my lyffte quarter of my body, all
that may be unarmed as for that quarter, and I woll lette bynde my
lyfft honde behynde me there hit shall nat helpe me, and ryght so I
35 shall do batayle with you.'

Than sir Mellyagaunce sterte up and seyde on hyght,

'Take hede, my lorde Arthur, of thys proffir, for I woll take hit.
And lette hym be dissarmed and bounden accordynge to hys proffir.'

'What sey ye?' seyde kynge Arthur unto sir Launcelot. 'Woll ye
40 abyde by youre proffir?'

'Ye, my lorde,' seyde sir Launcelot, 'for I woll never go fro that I
have onys sayde.'

Than the knyghtes parters of the fylde disarmed sir Launcelot,
firste hys hede and than hys lyffte arme and hys lyffte syde, and they

bounde his lyffte arme to hys lyffte syde fast behynde hys bak, withoute
shylde or onythynge. And anone they yode togydirs.

Wyte you well there was many a lady and many a knyght mervayled
of sir Launcelot [that] wolde jouparté hymselff in suche wyse.

Than sir Mellyagaunce com wyth swerde all on hyght, and sir   5
Launcelot shewed hym opynly hys bare hede and the bare lyffte syde.
And whan he went to have smytten hym uppon the bare hede, than
lyghtly he devoyded the lyffte legge and the lyffte syde and put hys
honde and hys swerde to that stroke, and so put hit on syde wyth
grete slyght. And than with grete force sir Launcelot smote hym on   10
the helmet such a buffett that the stroke carved the hed in two partyes.

Than there was no more to do, but he was drawyn oute of the fylde,
and at the grete instaunce of the knyghtes of the Table Rounde the
kynge suffird hym to be entered, and the mencion made uppon hym
who slewe hym and for what cause he was slayne.   15

And than the kynge and the quene made more of sir Launcelot, and
more was he cherysshed than ever he was aforehande.

V. THE HEALING OF SIR URRY

THAN, as the Freynshe boke makith mencion, there was a good knyght   (10)
in the londe of Hungré whos name was sir Urré. And he was an adven-   20
turys knyght, and in all placis where he myght here ony adventures
dedis and of worshyp there wold he be.

So hit happened in Spayne there was an erle, and hys sunnes name
was called sir Alpheus. And at a grete turnemente in Spayne thys sir
Urry, knyght of Hungré, and sir Alpheus of Spayne encountred togy-   25
dirs for verry envy, and so aythir undirtoke other to the utteraunce.
And by fortune thys sir Urry slew sir Alpheus, the erlys son of Spayne.
But thys knyght that was slayne had yevyn sir Urry, or ever he were
slayne, seven grete woundis, three on the hede and three on hys body,
an one uppon hys lyffte honde. And thys sir Alpheus had a modir   30
[whiche] was a grete sorseras; and she, for the despyte of hir sunnes
deth, wrought by her suttyle craufftis that sir Urry shulde never be hole,
but ever his woundis shulde one tyme fester and another tyme blede,
so that he shulde never be hole untyll the beste knyght of the worlde
had serched hys woundis. And thus she made her avaunte, where-   35
thorow hit was knowyn that this sir Urry sholde never be hole.

Than hys modir lete make an horse-lytter and put hym therein with
two palfreyes caryyng hym. And than she toke wyth hym hys syster, a
full fayre damesell whos name was Fyleloly, and a payge wyth hem to
kepe their horsis, and so they lad sir Urry thorow many contreyes.   40

For, as the Freynshe booke saythe, she lad hym so seven yere thorow all londis crystened and never cowde fynde no knyght that myght ease her sunne.

So she cam unto Scotlonde and into the bondes of Inglonde. And by
5 fortune she com unto the feste of Pentecoste untyll kynge Arthurs courte that at that tyme was holdyn at Carlehylle. And whan she cam there she made hit to be opynly knowyn how that she was com into that londe for to hele her sonne. Than kynge Arthur lette calle that lady and aske her the cause why she brought that hurte knyght
10 into that londe.

'My moste noble kynge,' seyde that lady, 'wyte you well I brought hym hyddir to be heled of hys woundis, that of all thys seven yere myght never be hole.'

And thus she tolde the kynge, and where he was wounded and with
15 whom, and how hys modir discoverde hit in her pryde how she had worought by enchauntemente that he sholde never be hole untyll the beste knyght of the worlde had serched hys woundis.

'And so I have passed all the londis crystynde thorow to have hym healed excepte thys londe, and gyff I fayle here in thys londe I woll
20 never take more payne uppon me. And that ys grete pité, for he was a good knyght and of grete nobeles.'

'What ys hys name?' seyde kynge Arthure.

'My good and gracious lorde,' she seyde, 'his name ys sir Urré of the Mounte.'

25 'In good tyme,' seyde the kynge. 'And sythyn ye ar com into thys londe, ye ar ryght wellcom. And wyte you welle, here shall youre son be healed and ever ony Crystyn man [may] heale hym. And for to gyff all othir men off worshyp a currayge, I myselff woll asay to handyll your sonne, and so shall all the kynges, dukis and erlis that ben here
30 presente at thys tyme, nat presumyng uppon me that I am so worthy to heale youre son be my dedis, but I woll corrayge othir men of worshyp to do as I woll do.'

And than the kynge commaunded all the kynges, dukes and erlis and all noble knyghtes of the Rounde Table that were there that tyme
35 presente to com into the medow of Carlehyll.

And so at that tyme there were but an hondred an ten of the Rounde Table, for forty knyghtes were that tyme away. And so here we muste begynne at kynge Arthur, as was kyndely to begynne at hym that was that tyme the moste man of worshyp crystynde.

(11) 40 Than kynge Arthur loked uppon sir Urré, and he thought he was a full lykly man whan he was hole. And than the kynge made to take hym downe of the lyttar and leyde hym uppon the erth, and anone there was layde a cussheon of golde that he shulde knele uppon. And than kynge Arthur sayde,

'Fayre knyght, me rewyth of thy hurte, and for to corrayge all other knyghtes I woll pray the sofftely to suffir me to handyll thy woundis.'

'My moste noble crystynd kynge, do ye as ye lyste,' seyde sir Urré, 'for I am at the mercy of God and at youre commaundemente.'

So than kynge Arthur softely handeled hym. And than som of hys woundis renewed uppon bledynge.   5

Than kynge Claryaunce of Northumbirlonde serched, and hit wolde nat be. And than sir Barraunte le Apres, that was called the Kynge with the Hundred Knyghtes, he assayed and fayled.

So ded kynge Uryence of the londe of Gore. So ded kynge Angwysh   10
of Irelonde, and so ded kynge Newtrys of Garloth. So ded kynge Carydos of Scotlonde. So ded the duke sir Galahalt the Haute Prynce. So ded sir Constantyne that was kynge Cadors son of Cornwayle. So ded duke Chalaunce of Claraunce. So ded the erle of Ulbawys. So ded the erle Lambayle. So ded the erle Arystanse.   15

Than cam in sir Gawayne wyth hys three sunnes, sir Gyngalyn, sir Florence, and sir Lovell (thes two were begotyn uppon sir Braundeles syster), and all they fayled. Than cam in sir Aggravayne, sir Gaherys, and sir Mordred, and the good knyght sir Gareth that was of verry knyghthod worth all the brethirn.   20

So cam in the knyghtes of sir Launcelottis kyn, but sir Launcelot was nat [that] tyme in the courte, for he was that tyme uppon hys adventures. Than sir Lyonell, sir Ector de Marys, sir Bors de Ganys, sir Blamoure de Ganys, sir Bleoberys de Gaynys, sir Gahalantyne, sir Galynodyn, sir Menadukc, ·sir Vyllars the Valyaunte, sir Hebes le   25
Renowné, all thes were of sir Launcelottis kynne, and all they fayled.

Than cam in sir Sagramour le Desyrus, sir Dodynas le Saveage, sir Dynadan, sir Brewne le Noyre that sir Kay named La Cote Male Tayle, and sir Kay le Senesciall, sir Kay d'Estraunges, sir Mellyot de Logris, sir Petipace of Wynchylsé, sir Galleron of Galway, sir Melyon of the   30
Mountayne, sir Cardoke, sir Uwayne les Avoutres, and sir Ozanna le Cure Hardy. Than cam in sir Ascamour, and sir Grummor and Grummorson, sir Crosseleme, sir Severause le Brewse that was called a passynge stronge knyght.

For, as the booke seyth, the chyff lady of the Lady off the Lake   35
fested sir Launcelot .and sir Severause le Brewse, and whan she had fested them both at sundry tymes, she prayde hem to gyff her a done, and ·anone they graunted her. And than she prayde sir Severause that he wolde promyse her never to do batayle ayenste sir Launcelot, and in the same wyse she prayde sir Launcelot never to do batayle ayenste   40
sir Severause, and so aythir promysed her. (For the Freynshe booke sayth that sir Severause had never corayge nor grete luste to do batayle ayenste no man but if hit we[re] ayenste gyauntis and ayenste dragons and wylde bestis.)

So leve we thys mater and speke we of them that at the kynges rekeyste were [there] at the hyghe feste, as knyghtes of the Rounde Table, for to serche sir Urré. And to thys entente the kynge ded hit, to wyte whych was the moste nobelyste knyght amonge them all.

5 Than cam in sir Agglovale, sir Durnor and sir Tor that was begotyn uppon the cowardis wyff, but he was begotyn afore Aryes wedded her (and kynge Pellynore begate them all: firste sir Tor, sir Agglovale, sir Durnor, sir Lamorak, the moste nobeleste knyght one of them that ever was in kynge Arthurs dayes as for a wordly knyght, and sir Per-
10 civale that was pyerles, excepte sir Galahad, in holy dedis. But they dyed in the queste of the Sangreall).

Than cam in sir Grylet le Fyze de Du, sir Lucan the Butlere, sir Bedyvere, hys brothir, sir Braundeles, sir Constantyne, sir Cadors son of Cornwayle that was kynge aftir Arthurs dayes, and sir Clegis, sir
15 Sadok, sir Dynas le Senesciall de Cornwayle, sir Fergus, sir Dryaunte, sir Lambegus, sir Clarrus off Cleremownte, sir Cloddrus, sir Hecty-mere, sir Edwarde of Carnarvan, sir Pryamus whych was crystynde by the meanys of sir Trystram, the noble knyght, and thes three were brethirn; sir Helayne le Blanke that was son unto sir Bors, for he begate
20 hym uppon kynge Brandygorys doughter, and sir Bryan de Lyste-noyse; sir Gauter, sir Raynolde, sir Gyllymere, were three brethirn whych sir Launcelot wan uppon a brydge in sir Kayes armys; sir Gwyarte le Petite, sir Bellyngere le Bewse that was son to the good knyght sir Alysaundir le Orphelyn that was slayne by the treson of
25 kynge Marke.

Also that traytoure kynge slew the noble knyght sir Trystram as he sate harpynge afore hys lady, La Beall Isode, with a trenchaunte glayve, for whos dethe was the moste waylynge of ony knyght that ever was in kynge Arthurs dayes, for there was never none so bewayled as was sir
30 Trystram and sir Lamerok, for they were with treson slayne: sir Trystram by kynge Marke, and sir Lamorake by sir Gawayne and hys brethirn.

And thys sir Bellynger revenged the deth of hys fadir, sir Alysaundir, and sir Trystram, for he slewe kynge Marke. And La Beall Isode dyed
35 sownyng uppon the crosse of sir Trystram, whereof was grete pité. And all that were with kynge Marke whych were of assente of the dethe of sir Trystram were slayne, as sir Andred and many othir.

Than cam sir Hebes, sir Morganoure, sir Sentrayle, sir Suppynabiles, sir Belyaunce le Orgulus that the good knyght sir Lamorak wan in
40 playne batayle, sir Neroveus and sir Plenoryus, two good knyghtes that sir Launcelot wanne, sir Darras, sir Harry le Fyze Lake, sir Ermynde, brother to kyng Hermaunce, for whom sir Palomydes faught at the Rede Cité with two brethirn; and sir Selyses of the Dolerous Towre, sir Edward of Orkeney, sir Ironsyde that was called the noble

knyght of the Rede Laundis, that sir Gareth wan for the love of da[m]e
Lyones; sir Arrok, sir Degrevaunt, sir Degrave Saunze Vylony that
faught wyth the gyaunte of the Blak Lowe; sir Epynogrys that was the
kynges son of Northumbirlonde, sir Pelleas that loved the lady Ettarde
(and he had dyed for her sake, had nat bene one of the ladyes of the   5
lake whos name was dame Nynyve; and she wedde sir Pelleas, and she
saved hym ever aftir, that he was never slayne by her dayes; and he
was a full noble knyght); and sir Lamyell of Cardyff that was a grete
lovear, sir Playne de Fors, sir Melyaus de Lyle, sir Boarte le Cure
Hardy that was kynge Arthurs son, sir Madore de la Porte, sir Coll-   10
grevaunce, sir Hervyse de la Foreyst Saveayge, sir Marrok the good
knyght that was betrayed with his wyff, for he made hym seven yere a
warwolff; sir Persaunt, sir Pertolope, hys brothir, that was called the
Grene Knyght, and sir Perymones, brother unto them bothe, whych
was called the Rede Knyght, that sir Gareth wanne whan he was   15
called Bewmaynes.

All thes hondred knyghtes and ten serched sir Urryes woundis by
the commaundemente of kynge Arthur.

'Mercy Jesu!' seyde kynge Arthur, 'where ys sir Launcelot du Lake,   (12)
that he ys nat here at thys tyme?'   20

And thus as they stood and spake of many thyngis, there one aspyed
sir Launcelot that com rydynge towarde them, and anone they tolde
the kynge.

'Pees,' seyde the kynge, 'lat no man say nothyng untyll he be com to
us.'   25

So whan sir Launcelot had aspyed kynge Arthur he descended
downe frome hys horse and cam to the kynge and salewed hym and
them all.

And anone as the damesell, sir Urryes syster, saw sir Launcelot, she
romed to her brothir thereas he lay in hys lyttar and seyde,   30

'Brothir, here ys com a knyght that my harte gyveth gretly unto.'

'Fayre syster,' seyde sir Urré, 'so doth my harte lyghte gretly ayenste
hym, and my harte gyvith me more unto hym than to all thes that hath
serched me.'

Than seyde kynge Arthur unto sir Launcelot, 'Sir, ye muste do as we   35
have done', and tolde hym what they had done and shewed hym them
all that had serched hym.

'Jesu defende me,' seyde sir Launcelot, 'whyle so many noble kyngis
and knyghtes have fayled, that I shulde presume uppon me to enchyve
that all ye, my lordis, myght nat enchyve.'   40

'Ye shall nat chose,' seyde kynge Arthur, 'for I commaunde you to do
as we all have done.'

'My moste renowmed lorde,' seyde sir Launcelot, 'I know well I
dare nat, nor may nat, disobey you. But and I myght or durste, wyte

you well I wolde nat take uppon me to towche that wounded knyght in that entent that I shulde passe all othir knyghtes. Jesu deffende me frome that shame!'

'Sir, ye take hit wronge,' seyde kynge Arthur, 'for ye shall nat do
5 hit for no presumpcion, but for to beare us felyshyp, insomuche as ye be a felow of the Rounde Table. And wyte you well,' seyde kynge Arthur, 'and ye prevayle nat and heale hym, I dare sey there ys no knyght in thys londe that may hele hym. And therefore I pray you do as we have done.'

10 And than all the kyngis and knyghtes for the moste party prayed sir Launcelot to serche hym. And than the wounded knyght, sir Urré, set hym up waykely and seyde unto sir Launcelot,

'Now, curteyse knyght, I requyre the, for Goddis sake, heale my woundis! For methynkis ever sytthyn ye cam here my woundis grevyth
15 me nat so muche as they ded.'

'A, my fayre lorde,' seyde sir Launcelot, 'Jesu wolde that I myght helpe you! For I shame sore with myselff that I shulde be thus requyred, for never was I able in worthynes to do so hyghe a thynge.'

Than sir Launcelot kneled downe by the wounded knyght, saiyng,
20 'My lorde Arthure, I muste do youre commaundemente, whych ys sore ayenste my harte.' And than he hylde up hys hondys and loked unto the este, saiynge secretely unto hymselff, 'Now, Blyssed Fadir and Son and Holy Goste, I beseche The of Thy mercy that my symple worshyp and honesté be saved, and Thou Blyssed Trynyté, Thou
25 mayste yeff me power to hele thys syke knyght by the grete vertu and grace of The, but, Good Lorde, never of myselff.'

And than sir Launcelot prayde sir Urré to lat hym se hys hede; and than, devoutly knelyng, he ransaked the three woundis, that they bled a lytyll; and forthwithall the woundis fayre heled and semed as they
30 had bene hole a seven yere. And in lyke wyse he serched hys body of other three woundis, and they healed in lyke wyse. And than the laste of all he serched hys honde, and anone hit fayre healed.

Than kynge Arthur and all the kynges and knyghtes kneled downe and gave thankynges and lovynge unto God and unto Hys Blyssed
35 Modir. And ever sir Launcelote wepte, as he had bene a chylde that had bene beatyn!

Than kyng Arthure lat ravyshe prystes and clarkes in the moste devoutiste wyse to brynge in sir Urré into Carlyle with syngyng and lovyng to God. And whan thys was done the kynge lat clothe hym in
40 ryche maner, and than was there but feaw bettir made knyghtes in all the courte, for he was passyngly well made and bygly.

Than kynge Arthur asked sir Urré how he felte hymselff.

'A! my good and gracious lorde, I felte myselffe never so lusty.'

'Than woll ye juste and do ony armys?' seyd kynge Arthur.

'Sir, and I had all that longed unto justis, I wolde be sone redy.'

Than kynge Arthur made a party [of] a hondred knyghtes to be (13)
ayenste an hondred, and so uppon the morn they justed for a dyamounde, but there justed none of the daungerous knyghtes. And so,
for to shortyn this tale, sir Urré and sir Lavayne justed beste that day, 5
for there was none of them but he overthrew and pulled down a thirty
knyght.

And than by assente of all the kynges and lordis sir Urré and sir
Lavayne were made knyghtes of the Table Rounde. And than sir
Lavayne keste hys love unto dame Fyleloly, sir Urré syster, and than 10
they were wedded with grete joy, and so kynge Arthur gaff to every of
them a barony of londis.

And this sir Urré wolde never go frome sir Launcelot, but he and
sir Lavayne awayted evermore uppon hym, and they were in all the
courte accounted for good knyghtes and full desyrous in armys. And 15
many noble dedis they ded, for they wolde have no reste but ever
sought uppon their dedis. Thus they lyved in all that courte wyth
grete nobeles and joy longe tymes.

But every nyght and day sir Aggravayne, sir Gawaynes brother,
awayted quene Gwenyver and sir Launcelot to put hem bothe to a 20
rebuke and a shame.

And so I leve here of this tale, and overlepe grete bookis of sir
Launcelot, what grete adventures he ded whan he was called 'le Shy
valere de Charyot'. For, as the Freynshe booke sayth, because of dispyte
that knyghtes and ladyes called hym 'the Knyght that rode in the 25
Charyot', lyke as he were juged to the jybett, therefore, in the despite
of all them that named hym so, he was caryed in a charyotte a twelve-
monethe; for but lytill aftir that he had slayne sir Mellyagaunte in the
quenys quarell, he never of a twelve-moneth com on horsebak. And,
as the Freynshe booke sayth, he ded that twelve-moneth more than 30
forty batayles.

And bycause I have loste the very mater of Shevalere de Charyot I
departe frome the tale of sir Launcelot; and here I go unto the morte
Arthur, and that caused sir Aggravayne.

AND HERE ON THE OTHIR SYDE FOLOWYTH *THE MOSTE PYTEUOUS* 35
TALE OF THE MORTE ARTHURE SAUNZ GWERDON PAR LE SHYVALERE
SIR THOMAS MALLEORRÉ, KNYGHT.

JESU, AYEDE LY PUR VOUTRE BONE MERCY! AMEN.

THE
MOST PITEOUS TALE
OF THE
MORTE ARTHUR SAUNZ
GUERDON

I. SLANDER AND STRIFE

In May, whan every harte floryshyth and burgenyth (for, as the season
ys lusty to beholde and comfortable, so man and woman rejoysyth and
gladith of somer commynge with his freyshe floures, for wynter wyth
hys rowghe wyndis and blastis causyth lusty men and women to cowre 5
and to syt by fyres), so thys season hit befelle in the moneth of May a
grete angur and unhapp⟨e⟩ that stynted nat tylle the floure of chyvalry
of |alle] the worlde was destroyed and slayne.

And all was longe uppon two unhappy knyghtis whych were named
sir Aggravayne and sir Mordred, that were brethirn unto sir Gawayne. 10
For thys sir Aggravayne and sir Mordred had ever a prevy hate unto
the quene, dame Gwenyver, and to sir Launcelot; and dayly and
nyghtly they ever wacched uppon sir Launcelot.

So hyt myssefortuned sir Gawayne and all hys brethirne were in
kynge Arthurs chambir, and than sir Aggravayne seyde thus opynly, 15
and nat in no counceyle, that manye knyghtis myght here:

'I mervayle that we all be nat ashamed bothe to se and to know how
sir Launcelot lyeth dayly and nyghtly by the quene. And all we know
well that hit ys so, and hit ys sha[m]efully suffird of us all that we shulde
suffir so noble a kynge as kynge Arthur ys to be shamed.' 20

Than spake sir Gawayne and seyde,

'Brothir, sir Aggravayne, I pray you and charge you, meve no such
maters no more afore me, for wyte you well, I woll nat be of youre
counceyle.'

'So God me helpe,' seyde sir Gaherys and sir Gareth, 'we woll nat 25
be knowyn of your dedis.'

'Than woll I!' seyde sir Mordred.

'I lyve you well,' seyde sir Gawayne, 'for ever unto all unhappynes,
sir, ye woll graunte. And I wolde that ye leffte [all thys,] and make you
nat so bysy, for I know,' seyde sir Gawayne, 'what woll falle of hit.' 30

'Falle whatsumever falle may,' seyde sir Aggravayne, 'I woll disclose hit to the kynge!'

'Nat be my counceyle,' seyde sir Gawayne, 'for, and there aryse
warre and wrake betwyxte sir Launcelot [and us], wyte you well,
brothir, there woll many kynges and grete lordis holde with sir Laun- 35
celot. Also, brothir, sir Aggravayne,' seyde sir Gawayne, 'ye muste
remembir how oftyntymes sir Launcelot hath rescowed the kynge and
the quene; and the beste of us all had bene full colde at the harte-roote
had nat sir Launcelot bene bettir than we, and that hathe he preved
hymselff full ofte. And as for my parte,' seyde sir Gawayne, 'I woll 40
never be ayenste sir Launcelot for one dayes dede, that was whan he

rescowed me frome kynge Carados of the Dolerous Towre and slew
hym and saved my lyff. Also, brother, sir Aggravayne and sir Mordred,
in lyke wyse sir Launcelot rescowed you bothe and three score and
two frome sir Tarquyne. And therefore, brothir, methynkis suche
5 noble dedis and kyndnes shulde be remembirde.'

'Do ye as ye lyste,' seyde sir [Aggrav]ayne, 'for I woll layne hit no
lenger.'

So wyth thes wordis cam in sir Arthur.

'Now, brothir,' seyde sir Gawayne, 'stynte youre stryff.'

10   'That woll I nat,' seyde sir Aggravayne and sir Mordred.

'Well, woll ye so?' seyde sir Gawayne. 'Than God spede you, for I
woll nat here of youre talis, nothir be of youre counceile.'

'No more woll I,' seyde sir Gaherys.

'Nother I,' seyde sir Gareth, 'for I shall never say evyll by that man
15 that made me knyght.'

And therewythall they three departed makynge grete dole.

'Alas!' seyde sir Gawayne and sir Gareth, 'now ys thys realme holy
destroyed and myscheved, and the noble felyshyp of the Rounde Table
shall be disparbeled.'

(2) 20   So they departed, and than kynge Arthure asked them what noyse
they made.

'My lorde,' seyde sir Aggravayne, 'I shall telle you, for I may kepe
hit no lenger. Here ys I and my brothir sir Mordred brake unto my
brothir sir Gawayne, sir Gaherys and to sir Gareth—for thys ys all, to
25 make hit shorte—[how] ⟨that⟩ we know all that sir Launcelot holdith
youre quene, and hath done longe; and we be your syster sunnes, we
may suffir hit no lenger. And all we wote that ye shulde be above sir
Launcelot, and ye ar the kynge that made hym knyght, and therefore
we woll preve hit that he is a traytoure to youre person.'

30   'Gyff hit be so,' seyde the kynge, 'wyte you well, he ys non othir.
But I wolde be lothe to begyn such a thynge but I myght have prevys
of hit, for sir Launcelot ys an hardy knyght, and all ye know that he ys
the beste knyght amonge us all, and but if he be takyn with the dede he
woll fyght with hym that bryngith up the noyse, and I know no knyght
35 that ys able to macch hym. Therefore, and hit be sothe as ye say, I
wolde that he were takyn with the dede.'

For, as the Freynshe booke seyth, the kynge was full lothe that such
a noyse shulde be uppon sir Launcelot and his quene; for the kynge
had a demyng of hit, but he wold nat here thereoff, for sir Launcelot
40 had done so much for hym and for the quene so many tymes that wyte
you well the kynge loved hym passyngly well.

'My lorde,' seyde sir Aggravayne, 'ye shall ryde to-morne an-
huntyng, and doute ye nat, sir Launcelot woll nat go wyth you. And
so whan hit drawith towarde nyght ye may sende the quene worde that

ye woll ly oute all that nyght, and so may ye sende for your cookis. And than, uppon payne of deth, that nyght we shall take hym wyth the quene, and we shall brynge hym unto you, quycke or dede.'

'I woll well,' seyde the kynge. 'Than I counceyle you to take with you sure felyshyp.' 5

'Sir,' seyde sir Aggravayne, 'my brothir sir Mordred and I woll take wyth us twelve knyghtes of the Rounde Table.'

'Beware,' seyde kynge Arthure, 'for I warne you, ye shall fynde hym wyght.'

'Lat us deale!' seyde sir Aggravayne and sir Mordred. 10

So on the morne kynge Arthure rode an-huntyng and sente worde to the quene that he wolde be oute all that nyght. Than sir Aggravayne and sir Mordred gate to them twelve knyghtes and hyd hemselff in a chambir in the castell of Carlyle. And thes were their namys: sir Collgrevaunce, sir Mador de la Porte, sir Gyngalyne, sir Mellyot de Logris, 15 sir Petipace of Wynchylsé, sir Galleron of Galoway, sir Melyon de la Mountayne, sir Ascomore, sir Gromoresom Erioure, sir Cursesalyne, sir Florence, and sir Lovell. So thes twelve knyghtes were with sir Mordred and sir Aggravayne, and all they were of Scotlonde, other ellis of sir Gawaynes kynne, other [well]-wyllers to hys brothir. 20

So whan the nyght cam sir Launcelot tolde sir Bors how he wolde go that nyght and speke wyth the quene.

'Sir,' seyde sir Bors, 'ye shall nat go thys nyght be my counceyle.'

'Why?' seyde sir Launcelot.

'Sir, for I drede me ever of sir Aggravayne that waytith uppon you 25 dayly to do you shame and us all. And never gaff my harte ayenste no goynge that ever ye wente to the quene so much as now, for I mystruste that the kynge ys oute thys nyght frome the quene [bycause peradventure he hath layne som wacche for you and the quene]. Therefore I drede me sore of som treson.' 30

'Have ye no drede,' seyde sir Launcelot, 'for I shall go and com agayne and make no taryynge.'

'Sir,' seyde sir Bors, 'that me repentis, for I drede me sore that youre goyng thys nyght shall wratth us all.'

'Fayre neveawe,' seyd sir Launcelot, 'I mervayle me much why ye 35 say thus, sytthyn the quene hath sente for me. And wyte you well, I woll nat be so much a cowarde, but she shall undirstonde I woll se her good grace.'

'God spede you well,' seyde sir Bors, 'and sende you sounde and sauff agayne!' 40

So sir Launcelot departed and toke hys swerde undir hys arme, and (3) so he walked in hys mantell, that noble knyght, and put hymselff in grete jouparté. And so he past on tylle he cam to the quenys chambir, and so lyghtly he was had into the chambir.

For, as the Freynshhe booke seyth, the quene and sir Launcelot were togydirs. And whether they were abed other at other maner of disportis, me lyste nat thereof make no mencion, for love that tyme was nat as love ys nowadayes.

5 But thus as they were togydir there cam sir Aggravayne and sir Mordred wyth twelve knyghtes with them of the Rounde Table, and they seyde with grete cryyng and scaryng voyce,

'Thou traytoure, sir Launcelot, now ar thou takyn!'

And thus they cryed wyth a lowde voyce, that all the courte myght
10 hyre hit. And thes fourtene knyghtes all were armed at all poyntis, as they shulde fyght in a batayle.

'Alas!' seyde quene Gwenyver, 'now ar we myscheved bothe!'

'Madame,' seyde sir Launcelot, 'ys there here ony armour within you that myght cover my body wythall? And if there be ony, gyff hit
15 me and I shall sone stynte their malice, by the grace of God!'

'Now, truly,' seyde the quyne, 'I have none armour nother helme, shylde, swerde, nother speare, wherefore I dred me sore oure longe love ys com to a myschyvus ende. For I here by their noyse there be many noble knyghtes, and well I wote they be surely armed, and ayenst
20 them ye may make no resistence. Wherefore ye ar lykly to be slayne, and than shall I be brente! For and ye myght ascape them,' seyde the quene, 'I wolde nat doute but that ye wolde rescowe me in what daunger that I ever stood in.'

'Alas!' seyde sir Launcelot, 'in all my lyff thus was I never bestad
25 that I shulde be thus shamefully slayne, for lake of myne armour.'

But ever sir Aggravayne and sir Mordred cryed,

'Traytour knyght, com oute of the quenys chambir! For wyte thou well thou arte besette so that thou shalt nat ascape.'

'A, Jesu mercy!' seyd sir Launcelot, 'thys shamefull cry and noyse I
30 may nat suffir, for better were deth at onys than thus to endure thys payne.'

Than he toke the quene in hys armys and kyssed her and seyde,

'Moste nobelest Crysten quene, I besech you, as ye have ben ever my speciall good lady, and I at all tymes your poure knyght and trew unto
35 my power, and as I never fayled you in ryght nor in wronge sytthyn the firste day kynge Arthur made me knyght, that ye woll pray for my soule if that I be slayne. For well I am assured that sir Bors, my nevewe, and all the remenaunte of my kynne, with sir Lavayne and sir Urré, that they woll nat fayle you to rescow you from the fyer. And therefore,
40 myne owne lady, recomforte youreselff, whatsomever com of me, that ye go with sir Bors, my nevew, and [sir Urré and] they all woll do you all the plesure that they may, and ye shall lyve lyke a quene uppon my londis.'

'Nay, sir Launcelot, nay!' seyde the quene. 'Wyte thou well that I woll ⟨nat⟩ lyve longe aftir thy dayes. But and ye be slayne I woll take my dethe as mekely as ever ded marter take hys dethe for Jesu Crystes sake.'

'Well, madame,' seyde sir Launcelot, 'syth hit ys so that the day ys com that oure love muste departe, wyte you well I shall selle my lyff as 5 dere as I may. And a thousandfolde,' seyde sir Launcelot, 'I am more hevyar for you than for myselff! And now I had levir than to be lorde of all Crystendom that I had sure armour uppon me, that men myght speke of my dedys or ever I were slayne.'

'Truly,' seyde the quene, 'and hit myght please God, I wolde that 10 they wolde take me and sle me and suffir you to ascape.'

'That shall never be,' seyde sir Launcelot, 'God deffende me frome such a shame! But, Jesu Cryste, be Thou my shylde and myne armoure!'

And therewith sir Launcelot wrapped hys mantel aboute hys arme (4) well and surely; and by than they had getyn a grete fourme oute of the 15 halle, and therewith they all russhed at the dore.

'Now, fayre lordys,' seyde sir Launcelot, 'leve youre noyse and youre russhynge, and I shall sette opyn thys dore, and tha[n] may ye do with me what hit lykith you.'

'Com of, than,' seyde they all, 'and do hit, for hit avaylyth the nat to 20 stryve ayenste us all! And therefore lat us into thys chambir, and we shall save thy lyff untyll thou com to kynge Arthur.'

Than sir Launcelot unbarred the dore, and with hys lyffte honde he hylde hit opyn a lytyll, that but one man myght com in at onys. And so there cam strydyng a good knyght, a much man and a large, and hys 25 name was called sir Collgrevaunce of Goore. And he wyth a swerde strake at sir Launcelot myghtyly, and so he put asyde the stroke, and gaff hym such a buffette uppon the helmet that he felle grovelyng ⌐dede⌐ wythin the chambir dore.

Than sir Launcelot with grete myght drew the knyght within the 30 chambir dore. And than sir Launcelot, wyth helpe of the quene and her ladyes, he was lyghtly armed in Collgrevaunce armoure. And ever stood sir Aggravayne and sir Mordred, cryyng,

'Traytoure knyght! Come forthe oute of the quenys chambir!'

'Sires, leve youre noyse,' seyde sir Launcelot, 'for wyte you well, sir 35 Aggravayne, ye shall nat preson me thys nyght! And therefore, and ye do be my counceyle, go ye all frome thys chambir dore and make you no suche cryyng and such maner of sclaundir as ye do. For I promyse you be my knyghthode, and ye woll departe and make no more noyse, I shall as to-morne appyere afore you all and before the 40 kynge, and than lat hit be sene whych of you all, other ellis ye all, that woll depreve me of treson. And there shall I answere you, as a knyght shulde, that hydir I cam to the quene for no maner of male engyne, and that woll I preve and make hit good uppon you wyth my hondys.'

'Fye uppon the, traytour,' seyde sir Aggravayne and sir Mordred, 'for we woll have the magré thyne hede and sle the, and we lyste! For we let the wyte we have the choyse of kynge Arthure to save the other sle the.'

5 'A, sirres,' seyde sir Launcelot, 'ys there none other grace with you? Than kepe youreselff!'

And than sir Launcelot sette all opyn the chambir dore, and myghtyly and knyghtly he strode in amonge them. And anone at the firste stroke he slew sir Aggravayne, and anone aftir twelve of hys felowys.

10 Within a whyle he had layde them down colde to the erthe, for there was none of the twelve knyghtes myght stonde sir Launcelot one buffet. And also he wounded sir Mordred, and therewithall he fled with all hys myght. And than sir Launcelot returned agayne unto the quene and seyde,

15 'Madame, now wyte you well, all oure trew love ys brought to an ende, for now wyll kyng Arthur ever be my foo. And therefore, madam, and hit lyke you that I may have you with me, I shall save you frome all maner adventures daungers.'

'Sir, that ys nat beste,' seyde the quene, 'mesemyth, for now ye have 20 don so much harme hit woll be beste that ye holde you styll with this. And if ye se that as to-morne they woll putte me unto dethe, than may ye rescowe me as ye thynke beste.'

'I woll well,' seyde sir Launcelot, 'for have ye no doute, whyle I am a man lyvyng I shall rescow you.'

25 And than he kyste her, and ayther of hem gaff othir a rynge, and so the quene he leffte there and wente untyll hys lodgynge.

(5) Whan sir Bors saw sir Launcelot he was never so glad of hys homecomynge.

'Jesu mercy!' seyde sir Launcelot, 'why be ye all armed? What 30 meanyth thys?'

'Sir,' seyde sir Bors, 'aftir ye were departed frome us we all that ben of youre blood and youre well-wyllars were so adreˡtchˡed that som of us lepe oute of oure beddis naked, and som in their dremys caught naked swerdys in their hondis. And therefore,' seyde sir Bors, 'we 35 demed there was som grete stryff on honde, and so we demed that [y]e were betrapped with som treson; and therefore we made us thus redy, what nede that ever [y]e were in.'

'My fayre nevew,' seyde sir Launcelot unto sir Bors, 'now shall ye wyte all that thys nyght I was more harde bestad than ever I was dayes 40 of my lyff. And thanked be God, I am myselff ascaped their daungere.' And so he tolde them all how and in what maner, as ye have harde toforehande. 'And therefore, my felowys,' seyde sir Launcelot, 'I pray you all that ye woll be of harte good, and helpe me in what nede that ever I stonde, for now ys warre comyn to us all.'

'Sir,' seyde sir Bors, 'all ys wellcom that God sendyth us, and as we have takyn much weale with you and much worshyp, we woll take the woo with you as we have takyn the weale.'

And therefore they seyde, all the good knyghtes,

'Loke ye take no discomforte! For there ys no bondys of knyghtes 5 undir hevyn but we shall be able to greve them as much as they [may] us, and therefore discomforte nat youreselff by no maner. And we shall gadir togyder all that we love and that lovyth us, and what that ye woll have done shall be done. And therefore lat us take the wo and the joy togydir.'   10

'Grauntmercy,' seyde sir Launcelot, 'of youre good comforte, for in my grete distresse, fayre nevew, ye comforte me gretely. But th[y]s, my fayre nevew, I wolde that ye ded, in all haste that ye may, [or] hit ys far dayes paste: that ye woll loke in their lodgynge that ben lodged nyghe here aboute the kynge, whych woll holde with me and whych 15 woll nat. For now I wolde know whych were my frendis fro my fooes.'

'Sir,' seyde sir Bors, 'I shall do my payne, and or hit be seven of the clok I shall wyte of such as ye have dou⟨t⟩ fore, who that woll holde with you.'   20

Than sir Bors called unto hym sir Lyonel, sir Ector de Marys, sir Blamour de Ganys, [sir Bleoberys de Ganys,] sir Gahalantyne, sir Galyhodyn, sir Galyhud, sir Menaduke, sir Vyllyers the Valyaunte, syr Hebes le Renowné, sir Lavayne, sir Urré of Hungry, sir Neroveus, sir Plenoryus (for thes two were knyghtes tha⟨t⟩ sir Launcelot wan up- 25 pon a brydge, and therefore they wolde never be ayenst hym), and sir Harry le Fyz Lake, and sir Selyses of the Dolerous Towre, sir Mellyas de Lyle, and sir Bellangere le Bewse that was sir Alysaundir le Orphelyne [sone]; bycause hys modir was [Alys la Beale Pelleryn, and she was] kyn unto sir Launcelot, he hylde wyth hym. So cam sir Palo- 30 mydes and sir Saphir, hys brothir; sir Clegis, sir Sadok, sir Dynas and sir Clarryus of Cleremount.

So thes two-and-twenty knyghtes drew hem togydirs, and by than they were armed and on horsebak they promysed sir Launcelot to do what he wolde. Than there felle to them, what of Northe Walys and 35 of Cornwayle, for sir Lamorakes sake and for sir Trystrames sake, to the numbir of a seven score knyghtes. Than spake sir Launcelot:

'Wyte you well, I have bene ever syns I cam to thys courte well-wylled unto my lorde Arthur and unto my lady quene Gwenyver unto my power. And thys nyght bycause my lady the quene sente for me to 40 speke with her, I suppose hit was made by treson; howbehit I dare largely excuse her person, natwithstondynge I was there b[e a fore-caste] nerehonde slayne but as Jesu provyded for me.'

And than that noble knyght sir Launcelot tolde hem how he was harde bestad in the quenys chambir, and how and in what maner he ascaped from them.

'And therefore wyte you well, my fayre lordis, I am sure there nys but warre unto me and to myne. And for cause I have slayne thys
5 nyght sir Aggravayne, sir Gawaynes brothir, and at the leste twelve of hys felowis, and for thys cause now am I sure of mortall warre. For thes knyghtes were sente by kynge Arthur to betray me, and therefore the kyng woll in thys hete and malice jouge the quene unto brennyng, and that may nat I suffir that she shulde be brente for my sake. For and I
10 may be harde and suffirde and so takyn, I woll feyght for the quene, that she ys a trew lady untyll her lorde. But the kynge in hys hete, I drede, woll nat take me as I ought to be takyn.'

(6)   'My lorde, sir Launcelot,' seyde sir Bors, 'be myne advyce, ye shall take the woo wyth the weall. And sytthyn hit ys fallyn as hit ys, I
15 counceyle you to kepe youreselff, for and ye woll youreselffe, there ys no felyshyp of knyghtes crystynde that shall do you wronge. And also I woll counceyle you, my lorde, that my lady quene Gwenyver, and she be in ony distres, insomuch as she ys in payne for youre sake, that ye knyghtly rescow her; for and ye ded ony other wyse all the worlde
20 wolde speke you shame to the worldis ende. Insomuch as ye were takyn with her, whether ye ded ryght othir wronge, hit ys now youre parte to holde wyth the quene, that she be nat slayne and put to a myschevous deth. For and she so dye, the shame shall be evermore youres.'

25   'Now Jesu deffende me from shame,' seyde sir Launcelot, 'and kepe and save my lady the quene from vylany and shamefull dethe, and that she never be destroyed in my defaute! Wherefore, my fayre lordy[s], my kyn and my fryndis,' seyde sir Launcelot, 'what woll ye do?'

And anone they seyde all with one voyce,
30 'We woll do as ye woll do.'

'Than I put thys case unto you,' seyde sir Launcelot, 'that my lorde, kynge Arthure, by evyll counceile woll to-morn in hys hete put my lady the quene unto the fyre and there to be brente, than, I pray you, counceile me what ys beste for me to do.'

35   Than they seyde all at onys with one voice,
'Sir, us thynkis beste that ye knyghtly rescow the quene. Insomuch as she shall be brente, hit ys for youre sake; and hit ys to suppose, and ye myght be handeled, ye shulde have the same dethe, othir ellis a more shamefuller dethe. And, sir, we say all that ye have rescowed her
40 frome her deth many tymys for other mennes quarels; therefore us semyth hit ys more youre worshyp that ye rescow the quene from thys quarell, insomuch that she hath hit for your sake.'

Than sir Launcelot stood stylle and sayde,
'My fayre lordis, wyte you well I wolde be lothe to do that thynge

that shulde dishonour you or my bloode; and wyte you well I wolde be full lothe that my lady the quene shu[l]de dye such a shamefull deth. But and hit be so that ye woll counceyle me to rescow her, I must do much harme or I rescow her, and peradventure I shall there destroy som of my beste fryndis, ⟨and⟩ [that shold moche repente me. And 5 peradventure there be som, and they coude wel bryng it aboute or disobeye my lord kynge Arthur, they wold sone come to me, the whiche I were loth to hurte.] And if so be that I may wynne the quene away, where shall I kepe her?'

'Sir, that shall be the leste care of us all,' seyde sir Bors, 'for how ded 10 the moste noble knyght sir Trystram? By youre good wyll, kept nat he with hym La Beall Isode nere three yere in Joyous Garde, the whych was done by youre althers avyce? And that same place ys youre owne, and in lyke wyse may ye do, and ye lyst, and take the quene knyghtly away with you, if so be that the kynge woll jouge her to be brente. 15 And in Joyous Garde may ye kepe her longe inowe untyll the hete be paste of the kynge, and than hit may fortune you to brynge the quene agayne to the kynge with grete worshyp, and peradventure ye shall have than thanke for youre bryngyng home where othir may happyn to have magré.' 20

'That ys hard for to do,' seyde sir Launcelot, 'for by sir Trystram I may have a warnynge: for whan by meanys of trety se sir Trystram brought agayne La Beall Isode unto kynge Marke from Joyous Garde, loke ye now what felle on the ende, how shamefully that false traytour kyng Marke slew hym as he sate harpynge afore hys lady, La Beall 25 Isode. Wyth a grounden glayve he threste hym in behynde to the harte, whych grevyth sore me,' seyde sir Launcelot, 'to speke of his dethe, for all the worlde may nat fynde such another knyght.'

'All thys ys trouthe,' seyde sir Bors, 'but there ys one thyng shall corrayge you and us all: ye know well that kynge Arthur and kynge 30 Marke were never lyke of cond[y]cions, for there was never yet man that ever coude preve kynge Arthure untrew of hys promyse.'

But so, to make shorte tale, the[y] were all condiscended that, for bettir othir for wars, if so were that the quene were brought on that morne to the fyre, shortely they all wolde rescow her. And so by the 35 advyce of sir Launcelot they put hem all in a wood as nyghe Carlyle as they myght, and there they abode stylle to wyte what the kynge wold do.

Now turne we agayne, that whan sir Mordred was ascaped frome sir (7) Launcelot he gate hys horse and cam to kynge Arthur sore wounded 40 and all forbled, and there he tolde the kynge all how hit was, and how they were all slayne save hymselff alone.

'A, Jesu, mercy! How may thys be?' seyde the kynge. 'Toke ye hym in the quenys chambir?'

'Yee, so God me helpe,' seyde sir Mordred, 'there we founde hym unarmed, and anone he slew sir Collgrevaunce and armed hym in hys armour.'

And so he tolde the kynge frome the begynnyng to the endynge.

5 'Jesu mercy!' seyde the kynge, 'he ys a mervaylous knyght of proues. And alas,' seyde the kynge, 'me sore repentith that ever sir Launcelot sholde be ayenste me, for now I am sure the noble felyshyp of the Rounde Table ys brokyn for ever, for wyth hym woll many a noble knyght holde. And now hit ys fallen so,' seyde the kynge, 'that I may
10 nat with my worshyp but my quene muste suffir dethe,' and was sore amoved.

So than there was made grete ordynaunce in thys ire, and the quene muste nedis be jouged to the deth. And the law was such in tho dayes that whatsomever they were, of what astate or degré, if they were
15 founden gylty of treson there shuld be none other remedy but deth, and othir the menour other the takynge wyth the dede shulde be causer of their hasty jougement. And ryght so was hit ordayned for quene Gwenyver: bycause sir Mordred was ascaped sore wounded, and the dethe of thirtene knyghtes of the Rounde Table, thes previs and
20 experyenses caused kynge Arthure to commaunde the quene to the fyre and there to be brente.

Than spake sir Gawayn and seyde,

'My lorde Arthure, I wolde counceyle you nat to be over hasty, but that ye wolde put hit in respite, thys jougemente of my lady the quene,
25 for many causis. One ys thys, thoughe hyt were so that sir Launcelot were founde in the quenys chambir, yet hit myght be so that he cam thydir for none evyll. For ye know, my lorde,' seyde sir Gawayne, 'that my lady the quene hath oftyntymes ben gretely beholdyn unto sir Launcelot, more than to ony othir knyght; for oftyntymes he hath
30 saved her lyff and done batayle for her whan all the courte refused the quene. And peradventure she sente for hym for goodnes and for none evyll, to rewarde hym for his good dedys that he had done to her in tymes past. And peraventure my lady the quene sente for hym to that entente, that sir Launcelot sholde a com prevaly to her, wenyng that
35 hyt had be beste in eschewyng [and dredyng] of slaundir; for oftyntymys we do many thynges that we wene for the beste be, and yet peradventure hit turnyth to the warste. For I dare sey,' seyde sir Gawayne, 'my lady, your quene, ys to you both good and trew. And as for sir Launcelot, I dare say he woll make hit good uppon ony knyght
40 lyvyng that woll put uppon hym vylany or shame, and in lyke wyse he woll make good for my lady the quene.'

'That I beleve well,' seyde kynge Arthur, 'but I woll nat that way worke with sir Launcelot, for he trustyth so much uppon hys hondis and hys myght that he doutyth no man. And therefore for my quene he

shall nevermore fyght, for she shall have the law. And if I may gete sir
Launcelot, wyte you well he shall have as shamefull a dethe.'

'Jesu defende me,' seyde sir Gawayne, 'that I never se hit nor know
hit.'

'Why say you so?' seyde kynge Arthur. 'For, perdé, ye have no 5
cause to love hym! For thys nyght last past he slew youre brothir sir
Aggravayne, a full good knyght, and allmoste he had slayne youre
othir brother, sir Mordred, and also there he slew thirtene noble
knyghtes. And also remembir you, sir Gawayne, he slew two sunnes
of youres, sir Florens and sir Lovell.'   10

'My lorde,' seyde sir Gawayne, 'of all thys I have a knowleche,
whych of her dethis sore repentis me. But insomuch as I gaff hem
warnynge and tolde my brothir and my sonnes aforehonde what
wolde falle on the ende, and insomuche as they wolde nat do be my
counceyle, I woll nat meddyll me thereoff, nor revenge me nothynge of 15
their dethys; for I tolde them there was no boote to stryve with sir
Launcelot. Howbehit I am sory of the deth of my brothir and of my
two sunnes, but they ar the causars of their owne dethe; for oftyntymes I warned my brothir sir Aggravayne, and I tolde hym the
perellis [the which ben now fallen].'   20

Than seyde kynge Arthur unto sir Gawayne,   (8)

'Make you redy, I pray you, in youre beste armour, wyth youre
brethirn, sir Gaherys and sir Ga[reth], to brynge my quene to the fyre
and there to have her jougement.'

'Nay, my moste noble kynge,' seyde sir Gawayne, 'that woll I never 25
do, for wyte you well I woll never be in that place where so noble a
quene as ys my lady dame Gwenyver shall take such a shamefull ende.
For wyte you well,' seyde sir Gawayne, 'my harte woll nat serve me for
to se her dye, and hit shall never be seyde that ever I was of youre
counceyle for her deth.'   30

'Than,' seyde the kynge unto sir Gawayne, 'suffir your brethirn sir
Gaherys and sir Gareth to be there.'

'My lorde,' seyde sir Gawayne, 'wyte you well they wyll be lothe to
be there present bycause of many adventures that ys lyke to falle, but
they ar yonge and full unable to say you nay.'   35

Than spake sir Gaherys and the good knyght sir Gareth unto kynge
Arthur,

'Sir, ye may well commaunde us to be there, but wyte you well
hit shall be sore ayenste oure wyll. But and we be there by youre
strayte commaundement, ye shall playnly holde us there excused: 40
we woll be there in pesyble wyse, and beare none harneyse of warre
uppon us.'

'In the name of God,' seyde the kynge, 'than make you redy, for she
shall have sone her jugemente.'.

'Alas,' seyde sir Gawayne, 'that ever I shulde endure to se this wofull day!'

So sir Gawayne turned hym and wepte hartely, and so he wente into hys chambir. And so the quene was lad furthe withoute Carlyle, and anone she was dispoyled into he[r] smokke. And than her gostely fadir was brought to her to be shryven of her myssededis. Than was there wepyng and waylynge and wryngyng of hondis of many lordys and ladyes; but there were but feaw in comparison that wolde beare ony armoure for to strengthe the dethe of the quene.

Than was there one that sir Launcelot had sente unto [that place], whych wente to aspye what tyme the quene shulde go unto her deth. And anone as he saw the quene dispoyled into her smok and shryvyn, than he gaff sir Launcelot warnynge anone. Than was there but spurryng and pluckyng up of horse, and ryght so they cam unto the fyre. And who that stoode ayenste them, there were they slayne; [there myght none withstande sir Launcelot.

So all that bare armes and withstoode them, there were they slayne], full many a noble knyght. For there was slayne sir Bellyas le Orgulus, sir Segwarydes, sir Gryfflet, sir Braundyles, sir Agglovale, sir Tor; sir Gauter, sir Gyllymer, sir Raynold, three brethirn, and sir Damas, sir Priamus, sir Kay le Straunge, sir Dryaunt, sir Lambegus, sir Hermynde, sir Pertolyp, sir Perymones, two brethern whych were called the Grene Knyght and the Rede Knyght.

And so in thys russhynge and hurlynge, as sir Launcelot thrange here and there, hit mysfortuned hym to sle sir Gaherys and sir Gareth, the noble knyght, for they were unarmed and unwares. As the Freynshe booke sayth, sir Launcelot smote sir Gaherys and sir Gareth uppon the brayne-pannes, wherethorow that they were slayne in the felde. Howbehit in very trouth sir Launcelot saw them [nat]. And so were they founde dede amonge the thyckyste of the prees.

Than sir Launcelot, whan he had thus done, and slayne and put to flyght all that wolde wythstonde hym, than he rode streyt unto quene Gwenyver and made caste a kurdyll and a gown uppon her, and than he made her to be sette behynde hym and prayde her to be of good chere. Now wyte you well the quene was glad that she was at that tyme ascaped frome the deth, and than she thanked God and sir Launcelot.

And so he rode hys way wyth the quene, as the Freynshe booke seyth, unto Joyous Garde, and there he kepte her as a noble knyght shulde. And many grete lordis and many good knyghtes were sente hym, and many full noble knyghtes drew unto hym. Whan they harde that kynge Arthure and sir Launcelot were at debate many knyghtes were glad, and many were sory of their debate.

II. THE VENGEANCE OF SIR GAWAIN

Now turne we agayne unto kynge Arthure, that whan hit was tolde (9)
hym how and in what maner the quene was taken away frome the fyre,
and whan he harde of the deth of his noble knyghtes, and in especiall
sir Gaherys and sir Gareth, than he sowned for verry pure sorow. And 5
whan he awooke of hys swoughe, than he sayde,

'Alas, that ever I bare crowne uppon my hede! For now have I loste
the fayryst felyshyp of noble knyghtes that ever hylde Crystyn kynge
togydirs. Alas, my good knyghtes be slayne and gone away fro me,
that now within thys two dayes I have loste nygh forty knyghtes and 10
also the noble felyshyp of sir Launcelot and hys blood, for now I may
nevermore holde hem togydirs with my worshyp. Now, alas, that ever
thys warre began!

'Now, fayre felowis,' seyde the kynge, 'I charge you that no man
telle sir Gawayne of the deth of hys two brethirne, for I am sure,' 15
seyde the kynge, 'whan he hyryth telle that sir Gareth ys dede, he wyll
go nygh oute of hys mynde. M[e]rci Jesu,' seyde the kynge, 'why slew
he sir Gaherys and sir Gareth? For I dare sey, as for sir Gareth, he
loved sir Launcelot of all men erthly.'

'That ys trouth,' seyde som knyghtes, 'but they were slayne in the 20
hurlynge, as sir Launcelot thrange in the thyckyst of the prees. And as
they were unarmed, he smote them and wyst nat whom that he smote,
and so unhappely they were slayne.'

'Well,' seyde Arthure, 'the deth of them woll cause the grettist
mortall warre that ever was, for I am sure that whan sir Gawayne know- 25
yth hereoff that sir Gareth ys slayne, I shall never have reste of hym
tyll I have destroyed sir Launcelottys kynne and hymselff bothe, othir
ellis he to destroy me. And therefore,' seyde the kynge, 'wyte you well,
my harte was never so hevy as hit ys now. And much more I am
soryar for my good knyghtes losse than for the losse of my fayre quene; 30
for quenys I myght have inow, but such a felyship of good knyghtes
shall never be togydirs in no company. And now I dare sey,' seyde
kynge Arthur, 'there was never Crystyn kynge that ever hylde such a
felyshyp togydyrs. And alas, that ever sir Launcelot and I shulde be at
debate! A, Aggravayne, Aggravayne!' seyde the kynge, 'Jesu forgyff 35
hit thy soule, for thyne evyll wyll that thou haddist and sir Mordred,
thy brothir, unto sir Launcelot hath caused all this sorow.'

And ever amonge thes complayntes the kynge wepte and sowned.

Than cam there one to sir Gawayne and tolde [hym] how the quene
was lad away with sir Launcelot, and nygh a four-and-twenty knyghtes 40
slayne.

'A, Jesu, save me my two brethirn!' seyde sir Gawayne, 'For full
well wyst I,' sayde sir Gawayne, 'that sir Launcelot wolde rescow her,

othir ellis he wolde dye in that fylde; and to say the trouth he were nat of worshyp but if he had rescowed the quene, insomuch as she shulde have be brente for his sake. And as in that,' seyde sir Gawayne, 'he hath done but knyghtly, and as I wolde have done myselff and I had
5 stonde in lyke case. But where ar my brethirn?' seyde sir Gawayne, 'I mervayle that I se nat of them.'

Than seyde that man, 'Truly, sir Gaherys and sir Gareth be slayne.'

'Jesu deffende!' seyd sir Gawayne. 'For all thys worlde I wolde nat that they were slayne, and in especiall my good brothir sir Gareth.'

10 'Sir,' seyde the man, 'he ys slayne, and that ys grete pité.'

'Who slew hym?' seyde sir Gawayne.

'Sir Launcelot,' seyde the man, 'slew hem both.'

'That may I nat beleve,' seyde sir Gawayne, 'that ever he slew my good brother sir Gareth, for I dare say my brothir loved hym bettir
15 than me and all hys brethirn and the kynge bothe. Also I dare say, an sir Launcelot had desyred my brothir sir Gareth with hym, he wolde have ben with hym ayenste the kynge and us all. And therefore I may never belyeve that sir Launcelot slew my brethern.'

'Veryly, sir,' seyde the man, 'hit ys noysed that he slew hym.'

(10) 20 'Alas,' seyde sir Gawayne, 'now ys my joy gone!'

And than he felle downe and sowned, and longe he lay there as he had ben dede. And whan he arose oute of hys swoughe he cryed oute sorowfully and seyde,

'Alas!'

25 And forthwith he ran unto the kynge, criyng and wepyng, and seyde, 'A, myne uncle kynge Arthur! My good brothir sir Gareth ys slayne, and so ys my brothir sir Gaherys, whych were two noble knyghtes.'

Than the kynge wepte and he bothe, and so they felle on sownynge. And whan they were revyved, than spake sir Gawayne and seyde,
30 'Sir, I woll goo and se my brother sir Gareth.'

'Sir, ye may nat se hym,' seyde the kynge, 'for I caused hym to be entered and sir Gaherys bothe, for I well undirstood that ye wolde make overmuche sorow, and the syght of sir Gareth shulde have caused youre double sorow.'

35 'Alas, my lorde,' seyde sir Gawayne, 'how slew he my brothir sir Gareth? I pray you telle me.'

'Truly,' seyde the kynge, 'I shall tell you as hit hath bene tolde me: sir Launcelot slew hym and sir Gaherys both.'

'Alas,' seyde sir Gawayne, 'they beare none armys ayenst hym,
40 neyther of them bothe.'

'I wote nat how hit was,' seyde the kynge, 'but as hit ys sayde, sir Launcelot slew them in the thyk prees and knew tham nat. And therefore lat us shape a remedy for to revenge their dethys.'

'My kynge, my lorde, and myne uncle,' seyde sir Gawayne, 'wyte you

well, now I shall make you a promyse whych I shall holde be my
knyghthode, that frome thys day forewarde I shall never fayle sir
Launcelot untyll that one of us have slayne that othir. And therefore I
requyre you, my lorde and kynge, dresse you unto the warres, for wyte
you well, I woll be revenged uppon sir Launcelot; and therefore, as ye   5
woll have my servyse and my love, now haste you thereto and assay
youre frendis. For I promyse unto God,' seyde sir Gawayn, 'for the
deth of my brothir, sir Gareth, I shall seke sir Launcelot thorowoute
seven kynges realmys, but I shall sle hym, other ellis he shall sle me.'

'Sir, ye shall nat nede to seke hym so far,' seyde the kynge, 'for as I   10
here say, sir Launcelot woll abyde me and us all wythin the castell of
Joyous Garde. And muche peple drawyth unto hym, as I here say.'

'That may I ryght well belyve,' seyde sir Gawayne; 'but my lorde,'
he sayde, 'assay your fryndis and I woll assay myne.'

'Hit shall be done,' seyde the kyng, 'and as I suppose I shall be   15
bygge inowghe to dryve hym oute of the bygyst toure of hys castell.'

So than the kynge sente lettirs and wryttis thorowoute all Inglonde,
both the lengthe and the brede, for to assomon all hys knyghtes. And
so unto kynge Arthure drew many knyghtes, deukes, and erlis, that he
had a grete oste, and whan they were assembeled the kynge enfourmed   20
hem how sir Launcelot had beraffte hym hys quene.

Than the kynge and all hys oste made hem redy to ley syege aboute
sir Launcelot where he lay within Joyous Garde.

And anone sir Launcelot harde thereof and purveyde hym off many
good knyghtes; ¹for with hym helde many knyghtes,¹ som for hys   25
owne sake and som for the quenys sake. Thus they were on bothe
partyes well furnysshed and garnysshed of all maner of thynge that
longed unto the warre. But kynge Arthurs oste was so grete that sir
Launcelottis oste wolde nat abyde hym in the fylde. For he was full
lothe to do batayle ayenste the kynge; but sir Launcelot drew hym   30
unto hys stronge castell with all maner of vytayle plenté, and as many
noble men as he myght suffyse within the towne and the castell.

Than cam kynge Arthure with sir Gawayne wyth a grete oste and
leyde syge all aboute Joyus Garde, both the towne and the castell. And
there they made stronge warre on bothe partyes, but in no wyse sir   35
Launcelot wolde ryde oute [nor go oute] of the castell of longe tyme;
and nother he wold nat suffir none of hys good knyghtes to issew oute,
nother of the towne nother of the castell, untyll fiftene wykes were
paste.

So hit felle uppon a day[e in hervest tyme] that sir Launcelot loked   40 (11)
over the wallys and spake on hyght unto kynge Arthure and to sir
Gawayne:

'My lordis bothe, wyte you well all thys ys in vayne that ye make at
thys syge, for here wynne ye no worshyp, but magré and dishonoure.

For and hit lyste me to com myselff oute and my good knyghtes, I
shulde full sone make an ende of thys warre.'

'Com forth,' seyde kynge Arthur unto sir Launcelot, 'and thou
darste, and I promyse the I shall mete the in myddis of thys fylde.'

5   'God deffende me,' seyde sir Launcelot, 'that ever I shulde encounter
wyth the moste noble kynge that made me knyght.'

'Now, fye uppon thy fayre langayge!' seyde the kynge, 'for wyte
thou well and truste hit, I am thy mortall foo and ever woll to my deth-
day; for thou haste slayne my good knyghtes and full noble men of my

10 blood, that shall I never recover agayne. Also thou haste layne be my
quene and holdyn her many wynters, and sytthyn, lyke a traytoure,
taken her away fro me by fors.'

'My moste noble lorde and kynge,' seyde sir Launcelot, 'ye may sey
what ye woll, for ye wote well wyth youreselff I woll nat stryve. But

15 theras ye say that I have slayne youre good knyghtes, I wote well that
I have done so, and that me sore repentith; but I was forced to do
batayle with hem in savyng of my lyff, othir ellis I muste have suffirde
hem to have slayne me. And as for my lady quene Gwenyver, excepte
youre person of your hyghnes and my lorde sir Gawayne, there nys no

20 knyght undir hevyn that dare make hit good uppon me that ever I was
traytour unto youre person. And where hit please you to say that I
have holdyn my lady, youre quene, yerys and wynters, unto that I
shall ever make a large answere, and prove hit uppon ony knyght that
beryth the lyff, excepte your person and sir Gawayne, that my lady,

25 quene Gwenyver, ys as trew a lady unto youre person as ys ony lady
lyvynge unto her lorde, and that woll I make good with my hondis.
Howbehyt hit hath lyked her good grace to have me in favoure and
cherysh me more than ony other knyght; and unto my power agayne I
have deserved her love, for oftyntymes, my lorde, ye have concented

30 that she sholde have be brente and destroyed in youre hete, and than
hit fortuned me to do batayle for her, and or I departed from her adversary they confessed there untrouthe, and she full worsshypfully
excused. And at suche tymes, my lorde Arthur,' seyde sir Launcelot,
'ye loved me and thanked me whan I saved your quene frome the fyre,

35 and than ye promysed me for ever to be my good lorde. And now
methynkith ye rewarde me evyll for my good servyse. And, my lorde,
mesemyth I had loste a grete parte of my worshyp in my knyghthod and
I had suffird my lady, youre quene, to have ben brente, and insomuche
as she shulde have bene brente for my sake; for sytthyn I have done

40 batayles for youre quene in other quarels than in myne owne quarell,
mesemyth now I had more ryght to do batayle for her in her ryght
quarell. And therefore, my good and gracious lorde,' seyde sir Launcelot,
'take your quene unto youre good grace, for she ys both tru and
good.'

'Fy on the, false recreayed knyght!' seyde sir Gawayn. 'For I lat the wyte: my lorde, myne uncle kynge Arthur shall have hys quene and the bothe magré thy vysayge, and sle you bothe and save you whether hit please hym.'

'Hit may well be,' seyde sir Launcelot, 'but wyte thou well, my 5 lorde sir Gawayne, and me lyste to com oute of thys castell ye shuld wyn me and the quene more harder than ever ye wan a stronge batayle.'

'Now, fy on thy proude wordis!' seyde sir Gawayne. 'As for my lady the quene, wyte thou well, I woll never say [of] her shame. But thou, false and recrayde knyght,' seyde sir Gawayne, 'what cause 10 haddist thou to sle my good brother sir Gareth that loved the more than me and all my kynne? And alas, thou madist hym knyght thyne owne hondis! Why slewest thou hym that loved the so well?'

'For to excuse me,' seyde sir Launcelot, 'hit boteneth me nat, but by Jesu, and by the feyth that I owghe unto the hyghe Order of Knyght- 15 hode, I wolde with as a good a wyll have slayne my nevew, sir Bors de Ganys, [at that tyme]. And alas, that ever I was so unhappy,' seyde sir Launcelot, 'that I had nat seyne sir Gareth and sir Gaherys!'

'Thou lyest, recrayed knyght,' seyde sir Gawayne, 'thou slewyste hem in the despite of me. And therefore wyte thou well, sir Launcelot, 20 I shall make warre uppon the, and all the whyle that I may lyve be thyne enemy!'

'That me repentes,' seyde sir Launcelot, 'for well I undirstonde hit boteneth me nat to seke none accordemente whyle ye, sir Gawayne, ar so myschevously sett. And if ye were nat, I wolde nat doute to have 25 the good grace of my lorde kynge Arthure.'

'I leve well, false recrayed knyght, for thou haste many longe dayes overlad me and us all, and destroyed many of oure good knyghtes.'

'Sir, ye say as hit pleasith you,' seyde sir Launcelot, 'yet may hit never be seyde on me and opynly preved that ever I be forecaste of 30 treson slew no goode knyght as ye, my lorde sir Gawayne, have done; and so ded I never but in my deffence, that I was dryven thereto in savyng of my lyff.'

'A, thou false knyght,' seyde sir Gawayne, 'that thou menyst by sir Lamorak. But wyte thou well, I slew hym!'   35

'Sir, ye slew hym nat youreselff,' seyde sir Launcelot, 'for hit had ben overmuch for you, for he was one of the beste knyghtes crystynde of his ayge. And hit was grete pité of hys deth!'

'Well, well, sir Launcelot,' seyde sir Gawayne, 'sytthyn thou en- (12) braydyst me of sir Lamorak, wyte thou well I shall never leve the tyll 40 I have the at suche avayle that thou shalt nat ascape my hondis.'

'I truste you well inowgh,' seyde sir Launcelot. 'And ye may gete me, I gett but lytyll mercy.'

But the Freynsh booke seyth kynge Arthur wolde have takyn hys

quene᷄ agayne and to have bene accorded with sir Launcelot, but sir
Gawayne wolde nat suffir hym by no maner of meane. And so sir
Gawayne made many men to blow uppon sir Launcelot, and so all at
onys they called hym 'false recrayed knyght'.

5   But whan sir Bors de Ganys, sir Ector de Marys and sir Lyonell
harde thys outecry they called unto them sir Palomydes and sir
Lavayne an sir Urré wyth many mo knyghtes of their bloode, and all
they wente unto sir Launcelot and seyde thus:

'My lorde, wyte you well we have grete scorne of the grete rebukis
10 that we have harde sir Gawayne sey unto you; wherefore we pray you
and charge you as ye woll have oure servyse, kepe us no lenger wythin
thys wallis, for we lat you wete playnly we woll ryde into the fylde and
do batayle wyth hem. For ye fare as a man that were aferde, and for all
their fayre speche hit woll nat avayle you, for wyte you well sir Gawayne
15 woll nevir suffir you to accorde wyth kynge Arthur. And therefore
fyght for youre lyff and ryght, and [ye] dare.'

'Alas,' seyde sir Launcelot, 'for to ryde oute of thys castell and to do
batayle I am full lothe.'

Than sir Launcelot spake on hyght unto kyng Arthur and sir
20 Gawayne:

'My lorde, I requyre you and beseche you, sytthyn that I am thus
requyred and conjoured to ryde into the fylde, that neyther you, my
lorde kyng Arthur, nother you, sir Gawayne, com nat into the
fylde.'

25 'What shall we do?' than seyde sir Gawayne. 'Is nat thys the kynges
quarell to fyght wyth the? And also hit ys my quarell to fyght wyth the
because of the dethe of my brothir, sir Gareth.'

'Than muste I nedys unto batayle,' seyde sir Launcelot. 'Now wyte
you well, my lorde Arthur and sir Gawayne, ye woll repent hit whan-
30 somever I do batayle wyth you.'

And so than they departed eythir frome othir; and than aythir party
made hem redy on the morne for to do batayle, and grete purveyaunce
was made on bothe sydys. And sir Gawayne lat purvey many knyghtes
for to wayte uppon sir Launcelot for to oversette hym and to sle hym.
35 And on the morn at underne kynge Arthure was redy in the fylde with
three grete ostys.

And than sir Launcelottis felyshyp com oute at the three gatis in full
good aray; and sir Lyonell cam in the formyst batayle, and sir Launcelot cam in the myddyll, and sir Bors com oute at the thirde gate. And
40 thus they cam in order and rule as full noble knyghtes. And ever sir
Launcelot charged all hys knyghtes in ony wyse to save kynge Arthure
and sir Gawayne.

(13)   Than cam forth sir Gawayne frome the kyngis oste and profirde to
juste. And sir Lyonel was a fyers knyght, and lyghtly he encountred

with hym, and there sir Gawayne smote sir Lyonell thorowoute the body, that he daysshed to the erth lyke as he had ben dede. And than sir Ector de Marys and other mo bare hym into the castell.

And anone there began a grete stowre and much people were slayne; and ever sir Launcelot ded what he myght to save the people on kynge 5 Arthurs party. For sir Bors and sir Palomydes and sir Saffir overthrew many knyghts, for they were dedely knyghtes, and sir Blamour de Ganys and sir Bleoberys, wyth sir Bellyngere le Bewse, thes six knyghtes ded much harme. And ever was kynge Arthur aboute sir Launcelot to have slayne hym, and ever sir Launcelot suffird hym and wolde nat 10 stryke agayne. So sir Bors encountirde wyth kynge Arthur, and sir Bors smote hym, and so he alyght and drew hys swerde and seyd to sir Launcelot,

'Sir, shall I make an ende of thys warre?' (For he mente to have slayne hym.) 15

'Nat so hardy,' seyde sir Launcelot, 'uppon payne of thy hede, that thou touch hym no more! For I woll never se that moste noble kynge that made me knyght nother slayne nor shamed.'

And therewithall sir Launcelot alyght of hys horse and toke up the kynge and horsed hym agayne, and seyd thus: 20

'My lorde the kynge, for Goddis love, stynte thys stryff, for ye gette here no worshyp and I wolde do myne utteraunce. But allwayes I forbeare you, and ye nor none off youres forberyth nat me. And therefore, my lorde, I pray you remembir what I have done in many placis, and now am I evyll rewarded.' 25

So whan kynge Arthur was on horsebak he loked on sir Launcelot; than the teerys braste oute of hys yen, thynkyng of the grete curtesy that was in sir Launcelot more than in ony other man. And therewith the kynge rod hys way and myght no lenger beholde hym, saiyng to hymselff, 'Alas, alas, that ᴿeverᴵ yet thys warre began!' 30

And than aythir party of the batayles wythdrew them to repose them, and buryed the dede and serched the wounded men, and leyde to their woundes soffte salves; and thus they endured that nyght tylle on the morne. And on the morne by undirn they made them redy to do batayle, and than sir Bors lad the vawarde. 35

So uppon the morn there cam sir Gawayne, as brym as ony boore, wyth a grete spere in hys honde. And whan sir Bors saw hym he thought to revenge hys brother, sir Lyonell, of the despite sir Gawayne gaff hym the other day. And so, as they that knew aythir other, feautred their spearis, and with all their myght of their horsis and themselff so 40 fyersly they mette togydirs and so felonsly that aythir bare other thorow, and so they felle bothe to the bare erthe.

And than the batayle joyned, and there was much slaughter on bothe partyes. Than sir Launcelot rescowed sir Bors and sent hym into the castell, but neyther sir Gawayne nother sir Bors dyed nat of their woundis, for they were well holpyn.

Than sir Lavayne and sir Urré prayde sir Launcelot to do hys payne and feyght as they do: 'For we se that ye forbeare and spare, and that 5 doth us much harme. And therefore we pray you spare nat youre enemyes no more than they do you.'

'Alas,' seyde sir Launcelot, 'I have no harte to fyght ayenste my lorde Arthur, for ever mesemyth I do nat as me ought to do.'

'My lorde,' seyde sir Palomydes, 'thoughe ye spare them never so 10 much all thys day they woll [never] can you thanke; and yf they may gete you at avayle ye ar but a dede man.'

So than sir Launcelot undirstoode that they seyde hym trouthe. Than he strayned hymselff more than he ded toforehonde, and bycause of hys nevew, sir Bors, was sore wounded he payned hymselff the more. 15 And so within a lytyll whyle, by evynsong tyme, sir Launcelottis party the bettir stood, for their horsis wente in blood paste the fyttlokkes, there were so many people slayne.

And than for verry pité sir Launcelot withhylde hys knyghtes and suffird kynge Arthurs party to withdraw them insyde. And so he with- 20 drew hys meyny into the castell, and aythir partyes buryed the dede and put salve unto the wounded men. So whan sir Gawayne was hurte, they on kynge Arthurs party were nat so orgulus as they were toforehonde to do batayle.

So of thys warre that was betwene kynge Arthure and sir Launcelot 25 hit was noysed thorow all Crystyn realmys, and so hit cam at the laste by relacion unto the Pope. And than the Pope toke a consideracion of the grete goodnes of kynge Arthur and of the hyghe proues off sir Launcelot, that was called the moste nobelyst knyght of the worlde. Wherefore the Pope called unto hym a noble clerke that at that tyme 30 was there presente (the Freynsh boke seyth hit was the Bysshop of Rochester), and the Pope gaff [hym bulles] undir leade, and sente hem unto the kynge, chargyng hym uppon payne of entirdytynge of all Inglonde that he take hys quene agayne and accorde with sir Launcelot.

(14) 35 So whan thys Bysshop was com unto Carlyle he shewed the kynge hys bullys, and whan the kynge undirstode them he wyste nat what to do: but full fayne he wolde have bene acorded with sir Launcelot, but sir Gawayn wolde nat suffir hym. But to have the quene he thereto agreed, but in no wyse he wolde suffir the kynge to accorde with sir 40 Launcelot; but as for the quene, he consented. So the Bysshop had of the kynge hys grete seale and hys assuraunce, as he was a trew and anoynted kynge, that sir Launcelot shulde go sauff and com sauff, and that the quene shulde nat be seyde unto of the kynge, nother of none other, for nothynge done of tyme paste. And of all thes

appoyntementes the Bysshop brought with hym sure wrytynge to shew unto sir Launcelot.

So whan the Bysshop was com to Joyous Garde, there he shewed sir Launcelot how he cam frome the Pope with wrytynge unto kyng Arthur and unto hym. And there he tolde hym the perelis, gyff he 5 wythhelde the quene frome the kynge.

'Sir, hit was never in my thought,' seyde sir Launcelot, 'to withholde the quene frome my lorde Arthur, but I kepe her for thys cause: insomuche as she shulde have be brente for my sake, mesemed hit was my parte to save her lyff and put her from that daungere tyll bettir 10 recover myght com. And now I thanke God,' seyde sir Launcelot, 'that the Pope hathe made he[r] pease. For God knowyth,' seyde sir Launcelot, 'I woll be a thousandefolde more gladder to brynge her agayne than ever I was of her takyng away, wyth thys I may be sure to com sauff and go sauff, and that the quene shall have her lyberté, and 15 never for nothyng that hath be surmysed afore thys tyme that she never frome thys stonde in no perell. For ellis,' seyde sir Launcelot, 'I dare adventure me to kepe her frome an harder showre than ever yet I had.'

'Sir, hit shall nat nede you,' seyde the Bysshop, 'to drede thus muche, for wyte yow well, the Pope muste be obeyed, and hit were nat the 20 Popis worshyp nother my poure honesté to know you distressed nother the quene, nother in perell nother shamed.'

And than he shewed sir Launcelot all hys wrytynge bothe frome the Pope and kynge Arthure.

'Thys ys sure ynow,' seyde sir Launcelot. 'For full well I dare truste 25 my lordys owne wrytyng and hys seale, for he was never shamed of hys promyse. Therefore,' seyde sir Launcelot unto the Bysshop, 'ye shall ryde unto the kynge afore and recommaunde me unto hys good grace, and lat hym have knowlccchynge that this same day eyght dayes, by the grace of God, I myselff shall brynge the quene unto hym. And than 30 sey ye to my moste redouted kynge that I woll sey largely for the quene, that I shall none excepte for drede nother for feare but the kynge hymselff and my lorde sir Gawayne; and that ys for the kyngis love more than for hymselff.'

So the Bysshop departed and cam to the kynge to Carlehyll, and tolde 35 hym all how sir Launcelot answerd hym; so that made the teares falle oute at the kyngis yen. Than sir Launcelot purveyed hym an hondred knyghtes, and all well clothed in grene velvet, and their horsis trapped in the same to the heelys, and every knyght hylde a braunche of olyff in hys honde in tokenyng of pees. And the quene had four-and-twenty 40 jantillwomen folowyng her in the same wyse. And sir Launcelot had twelve coursers folowyng hym, and on every courser sate a yonge jantylman; and all they were arayed in whyght velvet with sarpis of golde aboute their quatters, and the horse trapped in the same wyse down to the helys, wyth many owchys, isette with stonys and perelys in golde, to the numbir of a thousande. And in the same wyse was the quene arayed, and sir Launcelot in the same, of whyght clothe of golde tyssew.

5 And ryght so as ye have harde, as the Freynshe booke makyth mencion, he rode with the quene frome Joyus Garde to Carlehyll. And so sir Launcelot rode thorowoute Carlehylle, and so into the castell, that all men myght beholde hem. And there was many a wepyng ien.

And than sir Launcelot hymselff alyght and voyded hys horse, and 10 toke adowne the quene, and so lad her where kyng Arthur was in hys seate; and sir Gawayne sate afore hym, and many other grete lordys.

So whan sir Launcelot saw the kynge and sir Gawayne, than he lad the quene by the arme, and than he kneled downe and the quene bothe. Wyte you well, than was there many a bolde knyght wyth kynge 15 Arthur that wepte as tendirly as they had seyne all their kynne dede afore them!

So the kynge sate stylle and seyde no worde. And whan sir Launcelot saw hys countenaunce he arose up and pulled up the quene with hym, and thus he seyde full knyghtly:

(15) 20 'My moste redouted kynge, ye shall undirstonde, by the Popis commaundemente and youres I have brought to you my lady the quene, as ryght requyryth. And if there be ony knyght, of what degré that ever he be off, except your person, that woll sey or dare say but that she ys trew and clene to you, I here myselff, sir Launcelot du Lake, woll 25 make hit good uppon hys body that she ys a trew lady unto you.

'But, sir, lyars ye have lystened, and that hath caused grete debate betwyxte you and me. For tyme hath bene, my lorde Arthur, that [y]e were gretly pleased with me whan I ded batayle for my lady, youre quene; and full well ye know, my moste noble kynge, that she hathe be 30 put to grete wronge or thys tyme. And sytthyn hyt pleased you at many tymys that I shulde feyght for her, therefore mesemyth, my good lorde, I had more cause to rescow her from the fyer whan she sholde have ben brente for my sake.

'For they that tolde you tho talys were lyars, and so hit felle uppon 35 them: for by lyklyhode, had nat the myght of God bene with me, I myght never have endured with fourtene knyghtes, and they armed and afore purposed, and I unarmed and nat purposed; for I was sente unto my lady, youre quyne, I wote nat for what cause, but I was nat so sone within the chambir dore but anone sir Aggravayne and sir Mordred 40 called me traytoure and false recrayed knyght.'

'Be my fayth, they called the ryght!' seyde sir Gawayne.

'My lorde, sir Gawayne,' seyde sir Launcelot, 'in their quarell they preved nat hemselff the beste, nother in the ryght.'

'Well, well, sir Launcelot,' seyde the kynge, 'I have gyvyn you no cause to do to me as ye have done, for I have worshipt you and youres more than ony othir knyghtes.'

'My lorde,' seyde sir Launcelot, 'so ye be nat displeased, ye shall undirstonde that I and myne have done you oftyntymes bettir servyse than ony othir knyghtes have done, in many dyverce placis; and where ye have bene full ha[r]d bestadde dyvers tymes, I have rescowed you frome many daungers; and ever unto my power I was glad to please you and my lorde sir Gawayne. In justis and in turnementis and in batayles set, bothe on horsebak and on foote, I have oftyn rescowed you, and you, my lorde sir Gawayne, and many mo of youre knyghtes in many dyvers placis.

'For now I woll make avaunte,' seyde sir Launcelot. 'I woll that ye all wyte that as yet I founde never no maner of knyght but that I was over harde for hym and I had done myne utteraunce, God graunte mercy! Howbehit I have be macched with good knyghtes, as sir Trystram and sir Lamorak, but ever I had favoure unto them and a demyng what they were. And I take God to recorde, I never was wrothe nor gretly hevy wyth no good knyght and I saw hym besy and aboute to wyn worshyp; and glad I was ever whan I founde a good knyght that myght onythynge endure me on horsebak and on foote. Howbehit sir Carados of the Dolerous Toure was a full noble knyght and a passynge stronge man, and that wote ye, my lorde sir Gawayne; for he myght well be called a noble knyght whan he be fyne fors pulled you oute of your sadyll and bounde you overthwarte afore hym to hys sadyll-bow. And there, my lorde sir Gawayne, I rescowed you and slew hym afore your syght. Also I founde youre brothir, sir Gaherys, and sir Terquyn ledyng hym bounden afore hym; and there also I rescowed youre brothir and slew sir Terquyn and delyverde three score and four of my lorde Arthurs knyghtes oute of hys preson. And now I dare sey,' seyde sir Launcelot, 'I mette never wyth so stronge a knyght nor so well-fyghtyng as was sir Carados and sir Tarquyn, for they and I faught to the uttermest.

'And therefore,' seyde sir Launcelot unto sir Gawayne, 'mesemyth ye ought of ryght to remembir this; for, and I myght have youre good wyll, I wold truste to God for to have my lorde Arthurs good grace.'

'Sir, the kynge may do as he wyll,' seyde sir Gawayne, 'but wyte thou well, sir Launcelot, thou and I shall never be accorded whyle we lyve, for thou hast slayne three of my brethyrn. And two of hem thou slew traytourly and piteuously, for they bare none harneys ayenste the, nother none wold do.'

'Sir, God wolde they had ben armed,' seyde sir Launcelot, 'for than had they ben on lyve. And [wete you well, sir Gawayne, as] for Gareth, I loved no kynnesman I had more than I loved hym, and ever whyle I lyve,' seyde sir Launcelot, 'I woll bewayle sir Gareth hys dethe,

nat all only for the grete feare I have of you, but for many causys
whych causyth me to be sorowfull. One is that I made hym knyght;
another ys, I wote well he loved me aboven all othir knyghtes; and the
third ys, he was passyng noble and trew, curteyse and jantill and well-
5 condicionde. The fourthe ys, I wyste well, anone as I harde that sir
Gareth was dede, I knew well that I shulde never aftir have youre love,
my lorde sir Gawayne, but everlastyng warre betwyxt us. And also I
wyste well that ye wolde [cause] my noble lorde kynge Arthur for ever
to be my mortall foo. And as Jesu be my helpe, and be my knyghthode,
10 I slewe never sir Gareth nother hys brother be my wyllynge, but alas
that ever they were unarmed that unhappy day!

'But this much I shall offir me to you,' seyde sir Launcelot, 'if hit may
please the kyngis good grace and you, my lorde sir Gawayn: I shall
firste begyn at Sandwyche, and there I shall go in my shearte, bare-
15 foote; and at every ten myles ende I shall founde and gar make an
house of relygion, of what order that ye woll assygne me, with an holé
covente, to synge and rede day and nyght in especiall for sir Gareth
sake and sir Gaherys. And thys shall I perfourme [from Sandwyche
unto Carlyle; and every house shall have suffycyent lyvelod. And thys
20 shall I perfourme] whyle that I have ony lyvelod in Crystyndom, and
there ys none of all thes religious placis but they shall be perfourmed,
furnysshed and garnysshed with all thyngis as an holy place ought to be.
And thys were fayrar and more holyar and more perfyte to their
soulis than ye, my moste noble kynge, and you, sir Gawayne, to warre
25 uppon me, for thereby shall ye gete none avayle.'

Than all the knyghtes and ladyes that were there wepte as they were
madde, and the tearys felle on kynge Arthur hys chekis.

'Sir Launcelot,' seyde sir Gawayne, 'I have ryght well harde thy
langayge and thy grete proffirs. But wyt thou well, lat the kynge do as
30 hit pleasith hym, I woll never forgyff the my brothirs dethe, and in
especiall the deth of my brothir sir Gareth. And if myne uncle, kynge
Arthur, wyll accorde wyth the, he shall loose my servys, for wyte thou
well,' seyde sir Gawayne, 'thou arte bothe false to the kynge and to me.'

'Sir,' seyde sir Launcelot, 'he beryth nat the lyff that may make hit
35 good! And ye, sir Gawayne, woll charge me with so hyghe a thynge, ye
muste pardone me, for than nedis must I answere you.'

'Nay, nay,' seyde sir Gawayne, 'we ar paste that as at thys tyme, and
that causyth the Pope, for he hath charged myne uncle the kynge that
he shall take agayne his quene and to accorde wyth the, sir Launcelot,
40 as for thys season, and therefore thou shalt go sauff as thou com. But
in this londe thou shalt nat abyde paste a fiftene dayes, such somons I
gyff the, for so the kynge and we were condescended and accorded ar
thou cam. And ellis,' seyde sir Gawayn, 'wyte thou well, thou shulde
nat a comyn here but if hit were magré thyne hede. And if hit were nat

for the Popis commaundement,' seyde sir Gawayne, 'I shulde do
batayle with the myne owne hondis, body for body, and preve hit
uppon the that thou haste ben both false unto myne uncle, kynge
Arthur, and to me bothe; and that shall I preve on thy body, whan
thou arte departed fro hense, wheresomever that I fynde the!'   5

    Than sir Launcelotte syghed, and therewith the tearys felle on hys (17)
chekys, and than he seyde thus:

    'Moste nobelyst Crysten realme, whom I have loved aboven all
othir realmys! And in the I have gotyn a grete parte of my worshyp,
and now that I shall departe in thys wyse, truly me repentis that ever I 10
cam in thys realme, that I shulde be thus shamefully banysshyd, undeserved and causeles! But fortune ys so varyaunte, and the wheele so
mutable, that there ys no constaunte abydynge. And that may be preved
by many olde cronycles, as of noble Ector of Troy and Alysaunder, the
myghty conquerroure, and many mo other: whan they were moste in   15
her royalté, they alyght passyng lowe. And so faryth hit by me,' seyde
sir Launcelot, 'for in thys realme I had worshyp, and be me and myne
all the hole Rounde Table hath bene encreced more in worshyp, by me
and myne, than ever hit was by ony of you all.

    'And therefore wyte thou well, sir Gawayne, I may lyve uppon my   20
londis as well as ony knyght that here ys. And yf ye, my moste redoutted
kynge, woll com uppon my londys with sir Gawayne to warre uppon
me, I muste endure you as well as I may. But as to you, sir Gawayne, if
that ye com there, I pray you charge me nat wyth treson nother felony,
for and ye do, I muste answere you.'   25

    'Do thou thy beste,' seyde sir Gawayne, 'and therefore hyghe the
faste that thou were gone! And wyte thou well we shall sone com aftir,
and breke th[e] strengyst castell that thou hast, uppon thy hede!'

    'Hyt shall nat nede that,' seyde sir Launcelot, 'for and I were as
orgulous sette as ye ar, wyte you well I shulde mete you in myddys of   30
the fylde.'

    'Make thou no more langayge,' seyde sir Gawayne, 'but delyvir the
quene from the, and pyke the lyghtly oute of thys courte!'

    'Well,' seyde sir Launcelot, 'and I had wyste of thys shortecomyng,
I wolde a advysed me twyse or that I had com here. For and the quene   35
had be so dere unto me as ye noyse her, I durste have kepte her frome
the felyshyp of the beste knyghtes undir hevyn.'

    And than sir Launcelot seyde unto quene Gwenyver in hyryng of the
kynge and hem all,

    'Madame, now I muste departe from you and thys noble felyshyp   40
for ever. And sytthyn hit ys so, I besech you to pray for me, and I shall
pray for you. And telle ye me, and if ye be harde bestad by ony false
tunges, but lyghtly, my good lady, sende me worde; and if ony knyghtes
hondys undir the hevyn may delyver you by batayle, I shall delyver you.'

And therewithall sir Launcelot kyssed the quene, and than he seyde all opynly,

'Now lat se whatsomever he be in thys place that dare sey the quene ys nat trew unto my lorde Arthur, lat se who woll speke and he dare
5 speke.'

And therewith he brought the quene to the kynge, and than sir Launcelot toke hys leve and departed. And there was nother kynge, duke, erle, barowne, nor knyght, lady nor jantyllwoman, but all they wepte as people oute of mynde, excepte sir Gawayne. And whan thys
10 noble knyght sir Launcelot toke his horse to ryde oute of Carlehyll, there was sobbyng and wepyng for pure dole of hys departynge.

And so he toke his way to Joyous Garde, and than ever afftir he called hit the 'Dolerous [Garde]'. And thus departed sir Launcelot frome the courte for ever.

15 And so whan he cam to Joyous Garde he called hys felyshyp unto hym and asked them what they wolde do. Than they answerde all holé togydirs with one voyce, they wold do as he wolde do.

'Than, my fayre felowys,' seyde sir Launcelot, 'I muste departe oute of thys moste noble realme. And now I shall departe, hit grevyth me
20 sore, for I shall departe with no worship; fo[r] a fleymed man departith never oute of a realme with no worship. And that ys to me grete hevynes, for ever I feare aftir my dayes that men shall cronycle uppon me that I was fleamed oute of thys londe. And ellis, my fayre lordis, be ye sure, and I had nat drad shame, my lady quene Gwenyvere and I
25 shulde never have departed.'

Than spake noble knyghtes, as sir Palomydes and sir Saffyr, hys brothir, and sir Bellynger le Bewse, and sir Urré with sir Lavayne, with many other:

'Sir, and ye woll so be disposed to abyde in thys londe we woll
30 never fayle you; and if ye lyste nat abyde in thys londe, there ys none of the good knyghtes that here be that woll fayle you, for many causis. One ys, all we that be nat of your bloode shall never be wellcom unto the courte. And sytthyn hit lyked us to take a parte with you in youre distres in this realme, wyte you well hit shall lyke us as well to go in
35 othir contreyes with you and there to take suche parte as ye do.'

'My fayre lordys,' seyde sir Launcelot, 'I well undirstond you, and as I can, I thanke you. And ye shall undirstonde, suche lyvelode as I am borne unto I shall departe with you in thys maner of wyse: that ys for to say, I shall departe all my lyvelode and all my londis frely amonge
40 you, and myselff woll have as lytyll as ony of you; for, have I sufficiaunte that may longe unto my person, I woll aske none other ryches nother aray. And I truste to God to maynteyne you on my londys as well as ever ye were maynteyned.'

Than spake all the knyghtes at onys: 'Have he shame that woll leve

you! For we all undirstonde, in thys realme [woll be no] quyett, but
ever debate and stryff, now the felyshyp of the Rounde Table ys brokyn.
For by the noble felyshyp of the Rounde Table was kynge Arthur
upborne, and by their nobeles the kynge and all the realme was ever in
quyet and reste. And a grete parte,' they sayde all, 'was because of 5
youre moste nobeles, sir Launcelot.'

'Now, truly I thanke you all of youre good sayinge! Howbehit I (18)
wote well that in me was nat all the stabilité of thys realme, but in that
I myght I ded my dever. And well I am sure I knew many rebellyons'
in my dayes that by me and myne were peased; and that I trow we all 10
shall here of in shorte space, and that me sore repentith. For ever I
drede me,' seyde sir Launcelot, 'that sir Mordred woll make trouble,
for he ys passyng envyous and applyeth hym muche to trouble.'

And so they were accorded to departe wyth sir Launcelot to hys
landys. And to make shorte thys tale, they trussed and payed all that 15
wolde aske them; and holé an hondred knyghtes departed with sir
Launcelot at onys, and made their avowis they wolde never leve hym
for weale ne for woo.

And so they shypped at Cardyff, and sayled unto Benwyke: som men
calle hit Bayan and som men calle hit Beawme, where the wyne of 20
Beawme ys. But say the sothe, sir Launcelott and hys neveawis was
lorde of all Fraunce and of all the londis that longed unto Fraunce; he
and hys kynrede rejoysed hit all thorow sir Launcelottis noble proues.

And than he stuffed and furnysshed and garnysshed all his noble
townys and castellis. Than all the people of th[o] landis cam unto sir 25
Launcelot on foote and hondis. And so whan he had stabelyoshed all
those contreyes, he shortly called a parlement; and there he crowned
sir Lyonell kynge off Fraunce, and sir Bors he crowned hym kynge of
all kyng Claudas londis, and sir Ector de Marys, sir Launcelottis yonger
brother, he crowned hym kynge of Benwyke and kynge of all Gyan, 30
whych was sir Launcelottis owne londys. And he made sir Ector
prynce of them all.

And thus he departed hys londis and avaunced all hys noble knyghtes.
And firste he avaunced them off hys blood, as sir Blamour, he made
hym duke of Lymosyn in Gyan, and sir Bleoberys, he made hym duke 35
of Payters. And sir Gahalantyne, he made hym deuke of Overn; and
sir Galyodyn, he made hym deuke of Sentonge; and sir Galyhud, he
made hym erle of Perygot; and sir Menaduke, he made hym erle of
Roerge; and sir Vyllars the Valyaunt, he made hym erle of Bearne; and
sir Hebes le Renownes, he made hym erle of Comange; and sir Lavayne, 40
he made hym erle of Armynake; and sir Urré, he made hym erle of
Estrake; and sir Neroveus, he made hym erle of Pardyak; and sir
Plenoryus, he made hym erle of Foyse; and sir Selyses of the Dolerous
Toure, he made hym erle of Ma⟨r⟩sank; and sir Melyas de le Ile, he

made hym erle of Tursanke; and sir Bellyngere le Bewse, he made hym
erle of the Lawundis; and sir Palomydes, he made hym deuke of
Provynce; and sir Saffir, he made hym deuke of Landok. And sir
Clegys, he gaff hym the erle[dome] of Agente; and sir Sadok, he gaff
5 hym the erledom of Sarlat; and sir Dynas le Senesciall, he made hym
deuke of Angeoy; and sir Clarrus, he made hym duke of Normandy.

Thus sir Launcelot rewarded hys noble knyghtes, and many mo that
mesemyth hit were to longe to rehers.

III. THE SIEGE OF BENWICK

(19) 10 So leve we sir Launcelot in hys londis and hys noble knyghtes with
hym, and returne we agayne unto kynge Arthure and unto sir Gawayne
that made a grete oste aredy to the numbir of three score thousande.
And all thynge was made redy for shyppyng to passe over the see, to
warre uppon sir Launcelot and uppon hys londis. And so they shypped
15 at Cardyff.

And there kynge Arthur made sir Mordred chyeff ruler of all Ingelonde, and also he put the quene undir hys governaunce: bycause sir
Mordred was kynge Arthurs son, he gaff hym the rule off hys londe and
off hys wyff.

20 And so the kynge passed the see and landed uppon sir Launcelottis
londis, and there he brente and wasted, thorow the ve[n]geaunce of sir
Gawayne, all that they myght overrenne. So whan thys worde was
[com] unto sir Launcelot, that kynge Arthur and sir Gawayne were
landed uppon hys londis and made full grete destruccion and waste,
25 than spake sir Bors and seyde,

'My lorde, sir Launcelot, hit is shame that we suffir hem thus to
ryde over oure londys. For wyte you well, suffir ye hem as longe as ye
wyll, they woll do you no favoure and they may handyll you.'

Than seyde sir Lyonell that was ware and wyse, 'My lorde, sir
30 Launcelot, I woll gyff you thys counceyle: lat us kepe oure stronge-
walled townys untyll they have hunger and colde, and blow on their
nayles; and than lat us fresshly set uppon them and shrede hem downe
as shepe in a folde, that ever aftir alyauntis may take ensample how
the[y] lande uppon oure londys!'

35 Than spake kynge Bagdemagus to sir Launcelot and seyde, 'Sir,
youre curtesy woll shende us all, and youre curtesy hath waked all thys
sorow; for and they thus overryde oure londis, they shall by proces
brynge us all to nought whyle we thus in holys us hyde.'

Than seyde sir Galyhud unto sir Launcelot, 'Sir, here bene knyghtes
40 com of kyngis blod that woll nat longe droupe and dare within thys

wallys. Therefore gyff us leve, lyke as we ben knyghtes, to mete hem in the fylde, and we shall ⌐slee them⌐ and so deale wyth them that they shall curse the tyme that ever they cam into thys contrey.'

Than spake seven brethirn of Northe Walis whych were seven noble knyghtes, for a man myghte seke seven kyngis londis or he myght fynde such seven knyghtes. And thes seven noble knyghtes seyde all at onys,

'Sir Launcelot, for Crystis sake, late us ryde oute with sir Galyhud, for we were never wonte to coure in castels nother in noble townys.'

Than spake sir Launcelot, that was mayster and governoure of hem all, and seyde,

'My fayre lordis, wyte you well I am full lothe to ryde oute with my knyghtes for shedynge of Crysten blood; and yet my londis I undir-stonde be full bare for to sustayne any oste awhyle for the myghty warris that whylom made kyng Claudas uppon thys contrey and uppon my fadir, kyng Ban, and on myne uncle, kynge Bors. Howbehit we woll as at this tyme kepe oure stronge wallis. And I shall sende a mes-syngere unto my lorde Arthur a tretyse for to take, for better ys pees than allwayes warre.'

So sir Launcelot sente forthe a damesel wyth a dwarff with her, requyryng kynge Arthur to leve hys warryng uppon hys londys. And so he starte uppon a palferey, and a dwarffe ran by her syde, and whan she cam to the pavelon of kynge Arthur, there she alyght. And there mette her a jantyll knyght, sir Lucan the Butlere, and seyde,

'Fayre damesell, com ye frome sir Launcelot du Lake?'

'Yee, sir,' she seyde, 'therefore cam I hyddir to speke with my lorde the kynge.'

'Alas,' seyde sir Lucan, 'my lorde Arthure wolde accorde with sir Launcelot, but sir Gawayne woll nat suffir hym.' And than he seyde, 'I pray to God, damesell, that ye may spede ⌐well⌐, for all we that bene aboute the kynge wolde that Launcelot ded beste of ony knyght lyvynge.'

And so with thys sir Lucan lad the damesell to the kynge, where he sate with syr Gawayne, for to hyre what she wolde say. So whan she had tolde her tale the watir ran oute of the kyngis yen. And all the lordys were full glad for to advyce the kynge to be accorded with sir Launcelot, save all only sir Gawayne. And he seyde,

'My lorde, myne uncle, what woll ye do? Woll ye now turne agayne, now ye ar paste thys farre uppon youre journey? All the worlde woll speke of you vylany and shame.'

'Now,' seyde kynge Arthur, 'wyte you well, sir Gawayne, I woll do as ye advyse me; and yet mesemyth,' seyde kynge Arthur, 'hys fayre proffers were nat good to be reffused. But sytthyn I am com so far uppon thys journey, I woll that ye gyff the damesell her answere, for I may nat speke to her for pité: for her profirs ben so large.'

(20)   Than sir Gawayne seyde unto the damesell thus: 'Sey ye to sir
Launcelot that hyt ys waste laboure now to sew to myne uncle. For
telle hym, and he wolde have made ony laboure for pease, he sholde
have made hit or thys tyme, for telle hym now hit ys to late. And say to
5 hym that I, sir Gawayne, so sende hym word, that I promyse hym by
the faythe that I owghe to God and to knyghthode, I shall never leve
hym tylle he hathe slayne me or I hym!'

So the damesell wepte and departed, and so there was many a wepyng
yghe. And than sir Lucan brought the damesell to her palffrey; and so
10 she cam to sir Launcelot, where he was amonge all hys knyghtes, and
whan sir Launcelot had harde hir answere, than the tearys ran downe
by hys chekys. And than hys noble knyghtes com about hym and
seyde,

'Sir Launcelot, wherefore make ye suche chere? Now thynke what
15 ye ar and what men we ar, and lat us noble knyghtis macche hem in
myddis of the fylde.'

'That may be lyghtly done,' seyde sir Launcelot, 'but I was never so
lothe to do batayle. And therefore I pray you, sirres, as ye love me, be
ruled at thys tyme as I woll have you. For I woll allwayes fle that noble
20 kynge that made me knyght; and whan I may no farther, I muste
nedis deffende me. And that woll be more worshyp for me and us all
tha[n] to compare with that noble kynge whom we have all served.'

Than they hylde their langayge, and as that nyght they toke their
reste. And uppon the mornyng erly, in the dawnynge of the day, as
25 knyghtes loked oute, they saw the cité of Benwyke besyged rounde
aboute, and gan faste to sette up laddirs. And they within kepte them
oute of the towne and bete hem myghtyly frome the wallis.

Than cam forthe sir Gawayne, well armede, uppon a styff steede, and
he cam before the chyeff gate with hys speare in hys honde, cryynge:
30 'Where art thou, sir Launcelot? Ys there none of all your proude
knyghtes that dare breake a speare with me?'

Than sir Bors made hym redy, and cam forth oute of the towne. And
there sir Gawayne encountred with sir Bors, and at that tyme he smote
hym downe frome hys horse, and allmoste he had slayne hym. And so
35 sir Bors was rescowed and borne into the towne.

Than cam forthe sir Lyonell and thoughte to revenge hym; and
aythir feawtred their spearys and so ran togydirs, and there they mette
spiteously, but sir Gawayne had such a grace that he smote sir Lyonell
downe and wounded hym there passyngly sore. And than sir Lyonell
40 was rescowed and borne into the towne.

And thus sir Gawayne com every day, and fayled nat but that he
smote downe one knyght or othir. So thus they endured halff a yere, and
muche slaughter was of people on bothe partyes.

Than hit befelle uppon a day that sir Gawayne cam afore the gatis, armed at all pecis, on a noble horse, with a greate speare in hys honde, and than he cryed with a lowde voyce and seyde,

'Where arte thou now, thou false traytour, sir Launcelot? Why holdyst thou thyselff within holys and wallys lyke a cowarde? Loke oute, thou false traytoure knyght, and here I shall revenge uppon thy 5 body the dethe of my three brethirne!'

And all thys langayge harde sir Launcelot every deale. Than hys kynne and hys knyghtes drew aboute hym, and all they seyde at onys unto sir Launcelot,

'Sir, now muste you deffende you lyke a knyght, othir ellis ye be 10 shamed for ever, for now ye be called uppon treson, hit ys tyme for you to styrre! For ye have slepte over longe, and suffirde overmuche.'

'So God me helpe,' seyde sir Launcelot, 'I am ryght hevy at sir Gawaynes wordys, for now he chargith me with a grete charge. And therefore I wote as well as ye I muste nedys deffende me, other ellis to 15 be recreaunte.'

Than sir Launcelot bade sadyll hys strongest horse and bade let fecche hys armys and brynge all to the towre of the gate. And than sir Launcelot spake on hyght unto the kynge and seyde,

'My lorde Arthur, and noble kynge that made me knyght! Wyte you 20 well I am ryght hevy for youre sake that ye thus sewe uppon me. And allwayes I forbeare you, for and I wolde be vengeable I myght have mette you in myddys the fylde or thys tyme and thereto have made your boldiste knyghtes full tame. And now I have forborne you and suffirde you halff a yere, and sir Gawayne, to do what ye wolde do. 25 And now I may no lenger suffir to endure, but nedis I muste deffende myselff, insomuch as sir Gawayn hathe becalled me of treson: whych ys gretly ayenste my wyll that ever I shulde fyghte ayenste ony of youre blood, but now I may nat forsake hit: for I am dryvyn thereto as beste tylle a bay.'   30

Than sir Gawayne seyde unto sir Launcelotte,

'And thou darste do batayle, leve thy babelynge and com off, and lat us ease oure hartis!'

Than sir Launcelot armed hym and mownted uppon hys horse, and aythir of them gate greate spearys in their hondys. And so the oste 35 withoute stoode stylle all aparte, and the noble knyghtes of the cité cam a greate numbir, that whan kynge Arthur saw the numbir of men and knyghtes he mervaylde and seyde to hymself,

'Alas, that ever sir Launcelot was ayenst me! For now I se that he hath forborne me.'   40

And so the covenaunte was made, there sholde no man nyghe hem nother deale wyth them tylle the tone were dede other yolden.

Than sir Launcelot and sir Gawayne departed a great way in sundir, (21) and than they cam togydirs with all the[ir] horse myghtes as faste as they myght renne, and aythir smote othir in myddis of their shyldis. But the knyghtes were so stronge and their spearys so bygge that their horsis myght nat endure their buffettis, and so their horsis felle to the erthe. And than they avoyded their horsys and dressed their shyldis 5 afore them; than they cam togydirs and gaff many sad strokis on dyverse placis of their bodyes, that the bloode braste oute on many sydis.

Than had sir Gawayne suche a grace and gyffte that an holy man had gyvyn hym, that every day in the yere, frome undern tyll hyghe noone, 10 hys myght encresed tho three owres as much as thryse hys strength. And that caused sir Gawayne to wynne grete honoure. And for hys sake kynge Arthur made an ordynaunce that all maner off batayles for ony quarels that shulde be done afore kynge Arthur shulde begynne at undern; and all was done for sir Gawaynes love, that by lyklyhode if 15 sir Gawayne were on the tone parté, he shulde have the bettir in batayle whyle hys strengthe endured three owrys. But there were that tyme but feaw knyghtes lyvynge that knewe thys advauntayge that sir Gawayne had, but kynge Arthure all only.

So sir Launcelot faught wyth sir Gawayne, and whan sir Launcelot 20 felte hys myght evermore encrese, sir Launcelot wondred and drad hym sore to be shamed; for, as the Freynshe booke seyth, he wende, whan he felte sir Gawaynes double hys strengthe, that he had bene a fyende and none earthely man. Wherefore sir Launcelot traced and traverced, and coverde hymselff with hys shylde, and kepte hys myght 25 and hys brethe duryng three owrys. And that whyle sir Gawayne gaff hym many sad bruntis ⌐and many sad strokis,⌐ that all knyghtes that behylde sir Launcelot mervayled how he myght endure hym, but full lytyll undirstood they that travayle that sir Launcelot had to endure hym.

30 And than whan hit was paste noone sir Gawaynes strengthe was gone and ⟨he⟩ had no more but hys owne myght. Whan sir Launcelot felte hym so com downe, than he strecched hym up and strode nere sir Gawayne and seyde thus:

'Now I fele ye have done youre warste! And now, my lorde sir 35 Gawayn, I muste do my parte, for many a grete and grevous strokis I have endured you thys day with greate payne.'

And so sir Launcelot doubled hys strokis and gaff sir Gawayne suche a stroke uppon the helmet that sydelynge he felle downe uppon hys one syde. And sir Launcelot withdrew hym frome hym.

40 'Why wythdrawyst thou the?' seyde sir Gawayne. 'Turne agayne, false traytoure knyght, and sle me oute! For and thou leve me thus, anone as I am hole I shall do batayle with the agayne.'

'Sir,' seyde sir Launcelot, 'I shall endure you, be Goddis grace! But wyte thou well, sir Gawayne, I woll never smyte a felde knyght.'

And so sir Launcelot departed and wente unto the cité. And sir
Gawayne was borne unto kynge Arthurs pavylon, and anone lechys
were brought unto hym of the beste, and serched and salved hym with
souffte oynementis. And than sir Launcelot seyde,

'Now have good day, my lorde the kynge! For wyte you welle ye 5
wynne no worshyp at thes wallis, for and I wolde my knyghtes oute-
brynge, there shulde many a douty man dye. And therefore, my lorde
Arthur, remembir you of olde kyndenes, and howsomever I fare,
Jesu be youre gyde in all placis.'

'Now, alas,' seyde the kynge, 'that ever thys unhappy warre began! 10 (22)
For ever sir Launcelot forbearyth me in all placis, and in lyke wyse my
kynne, and that ys sene well thys day, what curtesy he shewed my
neveawe, sir Gawayne.'

Than kynge Arthur felle syke for sorow of sir Gawayne, that he was
so sore hurte, and bycause of the warre betwyxte hym and sir Launce- 15
lot. So aftir that they on kynge Arthurs party kepte the sege with
lytyll warre wythouteforthe, and they withinforthe kepte their wallys
and deffended them whan nede was.

Thus sir Gawayne lay syke and unsounde three wykes in hys tentis
with all maner of lechecrauffte that myght be had. And as sone as sir 20
Gawayne myght go and ryde, he armed hym at all poyntis and bestroode
a styff courser and gate a grete speare in hys honde, and so he cam
rydynge afore the chyeff gate of Benwyke. And there he cryed on
hyght and seyde,

'Where arte thou, sir Launcelot? Com forth, thou false traytoure 25
knyght and recrayed, for I am here, sir Gawayne, that woll preve thys
that I say uppon the!'

And all thys langayge sir Launcelot harde and sayde thus:

'Sir Gawayne, me repentis of youre fowle sayinge, that ye woll nat
cease your langayge. For ye wote well, sir Gawayne, I know youre 30
myght and all that ye may do, and well ye wote, sir Gawayne, ye may
nat greatly hurte me.'

'Com downe, traytoure knyght,' seyde he, 'and make hit good the
contrary wyth thy hondys! For hit myssehapped me the laste batayle
to be hurte of thy hondis, therefore, wyte thou well, I am com thys day 35
to make amendis, for I wene this day to ley the as low as thou laydest me.'

'Jesu deffende me,' seyde sir Launcelot, 'that ever I be so farre in
youre daunger as ye have bene in myne, for than my dayes were done.
But, Gawayne,' seyde sir Launcelot, 'ye shall nat thynke that I shall
tarry longe, but sytthyn that ye unknyghtly calle me thus of treson, ye 40
shall have bothe youre hondys fulle of me.'

And than sir Launcelot armed hym at all poyntis and mounted uppon
[his] horse and gate a grete speare in hys honde and rode oute at the
gate. And bothe their ostis were assembled, of them withoute and

within, and stood in aray full manly, and bothe partyes were charged to holde hem stylle to se and beholde the batayle of thes two noble knyghtes.

And than they layde their spearys in their restis and so cam togydir as
5 thundir. And sir Gawayne brake hys speare in an hondred peces to hys honde, and sir Launcelot smote hym with a gretter myght, that sir Gawaynes horse feete reysed, and so the horse and he felle to the erthe. Than sir Gawayne delyverly devoyded hys horse and put hys shylde afore hym, and egirly drew hys swerde and bade sir Launcelot, 'Alyght,
10 traytoure knyght!' and seyde,

'Gyff a marys sonne hath fayled me, wyte thou well a kyngis sonne and a quenys sonne shall nat fayle the!'

Than sir Launcelot devoyded hys horse and dressed hys shylde afore hym and drew hys swerde, and so cam egirly togydirs and gaff
15 many sad strokis, that all men on bothe partyes had wondir.

But whan sir Launcelot felte sir Gawaynes myght so mervaylously encres, he than wythhylde hys corayge and hys wynde, and so he kepte hym undir coverte of hys myght and of hys shylde: he traced and traverced here and there to breake sir Gawaynys strokys and hys
20 currayge. And ever sir Gawayne enforced hymselff wyth all hys myght and power to destroy sir Launcelot, for, as the Freynshe booke saythe, ever as sir Gawaynes myght encresed, ryght so encreced hys wynde and hys evyll wyll.

And thus he ded grete payne unto sir Launcelot three owres, that he
25 had much ado to defende hym. And whan the three owres were paste, that he felte sir Gawayne was com home to his owne propir strengthe, than sir Launcelot sayde,

'Sir, now I have preved you twyse that ye ar a full daungerous knyght and a wondirfull man of [your] myght! And many wondir
30 dedis have ye done in youre dᵣayeˡs, for by youre myght encresyng ye have desceyved many a full noble knyght. And now I fele that ye have done youre myghty dedis, now, wyte you well, I muste do my dedis!'

And than sir Launcelot strode nere sir Gawayne and doubled hys strokis, and ever sir Gawayne deffended hym myghtyly, but nevertheles
35 sir Launcelot smote such a stroke uppon hys helme and uppon the olde wounde that sir Gawayne sanke downe and sowned. And anone as he ded awake he waved and foyned at sir Launcelot as he lay, and seyde,

'Traytoure knyght, wyte thou well I am nat yet slayne. Therefore
40 com thou nere me and p[er]fo[rm]e thys batayle to the utteraunce!'

'I woll no more do than I have done,' seyde sir Launcelot. 'For whan I se you on foote I woll do batayle uppon you all the whyle I se you stande uppon youre feete; but to smyte a wounded man that may nat stonde, God defende me from such a shame!'.

And than he turned [hym and wente] hys way towarde the cité, and sir Gawayne evermore callyng hym 'traytoure knyght' and seyde,

'Traytoure knyght! Wyte thou well, sir Launcelot, whan I am hole I shall do batayle with you agayne, for I shall never leve the tylle the tone of us be slayne!'   5

Thus as thys syge endured and as sir Gawayne lay syke nerehande a moneth, and whan he was well recovirde and redy within three dayes to do batayle agayne with sir Launcelot, ryght so cam tydyngis unto kynge Arthur frome Inglonde that made kynge Arthur and all hys oste to remeve.   10

IV. THE DAY OF DESTINY

As sir Mordred was rular of all Inglonde, he lete make lettirs as thoughe   XXI (1) that they had com frome beyonde the see, and the lettirs specifyed that kynge Arthur was slayne in batayle with sir Launcelot. Wherefore sir Mordred made a parlemente, and called the lordys togydir, and there 15 he made them to chose ⌐hym⌐ kynge. And so was he crowned at Caunturbyry, and hylde a feste there fiftene dayes.

And aftirwarde he drew hym unto Wynchester, and there he toke quene Gwenyver, and seyde playnly that he wolde wedde her (which was hys unclys wyff and hys fadirs wyff). And so he made redy for the 20 feste, and a day prefyxte that they shulde be wedded; wherefore quene Gwenyver was passyng hevy. But she durst nat discover her harte, but spake fayre, and aggreed to sir Mordredys wylle.

And anone she desyred of sir Mordred to go to London to byghe all maner thynges tha[t] longed to the brydale. And bycause of her fayre 25 speche sir Mordred trusted her and gaff her leve; and so whan she cam to London she toke the Towre of London, and suddeynly in all haste possyble she stuffed hit with all maner of vytayle, and well garnysshed hit with men, and so kepte hit.

And whan sir Mordred wyst thys he was passynge wrothe oute of 30 mesure. And shorte tale to make, he layde a myghty syge aboute the Towre and made many assautis, and threw engynnes unto them, and shotte grete gunnes. But all myght nat prevayle, for quene Gwenyver wolde never, for fayre speache nother for foule, never to truste unto sir Mordred to com in hys hondis agayne.   35

Than cam the Bysshop of Caunturbyry, whych was a noble clerke and an holy man, and thus he seyde unto sir Mordred:

'Sir, what woll ye do? Woll ye firste displease God and sytthyn shame youreself and all knyghthode? For ys nat kynge Arthur youre uncle, and no farther but youre modirs brothir, and uppon her he 40 hymselffe begate you, uppon hys owne syster? Therefore how may ye wed youre owne fadirs wyff? And therefor, sir,' seyde the Bysshop, 'leve thys opynyon, other ellis I shall curse you with booke, belle and candyll.'

5 'Do thou thy warste,' seyde sir Mordred, 'and I defyghe the!'

'Sir,' seyde the Bysshop, 'wyte you well I shall nat feare me to do that me ought to do. And also ye noyse that my lorde Arthur ys slayne, and that ys nat so, and therefore ye woll make a foule warke in thys londe!'

10 'Peas, thou false pryste!' seyde sir Mordred, 'for and thou chauffe me ony more, I shall stryke of thy hede!'

So the Bysshop departed, and ded the cursynge in the moste orguluste wyse that myght be done. And than sir Mordred sought the Bysshop off Caunturbyry for to have slayne hym. Than the Bysshop 15 fledde, and tooke parte of hys good with hym, and wente nyghe unto Glassyngbyry. And there he was a preste-ermyte in a chapel, and lyved in poverté and in holy prayers; for well he undirstood that myschevous warre was at honde.

Than sir Mordred soughte uppon quene Gwenyver by lettirs and 20 sondis, and by fayre meanys and foule meanys, to have her to com oute of the Towre of London; but all thys avayled nought, for she answerd hym shortely, opynly and pryvayly, that she had levir sle herselff than to be maryed with hym.

Than cam there worde unto sir Mordred that kynge Arthure had 25 areysed the syge frome sir Launcelot and was commynge homwarde wyth a greate oste to be avenged uppon sir Mordred, wherefore sir Mordred made wryttes unto all the baronny of thys londe. And muche people drew unto hym; for than was the comyn voyce amonge them that with kynge Arthur was never othir lyff but warre and stryff, and 30 with sir Mordrede was grete joy and blysse. Thus was kynge Arthur depraved, and evyll seyde off; and many there were that kynge Arthur had brought up of nought, and gyffyn them londis, that myght nat than say hym a good worde.

Lo ye all Englysshemen, se ye nat what a myschyff here was? For he 35 that was the moste kynge and nobelyst knyght of the worlde, and moste loved the felyshyp of noble knyghtes, and by hym they all were upholdyn, and yet myght nat thes Englyshemen holde them contente with hym. Lo thus was the olde custom and usayges of thys londe, and men say that we of thys londe have nat yet loste that custom. Alas! 40 thys ys a greate defaughte of us Englysshemen, for there may no thynge us please no terme.

And so fared the peple at that tyme: they were better pleased with sir Mordred than they were with the noble kynge Arthur, and muche people drew unto sir Mordred and seyde they wold abyde wyth hym

for bettir and for wars. And so sir Mordred drew with a greate oste to
Dovir, for there he harde sey that kyng Arthur wolde aryve, and so he
thought to beate hys owne fadir fro hys owne londys. And the moste
party of all Inglonde hylde wyth sir Mordred, for the people were so
new-fangill.   5

And so as sir Mordred was at Dovir with hys oste, so cam kyng (2)
Arthur wyth a greate navy of shyppis and galyes and carykes, and there
was sir Mordred redy awaytyng uppon hys londynge, to lette hys
owne fadir to londe uppon the londe that he was kynge over.

Than there was launchyng of greate botis and smale, and full of 10
noble men of armys; and there was muche slaughtir of jantyll knyghtes,
and many a full bolde barown was layde full lowe, on bothe partyes.

But kynge Arthur was so currageous that there myght no maner of
knyght lette hym to lande, and hys knyghtes fyersely folowed hym.
And so they londed magré sir Mordredis hede and all hys power, and 15
put sir Mordred abak, ʳthat he fledde¹ and all hys people.

So whan thys batayle was done, kynge Arthure let serche hys people
that were hurte and dede. And than was noble sir Gawayne founde in
a greate boote, liynge more than halff dede. Whan kyng Arthur knew
that he was layde so low he wente unto hym and so fownde hym. And 20
there the kynge made greate sorow oute of mesure, and toke sir Gawayne
in hys armys, and thryse he there sowned. And than whan he was
waked, kyng Arthur seyde,

'Alas! sir Gawayne, my syster son, here now thou lyghest, the man
in the worlde that I loved moste. And now ys my joy gone! For now, 25
my nevew, sir Gawayne, I woll discover me unto you, tha⟨t⟩ in youre
person and in sir Launcelot I moste had my joy and myne affyaunce.
And now have I loste my joy of you bothe, wherefore all myne
erthely joy ys gone fro me!'

'A, myn uncle,' seyde sir Gawayne, 'now I woll that ye wyte that my 30
deth-dayes be com! And all I may wyte myne owne hastynes and my
wy[l]fulnesse, for thorow my wylfulnes I was causer of myne owne
dethe; for I was thys day hurte and smytten uppon myne olde wounde
that sir Launcelot gaff me, and I fele myselff that I muste nedis be dede
by the owre of noone. And thorow me and ⟨my⟩ pryde ye have all 35
thys shame and disease, for had that noble knyght, sir Launcelot, ben
with you, as he was and wolde have ben, thys unhappy warre had never
ben begunne; for he, thorow hys noble knyghthode and hys noble
bloode, hylde all youre cankyrde enemyes in subjeccion and daungere.
And now,' seyde sir Gawayne, 'ye shall mysse sir Launcelot. But alas 40
that I wolde nat accorde with hym! And there[fore], fayre unkle, I
pray you that I may have paupir, penne, and inke, that I may wryte
unto sir Launcelot a letter wrytten with myne owne honde.'

So whan pauper, penne and inke was brought, than sir Gawayne was sette up waykely by kynge Arthure, for he was shryven a lytyll afore. And than he toke hys penne and wrote thus, as the Freynshe booke makith mencion:

'Unto the, sir Launcelot, floure of all noble kynghtes that ever I
5 harde of or saw be my dayes, I, sir Gawayne, kynge Lottis sonne of Orkeney, and systirs sonne unto the noble kynge Arthur, sende the gretynge, lattynge the to have knowlecche that the tenth day of May I was smytten uppon the olde wounde that thou gaff me afore the cité of Benwyke, and thorow that wounde I am com to my dethe-day. And I
10 woll that all the worlde wyte that I, sir Gawayne, knyght of the Table Rounde, soughte my dethe, and nat thorow thy deservynge, but myne owne sekynge. Wherefore I beseche the, sir Launcelot, to returne agayne unto thys realme and se my toumbe and pray som prayer more other les for my soule. And thys same day that I wrote this same
15 sedull I was hurte to the dethe, whych wounde was fyrste gyffyn of thyn honde, sir Launcelot; for of a more nobelar man myght I nat be slayne.

'Also, sir Launcelot, for all the love that ever was betwyxte us, make no taryyng, but com over the see in all the goodly haste that ye
20 may, wyth youre noble knyghtes, and rescow that noble kynge that made the knyght, for he ys full straytely bestad wyth an false traytoure whych ys my halff-brothir, sir Mordred. For he hath crowned hymselff kynge, and wolde have wedded my lady, quene Gwenyver; and so had he done, had she nat kepte the Towre of London with stronge honde.
25 And so the tenth day of May last paste my lorde kynge Arthur and we all londed uppon them at Dover, and there he put that false traytoure, sir Mordred, to flyght. And so hit there mysfortuned me to be smytten uppon the strooke that ye gaff me of olde.

'And the date of thys lettir was wrytten but two owrys and an halff
30 afore my dethe, wrytten with myne owne honde and subscrybed with parte of my harte blood. And therefore I requyre the, moste famous knyght of the worlde, that thou wolte se my tumbe.'

And than he wepte and kynge Arthur both, and sowned. And whan they were awaked bothe, the kynge made sir Gawayne to resceyve hys
35 sacrament, and than sir Gawayne prayde the kynge for to sende for sir Launcelot and to cherysshe hym aboven all othir knyghtes.

And so at the owre of noone sir Gawayne yelded up the goste. And than the kynge lat entere hym in a chapell within Dover castell. And there yet all men may se the skulle of hym, and the same wounde is
40 sene that sir Launcelot gaff in batayle.

Than was hit tolde the kynge that sir Mordred had pyght a new fylde uppon Bareon Downe. And so uppon the morne kynge Arthur rode thydir to hym, and there was a grete batayle betwyxt hem, and muche people were slayne on bothe partyes. But at the laste kynge

Arthurs party stoode beste, and sir Mordred and hys party fledde unto Caunturbyry.

And than the kynge let serche all the downys for hys knyghtes that (3) werc slayne and entered them; and salved them with soffte salvys that full sore were wounded. Than much people drew unto kynge Arthur, 5 and than they sayde that sir Mordred warred uppon kynge Arthure wyth wronge.

And anone kynge Arthure drew hym wyth his oste downe by the seesyde westewarde, towarde Salusbyry. And there was a day assygned betwyxte kynge Arthur and sir Mordred, that they shulde mete uppon 10 a downe besyde Salesbyry and nat farre frome the seesyde. And thys day was assygned on Monday aftir Trynyté Sonday, whereof kynge Arthur was passyng glad that he myght be avenged uppon sir Mordred.

Than sir Mordred araysed muche people aboute London, for they of Kente, Southsex and Surrey, Esax, Suffolke and Northefolke helde the 15 moste party with sir Mordred. And many a full noble knyght drew unto hym and also [to] the kynge; but they that loved sir Launcelot drew unto sir Mordred.

So uppon Trynyté Sunday at nyght kynge Arthure dremed a wondirfull dreme, and in hys dreme hym semed that he saw uppon a chafflet a 20 chayre, and the chayre was faste to a whele, and thereuppon sate kynge Arthure ⌐in the rychest⌐ clothe of golde that myght be made. And the kynge thought there was undir hym, farre from hym, an hydeous depe blak watir, and therein was all maner of serpentis and wormes and wylde bestis fowle and orryble. And suddeynly the kynge thought that 25 the whyle turned up-so-downe, and he felle amonge the serpentes, and every beste toke hym by a lymme. And than the kynge cryed as he lay in hys bed,

'Helpe! helpe!'

And than knyghtes, squyars and yomen awaked the kynge, and than 30 he was so amased that he wyste nat where he was. And than so he awaked untylle hit was nyghe day, and than he felle on slumberynge agayne, nat slepynge nor thorowly wakynge.

So the kyng semed verryly that there cam sir Gawayne unto hym with a numbir of fayre ladyes wyth hym. So whan kyng Arthur saw 35 hym he seyde,

'Wellcom, my systers sonne, I wende ye had bene dede! And now I se the on lyve, much am I beholdyn unto Allmyghty Jesu. A, fayre nevew, what bene thes ladyes that hyder be com with you?'

'Sir,' seyde sir Gawayne, 'all thes be ladyes for whom I have foughten 40 for, whan I was man lyvynge. And all thes ar tho that I ded batayle fore in ryghteuous quarels, and God hath gyvyn hem that grace at their grete prayer, bycause I ded batayle [for] them for their ryght, that they shulde brynge me hydder unto you. Thus much hath gyvyn me leve

God for to warne you of youre dethe: for and ye fyght as to-morne
with sir Mordred, as ye bothe have assygned, doute ye nat ye shall be
slayne, and the moste party of youre people on bothe partyes. And for
the grete grace and goodnes that Allmyghty Jesu hath unto you, and
5 for pyté of you and many mo other good men there shall be slayne,
God hath sente me to you of Hys speciall grace to gyff you warnyng
that in no wyse ye do batayle as to-morne, but that ye take a tretyse for
a moneth-day. And proffir you largely, so that to-morne ye put in a
delay. For within a moneth shall com sir Launcelot with all hys noble
10 knyghtes, and rescow you worshypfully, and sle sir Mordred and all
that ever wyll holde wyth hym.'

Than sir Gawayne and all the ladyes vanysshed, and anone the kynge
called uppon hys knyghtes, squyars, and yomen, and charged them
wyghtly to fecche hys noble lordis and wyse bysshoppis unto hym.
15 And whan they were com the kynge tolde hem of hys avision: that sir
Gawayne had tolde hym and warned hym that and he fought on the
morn, he sholde be slayne. Than the kynge commaunded sir Lucan the
Butlere and hys brothir sir Bedyvere the Bolde, with two bysshoppis
wyth hem, and charged them in ony wyse to take a tretyse for a moneth-
20 day wyth sir Mordred:

'And spare nat, proffir hym londys and goodys as much as ye thynke
resonable.'

So than they departed and cam to sir Mordred where he had a
grymme oste of an hondred thousand, and there they entretyd sir
25 Mordred longe tyme. And at the laste sir Mordred was aggreed for to
have Cornwale and Kente by kynge Arthurs dayes; and afftir that all
Inglonde, after the dayes of kynge Arthur.

(4)   Than were they condescende that kynge Arthure and sir Mordred
shulde mete betwyxte bothe their ostis, and everych of them shulde
30 brynge fourtene persons. And so they cam wyth thys worde unto
Arthur. Than seyde he,

'I am glad that thys ys done'; and so he wente into the fylde.

And whan kynge Arthur shulde departe he warned all hys ⌐hoost⌐
that and they se ony swerde drawyn, 'loke ye com on fyersely and sle
35 that traytoure, sir Mordred, for ⌐I⌐ in no wyse truste hym'. In lyke
wyse sir Mordred warned hys oste that 'and ye se ony maner of swerde
drawyn, loke that ye com on fyersely and so sle all that ever before you
stondyth, for in no wyse I woll nat truste for thys tretyse'. And in the
same wyse seyde sir Mordred unto hys oste: 'for I know well my
40 fadir woll be avenged uppon me.'

And so they mette as their poyntemente was, and were agreed and
accorded thorowly. And wyne was fette, and [they] dranke togydir.
Ryght so cam oute an addir of a lytyll hethe-buysshe, and hit stange a
knyght in the foote. And so whan the knyght felte hym so stonge, he

loked downe and saw the adder; and anone he drew hys swerde to sle
the addir, and thought none othir harme. And whan the oste on bothe
partyes saw that swerde drawyn, than they blewe beamys, trumpettis,
and hornys, and shoutted grymly, and so bothe ostis dressed hem
togydirs. And kynge Arthur toke hys horse and seyde, 'Alas, this   5
unhappy day!' and so rode to hys party, and sir Mordred in lyke wyse.

And never syns was there seyne a more dolefuller batayle in no
Crysten londe, for there was but russhynge and rydynge, foynynge and
strykynge, and many a grym worde was there spokyn of aythir to
othir, and many a dedely stroke. But ever kynge Arthure rode thorow-   10
oute the bat[a]yle of sir Mordred many tymys and ded full nobely, as
a noble kynge shulde do, and at all tymes he faynted never. And sir
Mordred ded hys devoure that day and put hymselffe in grete perell.

And thus they fought all the longe day, and never stynted tylle the
noble knyghtes were layde to the colde erthe. And ever they fought   15
stylle tylle hit was nere [ny]ght, and by than was there an hondred
thousand leyde dede uppon the erthe. Than was kynge Arthure wode
wroth oute of mesure, whan he saw hys people so slayne frome hym.

And so he loked aboute hym and cowde se no mo of all hys oste and
good knyghtes leffte no mo on lyve but two knyghtes: the tone was   20
sir Lucan de Buttler and hys brother, sir Bedwere; and yette they were
full sore wounded.

'Jesu mercy!' seyde the kynge, 'where ar all my noble knyghtes
becom? Alas, that ever I shulde se thys doleful day! For now', seyde
kynge Arthur, 'I am com to myne ende. But wolde to God,' seyde he,   25
'that I wyste now where were that traytoure sir Mordred that hath
caused all thys myschyff.'

Than kynge Arthur loked aboute and was ware where stood sir
Mordred leanyng uppon hys swerde amonge a grete hepe of dede
men.   30

'Now, gyff me my speare,' seyde kynge Arthure unto sir Lucan, 'for
yondir I have aspyed the traytoure that all thys woo hath wrought.'

'Sir, latte hym be,' seyde sir Lucan, 'for he ys unhappy. And yf ye
passe this unhappy day y[e] shall be ryght well revenged. And, [good
lord, remembre ye of your nyghtes dreme and] what the spyryte of sir   35
Gawayne tolde you tonyght, and yet God of Hys grete goodnes hath
preserved you hyddirto. And for Goddes sake, my lorde, leve of thys,
for, blyssed be God, ye have won the fylde: for yet we ben here three
on lyve, and with sir Mordred ys nat one on lyve. And therefore if ye
leve of now, thys wycked day of Desteny ys paste!'   40

'Now tyde me dethe, tyde me lyff,' syde the kyng, 'now I se hym
yondir alone, he shall never ascape myne hondes! For at a bettir avayle
shall I never have hym.'

'God spyede you well!' seyde sir Bedyvere.

Than the kynge gate his speare in bothe hys hondis, and ran towarde sir Mordred, cryyng and saying,

'Traytoure, now ys thy dethe-day com!'

And whan sir Mordred saw kynge Arthur he ran untyll hym with
5 hys swerde drawyn in hys honde, and there kyng Arthur smote sir Mordred undir the shylde, with a foyne of hys speare, thorowoute the body more than a fadom. And whan sir Mordred felte that he had hys dethys wounde he threste hymselff with the myght that he had upp to the burre of kyng Arthurs speare, and ryght so he smote hys fadir,
10 kynge Arthure, with hys swerde holdynge in both hys hondys, uppon the syde of the hede, that the swerde perced the helmet and the tay of the brayne. And therewith Mordred daysshed downe starke dede to the erthe.

And noble kynge Arthure felle in a swoughe to the erthe, and there
15 he sowned oftyntymys, and sir Lucan and sir Bedwere offtetymys hove hym up. And so waykly betwyxte them they lad hym to a lytyll chapell nat farre frome the see, and whan the kyng was there, hym thought hym resonabely eased.

Than harde they people crye in the fylde.

20 'Now go thou, sir Lucan,' seyde the kyng, 'and do me to wyte what betokyns that noyse in the fylde.'

So sir Lucan departed, for he was grevously wounded in many placis; and so as he yode he saw and harkened by the moonelyght how that pyllours and robbers were com into the fylde to pylle and to robbe
25 many a full noble knyght of brochys and bees and of many a good rynge and many a ryche juell. And who that were nat dede all oute, there they slewe them for their harneys and their ryches.

Whan sir Lucan undirstood thys warke he cam to the kynge as sone as he myght, and tolde hym all what he had harde and seyne.

30 'Therefore be my rede,' seyde sir Lucan, 'hit ys beste that we brynge you to som towne.'

(5) 'I wolde hit were so,' seyde the kynge, 'but I may nat stonde, my hede worchys so. . . . A, sir Launcelot!' seyde kynge Arthure, 'thys day have I sore myssed the! And alas, that ever I was ayenste the!
35 For now have I my dethe, whereof sir Gawayne me warned in my dreame.'

Than sir Lucan toke up the kynge the tone party and sir Bedwere the othir parté, and in the lyfftyng up the kynge sowned, and in the lyfftynge sir Lucan felle in a sowne, that parte of hys guttis felle o[ut]e of
40 hys bodye, and therewith the noble knyght hys harte br[aste]. And whan the kynge awoke he behylde sir Lucan, how he lay fomyng at the mowth and parte of his guttes lay at hys fyete.

'Alas,' seyde the kynge, 'thys ys to me a fulle hevy syght, to se thys noble deuke so dye for my sake, for he wold have holpyn me that had

more nede of helpe than I! Alas, that he wolde nat complayne hym,
for hys harte was so sette to helpe me. Now Jesu have mercy uppon
hys soule!'

Than sir Bedwere wepte for the deth of hys brothir.

'Now leve thys mournynge and wepyng, jantyll knyght,' seyde the 5
kyng, 'for all thys woll nat avayle me. For wyte thou well, and I myght
lyve myselff, the dethe of sir Lucan wolde greve me evermore. But my
tyme passyth on faste,' seyde the kynge. 'Therefore,' seyde kynge
Arthur unto sir Bedwere, 'take thou here Excaliber, my good swerde,
and go wyth hit to yondir watirs syde; and whan thou commyste 10
there, I charge the throw my swerde in that water, and com agayne and
telle me what thou syeste there.'

'My lorde,' seyde sir Bedwere, 'youre commaundement shall be
done, and lyghtly brynge you worde agayne.'

So sir Bedwere departed. And by the way he behylde that noble 15
swerde, and the pomell and the hauffte was all precious stonys. And
than he seyde to hymselff, 'If I throw thys ryche swerde in the water,
thereof shall never com good, but harme and losse.' And than sir
Bedwere hyd Excalyber undir a tre, and so as sone as he myght he cam
agayne unto the kynge and seyde he had bene at the watir and had 20
throwen the swerde into the watir.

·   'What sawe thou there?' seyde the kynge.

'Sir,' he seyde, '[I] saw nothyng but wawis and wyndys.'

'That ys untruly seyde of the,' seyde the kynge. 'And therefore go
thou lyghtly agayne, and do my commaundemente; as thou arte to me 25
lyff and dere, spare nat, but throw hit in.'

Than sir Bedwer[e] returned agayne a[n]d toke the swerde in hys
honde; and ⟨y⟩et hym thought synne and [s]hame to throw away that
noble swerde. And so effte he hyd the swerde and returned agayne and
[t]olde the kynge that he had bene at the watir and done hys com- 30
maundement.

'What sawist thou there?' seyde the kyrg٥.

'Sir,' he seyde, 'I sy nothynge but watirs wap and wawys wanne.'

'A, traytour unto me and untrew,' seyde kyng Arthure, 'now hast
thou betrayed me twyse! Who wolde wene that thou that hast bene to 35
me so leve and dere, and also named so noble a knyght, that thou wolde
betray me for the ryches of thys swerde? But now go agayn lyghtly;
'for thy longe taryynge puttith me in grete jouperté of my lyff, for I
have takyn colde. And but if thou do now as I bydde the, if ever I
may se the, I shall sle the myne owne hondis, for thou woldist for my 40
rych swerde se me dede.'

Than sir Bedwere departed and wente to the swerde and lyghtly
toke hit up, and so he wente unto the watirs syde. And there he bounde
the gyrdyll aboute the hyltis, and threw the swerde as farre into the

watir as he myght. And there cam an arme and an honde above the
watir, and toke hit and cleyght hit, and shoke hit thryse and braun-
dysshed, and than vanysshed with the swerde into the watir.

So sir Bedyvere cam agayne to the kynge and tolde hym what he saw.

5 'Alas,' seyde the kynge, 'helpe me hens, for I drede me I have taryed
over [l]onge.'

Than sir Bedwere toke the kynge uppon hys bak and so wente with
hym to the watirs syde. And whan they were there, evyn faste by the
banke hoved a lytyll barge wyth many fayre ladyes in hit, and amonge
10 hem all was a quene, and all they had blak hoodis. And all they wepte
and shryked whan they saw kynge Arthur.

'Now put me into that barge,' seyde the kynge.

And so he ded sofftely, and there [re]sceyved hym three ladyes with
grete mournyng. And so they sette he[m d]owne, and in one of their
15 lappis kyng Arthure layde hys hede. And than the quene seyde,

'A, my dere brothir! Why [ha]ve ye taryed so longe frome me? Alas,
thys wounde on youre hede hath caught overmuch coulde!'

And anone they rowed fromward the londe, and sir Bedyvere
behylde all tho ladyes go frowarde hym. Than sir Bedwere cryed and
20 seyde,

'A, my lorde Arthur, what shall becom of me, now ye go frome me
and leve me here alone amonge myne enemyes?'

'Comforte thyselff,' seyde the kynge, 'and do as well as thou mayste,
for in me ys no truste for to truste in. For I muste into the vale of
25 Avylyon to hele me of my grevous wounde. And if thou here nevermore of me, pray for my soule!'

But ever the quene and ladyes wepte and shryked, that hit was pité
to hyre. And as sone as sir Bedwere had loste the syght of the barge he
wepte and wayled, and so toke the foreste and wente all that nyght.

30 And in the mornyng he was ware, betwyxte two holtis hore, of a
(6) chapell and an ermytage. Than was sir Bedwere fayne, and thyder he
wente, and whan he cam into the chapell he saw where lay an ermyte
grovelynge on all four, faste there by a tumbe was newe gravyn. Whan
the ermy[t]e saw sir Bedyvere he knewe hym well, for he was but
35 l[y]tyll tofore Bysshop of Caunturbery that sir Mordred fleamed.

'Sir,' seyde sir Bedyvere, 'what man ys there here entyred that ye
pray so faste fore?'

'Fayre sunne,' seyde the ermyte, 'I wote nat veryly but by demynge.
But thys same nyght, at mydnyght, here cam a numbir of ladyes and
40 brought here a dede corse and prayde me to entyre hym. And here
they offird an hondred tapers, and they gaff me a thousande besauntes.'

'Ala[s]!' seyde sir Bedyvere, '[th]at was my lo[r]de kynge Arthur,
whych lyethe here gravyn in thys chapell.'

Than sir Bedwere sowned, and whan he awooke he prayde the

ermyte tha⟨t⟩ he myght abyde with hym stylle, there to lyve with
fastynge and prayers:

'For from hens woll I never go,' seyde sir Bedyvere, 'be my wyll,
but all the dayes of my lyff here to pray for my lorde Arthur.'

'Sir, ye ar wellcom to me,' seyde the ermyte, 'for I know you bettir 5
than ye wene that I do: for ye ar sir Bedwere the Bolde, and the full
noble duke sir Lucan de Butler was you[r] brother.'

Than sir Bedwere tolde the ermyte all as ye have harde tofore, and
so he belaffte with the ermyte that was beforehande Bysshop of
Caunturbyry. And there sir Bedwere put uppon hym poure clothys, and 10
served the ermyte full lowly in fastyng and in prayers.

Thus of Arthur I fynde no more wrytten in bokis that bene auctorysed, nothir more of the verry sertaynté of hys dethe harde I never
rede, but thus was he lad away in a shyp wherein were three quenys;
that one was kynge Arthur syster, quene Morgan le Fay, the tother was 15
the quene of North Galis, and the thirde was the quene of the Waste
Londis. Also there was dame Nynyve, the chyff lady of the laake,
whych had wedded sir Pellyas, the good knyght; and thys lady had
done muche fo[r] kynge Arthure. (And thys dame Nynyve wolde
never suffir sir Pe[ll]eas to be in no place where he shulde be in daungere 20
of hys lyff, and so he lyved unto the uttermuste of hys dayes with her
in grete reste.)

Now more of the deth of kynge Arthur coude I never fynde, but
that thes ladyes brought hym to hys grave, and such one was entyred
there whych [the] ermyte bare wytnes that sometyme was Bysshop of 25
Caunturbyry. But yet the ermyte knew nat in sertayne that he was
veryly the body of [kyn]ge Arthur; for thys tale sir Bedwere, a knyght
of the Table Ro[un]de, made hit to be wrytten.

Yet som men say in many p[art]ys of Inglonde that kynge Arthure (7)
ys nat dede, but h[ad] by the wyll of oure Lorde Jesu into another place; 30
and men say that he shall com agayne, and he shall wynne the Holy
Crosse. Yet I woll nat say that hit shall be so, but rather I wolde sey:
here in thys worlde he chaunged hys lyff. And many men say that there
ys wrytten uppon the tumbe thys:

HIC IACET ARTHURUS, REX QUONDAM REXQUE FUTURUS   35

And thus leve I here sir Bedyvere with the ermyte that dwelled that
tyme in a chapell besydes Glassyngbyry, and there was hys ermytage.
And so they lyved in prayers and fastynges and grete abstynaunce.

And whan quene Gwenyver undirstood that kynge Arthure was
dede and all the noble knyghtes, sir Mordred and all the remanaunte, 40
than she stale away with fyve ladyes with her, and so she wente to
Amysbyry. And there she lete make herselff a nunne, and wered whyght
clothys and blak, and grete penaunce she toke uppon her, as ever ded

synfull woman in thys londe. And never creature coude make her
myry, but ever she lyved in fastynge, prayers, and almes-dedis, that all
maner of people mervayled how vertuously she was chaunged.

V. THE DOLOROUS DEATH AND
5 DEPARTING OUT OF THIS WORLD OF
SIR LAUNCELOT AND QUEEN
GUINEVERE

Now leve we the quene in Amysbery, a nunne in whyght clothys and
blak—and there she was abbas and rular, as reson w[o]lde—and now
(8) 10 turne we from her and speke we of sir Launcelot du Lake, that whan
he harde in hys contrey that sir Mordred was crowned kynge in Inglonde and made warre ayenst kyng Arthur, hys owne fadir, and wolde
lette hym to londe in hys owne londe (also hit was tolde hym how sir
Mordred had leyde a syge aboute the Towre of London, bycause the
15 [quen]e wold nat w[ed]de hym), than was sir Launcelot wrot[he o]ute
of mesure and seyde [to] hys kynnesmen,
'Alas! that double tra[yt]oure, sir Mordred, now me [rep]entith
that ever he ascaped [my] hondys, [fo]r much shame hath he done
unto my lorde Arthure. For I fele b[y th]ys dolefull letter that sir
20 Gawayne sente me, on whos soule Jesu have mercy, that my lorde
Arthur ys full harde bestad. Alas,' seyde sir Launcelot, 'that ever I
shulde lyve to hyre of that moste noble kynge that made me knyght
thus to be oversette with hys subjette in hys owne realme! And this
dolefull lettir that my lorde sir Gawayne hath sente me .afore hys
25 dethe, praynge me to se hys tumbe, wyte you well hys doleffull wordes
shall never go frome my harte. For he was a full noble knyght as ever
was born! And in an unhappy owre was I born that ever I shulde have
that myssehappe to sle firste sir Gawayne, sir Gaherys, the good
knyght, and myne owne frynde sir Gareth that was a full noble knyght.
30 Now, alas, I may sey I am unhappy th[at] ever I shulde do thus. And
yet, alas, myght I never have hap to sle that traytoure, sir Mordred!'
'Now leve youre complayntes,' seyde sir Bors, 'and firste revenge you
of the dethe of sir Gawayne, on whos soule Jesu have mercy! And hit
woll be well done that ye se hys tumbe, and secundly that ye revenge
35 my lorde Arthur and my lady quene Gwenyver.'
'I thanke you,' seyde sir Launcelot, 'for ever ye woll my worshyp.'
Than they made hem redy in all haste that myght be, with shyppis
and g[a]lyes, with hym and hys oste to pas into Inglonde. And so at the

laste he cam to Dover, and there he landed with seven kyngis, and the numbir was hedeous to beholde.

Than sir Launcelot spyrred of men of Dover where was the kynge becom. And anone the people tolde hym how he was slayne and sir Mordred to, with an hondred thousand that dyed uppon a day; and how sir Mordred gaff kynge Arthur the first batayle there at hys lond-ynge, and there was sir Gawayne slayne. 'And uppon the [mor]ne sir Mordred faught with the kynge on Baram Downe, and the[re t]he kyng put sir Mordred to the wars.'

'Alas,' seyde sir Launcelot, 'thys [i]s the hevyest tydyngis that ever cam [to] my harte! Now, f[a]yre sirres,' seyde sir Launcelot, 'shew me [th]e tumbe of sir Gawayne.'

And anone he was brought into the castel of Dover, and so they shewed hym the tumbe. Than sir Launcelot kneled downe by the tumbe and wepte, and prayde hartely for hys soule.

And that nyght he lete make a dole, [and] all that wolde com of the towne or of the contrey they had as much fleyssh and fysshe and wyne and ale, and every man and woman he dalt to twelve pence, com whoso wolde. Thus with hys owne honde dalte he thys money, in a mournyng gown; and ever he wepte hartely and prayde the people to pray for the soule of sir Gawayne.

And on the morn all the prystes and clarkes that myght be gotyn in the contrey and in the town were there, and sange massis of Requiem. And there offird first sir Launcelot, and he offird an hondred pounde, and than the seven kynges offirde, and every of them offirde fourty pounde. Also there was a thousand knyghtes, and every of them offirde a pounde; and the offeryng dured fro the morne to nyght.

And there sir Launcelot lay two nyghtes uppon hys tumbe, in prayers and in dolefull wepynge. Than, on the thirde day, sir Launcelot called the kyngis, deukes, and erlis, with the barownes and all hys noble knyghtes, and seyde [t]hus:

'My fayre lordis, I thanke you all of youre comynge into thys contrey with me. But wyte you well all, we ar com to late, and that shall repente me whyle I lyve, but ayenste deth may no man rebell. But sytthyn hit ys so,' seyde sir Launcelot, 'I woll myselffe ryde and syke my lady, quene Gwenyver. For, as I here sey, she hath had grete payne and muche disease, and I here say that she ys fledde into the weste. And therefore ye all shall abyde me here, and but if I com agayne within thes fyftene dayes, take youre shyppis and youre felyship and departe into youre contrey, for I woll do as I [sey y]ou.'

Than cam sir [B]ors and seyde, 'My lorde, sir Launcelot, [w]hat thynke ye for to d[o, n]ow for to ryde in thys realme? Wyte [yo]u well ye shall do fy[n]de feaw fryndis.'

'Be as be may as for ⟨th⟩at,' seyde sir Launcelot, 'kepe you stylle here,

for I woll furthe on my journey, and no man nor chylde shall go with
me.'

So hit was no boote to stryve, but he departed and rode westirly;
and there he sought a seven or eyght dayes. And at the laste he cam to
5 a nunry, and anone quene Gwenyver was ware of sir Launcelot as she
walked in the cloyster. And anone as she saw hym there, she sowned
thryse, that all ladyes and jantyllwomen had worke inowghe to hold the
quene frome the erthe. So whan she myght speke she called her ladyes
and jantillwomen to her, and than she sayde thus:

10 'Ye mervayle, fayre ladyes, why I make thys fare. Truly,' she seyde,
'hit ys for the syght of yondir knyght that yondir stondith. Wherefore
I pray you calle hym hyddir to me.'

Than sir Launcelot was brought before her; than the quene seyde to
all tho ladyes,

15 'Thorow thys same man and me hath all thys warre be wrought, and
the deth of the moste nobelest knyghtes of the worlde; for thorow
oure love that we have loved togydir ys my moste noble lorde slayne.
Therefore, sir Launcelot, wyte thou well I am sette in suche a plyght to
gete my soule ⌐hele⌐. And yet I truste, thorow Goddis grace and thorow
20 Hys Passion of Hys woundis wyde, that aftir my deth I may have a
syght of the blyss[ed] face of Cryste Jesu, and on Doomesday to sytte
on Hys ryght syde; [fo]r as synfull as ever I was, now ar seyntes in
hevyn. And there[f]ore, sir Launcelot, I requyre the and beseche the
hartily, for all the lo[v]e that ever was betwyxt us, that thou never se
25 me no more in the visayge. And I commaunde the, on Goddis behalff,
that thou forsake my company. And to thy kyngedom loke thou turne
agayne, and kepe well thy realme frome warre and wrake, for as well
as I have loved the heretofore, myne [har]tè woll nat serve now to se
the; for thorow the and me ys the f[lou]re of kyngis and [knyghtes]
30 destroyed. And therefore [go] thou to thy realme, [an]d there take ye
a wyff, and lyff with [hir wyth] joy and blys. [A]nd I pray the hartely to
pray for me [to] the Everlastynge Lorde [tha]t I may amende my
mysselyvyng.'

'Now, my swete madame,' seyde sir Launcelot, 'wolde ye that I
35 shuld turne agayne unto my contrey and thereto wedde a lady? Nay,
madame, wyte you well that shall I never do, for I shall never be so
false unto you of that I have promysed. But the selff desteny that ye
have takyn you to, I woll take me to, for the pleasure of Jesu, and ever
for you I caste me specially to pray.'

40 'A, sir Launcelot, if ye woll do so and holde thy promyse! But I may
never beleve you,' seyde the quene, 'but that ye woll turne to the worlde
agayne.'

'Well, madame,' seyde he, 'ye say as hit pleasith you, f⟨o⟩r yet wyste
ye me never false of my promyse. And God deffende but that I shulde

forsake the worlde as ye have done! For in the queste of the Sankgreall
I had that tyme forsakyn the vanytees of the worlde, had nat youre love
bene. And if I had done so at that tyme with my harte, wylle, and
thought, I had passed all the knyghtes that ever were in the Sankgreall
[excepte syr Galahad, my sone. And therfore, lady, sythen ye have 5
taken you to perfeccion, I must nedys take me to perfection, of ryght.
For I take recorde of God, in you I have had myn erthly joye, and yf I
had founden you now so dysposed, I had caste me to have had you
into myn owne royame. But sythen I fynde you thus desposed, I (10)
ensure you faythfully, I wyl ever take me to penaunce and praye whyle 10
my lyf lasteth, yf that I may fynde ony heremyte, other graye or whyte,
that wyl receyve me. Wherfore, madame, I praye you kysse me, and
never no more.'

'Nay,' sayd the quene, 'that shal I never do, but absteyne you from
suche werkes.'   15

And they departed; but there was never so harde an herted man but
he wold have wepte to see the dolour that they made, for there was
lamentacyon as they had be stungyn wyth sperys, and many tymes
they swouned. And the ladyes bare the quene to hir chambre.

And syr Launcelot awok, and went and took his hors, and rode al 20
that day and al nyght in a forest, wepyng. And atte last he was ware of
an ermytage and a chappel stode betwyxte two clyffes, and than he
herde a lytel belle rynge to masse. And thyder he rode and alyght, and
teyed his hors to the gate, and herd masse.

And he that sange masse was the Bysshop of Caunterburye. Bothe 25
the Bysshop and sir Bedwer knewe syr Launcelot, and they spake
togyders after masse. But whan syr Bedwere had tolde his tale al hole,
syr Launcelottes hert almost braste for sorowe, and sir Launcelot
threwe hys armes abrode, and sayd, 'Alas! Who may truste thys
world?'   30

And than he knelyd doun on his knee and prayed the Bysshop to
shryve hym and assoyle hym; and than he besought the Bysshop that
he myght be hys brother. Than the Bysshop sayd, 'I wyll gladly', and
there he put an habyte upon syr Launcelot. And there he servyd God
day and nyght with prayers and fastynges.   35

Thus the grete hoost abode at Dover. And than sir Lyonel toke
fyftene lordes with hym and rode to London to seke sir Launcelot;
and there syr Lyonel was slayn and many of his lordes. Thenne syr
Bors de Ganys made the grete hoost for to goo hoome ageyn, and syr
Boors, syr Ector de Maris, syr Blamour, syr Bleoboris, with moo other 40
of syr Launcelottes kynne, toke on hem to ryde al Englond overthwart
and endelonge to seek syr Launcelot.

So syr Bors by fortune rode so longe tyl he came to the same chapel
where syr Launcelot was. And so syr Bors herde a lytel belle knylle

that range to masse, and there he alyght and herde masse. And whan
masse was doon, the Bysshop, syr Launcelot and sir Bedwere came to
syr Bors, and whan syr Bors sawe sir Launcelot in that maner clothyng,
than he preyed the Bysshop that he myght be in the same sewte. And
5　so there was an habyte put upon hym, and there he lyved in prayers and
fastyng.

And wythin halfe a yere there was come syr Galyhud, syr Galyhodyn, sir Blamour, syr Bleoberis, syr Wyllyars, syr Clarrus, and sir
Gahallantyne. So al these seven noble knyghtes there abode styll. And
10　whan they sawe syr Launcelot had taken hym to suche perfeccion they
had no lust to departe but toke such an habyte as he had.

Thus they endured in grete penaunce syx yere. And than syr Launcelot took th' abyte of preesthode of the Bysshop, and a twelve-monthe
he sange masse. And there was none of these other knyghtes but they
15　redde in bookes and holpe for to synge masse, and range bellys, and
dyd lowly al maner of servyce. And soo their horses wente where they
wolde, for they toke no regarde of no worldly rychesses; for whan they
sawe syr Launcelot endure suche penaunce in prayers and fastynges
they toke no force what payne they endured, for to see the nobleste
20　knyght of the world take such abstynaunce that he waxed ful lene.

And thus upon a nyght there came a vysyon to syr Launcelot and
charged hym, in remyssyon of his synnes, to haste hym unto Almysbury: 'And by thenne thou come there, thou shalt fynde quene Guenever dede. And therfore take thy felowes with the, and purvey them of
25　an hors-bere, and fetche thou the cors of hir, and burye hir by her hus-
bond, the noble kyng Arthur.'

(11)　　So this avysyon came to Launcelot thryse in one nyght. Than syr
Launcelot rose up or day and tolde the heremyte.

'It were wel done,' sayd the heremyte, 'that ye made you redy and
30　that ye dyshobeye not the avysyon.'

Than syr Launcelot toke his seven felowes with hym, and on fote
they yede from Glastynburye to Almysburye, the whyche is lytel more
than thirty myle, and thyder they came within two dayes, for they were
wayke and feble to goo.

35　　And whan syr Launcelot was come to Almysburye within the nun-
erye, quene Guenever deyed but halfe an oure afore. And the ladyes
tolde syr Launcelot that quene Guenever tolde hem al or she passyd
that syr Launcelot had ben preest nere a twelve-monthe: 'and hyder he
cometh as faste as he may to fetche my cors, and besyde my lord kyng
40　Arthur he shal berye me.' Wherefore the quene sayd in heryng of hem
al, 'I beseche Almyghty God that I may never have power to see syr
Launcelot wyth my worldly eyen!'

'And thus,' said al the ladyes, 'was ever hir prayer these two dayes
tyl she was dede.'

Than syr Launcelot sawe hir vysage, but he wepte not gretelye, but syghed. And so he dyd al the observaunce of the servyce hymself, bothe the dyryge and on the morne he sange masse. And there was ordeyned an hors-bere, and so wyth an hondred torches ever brennyng aboute the cors of the quene and ever syr Launcelot with his eyght 5 felowes wente aboute the hors-bere, syngyng and redyng many an holy oryson, and frankensens upon the corps encensed.

Thus syr Launcelot and his eyght felowes wente on foot from Almysburye unto Glastynburye; and whan they were come to the chapel and the hermytage, there she had a dyryge wyth grete devocyon. And on 10 the morne the heremyte that somtyme was Bysshop of Canterburye sange the masse of Requyem wyth grete devocyon, and syr Launcelot was the fyrst that offeryd, and than als his eyght felowes. And than she was wrapped in cered clothe of Raynes, from the toppe to the too, in thirtyfolde; and after she was put in a webbe of leed, and than in a 15 coffyn of marbyl.

And whan she was put in th' erth syr Launcelot swouned, and laye longe stylle, whyle the hermyte came and awaked hym, and sayd,

'Ye be to blame, for ye dysplese God with suche maner of sorow-makyng.'   20

'Truly,' sayd syr Launcelot, 'I trust I do not dysplese God, for He knoweth myn entente: for my sorow was not, nor is not, for ony rejoysyng of synne, but my sorow may never have ende. For whan I remembre of hir beaulté and of hir noblesse, that was bothe wyth hyr kyng and wyth hyr, so whan I sawe his corps and hir corps so lye 25 togyders, truly myn herte wold not serve to susteyne my careful body. Also whan I remembre me how by my defaute and myn orgule and my pryde that they were bothe layed ful lowe, that were pereles that ever was lyvyng of Cristen people, wyt you wel,' sayd syr Launcelot, 'this remembred, of their kyndenes and myn unkyndenes, sanke so to myn 30 herte that I myght not susteyne myself.' So the Frensshe book maketh mencyon.

Thenne syr Launcelot never after ete but lytel mete, nor dranke, tyl (12) he was dede, for than he seekened more and more and dryed and dwyned awaye. For the Bysshop nor none of his felowes myght not 35 make hym to ete and lytel he dranke, that he was waxen by a kybbet shorter than he was, that the peple coude not knowe hym. For evermore, day and nyght, he prayed, but somtyme he slombred a broken slepe. Ever he was lyeng grovelyng on the tombe of kyng Arthur and quene Guenever, and there was no comforte that the Bysshop, nor syr 40 Bors, nor none of his felowes coude make hym, it avaylled not.

Soo wythin syx wekys after, syr Launcelot fyl seek and laye in his bedde. And thenne he sente for the Bysshop that there was heremyte, and al his trewe felowes. Than syr Launcelot sayd wyth drery steven,

'Syr Bysshop, I praye you gyve to me al my ryghtes that longeth to
a Crysten man.'

'It shal not nede you,' sayd the heremyte and al his felowes. 'It is
but hevynesse of your blood. Ye shal be wel mended by the grace of
5 God to-morne.'

'My fayr lordes,' sayd syr Launcelot, 'wyt you wel my careful body
wyll into th' erthe, I have warnyng more than now I wyl say. Therfore
gyve me my ryghtes.'

S⟨o⟩ whan he was howselyd and enelyd and had al that a Crysten
10 man ought to have, he prayed the Bysshop that his felowes myght bere
his body to Joyous Garde. (Somme men say it was Anwyk, and somme
men say it was Bamborow.)

'Howbeit,' sayd syr Launcelot, 'me repenteth sore, but I made myn
avowe somtyme that in Joyous Garde I wold be buryed. And bycause
15 of brekyng of myn avowe, I praye you al, lede me thyder.'

Than there was wepyng and wryngyng of handes among his felowes.

So at a seson of the nyght they al wente to theyr beddes, for they alle
laye in one chambre. And so after mydnyght, ayenst day, the Bysshop
that was hermyte, as he laye in his bedde aslepe, he fyl upon a grete
20 laughter. And therwyth al the felyshyp awoke and came to the Bysshop
and asked hym what he eyled.

'A, Jesu mercy!' sayd the Bysshop, 'why dyd ye awake me? I was
never in al my lyf so mery and so wel at ease.'

'Wherfore?' sayd syr Bors.

25 'Truly,' sayd the Bysshop, 'here was syr Launcelot with me, with mo
angellis than ever I sawe men in one day. And I sawe the angellys heve
up syr Launcelot unto heven, and the yates of heven opened ayenst
hym.'

'It is but dretchyng of swevens,' sayd syr Bors, 'for I doubte not syr
30 Launcelot ayleth nothynge but good.'

'It may wel be,' sayd the Bysshop. 'Goo ye to his bedde, and than
shall ye preve the soth.'

So whan syr Bors and his felowes came to his bedde they founde
hym starke dede; and he laye as he had smyled, and the swettest savour
35 aboute hym that ever they felte. Than was there wepynge and wryngyng of handes, and the grettest dole they made that ever made men.

And on the morne the Bysshop dyd his masse of Requyem, and
after the Bysshop and al the nine knyghtes put syr La⟨un⟩celot in the
same hors-bere that quene Guenevere was layed in tofore that she was
40 buryed. And soo the Bysshop and they al togyders wente wyth the
body of syr Launcelot dayly, tyl they came to Joyous Garde; and ever
they had an hondred torches brennyng aboute hym.

And so within fyftene dayes they came to Joyous Garde. And there
they layed his corps in the body of the quere, and sange and redde

many saulters and praye⟨r⟩s over hym and aboute hym. And ever his vysage was layed open and naked, that al folkes myght beholde hym; for suche was the custom in tho dayes that al men of worshyp shold so lye wyth open vysage tyl that they were buryed.

And ryght thus as they were at theyr servyce, there came syr Ector 5 de Maris that had seven yere sought al Englond, Scotlond and Walys, sekyng his brother, syr Launcelot. And whan syr Ector herde suche (13) noyse and lyghte in the quyre of Joyous Garde, he alyght and put his hors from hym and came into the quyre. And there he sawe men synge ⟨and⟩ wepe, and al they knewe syr Ector, but he knewe not them. 10 Than wente syr Bors unto syr Ector and tolde hym how there laye his brother, syr Launcelot, dede. And than syr Ector threwe hys shelde, swerde and helme from hym, and whan he behelde syr Launcelottes vysage he fyl doun in a swoun. And whan he waked it were harde ony tonge to telle the doleful complayntes that he made for his brother. 15

'A, Launcelot!' he sayd, 'thou were hede of al Crysten knyghtes! And now I dare say,' sayd syr Ector, 'thou sir Launcelot, there thou lyest, that thou were never matched of erthely knyghtes hande. And thou were the curtest knyght that ever bare shelde! And thou were the truest frende to thy lovar that ever bestrade hors, and thou were the 20 trewest lover, of a synful man, that ever loved woman, and thou were the kyndest man that ever strake wyth swerde. And thou were the godelyest persone that ever cam emonge prees of knyghtes, and thou was the mekest man and the jentyllest that ever ete in halle emonge ladyes, and thou were the sternest knyght to thy mortal foo that ever 25 put spere in the reeste.'

Than there was wepyng and dolour out of mesure.

Thus they kepte syr Launcelots corps on-lofte fyftene dayes, and than they buryed it with grete devocyon. And than at leyser they wente al with the Bysshop of Canterburye to his ermytage, and there they 30 were togyder more than a monthe.

Than syr Costantyn that was syr Cadores sone of Cornwayl was chosen kyng of Englond, and he was a ful noble knyght, and worshypfully he rulyd this royame. And than thys kyng Costantyn sent for the Bysshop of Caunterburye, for he herde saye where he was. And so he 35 was restored unto his bysshopryche and lefte that ermytage, and syr Bedwere was there ever stylle heremyte to his lyves ende.

Than syr Bors de Ganys, syr Ector de Maris, syr Gahalantyne, syr Galyhud, sir Galyhodyn, syr Blamour, syr Bleoberys, syr Wyllyars ⟨le⟩ Valyaunt, syr Clarrus of Cleremounte, al these knyghtes drewe them to 40 theyr contreyes. Howbeit kyng Costantyn wold have had them wyth hym, but they wold not abyde in this royame. And there they al lyved in their cuntreyes as holy men.

And somme Englysshe bookes maken mencyon that they wente

never oute of Englond after the deth of syr Launcelot—but that was but favour of makers. For the Frensshe book maketh mencyon—and is auctorysed—that syr Bors, syr Ector, syr Blamour and syr Bleoberis wente into the Holy Lande, thereas Jesu Cryst was quycke and deed. And anone as they had stablysshed theyr londes, for, the book saith, so syr Launcelot commaunded them for to do or ever he passyd oute of thys world, ⟨there⟩ these foure knyghtes dyd many bataylles upon the myscreantes, or Turkes. And there they ⟨dyed⟩ upon a Good Fryday for Goddes sake.

HERE IS THE ENDE OF THE HOOLE BOOK OF KYNG ARTHUR AND OF HIS NOBLE KNYGHTES OF THE ROUNDE TABLE, THAT WHAN THEY WERE HOLE TOGYDERS THERE WAS EVER AN HONDRED AND FORTY. AND HERE IS THE ENDE OF *The Deth of Arthur.*

I PRAYE YOU ALL JENTYLMEN AND JENTYLWYMMEN THAT REDETH THIS BOOK OF ARTHUR AND HIS KNYGHTES FROM THE BEGYNNYNG TO THE ENDYNGE, PRAYE FOR ME WHYLE I AM ON LYVE THAT GOD SENDE ME GOOD DELYVERAUNCE. AND WHAN I AM DEED, I PRAYE YOU ALL PRAYE FOR MY SOULE.

FOR THIS BOOK WAS ENDED THE NINTH YERE OF THE REYGNE OF KYNG EDWARD THE FOURTH, BY SYR THOMAS MALEORÉ, KNYGHT, AS JESU HELPE HYM FOR HYS GRETE MYGHT, AS HE IS THE SERVAUNT OF JESU BOTHE DAY AND NYGHT.]

NOTES AND GLOSSARY

NOTES[1]

I. THE TALE OF KING ARTHUR

MALORY's *Tale of King Arthur* describes the circumstances of Arthur's birth, his accession to the throne, the victories he won over hostile neighbours and vassals, the tragic life of Balin, the 'unhappy knight', the quests undertaken by Gawain, Torre, and Pellinor and a series of adventures which Gawain shares with Ywain (*Uwain*) and Marhalte. Two other themes are interwoven with these: the life and death of Merlin and the treacherous intrigues of Arthur's half-sister, Morgan le Fay.

Malory borrowed this varied collection of stories from a thirteenth-century French prose romance known today as *La Suite du Merlin*—a section of a vast recently reconstructed composition sometimes described as *Le Roman du Graal*. The *Suite du Merlin* has been preserved in two fourteenth-century manuscripts, both incomplete: British Museum Add. 38117 and Cambridge Add. 7071. The British Museum manuscript used to belong to Alfred Huth and is still referred to as the 'Huth MS.' Its publication by Gaston Paris and Jacob Ulrich in 1886 was the first major step towards the rediscovery of the Arthurian prose romances in the nineteenth century. An extract from it containing the story of Balin was published in 1942 by Miss M. D. Legge with my Introduction. The Cambridge manuscript, which first came to light in 1945 when I had the good fortune to identify it, is still unpublished except for a few extracts. This is all the more regrettable because there is every reason to believe that it is at present the nearest approach we have to Malory's source. It contains, among other things, the only known French version of the episode of the 'dolorous stroke'; the corresponding leaf in the British Museum manuscript is missing. A large fragment corresponding to the final part of Malory's *Tale*—the adventures of Gawain, Ywain, and Marhalte—was discovered some time ago by Eduard Wechssler in MS. Fr. 112 of the Bibliothèque nationale; and quite recently Dr. Fanni Bogdanow found in the municipal archives of Siena a short fragment corresponding to vol. ii, pp. 64–72 of Gaston Paris's edition. All these texts can occasionally be supplemented by the Spanish *Demanda del Sancto Grial*, two versions of which are now available in modern editions.

[1] The text preceding the notes on each romance consists mainly of extracts from the Commentary to my three-volume second edition of *The Works of Sir Thomas Malory* (Oxford, 1967). The notes, introduced by page- and line-references, are intended to be strictly explanatory. Unlike the original Commentary, they are only concerned with doubtful or difficult passages in the text. They would have been less complete and less accurate but for the expert help I received in the course of their preparation from Mrs. Sandra Ihle whose contribution I gratefully acknowledge. For all bibliographical and textual information, as well as for detailed comparisons of the text with its sources, reference should be made to pp. 1267–1663 of the three-volume edition and to the critical works listed there on pp. 1282–3, 1303–4, 1323, 1335–6, 1343, 1353–4, 1371–2, 1413, 1434–5, 1455, 1523–4, 1544–5, 1595–6, and 1627–8.

Of paramount interest to the literary historian is the way in which Malory dealt with the narrative structure of the French source of this work—a topic which I have discussed at some length in the Introduction and the Commentary of my three-volume edition of Malory's works. Two other aspects of the *Tale of King Arthur* deserve more than a passing mention: the treatment of the supernatural and the emphasis placed on the role of Arthur. The fairy kingdom of Logres which in the French romances lacked geographical definition, becomes a recognizable part of England with well-defined boundaries; and at the same time incidents which appealed to the French authors because of their fairy elements are reproduced with a stress on their realistic and human aspects. In the story of Arthur's fight with Accolon what impresses Malory is not the part played by the sword with its magic scabbard, but the seemingly monstrous fact that Accolon is fighting against his anointed lord. To make this more credible Malory blackens the character of Accolon so that the story becomes an example of a traitor's criminal behaviour, not of the power of witchcraft. On the other hand the virtual suppression of the Merlin–Niviene theme makes it possible to shift the entire emphasis from the story of a great magician to the chronicle of a great king. The tradition that lies behind the *Tale* was sufficiently 'Arthurian' in its orientation to enable the narrative to develop in this way. Malory's next book, *The Noble Tale of King Arthur and the Emperor Lucius*, and his last, *The Tale of the Death of King Arthur*, will provide further examples of his interest in the Arthurian tradition in the strict sense of the term, and this is what will distinguish them, among other things, from the five intervening romances in which Arthur will recede into the background and yield his place as a champion of Arthurian chivalry to other famous knights.

4. 9. *had lytyl ado to telle hym* = had little reason to tell him.

4. 20. *rode on more than a paas* = rode at a good speed.

4. 27. *every dele* = completely.

4. 32. *gete a child on her.* Cf. note **11.** 36.

4. 41. *wayte ye make not many questions* = take care not to ask too many questions.

5. 3–4. *to have distressid the kynges hooste* = to have attacked the king's army. The earliest example of this use of the verb 'to distress' quoted in the *Oxf. Eng. Dict.* comes from Caxton's *Fayttes of Armes and of Chyualrye*, Bk. 1, ch. 8 'men ynoughe for to dystresse bothe hym and his grete oost'.

5. 37. *by the feythe of my body* = by my faith (*my body* replacing the personal pronoun).

8. 17. *to the justes-ward* = towards the place of jousting.

8. 17. *sir Kay had lost his suerd* = Sir Kay missed (*or* realized that he had left behind) his sword. For an example of a similar use of the verb 'to lose' see note **669.** 32.

8. 43. *withoute ony payn* = without any effort. Cf. *Cursor Mundi*, line 14480: 'Fra þat time forth þai did þair paine þat he and lazar bath war slainne' (EETS edition).

11. 29. *in a maner* = thoroughly.

11. 36. *goten* = begotten. Cf. note **4. 32.**

12. 22. *ten so many* = ten times as many.

12. 29. *go unto the wers* = fare badly.

13. 6. *journeye* may well be an error for *tourney*, or simply Caxton's misprint. This portion of the text is missing in the Winchester MS.

14. 17. *eyght* is probably an error for VII.

16. 31–2. *he ledde the oste. He* refers to Arthur who is leading the army.

17. 7–8. *for welle nothyr wo* = for good or evil, for good or bad fortune.

24. 9. *woode* = trees.

24. 13. *there dressed twenty-one knyghtes* = twenty-one knights came forward (cf. note **415.** 15–16). Both Caxton's edition and the Winchester MS. have XL., but as there are only twenty-one names in the list and as the French source has XXI, it seems legitimate to amend XL to XXI.

27. 37. *in maner of* = in the capacity of.

28. 17. *the kynge saw the herte unboced.* Caxton prints *enbusshed.* The most likely meaning of 'unboced' is 'escaped into a thicket', but it could mean 'driven to extremities', 'hunted down'. (Late Latin *inboscare* 'to set in a bush or thicket' >Old French *embuscher, embuissier.*) Cf. note **82.** 2.

29. 4. *bettir worthy* = more worthy. For *bettir* used by itself in the same sense see note **204.** 32.

29. 9. *the kynge sat in a study* = the king reflected for a while.

31. 24. *hit ys in grete perell if ever he com agayne* = it is very doubtful whether he will ever come back.

33. 36. *I have loste the honoure* = I have been defeated.

34. 30. *The stynte of my londe a yere.* 'The loss of revenue from my land for a year' replaces the French *le meilleur chastiel que j'aie.*

35. 4. *No force* = That does not matter.

36. 16–17. *unto kynge Pellinore saw nat kynge Arthure* = with the result that King Pellinor could not see King Arthur. For an example of this use of *unto* cf. Richard Rolle's *English Psalter* as preserved in the Harleian MS (ed. Horstman, vol. ii, p. 228, *var.*) : 'Vnto þat rihtnes be turned in dome with quert' (xciii. 15). Puzzled by this construction Caxton substituted *that* for *unto.*

37. 16–17. *and som were four wekis olde and som lesse.* This could hardly have been the case if all the children had been born on the same day (1 May). Malory omits to mention that Arthur had ordered that all those born *in that month* (*en chelui mois*) be imprisoned.

37. 21–2. *as hit rehersith aftirward and towarde the ende of the* MORTE ARTHURE. This is probably a reference to the English alliterative *Morte Arthure*, the source of Malory's *Tale of King Arthur and the Emperor Lucius*, which was in all likelihood written before the *Tale of King Arthur* (see my OET second edition, pp. lii–liv and 1303).

38. 20–1. *withoute . . . trechory and withoute treson. Trechory* is the equivalent of the French *tricherie* ('deceit'). The French has *sans tricherie . . . et sans traïson.*

38. 29–30. *everych one aftir othir* = in turn.

38. 41. *be rew* = in turn. See Glossary, *s.v.* 'rew'.

39. 2. *their grace ys nat to helpe you* = they have not had the good fortune to help you.

39. 12. *put hymselff nat far in prees* = did not press forward.

39. 13. *if hys grace happed hym* = if fortune favoured him.

39. 21–2. *she thought he sholde nat be of no worship* = she thought he could not be a person of quality.

39. 24. *hit nedith nat you to put me to no more payne* = you need not trouble me any more.

40. 31. *The Lady of the Laake* is not Viviane (Malory's *Nyneve, Nyvene*), who is also called the Lady of the Lake, and who in the French romance brings up the young Lancelot and causes the death of Merlin. The damsel who asks for Balin's head is never described in Malory's source otherwise than as *une damoisiele.*

40. 34–5. *I have forgotyn the name of my swerde that ye gaff me.* The French source says 'I have forgotten *to ask you* the name of this sword' (*je vos obliai a demander le nom,* etc.).

40. 36–7. *that ys as muche to sey as Kutte Stele.* The French romance says that this is a Hebrew name which means 'cuts iron and steel' (*trenche fer et achier*), but the most likely source of the name is Virgil's *vulnificus chalybs* (*Aeneid,* viii. 445–6).

40. 41–2. *I take no force though I have both theire hedis* = I would willingly have both their heads.

41. 9. *Evyll be ye founde.* This may mean 'you came in an evil hour', or 'may you be cursed', by analogy with *well founde* (cf. note **262.** 1). The OET edition translates *founde* 'proved to be'.

41. 15. *sauffconduyghte* should probably be taken here in the French sense of 'protection' rather than in the usual English sense of 'guarantee of protection'. Cf. Robert of Gloucester, *Metrical chronicle* (ed. W. A. Wright, 1887), 10226: 'To vinde him gode borewes & sauf condut al so.'

42. 15–16. *thys same damesell that here stondith.* The damsel had in the meantime returned to court.

42. 30. *God wolde* = would to God.

44. 3. *the Castell of Four Stonys* is in the French the castle 'of four catapults' (*chastiel de quatre perrieres*).

44. 30. *in my defendaunte* = in self-defence. The phrase is modelled on *sur moi defendant.* Cf. *The Romances of Guy of Warwick and Rembrun his Son* (ed. Julius Zupitza), l. 6890: 'ʒif ich þi sone owhar a-slouʒ, It was me defendant nouʒ.'

46. 10–11. *Hit ys an evyll sygne . . . that thou arte a trew man, that,* etc. = It is a sign that you are not an honest man if, etc.

46. 34. *wounded hym freyshly* = severely wounded him. Cf. *The Romance of William of Palerne* (ed. W. W. Skeat, 1867), l. 1190: 'William ginnes ride fresly toward here fos.'

47. 6. *charged hem with hym* = entrusted him to them.

47. 22–3. *I have evill deserved hit agayne for hys kyndnesse* = I have not deserved that he should be kind in return.

48. 4. *in my defaute* = through my fault.

48. 16. *slayne and distressed.* 'Distressed' may mean here either 'harassed' ('killed and harassed') or 'defeated'. Cf. note 5. 3–4.

48. 29–30. *for because that* = because.

49. 10. *in the sygne of* = in the shape of.

49. 16. *how that whan* can be translated either 'that when' or 'how when'.

50. 17–18. *othir ellis I woll greve hym* = and hurt him if need be.

51. 28. *there fell many men aboute the damesell* = many men surrounded the damsel.

52. 2. *as hit tellith aftir in the SANKGREALL.* This may be a reference either to the Grail branch of the French romance—*La Queste del Saint Graal*— or its later, 'post Vulgate' form, or Malory's own Grail book. The reference suggests that from Malory's point of view the *Sankgreall* in its French or English version was a distinctly identifiable unit—a well-defined part of a series.

53. 27. *a grymme wepyn.* The 'grim' (i.e. formidable) weapon was, according to the French romance, a log of wood.

53. 29–30. *And whan Balyne was wepynles,* etc. He was obviously not 'weaponless' since he still had his other sword with him, the one with which he was to kill unwittingly his brother Balan. But any reference to that sword would have spoilt the motivation of the Dolorous Stroke theme.

54. 11. *nyghe of Joseph his kynne* = close kin to Joseph.

54. 34. *my promyse* = the promise made to me.

55. 11. *more than a paas* = at a good speed. Cf. note 4. 20.

55. 27. *I shold have passed my sorow* = I should have been spared my sorrow. The earliest example of this use of the verb 'to pass' in the *Oxf. Eng. Dict.* comes from Chapman's *Iliad* (iii. 114): 'An old man will consent to pass things past.'

56. 1–2. *'That blast',* said Balyn, *'is blowen for me, for I am the pryse, and yet am I not dede.'* The choice of words, based as it is on the Middle English *blawyng of prys* (cf. *Sir Gawain and the Green Knight,* 1362 and 1601), conveys much the same sense as the otherwise untranslatable pun: *Me tiennent il a pris qui cornent de prise.*

56. 4. *unto his syght* = to his face, in his presence. The 'good cheer' conceals a sinister design.

56. 35. *by cause of his two swerdys.* By this time Balin had only one sword left (the one that Malory ignored in describing the scene of the Dolorous Stroke). The phrase 'because of his two swords' was suggested by the French *chelui a deus espees* used in this instance as a substitute for a proper name.

56. 37. *they aventryd theyr speres.* This should mean 'levelled their spears', unless *aventryd* is a corruption of *afeautryd* ('set').

57. 22–3. *so ful hewen and bledde* = all gashed and covered with blood.

57. 27. *I aspyed wel your two swerdys.* See above, note **56.** 35.

57. 32. *That were wel done* = That would have been a good deed.

58. 17–18. *Launcelot de Lake fordyd that bed thorow his noblesse.* Lancelot destroyed the bed when the spell was broken by the magic action of his ring.

58. 26. *other ellis Galahad, hys sonne.* Malory here makes one sword out of two: the one which is to be handled by Lancelot who will inflict with it a mortal wound on Gawain (Balin's sword) and the one which Galahad will one day draw from a stone. The confusion is significant in that it reflects Malory's reluctance to differentiate between the 'goodness' of Lancelot and that of Galahad.

58. 39. *that ys in Englysh called Wynchester.* No such identification is found in Malory's French models. Caxton, in his Preface to *Le Morte Darthur*, describes Camelot as 'a city in Wales'.

58. 43–4. *THE BOOKE OF THE SANKGREALL.* Cf. note **52.** 2.

59. 14–15. *for the moste party of the barowns knew nat he was Uther Pendragon son,* etc. = because most of the barons did not know that he was Uther Pendragon's son, many kings and lords waged war upon him.

60. 17. *what by watir and by londe* = now by water, now by land.

60. 31. *twenty and eyght knyghtes.* This should be 48 so as to bring the total up to 148 and leave two seats vacant, the Siege Perilous and the seat which is to be occupied by Pellinor. Cf. Arthur's remark on p. 62 (ll. 41–2): 'What ys the cause that there ys two placis voyde in the segis?' But the figure 28 is repeated in ll. 33–4.

63. 37. *I may nat do therewith* = I cannot interfere.

65. 35. *he* refers to Gawain.

66. 8. *and felle over hym.* The lady purposely thrust herself forward to protect her lover.

66. 24–5. *he made hym to bere the one grehownde before hym on hys horse and the other behynde hym.* The object of this is to show *l'ochoison de la bataille* and so justify Gawain's behaviour.

66. 28–9. *Gawayne wente unto the castell.* Malory seems to forget that Gawain and Gaheris are already in the castle (cf. p. 65, l. 26).

67. 10. *what chere?* = how are things?

67. 32. *Merlion dud make kynge Arthure that sir Gawayne was sworne* = contrived with King Arthur that Sir Gawain was sworn.

67. 36–7. *there was sette a queste of ladyes uppon sir Gawayn. Queste* here means 'judgement', 'trial'.

69. 24. *lodgynge* = food and lodging.

69. 24. *as* = also.

70. 5. *onles that thou wolte geff me the brachette.* The dog is still in Abelleus's possession and Abelleus is merely asking Torre to let him keep it. *Geff* = 'grant possession'.

70. 17. *I am lothe of that gyffte I have gyvyn you* = I bitterly regret having granted you that boon.

72. 19–20. *Outelake of Wentelonde* is not to be confused with a character of the same name who plays a prominent part in the story of Arthur and Accolon.

72. 25. *and you bothe,* meaning 'and you too', refers to Outelake.

72. 25. *othir ellis that one of us to leve in the fylde* = or else that one of us should be left lying dead in the field.

75. 14–17.'*Madam*', *seyde kynge Pellynore*, etc. Is Pellinor blaming his daughter for having taken her life or is he telling Guinevere that it would have been foolish of him to risk his? Pellinor is addressing the queen, but he is also replying to her reproach and telling her why he did not save his daughter's life.

75. 15–16. *salf youre displesure* = may it not displease you.

75. 18–30. ' . . . *ye ought sore to repente hit*', *seyde Merlion*, '*for that lady was youre owne doughtir, begotyn of the lady of the Rule*', etc. This is an example of Malory's practice of solving a mystery at the earliest possible opportunity. In the French, Merlin deliberately refrains from telling Pellinor the whole truth.

75. 27–30. *ye shall se youre beste frende fayle you whan ye be in the grettist distresse that ever ye were othir shall be.* This is a summary of Merlin's prophecy about the death of Pellinor: Pellinor will be wounded in battle by Gawain; he will appeal for help to Torre, his son, who, failing to recognize him, will offer him no help; and Gawain will then return and cut off Pellinor's head: *he that ye sholde truste moste on of ony man on lyve, he shall leve you there ye shall be slayne.*

75. 33–76. 3. *Thus whan the queste was done of the whyght herte . . . . Explicit the wedding of kyng Arthur.* There is no such conclusion in Malory's source. Its interest lies less perhaps in the common device of recapitulation at the end of the story than in the definition it contains of the duties of knighthood as Malory saw them.

76. 33. *yonge Launcelot.* Lancelot was then one year old.

77. 4. *hardely . . . on my perelle* = indeed I can assure you.

77. 7–16. *And allwayes he lay aboute . . . departed and leffte Merlyon.* Malory does not explain how Merlin fell a victim to his own witchcraft: it was he who taught Nivene the 'subtyle worchyng' by which she acquired mastery over him.

77. 11–13. *Merlyon ded shew hir in a roche whereas was a grete wondir and wrought by enchauntement that went undir a grete stone* = Merlin showed her, in a rock, a great marvel which, wrought by enchantment, was underneath a great stone.

81. 10–15. *his squyre founde wretyn uppon the crosse that Bagdemagus sholde never retourne*, etc. This is a misreading of the French 'il jura seur la crois oiant le varlet que ja mais en la court le roi Artu ne retournera'. Malory must have mistaken *il jura seur la crois oiant le varlet* (= he swore on the cross in the presence of the squire) for *i truva seur la crois escrit li varlets* (= the squire found there written on the cross).

81. 19–21. *and there by the way he founde a braunche of holy herbe that was the signe of the Sancgreall*, etc. However tempting it may be to see in this reference to the 'holy herbe' a survival of an agrarian cult and possibly even a confirmation of the ritual theory of the origins of the Grail, it is nothing more than a mistranslation. Unfamiliar as he probably was with the word *branke* in the technical sense of 'subdivision of a cycle', Malory made the phrase *brankes del Graal* into 'a braunche of holy herbe that was the signe of the Sancgreall'.

81. 40. *the horses were so fre . . .* = so ready to go, so willing. Cf. *Paston Letters*, 802 : 'It shall never neede to prykke nor threte a free horse' (*Oxf. Eng. Dict.*, *s.v.* 'free' 20 *c*).

82. 2. *inboced* = driven to extremities, hunted down. The *Oxf. Eng. Dict.* (*s.v.* embossed) records no example of this meaning prior to 1641. Cf. note **28.** 17.

82. 8–10. *the kynge loked aboute the worlde and sawe before hym in a grete water a lytyll shippe*. A curious mistranslation of 'li rois, regarde *contre mont* (= upwards) la riviere et voit venir a val l'iaue une nef'.

83. 4–5. *he kepith frome hym . . . and therein sir Outlake dwellyth*. *He* refers to Outlake, *hym* to Damas.

83. 12–13. *no knyght woll fyght for hym*. This refers to Damas's attempt to persuade one of his neighbours to do battle for him.

83. 31. *Wyth this* = On this condition, that. Cf. p. 340 (l. 12) (*with that*).

85. 2. *as he was wounded* = wounded as he was.

85. 6–8. *he seyde that he wolde fyght . . . on the morne*. The French source explains how, having heard of the dispute between Damas and Outlake, Morgan turned it to her own advantage. Both Damas and Outlake come to her and ask her to find them champions, Damas because he lacks prowess, and Outlake because he is suffering from wounds received in battle. Morgan at once sees her chance and arranges a battle between Arthur and Accolon.

85. 42–4. *Whan Arthure behelde the grounde so sore bebledde he was dismayde. And than he demed treson, that his swerde was chonged, for his swerde bote nat steele as hit was wonte to do*. Malory does not say either here or later that Accolon lost no blood because he was protected by the magic scabbard.

87. 36–7. *Than sir Arthure remembirde hym and thought he scholde have sene this knyght* is a mistranslation of *et lors s'apensa li rois Artus qu' il savra que il est*. Malory has mistaken the future for the past, with the result that Arthur, instead of deciding to find out the knight's name recognizes him as an old acquaintance.

88. 6–9. The contradiction between ll. 6–7 (*this swerde hath bene in my kepynge* *the moste party of this twelve-month*) and ll. 7–8 (*Morgan le Fay sent hit me yestir-day*) is also found in Malory's source.

89. 3–30. *Than all the peple . . . brother Damas.* Malory must have felt that as Outlake was the victim of an injustice the case could not be settled without some material compensation such as a transfer of property from the offender to the victim.

91. 10. *there sholde no golde go for hir lyff* = no amount of gold would save her life.

91. 20–1. *she wyste welle that he was there. And anone she asked where he was.* I take this to mean that Morgan le Fay knew that Arthur was in the abbey and that when she arrived there she asked where in the abbey she could find him.

92. 7. *Whatsoever com of me* = Whatever may befall me.

92. 19. *there she come fro. She* = Morgan le Fay.

92. 23. *Saw ye of Arthure . . .?* = Did you see anything of Arthur?

92. 24–5. *we myght a stered of one stede* = if any one of us could have moved from his steed. The French has 'we had hardly enough strength to breathe', but Malory must have misread *metre fors nos alainnes* as *metre fors nes* (= even) *a. l. aune* (= to move from any one of our saddles).

92. 25. *amyvestyall.* No such word exists in either Old French or Middle English. The Huth MS. has in the corresponding place: 'nous n'aviens nes poissanche de metre fors nos alainnes, *ains estions del* tout aussi comme mors'. This was the sentence Malory had in front of him when he was looking for a suitable epithet to go with 'countenaunce'. It does not seem unreasonable to suppose that glancing at the passage without really reading it he saw the words *ains estions del* and promptly coined a new adjective—*amyvestyall* or *amivestiall.* Caxton rationalized it by changing it to *armyuestyall* which later editors have glossed 'martial' or 'warlike'.

93. 8–9. *lette hym wete I can do much more whan I se my tyme.* Judging by the French, this should mean that next time Morgan arranges a single combat between Arthur and one of her own knights Arthur will not come out of it alive.

93. 14–**94.** 17. *Whan the kynge had well rested hym,* etc. Malory is here combining two distinct episodes: that of Uwain's exile from the court and a later episode, that of the magic mantle. The adventure of the magic mantle leads to the discovery of Morgan's plot, which in its turn causes Arthur to banish Uwain, 'held suspect' because he is Morgan's son. In this way Malory's narrative acquires more coherence and unity than can be claimed for its source, and the threefold quest of adventures by Uwain, Gawain, and Marhalte appears as a natural outcome of the story of Morgan's treachery.

94. 13. *that ye be of counseyle* = that you are plotting (against me).

95. 5–6. *hit is to suppose* = it is likely.

95. 30. *to fecche his raunge* = to reach the right distance for charging. The earliest example of this use of the verb 'to fetch' in the *Oxf. Eng. Dict.* is dated 1547. It occurs in James Harrison's *Exhortation to the Scottes,* ed. J. A. H. Murray

p. 213: 'As one that intendeth to make a greate lepe, I muste bee forced to ronne back to fetche my course.'

96. 18. *fro hit was* = from the time when it was.

97. 12. *Arthurs syster-sonnes* = the sons of Arthur's sisters.

98. 8. *hir is me moste levyste.* *W*'s reading may mean 'her that is most dear to me' or, if *levyste* is to be taken as an adverb ('gladly', 'willingly', with the verb 'to have' understood), 'for it is her I should have most willingly'.

98. 28. *I may lay that on syde* = I may as well have none of that.

98. 36. *at the leste way* = leastways, at least.

99. 6. *I wolde do for hym* = I would willingly help him.

99. 16. *Woll we do welle?* = Shall we do the right thing?

99. 17. *Lette hit be putt uppon hym* = let it be entrusted to him.

99. 29–31. *Than com there two knyghtes all armed and cryed on hyght, 'Sir Gawayne, knyght of the courte of kynge Arthure! Make the redy in haste and juste with me!'* In the French two knights appear, but only one of them speaks. Hence the plural of the opening sentence and the singular of 'juste with *me*'.

99. 37–9. *I may nat fynde in my herte to be with hym, for ryght now here was one knyght that scomfyted ten knyghtes, and at the laste he was cowardly ledde away.* The lady thinks that Gawain is a coward because he has allowed a good knight to be defeated and carried away without even attempting to rescue him.

100. 8–9. *And so whan he loved hir there was cryed* = and so he loved her; and then there was cried, etc.

100. 33–4. *and whan he hath putt hem to the worse, than woll he suffir hem wylfully to take hym presonere because he wolde have a syght of this lady.* By a process of simplification and compression Malory has robbed this incident, perhaps deliberately, of its original significance. The French Pelleas submits, not, as in Malory, because he hopes to 'have a sight' of Ettard (Fr. 'Arcade'), but because he is anxious to obey the courtly convention which requires a knight to carry out any command given in the name of his lady. See note **101.** 5–15.

101. 4. The subject of 'asked' is clearly Gawain.

101. 5–15. *And as hit above rehersyth . . . on his horse bak.* Whereas the French writer thinks at this point that the knight is amply justified in besmirching his reputation for prowess in obedience to his lady, Malory endeavours to assure his readers that but for the expectation of a reward Pelleas would have preferred death. Cf. note **100.** 33–4.

101. 6. *to fare so with me* = to treat me.

101. 30–1. *and but if I ded so that I myght have a syght of hir, I had bene dede longe ar this tyme* = and had I not done this so that I might have sight of her, I should have died long since.

102. 23–4. *what that ye may do* = whatever you can do.

103. 7–19. *And than he toke his horse . . . and rode his way.* The French Pelleas places his sword, not 'across both their throats', but on the head of the bed, so that the sword becomes a symbol of both authority and forbearance; in Malory it is a token of an unfulfilled desire for vengeance.

103. 29–**104.** 38. *Than sir Gawayne and Ettarde . . . duryng their lyfe.* This denouement bears no resemblance to the French. There Gawain is seized with contrition at the sight of the sword and bitterly regrets his *mesfait.* Arcade tries to comfort him instead of blaming him as she does in Malory for his breach of trust. Reluctant though she is to part with her lover, she agrees to go back to Pelleas for Gawain's sake. On hearing this Pelleas forgives Gawain and returns with Arcade to her castle.

104. 23–4. *grete sorow oute of mynde* = sorrow beyond measure, unreasonably great.

105. 8. *wente uppon his gate* = went his way.

105. 20–**106.** 25. *'Sir', he seyde, 'I am a knyght of kynge Arthurs and knyght of the Table Rounde, and my name is sir Marhaute,'* etc. Malory is here at variance with his own ending of the *Tale of King Arthur,* for he says there that 'at the next feste' (i.e. after Marhalte had completed his quest and come to Arthur's court) 'sir Pelleas and sir Marhalt were made knyghtes of the Rounde Table'.

107. 40. *by their extorsion* = by using force. Cf. *Cursor Mundi* (EETS edition), l. 27825: 'O þis (couaitise) cums . . . reuelaic, theft, extorsium.'

108. 20. *in the defence* = in the battle for the defence.

108. 38–9. *as men outraged of reson* = as though they were out of their minds.

109. 36–9. *And grete joy had kynge Arthure of sir Pelleas and of sir Marhalte, but Pelleas loved never aftir sir Gawayne . . . for so hit rehersyth in the booke of Frensh.* Whereas in the French romance Pelleas and Gawain are reconciled, Malory's Pelleas remains hostile to 'that false knyght sir Gawain' (cf. p. 103. 26). The reference to the 'book of French' conceals a departure from the source.

109. 44–**110.** 1. *sir Pelleas . . . was one of the four that encheved the Sankgreal.* It is not clear whether Malory identifies Pelleas, the unfortunate lover of Lady Ettard, with King Pelles, or whether he is thinking of the Grail quest as the kind of adventure that would enhance a knight's reputation for prowess.

110. 10–13. *Who that woll make ony more lette hym seke other bookis,* etc. Whatever Malory's original intention was, it is clear that when he came to write the words 'who that woll make ony more', etc., he felt that—possibly through failure to obtain further material—his own work had come to an end. Moreover, *ony more* clearly means 'more tales' or 'another tale' rather than 'more of the same tale'. The phrase can legitimately be taken to refer, not to a possible completion of an unfinished work, but to further works on similar themes.

II. THE TALE OF THE NOBLE KING ARTHUR
AND THE EMPEROR LUCIUS

Malory's *Tale of the Noble King Arthur and the Emperor Lucius* is a shortened and modernized rendering of the English alliterative *Morte Arthure*—a four-teenth-century poem preserved in a single manuscript, Thornton A. 1. 17, in the library of Lincoln Cathedral. The manuscript, usually dated *c.* 1440, is not the one Malory used. There are, of course, a number of passages in which Malory's *Tale* agrees word for word with Thornton, but some of his variants clearly go back to an earlier state of the poem and supply either alliterating lines which are missing in the Thornton text or words and phrases which improve the sense, or even sentences which help to fill some gaps in the extant version.[1] There is also evidence to show that Malory's source was more closely related than the Thornton *Morte Arthure* to such works as the so-called 'Vulgate continuation' of the *Merlin*, Wace's *Brut*, and Geoffrey of Monmouth's *Historia*.

Since the Thornton copy of the alliterative poem is imperfect and often inferior to Malory's version, the differences between them do not necessarily represent Malory's alterations. What is obvious, however, is that Malory reduced the narrative to about half its original size,[2] not by means of indiscriminate omission, but by a careful elimination of passages which seemed to him to delay the action: monologues, dialogues, and descriptions of scenery.[3] He clearly aimed at a more direct narrative and in the endeavour to avoid all that was not essential to its progress[4] did not hesitate to omit such episodes as Arthur's council of war in Luxemburg,[5] the adventures of King Loth[6] and those of the Earl of Artele.[7] A no less consistent feature is the omission of some of the gruesome details of the battle-scenes. Just as Arthur's brutality in the *Morte Arthure* was in keeping with the traditional style of early epic, so whatever Malory did to soften Arthur's character was part of the process of adjustment to a new setting. This seems all the more likely when it is realized that the adjustment was a two-way process: if Arthur loses in Malory some of his epic characteristics, Lancelot, on the contrary, assumes those of an epic hero. No reader of Malory's *Tale* would gather from it that Lancelot had been from the beginning a courtly hero, that he had first appeared in medieval literature as a champion of *courtoisie*, and that it was as the protagonist of Chrétien de Troyes' *Conte de la Charrette* that he had won his world-wide fame. Earlier English adaptors of Arthurian romance had found little in him to support and illustrate their own conception and treatment of the Arthurian tradition; and it was no doubt for this reason that the author of the *Morte Arthure* had relegated him to comparative insignificance. Malory's attitude at the time when he wrote his *Tale of Arthur and Lucius* was not very different from that of other English writers: his mind dwelt on problems of human heroism, not on the subtle issues of courtly behaviour. And in order to restore Lancelot to fame he had to make him into a character more akin to the Gawain of the *Morte Arthure* than to the 'Knight of the Cart' of Chrétien's romance or, for that matter, to the Lancelot of his own *Book of Sir Launcelot and Queen Guinevere*. What a recent critic describes as 'the aggrandizement of Lancelot' is the expression of Malory's consistent preference for Lancelot—

---

[1] For detailed references see p. 1366 ff. of the three-volume edition.

[2] Caxton reduces Malory's account in almost exactly the same proportion.

[3] The following passages do not appear in Malory: *Morte Arthure*, 697–712, 1210–12, 1502–9, 1963–72, 2047–50, 2314–20.

[4] See notes 192. 22–193. 4; 205. 15–16; 218. 14–15, etc., in the three-volume edition.

[5] *Morte Arthure*, 2388–416.   [6] Ibid. 2081–95.   [7] Ibid. 2837–51.

a preference which persists throughout the whole of the *Quest of the Holy Grail* in defiance of the letter and the spirit of the French *Queste del Saint Graal.* But consistent preference does not necessarily produce consistent characterization, and it is not surprising, therefore, that the Lancelot of the *Tale of Arthur and Lucius* is not the Lancelot of later tales: when he does 'great deeds of arms' and successfully attacks the Emperor Lucius himself, he is fighting for his king, not for his 'sovereign lady'. For him as for Malory the great adventure of the 'French books' had not yet begun.

113. 16–19. '*Thou recrayed and coward knyghte, why feryst thou my countenaunce? There be in this halle, and they were sore aggreved, thou durste nat for a deukedom of londis loke in their facis.*' The meaning of Arthur's reply in Malory is: 'Why should you fear *my* countenance? There are many in this hall whom you would not dare look in the face if they were as sorely angered as I am.'

114. 42–3. *Poynte Tremble* = Pontremoli in the Apennines.

115. 15–16. *Thoughe my londis marche nyghe thyne enemyes.* Malory was thinking of France as Lancelot's kingdom.

116. 16. *as a man were rased of his wytte* = like a man who is out of his mind.

117. 43–4. *sir Cadore son of Cornuayle, that was at the tyme called sir Constantyne* = Sir Constantine, son of Sir Cador of Cornwall.

118. 3. *beleft* could be read as *he left.*

118. 34. *flowe oute of his mowth* — came pouring out of his mouth.

118. 38. *lugerande lokys* = locks of hair hanging loosely(?).

119. 4–5. *brennys hym up clene that all felle on pouder, both the fleysh and the bonys.* Malory probably mistook *brittenyd* (*MA* 802), meaning 'struck, broke into pieces', for *brennen* ('to burn') and so imagined that the dragon had set the bear on fire. To complete the picture he added *all felle on pouder, both the fleysh and the bonys.* This did not prevent him later on from translating *bryttenede* almost literally (p. 119. 16).

119. 41–2. *I wolde have done my payne* = I would have done my utmost (to rescue her).

120. 2. *colde strendys* = cold streams.

120. 3–4. *more tresoure, as I suppose, than is in all Fraunce aftir* = in the rest of France.

120. 21. *fastenys . . . oure horsis* = let our horses be fastened (*imperative plural*).

120. 21. *that none nyghe other* = so that neither should be near the other.

121. 40. *evyn infourmede* = well directed.

122. 4. *raught hym a buffette* — dealt him a parlous blow.

122. 34. *in harde bondis* = a prisoner, sorely beset.

122. 40. *So I have* = provided that I have, so long as I have.

122. 42. *the mounte of Arrabé* is a mountain in Wales to which Geoffrey of Monmouth refers as *mons Aravius.*

123. 32. *maysterlesse men* = unprotected (or unarmed) men.

123. 40. *he leffte* may be a misreading of *they leffte.*

125. 40. '*That is knyghtly spokyn*', *seyde sir Idres, and pulde up her brydyls.* The probable reason for the plural possessive pronoun *her* (= their) is that in the alliterative poem the subject of this sentence is *the Bretons.*

126. 36. *and I had wolde myself* = if I had been victorious.

126. 39. *and spoke* = and they spoke.

126. 39–40. *the grete prouesse that the messyngers ded that day thorow dedys of armys.* The context suggests that *ded* should be taken to mean 'showed', 'displayed'.

127. 3. *I pray the, sir, as thow lovys me*, etc., refers to Lancelot.

129. 2. *carpis grete wordis* = speaks boastfully.

129. 19–20. *umbelyclosed.* A blend of *umbelie* and *umbeclose*, both meaning 'to surround', 'to enclose'.

129. 23–5. *nere had sir Clegis, sir Cleremonde had nat bene, with the knyghthode of sir Launcelot: tho newe made knyghtes had be slayne everych one* = but for Sir Cleremonde and the gallantry of Sir Lancelot, Sir Clegis would have been taken prisoner and all the newly made knights would have been slain.

130. 30–1. *for I calle hit but foly to abyde whan knyghtes bene overmacched.* The argument is that honour comes before strategy, and that no knight should avoid a battle, no matter what the odds against him might be, even though 'wisdom' is a greater virtue than 'valour'.

130. 34–5. *knyghtes ons shamed recoverys hit never.* '*Hit*' stands for 'reputation'.

131. 7. *Sessoyne* = Soissons.

131. 35–7. *there he mette wyth the valyaunte Vyllers hymself that was vycounte of Rome, and there he smote hym thorow the shorte rybbys.* It would seem that the first 'he', like 'hymself', stands for the 'Welsh King', while the 'vycounte of Rome' is used in apposition to the 'valyaunte Vyllers', referred to as the 'vycounte' in l. 33.

132. 7. *all seyde that hit sawe* = all those who saw it said.

132. 26–7. *a syse . . . lyke* = the same size.

132. 43. *by good meanys* = with great skill.

133. 13–14. *worche for my soule* = pray for my soul *or* work for my salvation.

133. 23. *in that haste* = quickly, without delay.

133. 27. *sir Lovelys son.* Malory never mentions 'Lovel's son', and it is clear from the next paragraph (p. 133, l.34) that the knight who joined Lancelot and Gawain in their attack on Lucius was Lovel, not his son. But since in an earlier passage Lovel is described as *Idrus brother* and Idrus as *sir Uwaynes son*, the letters *ys* could be interpreted as an abbreviation of Y[waine]s.

134. 14–15. *they that woll accompany them with Sarezens, the man that wolde save them were lytyll to prayse* = whoever saved the people who followed the Saracens would deserve little praise.

134. 26. *all yode to the swerde* = all were put to the sword.

134. 43. *were honoured full noble men* = were held in honour as men of great nobility.

135. 15. *in a corde* = tied together.

135. 36–8. *entryth streyghte into Lushburne and so thorowe Flaundirs and than to Lorayne.* The route given in the alliterative poem is the normal route from Normandy to Tuscany. Malory adds a detour: instead of going straight to Luxemburg on his way south Arthur suddenly turns north towards Flanders and, according to Caxton, to Brabant. This at once calls to mind the itinerary followed by Henry V on his way from Fécamp to Agincourt. The triangle Soissons–Luxemburg–Flanders is an exaggerated replica of the triangle Amiens–Athies–Calais, which roughly describes the route chosen by Henry V. Malory, writing a history of Arthur's conquest of the Continent, could not help remembering the most remarkable English victory of the century. By strengthening the analogy he may have meant to enhance the significance of his work.

135. 44. *there was a cité.* MA gives the name of this city as *Meyes* (= Metz).

136. 34. *a woodis ease* = the edge of a wood. Cf. *Sir Gawain and the Green Knight*, 1178: 'by lynde woodez euez'.

137. 19. *so worched his wounde* = his wound ached so much.

137. 20–1. *blody berenne* = covered with blood.

138. 32. *Southlonde.* MA (2657) has Surylande (–Syria) which is probably the correct reading.

138. 40. *and thou be raught with that rought* = if you are caught by (with?) that company. This is a repetition of the warning contained in the previous sentence: *Raunsom woll they none aske.*

139. 6–9. *for thoughe my shylde . . . hele us bothe.* This may be paraphrased as follows: 'Although my armour is damaged, Sir Priamus is seriously wounded. But he has a remedy which will heal both his wounds and mine.'

139. 17. *th[at] mykyll fruyte in fallys.* (*fallys* = 'fallacy', 'deceit'). I am indebted to the late R. S. Loomis for the emendation in l. 17: 'It is full of the flower of the four good rivers that flow from Paradise, *in which* much fruit falls', and also for the emendation of *the* to *that*.

139. 36. *grype up your hertes* = have courage.

140. 17–18. *folke of the bestes* = horsemen (?).

141. 19. *by that* = when.

141. 33–4. *at all assemble many Saresyns were destroyed, for the soveraynes of Sessoyne were salved for ever.* MA's *that saluede was never* makes much better sense since the 'sovereigns of Soissons' are Saracens.

142. 1. *sowdyars* = mercenary troops.

142. 4. *at the gaynyste* = by the shortest (i.e. nearest) way.

143. 20–1. *kneled in their kyrtyls.* Malory has here changed the battlements of a castle (MA's *krynelles*) into a lady's gown (*kyrtyl*).

144. 9. *Virvyn* is either a misreading of *MA*'s *vnsene* or an attempt to coin a place-name, or both.

144. 31. *Petresaynte* (Pietrasanta?). The corresponding place-name in *MA* is *Pawnce*.

144. 36. *whan he tyme semed* = when he thought fit.

145. 26. *the myghty kynge Claudas* = the lands of the mighty King Claudas.

145. 28–9. *make your repeyre* = pay regular visits.

III. THE NOBLE TALE OF SIR LAUNCELOT DU LAKE

In the *Noble Tale of Sir Launcelot du Lake* Malory abandons Arthur in favour of his protagonist, Lancelot du Lake. He does so, according to his own admission, because 'in all tournaments, jousts and deeds of arms, both for life and death', Lancelot surpassed all other knights and 'increased marvellously in worship and honour'. Malory is not concerned in this work with the main theme of the French Lancelot romance. He knows that Lancelot loves Guinevere and that he rescued her from the stake, but he is content to give his readers the impression that apart from this and other feats of prowess Lancelot 'rested him with play and game'. When one of the numerous damsels encountered by Lancelot says: 'It is noised that you love Queen Guinevere', Lancelot denies the rumour: 'I may not warn people to speak of me what it pleaseth them.' He forces his defeated opponents to pay homage to the 'truest lady to her lord living' and he is even 'rumoured' to be indifferent to all women except one, who 'has him in great favour, above all other knights'. But the adventures he undertakes are not the ones that illustrate his characteristic role of Guinevere's lover; they are those of a 'knight adventurous' who lives for 'arms and tournaments'.

The *Tale* falls into three distinct sections of approximately equal length, each corresponding roughly to two folio leaves of Malory's 'French Book'. The three sections belong to three different parts of the text. It is tempting, but perhaps not very realistic, to speculate that Malory's source was simply a gathering of three sheets which had dropped out of a volume of the Prose *Lancelot*. The alternative, and the more likely, explanation is that he deliberately chose those three sections in order to give a reasonably continuous account of Lancelot's adventures and so avoid the necessity of interweaving a variety of different themes. In the first section Lancelot decides to 'prove himself in strange adventures' and, accompanied by Lionel, starts on a quest for new experiences. The next section describes how Lancelot killed Lionel's captor, Tarquyn, released the prisoners and, in order to conclude this adventure, assisted a damsel by disposing of another enemy of knighthood, Perys de Foreste Savage, a 'thief' and a 'ravisher of women', who 'distressed all ladies and gentlewomen'. Three days later Lancelot performs another noble deed: he frees the people of the Castle of Tintagel of the tyranny of two giants. The source of these stories is a later section of the Prose *Lancelot* (vol. v, pp. 87–102 and 204–14 of H. O. Sommer's edition). As for the remaining portion of the *Tale*, only the first few pages have a parallel in the extant versions of the *Lancelot* (Sommer, vol. v, pp. 306–10). Lancelot rescues Kay from four knights, overcomes three more knights (Gawtere, Glymere, and Reynolds), meets four knights of the Round Table—Sagremore, Ector, Gawain, and Uwain—defeats them all with one spear, rescues Melyot de Logrys[1] and saves his own life by killing Phelot who had framed an elaborate plot to capture him. Then, after a long journey through 'moors and mares', he tries to rescue a lady from Sir Pedyvere who, in spite of Lancelot's warning, cuts off her head and then throws himself upon Lancelot's mercy. The *Tale* is concluded by the hero's return to the court of King Arthur. All his former enemies 'bear record' of his chivalric deeds and so introduce into this curious anthology of adventures what Malory could not have found in his source: a sense of the ending. The last page of the *Tale* (from p. 172, l. 11 onwards) may well be entirely his own.

149. 32–3. *folowed hem three but one knyght* = only one knight followed the three of them.

151. 2. *do myne advauntage* = do whatever is in my power.

151. 44–**152.** 1. *withoute ony comforte.* 'Comforte' should be taken here, as in Middle English and Old French, in the moral sense.

154. 6–7. *he laffte me goodly* = he graciously accepted my surrender.

155. 35. *hym* probably refers to Madore de la Porte.

156. 41. *here is adventures fast by that fallyth for the* = there are here close by adventures that it would be proper for you to undertake.

157. 5. *so ye woll* = on condition that you will.

157. 16. *Gaherys* corresponds here to the French *Gaheriet*, to whom Malory usually refers as Gareth.

158. 25. *so be hit that thou be nat* = provided you are not.

161. 6–7. *knyghtes that bene adventures sholde nat be* etc. = knights that are adventurous should not be adulterers or lecherous.

163. 6–7. *as ye woll have my helpe* = if you wish me to help you.

170. 24. *toke hym on the hede* = hit him on the head.

170. 32. *for drede of more resseite* = for fear of another trap.

172. 8–10. *ye shall nevir reste one nyght thereas ye do another, and ye go to ony bedde the dede body shall lye with you* = you shall never stay more than one night in any one place, and whatever bed you go to the dead body shall lie with you.

172. 36–7. *sir Kay forsoke them and seyde he fought never with hem* = Sir Kay denied having ever fought with them.

---

[1] This episode in reminiscent of a passage in *Perlesvaus* (ll. 8156–8250 in W. A. Nitze's edition).

IV. THE TALE OF SIR GARETH OF ORKNEY

The *Book of Gareth* is to the critic Malory's most puzzling work. Its immediate source is unknown, but it has numerous parallels in earlier medieval romance. Points of similarity with Renaud de Beaujeu's *Guinglain* and its prose version by Claude Patin[1] have long since been known to critics; in both stories the plot hinges on an expedition the object of which is to rescue a lady. But some of the circumstances of the expedition are reminiscent of another French story, that of *La Cotte Mal Taillée*, which occurs in the French Prose *Tristan*: both La Cotte (or Brunor) and Gareth are young noblemen who conceal their high birth and begin their careers in a humble way. They are both ridiculed by Kay who gives them nicknames: 'Beaumains' to Gareth, 'La Cotte Mal Taillée' to Brunor. Then in both stories a lady in distress comes to Arthur's court to ask for protection against a redoubtable knight. The young man obtains Arthur's permission to undertake the adventure, but for a long time the lady scorns his attempts at fighting on her behalf and rebukes him in the rudest possible fashion. Finally, in both stories the lady begins to suspect that her champion is a man of high birth. The ending is a happy one: the young hero marries the lady he has rescued.

Gareth's other adventures are a curious mixture of literary reminiscences, among which the romances of Chrétien de Troyes figure prominently, and the real question is whether it was Malory who put these incidents together and made Gareth their protagonist, or whether the story had been in existence before his time. Gareth bears a striking resemblance to one of the minor characters in the French Prose *Lancelot*, Gauvain's youngest brother, Gaheret (*var.* Gaheriet of Gaheries, often confused with Guerrhes), whose two outstanding features are his beauty and his modesty. Noted though he is for his *hautes proueces*, Gaheret never boasted of them: *onques n'en dist nulle*. Malory's Gareth is likewise 'the goodlyest yonge man and the fayreste that ever they sawe; and he was large and longe and brode in the shuldyrs, well-vysaged, and the largyst and the fayreste-handid that ever man sye'. His modesty is amply illustrated by his behaviour with Lady Linet, for in spite of all her insults, which he bears with good grace, he refuses to disclose his noble origin. In the French romance Gaheret is further described as *li plus gratieus de touz les freres; il fut assez plains de chevalerie et hardis et legiers, et biaus et gens*.

Why, then, does Malory say that the nickname Beaumains was given to the young hero by Kay *in mockery*? Gareth's mother, the Queen of Orkney, confirms this. 'Sir Kay [she says] dud mok and scorne hym and gaff hym to name Bewmaynes. . . . Yet [she adds] Sir Kay named hym more ryghteously than he wende, for I dare sey he is as fayre an handid man and wel disposed, an he be on lyve, as ony lyvynge.' To explain these remarks it is enough to refer again to the French Gaheret *qui ot le brach destre plus lonc que l'autre*.[2] All the Queen does in protesting against the nickname is to turn the tables on

---

[1] Cf. *Romania*, vol. xv, pp. 22–4; and R. H. Wilson, 'The "Fair Unknown" in Malory', *PMLA*, vol. lviii, no. 1, part 1 (March 1939).

[2] MS. Add. 10293, f. 250^r, col. 2. Throughout this passage there is some confusion between the names of the two brothers, *Gaheret* and *Guerrhes*. That Kay used the name *Beaumains* 'in scorne' is further confirmed by the dwarf at 195. 43.

Kay: he thought he would hurt the young knight by reminding him that he had one arm longer than the other; in reality he paid him a compliment, for the nickname, ironical though it may sound if applied to Gareth's physical features, may be taken as a tribute to his moral character; he is 'fayre-handid', and even 'largest-handid', for he is the most generous man that ever lived.

Malory's source must, however, have contained a number of motifs which do not occur at all in the *Lancelot*, such as the 'disguised nobleman' mocked by Kay and rebuked by the lady for whom he is fighting, the *Joie de la Cort* theme, the dismissal of the victorious champion by a haughty and ambitious lady, the love affair interrupted by an intruder with a replaceable head, and finally a tournament at which the hero adopts a different disguise each day. All these traits must have reached Malory through some French 'romance of Gaheret', the specific form of which is entirely unknown today except through Malory's adaptation. Dispensing with the subtleties of the courtly code, this French *Gaheret* must have propounded the theory that 'a man of low birth cannot defeat a nobleman except by accident or by guile', and so championed the claims of knighthood as an aristocratic institution. And Malory must have found himself in harmony with his model; for his own work may well be said to belong to that rapidly shrinking tradition which treated chivalry as a quality inherent in rank and breeding, and firmly refused to yield to the threats of the most formidable 'kitchen-knaves'.

178. 4–5. *for myne herte gyvyth me to the gretly, that* etc. *That* here means 'because', even though Arthur is still unaware that Gareth comes *of men of worshyp.*

181. 43–4. *he was heled harde with the lyff* = his life was only just saved.

186. 28. *in thy daunger* = under an obligation to you.

187. 34. *my body* = myself.

190. 37. *sauff all only this passage* = except this one passage.

193. 27. *this is his taryynge* = this is the reason why he tarries.

194. 8. *so that ye woll kepe hit in cloce* = provided that you keep it a secret.

195. 8. *ryche of* = adorned with.

198. 32–3. *toke their bere* = gathered impetus by a run.

200. 35. *all her hertys* = all the damage done to her (i.e. 'all the trespasse that he hath done ayenst hir and hir landys', as stated in lines 19–20).

202. 25. *his lorde* = the dwarf's master (Gareth).

203. 14. *as for that thretynge* = for all those threats.

203. 21. *sufferynge* = patient.

203. 40. *I kepe no more of the dwarff* = I do not care any more about the dwarf.

204. 20–1. *sir Gareth thought many tymes: 'Jesu, wolde that the lady of this Castell Perelus were so fayre as she is!'* The fact that Gareth fails to recognize Lady Lyones at the feast given in his honour by Gryngamoure seems to suggest that Malory has omitted some link in the narrative, such as a mention of some 'enchantment' by means of which Lady Lyones could have changed her appearance in order to test Gareth's love for her.

204. 24. *he passed hymself farre in his reson* = he completely lost his self-control.

204. 32. *and ye were bettir than ye ar, ye were well bewared* (= bestowed) *uppon hym* = he would be a good match for you even if you were more worthy than you are.

207. 13. *by this done* = by the time that this was done.

208. 11–12. *I am called the Rede Knyght of the Rede Laundis, but my name is*, etc. 'I am called' introduces Ironside's nickname, and 'my name' his real name.

208. 14. *in playne batayle hande for hande* = in an open hand-to-hand fight, i.e. in single combat.

208. 33. *for the love of* = because of.

209. 20. *and smote hym* = by striking him.

209. 31. *Where have ye done* = Where have you put.

210. 4–5. *as though he myght nat have gone* = as if he could not walk.

211. 21. *to com off and to breff this tale* = to proceed briefly with this tale.

211. 38–9. *with unhappynesse* = unluckily.

212. 32. *at hir large* = free to come.

213. 4–5. *but as othir meane knyghtis* = any more than any ordinary knight would do.

213. 42. *encresyth my beawté muche more than hit is of myself* = makes me much more beautiful than I really am.

215. 14–15. *than com into the felde sir Perimones, the Grene Knyght, sir Persauntis brothir. Perimones the Grene Knyght* is a spurious character, a mixture of *Perimones* the Red Knight, the 'lord of the tower', defeated by Gareth much earlier on, and Pertolype, the *Green Knyght*, who has already appeared and defeated Lionel (p. 215. 8–11).

217. 1. *what maner a knyght* etc. This sentence could be read as direct speech.

218. 38. *as hit had bene wylde* = as if a storm were raging.

219. 37. *so well of etynge* = with such a good appetite (or possibly a synonym of the phrase used in the previous sentence: 'full knyghtly he ete', referring presumably to his behaviour at the meal).

220. 31–40. *Browne Knyght wythoute Pyté* is clearly identical with Breunis saunce Pyté. Malory makes him die at the hands of Gareth. In the *Tristram* book Breunis appears again as 'the perelust knyght that now lyvyth'.

221. 2–3. *they made hym good chere, for they myght none other do, for they were but poore* = poor as they were, they could do no more than make him good cheer.

223. 41. '*What, nevew?*' *seyde the kynge.* '*Is the wynde in that dore?*' This, to my knowledge, is the earliest example on record of the phrase *Is the wind in that door?* meaning 'Is the wind in that quarter?', 'Is that the tendency of affairs?' or simply: 'Is this what you want?' (Cf. *Oxf. Eng. Dict.*, *s.v.* 'door', 6 *c*.). It is used here in much the same sense as in Falstaff's remark in 1 *Henry IV* (Act

III, scene iii): 'How now, lad! Is the wind in that door, i' faith? Must we all march?'

225. 5. *hym* = Gareth.

V. THE BOOK OF SIR TRISTRAM DE LYONES

The French Prose *Romance of Tristan*, written about the year 1230 and preserved in a large number of manuscripts of the thirteenth, fourteenth, and fifteenth centuries, owed its immense popularity to the way in which it combined a traditional theme with a fashionable setting. It brought the story of Tristan and Iseult as it had been told by twelfth-century poets within the framework of the thirteenth-century Arthurian Cycle; and while it thus added to the poetical tradition of Tristan a vast amount of fresh material, it also shifted the emphasis from the original story of tragic love to the protagonist's adventures in the service of the Round Table. A large part of this vast composition consists of descriptions of tournaments, battles, and quests; knight-errantry is its inspiration and its *raison d'être*, and just as the life of a knight-errant is a succession of experiences designed to exhibit and test his valour, strength, and gallantry, so the Prose *Tristan* is essentially a long series of episodes centring upon the figure of a great knight who embodies the traditional virtues of Arthur's fellowship.

What is apparent to the reader unfamiliar with Malory's source is precisely what Malory liked least about it: the seemingly indiscriminate accumulation of adventures. There is evidence to show that the English author supplied from his own invention several lyrical passages such as the farewell scene before Tristram's departure from Ireland and the recognition scene in the garden. Isode 'felle downe in a swoune, and so lay a grete whyle. And whan she myght speke she seyde, "A, my lorde, sir Trystram! Blessed be God ye have your lyff." She is prepared to part with him to save him from Mark's vengeance: 'For Goddys sake, myne owne lorde, graunte kynge Marke hys wyll, and than draw you unto the court of kynge Arthure, for there ar ye beloved. And ever whan I may I shall sende unto you, and whan ye lyste ye may com unto me, and at all tymes early and late I woll be at youre commaundement, to lyve as poore a lyff as ever ded quyene or lady.' It is, of course, possible to set against these passages a number of equally moving scenes which Malory mercilessly cut out. Sometimes the only word he uses to describe the peace and happiness of his heroes is 'cheer': 'so he had all the chere that she myghte make hym'; or again: 'bycause sir Tristram had such chere and ryches and other pleasaunce . . . allmoost he hadde forsaken La Beale Isode.' Short remarks and phrases such as these often take the place of long monologues, and a number of lyrical speeches are omitted altogether. The reason for this is not far to seek. While anxious to reintroduce sentiment, Malory was not always in sympathy with the kind of sentiment he found in his source. His archaism did not go beyond the attempt to record the 'noble and gentle deeds' of Arthurian knights, and he was clearly unable to sympathize with the more authentic forms of *courtoisie*.

There is a still greater contrast between his outlook and that of the pre-courtly Tristan poems. The great tragic conception of the legend had been abandoned by the French prose-writer, and Malory had no means of knowing that it ever existed. With the notable exception of the episode of Tristram's madness, which is probably his finest and most subtle contribution to the story, he insists on making his heroes uniformly happy and, like the French prose-writer, builds their happiness on a wholesale condemnation of their enemies. The prose version with its clear-cut division of characters into heroes and villains, and the natural tendency to make the heroes happy and the villains miserable, was on the whole much after his own heart. His strong sense of the value of chivalry as the noblest human institution prompted him to go even further. There are numerous passages in his work stressing the chivalric temper of his characters and insisting on the advantages of being a 'true knight'. Phrases such as 'he was a true knight' or 'the High Order of Knighthood' are too common to be quoted, but it is important to note that they are in most cases absent from Malory's source and that he uses them in order to support the view, clearly expressed in the French Prose *Tristan*, that Tristram's love for Isode was fully justified because Tristram was a true knight and Mark an enemy of knighthood. Mark, says Lamorak, 'is a grete enemy to all good knyghtes, and that proveth wel, for he hath chaced oute of that contrey sir Trystram, that is the worshipfullest knyght that now is living, and all knightes speak of him worship. And for jealousnes of his queen he hath chaced him out of his countrey.'

If there is a leitmotif in Malory's adaptation it is the notion that 'all that the noble sir Tristram does is through clean knighthood'. When he and Isode are on their way to Cornwall and he hears of Lancelot's exploits he exclaims: 'Alas! . . . and I had nat this messayge in hande with this fayre lady, truly I wolde never stynte or I had founde sir Launcelot!' The 'message' is the task of bringing Isode to Cornwall. But for this, Tristram would have gone in search of Lancelot, leaving all else behind. It does not seem to matter to him that only a short while ago he and Isode drank the love potion, and that 'when that drynke was in their bodyes they loved aythir other so well that never hir love departed'. In the original Tristan story the potion was so made that it was impossible for the lovers to part once they had drunk it: if, says Eilhart, they had parted for half-a-day they would have fallen ill; if for a week they would have died. No such quality is ascribed to it either in the Prose Romance or in Malory: love is not allowed to interfere with the customs of knight-errantry. As a true knight-errant, what Tristram values above all is not the presence of his beloved, nor the joy of sharing every moment of his life with her, but the high privilege of fighting in her name. The service of love for him as for Lancelot is yet another form of self-assertion as a true champion of the 'High Order of Knighthood', and his fidelity to Isode is but another illustration of his dedication to the 'High Order'.

232. 9. *never jantylman more that ever we herde rede of.* 'Did' is understood between *jantylman* and *more*.

233. 1. *whatsomevir ye spende* = whatever the cost of the expedition.

233. 6. *for to avaunce my dedis* = to add to the number of my exploits.

236. 12. *forsake the* = refuse to encounter you. Cf. *Ancren Riwle* (ed. James Morton, 1853), p. 182: 'Nolde me tellen him alre monne dusigest, þet forsoke enne buffet, uor one speres wunde' (Mabel Day's edition, p. 81).

236. 14–15. *at my nevewys requeste* = at my uncle's request. This meaning of 'nephew' is not recorded in the *Oxf. Eng. Dict.* nor, so far as I am aware, in any published text.

240. 32–3. *sir Gawayne and his felowys nine.* Judging by the corresponding passage in Malory's source, the ninth companion must have been Gareth, not mentioned on the previous page.

242. 35. *he* = Tristram.

242. 38. *to compare ayenste me* = to appear before me.

243. 26. *wyth more* = moreover.

243. 43. *there agaynste* = in return.

244. 5. *moste and leste* = high and low.

250. 33. *thou madist no chere* = you did not seem disposed.

251. 19. *I shall know hir passyngly well that I shall love other truste* = I shall now know for certain whom I can love and trust.

254. 41–2. '*I have no doute of you . . . that and ye sholde have ado with sir Launcelot de Lake.*' Unless this is intended to be an incomplete sentence interrupted by Tristram's remark ('*As for sir Launcelot*', etc.) it should mean: 'I have no doubt *but that* you should', etc.

256. 42. *his parte his adversary* = the adversary of his party.

259. 5. *I undirtake for youre desyre shall be spedde* = I make myself responsible for the fulfilment of your wish.

260. 3. *if that she had bene fowler* = had she been less beautiful.

262. 1. *Well . . . founde* = Well met.

262. 44. *and sayde.* The subject of *sayde* may be either Galahalte or those who brought him the news of Lancelot's victory over Carados.

263. 6. *they* = Mark and Isode.

263. 23–4. *to put away hir thoughtes* = to try to forget her grief.

269. 15. *at avauntage* = at a disadvantage.

271. 32. *naked* = unarmed.

274. 38. *I was never ferde to renayne my lorde* = I have never disowned my lord out of fear.

279. 9. *to save his lyff* = to save the knight's life.

281. 33–4. *I . . . forgyff the myne evyll wyll* = I forgive you (modelled on the Old French: 'je vous pardonne mon mautalent').

287. 32–3. *And that was she that sir Breunys Saunze Pité toke the shylde frome.* Malory seems to have confused the shield sent to Lancelot by the Lady of the Lake with the one that Damsel Maledysaunte had brought to Arthur's court.

288. 32. *resseyved hym fayre* = graciously accepted his surrender.

291. 11. *there hit goth* = so be it.

298. 5. *beryth the lyff* = lives.

298. 16. *was harde byg for hym* = was too strong for him.

299. 6. *evyll wyll* here means 'wrath' (OF. *mautalent*).

300. 2. *sir Kay folowed hym, but he wolde none of hys felyship.* In Malory's source Tristram is treacherously attacked by Kay, Brandiles, and Tor, who want to prove the inferiority of Cornish knights. He naturally resents this as well as their unchivalrous behaviour.

303. 31. *as I slepte I slumbirde* = as I slept I dreamt.

304. 42. *he beryth the pryse of the worlde* = he is the best in the world.

308. 21. *savely and fayre* = graciously and taking due precautions ('safely').

311. 13. *all four* presumably includes Blioberis.

311. 43. *if case be* = if.

312. 7. *there yoode but ten away* = only ten survived.

312. 41. *What aray ys thys?* = What is happening here?

317. 17. *two yere afore* = for two years.

318. 27. Cf. p. 269. 15.

319. 17. *so many for so many* = equal numbers on each side.

321. 19–20. *hylde them passyng shorte* = pressed them very hard.

323. 34. *in veary purpose* = determined.

325. 26–7. *But in no wyse sir Trystram myght nat be knowyn with sir Palomydes.* Malory omits to explain this. According to his source, Tristram escaped recognition because he had been wounded in the face.

326. 5. *by forse of kynge Arthurs knyghtes* = with the help of King Arthur's knights. Cf. Robert Mannyng of Brunne, *Handlyng Synne* (EETS, 1901), l. 3363: 'With fors þey gun with hym fyght.'

327. 36–7. *And whan he was com he rode towarde sir Trystram.* The first 'he' stands for Gaheris, the second for Palomides.

332. 21–2. '. . . *ye shall nat do so*', seyde sir Uwayne, '*but ye shall have ado with me.*' 'ye shall nat do so but' = 'you shall not do otherwise than' or ' you cannot but'.

333. 11–18. *So sir Trystram endured there grete payne . . . that he had allmoste slayne hymselff.* The whole of this paragraph is Malory's own. But while it is clear that he uses the term *good delyveraunce* in the sense of 'release from prison', the passage need not have been *written* in prison. It may just as easily have been inspired by Malory's recollection of the 'pain' he had once endured as a prisoner.

333. 25–6. *at hys owne messe* = at his end of the table, among his peers. Gaheris was not to sit among the 'lower messes' at the end of the table reserved for inferiors.

333. 40. *hym* = Tristram.

334. 37. *there ys nat one here nother ye that shall thynk* = neither you nor anyone else here will think.

338. 19–20. *undir them bothe* stands for the French *entre eus deus* (= both of them), a construction which seems to have puzzled Malory more than once.

338. 39. *youre two sunnes.* 'Two' is probably an error for 'three'. Cf. l. 31.

340. 12. *with that* = on this condition, that.

342. 27. *with that shylde* refers to the shield Tristram received from Morgan le Fay, cf. p. 340. 13–44.

345. 32–6; **346.** 10–11. *'assygne me a day'* . . . *'I assygne you to mete me in the medowe by the ryver of Camelot'.* Tristram and Palomides seem to be talking at cross-purposes. Instead of assigning 'a day' Tristram assigns the place; he has therefore no reason to say later on (p. 346. 10–11) that Palomides has promised to meet him 'this day fourtenyght'.

347. 7–8. *hit is in adventure and ever ye scape his hondys* = it is doubtful whether you will survive his attack.

347. 36. *toke his wordis at* = considered his words to be.

348. 25. *And thus is he departed* refers to the unknown knight.

348. 27. *sir Trystram asked what was their namys.* 'His name' would make better sense. Dinadan's name is already known to Tristram (see l. 24).

348. 30–1, 36. *And there he reposed hym with a good man six dayes; he toke his leve at the wydow.* If Tristram *reposed hym with a good man* he could not have taken his leave *at the wydow.* The *wydow* is probably a reminiscence of an earlier passage (see l. 18) in which Dinadan and Kay tell Tristram that they are *lodged hereby in a wydows house.*

351. 8. *aythir gaff other the gre* = each said that the other was the victor.

351. 22. *I mervayle I hyre nat of hym.* Palomides fails to appear at the Perron Merlin because he is imprisoned in a castle (cf. p. 366. 11–13).

352. 12–20. *'Wellcom, sir Trystram!'* . . . *'wellcom to this courte.'* Although these speeches of welcome do not occur in the French Prose Romance, they are well in keeping with the spirit of a work which is not so much a Romance of Tristram and Isode as a story of Tristram's adventures. Equally characteristic is Malory's description of his hero's accomplishments: 'For of all maner of huntynge thou beryste the pryce, and of all mesures of blowynge thou arte the begynnynge, of all the termys of huntynge and hawkynge ye ar the begynner.' Such were to Malory's mind the virtues of an English gentleman— such, in fact, they have remained in some quarters to this day. And the fact that they are mentioned at the moment of Tristram's accession to the fellowship of the Round Table throws an interesting light on what Malory meant by knighthood.

353. 42. *ye ar disposed shamfully* = you are wicked.

356. 8–9. *hit is ever worshyp to a knyght to refuse that thynge that he may nat attayne.* This maxim expresses an attitude of mind incompatible with the belief in knight-errantry as a mode of life, but consistent with Malory's essentially practical view of knighthood. For a knight to attempt what 'he may nat attayne' is to do a disservice to the 'High Order'.

361. 7–8. *theym behoved for no good* = they thought it would be unfortunate.

361. 9. *hys owne hondys* = with his own hands.

363. 29–37. '*A, fayre lady, why love I the?*' etc. Malory merely summarizes his French source here, but in the process of condensation the courtly colouring is irretrievably lost. In the French, while deprecating the cruelty of love, its *tricherie* and *orgueill*, Palomides does not utter a word of reproach to his lady, Queen Isode. Her cruelty does not impair the state of grace for which the lover is indebted to her. Unrequited love may cause grief and anxiety, but its ennobling and enlightening effect is never questioned; to Palomides, as to any courtly lover, it remains the only source of his *clarté*.

363. 29. *fayryst of all othir* = fairer than any other.

367. 28–9. *harde yf that he ascape* = he will not easily escape.

368. 42. *I shall fynde you justynge inowghe* = I shall give you ample opportunity to joust.

370. 3. *I shall gyff you my beholdynge* = I shall look on.

372. 27–42. '*Nat so*', *seyde sir Dynadan. . . . So they departed.* This dialogue makes little sense because Malory has altered the motivation of Dinadan's refusal to fight in such a way as to conceal the real point of the argument, which was to expose the code of chivalry to Dinadan's subtle attack and hold it up to ridicule.

373. 14–15. *I sawe hym bettyr preved hande for hande* = I saw him defeated in single combat. 'Bettyr preved' here means euphemistically, 'put to a harder test'.

373. 34. *frome the justys* = some distance away from the place of the tournament.

375. 1. *put hym to such a dishonoure.* Unless *hym* is a corruption of *hem* (= them) it must refer to Gawain.

375. 10–11. *lat se: devyse how ye woll be revenged.* A word (*and?*) may have dropped out between *se* and *devyse.*

375. 41. *And sir Trystram toke suche a sorow.* Tristram is distressed at the thought of having to keep Mark company.

378. 13–15. *Ye ded the more wronge . . . for my fadir slew nat your fadir: hit was Balyn le Saveage*, etc. This is a reference to Malory's earlier work, *The Tale of King Arthur*, and one of many examples of confusion between Pellinor, Lamorak's father, and Pellam, the victim of Balin's 'dolorous stroke'.

379. 27–32. *Whan they undirstode . . . that ever were called murtherers.* Malory's French source makes it clear that Dalan—who was Mordred's and Agravain's friend—made them turn against Dinadan whose father had killed Dalan's father. It was thus that Mordred and Agravain were persuaded to attack Dinadan in spite of the fact that the latter had saved them from Breunis Saunze Pité.

380. 18–19. *as who saythe* = as much as to say.

382. 11–12. *the worste lay that ever harper songe.* This does not refer to the quality of the lay, but to the *mauvestie* of King Mark.

382. 26–7. *they devysed and caste many perellys of the grete strengthe of hir enemyes* = they imagined and anticipated many dangers with which they were threatened in view of their enemies' strength.

386. 9. *my woundis bene grene* = my wounds are recent. Cf. Robert of Gloucester, *Metrical Chronicle* (ed. W. A. Wright, 1887), l. 8670: 'To Winchestre he was ilad al mid is grene wounde.'

386. 38. *gaff . . . abak* = gave way.

388. 38. *hastely and uppon hede* = rashly and inconsiderately.

392. 12 17. *Than kynge Marke called a knyght . . . thou haddyste of thyne owne.* This knight was present at Alexander's meeting with his friends at Magance and came to tell Mark all that he had heard them say.

394. 24. *he had no foote to stonde* = he was too weak to stand up.

396. 1. *kepe the rome of this castell* = keep within the boundaries of this castle.

396. 28. *the pyce of erthe.* This refers to the undertaking given by Alexander (l. 18) to 'keep that piece of earth thereas the castle of La Beale Regarde was, a twelve-month and a day, from all manner of knights that would come'. The 'piece of earth' held by Alexander was, however, not the ground on which the castle stood, but a strip of land immediately adjoining it.

397. 16–17. *Harleuse le Berbuse.* In the *Tale of King Arthur* this knight is slain, while riding under Balin's protection, by Garlon, the invisible knight (pp. 50–1). But if the name is modelled on the French *Herlaus li Barbuz* of the Prose *Tristan*, it must have been first used by Malory in the *Tristram* section, and since there is abundant evidence to show that this was written after the *Tale of King Arthur*, the insertion of Harleuse's name in the latter work must be due not to Malory, but to one of his rubricators whose task it sometimes was to write in proper names in red ink. The Winchester MS. is an example of this process.

397. 27–8. *in her play tolde Alys* = told Alys with great joy.

400. 34. *aftir me* = as I tell you.

402. 42–3. *and smote of his hede. Than the Haute Prynce and quene Gwenyver went to souper.* Malory here repeats the words he used a page above (cf. p. 401. 4–5) to conclude another successful battle, quite regardless of the fact that only a short while before Galahalt, the Haute Prince, had partaken of a meal (ll. 32–3).

403. 5. *that had in gyffte an ilonde* = who had been granted possession of an island.

405. 13. *tho three kynges.* Presumably those mentioned on p. 404. 35–8.

405. 35. *Elyce, his sonne* = Elyce, son of Adrawns.

406. 18–19. *and nat so hardy in sir Gawaynes hede, nothir none of his bretherne, to do the wronge* = and let no hardy thought come into sir Gawain's head or that of any of his brothers.

409. 22–7. *'I ensure the, sir Dynadan,' seyde sir Launcelot, 'I shall no more mete with the'*, etc. This speech would seem to be more in keeping with Dinadan's behaviour than with Lancelot's, and its attribution to the latter may be an oversight.

410. 15–16. *he dradde perellys lest hit sholde be sir Launcelot disgysed* = he greatly feared lest, etc. *Perellys* seems to be used adverbially here, but the normal sense of 'dreading a peril' cannot be altogether excluded.

410. 17–18. *grete coystrons* = stout scullions.

415. 15–16. *Trystram dressed hym to the raunge* = Tristram advanced to the line of battle.

416. 13–15. *than he made suche purvyaunce that La Beall Isode sholde beholde the justis in a secrete place that was honeste for her astate.* The French says that Tristram and Isode were to come *freely* to the tournament. The Old French for 'freely' is *abandoneement*, but the adjective *abandonné* can mean 'secret'. Hence the confusion.

416. 23. *syses and mesures*. *Syses* is probably used here for emphasis, the meaning being identical with that of *mesures*.

431. 18. *What wolde ye?* = Why do you ask?

442. 30. *he had the speache* = he spoke out loud.

446. 37. *every man take kepe to his felow* = let every man look after his opponent.

448. 29–31. *And sir Trystram knew for whos love he doth all this dedys of armys, sone he wolde abate his corrage.* The situation is in keeping with the courtly code of behaviour. The lover owes his lady a debt of gratitude for the honour she has bestowed upon him by dominating his thoughts. What matters most to Tristram and Palomides—even more than Isode's love—is the privilege of devoting all their thoughts to her and of being inspired by her to perform deeds of valour.

451. 38. *at all ryghtes* = in every respect, fully. Cf. *Richard Cœur de Lion* (ed. E. K. Brunner, 1913), l. 3145: 'He was armd to alle ryghtes.'

454. 14. *I shall lacke you* = I shall miss you. The earliest example of this use of the verb 'to lack' in the *Oxf. Eng. Dict.* comes from *Othello*, III. iii. 318: 'Poore lady, shee'l run mad/When she shall lacke it.'

458. 19. *I hylde hym resonabely hote* = I pressed him quite hard.

460. 5–6. *there was none othir recover* = I could not have escaped death in any other way. Tristram knew that, like Marhalte, he was fighting for his life.

460. 6. *sir Marhalte dyed thorow false lechis*. There is no reference to this incident anywhere else in Malory or, to my knowledge, in any of his French sources.

462. 7. *'But I mervayled whye ye turned on oure party.'* Both the context and the source suggest that the speaker is Arthur.

462. 35–6. *sir Palomydes begynnyth to play his play* = Sir Palomides has begun to perform his valiant deeds.

464. 26. *ded of* = doffed.

465. 17–19. A characteristic anacoluthon. *La Beall Isode* appears to be both the subject and the direct object of *brought*.

465. 25–6. *he was as sorowful a parte to go frome the felyshyp of sir Trystram.* It is part of Malory's own conception of the story not to allow Palomides' love for Isode to affect his devotion to Tristram.

466. 13–14. *and hyt happyn an envyous man onys to wynne worshyp* = should it ever so happen that an evil-minded man were victorious.

473. 6. *had a graunte of sir Launcelot* = was granted his request by Sir Lancelot.

473. 7–8. *thoughe had nat desyred hym, he wolde have rydden with hem, other sone a com aftir hym* = even if Tristram had not invited him (*had nat desyred hym*), Lancelot would have either ridden with them or joined Tristram soon afterwards.

475. 40. *because* = in order to.

477. 12–13. *ever betwene* = meanwhile.

479. 16–17. *And furthwythall there was uppon the table all maner of meates and drynkes.* The French supplies an important detail: the dove, having brought the 'censer' into the dining hall, flies away. Two servants then bring in the tables. Malory, having omitted to mention that the dove flew out of the hall carrying the 'censer', gives the impression that the 'censer' supplied the 'meates and drynkes'.

479. 31–2. *shulde be brought oute of daunger.* 'To be brought out of danger' would seem to mean in this context 'delivered', 'set free', rather than 'saved from the perils which threaten one'.

479. 37–8. *and he shall nat wyte but that* = he will not know anything other than that he, etc.

480. 13. *secrete* = private or secret affairs. Cf. *Oxf. Eng. Dict.*, s.v. 'secret', sense I *n*.

481. 5–6. *I may not wyte thys to you* = I cannot blame you for this.

481. 38. *that ye spare hym* = that you find him.

482. 13. The second *he* = Bors.

483. 6–7. *what ye meane in thys contrey* = what you say about this country.

483. 24–5. *sir Boors semed* = it seemed to Sir Bors.

483. 39. *he* = the knight.

487. 16–17. *and so by course of kynde he slepte and dame Elayne bothe* = as Nature would have it, he slept and so did Dame Elaine.

488. 5. *yf ye were nat* = but for you.

488. 36. *gyff her an hete* = tell her what I think of her behaviour. I take 'hete' to mean 'reproach'.

491. 8. *in party of paymente* = by way of revenge.

495. 29. *sharpe showres* = great hardships.

498. 13–14. *on the brawne of the thyghe up unto the howghe-boone* = on the flesh of the thigh, reaching the back part of the knee-joint.

501. 30. *my name ys Le Shyvalere Ill Mafeete*, etc. The French *li chevaliers mesfait* could be translated 'the ill-made knight'. Hence Malory's use of the adverb *ill* which duplicates his transcription of the name.

501. 34. *I put a case* = supposing.

505. 34. *Camelot, that ys in Englyshe called Wynchester*. On this localization see note **621**. 27–8.

506. 33–4. *for thorow me ye bene marked of many good knyghtes*, etc. Malory's is the only version of the story in which Isode declines to go to the tournament for fear of causing Tristram *muche more laboure;* unlike most courtly ladies, she is unwilling to let him do too much fighting for her sake.

507. 43. *thou arte here naked and I am armede*. Cf. note **271**. 32.

510. 5. Cf. note **269**. 15.

510. 28. *all my evyll wyll God forgyff hyt you, and I do* = May God forgive you if (as) I do.

VI. THE QUEST OF THE HOLY GRAIL

Malory's *Tale of the Sankgreall* is the least obviously original of his works. Apart from omissions and minor alterations, it is to all intents and purposes a translation of the French *Queste del Saint Graal*, the fourth branch of the thirteenth-century Arthurian Prose Cycle. One is tempted to describe Malory's attitude to this work as that of a man to whom the quest of the Grail was primarily an *Arthurian* adventure and who regarded the intrusion of the Grail upon Arthur's kingdom not as a means of contrasting earthly and divine chivalry and condemning the former, but as an opportunity offered to the knights of the Round Table to achieve still greater glory in this world. He makes a lady in distress appeal to Sir Bors 'for kynge Arthures sake', not, as in the French, *sus la foi que tu doiz a Celui cui hom lige tu es at an qui servise tu t'es mis*. The same Sir Bors, when asked to explain the purpose of the Grail quest, says that 'he shall have much erthly worship that may bryng hit to an ende'. And so throughout the story Malory is primarily concerned with 'erthly worship' and the consequent attempt to secularize the Grail theme as much as the story will allow. Ignoring the contrast between *la chevaillierie celestiale* and *la seculiere*, Malory replaces the former by 'virtuous living', and even uses the phrase 'knyghtly dedys and vertuous lyvyng' to describe the duties of a good Christian. Naturally enough, when he comes to assess Lancelot's virtues and vices he finds himself unable to follow either the spirit or the letter of the French. Lancelot's main fault, according to Malory, is that 'he ys nat stable'; if he were, he would presumably have been worthy of achieving the Grail. His main virtue in the *Queste* was his readiness to repent; in Malory it is his reluctance to 'murder' his opponents in battle; and it is the absence of this same virtue that accounts for the condemnation of Lionel, a 'murtherer' who 'doth contrary to the Order of Knyghthode'.

But the substitution of the Arthurian for the Christian scale of values is perhaps best illustrated by the attempt to rehabilitate Lancelot. In the French *Queste* Lancelot was an example of earthly chivalry humbled in the endeavour to make itself worthy of divine grace, and Lancelot's humiliation was as necessary a part of the story as Galahad's triumph. Malory takes it upon himself to protect Lancelot against this treatment. Not only does he omit important passages which might reflect discredit on his hero, but he insists on Lancelot's past greatness and assigns to him a role which he could never have played in the original version. In Malory, as in the *Queste*, Lancelot is a repentant sinner; but he is far less conscious of his ultimate failure to achieve the quest than of his relative success in it. He thanks God for what he has seen in his search for the Grail; and what he has seen 'suffices him': he returns from his adventures with a feeling of having once more accomplished a great task. He even places on record, as only the Grail knights themselves could have done, 'the adventures of the Sangreall', adding the qualifying phrase 'that he had sene'.

The French *Queste* was a treatise on grace[1] with hardly a page or a line not intended for doctrinal exposition. It was written by someone who was clearly an expert in theological discussion, but whose mind never grasped the picturesque possibilities of the story, and whose language never extended to imaginative expression. The work was designed, as Pauphilet puts it, 'pour l'esprit et non pour les yeux'.[2] Hence, on the one hand, a remarkable precision in the expression and elucidation of thought, and, on the other, a complete indifference to physical reality. Form, colour, movement—those are things which the French author never seems to notice except in so far as they provide material for allegory. He carefully describes the colour of the horse symbolizing the fiend, just as he spares no detail in speaking of the priest's habit, because these objects serve his argument; but whatever cannot be used in this way, whether it be scenery or costume or character, is either ignored or sketched in conventional terms.

The fact that for this method of exposition Malory substitutes one which can in a very real sense be described as imaginative constitutes his main claim to originality. When he finds a conventional simile such as *comme une mote de terre* he replaces it by the remark: 'he myght nat stonde nother stirre no membir that he had'. The lion following Perceval does not merely, as in the French version, 'make great joy': he goes 'allwey aboute hym, fawnynge as a spaynell'. The long-winded and amorphous phraseology of the French *Queste* is transformed into crisp and spontaneous idiom. Instead of

'il estoit ore a ce menés que ceste mesaise qu'il a conmencie li plaist tant a souffrir et embelist qu'il n'essaia onques mais riens qui tant li pleust, et pour ce ne li greve riens qu'il face',

Malory writes simply: 'He toke hyt mekely and suffirde the payne', just as he uses the phrase 'for natural love' instead of literally translating *por ce qu'il le doit garder et aimer*. And no one will mistake the significance of the contrast between Malory's 'the wordis wente to hys herte' and the French *lez . . . paroles n'a il mie oubliees ne oubliera ja mais tant qu'il vive*. He may have misunderstood

[1] *Études Sur la Queste del Saint Graal*, p. 174.   [2] Loc. cit.

the Grail doctrine and confused the spiritual issue; for all this, it is through his version and not through the *Queste del Saint Graal* that the Grail has aquired in our imagination the significance and the power of a poetic symbol.

516. 16. *at the reverence of the hyghe feste* = in honour of the high feast.

518. 44. *the Hawte Prynce*. Confusion between Galahad and 'Galehoult li Haut Prince, li Sires des Longtaines Isles'—a prominent figure in the Prose *Lancelot* and in the *Tristan*.

519. 37. *that* = that which.

521. 2–3. *all thys mevynge of the kynge* = all that the king did.

521. 35. The phrase *crakynge and cryynge of thundir*, which characteristically combines rich alliteration with an onomatopoeic effect, was, like so many of Malory's descriptive phrases, suggested to him by the words he found in his source (*escrois de tonnere* = thunderstroke).

521. 38. *they were alyghted of the grace of the Holy Goste*. 'Alyghted' = 'illumined'.

522. 28. *hit forthynkith nat me a litill* = me not a little.

522. 34. *doute* = fear

523. 12. *hit ys nat to do* = it is not seemly.

523. 43. *hevy me* = grieve me.

526. 10. *lok . . . to hys woundys* = was treated for his wounds.

527. 18–19. *And so by fortune that tydynges com unto a worthy man that hyght Mondrames*. 'Mondrames' is a misreading of *Mordrains*, name given to Evalac on his baptism. Malory clearly fails to realize that the 'worthy man' to whom this sentence refers is Evalac.

528. 29. *may nat deare the* = may not resist thee.

528. 39. *that that coverde the body* = that which, etc.

531. 4. *of hys play* = of his wound.

531. 9. *turned into helpynge* = recovery.

531. 12–13. *And thys knyght and I were in the same quest of the Sankgreal*. In Malory's source this remark is addressed to the monks, but refers, as in Malory, to Melias. What makes it difficult to understand is that Galahad appears to be speaking to Melias while referring to him in the third person.

531. 14–17. Malory clearly intended the first remark ('for hys synne', etc.) to be addressed to Galahad and the second ('And I mervayle', etc.) to Melias.

531. 22. *to be overthrowyn* = to fall.

531. 23. *vertuous lyvynge* stands here for the French *chevaillierie celestiale* as contrasted with *la seculiere*.

531. 26. *hede of every synne* = the greatest of all sins.

531. 38–9. *a place that hyght Abblasowre*. The French author mentions no such 'place' but uses the word *vavasseur* from which Malory coined a new place-name.

532. 25. *and ye woll abyde by that* = if you perform this (task).

532. 26. *hast my nedys* = hasten the fulfillment of my task. The phrase is recorded in the *Oxf. Eng. Dict., s.v.* 'need', II 12. *b.*

534. 30–1. *f r the love of* = on account of.

536. 12. *Than percyved they bothe that he was sir Galahad.* In the French Galahad is not identified until Perceval, after a good deal of discussion, decides to ask the recluse who he is, and when Malory reaches this point in the story (pp. 540–1) he forgets that in his version the recognition has already taken place.

540. 12. *but as to sew knyghthode. But as* = except for.

540. 38–9. *Percyvale wente to the recluse and asked her if she knew that knyght with the whyght shylde.* See note **536.** 12.

541. 22. *change the lyff* = to die.

541. 31. *by ryght* = truly.

543. 5. *in the cité of Sarras.* By omitting to mention that the city of Sarras is 'vers les parties de Jerusalem' Malory suggests, perhaps intentionally, that it is within the boundaries of Arthur's kingdom.

544. 12–14. *'as ever y may do . . . that ye woll lende me that blacke steed'. 'I praye you'* or *'I requyre you'* is either understood or omitted before *that ye woll.*

545. 20. *inly black.* Unless *inly* is a mistranscription of *inkly* (= as ink) the most likely etymology is *Inde* (dark blue)+*ly.* The French source throws no light on this reading (*si noir que ce iert merveilles a veoir*).

545. 26. *rowghe watir whych rored.* 'Une riviere moult grant et moult rade.' Malory reproduces both the sense and the sound of the French *rade*: the former in *rowghe*, the latter in *rored*.

545. 30. *hym* = himself.

546. 8–10. *his shylde whych was brokyn . . . he was gretly chaffed with the serpente.* In the French Perceval's shield is not broken, but burnt by the flames which come out of the serpent's mouth. Hence the phrase *gretly chaffed.*

546. 30–1. *thou shalt nat be quytte for losyng of ony of thy membrys* = you will not get off with the loss of one or other of your limbs.

547. 1. *jantiller nature* = nobler nature.

549. 5. *whych was* = who would have been.

551. 36. *he conjoured* = he summoned the evil spirits in order to exorcize them.

552. 29–30. *all hys clothys and the heyre of hys backe* = his clothes with the hairshirt he wore on his back.

554. 40–**555.** 6. *and of the seven kynges and the two knyghtes the firste*, etc. The transition from Evelake's victories to Lancelot's genealogy cannot be understood without reference to the French. According to the *Estoire del Graal*, 'Nacien', the son of Nappus, was so named in memory of his great-grandfather 'Nascien d'Orberique', brother-in-law of Evelac. Nascien d'Orberique married Evelac's sister Flegentine, and their son Celidoine was the father of Nappus.

555. 6. *hit signyfieth*, etc. This is a reference to one of the passages omitted by Malory.

555. 7. *the seven felysship* = the company of seven.

555. 8. *he was signyfyed.* See note **555. 6.**

557. 8. *The turnamente was tokyn to se who sholde have moste knyghtes* = the tournament was intended to show who should have the greater number of knights.

557. 13. *erthely kynges and erthely knyghtes.* Malory's source has 'lez chevailliers terriens *et li celestial*'. The alteration accounts for the apparent inconsistency between this sentence and the next: '*Of thes* the erthely knyghtes were', etc.

557. 27–39. *thou turned to the synners*, etc. There is no justification either in the French *Queste* or in Malory's own version for saying that after his first experiences in the quest of the Grail Lancelot 'turned to the sinners'. This the hermit in the *Queste* plainly denies, and in fact contrasts Lancelot's pious attitude with the pride which had made him long for worldly successes.

558. 30–1. *hit ys in waste of all the remenaunte to recover hit.* In the French, *recovrer* is here used intransitively, with the sense of 'to succeed': 'if Galahad fails in the quest of the Grail, no one else will succeed in it'. Malory's *recover* cannot be taken in this sense since it has a direct object, and the most likely meaning is 'to secure'.

559. 10–11. *there rose up a grete crye for lacke of wynde that fayled them.* It is not clear whether *wynde* is used here in the sense of 'breath' or whether it is simply an imitation of the French *viande* (= food.). It may well be both. As at 545.26 and again at 603.43, Malory reproduces the sound rather than the sense of his original.

561. 19. *wortis* means 'roots', but the choice of the word was no doubt influenced by the French *orties* (= nettles) used in the corresponding place in Malory's source.

562. 32–4. *the more men desyre hit to take hit*, etc. Malory either took the French *asavorer* (= enjoy) to mean 'to desire'—a natural error—or simply misread *l'asavore* as *la desire*.

562. 44–**563.** 1. *she* refers to 'charity'.

563. 20. *nere were that he ys* = but for the fact that he is (*nere* = were it not).

564. 26–7. *in sygne of chastisemente.* Malory's *chastisemente*, although suggested by the French *chastiement*, should probably be taken to mean 'penance'.

566. 10. *And thou serve me to-morow. And* is here a copulative conjunction.

566. 13–19. The 'good man' who *departed them, that they towched none othir* sat, according to the French, in a *chayre* which separated the dry tree from the flowers.

568. 19. *creature.* A curious modernization of 'liege-man'.

569. 21. *the company of you and me ar departed* = our companionship has come to an end.

569. 30. *in the tombe.* The body, according to the *Queste*, was placed upon the tomb until morning. Hence the remark in l. 32: *we com hyre agayne to do hym servyse.*

570. 2. *for thou woldist nat do hit for to be holdyn chaste* = you would not do this (i.e. have pity on her) lest you might not be thought chaste [, not for the fear of punishment].

570. 6. *whych* refers to Lionel.

570. 10–11. *Now hast thou harde the tokyns of thy dreme?* = Do you understand now what your dream signifies?

570. 16. *in my defaught* = through my failure to take up the challenge.

571. 19–21. *natforthat he was nat uncounceyled,* etc. = He was nevertheless in no doubt (that he would rather they lost their souls than that they should have his).

572. 29. *evyll* = in an evil fashion.

573. 36. *to forgyff hym hys evyll wylle* = to forgive him.

574. 35. *he rescowed hym nat of hys evyll wylle* = his wrath did not abate.

575. 28–9. *Than behylde he sir Bors whych sate dressyng upward hymselff, which seyde.* The second 'which' refers to Collegrevaunce.

576. 24–5. *alyght a clowde betwyxte them in lykenes of a fayre and a mervaylous flame.* It is difficult to account for the change from *uns brandons de feu en semblance de foudre* to a 'cloud in likeness of a fire'.

578. 25–7. *he cam that nyght to the castell of Carbonecke. And so hit befelle hym that he was benyghted and cam unto an armytayge.* The apparent inconsistency is due to the fact that in the first sentence Malory mistook *a deus liues de Corbenyc* for *a Corbenyc.*

579. 16–17. *he asked them what they were. 'Sir,' seyde she, 'leve youre horse hyre, and I shall leve myne also.'* Galahad and the damsel seem to be talking at cross-purposes because Malory has omitted to translate the words *si demande a la damoisele se ele descendra* which immediately precede the damsel's reply.

580. 1. *two fayre lettirs.* The plural is probably due to a misunderstanding of the Old French use of the plural form *lettres.*

580. 13. *he* refers to the ship.

581. 38. *for the defens* is a reference to the warning contained in the letter which was found on the ship.

582. 1. *the body of hym* = he.

582. 17. *was bore in a towne.* I can think of no better explanation of Malory's *towne* than that he mistook the French *nue* for *uile* (*n* for *u* and *u* for *il*).

583. 29. *tofore we com to hym. we* may well be a misreading of *ye.*

584. 6. *all* (= all the trees) *that com oute of hit.*

584. 10. *he* = the tree.

584. 12. *all the plantis dyed thereoff* = all the trees that were planted from it died.

584. 35–42. *ever he mervayled and studyed who that sholde be, and what hys name myght be.* In Malory's sources Solomon's only concern is that the last of his descendants, Jesus Christ, should know that he had foreseen His advent. Since in Malory Solomon never explains this to his wife, her remark, *I shall lette make a shippe* seems irrelevant; it suggests that by building a ship of the best wood *and moste durable* Solomon could discover *what hys* (= Christ's) *name myght be.*

585. 15. *and sette hir uppon the beddis hede coverde with sylke.* The pronoun *hir* should refer to the crown which Solomon placed upon the bed ('au chevetz mist le roy *sa couronne*').

586. 7. *I ne am but Fayth and Belyve* = I am pure faith and belief.

586. 10. *He* (= the ship) *wente so faste.*

586. 12–13. *shall reste in thys bedde.* Malory's French source says 'se reposera en ce lit que tu as fait *et savra nouvelle de toy*'. Since the purpose of the ship is to let Solomon's descendants have *nouvelles de lui*, the omission of the words *et savra nouvelle de toy* makes the remark meaningless.

586. 44–**587.** 2. *no man that hath blood in hym ne shall never see that one party of the sheth whych was made of the tree of lyff.* Malory's *blood* is a misreading of the French *sans* meaning 'sense'. Malory has, in addition, omitted the most important part of the corresponding sentence which says: [no one . . . will ever see, etc.] *without remembering the blood of Abel.*

587. 9. *gryped aboute hit with his fyngirs a grete dele.* This should be taken to mean that Galahad gripped the hilt of the sword so well that his thumb went over his fingers; had he not done this, but merely gripped the sword firmly 'with his fingers', he would have failed in the test.

587. 12. *whych hath made* = because I have made.

588. 9–10. *He wolde nat suffir hem to regne no lenger* = He would not allow them (i.e. the ten knights) to hold out any longer.

588. 32. *magré her hede.* 'Her' obviously refers to Hernox's daughter.

589. 19–20. *toke hem to assente* = agreed.

590. 22–3, 29. *tofore ye have yolden the custum* = until you have complied with the custom.

592. 38. *turned up-so-downe* = was razed to the ground.

593. 6. *for hit ys nat for you* = there is no need for you to do this.

594. 29. *For much my herte gevith unto you.* This remark, put by Malory into Galahad's mouth, suggests that the latter was not merely anxious to know the stranger's name, but was drawn towards him because it was his father.

596. 1–2. *there cam a dwerf sodenly and smote hym the arme so sore that the suerd felle oute of his hand.* The 'dwerf' is a misreading of the French *main* for *nain*.

597. 29. *also many nyghtis* = as many nights.

597. 44–**598.** 2. *saw the hayre whych he had borne nyghe a yere; for that he forthoughte hym ryght muche that he had brokyn his promyse unto the ermyte.* It would seem that the sight of the hair-shirt which Lancelot had worn as penance for nearly a year should, on the contrary, have been gratifying to him. The French supplies the missing link: Lancelot on his awakening realizes that during his sleep which lasted twenty-four days he did not wear his hair-shirt.

598. 10–11. *encheved . . . in you* = completed so far as you are concerned.

598. 13–15. *Now I thanke God*, etc. Lancelot is not seen in Malory, as he so often is in the French *Queste*, in an attitude of abject humiliation. He knows that his former life was 'good'; and it matters little to him that because it was not 'best' the supreme reward of the Grail is denied him.

600. 16–17. *whych had layne blynde of longe tyme.* Mordrains (originally called Evelake) was struck blind because he approached the Grail 'so nyghe that oure Lorde was displeased with hym' (cf. p. 543).

600. 24–5. *For the fyre of the Holy Goste ys takyn*, etc. A mistranslation of *le feu du Saint Esperit est si en toy espris* (= 'aflame').

600. 28. *he* = Mordrains.

600. 38–9. *hit was a sygne of lechory that was that tyme muche used.* In the French the burning fountain is a symbol not of 'lechory', but of man's sinful nature, and the 'miracle of Galahad' is his ability to destroy it.

601. 5–7. *But he was fownder thereoff*, etc. The meaning is not clear. If 'he' means Lancelot, it is conceivable that some such words as 'not only' dropped out after *was*.

601. 6–7. *where sir Launcelot had fayled.* For an account of this episode, which is not in Malory, see *The Vulgate Version of the Arthurian Romances*, ed. Sommer, vol iv, pp. 175–7.

601. 18–19. *good awre* is a gallicism (*bon eür* confused, as indeed it was at an early date in French, with *bonne heure*) meaning here 'the good fortune to remove the souls of men from earthly suffering'.

601. 28–42. *And so he rode fyve dayes*, etc. Malory's source makes it five years, but if five years is perhaps too long a period to be dealt with in one line, five days is hardly enough for all the adventures of Logres to be 'encheved'. This is why Malory dismisses most of them with the remark that as Perceval inquired about Galahad he was told 'how the aventures of Logrus were encheved'. The effect of this alteration, however, is to separate Perceval from Galahad. Traces of the original version are still found in Malory's account: 'So on a day hit befelle that he (= Perceval) cam oute of a grete foreyste, and there mette *they* at travers with sir Bors which rode alone.' In the end Malory forgets that his Perceval is supposed to be riding alone and writes: 'he (= Bors) salewed *them* (i.e. Galahad and Perceval) and *they* yelded to hym honoure and good aventure'.

602. 1. *sowded* probably means here 'used', 'employed'. The corresponding word in the French text is *emploiee*.

602. 10. *swerde.* The 'sword' should be 'a wind'. The French has *ung vent*. If the word division is ignored and if *v* and *t* are mistaken respectively for *l* and *e*, *ung vent* may be read as *un gleve*.

602. 35–6. *There be two amonge you that be nat,* etc. There are *three* people at the table apart from the Grail knights: Pelles, his son, and his niece.

602. 43. *Succoured* is Malory's rendering of *sacra* (= consecrated): another example of the sound of the French determining the sense of the English.

603. 6. The *towell* is the French *touaille* ('veil').

603. 16. *and smote hymselff* = impressed its image.

603. 31. The phrase 'high order and meat' corresponds to the French *la haute viande*—'the holy food'.

604. 5. To make satisfactory sense this should read 'from which you took' (instead of 'and with you take') as in the French *Queste del Saint Graal: la nef ou tu preis l'espee.* But it is not certain whether the error first occurred in Malory or in one of the copies of his text.

604. 18. *he* = the maimed knight; *hym* = himself.

604. 24. There seems to be no satisfactory explanation of Malory's 'chief sons'. The French has *fillastres* (= stepsons).

604. 38, 40. *ryvage* = shore; *to the bourde* = in the midst of.

605. 7. *of* = for the sake of the.

605. 23–5. *he toke hit to sir Percivale and to sir Bors to go tofore, and sir Galahad com behynde.* Taken as it stands this might suggest that Perceval and Bors carried the Grail table while Galahad walked behind, but both the context (cf. ll. 26–7 and 32) and the source show that the three knights carried the table together.

605. 24. *to go tofore* = so that Sir Perceval and Sir Bors should carry the front part.

605. 32. *toke one parte ayenst sir Galahad* = held one side of it next to Sir Galahad.

606. 2. *fullfylled* = fed (Old French *repeu*).

606. 24. *made an ende* = completed it.

606. 40–2. *thou hast resembled me in to thynges,* etc. *To* is here a numeral.

607. 27–8. *rode a pace* = at a good speed.

608. 5. *my poure body* = my humble self.

VII. THE BOOK OF SIR LAUNCELOT AND QUEEN GUINEVERE

The first episodes of the *Book of Sir Launcelot and Queen Guinevere*—*The Poisoned Apple* and *The Fair Maid of Astolat*—belong to the French *Mort Artu,*[1] the last branch of the Arthurian Prose Cycle. They also occur, in shortened form, in the English *Le Morte Arthur*—a fifteenth-century stanzaic poem derived, directly or indirectly, from the same branch. The structure of Malory's source was characteristically 'interwoven': the narrative contained two major themes split into fragments and interlocked both with one another

---

[1] The complete title is *La Mort le Roi Artu.*

and with stories belonging to neither theme. That Malory preferred a more straightforward arrangement can be seen from his *Tale of King Arthur* and his *Noble Tale of Sir Launcelot*, in which he had set himself the task of extracting from his sources reasonably self-contained tales and of disentangling the interwoven threads of the French narrative. But it was not until he came to the *Book of Sir Launcelot and Queen Guinevere* that he fully mastered this method. In reading through the *Mort Artu* he must have felt that to avoid any 'loose ends' such as those which had so often appeared in his earlier adaptations, all the passages referring to theme *a* ('The Poisoned Apple') had to be pieced together and separated from all those referring to theme *b* ('The Fair Maid of Astolat'). The material which in the *Mort Artu* formed the sequence

$$a^1\, b^1 a^2 b^2 x b^2 y b^2\, z\, b^2\, m\, b^2\, n\, b^2\, p\, a^3\, a^6\, a^4\, b^3\, a^5$$

had to be rearranged in accordance with some such formula as

$$a^1\, a^2\, a^3\, a^4\, a^5\, a^6\, b^1\, b^2\, b^3$$

Only thus could the mingling of the two themes with one another and the intrusion of themes unrelated to either ($x\,y\,z\,m\,n$ and p) be successfully avoided.[1] But when this was done Malory must have realized that there was still a good deal left for him to do before he could produce a smooth and continuous narrative, and so he proceeded to supply the necessary links between passages which in his source had stood apart. In this way his version acquired the two main features which distinguish it from the French: (*a*) a rearrangement of episodes consistent with Malory's own narrative technique, and (*b*) a series of connecting passages designed to link together the episodes so rearranged.

That his immediate source differed in some minor points from the extant manuscripts of the *Mort Artu*, there can be little doubt. But nothing is less likely than that it was responsible for any of the important innovations found in Malory's version of the first two episodes of the Book. A French romance similar in structure and character to his would have been unlike any other French Arthurian work of the Middle Ages; and as long as there is no need to assume such an improbable development, it seems safe to say that of all medieval writers Malory was the first to re-tell the story of the Maid of Astolat in a manner alien to his French books and suited to modern taste.

The story of the *Knight of the Cart* presents a different problem. It was in order to illustrate the power of courtly love that Chrétien de Troyes had made Lancelot ready to suffer humiliation in the eyes of the world. Chrétien's purpose was to show that to Lancelot as the supreme example of a perfect knight any suffering that he might be called upon to bear for his lady's sake was welcome; and it was because he had hesitated for 'two whole steps' before entering the ignominious cart that Guinevere refused to speak to him after his victory over Meleagant. In the prose version the only one that was accessible to Malory—there is a marked change in the motivation of this incident. Unable as he was to understand how Guinevere's displeasure could

---

[1] Professor R. M. Lumiansky's claim in *Malory's Originality* (p. 217) that 'the Middle English poet did about nine-tenths of the unravelling' seems to ignore the fact that on his own admission in the English poem the two themes *a* and *b* alternate, in reverse order (b^1, a^1, b^2, a^2).

have been caused by so trifling an offence, the prose writer made an attempt to account for it on other grounds: Lancelot, we are told, had parted with her ring to Morgan le Fay and left the court without taking leave of the queen. Allusions to the ignominy of riding in a cart abound in the prose romance, but the knight's humiliation is not its central theme. Lancelot hesitates to accept the dwarf's offer not because he fears shame, but because he doubts whether the dwarf will keep his word. And all the significance which might still be attached to the symbol of the cart is destroyed when, on another occasion, in order to deliver the Lady of the Lake, first Gawain, then Arthur, Guinevere, and the whole court agree to be driven in a cart by a dwarf.

It is not surprising, therefore, to find that in Malory the original purpose of the episode of the cart is no longer recognizable. Even the appearance of the cart and its driver is changed: the misshapen dwarf's cart becomes a woodman's cart, driven by two men who use it to fetch wood for Meleagant. It is only because of the weight of his armour that Lancelot asks their leave to ride with them to Meleagant's castle—not because he is promised news of the queen. The exalted symbol of twelfth-century courtoisie is dissolved in realistic detail, just as the mysterious *Terre Foraine* of Chrétien and of the prose romance, the land from which no traveller returns, is transformed into a castle not far distant from Lambeth and the Thames. 'Than lepe ye up into the charyote', the carter says to Lancelot, 'and ye shall be there anone.' In less than two hours Lancelot reaches the castle where Guinevere is awaiting him 'at a bay-window'. The adventures which beset his path in the French story— the magic bed, the night in the maiden's castle, the Saint Cimentiere, the Pas des Perrons, the fight in the valley, the combat with the knight who reproached him with the shame of the cart, the Sword-Bridge which Lancelot crosses on his knees, oblivious of the torture he inflicts upon himself—all are dismissed, and Lancelot's journey is made swift and uneventful. But it is perhaps best that it should be so. The great examples of courtly heroism, of Lancelot's devotion to a sublime duty, of his infinite sense of sacrifice, would have gained little from Malory's prosaic context, as little as does the *Terre Foraine* from its localization within 'seven miles of Westminster'. For they belong to a world of their own, the very existence of which neither Malory nor any of his readers could have suspected—a distant realm surrounded by an invisible wall, accessible to none but the chosen few. Faithful to its initial purpose, courtly romance refused to make its secret known to the uninitiated, and so was able to fulfil, in the only way possible, the task of poetry at its highest.

611. 19. *opynne-mowthed.* The phrase could mean 'talkative', but it is more likely to be a mistranslation of the French *pour ce qu'il beast* (= was anxious) *le roi a vengier de sa honte.* Without the indirect object the verb *beer* meant 'to be open', 'to gape'. Cf. *Arthuriana*, vol. i (Oxford, Blackwell, 1929), p. 65.

612. 36. *ermytayge* = hermit.

612. 40. *defended me so hyghly* = sent me away so angrily.

613. 10–11. *the quene outewarde made no maner of sorow in shewyng to none of his bloode nor to none other* = the queen displayed no outward sign of sorrow either to any of Lancelot's relatives or to anyone else.

613. 23–4. *Sir Alyduke* appears in two earlier romances: *The Tale of Arthur and Lucius* and in *The Tale of Sir Launcelot* (cf. pp. 128–9, 130, and 159).

614. 29. *com never by her* = was in no way her doing.

614. 38. *in that degré* = in that (your) rank.

614. 39. *and ye ar sworne unto knyghthode als welle as we be.* Feudal practice would require that Mador should at this point repudiate his allegiance to Arthur as he does in the French romance (*se devest de toute la terre que il tenoit du roi*). From Malory's point of view equality of rank is enough to justify a contest between king and nobleman.

615. 29. *That* is to be understood as a duplication of *that* preceding *none*: 'that none will do battle for you'.

616. 1. *tho knyghtes wolde have you in suspeccion* — those knights who choose to suspect you.

616. 2–3. *he wolde nat a fayled you in youre ryght nother in youre wronge* = right or wrong, he would not have failed you.

620. 14–15. *to take a soppe of wyne* = to have some bread dipped in wine.

620. 21–30. Lancelot here defines the terms of his allegiance to Arthur and Guinevere: he says that he should be always 'on the king's side and on his lady the queen's side'. The reason for this is that as he was being knighted (cf. *The Vulgate Version of Arthurian Romances*, ed. Sommer, vol. iii, pp. 127–37) news was brought of an important adventure, and Arthur forgot—or did not have time—to give Lancelot his sword. The investiture was completed when Guinevere, on receiving homage from one of Lancelot's defeated opponents, sent her young champion a handsome, richly decorated sword. This episode is mentioned neither in Malory nor in the portion of the French Cycle which he used for his story of Mador, but he had probably read it in one of his 'French books'.

620. 39. *was had to lechecrauffte* = was put in the care of physicians, given treatment.

620. 42–**621.** 6. *And so hit befelle that the Damesell of the Lake*, etc. When in the *Mort Artu* Lancelot has defended the queen against the charge of having poisoned Mador's brother, his victory is accepted as evidence of the queen's innocence. Malory seems to find the evidence insufficient and brings in the Lady of the Lake to make the truth 'openly known'.

621. 22. *he* = Lancelot.

621. 27–8. *Camelott, otherwyse called Wynchester.* The identification is peculiar to Malory. Caxton seems to ignore it. He refers to Camelot as a town in Wales (cf. p. xiv above) where 'grete stones and mervayllous werkys of yron lyeng under the grounde, and ryal vautes' have been seen by many people.

622. 18. *of late com syn* = not long since.

622. 32–3. *to an olde barownes place that hyght sir Barnarde of Astolot.* Malory's identification of Astolat with Guildford, approximately a day's ride from London, makes it seem natural that Arthur should break the journey there on his way to Winchester.

631. 11–12. *ye have ryght* = you are right (in your choice), you have chosen well.

631. 28. *by meanys of syght* = as far as one can see.

631. 35. *knew the verry sertaynté* = knew for certain.

633. 32. *hit woll turne untyll angir* = it will result in vexation.

636. 23. *put a thynge in hys nose* = put something in his nose.

641. 13–14. *Therefore unto all ladyes I make my mone, yet for my soule ye pray and bury me at the leste.* Ye refers to Lancelot, not to *all ladyes.*

643. 18–19. *bothe for the strenge and for a bate.* I take this to mean that some of the dogs were trained for the chase and held by the *strenge*, or leash, while others were used for the kill.

643. 20–1. *had abated her dogge for the bowghe at a barayne hynde* = set her dog on a barren hind to bring it to the bow.

643. 23–4. *checked hit by the noyse of the hounde to have mette with the hynde at som watir* = came to a check because the cry of a hound told them that the hind had been brought to bay at a stream.

643. 27. *he* = she (OE. *heo*), as at 667. 12 and 701. 21.

643. 27–8. *wente to soyle.* The hind, to cool herself and also to kill the scent, lay in the shallows of the stream.

645. 40. *thes nine knyghtes.* The list contains ten names.

646. 43–**647.** 1. *And sir Lavayne smote . . . mo than twenty knyghtes. And yet, for all thys, sir Launcelot knew nat sir Gareth.* While Lancelot recognized Lavain, who had defeated twenty knights, he failed to recognize Gareth whom he knew and who had defeated as many as thirty opponents.

648. 38. *lusty* is used throughout this passage in the sense of 'merry', but in phrases like 'lusty heart' and 'lusty deeds' some of the other connotations of the word are also present.

649. 7. *wynter rasure.* A likely meaning is that given in the *Oxf. Eng. Dict.* under 3*b*: 'obliteration, effacement', but the earliest example quoted under this rubric is 'razure of oblivion' from *Measure for Measure* (v. i. 13).

649. 23–4. *for where they bethe sone accorded and hasty* = when such desires are quickly and hastily fulfilled.

649. 27–8. *than was love trouthe and faythefulnes* = love at that time was *trouthe and faythefulnes.* There should be no comma after *love*, which so many editors (including myself in 1947) have inadvertently inserted.

650. 26–7. *they bare none of hem no maner of knowlecchynge of their owne armys but playne whyght shyldis* = they bear no arms by which they could be recognized, but only plain white shields.

652. 4. *I take no force of my lyff nor deth* = it matters not whether I live or die.

653. 14. This reference to Lavain (instead of Gawain, as in the French source) is a link with Malory's own version of the story of Elaine, the Fair Maid of Astolat, whose brother is called Lavain. In the French Romance this episode occurs long after that of the Knight of the Cart.

653. 39–40. *A good man ys never in daungere but whan he ys in the daungere of a cowhard.* The first *daungere* has the modern sense of 'peril', the second the older sense of 'power'. Cf. Chaucer, *Prol.* 663, and Shakespeare, *Merchant of Venice*, IV. i. 180.

654. 3–5. '*Say me, carter,*' *seyde sir Launcelot,* '*what shall I gyff the to suffir me to lepe into thy charyote*', etc. A remark such as this is contrary to the whole of the French tradition which lies behind the story of the cart. In Chrétien de Troyes, as in the Prose *Lancelot*, when the dwarf driving the cart promises Lancelot that if he gets into it he will have news of the queen, Lancelot at first hesitates to accept the dwarf's offer, and in Chrétien's poem it is this hesitation that causes his disgrace. In the Prose Romance Lancelot's first reaction to the prospect of losing his honour is clearly indicated ('Et Lancelos dist au nain qu'il yra plus volentiers après la charrete que il ne monteroit ens'), but it has no effect on subsequent events, and it is not surprising that it should have been ignored altogether by a fifteenth-century adaptor such as Malory who knew nothing about the original meaning of the episode. Malory changes the scene into one of a dramatic dispute between a knight determined from the first to climb into the cart and two carters, one of whom loses his life.

654. 26–7. A cart was used in medieval times—and later—to convey criminals to the place of punishment. Cf. Chrétien de Troyes, *Le Chevalier de la Charrette* (ll. 335–46).

656. 2–3. *of every shamefull noyse of wysedom to lay adoune* = in order wisely to put an end to every shameful rumour.

656. 20. *he* = Mellyagaunce.

656. 21. *he* = Lancelot.

657. 4–5. *se unto them that they wanted nothynge* = look after them so that they should have all they wanted.

657. 34–5. *hys plesaunce and hys lykynge* = his pleasure and his joy.

658. 29. *in thys rumour* = as they were arguing.

658. 31. Cf. note **312.** 41.

658. 35. *hit was drawyn* = the curtain was drawn.

659. 2. *hit woll be takyn at youre handys* = your challenge will be accepted.

659. 5–6. *yet shulde ye be avysed to do batayle in a wronge quarell* = you should beware of doing battle on the wrong side.

659. 17. *they were sealed* = their challenges were sealed.

659. 25–6. *nother none for you* = and none shall be done to you.

659. 30. *fared with treson* = acted treacherously.

660. 5–6. *made suddaynly to put on syde sir Lavaynes horse* = suddenly contrived to have Sir Lavain's horse concealed. *Lavaynes* may well be a mistake for *Launcelots*, which the context clearly requires.

660. 6. *that they myght all undirstonde* = so that they should all think.

660. 27–8. *youre lady . . . shall be brente in youre defaute* = your lady . . . will be burnt because of your failure to appear (on the day set for the battle).

662. 7–8. *Than was the quene . . . sette . . . in the grete truste of hir champion* = Then the queen's defence was entrusted to her champion.

662. 25. *as ho seyth* = as if to say (Old French: *comme celle qui disoit*).

663. 35. *made her avaunte* = declared, made it known.

664. 15. *how hys modir discoverde* = how the mother of the man who had wounded Sir Urry revealed, etc.

665. 30–1. *Melyon of the Mountayne* is not, as has hitherto been assumed, distinct from Melyon de Tartare (*Merlyn*—or *Mellis*—*del Tertre* in the French Prose *Lancelot*) who appears on p. 489 (l. 31) of Malory's text. *Mountayne* is his translation of *tertre* and *tartare* his attempt to imitate its sound.

666. 9. *wordly knyght* = earthly knight (used in opposition to the knights who, like Perceval and Galahad, distinguished themselves in 'holy deeds').

666. 26–35. *Also that traytoure kynge slew the noble knyght sir Trystram . . . whereof was grete pité.* The story of the death of Tristan and Iseult as told in the French Prose Romance of Tristan is altered here in one important respect. In the French Prose version Iseult dies not of sorrow, but because Tristan strangles her in his last embrace—an idea typical of the prose writer's rational outlook. Malory, perhaps unknowingly, restores something of the original version of the story when he says that *La Beall Isode dyed sownyng uppon the crosse of sir Trystram.*

667. 7. *by her dayes* = in her lifetime.

667. 9–10. *sir Boarte le Cure Hardy that was kynge Arthurs son.* Malory refers to him in the *Tale of King Arthur* as 'Borre', following the French source of that work. Cf. p. 26.

667. 12. *he* = she. Cf. **643.** 27.

667. 35–**668.** 6. *Than seyde kynge Arthur unto sir Launcelot . . . a felow of the Rounde Table.* Lancelot wants to be acquitted of any charge of presumption in attempting to do what all the other knights have failed to do. Hence his hesitation. Arthur reassures him by saying: 'ye take hit wronge, for ye shall nat do hit for no presumpcion'.

669. 32. *the very mater of.* Literally: 'the genuine tale of the Knight of the Cart'. By this Malory probably means the French Prose *Lancelot* or at least the main portion of it preceding the last two branches of the Cycle—the *Queste del Saint Graal* and the *Mort Artu*. It is not clear whether 'I lost' is to be taken in the sense of 'I no longer possess', or 'I cannot find'. Cf. note **8.** 17.

669. 35. *And here on the othir syde folowyth*, etc. Only mechanical copying can account for the occurrence of the phrase *on the othir syde* since in the Winchester MS. the next 'book' begins on the same page.

VIII. THE TALE OF THE DEATH OF KING ARTHUR

The tragedy of the Round Table as Malory saw it was not just an example of the mutability of man's destiny nor the result of the failure of the 'worldly' knights to achieve the quest of the Grail. The final catastrophe was to Malory a human drama determined from first to last by the tragic clash of loyalties. With remarkable consistency he emphasized throughout the work the ties of friendship and affection between his protagonists—Gawain and Lancelot, Lancelot and Guinevere, Lancelot and Arthur. It is Lancelot's loyalty to Guinevere that causes him, in his anxiety to protect her, to act with such rashness as to destroy unwittingly the man he loves most—Gareth, Gawain's brother. It is not vindictiveness, as in the French romance, but genuine grief that turns Lancelot's truest friend, Gawain, into a mortal enemy. And above all, Arthur's affection for the two opponents and his deep sorrow at their fateful strife serve as a reminder, full of significance to the reader, but un-heeded by the protagonists, of the human greatness which is both the cause and the victim of their tragic folly.

Having transferred the tragedy of Arthurian knighthood to this essentially human plane, Malory could only make it convincing by emphasizing those emotions which, in his conception, had caused the catastrophe—the passionate feudal loyalty of man to man and the self-denying devotion of the knight-lover to his lady. Hence the burial scenes, so strikingly similar: Lancelot's visit to Gawain's tomb, where he 'kneled downe . . . and wepte, and prayde hartely for hys soule . . . and lay two nyghtes uppon hys tumbe', and a few pages further on the vision that 'charged hym, in remyssyon of his synnes, to haste hym unto Almysbury: "And by thenne thou come there, thou shalt fynde quene Guenever dede."' In aptness and depth of feeling there is nothing comparable to this in the whole of Malory's work; and if the rough outline of it was suggested to him by the English poem the emotional significance of the scene is inseparable from his own interpretation and treatment of the Death of Arthur theme.

In the French *Mort Artu* and in the English stanzaic *Le Morte Arthur*, both of which Malory used extensively, Lancelot dies of an illness caused by his life of penance. In neither of these texts is Lancelot's death in any way related to his grief; he falls ill as the result of his devotion to religious duty, not because in his sorrow he refuses food and drink and lies 'grovelyng on the tombe of kyng Arthur and quene Guenever'. It is as Guinevere's faithful lover that in Malory he becomes a hermit; it is not of the sins he committed against God, but of the sorrow he caused Guinevere and Arthur that in Malory he repents; and it is as her lover that Malory wants him to die, so that the 'dolorous death and departing' of the noblest of Arthur's knights should appear as the denouement of the noblest story of human love. At Joyous Gard as at the siege of Benwick, Lancelot's behaviour is marked by that heroic sense of loyalty which permeates the whole action. When Bors unhorses Arthur, Lancelot alights and helps him back into the saddle; and 'whan kynge Arthur was on horseback he loked on sir Launcelot, than the teerys braste oute of hys yen, thynkyng of the grete curtesy that was in sir Launcelot more than in any other man'. Forced at long last to meet Gawain in single combat Lancelot twice lays him low, and twice refuses to take his life. But just as Arthur's kingdom is threatened by Mordred, Gawain dies of his wound. On his death-bed he relents, bidding Arthur send for Lancelot; but it is all too late: what Arthurian knighthood has lost through the fatal encounter of the two truest friends can never be recovered. In lamenting the death of Gawain Arthur laments the fall of his realm, made inevitable by the fatal interplay of the noblest feelings.

There is no moral to be drawn from this, no comfort for those who live to see the Day of Destiny, no 'trust to trust in' for those who are left to mourn the dead: nothing but the knowledge that so must end the conflicts arising from sheer purity of heart. And in the silence of Salisbury Plain the death of the best of Arthur's knights and his own departure to Avalon appear as the only fitting ending to this tragic tale of human greatness—of love and loyalty for ever lost through their own passionate exuberance which,

> like a dome of many-coloured glass,
> Stains the white radiance of Eternity.

673. 9. *longe uppon* = due to.

673. 25–6. *we woll nat be knowyn of your dedis* = we shall not be party to your deeds.

673. 38. *the beste of us all had bene full colde at the harte-roote* = the best among us would long since have been dead.

674. 33. *but if* = unless.

674. 37–41. *For, as the Freynshe booke seyth,* etc. Neither the French romance nor the English poem has anything corresponding to this paragraph. On the eve of the first episode of the 'piteous tale' Malory is anxious to stress Arthur's affection for Lancelot and his reluctance that 'such a noyse shulde be uppon' him.

675. 26–7. *And never gaff my harte ayenste no goynge that ever ye wente to the quene so much as now.* The tautology is the result of a merger of two constructions. The preposition *ayenste* can govern a verbal noun (*goynge*) or a noun phrase (*that ever ye wente*). Malory has made it govern both.

676. 2–4. *whether they were abed other at other maner of disportis, me lyste nat there-of make no mencion, for love that tyme was nat as love ys nowadayes.* Conscious as he is of the difference between the 'old love' and 'love as it fareth nowadays', Malory follows neither *Le Morte Arthur* (1806: 'To bede he gothe with the quene') nor the French (p. 92: 'se coucha avec la roïne'), for they both might, in his view, convey the wrong idea of how in Arthur's time lovers were expected to behave.

678. 12. *he (fled)* = Mordred.

679. 14. *far dayes paste* = far on in the sky.

679. 19. *such as ye have dout fore* = those whose loyalty you doubt.

679. 33. *two-and-twenty knyghtes.* The list, as emended by the addition of the name of Bleoberys, includes twenty-four names.

679. 41. *made by* = made out to be.

679. 43. *but as* = had not.

680. 9–10. *and I may be harde and suffirde and so takyn* = if I may be heard and allowed to fight for the queen, and if my offer is accepted.

680. 15. *for and ye woll youreselffe* = will guard yourself.

681. 7. *the whiche* = whom; i.e. those who, like Gareth, would have willingly disobeyed King Arthur and joined Lancelot.

682. 10. *my quene muste suffir dethe.* In the *Mort Artu*, as in *Le Morte Arthur* (1920–5), the queen is sentenced to death by the barons, in Malory by Arthur: not because Malory's Arthur is less humane, but because Malory's conception of kingship includes prerogatives which would have been denied a feudal overlord.

682. 16. *othir the menour other the takynge wyth the dede* = either the behaviour of the accused or the capture *in flagrante delicto*. The distinction is similar to that between direct and circumstantial evidence.

682. 24. *put hit in respite, thys jougemente* = postpone this judgement.

682. 43. *worke with sir Launcelot* = behave towards Sir Lancelot.

683. 29–30. *of youre counceyle* = on your side.

684. 9. *for to strengthe* = to show support for.

684. 12. *dispoyled into* = stripped down to.

687. 2–3. *I shall never fayle sir Launcelot* = I shall never desist from my feud with Sir Lancelot.

687. 29–30. *For he was . . . but sir Launcelot* = And because he was . . . Sir Lancelot.

688. 20. *make hit good uppon me* = prove by combat with me.

688. 41–2. *in her ryght quarell.* 'My right quarrell' would have made better sense.

690. 3. *to blow uppon* = to defame.

691. 15. *hym* = King Arthur.

691. 16. *'Nat so hardy'* = 'Stay your hand.'

691. 21–5. *My lorde the kynge . . . and now am I evyll rewarded.* This speech comes as a natural sequel to Lancelot's earlier dialogue with Arthur, and gives point to the next paragraph: when, in answer to Lancelot's appeal, the king looks at him again, 'the teerys braste oute of hys yen'.

692. 9–10. *never so much* = no matter how much.

692. 10. *they woll never can you thanke* = they will never be grateful.

692. 20. *meyny* = retainers.

692. 26–8. *And than the Pope toke a consideracion of the grete goodnes of kynge Arthur and of the hyghe proues off sir Launcelot.* The reason given in the *Mort Artu* for the Pope's action is that the queen had not been proved guilty.

692. 43–4. *the quene shulde nat be seyde unto of the kynge, nother of none other, for* *nothynge done of tyme paste* = the queen should not be reproached either by the king or by anybody else with anything done in the past.

693. 17–18. *'I dare adventure me to kepe her frome an harder showre than'* = 'I venture to take it upon myself to save her by fighting the hardest battle that', etc.

693. 26–7. *shamed of hys promyse* = found untrue to his promise.

693. 29. *lat hym have knowlecchynge* = inform him.

693. 34. *hymselff* = Gawain.

695. 21–32. *Howbehit sir Carados . . . I faught to the uttermest.* In the *Mort Artu* Lancelot reminds Gawain of the first of these incidents, but not of the second, although both occur in the Prose *Lancelot*. Nor is either of them referred to in *Le Morte Arthur*. Malory is probably thinking of his own version of Lancelot's fight with Tarquyn (see pp. 157–8).

696. 15. *gar make* = cause to be built.

696. 18, 20, 21. The verb *perfourme*, which caused the omission of ll. 1–3 in the Winchester text, is used here in two different senses: 'to do' in ll. 18 and 20, and 'to bring to completion' in l. 21.

697. 12. *wheele* = wheel of Fortune.

697. 28. *uppon* = I swear by.

699. 19–21. *sayled unto Benwyke: som men calle hit Bayan and som men calle hit Beawme, where the wyne of Beawme ys.* 'Bayan' presumably stands for Bayonne and 'Beawme' for Beaune. In no other version is Benwick (Fr. *Benoic*) identified with either city. Of the two *Beawme* is the less appropriate since it is over two hundred and fifty miles from the nearest seaport.

699. 26. *on foote and hondis* = offering submission.

699. 27–32. *there he crowned sir Lyonnell . . . made sir Ector prynce of them all.* By 'France' Malory obviously means the kingdom of France as it was before the reconquest of Aquitaine and Normandy, and he takes *Gaunes* for the province of Guienne (*Gyan*), which at that time was an English dominion forming an irregular triangle with its base on the sea-board between Bayonne and the mouth of the Gironde, and its apex at Bergerac on the Dordogne. Many of the 'dukedoms' and 'earldoms' listed on pp. 699–700 formed part of that province.

699. 34–**700.** 6. *And firste he avaunced them off hys blood . . . made hym duke of Normandy.* The list of place-names covers, in addition to Normandy, a vast area stretching from the Bay of Biscay to the Rhône, and from the Loire to the Pyrenees and the Mediterranean. Apart from some well-known place-names such as Anjou, Auvergne, Béarn, Languedoc, Landes, Périgord (*Perygot*), and Poitiers (*Payters*), it includes the names of nine comparatively small fiefs: Agen (*Agente*), Armagnac (*Armynake*), Astarac (*Estrake*), Comminges (*Comange*), Marsan (*Marsank*), Pardiac (*Pardyak*), Rouergue (*Roerge*), Sarlat, and Tursan (*Tursanke*), six of which (Armagnac, Astarac, Comminges, Marsan, Pardiac, and Tursan) are situated within the area in which most of the military operations leading to the reconquest of Aquitaine in 1453 took place. Whether the occurrence of these place-names in Malory's text means that the author served in the south-west of France at the time of the reconquest is a problem which his next biographer might profitably investigate. It has recently received some attention in Professor William Matthews's study entitled *The Ill-Framed Knight*.

701. 21. *he* = she, as at 643. 27 and 667. 12.

702. 22. *compare* = contend.

702. 23. *they hylde their langayge* = they talked no more.

702. 26. *gan* = the besieging army began.

703. 11. *ye be called uppon* = you are accused. This is the earliest example of this use of the verb 'to call' recorded in the *Oxf. Eng. Dict.*

704. 20. *hys* = Gawain's.

706. 25. *hym* = himself.

707. 40. *no farther but youre modirs brothir*, etc. Malory stresses here Mordred's disloyalty, not Arthur's sin. Arthur's defeat on the battlefield is never treated in Malory as a punishment for his incest.

708. 28–**709.** 1. *than was the comyn voyce amonge them . . . for bettir and for wars.* The remark about popular discontent is most probably a comment on contemporary events. Malory's sources do not mention the *comyn voyce*.

709. 24–**710.** 37. *'Alas! sir Gawayne, my syster son' . . . sir Gawayne yelded up the goste.* While in the French romance Arthur dwells on the vicissitudes of Fortune and the blind cruelty of fate, in Malory he is acutely conscious of a sense of irretrievable loss. Gawain is to him primarily the man he loved most: 'in youre person and in sir Launcelot I moste had my joy and myne affyaunce'. Malory also adds the text of Gawain's letter, in which he elaborates the dual theme of Gawain's tragic guilt and of his affection for Lancelot, 'floure of all noble knyghtes . . . But alas that I wolde nat accorde with hym!'

710. 13–14. *more nother les* = long or short.

710. 14–15. *this same sedull* = this letter.

710. 29–30. *but two owrys and an halff afore my dethe.* Gawain's foreknowledge is taken for granted.

710. 41–**711.** 2. *Than was hit tolde the kynge . . . fledde unto Caunturbyry.* This battle, fought on the morning after Arthur's landing, is related in the English poem *before* Gawain's death (ll. 3094–3129). Malory has already used the passage once and the sentence on p. 711. 3 (*And than the kynge let serche*, etc.) repeats the one on p. 709. 17.

710. 41–2. *had pyght a new fylde* = had arranged a new field of battle.

710. 42. *Bareon Downe* = Barham Down, six miles south-east of Canterbury.

711. 14–16. *Than sir Mordred araysed muche people . . . helde the moste party with sir Mordred.* The reference to Kent, Sussex, Surrey, Essex, and Norfolk would seem to suggest that Malory had in mind a situation similar to that which obtained at the time of the Wars of the Roses when the strength of the Yorkists lay to a large extent in the south-eastern counties.

711. 32. *awaked* = remained awake.

712. 26. *by kynge Arthurs dayes* = during King Arthur's lifetime.

712. 41. *as their poyntemente was* = as was arranged between them.

713. 4–5. *dressed hem togydirs* = arrayed themselves against each other.

715. 33. *nothynge but watirs wap and wawys wanne.* Malory's *wanning waves* represent an attempt to turn the adjective *wanne* into a verb: the sense of 'receding (waning) waves' is, as it were, superimposed upon that of 'waves that grow dark' (wanning).

716. 36–7. *ye pray so faste* = you pray so earnestly.

717. 12–38. *Thus of Arthur I fynde no more wrytten in bokis that bene auctorysed,* etc. Here Malory departs from both his sources to give his own account of Arthur's death and of the legend of his survival, with an expression of scepticism about the way in which Arthur 'chaunged hys lyff' (l. 33). The probable meaning is that he changed his form of life.

718. 12. *hys owne* = Arthur's own.

718. 36. *'for ever ye woll my worshyp'* = 'for always you wish me to act honourably'.

719. 18. *he dalt to* = he gave.

719. 38. *but if* = unless.

720. 10. *why I make thys fare* = why I behave in this manner.

721. 14–15. *absteyne you from suche werkes* = refrain from such behaviour.

722. 16–17. *And soo their horses wente where they wolde, for they toke no regarde of no worldly rychesses.* This remark, absent from Malory's sources, seems to reflect the attitude of a man who knows from experience that the moment a knight has ceased to take care of his horse his worldly life is ended.

722. 22. *in remyssyon* = for the remission.

723. 14. *in cered clothe of Raynes* = waxed linen of Rennes (for which it was noted).

724. 9. *howselyd and enelyd* = received the Eucharist and the extreme unction.

724. 11–12, 43. *Somme men say it was Anwyk, and somme men say it was Bamborow.* The suggested identification of Joyous Gard with either Alnwick or Bamburgh may well have some connection with the author's own experiences. In 1462 he went to Northumberland with the forces of the Earl of Warwick who, with the support of the troops brought by Edward IV, besieged Bamburgh, Alnwick, and Dunstanburgh. Bamburgh surrendered on Christmas Eve, 1462, the siege of Alnwick ended on 30 January 1463, and the whole campaign, so far as Malory was concerned, must have lasted at least three months—from 30 October 1462 to 30 January 1463. Malory says that the journey from the hermitage to Joyous Gard took fifteen days (p. 724. 43). It is perhaps not without significance that this was almost exactly the time taken by Edward to reach York and that Warwick's expedition from London to Northumberland took about as long.

724. 14–15. '*And bycause of brekyng of myn avowe, I praye you al, lede me thyder.*'
Bycause of here means 'for fear of', 'for the sake of not'.

724. 44. *in the body of the quere* = in the centre of the chancel.

725. 21. *of a synful man* = of all sinful men.

726. 2. *favour of makers* = bias of poets.

726. 4. *was quycke and deed* = lived and died.

726. 9. *for Goddes sake* = in God's service.

726. 10–13. *Here is the ende of the hoole book of kyng Arthur and of his noble knyghtes of the Rounde Table, that whan they were hole togyders there was ever an hondred and forty. And here is the ende of The Deth of Arthur.* The title *Deth of Arthur* clearly refers to the last of Malory's works—*The Morte Arthur* as he calls it earlier on—not to the entire collection. 'The hoole book of kyng Arthur and of his noble knyghtes of the Rounde Table' is the series of works, some of which Malory may by this time have put together without necessarily giving them more unity or cohesion than they had when they were first composed.

Recent discoveries concerning Malory's life add poignancy to his appeal for 'good deliverance', for we now know that in the year in which the book—the 'whole book'—was completed Malory was excluded for the fourth and last time from the operation of a general pardon granted to the Lancastrians by Edward IV.

GLOSSARY

THE Glossary is based upon a revision of the one compiled by Professor G. L. Brook for my 1947 edition of *The Works of Sir Thomas Malory*. In the course of the revision I have expanded a number of entries and added many new ones, but I have endeavoured to avoid duplicating the glosses already supplied in the Notes. Easily recognizable words and phrases have been recorded only in so far as they differ in meaning from modern usage, and no account has been taken of the cases where they occur in their normal modern sense. Thus *avyce* has been glossed 'request', 'consent', but not 'advice', although this last meaning is found at least as frequently as either of the other two.

In the alphabetical arrangement *y* used as a vowel is treated as *i*, otherwise (replacing ȝ) as *y*.

A

a, *prep.* on.

a, *pron.* I; he.

a, *v.* unstressed form of 'have' used as an auxiliary.

abaysshe, abeyse, *v.* to lower; to beat down; to be astonished.

aba(y)sshed, *ppl. adj.* ashamed.

abate, *v.* to lessen; to cast down; *abated at*, set on.

abeyse. See *abaysshe*, v.

abyde, *v.,; abyde by*, to perform.

able, *adj.* of sufficient power.

ablemente, *sb.* warlike accoutrements and munitions.

abought, *v. pret.* paid for.

aboute, *adv.* in every direction; *lay aboute to*, was busy scheming; *be aboute to*, to be scheming; to be engaged in; to be admitted to.

abrode, *adv.* away; widely apart.

ac(c)ompte, *v.* to consider, to think.

accord, *sb.* reconciliation.

ac(c)orde, *v.* to reconcile, to be reconciled.

ac(c)orded, *ppl. adj.* agreed.

accounseyle, *adj.* plotting.

acombird, *pp.* encumbered.

acquyte, *v.* to requite; to repay; to defend; to excuse; *reflex.* to perform one's part.

actuall, *adj.* active, energetic.

actually, *adv.* vigorously.

admyrall. See *amerall*, sb.

adouted, *pp.* afraid.

adretched, *pp.* perturbed.

a(d)va(u)ntage, *sb.* profit; boasting.

a(d)venture, *sb.* chance; risk; danger; enterprise; chance occurrence; remarkable experience.

a(d)venture, *v.* to risk; *reflex.* to venture.

adventures(t), *adj.* adventurous, ready to undertake adventures; perilous.

advyce, advyse, *sb.* opinion.

a(d)vyse, *v. reflex.*, be a(d)vysed, to think.

a(d)vysemente. See *avysement*, sb.

a(d)vysyon, avision, *sb.* dream, vision.

advoutrer, *sb.* adulterer.

aferde, *ppl. adj.* afraid.

affyaunce, *sb.* trust.

affinité, *sb.* kinship.

affray, *sb.* disturbance.

afonned, *adj.* passionately in love.

aforne, *adv.* previously.

after, aftir, *prep.* along; according to; in view of.

agayne, ageyne, ayen, *prep.* against; in front of; near (the beginning of); *adv.* in return; in reply; back.

agayne-commynge, *sb.* return.

agaynesay, agaynesey, to speak against.

agaynewarde, *adv.* back.

agaynste. See *ayenste*, prep.

ageyne. See *agayne*.
aghenst. See *ayenste*, prep.
ayedé, *vb. 2 pl. imper.* (Fr.) help.
ayge, *sb.*; *within two ayges*, of military age.
ayre, *sb.* heir.
aknowyn, *ppl. adj.* cognizant; *be aknowyn of*, to acknowledge.
alyauntis, *sb. pl.* foreigners.
alygeaunce, *sb.* alleviation, relief.
alyghted, *pp.* illumined.
alledged, *pp.* lessened.
al(l) only, *adv.*; *sauff all only*, with the exception of.
allso. See *also*, adv. and conj.
allther(nexte). See *althers*, adj. gen. pl. and *althirnexte*, adv.
almeryes, *sb. pl.* ambries, libraries.
almes-dede, *sb.* charitable act.
alow, *v.* to praise, commend.
als, *adv.* also.
also, allso, *adv. and cj.* thus; now (introducing narrative); when; as soon as; just as.
althers, allther, *adj. gen. pl.* of all; *oure allther*, of us all; *youre althers*, of you all.
althirnexte, allthernexte, *adv.* nearest of all, next of all.
amased, *ppl. adj.* out of one's wits, bewildered.
amated, *pp.* confused.
ambular, *sb.* ambling horse.
amende, *v.* to mend; to cure; to adorn, improve.
amerall, admyrall, *sb.* Saracen emir or prince; *admyrallys noblys*, noble Saracen princes.
amyvestyall, *adj.* word of unknown meaning, probably coined by Malory.
amonge, *adv.* from time to time; *ever amonge*, every now and then.
amoved, *pp.* angry.
amownted, *pret.* mounted.
an, *prep.* on; engaged in.
an(d), *cj.* if.
anone, *adv.* at once, quickly; *anone as*, as soon as.
answere, *v.* to fight with.
anvylde, *sb.* anvil.
aparte, *adv.* in part.
apeche, appeyche, *v.* to accuse.
apoynted, *pp.* determined, resolved.
appayre, *v.* to impair, injure.

apparayled, *pp.* furnished.
appeyche. See *apeche*, v.
appele, *v.* to accuse.
appertenaunce, apportenaunce, *sb.* property rights, privileges belonging to an estate.
applye, *v. reflex.* set about.
appoynte, *v.* to arrange.
appoyntement, *sb.* agreement; arrangement.
apportenaunce. See *appertenaunce*, sb.
ar, *adv., cj., and prep.* before.
arace, *v.* to raze, demolish.
araged, *ppl. adj.* enraged, frenzied.
aray, *v.* to treat; to clothe; to equip; to discomfit, to rout.
aray. See *ar(r)ay*, sb.
araymente, *sb.* attire, clothing.
arayse, areyse, *v.* to raise, levy.
aredy, *adj.* ready, prepared.
areyse. See *arayse*, v.
arere, *v.* to raise, call to arms; to rear.
arest, *v.* to seize, commandeer.
areste, *sb.* capture.
aretted, *pp.* presumed.
aryve, *v.* to reach the shore.
armes, armys, *sb. pl.* warlike deeds.
armytayge, *sb.* hermitage.
armyte, *sb.* hermit.
ar(r)ay, *sb.* attire, clothing; preparation; state, condition; state of affairs.
arred, *pp.* erred.
ars, *sb.* buttocks.
arson, *sb.* saddle-bow.
arst(e), *adv.* previously; until then.
as, os, *cj.* as, as if; where; when; *as for, as in*, with regard to, in respect of; *but as*, but that.
asay. See *as(s)ay*, v.
ascawnce, *cj.* as if.
askynges, *sb. pl.* demands.
asoted, *ppl. adj.* infatuated.
aspye, *v.* to perceive, notice; to search; to learn, become aware; to become familiar with.
aspyes, *sb. pl.* secret watch.
as(s)ay, *v.* to attempt, try; to put to the test; to challenge, attack; to fight with; to appeal to.
assigne, *v.* to arrange.
assoyle, *v.* to absolve.
assomon, assumpne, *v.*; assomned assumned, *pp.* to summon.
assomons, *sb. pl.* bands, companies.

assot(t)ed, *ppl.* See *asoted.*
assumned, assumpne. See *asso-mon,* v.
as(s)ure, *sb.* azure, blue.
astat(t)e, *sb.* rank, position; lady of rank; state, condition; *pl.* classes, estates of the realm.
asto(o)ned, *pp.* dazed, stunned; astounded, dumbfounded.
asure. See *as(s)ure,* sb.
aswaged, *pp.* diminished.
at, *prep.* to, towards, in, into, by, from.
ataynte, *ppl. adj.* exhausted.
ato, a-to(o), *adv.* in two.
attayne, *v.* to prevail, be victorious.
attame, *v.* to cut into, pierce.
atte, assimilated form of *at the.*
attemte, *v.* to tempt.
attende, *v.* to lie in wait.
attyre, *v.* to equip.
audiens, *sb.* hearing; *in opyn audiens,* in the hearing of all.
au(l)ter, awter, *sb.* altar.
auncet(t)ryes, *sb. pl.* ancestors.
availle, avayle, *sb.* benefit, advantage.
availle, *v.* to benefit, be of advantage.
avalyd, *v. pret.* dismounted.
ava(u)nta(y)ge. See *a(d)va(u)ntage.*
avaunte, *sb.* boast, threat.
aventryd, *v. pret.* level, set (spear) in position for a charge.
aventure. See *adventure,* sb. and v.
avyce, avys(e), *sb.* request; consent.
avyse, *v.* to arrange; to perceive; to see, behold. See also *a(d)vyse.*
avysed, *ppl. adj.* informed; intending; wary; cautious; reluctant; *be avysed to do,* beware of doing; *I woll be avysed,* I will consider.
avysement, *sb.* counsel, deliberation, reflection.
avision, *sb.* See *a(d)vysyon.*
avoydaunce, *sb.* clearing, emptying.
avoyde, *v.* to go away, to withdraw, to withdraw from, to dismount from, to dismiss, to remove, to let slip.
avow(e), *sb.* vow, promise.
avowe, *v.* to admit, to promise.
awayte, *sb.; have you gretely in awayte,* watch you with suspicion.
aw(a)yte, *v.* to watch, to attend; *awayte on,* to look to; *awayte uppon,* to help.

awaywarde, *adv.* away.
awarde, *sb.* custody, care.
awghe. See *ow(gh)e,* v.
awyte. See *aw(a)yte,* v.
awke, *adj.* back-handed.
awkewarde, *adv.* with a backward stroke, sideways,
awne, *adj.* own.
awroke, *pp.* avenged.
awter. See *au(l)ter,* sb.
axe, *v.* to ask, to request; to demand.
ayen. See *agayne,* prep. and adv.
ayenst(e), agaynste, aghenst, *prep.* next to; against; opposite; towards; in; contrary to; shortly before; *there agaynste,* in return.

B

bacheler, *sb.* young knight.
backer, *adv. comp.* further back.
bayne, *sb.* bath.
bayte, *v.* to feed; to attack.
baly. See *b(e)aly,* sb.
bandes. See *bondys,* sb. pl.[1]
bankys, *sb. pl.* shores.
barayne, *adj.* barren, not pregnant.
barbys, *sb.* horse-armour.
barge, *sb.* boat.
barget, *sb.* small boat.
basnet, *sb.* light helmet, basinet.
batayl(l)e, *sb.* host, army; battalion; battle array.
bate, *sb.*[1] quarrel.
bate, *sb.*[2] bait, kill.
bate, *v.* to abate, cast down.
bavoure, *sb.* beaver, lower part of face-guard.
bawdy, *adj.* dirty, filthy.
bawme, *v.* to anoint, embalm.
be, *prep.* by, before; because of; judging by; according to.
beadis, *sb. pl.* prayers, devotions.
b(e)aly, *sb.* belly.
beamys, *sb. pl.* trumpets.
be(a)nded, *ppl. adj.* with bands; striped (in heraldry).
beate, *v.* to drive.
becalled, *pp.* accused.
becam, becom, *v. pret.* went, gone.
because, bycause, *cj.* in order that.
beclosed, *pp.* surrounded.
bedaysshed, *pp.* bedecked; adorned.
bede, *v.,* bodyn, *pp.,* to bid, to command, to invite.

bedrad, *ppl. adj.,* feared, dreadful.
bee, bye, *sb.* ring; bracelet.
beeke, *v.* to warm.
befurred, *pp.* wrapped up or dressed
in furs.
began, *v. pret.* entered.
begone, *ppl. adj.* covered.
behestis, *sb. pl.* vows; promises.
behyght. See *behote,* v.
behynde, *adv.* unpaid, in arrear; still
to come.
beholde, beholdynge, *ppl. adj., adj.*
beholden; indebted; bound.
behote, *v.;* **behyght,** *pret.* to hold
out hope of; to promise; to threaten
with.
behove, *v. theym behoved for no good,*
they thought it would be unfortunate.
belaffte, beleffte, beleft(e), *v. pret.*
remained; left.
belye, *v.* to slander.
bended. See *be(a)nded,* ppl. adj.
benomme, *pp.* deprived, taken away.
bente, *sb.* open, grassy place.
bere, *sb.* force, impetus.
beré, byry, *sb.* berry.
berenne, *pp.* covered; *blody berenne,*
covered with blood.
beryellys, *sb. pl.* burial-place.
besayne, bese(y)ne, bisene, *ppl.
adj.* equipped, dressed; *well besene,*
good-looking.
beseme, *v.* to seem, appear; to befit;
to be obliged.
besett(e), *v.* to bestow; to suit.
besy, bysy, *adj.* importunate; anxious,
striving; meddlesome; in earnest.
besyde(s), *prep. and adv.* near.
besparcled, *pp.* bespattered.
besprente, *v. pret.* sprinkled.
bestad(de), *pp.* beset with; *harde
bestad(de),* hard pressed, in difficulty.
beste-brethid, *ppl. adj.* best in wind.
beswette, *ppl. adj.* covered with
sweat.
betaughte, *v. pret.* commended, entrusted.
betyde, *v.* to obtain as one's lot.
betyme(s), *adv.* at once; early.
betoke. See *bitake,* v.
betoken, *v.* to signify; *betokenyth the
sygnes whereof,* is a sign that.
betrappe, *v.* to entrap, circumvent.

bettir-farynge, *adj.* bearing himself
better.
betwene, *adv.;* *ever betwene,* meanwhile.
betwyxte, *prep.* among; *seyde betwyxte,* said of the relations between.
bewared, *ppl. adj.* bestowed.
by, *prep.* near; before; concerning;
during; through; with regard to;
cj. by the time that, when; *by this
done,* by the time that this was done;
by that, when.
bycause. See *because,* cj.
byde, *v.;* **byddyn,** *pp.* to remain.
bye. See *bee,* sb.
byghte, *v.;* **bo(o)te,** *pret.* to bite.
bylled, *pp.* mown down.
byry. See *beré.*
bisene. See *bese(y)ne,* ppl. adj.
bysy. See *besy,* adj.
bitake, *v.;* **betoke, bytoke,** *pret.;*
betaken, bitaken, *pp.* to entrust,
commend.
byver, *v.* to tremble.
bledde, *v. pret.* stained with blood;
adj. covered with blood.
blyve, *adv.* promptly, quickly.
bloode, *sb.* kin, family; rank; *bloode
elders,* ancestors.
blow(e), *v.* to utter; to summon;
blow uppon, to defame; *blew to lodgyng,* ordered the fighting to cease
for the night.
bobbaunce, *sb.* boasting, pride.
body, *sb.;* *my body,* myself; *the body
of hym,* he; *with hys body,* in person.
bodyn. See *bede,* v.
boyes, *sb. pl.* contemptible fellows,
rascals.
boysh, boyshemente. See *buys(s)h,*
sb., *bu(y)shemente,* sb.
boy(s)teous, boystouse, *adj.* rude,
unpolished; raging; huge; rough,
strong.
bole, *sb.* boll.
bonde(n), *ppl. adj.* bound.
bondys, bundes, *sb. pl.*[1] bounds,
confines; *in harde bondis,* a prisoner;
sorely beset.
bondis, *sb. pl.*[2] stripes.
bondys, *sb. pl.*[3] bands, companies.
bone, *adj.* (Fr.) good.
booster, *sb.* braggart.
boote, *sb.*[1] use, remedy, course of

boote (*cont.*):
  action; *ther was none other boote*,
  there was no help for it.
boote, *sb.*²; botis, *pl.* boat.
boote. See *byghte, v.*
borow, *sb.*¹ fortified town.
borow, *sb.*² pledge.
borow, *v.* to rescue, release; *to borow
  oute*, to ransom.
bote. See *byghte, v.*
boteneth, *v. 3 sg. impers.* avails, helps.
botis. See *boote, sb.*²
bought,*pp.*; *evyl bought,* fully avenged.
bounde, *adj.* ready, attired.
bounden, *ppl. adj.* indebted.
bounté, bownté, *sb.* goodness, generosity; kindness, favour; worth,
  excellence.
b(o)urde, *sb.* board, table; side of a
  ship; floor-board, plank.
bourde, *v.* to jest.
bourder, *sb.* jester.
bourely, bowerly, *adj.* mighty, excellent.
bowe. See *bow(gh)e, v.*
bowe-draught, *sb.* bowshot.
bowerly. See *bourely,* adj.
bow(gh)e, *v.* to bend, bow; to submit.
bowghe, *sb. for the bowghe,* to bring
  to the bow.
bownté. See *bounté, sb.*
bowske. See *buske, v.* reflex.
boxe, *sb.* blow.
brace, *v.* to embrace; to fasten.
brachet, brachett(e), *sb.* bitch-
  hound.
bray, *sb.* conflict, encounter.
bray, *v.* to cry out.
brayde, *sb.* sudden movement.
brayde, *v.* to remove.
brayle, *sb.* body.
brayn(n)e-panne, *sb.* skull.
brake. See *breke, v.*
braste, brest, *v. pret.* broke; burst;
  gushed, poured; had the flesh torn.
brawne, *sb.* flesh, muscle.
brede, *sb.*¹ bread.
brede, *sb.*² breadth.
breff, *v.* to cut short, shorten.
breke, *sb.* breeches.
breke, *v.*; brake, *pret.*; brokyn, *pp.*
  to rush out; to leave; to lose; to dis-
  turb; to disclose, reveal; *brake hys
  faste,* had breakfast.

brekelys, *adj.* without breeches.
bren(ne), *v.*; brente, brenned, *pret.
  and pp. trans.* to burn; *intr.* to be
  burnt; to be strongly moved (with
  love or sorrow).
brese. See *bruse, v.*
brest. See *braste, v.* pret.
brethid, *ppl. adj.*; *bettir brethid,* in
  better wind.
brewte, *sb.* fame.
brym, *adj.* fierce.
brymme, *sb.* bank.
bryse. See *bruse, v.*
broche, *sb.* spit.
broche, *v.* to transfix, pierce.
brokyn. See *breke, v.*
bronde, *sb.* sword.
broute, *v. pret.* bought.
browes, *sb.* broth.
bruntis, *sb. pl.* sharp blows.
bruse, bryse, brese, *v.* to crush,
  hurt; to wound; to break.
brutyll, *adj.* fragile, easily destroyed.
buff, *sb.* chin-piece.
buffett(e), *sb.* blow.
buys(s)h, boysh, *sb.* mass of foliage,
  bush.
bu(y)shement(e), bu(y)sshement,
  boyshemente, inbusshemente,
  sb. ambush.
burbely, *adj.* bubbling.
burbelynge, *pres. part.* bubbling.
burde. See *b(o)urde, sb.*
burre, *sb.* broad ring on spear to protect the hand.
bushement. See *bu(y)shemente, sb.*
buske, bowske, *v. reflex.* to hasten;
  to prepare oneself; *busked up,*
  hoisted.
but,*prep. and cj.* except; than; nothing
  but, only; but that; unless; *but yf,
  but that,* unless; *but as,* except for;
  but that.
but, *sb.*¹ thick end.
but, *sb.*² mark, target; *full but,* directly (cf. Fr. 'de plain bout').

C

caban, *sb.* cabin.
cayser, *sb.* emperor.
caytyff, *sb. as adj.* miserable.
calle, *v.* to accuse; to consider.
can, *v.*; couthe, cowth(e),
  cow(u)de, *pret.* to know; to know

of; to have learnt; *can thanke*, express thanks.

Candilmasse. The feast of the purification of the Virgin Mary (2 February).

canellbone, *sb.* neck-bone.

cankyrde, *ppl. adj.* malignant.

cantel(l), *sb.* slice, strip.

care, *v.* to trouble, worry.

care. See *car(r)e,* sb.

carefull, *adj.* sorrowful.

carff, carve, *v. pret.* cut.

caryage, *sb.* baggage, equipment.

cary(c)k, *sb.* carrack, large ship.

caryot. See *charyot(t)e,* sb.

carle, *sb.* churl, evil fellow.

carpe, *v.* to speak.

car(r)e, *sb.* sorrow, trouble.

carve, See *carff,* v. pret.

case, *sb.*[1] plight; *I put a case,* supposing; *if case be,* if.

case, *sb.*[2] cover.

caste, *sb. pl.* quantity of bread made at one time.

caste, *v., inf., pret., and pp.* to be inclined; to think about, devise. *Reflex.* to intend, resolve; *caste on,* to don; *keste such a love,* loved so well.

caughte, *v. pret.* took, seized.

cause, *sb.* matter, affair; *pl.* cause, reason; *cause why,* because; *for cause,* because, in order that; *by cause,* because.

cerche. See *serch(e),* v.

cerclet, *sb.* ring, crown.

cered, *ppl. adj.* smeared or embalmed with wax.

cetyl, *v.* to withdraw, cause to retire.

cewe. See *sew(e),* v.

chacer, *sb.* hunter.

chaffed, *ppl. adj.* heated.

chafflet, *sb.* scaffold, platform.

champayne, champion, *sb.* open country.

change, *v.* relinquish; *change the lyff,* die.

charbuckkle, *sb.* precious stone.

charge, *sb.* injunction, command; business, responsibility; task; care, custody.

charge, *v.* to command; to load; to entrust.

charyot(t)e, caryot, *sb.* cart.

chartyrs, *sb. pl.* pardon.

chauffe, *v.* to anger.

chauffynge, *sb.* chafing; rubbing.

checke, *vb.* to overtake.

cheff, chyff, *adj.* chief; excellent.

cheff, *sb.* chief (in heraldry).

chek(k)e, *sb.* attack; advantage.

chere, chyre, *sb.* face; expression; disposition; cordial welcome, entertainment; *what chere?* how are things with you? *thou madist no chere,* you did not seem disposed.

chere, *v.* to encourage.

cherys(s)h, *v.* to love, esteem.

chest, *sb.* coffin.

chevalry. See *chyvalry,* sb.

cheve, *v.* to achieve.

chydde, *v. pret.* chided.

chyff. See *cheff,* adj.

chyld(e), *sb.* nobly-born youth; *pl.* chyldir.

chylde, *sb.* shield.

chyre. See *chere,* sb.

chyvalry, chevalry, shevalry, *sb.* knights; prowess; strength; reputation.

chyvetayn, *sb.* sovereign.

choppe, *v.* to strike, knock.

chorle, *sb.* churl, low-born fellow.

claffe, clave, *v. pret.* cut, cleaved; was split.

clatir, *v.* to chatter, talk.

clave. See *claffe,* v. pret.

clegge, *v.* to drag.

cleyght(e), *v. pret. and pp.* clasped, embraced; seized.

clene, *adj.* pure, innocent; excellent; complete, full.

clene, *adv.;* **clennyst,** *superl.* cleanly; well; completely.

clenyst-myghted, *adj.* strongest.

clenly, *adv.* cleanly; completely.

clennes, *sb.* purity.

clennyst. See *clene,* adv.

clepe, *v.* to call.

clere, *adj.* fair, beautiful.

clerencsse, *sb.* brightness, splendour.

clevid, *v. pret.* clung, stuck.

clyched, *v. pret.* clutched, seized.

clyerly, *adv.* openly.

clyppe, *v.* to embrace.

cloce, *sb.* secret.

clowys, *sb. pl.* cloughs, steep valleys.

cog, *sb.* broadly-built ship.

co(g)nyssaunce, cognysshauns, *sb.* badge, means of recognition, mark of distinction.

coyff(e), *sb.* coif, close-fitting cap.

coystron, *sb.* kitchen-knave, base-born fellow, scullion.

colys, *sb. pl.* cinders.

comberaunce, *sb.* inconvenience.

com(e), *v.*; com(e), cam(e) cum, *pret.*; com(myn), cam, *pp.*; to descend; to be done; *come of* (*f*), to befall; to desist; *of late com syn*, not long since.

comfortable, *adj.* pleasant, refreshing.

comynalté, *sb.* common people.

comyns, *sb. pl.* common people.

commaunde, *v.* to request; to entrust; to commend.

commaundemente, *sb.* right, authority; disposal.

commyn. See *com(e)*, v.

commons. See *comyns*, sb. pl.

compare, *v.* to vie, contend.

compaste, *v. pret.* reflected.

complevysshed, *pp.* accomplished.

complysshed, *pp.* filled.

conceyte, *sb.* judgement.

concente. See *consente*, v.

conclude, *v.* to decide; to agree.

conde(s)cended, *ppl. adj.* agreed.

condis(s)ion, condycion, *sb.* disposition, character; characteristic; quality.

conduyte, *sb.* safe-conduct; escort.

conduyte, *v.* to conduct, escort.

con(e)stable, *sb.* chief officer of a household.

conferme, *v.* to name.

confounded, *v. pret.* utterly defeated.

conyes, *sb. pl.* rabbits.

conyssaunce. See *co(g)nyssaunce*, sb.

conj(e)oure, *v.* to entreat, urge; to invoke spirits.

consente, concente, *v.* to agree; to decide.

constable. See *con(e)stable*, sb.

contrary, *adj. as adv.* unsuccessfully. See *falle.*

contrary, *v.* contradict.

co(n)versaunte, *adj.* living, dwelling.

cooper, *sb.* copper.

coorse, See *corse*, sb.

coote, *sb.* coat.

corage. See *corrayge*, v.

corde, *sb.* cord, rope; *in a corde*, tied together.

coryous, *adj.* careful, attentive.

corne-boote, *sb.* excellent remedy; full amends.

coronal(l), *sb.* coronet; gold circlet; round helmet.

corpus. See *corse*, sb.

corrage, cor(r)ayge, courage, curra(y)ge, *sb.* spirit, disposition; desire; ardour, vigour; encouragement.

corryage, corage, *v.* to encourage, to exhort.

corroure, curroure, *sb.* messenger.

corse, coorse, corpus, *sb.* corpse.

corseynte, *sb.* holy relic, body of a saint.

coste, *sb.* side.

coste, *v.* to follow.

couche, *v.* to lower (spear) for attack; to lie.

counceyle, counsel, counseyle, *sb.* advice, counsel; council; plan; secret; consent.

countenaunce, *sb.* pretence; appearance.

countir, *v.* to encounter, fight.

courage. See *corrage*, sb.

coure, cowre, *v.* to hide, cower.

cours(e), *sb.* charge, onset.

courser, *sb.* large, powerful horse; charger.

court(e)la(y)ge, *sb.* yard, piece of ground.

couthe, cowth(e), cow(u)de. See *can*, v.

covente, *sb.* convent.

cover, *v.* to relieve, cure.

coversaunte. See *co(n)versaunte*, adj.

coverte, *sb.* concealment.

covertly, *adv.* secretly.

covyn, *sb.* conspiracy, deceit.

coward. See *cowherde*, sb.[2]

cowde. See *couthe*, v. pret.

cowherde, *sb*[1]. coward; *adj.* cowardly.

cowherde, coward, *sb.*[2] cow-herd.

cowre. See *coure*, v.

cowth(e), cowude. See *can*, v.

craffte. See *cra(u)ffte*, sb.

cragge, *sb.* rock.

crake, *v.* to cry out.

cra(u)ffte, crauff, *sb.* magic, enchantment; deceit; art, occupation; force.

creature, *sb.*[1] creator; *resceayved his Creature*, received the sacrament.

creature, cryature, *sb.*[2] man, person.

credence, *sb.* message.

creyme, *sb.* anointing oil.

cryature. See *creature*, sb[2].

crysemed, *pp.* anointed with consecrated oil.

croked, *ppl. adj.* bent (with age).

crosse, *sb.* cross-roads.

croufte, *sb.* crypt, vault.

croupe, croupen, croupyr, *sb.*; crowpers, *pl.* hind-quarters.

cum. See *com(e)*, v.

cunnyngst, *adj. superl.* most learned.

curra(y)ge. See *corrage*, sb.

curroure. See *corroure*, sb.

cursednesse, *sb.* ill-luck.

cursynge, *sb.* excommunication.

curte(y)st, *adj. superl.* most courteous.

curtyll, *sb.* tunic, coat.

D

daffysshe, *adj.* spiritless, feeble; of no consequence.

day, *sb.* daylight; *pl.* lifetime.

dayssh(e), *sb.* blow.

daysshe, *v.* to fall.

dalt(e). See *de(a)le*, v.

dam(m)age, dommage, *sb.* suffering, injury; grief; matter for regret, pity; power to cause injury; *oute of the damage of your enemyes*, beyond the reach of your enemies.

dare, *v.* to remain motionless.

darf, *v.* need.

daunger(e) *sb.* power; captivity; debt, obligation; *in thy daunger*, beholden to thee; *in the daungere of*, in the power of; *I am . . . ascaped their daungere*, I am no longer at their mercy.

daungerous, *adj.* formidable, arrogant; powerful.

dawe, *v.* to dawn; to awaken, revive.

de(a)le, *v.*; dalt(e), *pret. and pp.* to fight, contend; to act; to do what is necessary; to manage, contrive; to give.

de(a)re, *v.* to harm; to resist (?)

debate, *sb.* strife, variance; resistance, argument.

debonayre, *adj.* gracious, useful.

ded(e). See *do*, v.

dede, deed, *adj.* dead.

ded(e)ly, *adj.* deathly; earthly, mortal; formidable; *dedly bedde*, death-bed.

dedys, *sb. pl.* deaths.

dedly. See *ded(e)ly*, adj.

deed. See *dede*, adj.

defaded, *ppl. adj.* faded, worn out.

defamed, *ppl. adj.* proclaimed, spoken of.

defau(gh)te, *sb.* lack, want; fault.

defendaunte, *sb.* self-defence.

defende. See *def(f)ende*, v.

deffame, *v.* to speak ill of, slander.

def(f)ence, *sb.* offence; *in the defence*, in the battle for the defence.

def(f)ende, *v.* to forbid; to repel, send away; to defend oneself against; to protect; to defend one's right to.

defyghe, *v.* to defy.

defoyle, defowle, *v.* to defile, to deflower; to put to shame; to afflict; to trample.

degré, *sb.* prize at a tournament; rank; situation; case.

dele, *sb.* portion; quantity; *every dele, dele*, completely.

dele. See *de(a)le*, v.

delyver, *v.* to set free; to kill, defeat; to entrust.

delyveraunce, *sb.* handing over; release (from prison).

delyverly, *adv.* adroitly; quickly.

demaynes, deme(a)nys, *sb. pl.* possession; behaviour, demeanour.

deme, *v.* to think; to suspect, guess; to atone.

demeanys. See *demaynes*, sb. pl.

demene, *v. reflex.*, to behave.

demenys. See *demaynes*, sb. pl.

demyng, *sb.* guessing, suspicion.

dente. See *dynte*, sb.

deore, *sb. pl.* deer.

departe, *v.* to divide; to share; to give; to separate; to part; to go; to put an end to; to come to an end.

departicion, *sb.* separation; departure.

depe, *adj.* extensive; covered with a deep layer of mud or sand.

depnes, *sb.* depth.
deprave, *v.* to disparage.
depreve, *v.* to convict.
dere, *adj.* valuable; brave.
dere. See *de(a)re,* v.
deserve, *v.* to earn; to repay.
desesed. See *diseased,* ppl. adj.
desyre, *v.* to ask.
despite. See *dispite,* sb.
destresse. See *distresse,* v.
destry, *v.* to lay waste.
dever, devoure, *sb.* duty, business; utmost effort, endeavour.
devyse, *sb.* desire, command; *pl.* conversation.
devyse, *v.* to arrange; to plot; to found; to imagine, conjecture.
devoyde, *v.* to remove; to get out of the way; to dismount.
devoure, *v.* to make away with, destroy.
devoure. See *dever,* sb.
devowrer, *sb.* destroyer.
dyght, *v. pret. and pp.* cut up, prepared; furnished.
dygnyté, *sb.* valour.
dyked, *ppl. adj.* protected with a ditch.
dyndled, *v. pret.* shook, trembled.
dynte, dente, *sb.* blow.
dyryge, *sb.* service for the dead.
disadventure, *sb.* misadventure.
dysceyvir, *v.* to separate.
discever. See *discover,* v.
dyscharge, discharge, *v.* to send away; to send away from; to abandon; to release (from an obligation); to exonerate.
discomfite(d), *pp.* vanquished, beaten.
discover, discever, *v.* to reveal; to betray; to distinguish; to reconnoitre.
discrece, *v.* to lessen.
dyscryve, *v.* to explain, interpret.
disease, *sb.* discomfort, trouble, anxiety.
diseased, desesed, *ppl. adj.* weary; ill.
dis(h)eryte, *v.* to deprive, dispossess.
dispayre, *sb.; sorowyng oute of dispayre,* lamenting his desperate plight.
disparbeled, *pp.* dispersed.
dispercle, *v.* to disperse.
disperysshe, *v.* to perish utterly.

dispite, despite, *sb.* contempt; injury, wrong; rebuff, insult; resentment, anger.
display, *v.* to draw, unfold.
dispoyle, *v.* to undress.
disporte, *sb.* amusement.
dissayved, *pp.* deceived.
dysseyvable, *adj.* deceitful.
distayned, *ppl. adj.* dishonoured.
distracke, *adj.* distracted.
distresse, destresse, *v.* to attack; to harass, defeat.
disworshyp, *sb.* disgrace, dishonour.
do, *v.*; **ded(e), dud,** *pret.*; **doon, do,** *pp.* to perform; to practise; to fight; to behave; to treat; to interfere; to attempt; to order; to put, place; to hold; to take up, bear; *ded of,* doffed; *do for,* to help; *do well,* to do the right thing.
doctour, *sb.* scholar.
dole, *sb.* distribution of gifts. See *do(o)le,* sb.
dolefull, *adj.* grievous, piteous; formidable, able to cause sorrow.
dolefully, *adv.* severely.
dolorous(e), dolerous(e), *adj.* unfortunate, sorrowing; grievous, heavy.
dombe. See *dom(m)e,* adj.
dome. See *do(o)me,* sb., *dom(m)e,* adj.
dommage. See *dam(m)age,* sb.
dom(m)e, dombe, doome, *adj.* dumb.
done, *sb.* gift, boon.
do(o)le, *sb.* sorrow, lamentation.
do(o)me, *sb.* decision; judgement.
doome. See *dom(m)e,* adj.
doon. See *do,* v.
dooted. See *doted,* ppl. adj.
dotage, *sb.* infatuation.
doted, dooted, *ppl. adj.* doting, stupid, foolish.
dou(b)t(e), dought, *sb.* fear; fearful thing.
douchery, *sb.* domain.
doughte, doute, dowte, *v.* to fear.
douteful, *adj.* redoubtable.
dowseperys, *sb. pl.* twelve peers.
dowte. See *doughte,* v.
draught, drawght, *sb.* course, way; current, recess.
draw(e), *v.* (*often reflexive*); **drow, drew(e),** *pret.* to go; to approach;

to resort, incline; to withdraw; to write; to adapt, translate.

drawght. See *draught*, sb.

drenche, *v.* to drown.

dresse, *v.* to prepare; to set in position; to lead, guide; to draw up; *reflex.* to rise; to prepare oneself, make ready; to array oneself; to go; to step forward, advance.

dretchyng, *sb.* trouble, confusion; make-believe.

drew(e). See *draw(e)*, v.

droupe, *v.* to sink down exhausted; to cower, lie hidden.

drow. See *draw(e)*, v.

dud. See *do*, v.

dunne, *adj.* dull brown.

durable, *adj.* persistent.

duras, *sb.* violence; affliction; hardship; pain, suffering.

dure, *v.* to endure, last; to exist.

durste, *v. pret.* dared.

dwelle, *v.* to linger.

dwere, *sb.* doubt.

dwyne, *v.* to waste, pine.

E

ease, *sb.*[1] health.

ease, evyse, *sb.*[2] edge, margin.

ease, *v.* to care for; to cure.

effte, *adv.* again.

elffe, *sb.* creature.

elis, ell(i)s, *adv.* else; otherwise; *othir ellis,* otherwise, apart from this.

elther, *adj. comp.* elder.

eme, *sb.* uncle.

empeyre, *v.* to grow weaker.

empyre, *sb.* rule.

empyreship, *sb.* office of emperor.

enbrayde, *v.* to upbraid.

encense, *v.* to burn.

enchace, *v.* to drive.

enchaff, *v.* to make warm; to inflame with passion.

encheve, enchy(e)ve, *v.* to achieve; to win, gain; to accomplish; to complete.

encres(e), encrece, *v.* to grow; to become stronger.

end(e)longe, enlonge, endlynge, *prep. and adv.* from end to end; straight on; along.

endewe, *v.* to endow.

endite, *v.* to write.

enelyd, *pp.* anointed, having received extreme unction.

enewed, *ppl. adj.* tinted, coloured.

enforce, enforse, *v. reflex.* to exert oneself, strive.

enformacion, *sb.* instruction.

engyn(n)e, *sb.* means, device; machination.

enlonge. See *end(e)longe*, prep. and adv.

enpoysen, enpoyson, *v.* to poison.

entent(e), *sb.* reason, intention; wish, object of desire; gist, contents; meaning, opinion.

entere, entyre, *v.* to bury.

enterement, *sb.* burial.

entermete, *v.* to concern oneself.

entirdytynge, *sb.* interdict.

entyre. See *entere*, v.

entromedled, *pp.* mingled.

envy, *sb.* displeasure; ill-will.

envyous, *adj.* evil-minded.

envyro(w)ne, *adv.* around, about.

eregned, *ppl. adj.* heretical.

erste, *adv.* hitherto, before.

erth, *sb.* piece of ground.

erthely, *adj.* mortal.

estate, *sb.* rank, order; pomp, ceremony.

esturys, *sb. pl.* rooms.

etynge, *sb.* appetite; *so well of etynge,* with such a good appetite.

even. See *evyn*, adv.

evenynge, *sb.* equal, match; *in the over evenynge,* having an unfair advantage over one's opponent.

every, everych(e), *adj. and pron.* each; *everych one aftir othir,* in turn.

evydence, *sb.* just claim.

evyl(l), yevil, yevell, *adj. and adv.* badly; ill; severely; dearly; *evyll wyll* (OF. *mautalent*) anger; malice.

evyn, even, *adv.* directly, straight; close, near; equally.

evyn, *sb.* eve, evening before.

evyse. See *ease*, sb.[2]

excepte, *cj.* unless.

excyte, *v.* to urge.

excussion, *sb.* execution.

exemple, *sb.*; *in an exemple that,* as if to show that.

exposycion, *sb.* explanation, interpretation.

expowne, *v.* to explain, interpret.

F

fa(a)re, *sb.* behaviour, bearing; fuss; commotion.

fade, *v.* to lose strength.

fadom, *sb.* cubit.

fayle, *v.* to lack; to be lacking; to lose; to miss; to cease; to abandon pursuit of.

fayne, *adj.* obliged.

fayne, *v. reflex.* to hesitate; to lack courage.

faynte, *v.* to grow tired; to falter, give way.

fair, fayre, *adv.* courteously, gently, kindly.

fayre, *sb.* fire.

fayrenes(se), *sb.* beauty; gentleness.

faytoure, *sb.* impostor.

famuste, *adj. superl.* most famous.

fantasy, *sb.* love.

fare, *v.* to act, behave; happen; *fare with,* to treat.

fare. See *fa(a)re,* sb.

farme, *sb.* fixed rent or tax.

farther, *v.* to help.

faste, *adv.* earnestly; firmly; soundly; quickly; soon; closely; near.

faughte, *sb.* fault, blame.

faught(e) *v.* to lack.

fauntekyn, *sb.* little child, infant.

favour, *sb.* bias, fancy.

fe(a)re, *v.* to frighten.

feaute. See *fewte,* sb.

feauter, fewter, *v.* to fix a spear in its rest.

feautyr, feawter, *sb.* rest or support for spear on saddle.

feawté, *sb.* fealty.

feawter. See *feautyr,* sb.

fecche, fette, *v.*; **fet(te),** *pret. and pp.* to fetch; to make; *to fecche his raunge,* to reach a suitable distance (for charging).

fee, *sb.* reward.

fe(e)r(r)ys, *sb. pl.* companions.

feffyd, *v. pret.* manned.

felaushyp. See *felyship,* v.

fele, *pron.* many.

felyship, felaushyp, *v.* to associate.

felle, *sb.* wild open country.

fel(l)on, *adj.* wicked, harmful.

ferde, *sb.* fear, terror.

fer(e), *sb.* companionship; *on fer, in re,* together.

fere. See *fe(a)re,* v.

fer(r)ys. See *fe(e)r(r)ys,* sb. pl.

fested, *ppl. adj.* present at the feast.

fet(te). See *fecche,* v.

fewte, feaute, *sb.* track.

fewter. See *feauter,* v.

fyaunce, *sb.* promise.

fyeble, *v.* to grow feeble.

fylde, *sb.; in the fylde,* killed.

fylth, *sb.* lust.

fyndynge, *sb.* provision.

fine, fyne, *adj.* main, superior.

fyse, *sb.* son.

flayne, *pp.* cut.

flakette, *sb.* vessel, flask.

flamand, *pres. part.* burning.

flange. See *flynge,* v.

flappe, *v.* to cut.

flasket, *sb.* vessel, flask.

flatlynge, *adv.* flat, at full length.

flawme, *v.* to flame, burn.

fleamed, flemyd, fleymed, *v. pret. and pp.* banished, put to flight.

fle(e)te, *v.* to float.

fleymed, flemyd. See *fleamed,* v. pret. and pp.

flete. See *fle(e)te,* v.

flynge, *v.,* **flange,** *pret.* to hasten; to draw.

flytte, *v.* to move, come.

floode, *sb.* water.

floter, *v.* to flutter, float.

foyle, *v.* to trample down (fig.).

foyne, *sb.* thrust.

foyne, *v.* to thrust.

foote-hote, *adv.* without pause.

foote-men, *sb. pl.* foot-soldiers.

for, *adv.* now; *cj.* because; that (weakened to expletive); *for that,* for.

for, fore, *prep.* on account of; about, concerning; against; in spite of; for fear of; in return for; *for me,* as far as I am concerned; *here is for me,* I am ready; *for of,* on account of; *for to,* in order to.

forbe(a)re, *v.*; **forbare,** *pret.*; **forborne,** *pp.* to bear with, have patience with; to leave alone.

forbled(de), *ppl. adj.* weak from loss of blood.

forborne. See *forbe(a)re,* v.

fordo, *v.* **fordyd,** *pret.* to render powerless; to put an end to; to destroy.

fore. See *for,* prep.

forecaste, *pp.* predestined.
forecaste, *sb.* design, plan.
forey, *v.* to forage in, to pillage.
forestage, *sb.* forecastle.
forewarde, *adj.* ready, eager.
forfare, *v.* to destroy.
forfende, *v. inf. and pp.* to deny,
  banish from.
forfete, *adj.* lost, ruined.
forfette, *sb.* offence.
forfoughtyn, *ppl. adj.* weary with
  fighting.
forhewyn, *ppl. adj.* cut to pieces.
forjuste, *v.* to defeat in jousting.
forlonde, *sb.* cape, promontory.
forsake, *v.* to refuse to encounter; to
  disown.
forstall, *v.* to intercept, cut off.
fo(r)ster, *sb.* forester.
forthynke, *v. reflex. and impers.* to
  regret; to grieve.
fortune, *sb.* chance.
fortune, *v.* to befall.
forwounded, *ppl. adj.* severely wounded.
foster. See *fo(r)ster*, sb.
foule, fowle, *adv.* evilly.
fourme, *sb.*[1] condition.
fourme, *sb.*[2] bench.
fourme, *v.* to make, create.
fowle. See *foule*, adv.
fowlys, *sb. pl.* birds.
frayke. See *freyke*, sb.
fraysted, *ppl. adj.* tried, experienced.
fre, *adj.* noble; generous; freely given;
  (of a horse) ready to go, willing.
freyke, frayke, *sb.* man, warrior.
frely, *adv.* bravely, nobly.
frende, *v. reflex.* to make friends.
frendly, *adv.* in a friendly way.
frycke, *adj.* strong, vigorous.
fro, frome, *prep.* away from; *cj.* from
  the time when; *a litill frome thens,*
  at some distance away.
fro(m)ward(e), *prep.* from, away
  from; *adv.* thither.
fruys(s)he, *v.* to dash, knock; to rush
  violently.
furyous, *adj.* eager.
furnysshe, *v.* to prepare (for).

G
gabbe, *v.* to lie.
gadde, *sb.* bar, rod.

gadlynges, *sb. pl.* fellows.
gadred, *v. pret.* gathered.
gaf(f). See *gyff(e)*, v.
gaynecommynge, *sb.* return.
gayneste, *adj. superl.* quickest, fastest;
  at the gaynyste, by the most direct
  route.
galyard, *adj.* valiant, gay.
galyottys, *sb. pl.* small boats.
game, *sb.* battle; amusement.
gan, *v. pret.* began.
gaper, *sb.* japer, jester.
gar, *v.* garte, *pret.* to command; to
  cause.
garneson, *sb.* reward.
garnyson, *sb.* defending force.
garnysshe, garnysh, *v.* to prepare
  for defence.
garte. See *gar*, v.
gastfull, *adj.* fearful, terrifying.
gate, ghate, *sb.* way, road.
gate. See *ge(e)te*, v.
ge(e)te, gett, *v.*; gate, *pret.*; goten,
  pp. to take, to seize, to obtain; to
  meet; to capture; to gain, win; to
  receive; to mount; to enter; to force
  down; to beget.
geff, geffyn. See *gyff*, cj., *gyff(e)*, v.
genytrottys, *sb. pl.* genitals.
gerde. See *gurde*, v.
gere, *sb.* armour, weapons.
germayne, jermayne, jarmayne,
  adj. closely akin; *cosyne germayne,*
  first cousin.
gesseraunte, jesseraunte, jesseraunce, *sb.* light coat of armour.
gete, gett. See *ge(e)te*, v.
gettles, *adj.* empty-handed.
geve, gevyn. See *gyff(e)*, v.
ghate. See *gate*, sb.
ghost, *sb.* life.
gyde, *v. reflex.* to find one's way.
gyeff. See *gyff(e)*, v.
gyff, geff, *cj.* if.
gyff(e), gyeff, geve, gyve, yeff,
  yeve, *v.*; gaf(f), *pret.*; geffyn,
  gyffyn, gevyn, yeffyn, *pp.* to appoint; to tell, inform; to warn; to
  incline; to be well-disposed.
gyffte, *sb.* right of giving.
gyrde. See *gurde*, v.
gyse, *sb.* habit, custom.
gysarne, gyserne, *sb.* battle-axe,
  halberd.

gyve. See *gyff(e)*, v.
glad, *v.* to gladden; to be glad.
glayve, *sb.* spear, lance.
glatys(s)aunte, glatissynge, *adj.* yelping.
glydyng, *pres. part.* sailing.
glystrand, *ppl. adj.* glittering, shining.
gloore, *v.* to stare.
gnaste, *v.* to gnash.
gobbettis, *sb. pl.* pieces.
godelye, goodly, *adj.* beautiful, handsome; courteous; *adv.* courteously, graciously.
gooldys, gouldes, *sb.* gules.
gorge, *sb.* throat.
gostly, *adj.* spiritual.
goten. See *ge(e)te*, v.
gouldes. See *gooldys*, sb.
governaunce, *sb.* care.
governe, *v. reflex.* to behave.
grace, *sb.* mercy; lot, fate; good fortune.
grame, *sb.* grief, harm.
grate. See *grete*, adj.
graunte, *sb.* agreement, acquiescence.
grauntesyre, *sb.* grandfather.
gravyn, *pp.* dug; buried.
gré, *sb.* victory, prize for victory; pre-eminence, mastery.
grece, *sb.*; *harte of grece*, fat deer.
grecis, *sb. pl.* steps, stairs.
grekynge, *sb.* dawn.
gres(e)ly, *adj.* terrible; *adv.* terribly.
gresylde, *adj.* grey, grizzly.
gresly. See *gres(e)ly*, adj. and adv.
grete, grate, *adj.*; **gretter,** *comp.*; **grettyste,** *superl.* large; boastful; severe; heavy.
grevaunces, *sb. pl.* sufferings.
greve, *adj.* severe.
greve, *sb.* thicket.
greve, gryff, *v.* to injure.
grymly, *adj.* fierce; severe.
grounden, *ppl. adj.* sharpened.
grucche, *v.* to grudge, grumble; to be unwilling.
grucchynge, *sb.* complaining; reluctance.
gummys, *sb. pl.* ointments, salves.
gunne, *sb.* projectile, cannon ball.
gurde, gyrde, *v.*; **gurde, gyrde, gerde,** *pret.* to strike; to rush.
guttys, *sb. pl.* entrails.

gwardonles, *adj.* without reward.
gwerdon, *sb.* reward; price.

H

haylese, *v.* to speak to, address.
haynxman, *sb.* servant, page.
hayre. See *here*, sb.
hakeney, *sb.* ambling horse, nag.
hale, *v.* to pull; *interj.* exclamation of sailors in hauling.
halff, *sb.* side.
halfendele, *sb.* half.
halow, *v.* to shout.
halse, *sb.* neck.
halse, *v.* to embrace.
hand(e). See *honde*, sb.
hande-brede, *sb.* handbreadth.
handels, hondils, *sb.* hilt.
handyll, *v.*; **hand(e)led** *pret. and pp.* to grasp; to clasp, embrace; to capture; to examine, touch.
hangers, *sb. pl.* testicles.
hansell, *sb.* gift.
hap(pe), *sb.* chance, fortune.
hap(pe), *v.* to befall; to happen, chance.
happely, *adv.* by a lucky chance.
happy, *adj.* lucky.
happyn, *v. trans.* to befall.
harberow, harborow. See *herborow*, sb. and v.
harde, *adj.* brave; difficult; poor; unlikely.
harde, *adv.* bravely; severely; extremely; with difficulty.
harde, *v. pret. and pp.* heard, understood.
hardé-herted, *ppl. adj.* brave.
hardely, *adv.* indeed.
hardy, *adj.* brave; violent.
hardynes(se), *sb.* valour; boldness, audacity.
harlot, *sb.* rascal.
harmys, *sb. pl.* wrongs, sufferings.
harneys(e), harnoys, harneysse, *sb.* arms, armour.
harneyst(e), *ppl. adj.* equipped; adorned.
harson, *sb.* saddle-bow.
harte. See *hert(e)*, sb.
harte-hole, *adj.* undismayed.
hartely, *adj.* deep, grievous.
harte-roote, bottom of the heart.

hatefull, *adj.* hostile.
hauffte, *sb.* handle.
haunte, *v.* to resort, frequent; to make use of, perform.
hauté, hawté, *adj.* proud; noble, high-born.
he, *pron.* it; she.
he(a)le, *sb.* strength, health; profit, advantage.
helde. See *holde*, v.
hele, *v.* to cover.
hele. See *he(a)le*, sb.
helme, *sb.* helmet; armed man.
helpynge, *sb.* recovery.
hem, *pron.* them.
hemynge, *sb.* coughing.
hemselff, *pron.* themselves.
hende, *adj.* courteous.
hente, *v.* to seize.
hepe, *sb.* group.
her, hir, *poss. adj.* their.
herberow. See *herborow*, sb. and v.
herbygeour, *sb.* harbinger, purveyor of lodgings.
herborgage, herbo(u)rage, *sb.* lodging.
herborow, herberow, *sb.* lodging.
herborow, herberow, harborow, harberow, *v.*; herbourde, *pp.* to procure lodging for, to lodge; to stay.
herbourage. See *herborgage*, sb.
here, heyre, hayre, *sb.* hair; hairshirt.
heretoforne, *adv.* before.
her(r)od, herowd, *sb.* herald.
hert(e), harte, *sb.*[1] courage; mind; person; thoughts, feelings.
herte, harte, *sb.*[2] hart.
hertely, hartely, *adj.* deep, grievous; *adv.* with feeling, sincerely, affectionately; earnestly; bitterly.
hertys, *sb. pl.* hurts, wrongs.
hete, *sb.*[1] anger.
hete, *sb.*[2] reproach.
hethynde, *adj.* heathen.
heve, *v.*; heve, hove, *pret.* to lift, raise.
hevy, *adj.* sad, sorrowful.
hevy, *v.* to grieve.
hevyly, *adv.* sadly.
hevynesse, *sb.* sorrow.
hew, *v. pret*; hewen, *pp.* hewed; gashed.

hic, *adv.* (Lat.) here.
hyde, *sb.*[1] skin.
hyde, *sb.*[2] heed.
hye. See *hy(gh)e*, v. reflex.
hy(g)he. *adj. and sb.* tall; great, notable; noble, gentle; loud; boastful; grave, serious; *the hygher hande*, victory; *on hyghe*, in height; *on hyghe, an hyghe*, high; loudly.
hy(gh)e, *v. reflex.* to hasten.
hyght, *sb.*; *(upp)on hyght*, aloud, loudly.
hyght(e), *v. pres. and pret.* to be called.
hyhe. See *hy(g)he*, adj. and sb.
hylde, *v.* to pour, shed.
hylde. See *holde*, v.
hyltis, *sb.* handle, hilt.
hir. See *her*, poss adj.
his, *poss. adj.* (used after proper name as equivalent of genitive inflexion): *Claudas his knyghtes*, Claudas's knights.
hit(te), *pron.* it.
holde, *sb.* stronghold.
holde, *v.*; helde, hylde, *pret.*; holde(n), *pp.* to grasp; to keep; to associate; to press; to fight; to withstand; to hold property; to celebrate; to consider; to deceive; to love, protect; *reflex.* to remain; *hylde ayenste* disapproved of; *hylde up*, held back.
hole, hool, *adj.* entire, whole; in good health; healed; *the hole barownes*, all the barons; *hole kynge of Ingelonde*, king of all England.
hole, holé, holy, *adv.* fully; *all hole togydirs*, all together.
hole, *sb.* window-opening, small window.
holsom, *adj.* suitable.
holt, *sb.* wood, copse.
honde, hand(e), *sb.* handle; side; *in hondis with*, at close quarters with; *on evyn hondis*; with honours even; *the better honde, the hygher hande*, victory; *unto your honde*, without exertion on your part; *hande for hande*, hand-to-hand; *hys owne hondys*, with his own hands; *hit woll be takyn at youre handys*, your challenge will be accepted.
honde-faste, *adj.* contracted, married.

hondils. See *handels*, sb.
hondredsom, sb. about a hundred.
hool. See *hole*, adj.
hooly, sb. holly.
hoote. See *hote*, adj.
hope, v. to think.
hore, adj. grey, bare; grey-headed.
horse, sb. horseman; *gen. sg.* horse's.
horse, v. to provide with a horse, to help on to horseback.
horse-bere, sb. horse-litter.
horse-mete, sb. food for horses.
hote, hoote, adj. passionate; angry; *adv.* passionately.
houseld, howseled, pp. shriven.
hove, v. to remain, wait; to float.
hove. See *heve*, v.
how, adv. why.
how, *interj.* exclamation of sailors in hauling.
howge, adj. great.
howseled. See *housled*, pp.
hurlynge, sb. commotion, disturbance.
hurtel, v. to rush, dash.
husbandeman, sb. countryman, peasant.

I

iacet, v. *3 pers. pres.* (Lat.) lies.
icleyght, pp. clasped.
idyght, pp. prepared.
idrawyn, pp. drawn.
ye(e), yen. See *y(gh)e*, sb.
yevell, yevil. See *evyl(l)*, adj. and adv.
yfared, pp. dealt.
ifounde, pp. met.
y(gh)e, yee, sb.; y(gh)en, iyen, eyen, *pl.* eye.
yghesyght, sb. look, gaze.
igyffyn, pp. given.
ihorsed, pp. horsed.
iyen. See *y(gh)e*, sb.
ylle, adv. grievously.
in, *prep.* in the power of; held by; by, near; because of; on; for; concerning; to.
inboced, *ppl. adj.* driven to extremity, hunted down.
inbusshemente. See *buyshemente*, sb.
inchaffed, *ppl. adj.* furious, excited.
inclyned, v.; *to be inclyned*, to seek.
incoronation, sb. coronation.
inde, sb. indigo.

infelyshyp, v. *reflex.* to join company.
infourmede, *ppl. adj.* placed, directed; *evyn infourmede*, well-directed.
inkly, adv. as ink.
inly(c)ke, inlyche, adv. alike; similarly.
inne, sb. lodging.
instaunce, sb. entreaty.
intyerly, adv. entirely, deeply.
into, *prep.* before; *cj.* until.
invenymed, pp. poisoned.
inward(e)ly, adv. deeply; at heart.
inwyth, *prep.* in, within.
isente, pp. sent.
isowdred, pp. joined.
issew, v. to come.
yssue, sb. gate; sally, sortie.
itaught, *ppl. adj.* taught, instructed.
ityed, pp. tied.
iwys, adv. indeed.

J

japer, sb. impostor; jester.
japyng, sb. jesting.
japis, sb. *pl.* trifles; jesting.
jarmayne, jermayne. See *germayne*, adj.
jesseraunce, jesseraunte. See *ges-seraunte*, sb.
joye, v. to rejoice.
joyne, v. to direct (towards).
jowke, v. to knock.
jurnay, sb. exploit, business, affair.
justenynge, sb. tournament.
justyse, sb. punishment.

K

keele, v. to cool.
ke(e)ne, adj. brave.
keep. See *kepe*, v.
kempys, sb. *pl.* champions.
ken, v. to tell; to show.
kene. See *ke(e)ne*, adj.
kepe, sb. heed, attention; *I take no kepe*, I do not care; *take kepe (un)to*, to look after.
kepe, keep, v. to guard, look after; to keep within; to conceal; to await; to want; to wish; *kepe of*, to care about.
kepyng(e), sb. care; defence.
kerve, v. to cut through.

kerver, *sb.* carver.
keste, kyst, *v. pret.* threw; felt.
keuerchoff, *sb.* kerchief.
kybbet, *sb.* cubit.
kyd(de), *ppl. adj.* famous, great.
kyll(e), *v.* to strike.
kynde, *adj.* natural, lawful; loving (ironical); *kynde elders*, ancestors.
kynde, *sb.* nature, disposition; family; right of birth.
kyndely, *adj.* natural.
kyndenes, *sb.* tenderness, affection.
kynred(e), *sb.* family.
kyrke, *sb.* church.
kyst. See *keste, v.* pret.
knave, *sb.* boy; servant.
knyghtly, *adv.* gallantly.
knylle, *v.* to ring.
knowynge, *adj.* skilled.
knowlecchynge, *sb.*; *lat hym have knowlecchynge*, let him know.
knowleche, *v.* to acknowledge.

L

lad, *pp.* carried.
lade, lode, *pp.* laden.
lay, *sb.* song.
lay(ne). See *ly(ghe), v.*
layne, *v.* to conceal.
layrge. See *large.*
laysshe, *v.* to strike.
langayge, *sb.* talk.
langeryng, *pres. part.* loitering.
langoure, *sb.* lamentation.
lappe, *v.* to wrap.
large, layrge, *adj., adv., and sb.* generous; generously; boastfully; *syxty myle large*, over a distance of sixty miles; *at large*, without restraint; *at hys large*, at liberty.
largely, *adv.* fully, freely; generously; boastfully.
largenesse, *sb.* generosity.
larges, *sb.* generosity.
laste, *cj.* lest.
laste, *adj. superl.* last; *the laste day*, yesterday.
laste, *v.* to reach, extend.
late, *adv.* recently, lately.
latyne, laton, *sb.* latten, brass.
laughte, *v. pret.* seized.
launde, lawnde, *sb.* glade; plain.
lawde, *sb.* praise.
lawnde. See *launde, sb.*

lazar cote, *sb.* hut for lepers.
leane. See *lene, v.*
learys, *sb. pl.* cheeks.
leche, *sb.* physician.
lechecrauffte, *sb.* skill in surgery.
lechés les alere (Fr.) let go.
lechourere, *sb.* debauchee.
leeff. See *leve,* adj.
leepe, *v.*; lepe, lope, *v. pret.*; lopyn, *pp.* leap; *leepe in*, came forward.
legeaunte, *sb.* liege lord.
ley. See *ly(ghe), v.*
leyde, *ppl. adj.* in their places.
leyne. See *ly(ghe), v.*
leyser, *sb.* leisure; opportunity.
lemman, *sb.* lover.
lende, *v.* to remain.
lendys, *sb. pl.* loins, buttocks.
lene, leane, *v.*; lente, *pret.* to lend; to give.
lepe, See *leepe, v.*
lerne, *v.* to teach; to direct, instruct.
lese. See *loose, v.*
leste, *adj. superl.* least, fewest.
let, *sb.* hindrance.
let(t)e, *v.*; lette, *pret.*; lette(d), *pp.* to prevent, hinder; to deprive; to resist; to remove.
leve, leeff, lyff *adj.*; lever, levir, *comp.*; levyste, *superl.* dear, beloved; willing; *lever*, rather.
leve, lyve, *v.* to believe.
leved, *ppl. adj.* leafy.
lever. See *leve,* adj.
levynge, *sb.* manner of life.
levir. See *leve,* adj.
levyste. See *leve,* adj.
lewde, *adj.* boorish, ill-mannered.
ley(ne), ly. See *ly(ghe), v.*
ly, *pron.* (Fr.) him.
lybarde, lybud, *sb.* leopard.
licence, lysence, *sb.* permission.
lyck(e)ly, lycly. See *lykly,* adj.
lycoure, *sb.* greed.
lycoures, *adj.* lecherous.
lyeffloode. See *lyvelod(e),* sb.
lyege, *adj.* entitled to (feudal) service; bound to render (feudal) service.
lyegemente, *sb.* alleviation.
lyen(e). See *ly(ghe), v.*
lyff. See *leve,* adj.
lyggyng(e), *ppl. adj.* lying.
ly(ghe), ley lay, *v.*; lyggys, *3 sg. pres.*; lay, *pret.*; ley(ne), layne,

ly(ghe) etc. (*cont.*):
 lyen(e), *pp.* to lie; to stay, remain; *lay aboute*, tried.
lyght, *adj.* active, nimble; wanton.
lyght, *v. pret.* mounted; came down.
lyghte, *v.* to grow light or cheerful.
lyghtly, *adv.* quickly.
lygnage, *sb.* family, descent.
lyke, *adj.* similar; likely; *adv.* equally; to judge by; as if; *lyke as* just as, as if.
lyke, *v.* to please.
lykynge, *adj.* pleasant.
lykynge, *sb.* rejoicing, pleasure.
lykly, lyck(e)ly, lycly, *adj.* good-looking.
lym-meale, *adv.* limb from limb.
lysence. See *licence*, sb.
lyst(e), *sb.* wish, desire.
lyst(e), *v.*; lyst(e), *pret.* to wish, to desire, want; (*impers.*) to please.
lythe, *sb.* joint.
lyve. See *leve*, v.
lyvelod(e), lyeffloode, *sb.* possessions, estates; endowment.
lode. See *lade*, pp.
lodgyng(e), *sb.* bed; food and lodging; rest.
loffte, *sb.* sky; (*upp*)*on loffte*, aloft; on horseback.
longe, *adj.* due; *longe* (*upp*)*on*, due to.
longe, *adv.*; lenger, *comp.*; lengist, *superl.* long; *longe and brode*, far and wide. See *overtwarte*, adv.
longe, *v.* to belong, to be fitting.
longis, *prep.* along, down.
longys, *sb. pl.* lungs.
longyng, *ppl. adj.* belonging.
lo(o)se, *sb.* fame, praise.
loose, lese, *v.*; loste, *pp.* to lose, to bring to ruin; to miss; to be unable to find (?).
lope, lopyn. See *leepe*, v.
lord(e)shyp, *sb.* protection, patronage; land, domain.
lorne, *pp.* lost, wasted.
lose. See *lo(o)se*, sb.
lose, *v*, to set free.
loste. See *loose*, v.
loth(e), *adj.* unwilling; hateful; *sey the lothe word*, to surrender.
lotles, *adj.* without harm.
louse. See *lowse*, v.
lovely, *adj.* loving.
lovynge, *sb.* praise.

lowe, *sb.* hill.
lowly, *adv.* humbly.
lowse, *adv.* loose, free.
lowse, louse, *v.* to set free.
lugerande, *ppl. adj.* hanging loosely (?).
lunes, *sb. pl.* leashes for a hawk.
luske, *sb.* sluggard.
lust(e), *sb.* pleasure; wish, desire.
lusty, *adj.* pleasing, gay, merry, hearty; pleasant; handsome.

M

maade. See *make*, v.
macche, *sb.* equal.
macche, matche, *v.* to prove a match; to fight with; to marry.
macchecolde, *pp.* machicolated.
mad(e). See *make*, v.
magré, *sb.* enmity, ill-will; defiance.
magré, magry, malgré, *prep.* in spite of; *magré hir hede*, against her will.
may, *v.* prevail, have one's way; can: have reason to.
mayles, *sb. pl.* mail-armour.
maymed, *ppl. adj.* wounded.
maymes, *sb. pl.* injuries.
maynelondis, *sb. pl.* wide territories.
maysterlesse, *adj.* unprotected, helpless.
maystir-man, *sb.* chief, leader.
ma(y)stry, *sb.* deed of prowess; game, contest; *pl.* violent behaviour.
make, *v.*; mad(e), maade, *pret.* to bid, command; to bring about, cause to happen; to contrive with; to declare, pretend; to describe, write; to take; to change; *made do*, commanded.
makeles, *adj.* peerless, unequalled.
maker, *sb.* narrator, poet.
makyng, *sb.* appearance.
male ease, *sb.* distress.
male engyn(n)e, *sb.* evil intention; deceit, guile.
malefortune, *sb.* misfortune.
malgré. See *magré*, prep.
malyce, *sb.* ill-will, power to harm.
malyncoly, *sb.* anger.
man, *sb.* anyone.
manhode, *sb.* humane feeling, compassion.

manne-handled, *pp.* encountered in battle.

marche, *v.* to border.

marche, marchis, *sb.*; marchys, *pl.* boundary, border; place; territory.

marys(e), *sb.*; mares, *pl.* marsh.

marke, *v.* to set a boundary; to notice.

mased, *ppl. adj.* stupefied.

masse-peny, *sb.* an offering of money made at mass.

mastry. See *ma(y)stry*, sb.

matche. See *macche*, v.

meane, *adj.* ordinary.

meane, *sb.* means, way; help; intermediary; *pl.* mediation, intervention; contriving, attempt.

meane, mene, *v.*[1]; mente, *pret.* to mention; to say.

meane, *v.*[2] to pity.

med(d)yll, med(d)el, *v.* to mingle; to have to do; to have intercourse; to fight; *meddel wyth*, to attack; to be a prey to.

medlé, medly, *sb.* mêlée; combat.

megir, *adj.* weak.

meke, *v. reflex.* to humble oneself.

membir, *sb.* limb.

mene. See *meane*, v.[1]

menour, *sb.* behaviour.

menyvere, *sb.* fur trimming.

mente. See *meane*, v.[1]

mesell, *sb.* serious illness.

mesemythe, *v. impers.* it seems to me.

messa(y)ge, *sb.* errand; messenger.

messe, *sb.* table.

messynge, *sb.* messenger.

mesure, *sb.* rule; moderation; *out of mesure*, without stint.

mete, *adj.* suitable, useful; close-fitting

mete, *sb.* food, meal.

mete-whyle, *sb.* meal-time.

methynke, *v. impers.* it seems to me.

mette, *v. pret.* dreamed.

meve, *v.* to carry; to suggest, propose; to persuade; *reflex.* to become excited.

mevear, *sb.* mover.

myckyll. See *mykyll*.

myghted, *adj.* having strength.

mykyll, mykel, myckyll, *adj.* much; great; *adv.* greatly.

mylde, *adj.* gentle; *as sb.* gentle person.

myne, *v.* to undermine, destroy.

myschevous, *adj.*; myschevuste, *superl.* shameful; wicked.

myschyff, *v.*; myscheved, *pp.* to hurt, harm; to afflict; to put to shame.

myschyff, myscheffe, *sb.* distress; wickedness.

myscomfort, *v. reflex.* to trouble.

myscreaunte, *sb.* unbeliever, infidel.

myssadventure, *sb.* ill-luck.

myssaye, *v.* to insult.

mysse, *sb.* injury, wrong.

mysse, *v.* to do without.

mysseadvysed, *ppl. adj.* ill-advised.

myssease, mysse-case, *sb.* distress, affliction.

myssecreature, *sb.* wicked person.

myssedo, *v.*; mysseded, *pret.* to harm, injure; to offend.

myssefortune, *sb.* mischance, mistake.

myssefortune, *v.* to happen unfortunately.

myssefortuned, *ppl. adj.* unfortunate.

myssehappe, *v. impers.* to befall unfortunately.

mysselyvyng, *sb.* evil life.

myssesay, *v.*; mysseseyde, *pret.* to insult.

myster, mystir, *sb.* need.

mo. See *mo(o)*, adj. comp.

moy(a)ne, *sb.* help; intervention.

mokkis, *sb. pl.* mockery.

molde, *sb.* earth, ground.

mone. See *mo(o)ne*, sb.

moneth-day, *sb.* the corresponding day of the following month.

mo(o), *adj. comp.* more in number; *mo other*, others.

mo(o)ne, *sb.* lamentation.

more, *adj. comp.* greater, taller, bigger; *adv.* again.

morne, *sb.*[1] morning.

morne, *sb.*[2] lamentation.

morte, *sb.* death.

morthir, *sb.* murder.

moste, *adj. superl.* greatest; *moste and leste*, high and low, all.

motis, *sb. pl.* notes of a horn.

mou, mow, *v.* must; may.

mountenaunce, mowntenaunce, *sb.* space of time.

muste, mutte, *v.* shall certainly.

N

nayed. See *nyghe*, v.²
naked, *adj.* unarmed; unsheathed.
named, *ppl. adj.* reputed; attributed.
nat(e), *adv.* not.
natforthan, notforthan, *adv.* nevertheless; *cj.* although.
natforthat, *adv.* nevertheless.
naturall, *adj.* humane; noble.
naught, nought, *adv.* not.
ne, *adv.* not; *cj.* nor; *ne . . . but,* nothing . . . but.
neyssh, *adj.* soft.
neyther, *adj.* lower, under.
neythir, *cj.* nor.
nere, *adv.* never, not at all.
nere, *v. pret.* were it not.
nerehonde, nerehande, *adv.* nearly; near at hand.
neve(a)w, *sb.* nephew; uncle.
Newerys, *sb.* New Year's.
new-fangill, *adj.* fond of new things.
nexte, *adj. superl.* nearest.
nyghe, *v.*¹ to approach.
nyghe, *v.*²; **nayed,** *pret.* to neigh.
nyghehonde, nyhonde, *adv.* near at hand; nearly.
nylle, *v. pres.* do not wish.
nymell, *adj.* agile.
nys, *v. pres.* is not.
nob(e)ley, *sb.* pomp, splendour.
noy, *v.* to harm, injure.
noyous, *adj.* troublesome, harmful.
noyse, *sb.* shouts of the crowd; scandal; rumour; complaint.
noyse, *v.* to report, describe; to defame, to spread rumours.
none, *adj.* no; *pron.* neither; *adv.* not.
noselynge, *adv.* headlong.
note, *sb.* business.
notforthan. See *natforthan*, adv.
nother, *pron.* neither; *cj.* nor.
nought, *adv.* See *naught*.
nourisshe, *v.* to nurse; *nourisshed broder,* foster-brother.
nourisshyng, *sb.* nursing, upbringing.
nouryture, nurture, *sb.* training, upbringing.
now, *adv.*; *now and now,* from time to time; *as now,* now, at present.
numbir, *sb.*; *oute of numbir,* without number.
nurture. See *nouryture*, sb.

O

o, *adj.* one. See also *on,* pron.
obeysaunce, obeissaunce, *sb.* rule.
obley, *sb.* wafer.
of(f), *prep.* at, about; by; from, out of; during, for the space of; for, to; into; on; with; because of; with regard to; in the person of.
offenser, *sb.* offender.
oldeness, *sb.* age.
olde-seyde, *ppl. adj.* ancient.
olyvaunte, *sb.* elephant.
on, one, *pron.* someone; *indef. art.* a.
on, one, *prep.* on; concerning; against; for; in; to.
one. See *on,* prep., *on,* pron.
one, *adv.* on.
ony, *adj. and pron.* any; some; either.
only. See *al(l) only*.
on-lofte, *adv.* above ground, unburied.
opynyon, *sb.* decision; intention; scheme.
opynne-mowthed, *ppl. adj.* talkative.
or, *cj. and prep.* before.
ordayne, ordeyne, *v.* to arrange; to command; to prepare; to appoint.
ordynaunce, *sb.* decision; command; battle-array, judgement.
ore, *sb.* oar.
orgule, *sb.* pride, haughtiness.
orgulyté, *sb.* pride.
orgul(o)us, *adj.*; **orguluste,** *superl.* proud, boastful; *adv.* proudly; *orgulous sette,* defiant.
os. See *as,* cj.
ostage, *sb.* pledge, security.
oste, *sb.* host, army.
ostré, ostry, *sb.* inn, lodging.
othirwhyle, *adv.* at other times.
otis, *sb. pl.* oats.
ought, *sb.* anything.
ought(e). See *oute,* adv., *ow(gh)e,* v.
oure, *pron. gen. pl.* of us; *oure all, all oure,* of us all.
oure, owre, *sb.* fortune; *in good owre,* fortunately.
oute, *adj.* outlying.
oute, ought, *adv.* outright, completely; outwardly, openly; away; *oute of,* beyond; *all oute,* altogether.
outecepte, *v.* to except.
out(e)rage, *v.* to commit excesses.

outerageous, *adj.* fierce, violent.
outerageousnes, *sb.* violence, ferocity.
oute-take, *prep.* except for.
oute-take, *v.* to except.
outrage. See *out(e)rage*, v.
overcast, *v. pret.* were entangled.
overcharge, *v.* to press hard.
overcom, *pp.* accomplished.
overfallen, *pp.* overcome.
overgete, *v.* to overtake.
overgovernyd, *pp.* ruled.
overheled, *ppl. adj.* covered.
overlad, *pp.* oppressed.
overlepe, *v.* to leave on one side; *overlepe unto*, to pass on to.
overlonge, *prep.* along.
overmacche, *v.* to defeat.
overpasse, *v.* to ignore.
overren(ne), *v.* to attack, overrun.
overryde, *v.*; overredyn, *pp.* to overthrow; to harry.
oversayne, *ppl. adj.* mistaken.
oversé, *v.* to take care; to peruse.
oversette, *ppl. adj.* defeated.
overslyppe, *v.* to pass.
overt(h)wart(e), overthawrte, ovirtwarte, *adj., adv., and prep.* crosswise; slanting; perverse, quarrelsome; across (his body); *at on overthwarte*, crosswise; *overtwarte and endelonge*, all over; *longe and overtwarte*, in every direction.
overthwortely, *adv.* askew, awry.
ovirbledde, *ppl. adj.* covered (with blood).
owchys, *sb. pl.* clasps, ornaments.
ow(gh)e, awghe, *v.*; ought(e), *pret.* to possess; to feel towards; to owe; *impers.* to be bound, to be incumbent upon.
owre. See *oure*, sb.

P

paas(e). See *pace*, sb.[1]
paase, *interj.* peace, silence.
pace, paas(e), *sb.*[1]; *a pace, a paas(e), a grete pace, more than a pace*, at a good speed.
pace, *sb.*[2] narrow or dangerous passage.
pageaunte, *sb.* scene; part; *play his pageaunte*, do his part.

paye, *v.* to please; to engage.
paylet, *sb.*; paylattes, *pl.* pallet, mattress.
payn(e), *sb.* exertion; trouble; distress; effort; penalty.
payne, *v. reflex.* to exert oneself, strive.
paynym, *sb.* heathen.
paytrels, *sb. pl.* breast-armour for horse.
palferey, *sb.* saddle-horse.
palle, *sb.* cloth.
paltokkys, *sb. pl.* short coats, jackets.
pappis, *sb. pl.* breast.
parage, *sb.* lineage, rank.
paramour(s), peramoures, *adv.* as a lover.
pardé. See *perde(us)*, adv.
parler, *sb.* room.
parte, *sb.* share; duty; side; lot, fortune; *a parte*, away, apart; *moost parte*, usually.
parte, *v.* to depart.
parté. See *party*, sb.
parter, *sb.* umpire.
party, parté, *sb.* part; side; behalf; region; direction; encounter; *a party*, in part; *the most party*, for the most part.
passe, *v.* to exceed; to leave; to go away; to escape; to overcome; to follow; to pass sentence; to continue; to survive; *passe thorow*, to cross from side to side, traverse; *passe as*, to become.
passyng(e), *adv.* very; too.
passyngly, *adv.* exceedingly.
paste, *prep.* above, more than.
pauper, paupir, *sb.* paper.
paveloun, pavelyon, pavilys, pavylon, *sb.* large tent.
pe(a)ce, pyce, *sb.* piece of flesh; piece of armour; *at all peacis*, fully.
peas. See *pees*, sb.[1]
pease, *v.* to appease.
peasab(e)ly, pesiblé, *adv.* easily; without opposition.
pece. See *pe(a)ce*, sb.
pees, peas, *sb.*[1] silence, peace.
pees, pyese, pyse, *sb.*[2] vessel.
penowne, *sb.* flag, banner.
pensell, *sb.* small pennon, lady's token.
pensyff, *adj.* thoughtful.
peradventure, *adv.* perhaps.

peramour(e), peramoures. See *paramour(s)*, adv.
perclose, *sb.* enclosure.
perde(us), pardé, *adv.* indeed, assuredly.
perelys, perelles, *sb. pl.* pearls.
perfay, *interj.* by my faith, truly.
perische, perish, peryssh, *v.* to hurt, destroy; to be destroyed.
perowne, perron, *sb.* large block of stone.
pesyble, *adj.* peaceable.
pesiblé. See *peasab(e)ly*, adv.
peté, *sb.* pity, compassion, mercy.
philozopher, phylozopher, *sb.* wise man.
pyce. See *pe(a)ce*, sb.
py(c)ke, *v. reflex*, to go, to depart; *pycked her way*, stole away.
pyese. See *pees*, sb.
pyght(e), *v. pret.* pitched, thrust.
pykyll, *sb.* pickle, sauce.
pylle, *v.* to plunder.
pyllour(e), *sb.* plunderer, robber.
pyloure, *sb.* pillar.
pynche, *v.* to seize, bite.
pyse. See *pees*, sb.
piteuously, pytewusly, *adv.* grievously, pitiably.
pytte, *sb.* grave.
place, *sb.* house.
play, *sb.* wound (OF. *playe*).
playne, *adj.* regular; open; honest, frank; *adv.* openly.
playne, *v.* to complain.
plante, *v.* to lay.
pleasaunce, *sb.* pleasure.
plenoure, *adv.* with the full number.
plyghte, *v. pret.* pledged, engaged.
pluckyng, *sb.* urging forward.
plumpe, *sb.* clump.
poy(y)nte, *sb.* part; position; *at al poyntes*, in every respect; *the poynte of the day*, daybreak.
poyntelynge, *adv.* point foremost.
poyntemente, *sb.* arrangements.
porte, *sb.* gate; entrance.
postren, *sb.* postern, side-door.
potestate, *sb.* potentate, ruler.
pousté, *sb.* power.
powder, *sb.* powdered spice, condiment.
power, *sb.* army; utmost.
powse, *sb.* pulse.

pray, *sb.* company of men; *sb. pl.* booty.
prayse, *v.* to welcome, value.
prease, prece, prees, *sb.* press of battle; crowd, throng; *in prees*, forward.
prece, prese, *v.* to press, follow; to urge, entreat.
prees. See *prease*, sb.
preff. See *preve*, v.
prese. See *prece*, v.
preson, *v.* to imprison.
presonment, *sb.* imprisonment.
prestly, *adv.* quickly, eagerly.
prevayle, *v.* to benefit, avail.
preve, preff, prove, *v.* to delare; to convict, find guilty; to learn; to be obvious; to make it good; to make trial of; to put to the test; to undertake; to strive; to show one's valour; *bettyr preved*, defeated.
preved, proved *ppl. adj.* well-tried, trusty.
prevy, pryvy, pryvé, *adj.* secret; confidential, trusted; *prevy with*, in the confidence of.
prevys, *sb. pl.* proof, evidence.
prevyté *sb.* secret contents.
pryce, *adj.* excellent.
pryce, pryse, *sb.* honour, glory; reward or symbol of victory; capture.
pry(c)ke, *v.* to ride on horseback; *reflex.* to advance.
prycker, *b.* horseman.
pryde, *sb.* reliance, confidence.
pryke. See *pry(c)ke*, v.
pryme, *sb.* first hour of the day.
pryse. See *pryce*, sb.
pryvy, pryvé. See *prevy*, adj.
proces, *sb.*; *by proces*, in course of time.
procurour, *sb.* procurator, administrator.
prof(f)yr, *v.* to challenge; to request.
profir, *sb.* offer.
prove, proved. See *preve*, v., *preved*, ppl. adj.
proveste, *sb.* chief magistrate.
provydence, *sb.* contriving; divine direction; provision.
puyssaunce, *sb.* power, force.
pur, *prep.* (Fr.) through.
purfilde, *pp.* trimmed.
purphile, *sb.* trimming.

purvey, *v.* to provide, arrange; to appoint, choose; *reflex.* to arrange; to prepare oneself.

purveyans, purv(e)yaunce, *sb.* preparation; provisions, food.

pusell, pusyll, *sb.* maid, virgin; chaste youth.

put, *v.*; put(te), *pret.*; putt, *pp.* to knock; to thrust; to drive; *put uppon*, accused; entrusted to; *put to the wors*, got the better of.

Q

quarel(l), *sb.*¹ short, heavy arrow.

quarell, *sb.*² cause for complaint, grievance.

quarters, *sb. pl.* thighs.

quere, quyre, *sb.* choir, chancel.

queste, *sb.* judicial inquiry, trial; enterprise.

queste, *v.* to bark, yelp.

questyng, *sb.* yelping.

quycke, quyk, *adj.* alive.

quyre. See *quere, sb.*

quyte, *v.*; quytte, *pp.* to repay, punish; *reflex.* to acquit oneself.

quyt(t)e, *adj.* free; rid.

quondam, *adv.* (Lat.) of yore.

R

race, *v.*¹ to snatch, pull.

race, *v.*² to rush.

rack. See *rak(e), sb.*

rad, *v. pret.* read.

raffte, *v. pret.* bereft, deprived.

ragynge, *sb.* violent desire.

rayed, *ppl. adj.* dressed.

rayge, *sb.* distress.

rayke, *v.* to go.

rayle, *v.* to flow, gush.

raynke. See *ren(c)k, sb.*

rak(e), rack, *sb.* feeding-rack.

random. See *ra(u)ndom, sb.*

ranke, *adj.* stout, strong.

ransake. See *rensake, v.*

rase, *v.* to cut, slash; *rase out*, to deprive.

rasure, *sb.* obliteration, effacement.

rathly, *adv.* quickly.

raught(e), *v. pret. and pp.* reached; seized; found; caught; gave.

raumpe, *v.* to strike, knock.

ra(u)ndom, rawndom, *sb.* force, violence.

raunge, *sb.* line of battle.

ravyshe, *v.*; to fetch, bring; *let (lat) ravyshe*, to send for.

ravysshed, *ppl. adj.* enraptured.

reales. See *releace, v.*

rebuke, *sb.* insult; *to put to a rebuke*, to defeat.

rebuke, *v.* to put to shame, defeat; to hurt; to insult.

rebukyng, *sb.* check, repulse.

rechace, *sb.* calling together of hounds.

recke, rek, *v.*; rought, *pret.* to care.

recomforte, *v.* to encourage, exhort; to revive; *reflex.* to take courage again.

recommaunde, *v.* to commend.

record(e), *sb.* support, witness; *by all record*, by all accounts.

recorde, *v.* to witness.

recountir, recounter, *sb.* encounter, fight.

recountir, *v.* to meet, fight.

recover, recovir, *sb.* recovery; escape from death; *good recover*, prompt release (from prison).

recover, recovir, *v.* to get up after a fall; to cure; to support; to find; *reflex.* to go, take refuge.

recr(e)ayed, recr(e)ayde, *ppl. adj.* cowardly, recreant.

recreaunte, *adj.* faint-hearted.

rede, *sb.* advice; *hit ys no rede*, it serves no purpose.

rede, *v.* to advise; to plan.

redounde, *v.* to re-echo, reverberate.

redouted, *ppl. adj.* dreaded; distinguished.

redresse, *v.* to re-form; to restore; to cure, heal; *reflex.* to prepare.

reed, *adv.* in red.

refygowred, *ppl. adj.* restored to vigour.

refreysshe, *v.* to succour; *reflex.* to rest.

refresshynge, *sb.* refreshment.

regeaunte, *ppl. adj.* ruling.

rehersall, *sb.* mention, record.

rehers(e), reherce, *v.* to mention; to report; to describe; to be narrated.

reyse, *v.* to rouse, stimulate.

rejoyse, *v.* to enjoy; to possess; to please.

rek. See *recke*, v.

rekeyst(e), *sb.* request.

rekles, *sb.* recluse.

rele, *v.* to waver, give way.

releace, reales, *v.* to abandon; to exonerate; to allow.

releve, *v.* to bring help; to rally; to comfort.

remanaunte, remenaunte, remanent, *sb.* rest, remainder.

remeve, *v.* to go away.

renayne, *v.* to name.

ren(c)k, raynke, *sb.* man.

rencountre, *sb.* encounter.

renk. See *ren(c)k*, sb.

ren(ne), *v.*; *renne from*, leave behind.

rennynge hound, *sb.* hunting dog employed to run down game.

renomed, *ppl. adj.* renowned, famous; reputed.

renommee, *sb.* reputation.

rensake, ransake, *v.* to search; to examine the wounds of.

rente, *v.* to tear to pieces.

repente, *v.* to regret; *impers. me repentys of*, I am sorry for.

reporte, *v. reflex.* to appeal for confirmation.

repreff, *sb.* reproof, shame.

repreve, *v.* to insult; to reprove; to suspend the punishment of.

requeste, *sb.* knightly quest.

requyre, *v.* to request, ask.

rere, *v.* to raise; to build.

rere-brace, *sb.* armour for the upper arm.

reremayne, *sb.* back-handed stroke.

rerewarde, *sb.* rear.

resyne, *v.* to entrust.

reson, *sb.* satisfaction; reasonable action; *by reson*, fitly, by right.

resorted, *v. pret.*; *resorted unto hym*, came begging him.

resortis, *sb. pl.* requests, entreaties.

resseite, resseyte, *sb.* place of rest, refuge, retreat.

reste, *sb.* safety, security.

restore, *v.* to compensate.

retray, *v. reflex.* to draw back.

r(e)ule. See *rule*, v.

reverence, *sb.* honour, reputation.

revers, *adv.* with back-handed blows.

rew, row, *sb.* row; order; *all be rew*, in turn; *on a rowe*, in succession.

rewarde, *v.* to award.

rewe, *v.*; ruys, rwyth, *3 sg.* to have pity; to grieve.

ryche, *adj.* beautiful; luxurious; powerful, mighty.

rychesse, *sb.* wealth, riches; ransom.

ryde, *v.*[1] to free.

ryde, *v.*[2] *pret.* rode.

rydge, *sb.* back.

ryght, *adv.* thereupon; *ryght so*, then.

ryghtes, *sb. pl.* correct observances; last sacrament.

ryght, *v.* to put right.

ryghteuouse, rightwys, ryghtwos, *adj.* rightful, just.

righteuously, *adv.* rightfully.

ryvage, *sb.* shore.

ryve, *v.*; roofe, rooff(e), rove, roff, *pret.* to stab; to split; to be split; to tear.

roche, *sb.* cliff; cave.

roff. See *ryve*, v.

royalté, *sb.* magnificence, pomp, splendour.

royame, *sb.* realm, kingdom.

rolled, *ppl. adj.* enrolled, included.

romaynes, *sb.* verse romance (the alliterative *Morte Arthure*).

rome, *sb.* boundaries.

rome, *v.*[1] to go.

rome, *v.*[2] to roar, cry.

roofe, rooff(e). See *ryve*, v.

rooted, *ppl. adj.* able to withstand assault.

rosshe, *v.* to knock.

rosteled, *v. pret.* fell.

rought. See *recke*, v.

route, rought(e) *sb.* band, company.

r(o)uthe, *sb.* pity.

rove, See *ryve*, v.

rowe. See *rew*, sb.

row(y)sshe. See *russhe*, v.

rude, *adj.* heavy.

rudely, *adv.* roughly, loudly.

ruys. See *rewe*, v.

rule, *sb.* charge, care; command; influence; good order, discipline.

rule, reule, *v.* to look after; to arrange; to persuade; *reflex.* to behave; *be ruled*, behave.

russhe, rowysshe, *v.* to fall violently; to pull; to knock; to cut.

ruthe. See *r(o)uthe*, sb.
rwyth. See *rewe*, v.

S

sable, *adj.* black.
sad(de), *adj.* heavy, severe; steadfast, valiant; thoughtful.
sadly, *adv.* firmly, closely, soundly.
say, *v.* to try (aphetic form of *assay*).
sakarynge, sakerynge, *sb.* consecration
salew, *v.* to greet, salute; to commend.
salf. See *sauff*, prep.
salve, *v.* to anoint.
same, *sb.*; *all in same*, together.
samyte, *sb.* rich silk.
Sank(e)greall, *sb.* Holy Grail.
sarezen, *sb.* heathen, pagan.
sarpis, *sb. pl.* chains (?).
sauf(f), *adv.* safely.
sauff. See *save*, v.
sauffconduyghte, *sb.* safe-conduct, guarantee of protection.
sauffgarde, *sb.* custody.
saulter, *sb.* psalm.
saunz, *prep.* without.
save, sauff, *v.* to protect; to fulfil; to spare.
Saveoure, *sb.* Eucharist.
savying, *sb.* protection.
savour(e), *sb.* scent; evil smell.
savoure, *v.* to smell offensively.
sawdon. See *sowdon,* sb.
sawe, *sb.* proverb, saying; speech; *pl.* message.
sawte, *sb.* attack, assault.
scape, *v.* to escape.
scathe, *sb.* injury.
scholde. See *shold(e)*, v. pret.
sclaundir, sclawndir, *sb.* scandal, uproar.
scomfyte, *v.* to defeat.
scowte-wacche, *sb.* sentinel.
scripture, *sb.* inscription.
sease, sece, *v.* to cease; to cause to cease.
se(a)son, *sb.* opportunity; proper time.
sece. See *sease*, v.
seche, *v.* to seek; to examine.
secrete, *sb.* confidence; *were aboute her secrete*, enjoyed her confidence.
sedull, *sb.* document, letter.
seek. See *seke*, adj.

se(e)kene, *v.* to become ill.
seyne, *ppl. adj.* manifest.
seynge, *sb.* seigneurie; *take seynge*, to establish one's authority.
seke, seek, syke, *adj.* ill.
seke, syke, *v.*; **sought(e),** *pret.*; **(i)sought,** *pp.* to search; to learn; to advance; to deserve; to provoke; *soughte uppon*, tempted, besought.
sekene. See *se(e)kene*, v.
semb(e)launte, *sb.* appearance; pretence.
semble, *adj.* false, hypocritical.
seme, *v.* to think; to appear.
semely, *adj.* handsome.
semyng(e), *sb.* appearance; thinking.
sendele, sendell, *sb.* fine silk or linen.
sensar, *sb.* censer.
senshyp, *sb.* censure.
septure, *sb.* sceptre.
serch(e), cerche, *v.* to collect; to examine; to find out; to attempt to heal (a wound); *serche for*, to probe.
sere, *adj.* dry, withered.
sere, *v.* to wrap in a cerecloth.
sertayne, *adv.* certainly; *sb.* certainty; certain number.
sertes, serteyse, *adv.* indeed.
servayge, *sb.* servitude, bondage.
serve, *v.* to treat; to permit.
seson. See *se(a)son*, sb.
seteled, *pp.* seated.
sette, *v.*; **set(te),** *pret.*; **sette,** *pp.* to appoint; to use, employ; to prepare, to sharpen; *reflex.* to sit; *sette by*, to care about.
sette, *ppl. adj.* fixed, rooted; minded, resolved.
setthen, sytthe(n), sytthyn, syth, *adv. and cj.* then, since then, since.
sevennyght, *sb.* week.
sew(e), cewe, *v.*; **swith,** *imper.* to pursue; to follow; to practise; to strive; to appeal.
sewear, *sb.* attendant at meal.
sewte, *sb.* dress, garb; sort, colour; attendance.
shafftemonde, *sb.* handbreadth.
shake, *sb.* speed; *a grete shake*, quickly.
sham(e)full, *adj.* mean, contemptible; scurrilous; contumacious.
shapyn, *ppl. adj.* in appearance.
shap(p)e, *v.*; **shope,** *pret.* to make; to plan; to aim a blow; to change.

shawe, *sb*. thicket, copse; *shawe of the wood*, small wood.
shende, *v*. **shente**, *pp*. to injure; to disgrace, ruin; to put to shame.
shene, *adj*. bright; beautiful.
shente. See *shende*, v.
shevalere, shyvalere, *sb*. knight; *shevalere de charyot*, knight of the cart.
shevalry. See *chyvalry*, sb.
shewyng, *sb*. appearance.
shipbourde, *sb*. side of a ship.
shypped, *ppl. adj*. on board ship.
shirly, *adv*. shrilly.
shytte, *ppl. adj*. shut up, enclosed.
shyvalere. See *shevalere*, sb.
shyver, *sb*. fragment.
shodde, *ppl. adj*. tipped, edged.
shold(e), scholde, solde, *v. pret*. would; could; did; were about to (equivalent to subjunctive after 'mesemythe').
shondeshyp, *sb*. shame, disgrace.
shooke, *v. pret*. hastened, advanced.
shope. See *shap(p)e*, v.
shorne, *pp*. cut, wounded.
shorte, *adj*.; *shorte rybbys*, lower ribs.
short(e)ly, *adv*. promptly, instantly.
shoter, *sb*. archer.
shotte, *v. pret*. launched.
shovyn, *pp*. set afloat.
showre, *sb*. misfortune; conflict. combat.
shrede, *v*. to cut, hack.
shrewde, shrewed, *adj*. poor, unsatisfactory; evil, mischievous.
shunte, *v*. to move aside; to hang back, steal away.
sybbe, *sb*. kin, relation.
sydelynge, *adv*. sideways.
sygnyfycasion, *sb*. significant thing.
syke. See *seke*, adj., *seke*, v.
syker, *adj*. sure, reliable; trusty, faithful.
sykerly, *adv*. certainly; thoroughly, carefully.
sykernesse, *sb*. agreement, assurance.
sykynge, *sb*. search.
sylden, *adv*. seldom.
syler, *sb*. canopy.
symple, *adj*. of low rank; slight, inadequate.
syn(e), syns, *adv.*, *prep.*, *and cj*. since; afterwards; *syn that*, since (then).

synattes, *sb. pl*. signets, small seals.
syns. See *syn(e)*.
syse, *sb*. correct method.
syth. See *syn(e)*.
sytte, *v*.; **syttande**, *pres. part*. to sit; to withstand.
sytthe(n), sytthyn. See *setthen*, adv. and cj.
syxtyfolde, *sb*. sixty thicknesses.
skaffoldys, *sb. pl*. platforms; stands.
skyffte, *sb*. lot, fate; effort.
skyffte, *v*. to divide; to arrange, manage.
skyfte, *adj*. rid.
skymme, *v*. to scour.
skyppe, *v*. to jump.
slad(e), *sb*. valley, glade.
slake, *v*. to abate.
slente, *v*. to slip, fall aslant.
sly, *adj*. skilful, expert.
sly(e)ve, *sb*. sash.
slyght, *sb*. skill.
slyly, *adv*. skilfully, dexterously; secretly.
slyppe, *v*. to pass on.
slyve. See *sly(e)ve*, sb.
slo(o)de, *v. pret*. fell.
small, *adj*. fine.
so, soo, *adv. and cj*. now; then; provided that, on condition that; that; *so that*, provided that.
sodde, *pp*. boiled.
soffte. See *so(u)ffte*, adj.
solde. See *shold(e)*, v. pret.
solempnité, *sb*. ceremony.
som, *adj*. any, a certain.
som. See *som(me)*, sb.
somever. See *whatsomever*, pron. and adj.
som(me), *sb*. number.
somons, *sb*. summons; terms.
sondis, *sb. pl*. messengers.
sondismen, *sb. pl*. messengers.
sondry. See *sundry*, adj.
soo. See *so*, adv. and cj.
sore, *adv*. grievously; deeply; closely; thoroughly; violently.
sorow, *sb*. trouble, difficulty.
sorte, *sb*. band.
sotte, *sb*. fool, dolt.
so(u)ffte, *adj*. steady.
sought(e). See *seke*, v.
sowde, *v*. to mend.

sowdyar, *sb.* soldier (who serves for pay).

sowdon, sowdan, sawdon, *sb.* sultan.

sowghe, *sb.* rushing sound.

sowghe. See *swow(gh)e*, sb.

sowne, *sb.*[1] sound.

sowne, *sb.*[2] swoon.

sowne, *v.* to swoon.

sowse, *v.* to immerse, plunge.

space, *sb.* space of time.

sparde, *v. pret.* barred.

spare, *v.* to refrain.

spare. See *spyrre*, v.

sparhawke, *sb.* sparrowhawk.

speciall, *adj.* dear, esteemed.

spede, *sb.* help.

spede, spyede, *v.*; spedde, *pp.* to fare; to succeed; to help, to achieve; to finish, dispatch; *reflex.* to hasten.

spedfull, *adj.* valiant.

speke, *v.* to say; *they speke you shame*, they blame you.

spende, *v.* to dispose of, make use of.

spendynge, *sb.* money to spend.

spere. See *spyrre*, v.

spy, *sb.* observation, watch; *have a spy uppon s.o.*, to watch s.o.

spycery, *sb.* spices.

spyede. See *spede*, v.

spynnesse, *sb. pl.* pinnaces.

spiritualités, *sb. pl.* consecrated ground.

spyrre, spurre, spare, spere, *v.* to ask; to find.

spite, *sb.* injury, wrong.

spyteuous, *adj.* contumacious, contemptuous.

spiteuously, *adv.* grievously; violently.

spore, *sb.* spur.

spore, *v.* to spur.

sprynge, *v.*; spronge, *pp.* to grow; to reveal.

spurre. See *spyrre*, v.

square, *adj.*; *four square*, cubic.

sqwatte, *v. pret.* knocked, crushed.

stabely, *adv.* firmly.

stable, *adj.* steadfast, settled.

stablisshe, stab(e)lysshe, *v.* to bring into settled order; to set in office or dignity.

stack. See *stake*, v. pret.

stadde, *ppl. adj.* attacked, beset.

stake, stack, *v. pret.* clung, stuck; was fixed.

stakir, *v.* to stagger, totter.

stale, *sb.* fixed position; body of armed men; *to kepe the stale*, to stand firm.

stale,.*v. pret.* stole.

stalke, *sb.* act of stalking game.

stalled, *pp.* established.

staryng, *ppl. adj.* loud.

starke, sterke, *adj.* thorough, arrant; *adv.* quite.

staunche, *v.* to be quenched.

ste(a)vyn, steven, *sb.* assignation; occasion; voice.

stede, *sb.*[1] place; *in the stede of*, instead of.

stede, styede, *sb.*[2] horse.

sterke, See *starke*, adj.

sterne, *adj.* resolute in battle, brave; high-spirited, fiery.

stevyn, steven. See *ste(a)vyn*, sb.

styede. See *stede*, sb.[2]

styew, *sb.* stove, heated room.

stylle, *adv.* continuously; always.

stylly, *adv.* silently.

stynte, *sb.* loss.

stynte, *v.*; stynte, *pret.* to cease; to put an end to.

stirre, *sb.* star.

sto(o)ne, *v.* to stun; to break, crush; to be crushed or stunned.

stoupe, stowpe, *v.* to fall.

stoure, stowre, *sb.* battle conflict.

stoute, *adj.* stern, firm.

stoutly, *adv.* vigorously.

stowpe. See *stoupe*, v.

stowre. See *stoure*, sb.

strayne, *v.* to exert.

strayte, strete, streyt(e), streyghte, *adj.* narrow; strict; confined, imprisoned; *adv.* severely, close(ly).

strayt(e)ly, *adv.* severely.

strake, *sb.* signal with hunting horn.

strake, *v.* to sound a note (on a horn).

strange, *adj.* wonderful.

strangely, *adv.* wonderfully, elaborately.

streyghte, *v. pret.* stretched.

streyghte, streyt(e). See *strayte*, adj. and adv.

streke, *sb.* blow.

stremys, *sb. pl.* currents, sea.

strendys, *sb. pl.* streams.
strene, *sb.* stock, family.
strenge, *sb.* leash.
strenger, **strengyst**. See *stronge*, adj.¹
strength, *sb.* stronghold.
strengthe, *v.* to secure, bring about.
strete. See *strayte*, adj. and adv.
stryff, *sb.* strife, contention.
strode, *v. pret.*; *strode uppon*, bestrode.
stronge, *adj.*¹; **strenger**, *comp.*; **strengyst**, *superl.* difficult, arduous; heavy.
stronge, *adj.*² strange.
strongely, *adv.* violently.
study, *sb.* thought.
stuff(e), *sb.* goods; forces.
stuff(e), *v.* to furnish with men and stores for defence.
sturdely, *adv.* roughly, violently.
sturre, *sb.* star.
subtylé, subtyle. See *suttelly*, adv., *suttyle*, adj.
sufferaunce, *sb.* forbearance; permission; will.
suffyse, *v.* to provide food for.
suffrygan, *sb.* (suffragan) bishop.
sundry, sondry, *adj.* different, separate (sometimes following its noun).
suppyngis, *sb. pl.* liquid food, broth.
suraunce, *sb.* assurance, agreement.
sureté, *sb.* assurance of safety; certainty of getting.
surmyse, *v.* to allege.
surmownte, *v.* to surpass, defeat.
sursynglys, *sb. pl.* girths for horses.
suttelyté, *sb.* cunning.
suttelly, subtylé, *adv.* skilfully.
suttyle, subtyle, *adj.* skilful, subtle.
swall, *v. pret.* swelled.
swalowe, *sb.* depth; whirlpool.
swamme, *v. pret.* floated.
swange, *v. pret.* drew.
swappe, *v.* to strike, knock.
swappyng, *sb.* clash.
swarffe, *sb.* sward, surface of the ground.
swevyn, *sb.* dream.
swith. See *sew(e)*, v.
swoghe. See *swow(ghe)*, sb.
sworne, *pp.* proclaimed.
swow(gh)e, swoughe, sowghe, swoghe, *sb.* swoon.

T

tacchis, tatchis, *sb. pl.* qualities; habits.
tay, *sb.* outer membrane.
tay, tey, *v.* to tie.
take, *v.*; **toke, took**, *pret.*; **takyn, tane**, *pp.* to take to; to betake; to receive; to accept (as a champion); to welcome; to practise; to call upon; to make; to give; to strike; *toke with*, gave; *toke up*, took prisoner.
tale, *sb.* number; *be tale*, in number.
talente, *sb.* desire.
tame, *v.* to cut through; to wound; to injure.
tane. See *take*, v.
tar(r)y, *v.*; **tarrynge**, *pres. part.* to continue, remain; to hinder, delay.
tatchis. See *tacchis*, sb. pl.
tatyr, *sb.* sharp point, jag.
teche, *v.*; **taughte**, *pp.* to lead, take.
tey. See *tay*, v.
tempte, *v.* to put to the test.
ten, *adj.* tenth.
tene, *sb.* sorrow, suffering.
terme, *sb.* (space of) time; *terme of his lyff*, for the rest of his life.
terme-day, *sb.* appointed day.
than, *adv. and cj.* then; when; *be than*, by the time that; by then.
that, *cj.* so that; because; unless; *how that*, that.
that, *pron. and adj.* such; those; that which, what; who; to whom; *that . . . he*, who; *that . . . hym*, whom; *that . . . hit*, *that . . . his*, whose; *that one*, one; *that other*, the other.
ther(e), *poss. adj.* their.
ther(e), *adv.* where.
thereaf(f)tir, *adv.* afterwards; in keeping.
ther(e)as, *adv. and cj.* there; where; to the place where; from the place where; whereas, although.
therefor(e), *adv.* on that account; thereto, to it.
therewithall, *adv.* thereupon.
therto, *adv.* moreover.
thycke, *adj.* heavy; *as sb.* thick part.
thynge, *sb. pl.* things, persons; *what thynge*, in whatever way.
thirle, thryle, *v.* to pierce; to run, flow.

thirste. See *threst(e)*, v. pret.

thirstelew, *adj.* thirsty.

this, thys, *adj. and pron.* these, the (*pl.*); this is.

tho, *adv.* then.

tho(o), *adj. and pron.* those.

thorowborne, *pp.* pierced.

th(o)rowoute, *prep. and adv.* through; because of.

thought(e), *sb.* grief, sorrow.

thralle, *sb.* thraldom.

thrange, *v. pret.* pressed.

threst(e), *v. pret.*; **thirste,** *pp.* pressed forward; rushed; pierced; thrust.

thryle. See *thirle*, v.

throoff, *v. pret.* prospered.

throwys, *sb. pl.* pains.

throwoute. See *th(o)rowoute*.

thrumbelyng, *adv.* in a heap.

tyde, *sb.* time.

tyde, *v.* to befall.

tyll, *v.* to tell.

tyll(e), *prep.* to; *tylle a bay*, at bay; *tyll that*, until.

tyme, *sb.* fit occasion; *be tyme*, quickly; *at thys tyme*, now; *at that tyme*, when; *in good tyme*, very good (cf. Fr. 'à la bonne heure').

tiraunte, tyr(r)aunte, *sb.* villain, ruffian.

tyred, *ppl. adj.* equipped, armed.

tyrraunte. See *tiraunte*, sb.

to, *prep.* at, towards; against; until; as far as; for; by means of; with regard to; in comparison with; comparable to; according to.

to. See *to(o)*, adj.

to-bete, *v. pret.* belaboured.

to-braste, *v. pret. and pp.* broke(n) in pieces, burst.

to-cracched, *ppl. adj.* badly scratched.

todir. See *tother*, adj. and pron.

to-dryve, *v.* to burst to pieces.

tofore, *prep., adv., and cj.* before, in front of; in the presence of; until.

toforehonde. See *tofornehande*, adv.

toforetyme, *adv.* previously.

toforne, *adv.* in front.

torfornehande, toforehonde, *adv.* previously.

togedyrs, togidirs, togydyr, togydirs, *adv.* together; against each other.

to-hew, *v. pret.* cut to pieces.

toke. See *take*, v.

tone, *adj. and pron.* one.

to(o), *adj.* two.

took. See *take*, v.

to-rongcled, *ppl. adj.* rugged (?).

to-rove, *v. pret.*; **to-ryven,** *pp.* split into pieces.

to-shevir, *v.* to break in pieces.

to-tatered, *ppl. adj.* jagged, pointed.

tother, todir, *adj. and pron.* other.

tou, *pron.* thou.

tourneye, *v.* to take part in a tournament.

toward(e), *prep. and adv.* supporting; *towarde and frowarde*, in all directions.

trace, *sb.* track.

trade, *v. pret.* trod.

tray, *sb.* pain, sorrow.

trayle, *v.* to flow slowly.

trayne, *sb.*[1] train (of a dress).

trayne, *sb.*[2] enticement, lure.

traytoures, *adj.* treacherous.

traytourly, *adv.* treacherously.

trappe, *sb.* trapdoor.

trapped, *ppl. adj.* adorned with trappings.

trapper, trap(o)ur, trappour(e), *sb.* trapping, covering for horse.

trase, *v.* to tread.

travayle, *sb.* labour, toil; difficulty.

travayle, traveille, *v.* to labour; to torment; to travel.

travayled, *ppl. adj.* tired.

travaillyng, *sb.* labour.

traveille. See *travayle*, v.

traveyse, *adv.* crosswise, athwart.

travers, *sb.*; *at travers*, crossways, transversely.

traverse, *v.* to move from side to side, dodge.

trencheaunte, *adj.* sharp.

trespasce, *v.* to offend.

treste, *sb.* appointed place; *at the treste*, lying in wait (?).

tretable, *adj.* tractable, manageable.

trete, *v.* to negotiate, to have dealings; to fight.

tretyse, *sb.* entreaty; agreement, compact.

tr(e)wage, tr(e)wayge, truage, *sb.* tribute.

tro(u)ncheo(u)n, truncheoune,

tro(u)ncheo(u)n etc. (*cont.*):
truncheon, *sb.* fragment, shaft (of spear).
trouth(e), trowthe, *sb.* faith, word; solemn promise; true account.
trow(e), *v.* to think, believe; to dream.
trowthe. See *trouth(e)*.
truage. See *tr(e)wage*, *sb.*
truncheon, truncheoune. See *tro(u)ncheo(u)n*, *sb.*
trusse, *v.* to carry off; to equip.
trwa(y)ge. See *tr(e)wage*, *sb.*
turne, *v.* to return; to change.
turvis, *sb. pl.* sods, pieces of turf.
twayne, tweyne, *adj.* two.
twelfth day, *sb.* Epiphany.
twenty, *adj.* twentieth.

U

umbelyclose, *v.* to surround.
umbir, *sb.* shade, shadow.
umbrell, *sb.* back of helmet.
umbrere, *sb.* visor of helmet.
unavysed, *adv.* rashly, unwarily.
unbecaste, *v. pret.* cast.
unbethought, *v. reflex.* called to mind.
unboced, *ppl. adj.* escaped into a thicket.
uncounceyled, *ppl. adj.* undecided, uncertain.
uncouth, *adj.* strange.
uncurteyse, *adj.* dishonourable.
under, undir, *prep.* beneath the shelter of; conditionally on, in addition to; *under God*, in the world.
underne, undirn, undyrn, *sb.* about 9 p.m. or later; evening.
undirtake, *v.* to be responsible; to seize, afflict.
ungerde, *v. pret.* took off.
ungoodly, *adv.* discourteously.
unhappe, *sb.* ill-fortune.
unhappy, *adj.* troublesome, objectionable; harmful; unlucky; disastrous.
unhappynes, *sb.* misfortune; mischief, evil.
unhylle, *v.* to uncover.
unkyndely, *adj.* unnatural.
unkyndenesse, *sb.* ill-feeling.
unlace, *v.* to unfasten.
unlyckly, *adj.* unsuitable, unseemly.
unmaymed, *ppl. adj.* uninjured.

unmesurabely, *adv.* excessively.
unnailled, *ppl. adj.* unfastened.
unneth(e), *adv.* with difficulty; hardly.
unsyker, *adj.* unstable, uncertain.
unsounde, *adj.* ill, unwell.
untyl(l), *prep.* to.
unto, unte, *prep. and cj.* as far as; until; toward; to, in; on; at; for; compared with; with regard to; in accordance with; *unto that*, until.
untrouthe, *sb.* wickedness, wicked deeds.
unwarely, *adv.* without warning, unawares.
unwares, *adj.* unaware.
unwympeled, *v. reflex. pret.*; *unwympeled her*, removed her veil.
unwrayste, *v. pret.* unfastened.
upborne, *ppl. adj.* supported.
up(p)on, *prep.* from; against; for; concerning; on pain of; to the decision of.
upryght, *adv.* at full length.
up-so-downe, *adv.* upside down; *turn up-so-downe*, to raze to the ground.
upwarde, *adv.* at full length.
usurppe, *v.* to encroach forcibly.
utas, *sb.* octave, eighth day after festival.
utteraunce, *sb.* utmost; end, finish; fullest extent.
utteryst(e), *sb.* utmost.
uttermuste, uttermoste, uttermest, uttirmust, *sb.* end; utmost.
uttir, *adj.* deadly; *adv.* further away.

V

valyaunte, *adj.* excellent, worthy.
varyaunte, *adj.* variable.
varlet, verlatte, *sb.* servant, attendant.
vauntage, *sb.* disadvantage.
vawarde, voward, *sb.* vanguard.
vawmbrace, *sb.* armour for forearm.
veary. See *ver(r)y*, *adj.*
velony. See *vilony*, *sb.*
venery, *sb.* hunting.
vengeabely, *adv.* vindictively, cruelly.
vengeable, *adj.* revengeful.
vergyne, *sb.* chaste man or woman.
very. See *ver(r)y*, *adj.*
veryly, *adv.* fully, really.

verlatte. See *varlet*, sb.

vermayne, *sb.* noxious animal.

vernacle, *sb.* vernicle, St Veronica's kerchief.

ver(r)y, verrey, veary, *adj.* true; undoubted.

vertue, *sb.* power, ability.

vycounte. See *vy(s)counte*, sb.

vygyle, *sb.* eve.

vigoure, *sb.* figure, image.

vylaunce, *adj.* wicked, evil; grievous, severe.

vylaunsly, *adv.* wickedly; insultingly.

vilony, velony, *sb.* wickedness.

vysage, *v.* to stare at.

vysayge, *sb.* face; *magré thy vysayge*, in spite of you.

vy(s)counte, *sb.* lord, ruler.

vitayle, *sb.* food.

voyde, *adj.* empty; riderless (horse).

voyde, *v.* to leave; to go away; to dismount from.

voutre, *poss. adj.* (Fr.) your.

voward. See *vawarde*, sb.

W

wacche, *v.* to lie awake; to lie in wait; to guard.

wage, *v.* to engage, hire; to fight.

wagge, *v.* to shake; to totter.

way, wey, *sb.*; *their wayes, on hir wayes, in hir wayes*, on their way; *by weyes*, on the way.

waycche, *sb.* watch.

wayte, *sb.* watch, waiting; watchman.

wayte, *v.*[1] to watch, be careful; to look; *wayte uppon*, to guard; to escort, attend; to lie in wait for; to keep hostile watch against; *wayte on*, to protect; *wayte wyth*, to treat with; *wayte wyth a hurte*, to attack; *wayte betwyxte*, to observe the behaviour of.

wayte, *v.*[2] to treat.

wallap, walop, *v.* to gallop.

waltred, waltyrde, *v. pret.* tossed about; tumbled, rolled.

wanhope, *sb.* despair.

wanne, *v.* to become dark.

wan(ne). See *wynne*, v.

wap, *v.* to lap.

waraunte. See *war(r)aunte*, sb., *war(r)aunte*, v.

warde, *sb.* body of guards.

warde. See *toward(e)*, prep.

wardeyn, *sb.* governor.

ware, *adj.* aware; aware of; cautious.

waryson, *sb.* reward.

warke. See *worke*, sb.

warly, *adj.* warlike.

warlow, werlow, *sb.* monster.

warne, *v.* to prevent; to refuse to accept; to command; to assure, inform.

war(r)aunte, *sb.* protector, champion.

war(r)aunte, *v.* to promise; to afford protection; to save.

warre, wars, wers(e), *adj. comp. as sb.* worse, inferior one; *as sb.* defeat; *putt to the warre (wars)*, defeated; *had the werse*, was defeated.

watir, watyr, *sb.* sea; lake; river.

wawis, *sb. pl.* waves.

waxe, wexe, *v.*; waxed, waxte, wexed, woxe, *pret.*; waxen, wexen, woxen, *pp.* to become.

webbe, *sb.* sheet.

weete, weyte. See *wyte*, v.[1]

well. See *woll*, v.

well-beseyne, *ppl. adj.* good-looking.

well-brethed, *ppl. adj.* sound in wind, not easily made out of breath.

well-condyssyonde, *ppl. adj.* full of good qualities.

welle-stremys, *sb. pl.* streams flowing from springs.

well-farynge, *ppl. adj.* handsome, well-favoured.

well-ruled, *ppl. adj.* well-behaved.

well vysaged, *ppl. adj.* good-looking.

well-wyllar, well-wyller, *sb.* well-wisher.

well-wylled, *ppl. adj.* well-disposed.

well-wyllynge, *ppl. adj.* well-disposed.

weltryng, *ppl. adj.* rolling about.

wene, wyne, *v.*; wennys, *3 sg. pres.*; went(e), wende, *pret.* to think, expect.

wery, *adj. as sb.* fatigue.

werke. See *worke*, sb.

werlow. See *warlow*, sb.

werre, *v.* to make war.

wers. See *warre*, adj. comp.

westirly, *adv.* westward.

wete. See *wyte*, v.[1]

wetynge. See *wyt(t)ynge*, sb.
wexe(d), wexen. See *waxe*, v.
whatsomever, whatsumever, *pron. and adj.* whatever; who; *what tyme somever*, whatever time.
wher(e), *adv.* wherever; *where that*, wherever.
where. See *whethir*, pron. and cj.
whereas, *adv.* where.
whereby, *adv.* why.
whereof, *adv.* from which.
wheresomever, *adv.* wherever.
wherethorow, *adv. and prep.* whereupon; therefore; on account of.
whethir, whother, *adv.* whither.
whethir, where, *pron. and cj.* which (of two); whichever; whether; even if; *whether as*, whichever.
whethirsomever, *pron.* whichever.
why, whyghe, *adv.*; *for why*, because, for.
which, *pron.* who; *which his*, whose.
whyghe. See *why*, adv.
whyght. See *wyght*, adj.
whyghtsauff, *v.* to vouchsafe, be willing.
whyle, *cj.* until; *sb.* time; *whyle that*, as long as.
whyrle, whorle, *v.* to rush; to jump.
who, *pron.* whoever; *who that*, whoever.
who(o), *interj.* stop!
whorle. See *whyrle*, v.
whoso, *pron.* whoever.
whosomever, *pron.* whoever.
whother. See *whether*, adv.
wydewhere, *adv.* far and wide.
wyght, whyght, *adj.* strong, stalwart.
wyght, *sb.*¹ blame.
wyght(e), *sb.*² creature.
wyght(e). See *wyte*, v.¹ and v.², *wyte*, sb.
wyghty, *adj.* strong.
wyghtly, *adv.* quickly.
wyghtnesse, *sb.* strength.
wyke, *sb.* week.
wylde, *adj.* mad, frenzied; fierce; stormy.
wyld(e) woode, *adj.* stark mad.
wylfully, *adv.* voluntarily, without resistance.
wylfulness, *sb.* stubbornness.
wyll(e), *sb.* pleasure; desire; intention; good will; *evyll wyll* (OF. *maltalent*), anger; *in wyll(e)*, intending; willing; *be my wylle*, willingly.
wyllfull, *adj.* voluntary.
wyllynge, *ppl. adj.* desirous.
wyllynge, *sb.* wish, intention.
wylsom, *adj.* lonely, dreary.
wympled, *ppl. adj.* veiled.
wynde, *v.*¹ to turn, go.
wynde, *v.*² to exhaust the breath of.
wyne. See *wene*, v.
wynne, *v.*; won, wan(ne), *pret.*; wonne, *pp.* to gain; to conquer; to profit; to defeat; to spring; to arrive; to come; *to wynne away*, to come away,
wyntir, *sb. pl.* years.
wyse, *adj.* careful.
wyse, *sb.* way; *in ony wyse*, at any rate.
wyse-fyghtynge, *adj.* skilful in fighting.
wysshe, *v. pret.* washed.
wyst(e). See *wyte*, v.¹
wytche, *sb.* sorcerer.
wyte, wyght, *sb.* blame.
wyte, wyghte, wytte, we(e)te, weyte, *v.*¹; wote, *pres. ind.*; wyste, *pret.* to know, to find out.
wyte, wyght(e), *v.*² to blame, to blame for.
with, wyt(h), *prep.* on behalf of; by; against; *with that*, provided that; thereupon; *wyth this*, on this condition that.
withal(l), *prep. and adv.* with (emphatic form following its object); then; besides, moreover; *I may not do withall*, I cannot help it.
withholde, *v.*; withhylde, *pret.*; withholdyn, *pp.* to keep in one's service; to detain; *be withholdyn(g) with*, to be in the service of.
within, *prep.* in the house of.
withinfurthe, withinforthe, *adv.* inside.
withoute, *adv., prep., and cj.* outside; unless.
withoutefurth, wythouteforthe, *adv.* without, outside.
withsey, *v.* to contradict, disobey.
withturne, *v.* to turn.
wytynge. See *wyt(t)ynge*, sb.
wytte, witte, *sb.* skill; knowledge;

wits, reason; good sense. See *wyte*, v.[1]

wytty, *adj.* wise.

wyttyly, *adv.* skilfully.

wyt(t)ynge, wetynge, *sb.* knowledge; *unto my wytynge*, as far as I know.

wyttyngly, *adv.* knowingly.

wode. See *wood(e)*, adj. and adv.

wolde, *pp.* prevailed.

woll, wyll, well, *v. 1 sg.*; **wold(e),** *pret. and pp.* wish, wish for, desire; intend; be about to; feel towards; *I wyll wel*, I readily agree; *wolde*, should.

wombe, *sb.* belly.

won. See *wynne*, v.

wondir, *adj. and adv.* wonderful; very.

wondirfully, *adv.* with wonder or admiration.

wondirly, *adv.* wonderfully; very.

wonne. See *wynne*, v.

wood(e), wode, *adj. and adv.* mad, angry, fierce; fiercely, violently; *wood wroth*, violently angry.

woodenesse. See *woodnes*, sb.

woodly, *adv.* fiercely.

woodnes, woodenesse, *sb.* anger, rage.

woodshaw, *sb.* thicket.

wordly, *adj.* earthly; *wordly knyght*, earthly knight (OF. *chevalier terrien*).

worke, warke, werke, *sb.* deed; affair, matter; difficulty; trouble, affliction.

worme, *sb.* dragon.

worship, worshyp, *sb.* honour, glory; praise; repute, standing.

worship, worshyp, *v.* to bring honour to; to ennoble.

worst, *adj. superl. as sb.* defeat.

worth, *adj.* worthy, excellent.

worthe, *v.* to befall.

wortis, *sb. pl.* roots.

wote. See *wyte*, v.[1]

wowe, *v.* to woo.

woxe(n). See *waxe*, v.

wrake, *sb.* harm, injury; hostility, strife.

wraste, *v. pret.* pulled.

wrath. See *wroth(e)*, v. pret.

wratth, wretth, *v.* to anger; to cause injury to.

wrytte, *sb.* document, writing; summons.

wrokyn, *pp.* vented.

wroth(e), wrath, *v. pret.* twisted.

wroth(e), *adj.*; **wrotther,** *comp.* angry.

Y

yarde, *sb.* branch.

yate, *sb.* gate.

yede. See *yo(o)de*, v. pret.

yeete, *v. pret.* ate.

yeff(yn). See *gyff(e)*, v.

yef(f)te, *sb.* gift.

yelde, *v.*; **yelde(d),** *pret.*; **yoldyn, yolden, yelden,** *pp.* to pay; to give up; to comply with; *reflex.* to go.

yeode. See *yo(o)de*, v. pret.

yeve. See *gyff(e)*, v.

yolden, yoldyn. See *yelde*, v.

yoman, *sb.* low-born man, servant.

yon, *adj.* those.

yo(o)de, ye(o)de, *v. pret.* went; fell; broke; *yoode away*, survived; *be yode to the swerde*, to be put to the sword.

PRINTED IN GREAT BRITAIN
AT THE UNIVERSITY PRESS, OXFORD
BY VIVIAN RIDLER
PRINTER TO THE UNIVERSITY